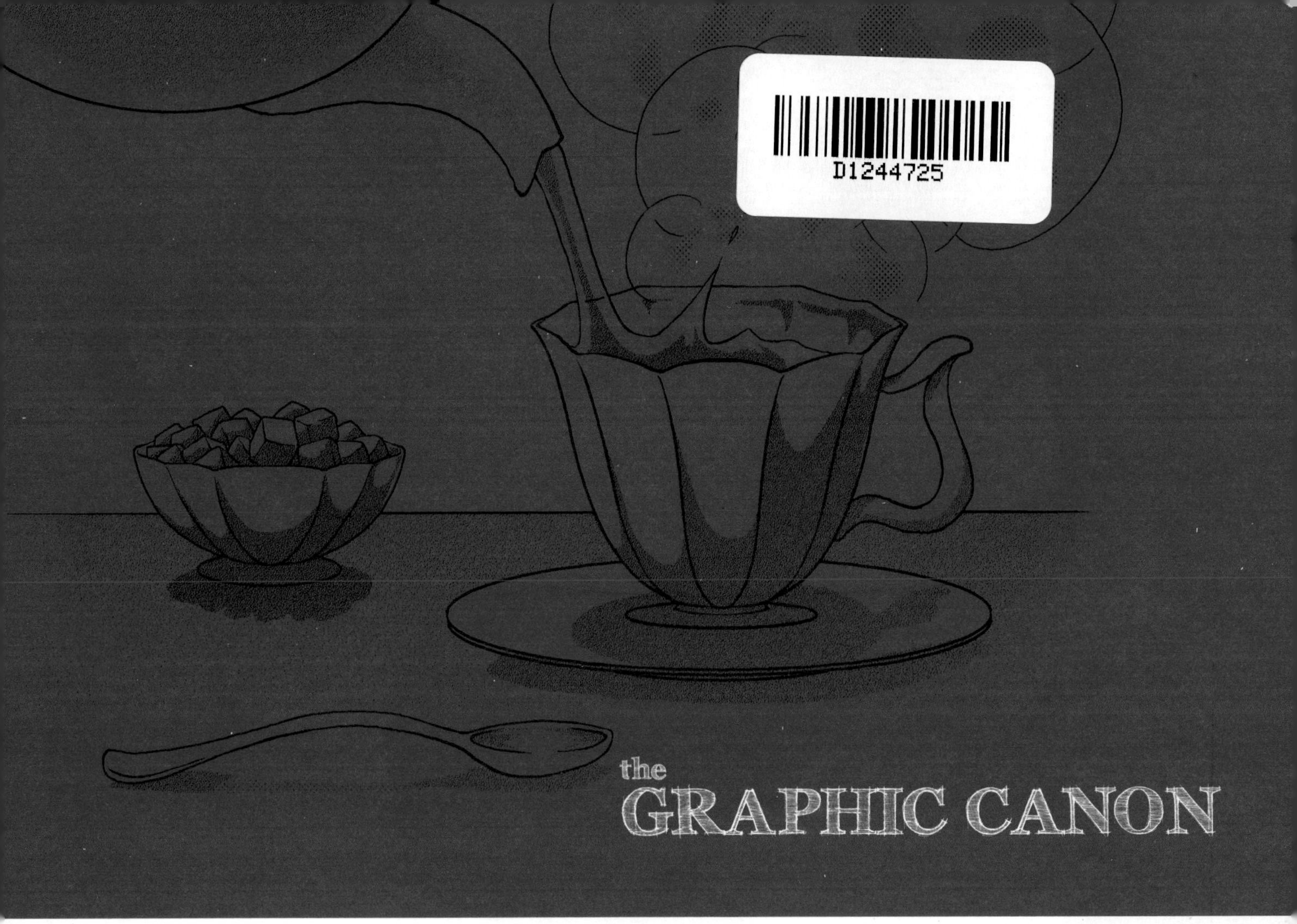

the GRAPHIC CANON

Volume 3

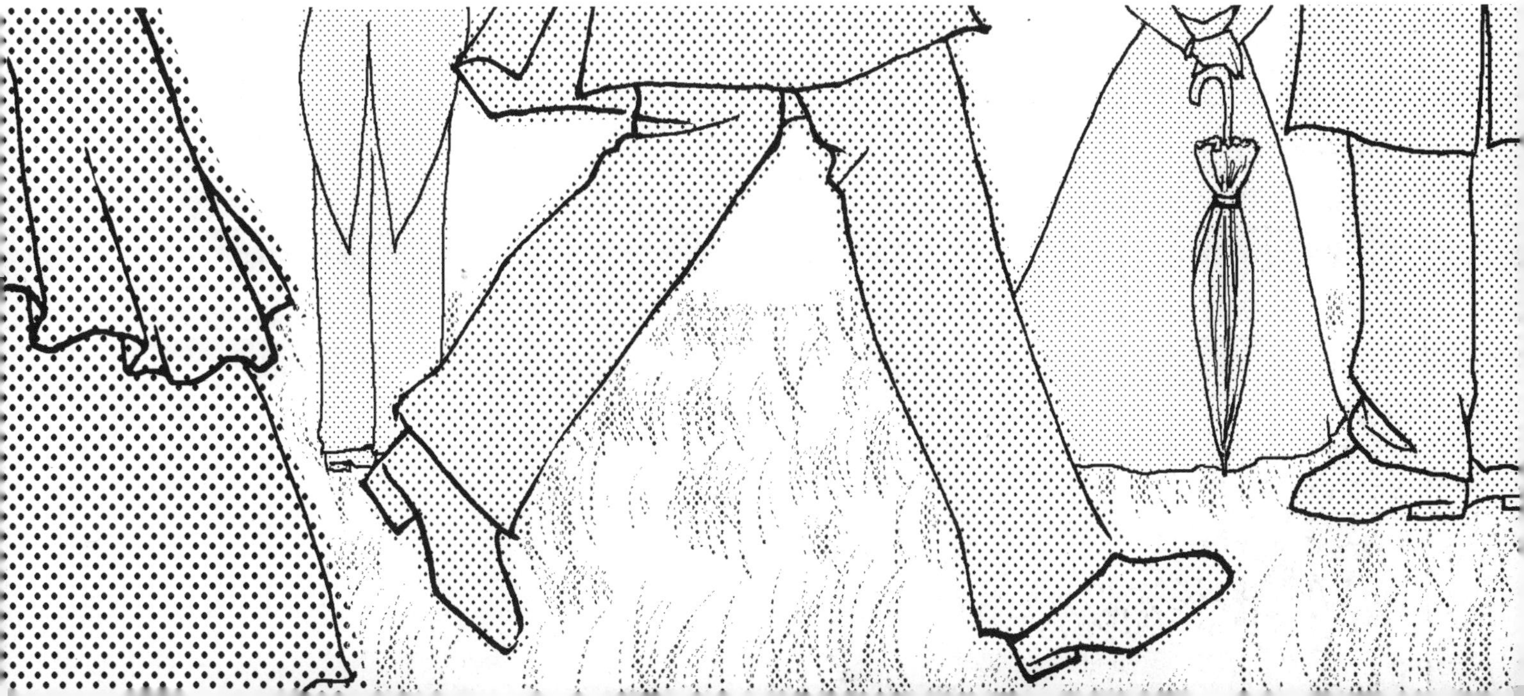

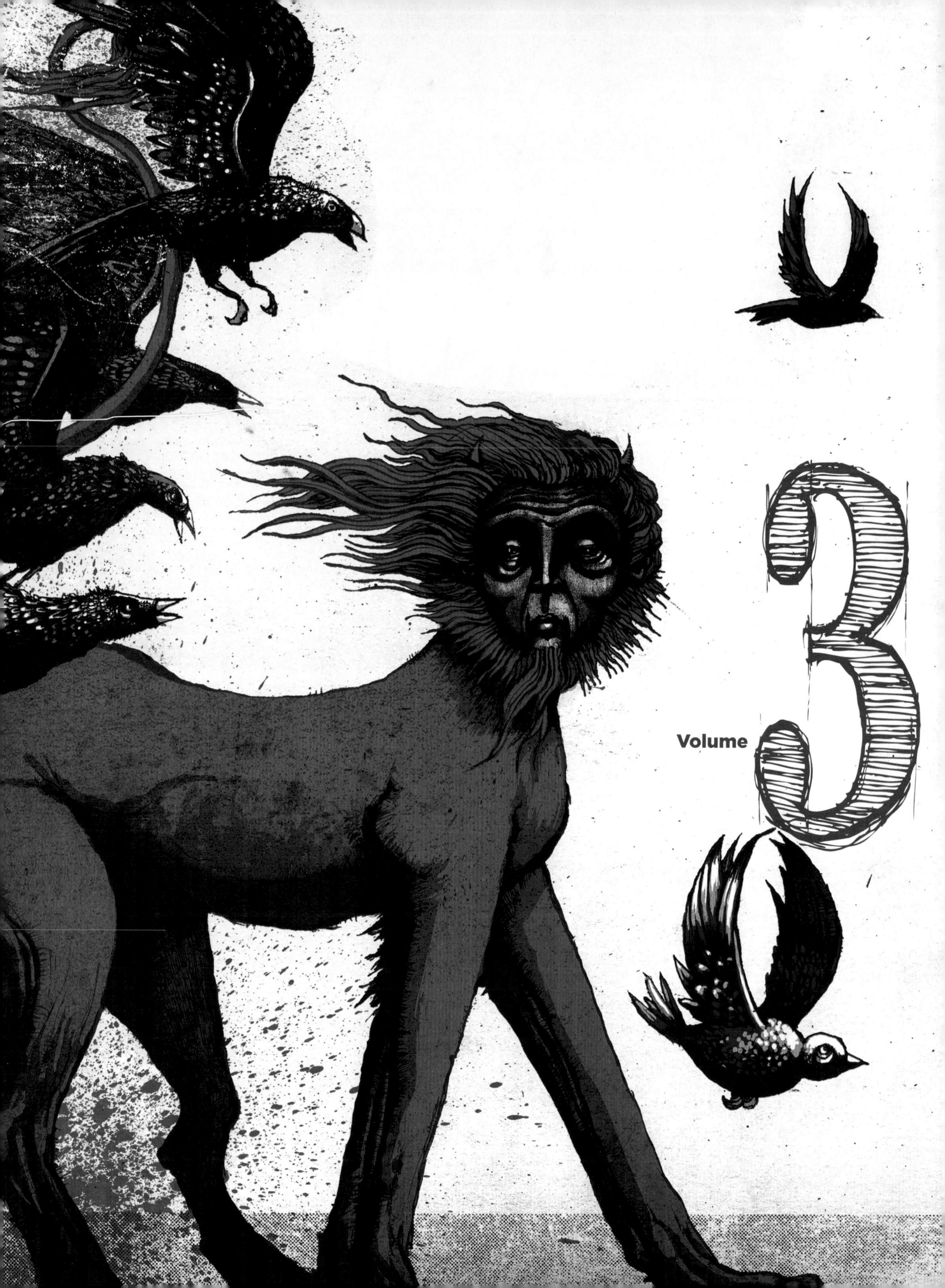
Volume 3

FROM *HEART OF DARKNESS*
TO HEMINGWAY
TO *INFINITE JEST*

the GRAPHIC CANON

Edited by
RUSS KICK

SEVEN STORIES PRESS
New York

For permissions information see page 562.

A SEVEN STORIES PRESS FIRST EDITION

SEVEN STORIES PRESS
140 Watts Street
New York, NY 10013
www.sevenstories.com

College professors may order examination copies of Seven Stories Press titles for a free six-month trial period. To order, visit www.sevenstories.com/textbook or send a fax on school letterhead to (212) 226-1411.

Book design by Stewart Cauley, New York
Cover art by Gustavo Rinaldi
Back cover art by Onsmith
Inside back cover art by Joy Kolitsky

Library of Congress Cataloging-in-Publication Data
The Graphic Canon, volume 3 : from Heart of Darkness to Hemingway to Infinite Jest / Edited by Russ Kick. —A Seven Stories Press First Edition.
pages cm
Includes index.
ISBN 978-1-60980-380-3 (pbk.)
1. Literature—Adaptations.
2. Graphic novels in education.
3. Graphic novels.
I. Kick, Russell.
PN6714.G737 2013
741.5'69—dc23
2012049460

Printed in Hong Kong

9 8 7 6 5 4 3 2 1

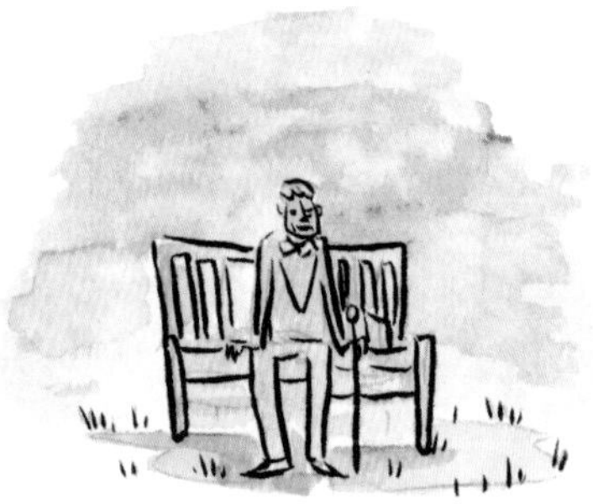

CONTENTS

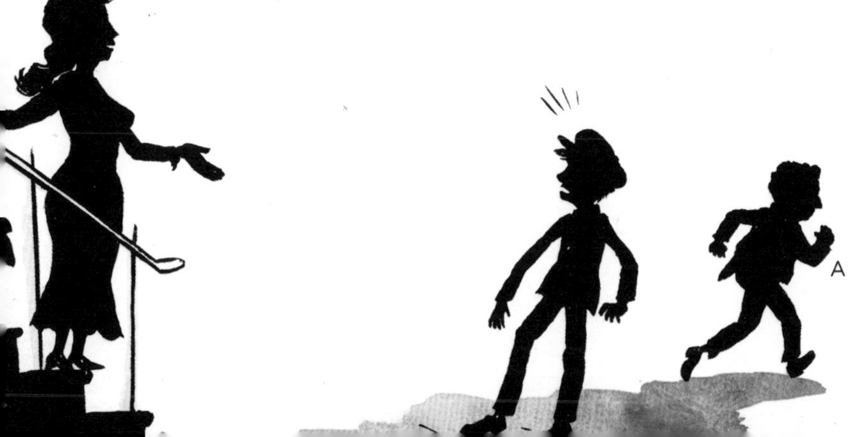

SMASH

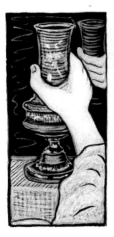

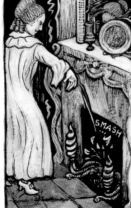

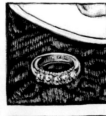

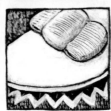

EDITOR'S INTRODUCTION TO VOLUME 3

HERE WE ARE AT THE TWENTIETH CENTURY. IF YOU'VE followed us from a previous volume of *The Graphic Canon*, you'll see that we're going chronologically, with comics artists, illustrators, and a few other types of artists adapting the great works of literature from *The Epic of Gilgamesh* (circa 1000 BCE) to the end of the 1700s in Volume 1, then the entire nineteenth century in Volume 2. If this is your first volume, rest assured that it's the perfect place to begin, a self-contained visual trip through the literature of the twentieth century.

Technically, the proceedings begin with three works published in 1899. But that's not simply because we ran out of room in Volume 2 (which we did). That volume closed tidily with a Civil War story from Ambrose Bierce and a masterpiece of *fin de siècle* decadence from Oscar Wilde. This volume opens appropriately with works that, although they jumped the gun slightly, have more in common with the twentieth century than the preceding one. The techniques, attitudes, and impact of *Heart of Darkness*, *The Awakening*, and *The Interpretation of Dreams* put them squarely in the 1900s. And, really, you couldn't ask for a better, more varied set of artwork to sound the starting gun—Matt Kish's stylized full-page illustrations, Rebecca Migdal's atmospheric comic done in white acrylic on black board, and Tara Seibel's utterly unique combination of illustration, type and hand-lettering, and design and layout.

The first work here truly published in the twentieth century is the "children's classic" *The Wonderful Wizard of Oz* from 1900, represented by yet another approach—dioramas built, photographed, and digitally souped-up by Graham Rawle. It just keeps going from there. We have two men who seem quintessentially nineteenth century, but kept going well into the twentieth: H. G. Wells and Rudyard Kipling. Three extremely varied writers—Jack London, Maxim Gorky, Saki—

keep the century rolling. Then it's onto the Modernists, lots of them. Which of course leads us to the Postmodernists. The Beats are here. As well as Orwell, Nabokov, and Steinbeck. French women of letters are represented by Anaïs Nin and Colette, while Langston Hughes and Zora Neale Hurston bring in the Harlem Renaissance. Black Elk, Kahlil Gibran, Hermann Hesse, and Aldous Huxley provide much-needed doses of spirituality in the often bleak landscape of twentieth-century lit. Magical realism, Existentialism, jazz, Southern Gothic, avant-garde science fiction, hard-boiled detective fiction, war poetry, theoretical physics . . . all this and more appear in these pages.

All three volumes of *The Graphic Canon* were edited simultaneously, as a single project, so what went for the first two books goes for this one: I asked the artists to stay true to the literary works as far as plot, characters, and text, but visually they had free reign. Any style, any media, any approach. Spare. Dense. Lush. Fragmented. Seamless. Experimental. Old school. Monochrome. Saturated. Pen and ink. Markers. Digital. Silk-screened. Painted. Sequential art. Full-page illustrations. Unusual hybrids of words and images. Images without words. And in one case, words without images.

The *Canon* was always meant as an art project, part of the ages-old tradition of visual artists using classic works of literature as their springboard. It was also conceived as a celebration of literature, a way to present dramatic new takes on the greatest stories ever told. It turned into a lot more—a survey of Western literature (with some Asian and indigenous works represented), an encyclopedia of ways to merge images and text, a showcase for some of the best (and often underexposed) comics artists and illustrators. And a kicky examination of love, sex, death, violence, revolution, money, drugs, religion, family, (non)conformity, longing, transcendence, and other aspects of the human condition that literature and art have always wrestled with.

the GRAPHIC CANON   Volume 3

Joseph Conrad

ILLUSTRATIONS BY **Matt Kish**

VOLUME 3 OF *THE GRAPHIC CANON* IS ALL ABOUT the twentieth century, and *Heart of Darkness* is the perfect way to start: Its publication history, style, and themes make it a bridge between the nineteenth and twentieth centuries. It was first serialized in a British magazine in 1899, then published in book form in 1902. Written by one of the great English-language novelists, the Polish-born Joseph Conrad (for whom English was a third language, after French and Polish), it follows Charles Marlow as he sails down an African river—presumably the Congo—on a mission for a Belgian trading company. He's on a quest to find the company's main ivory trader in the region, the charismatic Renaissance man Kurtz, whose communications with headquarters have become odd—and who may or may not be very ill—and to bring him and the ivory back to home base.

At the time, the area was laughably known as the Congo Free State but was actually a colony of Belgium's King Leopold II, who had elaborately deceived the international community in order to bring this large chunk of central Africa under his personal control. He proceeded to enslave the population, forcing them to harvest ivory and rubber. Men, women, and children who didn't meet their quotas had their hands cut off. Women and girls were raped with impunity. Whole villages were uprooted and forced to resettle. Conrad based the novella on his own experiences and observations during a six-month stint traveling by foot and riverboat in the Congo.

The work he produced is complex, layered, and ambiguous, leading to numerous interpretations and endless debate. Although it deals with atrocities, it's not a straightforward tut-tutting. The tale is told by a nameless narrator, who is hearing it from Marlow himself, as they and three others ride in a boat along the Thames. Thus we have two levels of narration. How do we know the accuracy of what Marlow is telling us? And how do we know that it's what Marlow is really saying, since we're actually hearing it relayed by the narrator, who claims to be quoting Marlow? Because of this unreliability, and other reasons, *Heart of Darkness* is seen as a forerunner of Modernism and Postmodernism. Some observers feel that the book at its core is racist, colonialist, and sexist, but maybe it's just the flawed Marlow who is those things. There's no doubt that one of its themes is the darkness that lies within all so-called civilized people.

Heart of Darkness formed the basis for the classic film *Apocalypse Now*, which transferred the setting from colonial Africa to wartime Vietnam and Cambodia, changing a number of plot elements, most notably the ending. Now librarian and self-trained artist Matt Kish presents a new visual take on this harsh tale. Matt originally caused a sensation when, with no fanfare and simply for his own enjoyment, he decided to create an illustration for each page of *Moby-Dick*. (They have since been collected into a hefty book from Tin House, and you can see a dozen of them in Volume 2 of *The Graphic Canon*.) When I approached Matt about doing something new for this anthology, he enthusiastically wanted to apply a similar approach to another of his favorite works. He has since gone on to create an illustration for each of *Heart of Darkness*'s hundred pages, but the ten stunning images you see here are the first of his original creations.

SOURCE

Conrad, Joseph. *Heart of Darkness: Complete, Authoritative Text with Biographical and Historical Contexts, Critical History, and Essays from Five Contemporary Critical Perspectives. 2nd ed.* Edited by Ross C. Murfin. Boston: Bedford Books, 1996.

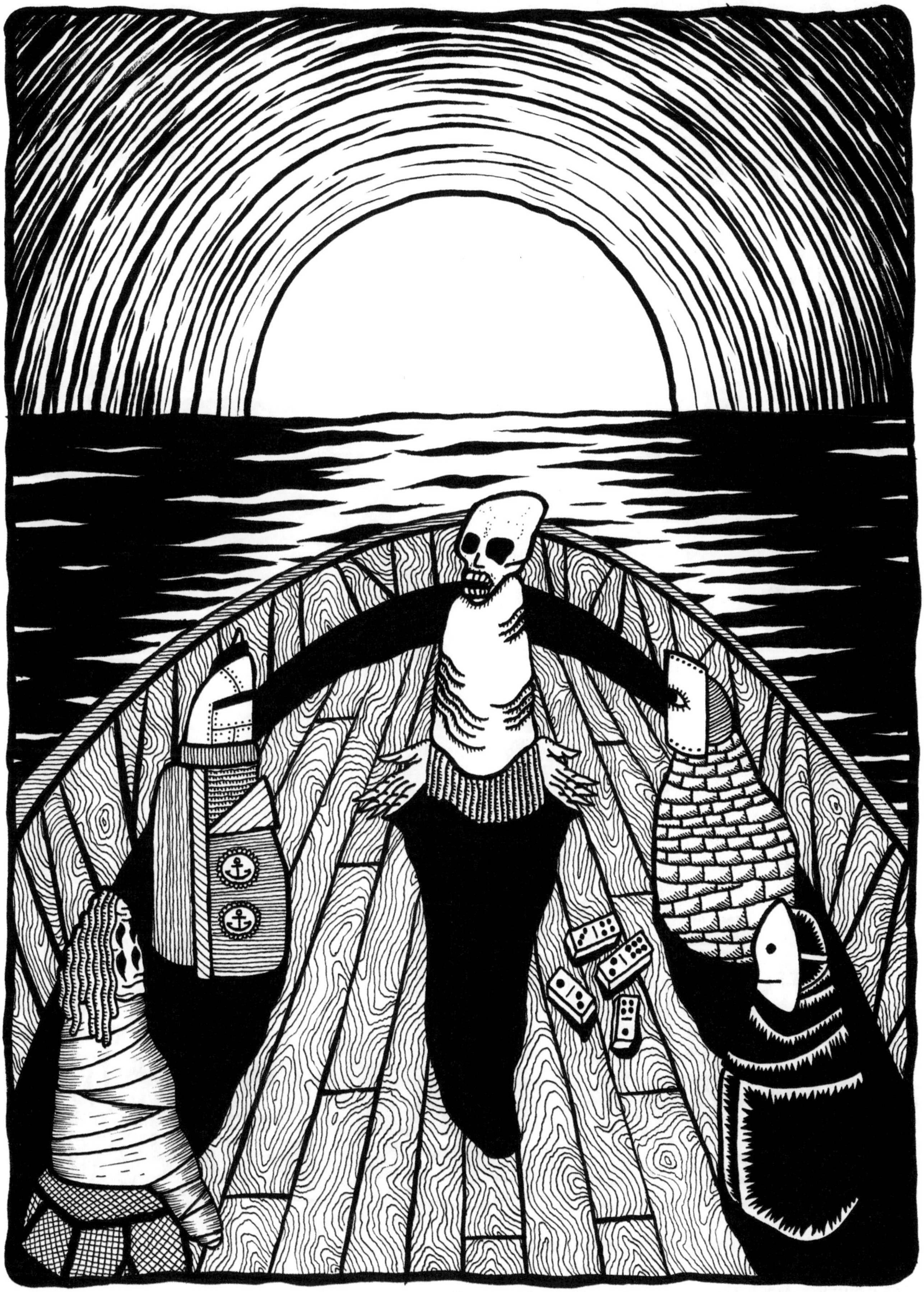

"'And this also,' said Marlow suddenly, 'has been one of the dark places of the earth.'" [page 3]

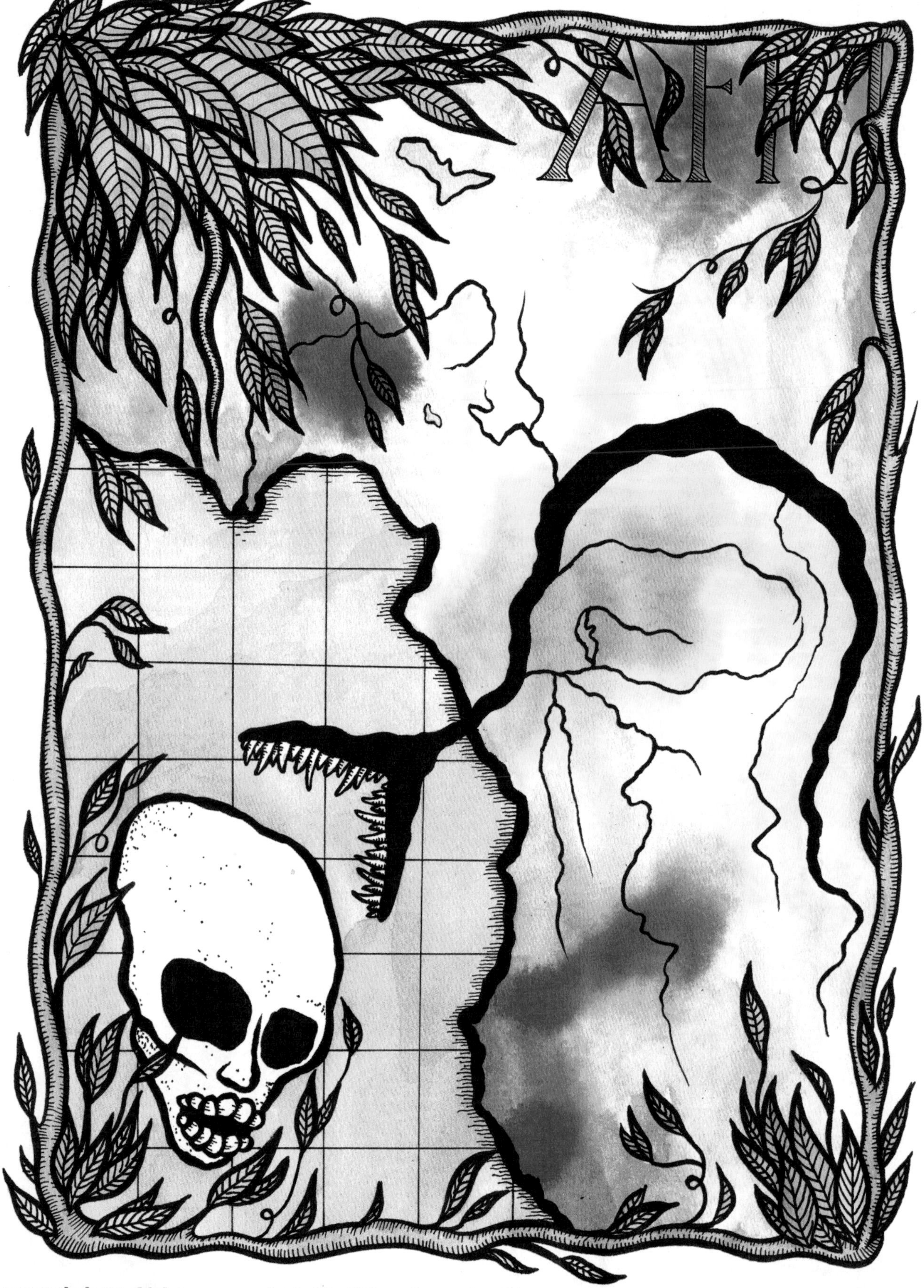

". . . on one end a large shining map, marked with all the colours of a rainbow. There was a vast amount of red—good to see at any time, because one knows that some real work is done in there, a deuce of a lot of blue, a little green, smears of orange, and, on the East Coast, a purple patch, to show where the jolly pioneers of progress drink the jolly lager-beer. However, I wasn't going into any of these. I was going into the yellow. Dead in the centre. And the river was there—fascinating—deadly—like a snake." [page 10]

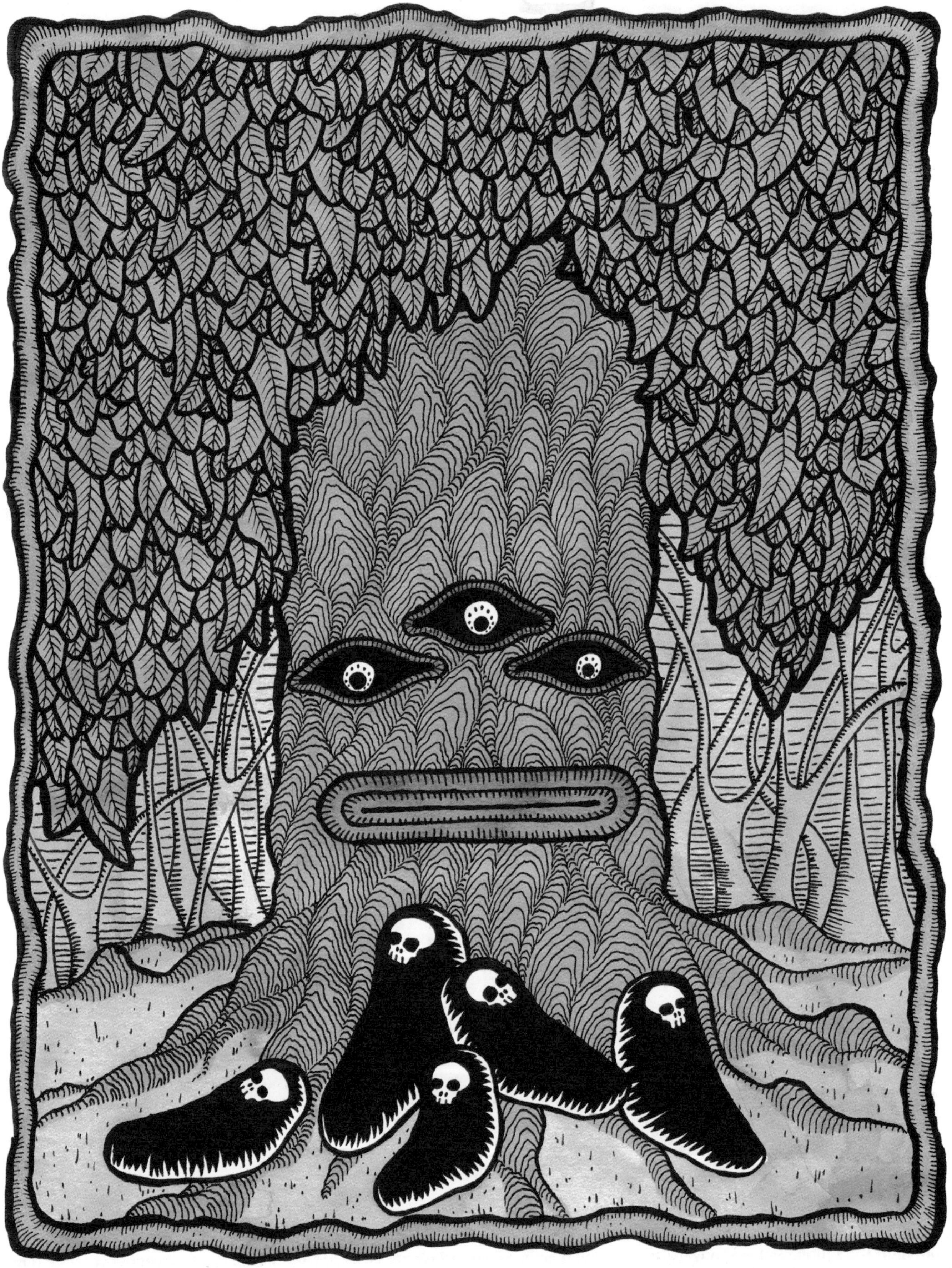

"They were dying slowly—it was very clear. They were not enemies, they were not criminals, they were nothing earthly now—nothing but black shadows of disease and starvation, lying confusedly in the greenish gloom." [page 19]

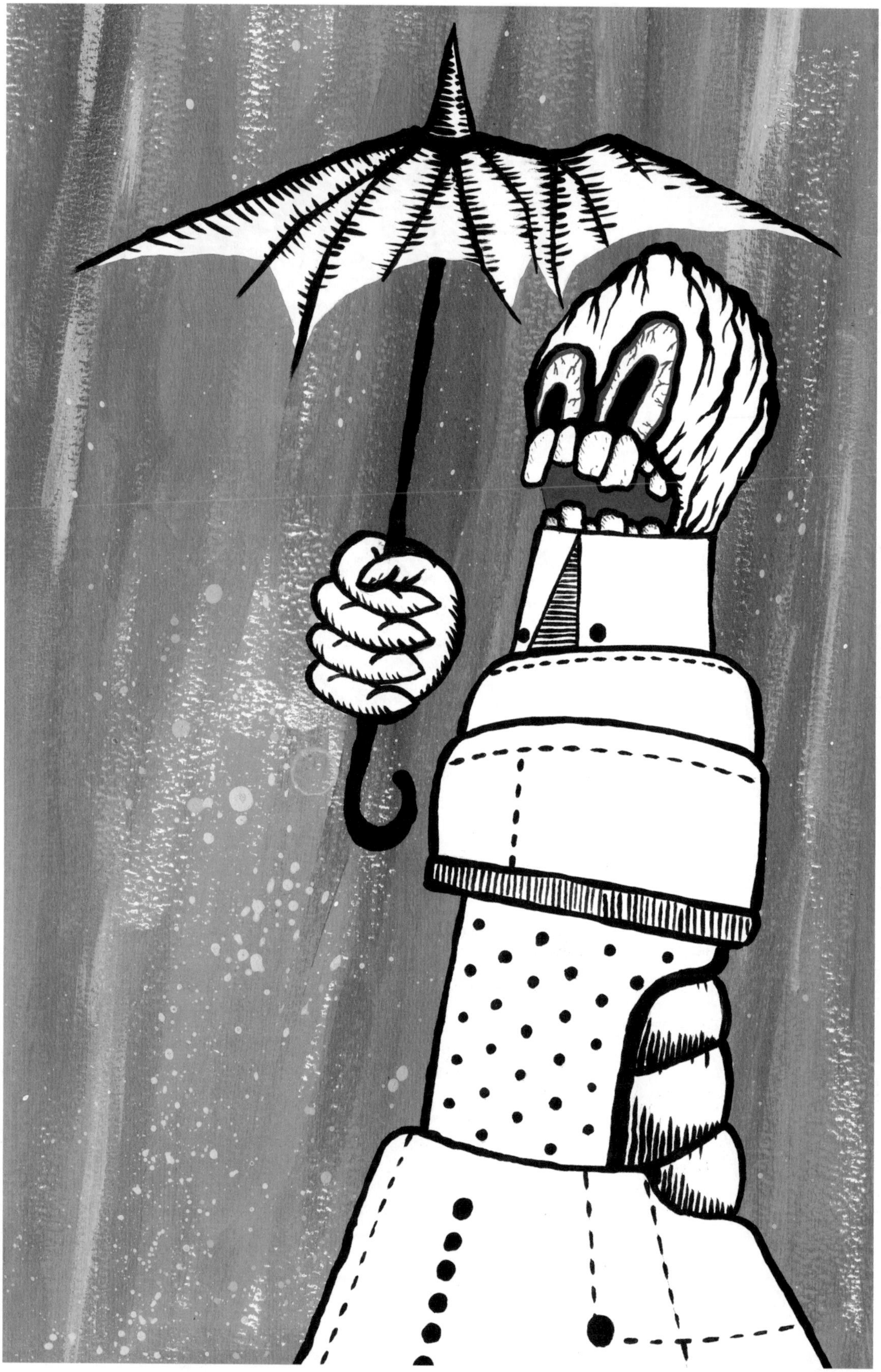

"When near the buildings I met a white man, in such an unexpected elegance of get-up that in the first moment I took him for a sort of vision. I saw a high starched collar, white cuffs, a light alpaca jacket, snowy trousers, a clean necktie, and varnished boots. No hat. Hair parted, brushed, oiled, under a green-lined parasol held in a big white hand. He was amazing . . ." [page 20]

"Going up that river was like travelling back to the earliest beginnings of the world, when vegetation rioted on the earth and the big trees were kings. An empty stream, a great silence, an impenetrable forest. The air was warm, thick, heavy, sluggish. There was no joy in the brilliance of sunshine. The long stretches of the waterway ran on, deserted, into the gloom of over-shadowed distances." [page 41]

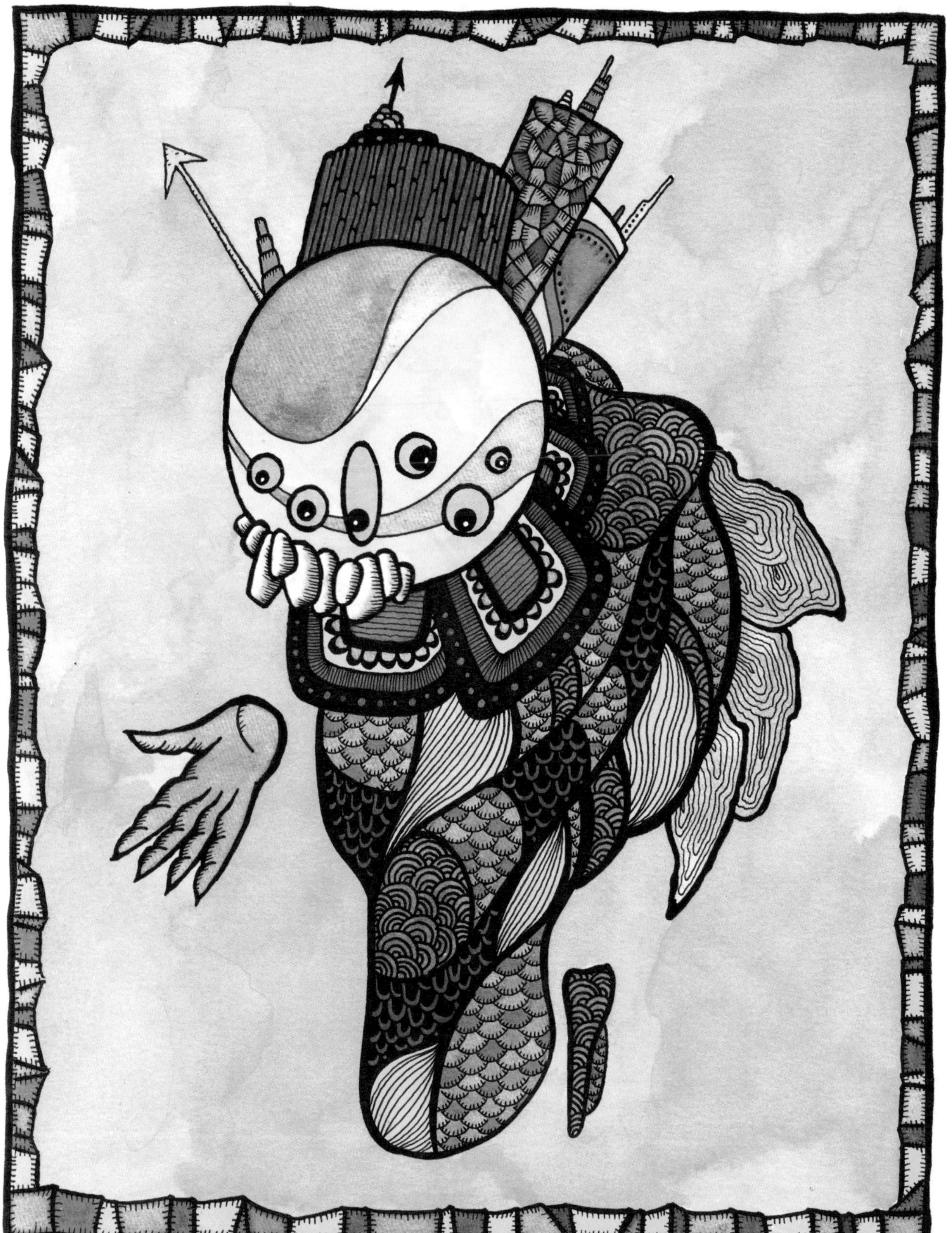

"He looked like a harlequin. His clothes had been made of some stuff that was brown holland probably, but it was covered with patches all over, with bright patches, blue, red, and yellow—patches on the back, patches on the front, patches on elbows, on knees; coloured binding around his jacket, scarlet edging at the bottom of his trousers; and the sun-shine made him look extremely gay and wonderfully neat withal, because you could see how beautifully all this patching had been done. A beardless, boyish face, very fair, no features to speak of, nose peeling, little blue eyes, smiles and frowns chasing each other over that open countenance like sunshine and shadow on a wind-swept plain." [page 67]

"'You can't judge Mr. Kurtz as you would an ordinary man.'" [page 71]

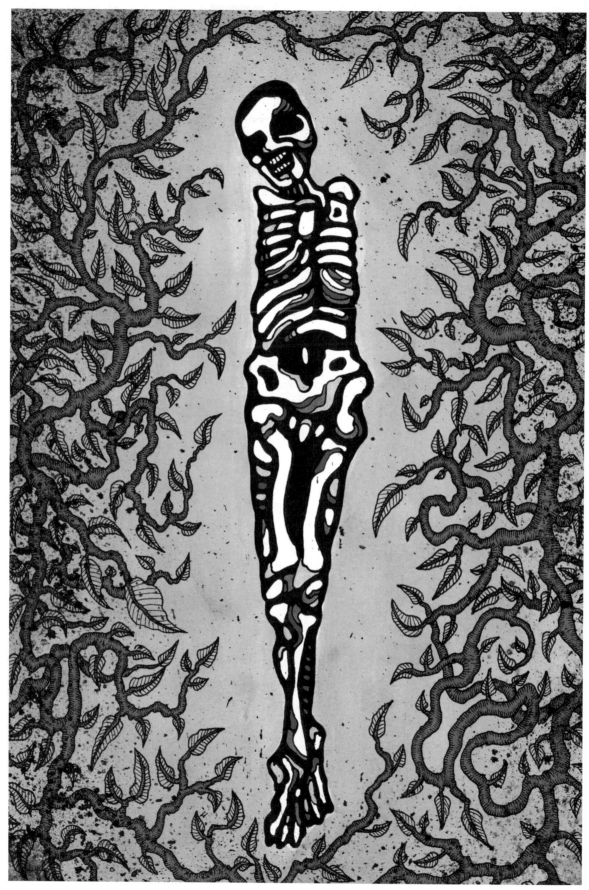

"'The horror! The horror!'" [page 90]

HEART OF DARKNESS JOSEPH CONRAD MATT KISH

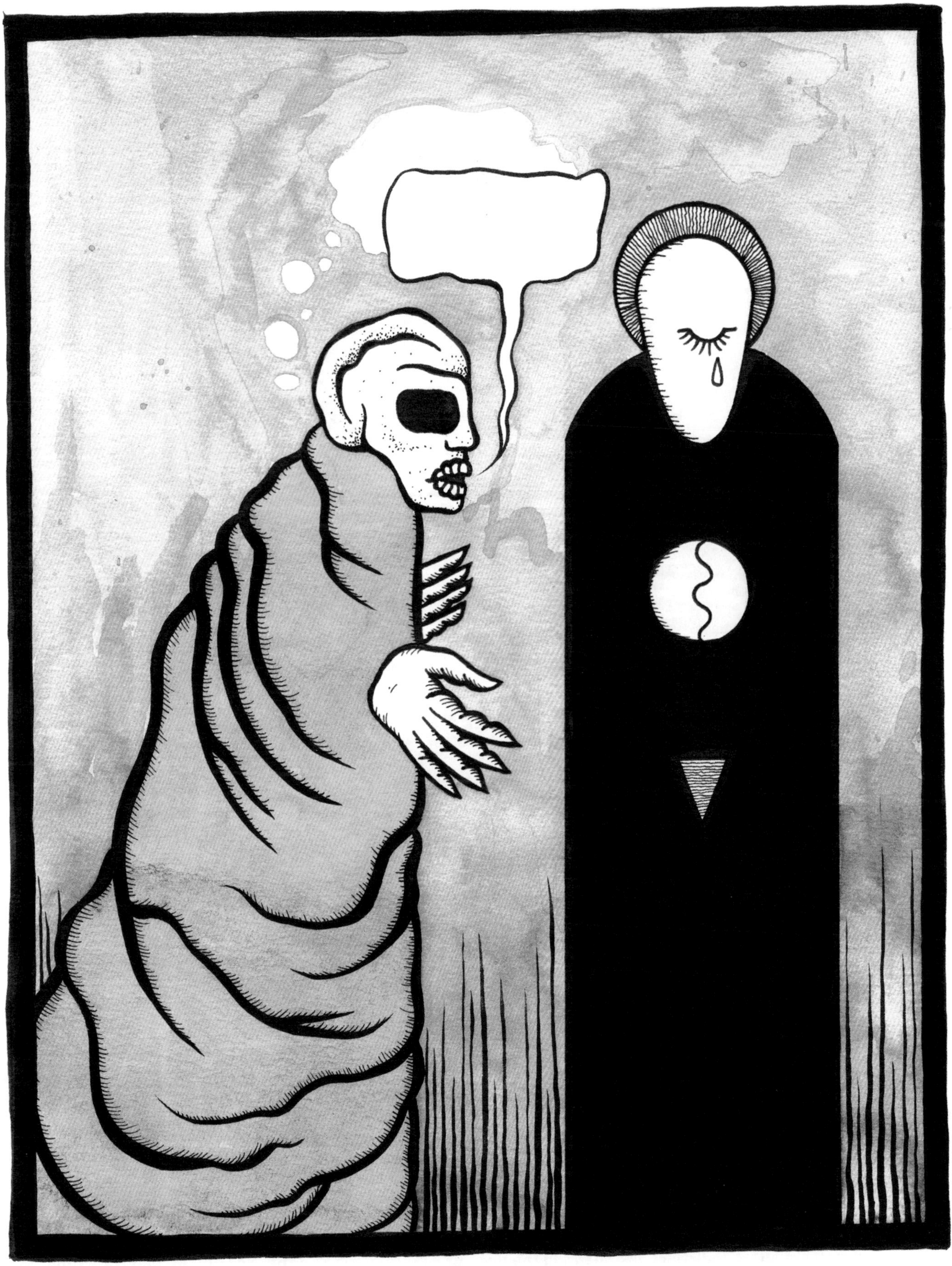

"'His last word—to live with,' she insisted. 'Don't you understand I loved him—I loved him—I loved him!'
I pulled myself together and spoke slowly.
'The last word he pronounced was—your name.'"
[page 99]

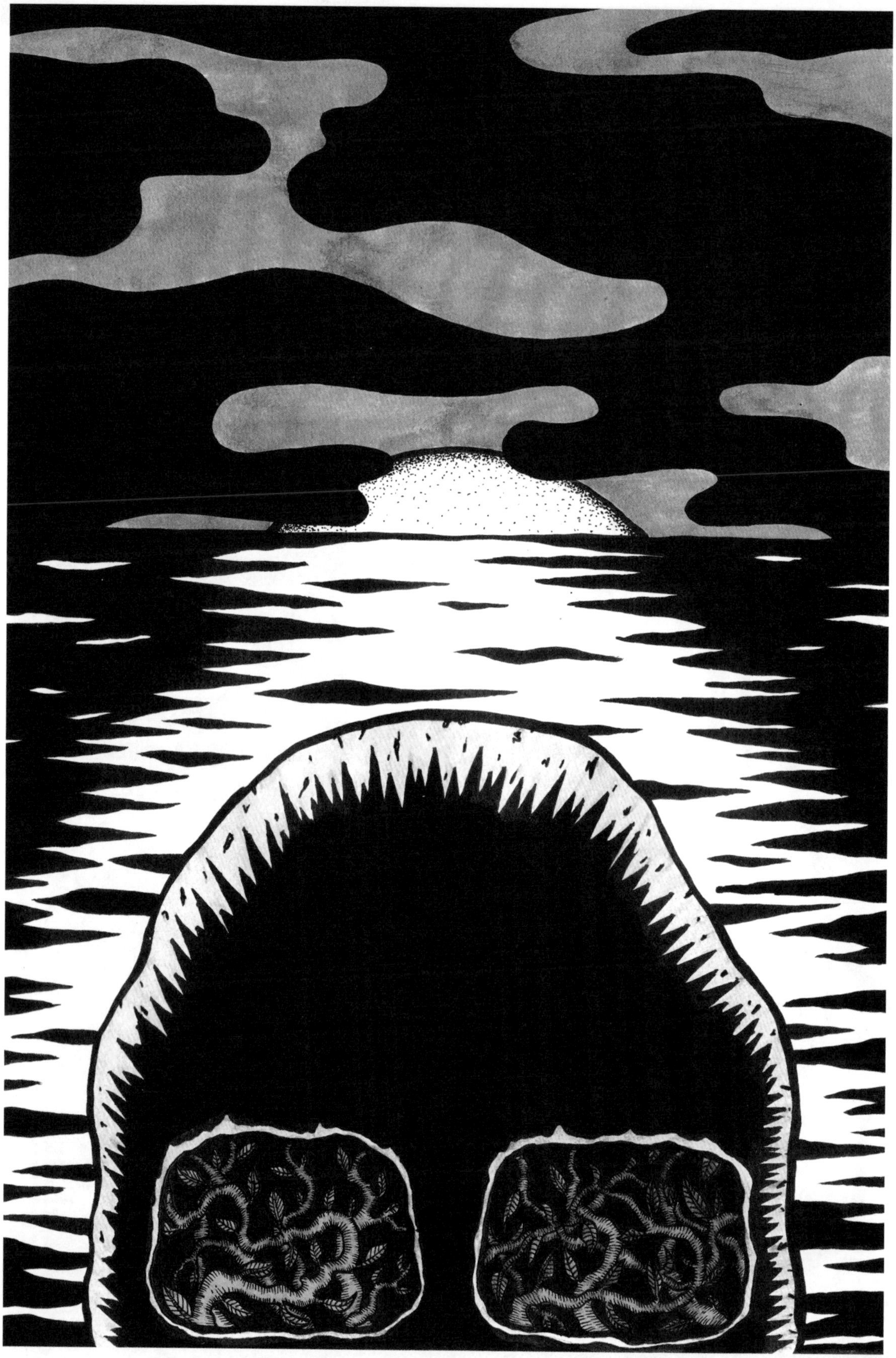

Marlow ceased, and sat apart, indistinct and silent, in the pose of a meditating Buddha. Nobody moved for a time. "We have lost the first of the ebb," said the Director suddenly. I raised my head. The offing was barred by a black bank of clouds, and the tranquil waterway leading to the uttermost ends of the earth flowed sombre under an overcast sky—seemed to lead into the heart of an immense darkness. [page 100]

The Awakening

Kate Chopin

ART/ADAPTATION BY **Rebecca Migdal**

KATE CHOPIN HAD QUITE A LITERARY CAREER GOING in the 1890s. A St. Louis native transplanted to New Orleans, her scads of short stories—many of which focus on women searching for identity and independence—were published in the country's most prestigious magazines and lauded by critics. She wasn't afraid to inject some controversial material into her work either, writing memorably about a child of mixed race, a woman surprised to find herself relieved upon hearing of her husband's death, even some subtle lesbian subtext in a few stories (too subtle for most people of that era to pick up on). But she stepped over society's line with her second novel, *The Awakening*.

Published in 1899, it tells of Edna Pontellier, who is dissatisfied and upset with her roles as wife to a dickish husband and as mother of two children. She expands her vistas in various ways, including welcoming the attentions of a certain charmer. Critics, the public, and even some fellow writers reacted with shock and disgust. They savaged the book as if it were the foulest pornography, and Chopin's career was destroyed. Her publisher canceled her upcoming collection of short stories. She never wrote another novel, and only a few of her stories were published afterward. This ridiculous turn of events damaged her literary reputation, though it has since recovered quite a bit. Her best stories are widely anthologized, and *The Awakening* is now recognized as a classic. Still, Chopin has never quite gotten the recognition she deserves. One of her biographers, Per Seyersted, wrote:

She was the first woman writer in her country to accept passion as a legitimate subject for serious, outspoken fiction. Revolting against tradition and authority; with a daring which we can hardly fathom today; with an uncompromising honesty and no trace of sensationalism, she undertook to give the unsparing truth about woman's submerged life. She was something of a pioneer in the amoral treatment of sexuality, of divorce, and of woman's urge for an existential authenticity. She is in many respects a modern writer, particularly in her awareness of the complexities of truth and the complications of freedom.

Chopin's fate has always bothered me greatly, and I was overjoyed when the multi-talented Rebecca Migdal—comics artist, performance artist, singer-songwriter, filmmaker, art director—chose to adapt *The Awakening* in full. Well, at fourteen pages it had to be somewhat abridged—or shall we say "streamlined"?—but you still get the story from beginning to upsetting end. And you get it in Rebecca's gorgeous, atmospheric treatment. She says:

It has long been my own aspiration to create work with honesty and realism, in particular from a feminine perspective, and with a touch of otherworldly magic; in illustrating Chopin I have been privileged to sit at the feet of a master.

I chose to employ the technique of painting in white acrylic on blackboard for several reasons. First, the results mimic somewhat the look of aquatint etching, a process I adore, and I hoped this would lend a historical quality to the look of the art. Secondly, I liked the idea of the figures emerging from the dark ground, just as Edna is emerging into greater consciousness throughout the story. And like Chopin's masterwork, the tiny paintings are dark and finely modeled. In allowing certain details to show themselves while others recede into blackness, I was able to echo Chopin's way of touching delicately on thoughts and objects and expressions—casting pinpoints of light here and there, in order to reveal a world much stranger and more marvelous than the world of the obvious and the expected in which we walk day by day, blind to the tragedies and passions of those around us.

SOURCES

The Kate Chopin International Society, http://www.katechopin.org.

Seyersted, Per. *Kate Chopin: A Critical Biography*. Baton Rouge: Louisiana State University Press, 1969.

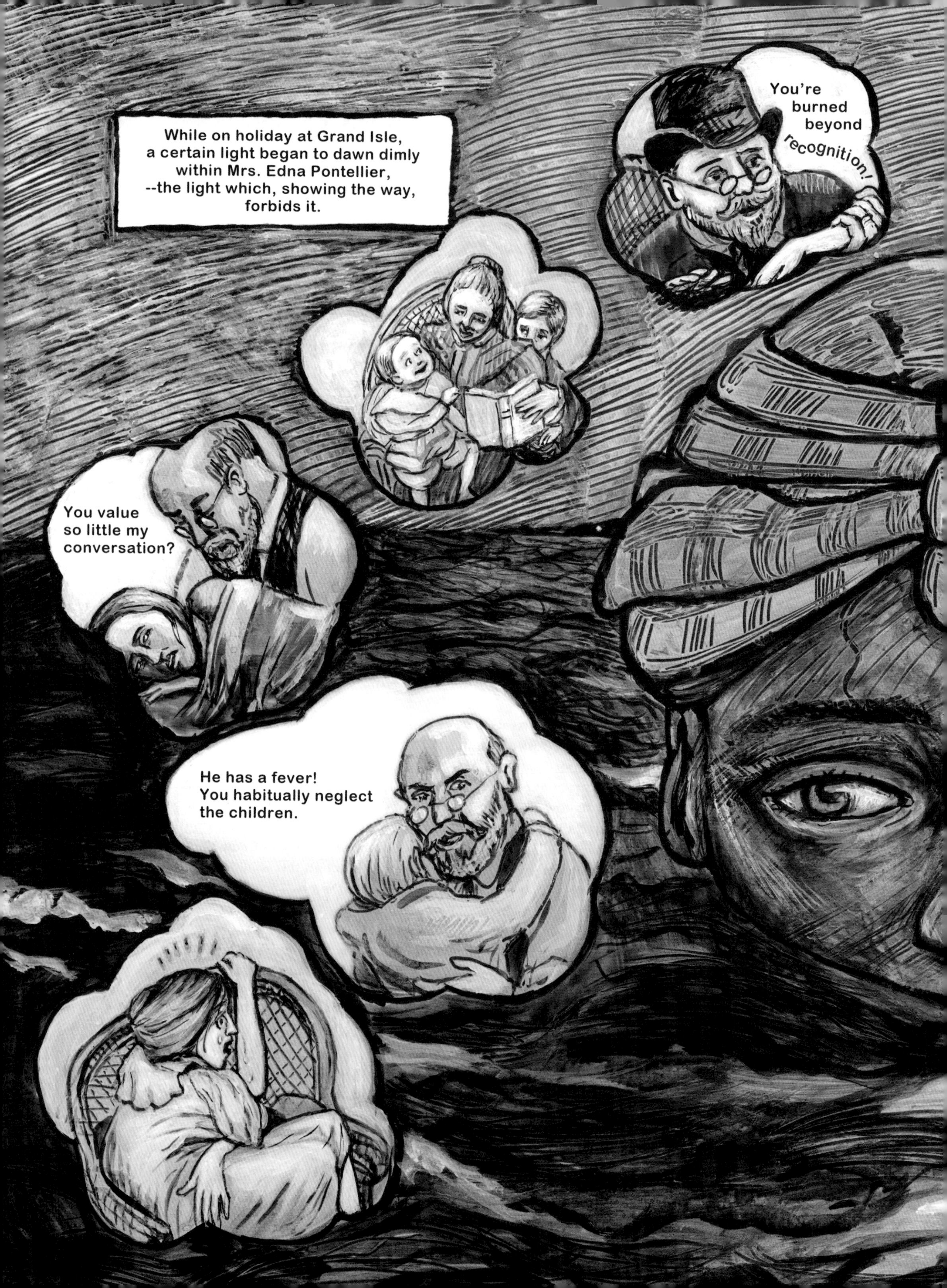
While on holiday at Grand Isle, a certain light began to dawn dimly within Mrs. Edna Pontellier, --the light which, showing the way, forbids it.
You're burned beyond recognition!
You value so little my conversation?
He has a fever! You habitually neglect the children.

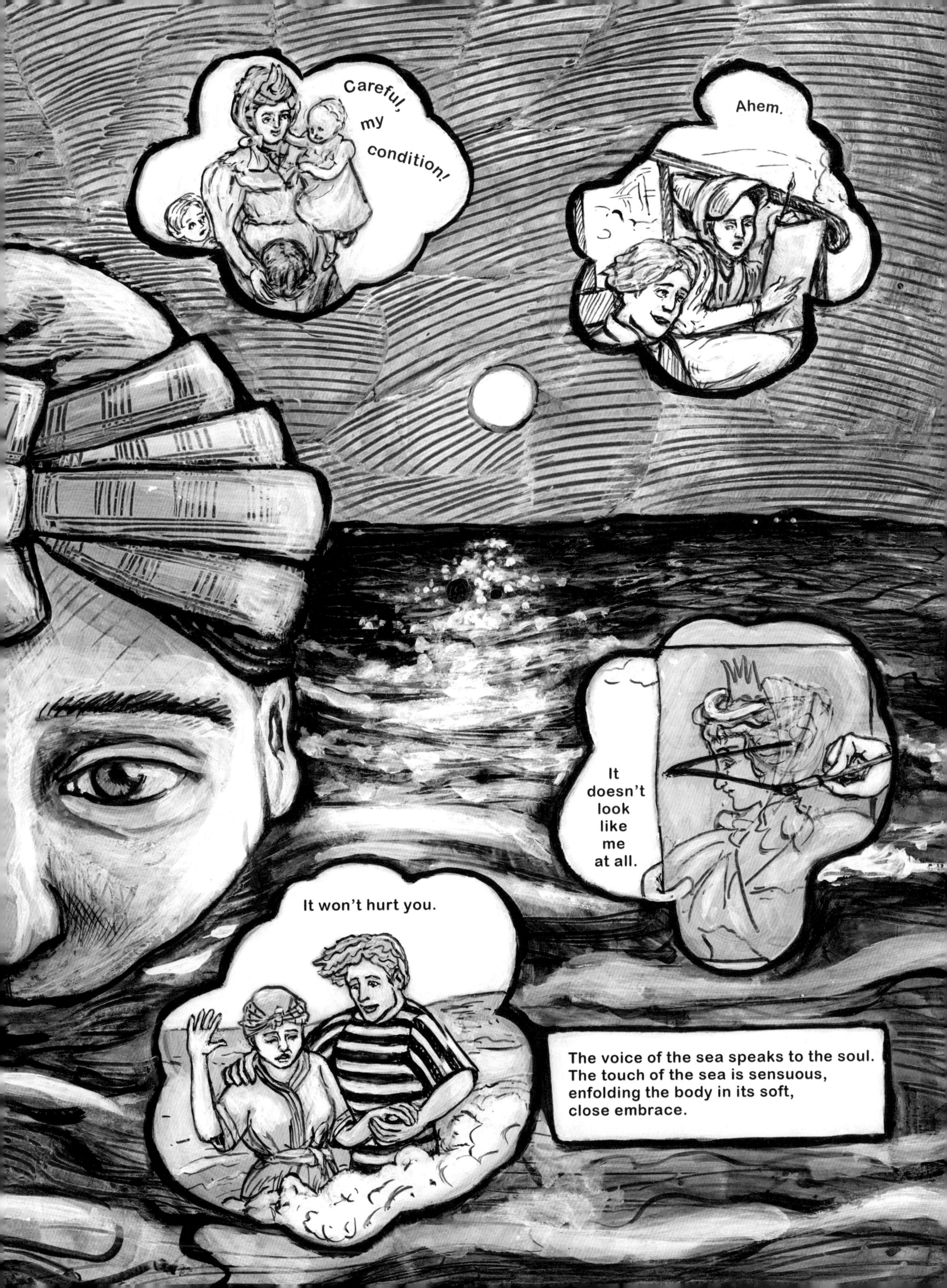
Careful, my condition!
Ahem.
It doesn't look like me at all.
It won't hurt you.
The voice of the sea speaks to the soul. The touch of the sea is sensuous, enfolding the body in its soft, close embrace.

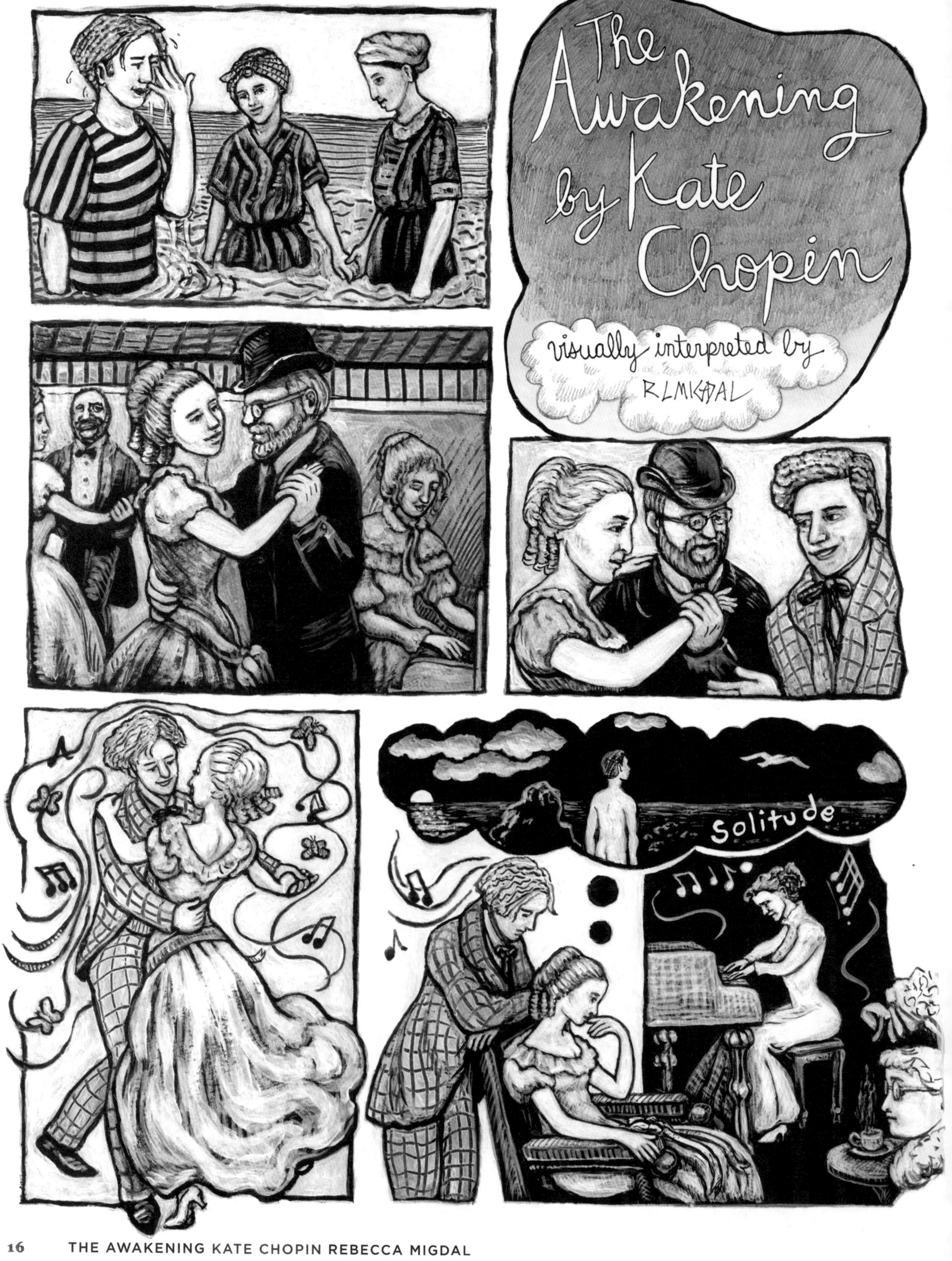
The Awakening by Kate Chopin
visually interpreted by
RLMIGDAL
solitude

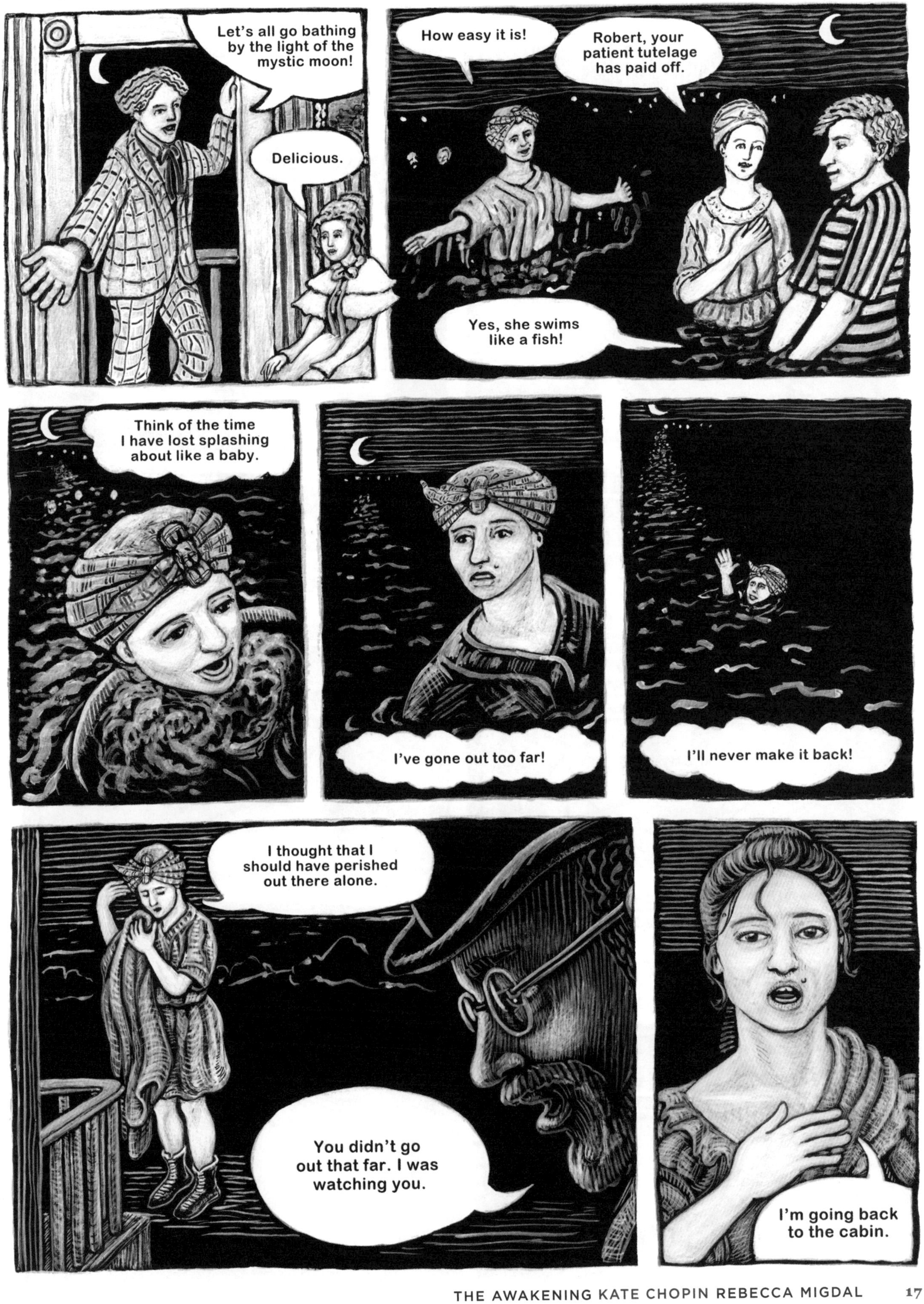
Let's all go bathing by the light of the mystic moon!
Delicious.
How easy it is!
Robert, your patient tutelage has paid off.
Yes, she swims like a fish!
Think of the time I have lost splashing about like a baby.
I've gone out too far!
I'll never make it back!
I thought that I should have perished out there alone.
You didn't go out that far. I was watching you.
I'm going back to the cabin.

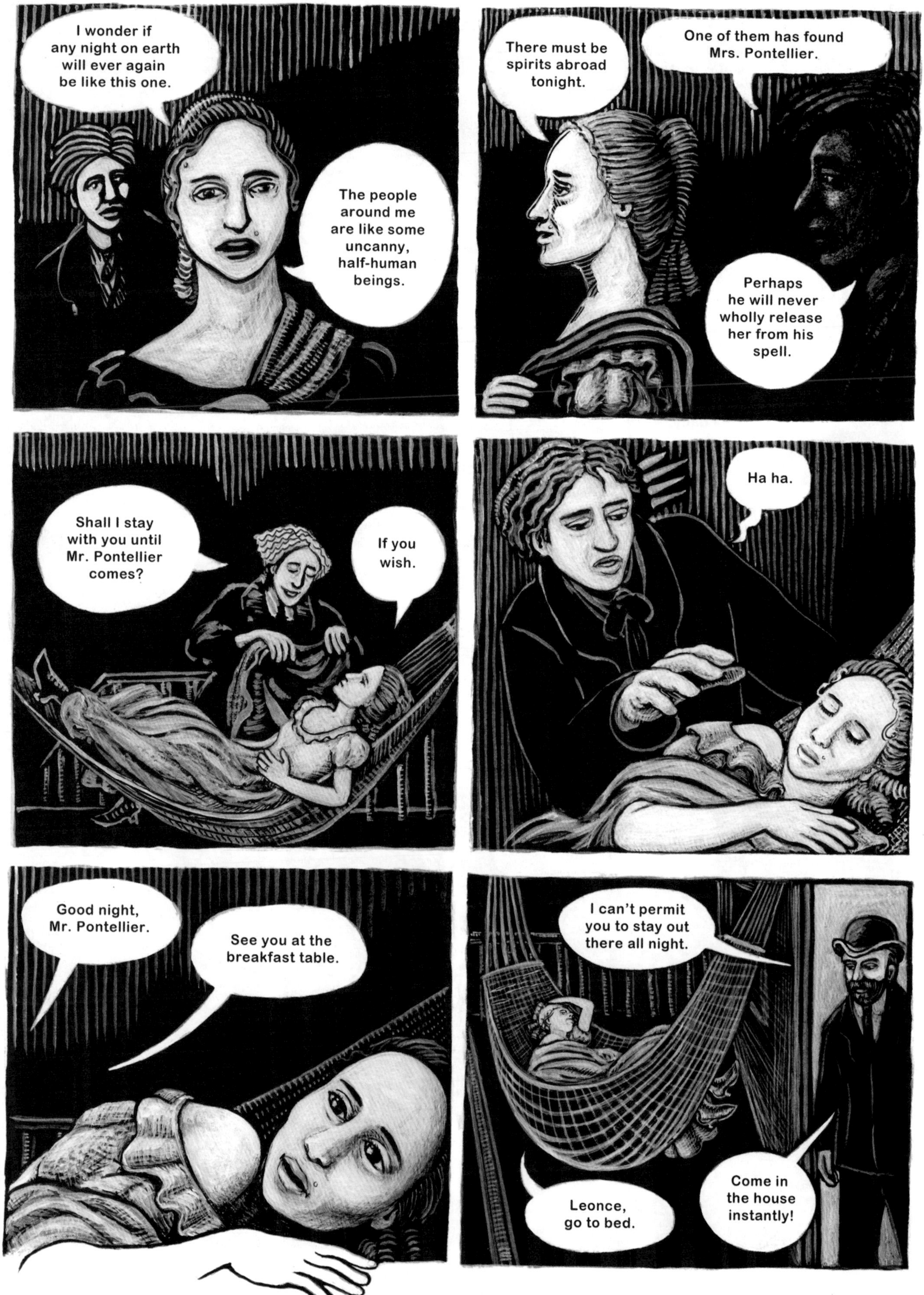
I wonder if any night on earth will ever again be like this one.
The people around me are like some uncanny, half-human beings.
There must be spirits abroad tonight.
One of them has found Mrs. Pontellier.
Perhaps he will never wholly release her from his spell.
Shall I stay with you until Mr. Pontellier comes?
If you wish.
Ha ha.
Good night, Mr. Pontellier.
See you at the breakfast table.
I can't permit you to stay out there all night.
Leonce, go to bed.
Come in the house instantly!

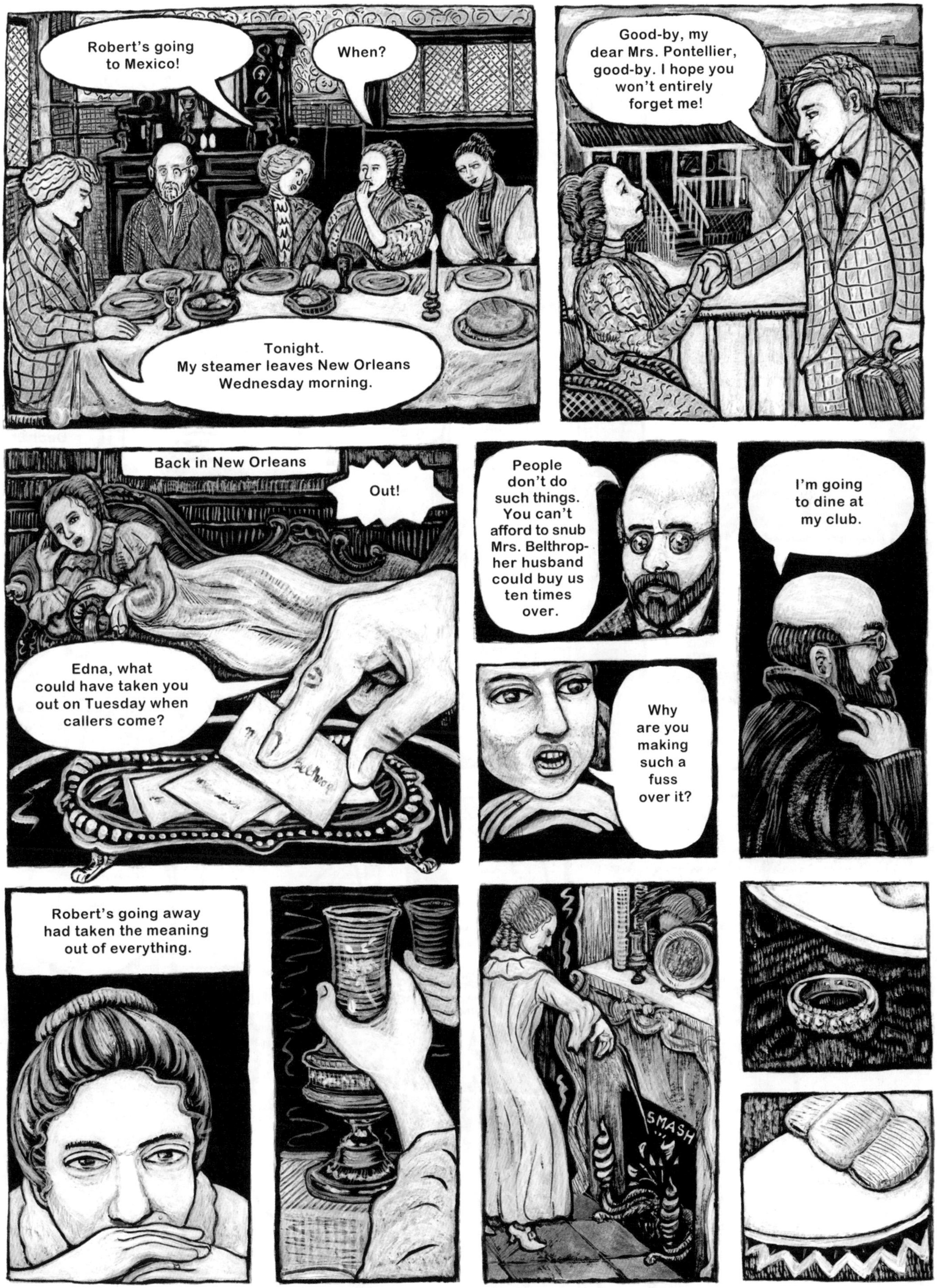
Robert's going to Mexico!
When?
Tonight. My steamer leaves New Orleans Wednesday morning.
Good-by, my dear Mrs. Pontellier, good-by. I hope you won't entirely forget me!
Back in New Orleans
Out!
Edna, what could have taken you out on Tuesday when callers come?
People don't do such things. You can't afford to snub Mrs. Belthrop- her husband could buy us ten times over.
Why are you making such a fuss over it?
I'm going to dine at my club.
Robert's going away had taken the meaning out of everything.
SMASH

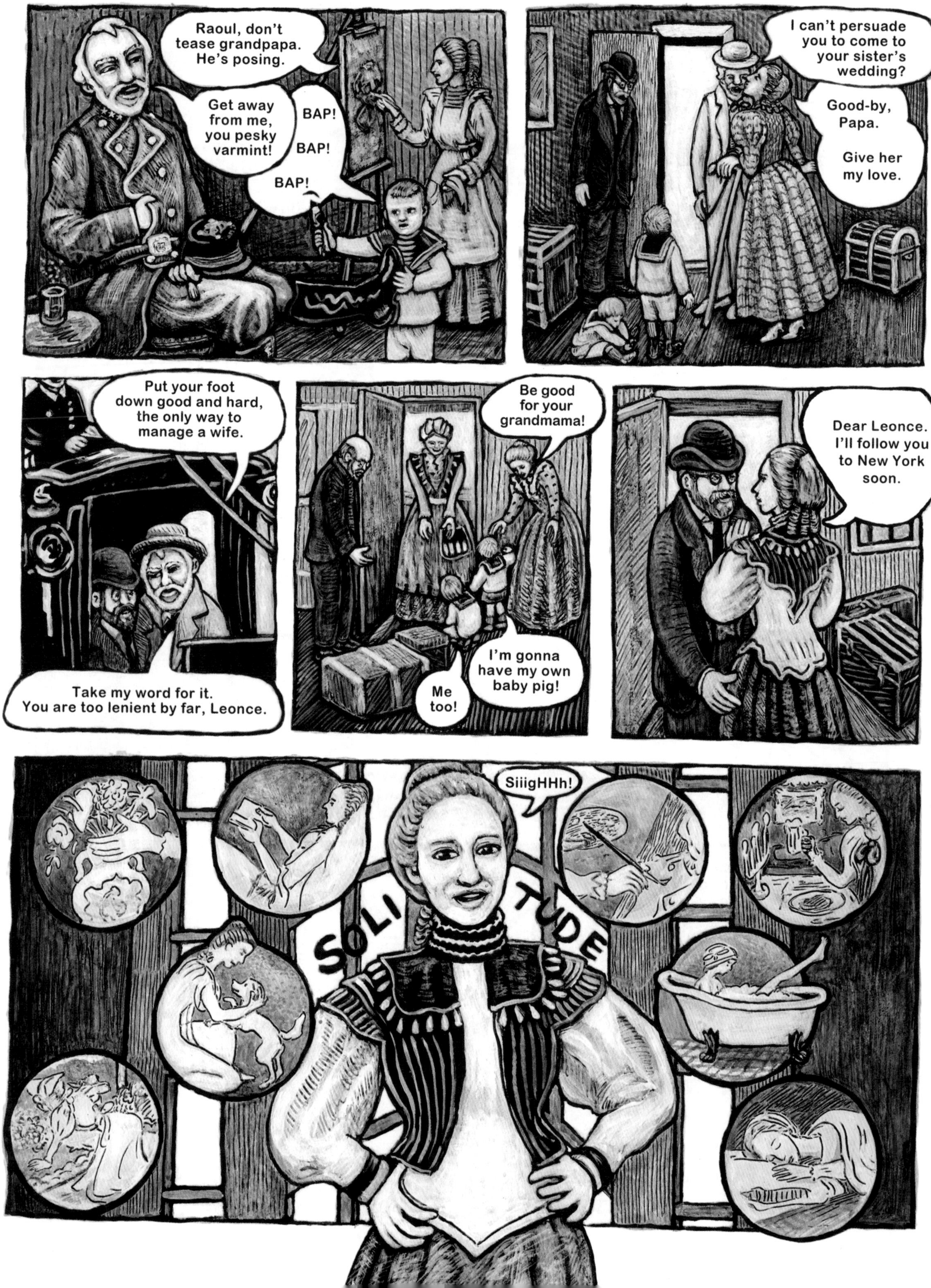
Raoul, don't tease grandpapa. He's posing.
Get away from me, you pesky varmint!
BAP!
BAP!
BAP!
I can't persuade you to come to your sister's wedding?
Good-by, Papa.
Give her my love.
Put your foot down good and hard, the only way to manage a wife.
Take my word for it. You are too lenient by far, Leonce.
Be good for your grandmama!
I'm gonna have my own baby pig!
Me too!
Dear Leonce. I'll follow you to New York soon.
SiiigHHh!
SOLI TUDE

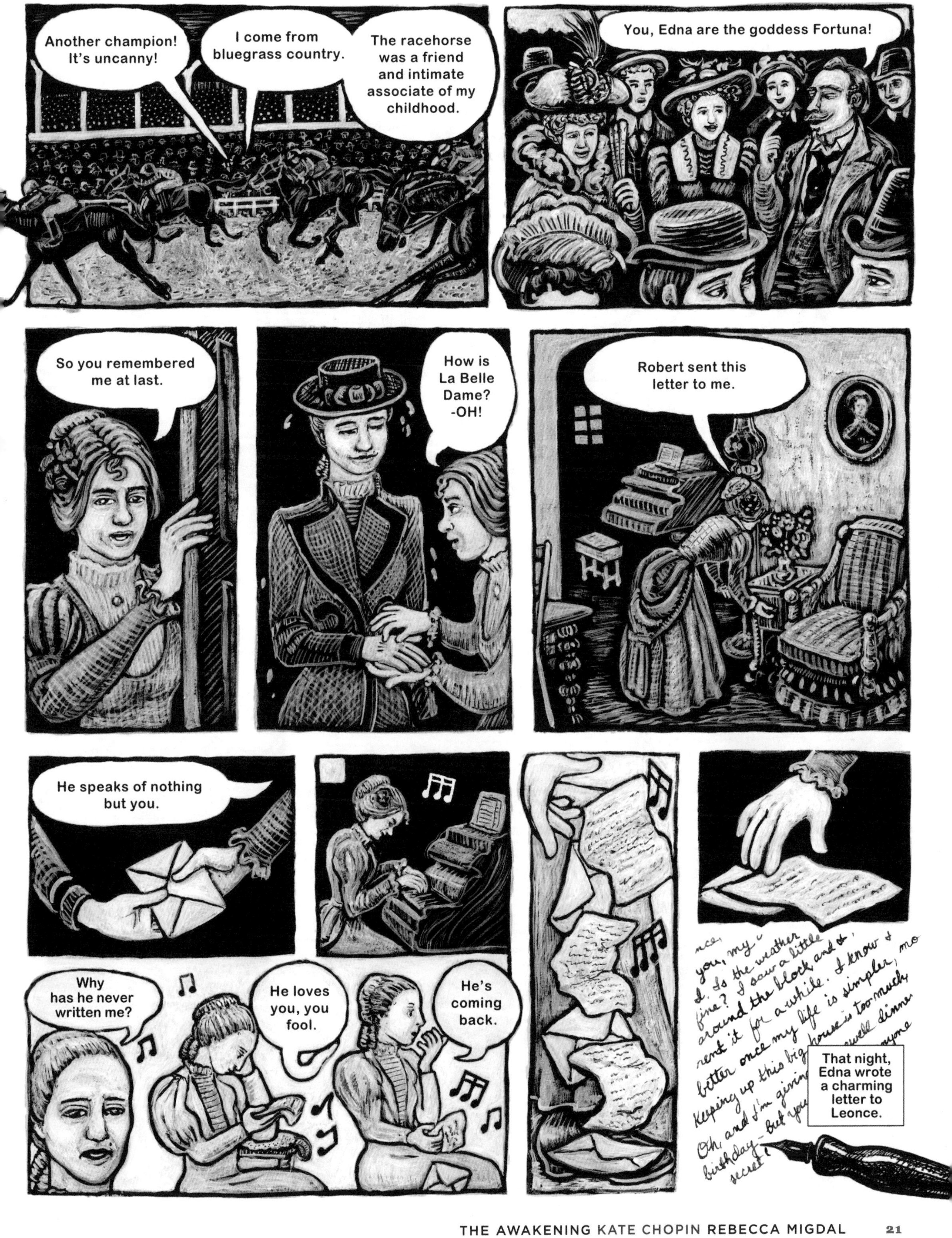
Another champion! It's uncanny!
I come from bluegrass country.
The racehorse was a friend and intimate associate of my childhood.
You, Edna are the goddess Fortuna!
So you remembered me at last.
How is La Belle Dame? -OH!
Robert sent this letter to me.
He speaks of nothing but you.
Why has he never written me?
He loves you, you fool.
He's coming back.
That night, Edna wrote a charming letter to Leonce.

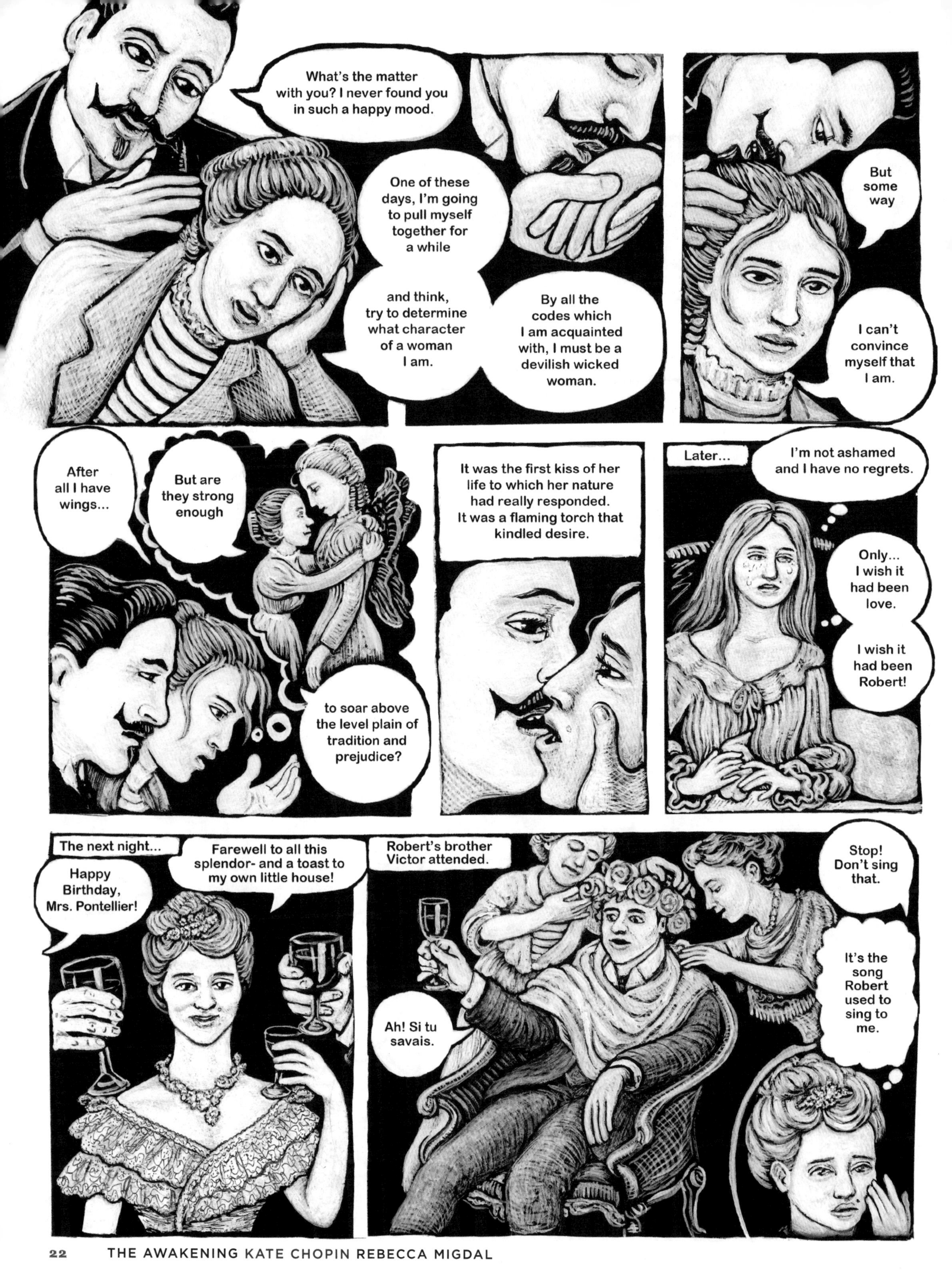

What's the matter with you? I never found you in such a happy mood.
One of these days, I'm going to pull myself together for a while
and think, try to determine what character of a woman I am.
By all the codes which I am acquainted with, I must be a devilish wicked woman.
But some way
I can't convince myself that I am.
After all I have wings...
But are they strong enough
to soar above the level plain of tradition and prejudice?
It was the first kiss of her life to which her nature had really responded. It was a flaming torch that kindled desire.
Later...
I'm not ashamed and I have no regrets.
Only... I wish it had been love.
I wish it had been Robert!
The next night...
Happy Birthday, Mrs. Pontellier!
Farewell to all this splendor- and a toast to my own little house!
Robert's brother Victor attended.
Ah! Si tu savais.
Stop! Don't sing that.
It's the song Robert used to sing to me.

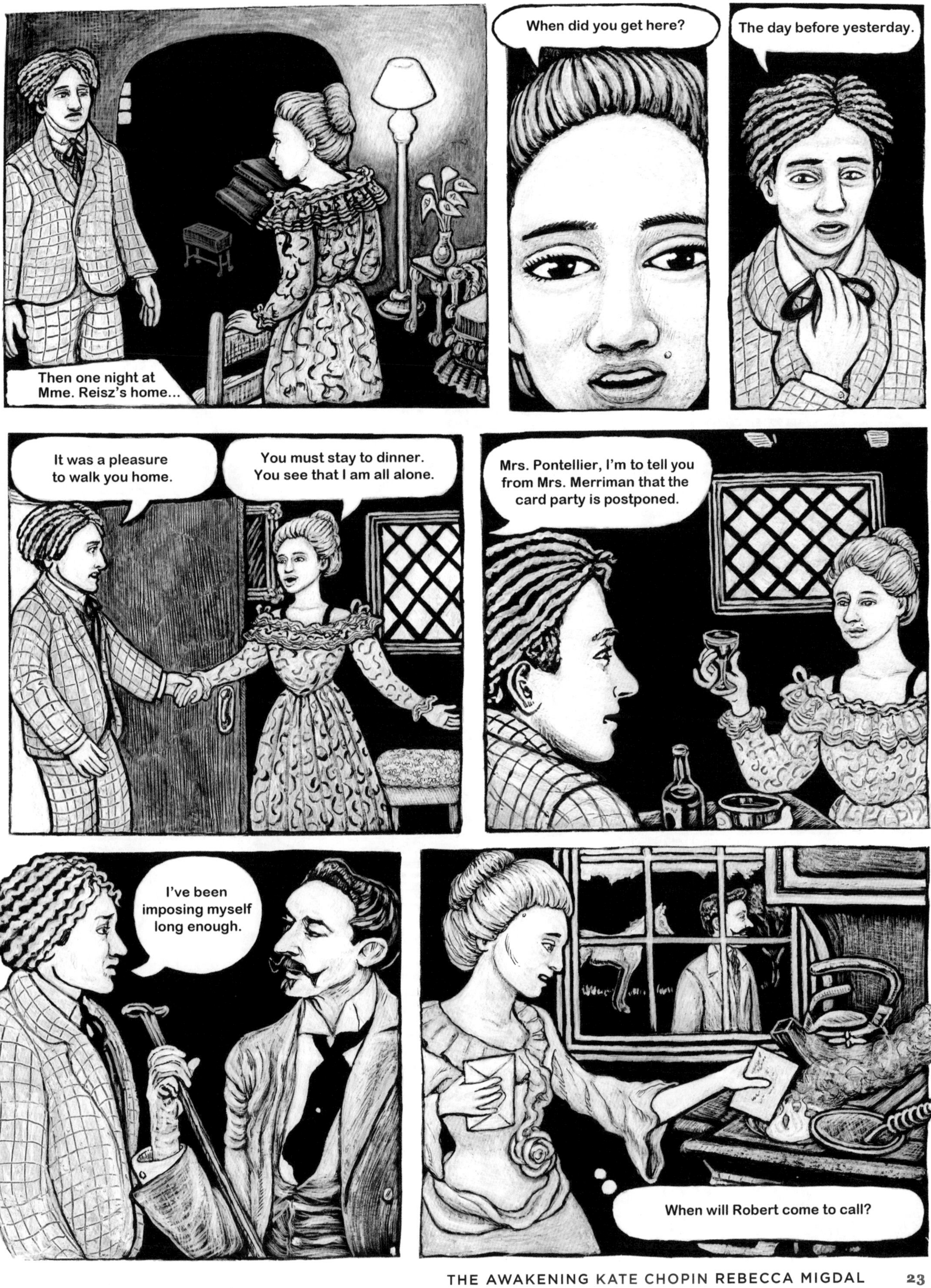
Then one night at Mme. Reisz's home...
When did you get here?
The day before yesterday.
It was a pleasure to walk you home.
You must stay to dinner. You see that I am all alone.
Mrs. Pontellier, I'm to tell you from Mrs. Merriman that the card party is postponed.
I've been imposing myself long enough.
When will Robert come to call?

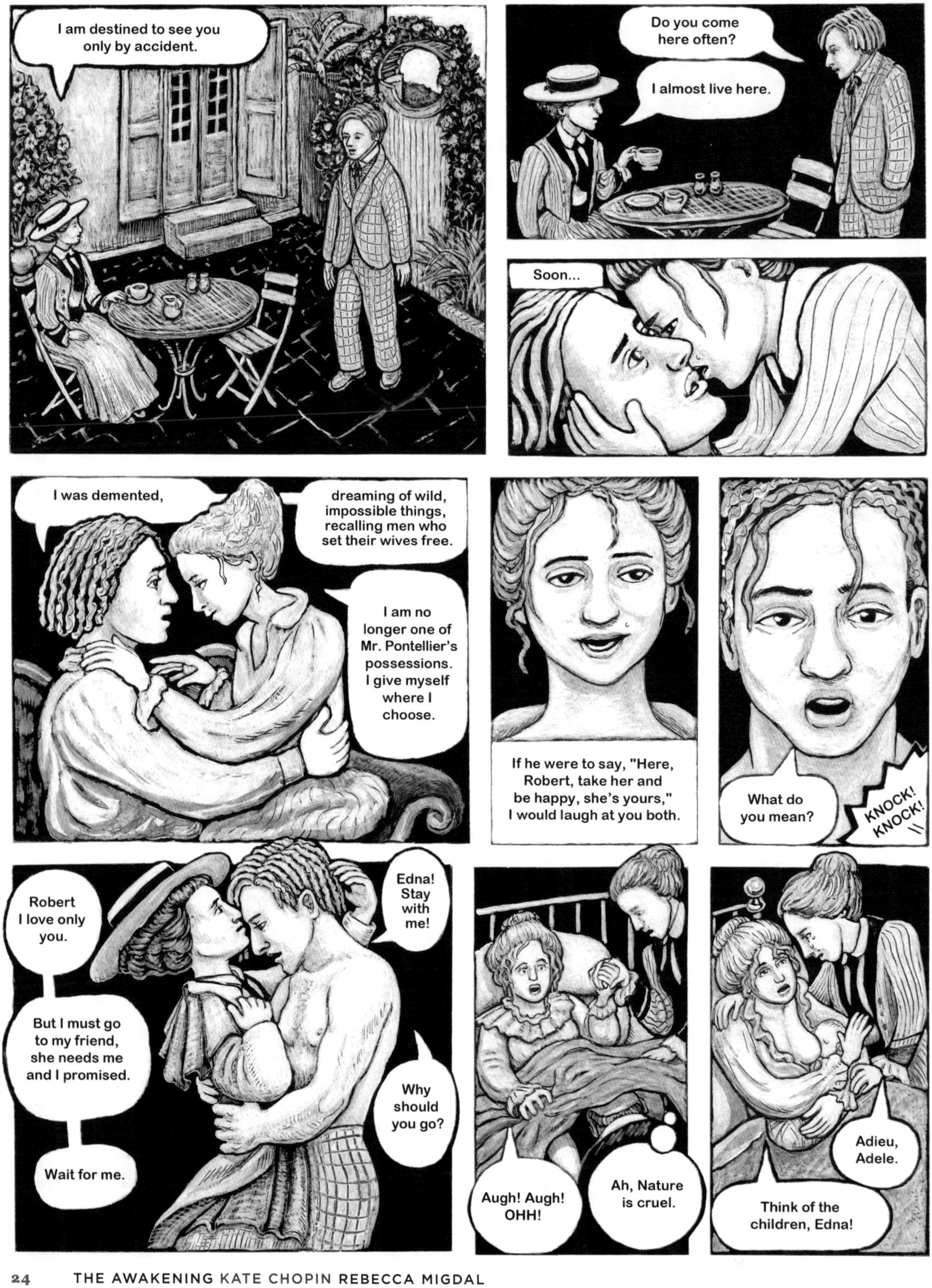

I am destined to see you only by accident.
Do you come here often?
I almost live here.
Soon...
I was demented,
dreaming of wild, impossible things, recalling men who set their wives free.
I am no longer one of Mr. Pontellier's possessions. I give myself where I choose.
If he were to say, "Here, Robert, take her and be happy, she's yours," I would laugh at you both.
What do you mean?
KNOCK! KNOCK!
Robert I love only you.
But I must go to my friend, she needs me and I promised.
Wait for me.
Edna! Stay with me!
Why should you go?
Augh! Augh! OHH!
Ah, Nature is cruel.
Adieu, Adele.
Think of the children, Edna!

Robert?

Robert, where are you?

Despondency came on her there in the wakeful night, and it never lifted.

Dearest Edna, I love you. Good by. because I love you. —Robert

She had come to Grand Isle alone, with no other purpose than to rest.

There was no one thing that she wanted. She even realized that there would come a day when the thought of Robert would melt out of her existence, and leave her alone.

Her children appeared before her as antagonists who had overcome her, who sought to drag her down in soul's slavery for the rest of her days. But she knew how to evade them.

The strength in her arms and legs was almost gone.

The old terror flamed up again for an instant, then sank away.

They need not have thought that they could possess her, body and soul.

THE AWAKENING KATE CHOPIN REBECCA MIGDAL   25

The Interpretation of Dreams

Sigmund Freud

ART/ADAPTATION BY **Tara Seibel**

A NUMBER OF SIGMUND FREUD'S BOOKS ARE NOT only science classics but have crossed into the literary canon as well. A practicing neurologist in 1880s Austria, Freud became convinced that many physiological problems were caused by traumatic childhood events and the unpleasant emotions associated with those events. He felt that the ongoing repression of these emotions (as well as suppressed desires) was the primary basis for neurosis, so he created the approach known as psychoanalysis to trigger the recollection and processing of those events, emotions, and desires. One of its popular techniques is free association, in which the patient is encouraged to say whatever comes to mind. Another technique is dream interpretation. Freud's 1899 work *The Interpretation of Dreams* solidified the notion that dreams use symbolism and distortion to smuggle unacceptable desires (and sometimes unacceptable memories) past the conscious watchdog mind. And because Freud often uses his own dreams as examples, it is "in part a record of Freud's epic self-analysis," as his biographer Richard Wollheim wrote.

Freud's impact is incalculable. He either created or refined and popularized notions of repressed memories, the Oedipus Complex, the libido, sublimation of sexual energies, free association, neurosis, the pleasure principle, the death drive, penis envy, castration anxiety, the Freudian slip, couch therapy, the conscious and unconscious minds, and the id, the ego, and the superego. Though psychoanalysis has been drastically modified and even largely abandoned, it held heavy sway as a mental-health approach throughout much of the twentieth century. Freud's ideas also greatly influenced literary theory, cultural criticism, and the arts (including the Surrealists and Alfred Hitchcock).

I would be remiss if I didn't report a fact that still doesn't get much play. The Freud myth—the idea of him as a towering intellectual whose ideas are absolutely true and who helped many people—is deeply embedded in our culture, but is indeed a myth. Freud was a vicious person who brooked no dissent within his psychoanalytic circle and who bullied his patients; he plagiarized and appropriated the work of others; he was a misogynist. To my mind the most damning thing is that Freud constantly lied about his track record. We know this for a fact. We now have access to his private case notes, his personal journals, his letters to colleagues, and other once-private documents, and we know that he flat-out lied in his famous published case histories. While publicly claiming to have cured his patients—to have "restored" their personalities—he was privately admitting that he hadn't been able to help them. (For more on this, see *Unauthorized Freud*, a collection of documented articles by academics.)

Tara Seibel, who worked closely with legendary comics writer Harvey Pekar during the last part of his life, has integrated illustrations, text (typed and handwritten), and patterns and flourishes into a visually astounding presentation of the written word. I'd love to see entire books designed like this. . . .

SOURCES

Crews, Frederick. *Unauthorized Freud: Doubters Confront a Legend.* New York: Viking, 1998.

Wollheim, Richard. *Sigmund Freud.* Cambridge: Cambridge University Press, 1995.

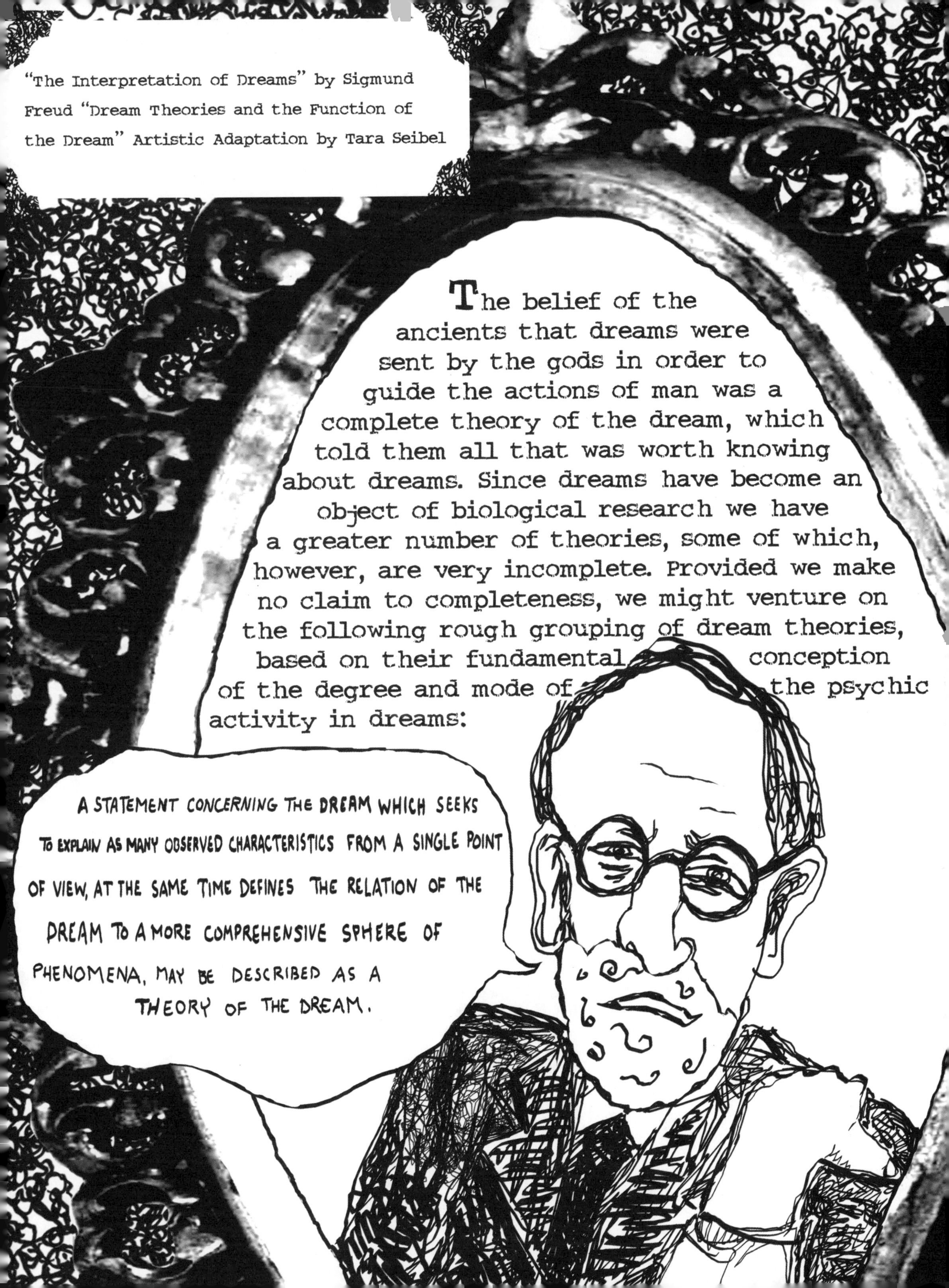
"The Interpretation of Dreams" by Sigmund Freud "Dream Theories and the Function of the Dream" Artistic Adaptation by Tara Seibel
The belief of the ancients that dreams were sent by the gods in order to guide the actions of man was a complete theory of the dream, which told them all that was worth knowing about dreams. Since dreams have become an object of biological research we have a greater number of theories, some of which, however, are very incomplete. Provided we make no claim to completeness, we might venture on the following rough grouping of dream theories, based on their fundamental conception of the degree and mode of the psychic activity in dreams:
A STATEMENT CONCERNING THE DREAM WHICH SEEKS TO EXPLAIN AS MANY OBSERVED CHARACTERISTICS FROM A SINGLE POINT OF VIEW, AT THE SAME TIME DEFINES THE RELATION OF THE DREAM TO A MORE COMPREHENSIVE SPHERE OF PHENOMENA, MAY BE DESCRIBED AS A THEORY OF THE DREAM.

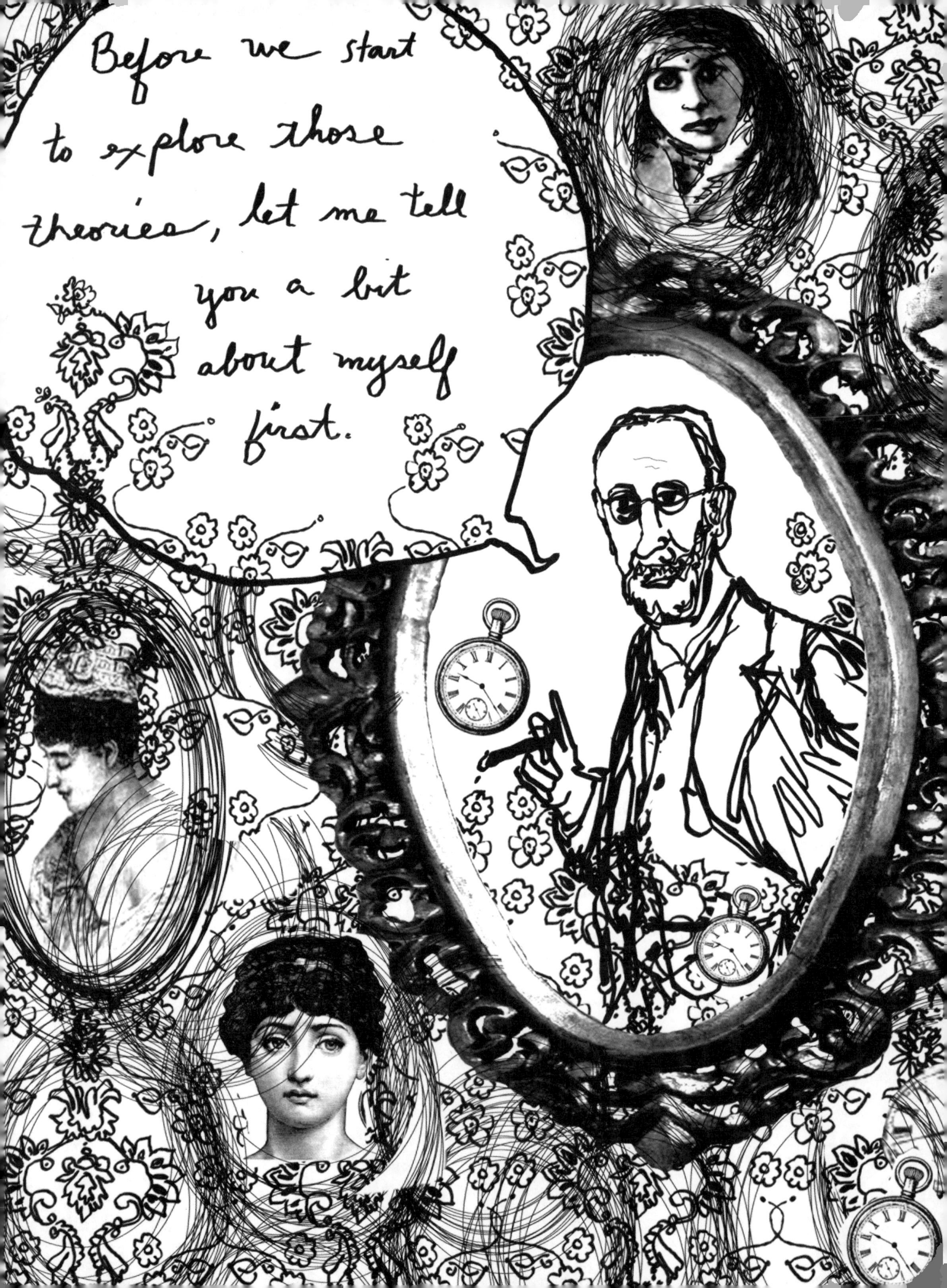
Before we start to explore those theories, let me tell you a bit about myself first.

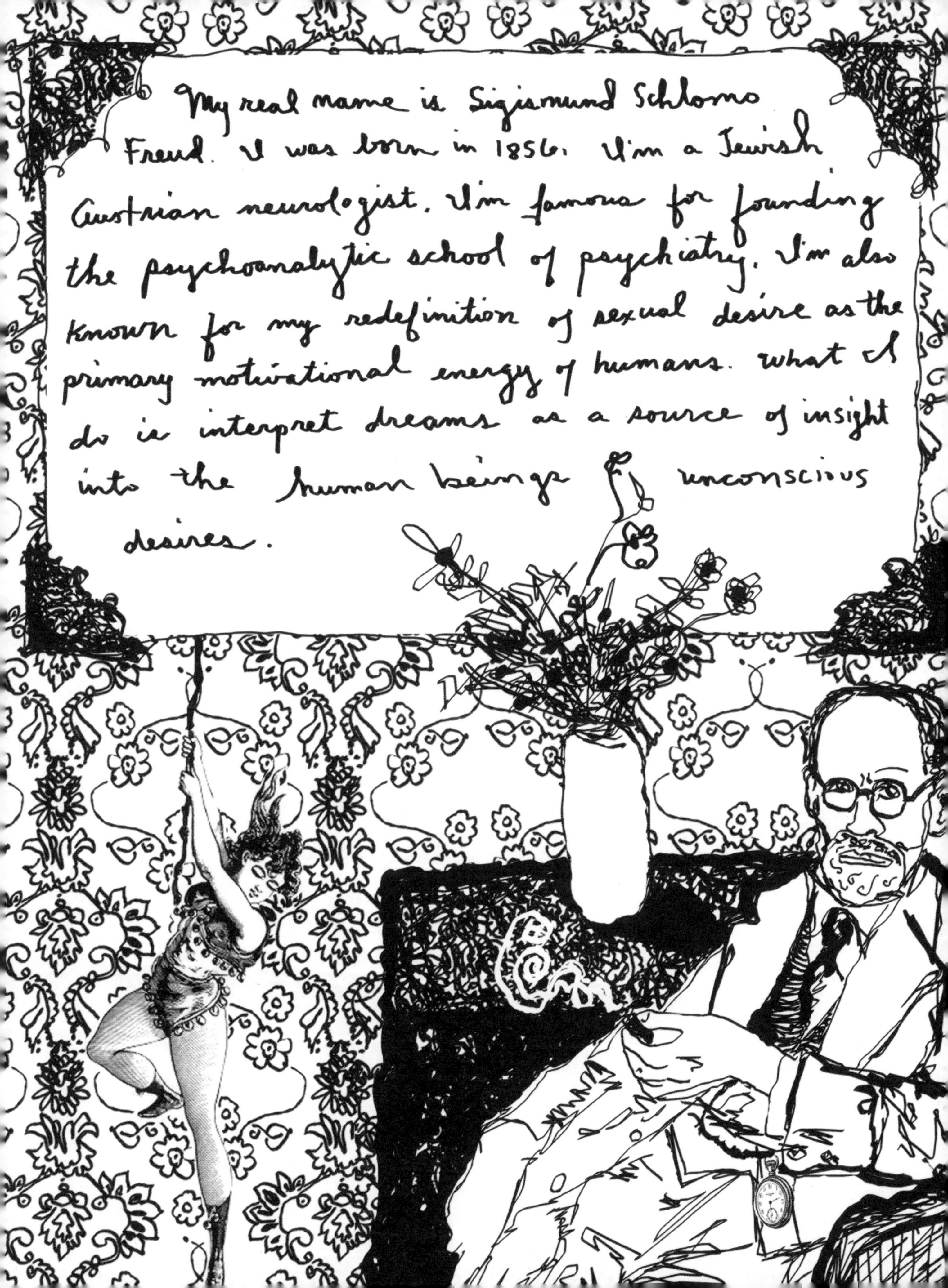
My real name is Sigismund Schlomo Freud. I was born in 1856. I'm a Jewish Austrian neurologist. I'm famous for founding the psychoanalytic school of psychiatry. I'm also known for my redefinition of sexual desire as the primary motivational energy of humans. What I do is interpret dreams as a source of insight into the human beings unconscious desires.

Dream Theories

The conception of the dream as an incomplete, partial waking state, or traces of the influence of this conception, will of course be found in the works of all the modern physiologists and philosophers. It is most completely represented by Maury. It often seems as though this author conceives the state of being awake or asleep as susceptible of shifting from one anatomical region to another; each anatomical region seeming to him to be connected with a definite psychic function. Here I will merely suggest that even if the theory of partial waking were confirmed, its finer superstructure would still call for exhaustive consideration.

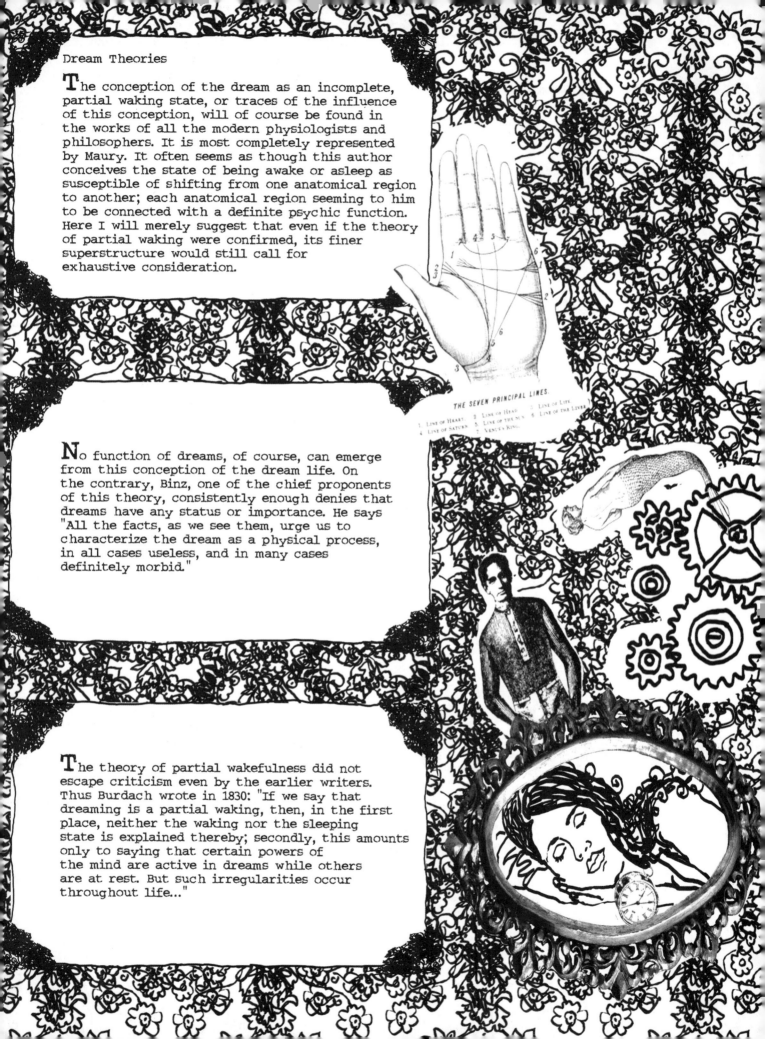

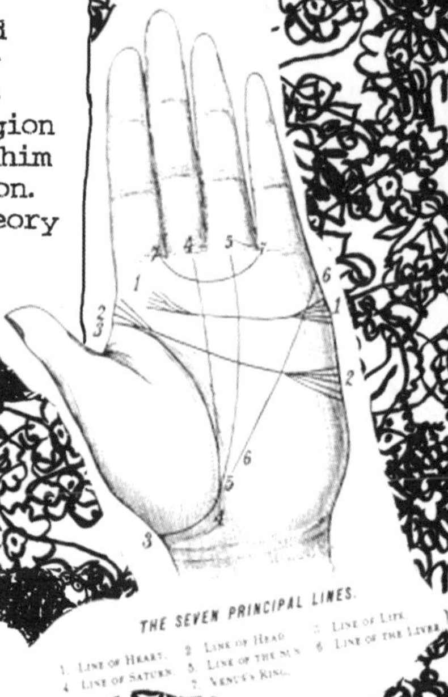
THE SEVEN PRINCIPAL LINES.
1. Line of Heart. 2. Line of Head 3. Line of Life.
4. Line of Saturn. 5. Line of the Sun 6. Line of the Liver.
7. Venus's Ring.

No function of dreams, of course, can emerge from this conception of the dream life. On the contrary, Binz, one of the chief proponents of this theory, consistently enough denies that dreams have any status or importance. He says "All the facts, as we see them, urge us to characterize the dream as a physical process, in all cases useless, and in many cases definitely morbid."

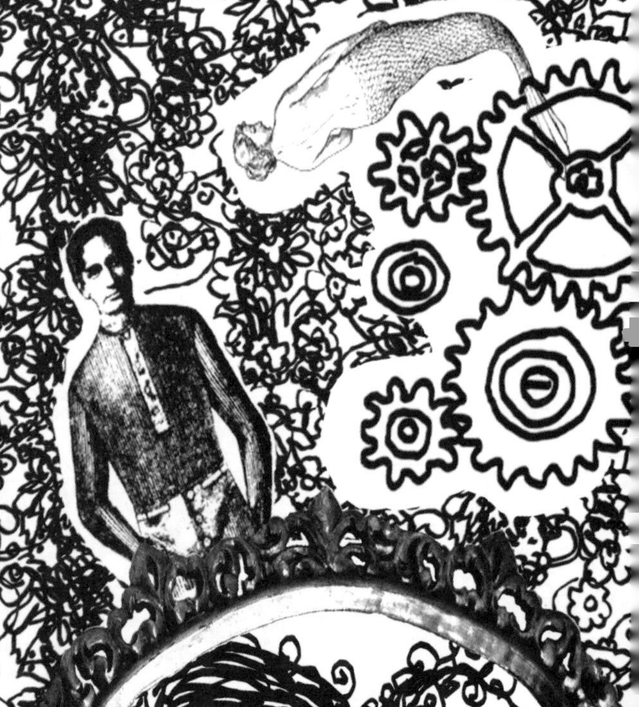

The theory of partial wakefulness did not escape criticism even by the earlier writers. Thus Burdach wrote in 1830: "If we say that dreaming is a partial waking, then, in the first place, neither the waking nor the sleeping state is explained thereby; secondly, this amounts only to saying that certain powers of the mind are active in dreams while others are at rest. But such irregularities occur throughout life..."

The prevailing dream theory which conceives the dream as a "physical" process finds a certain support in a very interesting conception of the dream which was first propounded by Robert in 1866, and which is seductive because it assigns to the dream a function or a useful result. "For this reason we cannot usually explain our dreams, since their causes are to be found in sensory impressions of the preceding day which have not attained sufficient recognition on the part of the dreamer."Robert therefore conceives the dream "as a physical process of elimination which in its psychic reaction reaches the consciousness."

Yves Delage, bases his theory on the same characteristics of the dream characteristics which are perceptible in the selection of the dream material, and it is instructive to observe how a trifling twist in the conception of the same things gives a final result entirely different in its bearings. Delage, having lost through death a person very dear to him, found that we either do not dream at all of what occupies us intently during the day, or that we begin to dream of it only after it is overshadowed by the other interests of the day.

The refreshing and healing activity of dreams is even more impressively described by Purkinje "The productive dreams in particular would perform these functions. These are the unconstrained play of the imagination, and have no connection with the events of the day. The mind is loth to continue the tension of the waking life, but wishes to relax it and recuperate from it. It creates, in the first place conditions opposed to those of the waking state. It cures sadness by joy, worry by hope and cheerfully distracting images, hatred by love and friendliness, and fear by courage and confidence; it appeases doubt by conviction and firm belief, and vain expectation by realization.

The Wonderful Wizard of Oz

L. Frank Baum

PHOTO-DIORAMAS BY **Graham Rawle**

LOUIS FRANK BAUM ALREADY HAD A COUPLE OF children's books under his belt—including the smash hit *Father Goose: His Book*—when he wrote the greatest American children's novel. Much like Lewis Carroll and *Alice's Adventures in Wonderland*, it started one day when Baum was telling several children—in this case, his own—tales of his own devising. "[S]uddenly this one moved right in and took possession," he wrote years later. "I shooed the children away and grabbed a piece of paper that was lying there on the rack and began to write. It really seemed to write itself. Then I couldn't find any regular paper so I took anything at all, even a bunch of old envelopes."

The original 1900 edition of *The Wonderful Wizard of Oz* was lavish, with beautiful binding, twenty-four color plates, and more than one hundred color illustrations by W. W. Denslow. It's still regarded as one of the most beautiful children's books ever published. It was an instant success, with 90,000 copies in print by the following January. In 1902, a quasi-Vaudeville musical extravaganza based on the book brought further fame and fortune to Baum. The sequel, *The Marvelous Land of Oz*, was an equally big hit, and Baum proceeded to write over a dozen more *Oz* books, including two published posthumously, in addition to other works for children. (Just as Arthur Conan Doyle had done with Sherlock Holmes, Baum at one point brought the *Oz* series to a close but was forced by public demand—to say nothing of personal financial demands—to resurrect it.)

In 1939, MGM released a movie based on the most successful children's book of the time. You may have seen it. Those images of Dorothy, Toto, the Tin Man, the Scarecrow, the Cowardly Lion, the Munchkins, the witches, and the Wizard are permanently engraved into our brains. But that's only one way to envision the story. For his highly lauded version, British artist Graham Rawle erased Judy Garland & Company from his memory and built dioramas based on the novel filtered through his wild sensibilities. He lit and photographed them, sometimes adding collaged elements in postproduction, making dramatic, funny, and nightmarish new visions of Baum's creations for an oversized hardcover edition that contains the full text and dozens of photo-dioramas.

The process was laborious. Graham spent two years on the project, with each photo taking about a week. The obvious exception is the mind-frying panorama of the Emerald City. Graham explains:

> The buildings are made out of a variety of food containers, household items, plumbing accessories, Christmas decorations, and bits of old modeling kits, all painted green and sprinkled with glitter and fake gems. After several months (and an incredibly complex lighting setup) I had a picture but it just didn't feel right so I started all over again. Initially I had photographed the whole thing as one big diorama, but later decided to light and shoot each building separately and assemble the cityscape as a digital image. I think by the end I had nearly 200 Photoshop layers.

Graham returns Dorothy's famous slippers to their original silver (they were changed to ruby red for the film in order to better show off the miracles of Technicolor), and brings back characters barred from the movie, including the aggressive Hammerheads.

SOURCE

Baum, L. Frank. *The Annotated Wizard of Oz*. Cenn. ed. Edited, with an introduction and notes by Michael Patrick Hearn. New York: W. W. Norton & Company, 2000.

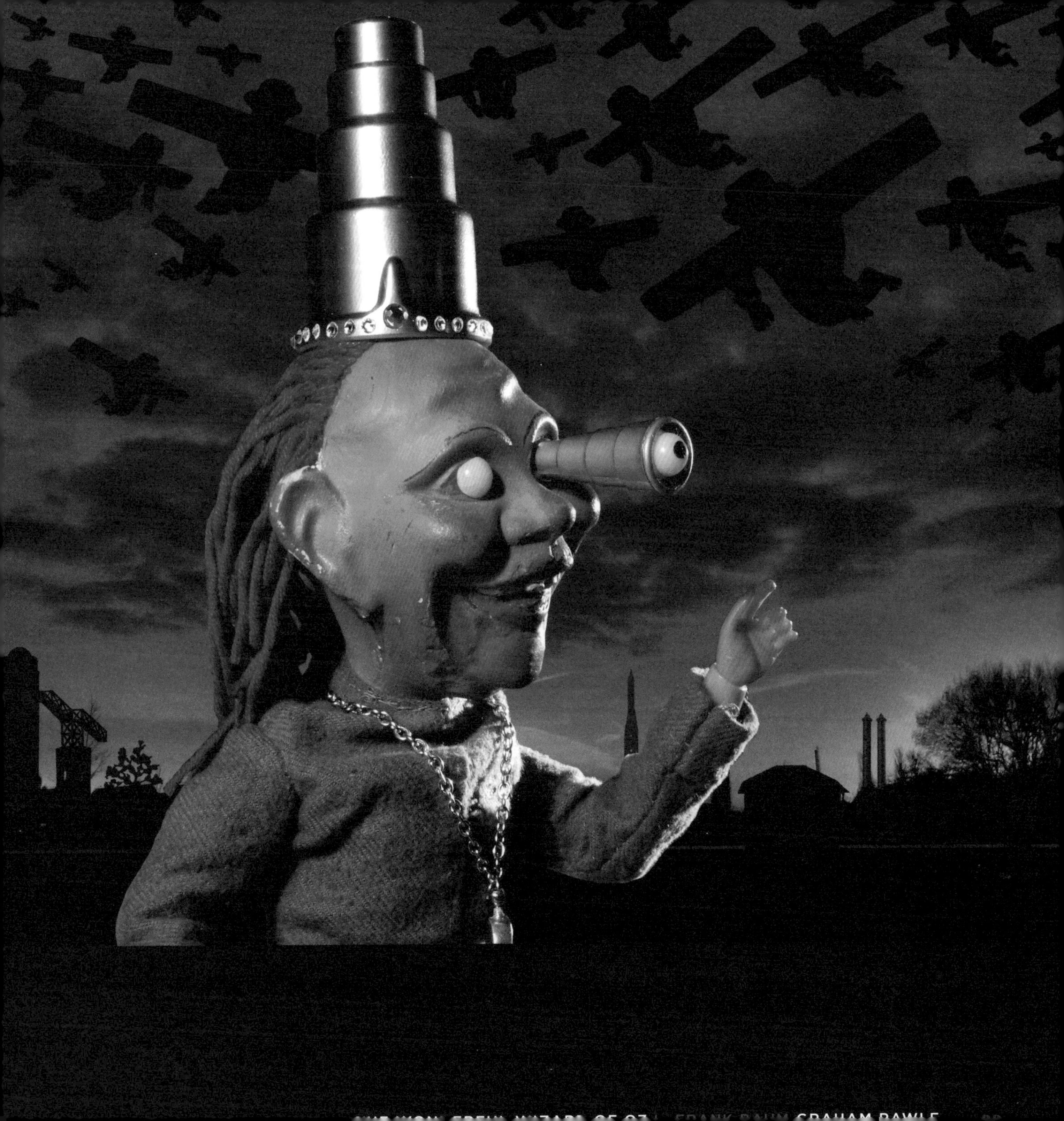

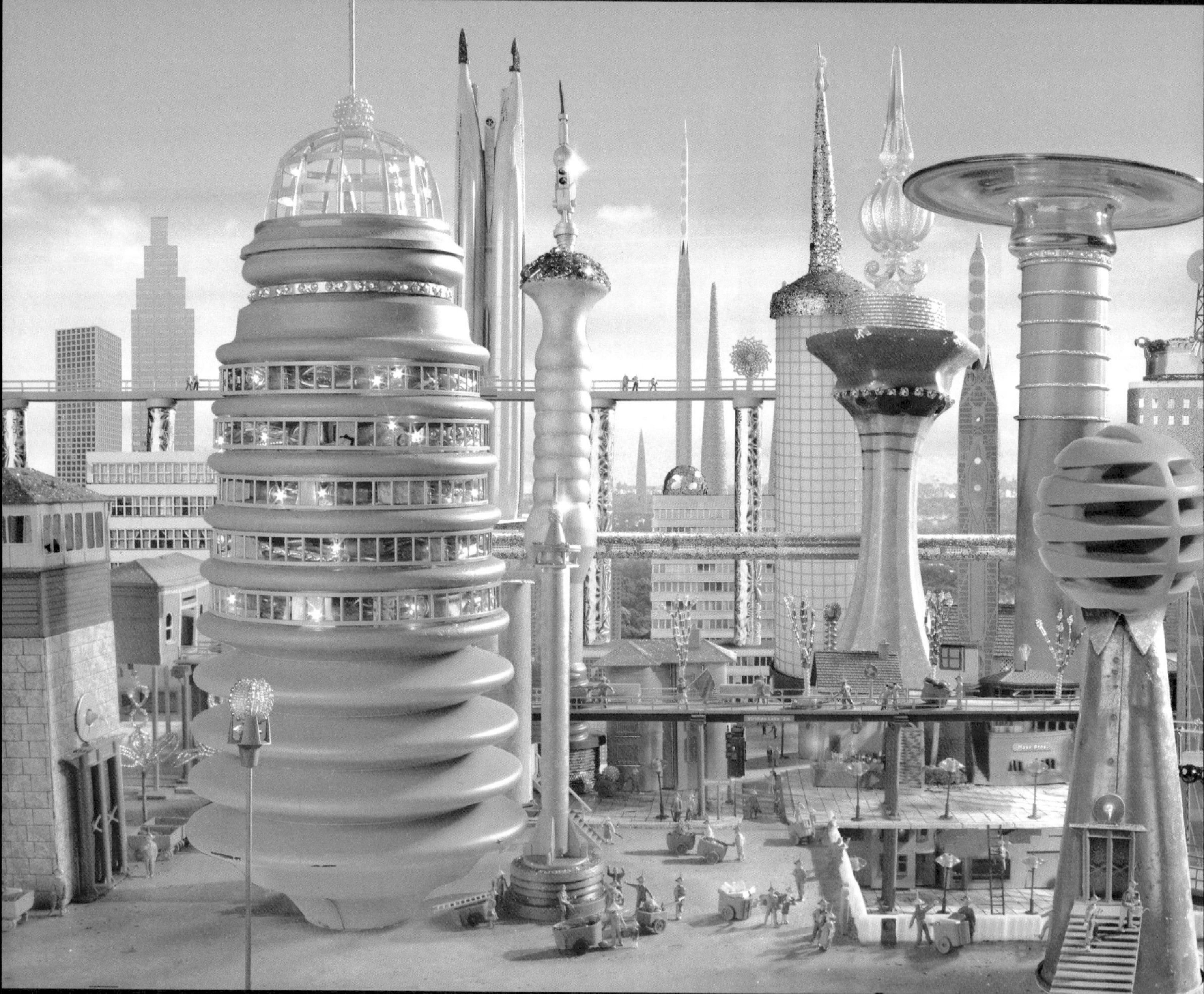

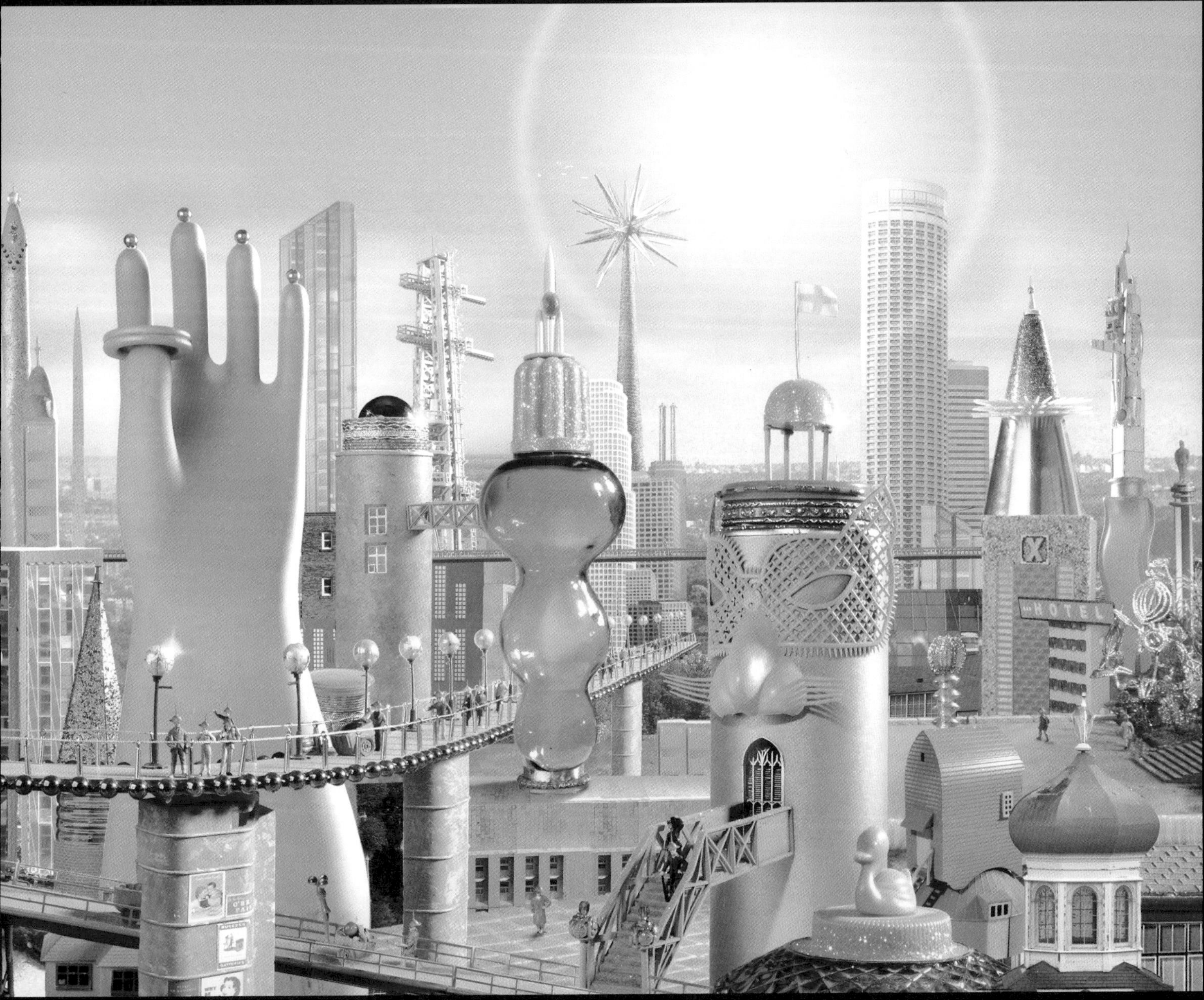
HOTEL

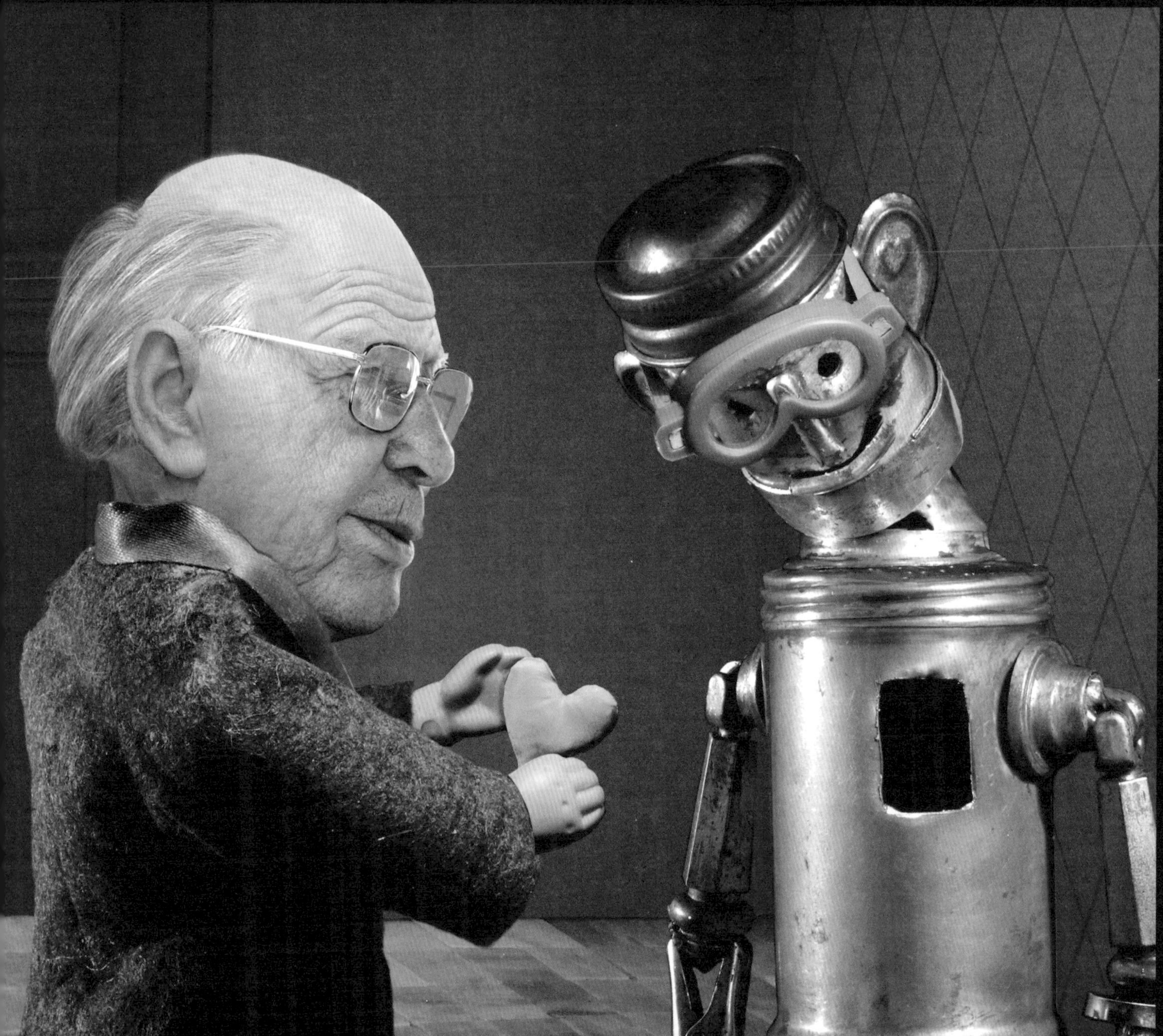

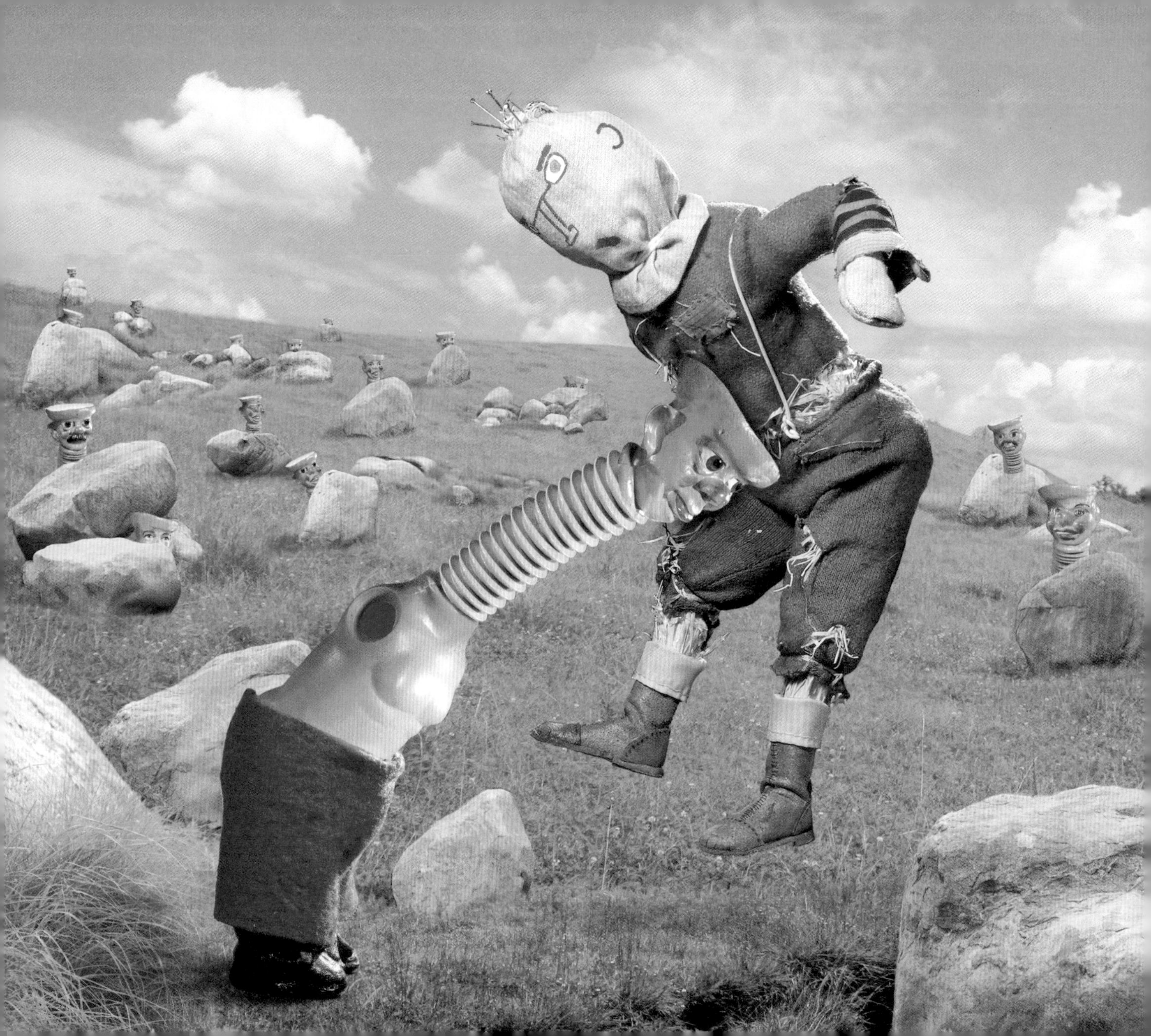

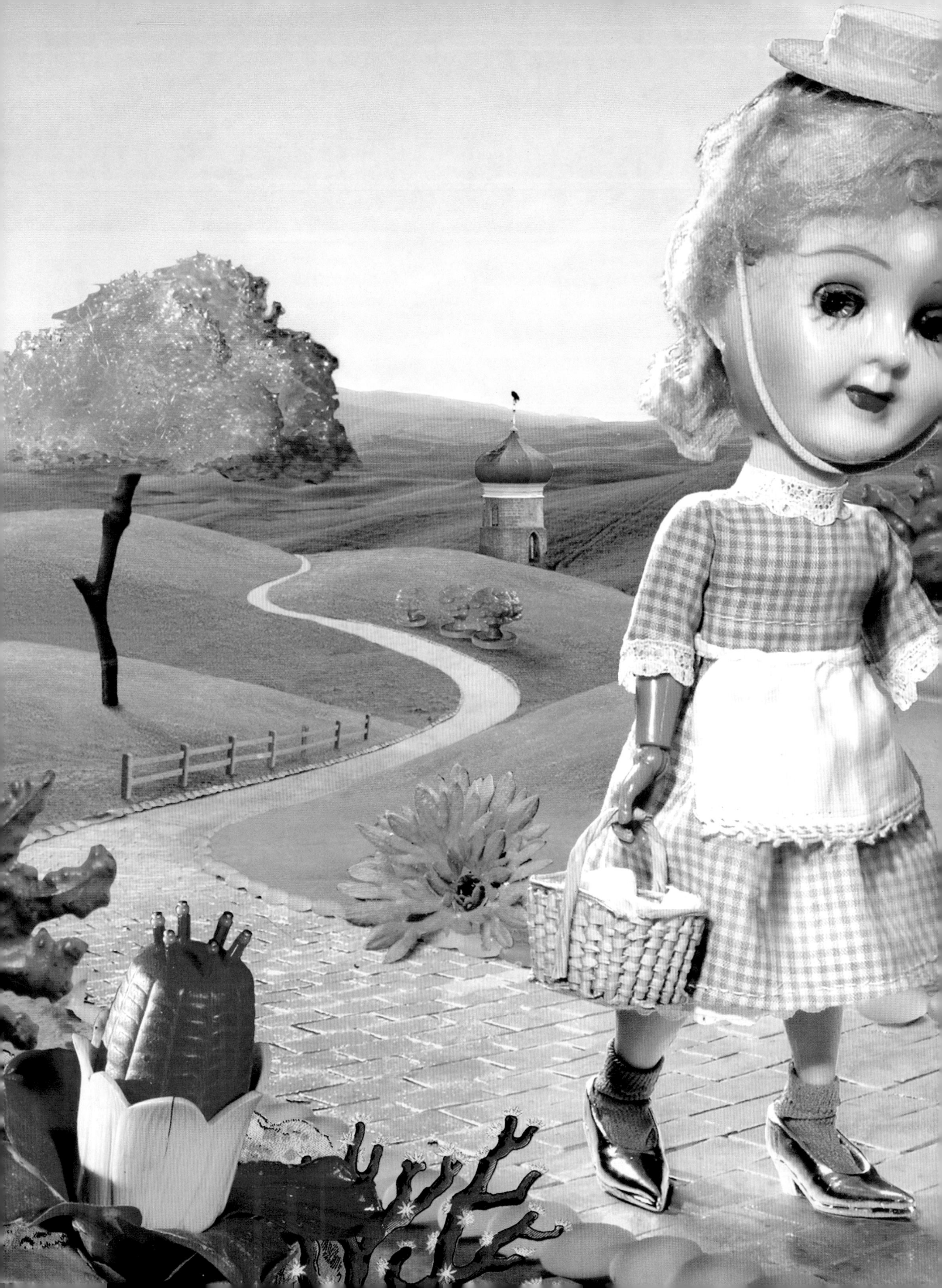

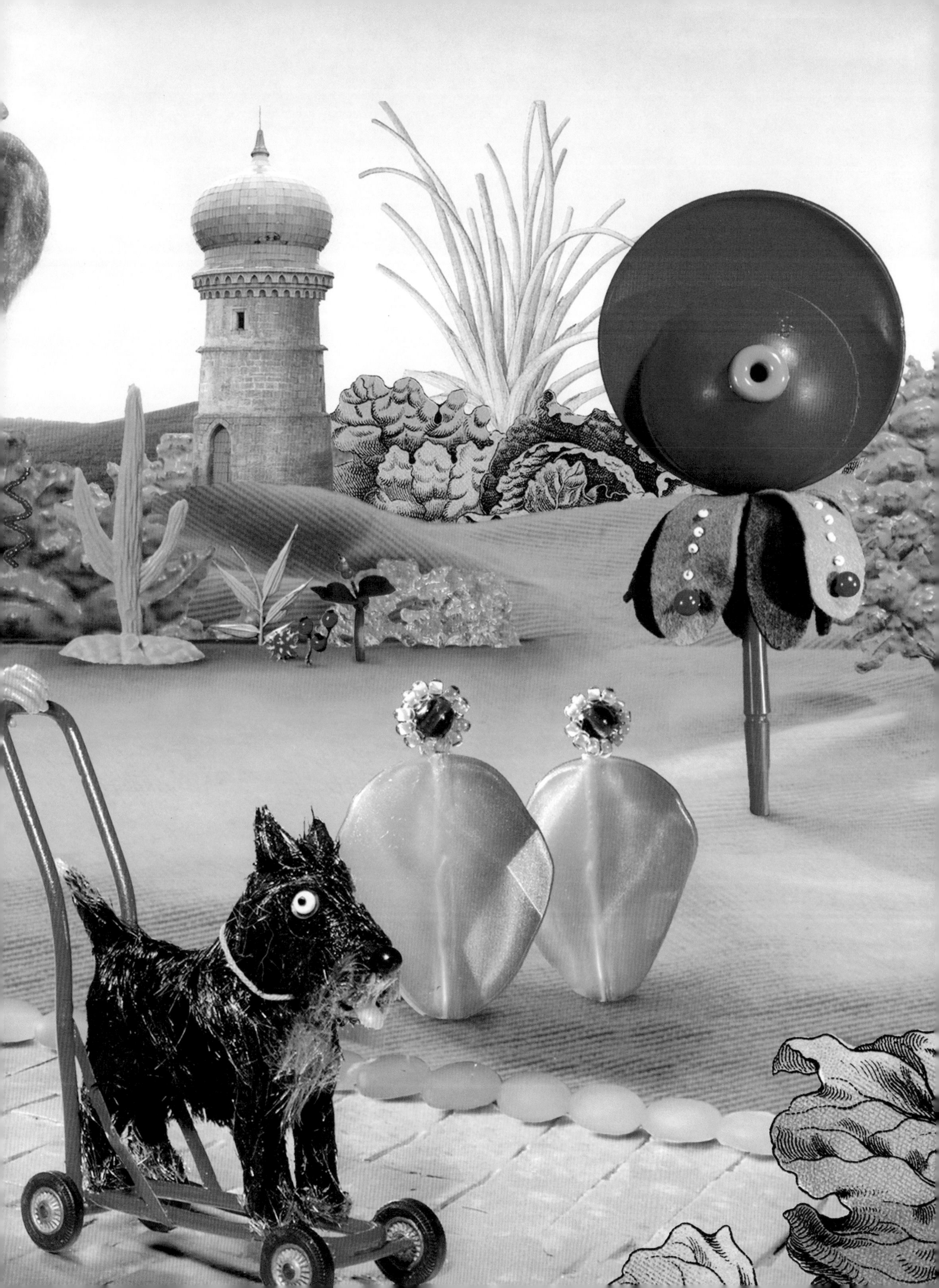

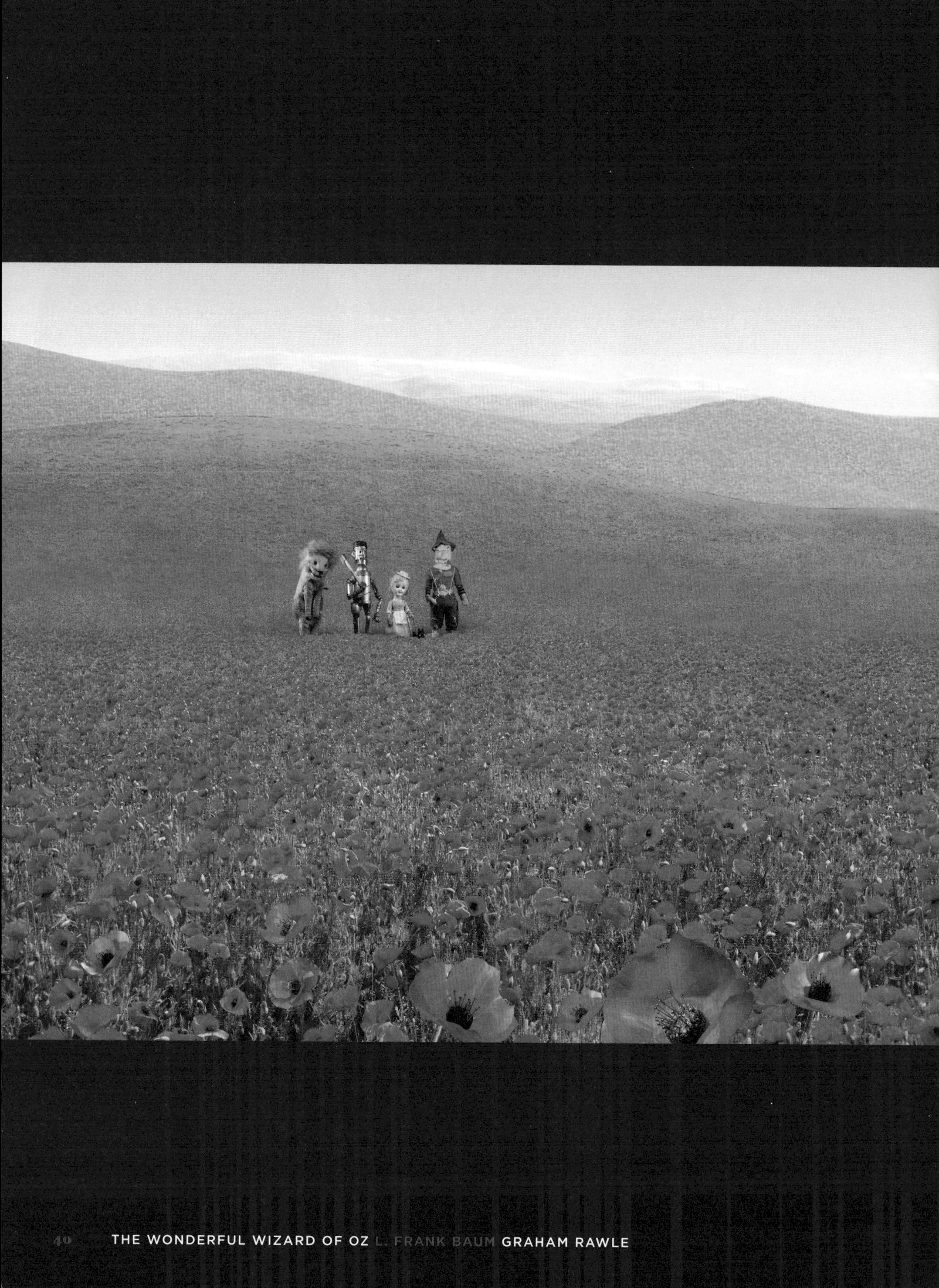

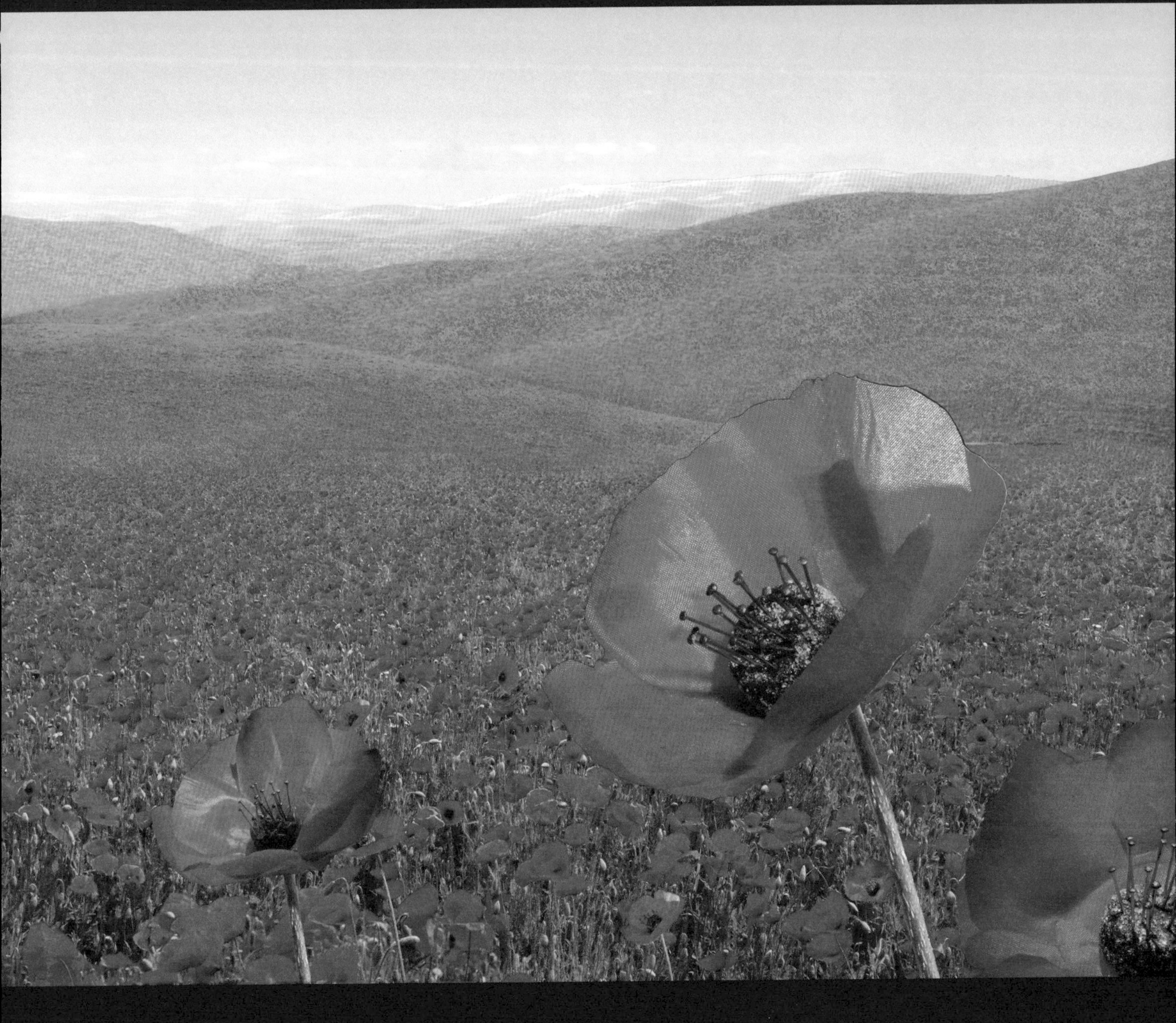

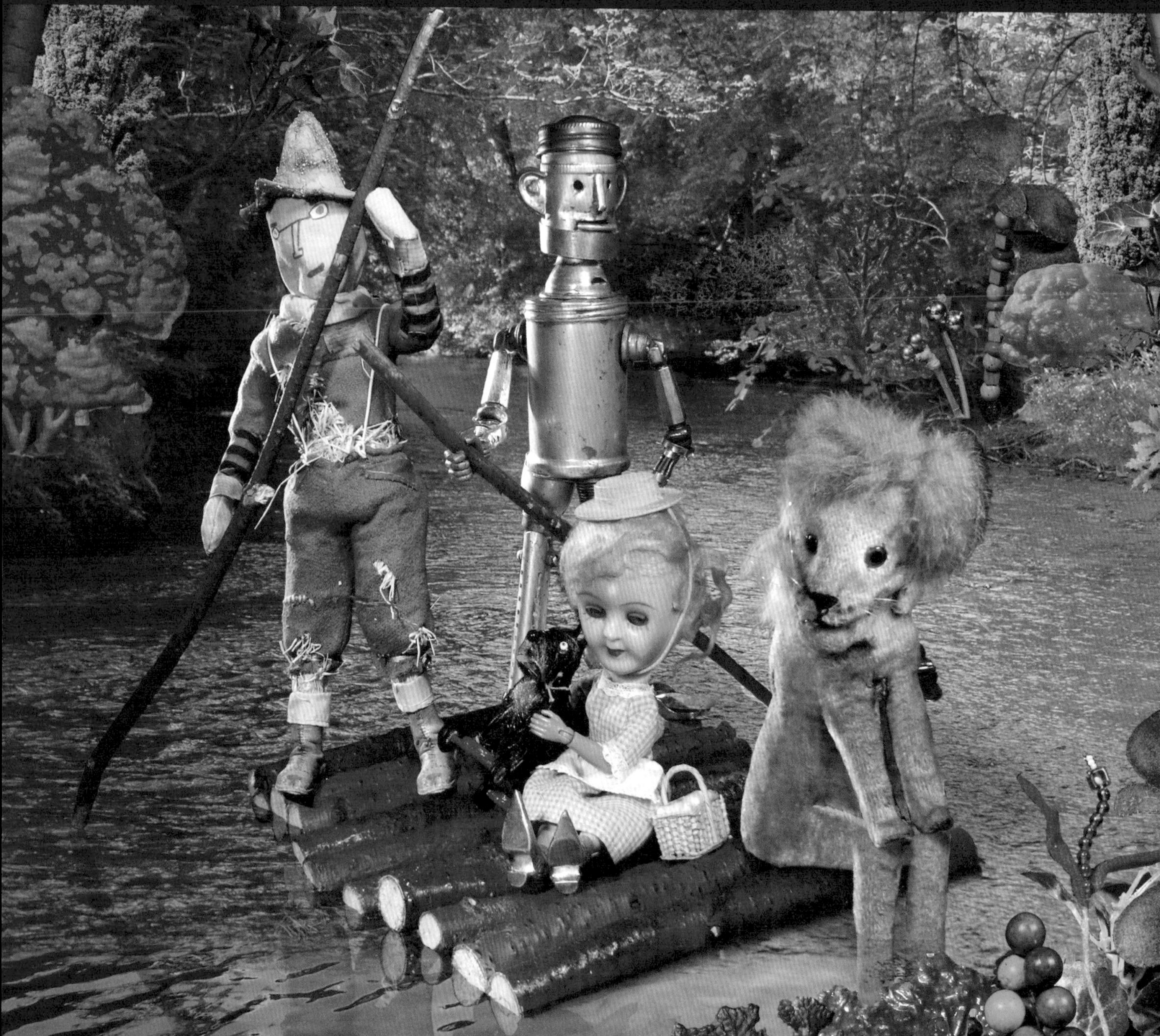

"The New Accelerator"

H. G. Wells

ART/ADAPTATION BY **Cole Johnson**

WE ASSOCIATE H. G. WELLS MOSTLY WITH HIS three 1890s proto-science fiction novels—*The Time Machine, The Invisible Man,* and *The War of the Worlds*—but he was an extremely prolific writer who ceaselessly cranked out prose until his death in 1946: more than fifty novels, seventy nonfiction books, and ninety short stories. He wrote histories, textbooks, political tracts, science fact, predictions, dystopias, utopias. . . . He thought a single world government was desirable and inevitable, and he tried to help make it happen through some of his books and lectures. "I am extravagantly obsessed by the things that might be, and impatient with the present," he wrote. "I want to go ahead of Father Time with a scythe of my own." Sci-fi, of course, provided him with the perfect vehicle for expressing and exploring his obsession with what might be.

When you hear the title of his 1901 short story "The New Accelerator," it's easy to picture some mechanical gizmo, a bit of steampunk tech that moves really fast. But the tale is more like something out of Philip K. Dick. Austin artist Cole Johnson nails both the Edwardian look and the proto-Dickian strangeness of this story. He explains:

I was asked to choose a story by H. G. Wells or Jules Verne to represent the early days of science fiction. I wasn't familiar with "The New Accelerator" but knew I wanted to adapt it as soon as I started reading. I was struck by the duality in the narrator's attitude toward drugs—the idea that they could "make [one] incredibly strong and alert or a helpless log," that they could alternately calm or madden a man. "The strange armoury of phials the doctors use" was at once a source of wonder and caution as the chemist inevitably used himself as the experimental subject. In adapting the work, I wanted to leave the drug's effect ambiguous. Was it truly warping time itself or were our two heroes simply high as gods?

43

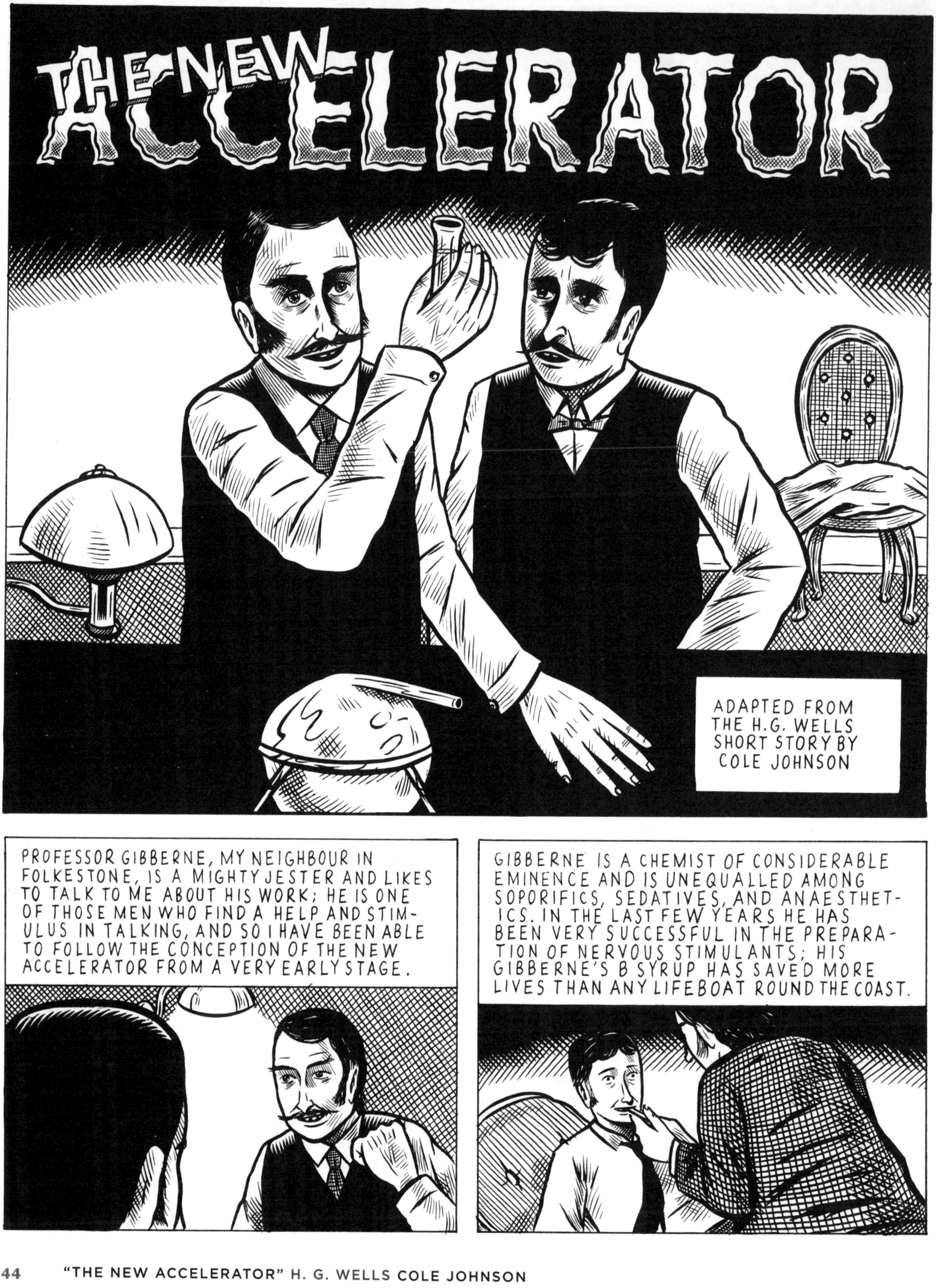
THE NEW ACCELERATOR
ADAPTED FROM THE H.G. WELLS SHORT STORY BY COLE JOHNSON
PROFESSOR GIBBERNE, MY NEIGHBOUR IN FOLKESTONE, IS A MIGHTY JESTER AND LIKES TO TALK TO ME ABOUT HIS WORK; HE IS ONE OF THOSE MEN WHO FIND A HELP AND STIMULUS IN TALKING, AND SO I HAVE BEEN ABLE TO FOLLOW THE CONCEPTION OF THE NEW ACCELERATOR FROM A VERY EARLY STAGE.
GIBBERNE IS A CHEMIST OF CONSIDERABLE EMINENCE AND IS UNEQUALLED AMONG SOPORIFICS, SEDATIVES, AND ANAESTHETICS. IN THE LAST FEW YEARS HE HAS BEEN VERY SUCCESSFUL IN THE PREPARATION OF NERVOUS STIMULANTS; HIS GIBBERNE'S B SYRUP HAS SAVED MORE LIVES THAN ANY LIFEBOAT ROUND THE COAST.

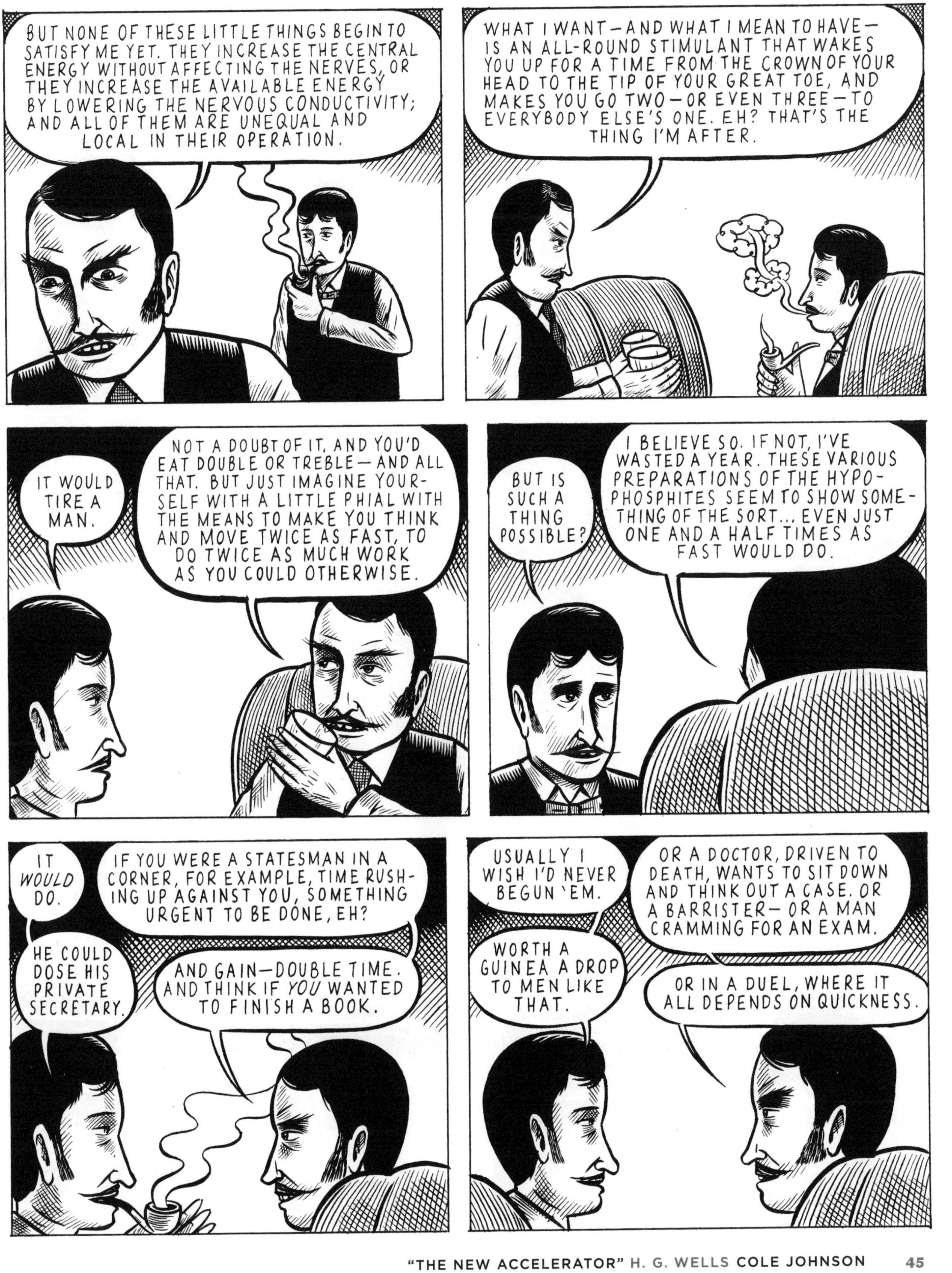
BUT NONE OF THESE LITTLE THINGS BEGIN TO SATISFY ME YET. THEY INCREASE THE CENTRAL ENERGY WITHOUT AFFECTING THE NERVES, OR THEY INCREASE THE AVAILABLE ENERGY BY LOWERING THE NERVOUS CONDUCTIVITY; AND ALL OF THEM ARE UNEQUAL AND LOCAL IN THEIR OPERATION.
WHAT I WANT—AND WHAT I MEAN TO HAVE—IS AN ALL-ROUND STIMULANT THAT WAKES YOU UP FOR A TIME FROM THE CROWN OF YOUR HEAD TO THE TIP OF YOUR GREAT TOE, AND MAKES YOU GO TWO—OR EVEN THREE—TO EVERYBODY ELSE'S ONE. EH? THAT'S THE THING I'M AFTER.
IT WOULD TIRE A MAN.
NOT A DOUBT OF IT. AND YOU'D EAT DOUBLE OR TREBLE—AND ALL THAT. BUT JUST IMAGINE YOURSELF WITH A LITTLE PHIAL WITH THE MEANS TO MAKE YOU THINK AND MOVE TWICE AS FAST, TO DO TWICE AS MUCH WORK AS YOU COULD OTHERWISE.
BUT IS SUCH A THING POSSIBLE?
I BELIEVE SO. IF NOT, I'VE WASTED A YEAR. THESE VARIOUS PREPARATIONS OF THE HYPOPHOSPHITES SEEM TO SHOW SOMETHING OF THE SORT... EVEN JUST ONE AND A HALF TIMES AS FAST WOULD DO.
IT *WOULD* DO.
IF YOU WERE A STATESMAN IN A CORNER, FOR EXAMPLE, TIME RUSHING UP AGAINST YOU, SOMETHING URGENT TO BE DONE, EH?
HE COULD DOSE HIS PRIVATE SECRETARY.
AND GAIN—DOUBLE TIME. AND THINK IF *YOU* WANTED TO FINISH A BOOK.
USUALLY I WISH I'D NEVER BEGUN 'EM.
OR A DOCTOR, DRIVEN TO DEATH, WANTS TO SIT DOWN AND THINK OUT A CASE. OR A BARRISTER—OR A MAN CRAMMING FOR AN EXAM.
WORTH A GUINEA A DROP TO MEN LIKE THAT.
OR IN A DUEL, WHERE IT ALL DEPENDS ON QUICKNESS.

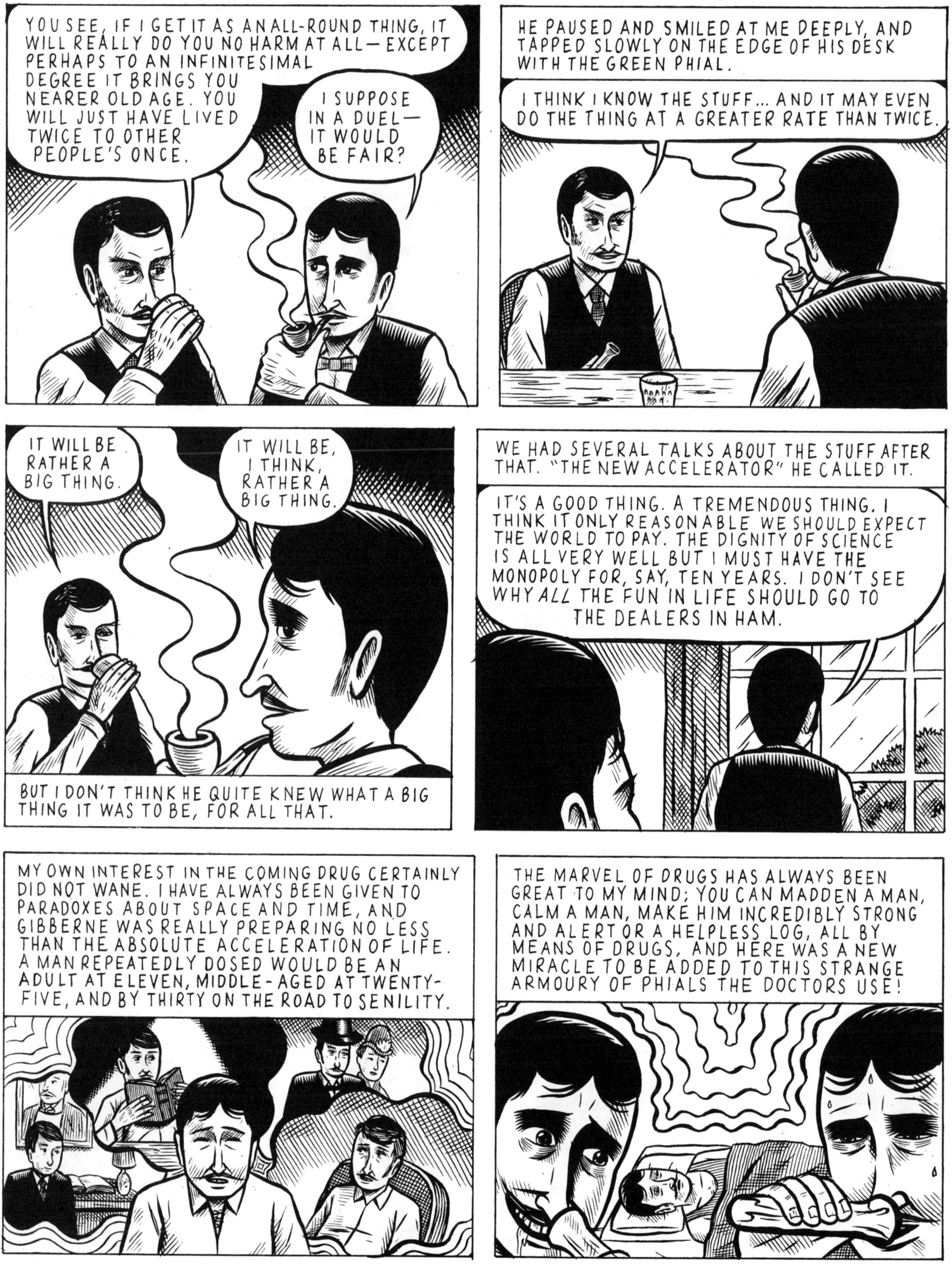
YOU SEE, IF I GET IT AS AN ALL-ROUND THING, IT WILL REALLY DO YOU NO HARM AT ALL — EXCEPT PERHAPS TO AN INFINITESIMAL DEGREE IT BRINGS YOU NEARER OLD AGE. YOU WILL JUST HAVE LIVED TWICE TO OTHER PEOPLE'S ONCE.
I SUPPOSE IN A DUEL — IT WOULD BE FAIR?
HE PAUSED AND SMILED AT ME DEEPLY, AND TAPPED SLOWLY ON THE EDGE OF HIS DESK WITH THE GREEN PHIAL.
I THINK I KNOW THE STUFF... AND IT MAY EVEN DO THE THING AT A GREATER RATE THAN TWICE.
IT WILL BE RATHER A BIG THING.
IT WILL BE, I THINK, RATHER A BIG THING.
BUT I DON'T THINK HE QUITE KNEW WHAT A BIG THING IT WAS TO BE, FOR ALL THAT.
WE HAD SEVERAL TALKS ABOUT THE STUFF AFTER THAT. "THE NEW ACCELERATOR" HE CALLED IT.
IT'S A GOOD THING. A TREMENDOUS THING. I THINK IT ONLY REASONABLE WE SHOULD EXPECT THE WORLD TO PAY. THE DIGNITY OF SCIENCE IS ALL VERY WELL BUT I MUST HAVE THE MONOPOLY FOR, SAY, TEN YEARS. I DON'T SEE WHY *ALL* THE FUN IN LIFE SHOULD GO TO THE DEALERS IN HAM.
MY OWN INTEREST IN THE COMING DRUG CERTAINLY DID NOT WANE. I HAVE ALWAYS BEEN GIVEN TO PARADOXES ABOUT SPACE AND TIME, AND GIBBERNE WAS REALLY PREPARING NO LESS THAN THE ABSOLUTE ACCELERATION OF LIFE. A MAN REPEATEDLY DOSED WOULD BE AN ADULT AT ELEVEN, MIDDLE-AGED AT TWENTY-FIVE, AND BY THIRTY ON THE ROAD TO SENILITY.
THE MARVEL OF DRUGS HAS ALWAYS BEEN GREAT TO MY MIND; YOU CAN MADDEN A MAN, CALM A MAN, MAKE HIM INCREDIBLY STRONG AND ALERT OR A HELPLESS LOG, ALL BY MEANS OF DRUGS, AND HERE WAS A NEW MIRACLE TO BE ADDED TO THIS STRANGE ARMOURY OF PHIALS THE DOCTORS USE!

IT WAS THE 10th OF AUGUST WHEN HE TOLD ME THE NEW ACCELERATOR WAS DONE AND WAS NOW A TANGIBLE REALITY IN THE WORLD. HIS EYES WERE UNUSUALLY BRIGHT AND HIS FACE FLUSHED, AND I NOTED EVEN THE SWIFT ALACRITY OF HIS STEP.

IT'S DONE.

EH?

IT'S MORE THAN DONE. COME UP TO MY HOUSE AND SEE.

REALLY?

AND IT DOES—TWICE?

IT DOES MORE, MUCH MORE. IT SCARES ME. COME UP AND SEE THE STUFF. TASTE IT! TRY IT! IT'S THE MOST AMAZING STUFF ON EARTH.

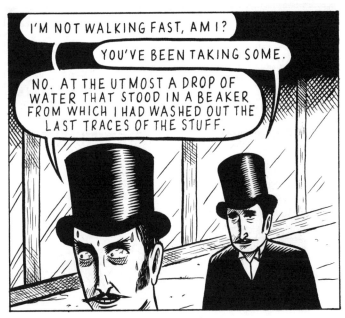

I'M NOT WALKING FAST, AM I?

YOU'VE BEEN TAKING SOME.

NO. AT THE UTMOST A DROP OF WATER THAT STOOD IN A BEAKER FROM WHICH I HAD WASHED OUT THE LAST TRACES OF THE STUFF.

I TOOK SOME LAST NIGHT, YOU KNOW. BUT THAT IS ANCIENT HISTORY NOW.

AND IT GOES TWICE?

IT GOES A THOUSAND TIMES, MANY THOUSAND TIMES!

IT THROWS ALL SORTS OF LIGHT ON NERVOUS PHYSIOLOGY, IT KICKS THE THEORY OF VISION INTO A PERFECTLY NEW SHAPE! HEAVEN KNOWS HOW MANY THOUSAND TIMES. WE'LL TRY ALL THAT AFTER— THE THING IS TO TRY THE STUFF NOW.

TRY THE STUFF?

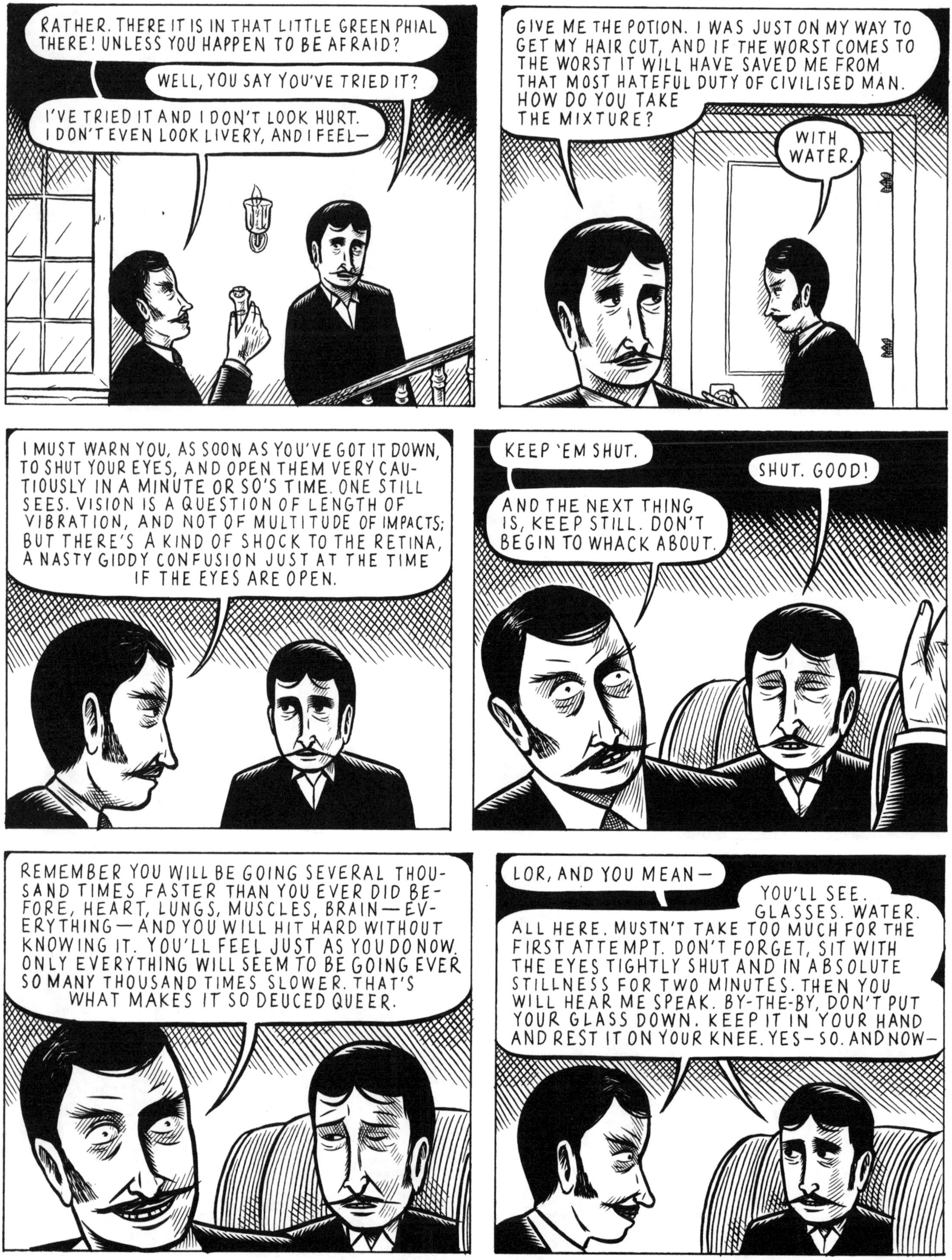
RATHER. THERE IT IS IN THAT LITTLE GREEN PHIAL THERE! UNLESS YOU HAPPEN TO BE AFRAID?
WELL, YOU SAY YOU'VE TRIED IT?
I'VE TRIED IT AND I DON'T LOOK HURT. I DON'T EVEN LOOK LIVERY, AND I FEEL—
GIVE ME THE POTION. I WAS JUST ON MY WAY TO GET MY HAIR CUT, AND IF THE WORST COMES TO THE WORST IT WILL HAVE SAVED ME FROM THAT MOST HATEFUL DUTY OF CIVILISED MAN. HOW DO YOU TAKE THE MIXTURE?
WITH WATER.
I MUST WARN YOU, AS SOON AS YOU'VE GOT IT DOWN, TO SHUT YOUR EYES, AND OPEN THEM VERY CAUTIOUSLY IN A MINUTE OR SO'S TIME. ONE STILL SEES. VISION IS A QUESTION OF LENGTH OF VIBRATION, AND NOT OF MULTITUDE OF IMPACTS; BUT THERE'S A KIND OF SHOCK TO THE RETINA, A NASTY GIDDY CONFUSION JUST AT THE TIME IF THE EYES ARE OPEN.
KEEP 'EM SHUT.
SHUT. GOOD!
AND THE NEXT THING IS, KEEP STILL. DON'T BEGIN TO WHACK ABOUT.
REMEMBER YOU WILL BE GOING SEVERAL THOUSAND TIMES FASTER THAN YOU EVER DID BEFORE, HEART, LUNGS, MUSCLES, BRAIN—EVERYTHING—AND YOU WILL HIT HARD WITHOUT KNOWING IT. YOU'LL FEEL JUST AS YOU DO NOW. ONLY EVERYTHING WILL SEEM TO BE GOING EVER SO MANY THOUSAND TIMES SLOWER. THAT'S WHAT MAKES IT SO DEUCED QUEER.
LOR, AND YOU MEAN—
YOU'LL SEE. GLASSES. WATER. ALL HERE. MUSTN'T TAKE TOO MUCH FOR THE FIRST ATTEMPT. DON'T FORGET, SIT WITH THE EYES TIGHTLY SHUT AND IN ABSOLUTE STILLNESS FOR TWO MINUTES. THEN YOU WILL HEAR ME SPEAK. BY-THE-BY, DON'T PUT YOUR GLASS DOWN. KEEP IT IN YOUR HAND AND REST IT ON YOUR KNEE. YES—SO. AND NOW—

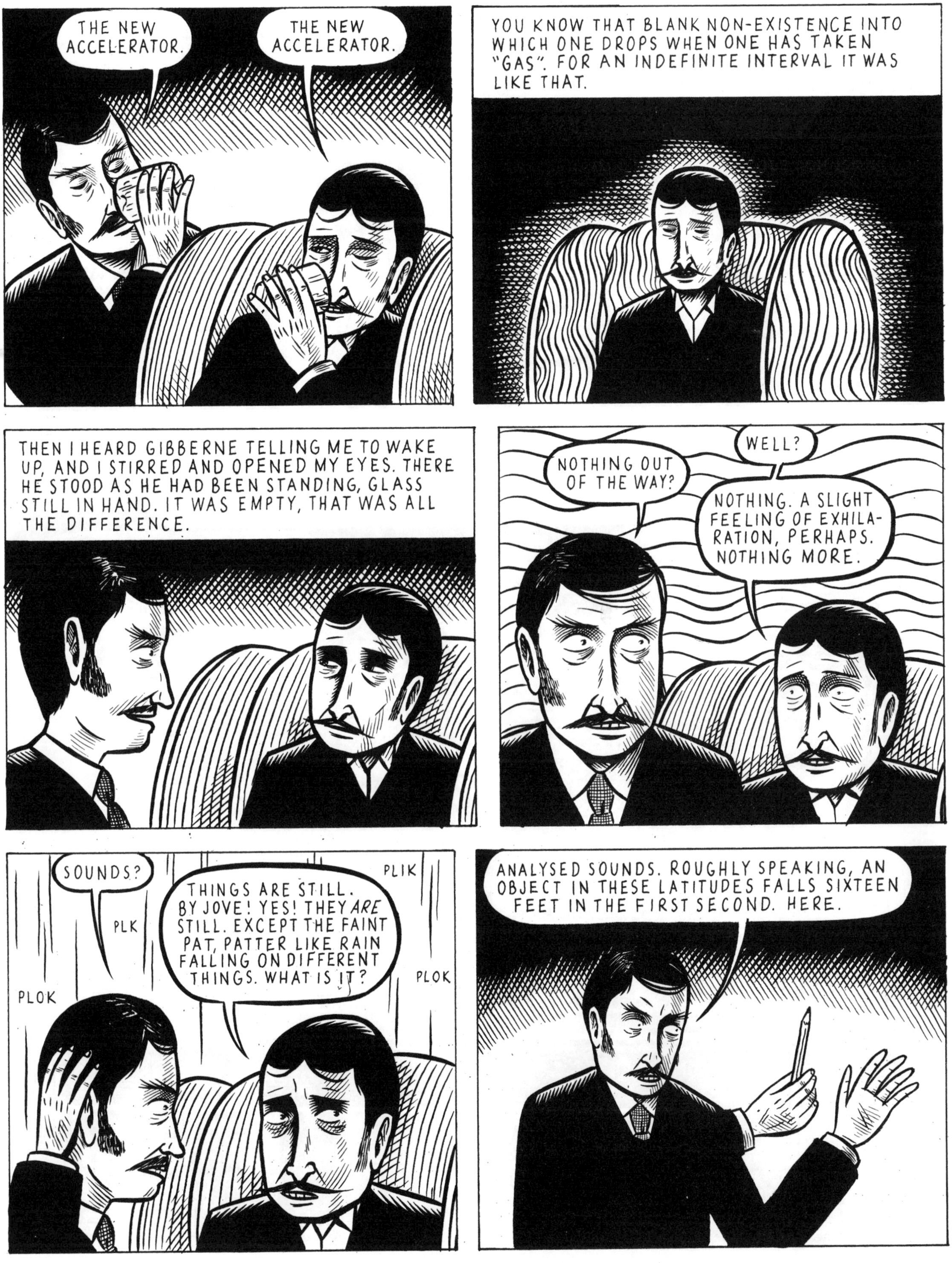
THE NEW ACCELERATOR.
THE NEW ACCELERATOR.
YOU KNOW THAT BLANK NON-EXISTENCE INTO WHICH ONE DROPS WHEN ONE HAS TAKEN "GAS". FOR AN INDEFINITE INTERVAL IT WAS LIKE THAT.
THEN I HEARD GIBBERNE TELLING ME TO WAKE UP, AND I STIRRED AND OPENED MY EYES. THERE HE STOOD AS HE HAD BEEN STANDING, GLASS STILL IN HAND. IT WAS EMPTY, THAT WAS ALL THE DIFFERENCE.
WELL?
NOTHING OUT OF THE WAY?
NOTHING. A SLIGHT FEELING OF EXHILA-RATION, PERHAPS. NOTHING MORE.
SOUNDS?
PLIK
THINGS ARE STILL. BY JOVE! YES! THEY *ARE* STILL. EXCEPT THE FAINT PAT, PATTER LIKE RAIN FALLING ON DIFFERENT THINGS. WHAT IS IT?
PLK
PLOK
PLOK
ANALYSED SOUNDS. ROUGHLY SPEAKING, AN OBJECT IN THESE LATITUDES FALLS SIXTEEN FEET IN THE FIRST SECOND. HERE.

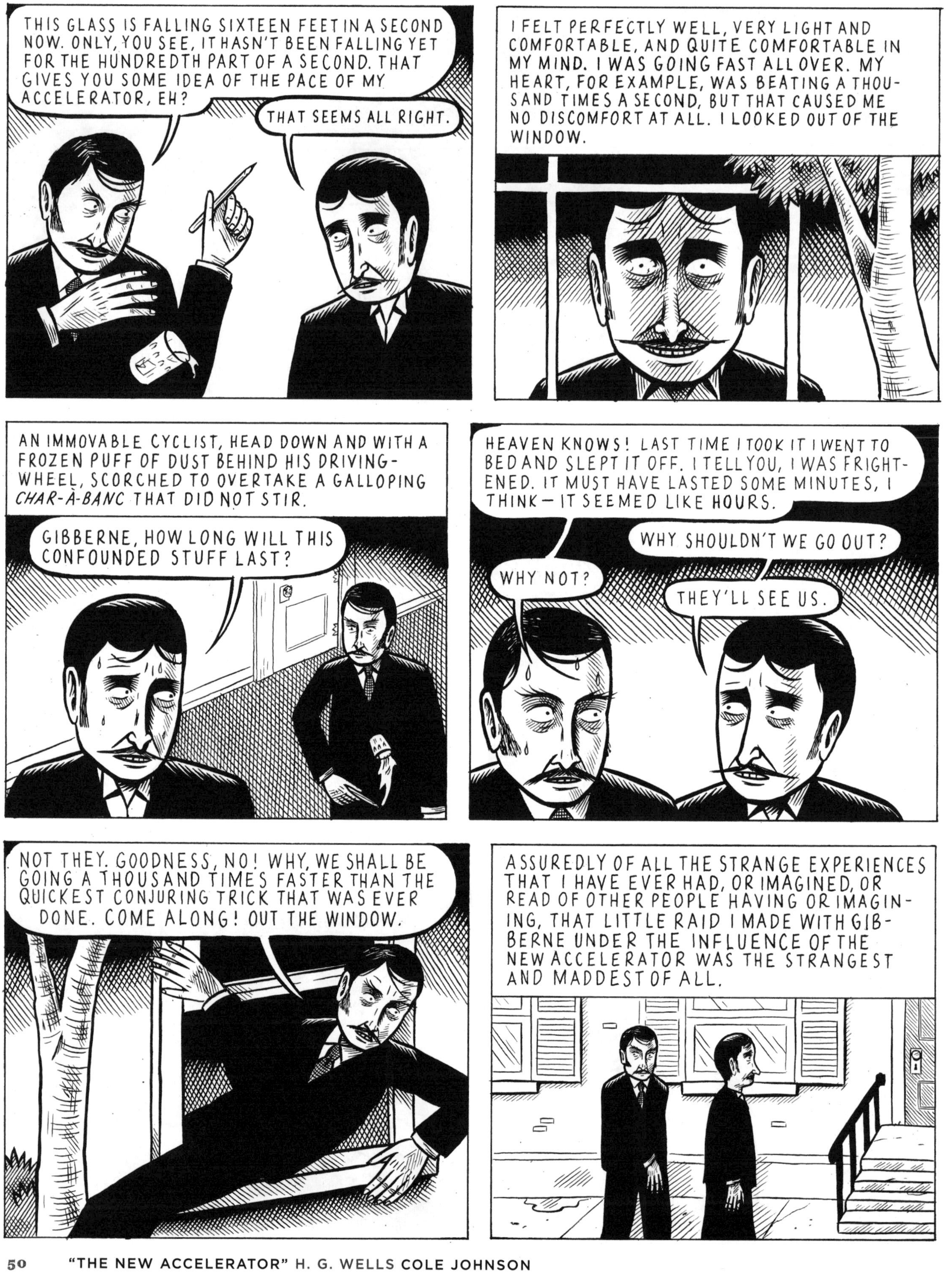

THIS GLASS IS FALLING SIXTEEN FEET IN A SECOND NOW. ONLY, YOU SEE, IT HASN'T BEEN FALLING YET FOR THE HUNDREDTH PART OF A SECOND. THAT GIVES YOU SOME IDEA OF THE PACE OF MY ACCELERATOR, EH?
THAT SEEMS ALL RIGHT.
I FELT PERFECTLY WELL, VERY LIGHT AND COMFORTABLE, AND QUITE COMFORTABLE IN MY MIND. I WAS GOING FAST ALL OVER. MY HEART, FOR EXAMPLE, WAS BEATING A THOUSAND TIMES A SECOND, BUT THAT CAUSED ME NO DISCOMFORT AT ALL. I LOOKED OUT OF THE WINDOW.
AN IMMOVABLE CYCLIST, HEAD DOWN AND WITH A FROZEN PUFF OF DUST BEHIND HIS DRIVING-WHEEL, SCORCHED TO OVERTAKE A GALLOPING *CHAR-À-BANC* THAT DID NOT STIR.
GIBBERNE, HOW LONG WILL THIS CONFOUNDED STUFF LAST?
HEAVEN KNOWS! LAST TIME I TOOK IT I WENT TO BED AND SLEPT IT OFF. I TELL YOU, I WAS FRIGHTENED. IT MUST HAVE LASTED SOME MINUTES, I THINK — IT SEEMED LIKE HOURS.
WHY SHOULDN'T WE GO OUT?
WHY NOT?
THEY'LL SEE US.
NOT THEY. GOODNESS, NO! WHY, WE SHALL BE GOING A THOUSAND TIMES FASTER THAN THE QUICKEST CONJURING TRICK THAT WAS EVER DONE. COME ALONG! OUT THE WINDOW.
ASSUREDLY OF ALL THE STRANGE EXPERIENCES THAT I HAVE EVER HAD, OR IMAGINED, OR READ OF OTHER PEOPLE HAVING OR IMAGINING, THAT LITTLE RAID I MADE WITH GIBBERNE UNDER THE INFLUENCE OF THE NEW ACCELERATOR WAS THE STRANGEST AND MADDEST OF ALL.

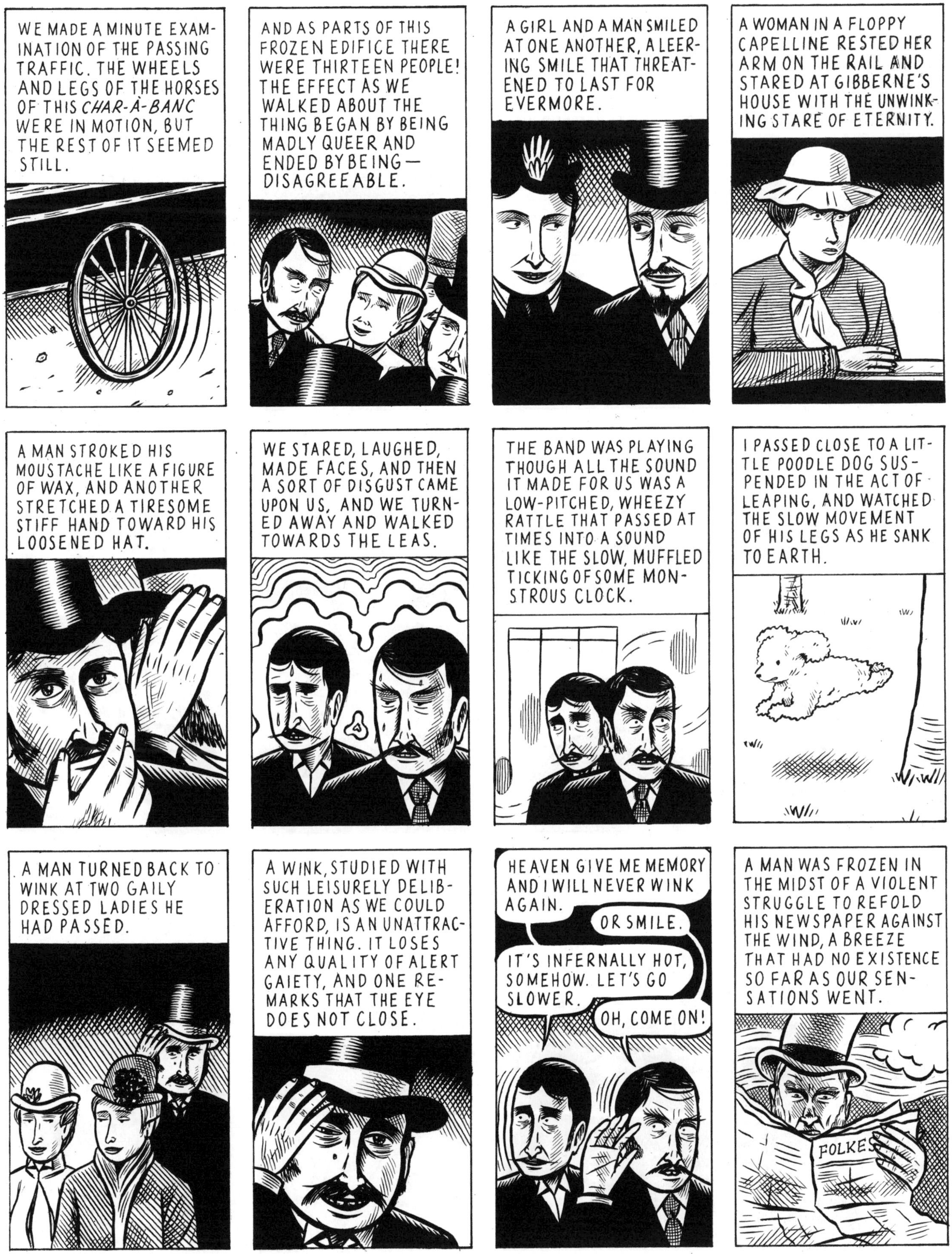
WE MADE A MINUTE EXAMINATION OF THE PASSING TRAFFIC. THE WHEELS AND LEGS OF THE HORSES OF THIS *CHAR-À-BANC* WERE IN MOTION, BUT THE REST OF IT SEEMED STILL.
AND AS PARTS OF THIS FROZEN EDIFICE THERE WERE THIRTEEN PEOPLE! THE EFFECT AS WE WALKED ABOUT THE THING BEGAN BY BEING MADLY QUEER AND ENDED BY BEING— DISAGREEABLE.
A GIRL AND A MAN SMILED AT ONE ANOTHER, A LEERING SMILE THAT THREATENED TO LAST FOR EVERMORE.
A WOMAN IN A FLOPPY CAPELLINE RESTED HER ARM ON THE RAIL AND STARED AT GIBBERNE'S HOUSE WITH THE UNWINKING STARE OF ETERNITY.
A MAN STROKED HIS MOUSTACHE LIKE A FIGURE OF WAX, AND ANOTHER STRETCHED A TIRESOME STIFF HAND TOWARD HIS LOOSENED HAT.
WE STARED, LAUGHED, MADE FACES, AND THEN A SORT OF DISGUST CAME UPON US, AND WE TURNED AWAY AND WALKED TOWARDS THE LEAS.
THE BAND WAS PLAYING THOUGH ALL THE SOUND IT MADE FOR US WAS A LOW-PITCHED, WHEEZY RATTLE THAT PASSED AT TIMES INTO A SOUND LIKE THE SLOW, MUFFLED TICKING OF SOME MONSTROUS CLOCK.
I PASSED CLOSE TO A LITTLE POODLE DOG SUSPENDED IN THE ACT OF LEAPING, AND WATCHED THE SLOW MOVEMENT OF HIS LEGS AS HE SANK TO EARTH.
A MAN TURNED BACK TO WINK AT TWO GAILY DRESSED LADIES HE HAD PASSED.
A WINK, STUDIED WITH SUCH LEISURELY DELIBERATION AS WE COULD AFFORD, IS AN UNATTRACTIVE THING. IT LOSES ANY QUALITY OF ALERT GAIETY, AND ONE REMARKS THAT THE EYE DOES NOT CLOSE.
HEAVEN GIVE ME MEMORY AND I WILL NEVER WINK AGAIN.
OR SMILE.
IT'S INFERNALLY HOT, SOMEHOW. LET'S GO SLOWER.
OH, COME ON!
A MAN WAS FROZEN IN THE MIDST OF A VIOLENT STRUGGLE TO REFOLD HIS NEWSPAPER AGAINST THE WIND, A BREEZE THAT HAD NO EXISTENCE SO FAR AS OUR SENSATIONS WENT.
FOLKES

THERE'S THAT INFERNAL OLD WOMAN!

WHAT OLD WOMAN?

LIVES NEXT DOOR WITH A YAPPING LAPDOG. GODS! THE TEMPTATION IS STRONG!

THERE IS SOMETHING VERY BOYISH AND IMPULSIVE ABOUT GIBBERNE AT TIMES. HE SNATCHED THE ANIMAL OUT OF VISIBLE EXISTENCE AND WAS RUNNING VIOLENTLY WITH IT TOWARDS THE CLIFF OF THE LEAS.

GIBBERNE, PUT IT DOWN! IF YOU RUN LIKE THAT YOU'LL SET YOUR CLOTHES ON FIRE. YOUR LINEN TROUSERS ARE GOING BROWN FROM THE FRICTION OF THE AIR!

WHAT?

FRICTION. GOING TOO FAST LIKE METEORITES AND THINGS. AND GIBBERNE! YOU CAN SEE PEOPLE STIRRING SLIGHTLY. THE STUFF'S WORKING OFF! PUT THAT DOG DOWN!

HE HURLED THE DOG AWAY FROM HIM AND IT WENT SPINNING UPWARD, STILL INANIMATE,

AND HUNG AT LAST OVER THE GROUPED PARASOLS OF A KNOT OF CHATTERING PEOPLE.

BY JOVE! I BELIEVE IT IS! A SORT OF HOT PRICKING AND—YES. THAT MAN'S MOVING HIS POCKET-HANDKERCHIEF! PERCEPTIBLY. WE MUST GET OUT OF THIS SHARP.

BUT WE COULD NOT GET OUT OF IT SHARPLY ENOUGH. LUCKILY, PERHAPS! FOR WE MIGHT HAVE RUN, AND IF WE HAD RUN WE SHOULD, I BELIEVE, HAVE BURST INTO FLAMES.

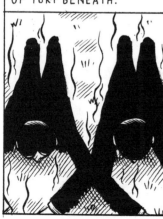

THE EFFECT OF THE ACCELERATOR PASSED LIKE THE DRAWING OF A CURTAIN. WE FLOPPED DOWN, SCORCHING THE PATCH OF TURF BENEATH.

THE WHOLE WORLD HAD COME ALIVE AGAIN, WAS GOING AS FAST AS WE WERE, OR RATHER WE WERE GOING NO FASTER THAN THE REST OF THE WORLD.

THE LITTLE DOG, WHICH HAD SEEMED TO HANG FOR A MOMENT WHEN THE FORCE OF GIBBERNE'S ARM WAS EXPENDED, FELL WITH A SWIFT ACCELERATION CLEAN THROUGH A LADY'S PARASOL!

THAT WAS THE SAVING OF US. I DOUBT IF A SOLITARY PERSON REMARKED OUR SUDDEN APPEARANCE AMONG THEM. PLOP! WE MUST HAVE APPEARED ABRUPTLY.

"THE NEW ACCELERATOR" H. G. WELLS COLE JOHNSON

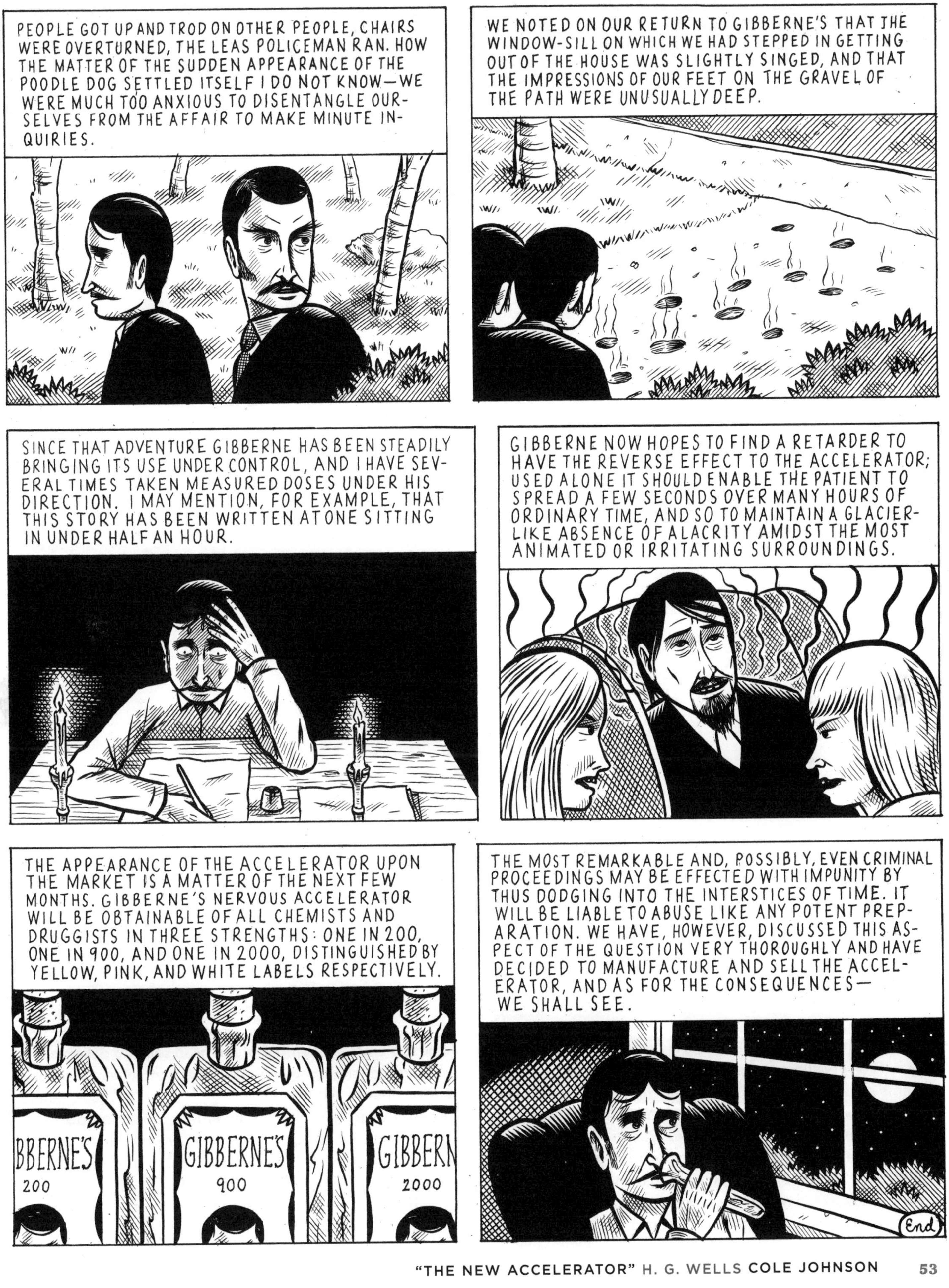
PEOPLE GOT UP AND TROD ON OTHER PEOPLE, CHAIRS WERE OVERTURNED, THE LEAS POLICEMAN RAN. HOW THE MATTER OF THE SUDDEN APPEARANCE OF THE POODLE DOG SETTLED ITSELF I DO NOT KNOW—WE WERE MUCH TOO ANXIOUS TO DISENTANGLE OURSELVES FROM THE AFFAIR TO MAKE MINUTE INQUIRIES.
WE NOTED ON OUR RETURN TO GIBBERNE'S THAT THE WINDOW-SILL ON WHICH WE HAD STEPPED IN GETTING OUT OF THE HOUSE WAS SLIGHTLY SINGED, AND THAT THE IMPRESSIONS OF OUR FEET ON THE GRAVEL OF THE PATH WERE UNUSUALLY DEEP.
SINCE THAT ADVENTURE GIBBERNE HAS BEEN STEADILY BRINGING ITS USE UNDER CONTROL, AND I HAVE SEVERAL TIMES TAKEN MEASURED DOSES UNDER HIS DIRECTION. I MAY MENTION, FOR EXAMPLE, THAT THIS STORY HAS BEEN WRITTEN AT ONE SITTING IN UNDER HALF AN HOUR.
GIBBERNE NOW HOPES TO FIND A RETARDER TO HAVE THE REVERSE EFFECT TO THE ACCELERATOR; USED ALONE IT SHOULD ENABLE THE PATIENT TO SPREAD A FEW SECONDS OVER MANY HOURS OF ORDINARY TIME, AND SO TO MAINTAIN A GLACIER-LIKE ABSENCE OF ALACRITY AMIDST THE MOST ANIMATED OR IRRITATING SURROUNDINGS.
THE APPEARANCE OF THE ACCELERATOR UPON THE MARKET IS A MATTER OF THE NEXT FEW MONTHS. GIBBERNE'S NERVOUS ACCELERATOR WILL BE OBTAINABLE OF ALL CHEMISTS AND DRUGGISTS IN THREE STRENGTHS: ONE IN 200, ONE IN 900, AND ONE IN 2000, DISTINGUISHED BY YELLOW, PINK, AND WHITE LABELS RESPECTIVELY.
BBERNE'S
200
GIBBERNE'S
900
GIBBERN
2000
THE MOST REMARKABLE AND, POSSIBLY, EVEN CRIMINAL PROCEEDINGS MAY BE EFFECTED WITH IMPUNITY BY THUS DODGING INTO THE INTERSTICES OF TIME. IT WILL BE LIABLE TO ABUSE LIKE ANY POTENT PREPARATION. WE HAVE, HOWEVER, DISCUSSED THIS ASPECT OF THE QUESTION VERY THOROUGHLY AND HAVE DECIDED TO MANUFACTURE AND SELL THE ACCELERATOR, AND AS FOR THE CONSEQUENCES—WE SHALL SEE.
End

"Reginald"

Saki

ART/ADAPTATION BY **Sonia Leong**

H. H. MUNRO—BETTER KNOWN AS SAKI—PUBLISHED over 150 very short stories and sketches, perfectly cut little gems of droll, mordant wit, usually first appearing in British newspapers. He's often compared to Oscar Wilde, P. G. Wodehouse (creator of Jeeves and Wooster), O. Henry (but with more bite), and Dorothy Parker. The Penguin Classics edition of his complete works explains: "Macabre, acid, and very funny, Saki's work drives a knife into the upper crust of English Edwardian life." Many of his stories feature Reginald, a handsome, effete member of the posh set who delights in upsetting and terrorizing his fellow aristocrats. Munro died on the front lines of World War I, cut down by a German sniper.

Sonia Leong came to my attention with her spot-on manga adaptation of *Romeo and Juliet*. When I approached her about contributing to *The Graphic Canon*, she wanted to do the first Reginald story, circa 1904. With manga's penchant for pretty boys, it's the perfect style for Saki's scandalous dandy.

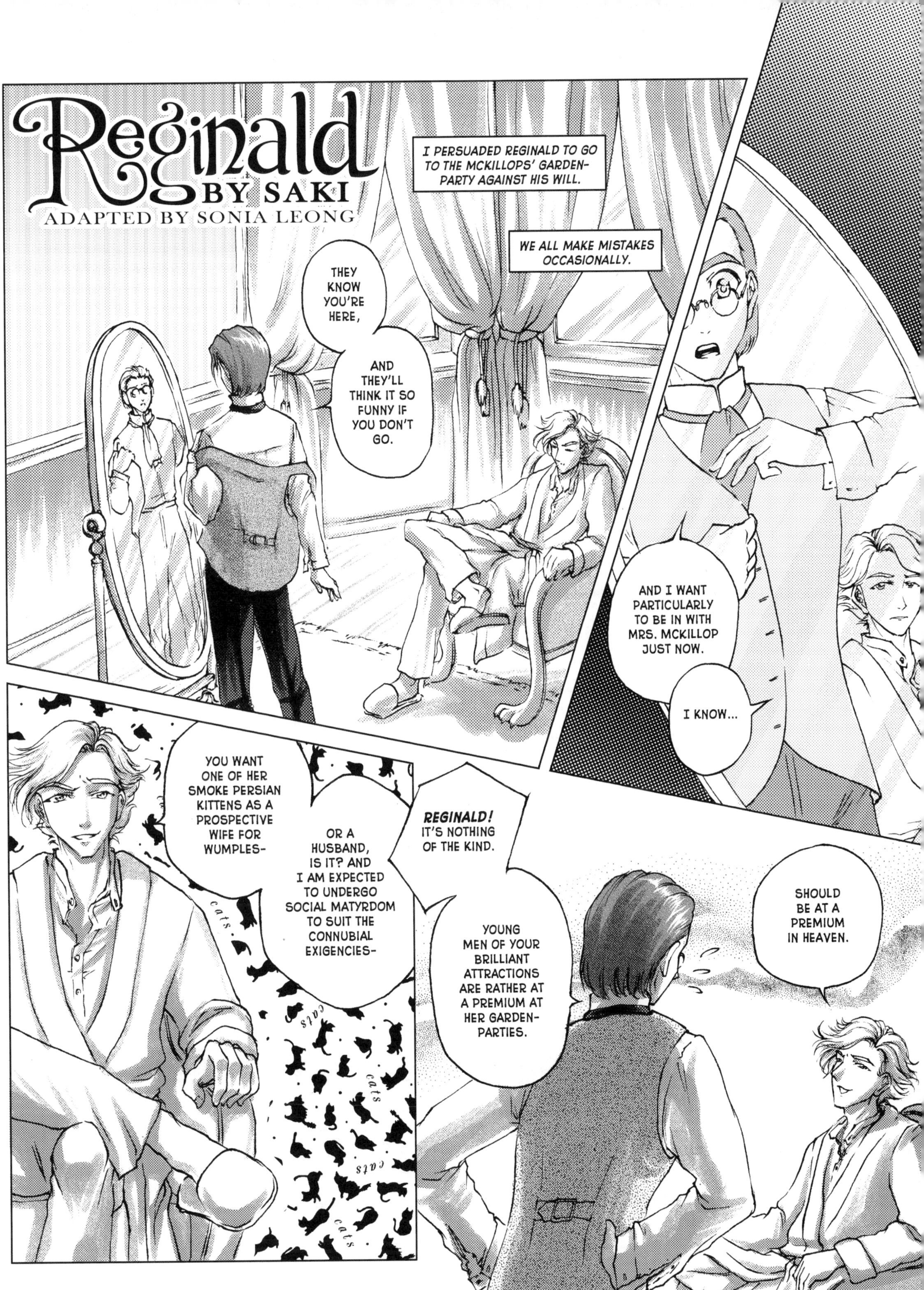
Reginald
BY SAKI
ADAPTED BY SONIA LEONG
I PERSUADED REGINALD TO GO TO THE MCKILLOPS' GARDEN-PARTY AGAINST HIS WILL.
WE ALL MAKE MISTAKES OCCASIONALLY.
THEY KNOW YOU'RE HERE,
AND THEY'LL THINK IT SO FUNNY IF YOU DON'T GO.
AND I WANT PARTICULARLY TO BE IN WITH MRS. MCKILLOP JUST NOW.
I KNOW...
YOU WANT ONE OF HER SMOKE PERSIAN KITTENS AS A PROSPECTIVE WIFE FOR WUMPLES-
OR A HUSBAND, IS IT? AND I AM EXPECTED TO UNDERGO SOCIAL MATYRDOM TO SUIT THE CONNUBIAL EXIGENCIES-
REGINALD! IT'S NOTHING OF THE KIND.
YOUNG MEN OF YOUR BRILLIANT ATTRACTIONS ARE RATHER AT A PREMIUM AT HER GARDEN-PARTIES.
SHOULD BE AT A PREMIUM IN HEAVEN.

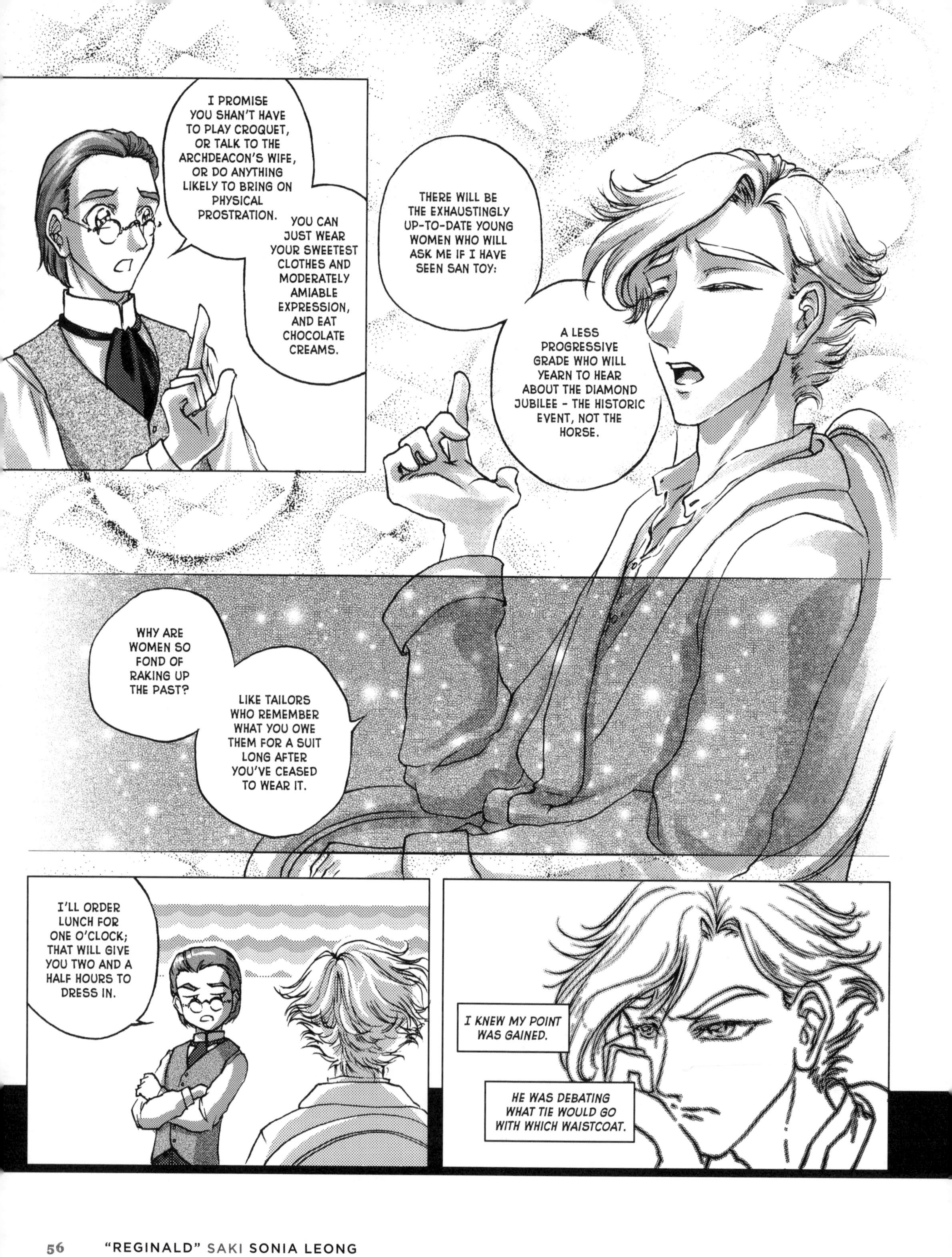
I PROMISE YOU SHAN'T HAVE TO PLAY CROQUET, OR TALK TO THE ARCHDEACON'S WIFE, OR DO ANYTHING LIKELY TO BRING ON PHYSICAL PROSTRATION.
YOU CAN JUST WEAR YOUR SWEETEST CLOTHES AND MODERATELY AMIABLE EXPRESSION, AND EAT CHOCOLATE CREAMS.
THERE WILL BE THE EXHAUSTINGLY UP-TO-DATE YOUNG WOMEN WHO WILL ASK ME IF I HAVE SEEN SAN TOY:
A LESS PROGRESSIVE GRADE WHO WILL YEARN TO HEAR ABOUT THE DIAMOND JUBILEE - THE HISTORIC EVENT, NOT THE HORSE.
WHY ARE WOMEN SO FOND OF RAKING UP THE PAST?
LIKE TAILORS WHO REMEMBER WHAT YOU OWE THEM FOR A SUIT LONG AFTER YOU'VE CEASED TO WEAR IT.
I'LL ORDER LUNCH FOR ONE O'CLOCK; THAT WILL GIVE YOU TWO AND A HALF HOURS TO DRESS IN.
I KNEW MY POINT WAS GAINED.
HE WAS DEBATING WHAT TIE WOULD GO WITH WHICH WAISTCOAT.

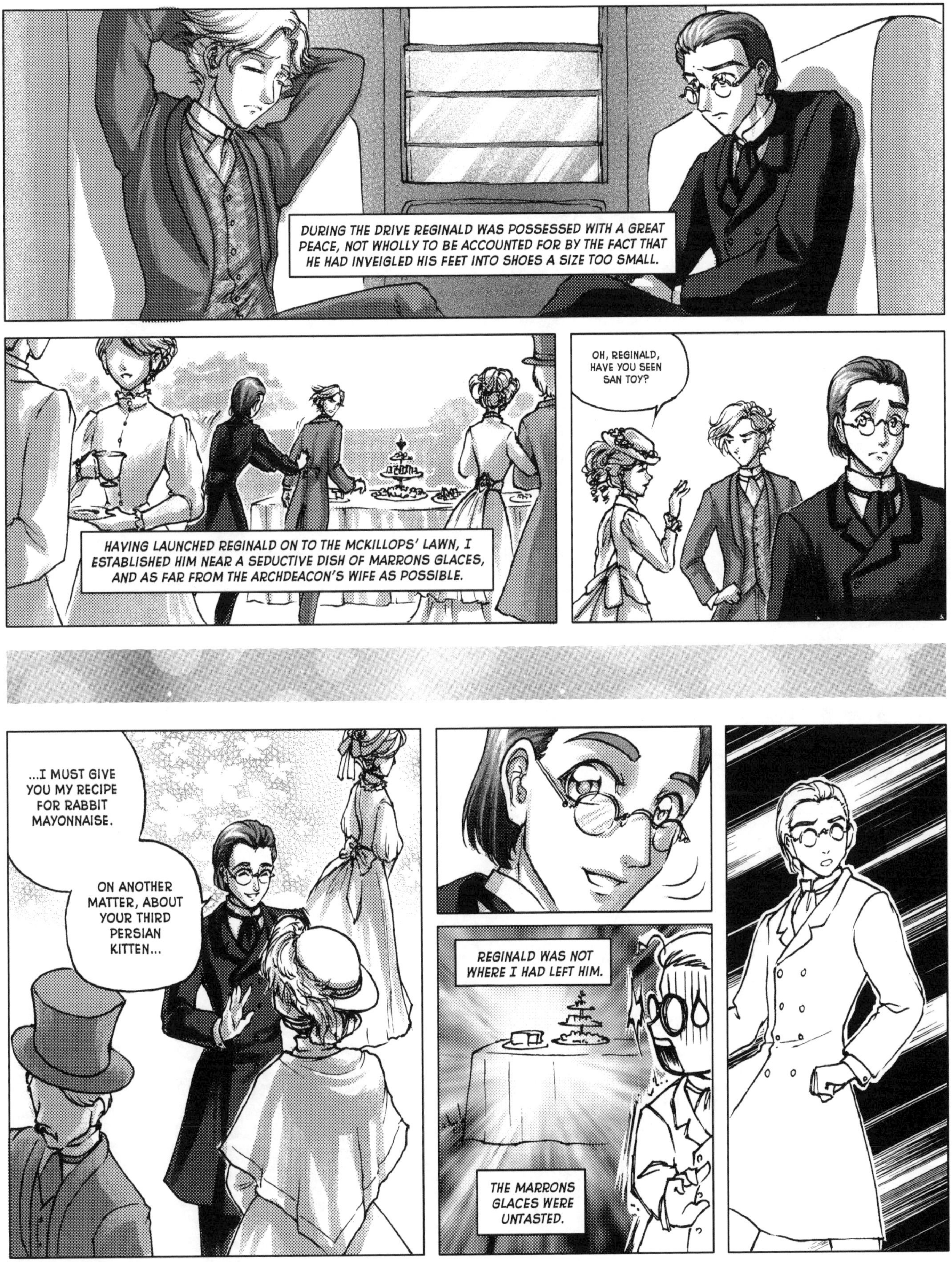
DURING THE DRIVE REGINALD WAS POSSESSED WITH A GREAT PEACE, NOT WHOLLY TO BE ACCOUNTED FOR BY THE FACT THAT HE HAD INVEIGLED HIS FEET INTO SHOES A SIZE TOO SMALL.
HAVING LAUNCHED REGINALD ON TO THE MCKILLOPS' LAWN, I ESTABLISHED HIM NEAR A SEDUCTIVE DISH OF MARRONS GLACES, AND AS FAR FROM THE ARCHDEACON'S WIFE AS POSSIBLE.
OH, REGINALD, HAVE YOU SEEN SAN TOY?
...I MUST GIVE YOU MY RECIPE FOR RABBIT MAYONNAISE.
ON ANOTHER MATTER, ABOUT YOUR THIRD PERSIAN KITTEN...
REGINALD WAS NOT WHERE I HAD LEFT HIM.
THE MARRONS GLACES WERE UNTASTED.

OLD COLONEL MENDOZA WAS ESSAYING TO TELL HIS STORY OF HOW HE INTRODUCED GOLF TO INDIA. REGINALD WAS IN DANGEROUS PROXIMITY.

WHEN I WAS AT POONA IN '76—

MY DEAR COLONEL!

SUCH A GIVE-AWAY FOR ONE'S AGE! I WOULDN'T ADMIT TO BEING ON THIS PLANET IN '76.

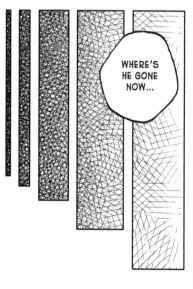

WHERE'S HE GONE NOW...

AH, WITH THE YOUNG RAMPAGE BOY...

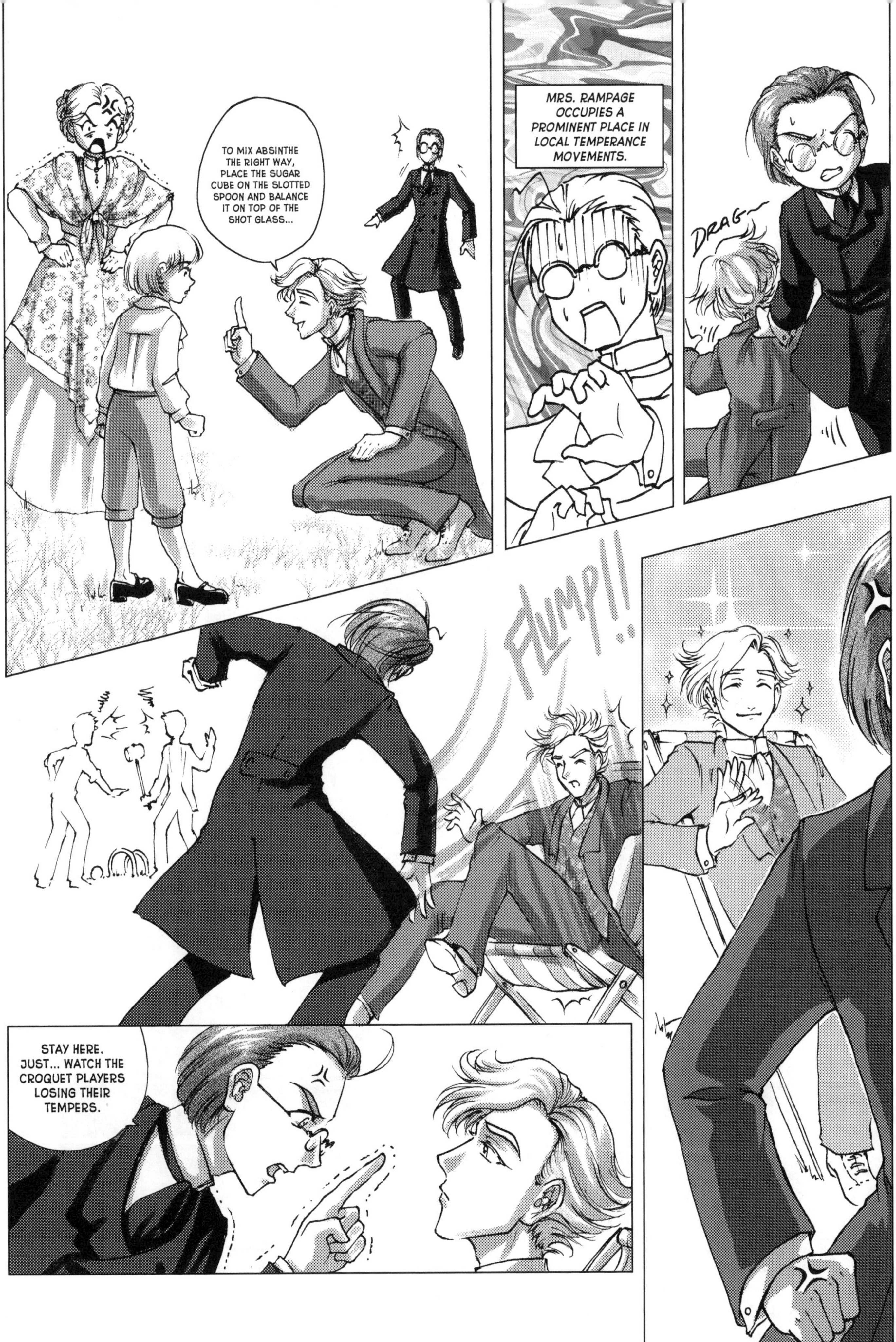
TO MIX ABSINTHE THE RIGHT WAY, PLACE THE SUGAR CUBE ON THE SLOTTED SPOON AND BALANCE IT ON TOP OF THE SHOT GLASS...
MRS. RAMPAGE OCCUPIES A PROMINENT PLACE IN LOCAL TEMPERANCE MOVEMENTS.
DRAG~
FLUMP!!
STAY HERE. JUST... WATCH THE CROQUET PLAYERS LOSING THEIR TEMPERS.

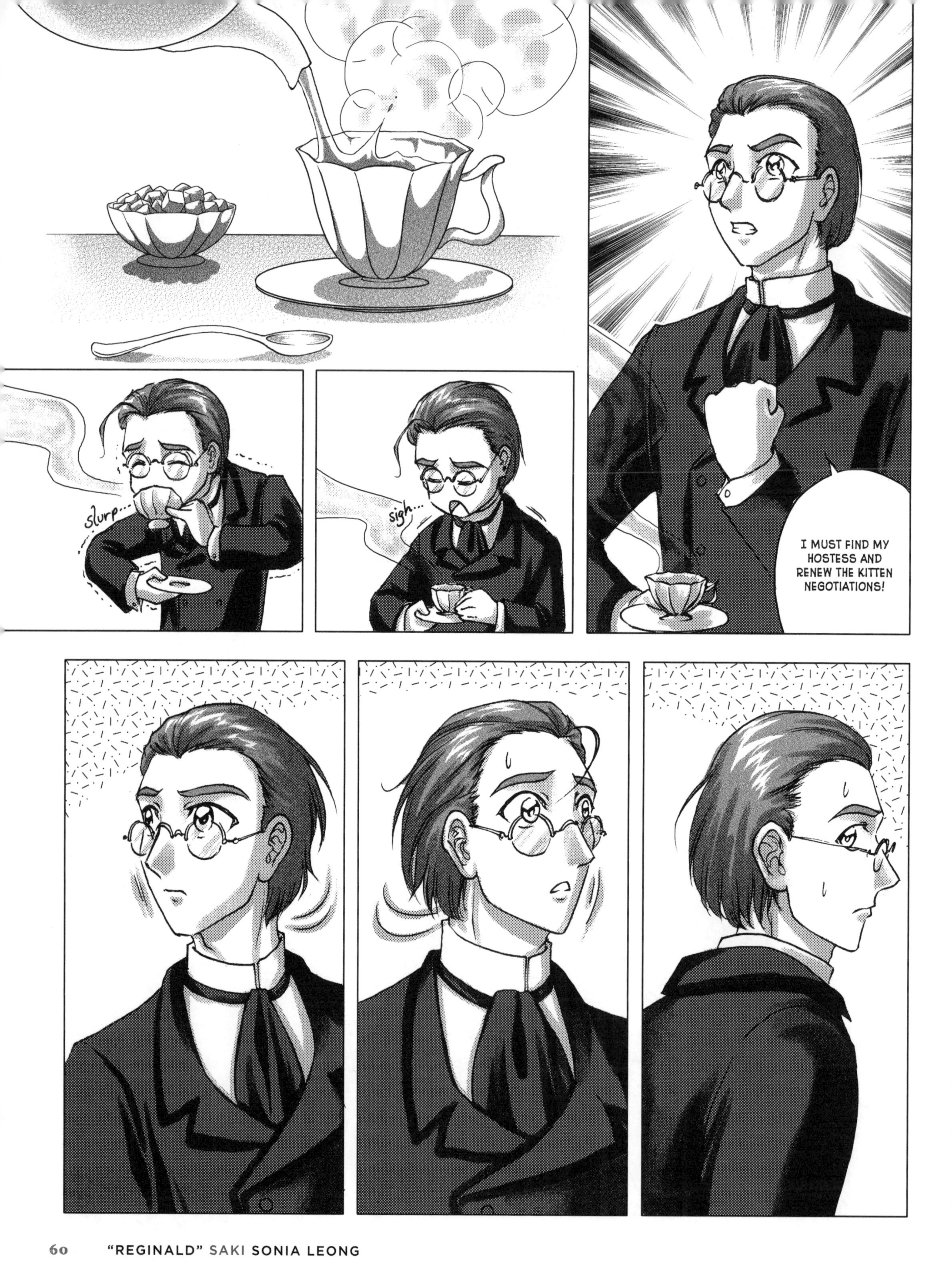
slurp...
sigh...
I MUST FIND MY HOSTESS AND RENEW THE KITTEN NEGOTIATIONS!

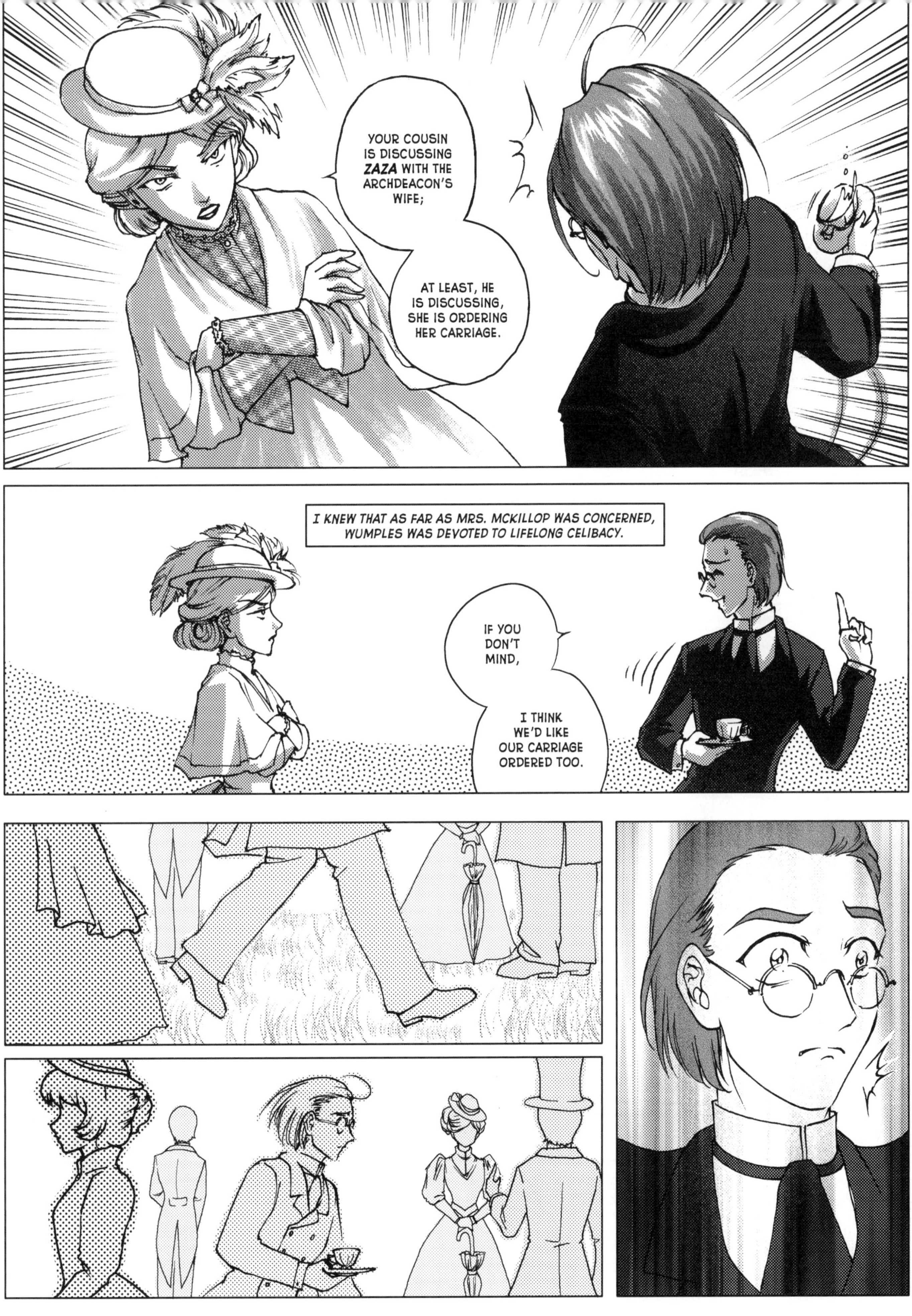
YOUR COUSIN IS DISCUSSING ZAZA WITH THE ARCHDEACON'S WIFE;
AT LEAST, HE IS DISCUSSING, SHE IS ORDERING HER CARRIAGE.
I KNEW THAT AS FAR AS MRS. MCKILLOP WAS CONCERNED, WUMPLES WAS DEVOTED TO LIFELONG CELIBACY.
IF YOU DON'T MIND,
I THINK WE'D LIKE OUR CARRIAGE ORDERED TOO.

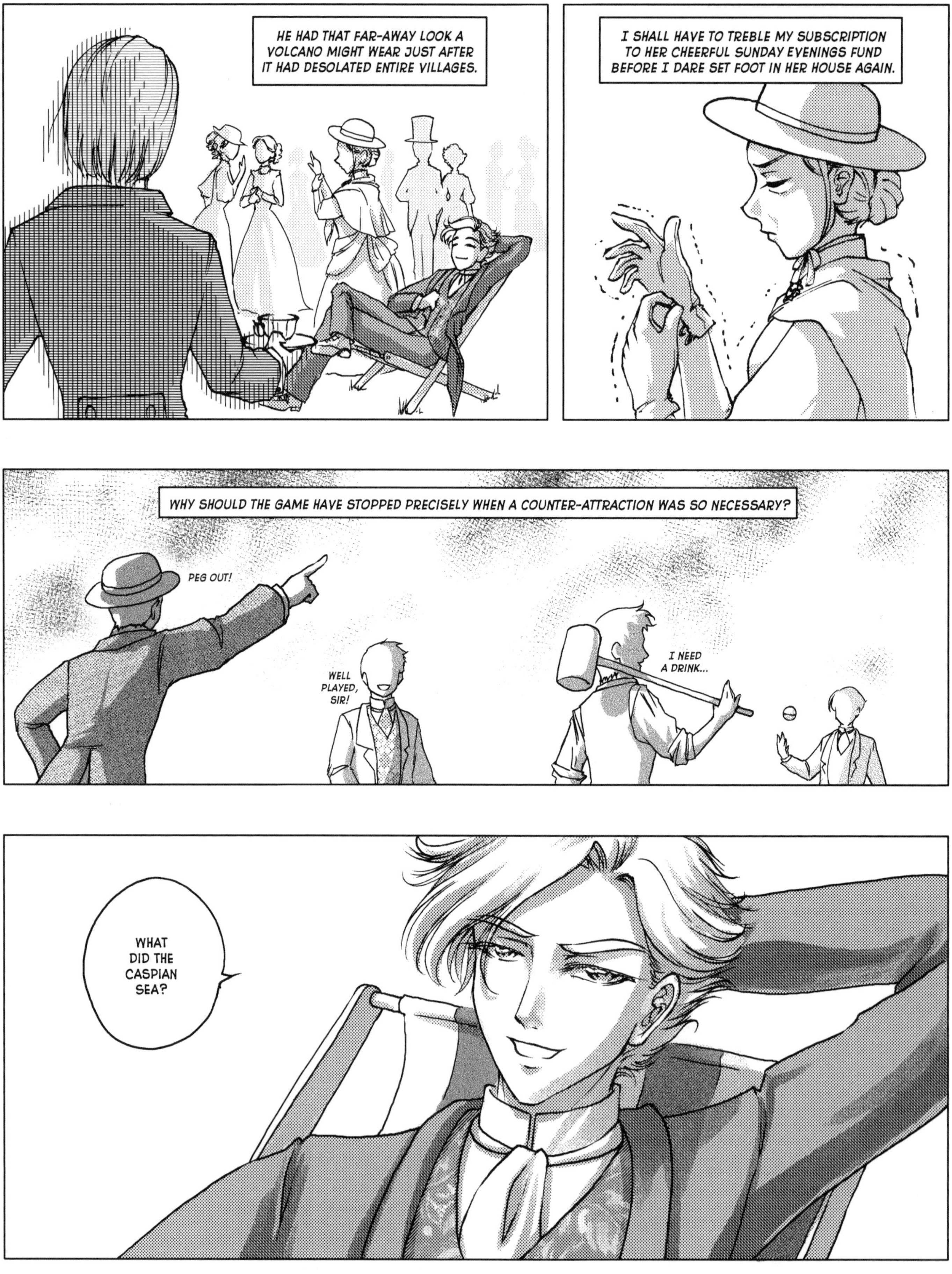
HE HAD THAT FAR-AWAY LOOK A VOLCANO MIGHT WEAR JUST AFTER IT HAD DESOLATED ENTIRE VILLAGES.
I SHALL HAVE TO TREBLE MY SUBSCRIPTION TO HER CHEERFUL SUNDAY EVENINGS FUND BEFORE I DARE SET FOOT IN HER HOUSE AGAIN.
WHY SHOULD THE GAME HAVE STOPPED PRECISELY WHEN A COUNTER-ATTRACTION WAS SO NECESSARY?
PEG OUT!
WELL PLAYED, SIR!
I NEED A DRINK...
WHAT DID THE CASPIAN SEA?

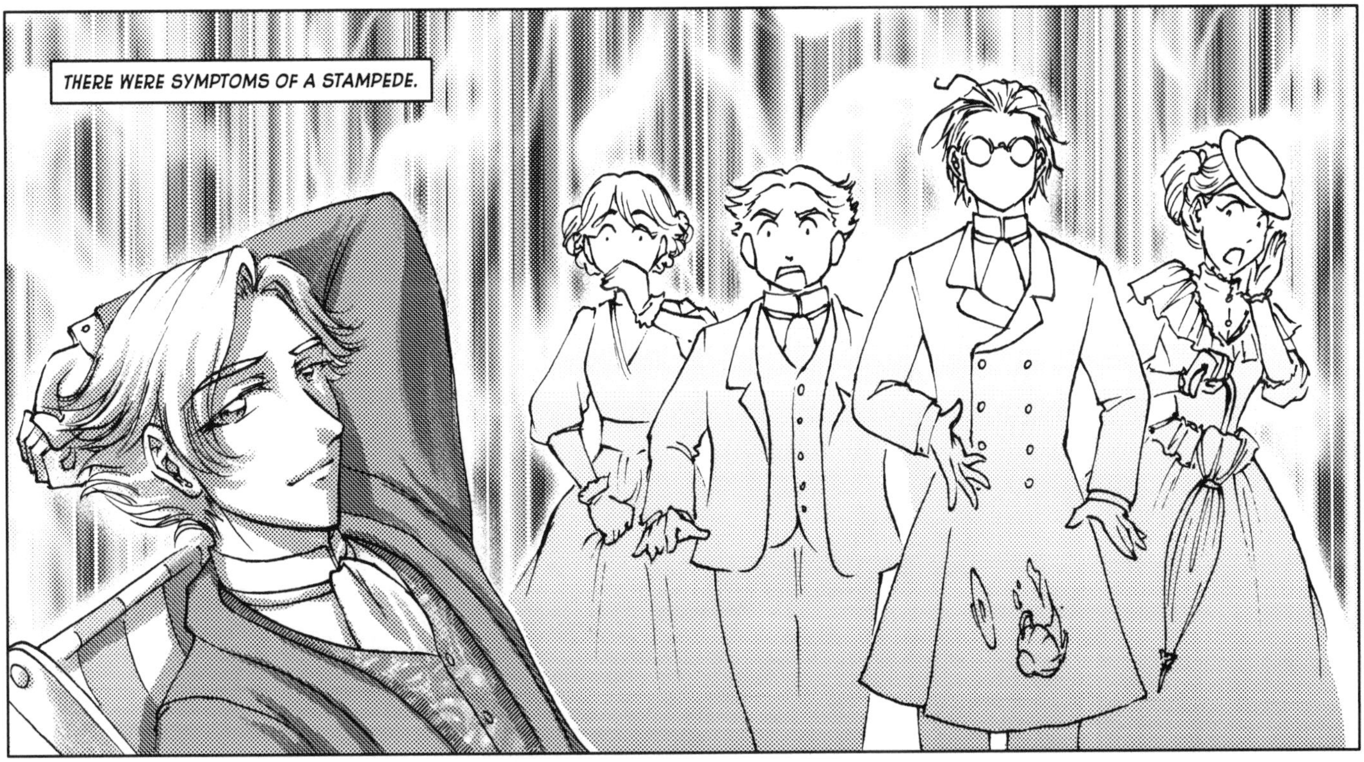
THERE WERE SYMPTOMS OF A STAMPEDE.

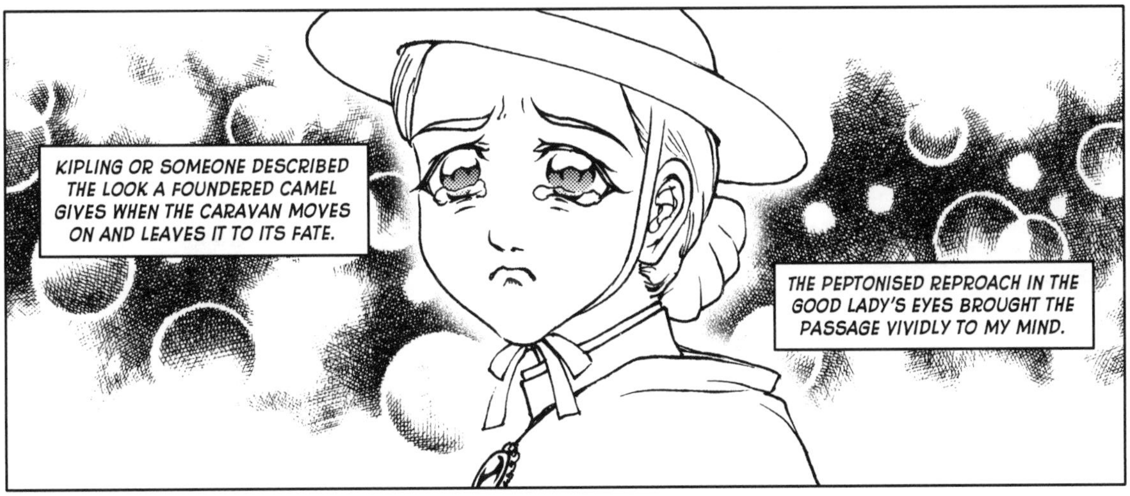
KIPLING OR SOMEONE DESCRIBED THE LOOK A FOUNDERED CAMEL GIVES WHEN THE CARAVAN MOVES ON AND LEAVES IT TO ITS FATE.
THE PEPTONISED REPROACH IN THE GOOD LADY'S EYES BROUGHT THE PASSAGE VIVIDLY TO MY MIND.

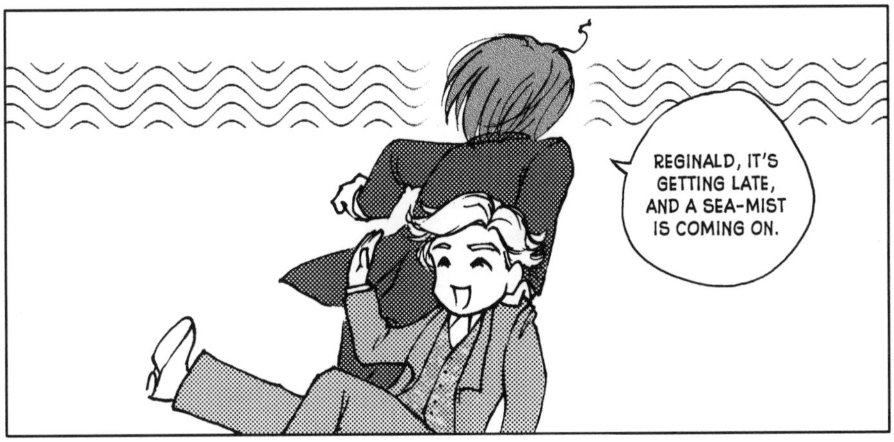
REGINALD, IT'S GETTING LATE, AND A SEA-MIST IS COMING ON.

NEVER, NEVER AGAIN, WILL I TAKE YOU TO A GARDEN-PARTY.

YOU BEHAVED ABOMINABLY... WHAT DID THE CASPIAN SEE?

I BELIEVE AN APRICOT TIE WOULD HAVE GONE BETTER WITH THE LILAC WAISTCOAT.

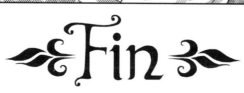

Three Panel Review
Lisa Brown

A ROOM WITH A VIEW by E.M. Forster
George is UNCONVENTIONAL
3.1.11
Cecil is a BORE.
Yawn.
© 2011 LISA M. BROWN | DIST. BY TRIBUNE MEDIA SERVICES, INC.
How to choose?

Mother

Maxim Gorky

ART/ADAPTATION BY **Stephanie McMillan**

MAXIM GORKY'S HIGH PLACE IN THE RUSSIAN literary pantheon isn't because he had the pure literary chops of Tolstoy, Dostoevsky, or Chekhov, but instead because of his choice of style and theme. He wrote persuasively and movingly of the plight of the workers in Tsarist Russia and of the need for organization and revolution. The nine-volume *Kratkaya literaturnaya entsiklopediya* dubbed him "the founder of socialist realism and originator of Soviet literature." Gorky was a member of the Bolshevik Party and put his writing talents—for novels, plays, poetry, and essays—to use furthering the cause.

His 1907 novel *Mother* is often considered his masterpiece. It would've been too obvious if Gorky had made the young, male revolutionary hero, Pavel Vlasov, the protagonist of the book. Instead, the main character is his mother, Pelagea Nilovna, who undergoes a radical political awakening, from abused worker and wife to fully conscious revolutionary. *The Handbook of Russian Literature* says that "it is difficult to name a work of Russian literature which has had more influence, political as well as literary." James Baldwin—author of the classics *Go Tell It on the Mountain* and *Giovanni's Room*—wrote that "the reasons for this resounding popularity are evident on every brave and bitter page. . . . It is rich in struggle, tears, courage, and good old-fashioned mother love."

Stephanie McMillan is a political/environmental cartoonist whose work includes the weekly *Code Green*, the daily *Minimum Security*, and the graphic novel *As the World Burns: 50 Simple Things You Can Do to Stay in Denial* (with Derrick Jensen). Her abbreviated adaptation starts on the day of the mass demonstration and continues through the end of the novel. She explains:

I chose *Mother* because it has deeply influenced and inspired revolutionaries all over the world since its writing in 1907. Gorky is considered the bridge between Russian classical literature and Soviet literature, and *Mother* is the first Russian novel about the working class and its struggle for emancipation. It's based on true events: the May Day demonstration in Sormovo in 1902 and its aftermath. But the ideals, emotions, and politics it expresses are internationally relevant and still timely. I wanted to help re-popularize this novel as a great example of political art (and to affirm the necessity of political art in a culture that demands art be apolitical); also so that it can inspire a new generation of revolutionaries-in-the-making.

SOURCES

Baldwin, James. *The Cross of Redemption: Uncollected Writings.* Edited by Randall Kenan. New York: Vintage, 2011.

Terras, Richard, ed. *Handbook of Russian Literature*. New Haven, CT: Yale University Press, 1990.

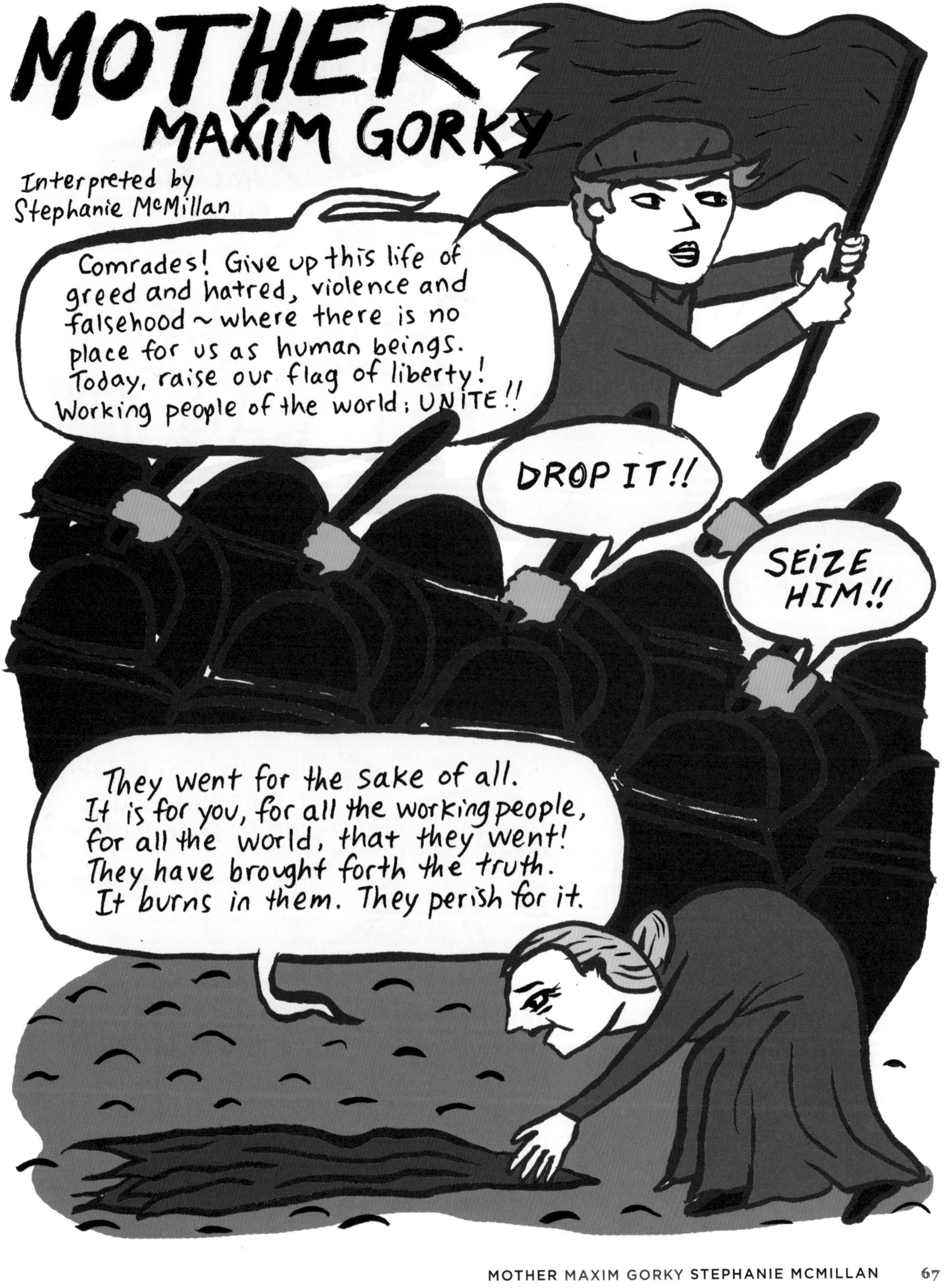
MOTHER
MAXIM GORKY
Interpreted by Stephanie McMillan
Comrades! Give up this life of greed and hatred, violence and falsehood ~ where there is no place for us as human beings. Today, raise our flag of liberty! Working people of the world: UNITE!!
DROP IT!!
SEIZE HIM!!
They went for the sake of all. It is for you, for all the working people, for all the world, that they went! They have brought forth the truth. It burns in them. They perish for it.

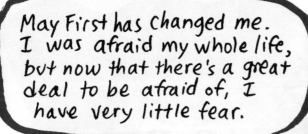

May First has changed me. I was afraid my whole life, but now that there's a great deal to be afraid of, I have very little fear.

Pavel will be tried?

Yes. They've decided on a trial.

What'll he get?

Hard labor, or exile for life.

When he started this, did he know what was in store for him?

Yes. He knew he might be struck with a bayonet, or exiled into hard labor, but he felt it was necessary to go, so he went. If his mother had lain across his path, he would have stepped over her body and gone his way.

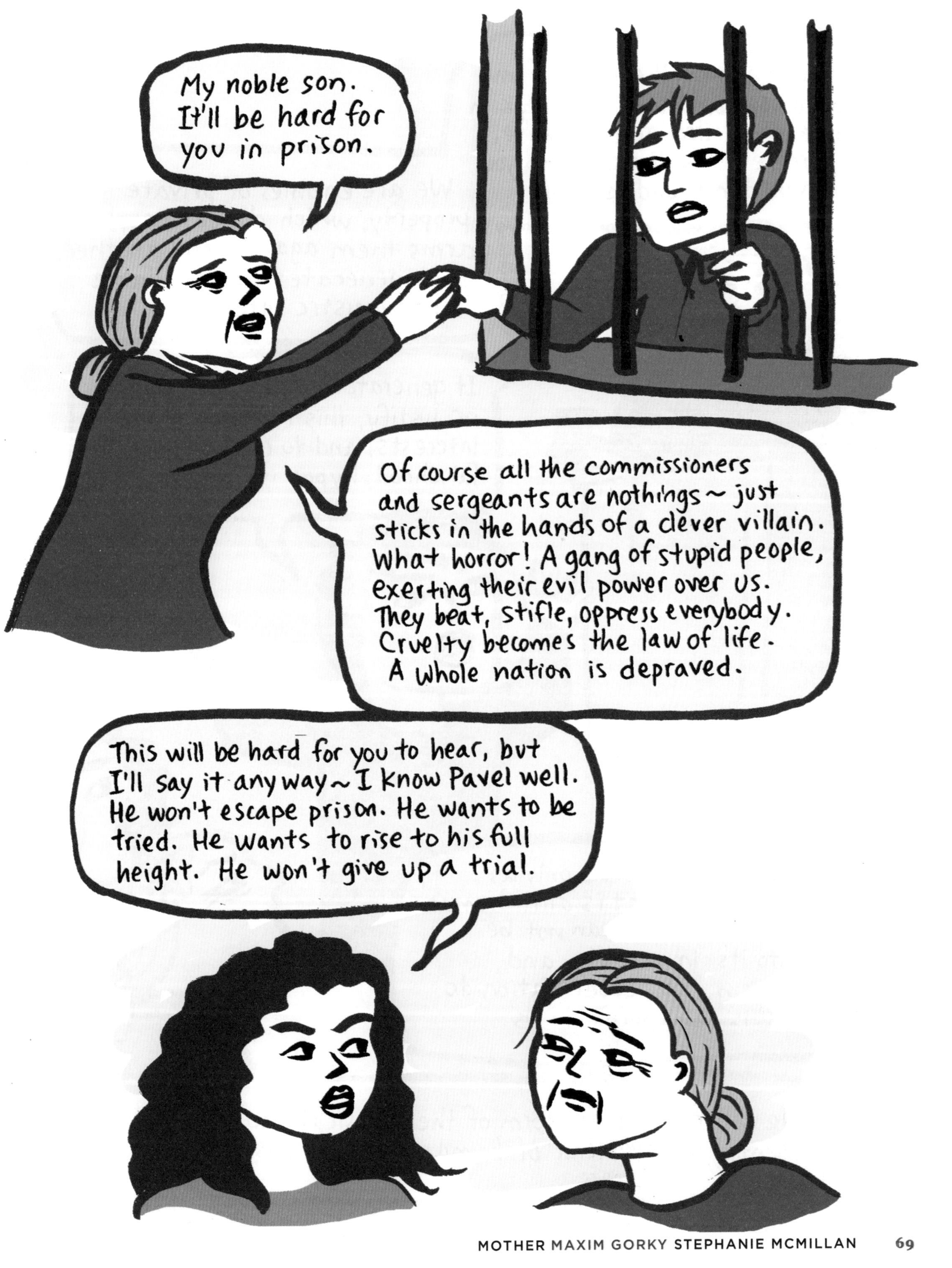
My noble son. It'll be hard for you in prison.
Of course all the commissioners and sergeants are nothings ~ just sticks in the hands of a clever villain. What horror! A gang of stupid people, exerting their evil power over us. They beat, stifle, oppress everybody. Cruelty becomes the law of life. A whole nation is depraved.
This will be hard for you to hear, but I'll say it anyway ~ I know Pavel well. He won't escape prison. He wants to be tried. He wants to rise to his full height. He won't give up a trial.

I recognize only the court of my organization, and will not speak in my defense. I decline a defense. I will merely try to explain to you what you don't understand.
We are enemies of private property, which divides people, arms them against one another, and generates irreconcilable antagonistic interests.
It generates lies to cover up, or justify, this conflict of interests, and to corrupt all with falsehood, hypocrisy, and malice.
A society that regards us only as tools for its enrichment is anti-human. It is hostile to us. We can not be reconciled to its immorality and lying cynicism. Its cruel relation to individuals is repugnant to us.
We will fight every form of the physical and mental enslavement of humanity by the system.

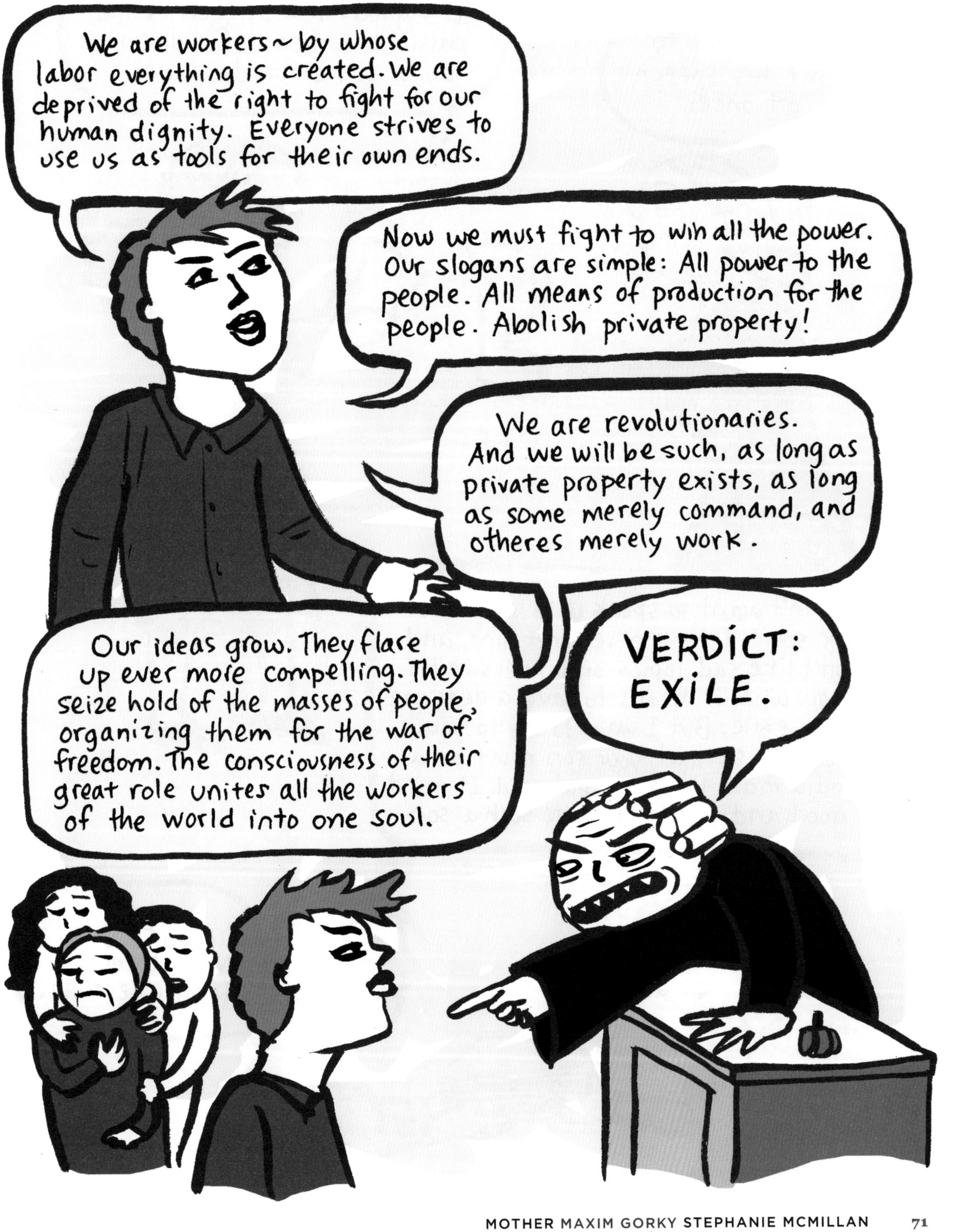
We are workers ~ by whose labor everything is created. We are deprived of the right to fight for our human dignity. Everyone strives to use us as tools for their own ends.
Now we must fight to win all the power. Our slogans are simple: All power to the people. All means of production for the people. Abolish private property!
We are revolutionaries. And we will be such, as long as private property exists, as long as some merely command, and otheres merely work.
Our ideas grow. They flare up ever more compelling. They seize hold of the masses of people, organizing them for the war of freedom. The consciousness of their great role unites all the workers of the world into one soul.
VERDICT: EXILE.

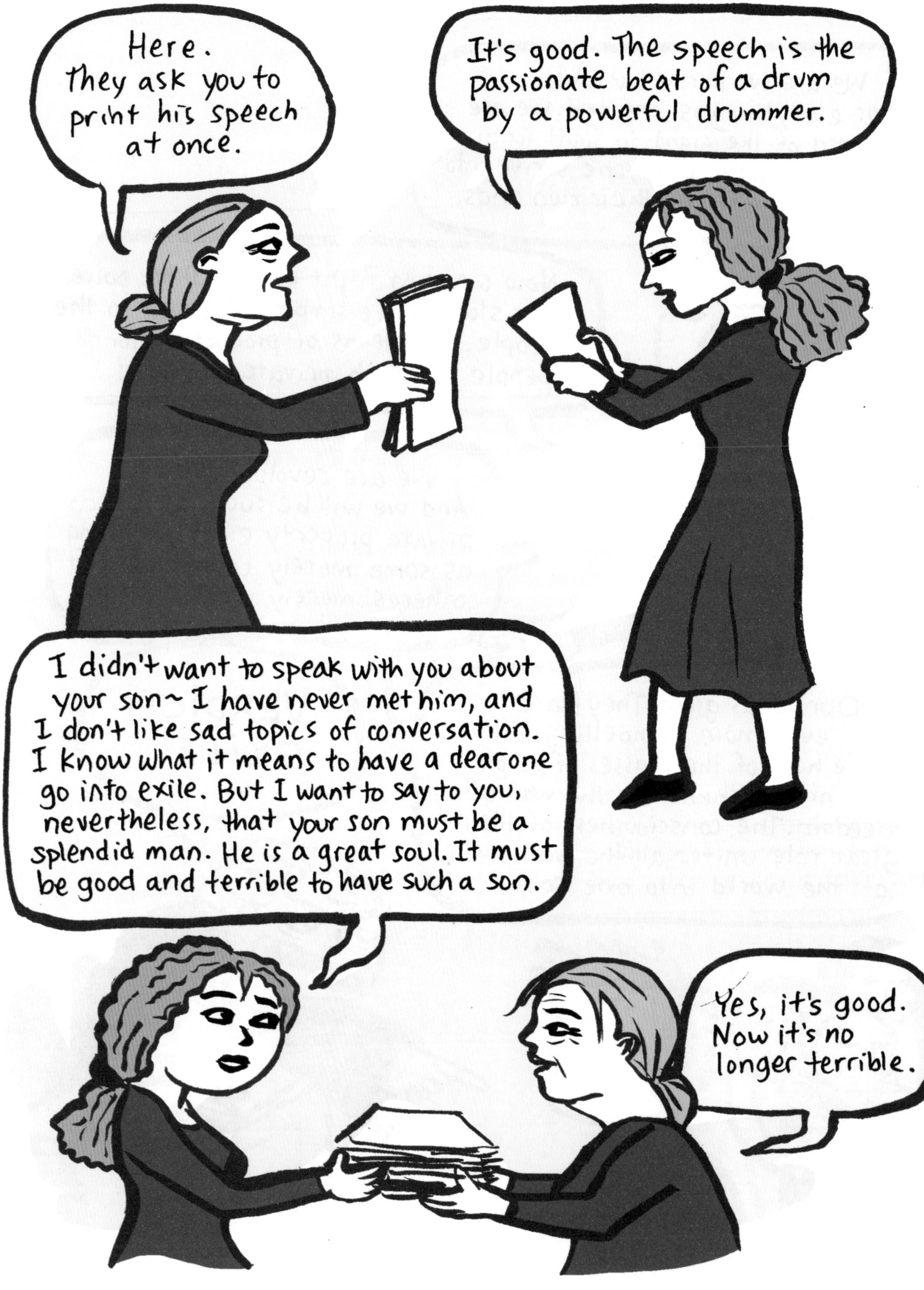
Here. They ask you to print his speech at once.
It's good. The speech is the passionate beat of a drum by a powerful drummer.
I didn't want to speak with you about your son~ I have never met him, and I don't like sad topics of conversation. I know what it means to have a dearone go into exile. But I want to say to you, nevertheless, that your son must be a splendid man. He is a great soul. It must be good and terrible to have such a son.
Yes, it's good. Now it's no longer terrible.

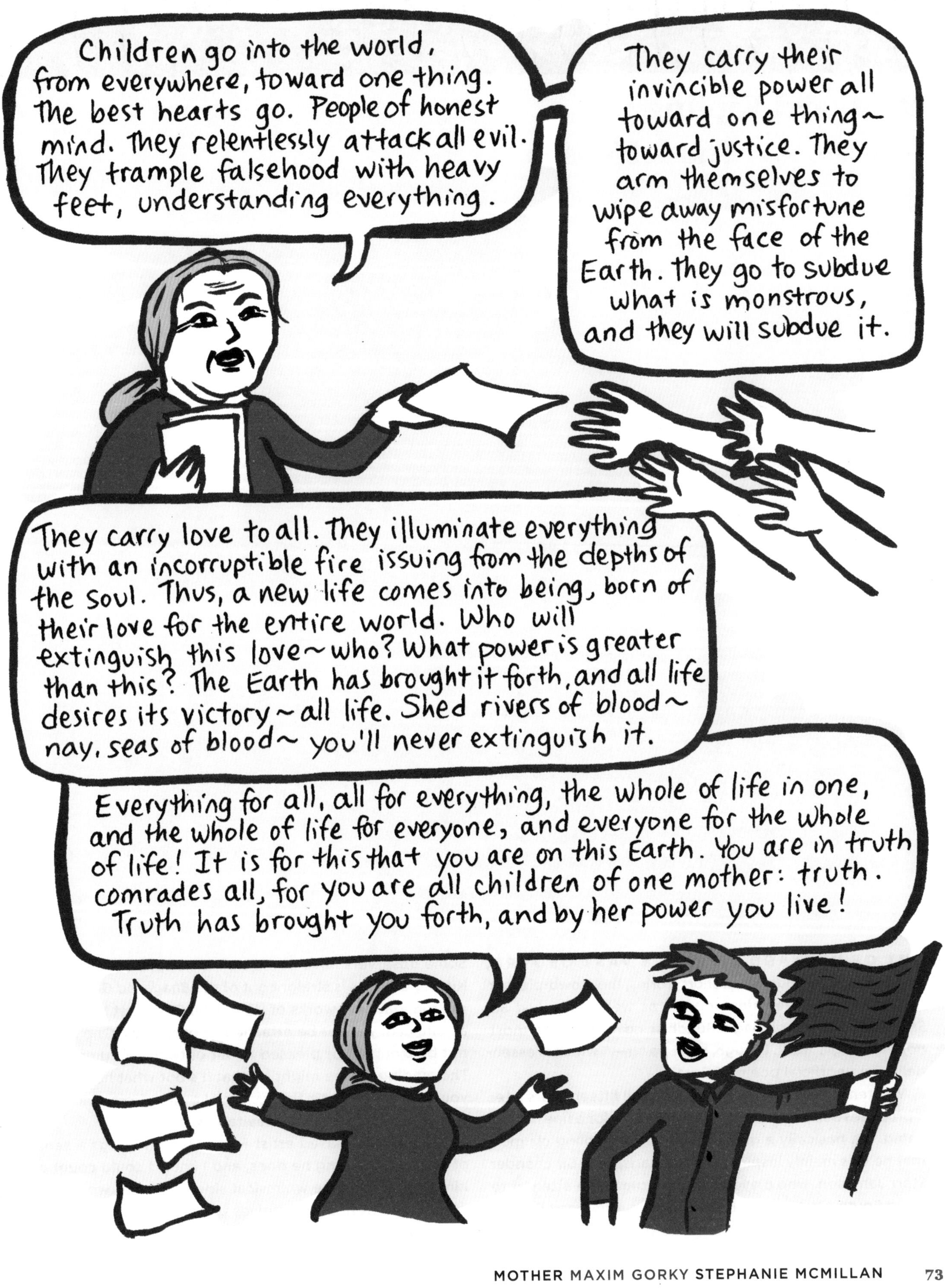
Children go into the world, from everywhere, toward one thing. The best hearts go. People of honest mind. They relentlessly attack all evil. They trample falsehood with heavy feet, understanding everything.
They carry their invincible power all toward one thing~ toward justice. They arm themselves to wipe away misfortune from the face of the Earth. They go to subdue what is monstrous, and they will subdue it.
They carry love to all. They illuminate everything with an incorruptible fire issuing from the depths of the soul. Thus, a new life comes into being, born of their love for the entire world. Who will extinguish this love~ who? What power is greater than this? The Earth has brought it forth, and all life desires its victory~ all life. Shed rivers of blood~ nay, seas of blood~ you'll never extinguish it.
Everything for all, all for everything, the whole of life in one, and the whole of life for everyone, and everyone for the whole of life! It is for this that you are on this Earth. You are in truth comrades all, for you are all children of one mother: truth. Truth has brought you forth, and by her power you live!

Rudyard Kipling

ART/ADAPTATION BY **Frank Hansen**

OUT OF RUDYARD KIPLING'S VAST OEUVRE, including lots of underrated short stories, the crowd-pleaser *The Jungle Book* remains popular, as well as his *Just So Stories* and the espionage/Buddhist novel *Kim*. His most popular single work, though, must be "If—," which is essentially the unofficial poem of Britain.

Written in 1895 but not published until fifteen years later, it proposes some of the qualities that make for a fine human being. It's basically a moral guide to life. Kipling claimed that he was mainly inspired by the charismatic Sir Leander Starr Jameson, who played a crucial role in the attempt to bring South Africa under British control, and many Britons see the poem as a celebration of the greatest English traits.

Some observers have noted that the approach to life that Kipling outlines is straight out of the *Bhagavad Gita*, one of the foundational works of Hinduism. One must try as hard as one can, yet not be attached to outcomes. One should not be troubled or pleased about outward circumstances. The guiding theme might be that it's not what happens to you that counts—it's that you make the effort, and react with equanimity to life's inevitables.

Los Angeles-based artist Frank Hansen brings a sense of fun to everything he does, and I knew I could count on him to draw out the whimsical side of a great work of literature. Sure enough, he gives us a light-hearted take on Rud's earnest manual for living.

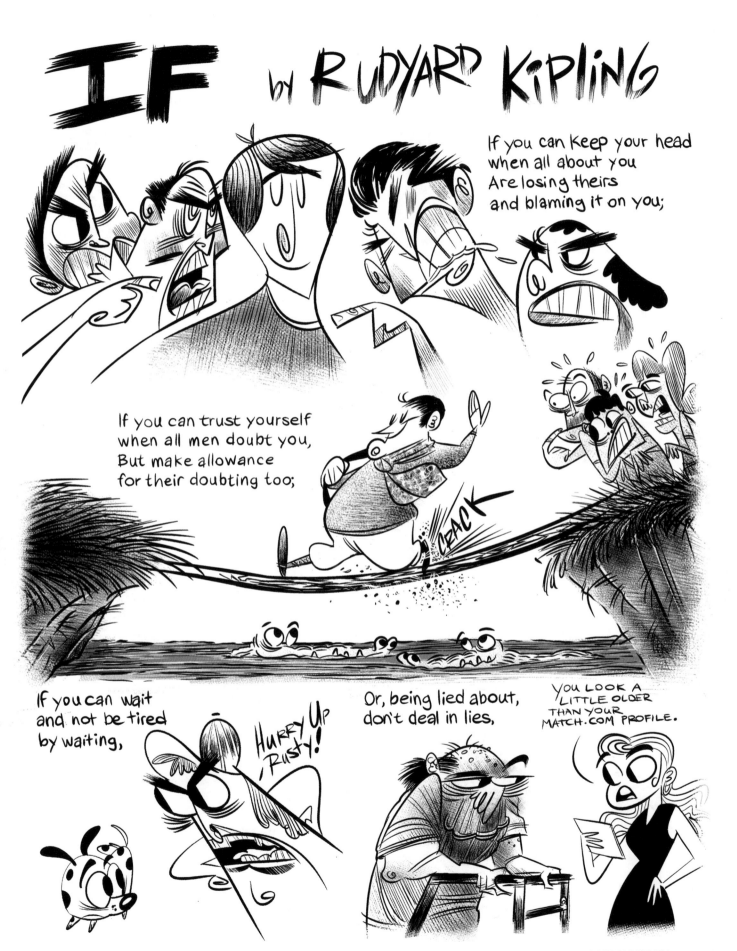

IF by RUDYARD KIPLING

If you can keep your head when all about you Are losing theirs and blaming it on you;

If you can trust yourself when all men doubt you, But make allowance for their doubting too;

CRACK

If you can wait and not be tired by waiting,

HURRY UP, RUSTY!

Or, being lied about, don't deal in lies,

YOU LOOK A LITTLE OLDER THAN YOUR MATCH.COM PROFILE.

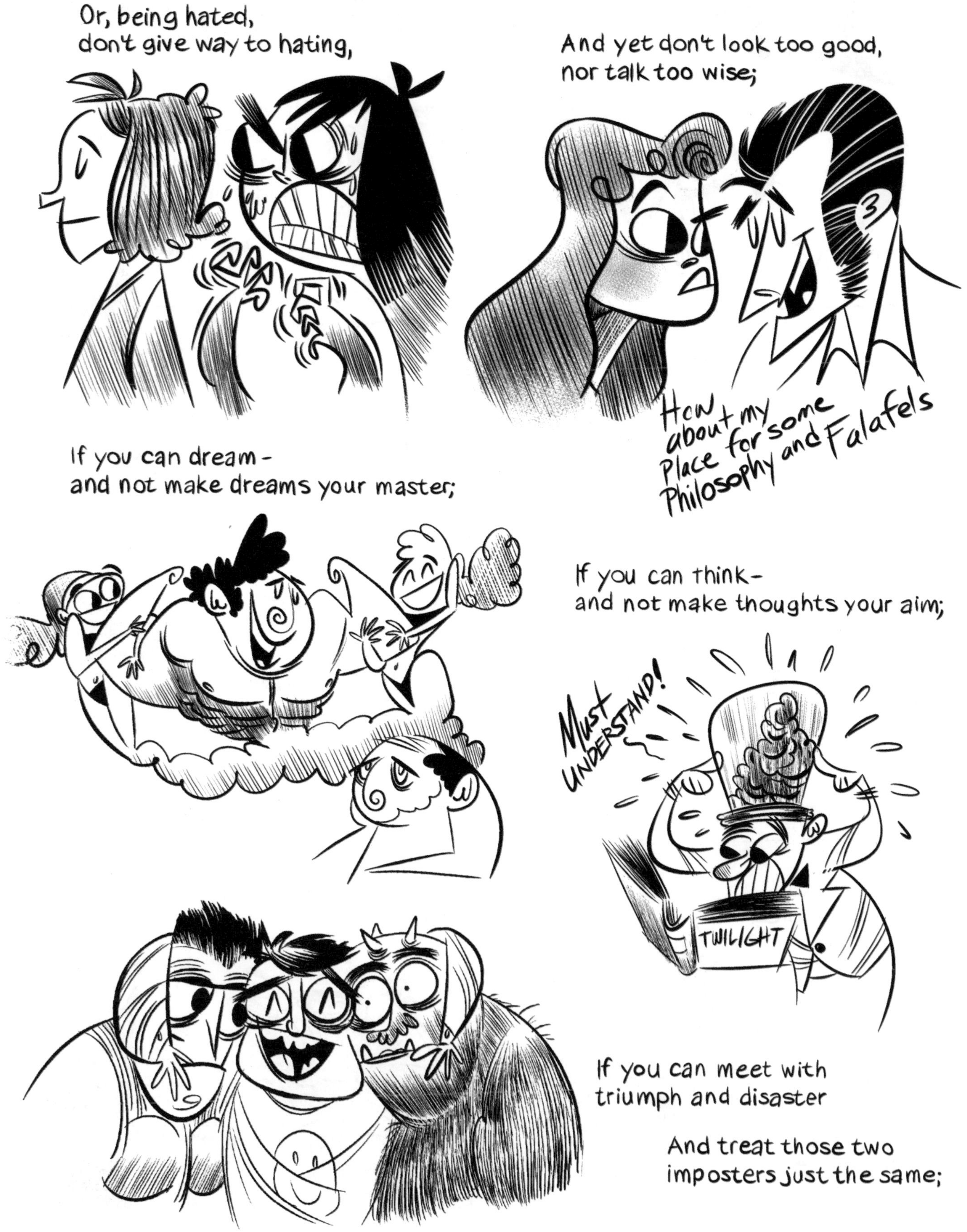
Or, being hated,
don't give way to hating,
And yet don't look too good,
nor talk too wise;
How about my place for some Philosophy and Falafels
If you can dream -
and not make dreams your master;
If you can think -
and not make thoughts your aim;
MUST UNDERSTAND!
TWILIGHT
If you can meet with
triumph and disaster
And treat those two
imposters just the same;

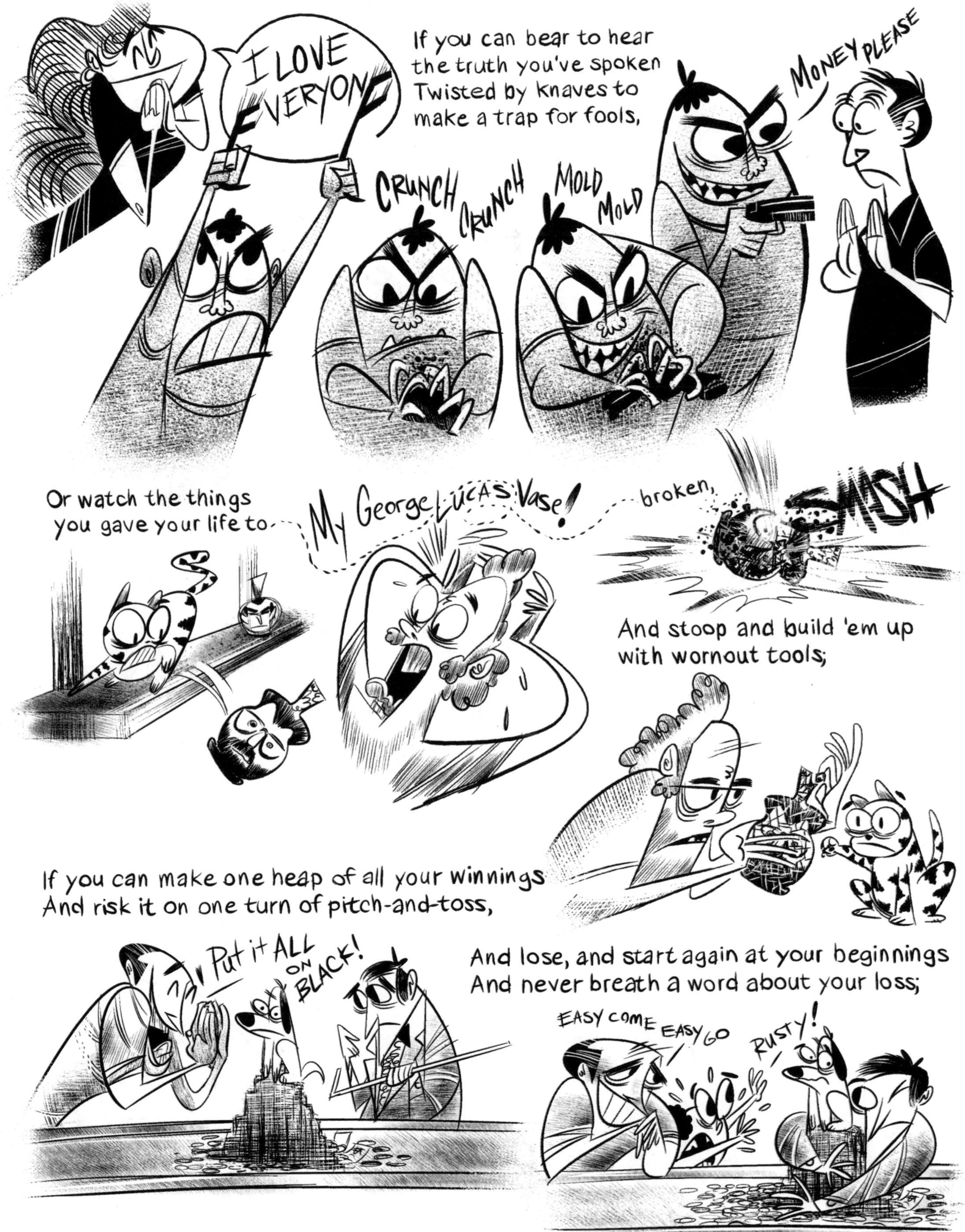
I LOVE EVERYONE
If you can bear to hear the truth you've spoken
Twisted by knaves to make a trap for fools,
CRUNCH CRUNCH
MOLD MOLD
MONEY PLEASE
Or watch the things you gave your life to
My George Lucas Vase!
broken,
SMASH
And stoop and build 'em up with wornout tools;
If you can make one heap of all your winnings
And risk it on one turn of pitch-and-toss,
Put it ALL ON BLACK!
And lose, and start again at your beginnings
And never breath a word about your loss;
EASY COME EASY GO
RUSTY!

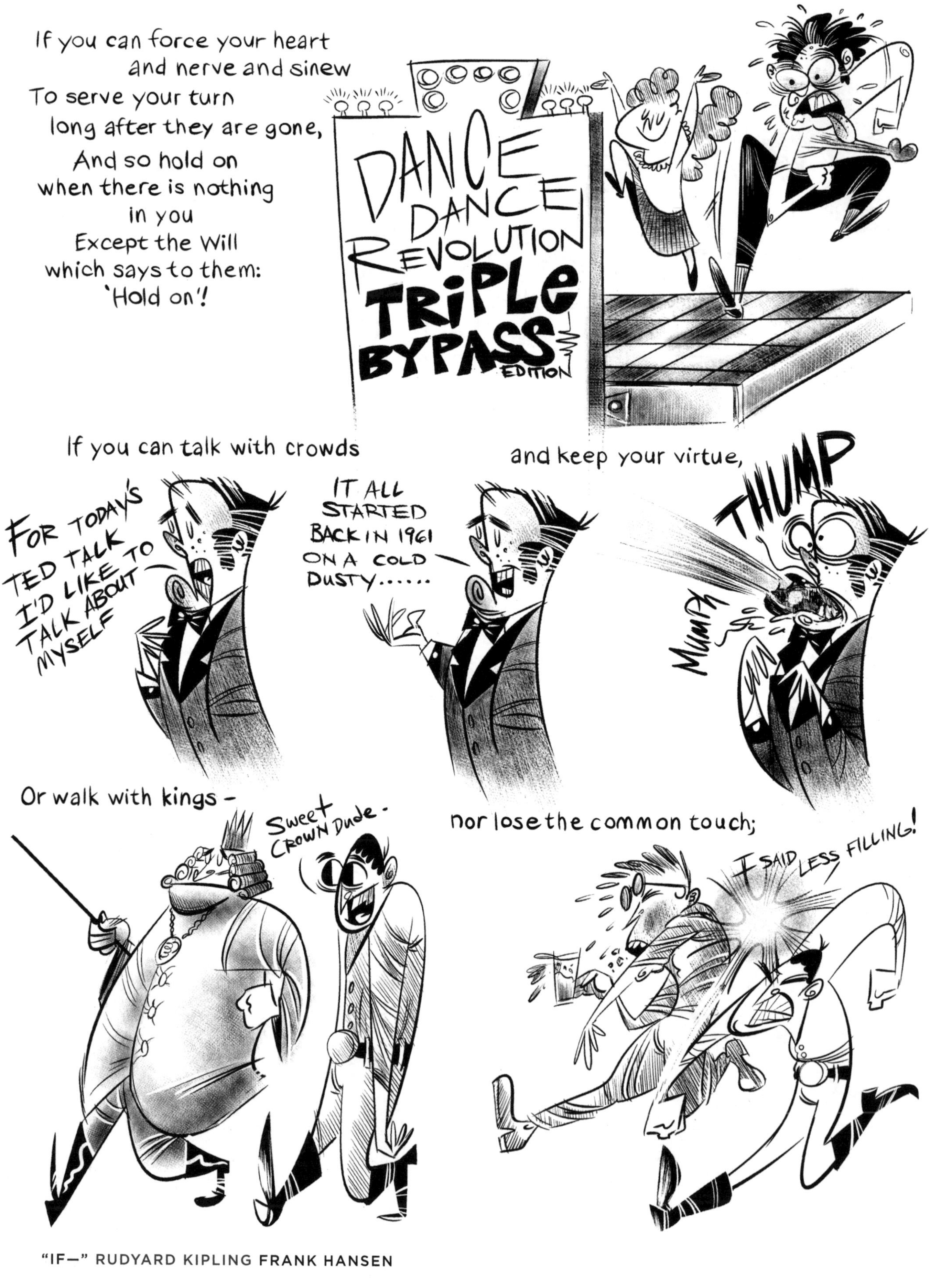

If you can force your heart and nerve and sinew
To serve your turn long after they are gone,
And so hold on when there is nothing in you
Except the Will which says to them: 'Hold on'!
DANCE DANCE REVOLUTION TRIPLE BYPASS EDITION
If you can talk with crowds
FOR TODAY'S TED TALK I'D LIKE TO TALK ABOUT MYSELF
IT ALL STARTED BACK IN 1961 ON A COLD DUSTY......
and keep your virtue,
THUMP
Or walk with kings -
Sweet CROWN Dude.
nor lose the common touch;
I SAID LESS FILLING!

If neither foes nor loving friends can hurt you;

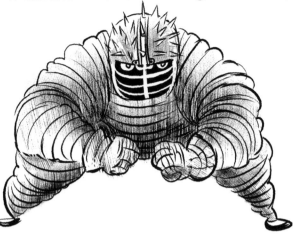

If all men count with you, but none too much;

If you can fill the unforgiving minute With sixty seconds' worth of distance run –

Yours is the Earth and everything that's in it, And - which is more - you'll be a Man my son!

Fmhansen.com

John Barleycorn

Jack London

ART/ADAPTATION BY **John Pierard**

LIKE H. G. WELLS, JACK LONDON WROTE PROLIFI-
cally—around thirty novels, boatloads of short stories, and
works in numerous other areas—but is known for just a handful
of writings, mainly *The Call of the Wild*, *White Fang*, *The Sea-
Wolf*, and "To Build a Fire." Like Ernest Hemingway, he was a man
of adventure and alcohol. Booze played such a large role in his life
that in 1912 he wrote his autobiography around it. Published the
next year, *John Barleycorn* recounts London's entire life through
this blurry lens. (The title is a reference to the English folksong
that personifies barley, the grain often used to make alcohol.) It
was meant as an anti-alcohol statement—and indeed, the temperance movement seized on it—and as an apology to his wife.

London was drinking sizeable quantities of beer at age
five, and was downing wine at seven. Alcohol was always
around, and he always partook. Not because he was born
with a craving, not because he liked the taste, and not
because he enjoyed the effects. It was a social thing, an
integral part of male bonding:

Not only had it always been accessible, but every interest of my developing life had drawn me to it. A newsboy
on the streets, a sailor, a miner, a wanderer in far lands,
always where men came together to exchange ideas, to
laugh and boast and dare, to relax, to forget the dull toil
of tiresome nights and days, always they came together
over alcohol. The saloon was the place of congregation.
Men gathered to it as primitive men gathered about the
fire of the squatting place or the fire at the mouth of
the cave.

John Pierard has a nicely varied career, having illustrated children's books, classic literature, and sex magazines
including the legendary *Screw*. In the first of three adaptations for this volume, he focuses on London's brush with
the Grim Reaper via John Barleycorn—the time he almost
drank himself to death on free whiskey.

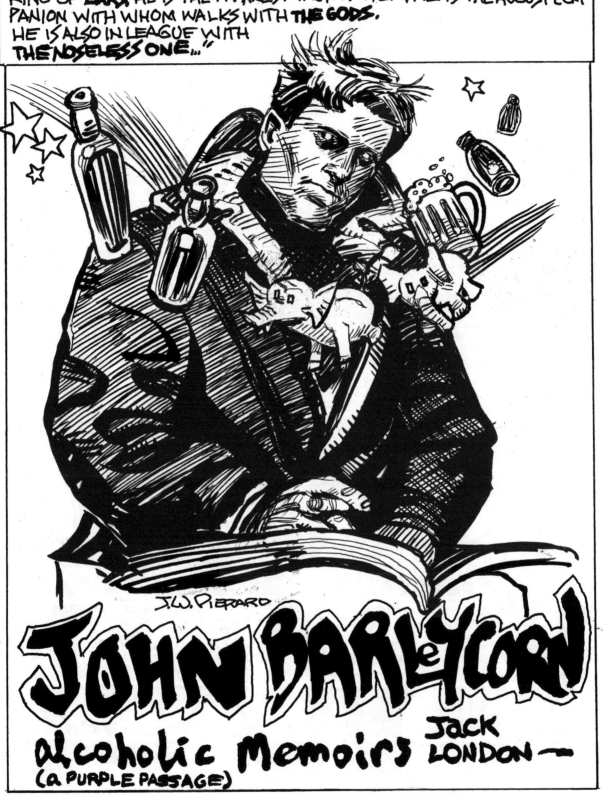

"I AM I WAS I AM NOT. I AM NEVER LESS HIS FRIEND THAN WHEN HE IS WITH ME, AND WHEN I SEEM MOST HIS **FRIEND**, HE IS THE KING OF **LIARS**. HE IS THE FRANKEST TRUTH SAYER, HE IS THE AUGUST COMPANION WITH WHOM WALKS WITH **THE GODS**. HE IS ALSO IN LEAGUE WITH **THE NOSELESS ONE**..."

J.W. PIERARD

JOHN BARLeYCORN

alcoholic memoirs JACK LONDON —
(a PURPLE PASSAGE)

ALCOHOL; I KNOW FROM MY EARLIEST EXPERIENCES THAT I DID NOT CARE FOR THE TASTE OF IT. I WORKED IN A CANNERY AS A BOY. I KNEW FROM MY VORACIOUS READING HABIT THAT THERE WAS MORE TO LIFE.

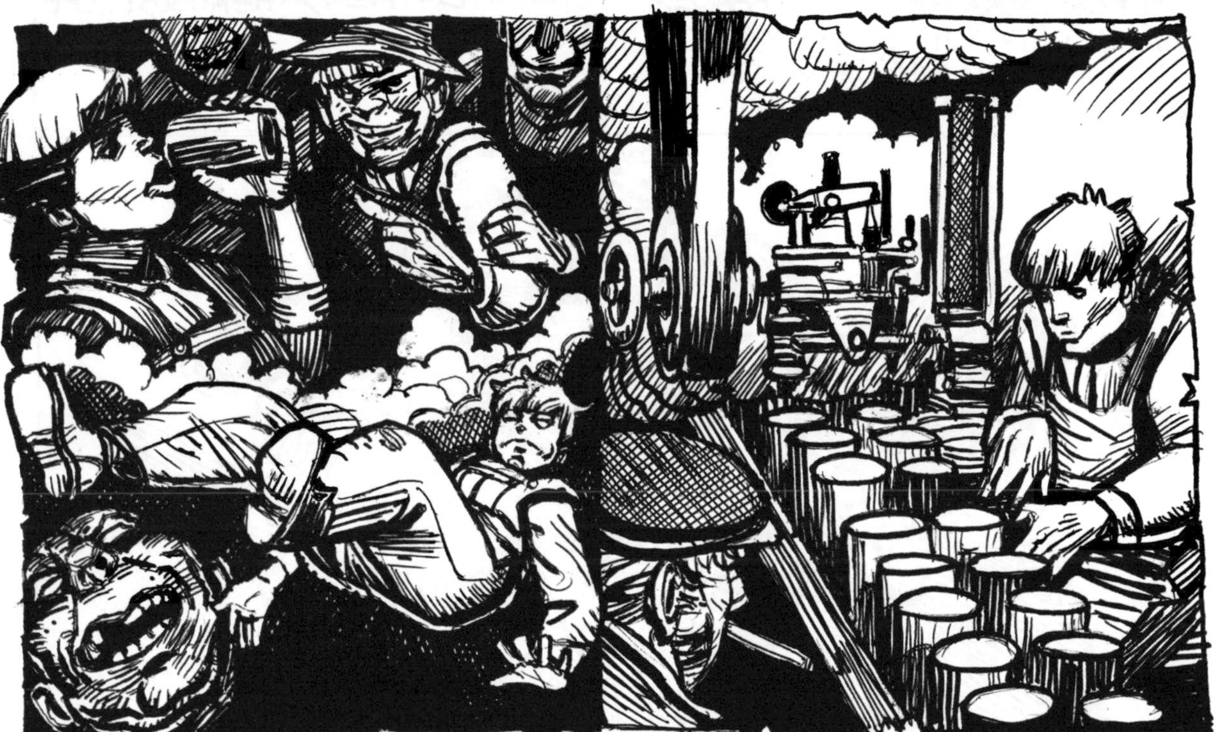

I DRANK IN THE MANY WATERFRONT SALOONS WITH MEN. DRINK WAS THE BADGE OF MANHOOD. THROUGH THIS ASSOCIATION THE WORLD OPENED UP FOR ME. I HAD MANY ADVENTURES...

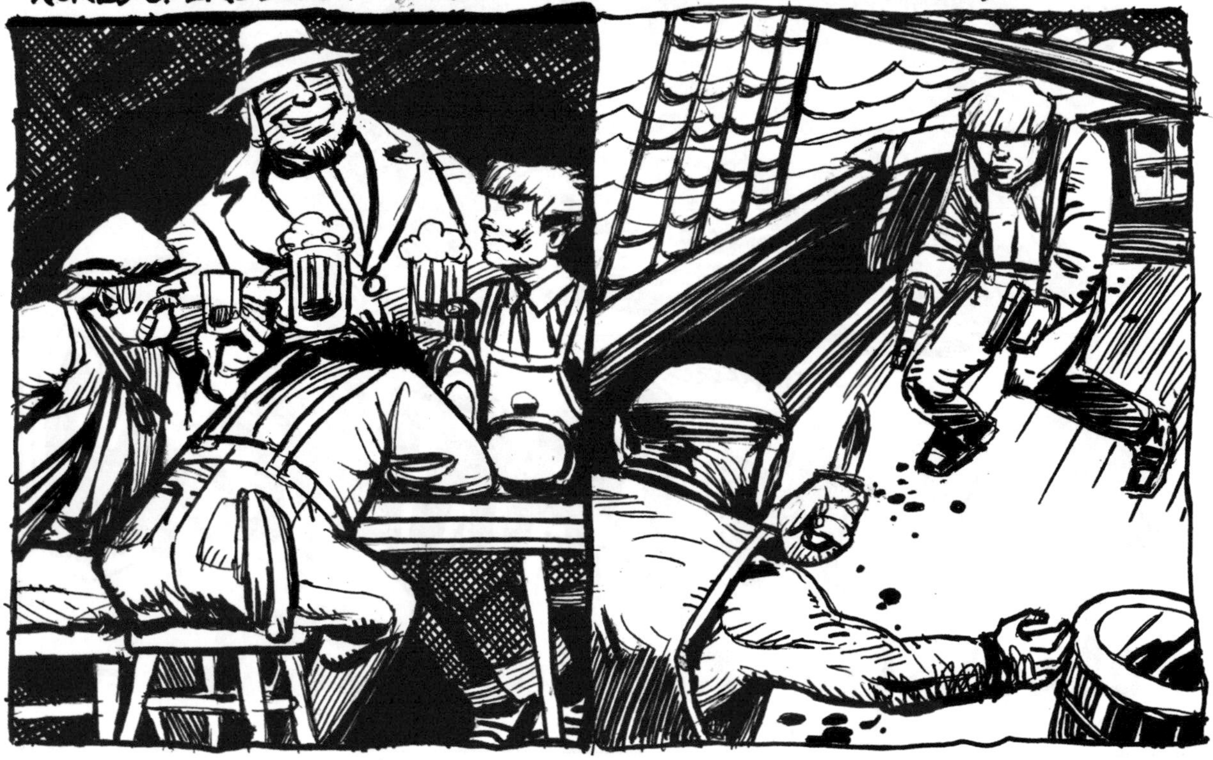

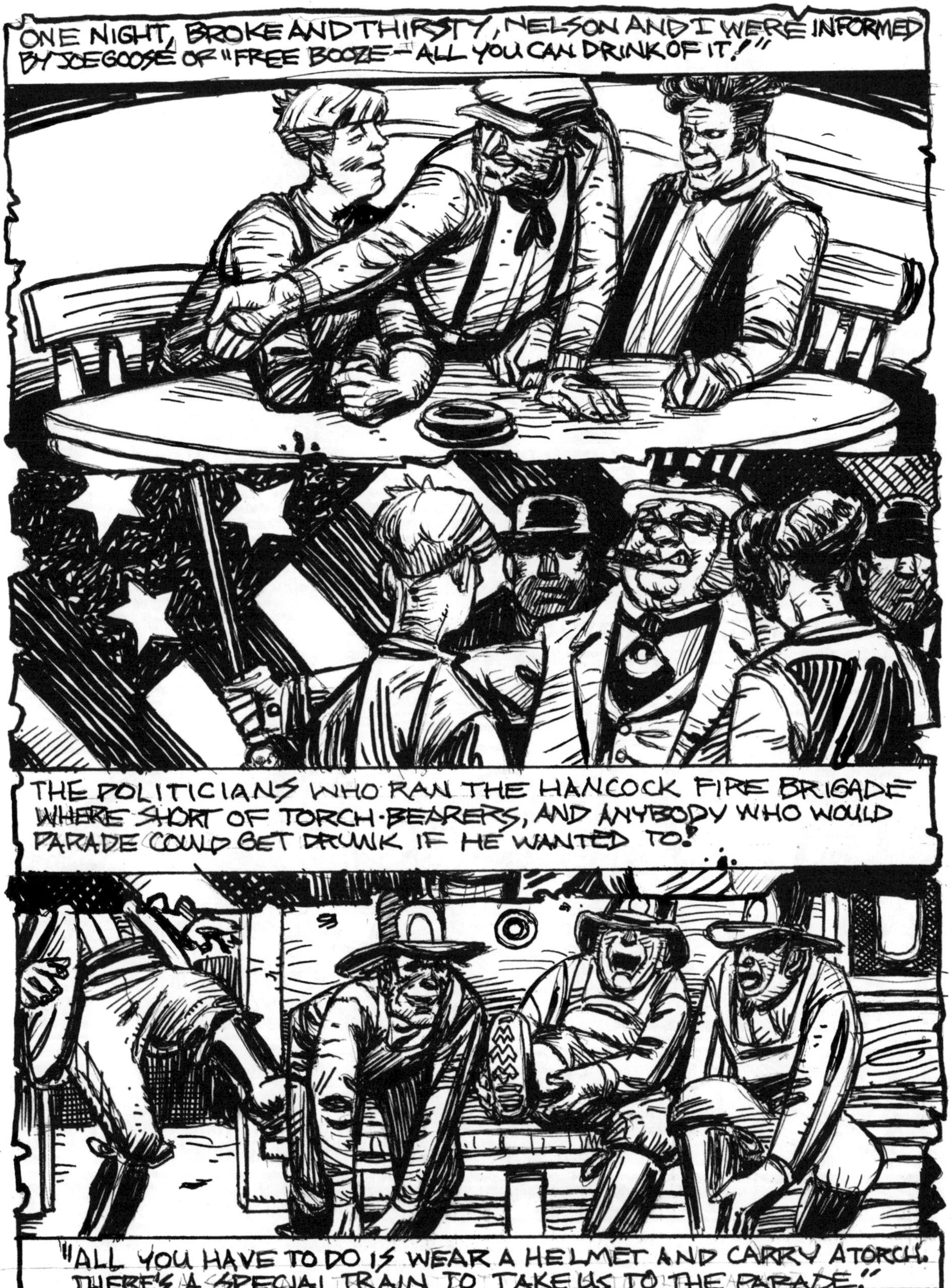
ONE NIGHT, BROKE AND THIRSTY, NELSON AND I WERE INFORMED BY JOE GOOSE OF "FREE BOOZE — ALL YOU CAN DRINK OF IT!"
THE POLITICIANS WHO RAN THE HANCOCK FIRE BRIGADE WHERE SHORT OF TORCH-BEARERS, AND ANYBODY WHO WOULD PARADE COULD GET DRUNK IF HE WANTED TO!
"ALL YOU HAVE TO DO IS WEAR A HELMET AND CARRY A TORCH. THERE'S A SPECIAL TRAIN TO TAKE US TO THE PARADE."

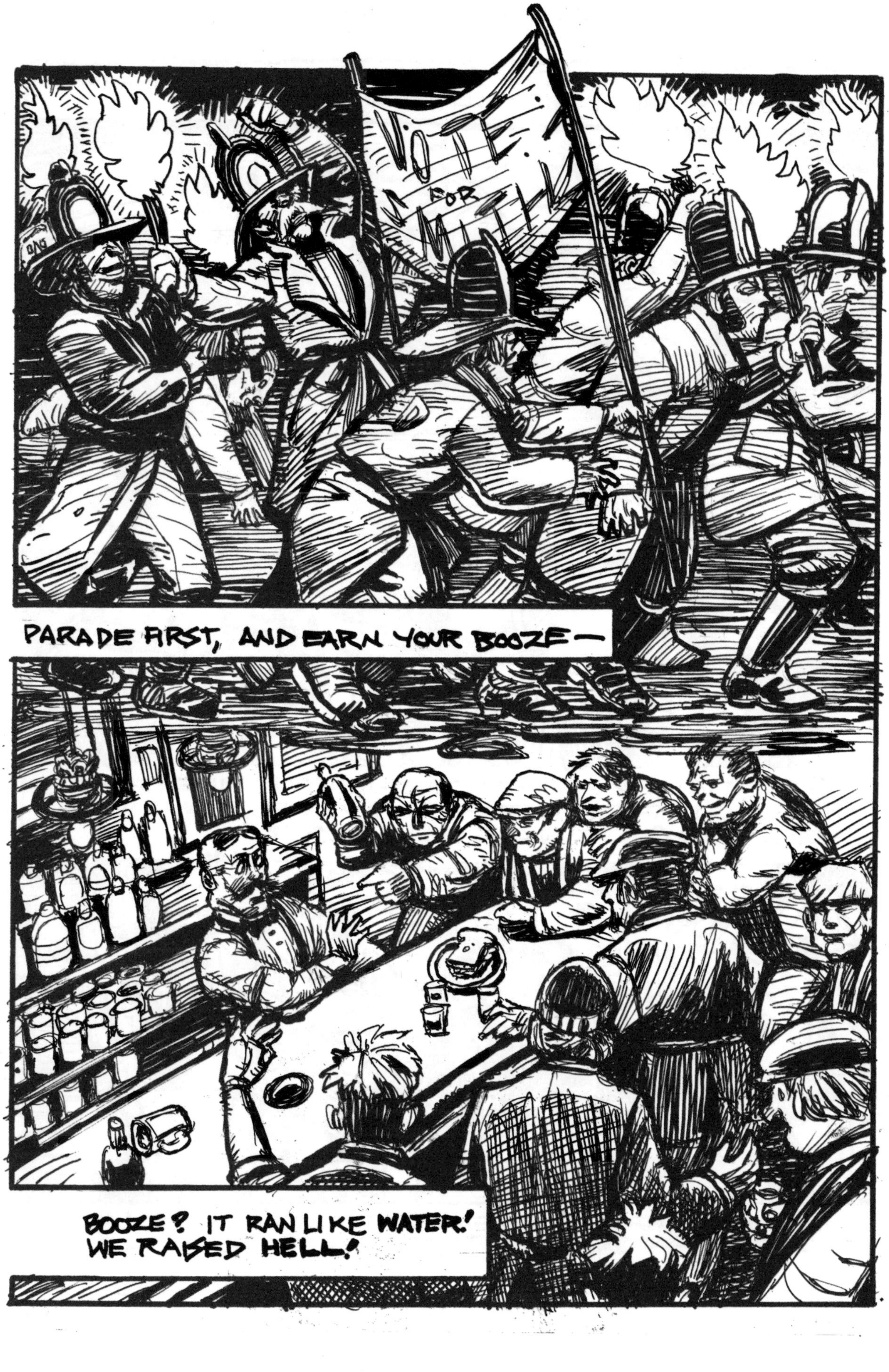
VOTE FOR SMITH
PARADE FIRST, AND EARN YOUR BOOZE—
BOOZE? IT RAN LIKE WATER! WE RAISED HELL!

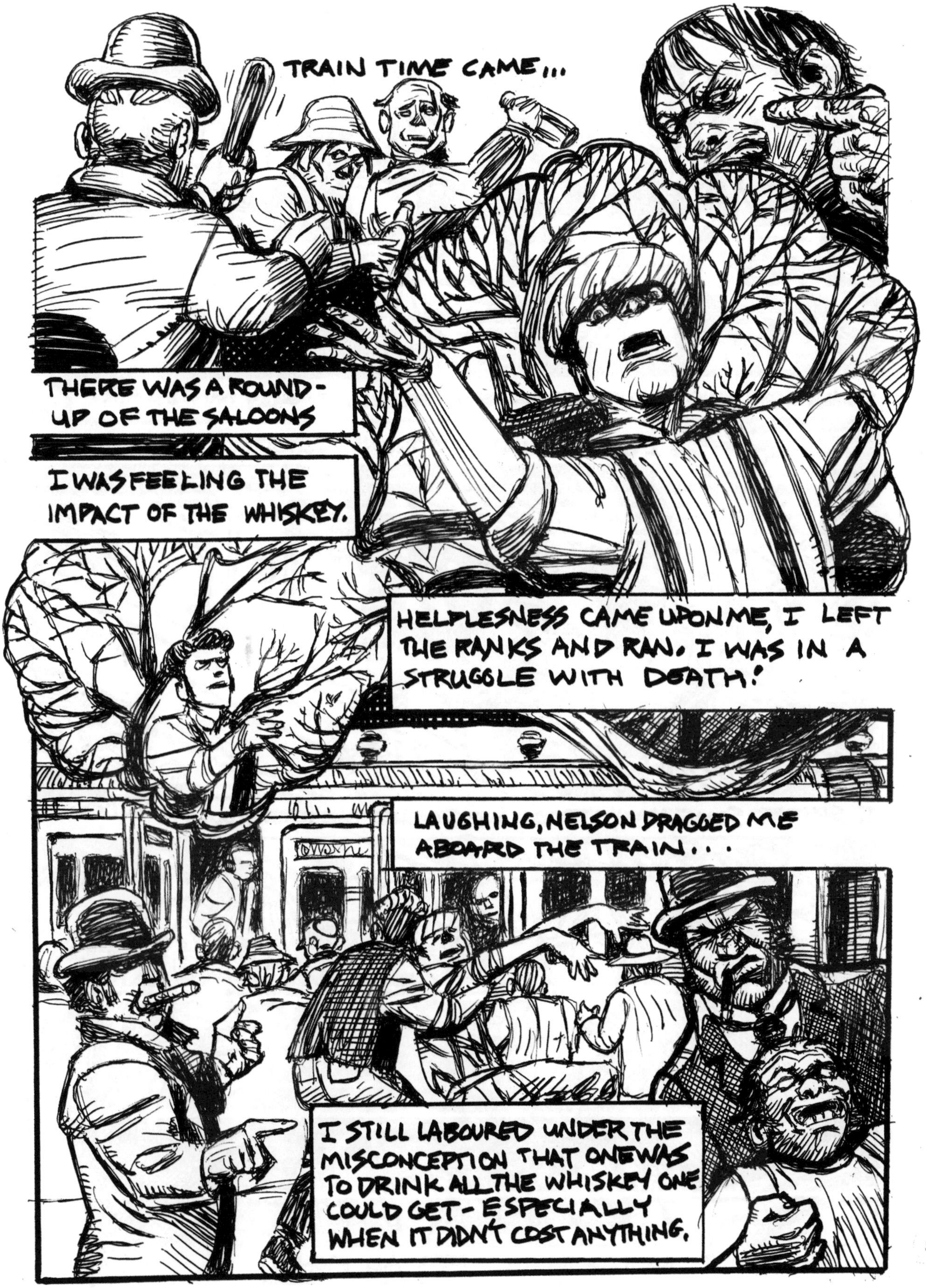
TRAIN TIME CAME...
THERE WAS A ROUND-UP OF THE SALOONS
I WAS FEELING THE IMPACT OF THE WHISKEY.
HELPLESNESS CAME UPON ME, I LEFT THE RANKS AND RAN. I WAS IN A STRUGGLE WITH DEATH!
LAUGHING, NELSON DRAGGED ME ABOARD THE TRAIN...
I STILL LABOURED UNDER THE MISCONCEPTION THAT ONE WAS TO DRINK ALL THE WHISKEY ONE COULD GET - ESPECIALLY WHEN IT DIDN'T COST ANYTHING.

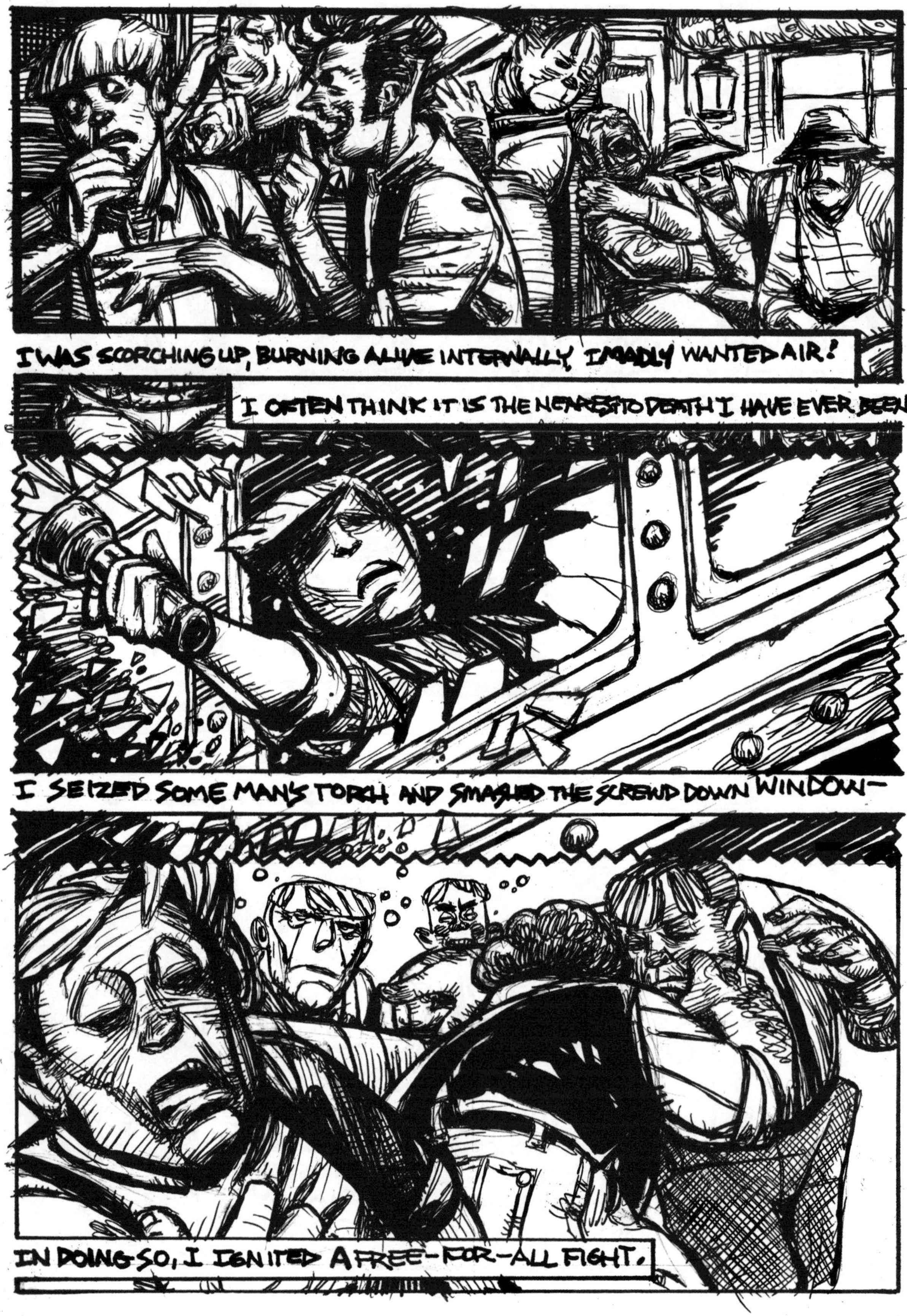
I WAS SCORCHING UP, BURNING ALIVE INTERNALLY, I MADLY WANTED AIR!
I OFTEN THINK IT IS THE NEAREST TO DEATH I HAVE EVER BEEN.
I SEIZED SOME MAN'S TORCH AND SMASHED THE SCREWED DOWN WINDOW-
IN DOING SO, I IGNITED A FREE-FOR-ALL FIGHT.

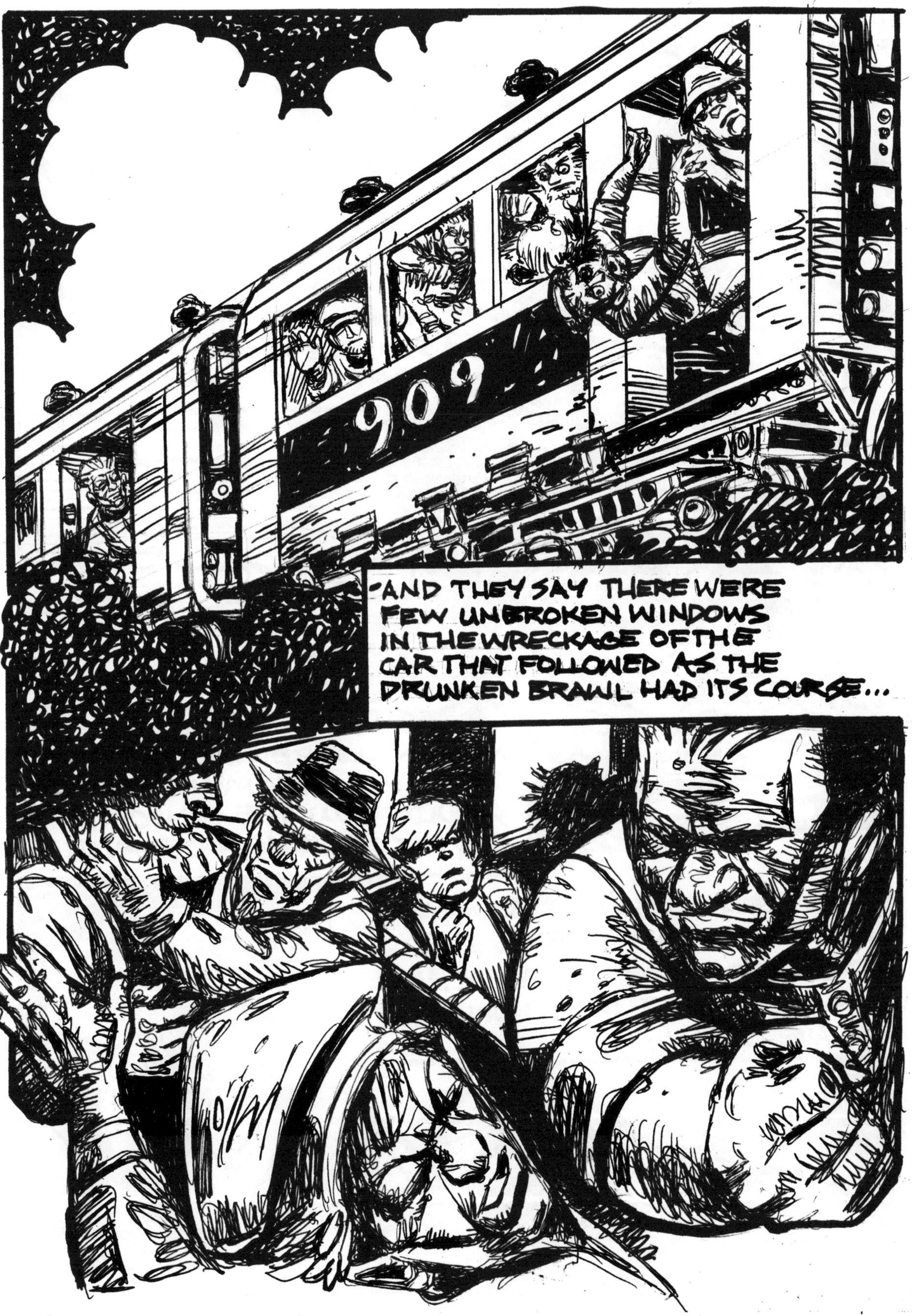
AND THEY SAY THERE WERE FEW UNBROKEN WINDOWS IN THE WRECKAGE OF THE CAR THAT FOLLOWED AS THE DRUNKEN BRAWL HAD ITS COURSE...

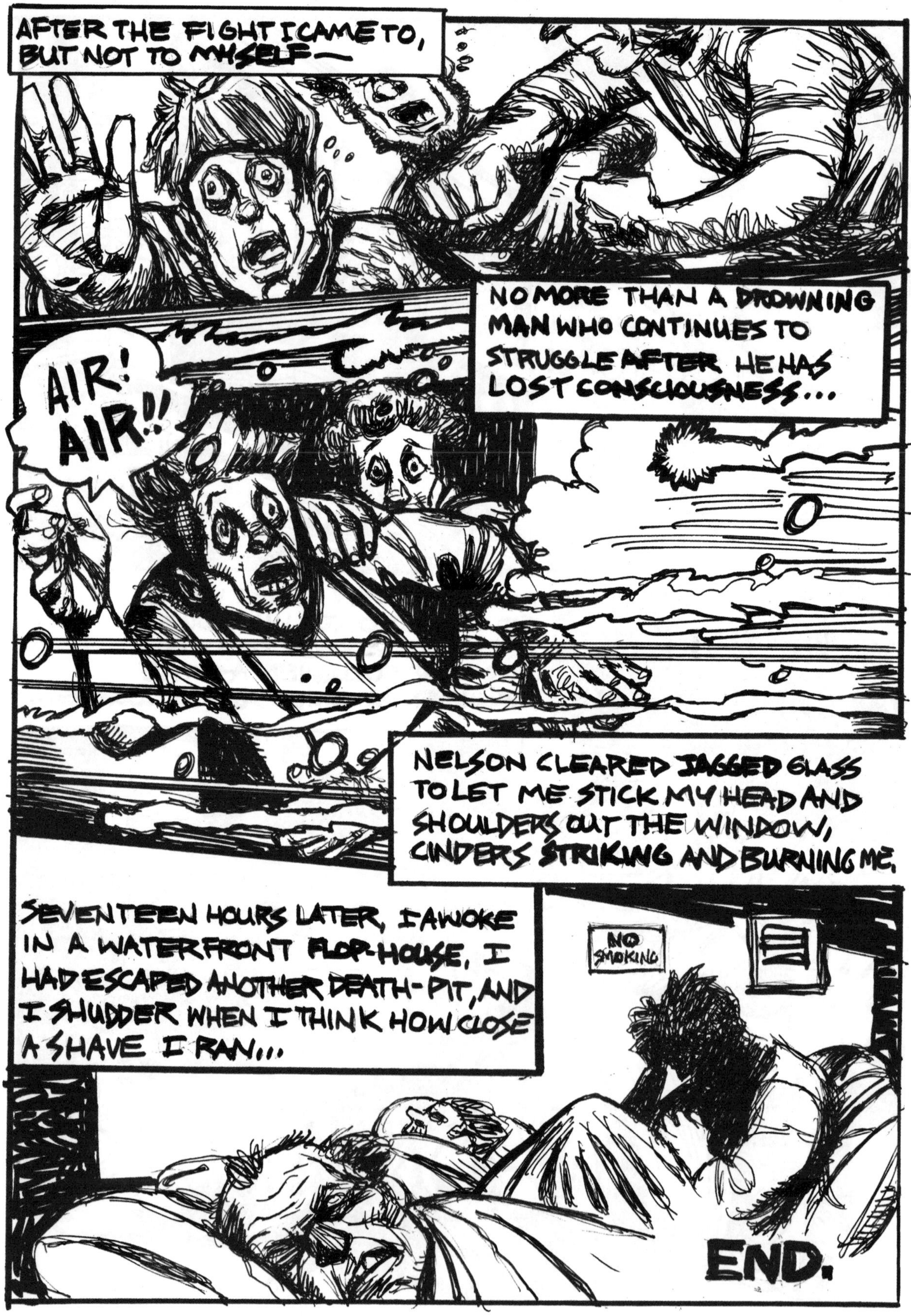
AFTER THE FIGHT I CAME TO, BUT NOT TO MYSELF—
NO MORE THAN A DROWNING MAN WHO CONTINUES TO STRUGGLE AFTER HE HAS LOST CONSCIOUSNESS...
AIR! AIR!!
NELSON CLEARED JAGGED GLASS TO LET ME STICK MY HEAD AND SHOULDERS OUT THE WINDOW, CINDERS STRIKING AND BURNING ME.
SEVENTEEN HOURS LATER, I AWOKE IN A WATERFRONT FLOP-HOUSE. I HAD ESCAPED ANOTHER DEATH-PIT, AND I SHUDDER WHEN I THINK HOW CLOSE A SHAVE I RAN...
NO SMOKING
END.

"Araby" (from Dubliners)

James Joyce

ART/ADAPTATION BY **Annie Mok**

BEFORE HE TURNED LITERATURE ON ITS EAR WITH *Ulysses*—and completely smashed it to smithereens with *Finnegans Wake*—James Joyce wrote one of literature's greatest collection of short stories. The fifteen stories in *Dubliners* are not experimental but are instead perfectly cut little gems written in a spare, direct style. Even though most of them seem like simple, if depressing, slices-of-life, there's a lot going on under the surface—things suggested, hinted at, but never revealed, enough to keep academics writing for a hundred years.

As the title suggests, all the stories are set in Joyce's hometown of Dublin, around the turn of the twentieth century, and they do not paint a flattering portrait of Ireland's capitol. It's a poor, bleak, stifling place, and all of its denizens have dreams—of love, of material success, of leaving Dublin—that never materialize. Alcoholism is widespread; poverty is pervasive; Catholicism only makes things worse. Most of these stories were written in 1904 and 1905, though the collection wasn't published until

1914 due to a staggering number of rejections, as well as publishers who backed out after being scared by the book's earthier parts. When *Dubliners* finally entered the world, its frank depiction of life among the lower classes and its many references to actual people and places caused quite a stir.

Though the collection as a whole is an endlessly debated and dissected classic, a few of the stories are considered absolute stand-outs, and "Araby" is one of them. Illustrator Annie Mok draws and writes comics—she also edited the fantastic anthology *Ghost Comics*—and has turned a good bit of her attention to the early works of Joyce. This adaptation of "Araby" was done specifically for *The Graphic Canon* and marks the first time that a story from *Dubliners* has been given the graphic treatment. Annie has also produced a minicomic containing a portion of Joyce's *A Portrait of the Artist as a Young Man* and even a comic strip with a snippet from Joyce's stunning, gloriously filthy love letters to his life partner, Nora.

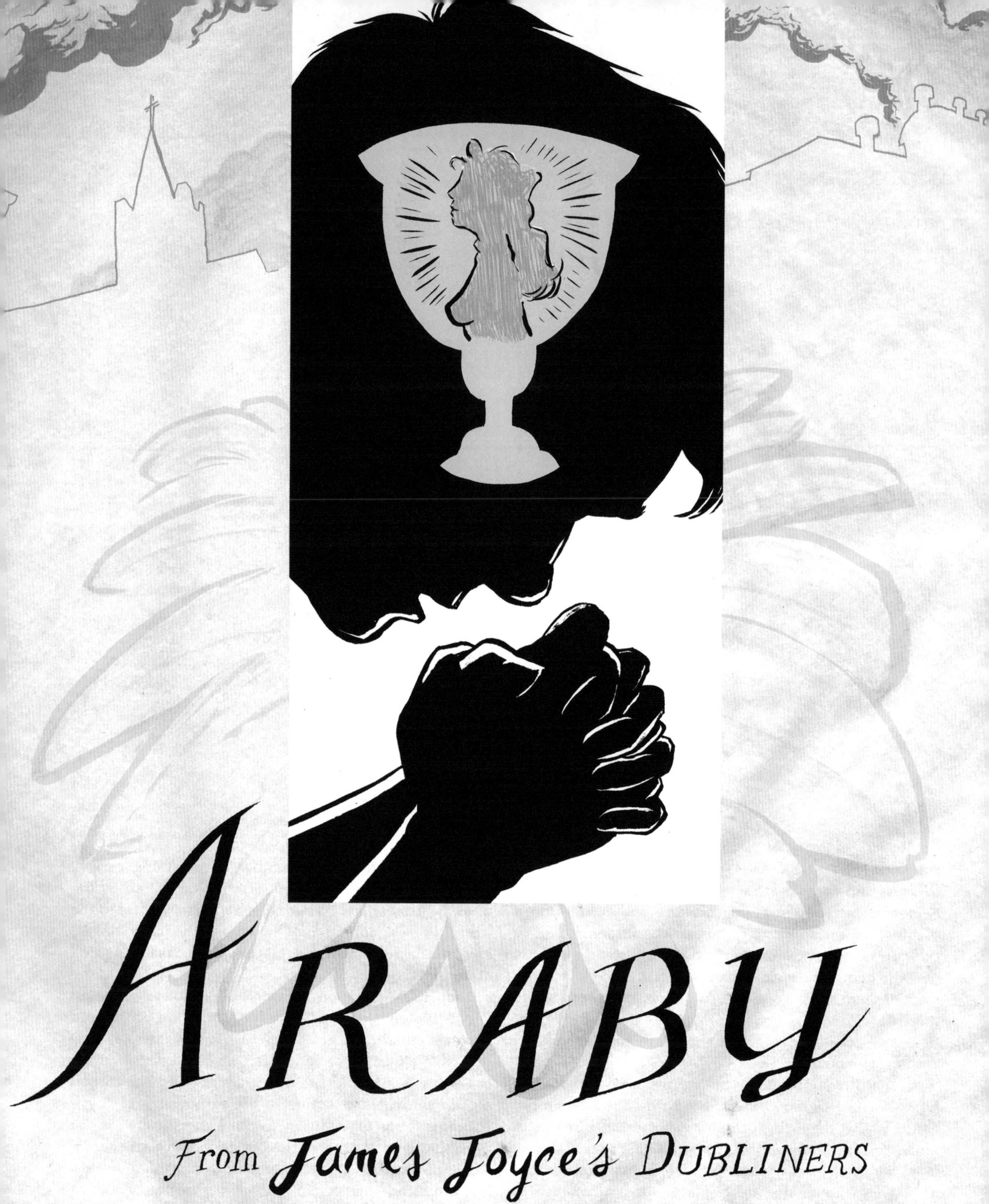

ARABY

From James Joyce's DUBLINERS

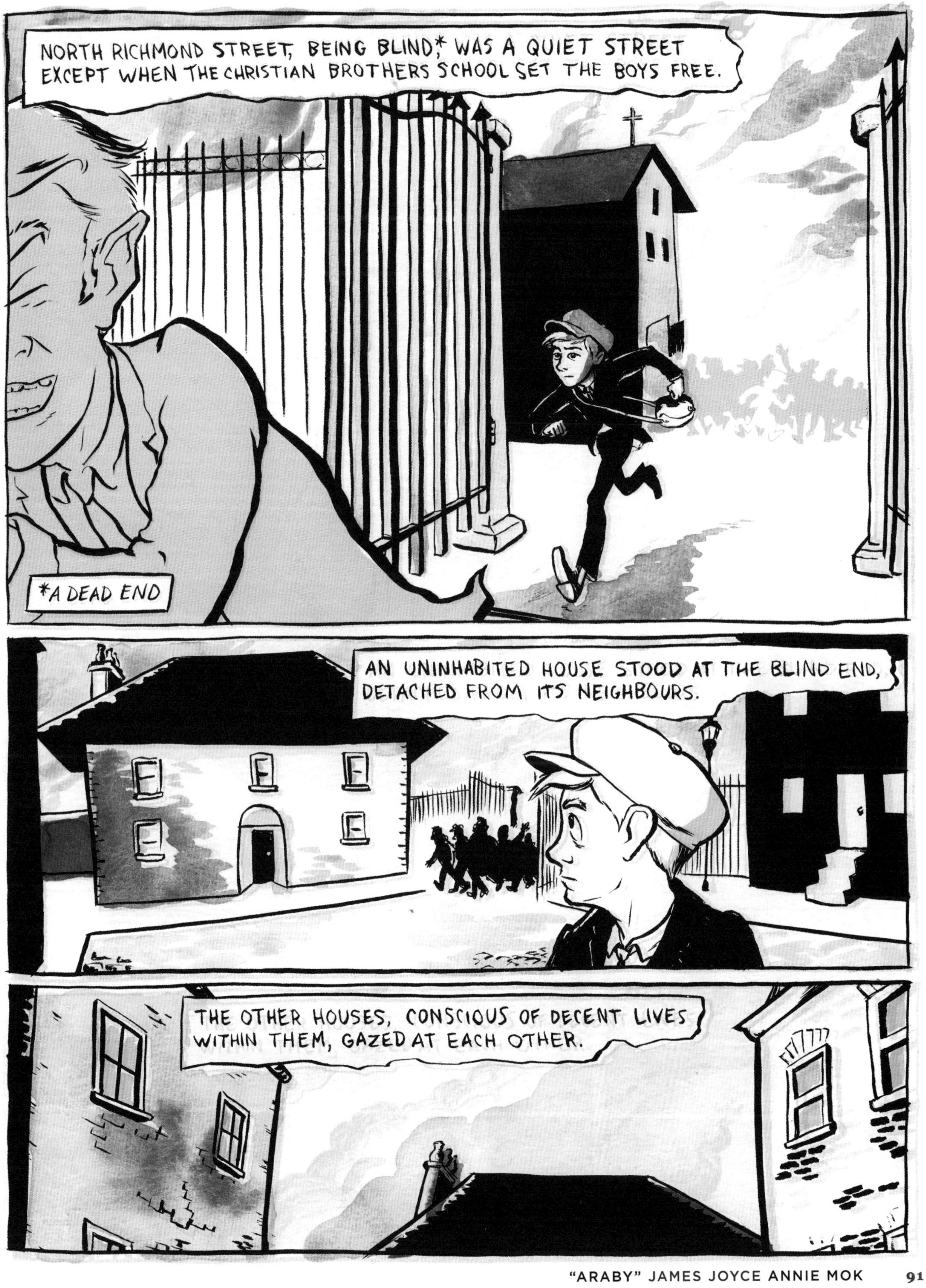
NORTH RICHMOND STREET, BEING BLIND,* WAS A QUIET STREET EXCEPT WHEN THE CHRISTIAN BROTHERS SCHOOL SET THE BOYS FREE.
*A DEAD END
AN UNINHABITED HOUSE STOOD AT THE BLIND END, DETACHED FROM ITS NEIGHBOURS.
THE OTHER HOUSES, CONSCIOUS OF DECENT LIVES WITHIN THEM, GAZED AT EACH OTHER.

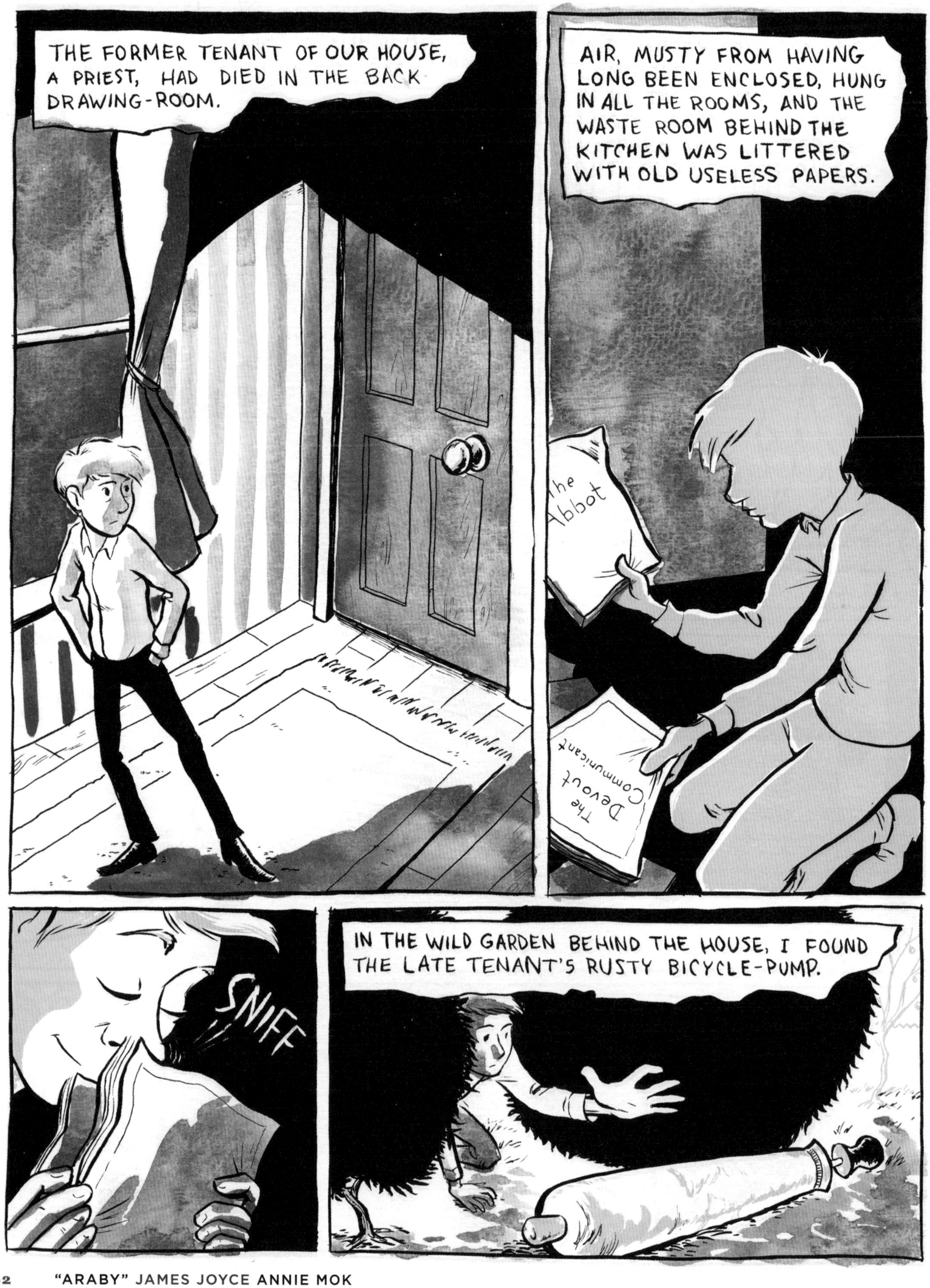
THE FORMER TENANT OF OUR HOUSE, A PRIEST, HAD DIED IN THE BACK DRAWING-ROOM.
AIR, MUSTY FROM HAVING LONG BEEN ENCLOSED, HUNG IN ALL THE ROOMS, AND THE WASTE ROOM BEHIND THE KITCHEN WAS LITTERED WITH OLD USELESS PAPERS.
The Abbot
The Devout Communicant
SNIFF
IN THE WILD GARDEN BEHIND THE HOUSE, I FOUND THE LATE TENANT'S RUSTY BICYCLE-PUMP.

HE HAD BEEN A VERY CHARITABLE PRIEST; HE HAD LEFT ALL HIS MONEY TO INSTITUTIONS AND HIS FURNITURE TO HIS SISTER.

PFFT

WHEN THE SHORT DAYS OF WINTER CAME, DUSK FELL WELL BEFORE WE HAD EATEN OUR DINNERS. OUR SHOUTS ECHOED IN THE SILENT STREET.

THE COLD AIR STUNG US AND WE PLAYED TILL OUR BODIES GLOWED.

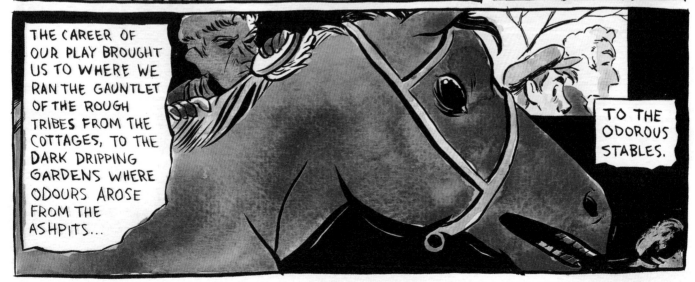

THE CAREER OF OUR PLAY BROUGHT US TO WHERE WE RAN THE GAUNTLET OF THE ROUGH TRIBES FROM THE COTTAGES, TO THE DARK DRIPPING GARDENS WHERE ODOURS AROSE FROM THE ASHPITS...

TO THE ODOROUS STABLES.

"ARABY" JAMES JOYCE ANNIE MOK   93

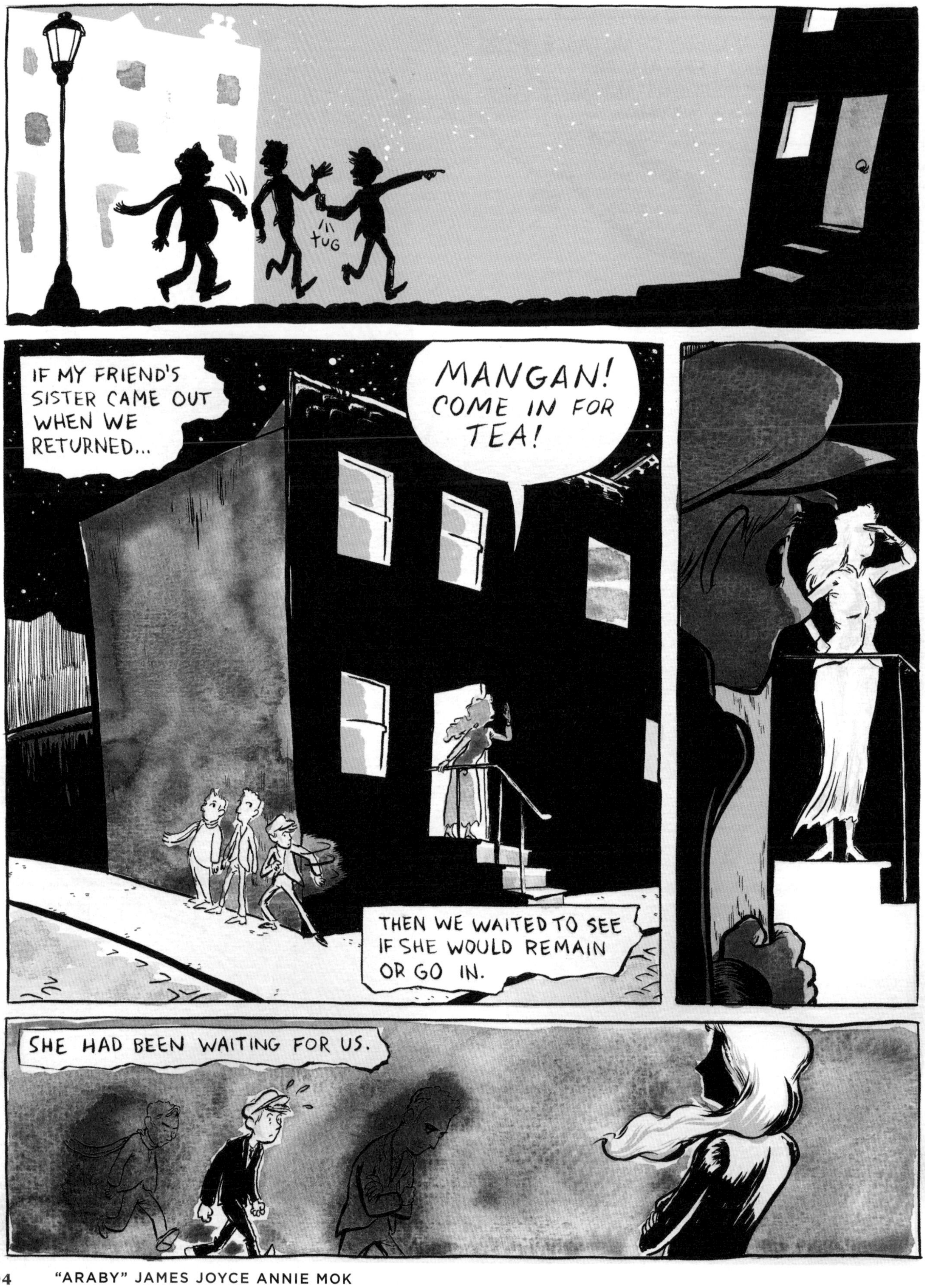
TUG
IF MY FRIEND'S SISTER CAME OUT WHEN WE RETURNED...
MANGAN! COME IN FOR TEA!
THEN WE WAITED TO SEE IF SHE WOULD REMAIN OR GO IN.
SHE HAD BEEN WAITING FOR US.

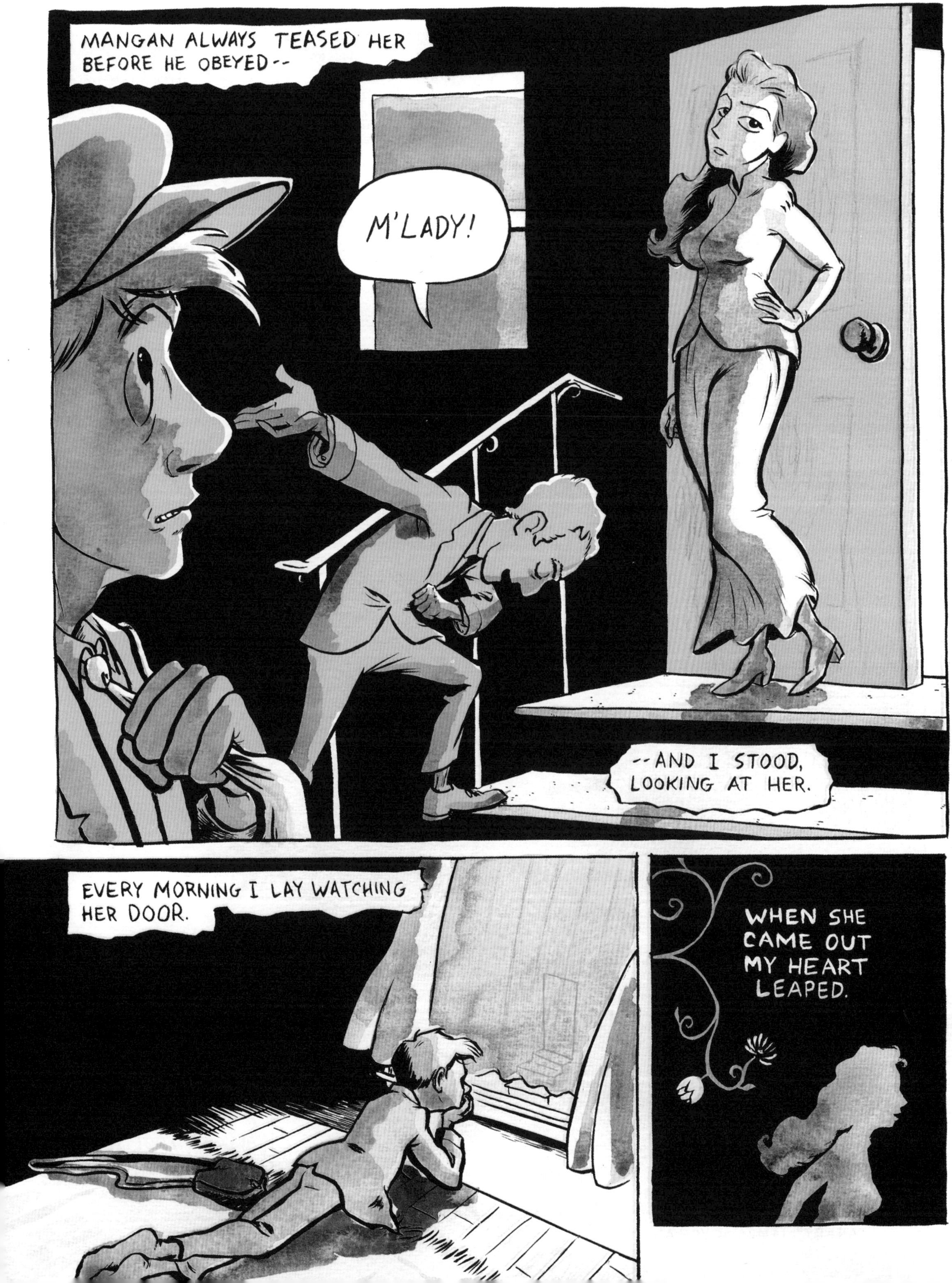
MANGAN ALWAYS TEASED HER BEFORE HE OBEYED--
M'LADY!
--AND I STOOD, LOOKING AT HER.
EVERY MORNING I LAY WATCHING HER DOOR.
WHEN SHE CAME OUT MY HEART LEAPED.

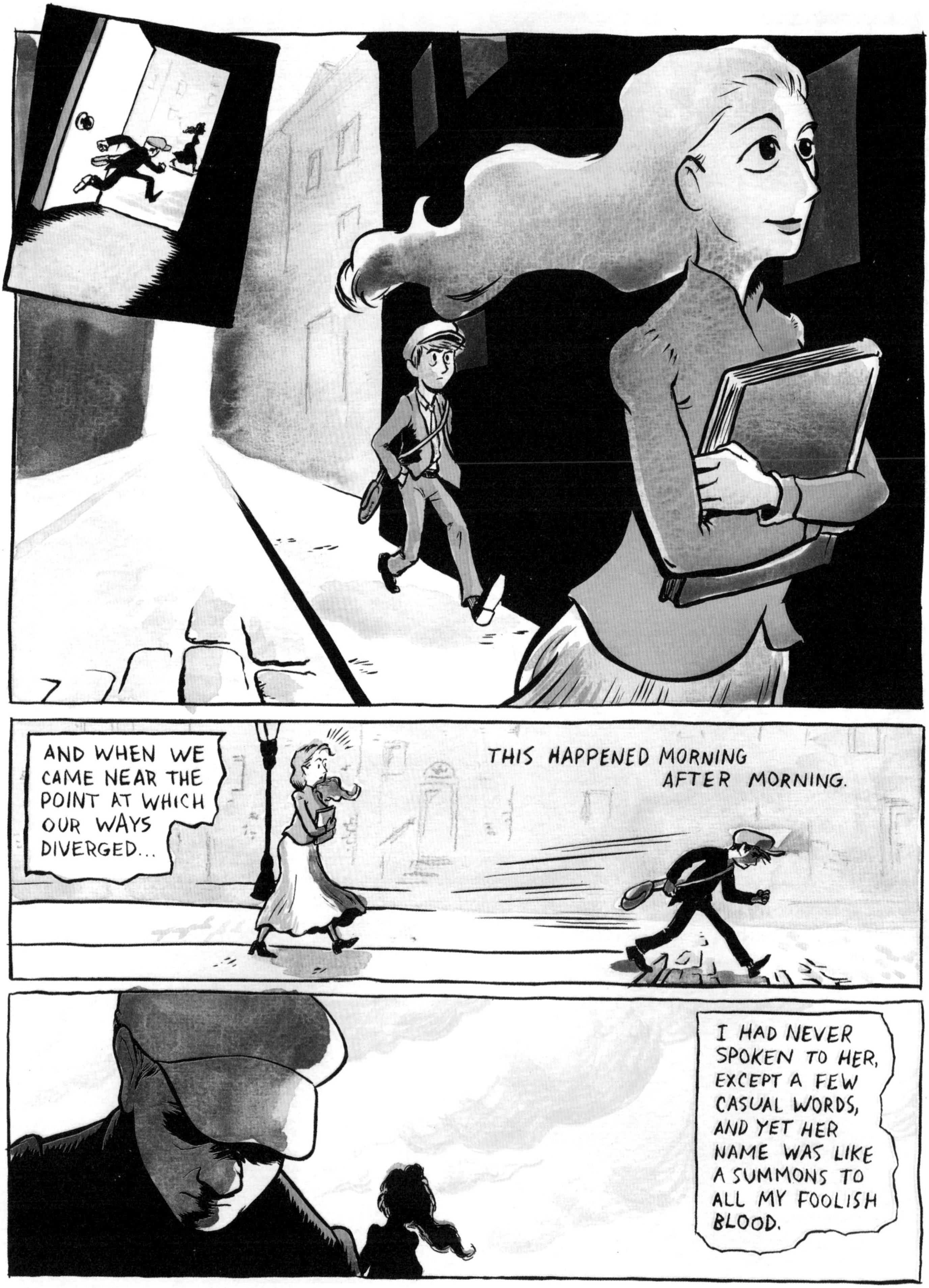
AND WHEN WE CAME NEAR THE POINT AT WHICH OUR WAYS DIVERGED...
THIS HAPPENED MORNING AFTER MORNING.
I HAD NEVER SPOKEN TO HER, EXCEPT A FEW CASUAL WORDS, AND YET HER NAME WAS LIKE A SUMMONS TO ALL MY FOOLISH BLOOD.

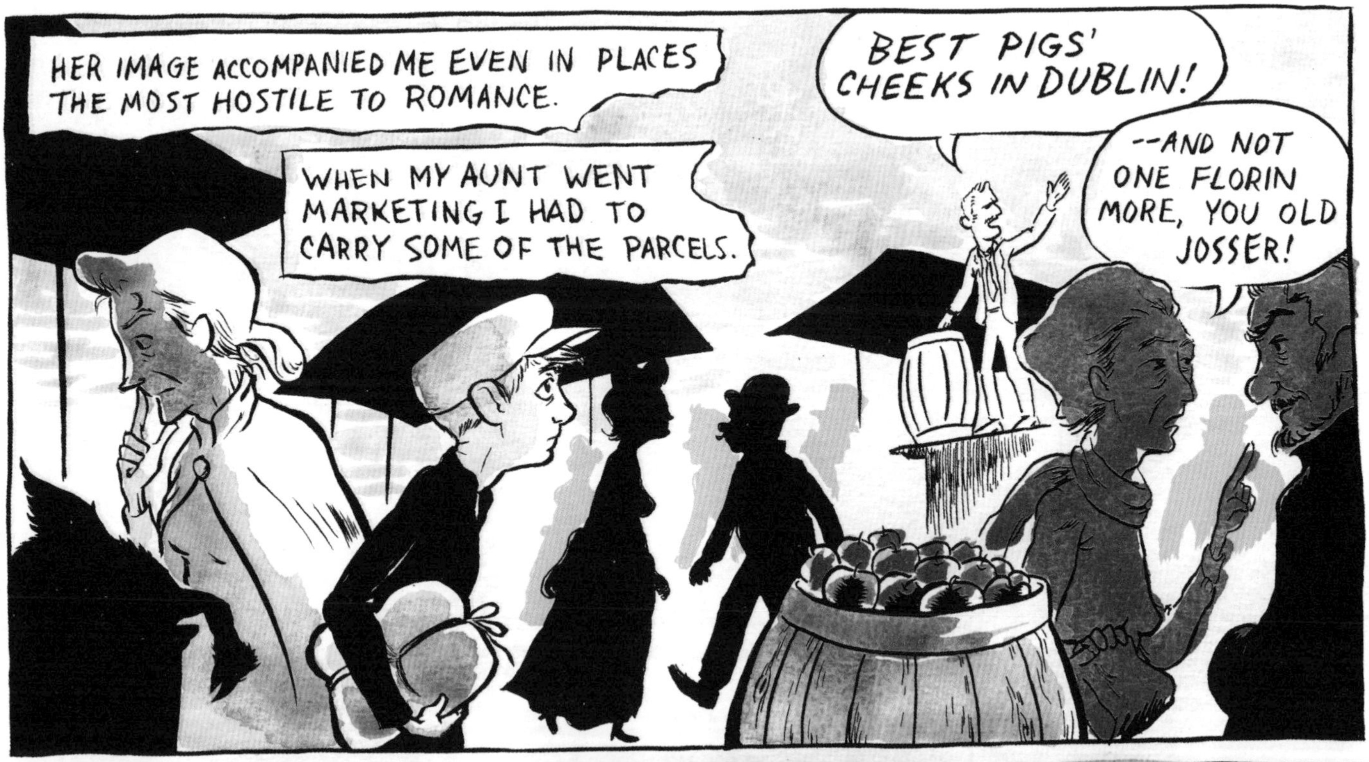
HER IMAGE ACCOMPANIED ME EVEN IN PLACES THE MOST HOSTILE TO ROMANCE.
WHEN MY AUNT WENT MARKETING I HAD TO CARRY SOME OF THE PARCELS.
BEST PIGS' CHEEKS IN DUBLIN!
--AND NOT ONE FLORIN MORE, YOU OLD JOSSER!

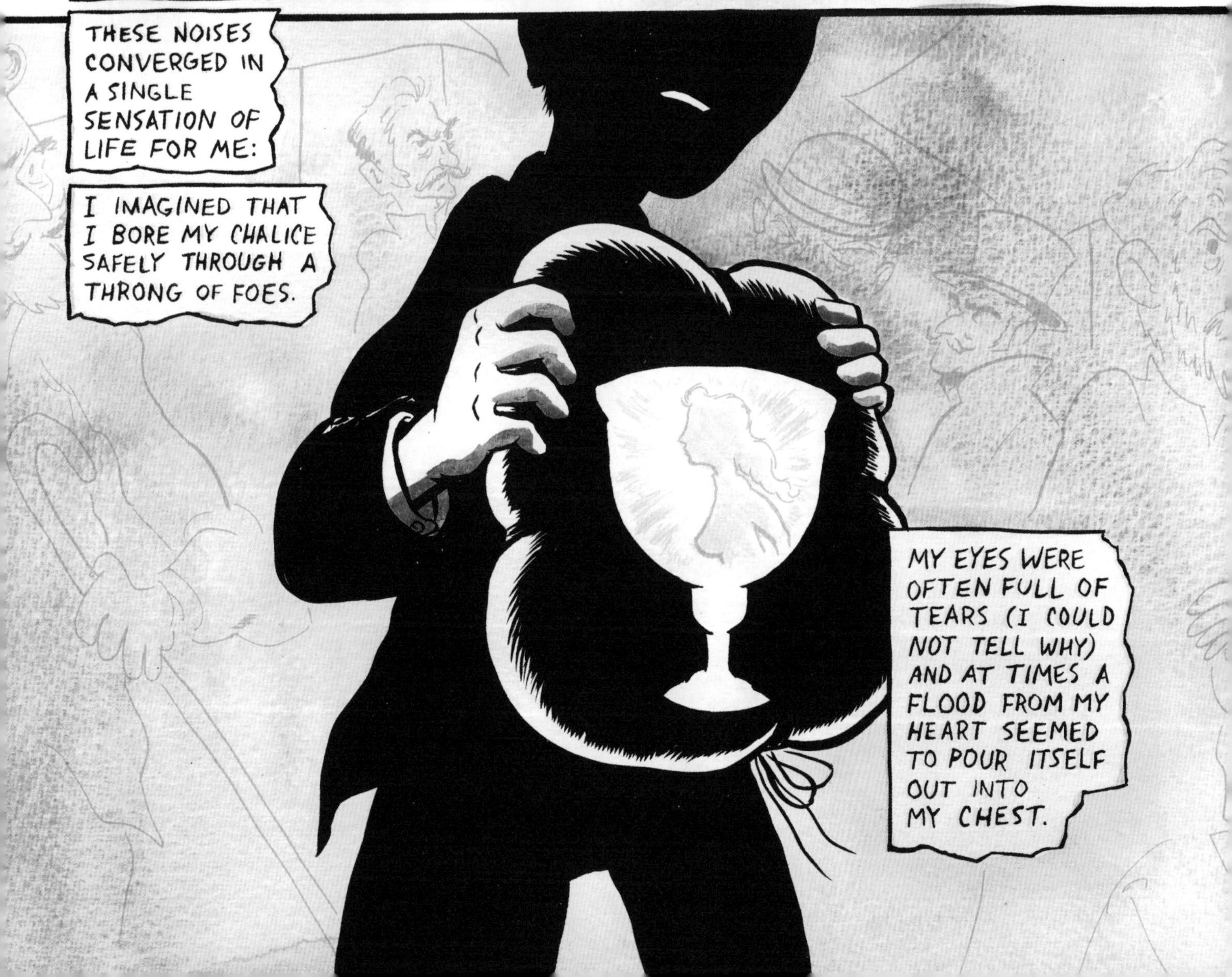
THESE NOISES CONVERGED IN A SINGLE SENSATION OF LIFE FOR ME:
I IMAGINED THAT I BORE MY CHALICE SAFELY THROUGH A THRONG OF FOES.
MY EYES WERE OFTEN FULL OF TEARS (I COULD NOT TELL WHY) AND AT TIMES A FLOOD FROM MY HEART SEEMED TO POUR ITSELF OUT INTO MY CHEST.

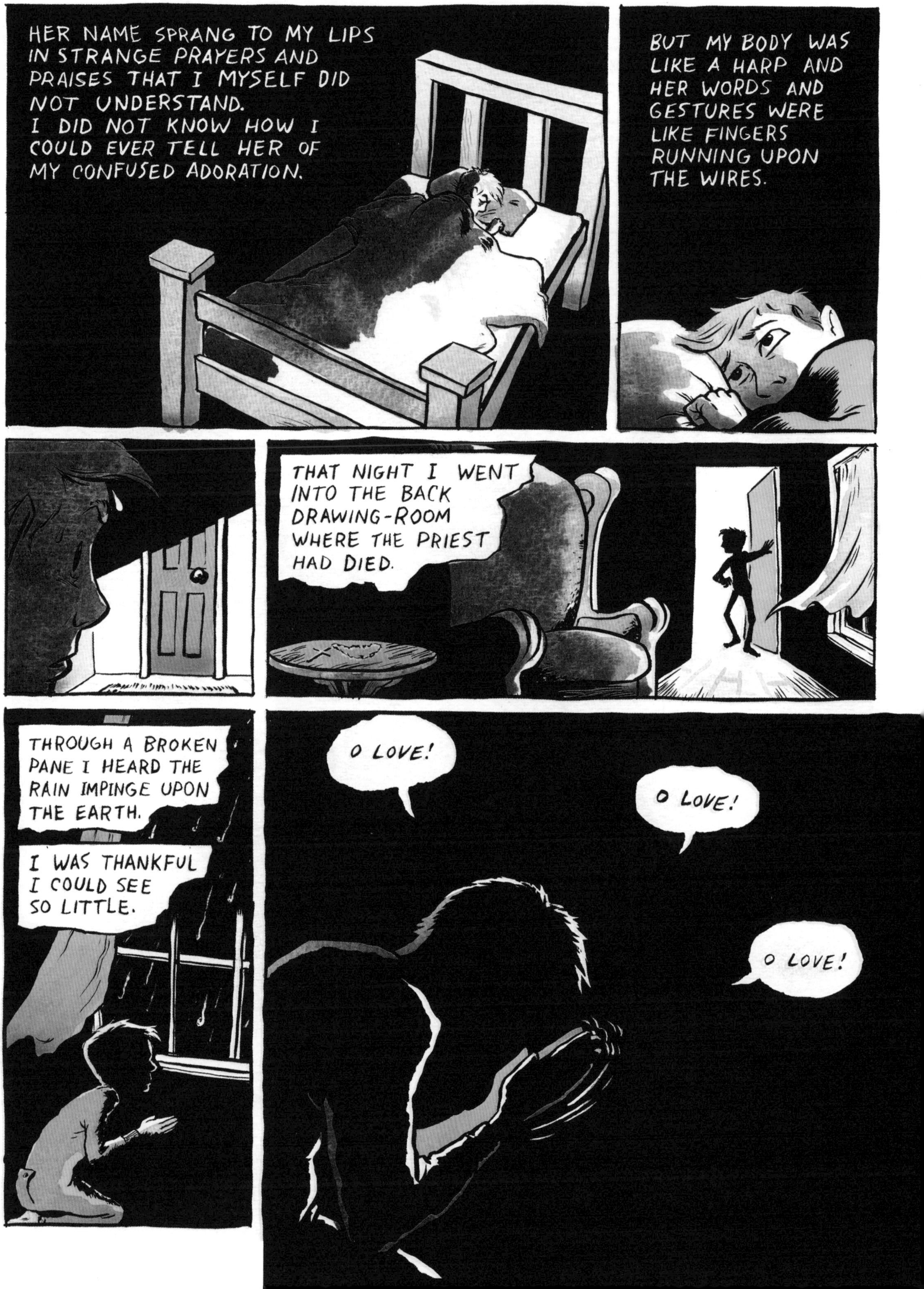
HER NAME SPRANG TO MY LIPS IN STRANGE PRAYERS AND PRAISES THAT I MYSELF DID NOT UNDERSTAND.
I DID NOT KNOW HOW I COULD EVER TELL HER OF MY CONFUSED ADORATION.
BUT MY BODY WAS LIKE A HARP AND HER WORDS AND GESTURES WERE LIKE FINGERS RUNNING UPON THE WIRES.
THAT NIGHT I WENT INTO THE BACK DRAWING-ROOM WHERE THE PRIEST HAD DIED.
THROUGH A BROKEN PANE I HEARD THE RAIN IMPINGE UPON THE EARTH.
I WAS THANKFUL I COULD SEE SO LITTLE.
O LOVE!
O LOVE!
O LOVE!

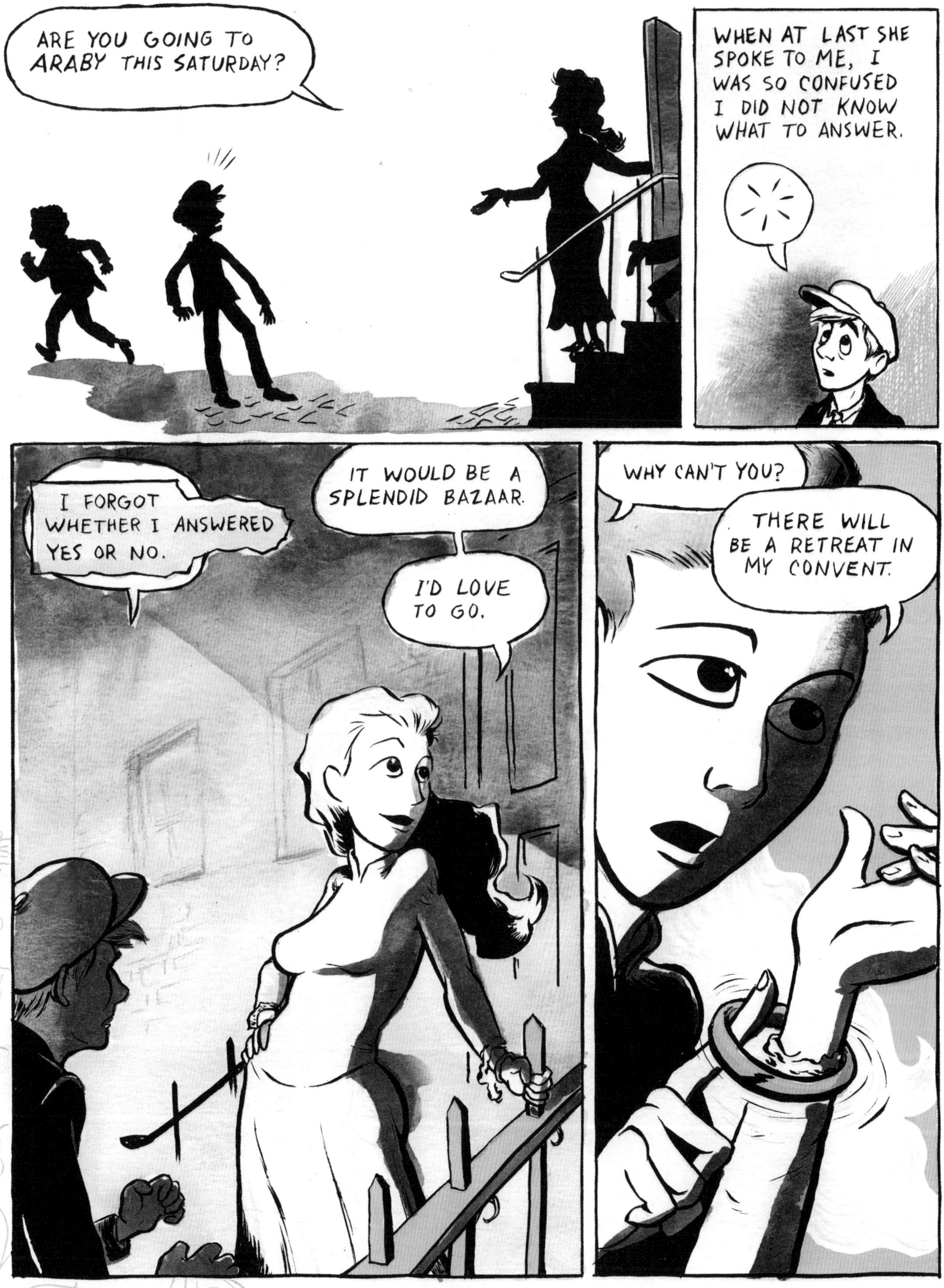
ARE YOU GOING TO ARABY THIS SATURDAY?
WHEN AT LAST SHE SPOKE TO ME, I WAS SO CONFUSED I DID NOT KNOW WHAT TO ANSWER.
I FORGOT WHETHER I ANSWERED YES OR NO.
IT WOULD BE A SPLENDID BAZAAR.
I'D LOVE TO GO.
WHY CAN'T YOU?
THERE WILL BE A RETREAT IN MY CONVENT.

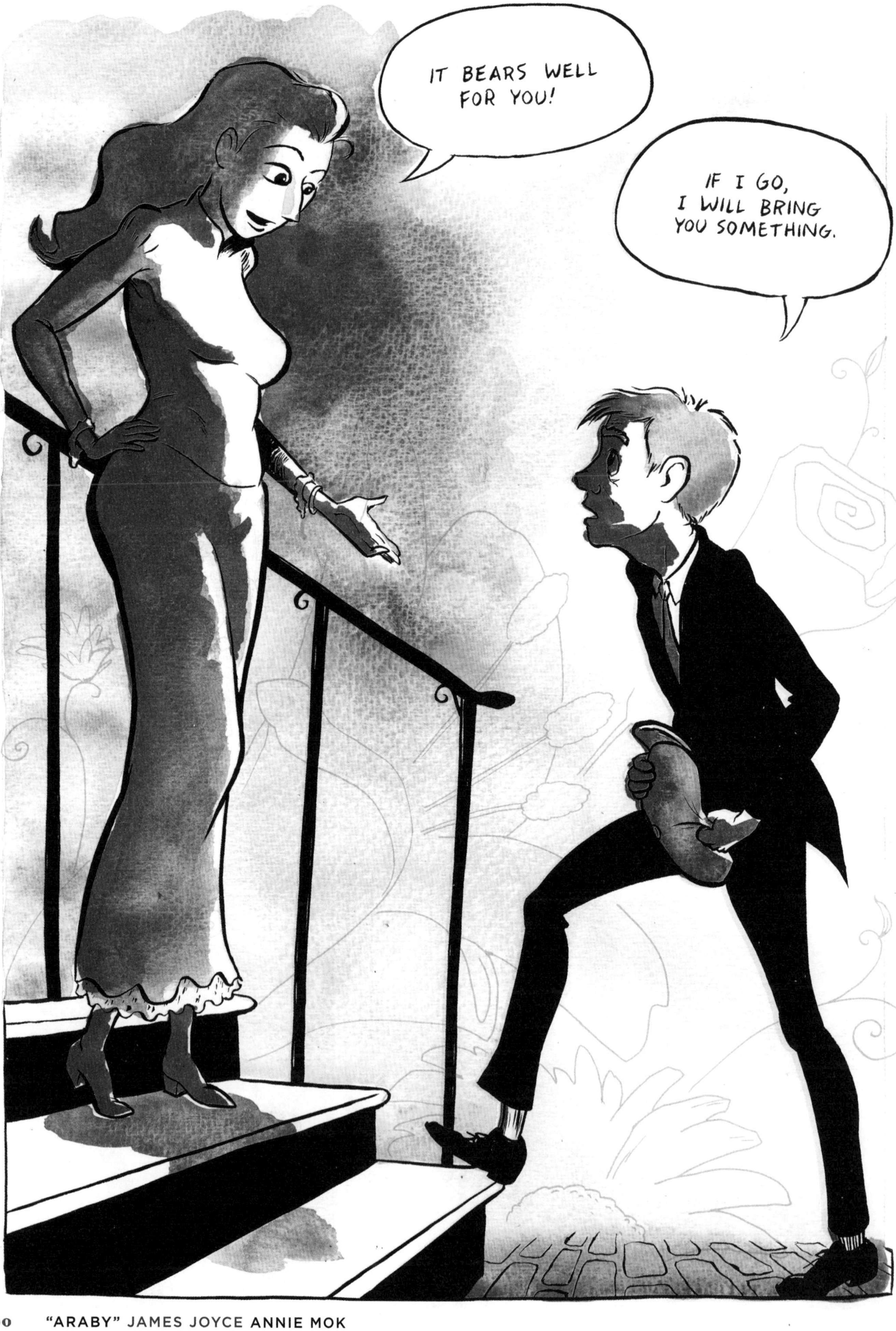
IT BEARS WELL FOR YOU!
IF I GO, I WILL BRING YOU SOMETHING.

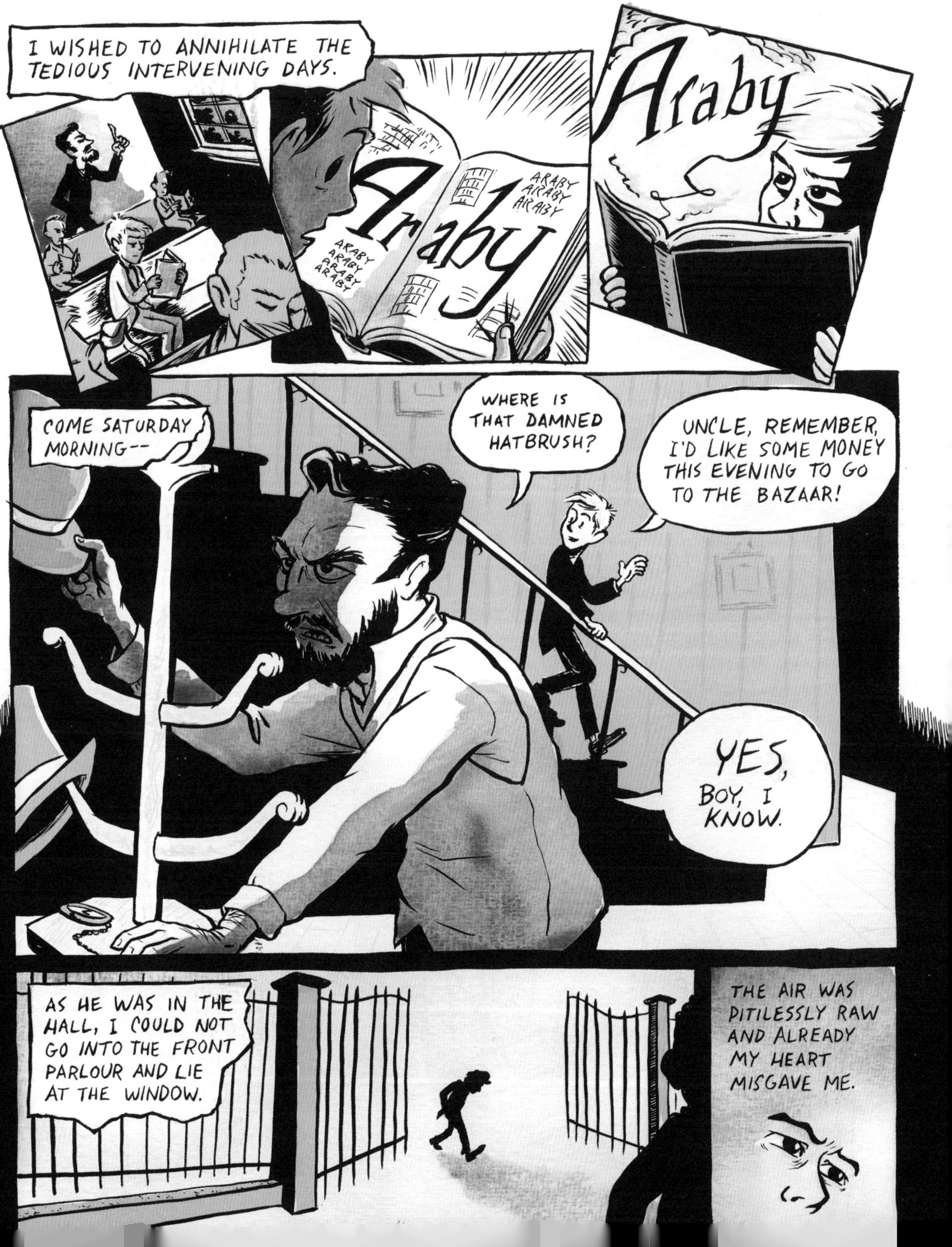
I WISHED TO ANNIHILATE THE TEDIOUS INTERVENING DAYS.
ARABY ARABY ARABY ARABY
Araby
ARABY ARABY ARABY
Araby
COME SATURDAY MORNING--
WHERE IS THAT DAMNED HATBRUSH?
UNCLE, REMEMBER, I'D LIKE SOME MONEY THIS EVENING TO GO TO THE BAZAAR!
YES, BOY, I KNOW.
AS HE WAS IN THE HALL, I COULD NOT GO INTO THE FRONT PARLOUR AND LIE AT THE WINDOW.
THE AIR WAS PITILESSLY RAW AND ALREADY MY HEART MISGAVE ME.

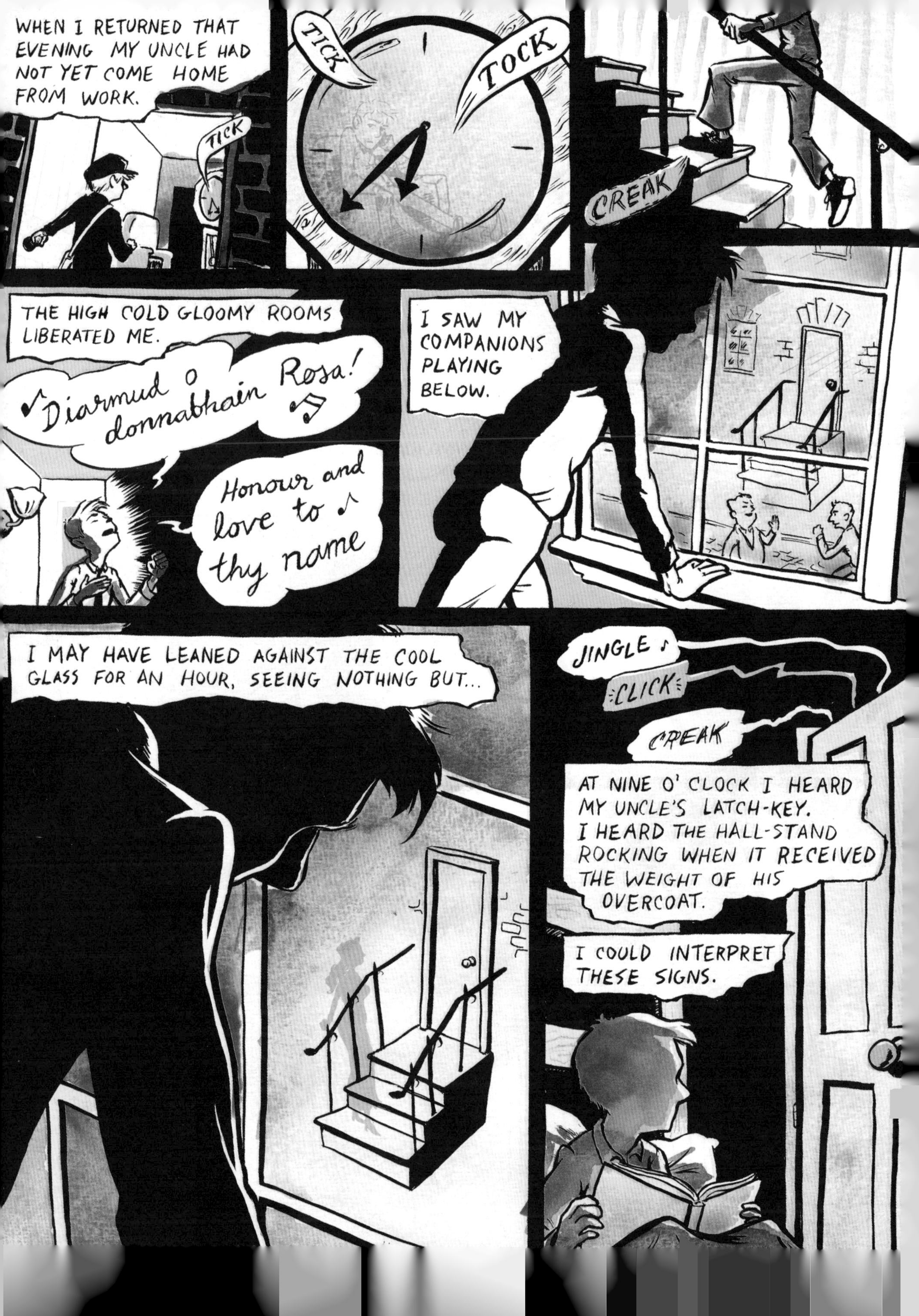
WHEN I RETURNED THAT EVENING MY UNCLE HAD NOT YET COME HOME FROM WORK.
TICK
TICK
TOCK
CREAK
THE HIGH COLD GLOOMY ROOMS LIBERATED ME.
Diarmud O donnabhain Rosa!
Honour and love to thy name
I SAW MY COMPANIONS PLAYING BELOW.
I MAY HAVE LEANED AGAINST THE COOL GLASS FOR AN HOUR, SEEING NOTHING BUT...
JINGLE
CLICK
CREAK
AT NINE O' CLOCK I HEARD MY UNCLE'S LATCH-KEY. I HEARD THE HALL-STAND ROCKING WHEN IT RECEIVED THE WEIGHT OF HIS OVERCOAT.
I COULD INTERPRET THESE SIGNS.

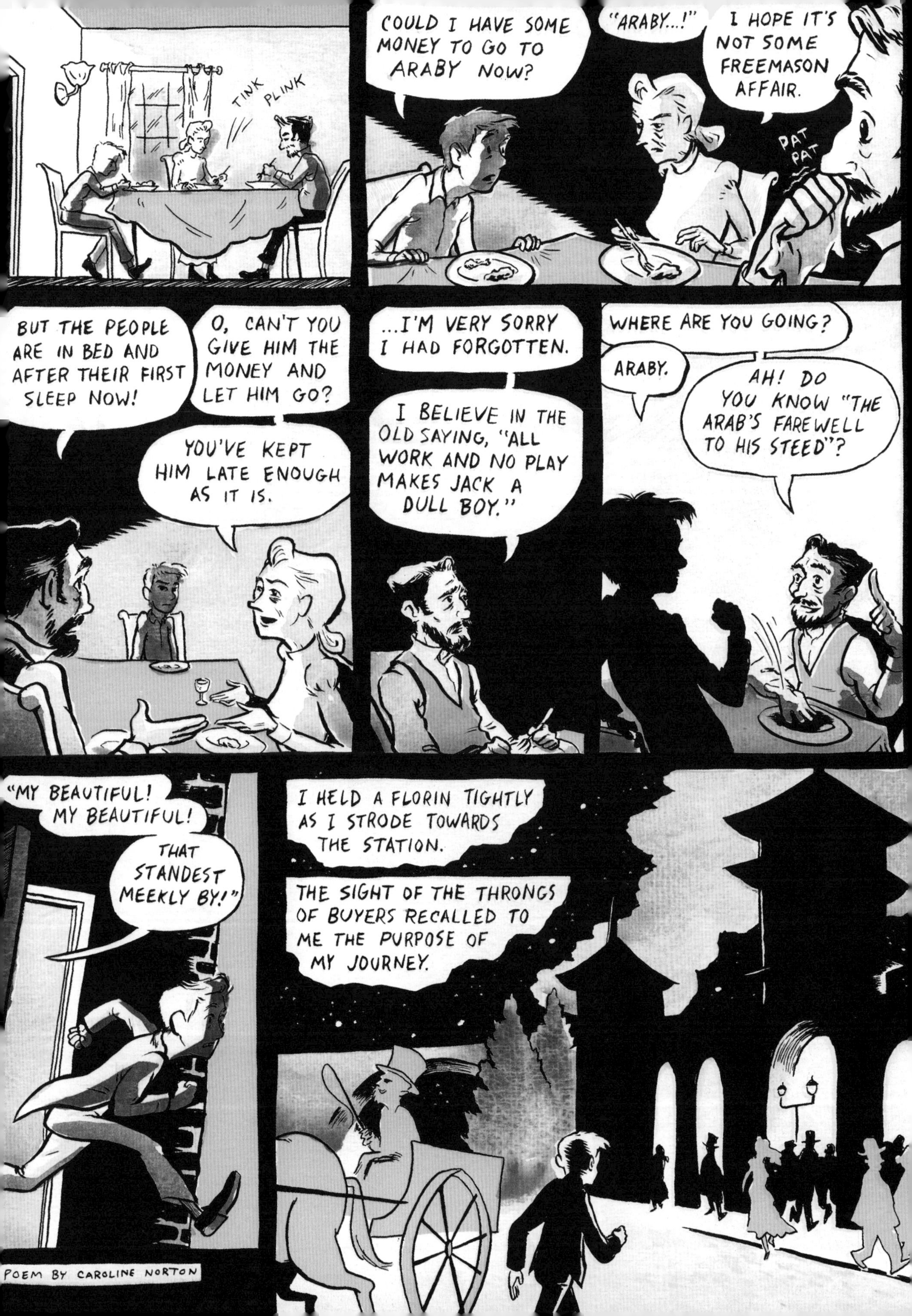
TINK
PLINK
COULD I HAVE SOME MONEY TO GO TO ARABY NOW?
"ARABY...!"
I HOPE IT'S NOT SOME FREEMASON AFFAIR.
PAT PAT
BUT THE PEOPLE ARE IN BED AND AFTER THEIR FIRST SLEEP NOW!
O, CAN'T YOU GIVE HIM THE MONEY AND LET HIM GO?
YOU'VE KEPT HIM LATE ENOUGH AS IT IS.
...I'M VERY SORRY I HAD FORGOTTEN.
I BELIEVE IN THE OLD SAYING, "ALL WORK AND NO PLAY MAKES JACK A DULL BOY."
WHERE ARE YOU GOING?
ARABY.
AH! DO YOU KNOW "THE ARAB'S FAREWELL TO HIS STEED"?
"MY BEAUTIFUL! MY BEAUTIFUL!
THAT STANDEST MEEKLY BY!"
POEM BY CAROLINE NORTON
I HELD A FLORIN TIGHTLY AS I STRODE TOWARDS THE STATION.
THE SIGHT OF THE THRONGS OF BUYERS RECALLED TO ME THE PURPOSE OF MY JOURNEY.

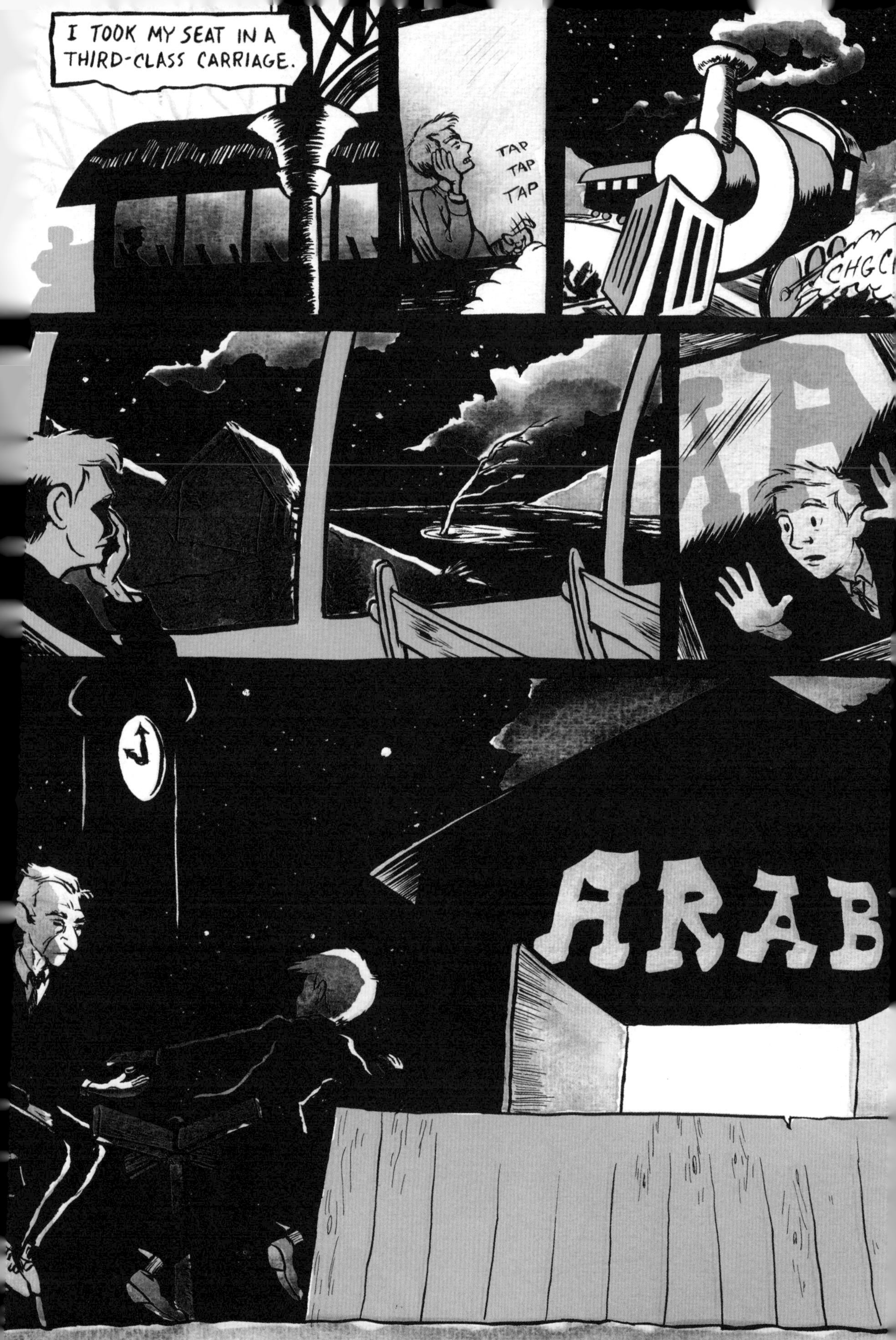
I TOOK MY SEAT IN A THIRD-CLASS CARRIAGE.
TAP
TAP
TAP
CHGC
ARAB

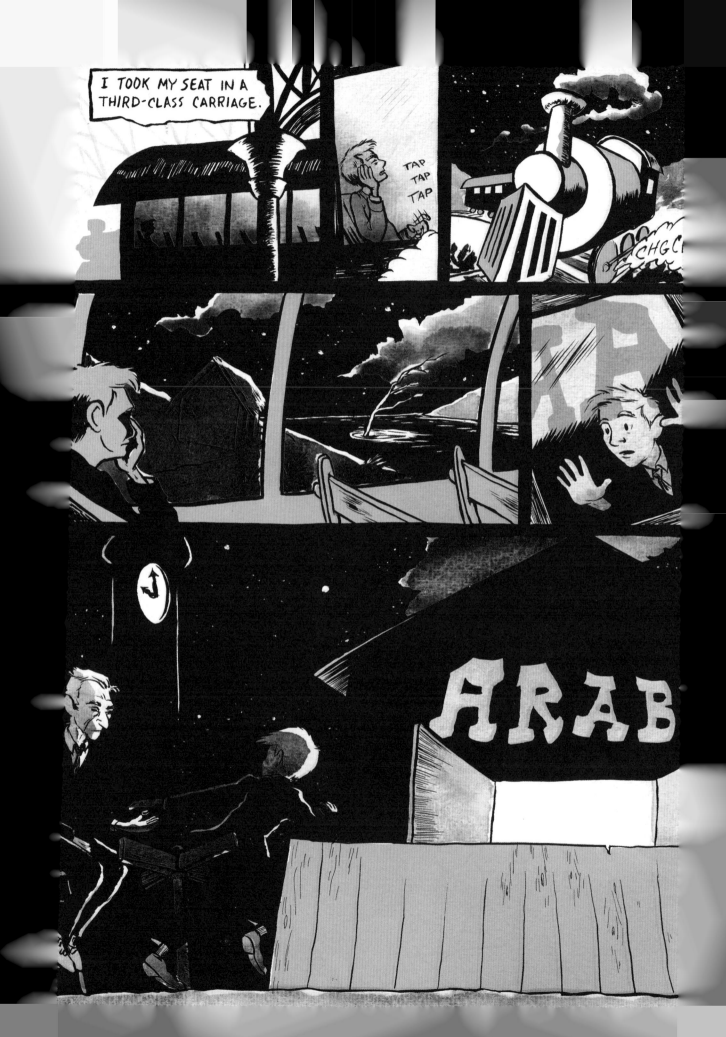

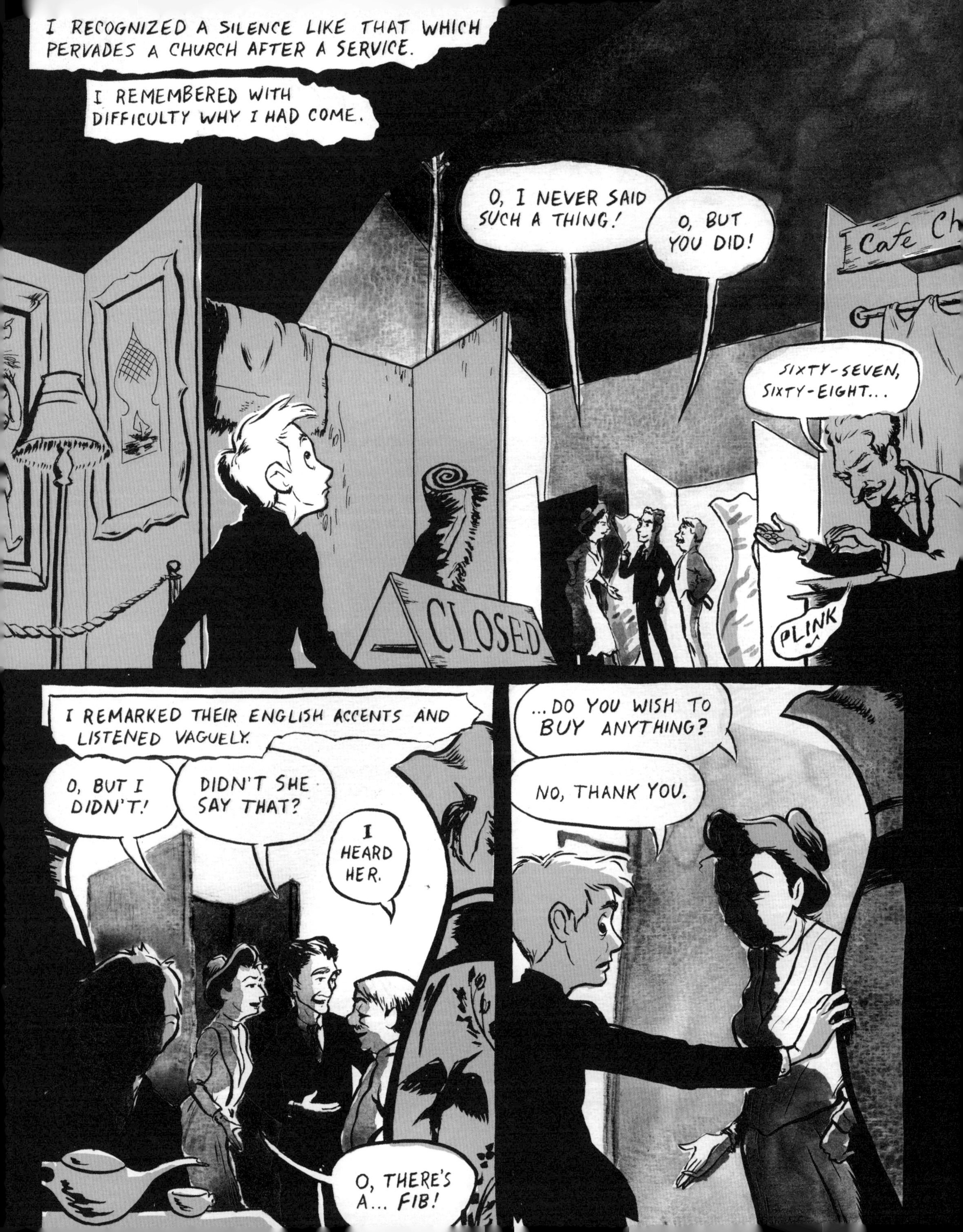
I RECOGNIZED A SILENCE LIKE THAT WHICH PERVADES A CHURCH AFTER A SERVICE.
I REMEMBERED WITH DIFFICULTY WHY I HAD COME.
O, I NEVER SAID SUCH A THING!
O, BUT YOU DID!
Cafe Ch
SIXTY-SEVEN, SIXTY-EIGHT...
CLOSED
PLINK
I REMARKED THEIR ENGLISH ACCENTS AND LISTENED VAGUELY.
O, BUT I DIDN'T!
DIDN'T SHE SAY THAT?
I HEARD HER.
O, THERE'S A... FIB!
...DO YOU WISH TO BUY ANYTHING?
NO, THANK YOU.

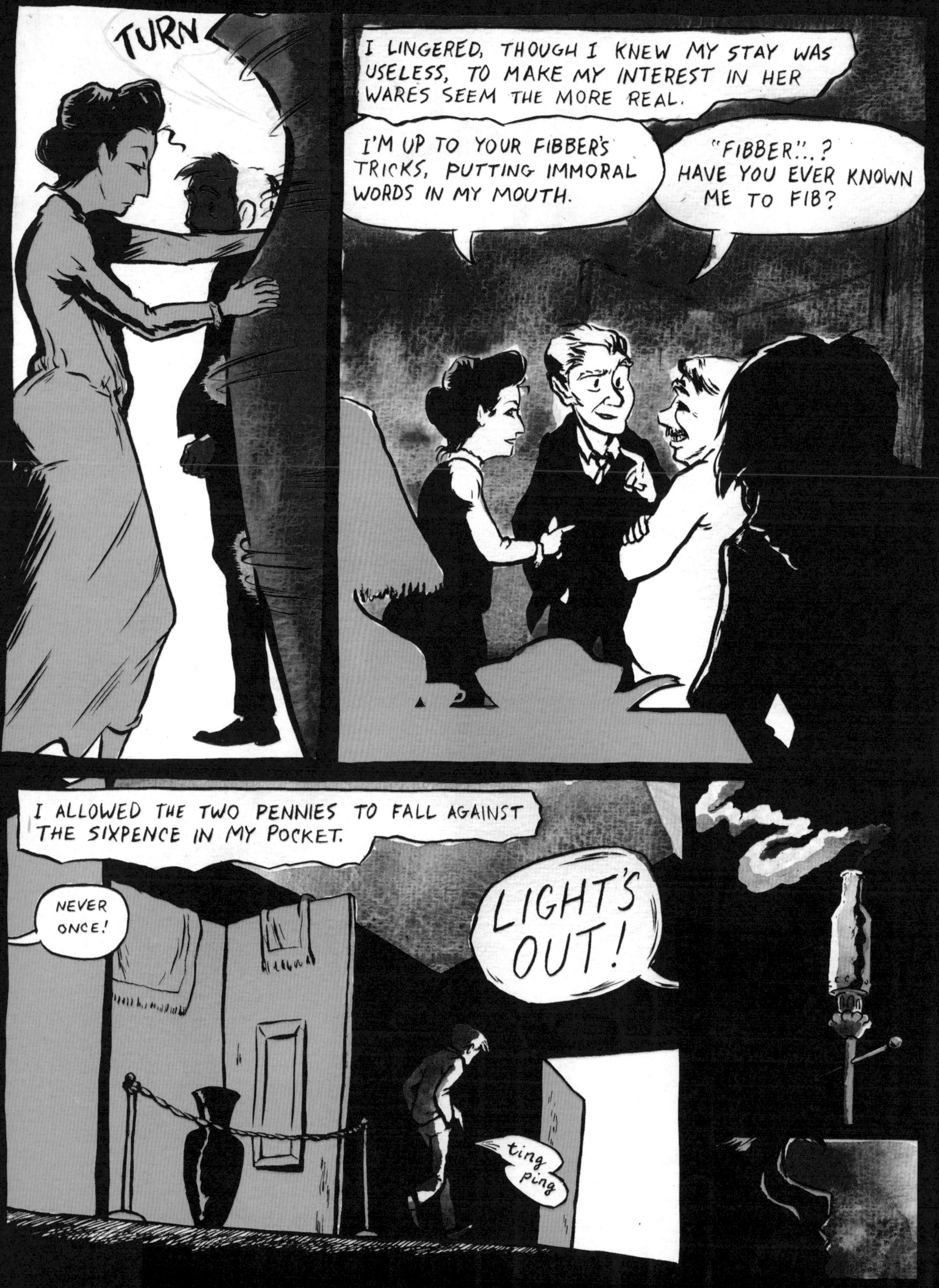
TURN
I LINGERED, THOUGH I KNEW MY STAY WAS USELESS, TO MAKE MY INTEREST IN HER WARES SEEM THE MORE REAL.
I'M UP TO YOUR FIBBER'S TRICKS, PUTTING IMMORAL WORDS IN MY MOUTH.
"FIBBER"..? HAVE YOU EVER KNOWN ME TO FIB?
I ALLOWED THE TWO PENNIES TO FALL AGAINST THE SIXPENCE IN MY POCKET.
NEVER ONCE!
LIGHT'S OUT!
ting ping

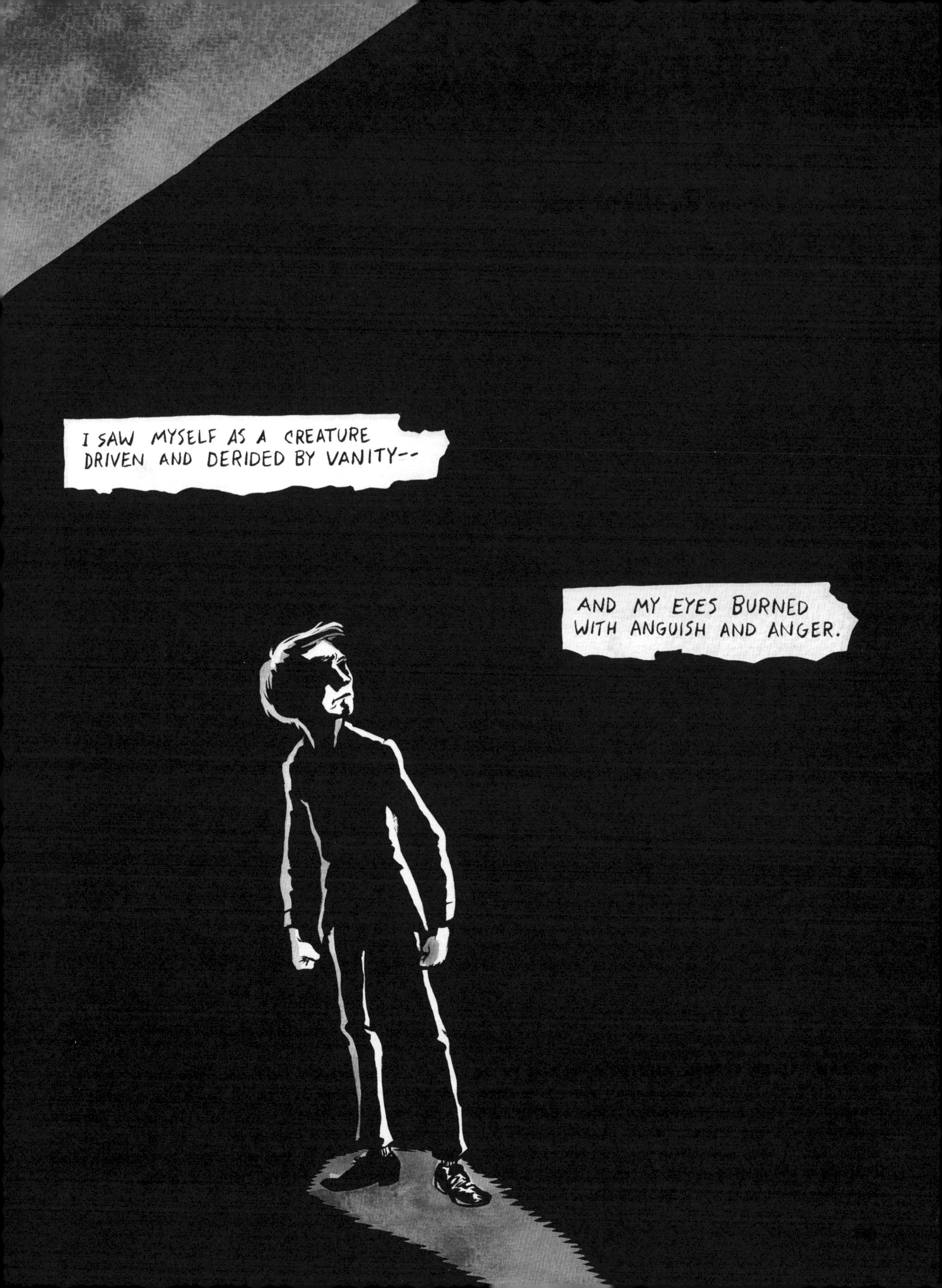
I SAW MYSELF AS A CREATURE DRIVEN AND DERIDED BY VANITY--
AND MY EYES BURNED WITH ANGUISH AND ANGER.

"The Metamorphosis"

Franz Kafka

ART/ADAPTATION BY **R. Sikoryak**

DREAD. ALIENATION. ANXIETY. *PEANUTS* IS heavy stuff. You thought I was talking about "The Metamorphosis"? That, too. Franz Kafka's famous 1915 novella about a man, Gregor Samsa, who inexplicably wakes up as a giant bug is a key work about the confusion and disgust of living in the modern world. So too is Charles Schulz's legendary comic strip, and R. Sikoryak makes such parallels hilariously apparent in his *Masterpiece Comics* series. He ingeniously mashes up a classic comic and a classic work of lit—*Dennis the Menace* with *Hamlet*, *Ziggy* with *Candide*, *Batman* with *Crime and Punishment*—and suddenly you see that these two works from very different branches of art were dealing with the same themes all along.

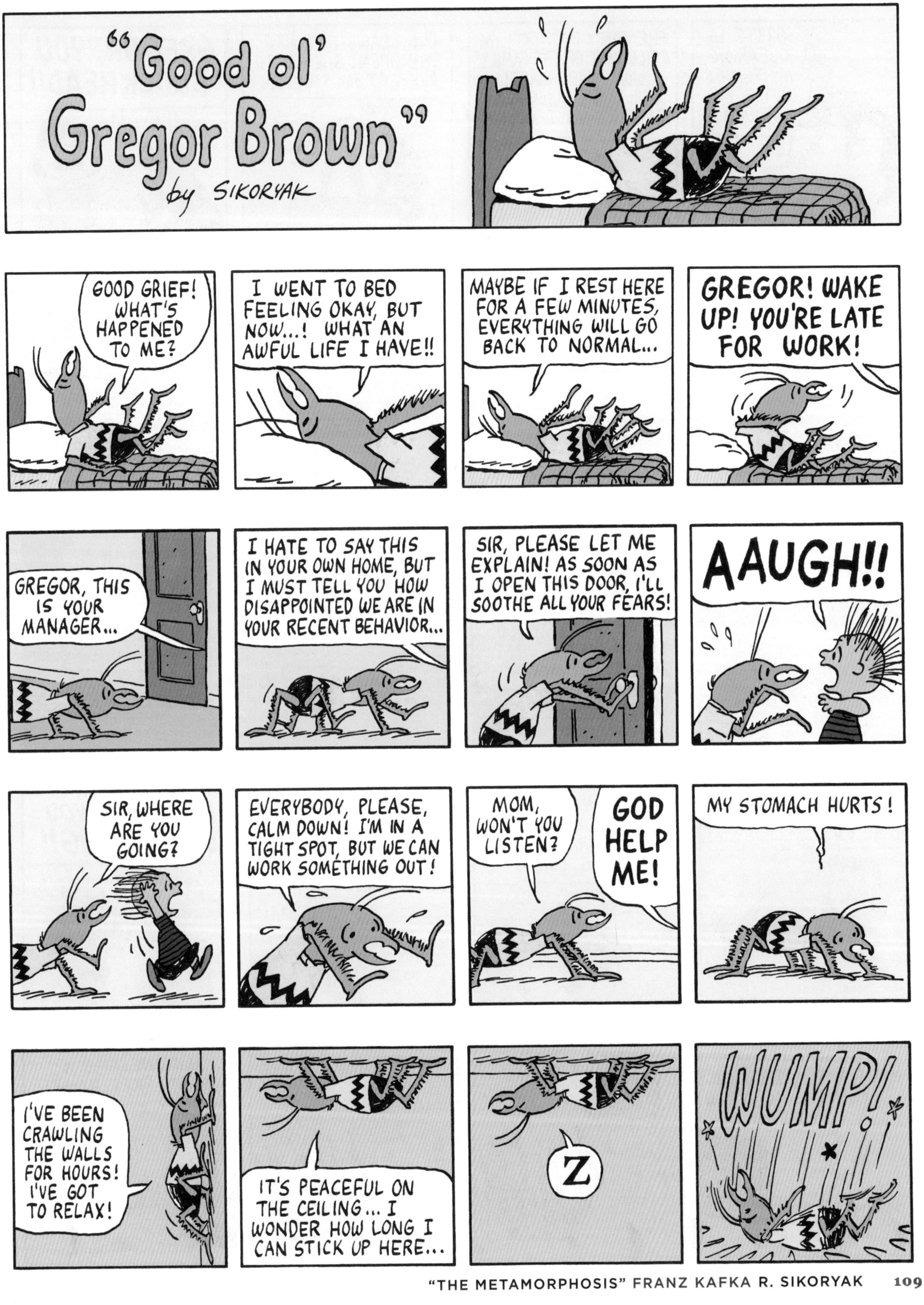
"Good ol' Gregor Brown"
by SIKORYAK
GOOD GRIEF! WHAT'S HAPPENED TO ME?
I WENT TO BED FEELING OKAY, BUT NOW...! WHAT AN AWFUL LIFE I HAVE!!
MAYBE IF I REST HERE FOR A FEW MINUTES, EVERYTHING WILL GO BACK TO NORMAL...
GREGOR! WAKE UP! YOU'RE LATE FOR WORK!
GREGOR, THIS IS YOUR MANAGER...
I HATE TO SAY THIS IN YOUR OWN HOME, BUT I MUST TELL YOU HOW DISAPPOINTED WE ARE IN YOUR RECENT BEHAVIOR...
SIR, PLEASE LET ME EXPLAIN! AS SOON AS I OPEN THIS DOOR, I'LL SOOTHE ALL YOUR FEARS!
AAUGH!!
SIR, WHERE ARE YOU GOING?
EVERYBODY, PLEASE, CALM DOWN! I'M IN A TIGHT SPOT, BUT WE CAN WORK SOMETHING OUT!
MOM, WON'T YOU LISTEN?
GOD HELP ME!
MY STOMACH HURTS!
I'VE BEEN CRAWLING THE WALLS FOR HOURS! I'VE GOT TO RELAX!
IT'S PEACEFUL ON THE CEILING... I WONDER HOW LONG I CAN STICK UP HERE...
Z
WUMP!

GRETE IS CLEARING MY THINGS OUT OF MY ROOM!

SHE CAN'T DO THAT! I'M STILL PART OF THE FAMILY! I WON'T HIDE QUIETLY WHILE SHE TAKES AWAY EVERYTHING I LOVE!

I'LL CRAWL OUT INTO THE OPEN! SHE HAS TO RESPECT MY RIGHTS!

GREGOR, YOU BLOCKHEAD!!

I DIDN'T MEAN TO UPSET GRETE LIKE THAT!

UH-OH, HERE COMES DAD! I HOPE HE'S NOT ANGRY AT ME!

HEY, WHAT'S HE DOING WITH ALL THOSE APPLES?

BONK!

I CAN'T SLEEP...

I'VE BECOME A BURDEN ON THE FAMILY... THEY CAN'T BE BOTHERED WITH ME... NOTHING SATISFIES MY DESIRES... MY OLD WAY OF LIFE IS JUST A DISTANT MEMORY...

⌖ SIGH ⌖

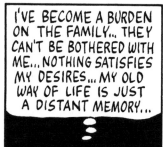

THAT MUSIC!... I... I NEVER REALIZED HOW BEAUTIFUL GRETE'S PLAYING IS...!

FINALLY, I'VE FOUND SOMETHING WORTHWHILE! I'VE GOT TO SHOW HER MY APPRECIATION! I'LL DO ANYTHING FOR HER!

GET LOST, YOU STUPID BUG!!

BRIGHT AND EARLY, THE MAID ENTERS THE BROWN HOUSEHOLD...

!

HAPPINESS IS A PEST-FREE HOME!

"THE METAMORPHOSIS" FRANZ KAFKA R. SIKORYAK

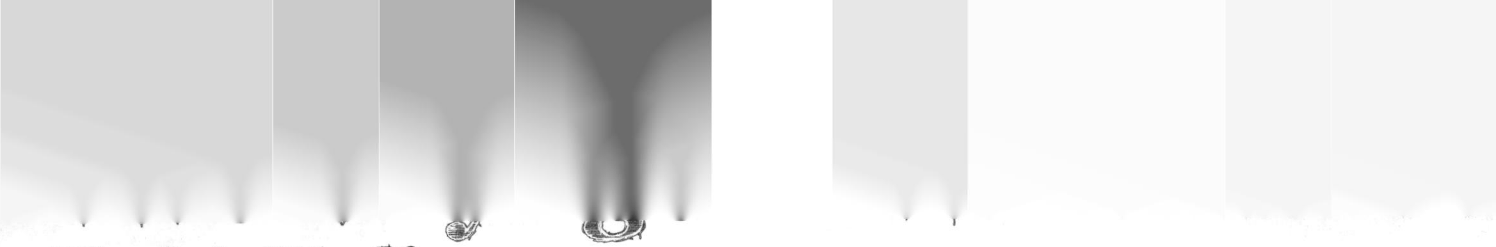

Virginia Woolf

ART/ADAPTATION BY **Caroline Picard**

WITH HER FIRST NOVEL *THE VOYAGE OUT* (1915)— which took her five years and at least five completely different drafts to complete—Virginia Woolf started experimenting with form and plot, helping lead the way to Modernism. As a group of British travelers sail to an English colony in South America, the journey becomes more menacing, more threatening, which mirrors the scary unknowns cropping up in the lives of the travelers. Our social constructs are really worthless attempts to put order on a chaotic, frightening world in which death and the unknown always lurk. "[O]ne never knows what any one feels. We're all in the dark. We try to find out, but can you imagine anything more ludicrous than one person's opinion of another person? One goes along thinking one knows; but one really doesn't know." At the center of this bleak take on life is Rachel, who's led an extraordinarily sheltered existence in England. Her aunt Helen tries to educate her about the ways of the world, especially love.

Caroline Picard brings her uniquely sinuous, flowing style to a key scene from the novel. As with her adaptation of the Incan play *Apu Ollantay* in Volume 1, each page is a unified piece that looks like a single full-page work of art. Yet, despite the lack of panels as such, a sequential story winds its way across each page.

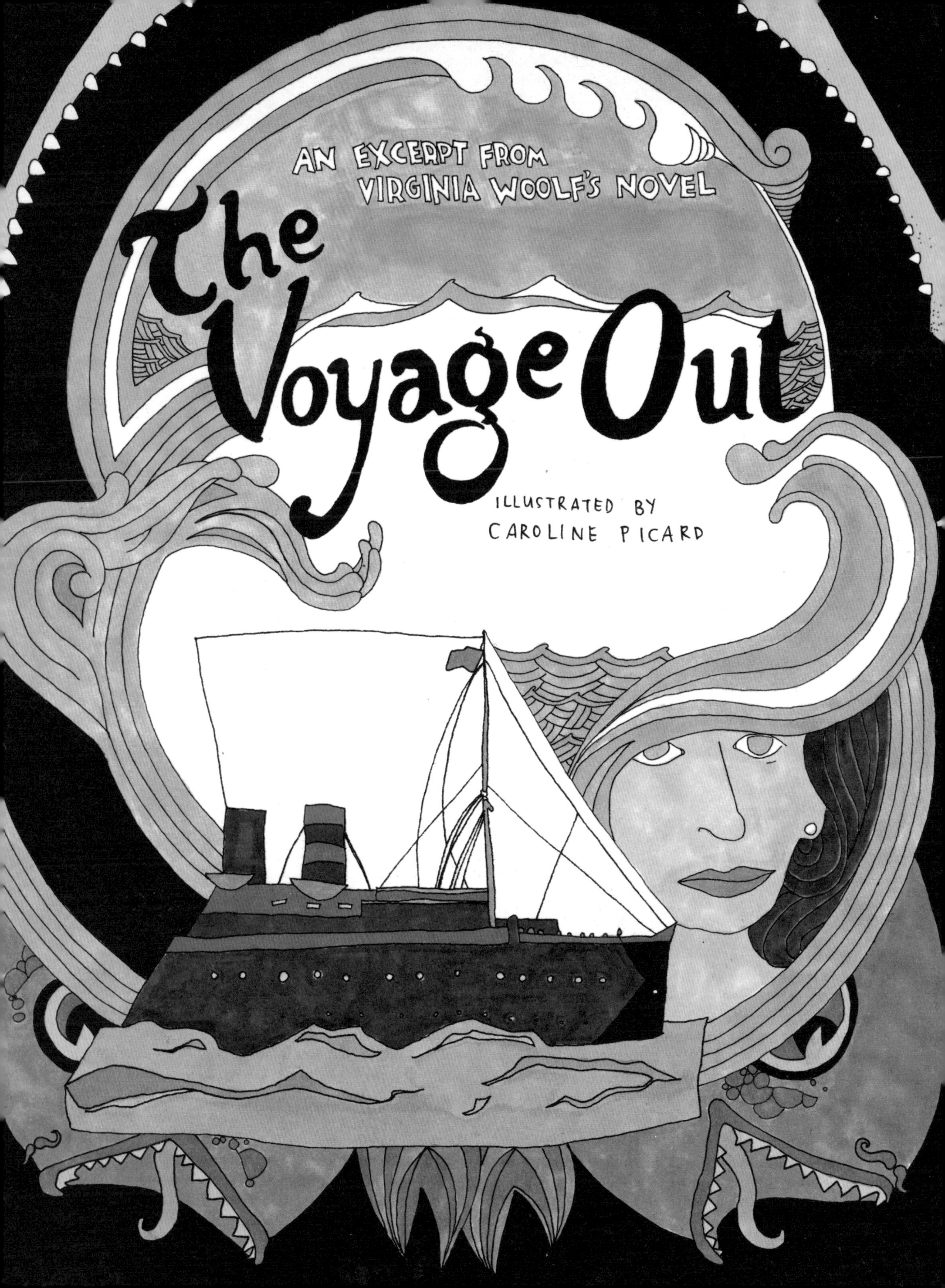
AN EXCERPT FROM VIRGINIA WOOLF'S NOVEL
The Voyage Out
ILLUSTRATED BY
CAROLINE PICARD

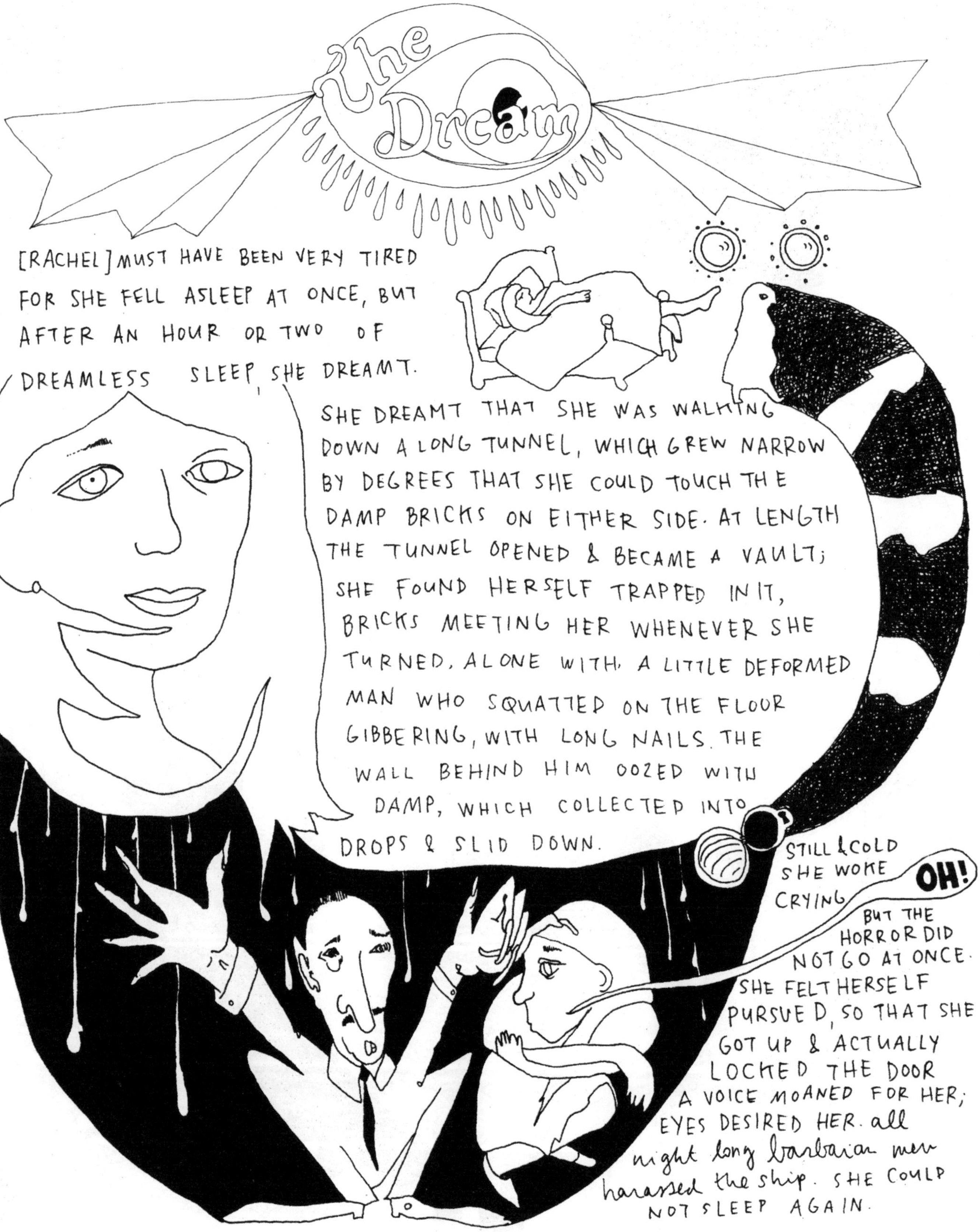
The Dream
[RACHEL] MUST HAVE BEEN VERY TIRED FOR SHE FELL ASLEEP AT ONCE, BUT AFTER AN HOUR OR TWO OF DREAMLESS SLEEP, SHE DREAMT.
SHE DREAMT THAT SHE WAS WALKING DOWN A LONG TUNNEL, WHICH GREW NARROW BY DEGREES THAT SHE COULD TOUCH THE DAMP BRICKS ON EITHER SIDE. AT LENGTH THE TUNNEL OPENED & BECAME A VAULT; SHE FOUND HERSELF TRAPPED IN IT, BRICKS MEETING HER WHENEVER SHE TURNED, ALONE WITH A LITTLE DEFORMED MAN WHO SQUATTED ON THE FLOOR GIBBERING, WITH LONG NAILS. THE WALL BEHIND HIM OOZED WITH DAMP, WHICH COLLECTED INTO DROPS & SLID DOWN.
STILL & COLD SHE WOKE CRYING
OH!
BUT THE HORROR DID NOT GO AT ONCE. SHE FELT HERSELF PURSUED, SO THAT SHE GOT UP & ACTUALLY LOCKED THE DOOR. A VOICE MOANED FOR HER; EYES DESIRED HER. all night long barbarian men harassed the ship. SHE COULD NOT SLEEP AGAIN.

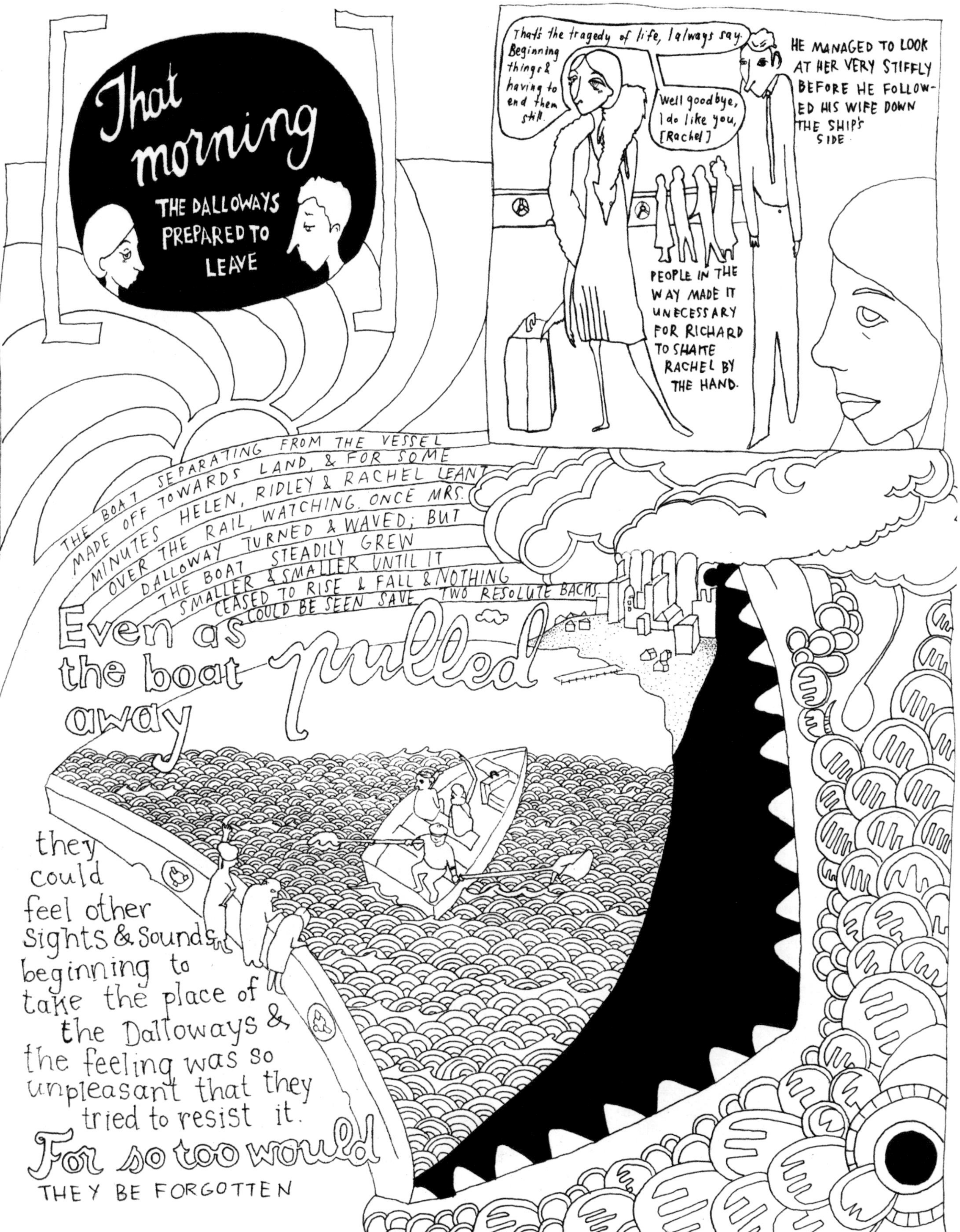

That morning
THE DALLOWAYS PREPARED TO LEAVE
That's the tragedy of life, I always say. Beginning things & having to end them still.
Well goodbye, I do like you, [Rachel]
HE MANAGED TO LOOK AT HER VERY STIFFLY BEFORE HE FOLLOWED HIS WIFE DOWN THE SHIP'S SIDE
PEOPLE IN THE WAY MADE IT UNECESSARY FOR RICHARD TO SHAKE RACHEL BY THE HAND.
THE BOAT SEPARATING FROM THE VESSEL MADE OFF TOWARDS LAND, & FOR SOME MINUTES HELEN, RIDLEY & RACHEL LEANT OVER THE RAIL, WATCHING. ONCE MRS. DALLOWAY TURNED & WAVED; BUT THE BOAT STEADILY GREW SMALLER & SMALLER UNTIL IT CEASED TO RISE & FALL & NOTHING COULD BE SEEN SAVE TWO RESOLUTE BACKS.
Even as the boat pulled away
they could feel other sights & sounds beginning to take the place of the Dalloways & the feeling was so unpleasant that they tried to resist it.
For so too would THEY BE FORGOTTEN

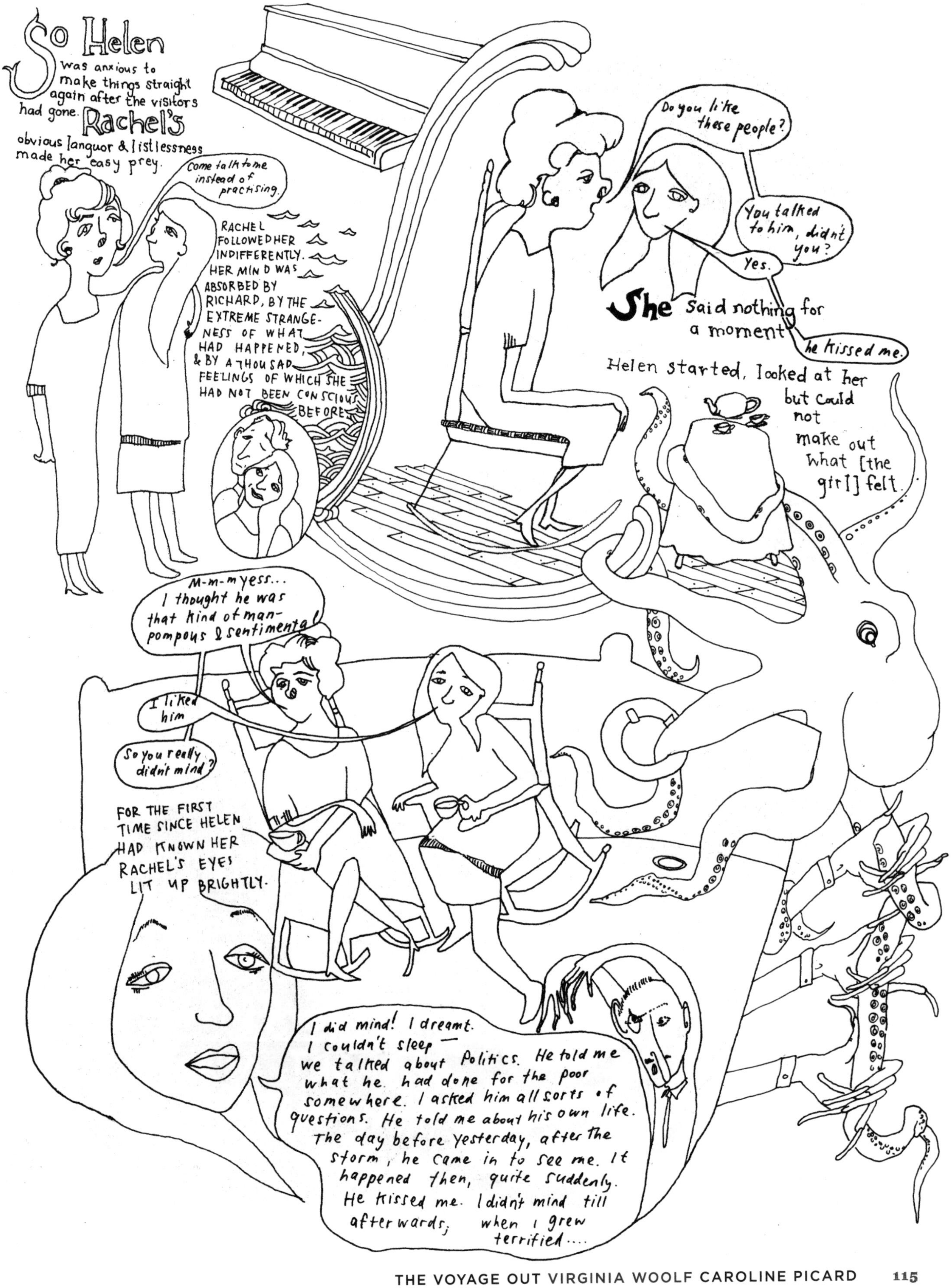
So Helen was anxious to make things straight again after the visitors had gone. Rachel's obvious languor & listlessness made her easy prey.
Come talk to me instead of practising.
RACHEL FOLLOWED HER INDIFFERENTLY. HER MIND WAS ABSORBED BY RICHARD, BY THE EXTREME STRANGENESS OF WHAT HAD HAPPENED, & BY A THOUSAD FEELINGS OF WHICH SHE HAD NOT BEEN CONSCIOUS BEFORE.
Do you like these people?
You talked to him, didn't you?
Yes.
She said nothing for a moment
he kissed me.
Helen started, looked at her but could not make out what [the girl] felt.
M-m-myess... I thought he was that kind of man- pompous & sentimental
I liked him
So you really didn't mind?
FOR THE FIRST TIME SINCE HELEN HAD KNOWN HER RACHEL'S EYES LIT UP BRIGHTLY.
I did mind! I dreamt. I couldn't sleep— we talked about Politics. He told me what he had done for the poor somewhere. I asked him all sorts of questions. He told me about his own life. The day before yesterday, after the storm, he came in to see me. It happened then, quite suddenly. He kissed me. I didn't mind till afterwards, when I grew terrified....

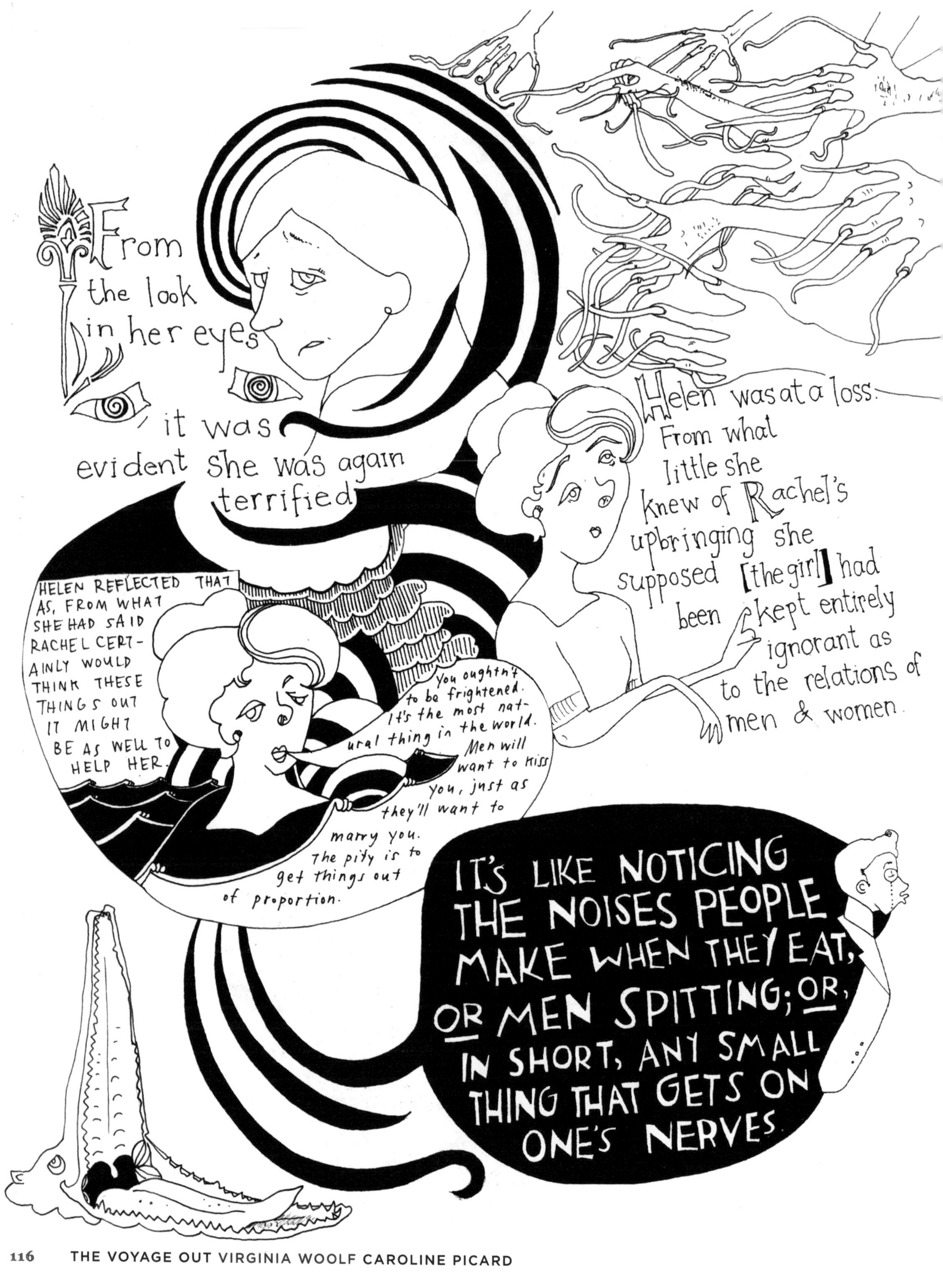
From the look in her eyes it was evident she was again terrified
Helen was at a loss. From what little she knew of Rachel's upbringing she supposed [the girl] had been kept entirely ignorant as to the relations of men & women.
HELEN REFLECTED THAT AS, FROM WHAT SHE HAD SAID RACHEL CERTAINLY WOULD THINK THESE THINGS OUT IT MIGHT BE AS WELL TO HELP HER.
You oughtn't to be frightened. It's the most natural thing in the world. Men will want to kiss you, just as they'll want to marry you. The pity is to get things out of proportion.
IT'S LIKE NOTICING THE NOISES PEOPLE MAKE WHEN THEY EAT, OR MEN SPITTING; OR, IN SHORT, ANY SMALL THING THAT GETS ON ONE'S NERVES.

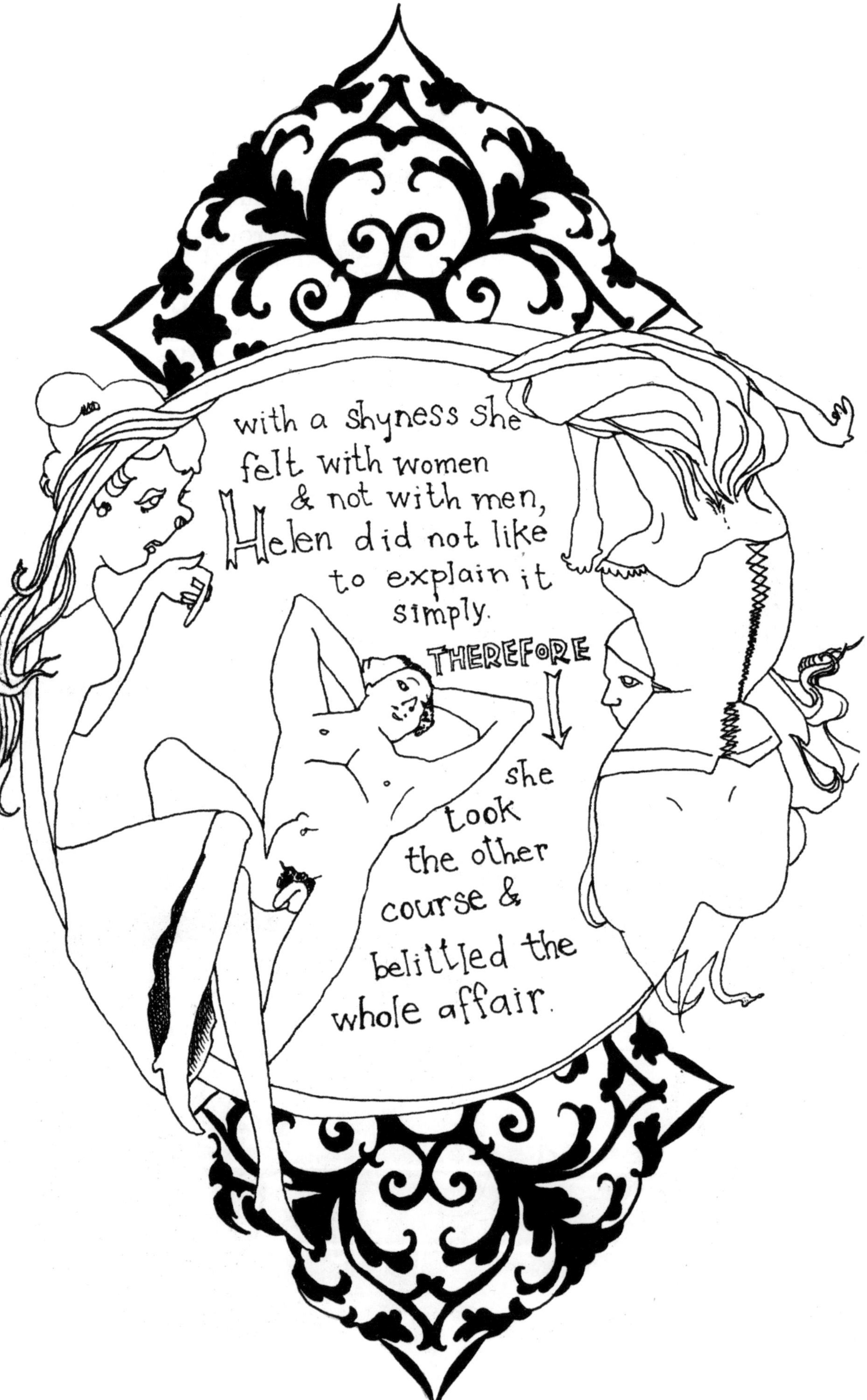
with a shyness she felt with women & not with men, Helen did not like to explain it simply.
THEREFORE
she took the other course & belittled the whole affair.

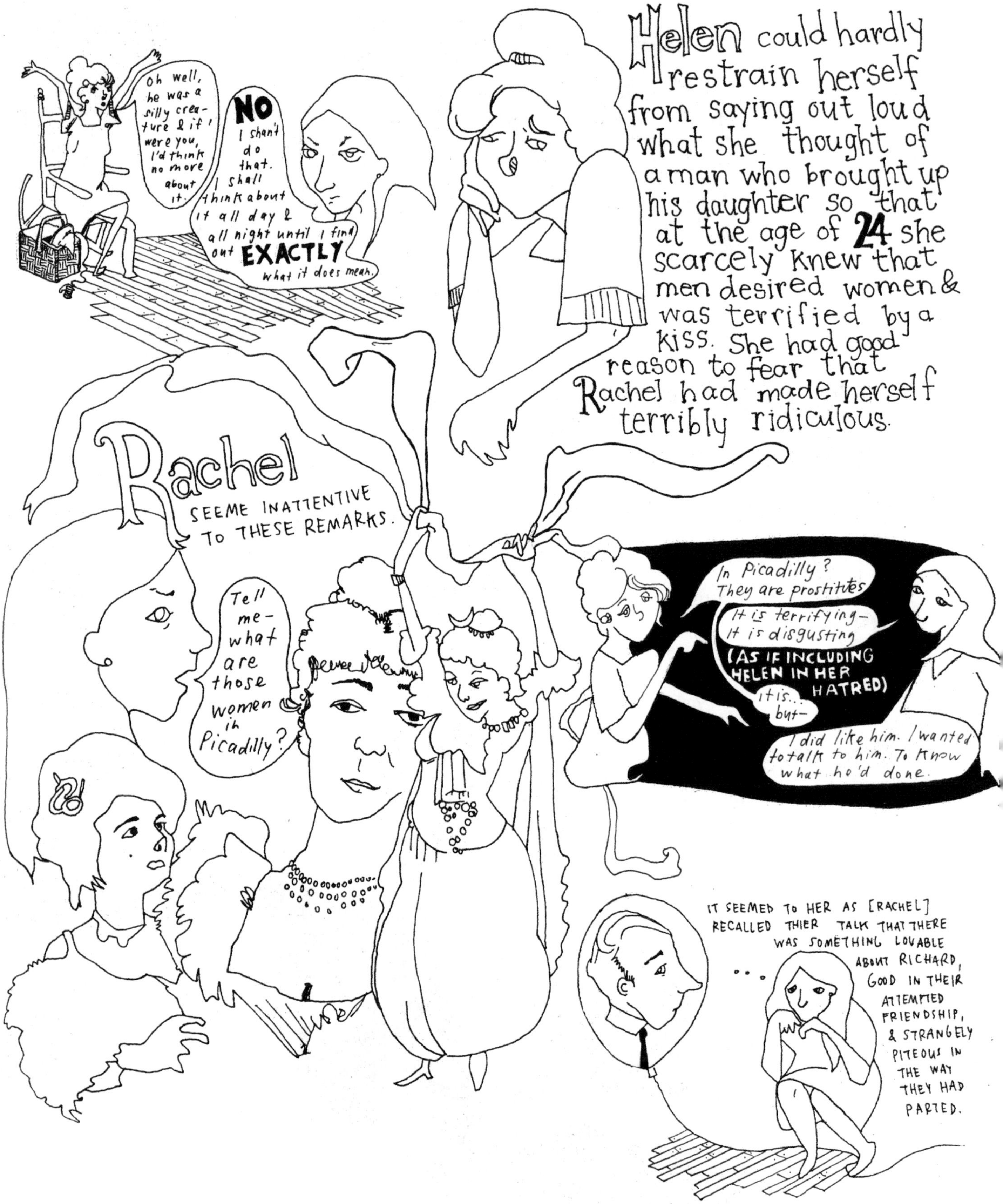
Oh well, he was a silly creature & if I were you, I'd think no more about it.
NO I shan't do that. I shall think about it all day & all night until I find out EXACTLY what it does mean.
Helen could hardly restrain herself from saying out loud what she thought of a man who brought up his daughter so that at the age of 24 she scarcely knew that men desired women & was terrified by a kiss. She had good reason to fear that Rachel had made herself terribly ridiculous.
Rachel SEEME INATTENTIVE TO THESE REMARKS.
Tell me - what are those women in Picadilly?
In Picadilly? They are prostitutes
It is terrifying - it is disgusting
(AS IF INCLUDING HELEN IN HER HATRED)
it is... but-
I did like him. I wanted to talk to him. To know what he'd done.
IT SEEMED TO HER AS [RACHEL] RECALLED THIER TALK THAT THERE WAS SOMETHING LOVABLE ABOUT RICHARD, GOOD IN THEIR ATTEMPTED FRIENDSHIP, & STRANGELY PITEOUS IN THE WAY THEY HAD PARTED.
...

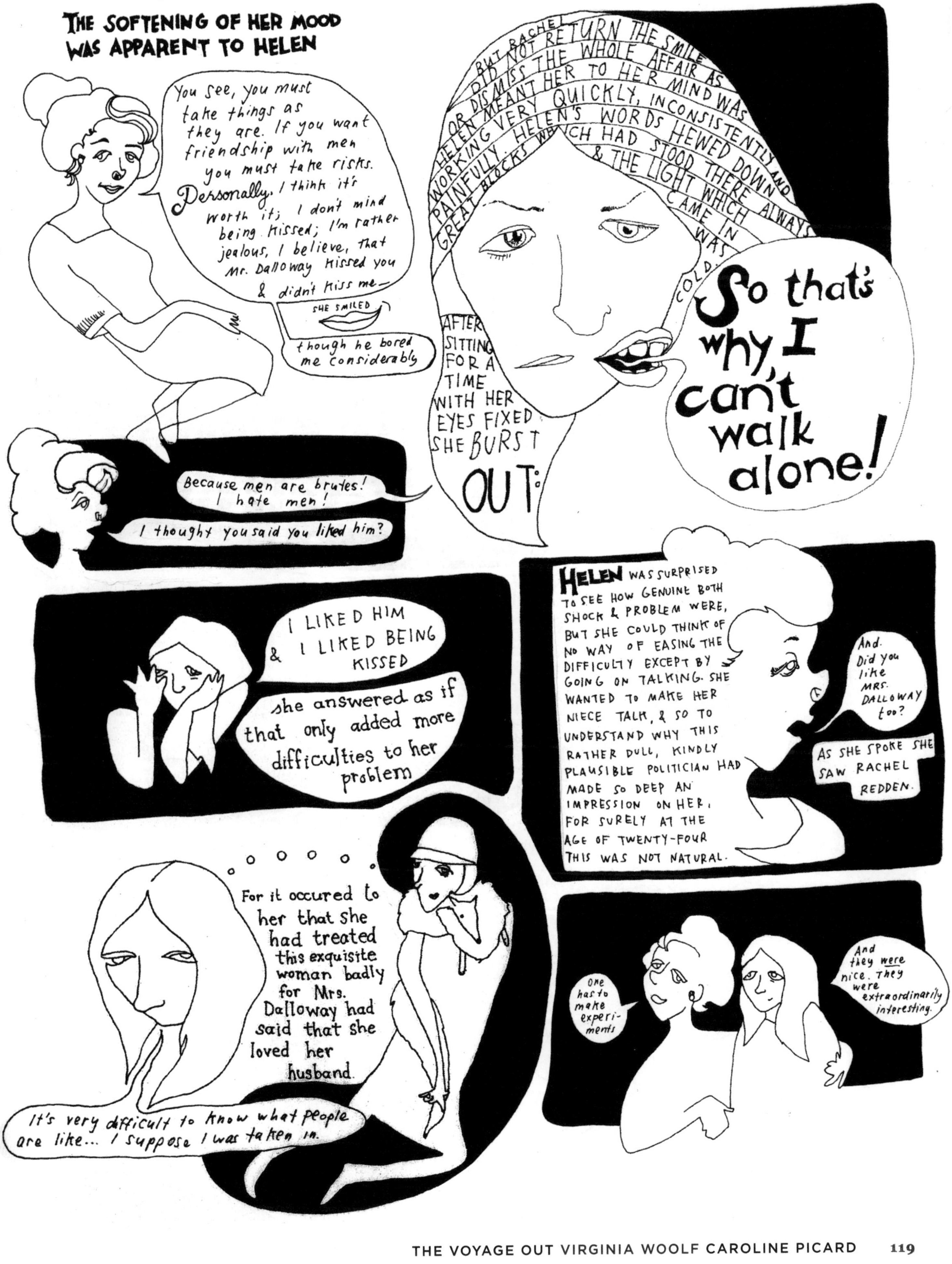
THE SOFTENING OF HER MOOD WAS APPARENT TO HELEN
You see, you must take things as they are. If you want friendship with men you must take risks. Personally, I think it's worth it; I don't mind being kissed; I'm rather jealous, I believe, that Mr. Dalloway kissed you & didn't kiss me—
SHE SMILED
though he bored me considerably
BUT RACHEL
DID NOT RETURN THE SMILE
OR DISMISS THE WHOLE AFFAIR AS
HELEN MEANT HER TO HER MIND WAS
WORKING VERY QUICKLY, INCONSISTENTLY AND
PAINFULLY. HELEN'S WORDS HEWED DOWN
GREAT BLOCKS W
CH HAD STOOD THERE ALWAYS
& THE LIGHT WHICH CAME IN WAS COLD.
AFTER SITTING FOR A TIME WITH HER EYES FIXED SHE BURST OUT:
So that's why I can't walk alone!
Because men are brutes! I hate men!
I thought you said you liked him?
I LIKED HIM & I LIKED BEING KISSED
she answered as if that only added more difficulties to her problem
HELEN WAS SURPRISED TO SEE HOW GENUINE BOTH SHOCK & PROBLEM WERE, BUT SHE COULD THINK OF NO WAY OF EASING THE DIFFICULTY EXCEPT BY GOING ON TALKING. SHE WANTED TO MAKE HER NIECE TALK, & SO TO UNDERSTAND WHY THIS RATHER DULL, KINDLY PLAUSIBLE POLITICIAN HAD MADE SO DEEP AN IMPRESSION ON HER, FOR SURELY AT THE AGE OF TWENTY-FOUR THIS WAS NOT NATURAL.
And. Did you like MRS. DALLOWAY too?
AS SHE SPOKE SHE SAW RACHEL REDDEN.
For it occured to her that she had treated this exquisite woman badly for Mrs. Dalloway had said that she loved her husband.
It's very difficult to know what people are like... I suppose I was taken in.
One has to make experiments
And they were nice. They were extraordinarily interesting.

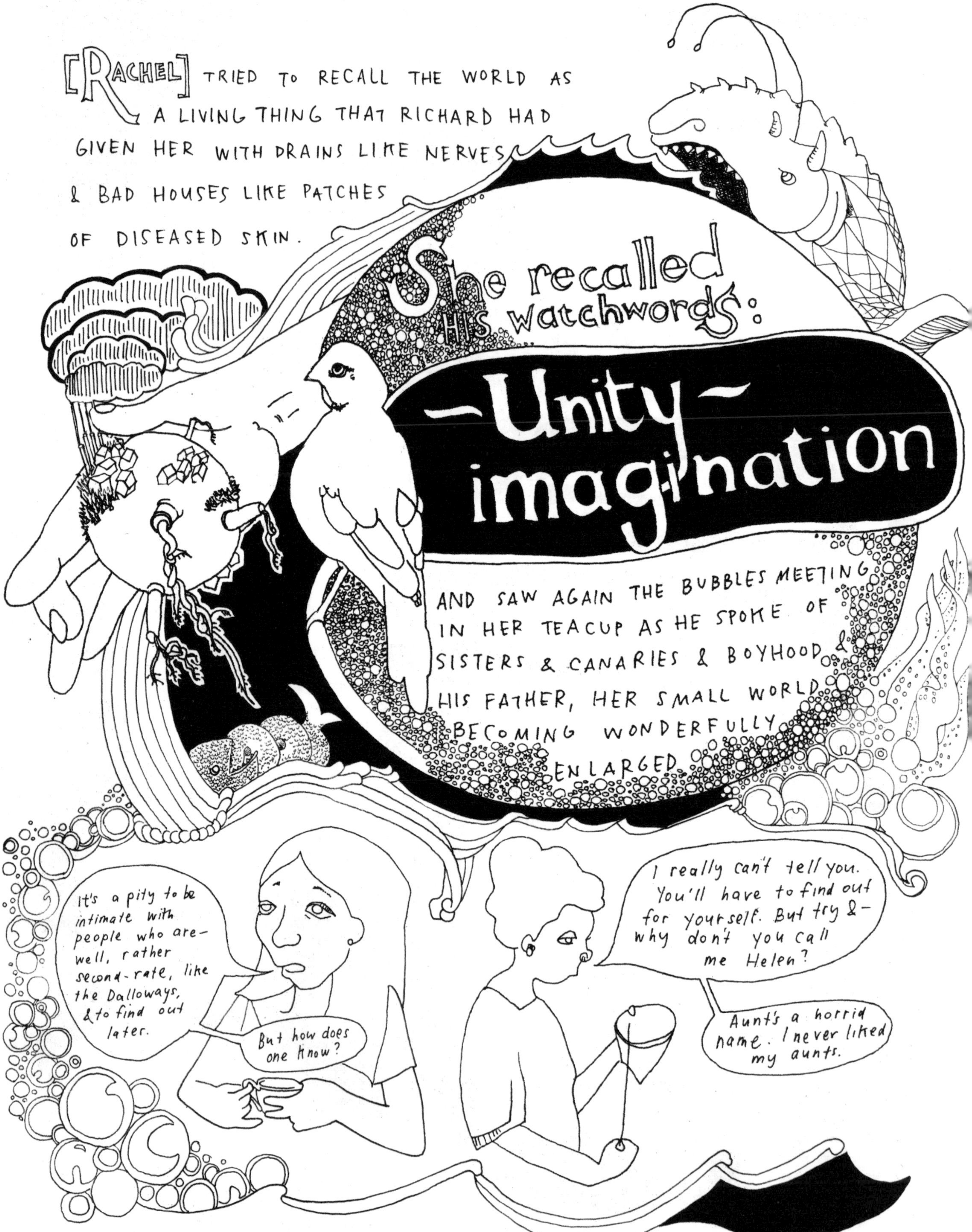
[RACHEL] TRIED TO RECALL THE WORLD AS A LIVING THING THAT RICHARD HAD GIVEN HER WITH DRAINS LIKE NERVES & BAD HOUSES LIKE PATCHES OF DISEASED SKIN.
She recalled his watchwords:
-Unity-
imagination
AND SAW AGAIN THE BUBBLES MEETING IN HER TEACUP AS HE SPOKE OF SISTERS & CANARIES & BOYHOOD & HIS FATHER, HER SMALL WORLD BECOMING WONDERFULLY ENLARGED.
It's a pity to be intimate with people who are- well, rather second-rate, like the Dalloways, & to find out later.
But how does one know?
I really can't tell you. You'll have to find out for yourself. But try &- why don't you call me Helen?
Aunt's a horrid name. I never liked my aunts.

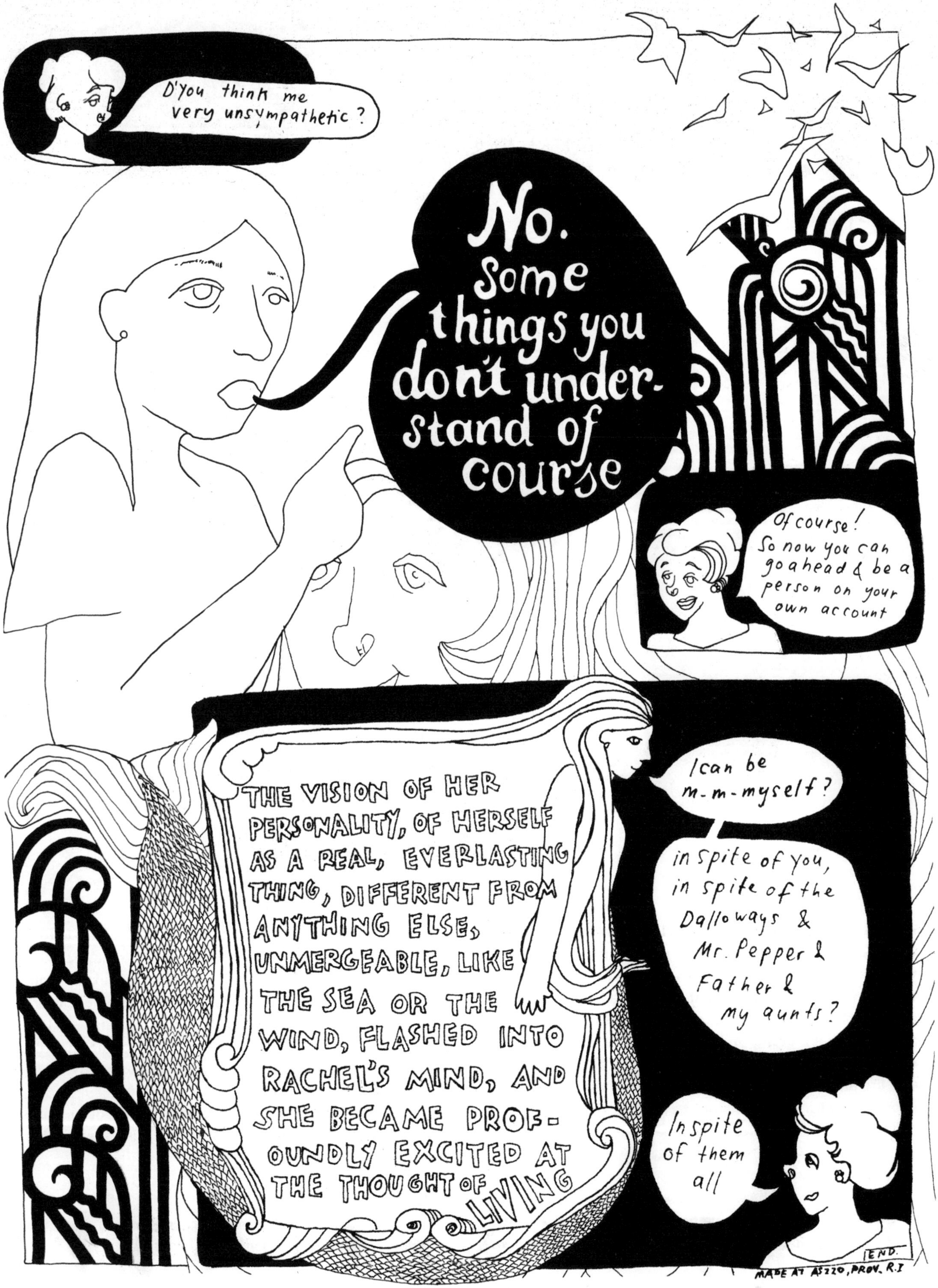
D'you think me very unsympathetic?
No. Some things you don't under-stand of course
Of course! So now you can go ahead & be a person on your own account
THE VISION OF HER PERSONALITY, OF HERSELF AS A REAL, EVERLASTING THING, DIFFERENT FROM ANYTHING ELSE, UNMERGEABLE, LIKE THE SEA OR THE WIND, FLASHED INTO RACHEL'S MIND, AND SHE BECAME PROF-OUNDLY EXCITED AT THE THOUGHT OF LIVING
I can be m-m-myself?
in spite of you, in spite of the Dalloways & Mr. Pepper & Father & my aunts?
In spite of them all
END.
MADE AT AS220, PROV. R.I

"The Love Song of J. Alfred Prufrock"

T. S. Eliot

ART/ADAPTATION BY **Anthony Ventura**

SEVEN YEARS BEFORE HE EXPLODED POETRY WITH "The Waste Land" in 1922, T. S. Eliot published his first masterpiece of verse. "The Love Song of J. Alfred Prufrock" is about disenchantment and despair, but being told in a stream-of-consciousness style, it can be hard to say precisely what's going on here. The overall gist is that the middle-aged Prufrock is insecure, fearful, and dissatisfied with life and, more specifically, he's upset that so much of what passes for love turns out to be lust. UCLA professor Michael North explained:

> Like Augustine, Eliot sees sex as the tyranny of one part of the body over the whole. Though Eliot is far too circumspect to name this part, he figures its power in his poetry by the rebelliousness of mere members: hands, arms, eyes.

Sexual desire pulls the body apart, so that to give in to it is to suffer permanent dismemberment. This may account for the odd combination in Eliot's work of sexual ennui and libidinous violence. The tyranny of one part scatters all the others, reducing the whole to impotence. In this way, the violence of sex robs the individual of the integrity necessary to action.

For this volume, Anthony Ventura has made bold, magazine-style spreads for three classic Modernist poems. This is the first of them.

SOURCE

North, Michael. *The Political Aesthetic of Yeats, Eliot, and Pound.* Cambridge: Cambridge University Press, 1991.

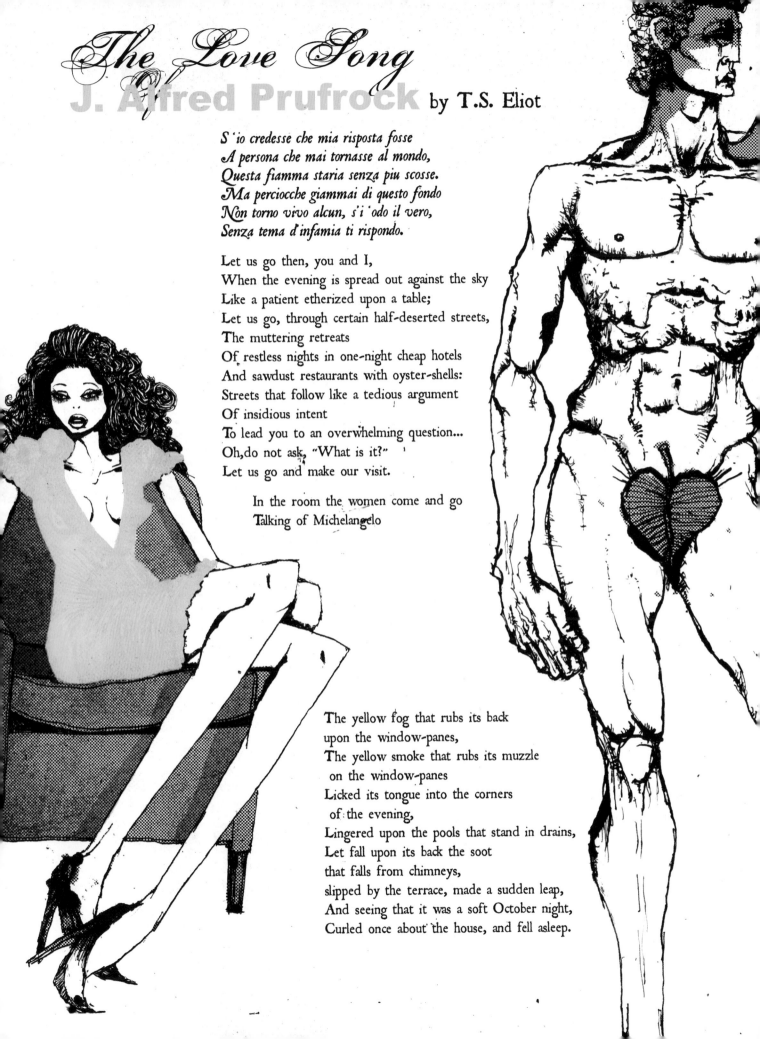

The Love Song Of J. Alfred Prufrock by T.S. Eliot

S 'io credesse che mia risposta fosse
A persona che mai tornasse al mondo,
Questa fiamma staria senza piu scosse.
Ma perciocche giammai di questo fondo
Non torno vivo alcun, s'i 'odo il vero,
Senza tema d'infamia ti rispondo.

Let us go then, you and I,
When the evening is spread out against the sky
Like a patient etherized upon a table;
Let us go, through certain half-deserted streets,
The muttering retreats
Of restless nights in one-night cheap hotels
And sawdust restaurants with oyster-shells:
Streets that follow like a tedious argument
Of insidious intent
To lead you to an overwhelming question...
Oh,do not ask, "What is it?"
Let us go and make our visit.

In the room the women come and go
Talking of Michelangelo

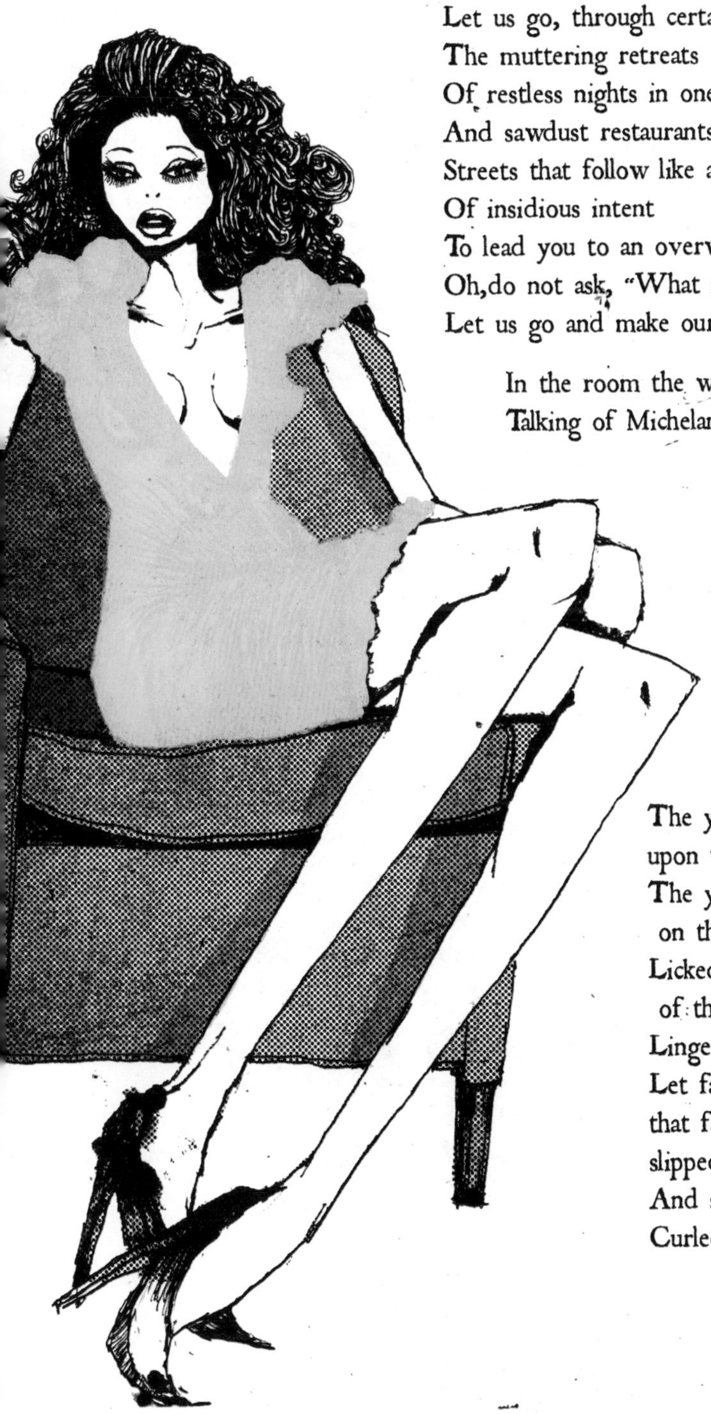

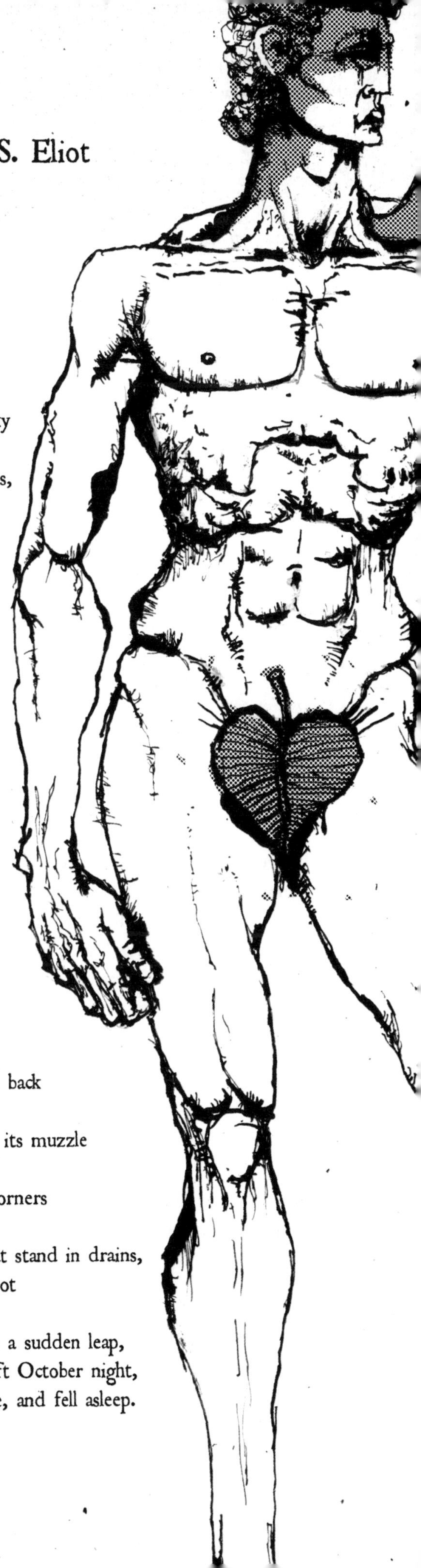

The yellow fog that rubs its back
upon the window-panes,
The yellow smoke that rubs its muzzle
on the window-panes
Licked its tongue into the corners
of the evening,
Lingered upon the pools that stand in drains,
Let fall upon its back the soot
that falls from chimneys,
slipped by the terrace, made a sudden leap,
And seeing that it was a soft October night,
Curled once about the house, and fell asleep.

And indeed there will be time
For the yellow smoke that slides along the street,
Rubbing its back upon the windowpanes;
There will be time, there will be time
To prepare a face to meet the faces that you meet;
There will be time to murder and create,
And time for all the works and days of hands
That lift and drop a question on your plate;
Time for you and time for me,
And time yet for a hundred indecisions,
And for a hundred visions and revisions,
Before the taking of a toast and tea.

In the room the women come and go
Talking of Michelangelo.

And indeed there will be time
To wonder, "Do I dare?" and, "Do I dare?"
Time to turn back and descend the stair,
With a bald spot in the middle of my hair—
[They will say: "How his hair is growing thin!"]
My morning coat, my collar mounting firmly to the chin,
My necktie rich and modest, but asserted by a simple pin—
[They will say: "But how his arms and legs are thin!"]
Do I dare
Disturb the universe?
In a minute there is time
For decisions and revisions which a minute will reverse.

For I have known them all already, known them all—
Have known the evenings, mornings, afternoons,
I have measured out my life with coffee spoons;
I know the voices dying with a dying fall
Beneath the music from a farther room.
So how should I presume?

And I have known the eyes already, known them all:
The eyes that fix you in a formulated phrase,
And when I am formulated, sprawling on a pin,
When I am pinned and wriggling on the wall,
Then how should I begin
To spit out all the butt-ends of my days and ways?
And how should I presume?

And I have known the arms already, known them all—
Arms that are braceleted and white and bare
[But in the lamplight, downed with light brown hair!]
Is it perfume from a dress
That makes me so digress?
Arms that lie along a table, or wrap about a shawl.
And should I then presume?
And how should I begin?

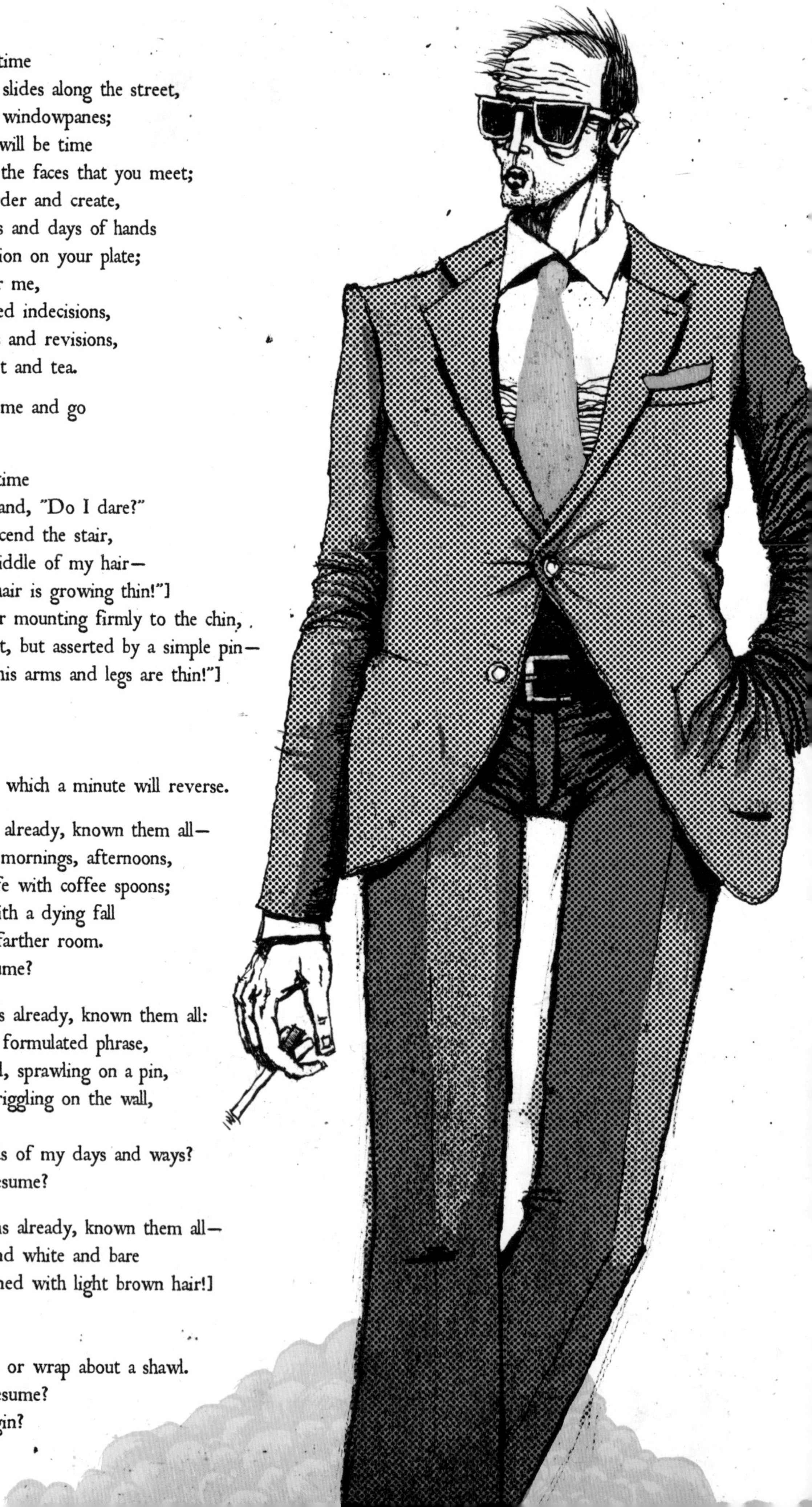

. . . . .

Shall I say, I have gone at dusk through narrow streets
And watched the smoke that rises from the pipes
Of lonely men in shirt-sleeves, leaning out of windows? ...

I should have been a pair of ragged claws
Scuttling across the floors of silent seas.

And the afternoon, the evening, sleeps so peacefully!
Smoothed by long fingers,
Asleep... tired... or it malingers,
Stretched on the floor, here beside you and me.
Should I, after tea and cakes and ices,
Have the strength to force the moment to its crisis?
But though I have wept and fasted, wept and prayed,
Though I have seen my head [grown slightly bald] brought in upon a platter,
I am no prophet—and here's no great matter;
I have seen the moment of my greatness flicker,
And I have seen the eternal Footman hold my coat, and snicker,
And in short, I was afraid.

And would it have been worth it, after all,
After the cups, the marmalade, the tea,
Among the porcelain, among some talk of you and me,
Would it have been worth while,
To have bitten off the matter with a smile,
To have squeezed the universe into a ball
To roll it toward some overwhelming question,

To say: "I am Lazarus, come from the dead,
Come back to tell you all, I shall tell you all"—
If one, settling a pillow by her head,
Should say: "That is not what I meant at all.
That is not it, at all."

THAT IS NOT WHAT I MEANT AT ALL.

And would it have been worth it, after all,
Would it have been worth while,
After the sunsets and the dooryards and the sprinkled streets,
After the novels, after the teacups, after the skirts that trail along the floor—
And this, and so much more?—
It is impossible to say just what I mean!
But as if a magic lantern threw the nerves in patterns on a screen:
Would it have been worth while
If one, settling a pillow or throwing off a shawl,
And turning toward the window, should say:
"That is not it at all,
That is not what I meant, at all."

. . . . .

No! I am not Prince Hamlet,
nor was meant to be;
Am an attendant lord, one that will do
To swell a progress, start a scene or two,
Advise the prince; no doubt, an easy tool,
Deferential, glad to be of use,
Politic, cautious, and meticulous;
Full of high sentence, but a bit obtuse;
At times, indeed, almost ridiculous—
Almost, at times, the Fool.

I grow old... I grow old...
I shall wear the bottoms of my trousers rolled.

Shall I part my hair behind? Do I dare to eat a peach?
I shall wear white flannel trousers, and walk upon the beach.
I have heard the mermaids singing, each to each.

I do not think that they will sing to me.

I have seen them riding seaward on the waves
Combing the white hair of the waves blown back
When the wind blows the water white and black.

We have lingered in the chambers of the sea
By sea-girls wreathed with seaweed red and brown
Till human voices wake us, and we drown.

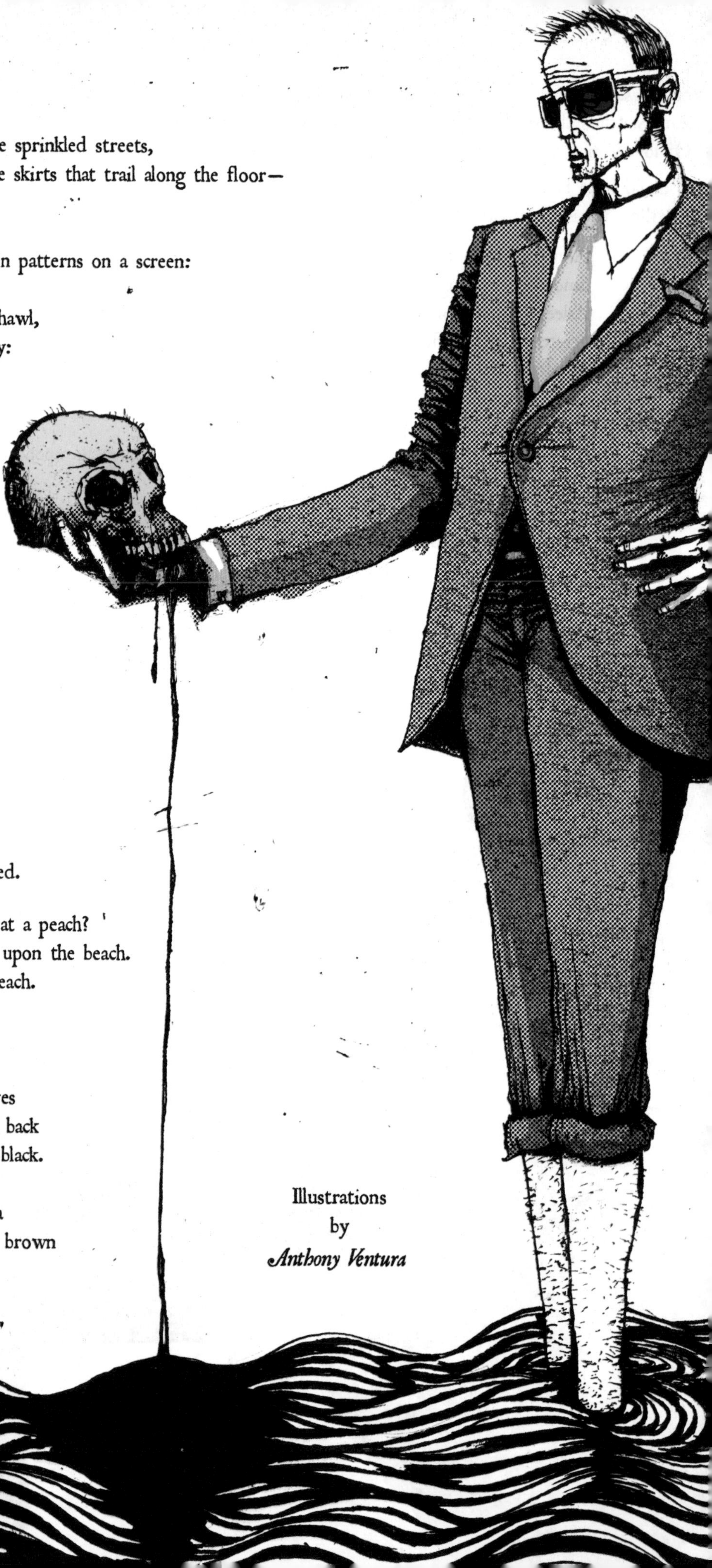

Illustrations
by
Anthony Ventura

"The Mowers"

D. H. Lawrence

ART/ADAPTATION BY **Bishakh Som**

NOVELIST AND POET D. H. LAWRENCE WAS ONE OF literature's wildmen of ideas, if not actions. He was upset about the effects of intellectualism and industrialism—the ways they push us away from our own bodies, our instincts, our basic nature. He summed up his outlook perfectly in a letter he wrote in 1913:

> My great religion is a belief in the blood, the flesh, as being wiser than the intellect. We can go wrong in our minds. But what our blood feels and believes and says, is always true. The intellect is only a bit and a bridle. What do I care about knowledge. All I want is to answer to my blood, direct, without fribbling intervention of mind, or moral, or what-not.

Two years later, several of his poems were published in the landmark anthology *Some Imagist Poets*, which helped usher in Modernism. Among the poems is "The Mowers," narrated by a woman with a Nottinghamshire dialect. Comics artist and painter Bishakh Som—part of the Hi-Horse collective—gives it a tender, rural feel with his beautifully pale tones.

SOURCE

Boulton, James T., ed. *The Selected Letters of D. H. Lawrence.* Cambridge: Cambridge University Press, 1997.

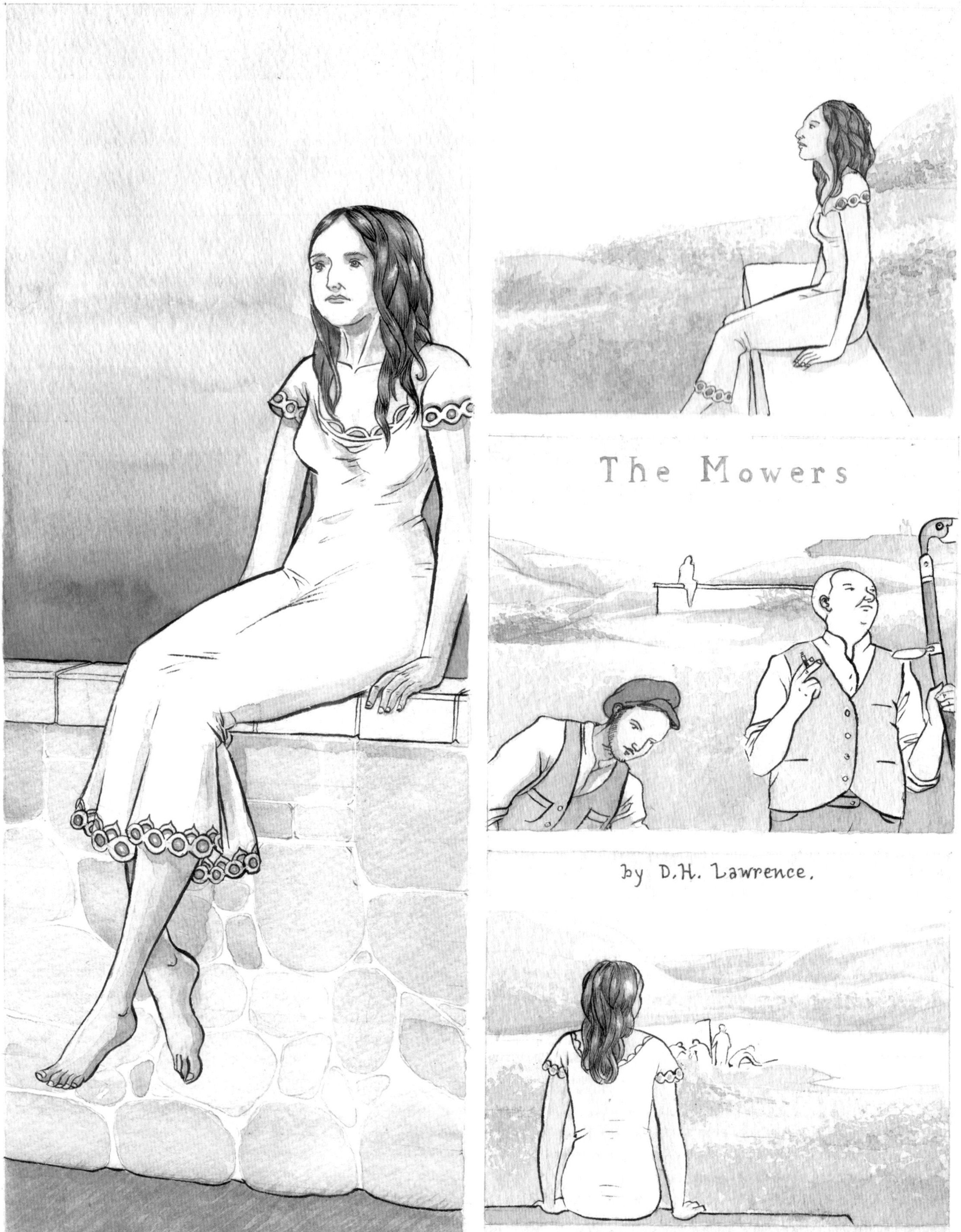
The Mowers
by D.H. Lawrence.
adapted by Bishakh k Som.

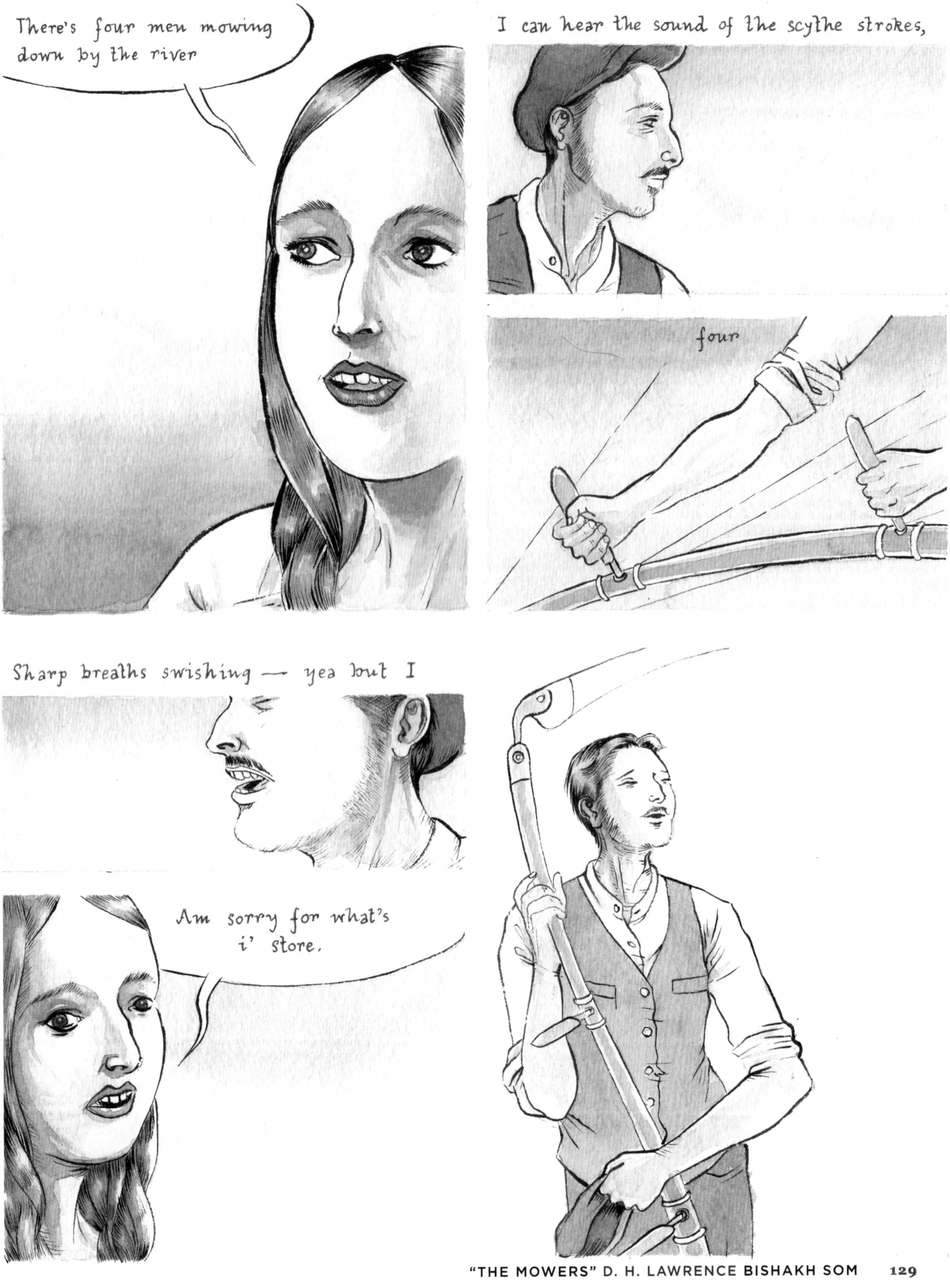
There's four men mowing down by the river
I can hear the sound of the scythe strokes,
four
Sharp breaths swishing — yea but I
Am sorry for what's i' store.

The first man out o' the four that's mowin'

is mine,

I mun claim him once for all.

But I'm sorry for him, on his young feet, knowin'

None o' the trouble

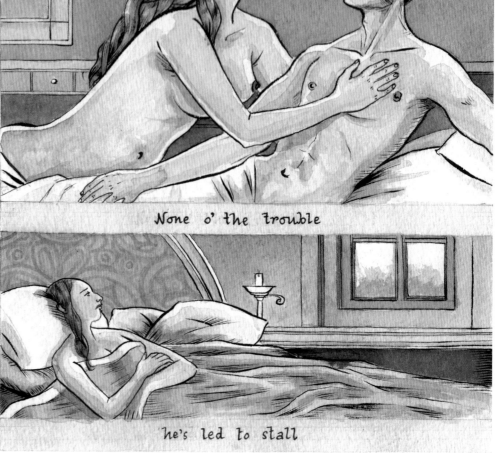

he's led to stall

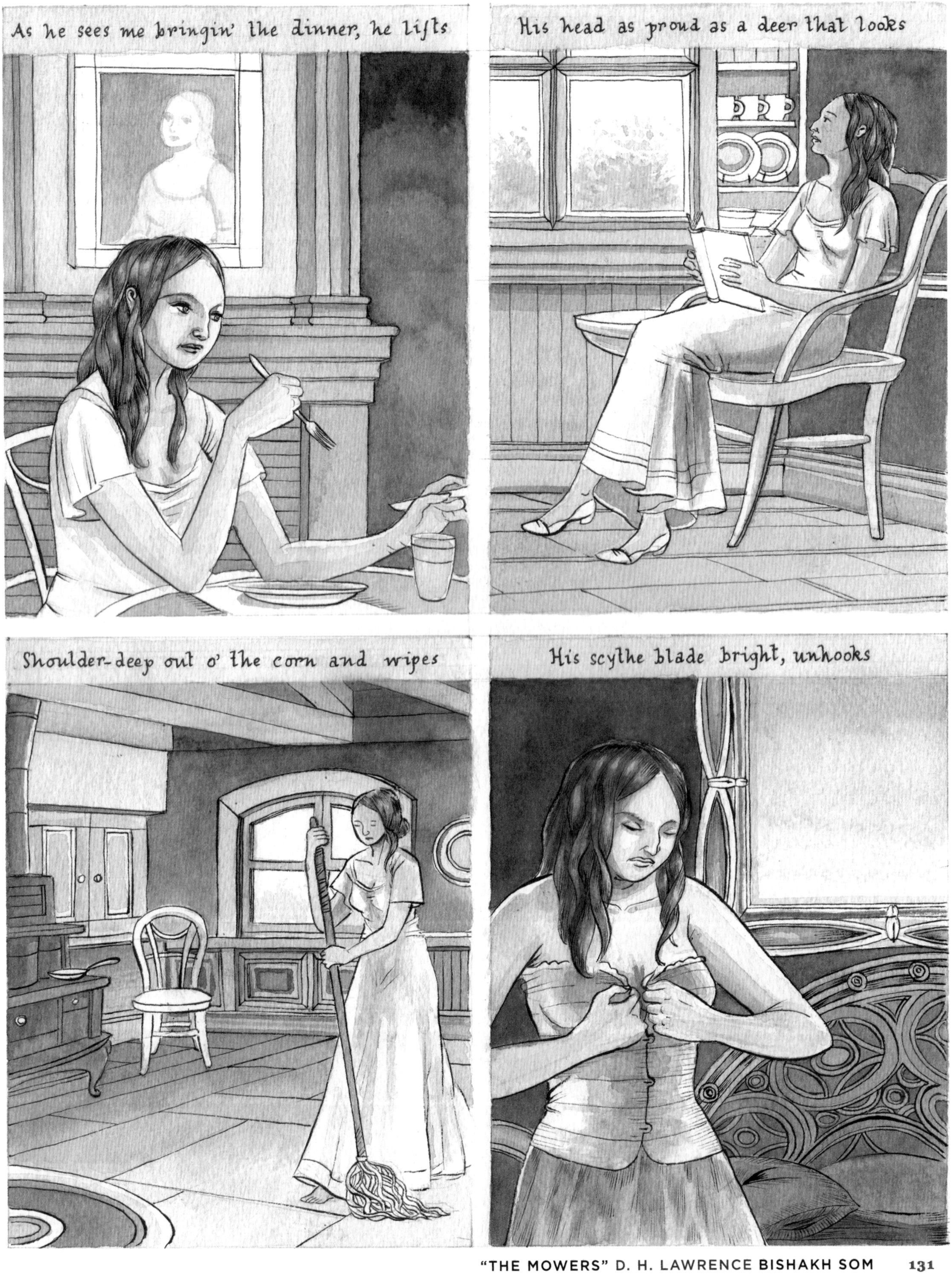
As he sees me bringin' the dinner, he lifts
His head as proud as a deer that looks
Shoulder-deep out o' the corn and wipes
His scythe blade bright, unhooks

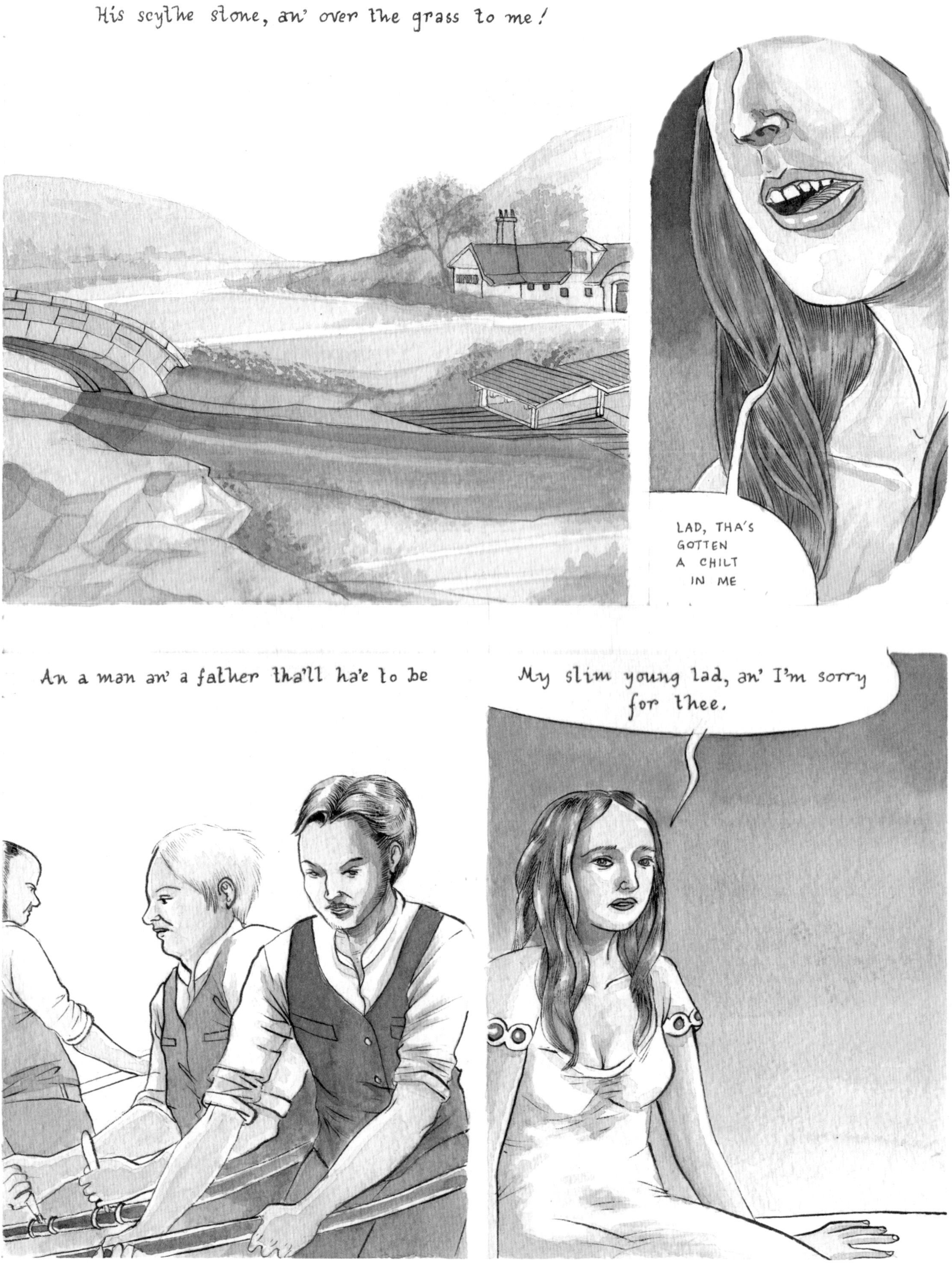

His scythe stone, an' over the grass to me!
LAD, THA'S GOTTEN A CHILT IN ME
An a man an' a father tha'll ha'e to be
My slim young lad, an' I'm sorry for thee.

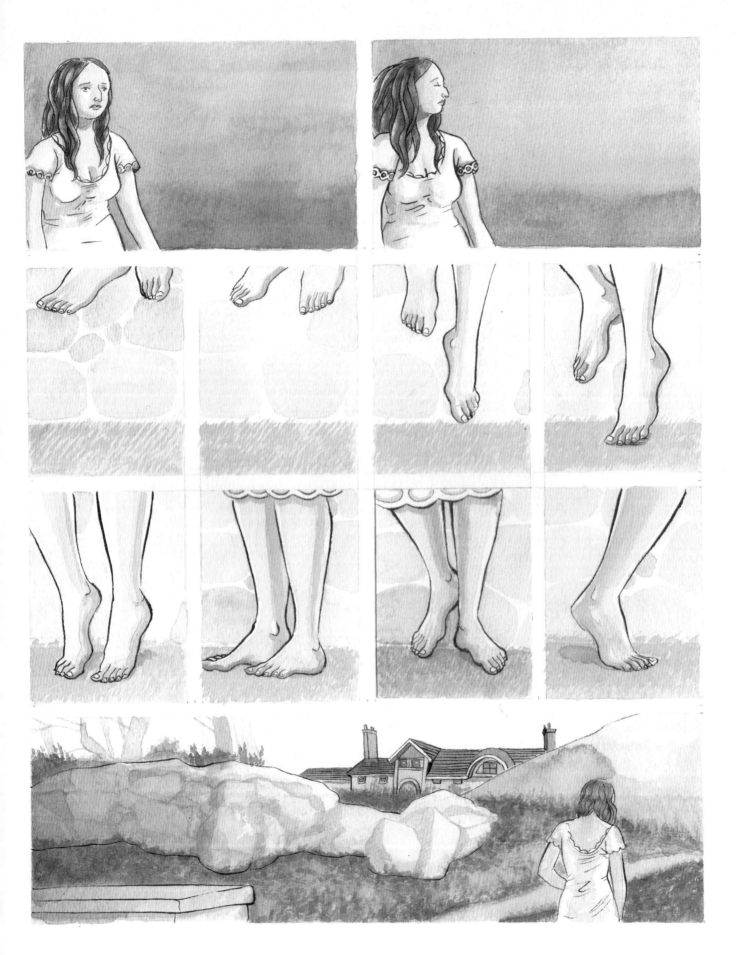

"Sea Iris"

H. D.

ART/ADAPTATION BY **Bishakh Som**

HILDA DOOLITTLE—WHO PUBLISHED UNDER HER initials—pushed the envelope in both her art and life. "She developed new lyric, mythic, and mystical forms in poetry and prose, and an alternative bisexual lifestyle that were little appreciated until the 1980s," wrote professor Bonnie Kime Scott. She also edited an influential literary journal, translated works from ancient Greek, was twice engaged to Ezra Pound, and became a patient of none other than Sigmund Freud. Like her poet-peers D. H. Lawrence and Edna St. Vincent Millay, she led a larger-than-life life.

Like Georgia O'Keeffe, H. D. used flower imagery to erotic effect. As with many of her poems, "Sea Iris" is lush with plant life—moss, myrrh, camphor, twigs. . . . It's part of a series of poems she wrote on plants that live on the seashore, in the zone between ocean and land. Several of these poems were published in *Some Imagist Poets*, the groundbreaking 1915 anthology that also included Lawrence's "The Mowers," which Bishakh Som has adapted in the preceding pages. This time using gentle, dreamy colors, he personifies the sea iris, who has a very good reason to come ashore, bringing the beautiful ocean with her.

SOURCE

Scott, Bonnie Kime. "H. D." In *The Oxford Companion to Women's Writing in the United States*. Edited by Cathy N. Davidson and Linda Wagner-Martin. Oxford: Oxford University Press, 1995.

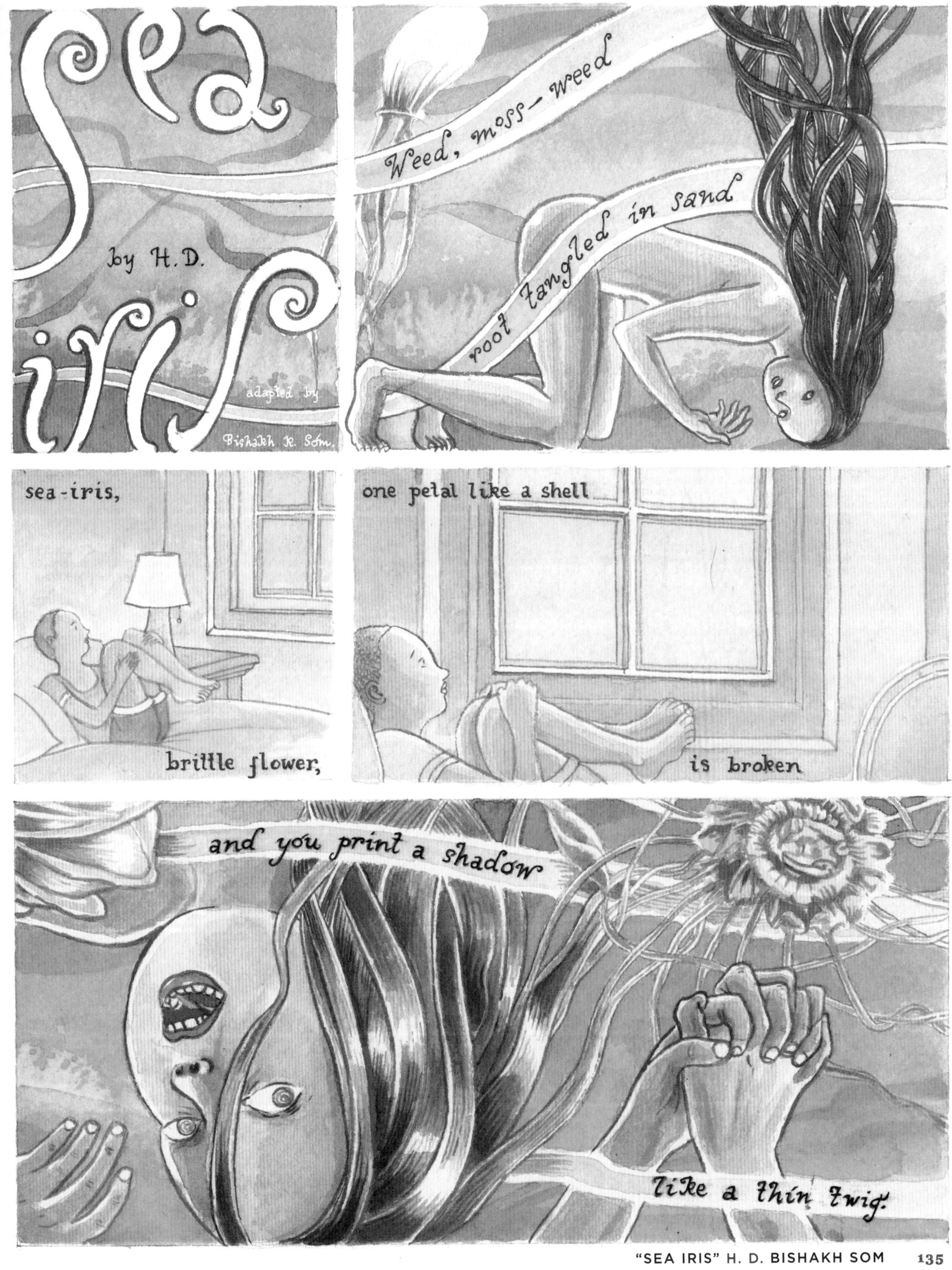
Sea
by H.D.
iris
adapted by
Bishakh K. Som.
Weed, moss-weed
root tangled in sand
sea-iris,
brittle flower,
one petal like a shell
is broken
and you print a shadow
like a thin twig.

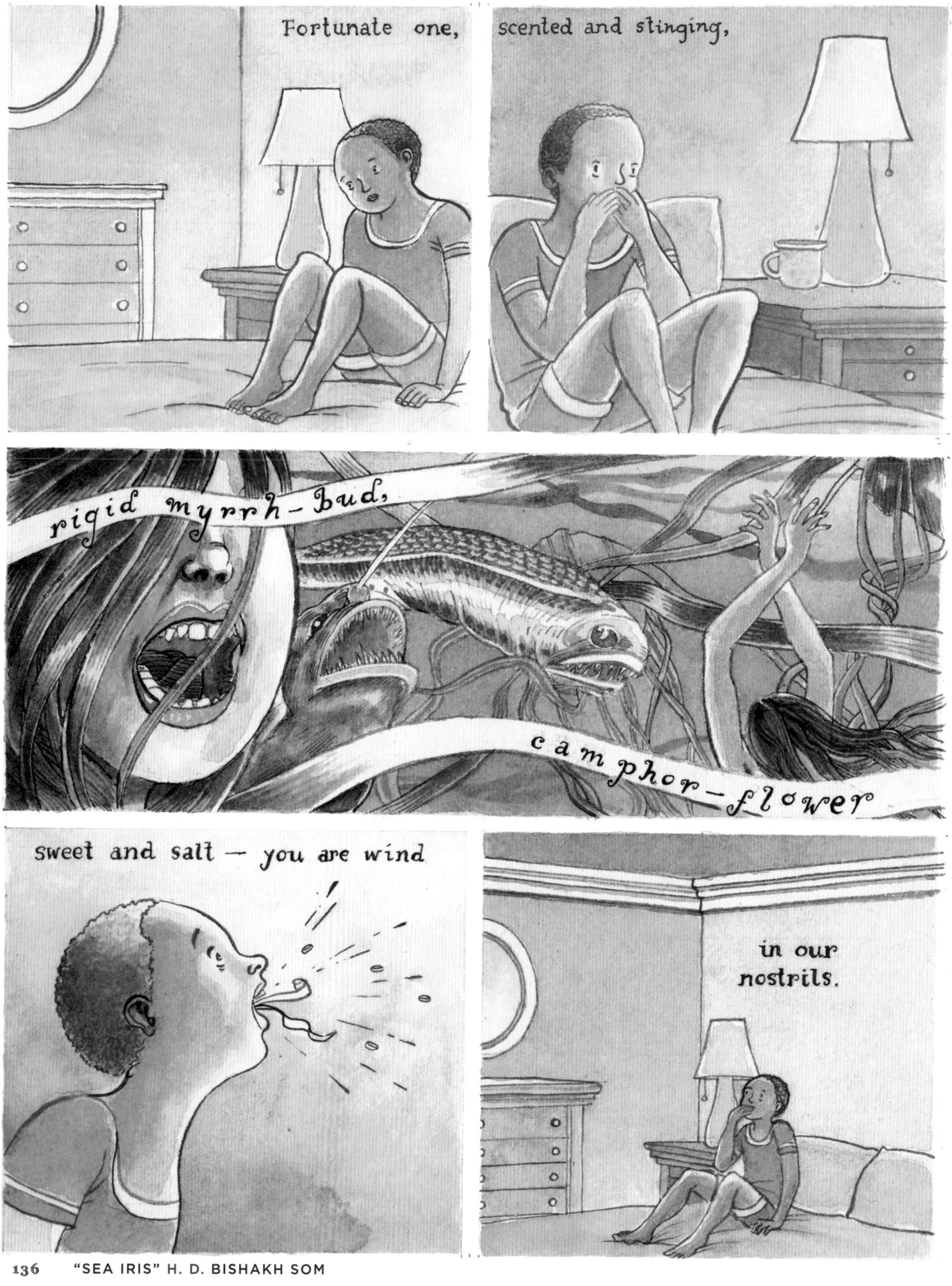
Fortunate one,
scented and stinging,
rigid myrrh-bud,
camphor-flower
sweet and salt — you are wind
in our nostrils.

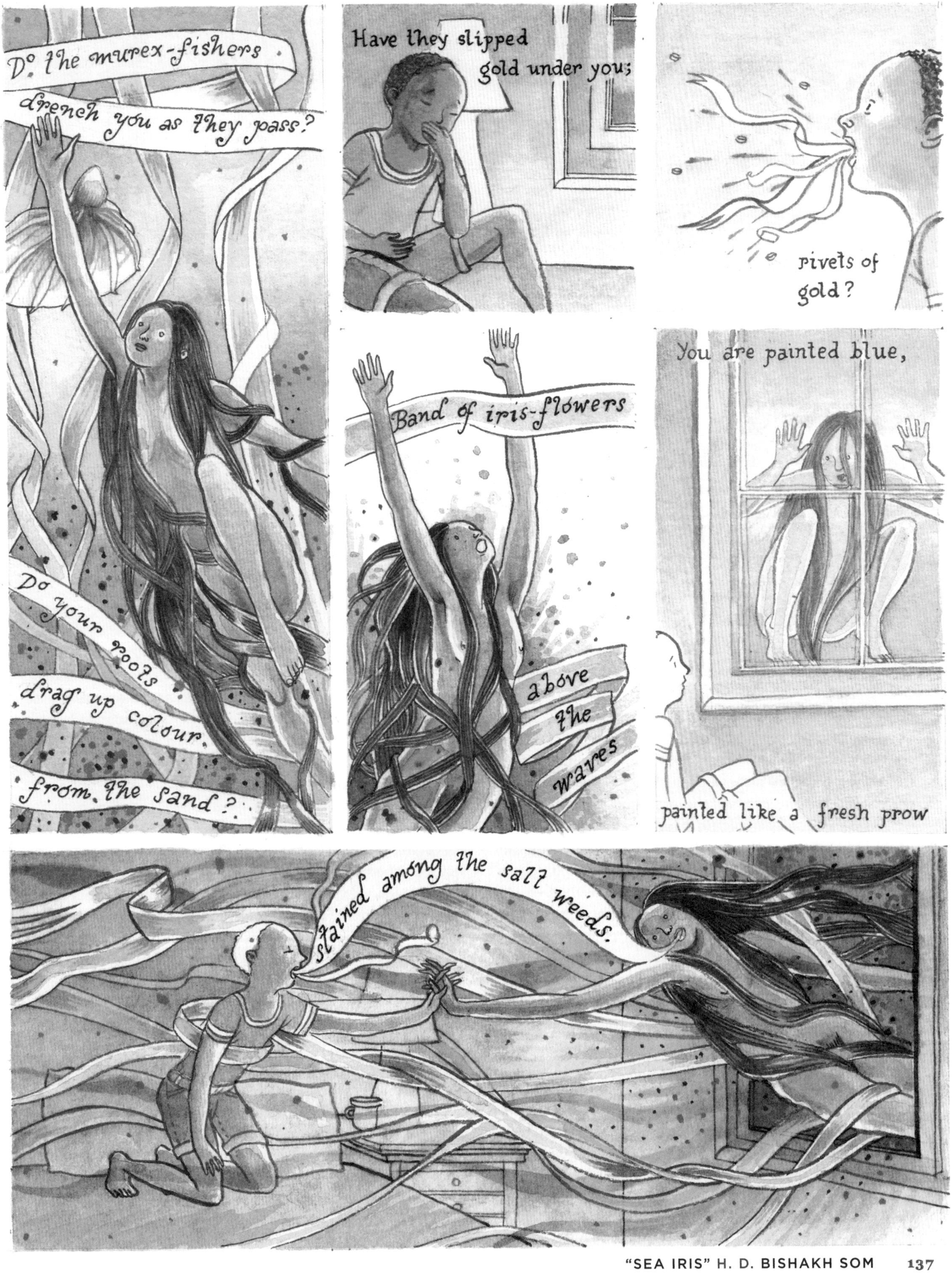
Do the murex-fishers
drench you as they pass?
Do your roots
drag up colour
from the sand?
Have they slipped
gold under you;
rivets of
gold?
Band of iris-flowers
above
the
waves
You are painted blue,
painted like a fresh prow
stained among the salt weeds.

"A Matter of Colour"

Ernest Hemingway

ART/ADAPTATION BY **Dan Duncan**

ONE OF LITERATURE'S BADBOYS, THE HARD-DRINKING, self-destructive man of action Ernest Hemingway led an outsize life filled with violence and adventure. Wounded as an ambulance driver in World War I, he covered further conflicts as a correspondent, always diving right into the front lines, bullets whizzing by his head. He was obsessed with bullfights and boxing, and engaged in fisticuffs with writers who pissed him off. He loved big-game hunting and deep-sea fishing, once admitting in a moment of candor: "I spend a hell of a lot of time killing animals and fish so I won't kill myself." But eventually—at age sixty-one—he did. Like his father before him, he fatally shot himself in the head.

Hemingway's wild, wild life and over-the-top machismo threaten to overshadow his writings, which include instant classics such as *The Sun Also Rises*, *A Farewell to Arms*, *For Whom the Bell Tolls* (one of my all-time favorite books), *The Old Man and the Sea* (which won him a Pulitzer and a belated Nobel), the short stories "The Snows of Kilimanjaro" and "The Short, Happy Life of Francis Macomber," and the memoir *A Moveable Feast*. Drawing on his early career as a reporter, he developed a lean, spare writing style—famously comprised of "short, declarative sentences," a lack of adverbs, and almost no statements of what characters are thinking or feeling, only what they're doing and saying—that became his hallmark, although his writing was more flexible than most observers imply.

For the adaptation that follows, we have a special treat, a rare early story from the man. Hemingway's first two published short stories appeared in his high-school newspaper and have rarely been included in collections. Even the so-called *The Complete Short Stories of Ernest Hemingway* doesn't contain them. To my knowledge, these rarities have been reprinted only twice, in a small, obscure 1992 book that was published by Hemingway's high school in Oak Park, Illinois, and three years later in *Ernest Hemingway: The Collected Stories*, which was published only in the UK. These germinal stories obviously aren't Hemingway at his finest, but they're fascinating because they already deal with some of the violent themes—boxing, hunting, guns, and suicide—that would dominate his life's work (and his life in general). "A Matter of Colour," from 1916, is by far the better of these first two stories, crackling with energy as a salty old trainer spins a slang-drenched tale from early in his career. It's just an excuse to tell an old joke, but young Hem does it with panache. (The non-American spelling of "Colour" is Hemingway's.)

Dan Duncan has drawn for Marvel and IDW, among many others, and he had just landed a plum gig drawing *Teenage Mutant Ninja Turtles* when I approached him about *The Graphic Canon*. Although pressed for time, he said he simply couldn't pass up the chance to adapt a Hemingway story about boxing. And the fact that the boxer's name, Dan Morgan, is so close to his own only helped seal the deal.

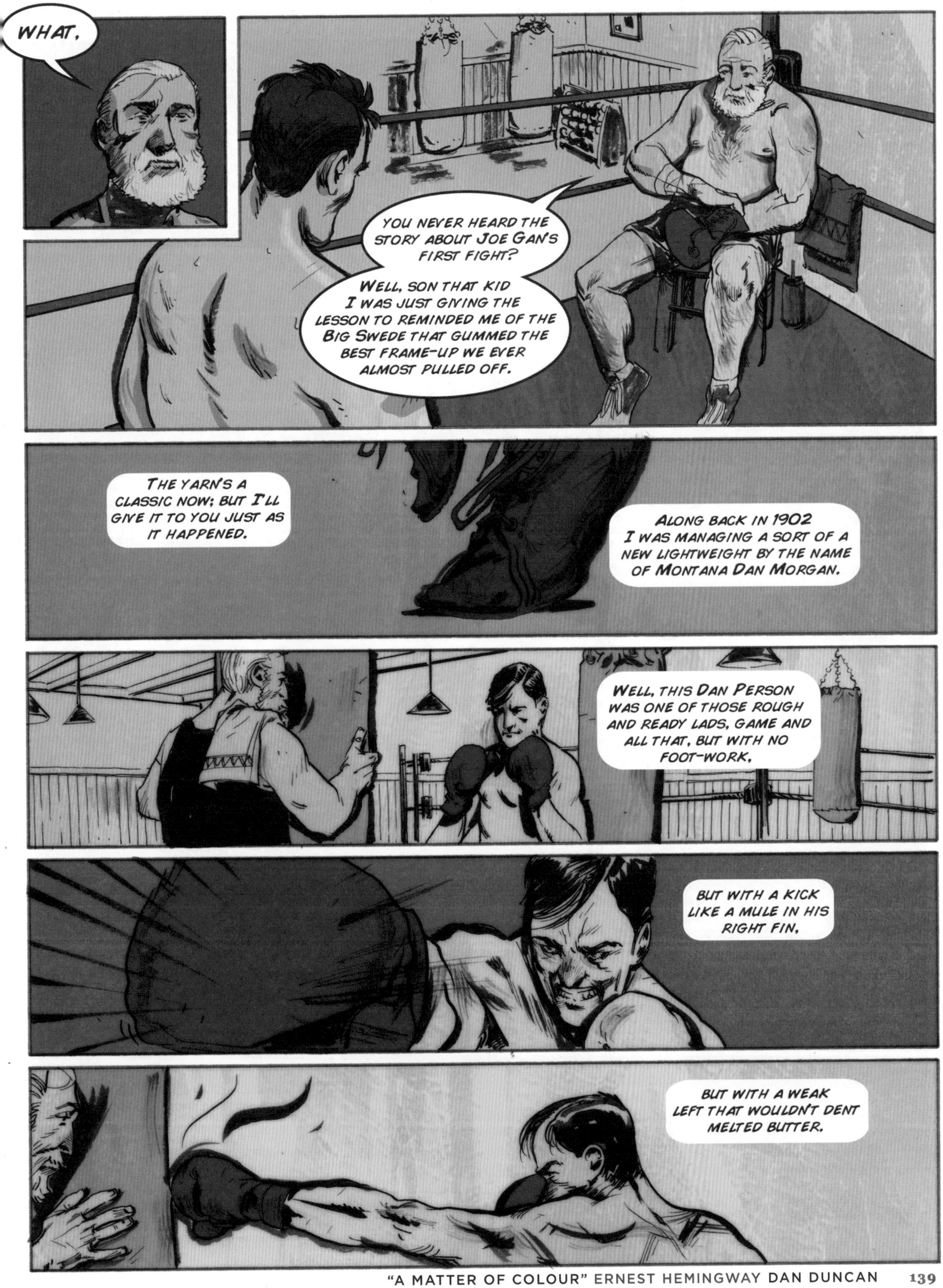
WHAT.
YOU NEVER HEARD THE STORY ABOUT JOE GAN'S FIRST FIGHT?
WELL, SON THAT KID I WAS JUST GIVING THE LESSON TO REMINDED ME OF THE BIG SWEDE THAT GUMMED THE BEST FRAME-UP WE EVER ALMOST PULLED OFF.
THE YARN'S A CLASSIC NOW; BUT I'LL GIVE IT TO YOU JUST AS IT HAPPENED.
ALONG BACK IN 1902 I WAS MANAGING A SORT OF A NEW LIGHTWEIGHT BY THE NAME OF MONTANA DAN MORGAN.
WELL, THIS DAN PERSON WAS ONE OF THOSE ROUGH AND READY LADS, GAME AND ALL THAT, BUT WITH NO FOOT-WORK,
BUT WITH A KICK LIKE A MULE IN HIS RIGHT FIN,
BUT WITH A WEAK LEFT THAT WOULDN'T DENT MELTED BUTTER.

I'D GOTTEN ALONG PRETTY WELL WITH THE BIRD,

AND WE'D COLLECTED SUNDRY SHEKELS

FIGHTING DOCKWALLOPERS AND STEVEDORES AND PRELIMINARY BOYS OUT AT THE OLD OLYMPIC CLUB.

DAN WAS GETTING TO BE QUITE A SIZABLE SCRAPPER,

AND BY USING HIS STRONG RIGHT MITT AND STALLING ALONG, HE MANAGED TO ACHIEVE QUITE A REPUTATION.

DAN MORGAN vs JIM O'ROURKE

20 Rounds

OLYMPIC

MORGAN   SEATS $2   O'ROURKE

FRIDAY 8 PM

SO I MATCHED THE LAD WITH JIM O'ROURKE, THE OLD TRIAL HORSE,

AND THE BOY MANAGED TO HANG ONE ON JIM'S JAW THAT WAS GOOD FOR THE TEN-SECOND ANESTHETIC.

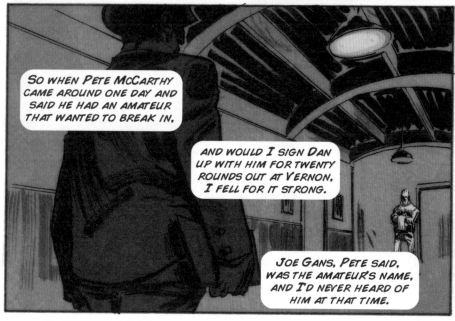

SO WHEN PETE McCARTHY CAME AROUND ONE DAY AND SAID HE HAD AN AMATEUR THAT WANTED TO BREAK IN,

AND WOULD I SIGN DAN UP WITH HIM FOR TWENTY ROUNDS OUT AT VERNON, I FELL FOR IT STRONG.

JOE GANS, PETE SAID, WAS THE AMATEUR'S NAME, AND I'D NEVER HEARD OF HIM AT THAT TIME.

I THOUGHT THAT IT WAS KIND OF STRANGE WHEN PETE CAME AROUND WITH A CONTRACT THAT HAD A $500 FORFEIT CLAUSE IN IT FOR NON-APPEARENCE,

BUT WE INTENDED TO APPEAR ALRIGHT, SO I SIGNED UP.

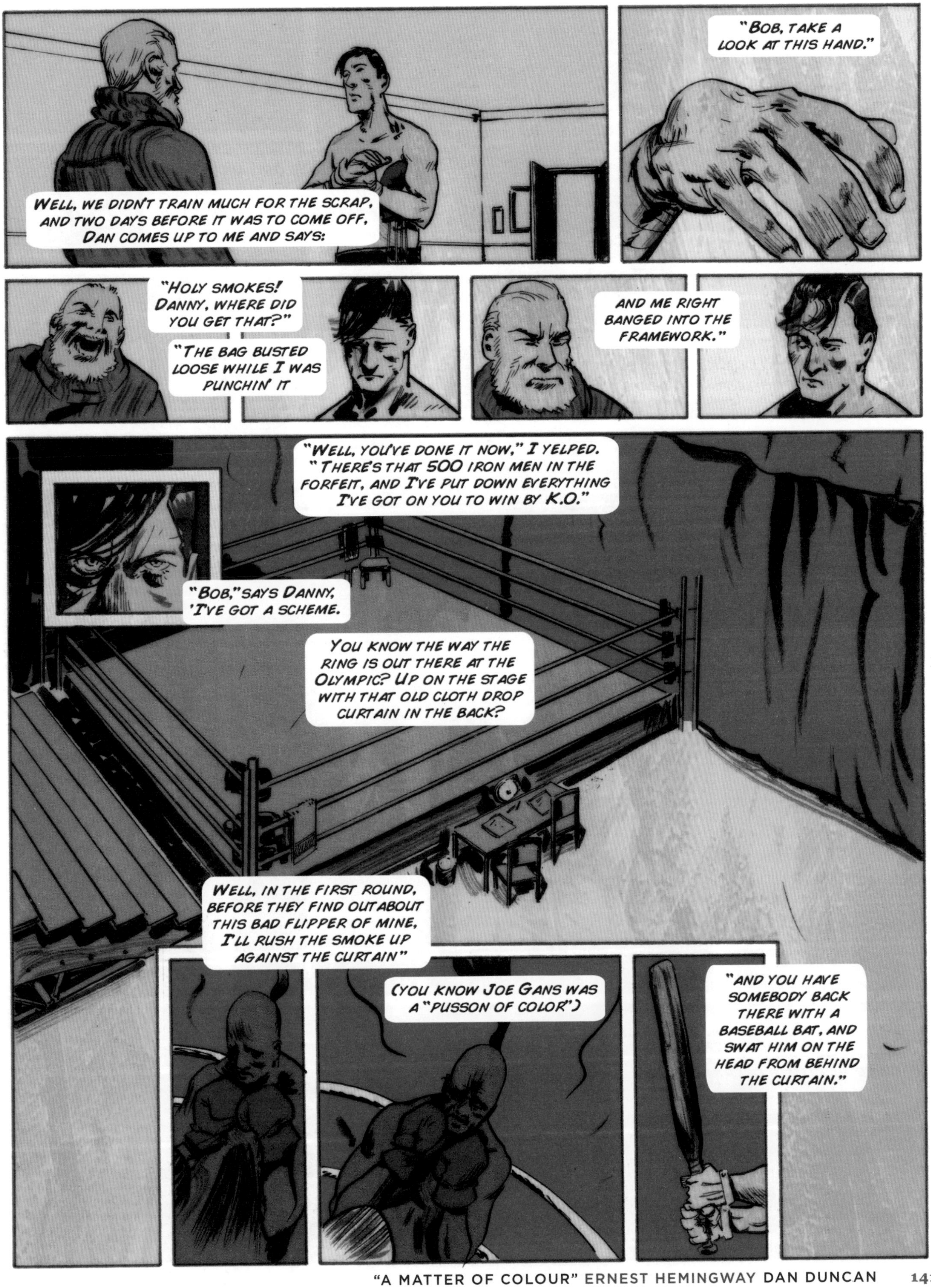
WELL, WE DIDN'T TRAIN MUCH FOR THE SCRAP, AND TWO DAYS BEFORE IT WAS TO COME OFF, DAN COMES UP TO ME AND SAYS:
"BOB, TAKE A LOOK AT THIS HAND."
"HOLY SMOKES! DANNY, WHERE DID YOU GET THAT?"
"THE BAG BUSTED LOOSE WHILE I WAS PUNCHIN' IT
AND ME RIGHT BANGED INTO THE FRAMEWORK."
"WELL, YOU'VE DONE IT NOW," I YELPED. "THERE'S THAT 500 IRON MEN IN THE FORFEIT, AND I'VE PUT DOWN EVERYTHING I'VE GOT ON YOU TO WIN BY K.O."
"BOB," SAYS DANNY, 'I'VE GOT A SCHEME.
YOU KNOW THE WAY THE RING IS OUT THERE AT THE OLYMPIC? UP ON THE STAGE WITH THAT OLD CLOTH DROP CURTAIN IN THE BACK?
WELL, IN THE FIRST ROUND, BEFORE THEY FIND OUT ABOUT THIS BAD FLIPPER OF MINE, I'LL RUSH THE SMOKE UP AGAINST THE CURTAIN"
(YOU KNOW JOE GANS WAS A "PUSSON OF COLOR")
"AND YOU HAVE SOMEBODY BACK THERE WITH A BASEBALL BAT, AND SWAT HIM ON THE HEAD FROM BEHIND THE CURTAIN."

SAY! I COULD HAVE THROWN A FIT. IT WAS SO BLAME SIMPLE.

SO I GOES OUT AND PAWNS MY WATCH TO PUT ANOTHER TWENTY DOWN ON DAN TO WIN BY A KNOCKOUT.

WE JUST COULDN'T LOSE, YOU SEE. IT COMES OFF SO QUICK NOBODY GETS WISE. THEN WE COLLECTS AND BEATS IT!

THEN WE WENT OUT TO VERNON AND I HIRED A BIG HUSKY SWEDE TO DO THE SLAPSTICK ACT.

THE DAY OF THE FIGHT DAWNED BRIGHT AND CLEAR, AS THE SPORTING WRITERS SAY, ONLY IT WAS FOGGY,

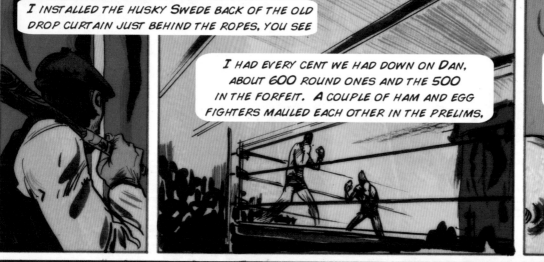

I INSTALLED THE HUSKY SWEDE BACK OF THE OLD DROP CURTAIN JUST BEHIND THE ROPES, YOU SEE

I HAD EVERY CENT WE HAD DOWN ON DAN, ABOUT 600 ROUND ONES AND THE 500 IN THE FORFEIT. A COUPLE OF HAM AND EGG FIGHTERS MAULED EACH OTHER IN THE PRELIMS,

AND THEN THE BELL RINGS FOR OUR SHOW.

I TIED DAN'S GLOVES ON, GIVES HIM A CHEW OF GUM AND MY BLESSING, AND HE CLIMBS OVER THE ROPES INTO THE SQUARED CIRCLE.

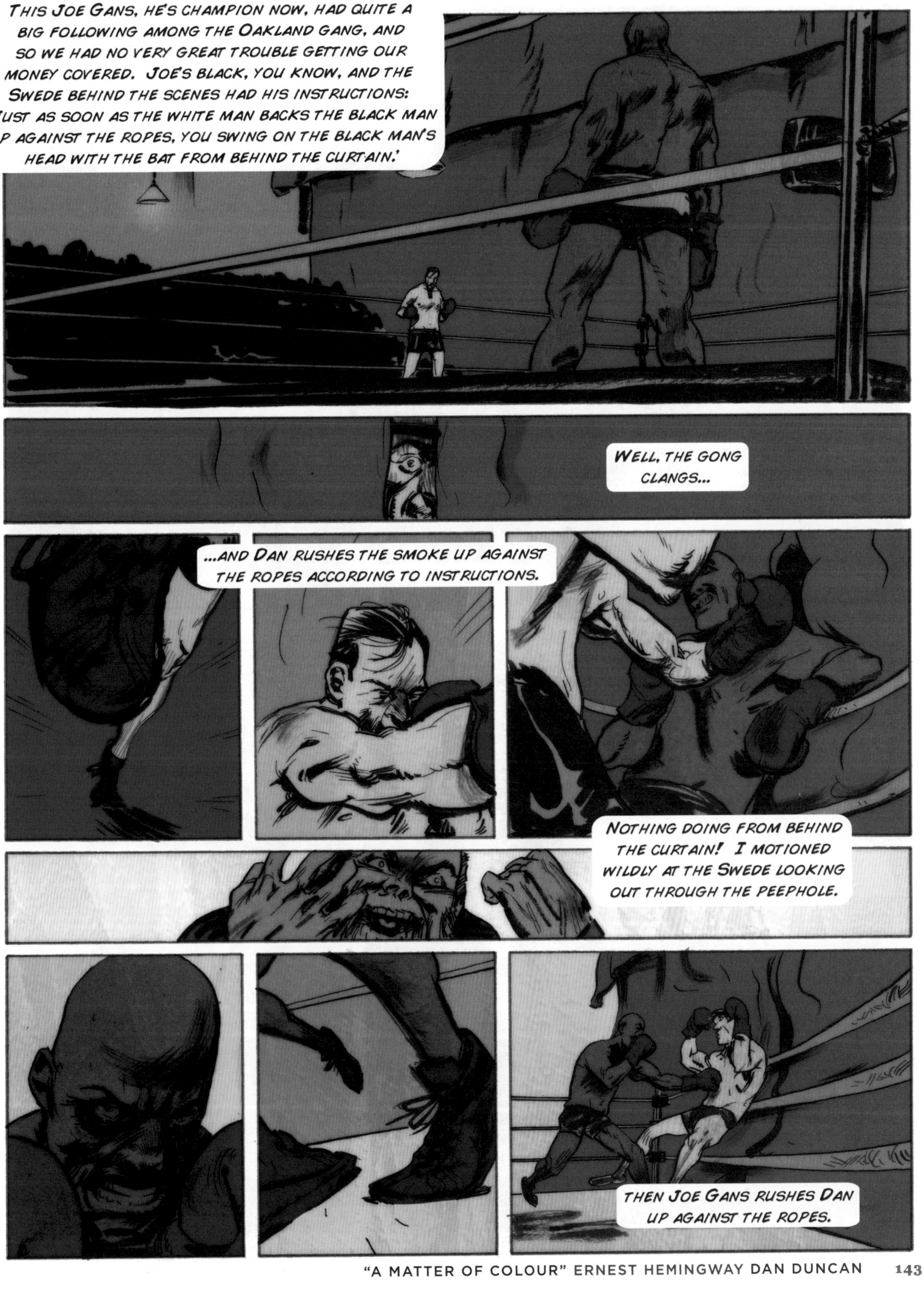
THIS JOE GANS, HE'S CHAMPION NOW, HAD QUITE A BIG FOLLOWING AMONG THE OAKLAND GANG, AND SO WE HAD NO VERY GREAT TROUBLE GETTING OUR MONEY COVERED. JOE'S BLACK, YOU KNOW, AND THE SWEDE BEHIND THE SCENES HAD HIS INSTRUCTIONS: 'JUST AS SOON AS THE WHITE MAN BACKS THE BLACK MAN UP AGAINST THE ROPES, YOU SWING ON THE BLACK MAN'S HEAD WITH THE BAT FROM BEHIND THE CURTAIN.'
WELL, THE GONG CLANGS...
...AND DAN RUSHES THE SMOKE UP AGAINST THE ROPES ACCORDING TO INSTRUCTIONS.
NOTHING DOING FROM BEHIND THE CURTAIN! I MOTIONED WILDLY AT THE SWEDE LOOKING OUT THROUGH THE PEEPHOLE.
THEN JOE GANS RUSHES DAN UP AGAINST THE ROPES.

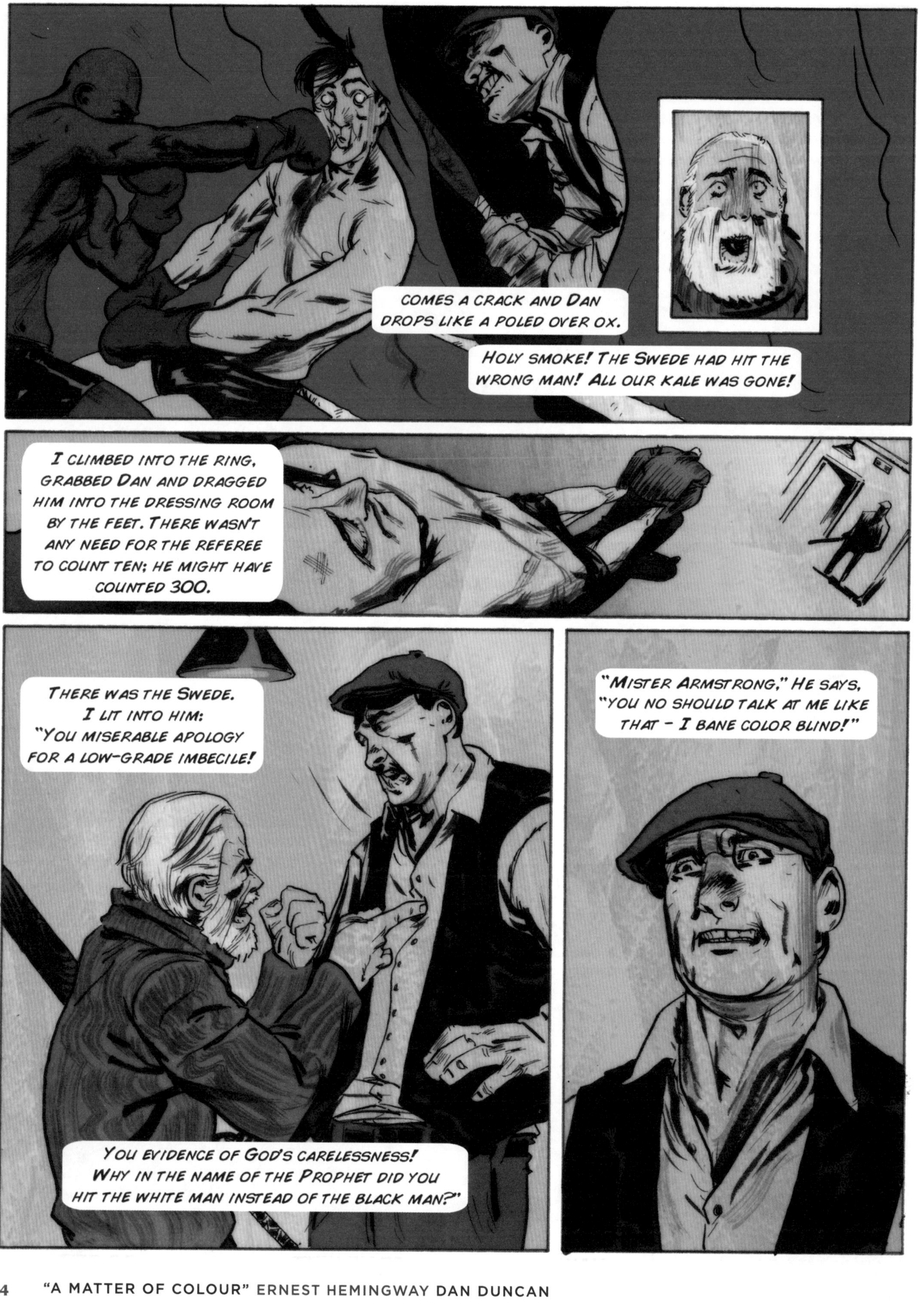
COMES A CRACK AND DAN DROPS LIKE A POLED OVER OX.
HOLY SMOKE! THE SWEDE HAD HIT THE WRONG MAN! ALL OUR KALE WAS GONE!
I CLIMBED INTO THE RING, GRABBED DAN AND DRAGGED HIM INTO THE DRESSING ROOM BY THE FEET. THERE WASN'T ANY NEED FOR THE REFEREE TO COUNT TEN; HE MIGHT HAVE COUNTED 300.
THERE WAS THE SWEDE. I LIT INTO HIM: "YOU MISERABLE APOLOGY FOR A LOW-GRADE IMBECILE!
YOU EVIDENCE OF GOD'S CARELESSNESS! WHY IN THE NAME OF THE PROPHET DID YOU HIT THE WHITE MAN INSTEAD OF THE BLACK MAN?"
"MISTER ARMSTRONG," HE SAYS, "YOU NO SHOULD TALK AT ME LIKE THAT - I BANE COLOR BLIND!"

The Madman

Kahlil Gibran

ART/ADAPTATION BY **Matt Wiegle**

KAHLIL GIBRAN'S 1923 BOOK *THE PROPHET* IS ONE of the all-time megasellers—translated into more than forty languages, with over one hundred million copies sold. Pretty amazing for a lad from Lebanon, who had difficulty reading and writing his native Arabic, never mind his second language, English. Early on, Gibran's drawings and paintings were the toast of his family's adopted city of Boston, but it was his wise writings that earned him lasting worldwide acclaim.

Gibran was born in 1883 in what is now Lebanon, into a Catholic family. His early stories about women who pursue true love despite arranged marriages—as well as other characters who buck cultural and religious norms, often going against lying or unfeeling clergymen—got him excommunicated and exiled, and his books were publicly burned in Beirut. He became what we would today call "spiritual but not religious," and his works—poetry, prose poetry, fables, parables, etc.—are filled with genuine wisdom, a great concern with love, dashes of cynicism, and a heavy debt to the style of the King James Bible, which Gibran studied intently. *The Prophet*, a series of twenty-four lyrical essays on the deeper meaning of friendship, marriage, food, clothes, children, crime, pain, and more, rings with great lines:

Love one another but make not a bond of love:
Let it rather be a moving sea between the shores of your
    souls.
Fill each other's cup but drink not from one cup.

. . .

Your children are not your children.
They are the sons and daughters of Life's longing for itself.
They come through you but not from you,
And though they are with you, yet they belong not to you. . . .
You may strive to be like them, but seek not to make them
    like you.
For life goes not backward nor tarries with yesterday.

While *The Prophet* is filled with great sentiments, the first book Gibran wrote in English—*The Madman* (1918), a slim collection of fables dealing with living an authentic life free of self-delusion—is brimming with fantastic visuals. It was crying out for graphic adaptation, and the endlessly inventive, Ignatz Award–winning Matt Wiegle answered that call perfectly, just as he did with a slice of the Hindu epic *Mahabharata* in Volume 1.

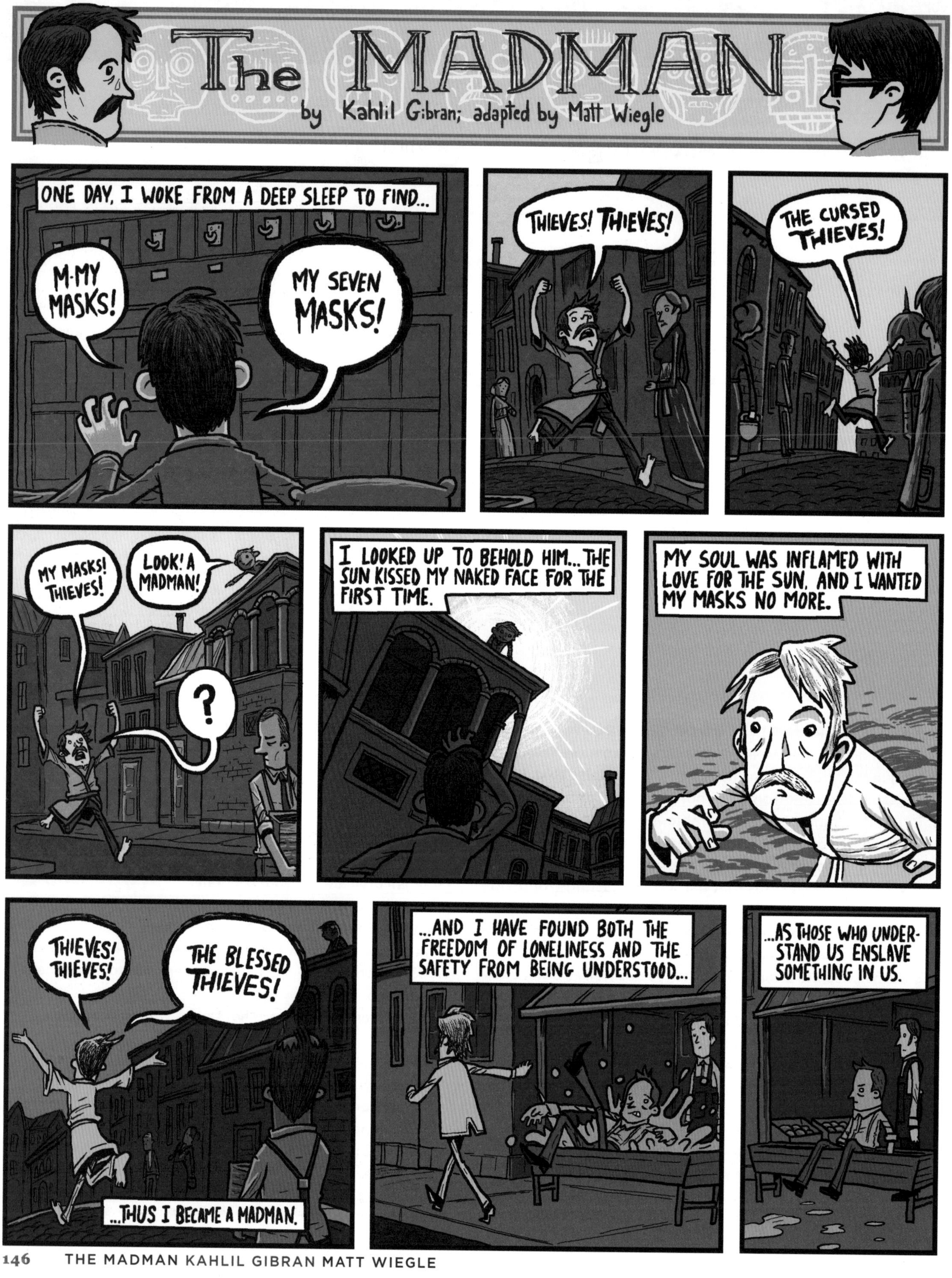
The MADMAN
by Kahlil Gibran; adapted by Matt Wiegle
ONE DAY, I WOKE FROM A DEEP SLEEP TO FIND...
M-MY MASKS!
MY SEVEN MASKS!
THIEVES! THIEVES!
THE CURSED THIEVES!
MY MASKS! THIEVES!
LOOK! A MADMAN!
?
I LOOKED UP TO BEHOLD HIM... THE SUN KISSED MY NAKED FACE FOR THE FIRST TIME.
MY SOUL WAS INFLAMED WITH LOVE FOR THE SUN, AND I WANTED MY MASKS NO MORE.
THIEVES! THIEVES!
THE BLESSED THIEVES!
...THUS I BECAME A MADMAN.
...AND I HAVE FOUND BOTH THE FREEDOM OF LONELINESS AND THE SAFETY FROM BEING UNDERSTOOD...
...AS THOSE WHO UNDERSTAND US ENSLAVE SOMETHING IN US.

THE EYE

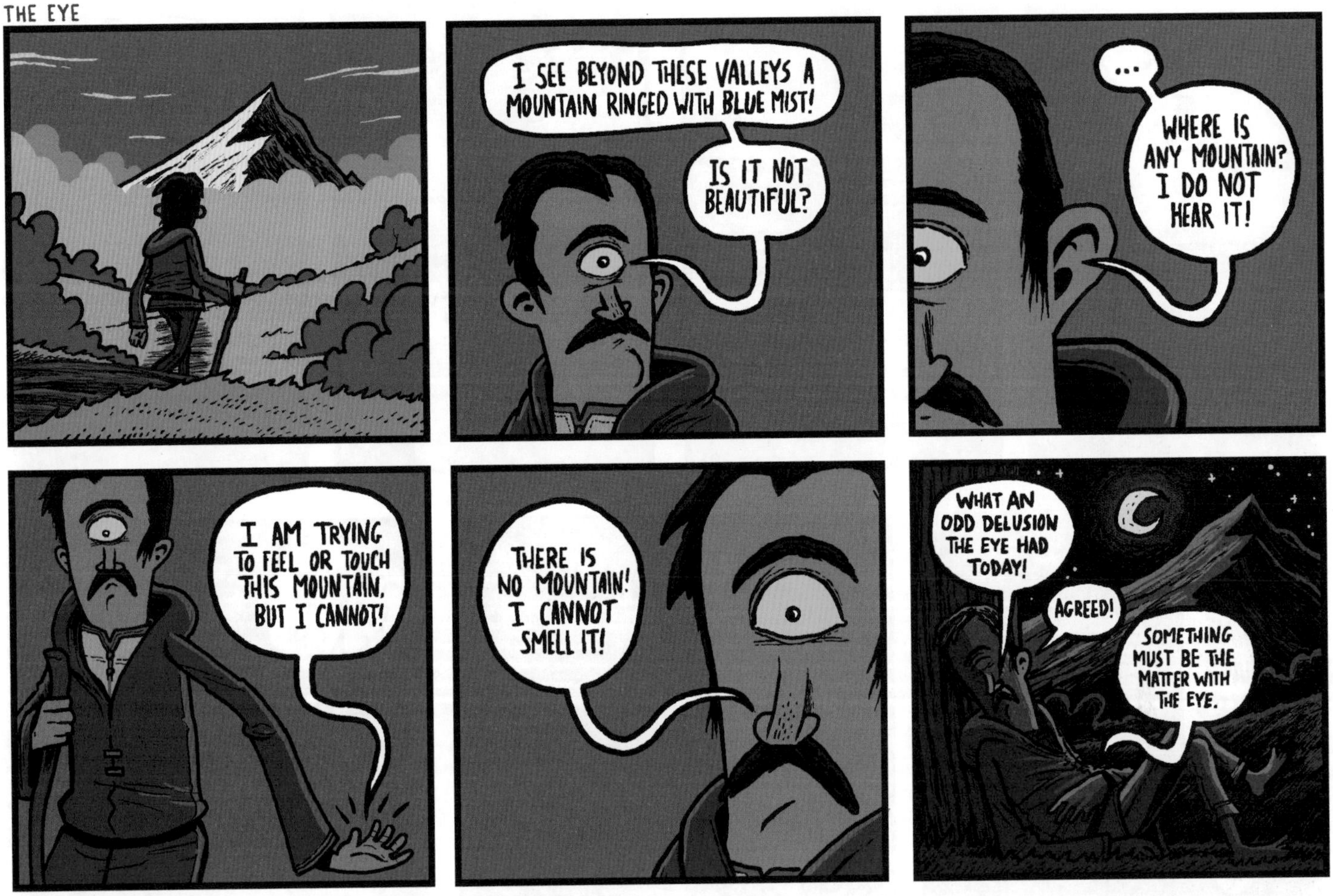

I SEE BEYOND THESE VALLEYS A MOUNTAIN RINGED WITH BLUE MIST!
IS IT NOT BEAUTIFUL?
...
WHERE IS ANY MOUNTAIN? I DO NOT HEAR IT!
I AM TRYING TO FEEL OR TOUCH THIS MOUNTAIN, BUT I CANNOT!
THERE IS NO MOUNTAIN! I CANNOT SMELL IT!
WHAT AN ODD DELUSION THE EYE HAD TODAY!
AGREED!
SOMETHING MUST BE THE MATTER WITH THE EYE.

THE SCARECROW

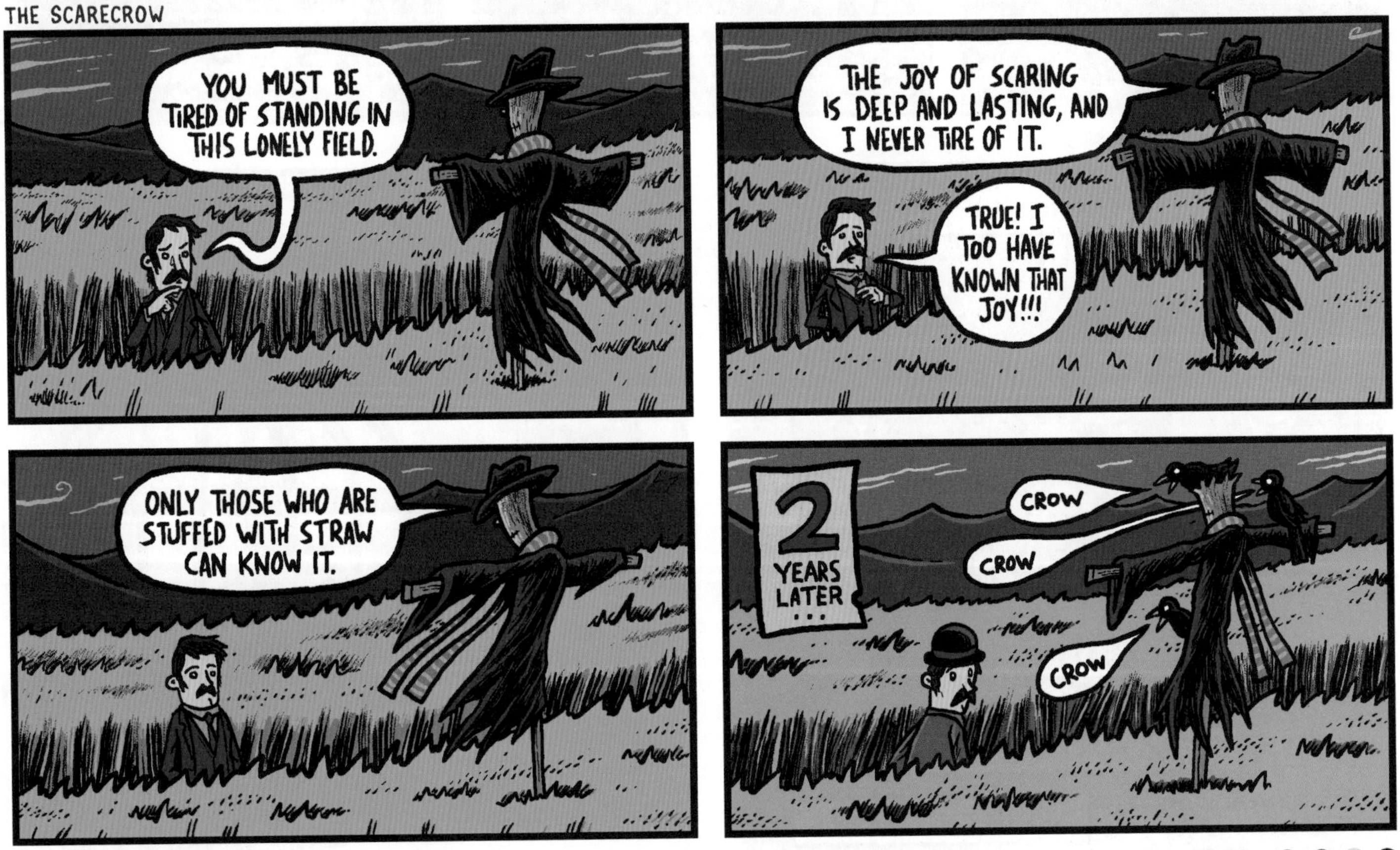

YOU MUST BE TIRED OF STANDING IN THIS LONELY FIELD.
THE JOY OF SCARING IS DEEP AND LASTING, AND I NEVER TIRE OF IT.
TRUE! I TOO HAVE KNOWN THAT JOY!!!
ONLY THOSE WHO ARE STUFFED WITH STRAW CAN KNOW IT.
2 YEARS LATER ...
CROW
CROW
CROW

"LET ME NOT BE TOO PROUD OF MY SAFETY. EVEN A THIEF IN A JAIL IS SAFE FROM ANOTHER THIEF." —THE MADMAN

THE FOX

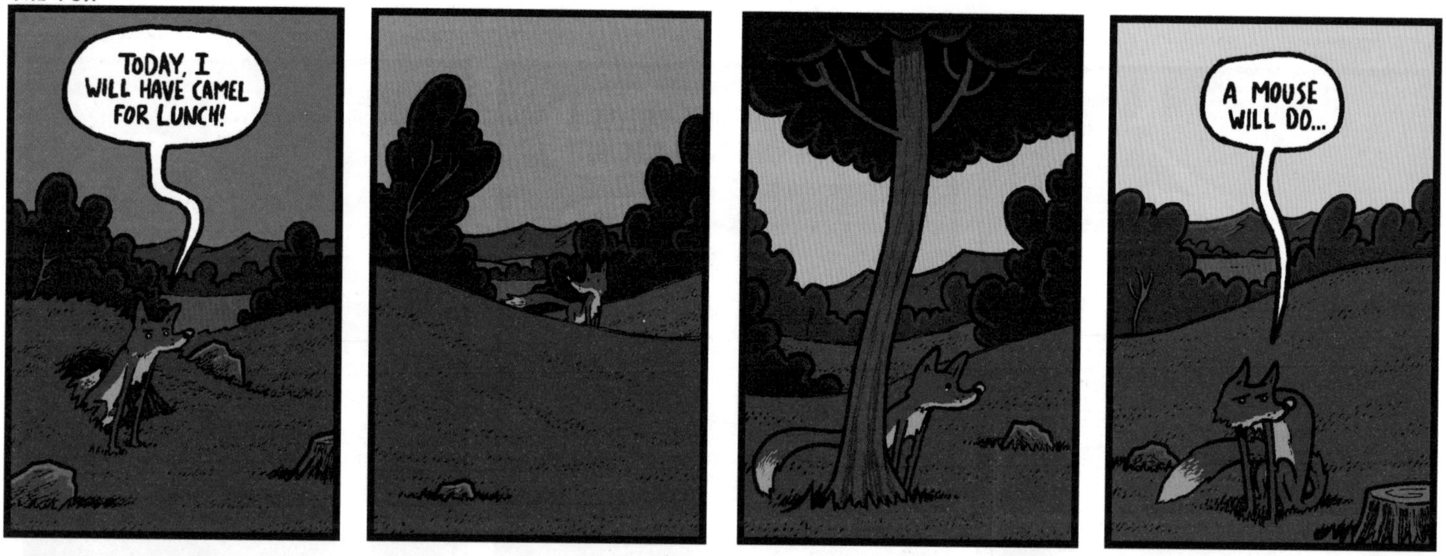
TODAY, I WILL HAVE CAMEL FOR LUNCH!
A MOUSE WILL DO...

THE NEW PLEASURE

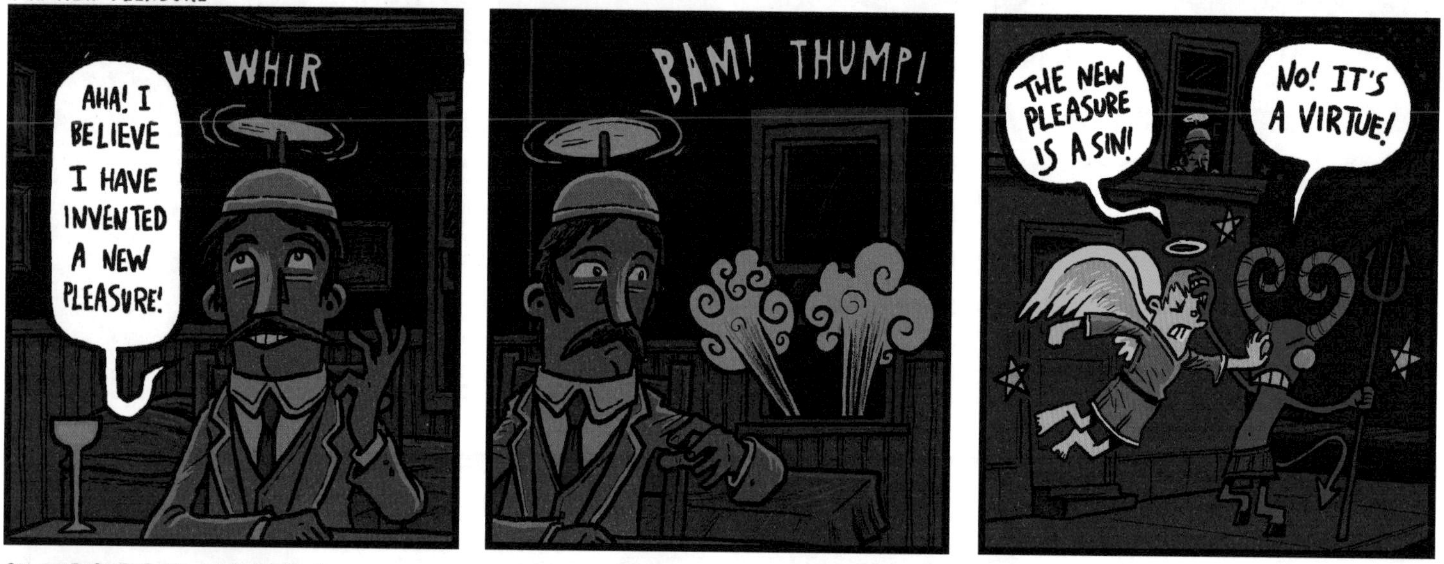
WHIR
AHA! I BELIEVE I HAVE INVENTED A NEW PLEASURE!
BAM! THUMP!
THE NEW PLEASURE IS A SIN!
NO! IT'S A VIRTUE!

ON THE STEPS OF THE TEMPLE

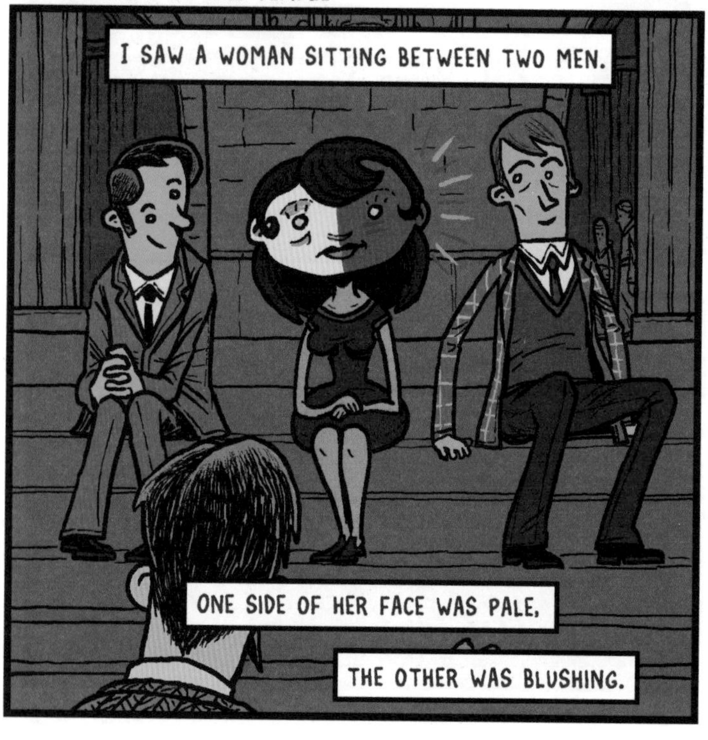
I SAW A WOMAN SITTING BETWEEN TWO MEN.
ONE SIDE OF HER FACE WAS PALE,
THE OTHER WAS BLUSHING.

THE TWO CAGES

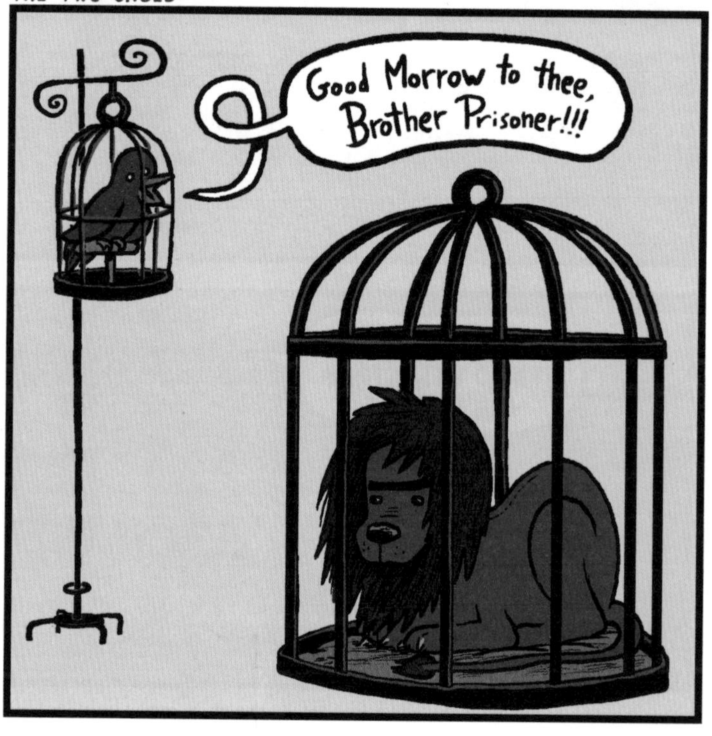
Good Morrow to thee, Brother Prisoner!!!

THE ANTS

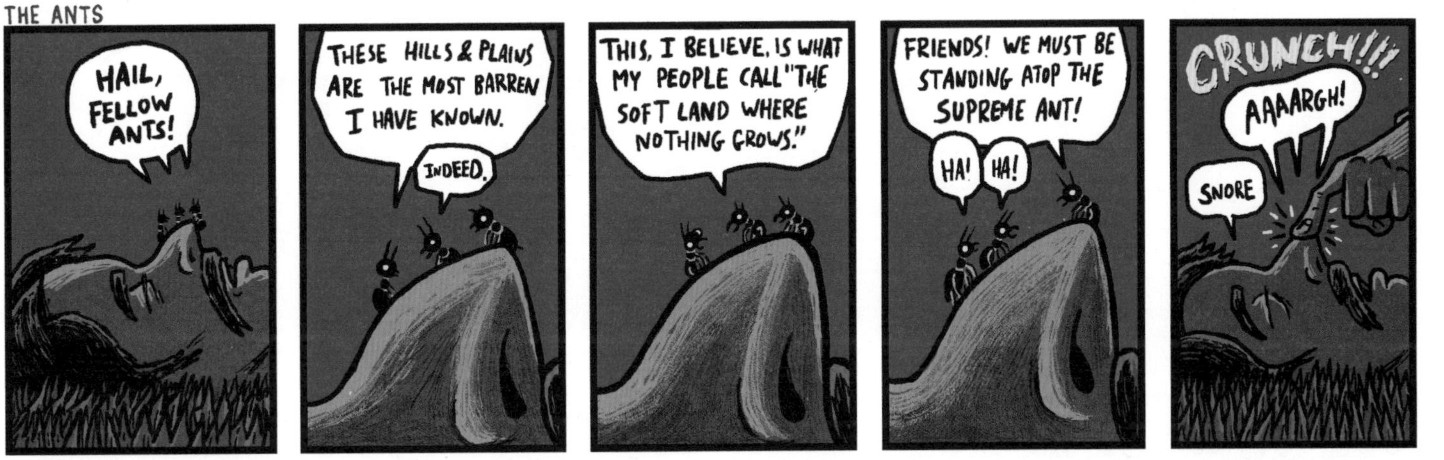
HAIL, FELLOW ANTS!
THESE HILLS & PLAINS ARE THE MOST BARREN I HAVE KNOWN.
INDEED.
THIS, I BELIEVE, IS WHAT MY PEOPLE CALL "THE SOFT LAND WHERE NOTHING GROWS."
FRIENDS! WE MUST BE STANDING ATOP THE SUPREME ANT!
HA!
HA!
CRUNCH!!!
SNORE
AAAARGH!

THE GRAVE-DIGGER

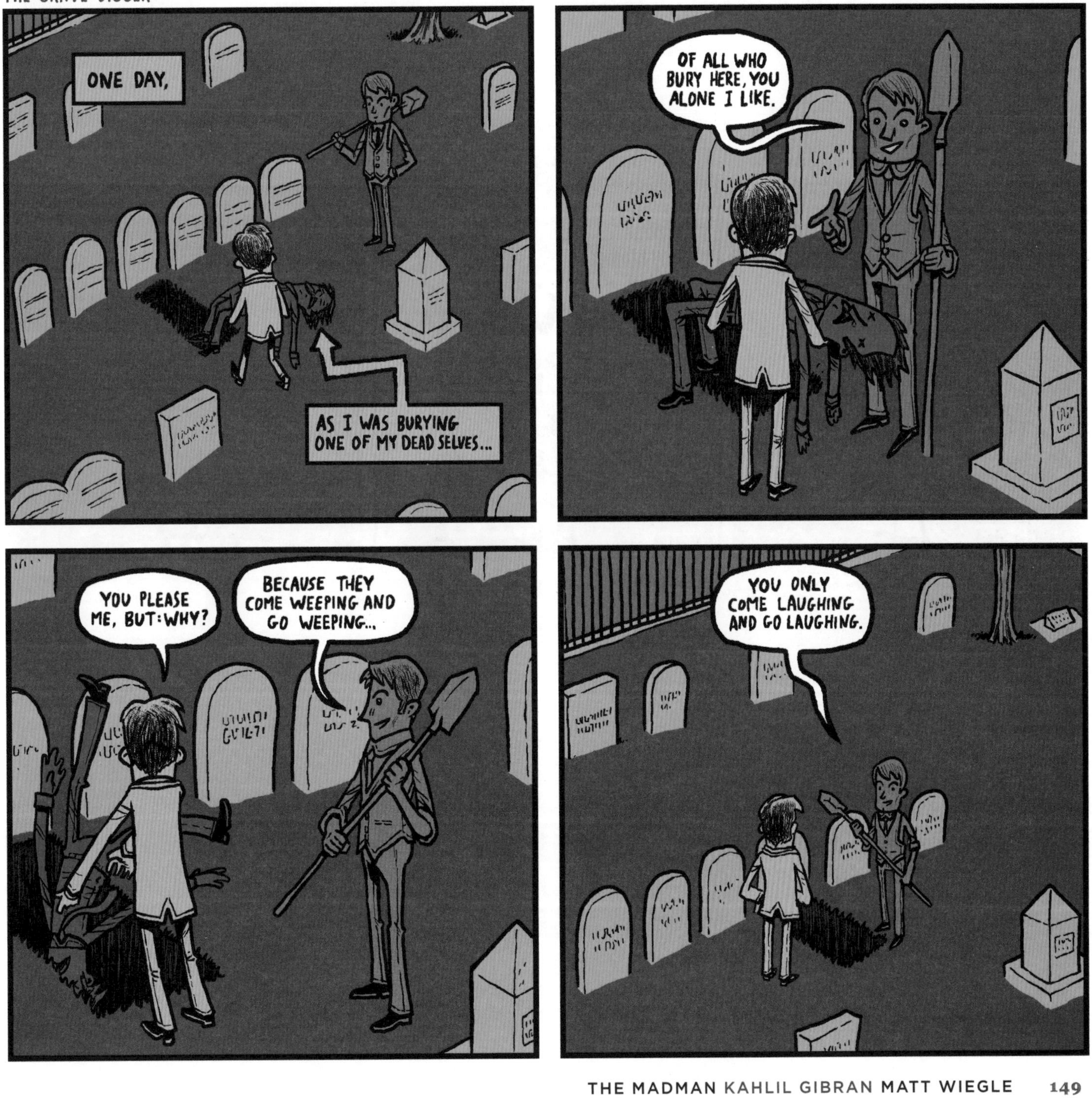
ONE DAY,
AS I WAS BURYING ONE OF MY DEAD SELVES...
OF ALL WHO BURY HERE, YOU ALONE I LIKE.
YOU PLEASE ME, BUT: WHY?
BECAUSE THEY COME WEEPING AND GO WEEPING...
YOU ONLY COME LAUGHING AND GO LAUGHING.

Three Panel Review
Lisa Brown

THE CATCHER IN THE RYE
by J.D. Salinger
Everyone around me is a PHONY.
What the hellya reading?
Goddamn book.
DINESON OUT OF AFRI
Except my brother ALLIE.
© LISA M. BROWN
Who is DEAD.
CENTRAL PARK WEST

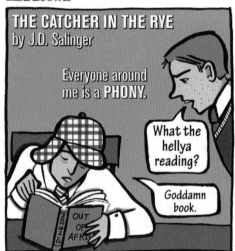

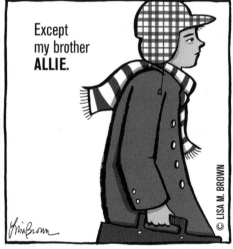

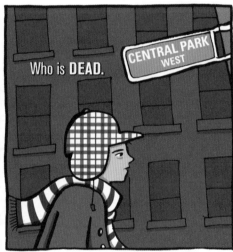

Sherwood Anderson

ART/ADAPTATION BY Ted Rall

A GENRE-BENDER UNLIKE ANY OTHER, *WINESBURG,* *Ohio* is among the quietest and yet most unsettling of America's twentieth-century masterpieces. Not, strictly speaking, a novel, it is closer to a novel than a short-story collection because of the strong unifying elements of the locale and the seamlessness of the narration. The life of the town is not explained but rather is revealed through accounts of the histories of each character's struggles. The book is a slim, incantatory, episodic work that captures a critical moment in our nation's history at the dawn of the modern age, when great fortunes were made and lost and we left behind our rural past for our industrialized future.

Anderson wrote "Hands" first, around 1915, and then the rest of the book, which was published in 1919, when the author was in his early forties. Though it was the book that made him famous and has something of the feel of a first book, it was actually his fourth, preceded by two novels and a collection of poems. In the introduction to the first Modern Library edition of 1947, Ernst Boyd describes *Winesburg, Ohio* as an exemplar of "a literature of revolt against the great illusion of American civilization, the illu-sion of optimism." But the author himself described the book only as "an effort to treat the lives of simple ordinary people in an American middle western town with sympathy and understanding." He wasn't a polemicist attacking the status quo so much as a writer attempting to show the lives of people he knew well.

Ted Rall is a fiercely progressive columnist and political cartoonist whose syndicated work appears in over one hundred newspapers. He's created several graphic novels and written nonfiction books, including *The Anti-American Manifesto*. Drawn to Anderson's focus on the common people and his distrust of industrialization, Ted chose to work with *Winesburg*, zeroing in on its first story.

SOURCES

Anderson, Sherwood. *Winesburg, Ohio*. Introduction by Ernest Boyd. New York: Modern Library (Random House), 1919.

Townsend, Kim. *Sherwood Anderson*. New York: Houghton Mifflin, 1987.

—Dan Simon

WING BIDDLEBAUM, FOREVER FRIGHTENED AND BESET BY A GHOSTLY BAND OF DOUBTS, DID NOT THINK OF HIMSELF AS IN ANY WAY A PART OF THE LIFE OF THE TOWN WHERE HE HAD LIVED FOR TWENTY YEARS. AMONG ALL THE PEOPLE OF WINESBURG BUT ONE HAD COME CLOSE TO HIM.

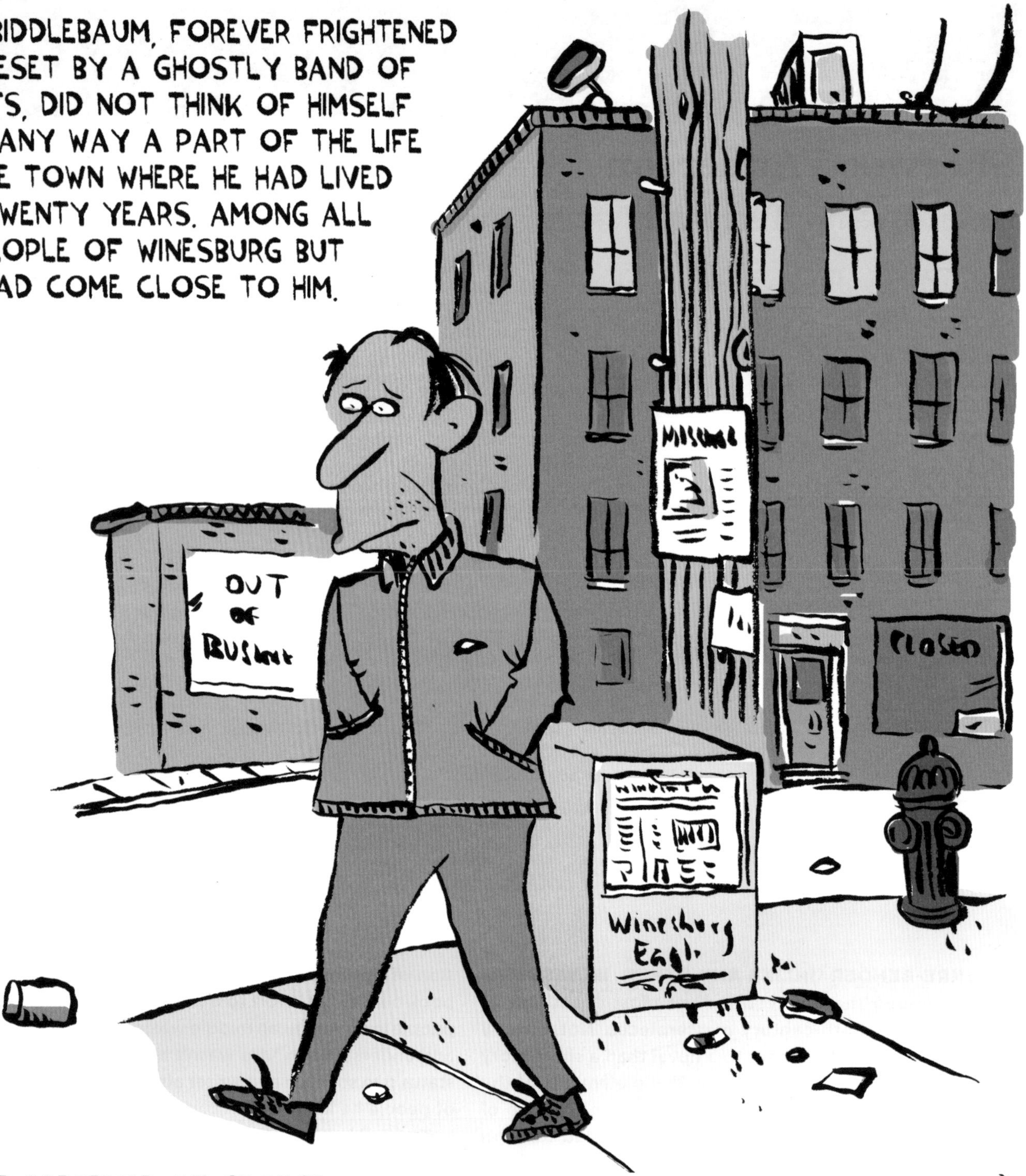
OUT
OF
CLOSED

IN THE PRESENCE OF GEORGE WILLARD, WING BIDDLEBAUM, WHO FOR TWENTY YEARS HAD BEEN THE TOWN MYSTERY, LOST SOMETHING OF HIS TIMIDITY, AND HIS SHADOWY PERSONALITY, SUBMERGED IN A SEA OF DOUBTS, CAME FORTH TO LOOK AT THE WORLD.

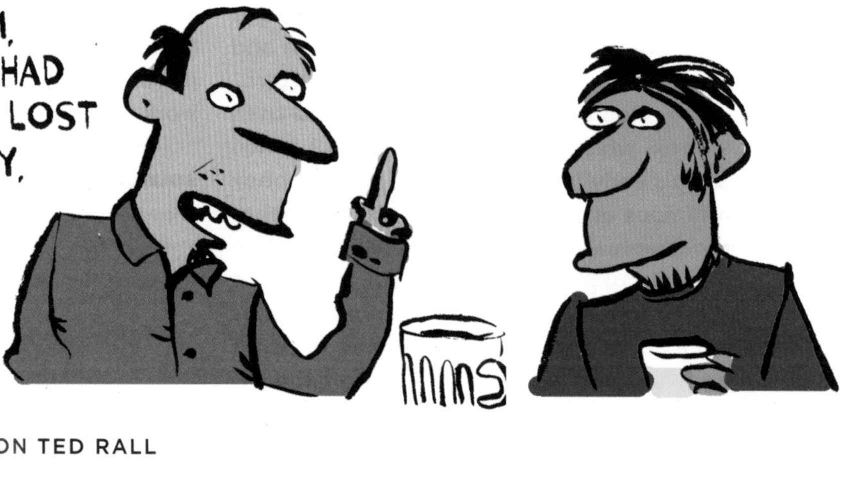

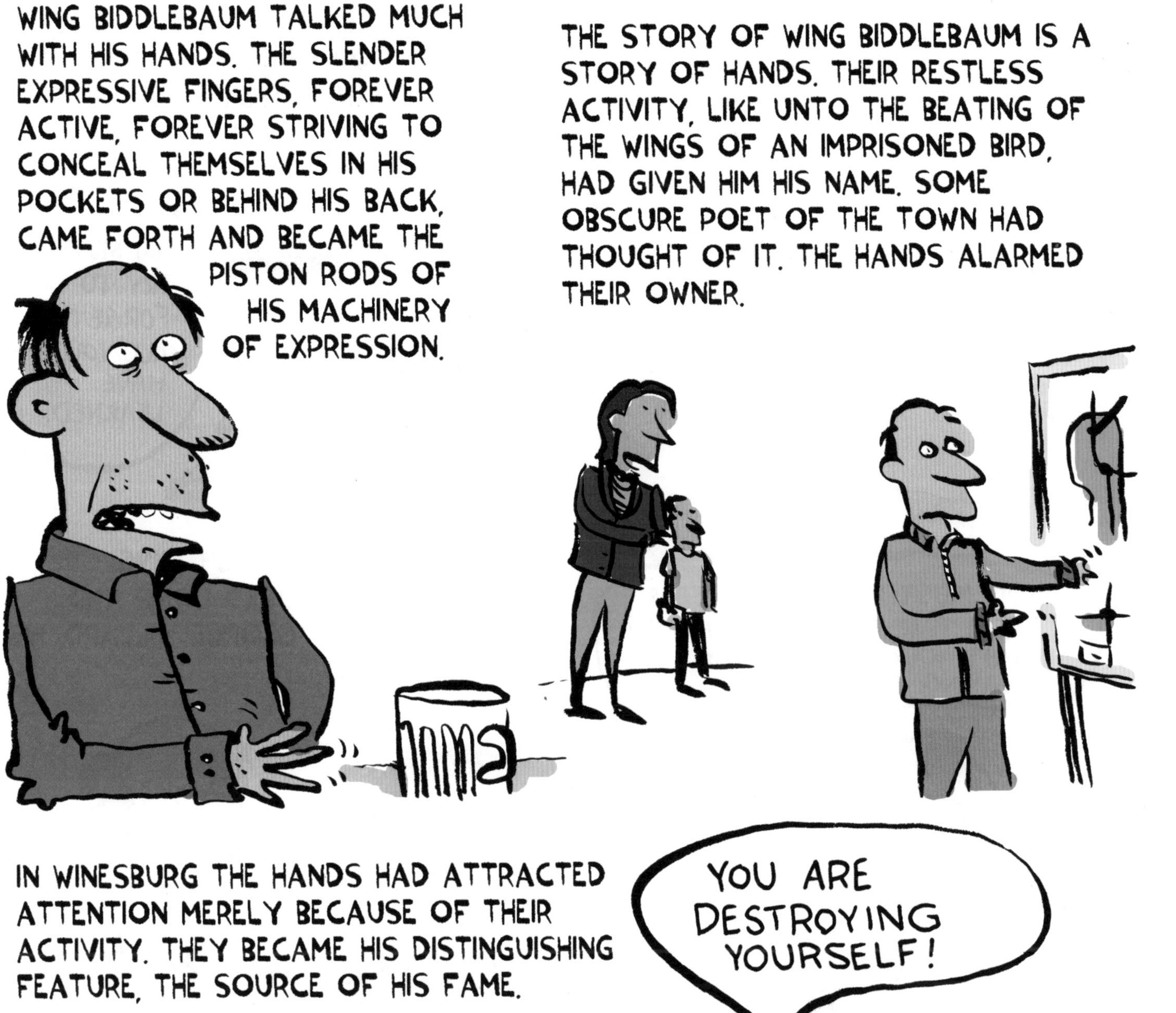
WING BIDDLEBAUM TALKED MUCH WITH HIS HANDS. THE SLENDER EXPRESSIVE FINGERS, FOREVER ACTIVE, FOREVER STRIVING TO CONCEAL THEMSELVES IN HIS POCKETS OR BEHIND HIS BACK, CAME FORTH AND BECAME THE PISTON RODS OF HIS MACHINERY OF EXPRESSION.
THE STORY OF WING BIDDLEBAUM IS A STORY OF HANDS. THEIR RESTLESS ACTIVITY, LIKE UNTO THE BEATING OF THE WINGS OF AN IMPRISONED BIRD, HAD GIVEN HIM HIS NAME. SOME OBSCURE POET OF THE TOWN HAD THOUGHT OF IT. THE HANDS ALARMED THEIR OWNER.
IN WINESBURG THE HANDS HAD ATTRACTED ATTENTION MERELY BECAUSE OF THEIR ACTIVITY. THEY BECAME HIS DISTINGUISHING FEATURE, THE SOURCE OF HIS FAME.
YOU ARE DESTROYING YOURSELF!

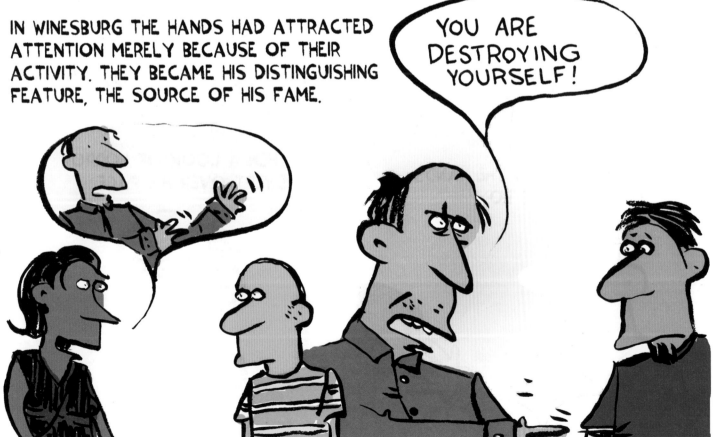

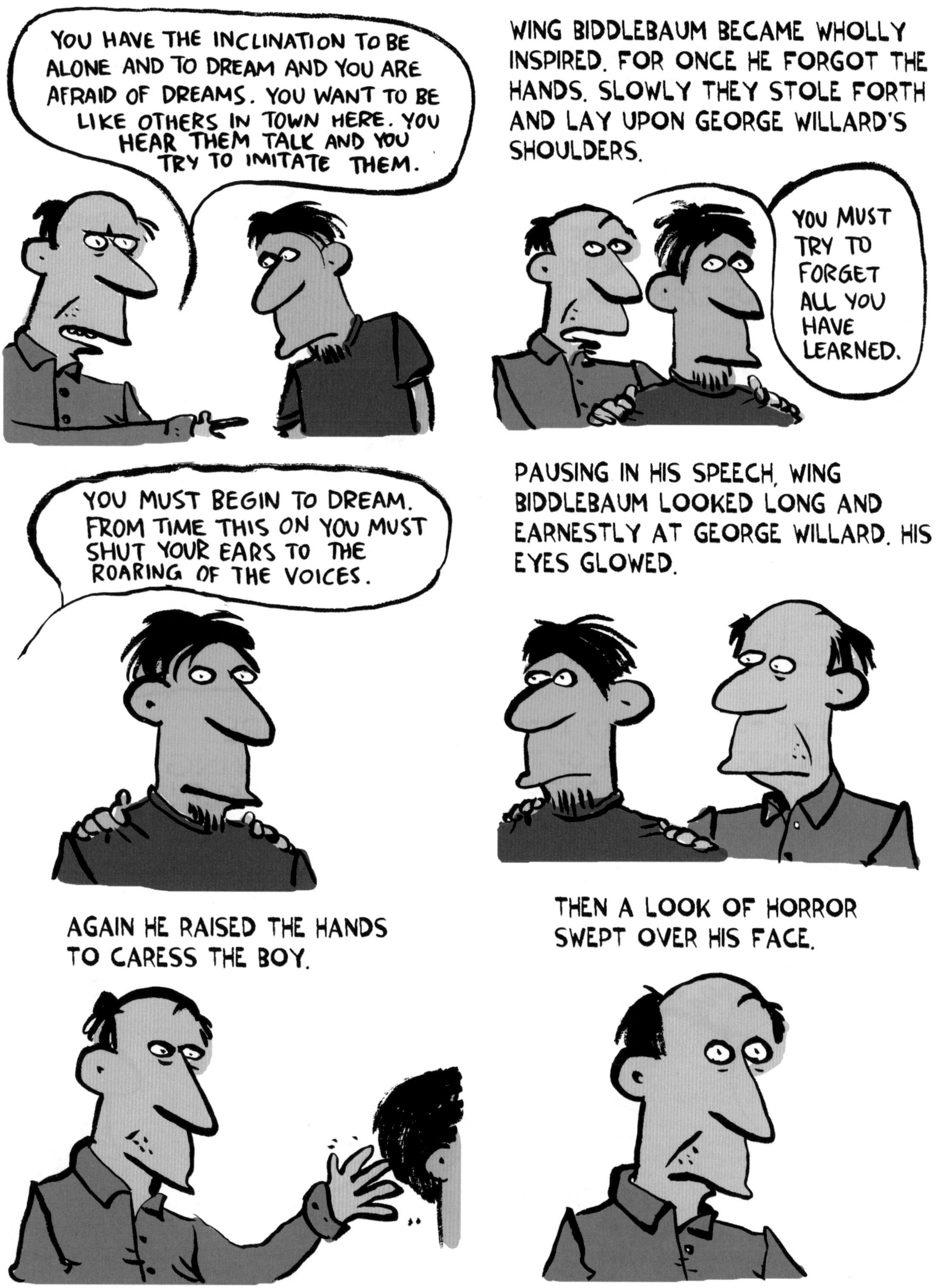
YOU HAVE THE INCLINATION TO BE ALONE AND TO DREAM AND YOU ARE AFRAID OF DREAMS. YOU WANT TO BE LIKE OTHERS IN TOWN HERE. YOU HEAR THEM TALK AND YOU TRY TO IMITATE THEM.
WING BIDDLEBAUM BECAME WHOLLY INSPIRED. FOR ONCE HE FORGOT THE HANDS. SLOWLY THEY STOLE FORTH AND LAY UPON GEORGE WILLARD'S SHOULDERS.
YOU MUST TRY TO FORGET ALL YOU HAVE LEARNED.
YOU MUST BEGIN TO DREAM. FROM TIME THIS ON YOU MUST SHUT YOUR EARS TO THE ROARING OF THE VOICES.
PAUSING IN HIS SPEECH, WING BIDDLEBAUM LOOKED LONG AND EARNESTLY AT GEORGE WILLARD. HIS EYES GLOWED.
AGAIN HE RAISED THE HANDS TO CARESS THE BOY.
THEN A LOOK OF HORROR SWEPT OVER HIS FACE.

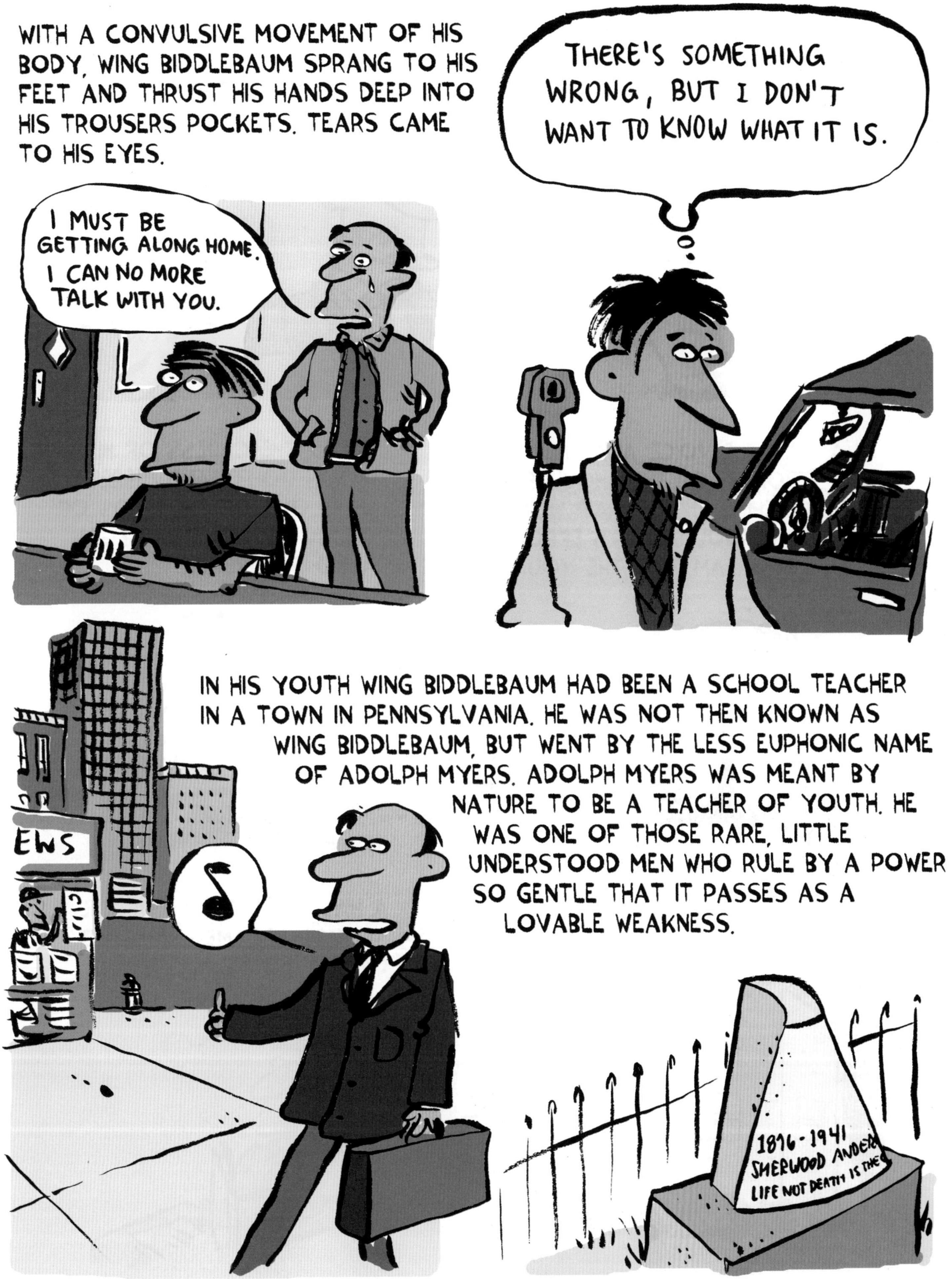
WITH A CONVULSIVE MOVEMENT OF HIS BODY, WING BIDDLEBAUM SPRANG TO HIS FEET AND THRUST HIS HANDS DEEP INTO HIS TROUSERS POCKETS. TEARS CAME TO HIS EYES.
I MUST BE GETTING ALONG HOME. I CAN NO MORE TALK WITH YOU.
THERE'S SOMETHING WRONG, BUT I DON'T WANT TO KNOW WHAT IT IS.
IN HIS YOUTH WING BIDDLEBAUM HAD BEEN A SCHOOL TEACHER IN A TOWN IN PENNSYLVANIA. HE WAS NOT THEN KNOWN AS WING BIDDLEBAUM, BUT WENT BY THE LESS EUPHONIC NAME OF ADOLPH MYERS. ADOLPH MYERS WAS MEANT BY NATURE TO BE A TEACHER OF YOUTH. HE WAS ONE OF THOSE RARE, LITTLE UNDERSTOOD MEN WHO RULE BY A POWER SO GENTLE THAT IT PASSES AS A LOVABLE WEAKNESS.
EWS
1876 - 1941
SHERWOOD ANDER
LIFE NOT DEATH IS THE

WITH THE BOYS OF HIS SCHOOL, ADOLPH MYERS HAD WALKED IN THE EVENING OR HAD SAT TALKING UNTIL DUSK UPON THE SCHOOLHOUSE STEPS LOST IN A KIND OF DREAM. HERE AND THERE WENT HIS HANDS, CARESSING THE SHOULDERS OF THE BOYS, PLAYING ABOUT THE TOUSLED HEADS.

IN A WAY THE VOICE AND THE HANDS, THE STROKING OF THE SHOULDERS AND THE TOUCHING OF THE HAIR WERE A PART OF THE SCHOOLMASTER'S EFFORT TO CARRY A DREAM INTO THE YOUNG MINDS.

UNDER THE CARESS OF HIS HANDS DOUBT AND DISBELIEF WENT OUT OF THE MINDS OF THE BOYS AND THEY BEGAN ALSO TO DREAM.

AND THEN THE TRAGEDY.

A HALF-WITTED BOY OF THE SCHOOL BECAME ENAMORED OF THE YOUNG MASTER.

GEO. L. ERWIT ELEMENTARY SCHOOL

"HANDS" SHERWOOD ANDERSON TED RALL

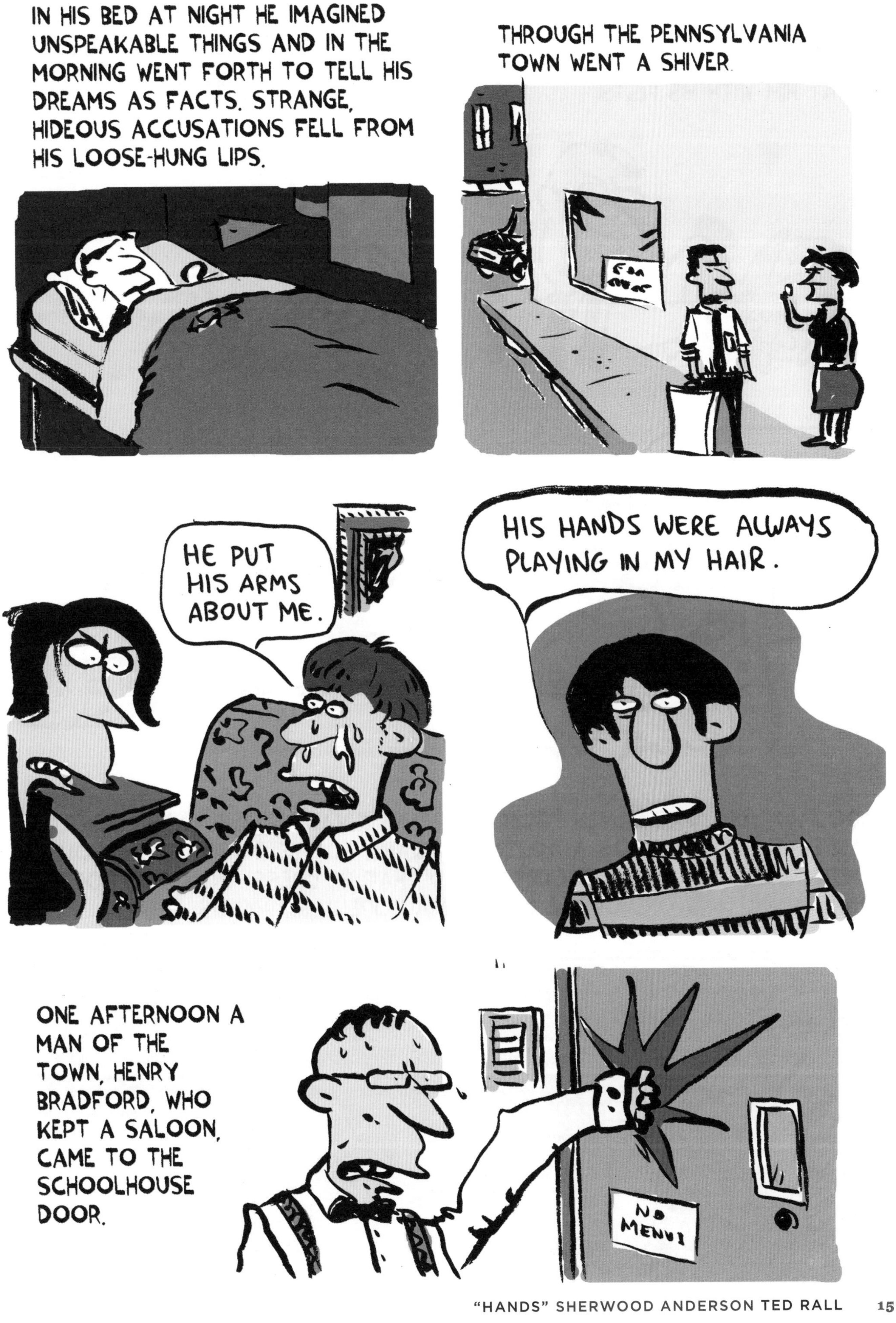
IN HIS BED AT NIGHT HE IMAGINED UNSPEAKABLE THINGS AND IN THE MORNING WENT FORTH TO TELL HIS DREAMS AS FACTS. STRANGE, HIDEOUS ACCUSATIONS FELL FROM HIS LOOSE-HUNG LIPS.
THROUGH THE PENNSYLVANIA TOWN WENT A SHIVER.
HE PUT HIS ARMS ABOUT ME.
HIS HANDS WERE ALWAYS PLAYING IN MY HAIR.
ONE AFTERNOON A MAN OF THE TOWN, HENRY BRADFORD, WHO KEPT A SALOON, CAME TO THE SCHOOLHOUSE DOOR.
NO MENU!

CALLING ADOLPH MYERS INTO THE SCHOOL YARD HE BEGAN TO BEAT HIM WITH HIS FISTS.

AS HIS HARD KNUCKLES BEAT DOWN INTO THE FRIGHTENED FACE OF THE SCHOOLMASTER, HIS WRATH BECAME MORE AND MORE TERRIBLE.

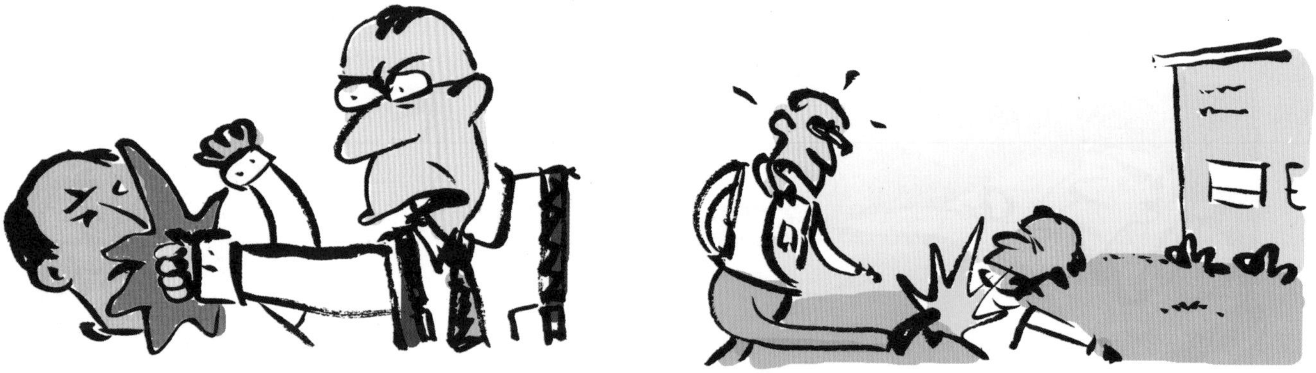

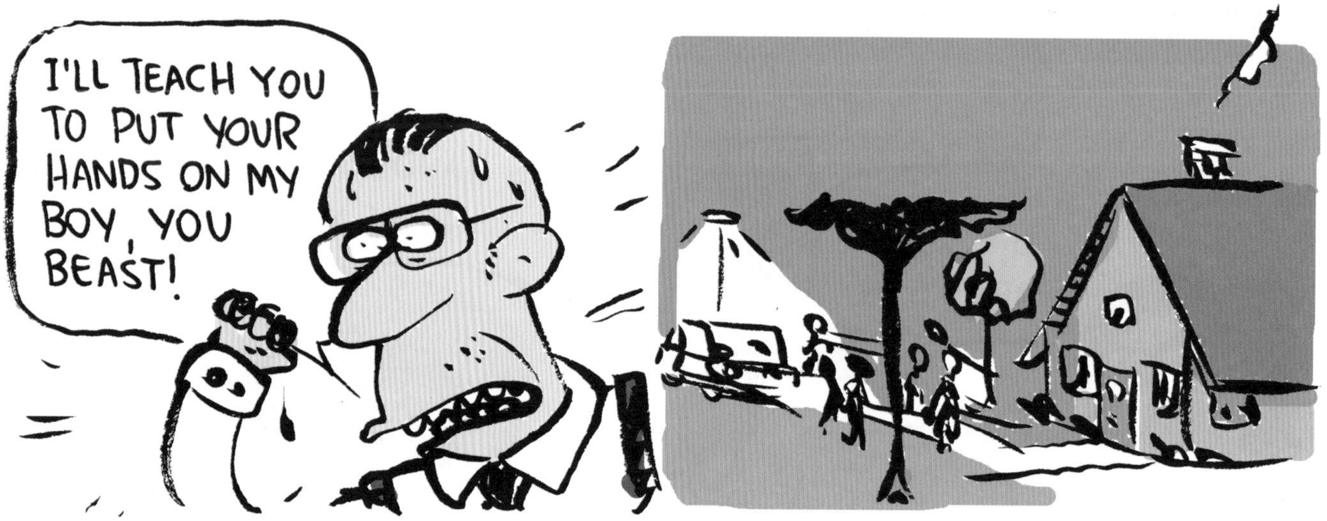
I'LL TEACH YOU TO PUT YOUR HANDS ON MY BOY, YOU BEAST!

ADOLPH MYERS WAS DRIVEN FROM THE PENNSYLVANIA TOWN IN THE NIGHT. WITH LANTERNS IN THEIR HANDS A DOZEN MEN CAME TO THE DOOR OF THE HOUSE WHERE HE LIVED ALONE AND COMMANDED THAT HE DRESS AND COME FORTH. IT WAS RAINING AND ONE OF THE MEN HAD A ROPE IN HIS HANDS.

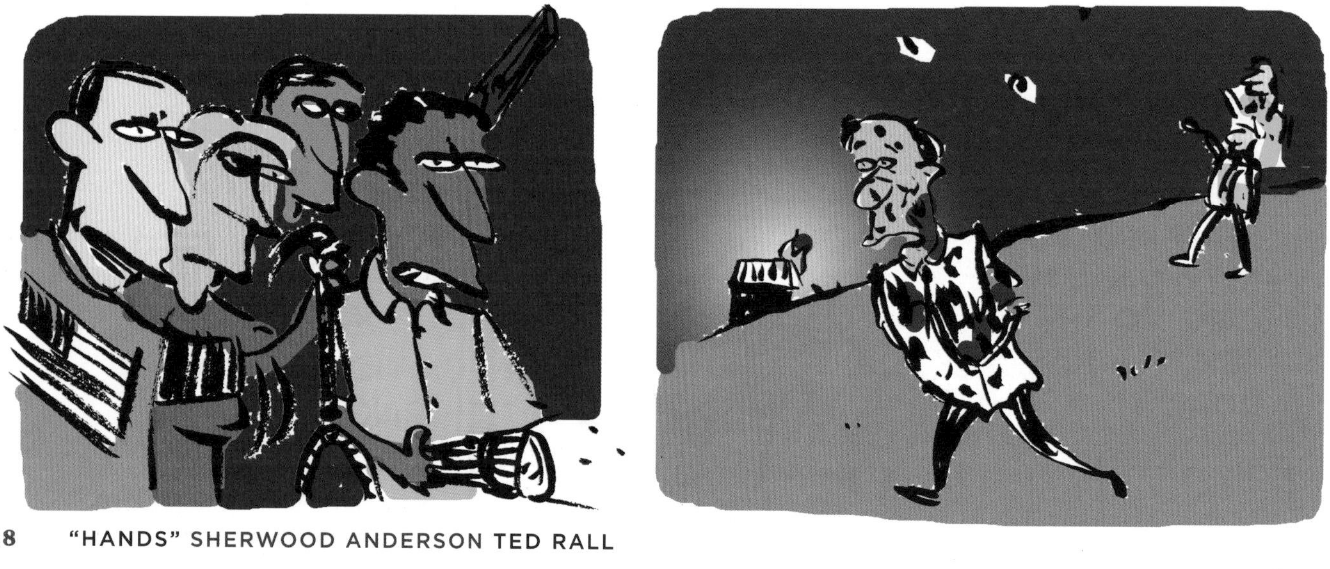

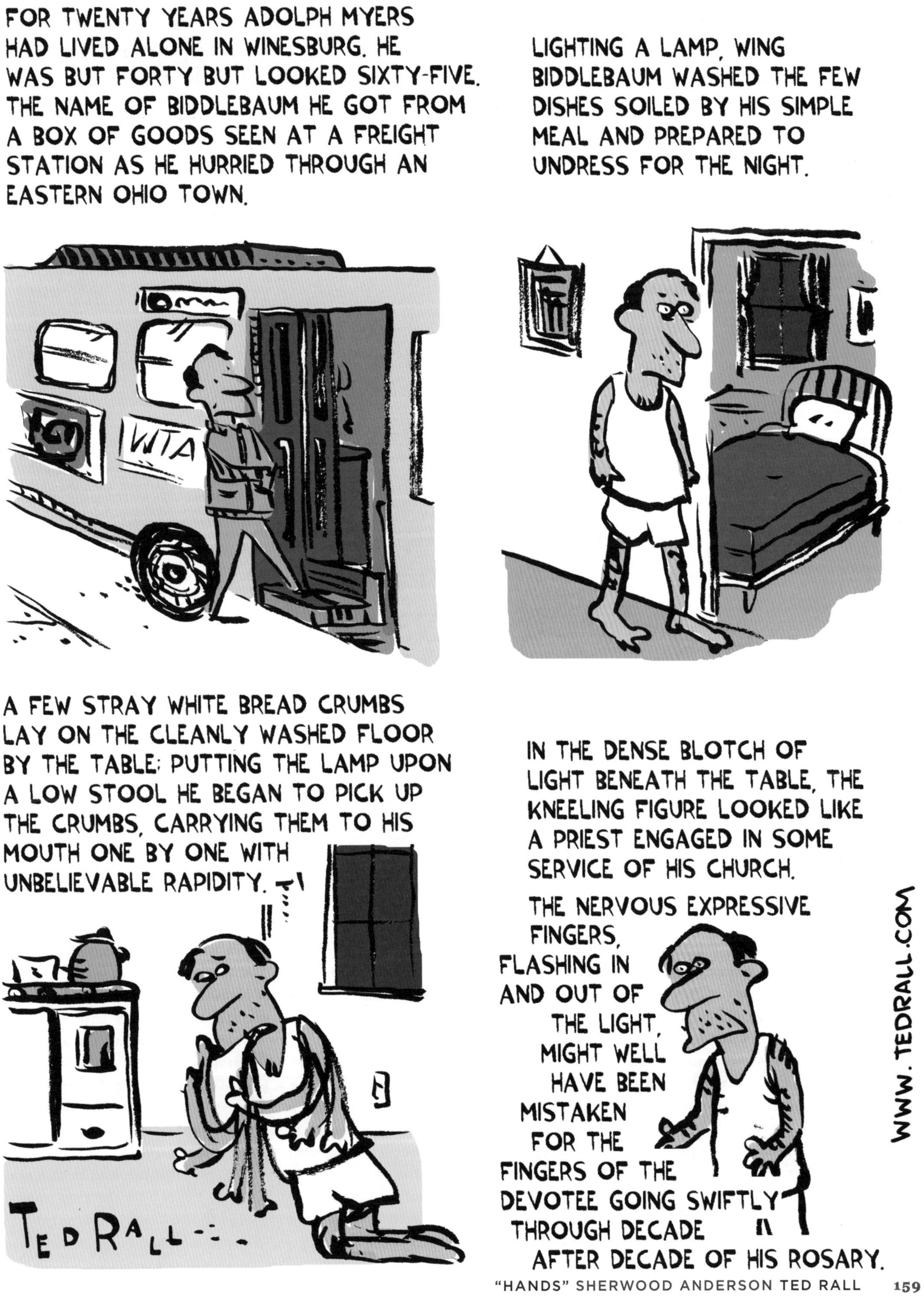
FOR TWENTY YEARS ADOLPH MYERS HAD LIVED ALONE IN WINESBURG. HE WAS BUT FORTY BUT LOOKED SIXTY-FIVE. THE NAME OF BIDDLEBAUM HE GOT FROM A BOX OF GOODS SEEN AT A FREIGHT STATION AS HE HURRIED THROUGH AN EASTERN OHIO TOWN.
WTA
LIGHTING A LAMP, WING BIDDLEBAUM WASHED THE FEW DISHES SOILED BY HIS SIMPLE MEAL AND PREPARED TO UNDRESS FOR THE NIGHT.
A FEW STRAY WHITE BREAD CRUMBS LAY ON THE CLEANLY WASHED FLOOR BY THE TABLE; PUTTING THE LAMP UPON A LOW STOOL HE BEGAN TO PICK UP THE CRUMBS, CARRYING THEM TO HIS MOUTH ONE BY ONE WITH UNBELIEVABLE RAPIDITY.
TED RALL
IN THE DENSE BLOTCH OF LIGHT BENEATH THE TABLE, THE KNEELING FIGURE LOOKED LIKE A PRIEST ENGAGED IN SOME SERVICE OF HIS CHURCH.
THE NERVOUS EXPRESSIVE FINGERS, FLASHING IN AND OUT OF THE LIGHT, MIGHT WELL HAVE BEEN MISTAKEN FOR THE FINGERS OF THE DEVOTEE GOING SWIFTLY THROUGH DECADE AFTER DECADE OF HIS ROSARY.
WWW.TEDRALL.COM

The Dreaming of the Bones

W. B. Yeats

ART/ADAPTATION BY **Lauren Weinstein**

MASTER POET AND PLAYWRIGHT W. B. YEATS, in addition to being a practicing mystic, was also a fiercely loyal Irishman. His one-act play *The Dreaming of the Bones* concerns the ghosts of two lovers trapped in an in-between state. But these aren't just any two spirits. The man is Diarmait Mac Murchada, a twelfth-century Irish chieftain. The woman is Derbforgaill, whom he married after stealing her from another chieftain. The jilted chieftain attacked Mac Murchada's forces and ousted him. To win back his kingdom, Mac Murchada enlisted the aid of King Henry II of England and of Norman warriors from Wales, thus bringing those forces into the Emerald Isle and starting all of that country's woes.

When Yeats wrote the playlet in 1919, the Irish were still struggling for independence from England. And here are the ghosts of the two lovers who started the whole mess 750 years prior, seeking forgiveness from one of their countrymen so that they may be released from their limbo.

Lauren Weinstein's work has been published in loads of prestigious anthologies, as well as the magazine *Bookforum*, which first ran the following comic under the title "Upon a Hill." It's a loose take on *The Dreaming of the Bones*. The central premise—the long-suffering ghosts of Mac Murchada and Derbforgaill asking for forgiveness— is the same. In the actual play, though, the young man on the road is an Irish resistance fighter, and in the end [**spoiler alert:**] he decides not to forgive the two lovers, even though he almost yields to the "terrible temptation" to absolve them.

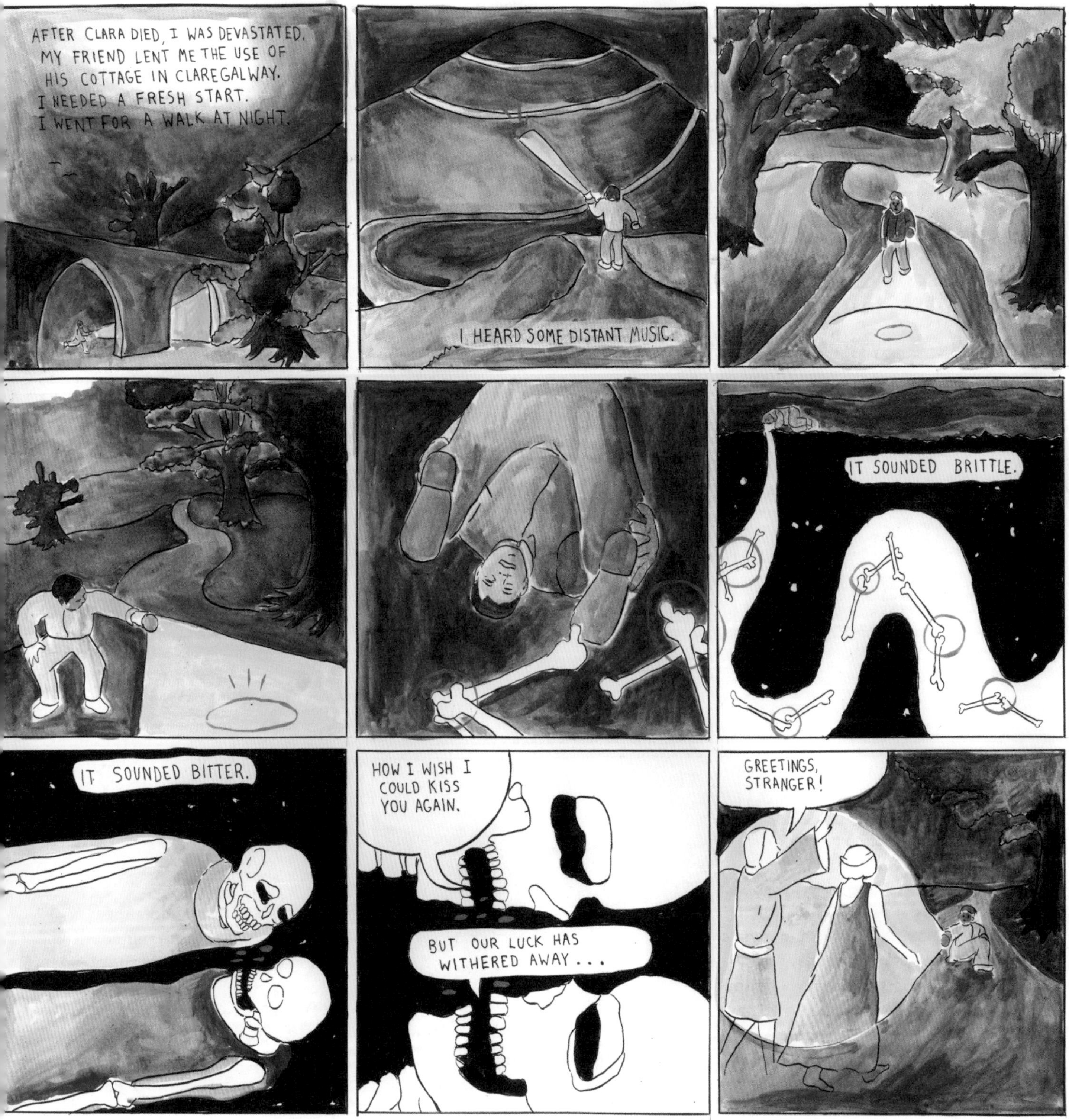
AFTER CLARA DIED, I WAS DEVASTATED. MY FRIEND LENT ME THE USE OF HIS COTTAGE IN CLAREGALWAY. I NEEDED A FRESH START. I WENT FOR A WALK AT NIGHT.
I HEARD SOME DISTANT MUSIC.
IT SOUNDED BRITTLE.
IT SOUNDED BITTER.
HOW I WISH I COULD KISS YOU AGAIN.
BUT OUR LUCK HAS WITHERED AWAY . . .
GREETINGS, STRANGER!

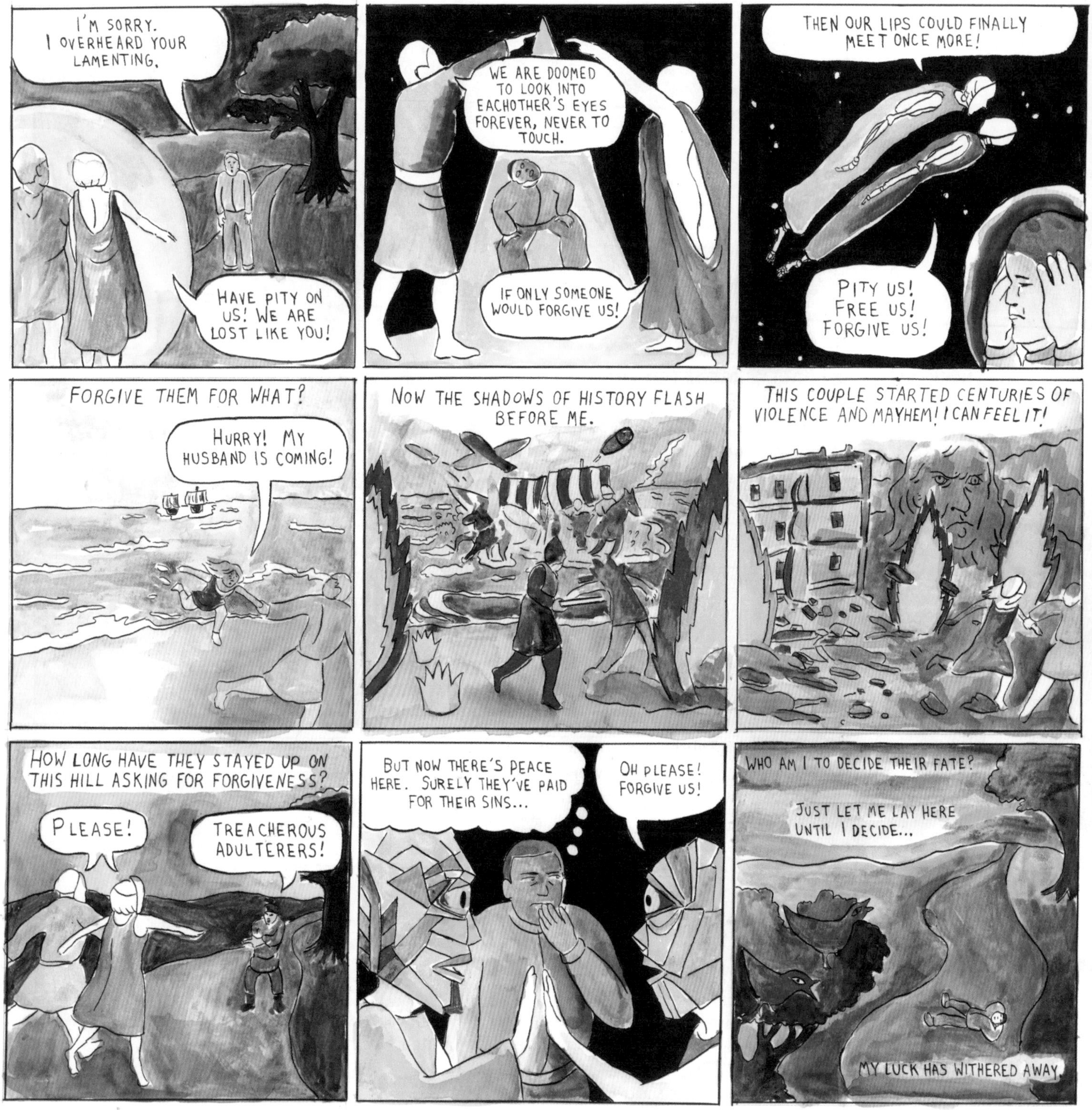
I'M SORRY. I OVERHEARD YOUR LAMENTING.
HAVE PITY ON US! WE ARE LOST LIKE YOU!
WE ARE DOOMED TO LOOK INTO EACHOTHER'S EYES FOREVER, NEVER TO TOUCH.
IF ONLY SOMEONE WOULD FORGIVE US!
THEN OUR LIPS COULD FINALLY MEET ONCE MORE!
PITY US! FREE US! FORGIVE US!
FORGIVE THEM FOR WHAT?
HURRY! MY HUSBAND IS COMING!
NOW THE SHADOWS OF HISTORY FLASH BEFORE ME.
THIS COUPLE STARTED CENTURIES OF VIOLENCE AND MAYHEM! I CAN FEEL IT!
HOW LONG HAVE THEY STAYED UP ON THIS HILL ASKING FOR FORGIVENESS?
PLEASE!
TREACHEROUS ADULTERERS!
BUT NOW THERE'S PEACE HERE. SURELY THEY'VE PAID FOR THEIR SINS...
OH PLEASE! FORGIVE US!
WHO AM I TO DECIDE THEIR FATE?
JUST LET ME LAY HERE UNTIL I DECIDE...
MY LUCK HAS WITHERED AWAY.

Chéri

Colette

ILLUSTRATION BY **Molly Crabapple**

WHEN THINKING OF SEXUALLY LIBERATED FRENCH women of letters, Anaïs Nin, Simone de Beauvoir, and Anne Desclos (a.k.a. Pauline Réage, author of *Story of O*) come easily to mind, but decades before they put pen to paper, Sidonie-Gabrielle Colette—known simply by her last name—was already making her scandalous mark. Married three times, carrying on openly with numerous lovers of all genders (among them were Josephine Baker and Colette's own teenage stepson), and at one point baring flesh as a performer at the legendary Moulin Rouge and other Paris music halls, this country girl from provincial France never stopped shaking up the establishment.

And then there were her books. "She published nearly eighty volumes of fiction, memoir, drama, essays, criticism, and reportage, among them perhaps a dozen masterpieces," wrote her biographer Judith Thurman, who said that Colette was "a pagan whose life and appetites were Olympian in their vitality." Colette referred to herself as an "erotic militant." Her primary themes were indeed sex, lust, and love—and all their complications—but she's also much admired for her evocations of nature and of childhood, and she even wrote the libretto for one of Ravel's operas. Her *New York Times* obituary noted: "A passionate lover of animals, especially cats, she was the author of 'Dialogue des bêtes.' This conversation-piece between a cat and a dog caused her to be compared with Rudyard Kipling as an animal writer. . . . Another novel, 'La Vagabonde,' was chosen in one critical rating as one of the dozen best French novels of the century."

During her stint as a journalist, she reported from the front lines of World War I (unheard of for a woman at the time) and broke the silence surrounding domestic violence. She was awarded many of France's highest literary/cultural honors, becoming the second female grand officer of the Legion of Honor, the first female president of the Goncourt Academy, and an awardee of the Grand Medal of the City of Paris, among other accolades.

Colette is best known to the English-speaking world for a smattering of works: her 1944 novella *Gigi*, the basis for the musical that won the 1958 Academy Award for Best Picture; *Chéri* (1920), in which a middle-aged courtesan initiates a young man into the ways of the world; and the megaselling, risqué (but not explicit) *Claudine* series of four novels from the first years of the twentieth century.

Artist Molly Crabapple knows something herself about making waves in society. She once locked herself in a hotel room for five days, using each waking moment to cover every square inch of the walls with art (the walls were themselves covered with huge sheets of butcher paper). Short-circuiting the age-old benefactor system in the fine arts, she raised over $65,000 through a Kickstarter campaign to produce a series of nine huge canvas paintings depicting the worldwide financial meltdown and the predatory capitalist system that caused it. She freely supplied the Occupy Wall Street movement with memorable graphics that were used on protest signs around the world, and she founded Dr. Sketchy's Anti-Art School, with worldwide chapters, allowing anyone regardless of talent or training to "draw glamorous underground performers in an atmosphere of boozy conviviality." In Volume 1 of *The Graphic Canon*, she illustrated one of her favorite novels, *Dangerous Liaisons*, and here she gives us an image from another of her favorites, also French: *Chéri*.

SOURCES

Colette. *The Complete Claudine*. Introduction by Judith Thurman. New York: Farrar, Straus and Giroux, 2001.

Taylor, Karen L. *Facts on File Companion to the French Novel*. New York: Facts on File, Inc., 2007.

Molly Crabapp

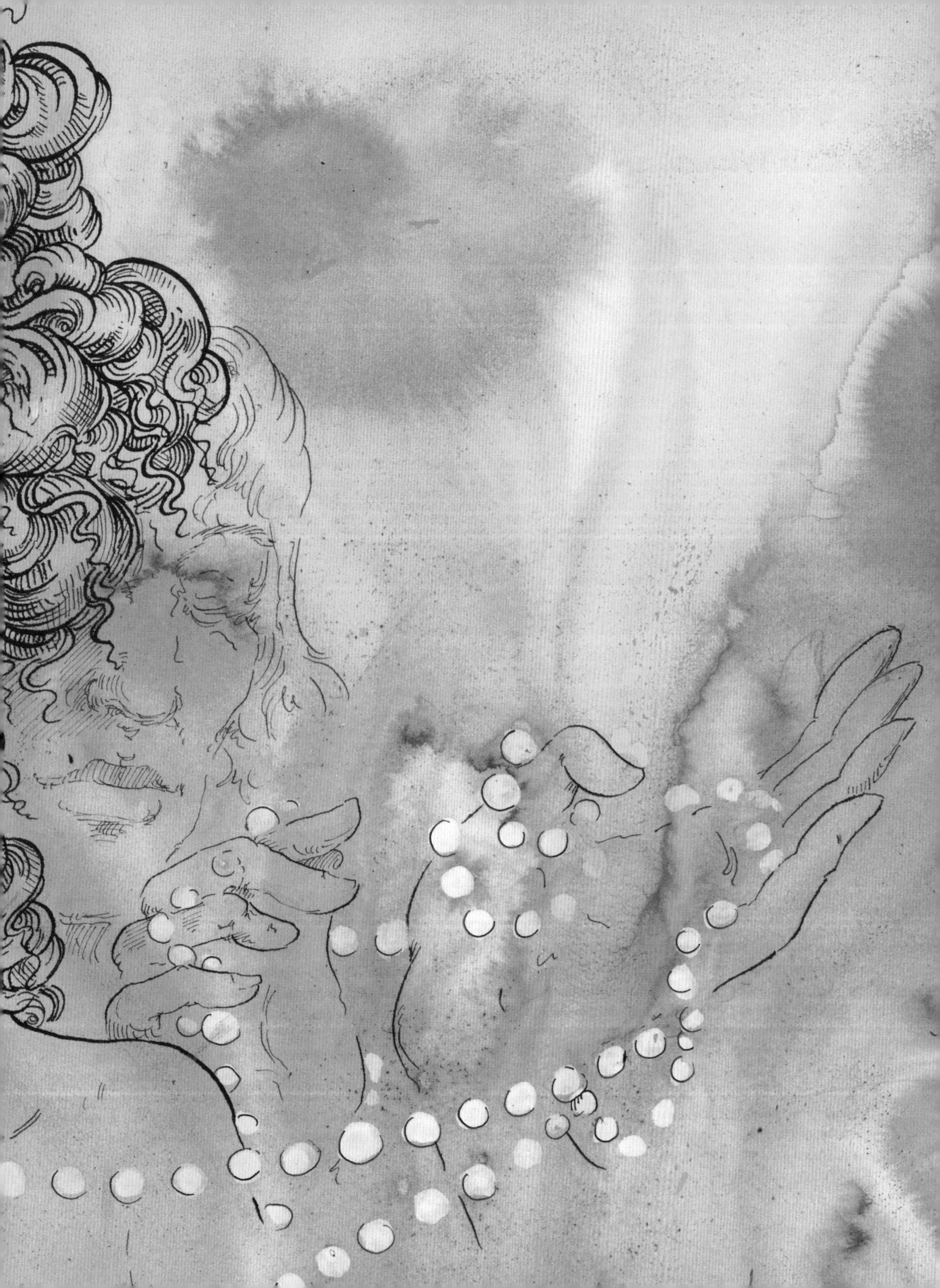

The Age of Innocence

Edith Wharton

ART/ADAPTATION BY **C. Frakes**

PERHAPS THE MOST LAUDED AMERICAN WOMAN of letters of her time, Edith Wharton wrote novels on many themes, but she's best known for her unflattering portraits of New York's blue bloods in the Gilded Age of the 1870s. Preeminent among these is her Pulitzer Prize–winning 1920 tome, *The Age of Innocence*. Newland Archer is about to enter into a predictable, upper-crust marriage to May Welland, but he finds himself dazzled and drawn to his fiancée's worldly, unorthodox cousin, Ellen Olenska, just back from Europe. C. Frakes gives us a beautifully colored, condensed version of the tale, with one-page takes on six key chapters. She writes:

Before getting into comics, I thought that I was going to be a costumer, and I was for two productions with the Tacoma Opera. *Age of Innocence* had been described to me before as half criticism on manners, half runway show—clothing plays a large part in the story, and works as a metaphor for the restrictiveness of New York society. When working on the comic, most of my research was on clothing. I learned a lot about the importance of hats and gloves, and also tried to "tag" each character with color—May starts out dressed in white, but goes from pink to red as her manipulative character starts to emerge.

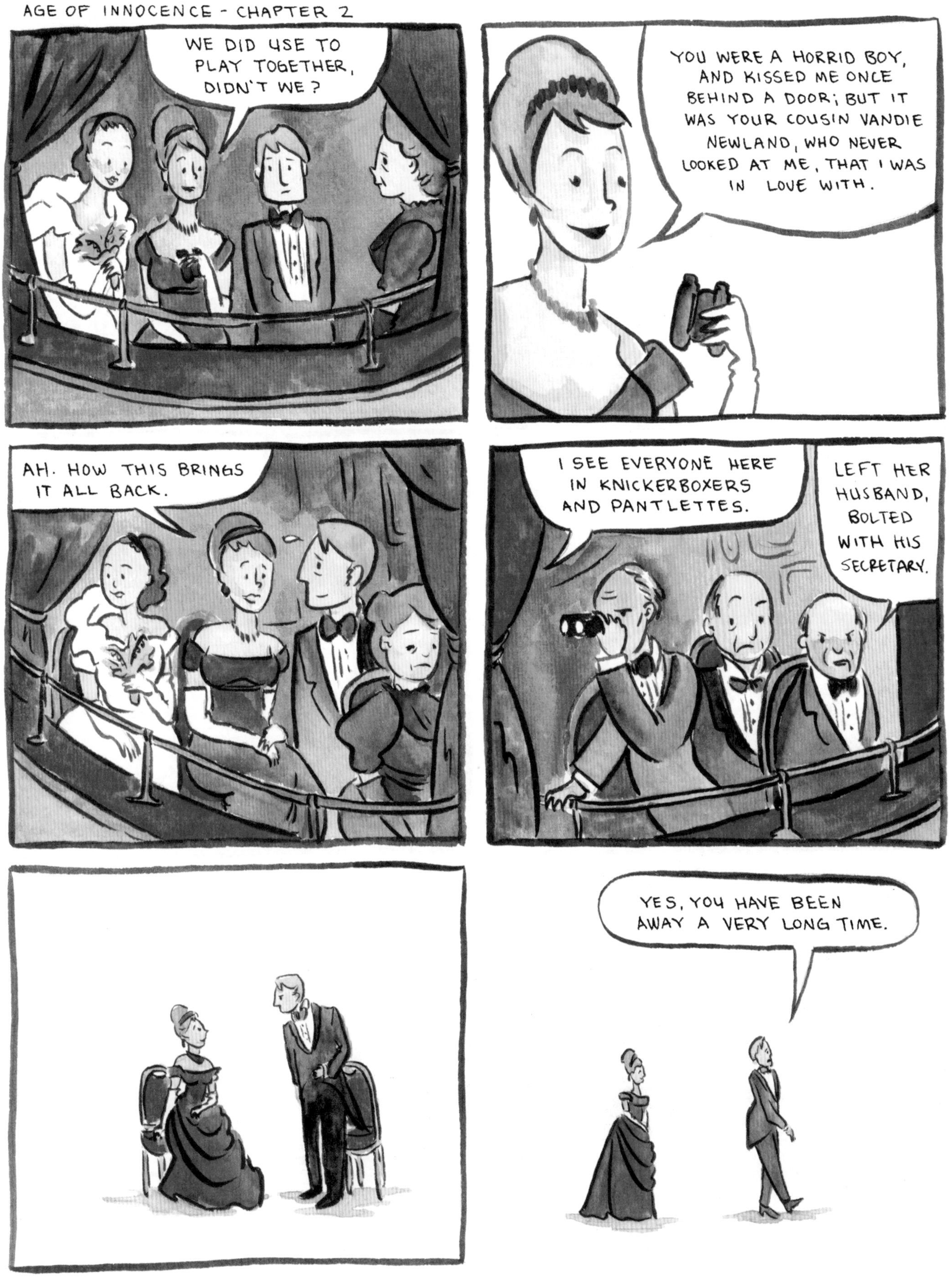
AGE OF INNOCENCE - CHAPTER 2
WE DID USE TO PLAY TOGETHER, DIDN'T WE?
YOU WERE A HORRID BOY, AND KISSED ME ONCE BEHIND A DOOR; BUT IT WAS YOUR COUSIN VANDIE NEWLAND, WHO NEVER LOOKED AT ME, THAT I WAS IN LOVE WITH.
AH. HOW THIS BRINGS IT ALL BACK.
I SEE EVERYONE HERE IN KNICKERBOXERS AND PANTLETTES.
LEFT HER HUSBAND, BOLTED WITH HIS SECRETARY.
YES, YOU HAVE BEEN AWAY A VERY LONG TIME.

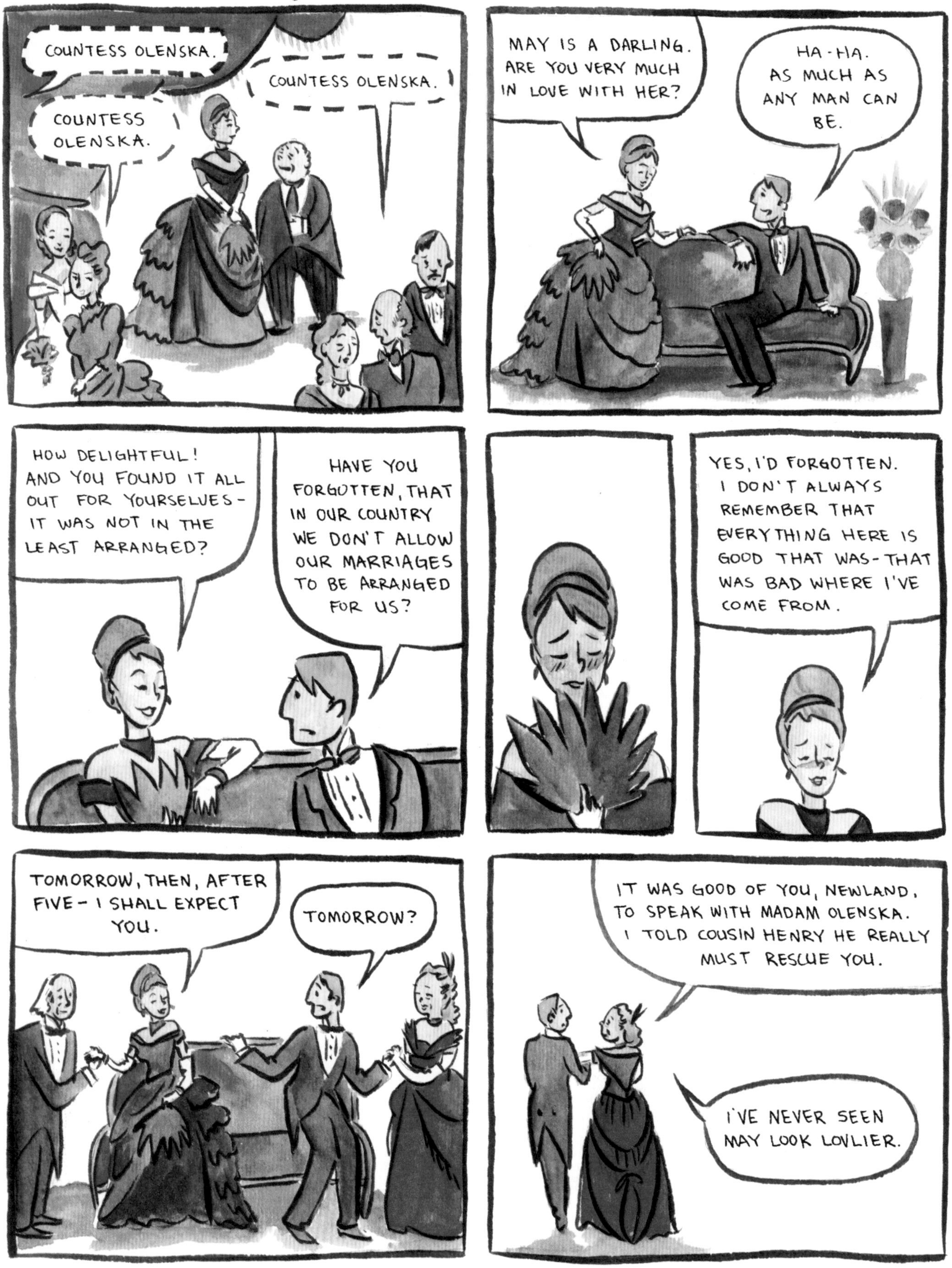
COUNTESS OLENSKA.
COUNTESS OLENSKA.
COUNTESS OLENSKA.
MAY IS A DARLING. ARE YOU VERY MUCH IN LOVE WITH HER?
HA-HA. AS MUCH AS ANY MAN CAN BE.
HOW DELIGHTFUL! AND YOU FOUND IT ALL OUT FOR YOURSELVES - IT WAS NOT IN THE LEAST ARRANGED?
HAVE YOU FORGOTTEN, THAT IN OUR COUNTRY WE DON'T ALLOW OUR MARRIAGES TO BE ARRANGED FOR US?
YES, I'D FORGOTTEN. I DON'T ALWAYS REMEMBER THAT EVERYTHING HERE IS GOOD THAT WAS - THAT WAS BAD WHERE I'VE COME FROM.
TOMORROW, THEN, AFTER FIVE - I SHALL EXPECT YOU.
TOMORROW?
IT WAS GOOD OF YOU, NEWLAND, TO SPEAK WITH MADAM OLENSKA. I TOLD COUSIN HENRY HE REALLY MUST RESCUE YOU.
I'VE NEVER SEEN MAY LOOK LOVLIER.

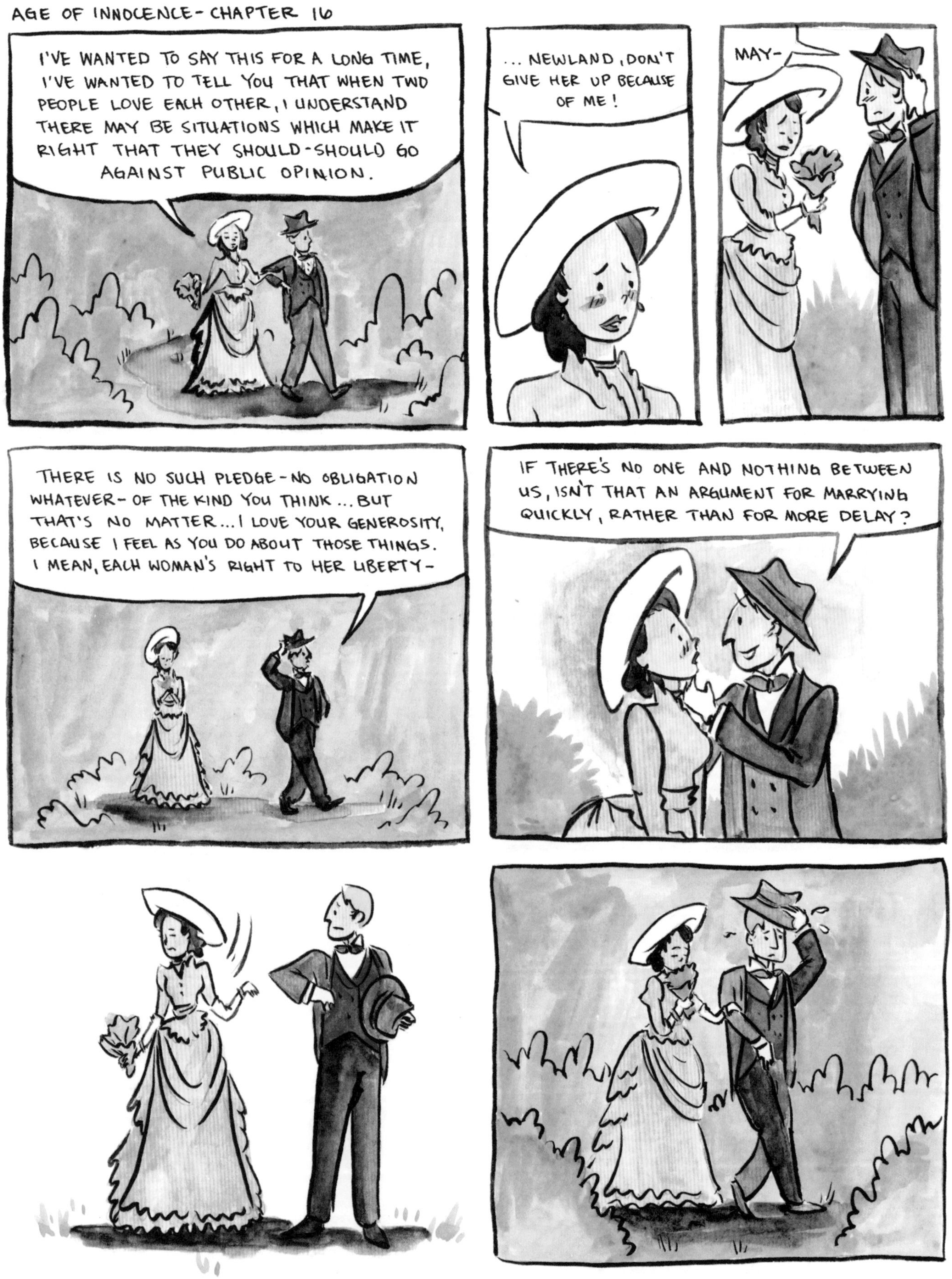
AGE OF INNOCENCE - CHAPTER 16
I'VE WANTED TO SAY THIS FOR A LONG TIME, I'VE WANTED TO TELL YOU THAT WHEN TWO PEOPLE LOVE EACH OTHER, I UNDERSTAND THERE MAY BE SITUATIONS WHICH MAKE IT RIGHT THAT THEY SHOULD-SHOULD GO AGAINST PUBLIC OPINION.
... NEWLAND, DON'T GIVE HER UP BECAUSE OF ME!
MAY-
THERE IS NO SUCH PLEDGE - NO OBLIGATION WHATEVER - OF THE KIND YOU THINK ... BUT THAT'S NO MATTER ... I LOVE YOUR GENEROSITY, BECAUSE I FEEL AS YOU DO ABOUT THOSE THINGS. I MEAN, EACH WOMAN'S RIGHT TO HER LIBERTY-
IF THERE'S NO ONE AND NOTHING BETWEEN US, ISN'T THAT AN ARGUMENT FOR MARRYING QUICKLY, RATHER THAN FOR MORE DELAY?

AGE OF INNOCENCE- CHAPTER 28

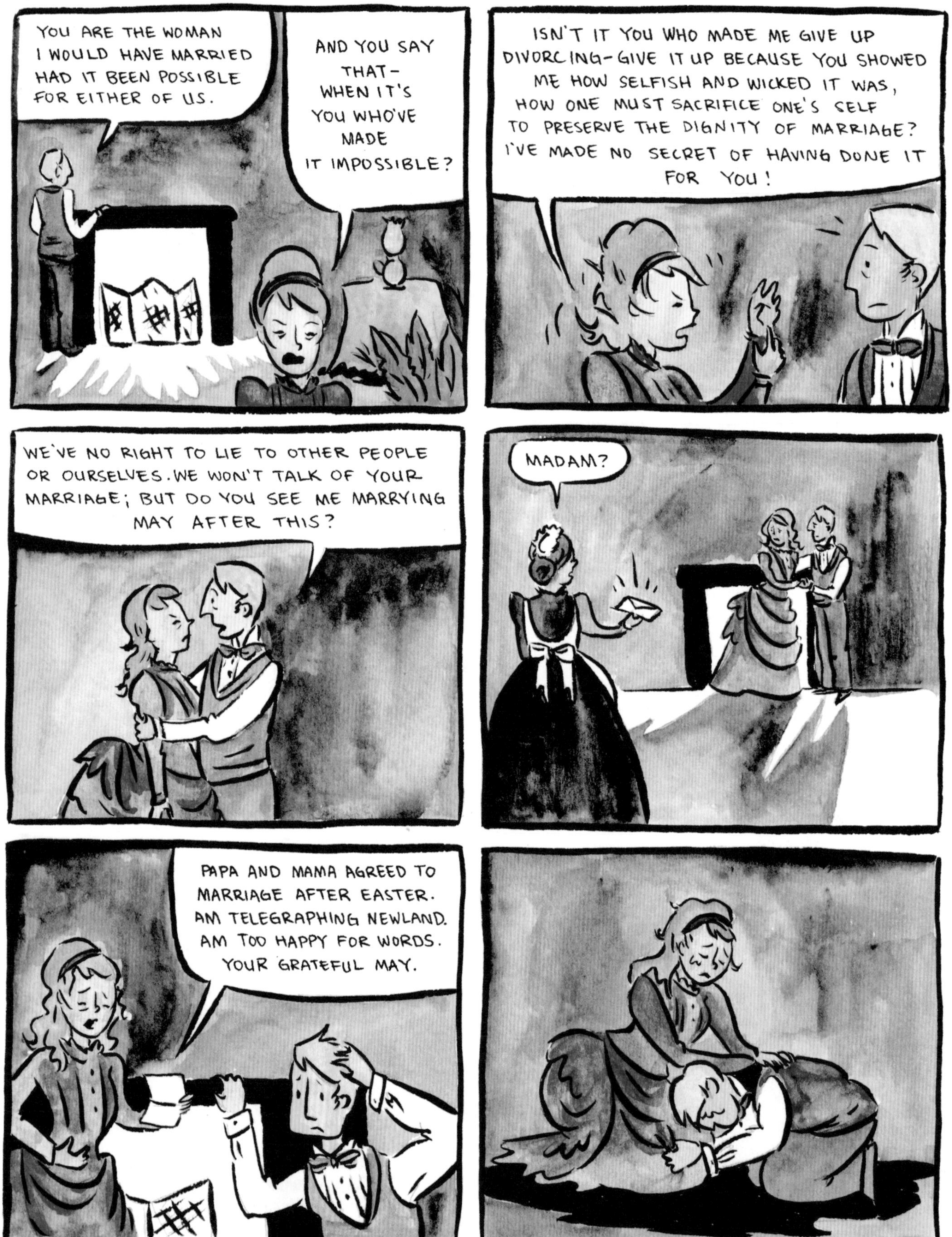
YOU ARE THE WOMAN I WOULD HAVE MARRIED HAD IT BEEN POSSIBLE FOR EITHER OF US.
AND YOU SAY THAT- WHEN IT'S YOU WHO'VE MADE IT IMPOSSIBLE?
ISN'T IT YOU WHO MADE ME GIVE UP DIVORCING- GIVE IT UP BECAUSE YOU SHOWED ME HOW SELFISH AND WICKED IT WAS, HOW ONE MUST SACRIFICE ONE'S SELF TO PRESERVE THE DIGNITY OF MARRIAGE? I'VE MADE NO SECRET OF HAVING DONE IT FOR YOU!
WE'VE NO RIGHT TO LIE TO OTHER PEOPLE OR OURSELVES. WE WON'T TALK OF YOUR MARRIAGE; BUT DO YOU SEE ME MARRYING MAY AFTER THIS?
MADAM?
PAPA AND MAMA AGREED TO MARRIAGE AFTER EASTER. AM TELEGRAPHING NEWLAND. AM TOO HAPPY FOR WORDS. YOUR GRATEFUL MAY.

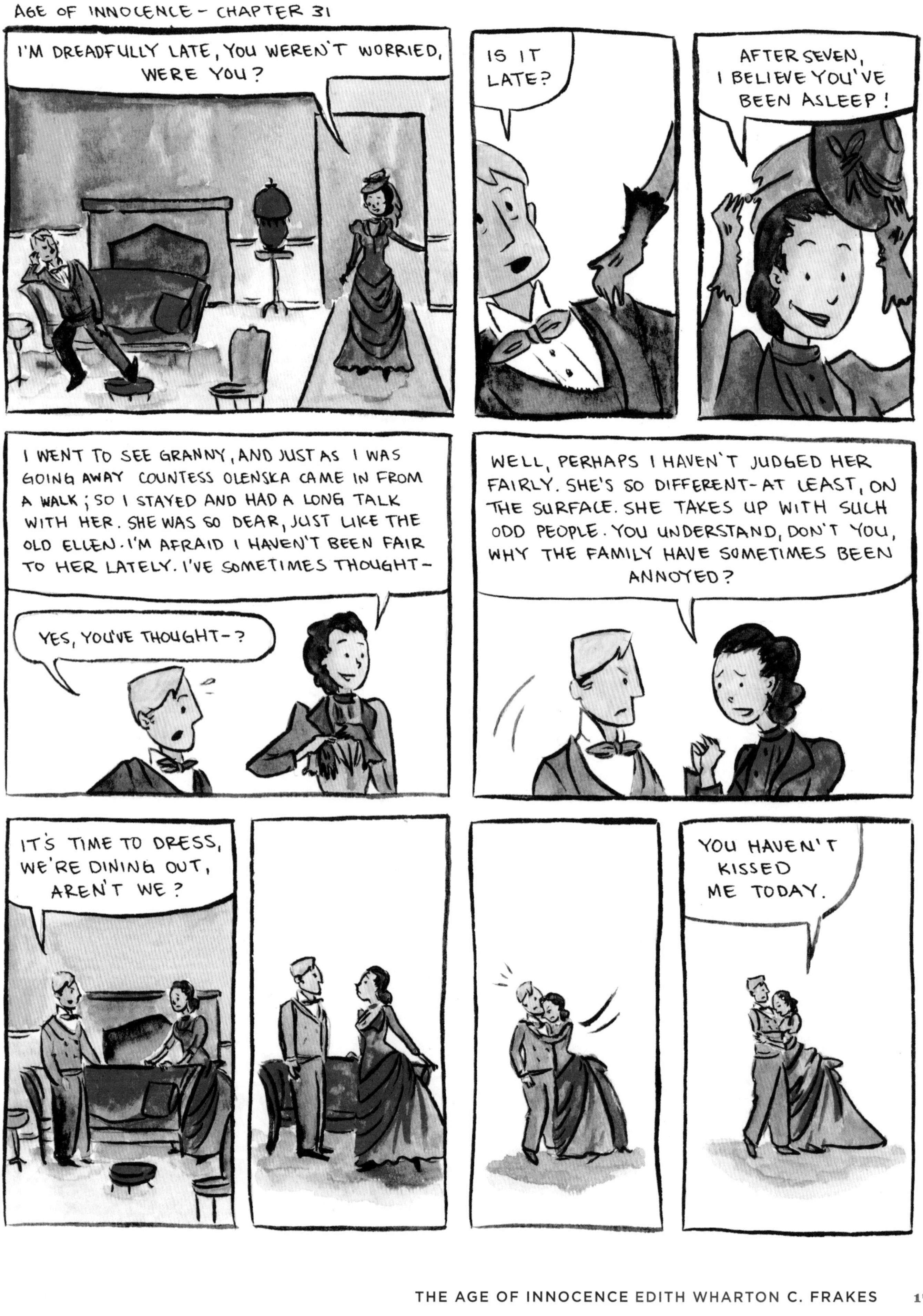
AGE OF INNOCENCE - CHAPTER 31
I'M DREADFULLY LATE, YOU WEREN'T WORRIED, WERE YOU?
IS IT LATE?
AFTER SEVEN, I BELIEVE YOU'VE BEEN ASLEEP!
I WENT TO SEE GRANNY, AND JUST AS I WAS GOING AWAY COUNTESS OLENSKA CAME IN FROM A WALK; SO I STAYED AND HAD A LONG TALK WITH HER. SHE WAS SO DEAR, JUST LIKE THE OLD ELLEN. I'M AFRAID I HAVEN'T BEEN FAIR TO HER LATELY. I'VE SOMETIMES THOUGHT-
YES, YOU'VE THOUGHT-?
WELL, PERHAPS I HAVEN'T JUDGED HER FAIRLY. SHE'S SO DIFFERENT- AT LEAST, ON THE SURFACE. SHE TAKES UP WITH SUCH ODD PEOPLE. YOU UNDERSTAND, DON'T YOU, WHY THE FAMILY HAVE SOMETIMES BEEN ANNOYED?
IT'S TIME TO DRESS, WE'RE DINING OUT, AREN'T WE?
YOU HAVEN'T KISSED ME TODAY.

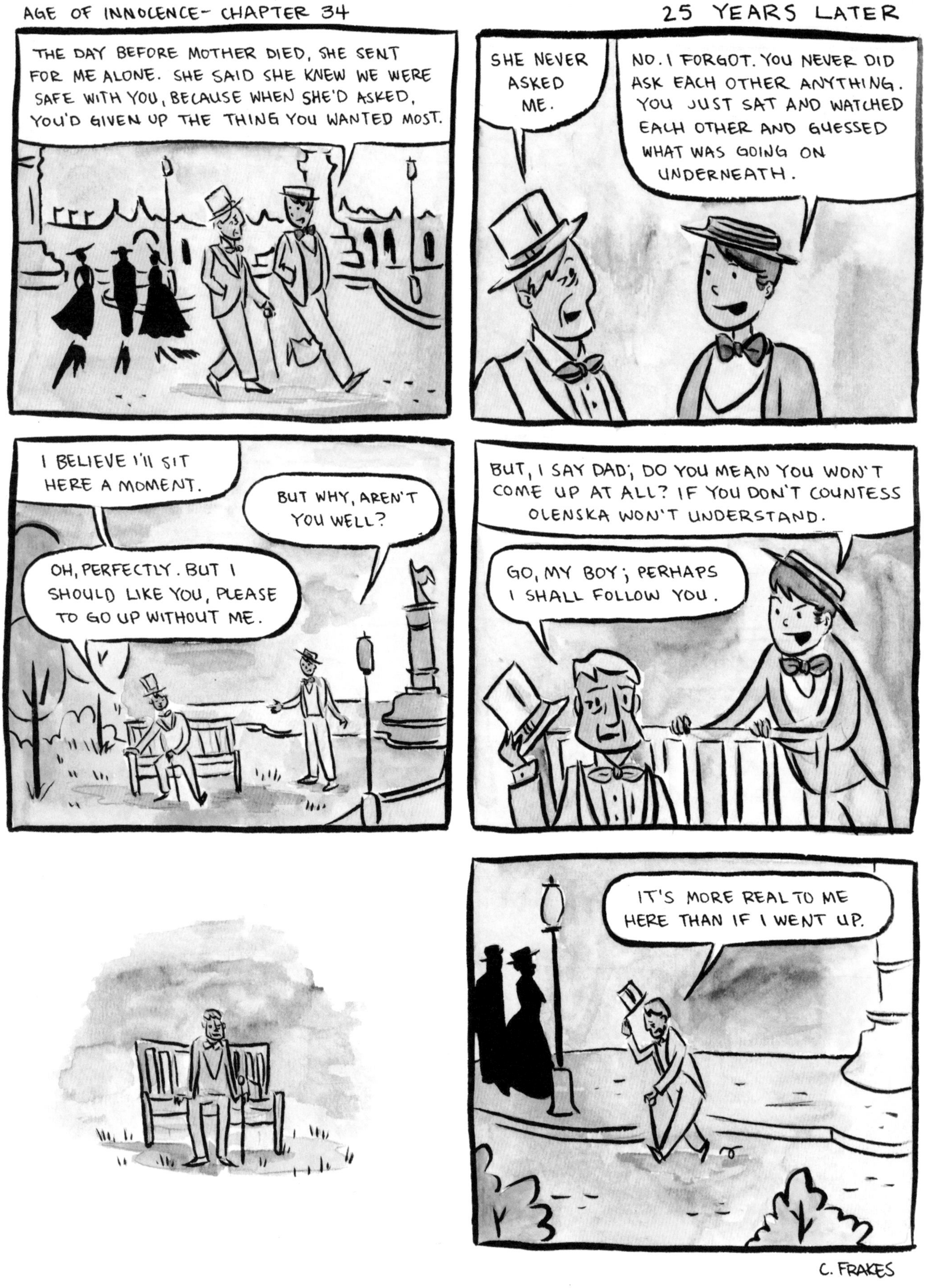
AGE OF INNOCENCE- CHAPTER 34
25 YEARS LATER
THE DAY BEFORE MOTHER DIED, SHE SENT FOR ME ALONE. SHE SAID SHE KNEW WE WERE SAFE WITH YOU, BECAUSE WHEN SHE'D ASKED, YOU'D GIVEN UP THE THING YOU WANTED MOST.
SHE NEVER ASKED ME.
NO. I FORGOT. YOU NEVER DID ASK EACH OTHER ANYTHING. YOU JUST SAT AND WATCHED EACH OTHER AND GUESSED WHAT WAS GOING ON UNDERNEATH.
I BELIEVE I'LL SIT HERE A MOMENT.
BUT WHY, AREN'T YOU WELL?
OH, PERFECTLY. BUT I SHOULD LIKE YOU, PLEASE TO GO UP WITHOUT ME.
BUT, I SAY DAD; DO YOU MEAN YOU WON'T COME UP AT ALL? IF YOU DON'T COUNTESS OLENSKA WON'T UNDERSTAND.
GO, MY BOY; PERHAPS I SHALL FOLLOW YOU.
IT'S MORE REAL TO ME HERE THAN IF I WENT UP.
C. FRAKES

"Dulce et Decorum Est"

Wilfred Owen

ADAPTATION BY **Jason Cobley**

LINE WORK BY **John Blake**

COLORING BY **Michael Reid**

LETTERING BY **Greg Powell**

WILFRED OWEN FOUGHT IN THE FIELD AND IN THE trenches during World War I, and the poetry he wrote is widely regarded as the finest to have sprung from that maelstrom. While recuperating from shell-shock (and from having his best friend blown to pieces right beside him), the young British poet-turned-soldier began writing unflinching, unromantic verse about the realities of war. No visions of grand heroics here—just brutal reportage of young men sent into a slaughterhouse. ("I have suffered seventh hell," he wrote to his mother.) After recovering for a year, during which he wrote most of his mature poems—including "Dulce et Decorum Est" and "Anthem for Doomed Youth"—Owen was sent back to the front. While taking part in an assault on German lines, he was killed exactly one week before the Armistice that ended the war. He was twenty-five.

Only five of his poems were published during his lifetime, the vast majority arriving posthumously, including "Dulce et Decorum Est," written in 1917 but not published until 1920. Collections of his poems (and several biographies and studies) remain in print to this day, testifying to the unfortunate timelessness of the subject of war's horrors.

Adapter Jason Cobley, artist John Blake, colorist Michael Reid, and letterer Greg Powell put forth a team effort to provide this gruesome adaptation of Owen's unsparing account of watching a comrade die horribly from an asphyxiating gas (most likely chlorine, which forms hydrochloric acid when coming into contact with moisture in the lungs and eyes).

SOURCE

Hibberd, Dominic. *Wilfred Owen: A New Biography*. Chicago: Ivan R. Dee, 2003.

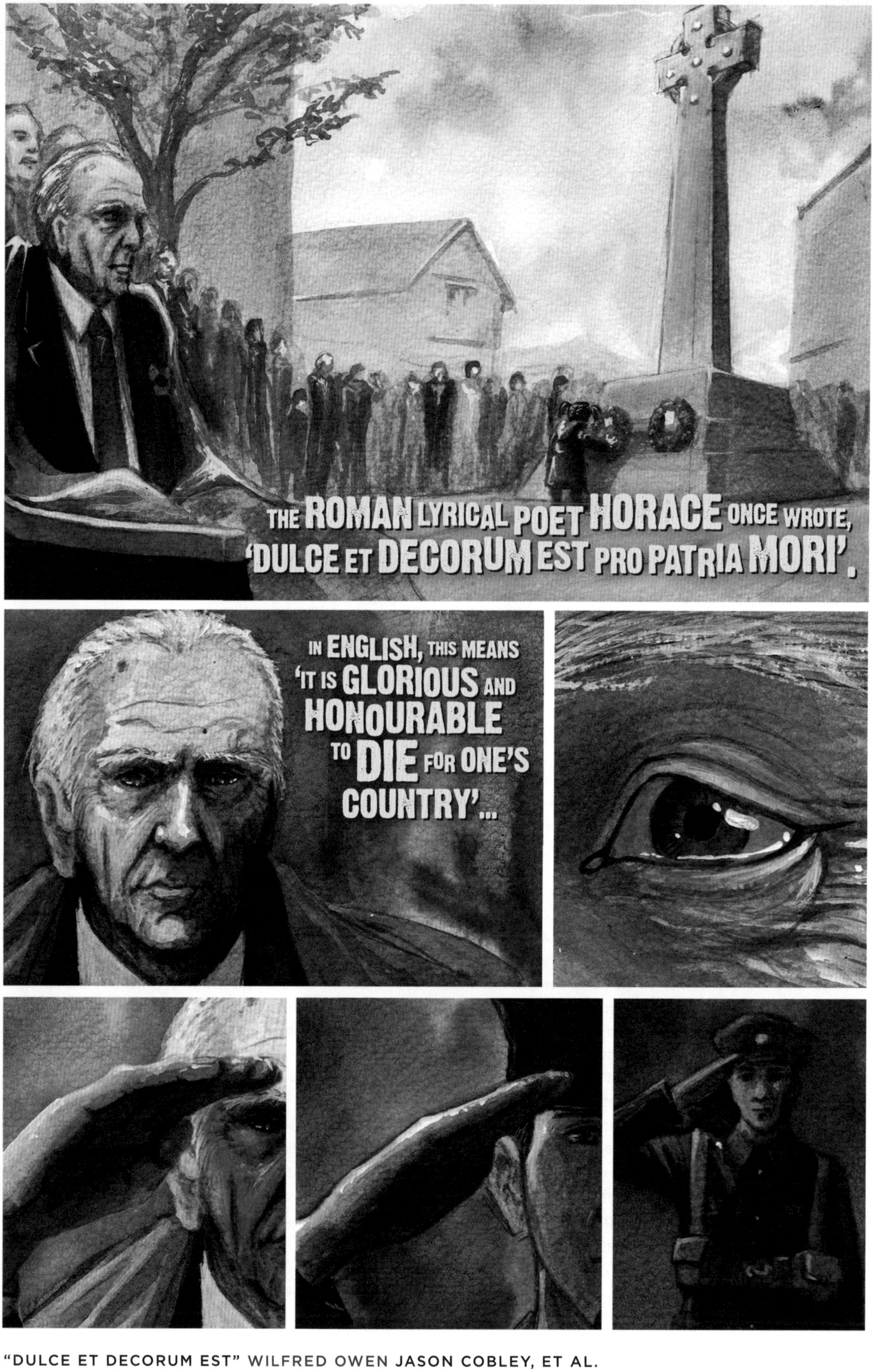
THE ROMAN LYRICAL POET HORACE ONCE WROTE,
'DULCE ET DECORUM EST PRO PATRIA MORI'.
IN ENGLISH, THIS MEANS 'IT IS GLORIOUS AND HONOURABLE TO DIE FOR ONE'S COUNTRY'...

'DULCE ET DECORUM EST'

BY WILFRED OWEN.

BENT DOUBLE, LIKE OLD BEGGARS UNDER SACKS,

KNOCK-KNEED, COUGHING LIKE HAGS, WE CURSED THROUGH SLUDGE,

TILL ON THE HAUNTING FLARES WE TURNED OUR BACKS

AND TOWARDS OUR DISTANT REST BEGAN TO TRUDGE.

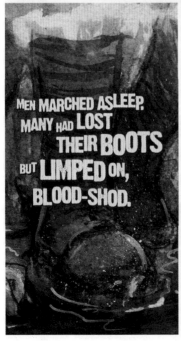

MEN MARCHED ASLEEP. MANY HAD LOST THEIR BOOTS BUT LIMPED ON, BLOOD-SHOD.

ALL WENT LAME; ALL BLIND; DRUNK WITH FATIGUE; DEAF EVEN TO THE HOOTS

OF TIRED, OUTSTRIPPED FIVE-NINES THAT DROPPED BEHIND.

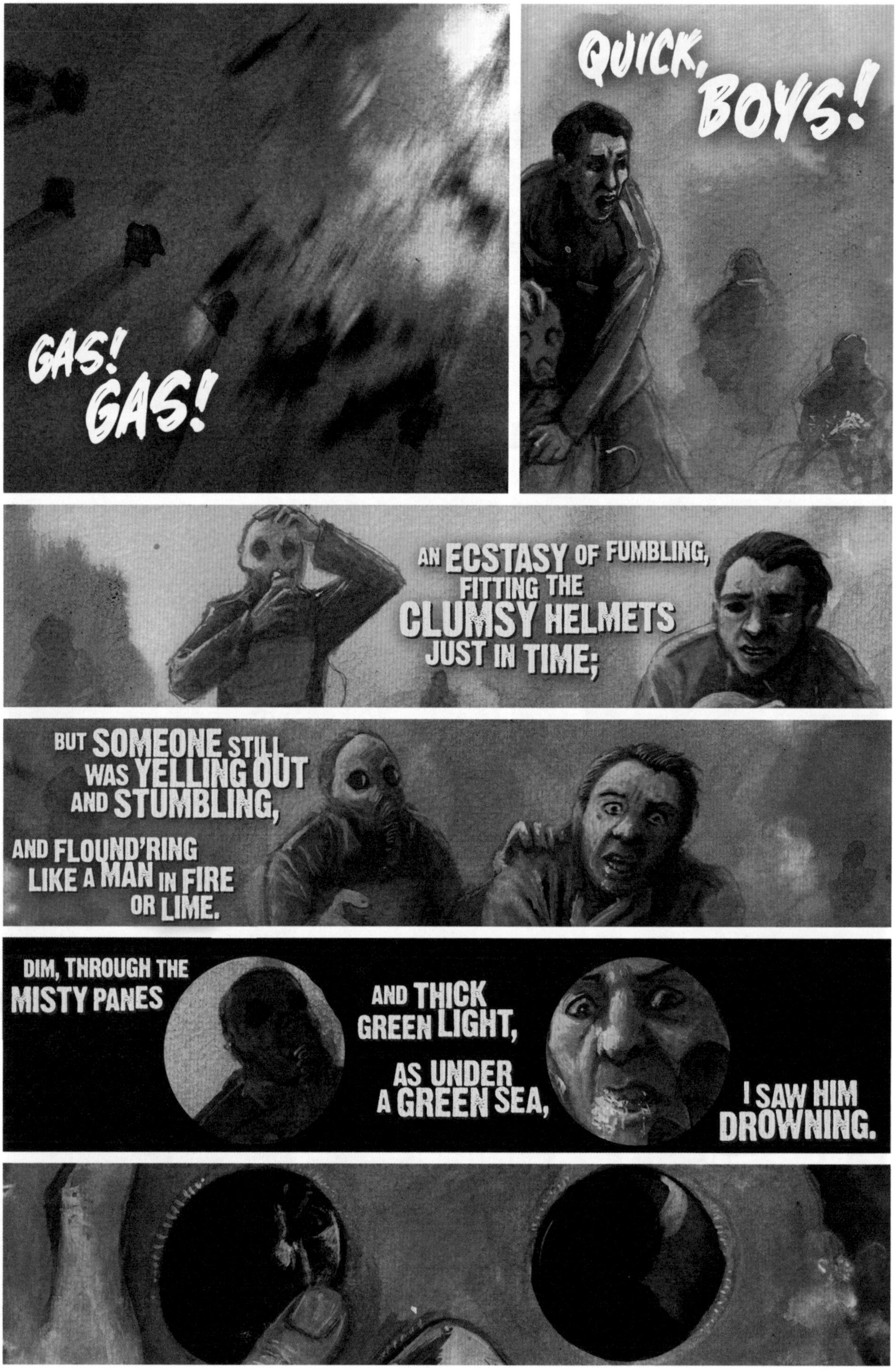
GAS! GAS!
QUICK, BOYS!
AN ECSTASY OF FUMBLING, FITTING THE CLUMSY HELMETS JUST IN TIME;
BUT SOMEONE STILL WAS YELLING OUT AND STUMBLING,
AND FLOUND'RING LIKE A MAN IN FIRE OR LIME.
DIM, THROUGH THE MISTY PANES
AND THICK GREEN LIGHT,
AS UNDER A GREEN SEA,
I SAW HIM DROWNING.

IN ALL MY **DREAMS,** BEFORE MY **HELPLESS SIGHT,** HE **PLUNGES** AT **ME,**

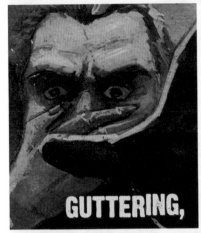

GUTTERING,

CHOKING,

DROWNING.

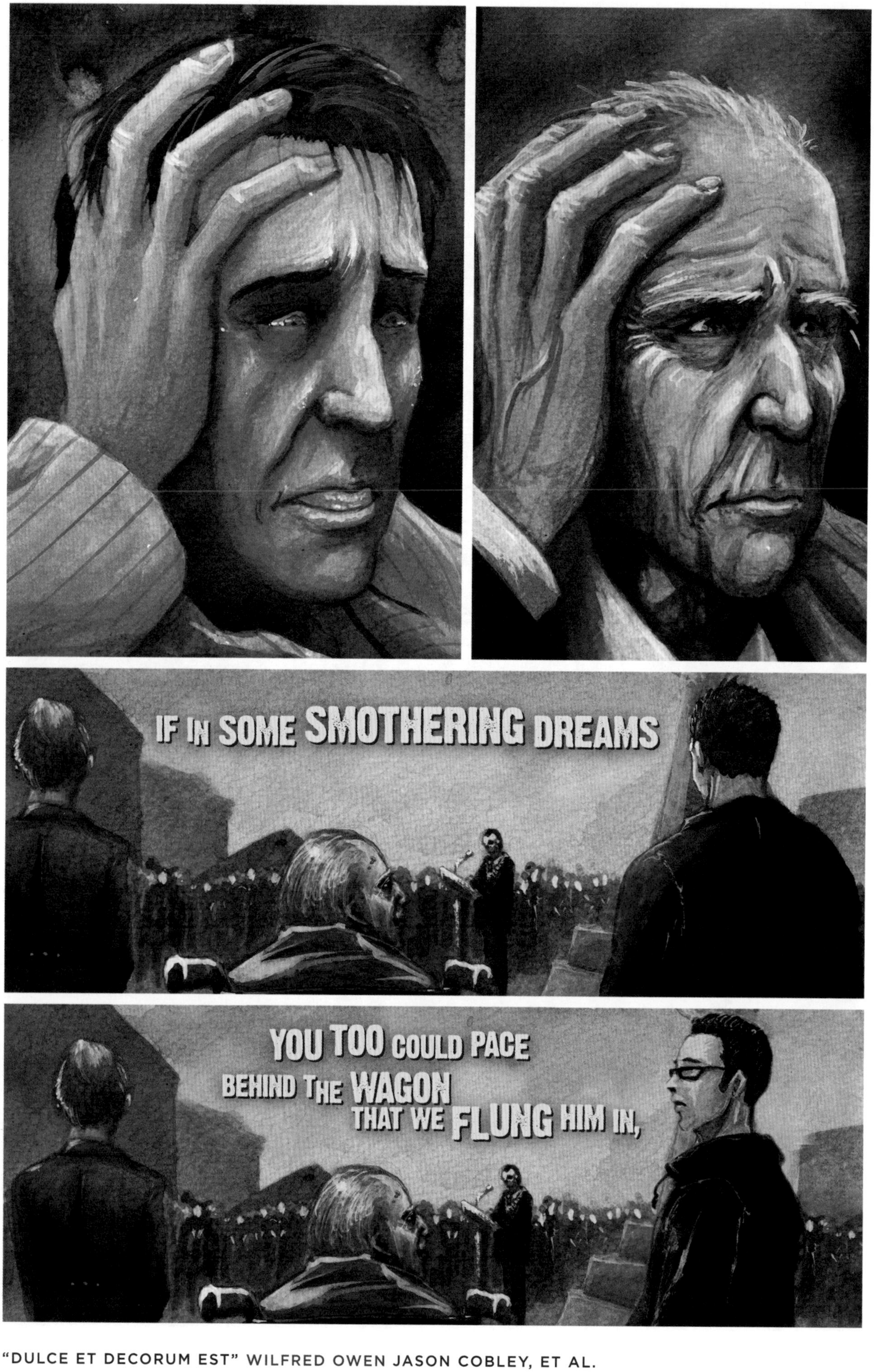
IF IN SOME SMOTHERING DREAMS
YOU TOO COULD PACE
BEHIND THE WAGON
THAT WE FLUNG HIM IN,

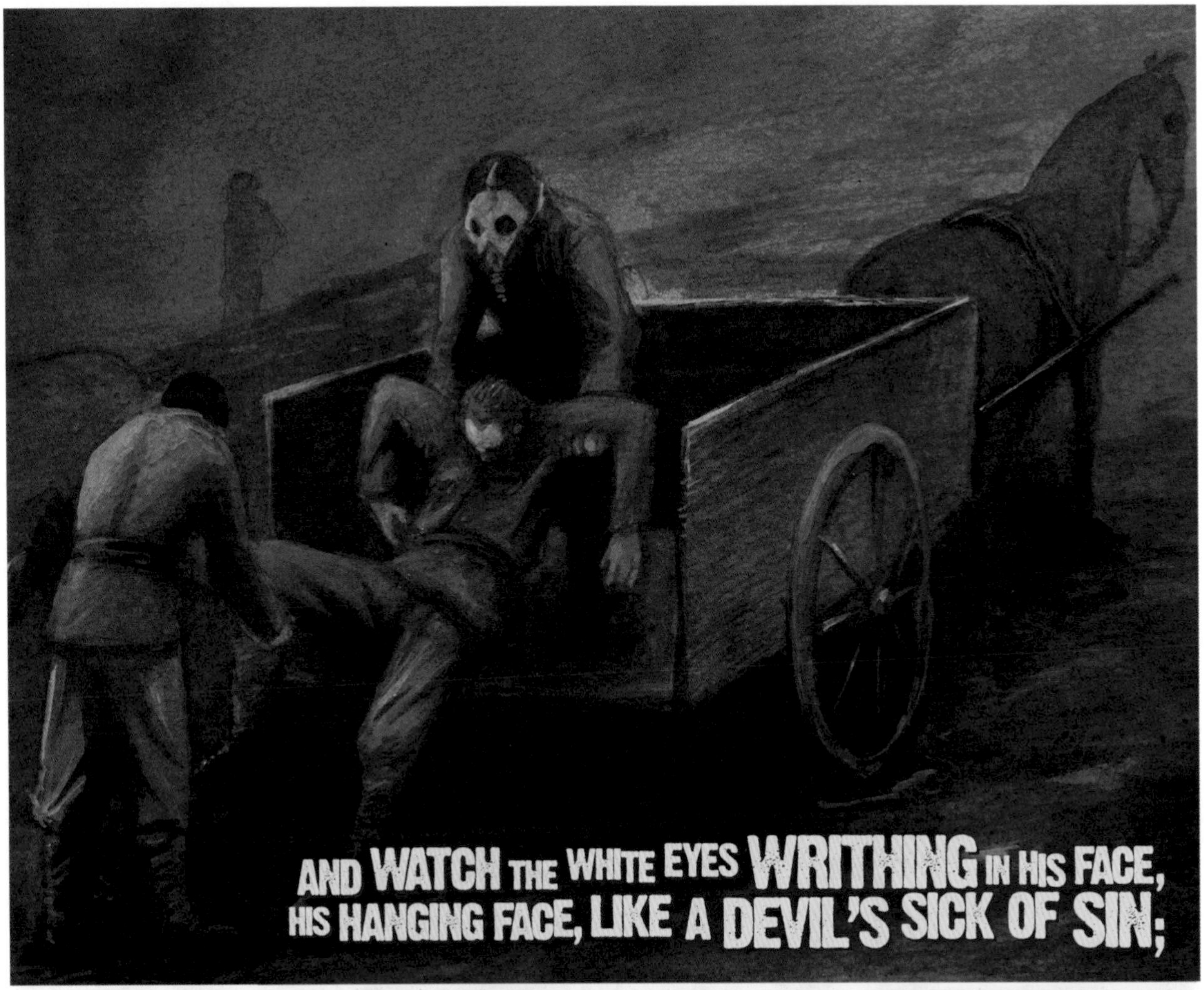
AND WATCH THE WHITE EYES WRITHING IN HIS FACE,
HIS HANGING FACE, LIKE A DEVIL'S SICK OF SIN;

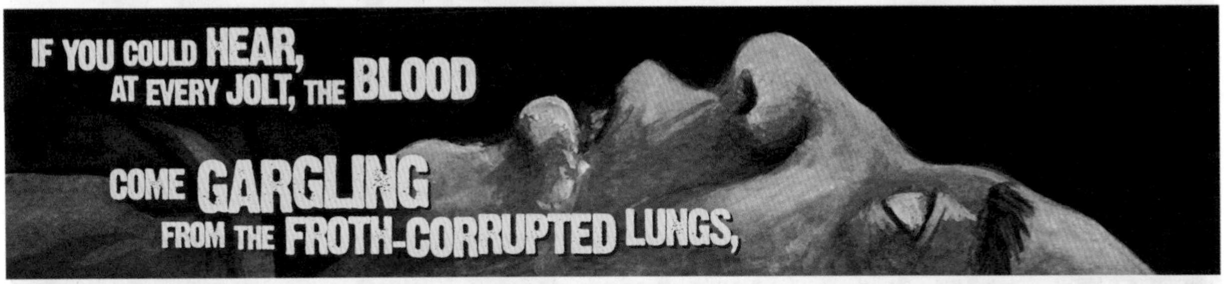
IF YOU COULD HEAR,
AT EVERY JOLT, THE BLOOD
COME GARGLING
FROM THE FROTH-CORRUPTED LUNGS,

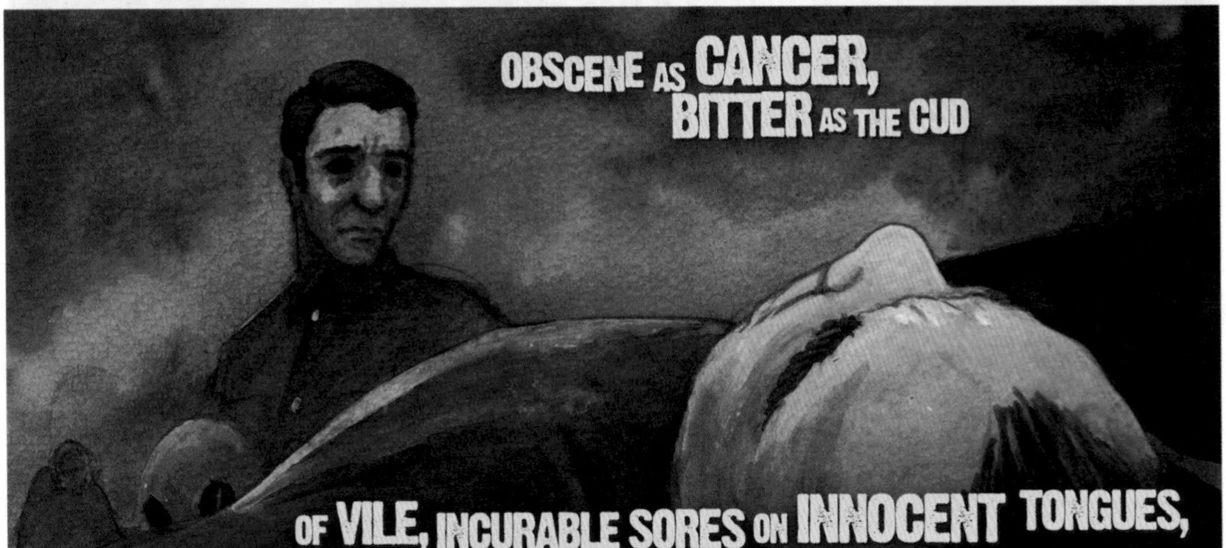
OBSCENE AS CANCER,
BITTER AS THE CUD
OF VILE, INCURABLE SORES ON INNOCENT TONGUES,

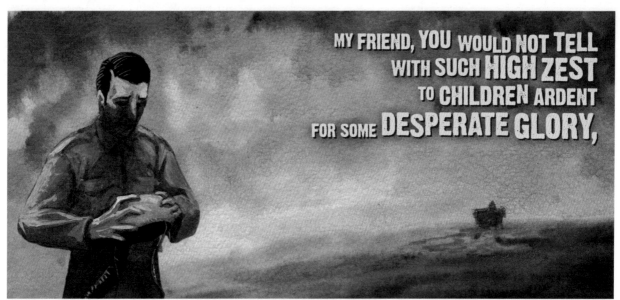

MY FRIEND, YOU WOULD NOT TELL WITH SUCH HIGH ZEST TO CHILDREN ARDENT FOR SOME DESPERATE GLORY,

THE OLD LIE:

DULCE ET DECORUM EST PRO PATRIA MORI.

ADAPTATION: JASON COBLEY
LINEWORK: JOHN BLAKE
COLOURING: MICHAEL REID
LETTERING: GREG POWELL

W. B. Yeats

ART/ADAPTATION BY **Anthony Ventura**

WILLIAM BUTLER YEATS, ONE OF THE TWENTIETH century's greatest poets (not to mention a heavyweight playwright) and winner of the Nobel Prize in Literature, is typically regarded as a Modernist, but his overt mystical leanings mean that he doesn't fit comfortably in that category. He was a member of the Order of the Golden Dawn, one of the most infamous occult/magickal secret societies, and it's thought that he helped create the most popular Tarot deck, the Rider-Waite. He studied (and practiced) numerous mystical belief systems, conducted séances, and wrote a classic work of esotericism, *A Vision*. His wife provided the nucleus of this work with several days' worth of channeled arcana via automatic writing; Yeats then spent years expounding on this material to build a comprehensive spiritual belief system.

That idiosyncratic system underlies one of the most popular, most reprinted poems of the twentieth century, "The Second Coming." It tells of the violent, anarchic end of our current age and the beginning of another. The title and the start of the second verse give us false hope: Surely Jesus is about to return. Surely we're about to witness a (R)evelation and the establishment of a peaceful kingdom on Earth. Nope. No dawning age of peace and prosperity. Instead, it's more brutality, more unending war, genocide, and hatred. A Second Coming is about to happen, but it's not Jesus returning; rather, a monstrosity is revealed—the Sphinx rising from the desert sands and lumbering to the Holy Land. The alarming, apocalyptic tone—and the bleak view of human nature—is soul-crushing.

This short poem, published in 1920, has given us several famous phrases: "the center cannot hold," "things fall apart," "rough beast," and "slouching toward Bethlehem." Again, Anthony Ventura has created a magazine-style spread for a classic poem, and he's filled this one with appropriately visceral, threatening images.

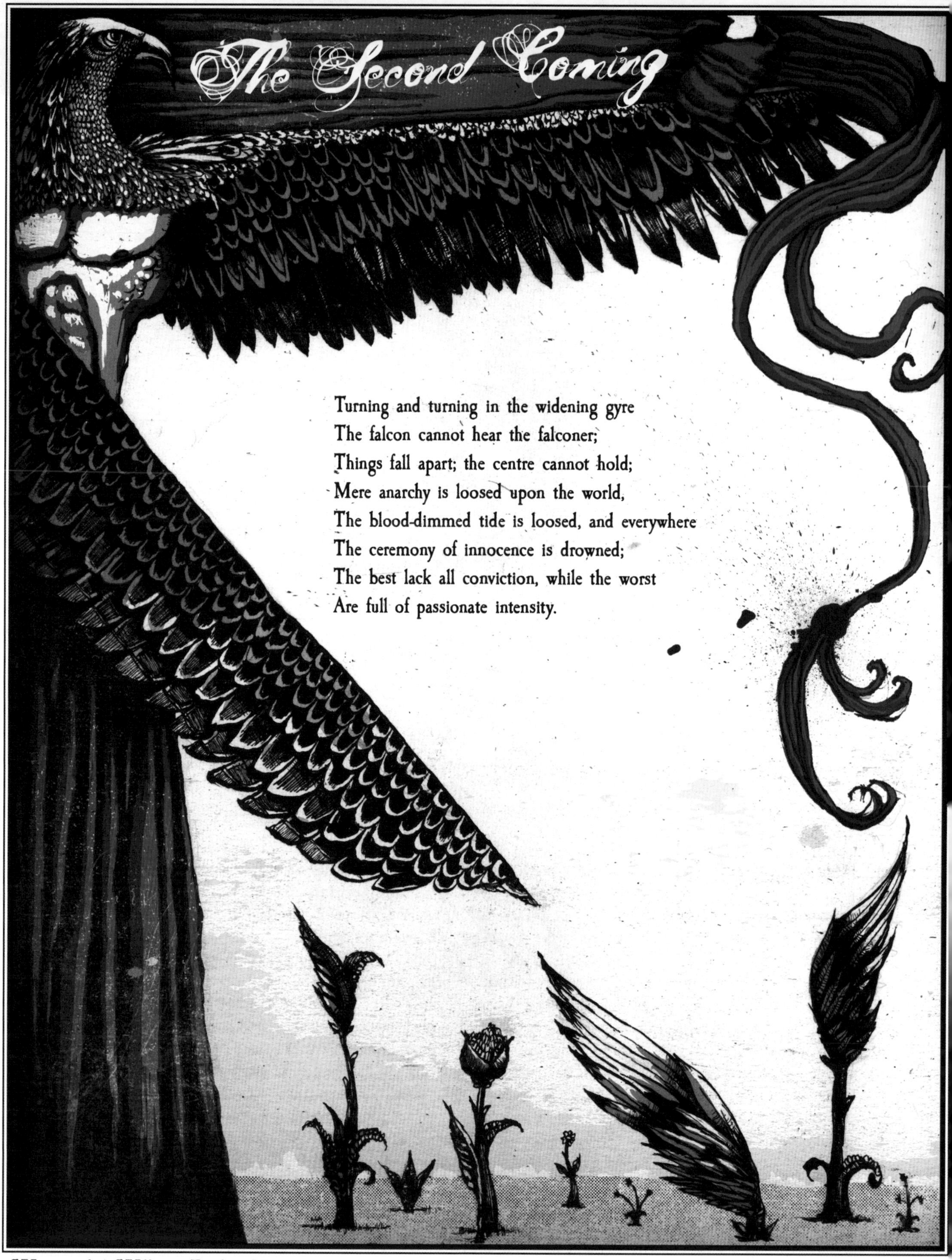
The Second Coming
Turning and turning in the widening gyre
The falcon cannot hear the falconer;
Things fall apart; the centre cannot hold;
Mere anarchy is loosed upon the world,
The blood-dimmed tide is loosed, and everywhere
The ceremony of innocence is drowned;
The best lack all conviction, while the worst
Are full of passionate intensity.

Written by William Butler Yeats

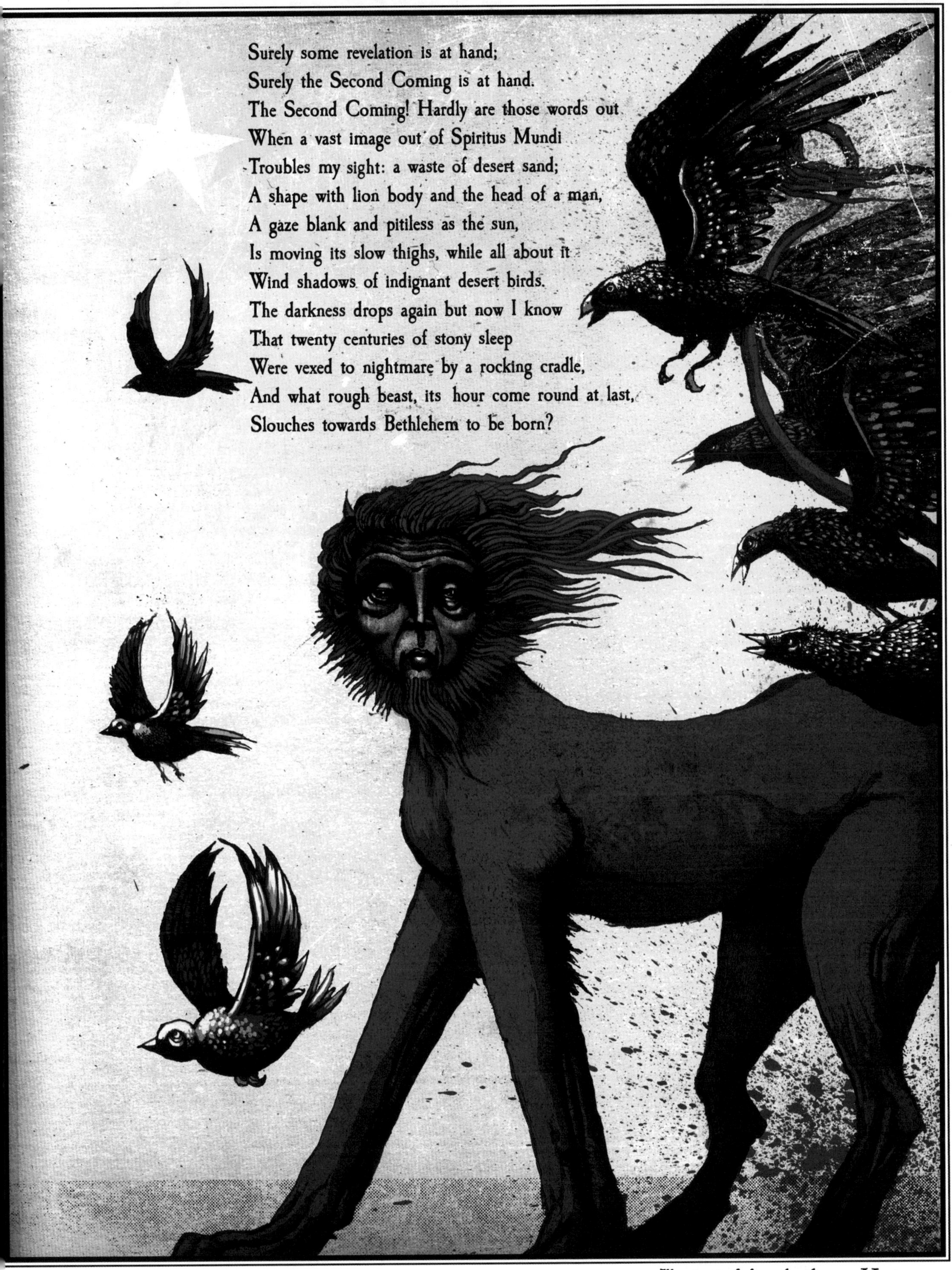
Surely some revelation is at hand;
Surely the Second Coming is at hand.
The Second Coming! Hardly are those words out
When a vast image out of Spiritus Mundi
Troubles my sight: a waste of desert sand;
A shape with lion body and the head of a man,
A gaze blank and pitiless as the sun,
Is moving its slow thighs, while all about it
Wind shadows of indignant desert birds.
The darkness drops again but now I know
That twenty centuries of stony sleep
Were vexed to nightmare by a rocking cradle,
And what rough beast, its hour come round at last,
Slouches towards Bethlehem to be born?

Illustrated by Anthony Ventura.

"The Penitent" and "The Singing-Woman from the Wood's Edge"

Edna St. Vincent Millay

ART/ADAPTATIONS BY **Joy Kolitsky**

FEROCIOUSLY INTELLIGENT, MULTI-TALENTED, and independent, Edna St. Vincent Millay is one of those literary figures—like Lord Byron and Hemingway—whose outsize life threatens to overshadow her writing. She acted, played piano beautifully, wrote song lyrics and an opera libretto, engaged in radical left-wing politics, and composed Pulitzer Prize–winning poetry that fused Modernist (and modern) outlooks with strong, traditional senses of rhythm, rhyme, and structure (she was particularly adept at the sonnet). And she was determined to live life to the fullest; one of her most famous poems, the quatrain "First Fig," goes like this:

> My candle burns at both ends;
> It will not last the night;
> But ah, my foes, and oh, my friends—
> It gives a lovely light.

In the biography *Savage Beauty*, Nancy Milford wrote:

> Edna St. Vincent Millay became the herald of the New Woman. She smoked in public when it was against the law for women to do so, she lived in Greenwich Village during the halcyon days of that starry bohemia, she slept with men and women and wrote about it in lyrics and sonnets that blazed with wit and a sexual daring that captivated the nation:

> I shall forget you presently, my dear,
> So make the most of this, your little day,
> Your little month, your little half a year,
> Ere I forget, or die, or move away,
> And we are done forever; by and by
> I shall forget you, as I said . . .

"Renascence"—the poem that first brought her national attention, in 1912 at the tender age of twenty—is a mystical poem for the ages, about a transcendent experience of oneness leading to a spiritual death and rebirth. She switched gears in the years leading up to 1920, writing beautifully crafted, brazen poems about female sexuality and independence. It is two of these poems—"The Penitent" and "The Singing-Woman from the Wood's Edge"— that Joy Kolitsky chose to adapt. When I found Joy's illustrations for *The New York Times Book Review*, *The Progressive*, children's books, and her own line of greeting cards, I was convinced she would turn in something amazing; and I was right.

SOURCE

Milford, Nancy. *Savage Beauty: The Life of Edna St. Vincent Millay.* New York: Random House, 2001.

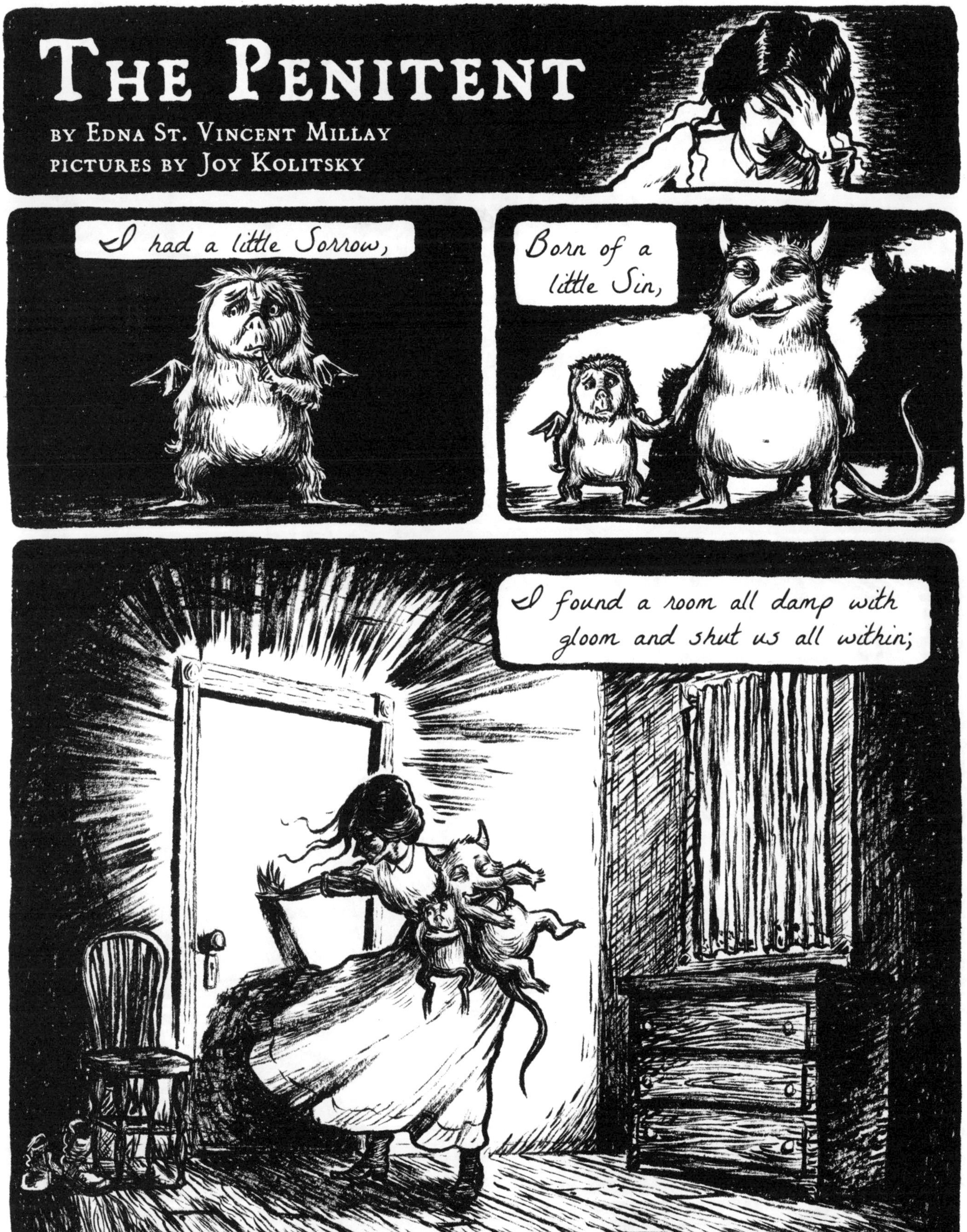
THE PENITENT
BY EDNA ST. VINCENT MILLAY
PICTURES BY JOY KOLITSKY
I had a little Sorrow,
Born of a little Sin,
I found a room all damp with gloom and shut us all within;

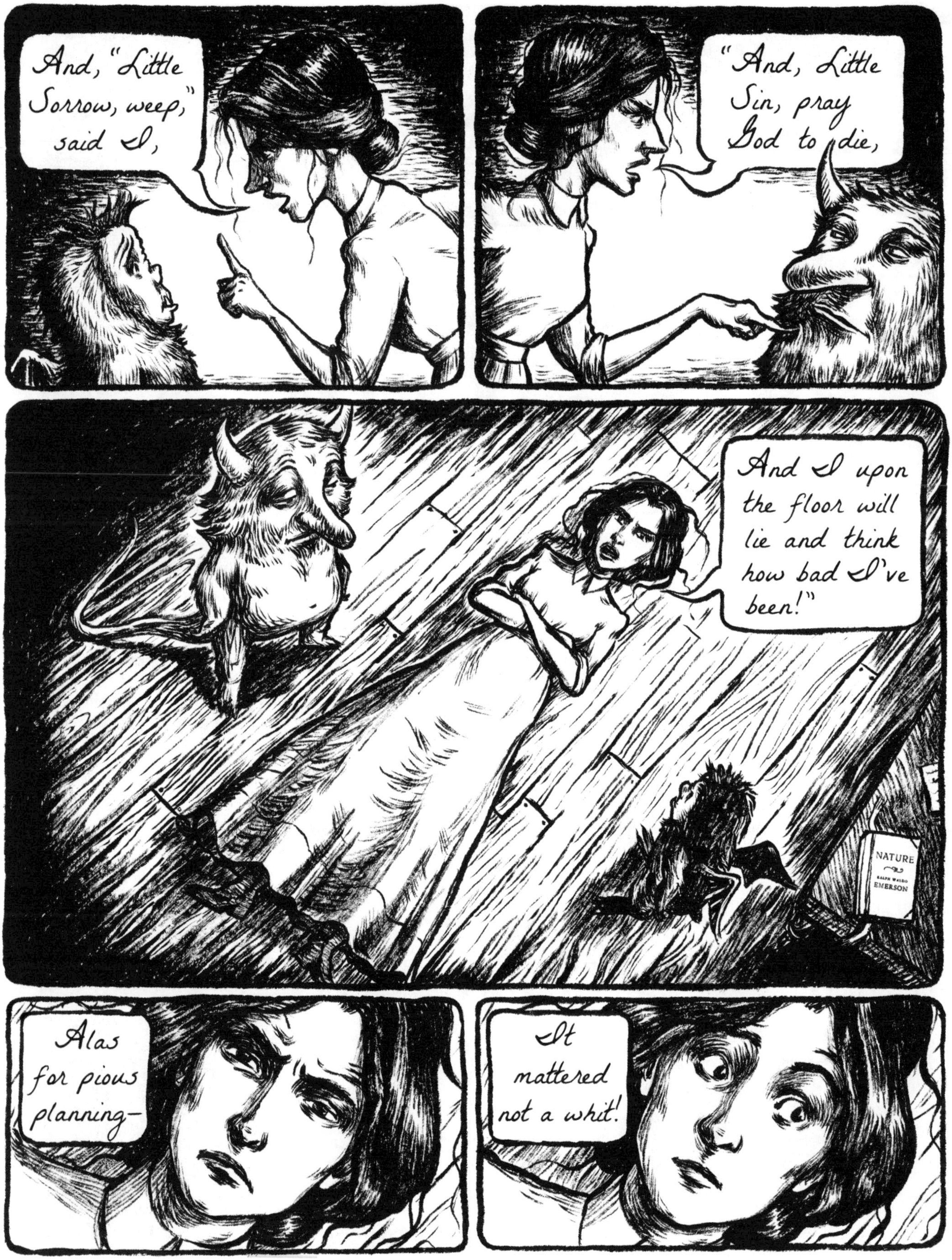
And, "Little Sorrow, weep," said I,
"And, Little Sin, pray God to die,
And I upon the floor will lie and think how bad I've been!"
NATURE
RALPH WALDO EMERSON
Alas for pious planning—
It mattered not a whit!

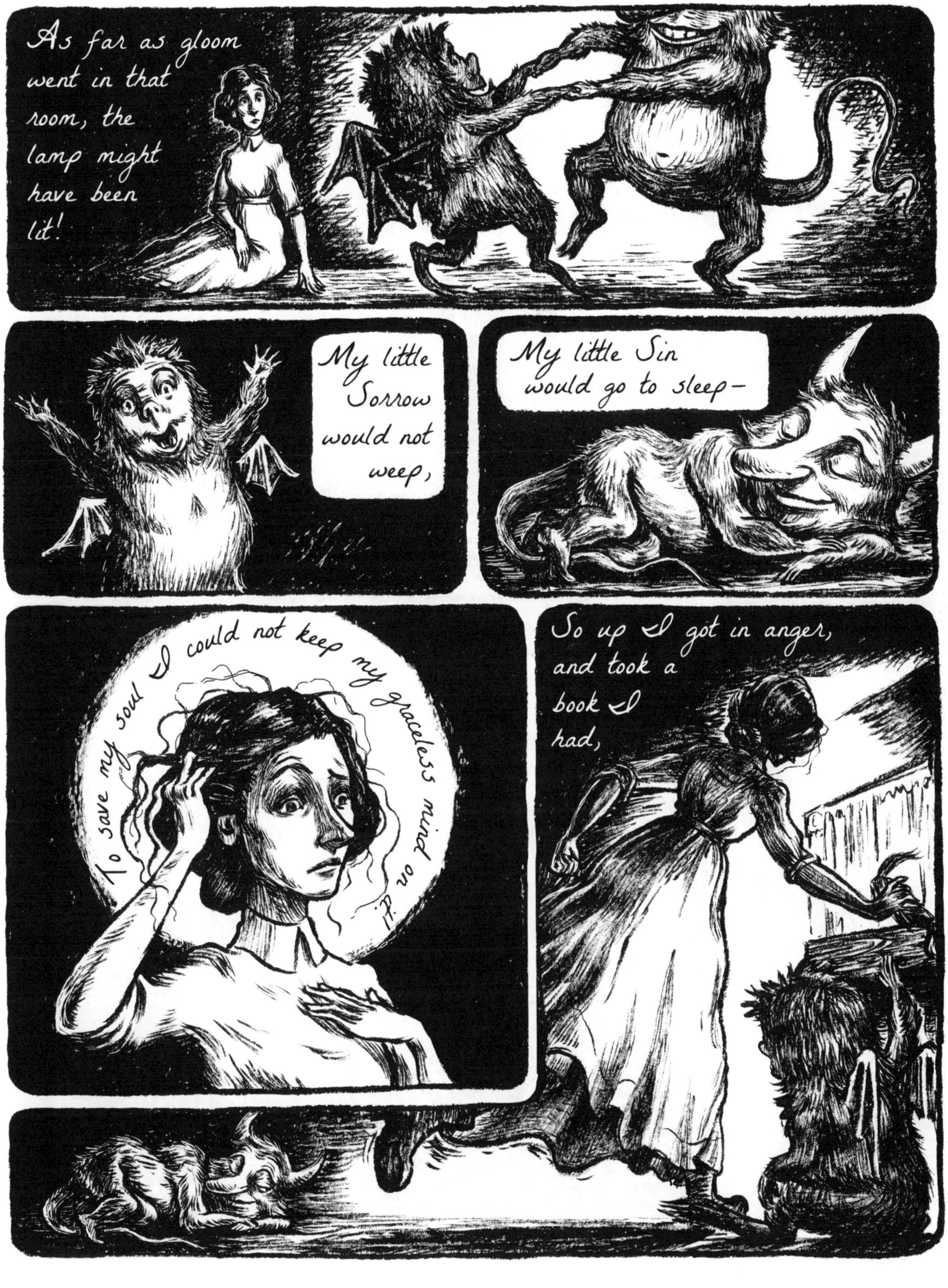
As far as gloom went in that room, the lamp might have been lit!
My little Sorrow would not weep,
My little Sin would go to sleep—
To save my soul I could not keep my graceless mind on it.
So up I got in anger, and took a book I had,

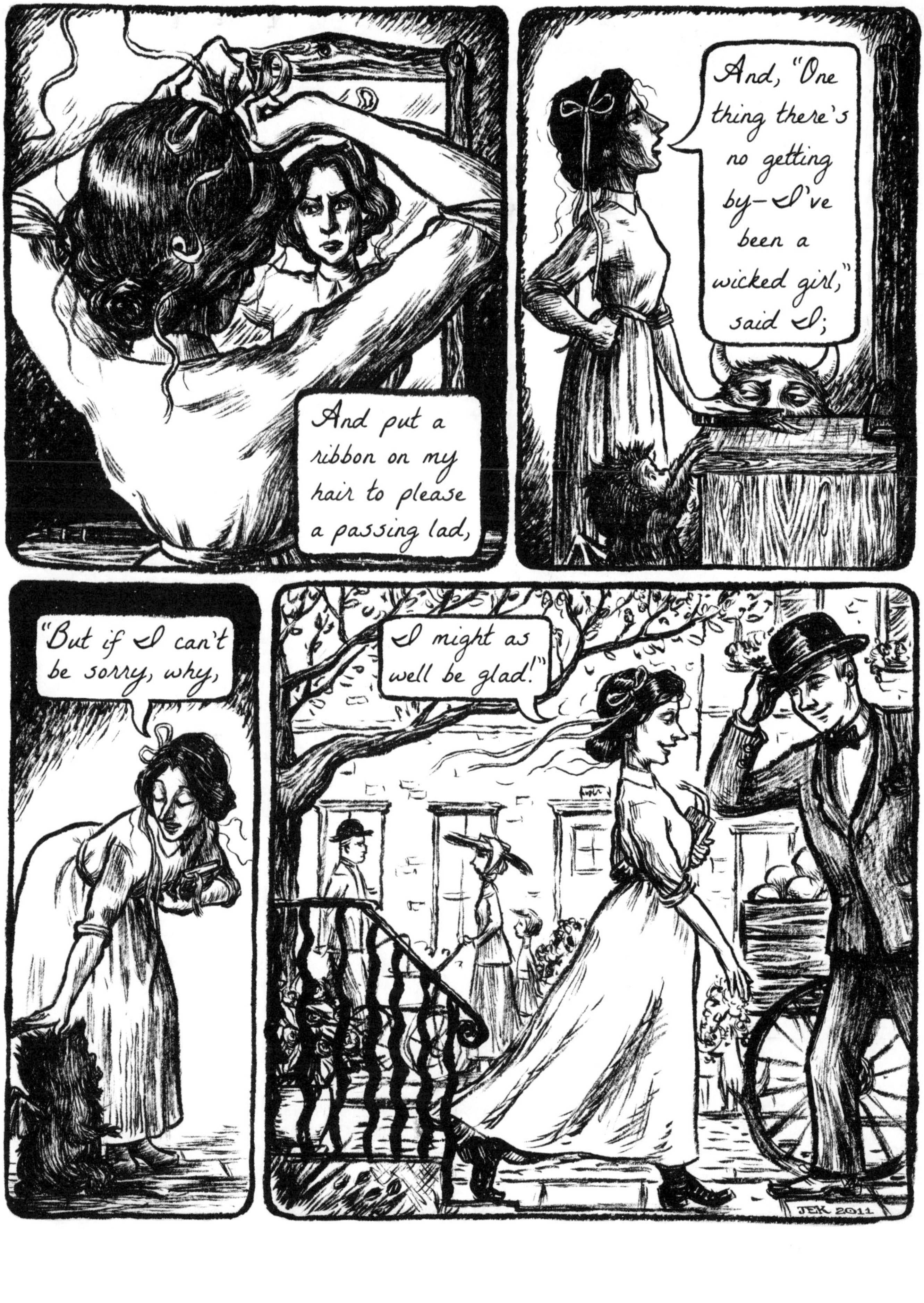
And put a ribbon on my hair to please a passing lad,
And, "One thing there's no getting by—I've been a wicked girl," said I;
"But if I can't be sorry, why,
I might as well be glad!"
JEK 2011

The Singing-Woman From the Wood's Edge

by Edna St. Vincent Millay • pictures by Joy Kolitsky

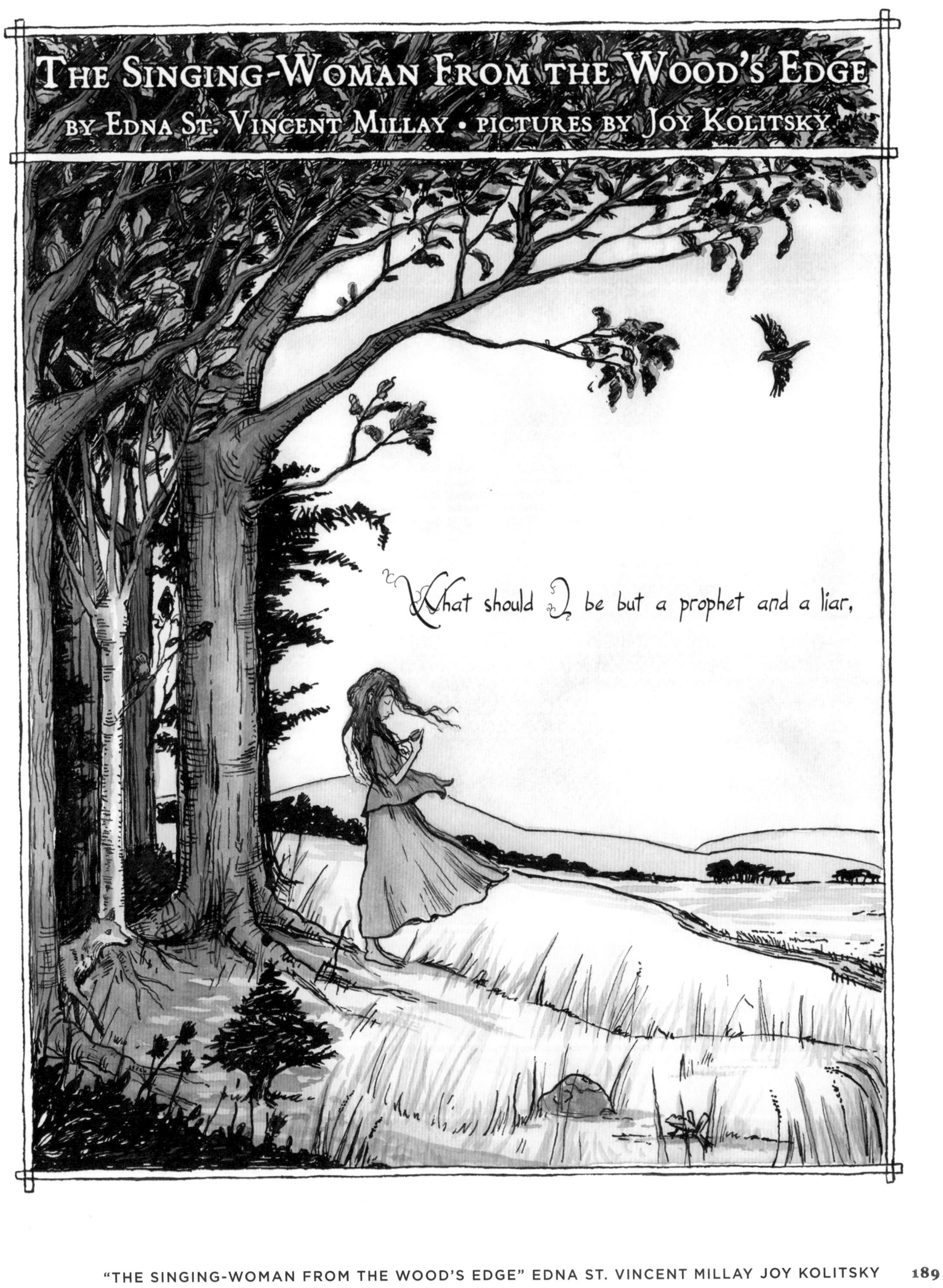
What should I be but a prophet and a liar,

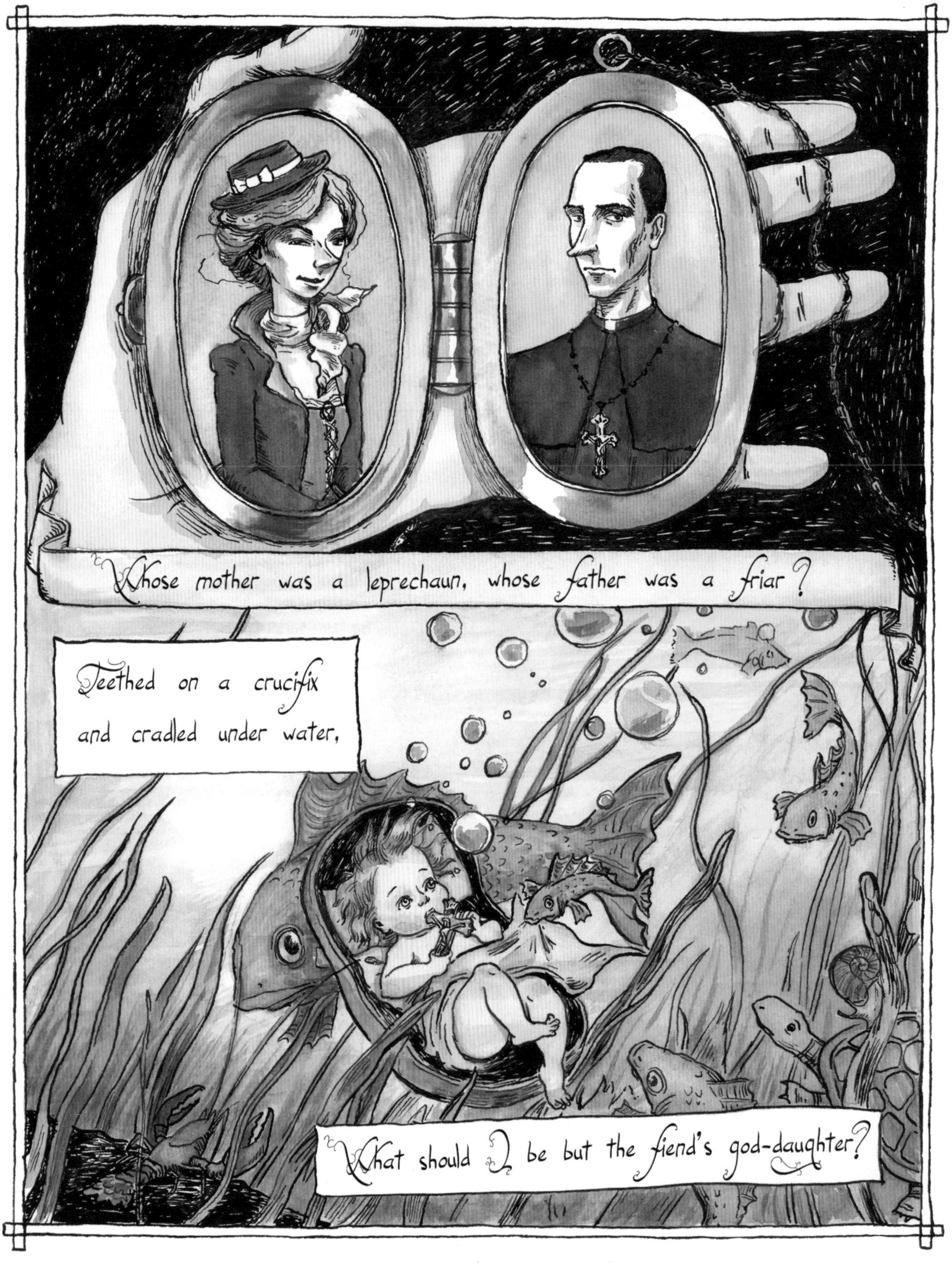
Whose mother was a leprechaun, whose father was a friar?
Teethed on a crucifix and cradled under water,
What should I be but the fiend's god-daughter?

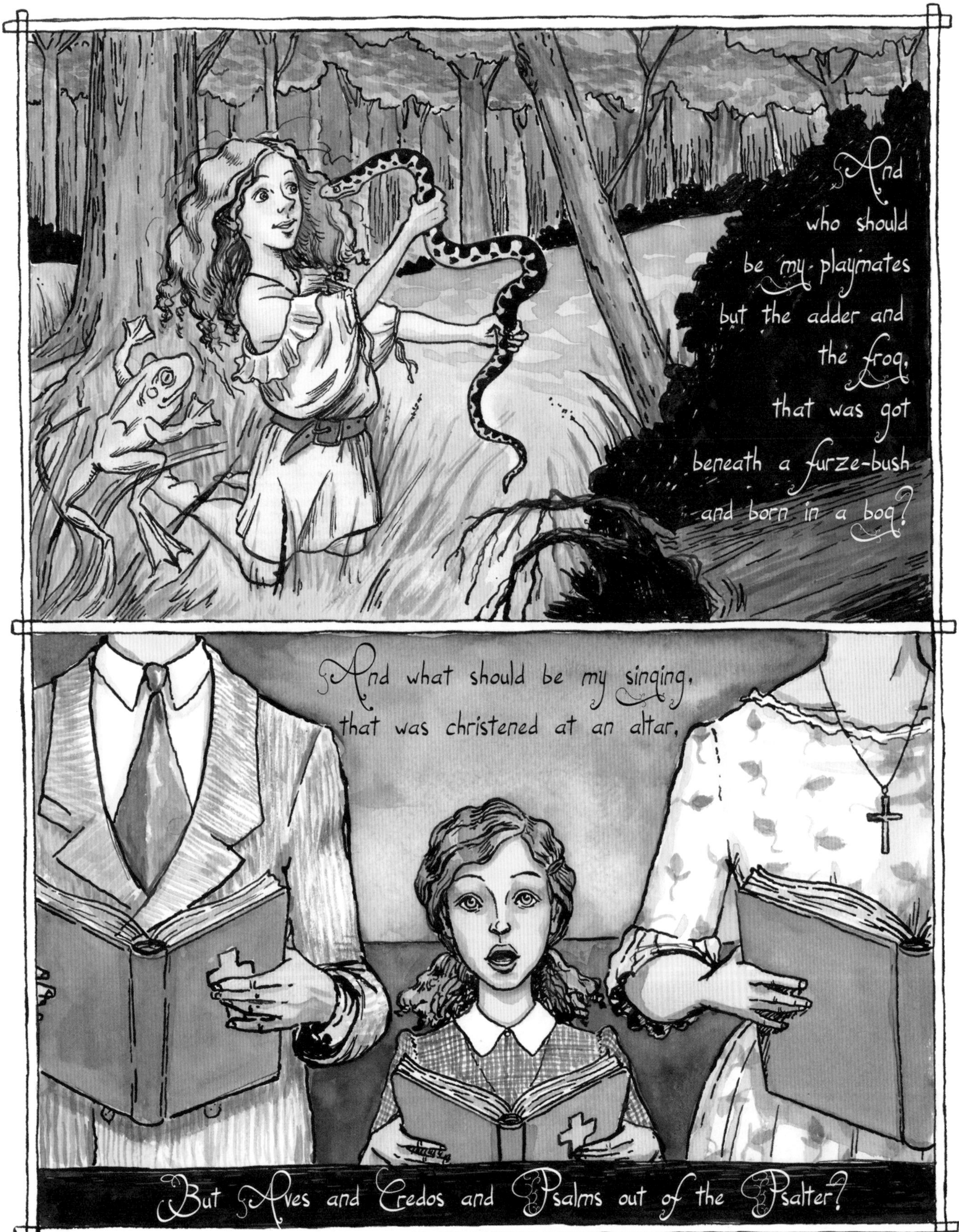
And
who should
be my playmates
but the adder and
the frog,
that was got
beneath a furze-bush
and born in a bog?
And what should be my singing,
that was christened at an altar,
But Aves and Credos and Psalms out of the Psalter?

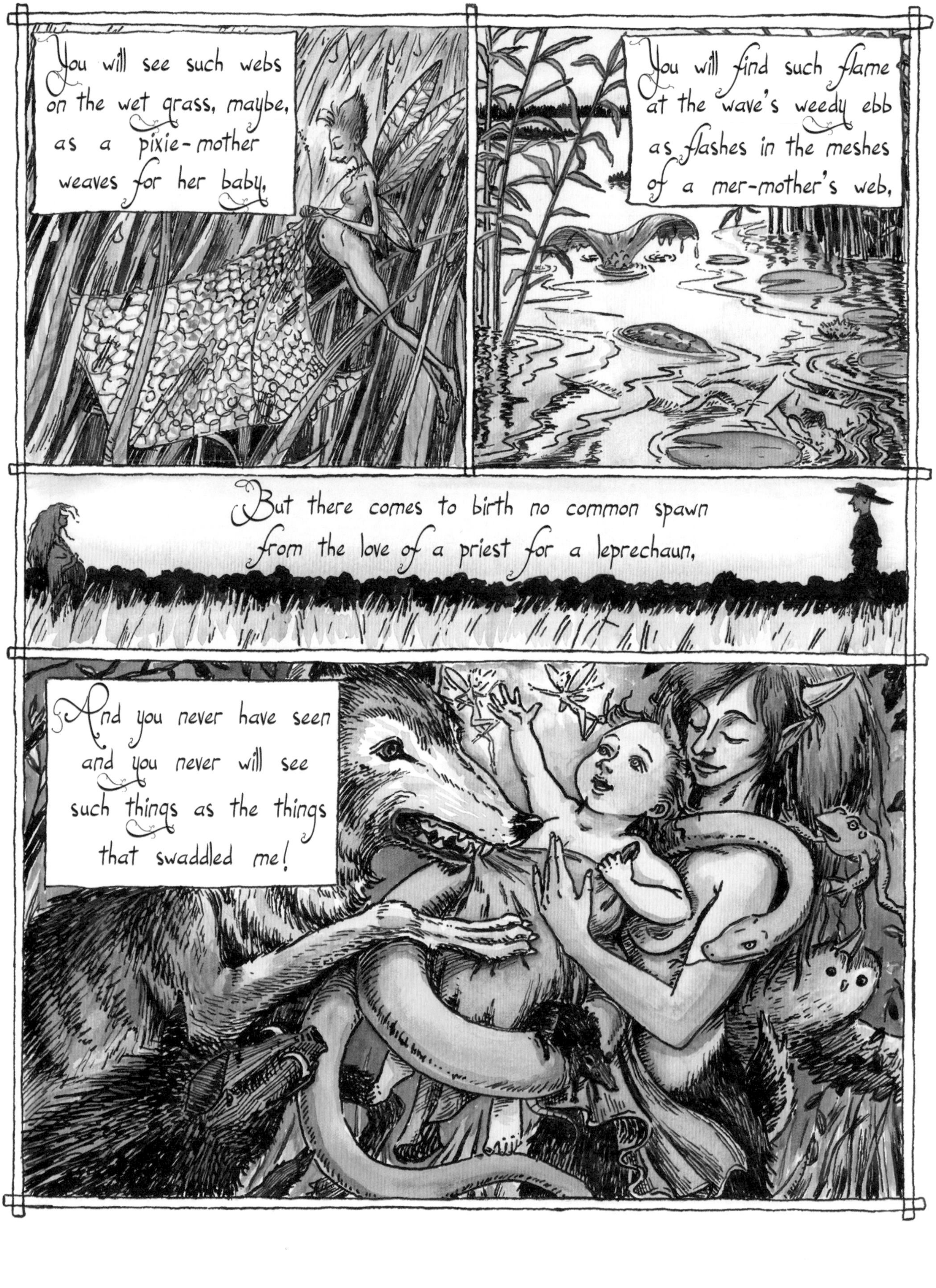
You will see such webs on the wet grass, maybe, as a pixie-mother weaves for her baby,
You will find such flame at the wave's weedy ebb as flashes in the meshes of a mer-mother's web,
But there comes to birth no common spawn from the love of a priest for a leprechaun,
And you never have seen and you never will see such things as the things that swaddled me!

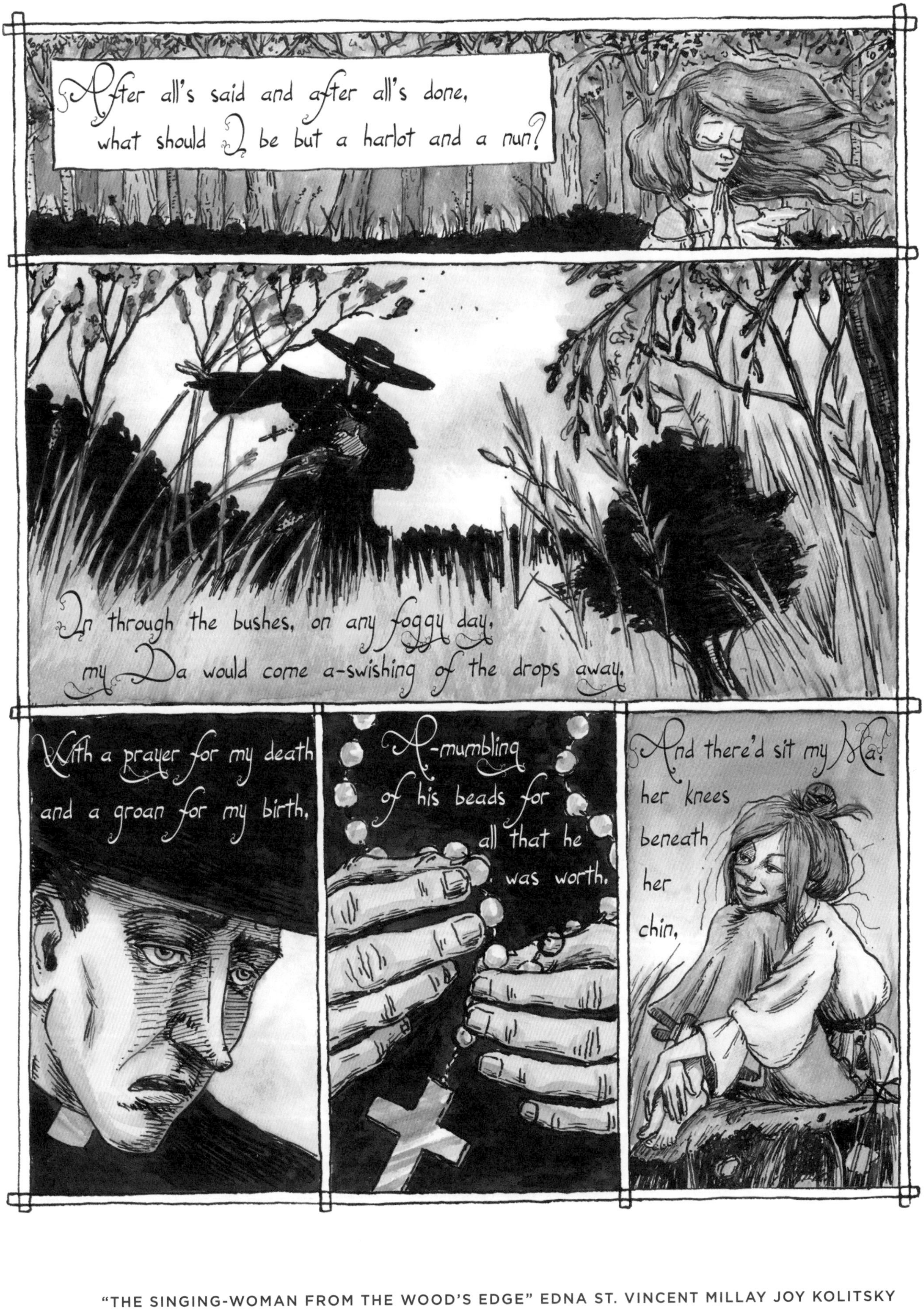
After all's said and after all's done,
what should I be but a harlot and a nun?
In through the bushes, on any foggy day,
my Da would come a-swishing of the drops away,
With a prayer for my death
and a groan for my birth,
A-mumbling
of his beads for
all that he
was worth.
And there'd sit my Ma,
her knees
beneath
her
chin,

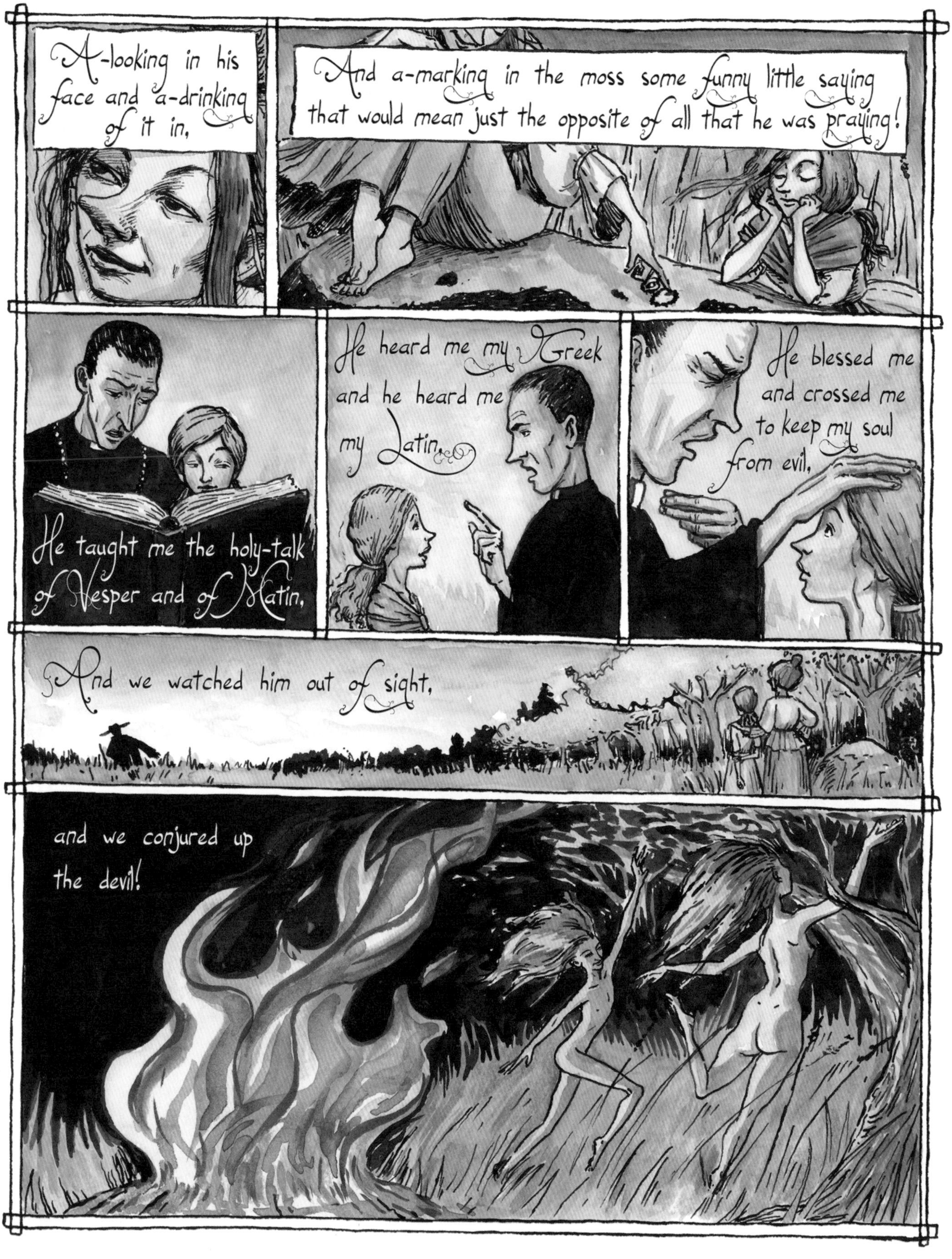
A-looking in his face and a-drinking of it in,
And a-marking in the moss some funny little saying that would mean just the opposite of all that he was praying!
He taught me the holy-talk of Vesper and of Matin,
He heard me my Greek and he heard me my Latin,
He blessed me and crossed me to keep my soul from evil,
And we watched him out of sight,
and we conjured up the devil!

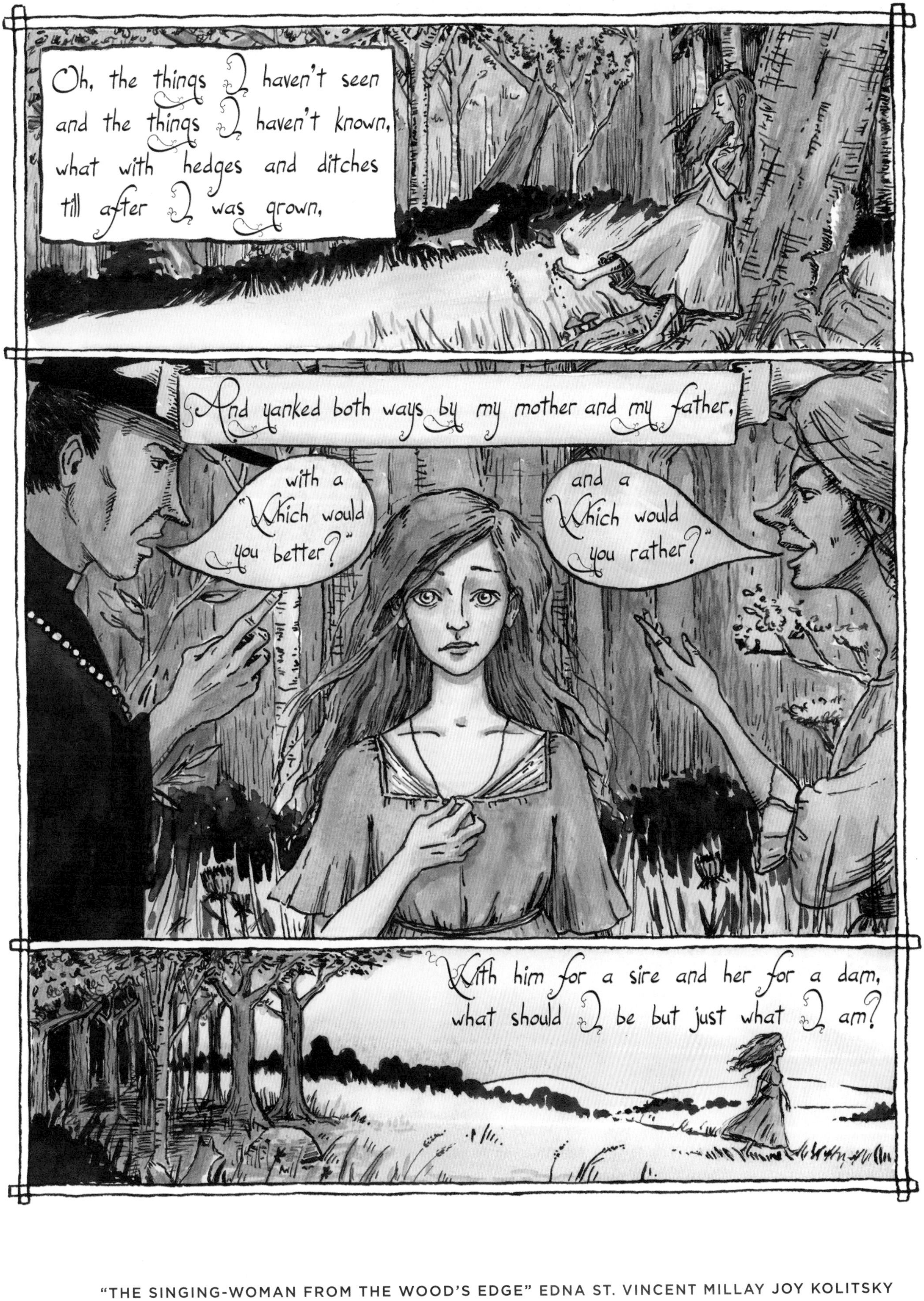
Oh, the things I haven't seen and the things I haven't known, what with hedges and ditches till after I was grown,
And yanked both ways by my mother and my father,
with a "Which would you better?"
and a "Which would you rather?"
With him for a sire and her for a dam, what should I be but just what I am?

"The Top" and "Give It Up!"

Franz Kafka

ART/ADAPTATIONS BY **Peter Kuper**

THE PRIDE OF PRAGUE, FRANZ KAFKA SPECIALIZED in unsettling works about everyday people caught in absurd, harrowing situations over which they have no control. In "The Metamorphosis," Gregor Samsa wakes up one morning as a loathsome giant insect. In *The Trial*, Joseph K. is unexpectedly arrested with no explanation and never told the charges against him nor how to defend himself. Similarly, *The Castle* relates a man's attempts to get answers from a mysterious, unapproachable bureaucracy.

In addition to the above works, Kafka wrote at least three dozen short stories, and, in the last few years of his life, over seventy vignettes, parables, and microfictions, most taking up less than a page. "The Top" is a tantalizing morsel, a single paragraph conjuring up a children's world that adults can only try to enter, and whose rules of play they must strain to comprehend. Also only a paragraph long, "Give It Up!" is among the very last of Kafka's writings, the story of a man who loses his way to the station after realizing it is much later than he realized. He asks a policeman for help. Assessing the situation, the policeman, instead of helping, utters the title phrase.

Cofounder of *World War 3 Illustrated* and regular contributor to *Mad*, Peter Kuper—whose art often seethes with sociopolitical commentary—graphically adapted nine of Kafka's short morsels in his black-and-white collection *Give It Up!* Two of them are presented here, newly colored by Peter especially for *The Graphic Canon*.

SOURCES

Kafka, Franz. *The Complete Stories*. New York: Schocken, 1983.

Pawel, Ernst. *The Nightmare of Reason: A Life of Franz Kafka*. New York: Farrar, Straus and Giroux, 1984.

—Dan Simon and Russ Kick

the TOP

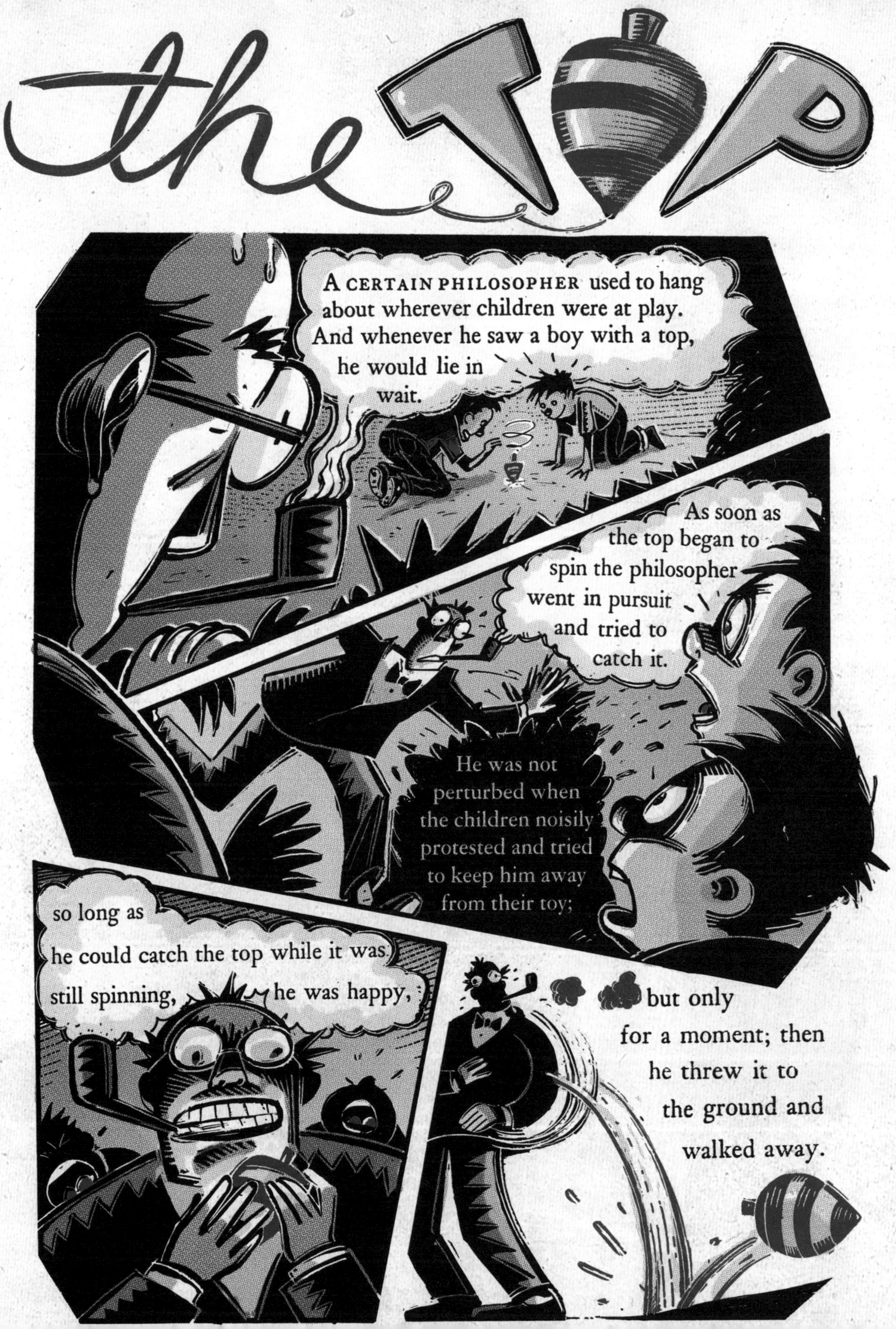
A CERTAIN PHILOSOPHER used to hang about wherever children were at play. And whenever he saw a boy with a top, he would lie in wait.
As soon as the top began to spin the philosopher went in pursuit and tried to catch it.
He was not perturbed when the children noisily protested and tried to keep him away from their toy;
so long as he could catch the top while it was still spinning, he was happy,
but only for a moment; then he threw it to the ground and walked away.

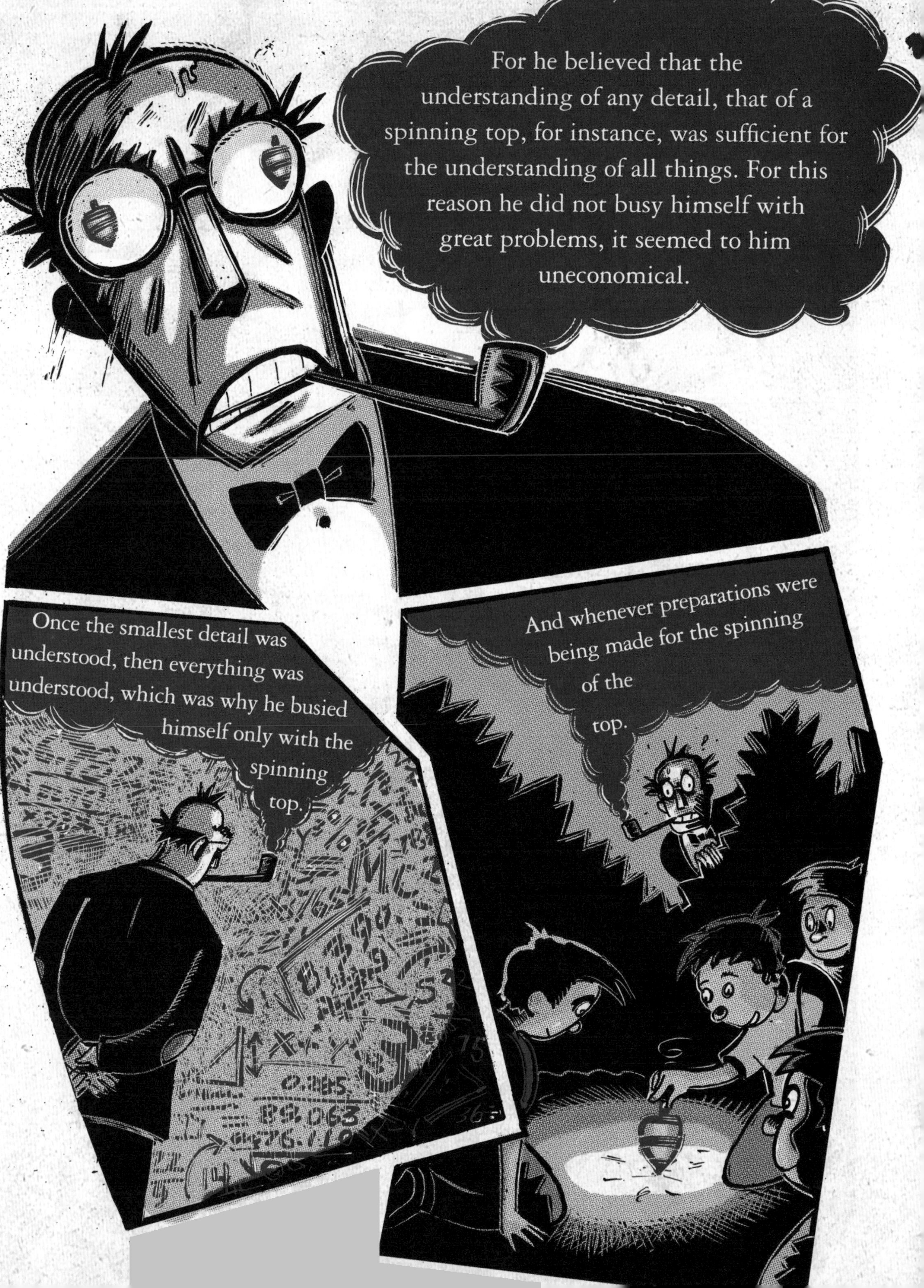
For he believed that the understanding of any detail, that of a spinning top, for instance, was sufficient for the understanding of all things. For this reason he did not busy himself with great problems, it seemed to him uneconomical.
Once the smallest detail was understood, then everything was understood, which was why he busied himself only with the spinning top.
And whenever preparations were being made for the spinning of the top.

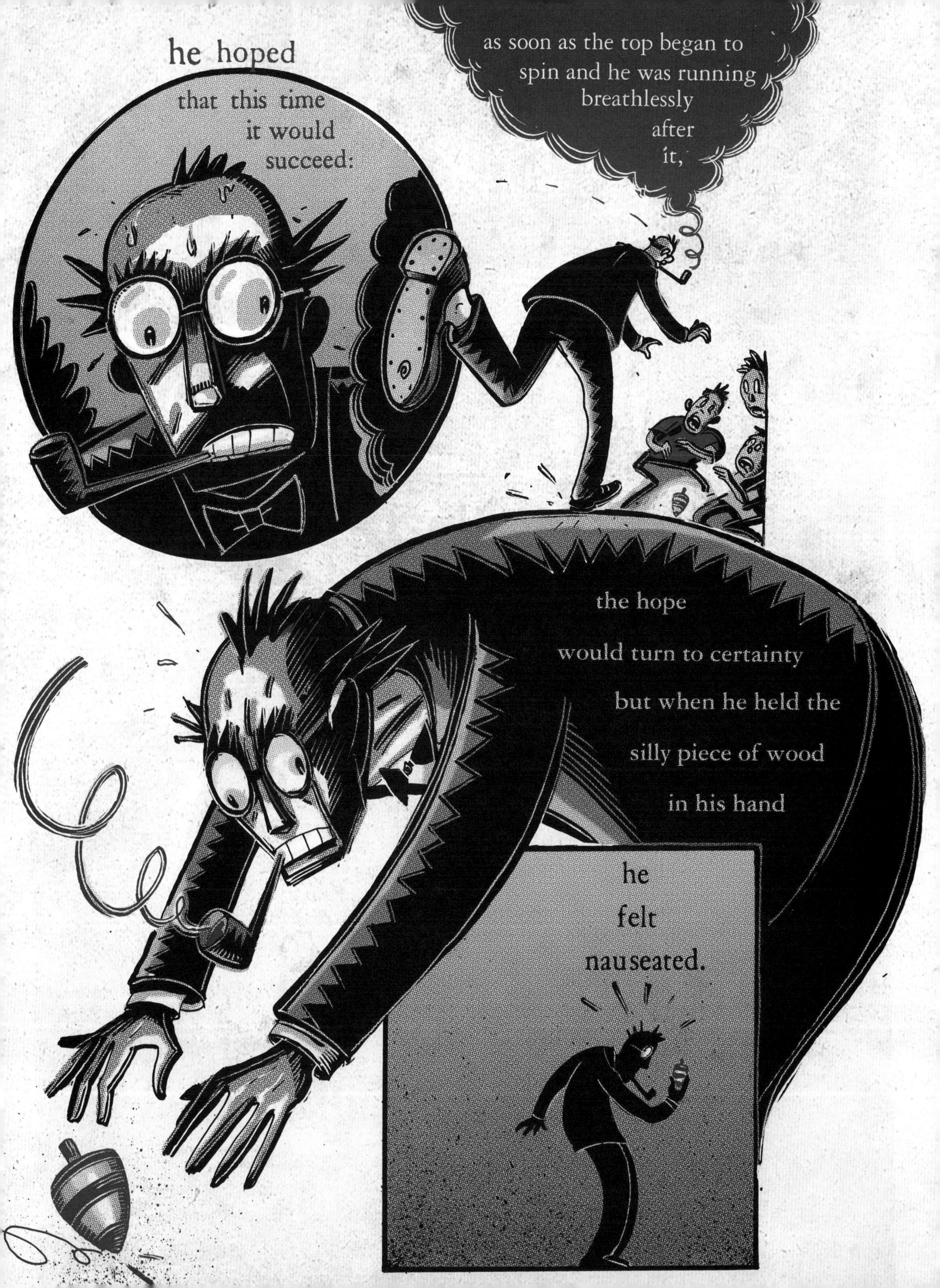
he hoped
that this time it would succeed:
as soon as the top began to spin and he was running breathlessly after it,
the hope would turn to certainty but when he held the silly piece of wood in his hand
he felt nauseated.

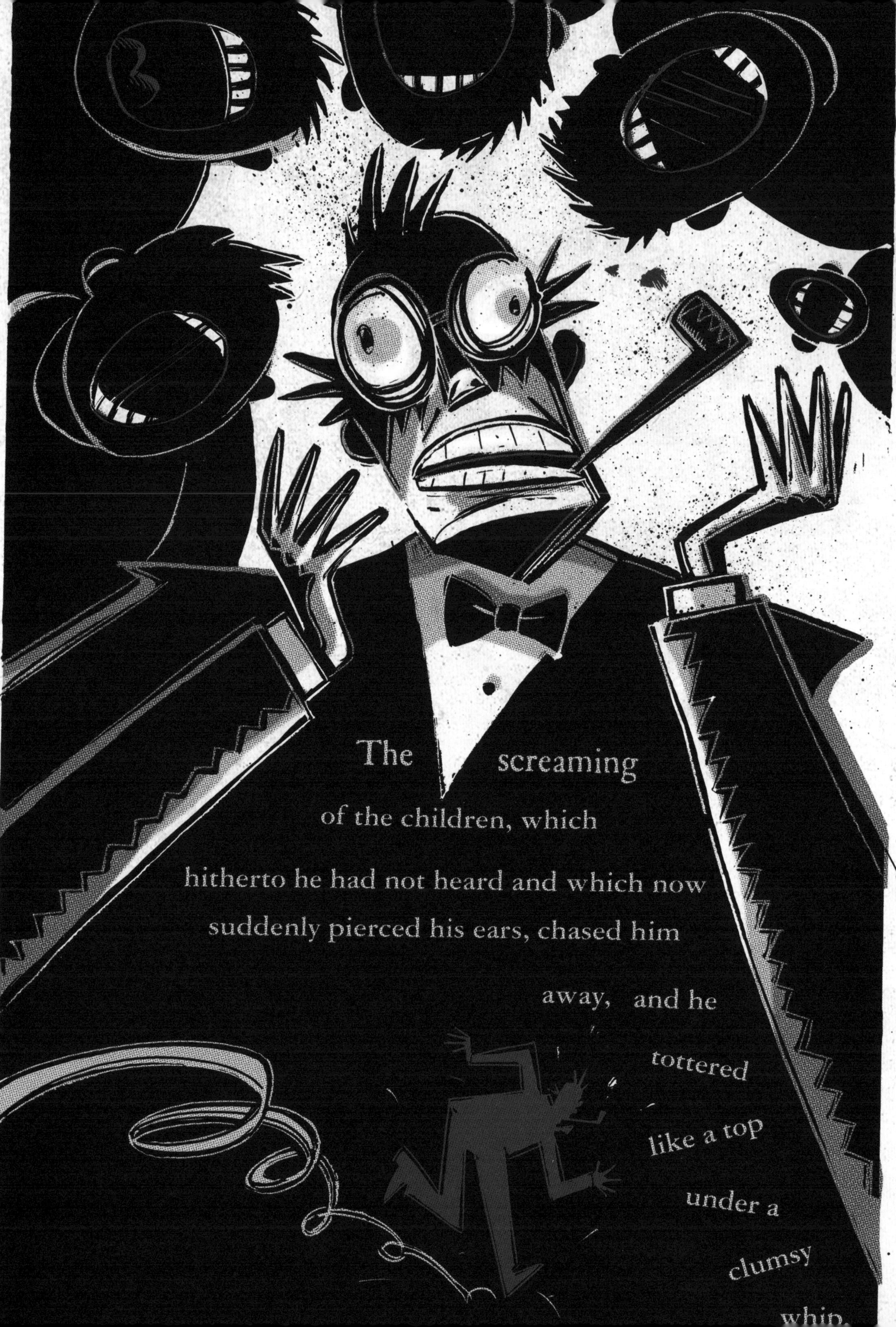

The screaming of the children, which hitherto he had not heard and which now suddenly pierced his ears, chased him away, and he tottered like a top under a clumsy whip.

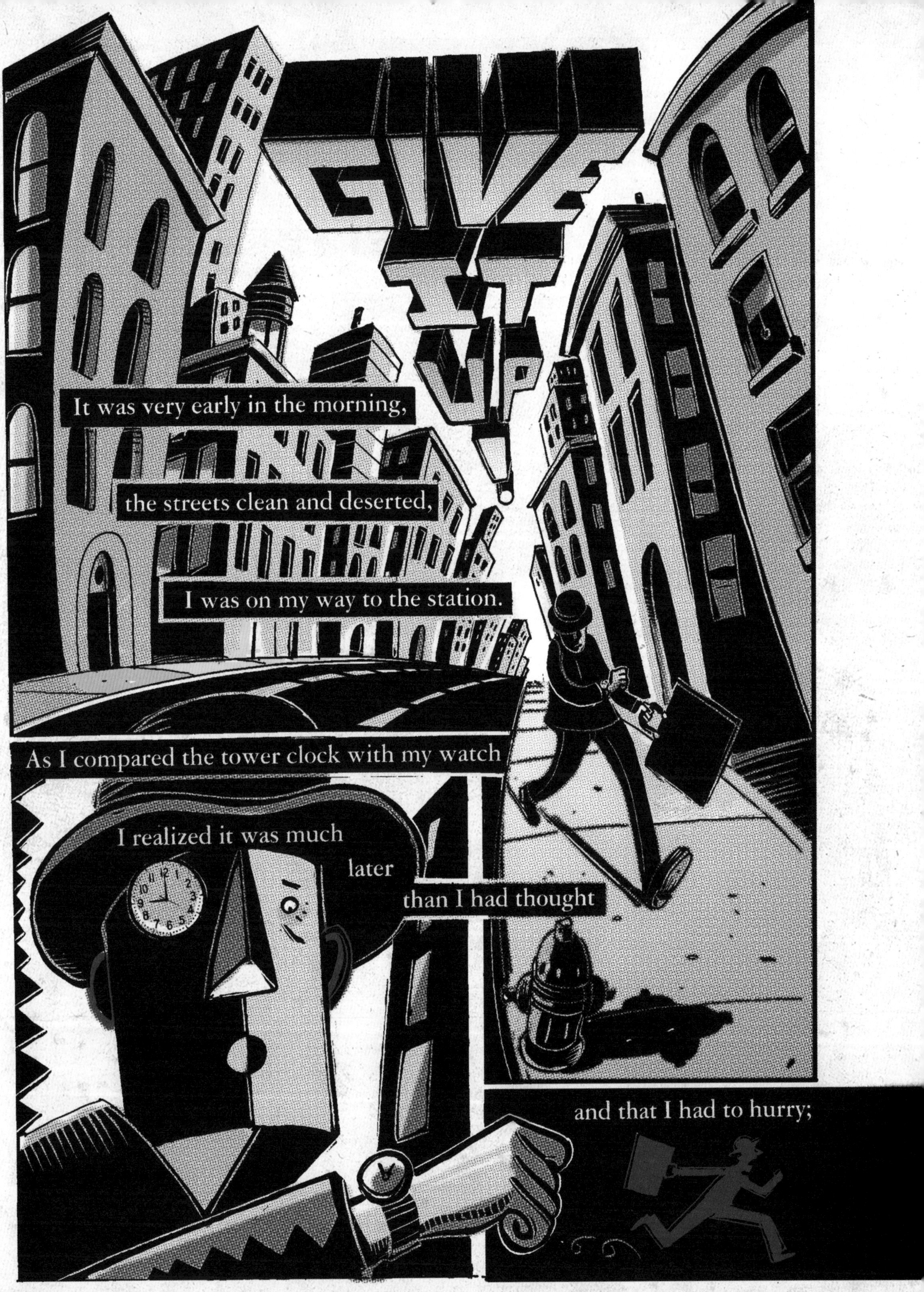
GIVE IT UP
It was very early in the morning,
the streets clean and deserted,
I was on my way to the station.
As I compared the tower clock with my watch
I realized it was much
later
than I had thought
and that I had to hurry;

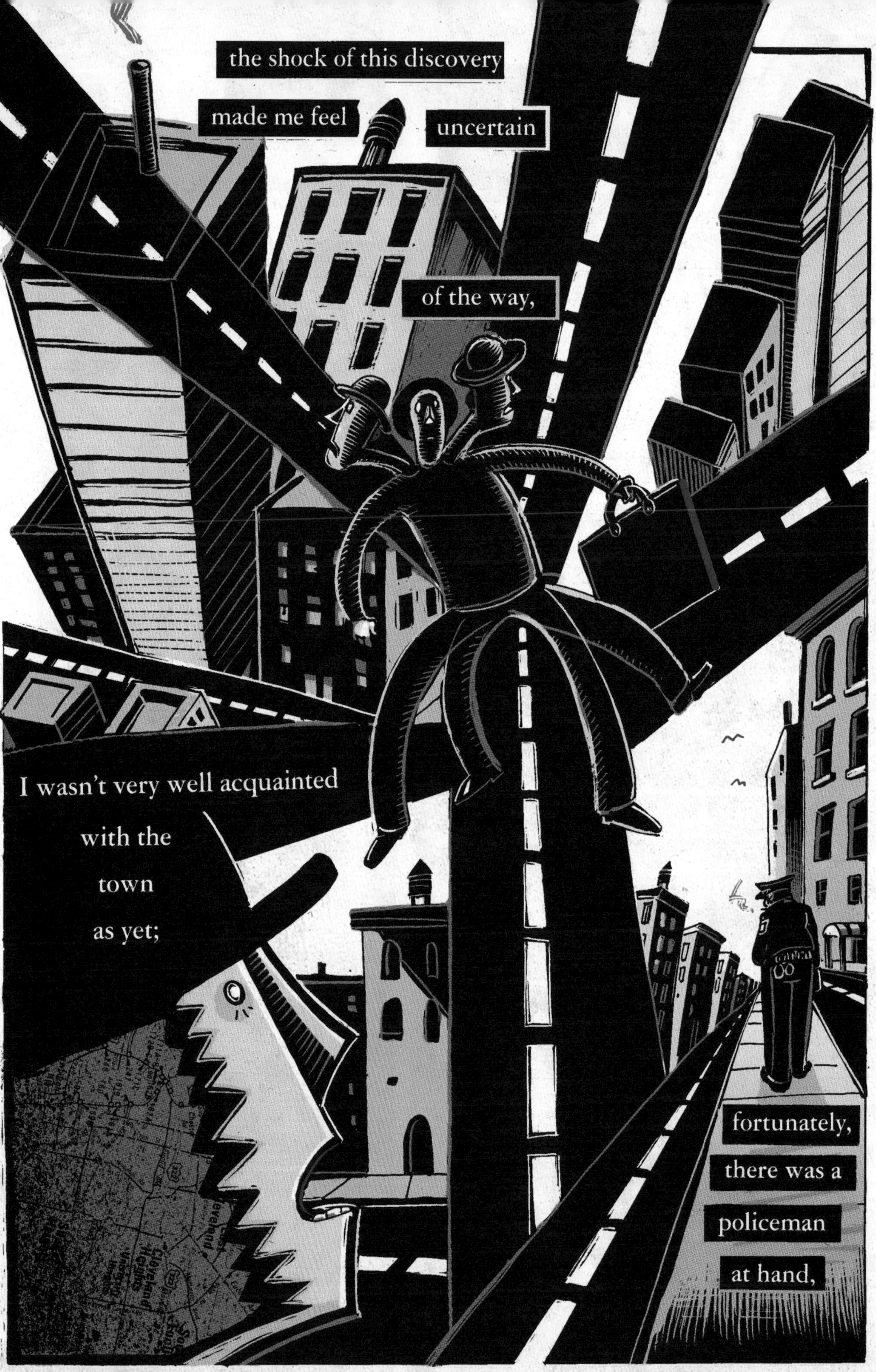
the shock of this discovery
made me feel
uncertain
of the way,
I wasn't very well acquainted
with the
town
as yet;
fortunately,
there was a
policeman
at hand,

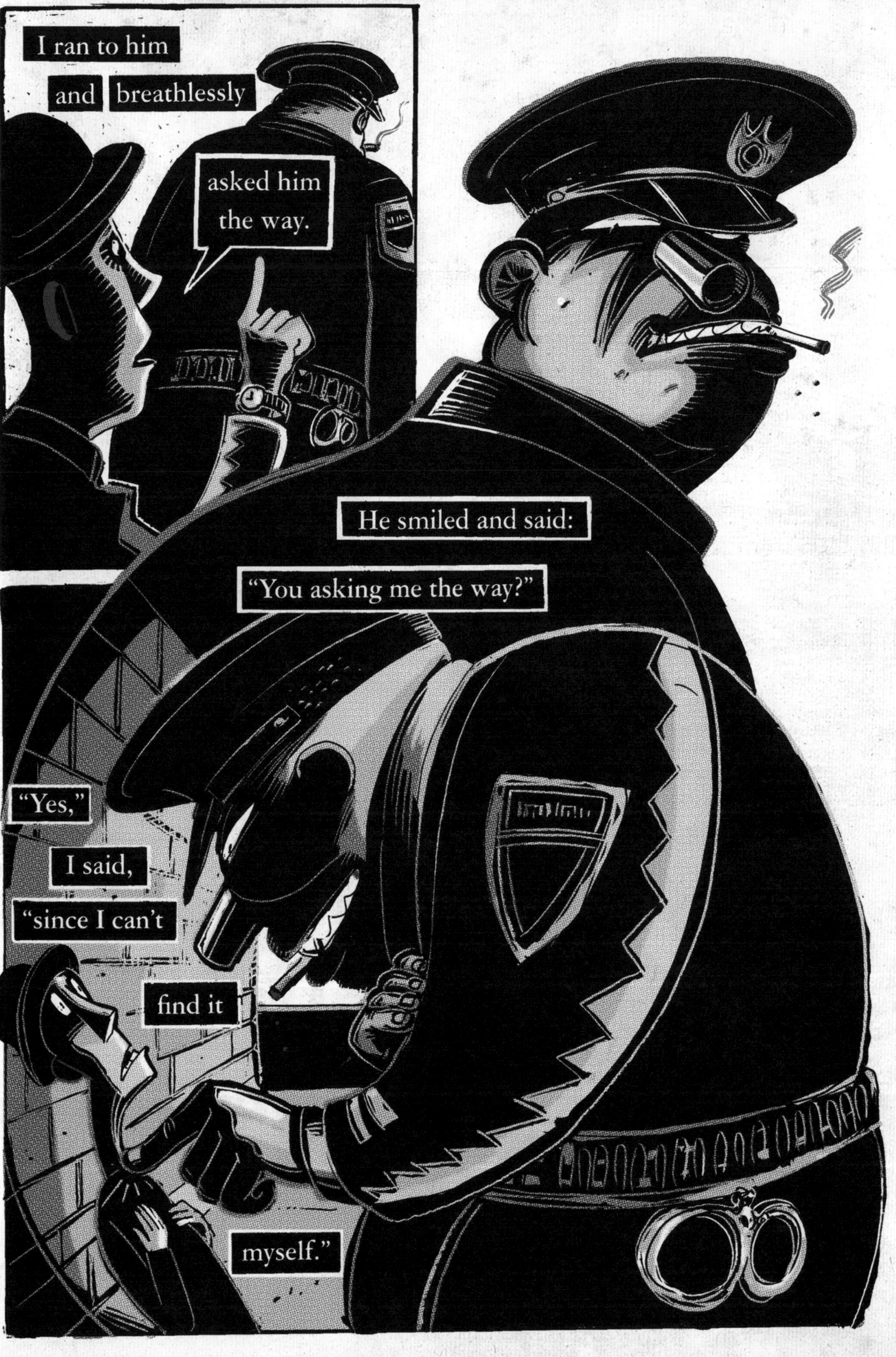
I ran to him
and breathlessly
asked him the way.
He smiled and said:
"You asking me the way?"
"Yes,"
I said,
"since I can't
find it
myself."

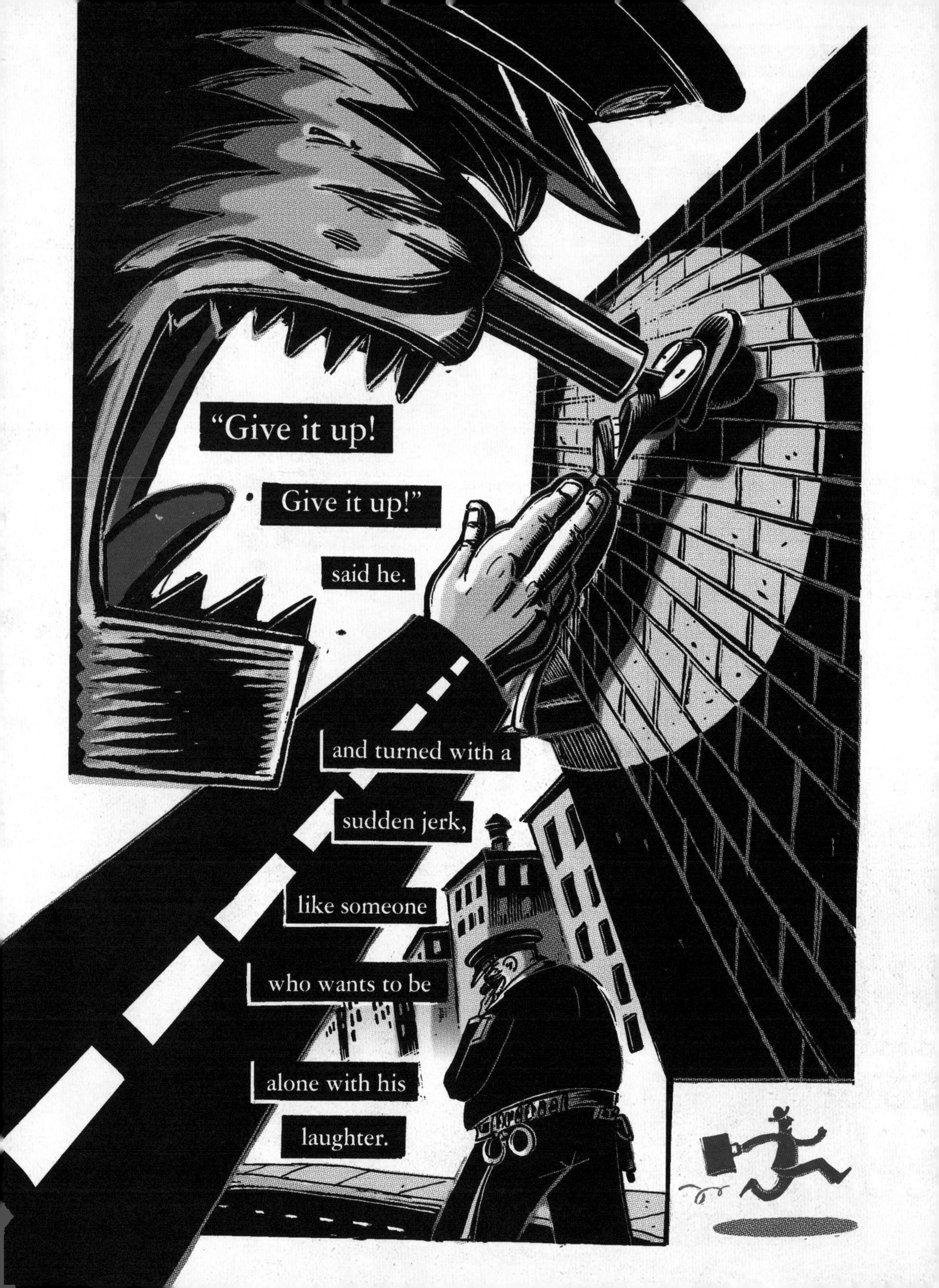
"Give it up!
Give it up!"
said he.
and turned with a
sudden jerk,
like someone
who wants to be
alone with his
laughter.

Three Panel Review
Lisa Brown

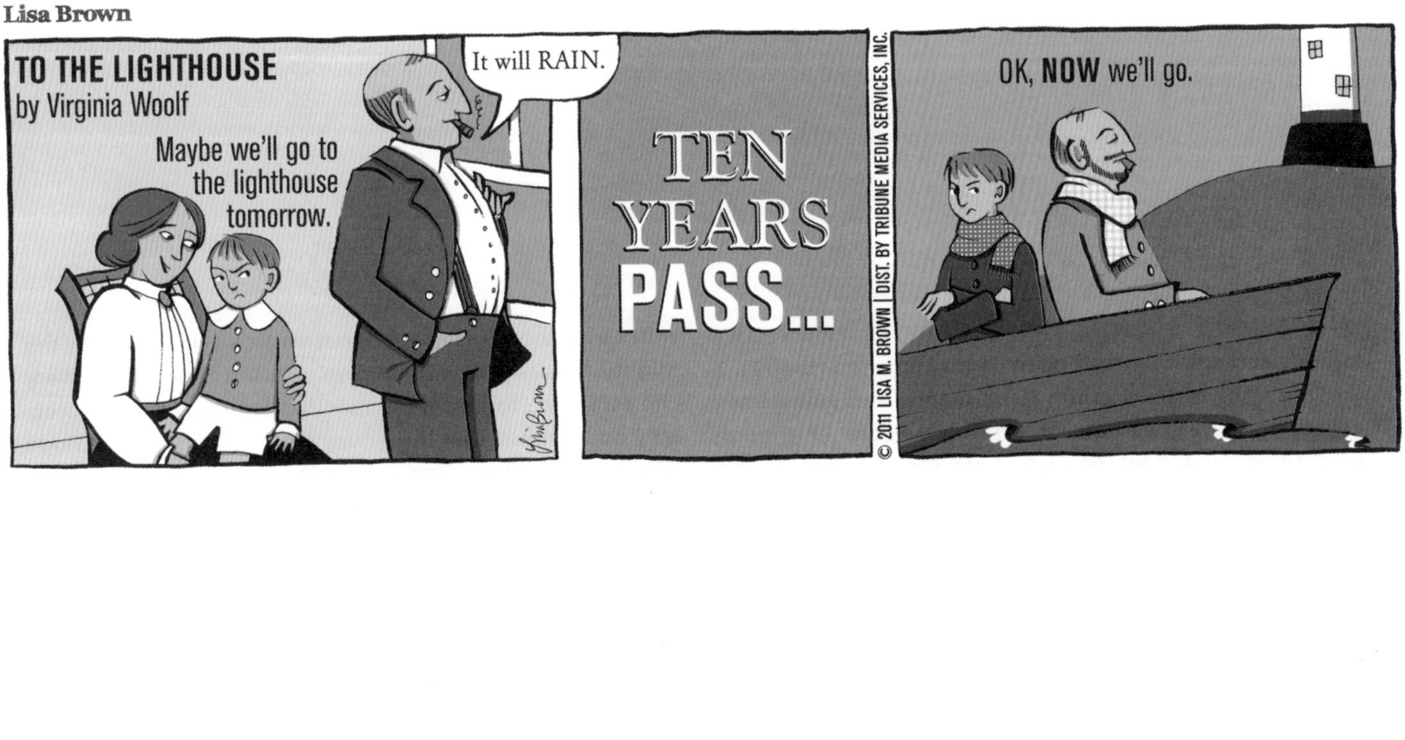
TO THE LIGHTHOUSE
by Virginia Woolf
Maybe we'll go to the lighthouse tomorrow.
It will RAIN.
TEN YEARS PASS...
© 2011 LISA M. BROWN | DIST. BY TRIBUNE MEDIA SERVICES, INC.
OK, NOW we'll go.

"The Negro Speaks of Rivers"

Langston Hughes

ART/ADAPTATION BY **Jenny Tondera**

"THE NEGRO SPEAKS OF RIVERS" IS THE MOST famous and anthologized poem from Langston Hughes, a leading light of the Harlem Renaissance and sometimes called "the Poet Laureate of the Negro Race." (Although best known as a poet, he also wrote short stories, novels, histories, plays, and operas.) Amazingly, he was only eighteen years old when he wrote it, and it belongs to that special breed of classic works that were written spontaneously in less than a day. Hughes had just graduated high school—where he had penned poetry for the school magazine—and was reluctantly on a train ride from Cleveland to his father's home in Mexico. As he crossed the Mississippi River outside St. Louis at sunset, his muse spoke to him, so he pulled an envelope from his pocket and spent about fifteen minutes writing this classic work of American literature on the back. It was published in 1921 in *The Crisis*, the magazine of the National Association for the Advancement of Colored People, edited by W. E. B. Du Bois.

Young Hughes packed a good deal into this short verse, tying the history of black people to a series of major rivers. Starting with the Euphrates in Mesopotamia, the cradle of civilization where the human race began, the poem moves to the Congo, running through western central Africa, and then to the Nile in Egypt, with an overt reference to the building of the ancient pyramids, which was accomplished with slave labor. Finally, the narrative arrives in the US, by the mighty Mississippi, with its own winding history of slavery. The reference to Lincoln is specifically about a story, probably apocryphal, that the future president visited the huge slave market in New Orleans as a young man, causing him to turn against slavery. With its references to blood—which also flows—and to Hughes's soul, plus his omnipresent identification with the entire black race, perhaps the entire human race since its beginning (shades of Walt Whitman's God-like "I"), this brief poem contains a deep and epic sweep.

Philadelphia graphic designer and artist Jenny Tondera—who's done work for Urban Outfitters and the University of Notre Dame, among others—has applied an unusual multilayered approach, resulting in a piece unlike anything else in *The Graphic Canon*. "For the imagery," she explains, "I abstracted stills from a film that the US government released mid-century, about people living along the Mississippi River. The inspiration for the typography came from the typography in title sequences of 1920s films, referencing the period when 'The Negro Speaks of Rivers' was first published."

SOURCE

Leach, Laurie F. *Langston Hughes: A Biography*. Westport, CT: Greenwood Press, 2004.

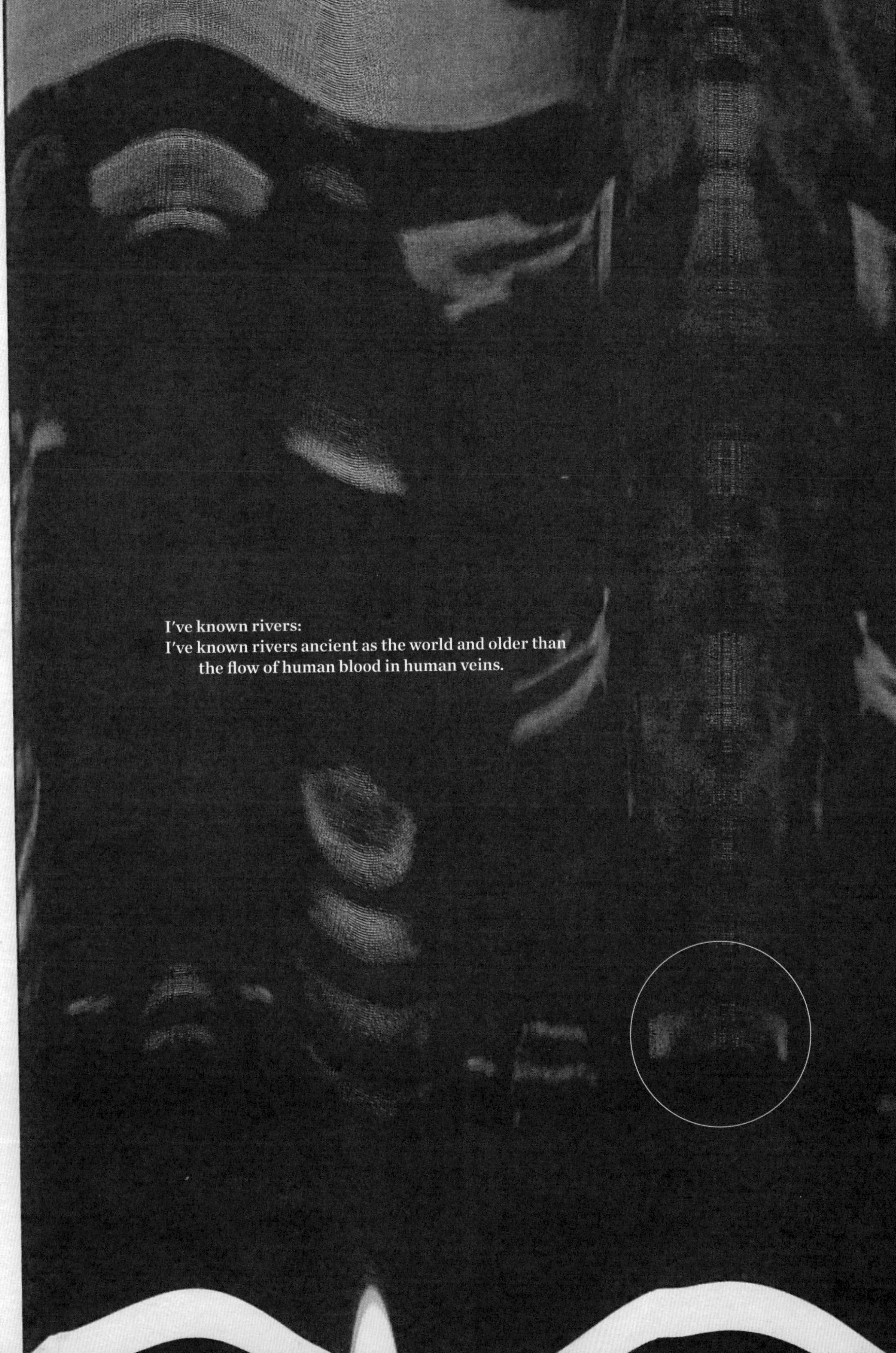

I've known rivers:
I've known rivers ancient as the world and older than
the flow of human blood in human veins.

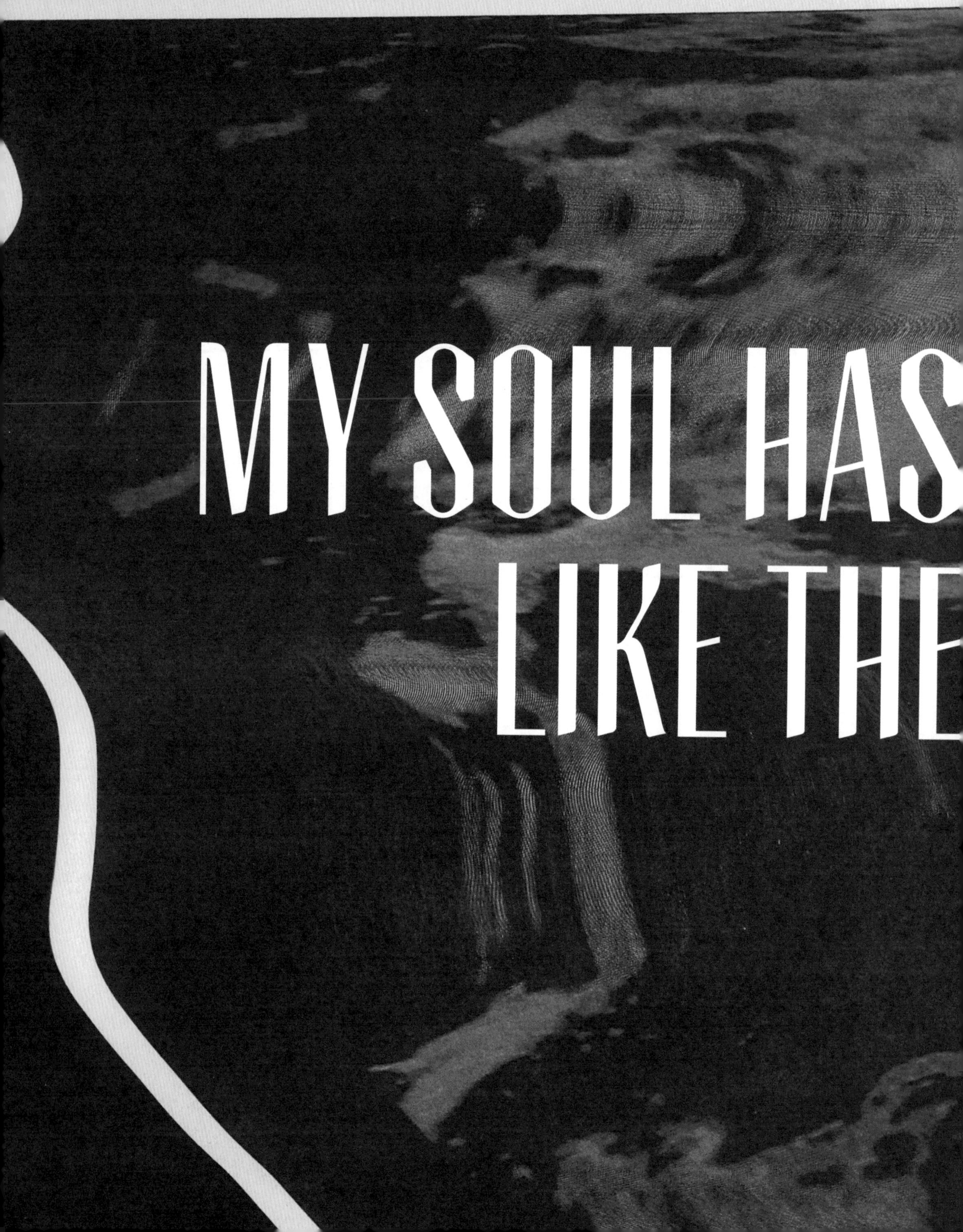
MY SOUL HAS
LIKE THE

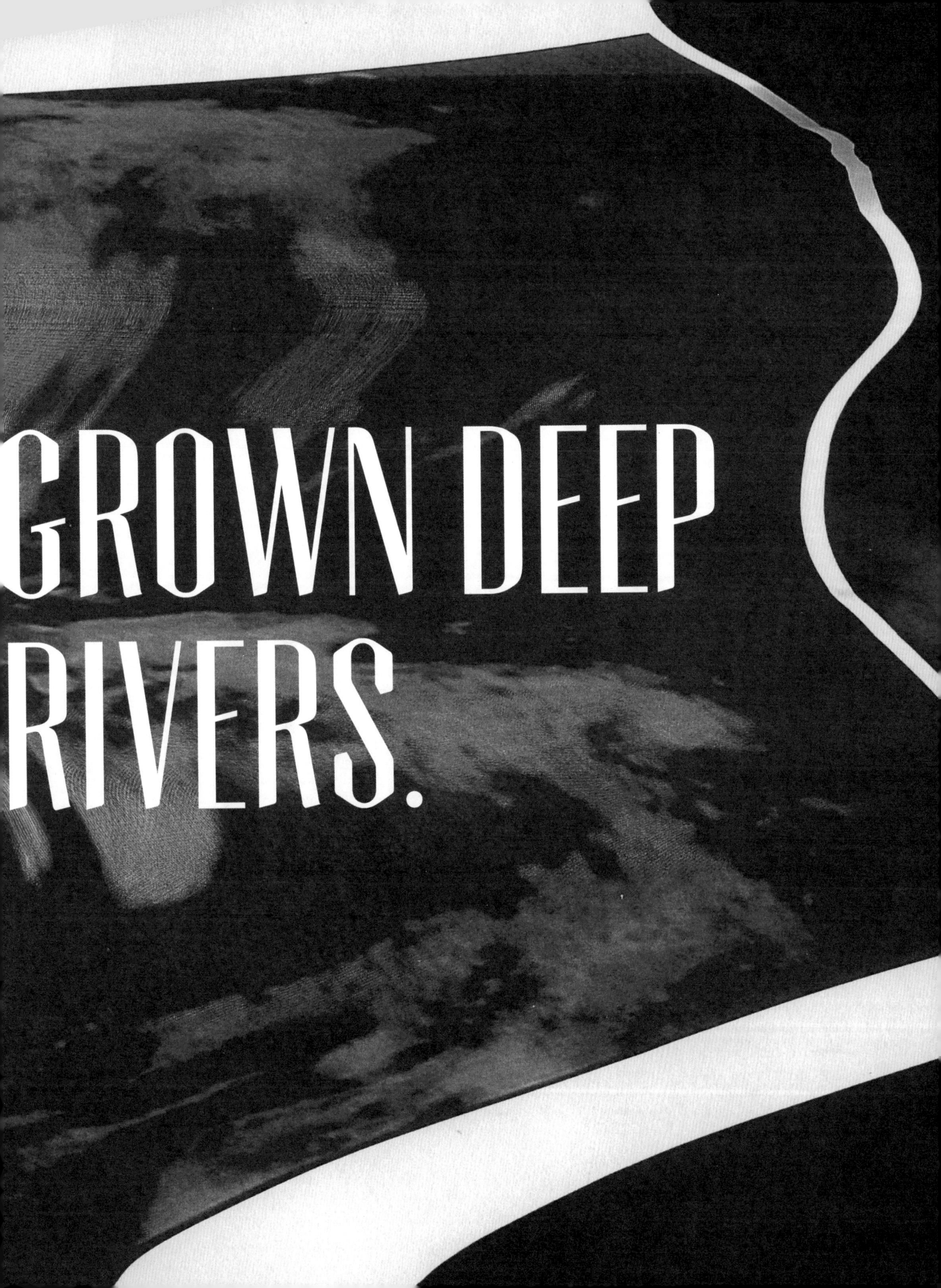
GROWN DEEP
RIVERS.

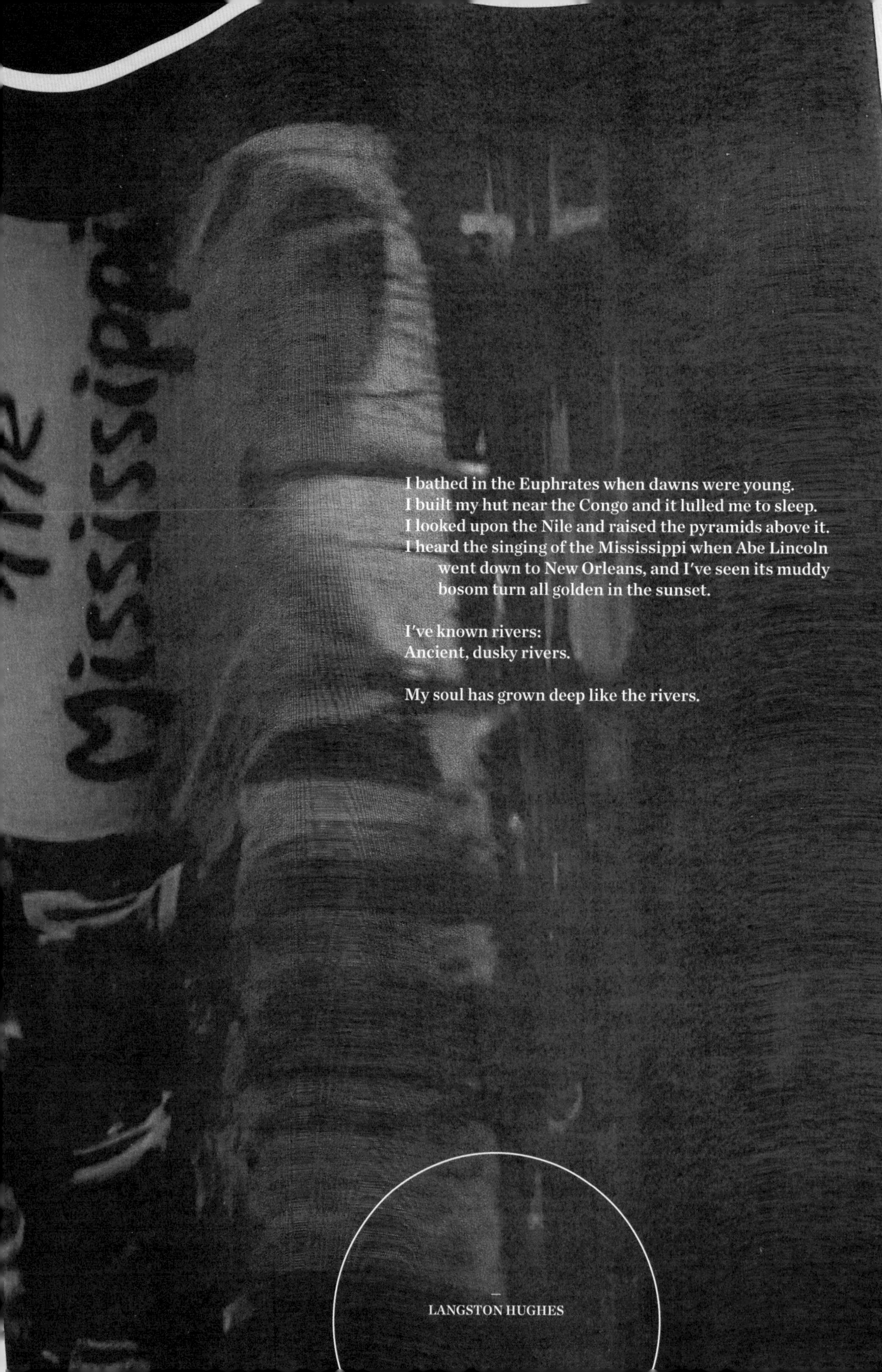

I bathed in the Euphrates when dawns were young.
I built my hut near the Congo and it lulled me to sleep.
I looked upon the Nile and raised the pyramids above it.
I heard the singing of the Mississippi when Abe Lincoln
went down to New Orleans, and I've seen its muddy
bosom turn all golden in the sunset.

I've known rivers:
Ancient, dusky rivers.

My soul has grown deep like the rivers.

—

LANGSTON HUGHES

"Rain"

W. Somerset Maugham

ART/ADAPTATION BY **Lance Tooks**

"SOMERSET MAUGHAM LIVED FOR NEARLY NINETY-two years, wrote seventy-eight books and kept his faithful audience from the late Victorian era to the early twenty-first century," wrote his biographer Jeffrey Myers. "[He] was adept at every kind of work he ever did: as an anthologist and as a writer of novels, stories, stage and screen plays, art and travel books, autobiographies, reportage and essays; and as a doctor, linguist, secret agent, war propagandist, government adviser, art connoisseur, art philanthropist and presenter of his films." Obviously, someone needs to create a graphic biography of this man. Maugham's best-known work is the novel *Of Human*

Bondage, and the most famous of his short stories is "Rain," which was made into a play and a movie. Anthony Burgess—author of *A Clockwork Orange*—claimed that Maugham wrote some of the best short stories in the English language.

Lance Tooks combines images and lots of text in a unique way, creating works that are more than stories accompanied by illustrations, but aren't exactly sequential comics in the standard sense. When I approached him about contributing to *The Graphic Canon,* he chose two short stories: Mary Shelley's "The Mortal Immortal" (in Volume 2) and Maugham's controversial tale of a prostitute and a missionary.

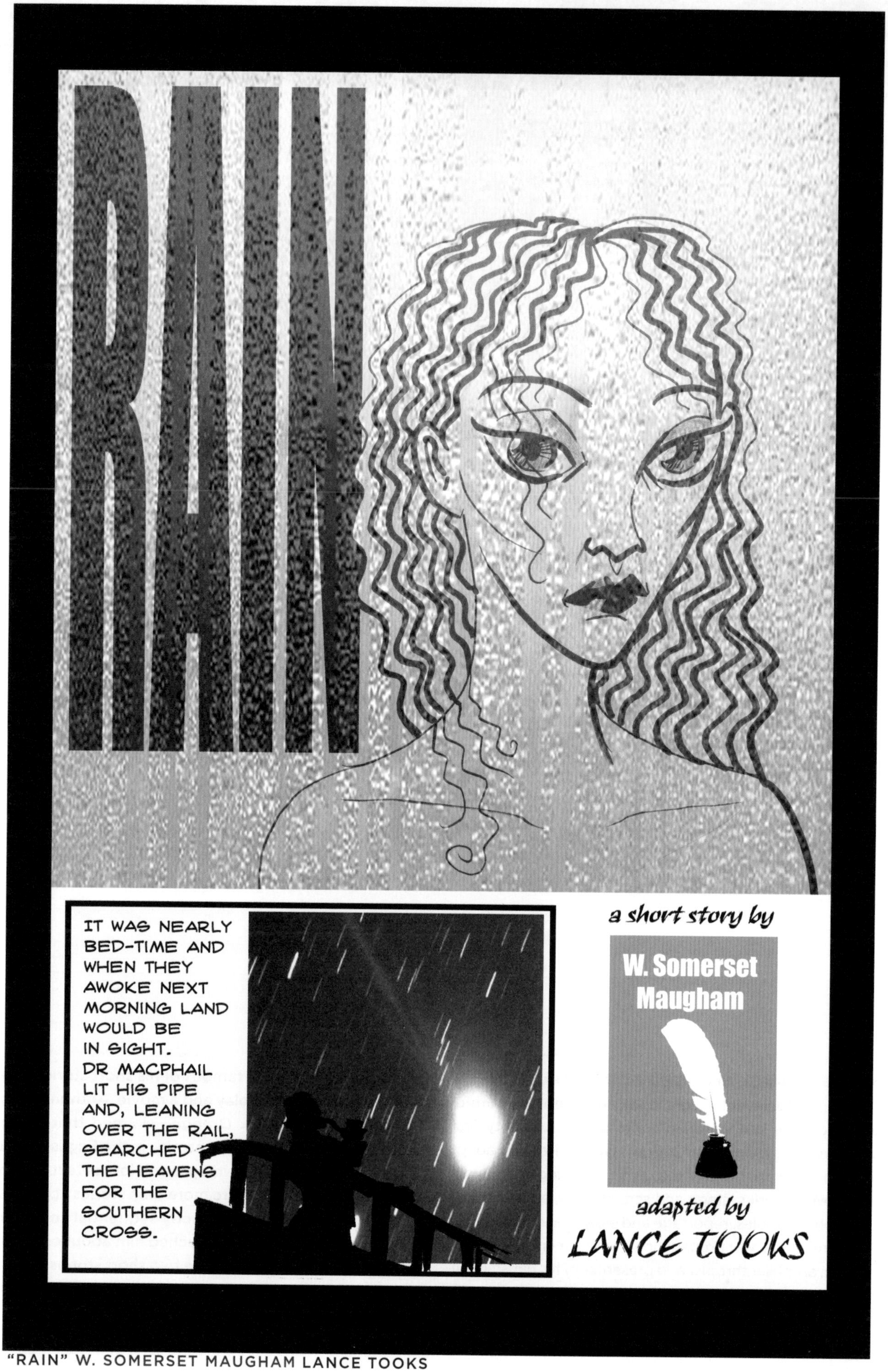
RAIN
IT WAS NEARLY BED-TIME AND WHEN THEY AWOKE NEXT MORNING LAND WOULD BE IN SIGHT. DR MACPHAIL LIT HIS PIPE AND, LEANING OVER THE RAIL, SEARCHED THE HEAVENS FOR THE SOUTHERN CROSS.
a short story by
W. Somerset Maugham
adapted by
LANCE TOOKS

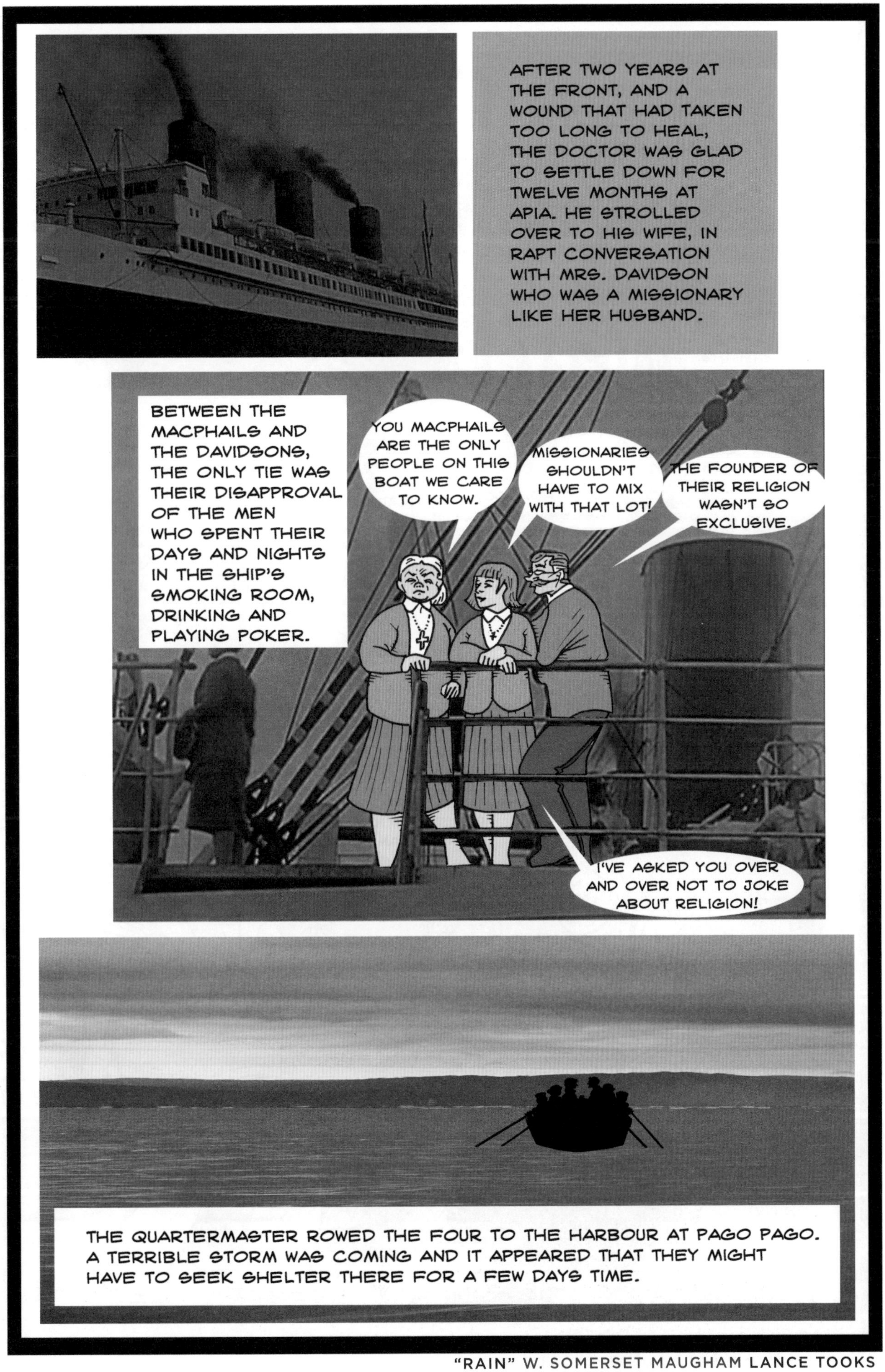
AFTER TWO YEARS AT THE FRONT, AND A WOUND THAT HAD TAKEN TOO LONG TO HEAL, THE DOCTOR WAS GLAD TO SETTLE DOWN FOR TWELVE MONTHS AT APIA. HE STROLLED OVER TO HIS WIFE, IN RAPT CONVERSATION WITH MRS. DAVIDSON WHO WAS A MISSIONARY LIKE HER HUSBAND.
BETWEEN THE MACPHAILS AND THE DAVIDSONS, THE ONLY TIE WAS THEIR DISAPPROVAL OF THE MEN WHO SPENT THEIR DAYS AND NIGHTS IN THE SHIP'S SMOKING ROOM, DRINKING AND PLAYING POKER.
YOU MACPHAILS ARE THE ONLY PEOPLE ON THIS BOAT WE CARE TO KNOW.
MISSIONARIES SHOULDN'T HAVE TO MIX WITH THAT LOT!
THE FOUNDER OF THEIR RELIGION WASN'T SO EXCLUSIVE.
I'VE ASKED YOU OVER AND OVER NOT TO JOKE ABOUT RELIGION!
THE QUARTERMASTER ROWED THE FOUR TO THE HARBOUR AT PAGO PAGO. A TERRIBLE STORM WAS COMING AND IT APPEARED THAT THEY MIGHT HAVE TO SEEK SHELTER THERE FOR A FEW DAYS TIME.

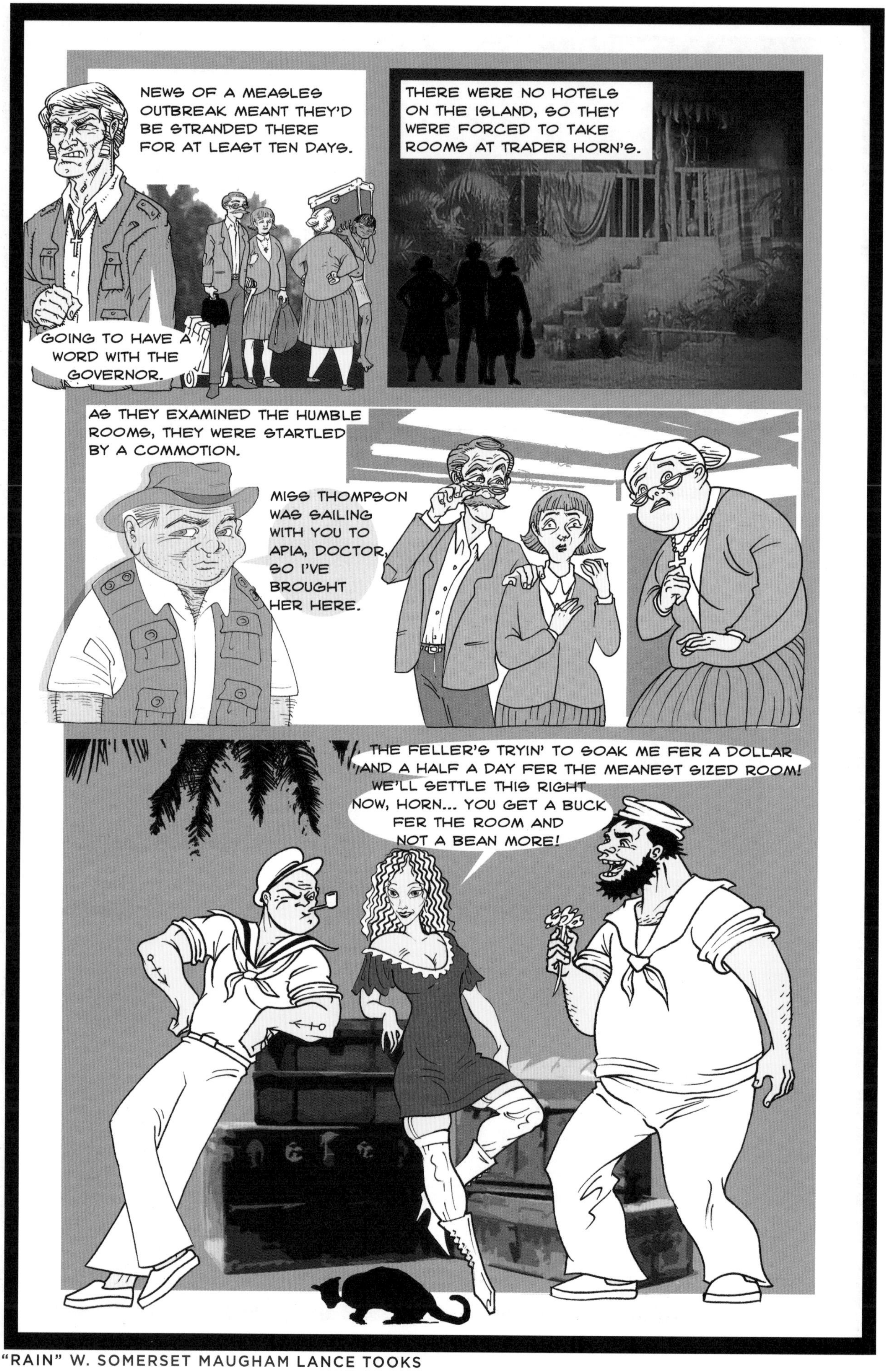
NEWS OF A MEASLES OUTBREAK MEANT THEY'D BE STRANDED THERE FOR AT LEAST TEN DAYS.
GOING TO HAVE A WORD WITH THE GOVERNOR.
THERE WERE NO HOTELS ON THE ISLAND, SO THEY WERE FORCED TO TAKE ROOMS AT TRADER HORN'S.
AS THEY EXAMINED THE HUMBLE ROOMS, THEY WERE STARTLED BY A COMMOTION.
MISS THOMPSON WAS SAILING WITH YOU TO APIA, DOCTOR, SO I'VE BROUGHT HER HERE.
THE FELLER'S TRYIN' TO SOAK ME FER A DOLLAR AND A HALF A DAY FER THE MEANEST SIZED ROOM!
WE'LL SETTLE THIS RIGHT NOW, HORN... YOU GET A BUCK FER THE ROOM AND NOT A BEAN MORE!

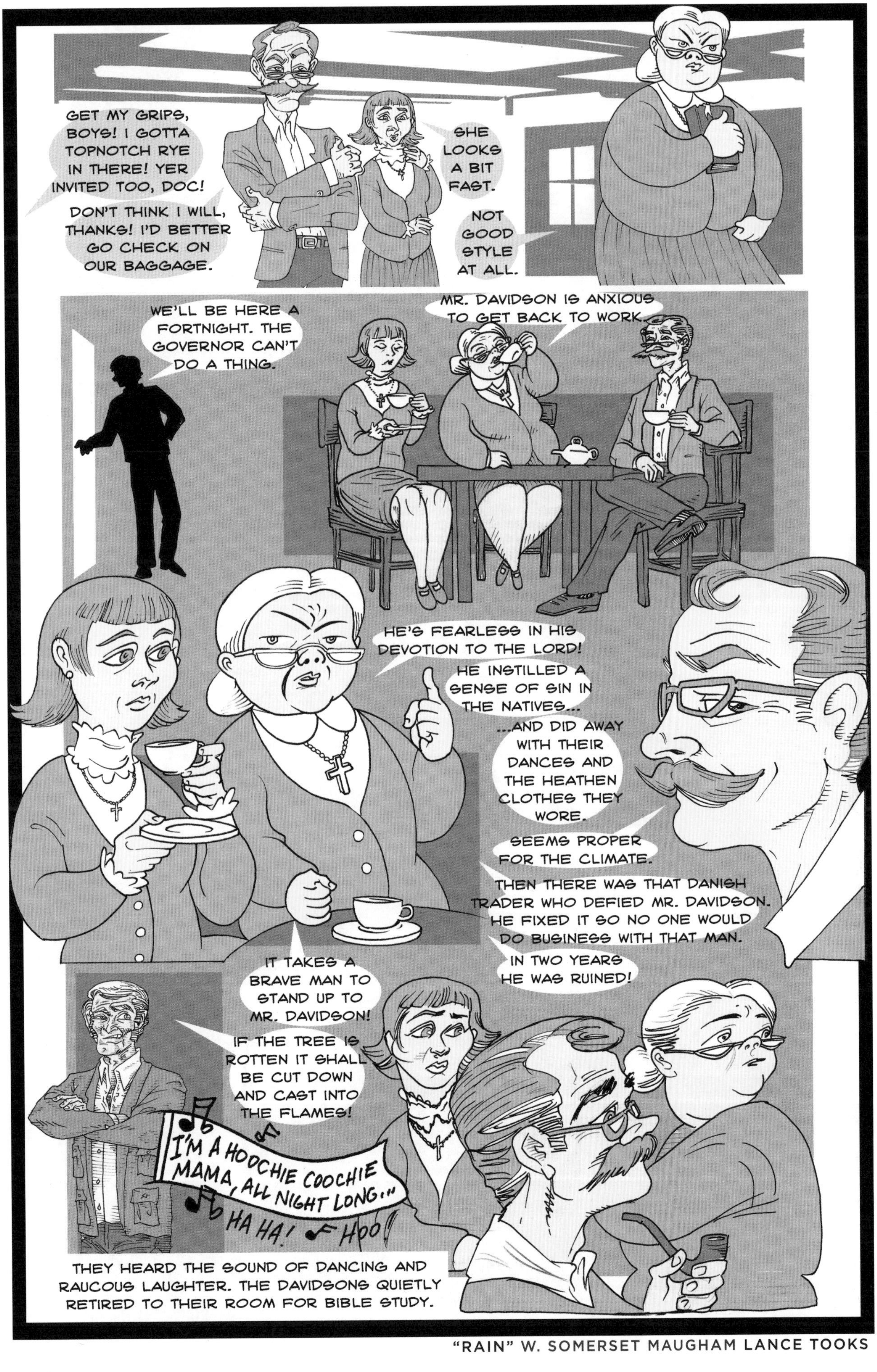
GET MY GRIPS, BOYS! I GOTTA TOPNOTCH RYE IN THERE! YER INVITED TOO, DOC!
DON'T THINK I WILL, THANKS! I'D BETTER GO CHECK ON OUR BAGGAGE.
SHE LOOKS A BIT FAST.
NOT GOOD STYLE AT ALL.
WE'LL BE HERE A FORTNIGHT. THE GOVERNOR CAN'T DO A THING.
MR. DAVIDSON IS ANXIOUS TO GET BACK TO WORK.
HE'S FEARLESS IN HIS DEVOTION TO THE LORD!
HE INSTILLED A SENSE OF SIN IN THE NATIVES...
...AND DID AWAY WITH THEIR DANCES AND THE HEATHEN CLOTHES THEY WORE.
SEEMS PROPER FOR THE CLIMATE.
THEN THERE WAS THAT DANISH TRADER WHO DEFIED MR. DAVIDSON. HE FIXED IT SO NO ONE WOULD DO BUSINESS WITH THAT MAN.
IN TWO YEARS HE WAS RUINED!
IT TAKES A BRAVE MAN TO STAND UP TO MR. DAVIDSON!
IF THE TREE IS ROTTEN IT SHALL BE CUT DOWN AND CAST INTO THE FLAMES!
I'M A HOOCHIE COOCHIE MAMA, ALL NIGHT LONG...
HA HA! HOO!
THEY HEARD THE SOUND OF DANCING AND RAUCOUS LAUGHTER. THE DAVIDSONS QUIETLY RETIRED TO THEIR ROOM FOR BIBLE STUDY.

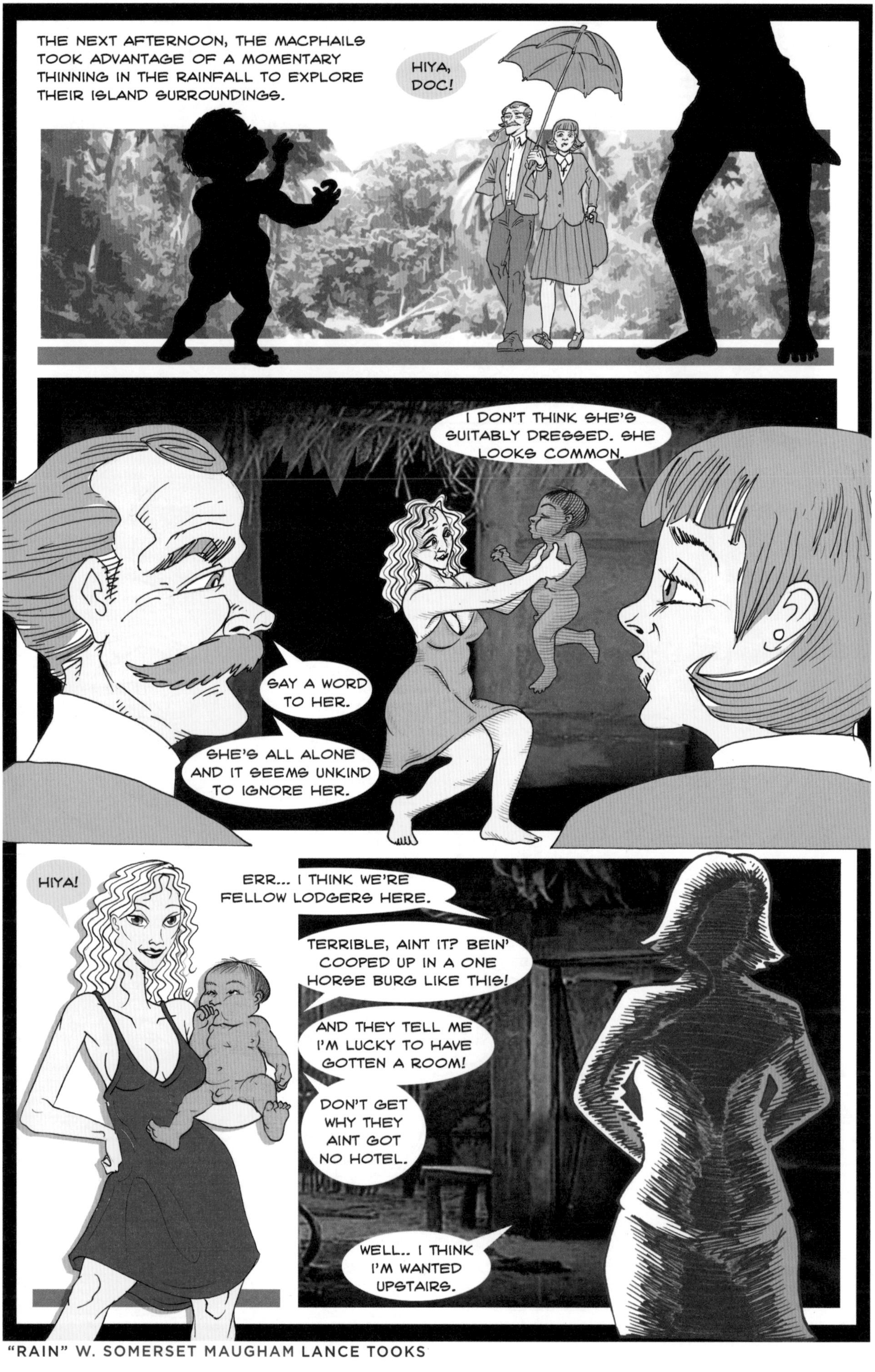
THE NEXT AFTERNOON, THE MACPHAILS TOOK ADVANTAGE OF A MOMENTARY THINNING IN THE RAINFALL TO EXPLORE THEIR ISLAND SURROUNDINGS.
HIYA, DOC!
I DON'T THINK SHE'S SUITABLY DRESSED. SHE LOOKS COMMON.
SAY A WORD TO HER.
SHE'S ALL ALONE AND IT SEEMS UNKIND TO IGNORE HER.
HIYA!
ERR... I THINK WE'RE FELLOW LODGERS HERE.
TERRIBLE, AINT IT? BEIN' COOPED UP IN A ONE HORSE BURG LIKE THIS!
AND THEY TELL ME I'M LUCKY TO HAVE GOTTEN A ROOM!
DON'T GET WHY THEY AINT GOT NO HOTEL.
WELL.. I THINK I'M WANTED UPSTAIRS.

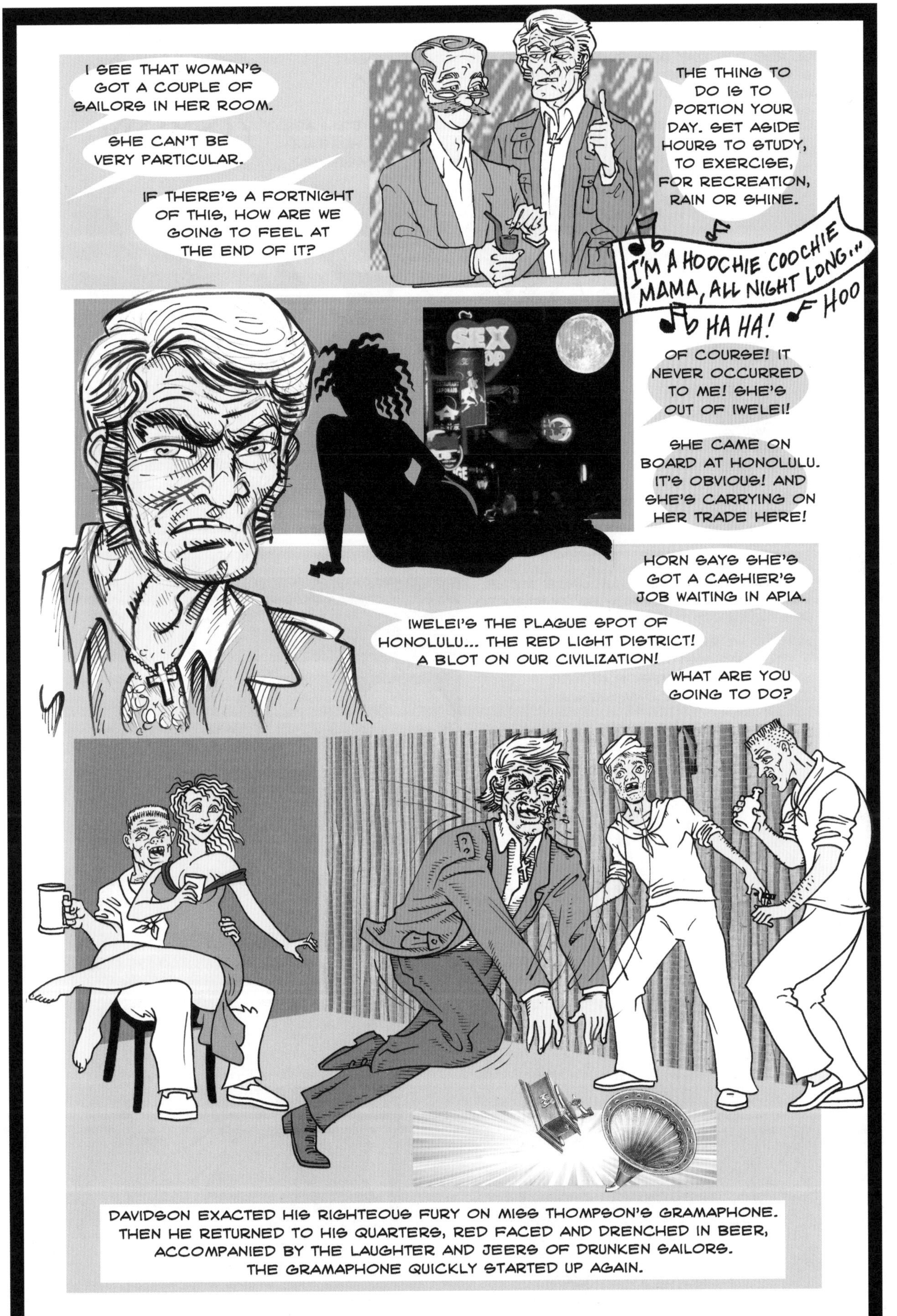
I SEE THAT WOMAN'S GOT A COUPLE OF SAILORS IN HER ROOM.
SHE CAN'T BE VERY PARTICULAR.
IF THERE'S A FORTNIGHT OF THIS, HOW ARE WE GOING TO FEEL AT THE END OF IT?
THE THING TO DO IS TO PORTION YOUR DAY. SET ASIDE HOURS TO STUDY, TO EXERCISE, FOR RECREATION, RAIN OR SHINE.
I'M A HOOCHIE COOCHIE MAMA, ALL NIGHT LONG...
HA HA! HOO
OF COURSE! IT NEVER OCCURRED TO ME! SHE'S OUT OF IWELEI!
SHE CAME ON BOARD AT HONOLULU. IT'S OBVIOUS! AND SHE'S CARRYING ON HER TRADE HERE!
HORN SAYS SHE'S GOT A CASHIER'S JOB WAITING IN APIA.
IWELEI'S THE PLAGUE SPOT OF HONOLULU... THE RED LIGHT DISTRICT! A BLOT ON OUR CIVILIZATION!
WHAT ARE YOU GOING TO DO?
DAVIDSON EXACTED HIS RIGHTEOUS FURY ON MISS THOMPSON'S GRAMAPHONE. THEN HE RETURNED TO HIS QUARTERS, RED FACED AND DRENCHED IN BEER, ACCOMPANIED BY THE LAUGHTER AND JEERS OF DRUNKEN SAILORS. THE GRAMAPHONE QUICKLY STARTED UP AGAIN.

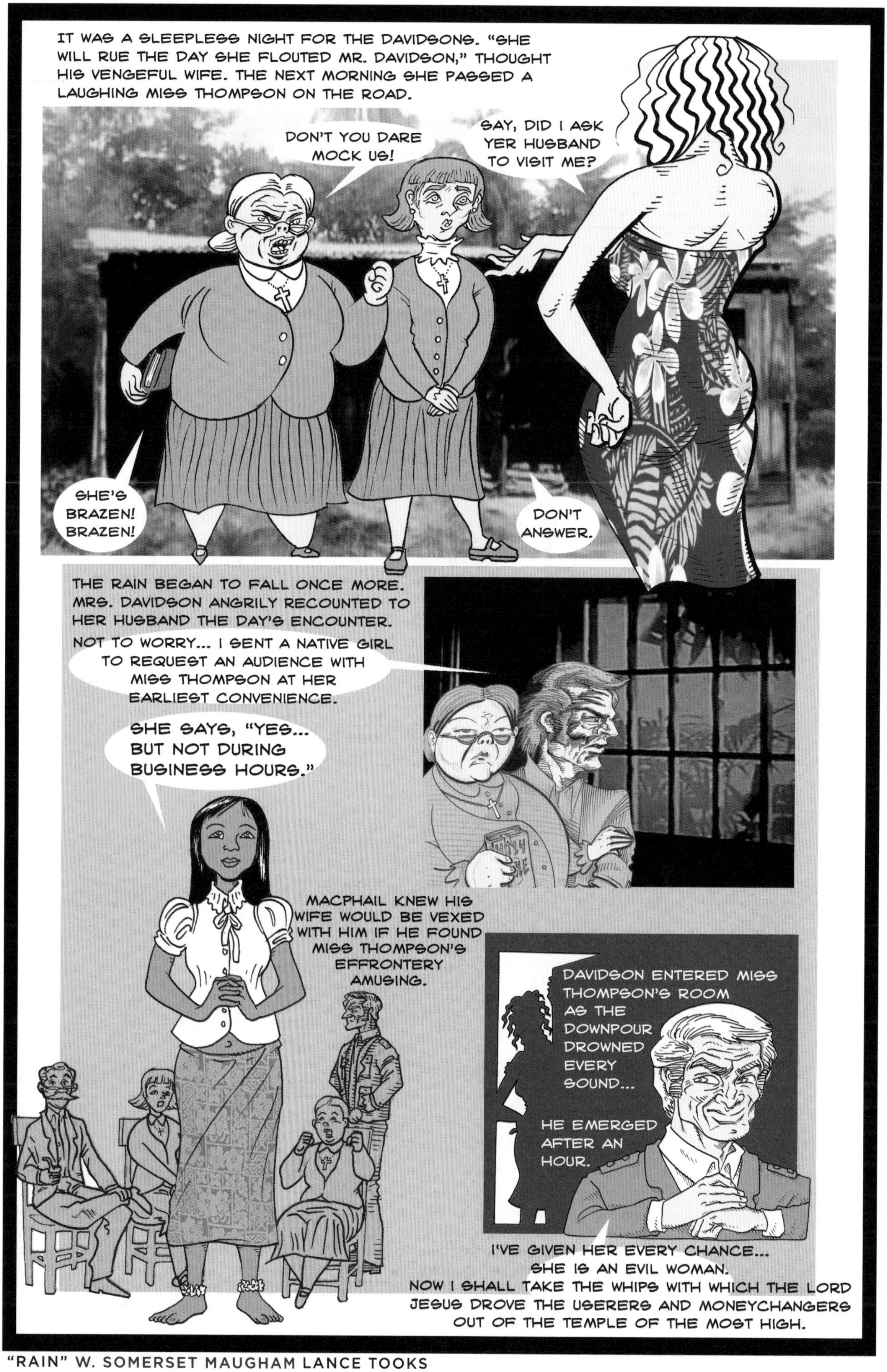
IT WAS A SLEEPLESS NIGHT FOR THE DAVIDSONS. "SHE WILL RUE THE DAY SHE FLOUTED MR. DAVIDSON," THOUGHT HIS VENGEFUL WIFE. THE NEXT MORNING SHE PASSED A LAUGHING MISS THOMPSON ON THE ROAD.
DON'T YOU DARE MOCK US!
SAY, DID I ASK YER HUSBAND TO VISIT ME?
SHE'S BRAZEN! BRAZEN!
DON'T ANSWER.
THE RAIN BEGAN TO FALL ONCE MORE. MRS. DAVIDSON ANGRILY RECOUNTED TO HER HUSBAND THE DAY'S ENCOUNTER.
NOT TO WORRY... I SENT A NATIVE GIRL TO REQUEST AN AUDIENCE WITH MISS THOMPSON AT HER EARLIEST CONVENIENCE.
SHE SAYS, "YES... BUT NOT DURING BUSINESS HOURS."
MACPHAIL KNEW HIS WIFE WOULD BE VEXED WITH HIM IF HE FOUND MISS THOMPSON'S EFFRONTERY AMUSING.
DAVIDSON ENTERED MISS THOMPSON'S ROOM AS THE DOWNPOUR DROWNED EVERY SOUND...
HE EMERGED AFTER AN HOUR.
I'VE GIVEN HER EVERY CHANCE... SHE IS AN EVIL WOMAN.
NOW I SHALL TAKE THE WHIPS WITH WHICH THE LORD JESUS DROVE THE USERERS AND MONEYCHANGERS OUT OF THE TEMPLE OF THE MOST HIGH.

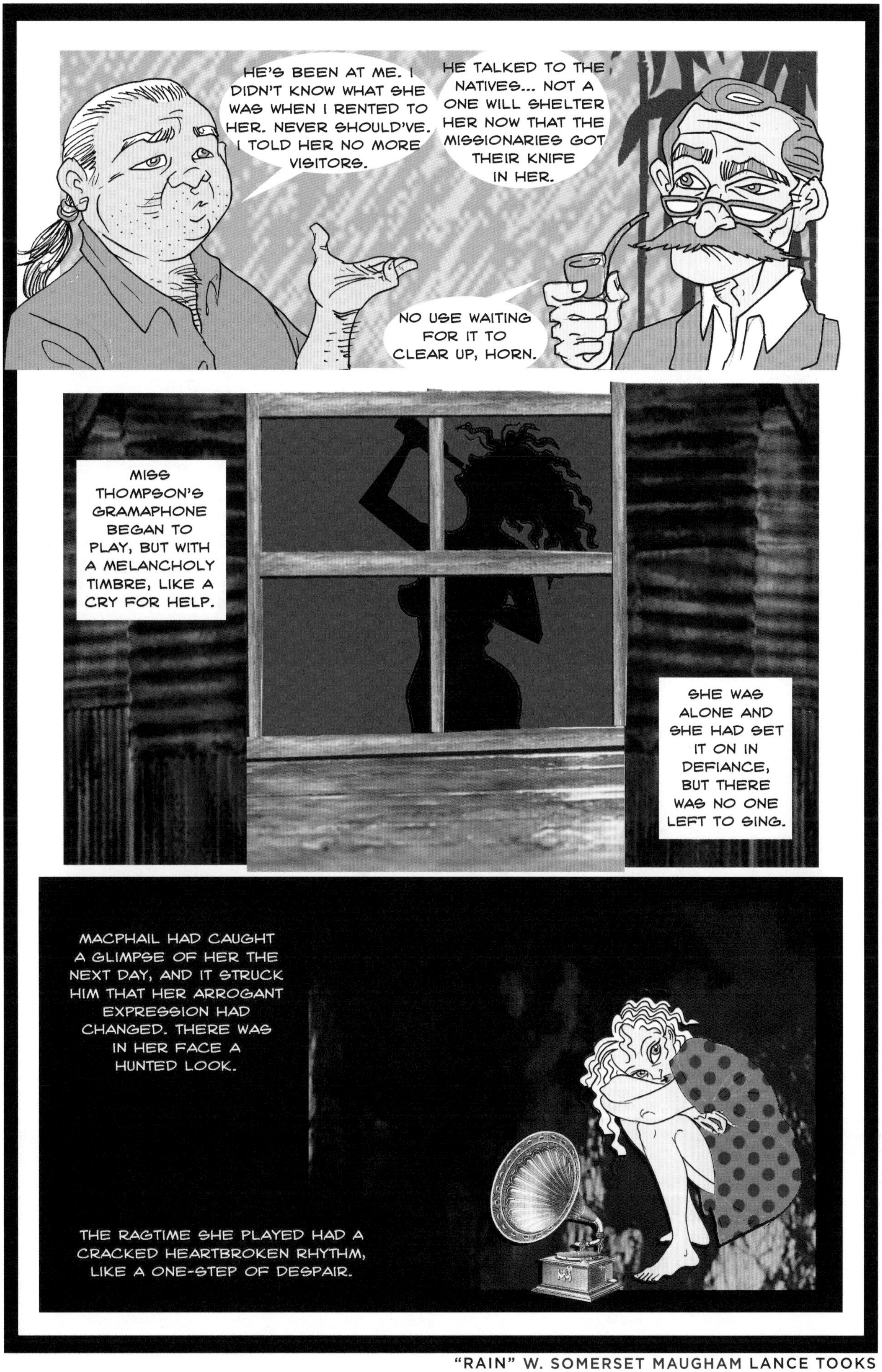
HE'S BEEN AT ME. I DIDN'T KNOW WHAT SHE WAS WHEN I RENTED TO HER. NEVER SHOULD'VE. I TOLD HER NO MORE VISITORS.
HE TALKED TO THE NATIVES... NOT A ONE WILL SHELTER HER NOW THAT THE MISSIONARIES GOT THEIR KNIFE IN HER.
NO USE WAITING FOR IT TO CLEAR UP, HORN.
MISS THOMPSON'S GRAMAPHONE BEGAN TO PLAY, BUT WITH A MELANCHOLY TIMBRE, LIKE A CRY FOR HELP.
SHE WAS ALONE AND SHE HAD SET IT ON IN DEFIANCE, BUT THERE WAS NO ONE LEFT TO SING.
MACPHAIL HAD CAUGHT A GLIMPSE OF HER THE NEXT DAY, AND IT STRUCK HIM THAT HER ARROGANT EXPRESSION HAD CHANGED. THERE WAS IN HER FACE A HUNTED LOOK.
THE RAGTIME SHE PLAYED HAD A CRACKED HEARTBROKEN RHYTHM, LIKE A ONE-STEP OF DESPAIR.

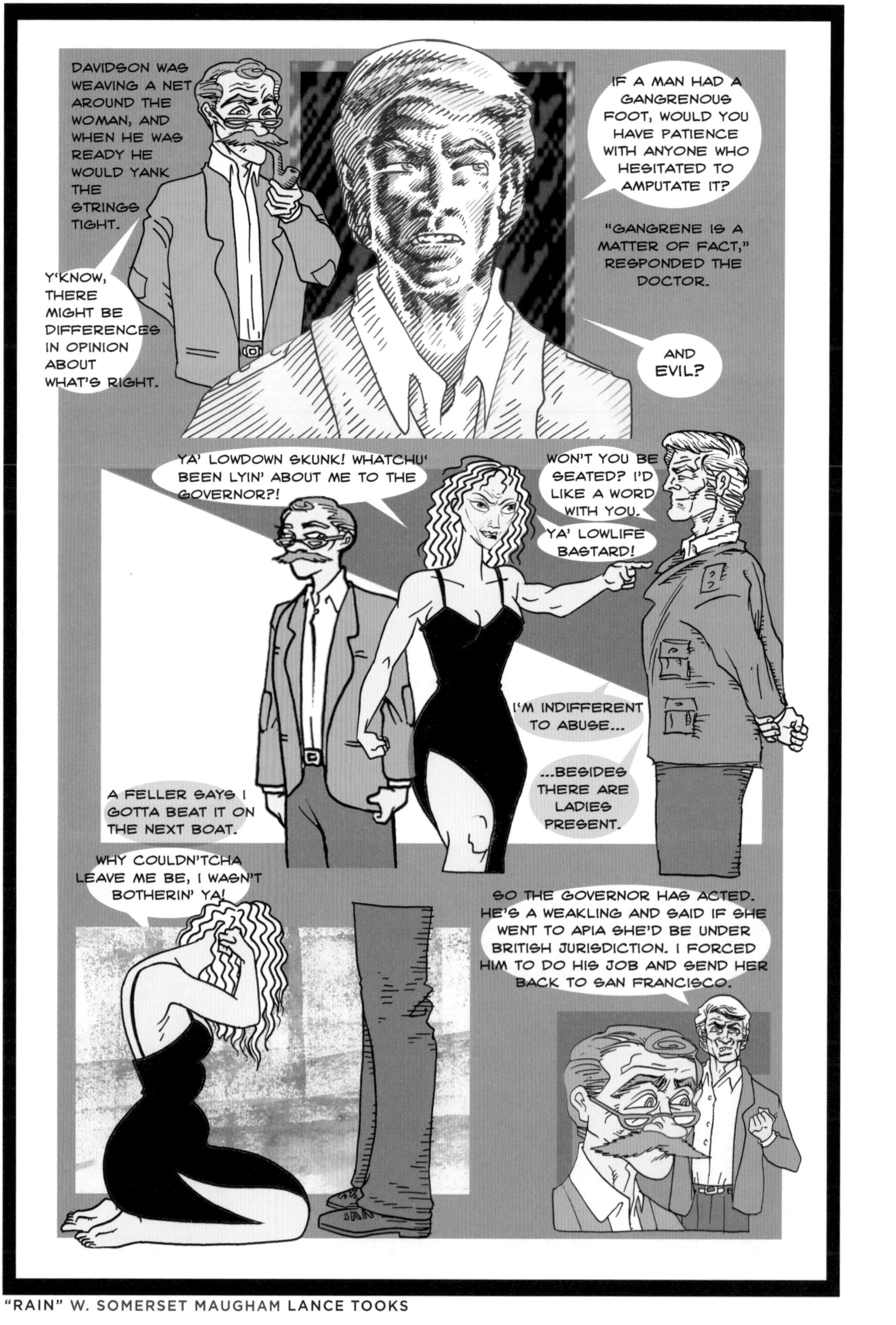

DAVIDSON WAS WEAVING A NET AROUND THE WOMAN, AND WHEN HE WAS READY HE WOULD YANK THE STRINGS TIGHT.
IF A MAN HAD A GANGRENOUS FOOT, WOULD YOU HAVE PATIENCE WITH ANYONE WHO HESITATED TO AMPUTATE IT?
"GANGRENE IS A MATTER OF FACT," RESPONDED THE DOCTOR.
Y'KNOW, THERE MIGHT BE DIFFERENCES IN OPINION ABOUT WHAT'S RIGHT.
AND EVIL?
YA' LOWDOWN SKUNK! WHATCHU' BEEN LYIN' ABOUT ME TO THE GOVERNOR?!
WON'T YOU BE SEATED? I'D LIKE A WORD WITH YOU.
YA' LOWLIFE BASTARD!
I'M INDIFFERENT TO ABUSE...
...BESIDES THERE ARE LADIES PRESENT.
A FELLER SAYS I GOTTA BEAT IT ON THE NEXT BOAT.
WHY COULDN'TCHA LEAVE ME BE, I WASN'T BOTHERIN' YA!
SO THE GOVERNOR HAS ACTED. HE'S A WEAKLING AND SAID IF SHE WENT TO APIA SHE'D BE UNDER BRITISH JURISDICTION. I FORCED HIM TO DO HIS JOB AND SEND HER BACK TO SAN FRANCISCO.

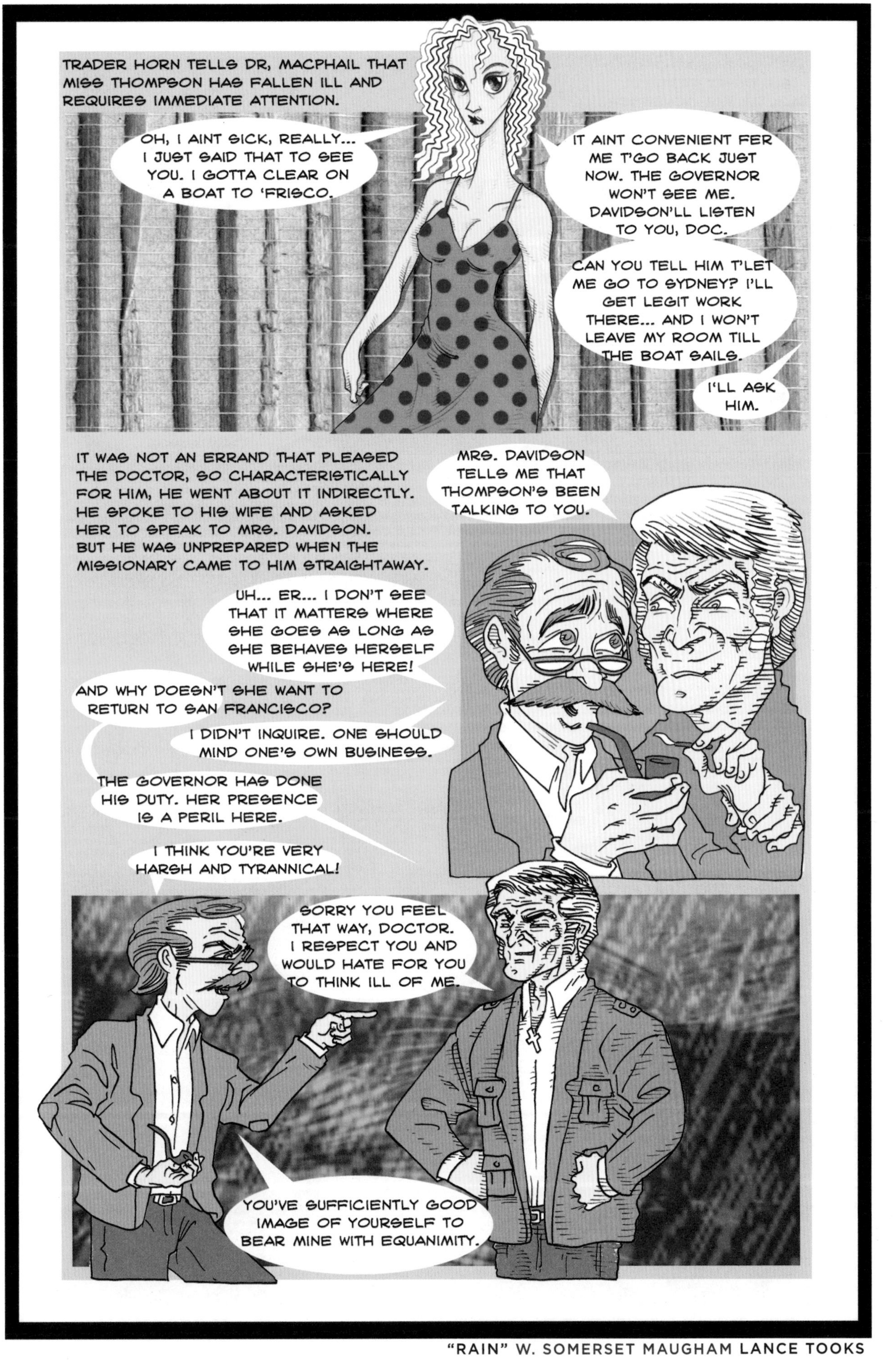
TRADER HORN TELLS DR, MACPHAIL THAT MISS THOMPSON HAS FALLEN ILL AND REQUIRES IMMEDIATE ATTENTION.
OH, I AINT SICK, REALLY... I JUST SAID THAT TO SEE YOU. I GOTTA CLEAR ON A BOAT TO 'FRISCO.
IT AINT CONVENIENT FER ME T'GO BACK JUST NOW. THE GOVERNOR WON'T SEE ME. DAVIDSON'LL LISTEN TO YOU, DOC.
CAN YOU TELL HIM T'LET ME GO TO SYDNEY? I'LL GET LEGIT WORK THERE... AND I WON'T LEAVE MY ROOM TILL THE BOAT SAILS.
I'LL ASK HIM.
IT WAS NOT AN ERRAND THAT PLEASED THE DOCTOR, SO CHARACTERISTICALLY FOR HIM, HE WENT ABOUT IT INDIRECTLY. HE SPOKE TO HIS WIFE AND ASKED HER TO SPEAK TO MRS. DAVIDSON. BUT HE WAS UNPREPARED WHEN THE MISSIONARY CAME TO HIM STRAIGHTAWAY.
MRS. DAVIDSON TELLS ME THAT THOMPSON'S BEEN TALKING TO YOU.
UH... ER... I DON'T SEE THAT IT MATTERS WHERE SHE GOES AS LONG AS SHE BEHAVES HERSELF WHILE SHE'S HERE!
AND WHY DOESN'T SHE WANT TO RETURN TO SAN FRANCISCO?
I DIDN'T INQUIRE. ONE SHOULD MIND ONE'S OWN BUSINESS.
THE GOVERNOR HAS DONE HIS DUTY. HER PRESENCE IS A PERIL HERE.
I THINK YOU'RE VERY HARSH AND TYRANNICAL!
SORRY YOU FEEL THAT WAY, DOCTOR. I RESPECT YOU AND WOULD HATE FOR YOU TO THINK ILL OF ME.
YOU'VE SUFFICIENTLY GOOD IMAGE OF YOURSELF TO BEAR MINE WITH EQUANIMITY.

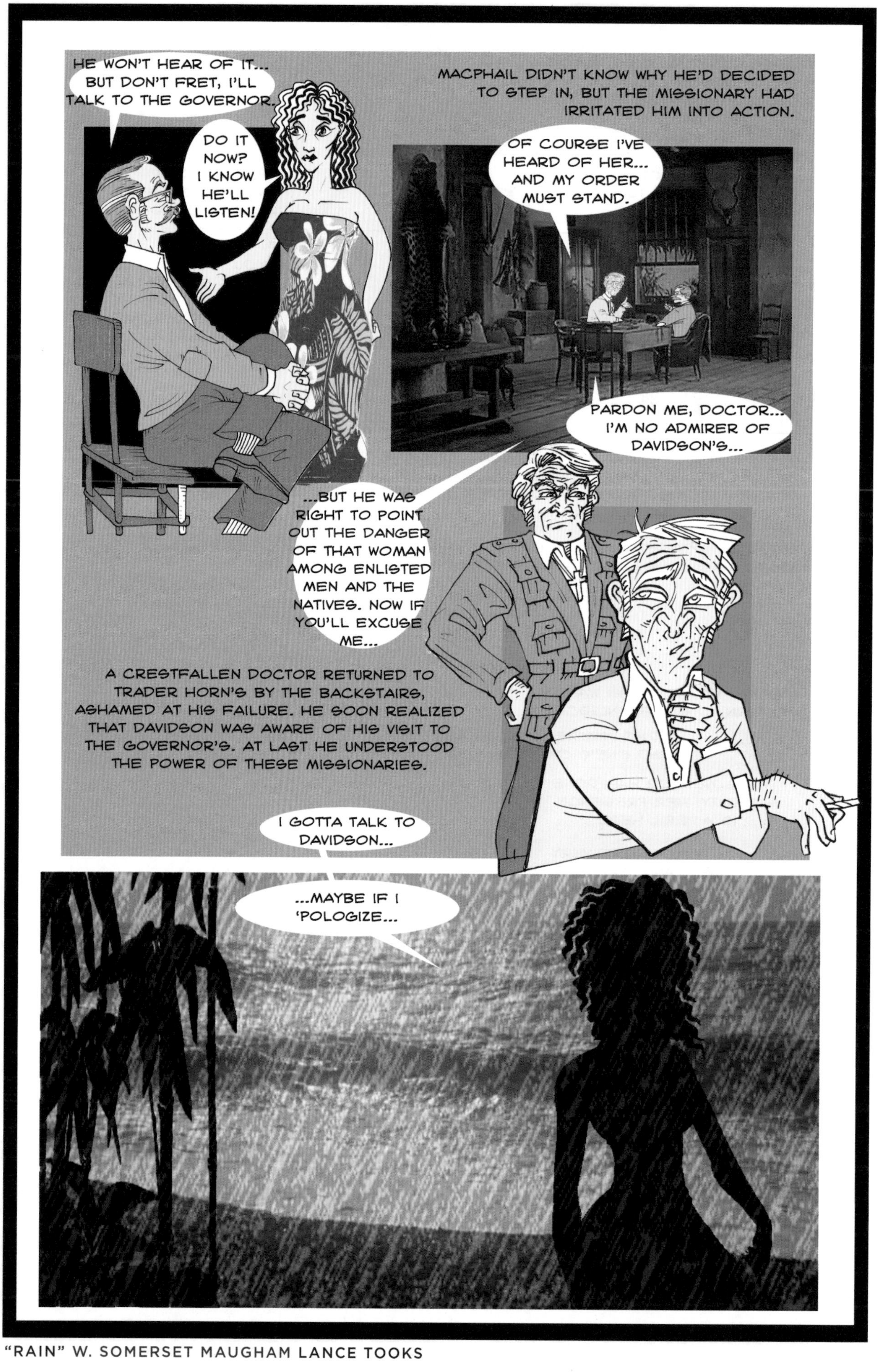
HE WON'T HEAR OF IT... BUT DON'T FRET, I'LL TALK TO THE GOVERNOR.
DO IT NOW? I KNOW HE'LL LISTEN!
MACPHAIL DIDN'T KNOW WHY HE'D DECIDED TO STEP IN, BUT THE MISSIONARY HAD IRRITATED HIM INTO ACTION.
OF COURSE I'VE HEARD OF HER... AND MY ORDER MUST STAND.
PARDON ME, DOCTOR... I'M NO ADMIRER OF DAVIDSON'S...
...BUT HE WAS RIGHT TO POINT OUT THE DANGER OF THAT WOMAN AMONG ENLISTED MEN AND THE NATIVES. NOW IF YOU'LL EXCUSE ME...
A CRESTFALLEN DOCTOR RETURNED TO TRADER HORN'S BY THE BACKSTAIRS, ASHAMED AT HIS FAILURE. HE SOON REALIZED THAT DAVIDSON WAS AWARE OF HIS VISIT TO THE GOVERNOR'S. AT LAST HE UNDERSTOOD THE POWER OF THESE MISSIONARIES.
I GOTTA TALK TO DAVIDSON...
...MAYBE IF I 'POLOGIZE...

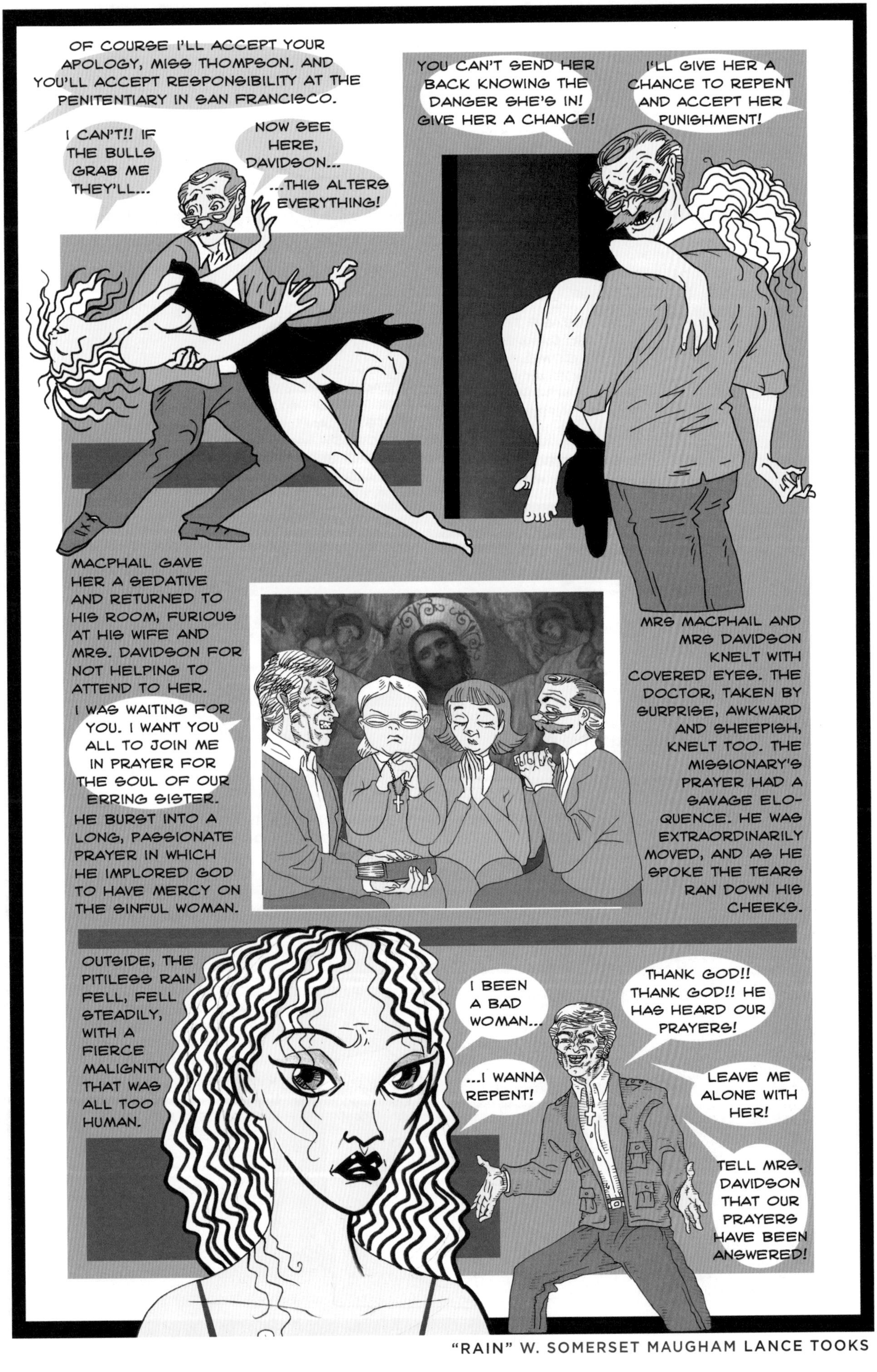
OF COURSE I'LL ACCEPT YOUR APOLOGY, MISS THOMPSON. AND YOU'LL ACCEPT RESPONSIBILITY AT THE PENITENTIARY IN SAN FRANCISCO.
I CAN'T!! IF THE BULLS GRAB ME THEY'LL...
NOW SEE HERE, DAVIDSON...
...THIS ALTERS EVERYTHING!
YOU CAN'T SEND HER BACK KNOWING THE DANGER SHE'S IN! GIVE HER A CHANCE!
I'LL GIVE HER A CHANCE TO REPENT AND ACCEPT HER PUNISHMENT!
MACPHAIL GAVE HER A SEDATIVE AND RETURNED TO HIS ROOM, FURIOUS AT HIS WIFE AND MRS. DAVIDSON FOR NOT HELPING TO ATTEND TO HER.
I WAS WAITING FOR YOU. I WANT YOU ALL TO JOIN ME IN PRAYER FOR THE SOUL OF OUR ERRING SISTER.
HE BURST INTO A LONG, PASSIONATE PRAYER IN WHICH HE IMPLORED GOD TO HAVE MERCY ON THE SINFUL WOMAN.
MRS MACPHAIL AND MRS DAVIDSON KNELT WITH COVERED EYES. THE DOCTOR, TAKEN BY SURPRISE, AWKWARD AND SHEEPISH, KNELT TOO. THE MISSIONARY'S PRAYER HAD A SAVAGE ELO-QUENCE. HE WAS EXTRAORDINARILY MOVED, AND AS HE SPOKE THE TEARS RAN DOWN HIS CHEEKS.
OUTSIDE, THE PITILESS RAIN FELL, FELL STEADILY, WITH A FIERCE MALIGNITY THAT WAS ALL TOO HUMAN.
I BEEN A BAD WOMAN...
...I WANNA REPENT!
THANK GOD!! THANK GOD!! HE HAS HEARD OUR PRAYERS!
LEAVE ME ALONE WITH HER!
TELL MRS. DAVIDSON THAT OUR PRAYERS HAVE BEEN ANSWERED!

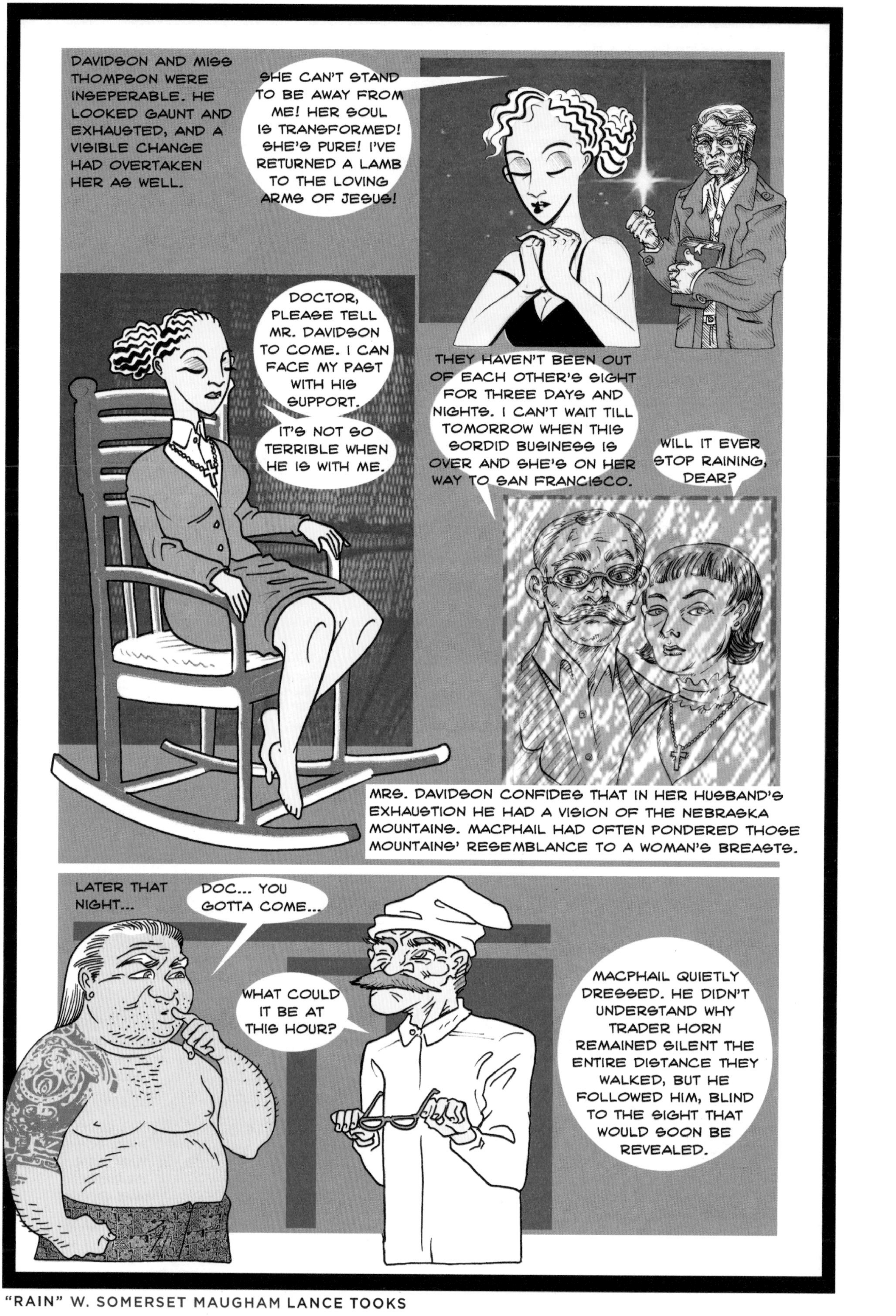
DAVIDSON AND MISS THOMPSON WERE INSEPERABLE. HE LOOKED GAUNT AND EXHAUSTED, AND A VISIBLE CHANGE HAD OVERTAKEN HER AS WELL.
SHE CAN'T STAND TO BE AWAY FROM ME! HER SOUL IS TRANSFORMED! SHE'S PURE! I'VE RETURNED A LAMB TO THE LOVING ARMS OF JESUS!
DOCTOR, PLEASE TELL MR. DAVIDSON TO COME. I CAN FACE MY PAST WITH HIS SUPPORT.
IT'S NOT SO TERRIBLE WHEN HE IS WITH ME.
THEY HAVEN'T BEEN OUT OF EACH OTHER'S SIGHT FOR THREE DAYS AND NIGHTS. I CAN'T WAIT TILL TOMORROW WHEN THIS SORDID BUSINESS IS OVER AND SHE'S ON HER WAY TO SAN FRANCISCO.
WILL IT EVER STOP RAINING, DEAR?
MRS. DAVIDSON CONFIDES THAT IN HER HUSBAND'S EXHAUSTION HE HAD A VISION OF THE NEBRASKA MOUNTAINS. MACPHAIL HAD OFTEN PONDERED THOSE MOUNTAINS' RESEMBLANCE TO A WOMAN'S BREASTS.
LATER THAT NIGHT...
DOC... YOU GOTTA COME...
WHAT COULD IT BE AT THIS HOUR?
MACPHAIL QUIETLY DRESSED. HE DIDN'T UNDERSTAND WHY TRADER HORN REMAINED SILENT THE ENTIRE DISTANCE THEY WALKED, BUT HE FOLLOWED HIM, BLIND TO THE SIGHT THAT WOULD SOON BE REVEALED.

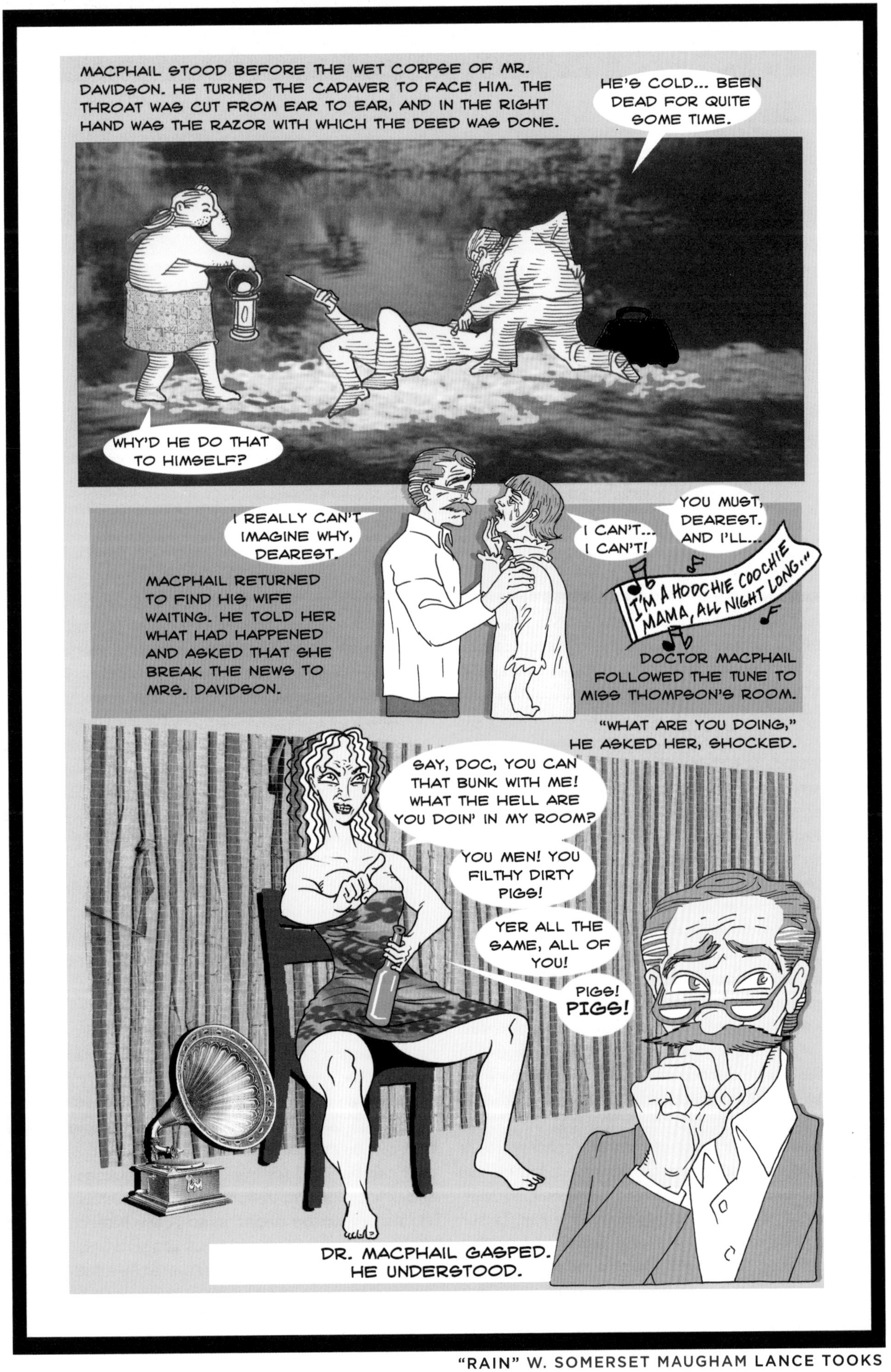
MACPHAIL STOOD BEFORE THE WET CORPSE OF MR. DAVIDSON. HE TURNED THE CADAVER TO FACE HIM. THE THROAT WAS CUT FROM EAR TO EAR, AND IN THE RIGHT HAND WAS THE RAZOR WITH WHICH THE DEED WAS DONE.
HE'S COLD... BEEN DEAD FOR QUITE SOME TIME.
WHY'D HE DO THAT TO HIMSELF?
I REALLY CAN'T IMAGINE WHY, DEAREST.
MACPHAIL RETURNED TO FIND HIS WIFE WAITING. HE TOLD HER WHAT HAD HAPPENED AND ASKED THAT SHE BREAK THE NEWS TO MRS. DAVIDSON.
I CAN'T... I CAN'T!
YOU MUST, DEAREST. AND I'LL...
I'M A HOOCHIE COOCHIE MAMA, ALL NIGHT LONG...
DOCTOR MACPHAIL FOLLOWED THE TUNE TO MISS THOMPSON'S ROOM.
"WHAT ARE YOU DOING," HE ASKED HER, SHOCKED.
SAY, DOC, YOU CAN THAT BUNK WITH ME! WHAT THE HELL ARE YOU DOIN' IN MY ROOM?
YOU MEN! YOU FILTHY DIRTY PIGS!
YER ALL THE SAME, ALL OF YOU!
PIGS! PIGS!
DR. MACPHAIL GASPED. HE UNDERSTOOD.

Ulysses

James Joyce

ART/ADAPTATION BY **Robert Berry** WITH **Josh Levitas**

WIDELY CONSIDERED THE GREATEST, MOST important novel of the twentieth century, *Ulysses*'s basic plot is disarmingly simple—we follow the fairly typical day of two men as they run errands, eat and drink, and otherwise wander about Dublin. But on this seemingly straightforward slice-of-life foundation, James Joyce erected one of the most complex, experimental, and, at times, daunting works of art ever created. The styles he uses are dense and rich and often unexpected: many are parodies and pastiches; puns and other wordplay abound. One chapter is written as newspaper headlines; part of another chapter is in the form of a play. Entire books have been written to explain Joyce's endless allusions—historical, political, theological, literary. Then there are the stream-of-consciousness sections, giving us the unstructured, unfiltered chain of thoughts of a given character. The novel famously ends with Molly Bloom's stream of consciousness—over 24,000 words and only two punctuation marks. She's thinking quite a bit about relationships (including hers with Leopold), love, and sex. The saltiness of this final chapter is part of the reason that *Ulysses* ran into over a decade of legal problems, banned for years after its 1922 publication. Copies were literally burned by authorities in Britain and in the US.

But underneath all the pyrotechnics and controversy is a warm, touching look at two men who have a father–son dynamic going: Leopold Bloom, an ad canvasser, middle-aged, half-Jewish, always checking out the ladies, father of a deceased child, carrying on a long-distance love affair while his wife, Molly, has an affair with a local man. Then there's the younger Stephen Dedalus—the main character of Joyce's earlier book, *A Portrait of the Artist as a Young Man*—who's much less likeable. Aloof, cerebral, a struggling poet who teaches history at a boys' school, in mourning over the death of his mother almost a year ago. He's the focus of the first three sections of *Ulysses*. Then the narrative doubles back to 8:00 a.m. that morning and follows Leopold's day. This is where the following excerpt begins.

Rob Berry is a classically trained painter who became intrigued by the storytelling potential of comics. He switched art forms—though he still often uses watercolors to color his ink work—and decided to tackle one of the most difficult novels around. In an interview, he explained:

> It seems to me that if comics are to expand as art form, to grow in their potential as a familiar but unique storytelling medium, we need to show a new audience what it can do; how it can make novels like this one a bit easier to "see" without simplifying the original material.

Thus was born *Ulysses* "*Seen*," Rob's epic project, with his production partner Josh Levitas, to graphically adapt the entire book, posting portions online serially and releasing them as apps for the iPad and other devices. He estimates that it will take a good ten years to complete. He wants to focus on the potential of digital publishing, especially as it can be used for hypertext connections, annotations, and discussion. I'm delighted that he's let us include some of this project on paper, specifically fifteen pages of the "Calypso" episode, showing us Leopold and Molly's morning. We catch up with "Poldy" after he's fed their cat and decided to go to the nearby butcher shop to fetch a pork kidney for breakfast.

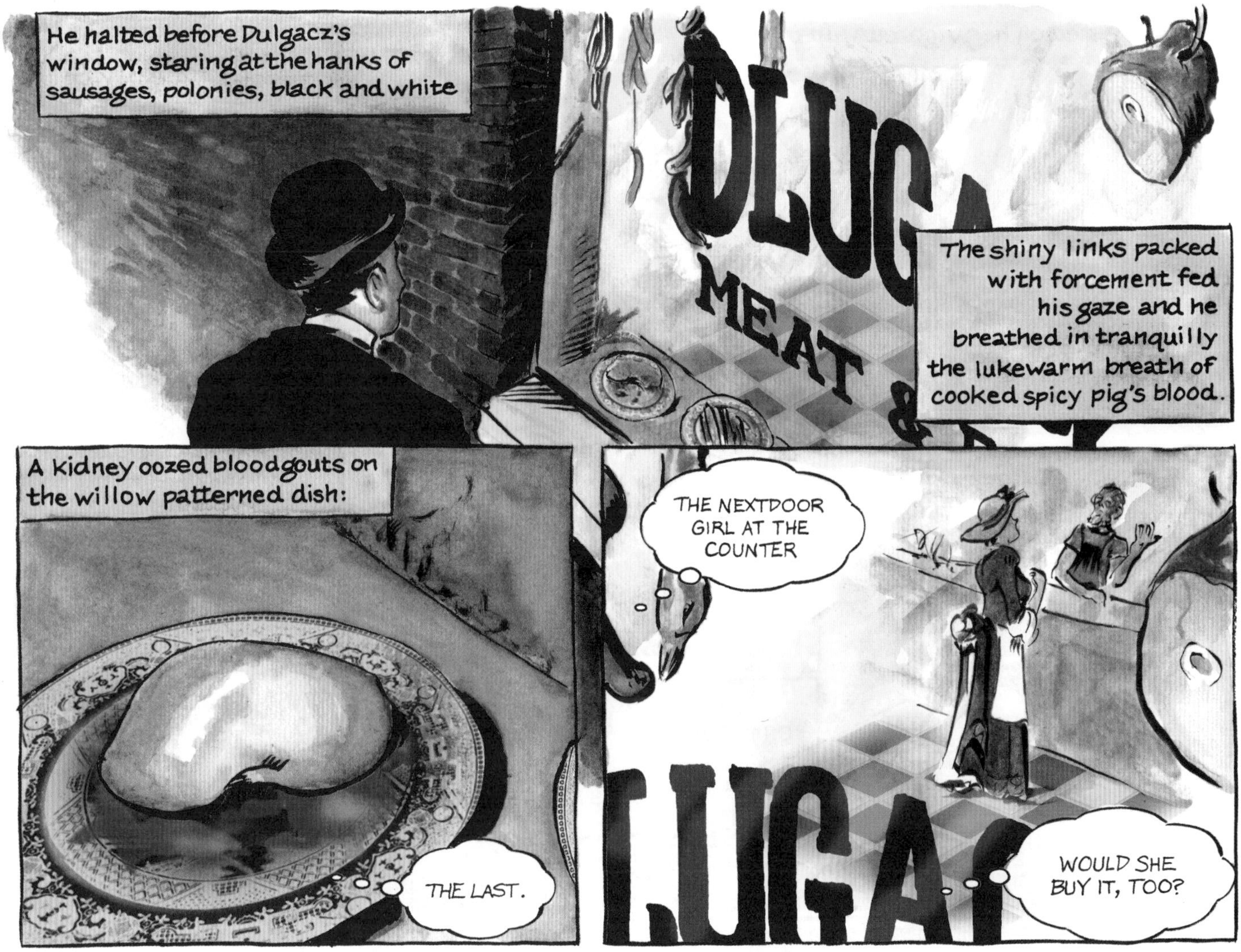
He halted before Dulgacz's window, staring at the hanks of sausages, polonies, black and white
DLUG
MEAT &
The shiny links packed with forcement fed his gaze and he breathed in tranquilly the lukewarm breath of cooked spicy pig's blood.
A kidney oozed bloodgouts on the willow patterned dish:
THE LAST.
THE NEXTDOOR GIRL AT THE COUNTER
LUGA
WOULD SHE BUY IT, TOO?

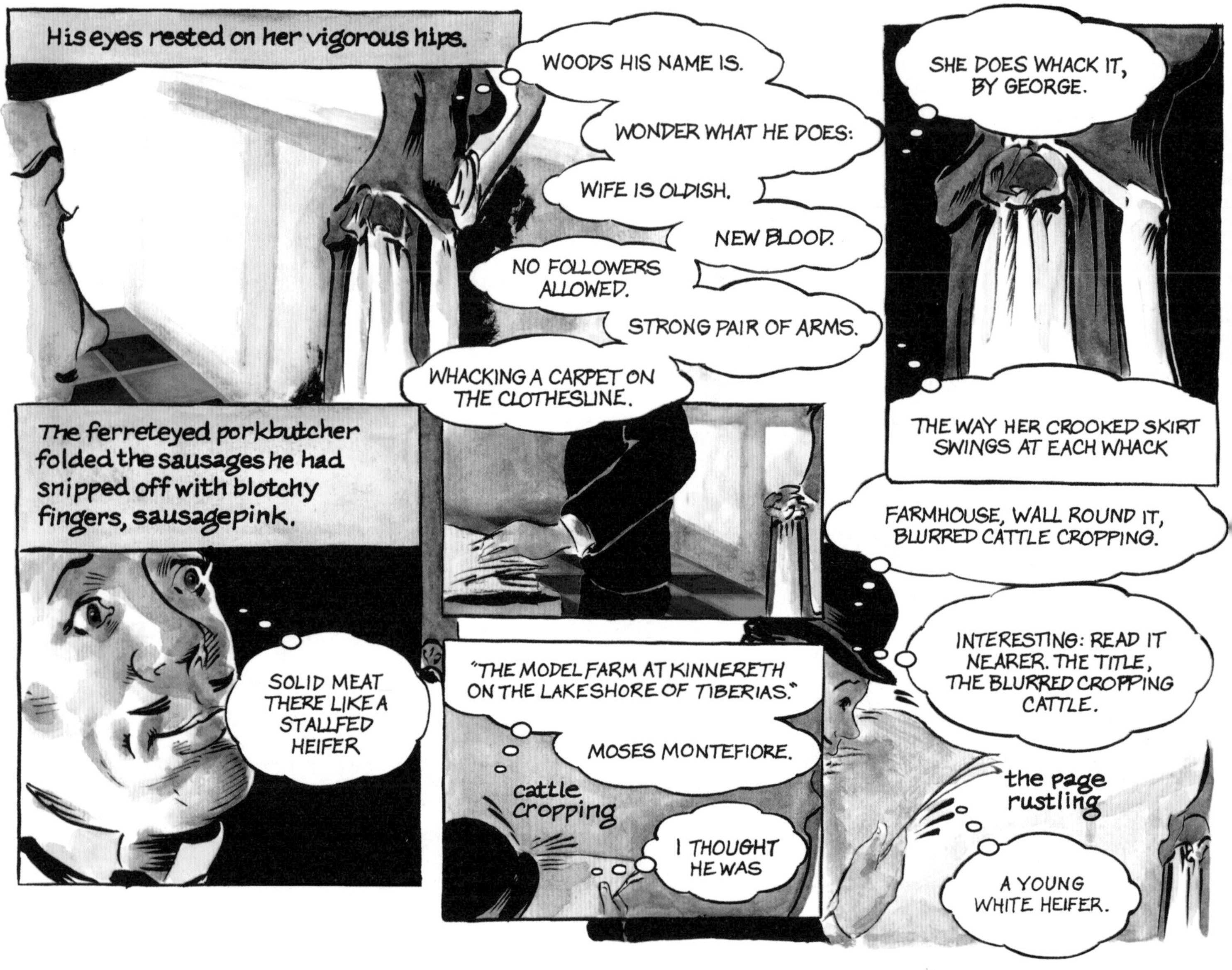

His eyes rested on her vigorous hips.
WOODS HIS NAME IS.
WONDER WHAT HE DOES:
WIFE IS OLDISH.
NEW BLOOD.
NO FOLLOWERS ALLOWED.
STRONG PAIR OF ARMS.
WHACKING A CARPET ON THE CLOTHESLINE.
SHE DOES WHACK IT, BY GEORGE.
THE WAY HER CROOKED SKIRT SWINGS AT EACH WHACK
The ferreteyed porkbutcher folded the sausages he had snipped off with blotchy fingers, sausagepink.
SOLID MEAT THERE LIKE A STALLFED HEIFER
FARMHOUSE, WALL ROUND IT, BLURRED CATTLE CROPPING.
"THE MODEL FARM AT KINNERETH ON THE LAKESHORE OF TIBERIAS."
MOSES MONTEFIORE.
INTERESTING: READ IT NEARER. THE TITLE, THE BLURRED CROPPING CATTLE.
cattle cropping
I THOUGHT HE WAS
the page rustling
A YOUNG WHITE HEIFER.

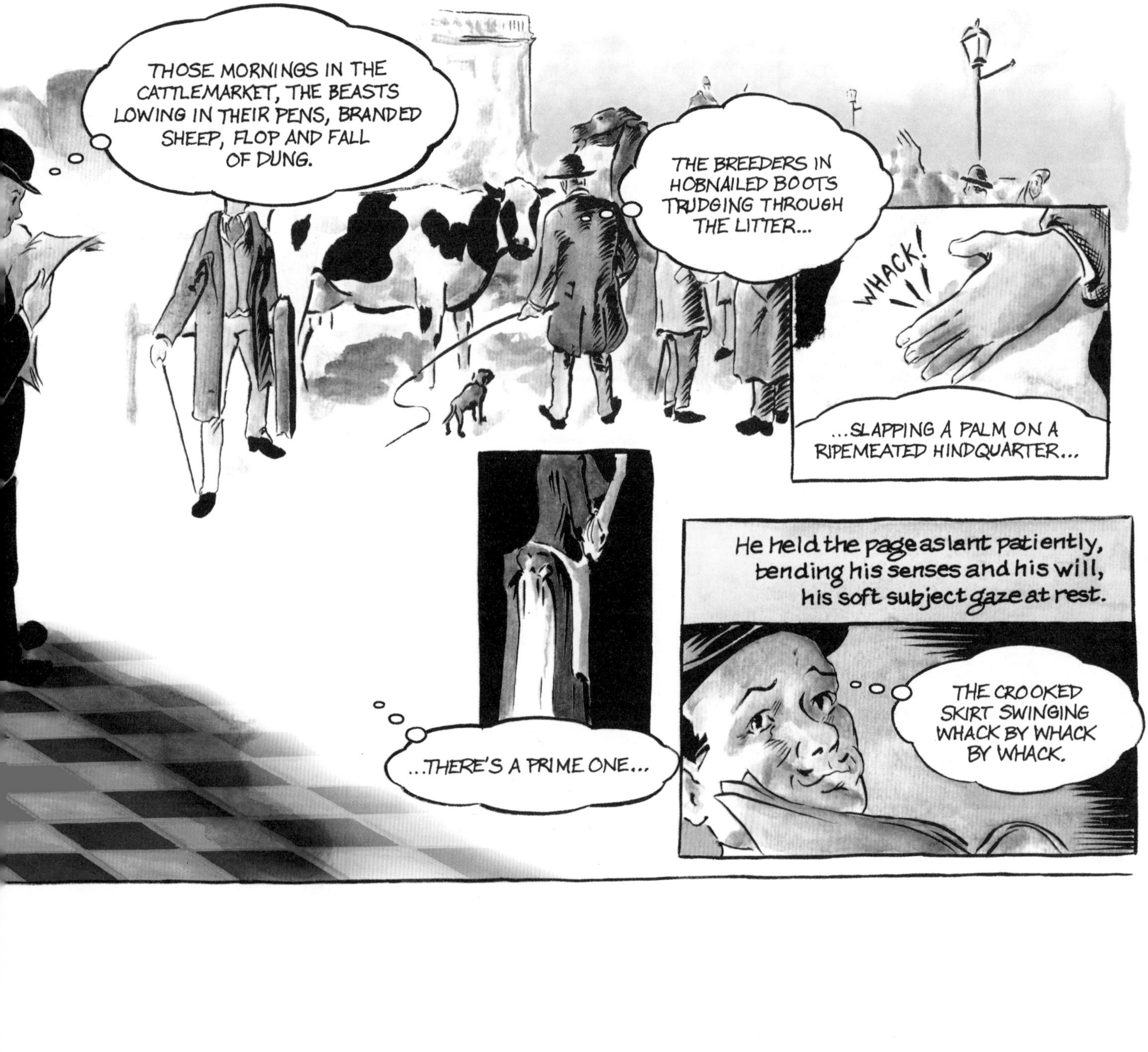
THOSE MORNINGS IN THE CATTLEMARKET, THE BEASTS LOWING IN THEIR PENS, BRANDED SHEEP, FLOP AND FALL OF DUNG.
THE BREEDERS IN HOBNAILED BOOTS TRUDGING THROUGH THE LITTER...
WHACK!
...SLAPPING A PALM ON A RIPEMEATED HINDQUARTER...
...THERE'S A PRIME ONE...
He held the page aslant patiently, bending his senses and his will, his soft subject gaze at rest.
THE CROOKED SKIRT SWINGING WHACK BY WHACK BY WHACK.

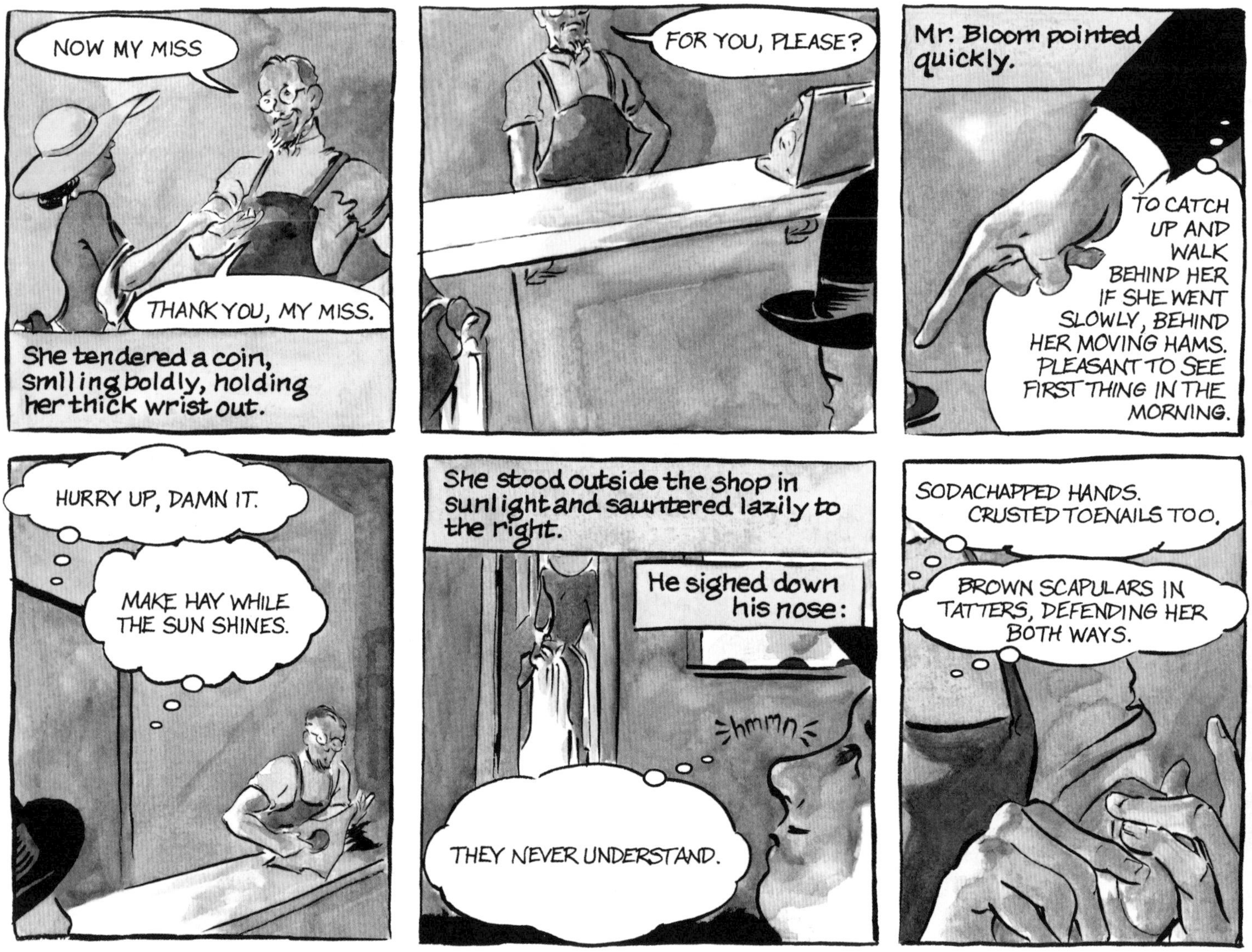

NOW MY MISS
THANK YOU, MY MISS.
She tendered a coin, smiling boldly, holding her thick wrist out.
FOR YOU, PLEASE?
Mr. Bloom pointed quickly.
TO CATCH UP AND WALK BEHIND HER IF SHE WENT SLOWLY, BEHIND HER MOVING HAMS. PLEASANT TO SEE FIRST THING IN THE MORNING.
HURRY UP, DAMN IT.
MAKE HAY WHILE THE SUN SHINES.
She stood outside the shop in sunlight and sauntered lazily to the right.
He sighed down his nose:
hmmn
THEY NEVER UNDERSTAND.
SODACHAPPED HANDS. CRUSTED TOENAILS TOO.
BROWN SCAPULARS IN TATTERS, DEFENDING HER BOTH WAYS.

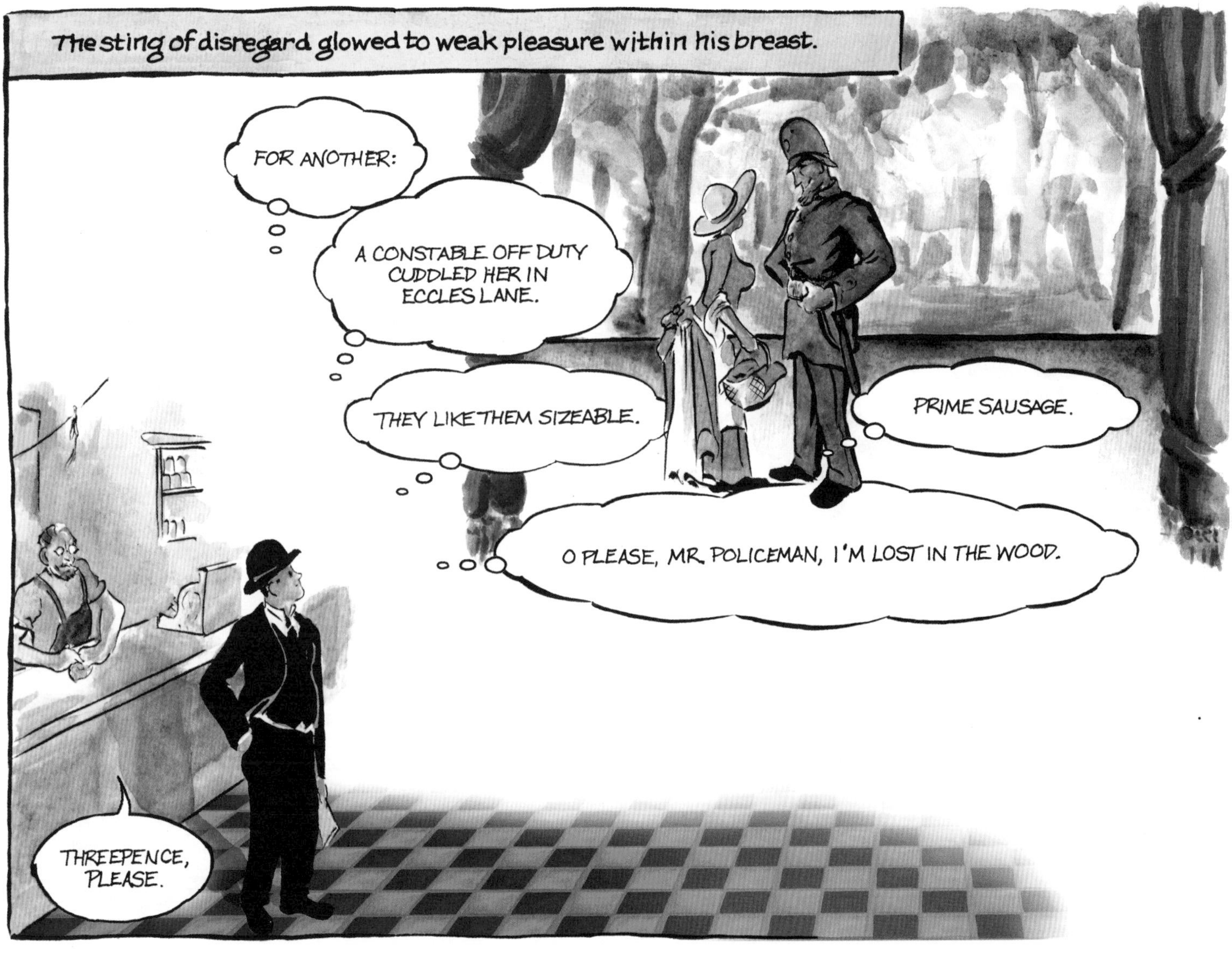
The sting of disregard glowed to weak pleasure within his breast.
FOR ANOTHER:
A CONSTABLE OFF DUTY CUDDLED HER IN ECCLES LANE.
THEY LIKE THEM SIZEABLE.
PRIME SAUSAGE.
O PLEASE, MR. POLICEMAN, I'M LOST IN THE WOOD.
THREEPENCE, PLEASE.

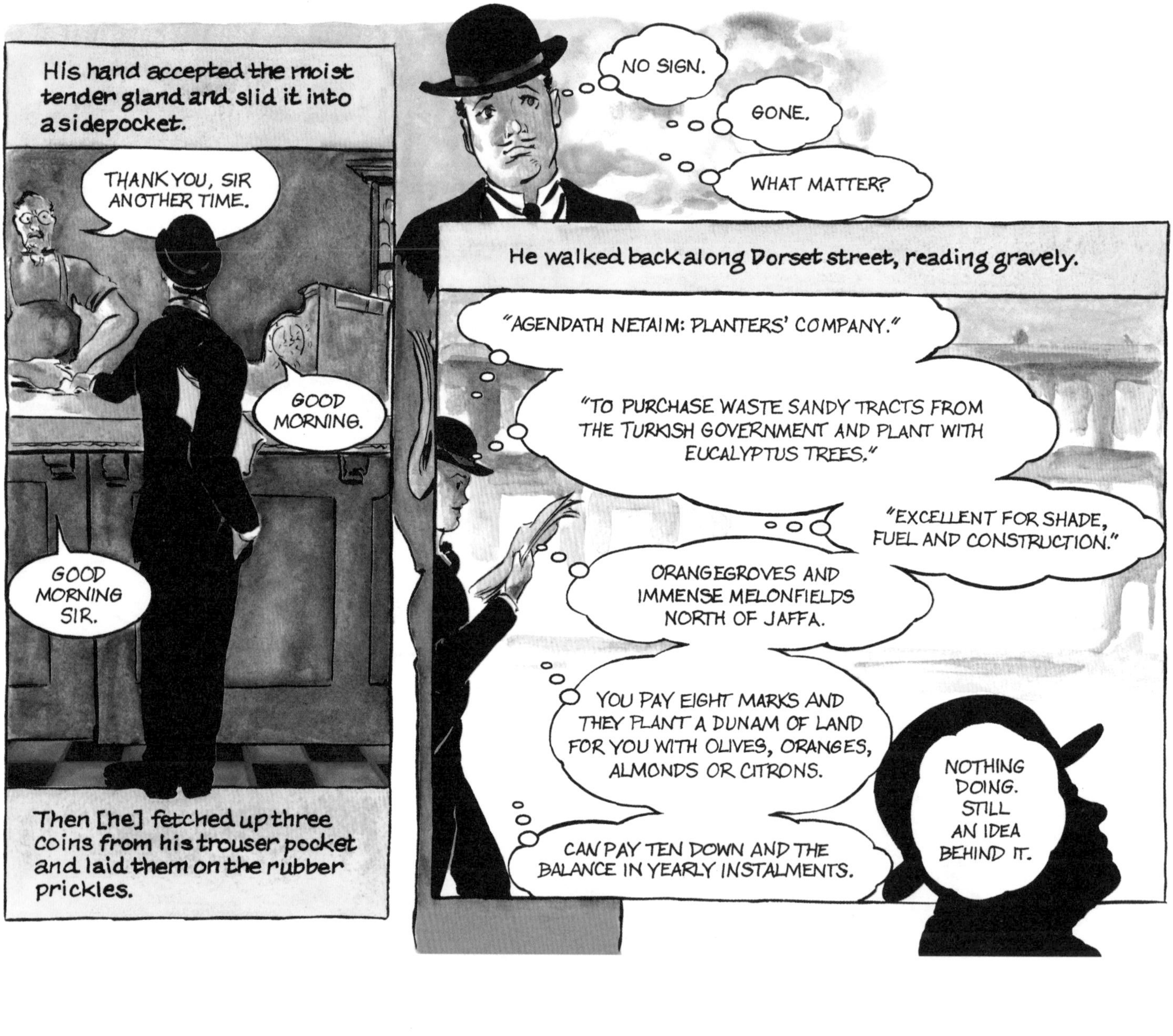

His hand accepted the moist tender gland and slid it into a sidepocket.
THANK YOU, SIR ANOTHER TIME.
GOOD MORNING.
GOOD MORNING SIR.
Then [he] fetched up three coins from his trouser pocket and laid them on the rubber prickles.
NO SIGN.
GONE.
WHAT MATTER?
He walked back along Dorset street, reading gravely.
"AGENDATH NETAIM: PLANTERS' COMPANY."
"TO PURCHASE WASTE SANDY TRACTS FROM THE TURKISH GOVERNMENT AND PLANT WITH EUCALYPTUS TREES."
"EXCELLENT FOR SHADE, FUEL AND CONSTRUCTION."
ORANGEGROVES AND IMMENSE MELONFIELDS NORTH OF JAFFA.
YOU PAY EIGHT MARKS AND THEY PLANT A DUNAM OF LAND FOR YOU WITH OLIVES, ORANGES, ALMONDS OR CITRONS.
CAN PAY TEN DOWN AND THE BALANCE IN YEARLY INSTALMENTS.
NOTHING DOING. STILL AN IDEA BEHIND IT.

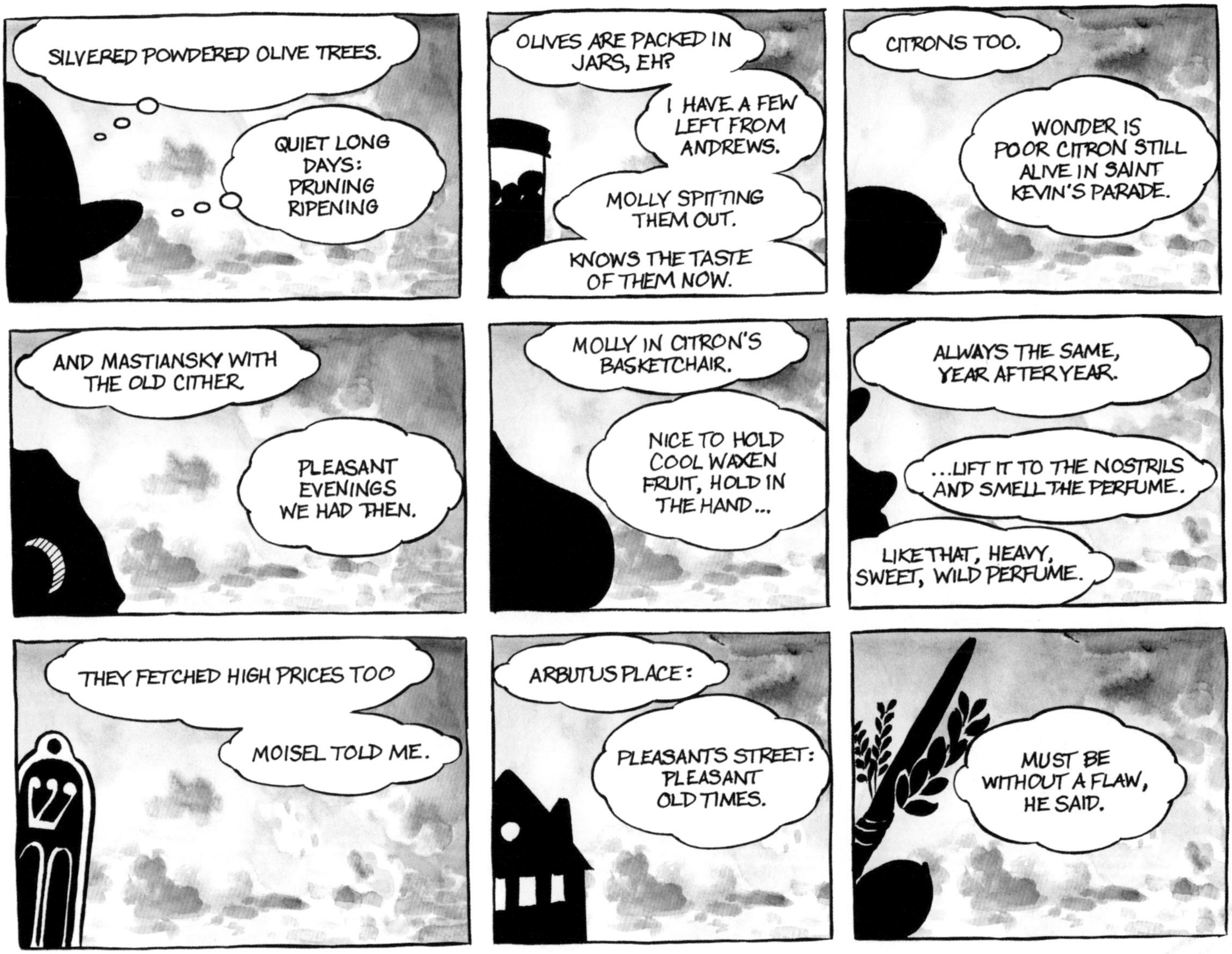
SILVERED POWDERED OLIVE TREES.
QUIET LONG DAYS: PRUNING RIPENING
OLIVES ARE PACKED IN JARS, EH?
I HAVE A FEW LEFT FROM ANDREWS.
MOLLY SPITTING THEM OUT.
KNOWS THE TASTE OF THEM NOW.
CITRONS TOO.
WONDER IS POOR CITRON STILL ALIVE IN SAINT KEVIN'S PARADE.
AND MASTIANSKY WITH THE OLD CITHER.
PLEASANT EVENINGS WE HAD THEN.
MOLLY IN CITRON'S BASKETCHAIR.
NICE TO HOLD COOL WAXEN FRUIT, HOLD IN THE HAND...
ALWAYS THE SAME, YEAR AFTER YEAR.
...LIFT IT TO THE NOSTRILS AND SMELL THE PERFUME.
LIKE THAT, HEAVY, SWEET, WILD PERFUME.
THEY FETCHED HIGH PRICES TOO
MOISEL TOLD ME.
ARBUTUS PLACE:
PLEASANTS STREET: PLEASANT OLD TIMES.
MUST BE WITHOUT A FLAW, HE SAID.

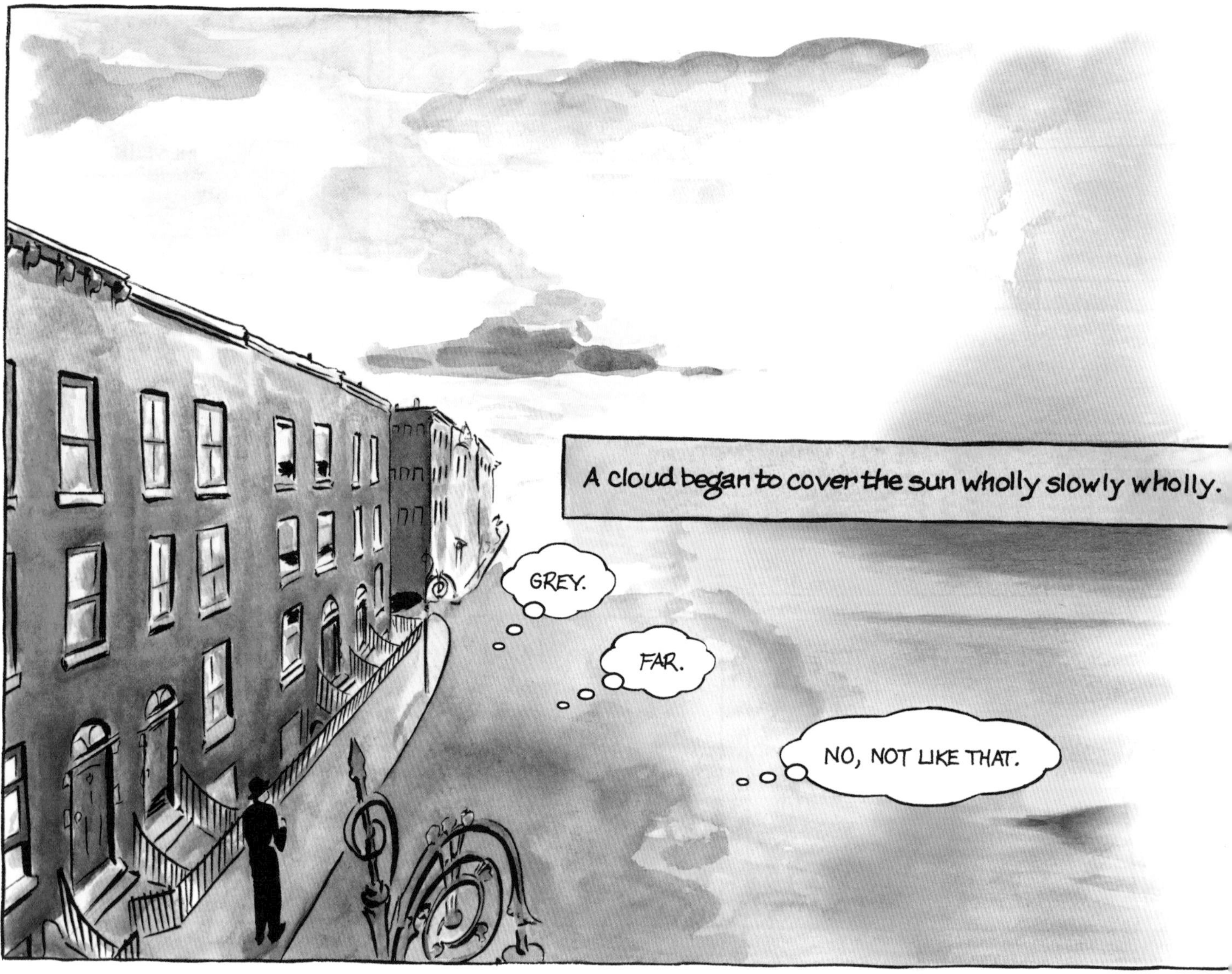
A cloud began to cover the sun wholly slowly wholly.
GREY.
FAR.
NO, NOT LIKE THAT.

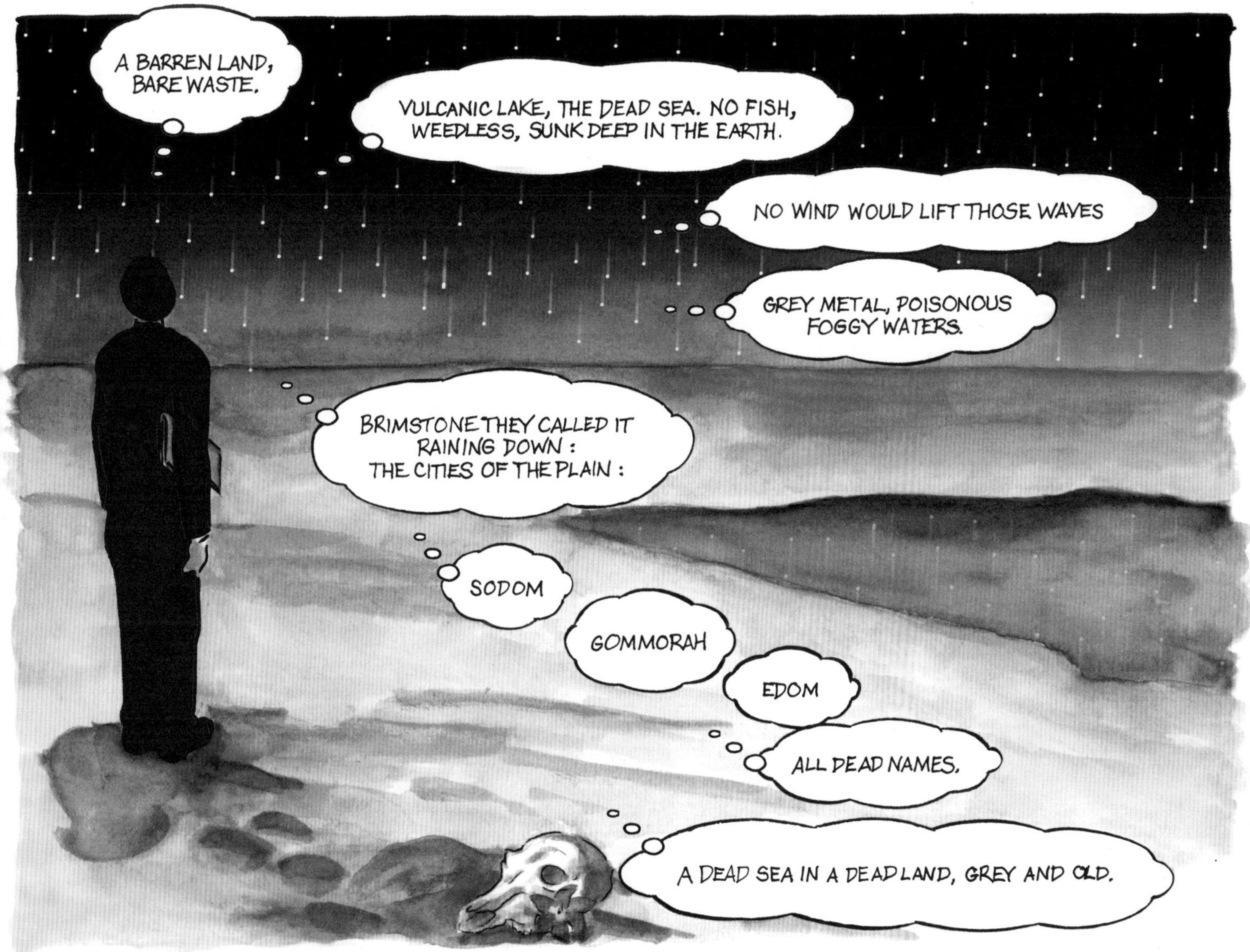
A BARREN LAND, BARE WASTE.
VULCANIC LAKE, THE DEAD SEA. NO FISH, WEEDLESS, SUNK DEEP IN THE EARTH.
NO WIND WOULD LIFT THOSE WAVES
GREY METAL, POISONOUS FOGGY WATERS.
BRIMSTONE THEY CALLED IT RAINING DOWN : THE CITIES OF THE PLAIN :
SODOM
GOMMORAH
EDOM
ALL DEAD NAMES.
A DEAD SEA IN A DEAD LAND, GREY AND OLD.

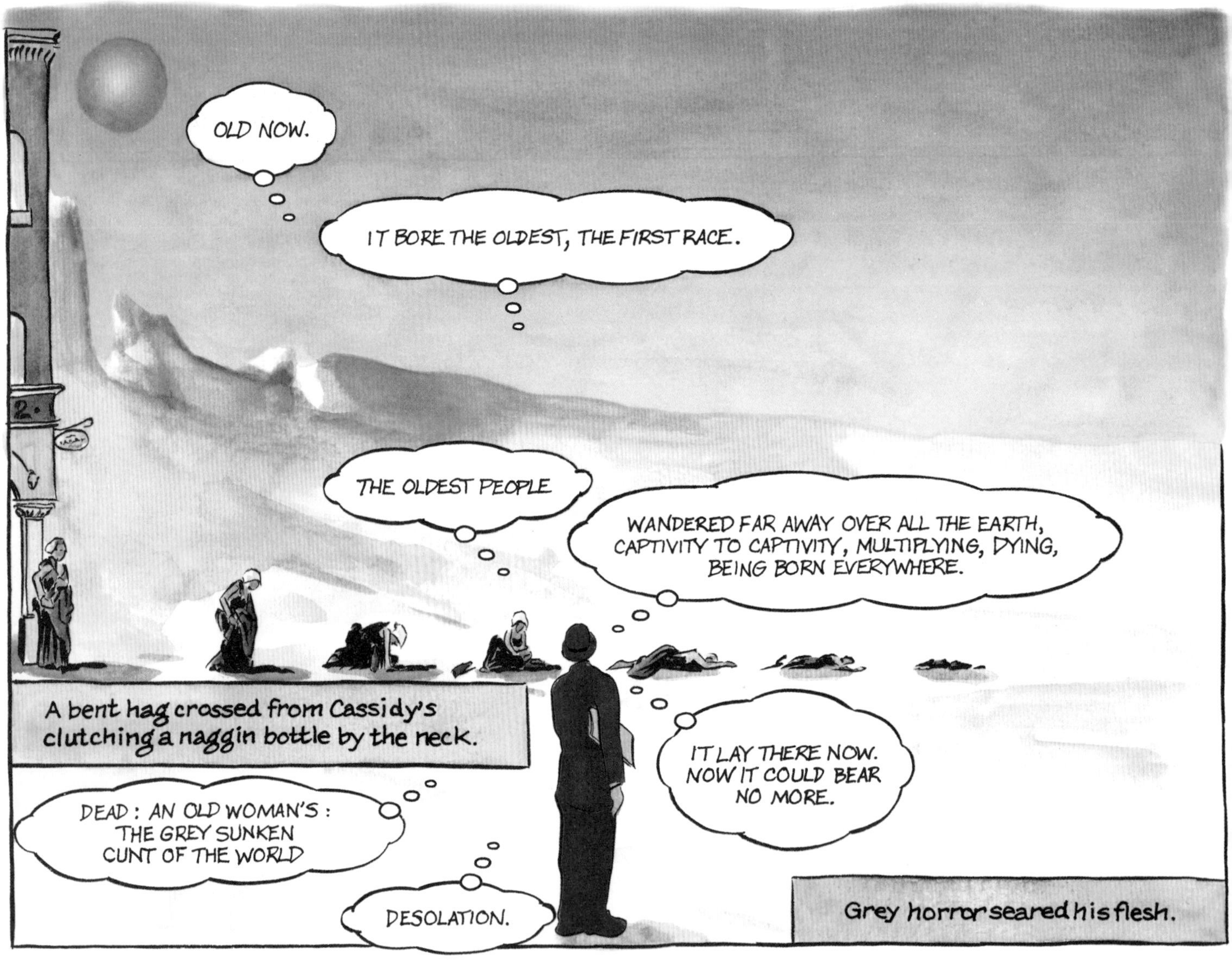
OLD NOW.
IT BORE THE OLDEST, THE FIRST RACE.
THE OLDEST PEOPLE
WANDERED FAR AWAY OVER ALL THE EARTH, CAPTIVITY TO CAPTIVITY, MULTIPLYING, DYING, BEING BORN EVERYWHERE.
A bent hag crossed from Cassidy's clutching a naggin bottle by the neck.
IT LAY THERE NOW. NOW IT COULD BEAR NO MORE.
DEAD : AN OLD WOMAN'S : THE GREY SUNKEN CUNT OF THE WORLD
DESOLATION.
Grey horror seared his flesh.

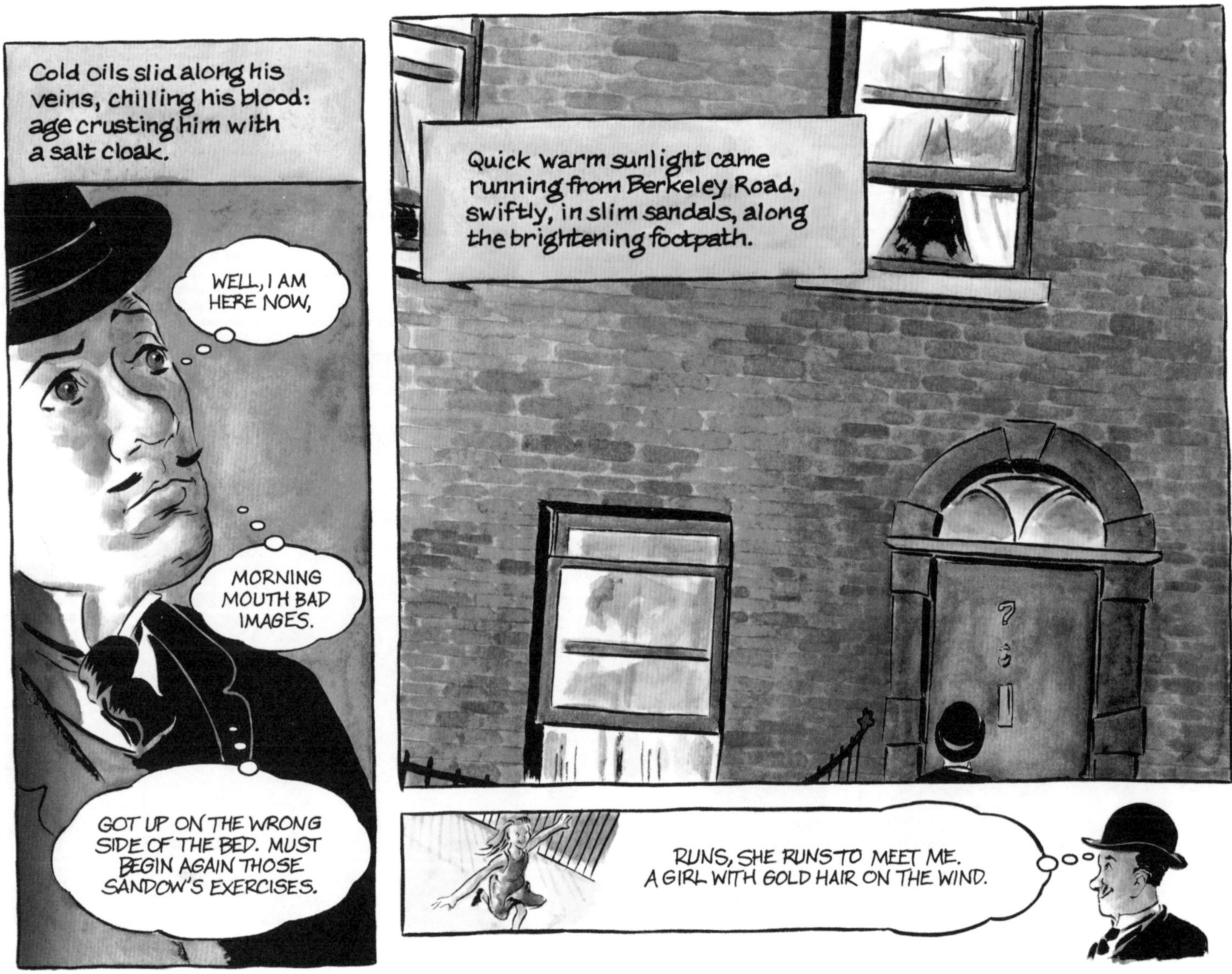
Cold oils slid along his veins, chilling his blood: age crusting him with a salt cloak.
WELL, I AM HERE NOW,
MORNING MOUTH BAD IMAGES.
GOT UP ON THE WRONG SIDE OF THE BED. MUST BEGIN AGAIN THOSE SANDOW'S EXERCISES.
Quick warm sunlight came running from Berkeley Road, swiftly, in slim sandals, along the brightening footpath.
RUNS, SHE RUNS TO MEET ME. A GIRL WITH GOLD HAIR ON THE WIND.

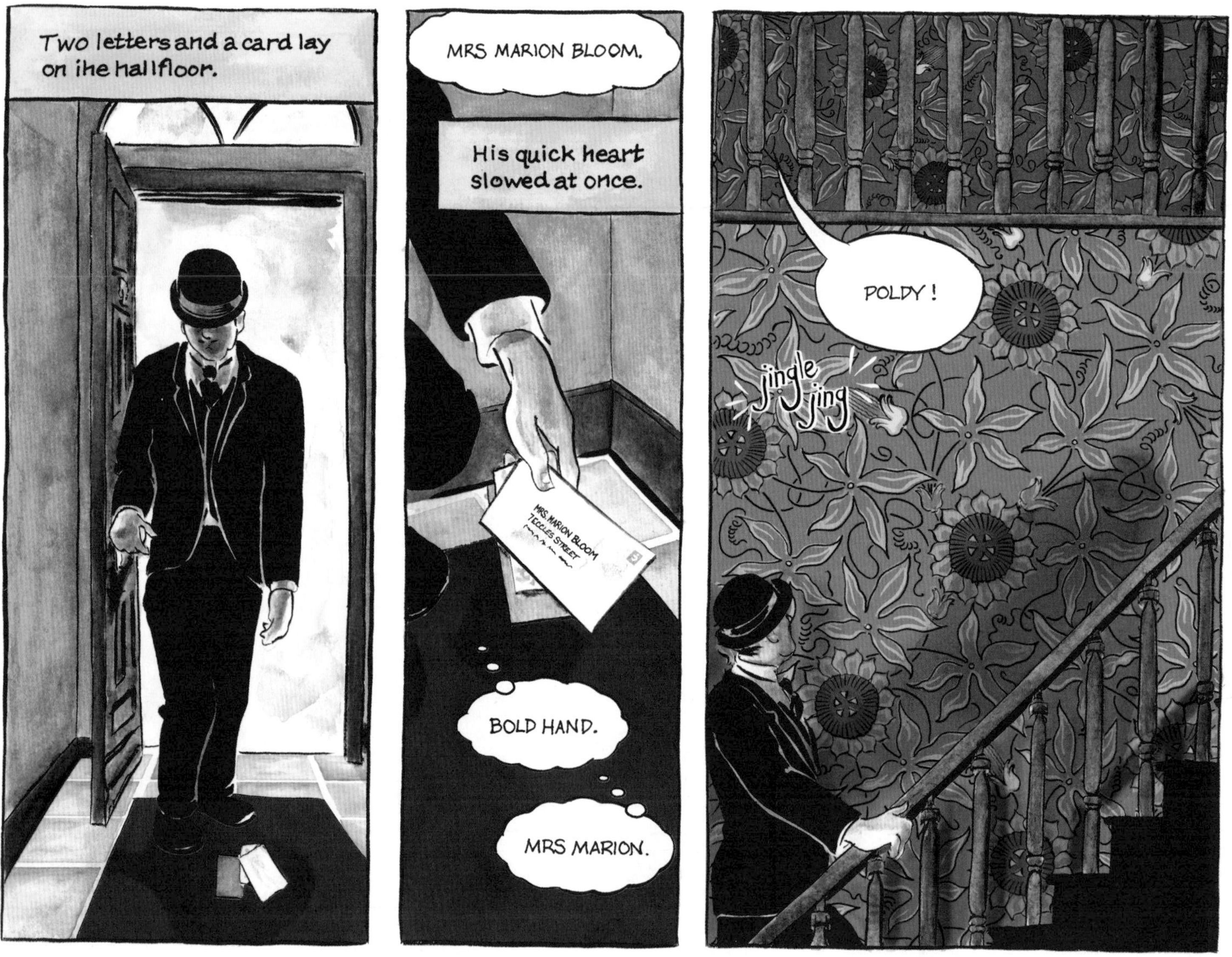
Two letters and a card lay on the hallfloor.
MRS MARION BLOOM.
His quick heart slowed at once.
BOLD HAND.
MRS MARION.
POLDY!
jingle jing

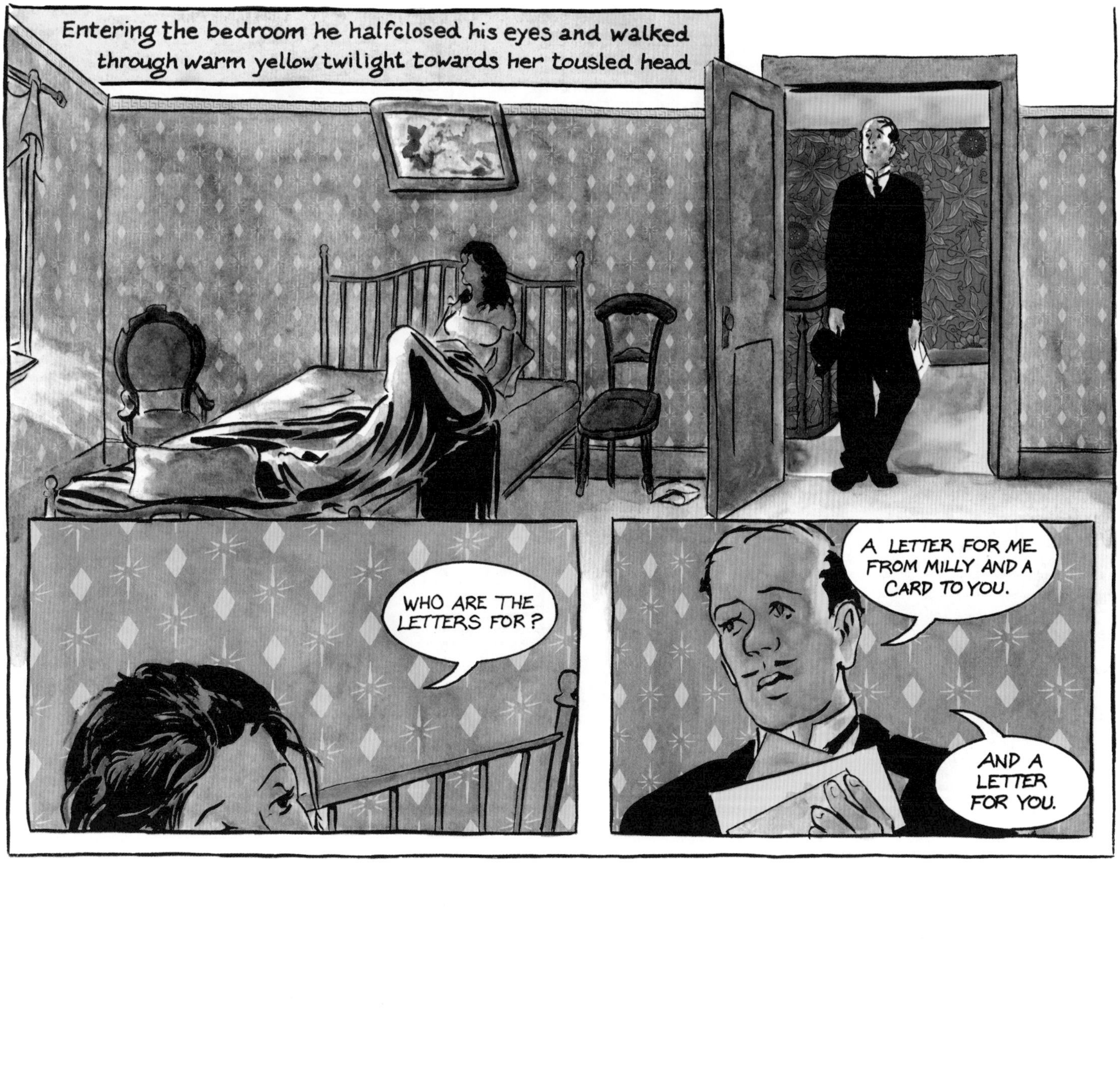
Entering the bedroom he halfclosed his eyes and walked through warm yellow twilight towards her tousled head
WHO ARE THE LETTERS FOR?
A LETTER FOR ME FROM MILLY AND A CARD TO YOU.
AND A LETTER FOR YOU.

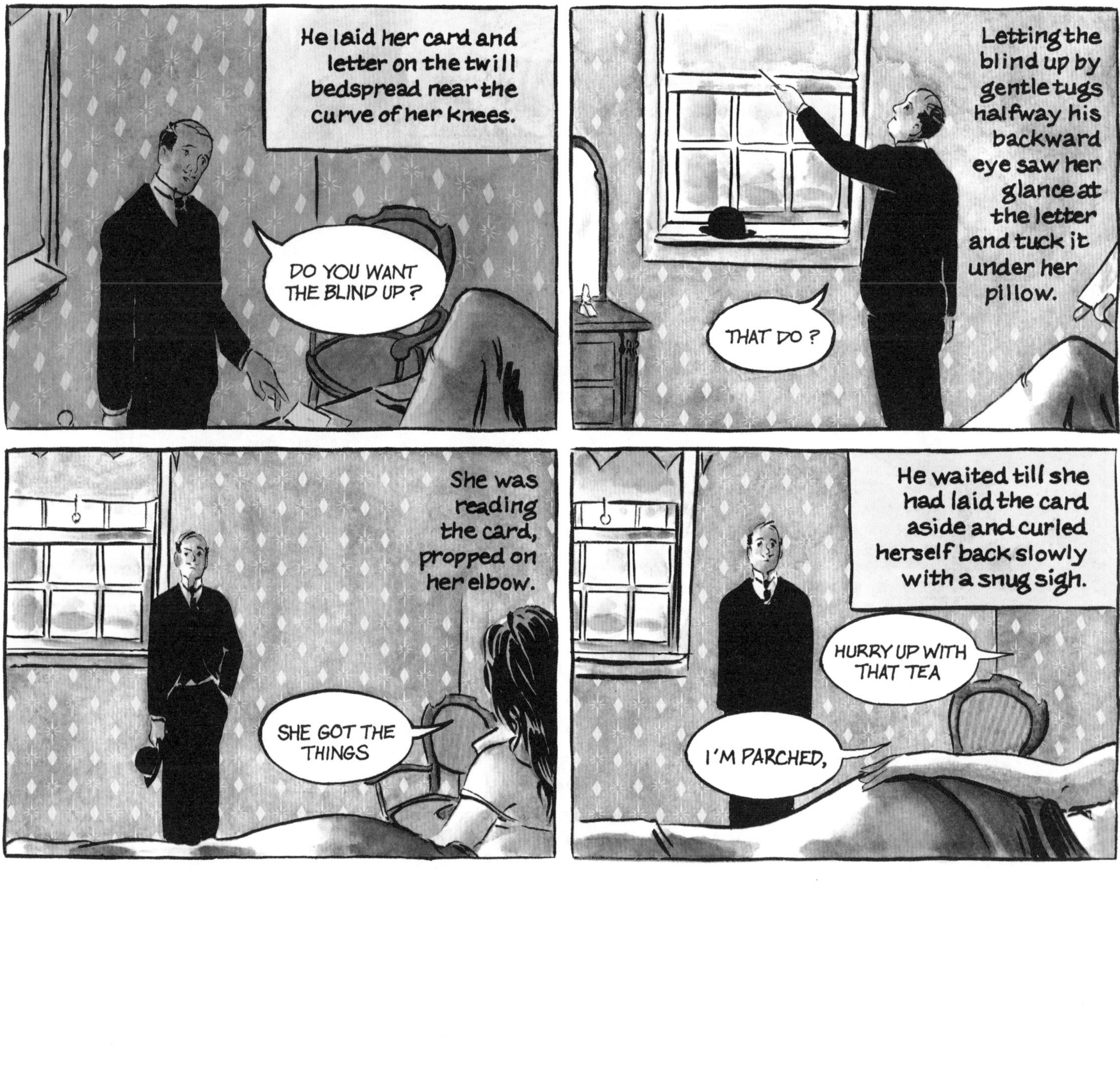
He laid her card and letter on the twill bedspread near the curve of her knees.
DO YOU WANT THE BLIND UP?
Letting the blind up by gentle tugs halfway his backward eye saw her glance at the letter and tuck it under her pillow.
THAT DO?
She was reading the card, propped on her elbow.
SHE GOT THE THINGS
He waited till she had laid the card aside and curled herself back slowly with a snug sigh.
HURRY UP WITH THAT TEA
I'M PARCHED.

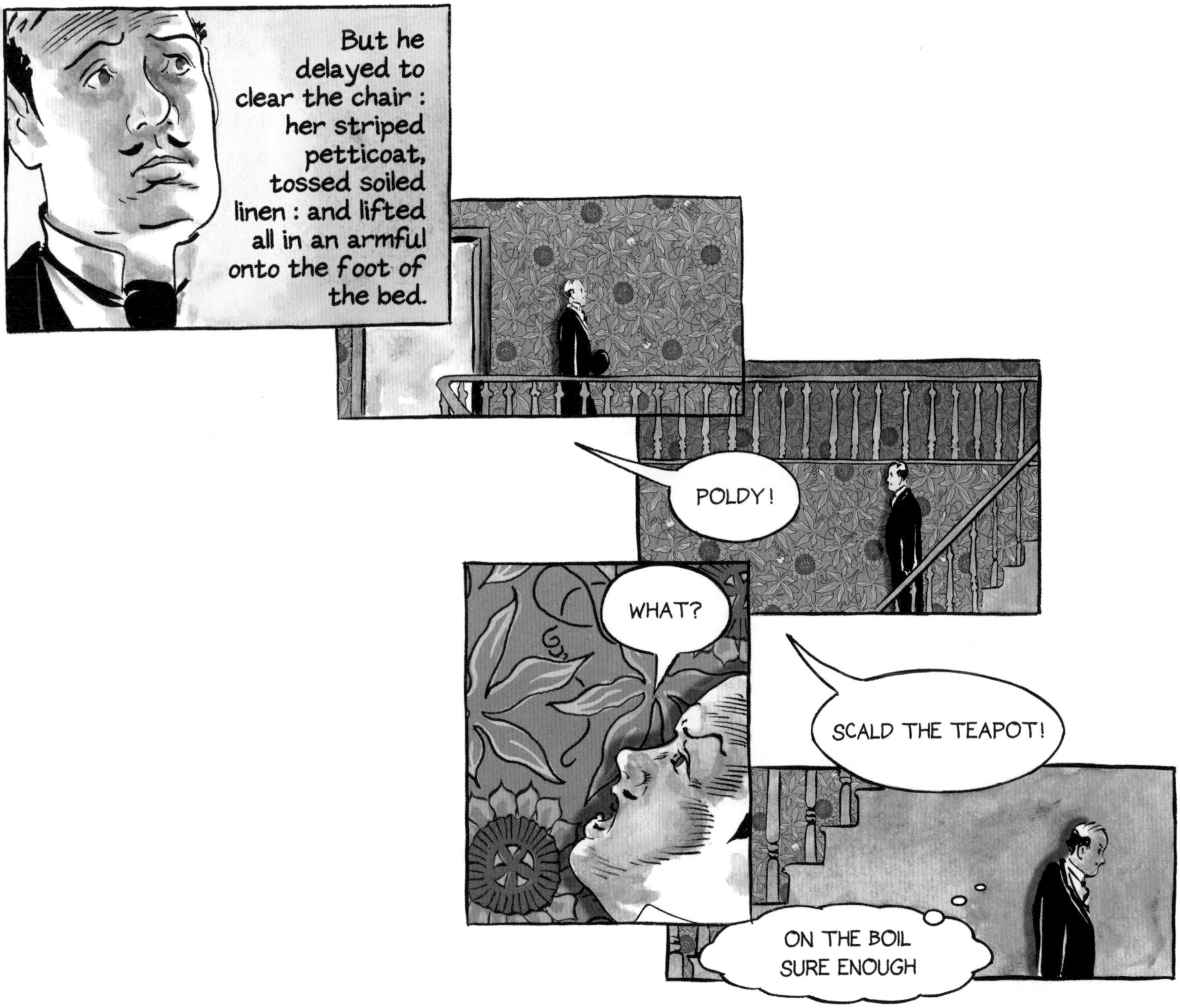
But he delayed to clear the chair : her striped petticoat, tossed soiled linen : and lifted all in an armful onto the foot of the bed.
POLDY!
WHAT?
SCALD THE TEAPOT!
ON THE BOIL SURE ENOUGH

James Joyce

ART/ADAPTATION BY **David Lasky**

AS MENTIONED IN THE PREVIOUS EXCERPT FROM Robert Berry's ongoing adaptation of *Ulysses*, James Joyce's masterpiece is physically huge and textually dense. It's famous for being a book that many start but few finish. Rob estimates taking at least a decade to adapt the whole thing.

Comics artist David Lasky took a different approach. In 1993, he created a twelve-page minicomic for *Ulysses*. The entire book in thirty-six panels. Yes, his tongue was planted firmly in cheek, but at the same time he remained remarkably faithful to the book, not just the narrative, but also the humor that pervades the novel. This isn't a parody but rather a bare-bones telling of the story itself. When you strip away the streams of consciousness, the digressions, the debates, the dialogue, and all the literary wizardry, you have a fairly straightforward story of nineteen hours in the busy lives of two Dubliners. The tower, the funeral,

the newspaper office, the pub, the museum, the library, the beach, the hospital, the brothel, Molly's soliloquy and her final words (also the book's final words) . . . they're all here in super-condensed form. Each pair of panels presents highlights from one of the book's eighteen sections (or chapters). Naturally, some bits got chopped—Leopold's visit to the butcher shop, Stephen getting punched out by a soldier—but still, you're not gonna get more *Ulysses* in less space than this!

David is the winner of a Xeric grant and a nominee for a Harvey and multiple Ignatz awards, as well as the artist of the stunning *Don't Forget This Song* (a graphic biography of the Carter Family, the first family of country music, written by Frank M. Young). His minicomic of *Ulysses* has itself become a classic, and he allowed us to include it here, even reworking the layout to fit the pages (thus, standing now at seven pages instead of twelve).

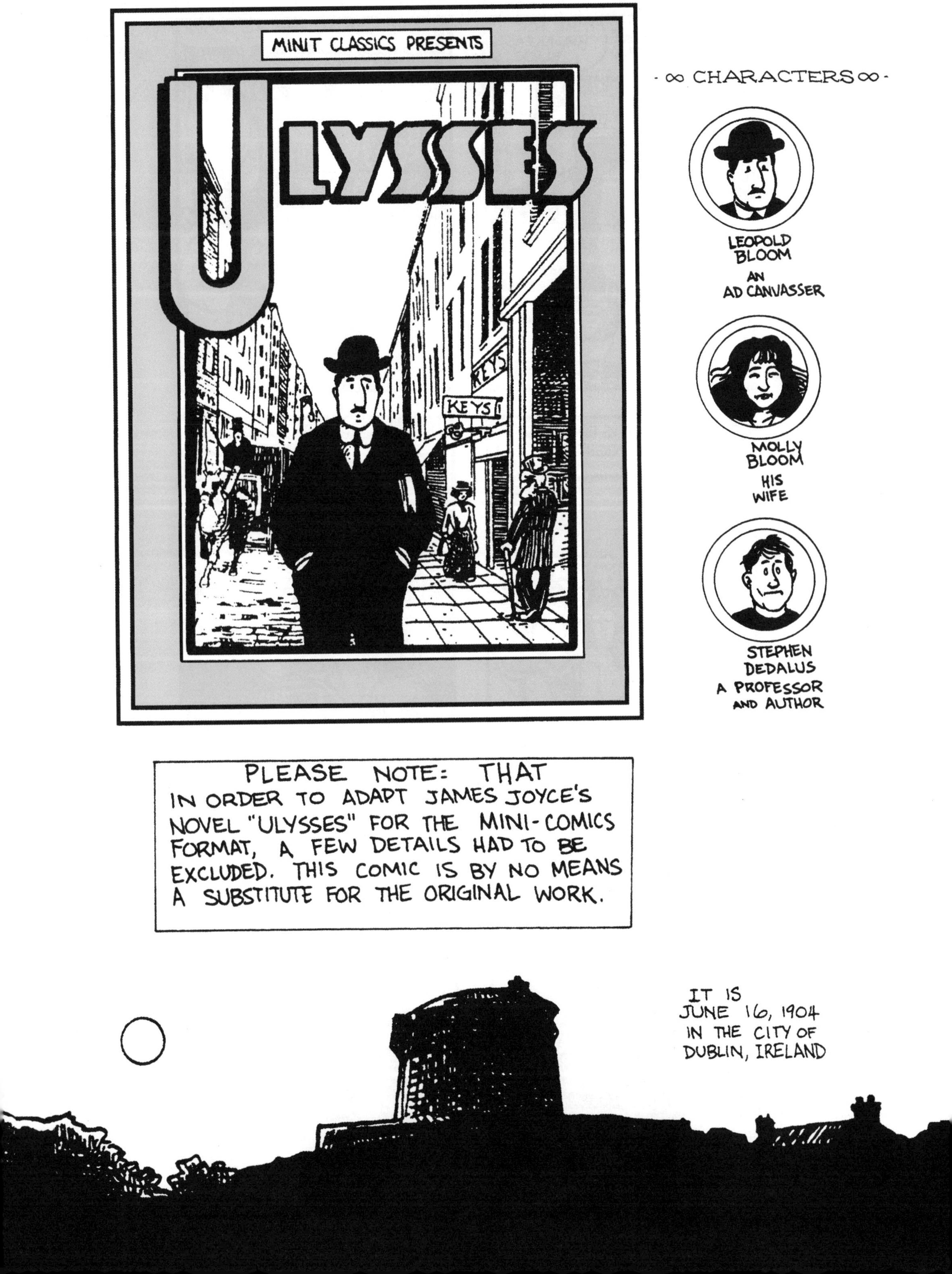
MINIT CLASSICS PRESENTS
ULYSSES
KEYS
KEYS
∞ CHARACTERS ∞
LEOPOLD BLOOM
AN AD CANVASSER
MOLLY BLOOM
HIS WIFE
STEPHEN DEDALUS
A PROFESSOR AND AUTHOR
PLEASE NOTE: THAT IN ORDER TO ADAPT JAMES JOYCE'S NOVEL "ULYSSES" FOR THE MINI-COMICS FORMAT, A FEW DETAILS HAD TO BE EXCLUDED. THIS COMIC IS BY NO MEANS A SUBSTITUTE FOR THE ORIGINAL WORK.
IT IS JUNE 16, 1904 IN THE CITY OF DUBLIN, IRELAND

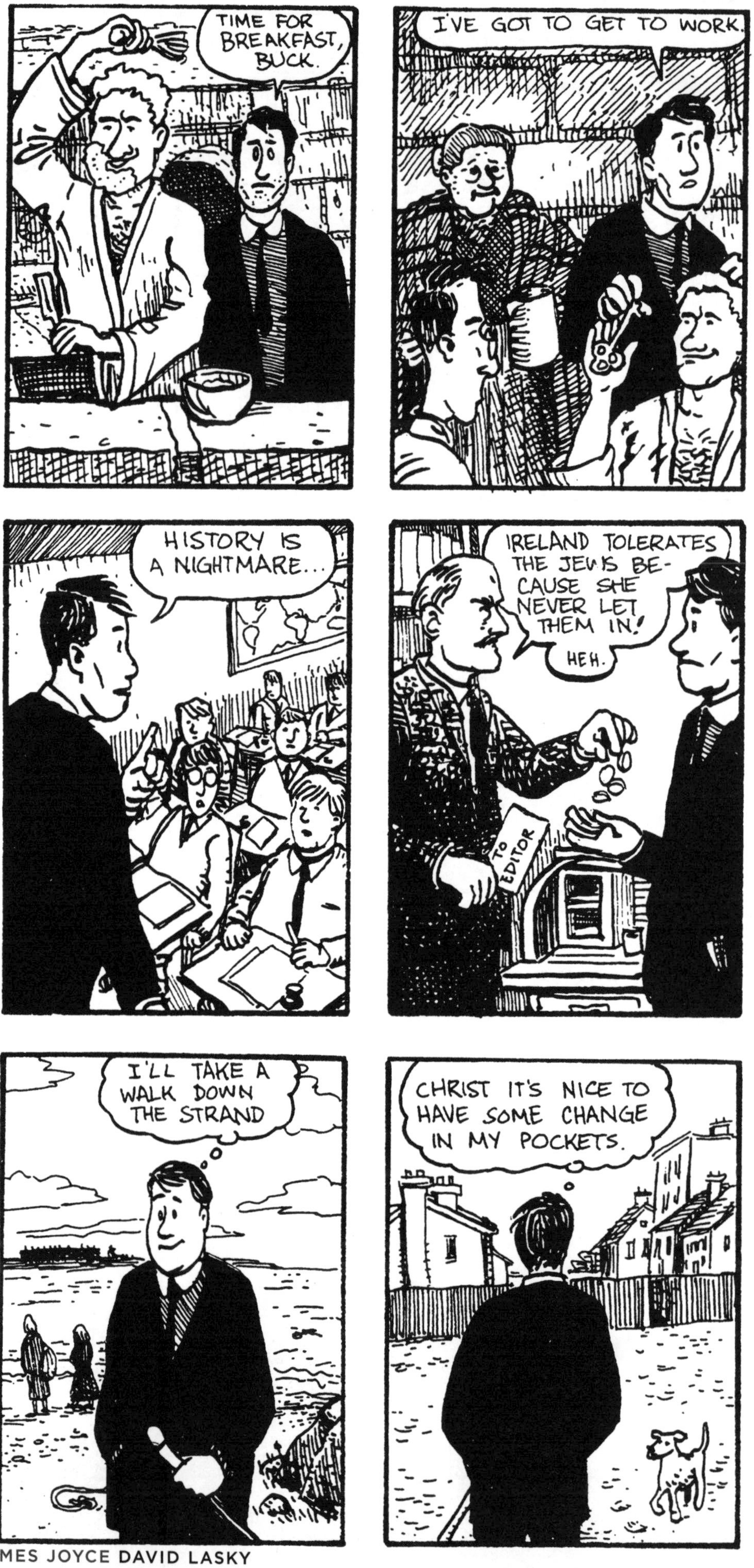
TIME FOR BREAKFAST, BUCK.
I'VE GOT TO GET TO WORK.
HISTORY IS A NIGHTMARE...
IRELAND TOLERATES THE JEWS BECAUSE SHE NEVER LET THEM IN!
HEH.
TO EDITOR
I'LL TAKE A WALK DOWN THE STRAND
CHRIST IT'S NICE TO HAVE SOME CHANGE IN MY POCKETS.

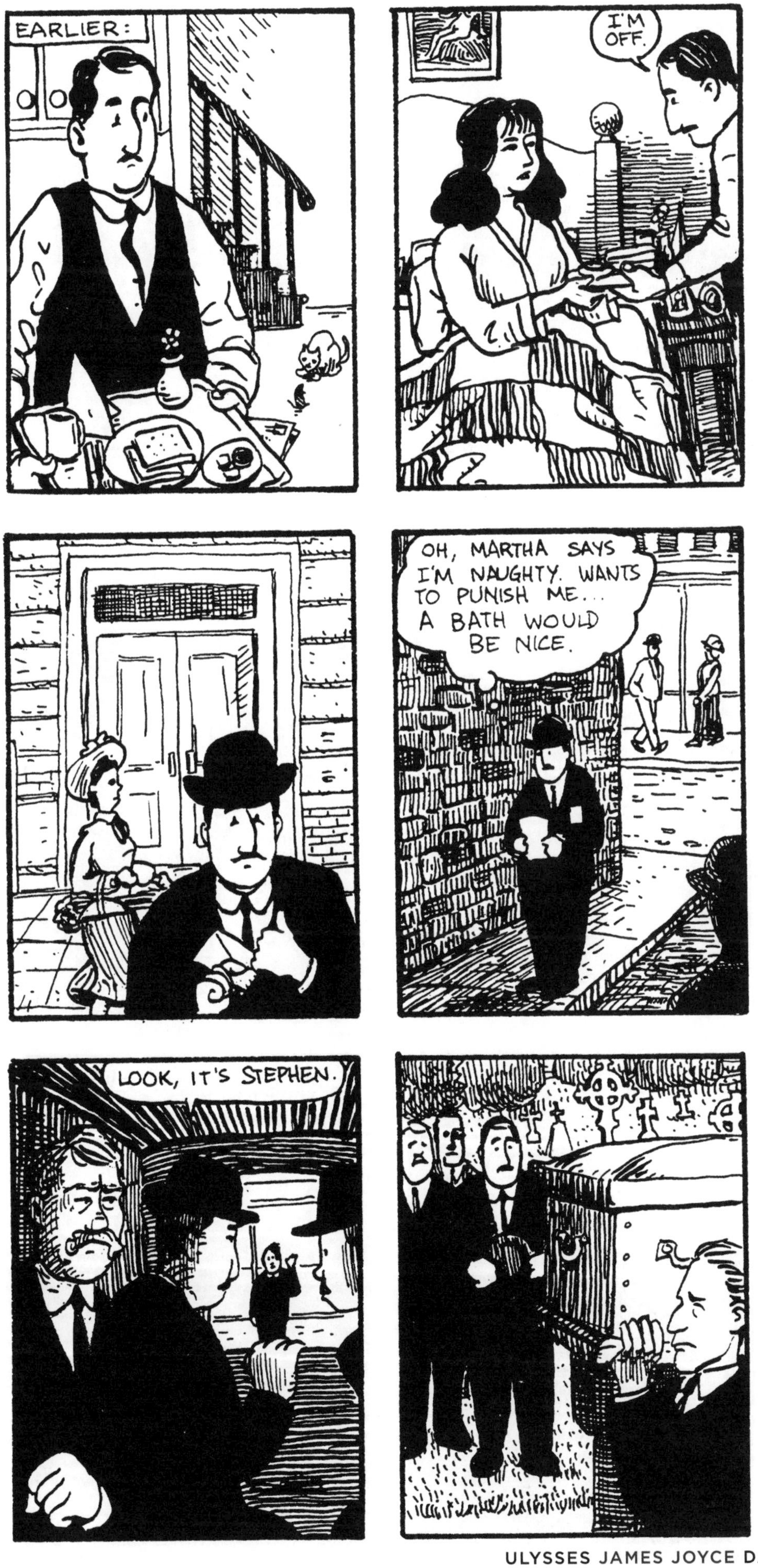
EARLIER:
I'M OFF.
OH, MARTHA SAYS I'M NAUGHTY. WANTS TO PUNISH ME... A BATH WOULD BE NICE.
LOOK, IT'S STEPHEN.

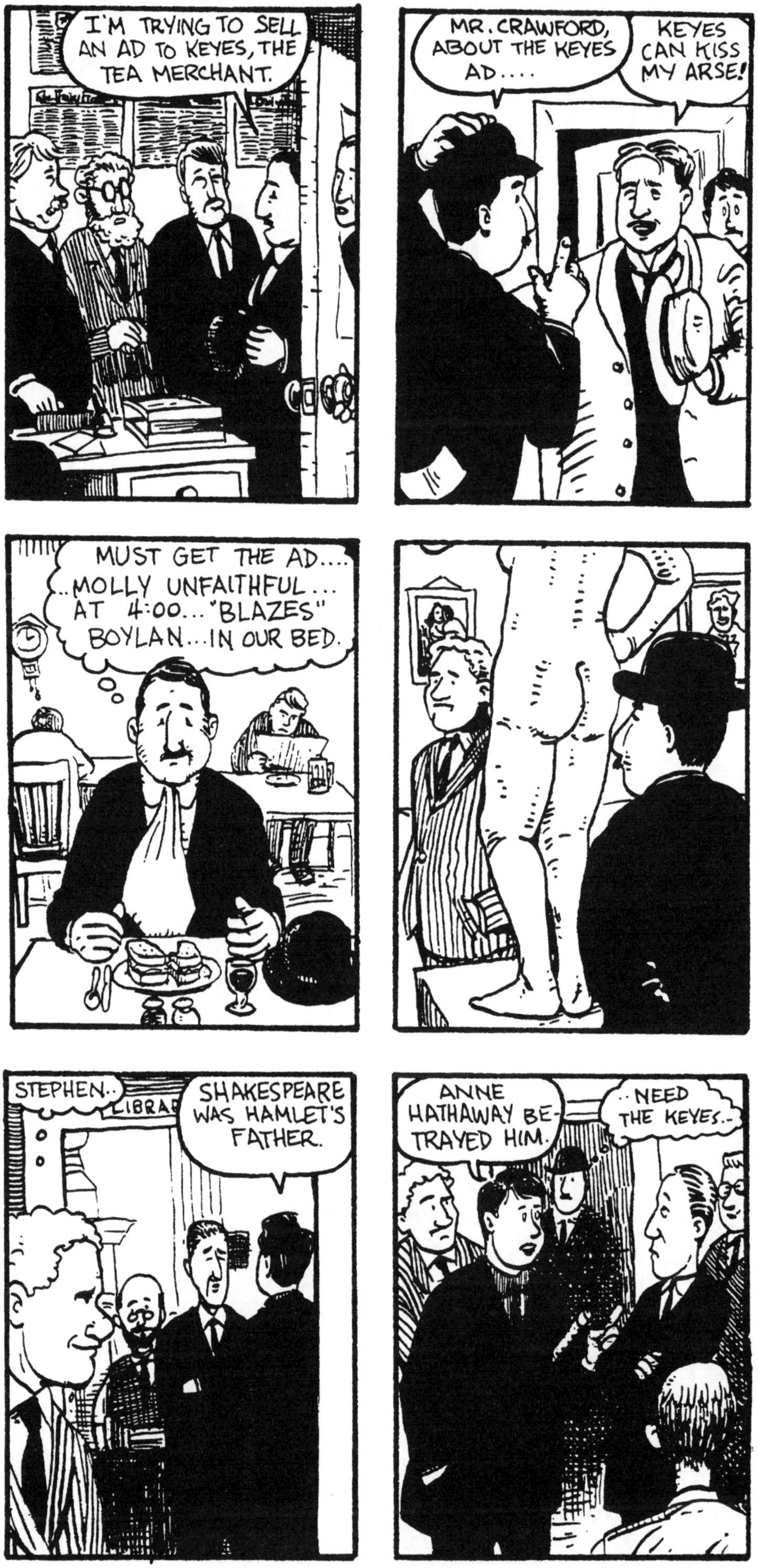
I'M TRYING TO SELL AN AD TO KEYES, THE TEA MERCHANT.
MR. CRAWFORD, ABOUT THE KEYES AD....
KEYES CAN KISS MY ARSE!
MUST GET THE AD.... ..MOLLY UNFAITHFUL... AT 4:00... "BLAZES" BOYLAN... IN OUR BED.
STEPHEN..
LIBRAR
SHAKESPEARE WAS HAMLET'S FATHER.
ANNE HATHAWAY BETRAYED HIM.
..NEED THE KEYES..

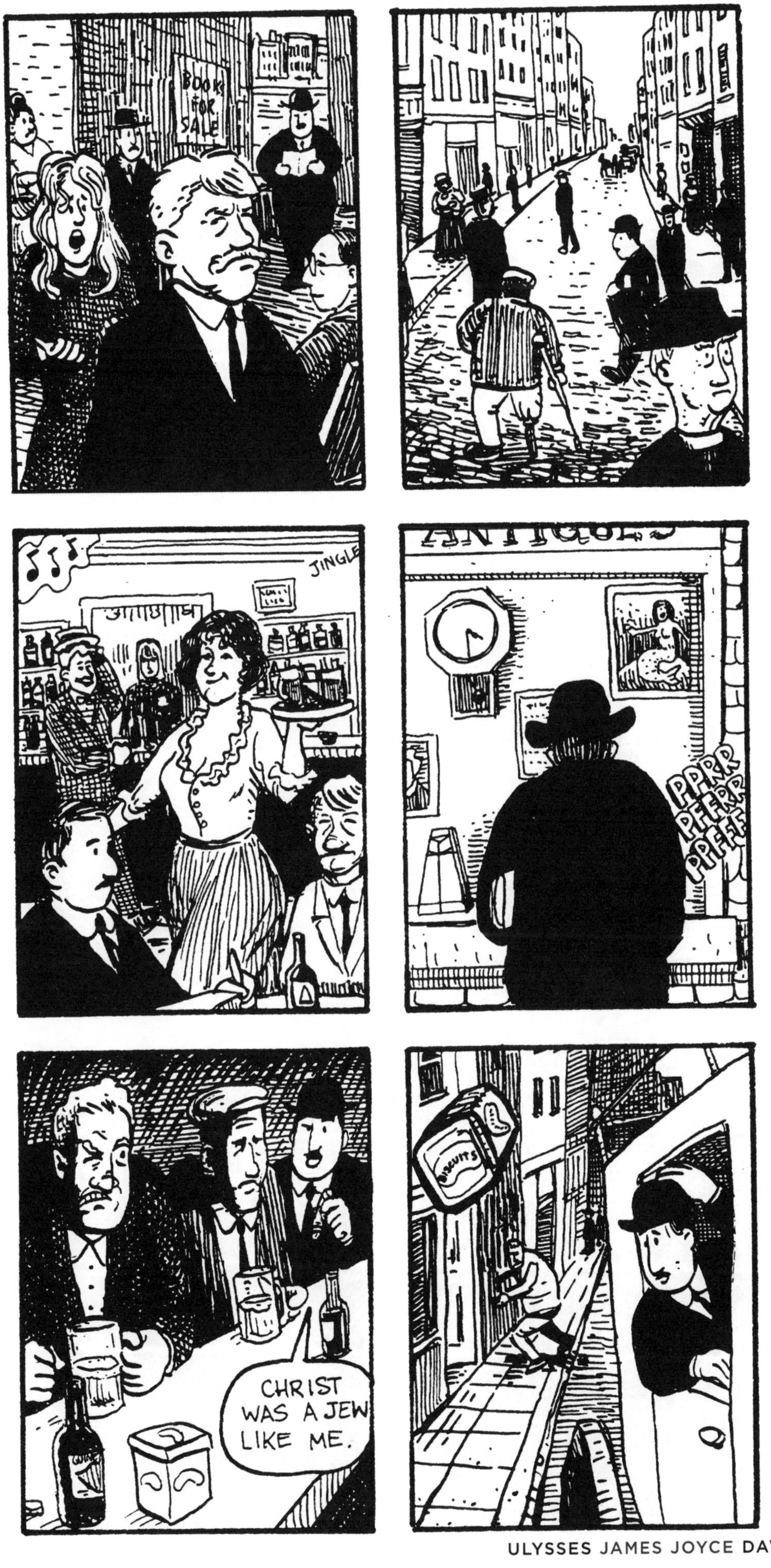
BOOK FOR SALE
JINGLE
PPRR
PFFRR
PPFFF
CHRIST WAS A JEW LIKE ME.
BISCUITS

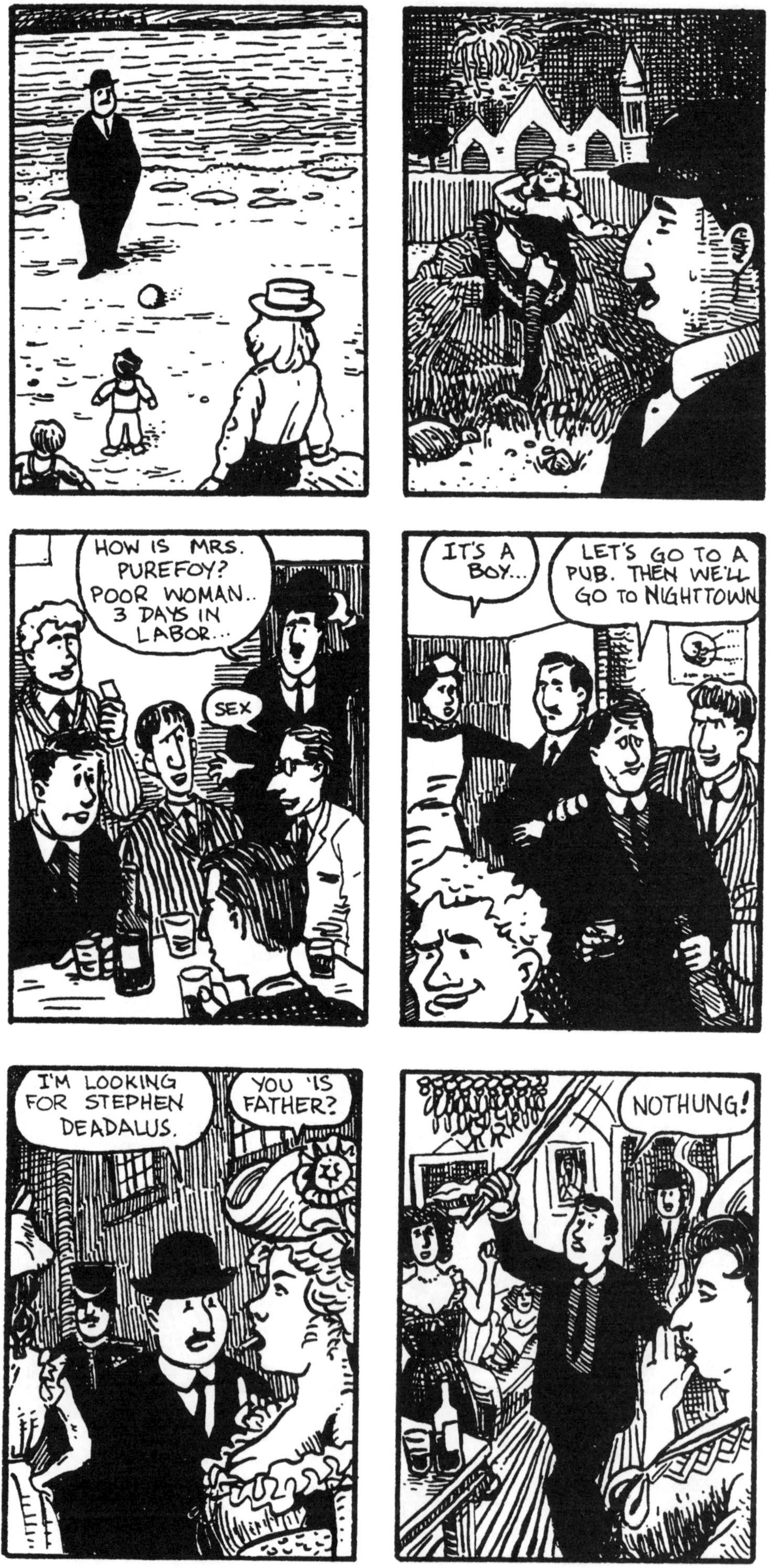
HOW IS MRS. PUREFOY? POOR WOMAN.. 3 DAYS IN LABOR...
SEX
IT'S A BOY...
LET'S GO TO A PUB. THEN WE'LL GO TO NIGHTTOWN
I'M LOOKING FOR STEPHEN DEADALUS.
YOU 'IS FATHER?
NOTHUNG!

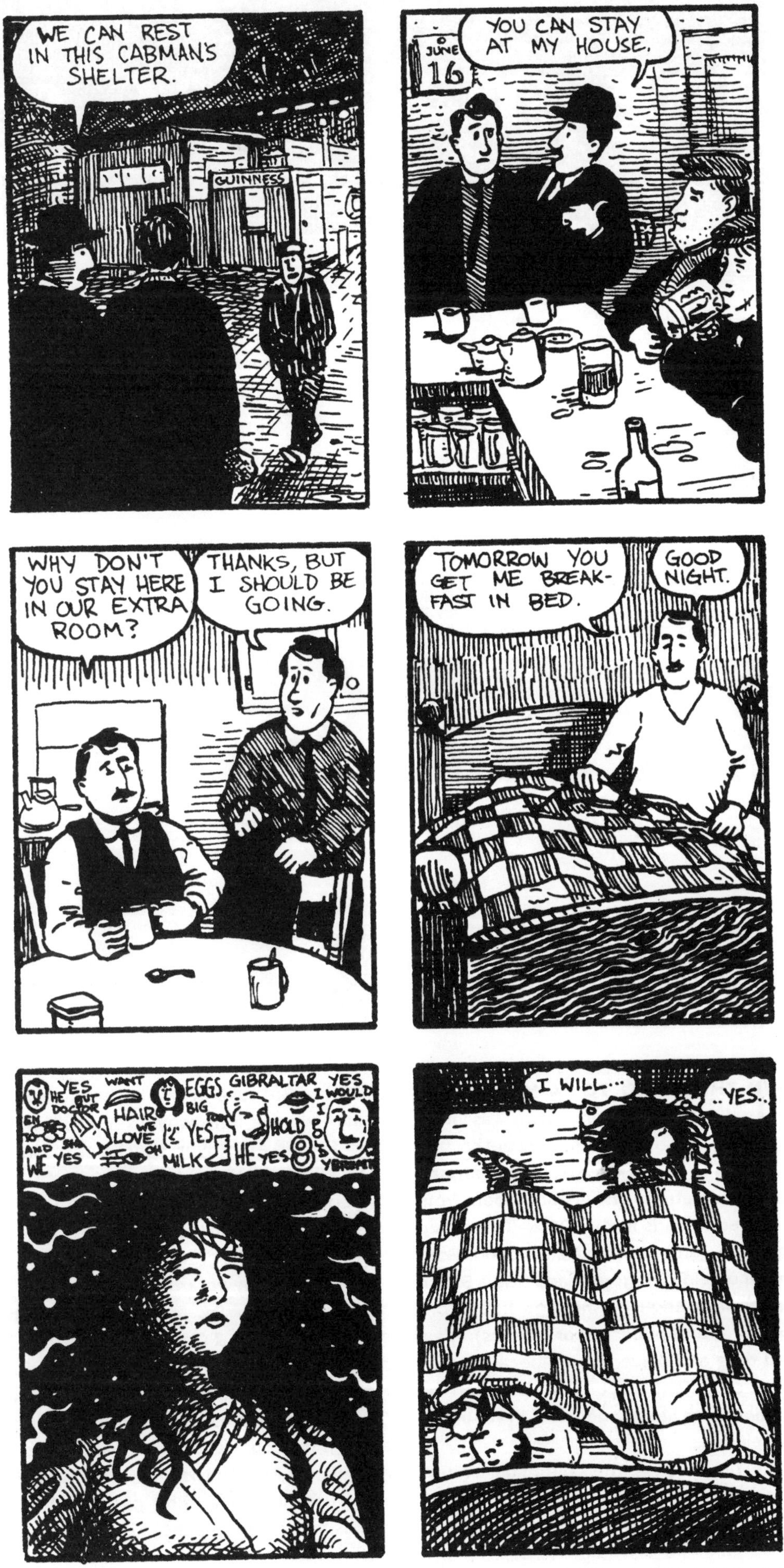
WE CAN REST IN THIS CABMAN'S SHELTER.
GUINNESS
JUNE 16
YOU CAN STAY AT MY HOUSE.
WHY DON'T YOU STAY HERE IN OUR EXTRA ROOM?
THANKS, BUT I SHOULD BE GOING.
TOMORROW YOU GET ME BREAK-FAST IN BED.
GOOD NIGHT.
YES WANT EGGS GIBRALTAR YES
HE BUT DOCTOR
I WOULD
HAIR BIG
WE LOVE YES
HOLD
AND
WE YES OH MILK HE YES
I WILL...
..YES..

"Living on $1,000 a Year in Paris"

Ernest Hemingway

ART/ADAPTATION BY **Steve Rolston**

AS MENTIONED IN THE INTRO TO "A MATTER OF Colour" earlier in this volume, Ernest Hemingway was larger than life, and part of his mystique comes from the fact that he and his then-wife Hadley Richardson were among the influential group of expatriate writers and poets from the US and UK who lived in Paris in the 1920s. This group included Gertrude Stein, James Joyce, Ezra Pound, Ford Madox Ford, F. Scott and Zelda Fitzgerald, and Sylvia Beach (founder of the legendary English-language bookstore Shakespeare & Company, and publisher of *Ulysses*). It's a highly romanticized time and place, mainly because, well, it was a highly romantic time and place—Paris between the wars, the Left Bank filled with literary geniuses in voluntary exile from their homelands.

Hemingway, then in his early twenties, didn't have much money to support his wife and infant son, but that wasn't such a problem—you didn't need much to live in Paris at the time. Because of the exchange rate, North American dollars went a long way. In the following report that he filed for his employer, the *Toronto Star*, on February 4, 1922, Hem mentions the figure $1,000 in the title. That's the equivalent of around $13,500 now. If a person could live comfortably on that in the Paris of today, I'd be writing this from the Eiffel Tower.

Steve Rolston works in the videogame industry, and has drawn comics for DC, Dark Horse, and Oni. His first professional gig, *Queen & Country* (with writer Greg Rucka), won an Eisner Award and was nominated for two others. He brings a delectably crisp style to Hemingway's guide to the City of Light. The locations, interiors, and fashions you see are highly accurate, as Steve used period photographs for reference. (Among the lucky denizens of Paris, you'll spot the artist himself [and his girlfriend], who, like Hitchcock, makes cameo appearances in his own works.)

Living on $1000 a Year in Paris

WRITTEN BY ERNEST HEMINGWAY
ILLUSTRATED BY STEVE ROLSTON

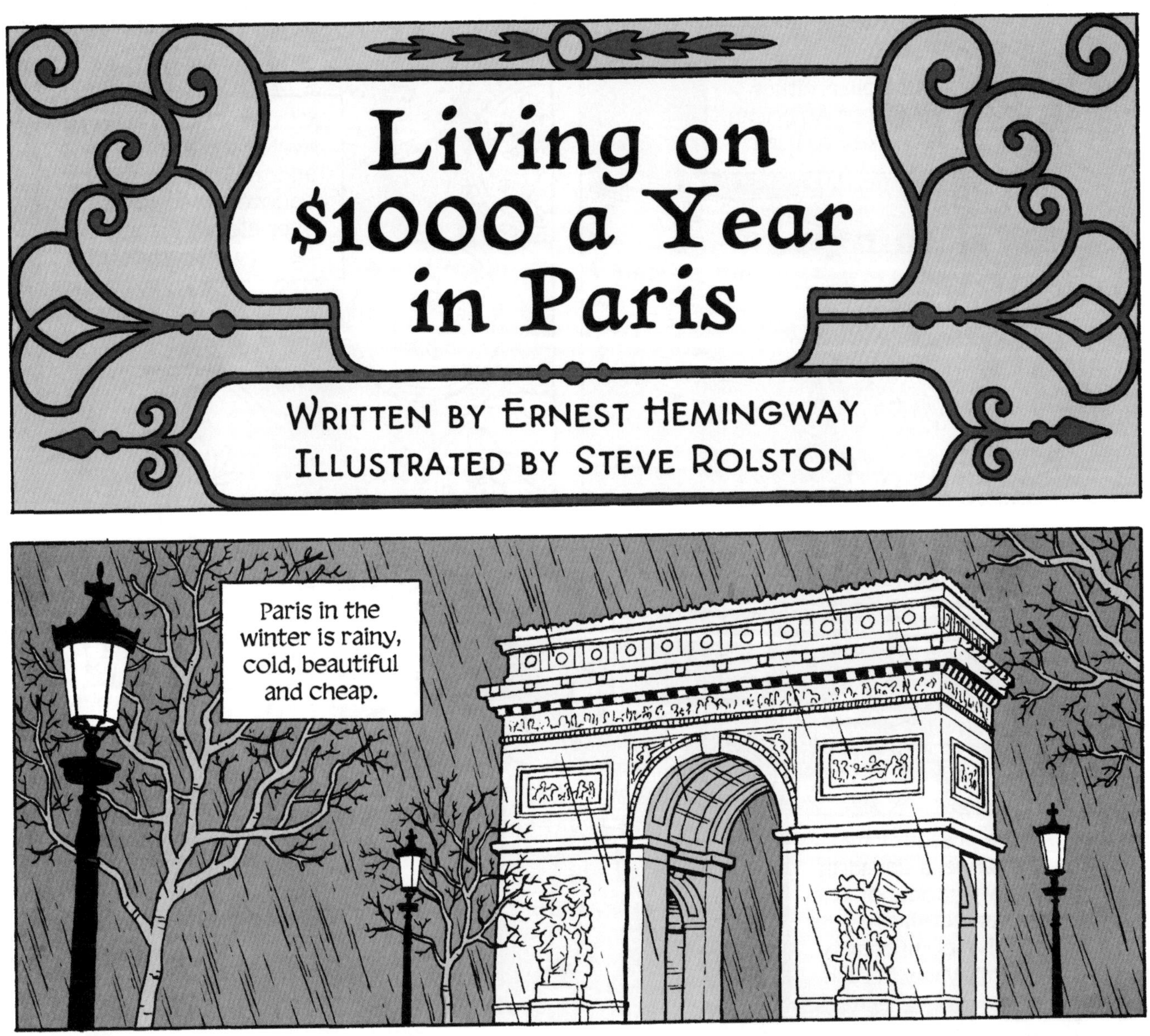
Paris in the winter is rainy, cold, beautiful and cheap.

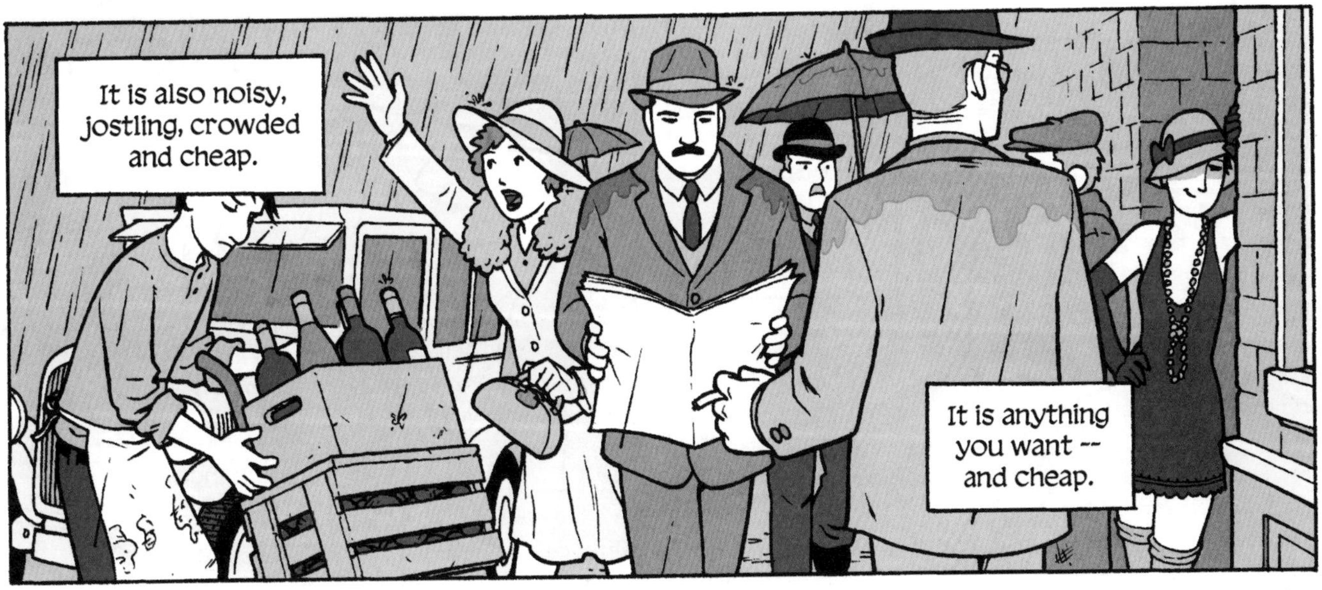
It is also noisy, jostling, crowded and cheap.
It is anything you want -- and cheap.

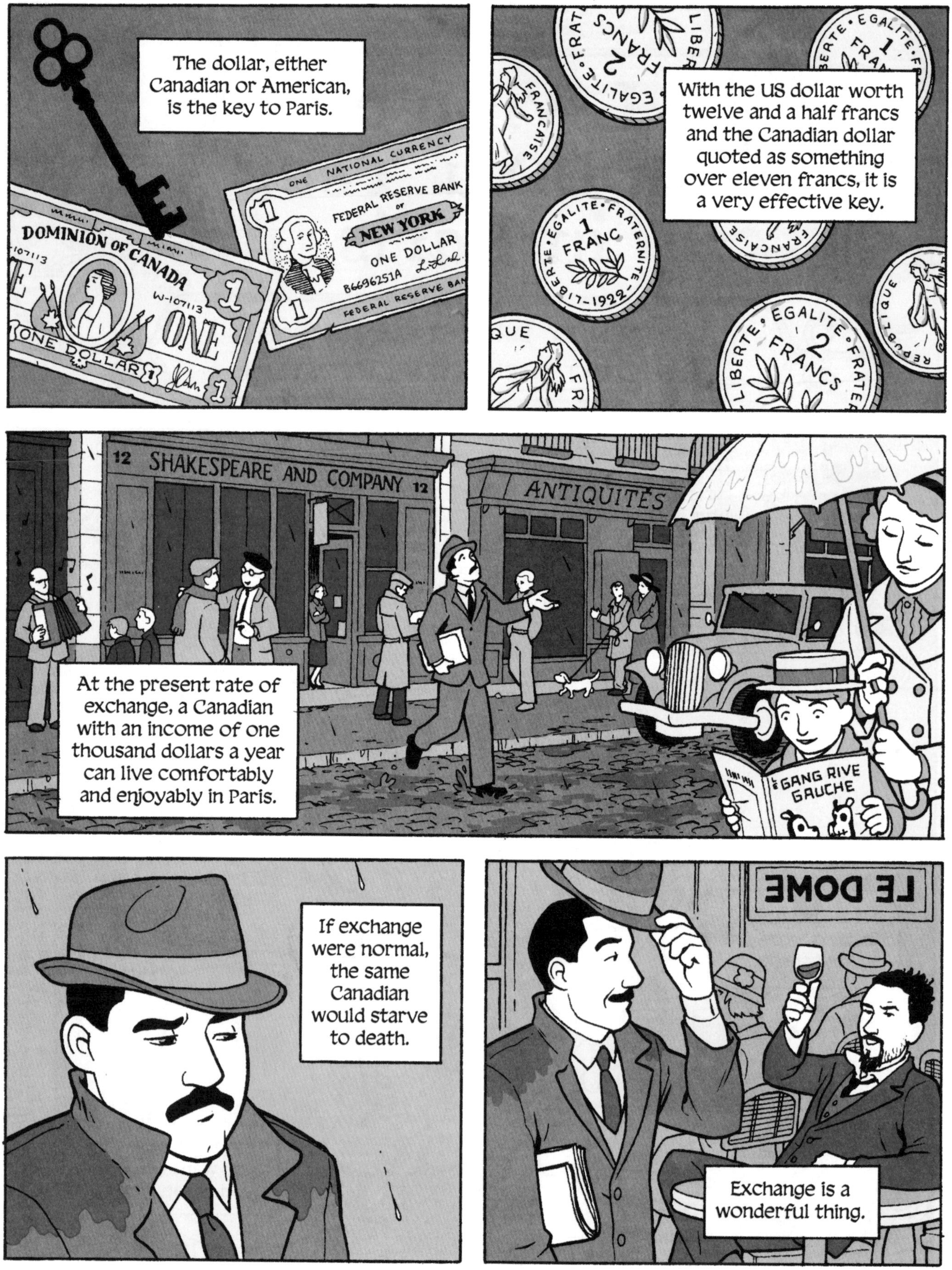
The dollar, either Canadian or American, is the key to Paris.
DOMINION OF CANADA
ONE DOLLAR
NATIONAL CURRENCY
FEDERAL RESERVE BANK OF NEW YORK
ONE DOLLAR
With the US dollar worth twelve and a half francs and the Canadian dollar quoted as something over eleven francs, it is a very effective key.
12 SHAKESPEARE AND COMPANY 12
ANTIQUITÉS
At the present rate of exchange, a Canadian with an income of one thousand dollars a year can live comfortably and enjoyably in Paris.
GANG RIVE GAUCHE
If exchange were normal, the same Canadian would starve to death.
LE DOME
Exchange is a wonderful thing.

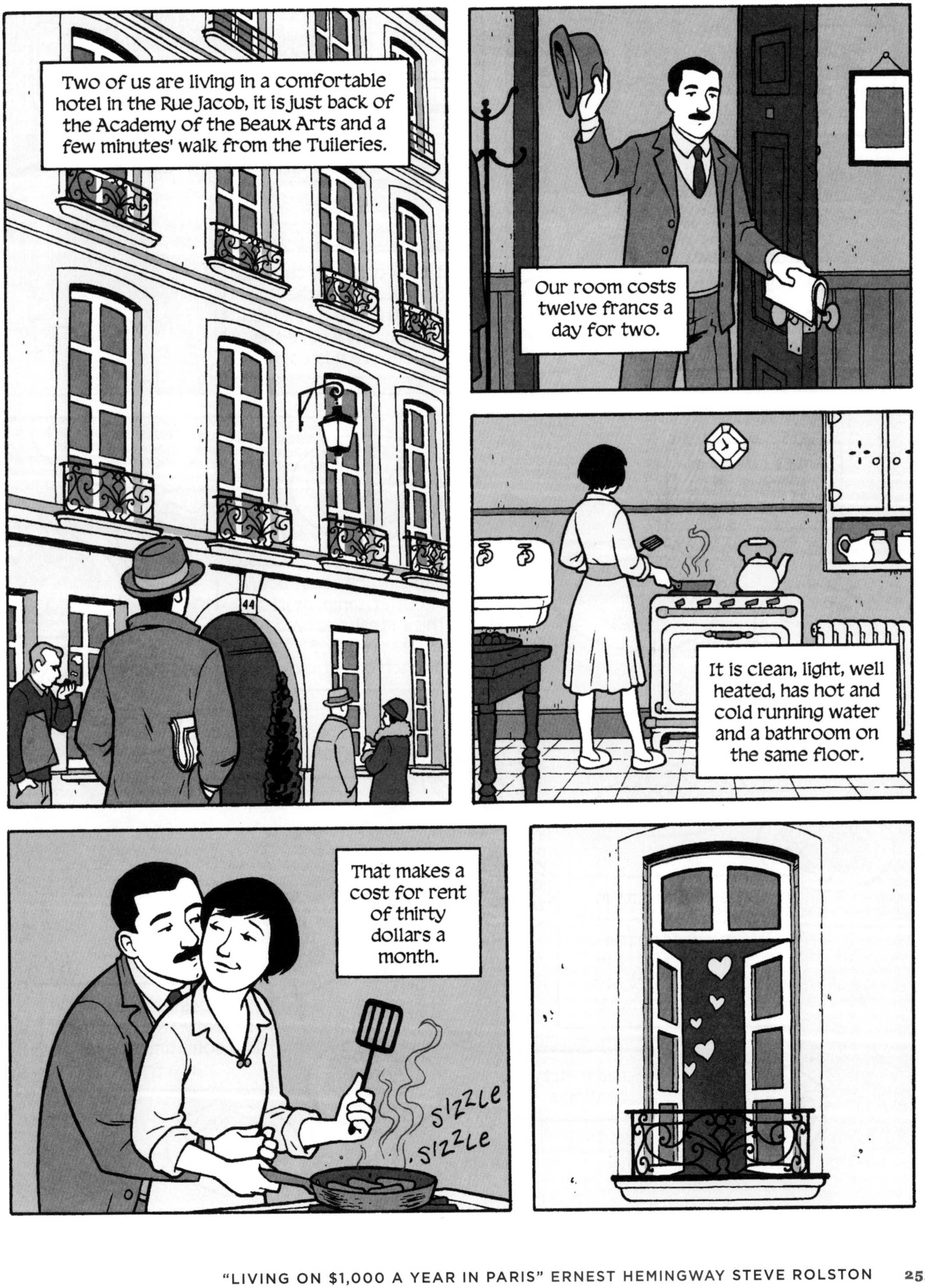
Two of us are living in a comfortable hotel in the Rue Jacob, it is just back of the Academy of the Beaux Arts and a few minutes' walk from the Tuileries.
44
Our room costs twelve francs a day for two.
It is clean, light, well heated, has hot and cold running water and a bathroom on the same floor.
That makes a cost for rent of thirty dollars a month.
SIZZLE
SIZZLE

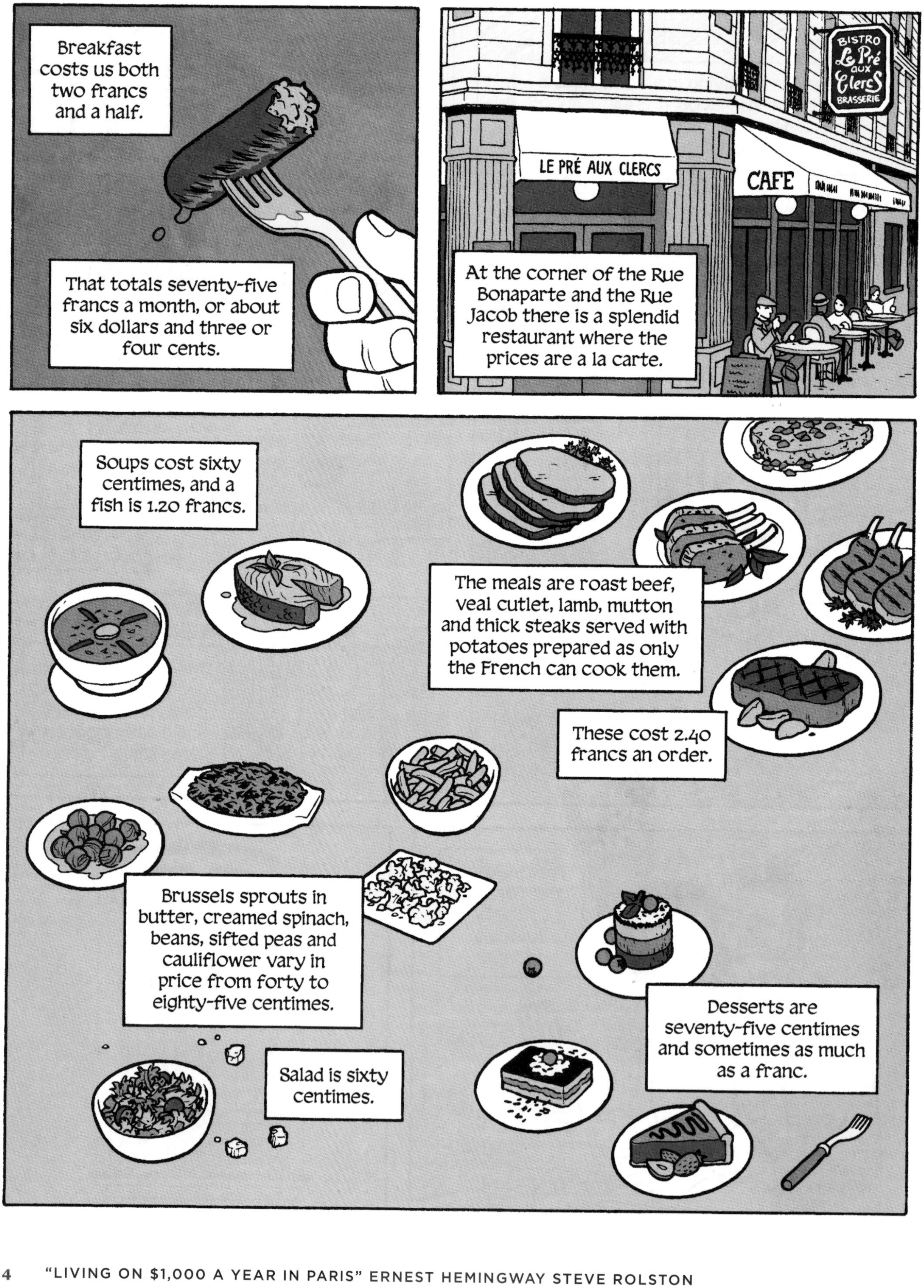

Breakfast costs us both two francs and a half.
That totals seventy-five francs a month, or about six dollars and three or four cents.
BISTRO Le Pré aux Clercs BRASSERIE
LE PRÉ AUX CLERCS
CAFE
At the corner of the Rue Bonaparte and the Rue Jacob there is a splendid restaurant where the prices are a la carte.
Soups cost sixty centimes, and a fish is 1.20 francs.
The meals are roast beef, veal cutlet, lamb, mutton and thick steaks served with potatoes prepared as only the French can cook them.
These cost 2.40 francs an order.
Brussels sprouts in butter, creamed spinach, beans, sifted peas and cauliflower vary in price from forty to eighty-five centimes.
Salad is sixty centimes.
Desserts are seventy-five centimes and sometimes as much as a franc.

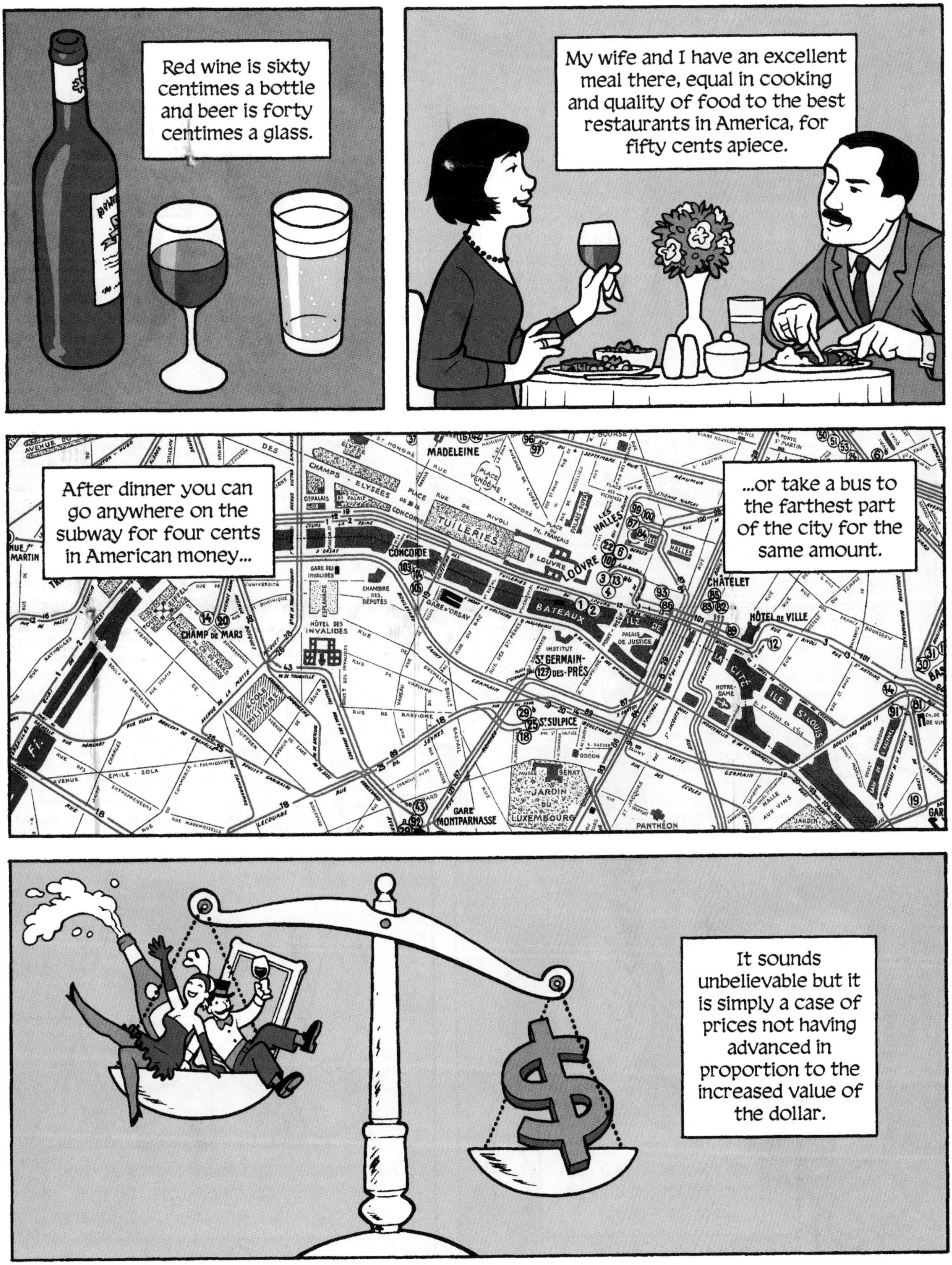
Red wine is sixty centimes a bottle and beer is forty centimes a glass.
My wife and I have an excellent meal there, equal in cooking and quality of food to the best restaurants in America, for fifty cents apiece.
After dinner you can go anywhere on the subway for four cents in American money...
...or take a bus to the farthest part of the city for the same amount.
MADELEINE
TUILERIES
CONCORDE
LOUVRE
HALLES
CHÂTELET
HÔTEL DE VILLE
BATEAUX
CHAMP DE MARS
HÔTEL DES INVALIDES
ST GERMAIN-DES-PRÉS
ST SULPICE
GARE MONTPARNASSE
JARDIN DU LUXEMBOURG
PANTHÉON
It sounds unbelievable but it is simply a case of prices not having advanced in proportion to the increased value of the dollar.

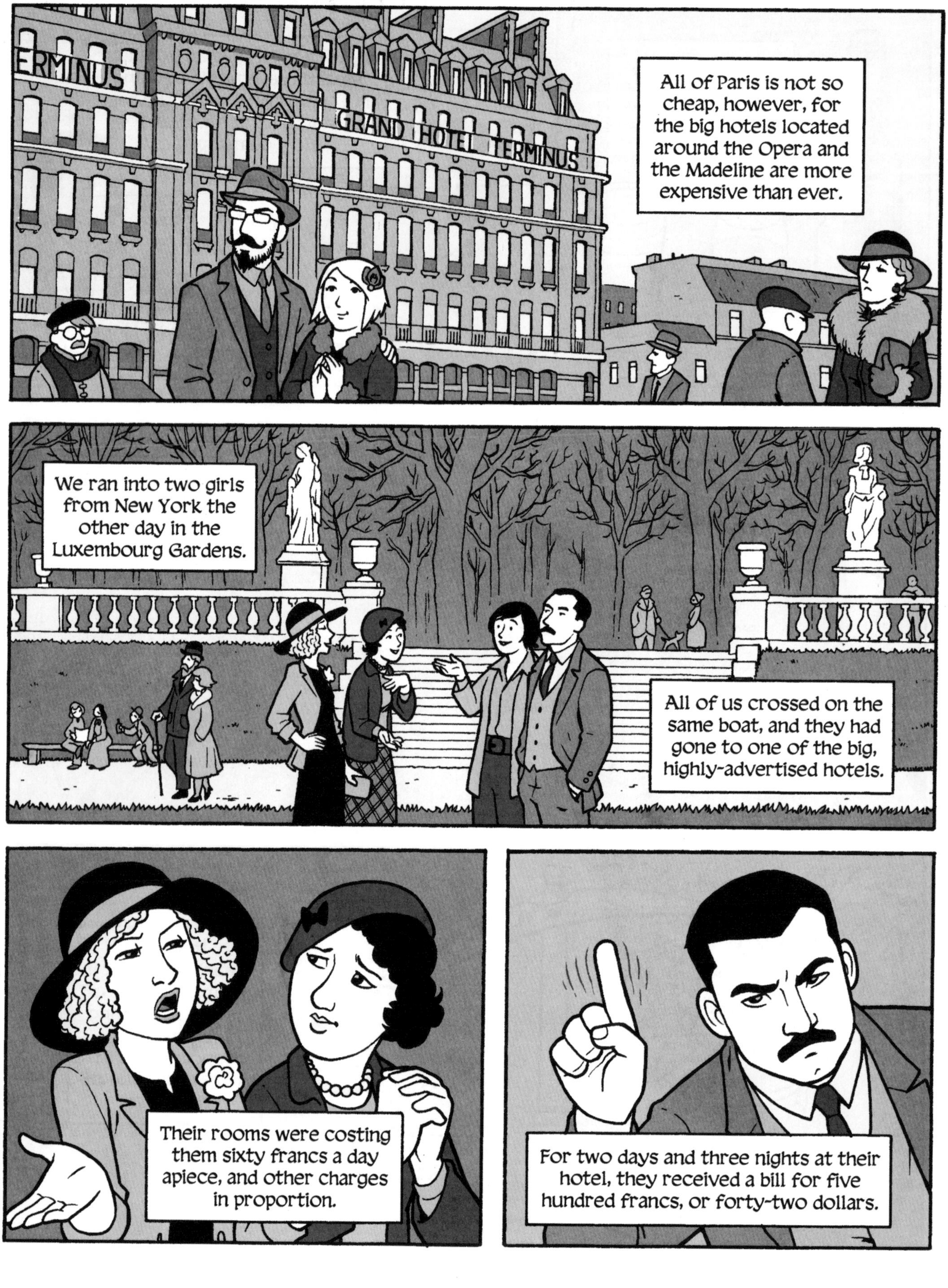
ERMINUS
GRAND HOTEL TERMINUS
All of Paris is not so cheap, however, for the big hotels located around the Opera and the Madeline are more expensive than ever.
We ran into two girls from New York the other day in the Luxembourg Gardens.
All of us crossed on the same boat, and they had gone to one of the big, highly-advertised hotels.
Their rooms were costing them sixty francs a day apiece, and other charges in proportion.
For two days and three nights at their hotel, they received a bill for five hundred francs, or forty-two dollars.

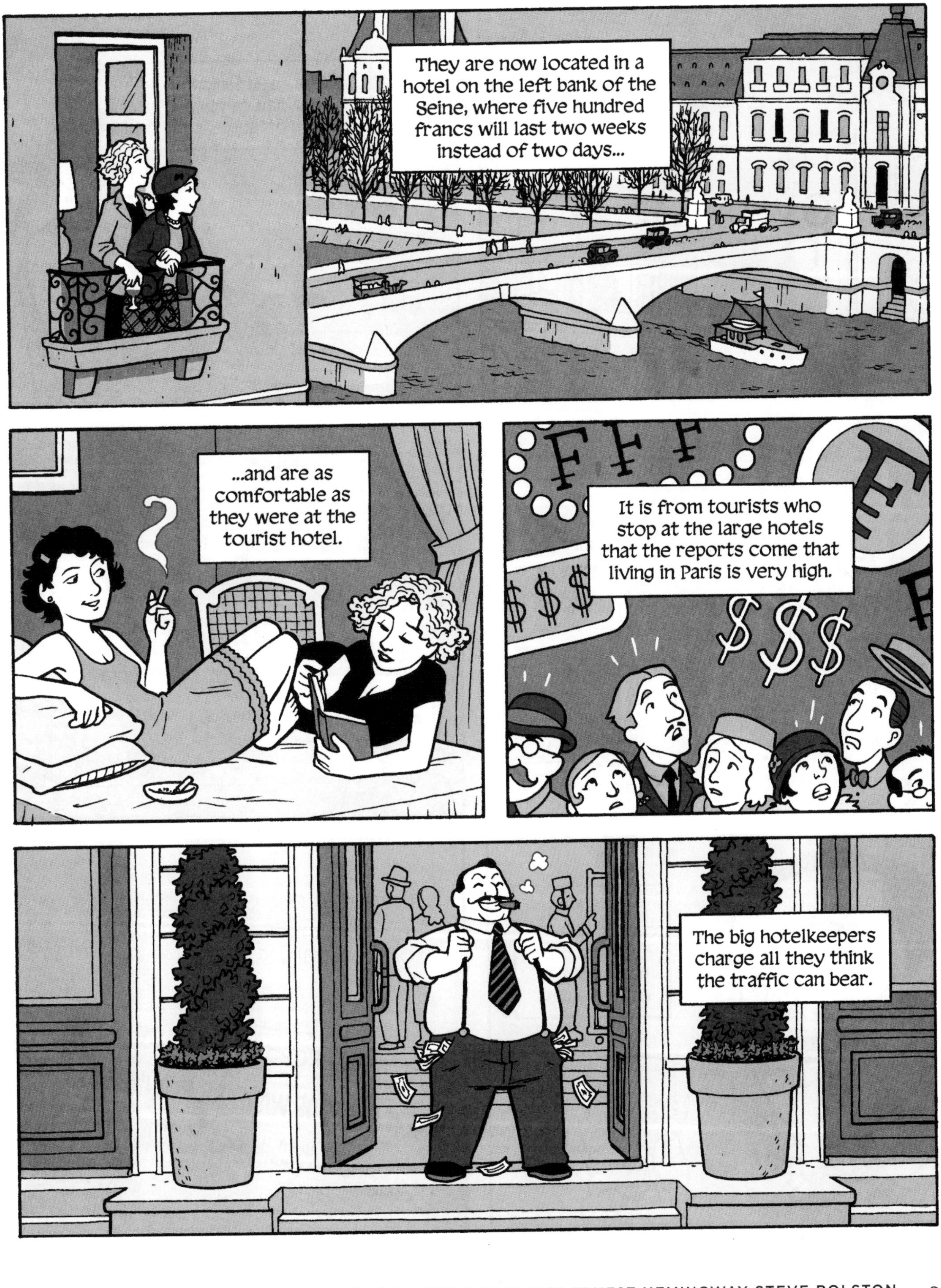
They are now located in a hotel on the left bank of the Seine, where five hundred francs will last two weeks instead of two days...
...and are as comfortable as they were at the tourist hotel.
It is from tourists who stop at the large hotels that the reports come that living in Paris is very high.
The big hotelkeepers charge all they think the traffic can bear.

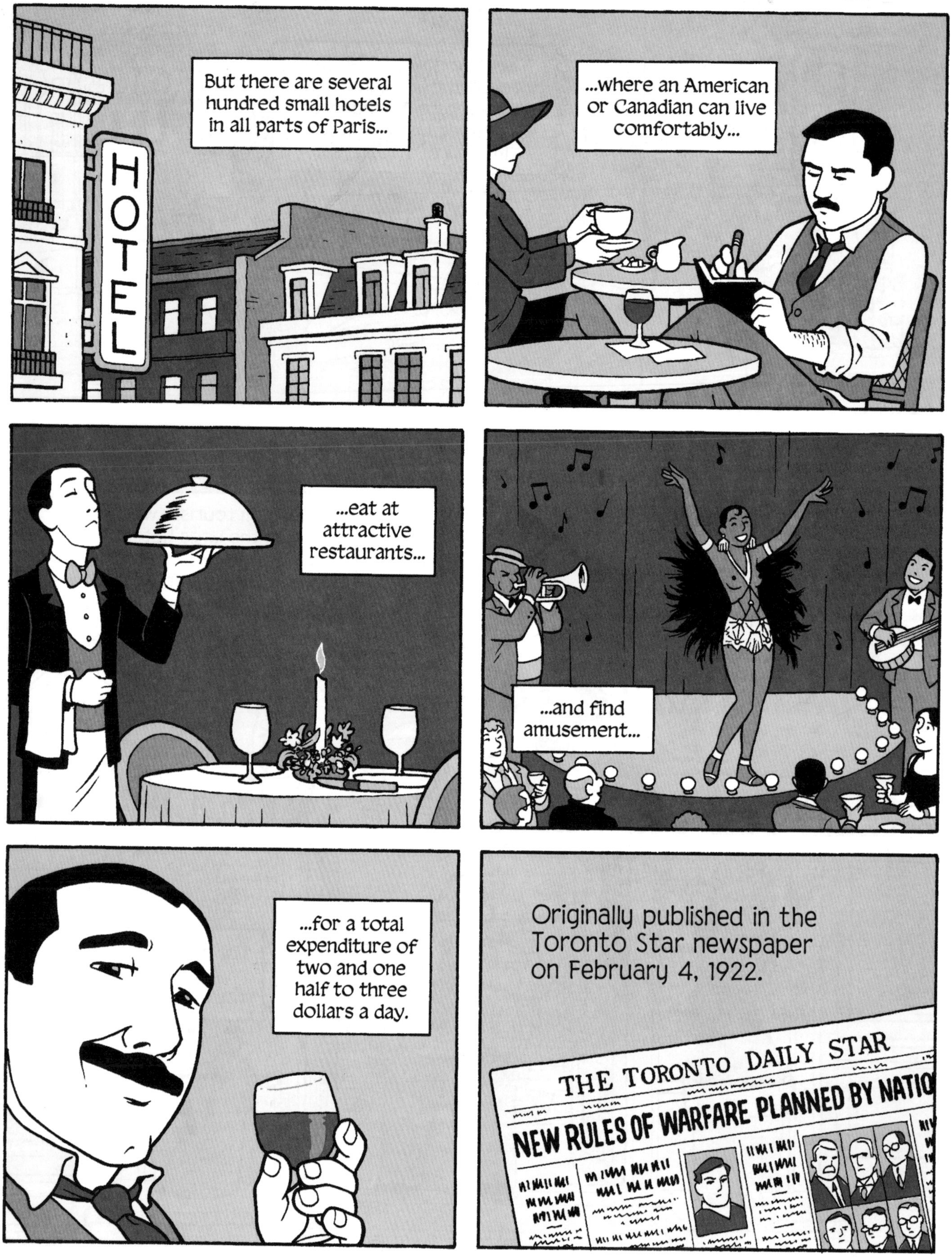
But there are several hundred small hotels in all parts of Paris...
HOTEL
...where an American or Canadian can live comfortably...
...eat at attractive restaurants...
...and find amusement...
...for a total expenditure of two and one half to three dollars a day.
Originally published in the Toronto Star newspaper on February 4, 1922.
THE TORONTO DAILY STAR
NEW RULES OF WARFARE PLANNED BY NATIO

"The Emperor of Ice-Cream"

Wallace Stevens

ART/ADAPTATION BY **Anthony Ventura**

WALLACE STEVENS IS AN ANOMALY. IN OUR cultural imagination, we see poets as wild men like Rimbaud and the Romantics, mystical visionaries like Blake and Yeats, or sensitive souls like Dickinson and Dylan Thomas. Wallace Stevens was an insurance executive.

He worked as a vice president at the Hartford Accident and Indemnity Company until his death, writing some of the century's finest poetry on company stationery or on the backs of envelopes while at work; some verses were dictated to his secretary. A sensitive, finely attuned poet's soul definitely resided in this staid executive and family man, whose first book of poetry was published when he was forty-four. In one of his best-known poems, "Thirteen Ways of Looking at a Blackbird," the Pulitzer winner writes:

> I do not know which to prefer,
> The beauty of inflections
> Or the beauty of innuendoes,
> The blackbird whistling
> Or just after.

As with many Modernists, his finely crafted poetry is often tough to understand, and interpretations can vary wildly. The short poem "The Emperor of Ice-Cream," one of his most celebrated, has triggered a lot of theorizing since its 1922 publication. What is seems to boil down to is that the first room/stanza is about life—boisterous, gaudy life—and the second room/stanza is about death—cold, dumb death. By saying "Let be be finale of seem," Stevens is siding with life: Let what is trump what only might be. Make your doings in this world more important than any theoretical next world. Carpe diem. My favorite explanation for the central phrase (and title) of the poem is that life is like ice cream—sweet and enjoyable but transitory. Better go ahead and eat it, because otherwise it's going to melt. And if life is ice cream, who would be the ruler/emperor of ice cream? Death, of course.

In this adaptation, Anthony Ventura provides another striking magazine-style layout for a classic poem.

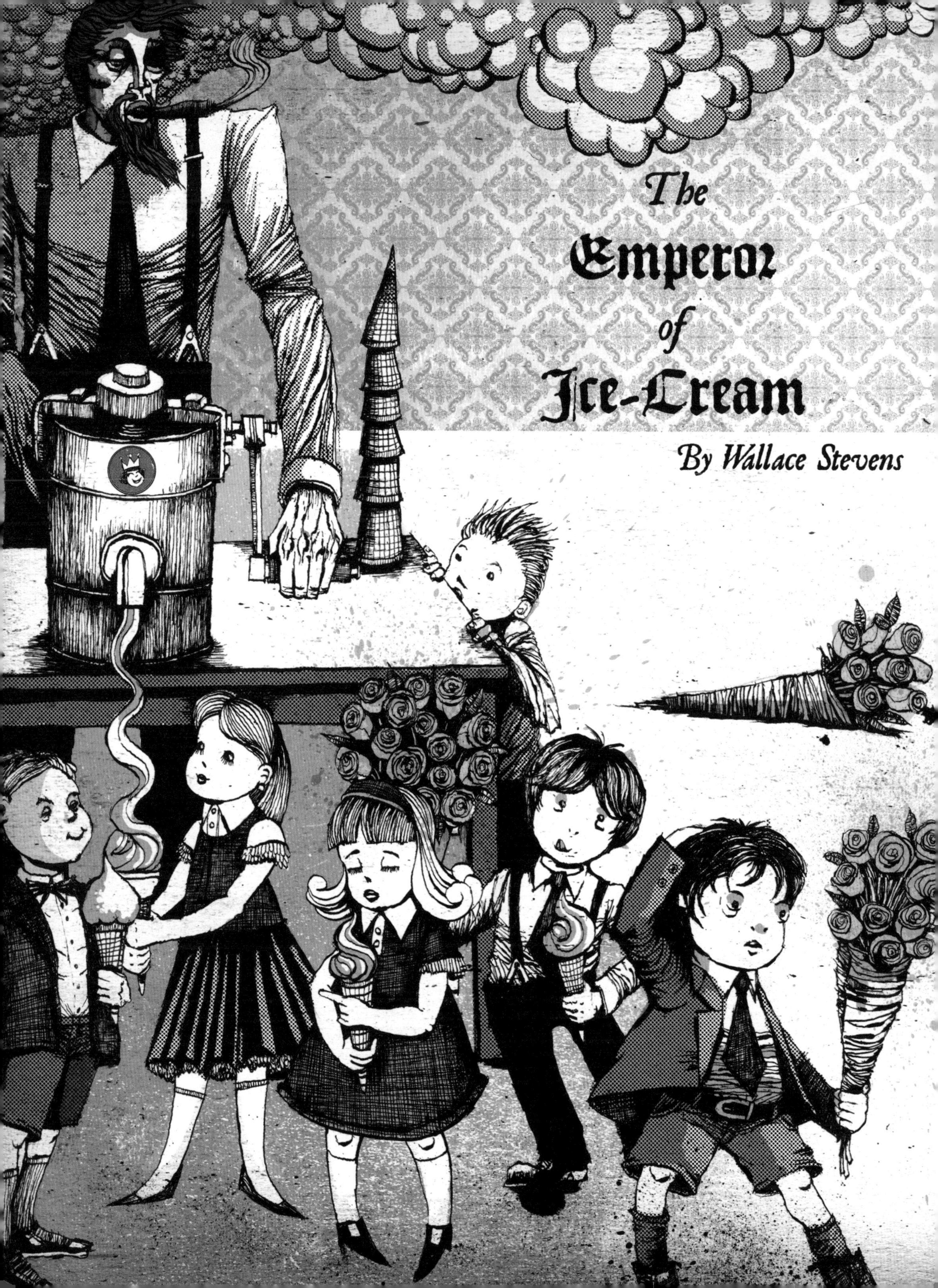
The Emperor of Ice-Cream
By Wallace Stevens

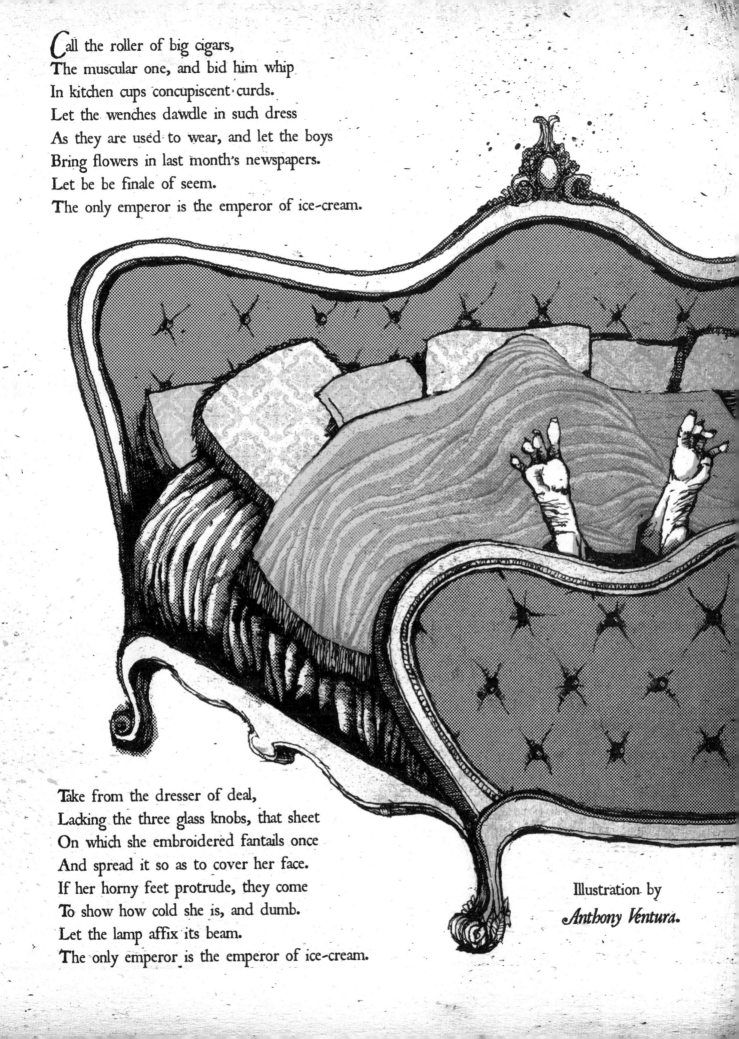

Call the roller of big cigars,
The muscular one, and bid him whip
In kitchen cups concupiscent curds.
Let the wenches dawdle in such dress
As they are used to wear, and let the boys
Bring flowers in last month's newspapers.
Let be be finale of seem.
The only emperor is the emperor of ice-cream.

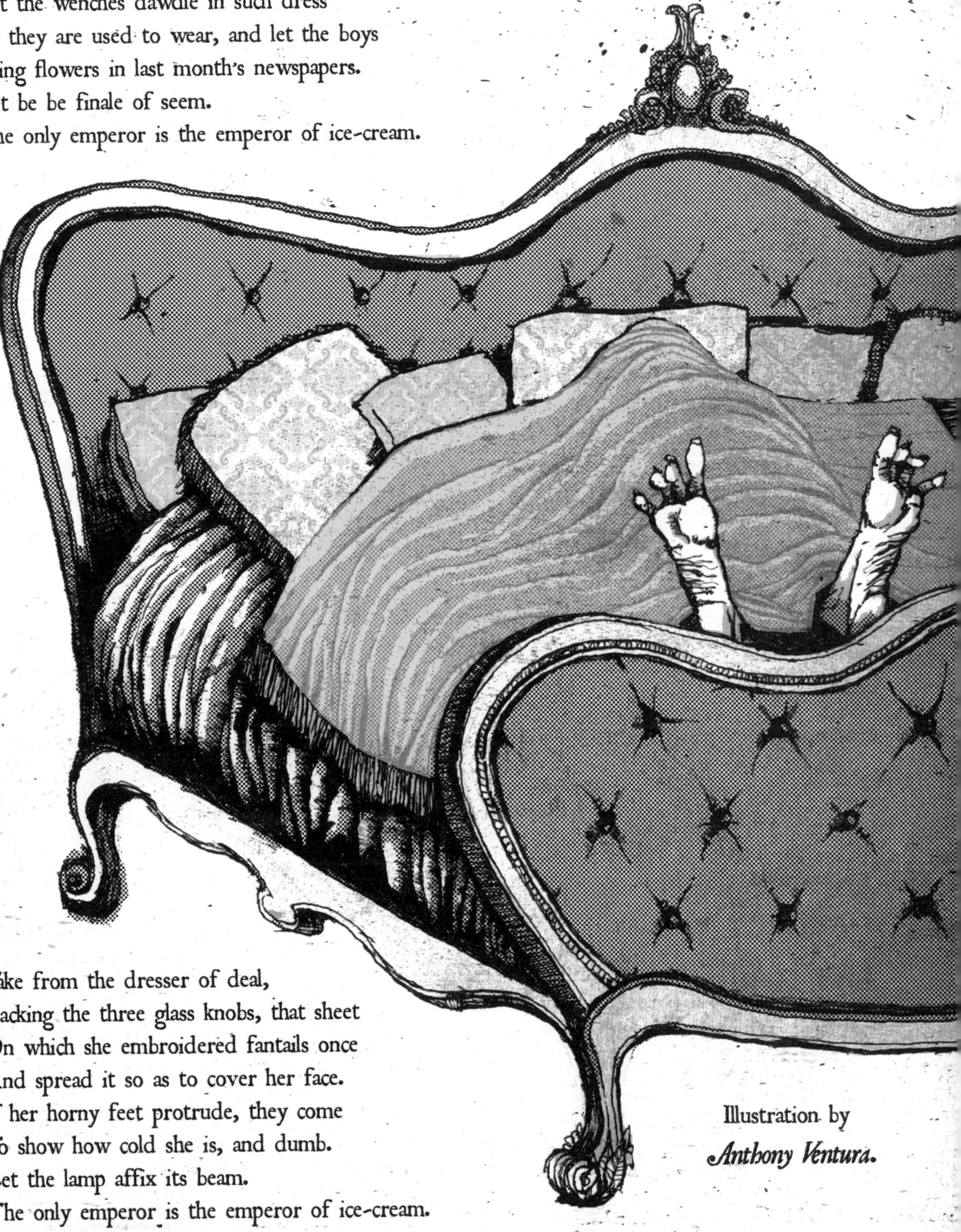

Take from the dresser of deal,
Lacking the three glass knobs, that sheet
On which she embroidered fantails once
And spread it so as to cover her face.
If her horny feet protrude, they come
To show how cold she is, and dumb.
Let the lamp affix its beam.
The only emperor is the emperor of ice-cream.

Illustration by
Anthony Ventura.

"The Hill"

William Faulkner

ART/ADAPTATION BY **Kate Glasheen**

UBER-CRITIC AND PROFESSOR OF WESTERN literature Harold Bloom has declared:

> By universal consent of critics and common readers, Faulkner is now recognized as the strongest American novelist of the twentieth century, clearly surpassing Hemingway and Fitzgerald, and standing as an equal in that sequence that includes Hawthorne, Melville, Mark Twain, and Henry James.

Born in Mississippi, Faulkner set pretty much all of his fiction—including the masterpieces *The Sound and the Fury*, *As I Lay Dying*, and *Absalom! Absalom!*—in the American South, racking up two Pulitzers and a Nobel in the process. He was no slouch at the short story either, and his "Barn Burning" and "A Rose for Emily" are two of the most anthologized in the English language, despite the latter's macabre subject matter, with a heavy implication of necrophilia.

While Faulkner's first two short stories were published in the literary magazine of his alma mater, the University of Mississippi, neither of them appears in his anthologies. They're not in *Collected Stories*, *The Uncollected Stories*, or Modern Library's *Selected Stories*. As far as I can tell, they've been reprinted a single time, in a slim 1962 volume that specifically gathered his college prose and poetry. It's

understandable why the 1919 story, "Landing in Luck," is MIA—it just isn't very good. But "The Hill," appearing three years later, is something else entirely. Not really a short story, more of a sketch, at times almost a prose poem, this short piece is reflective, experimental, and charming in a quiet, downbeat way. It indicates some of the themes and approaches Faulkner would later explore more fully.

Kate Glasheen did extraordinary work illustrating *Hybrid Bastards!* (written by Tom Pinchuk), a graphic novel in which the lascivious god Zeus creates monstrous, zany offspring due to his dalliances with a car, an apple, a mail box, a refrigerator, a vacuum, a stack of bricks. . . . Because of the rarity of "The Hill," I asked Kate if she would incorporate the full text into her adaptation. She obliged, turning in a tour de force. Although there is a rural stillness to the piece overall, Faulkner packed it with powerful, unexpected visuals, and Kate homed in on these, bringing each into full view with nine full-page paintings.

SOURCES

Bloom, Harold, ed. *Bloom's Modern Critical Views: William Faulkner* (new edition). New York: Infobase Publishing, 2008.

Faulkner, William. *William Faulkner: Early Prose and Poetry*. Carvel Collins, editor. Boston: Little, Brown, 1962.

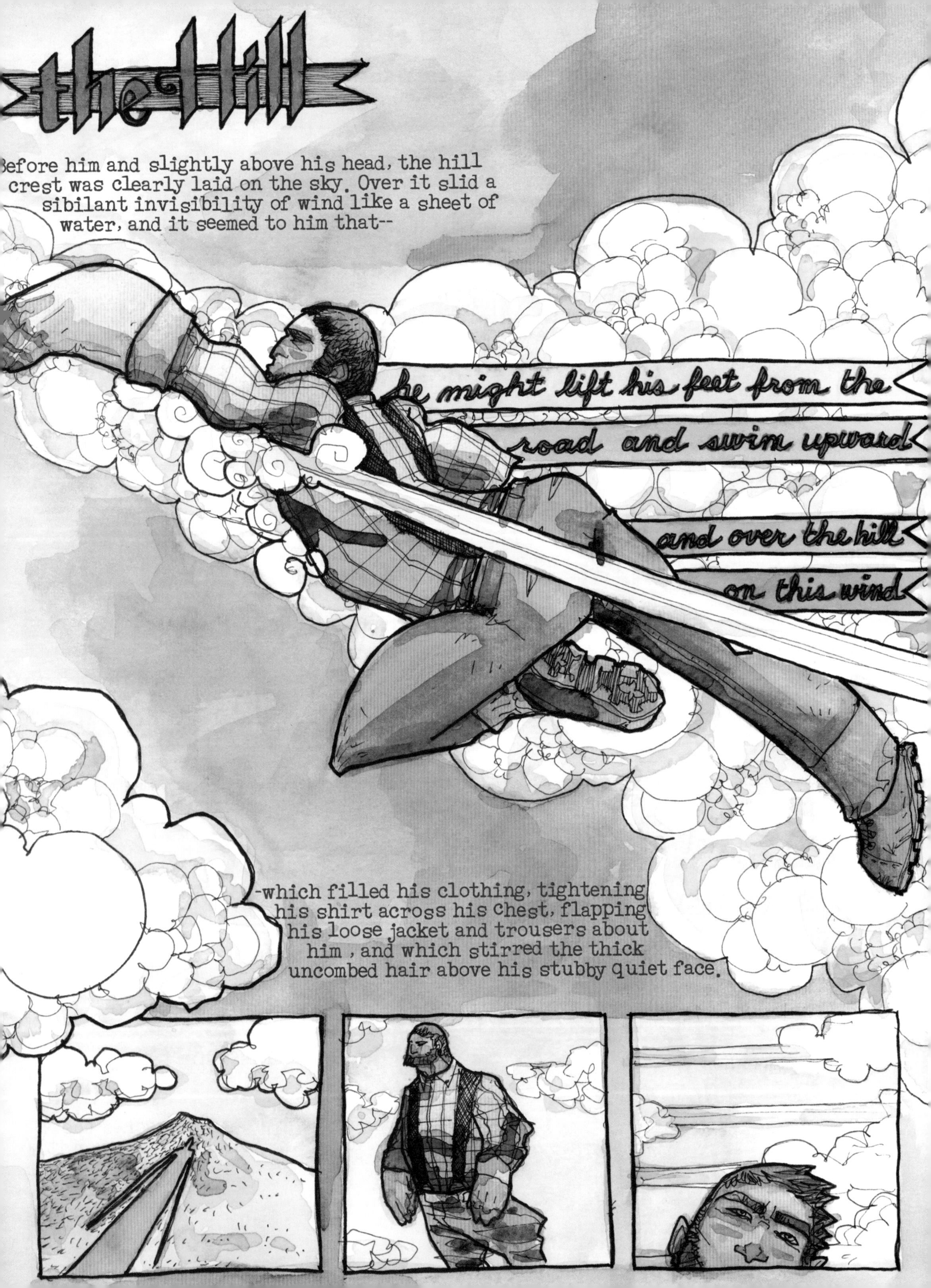
the Hill
Before him and slightly above his head, the hill crest was clearly laid on the sky. Over it slid a sibilant invisibility of wind like a sheet of water, and it seemed to him that--
he might lift his feet from the
road and swim upward
and over the hill
on this wind
-which filled his clothing, tightening his shirt across his chest, flapping his loose jacket and trousers about him , and which stirred the thick uncombed hair above his stubby quiet face.

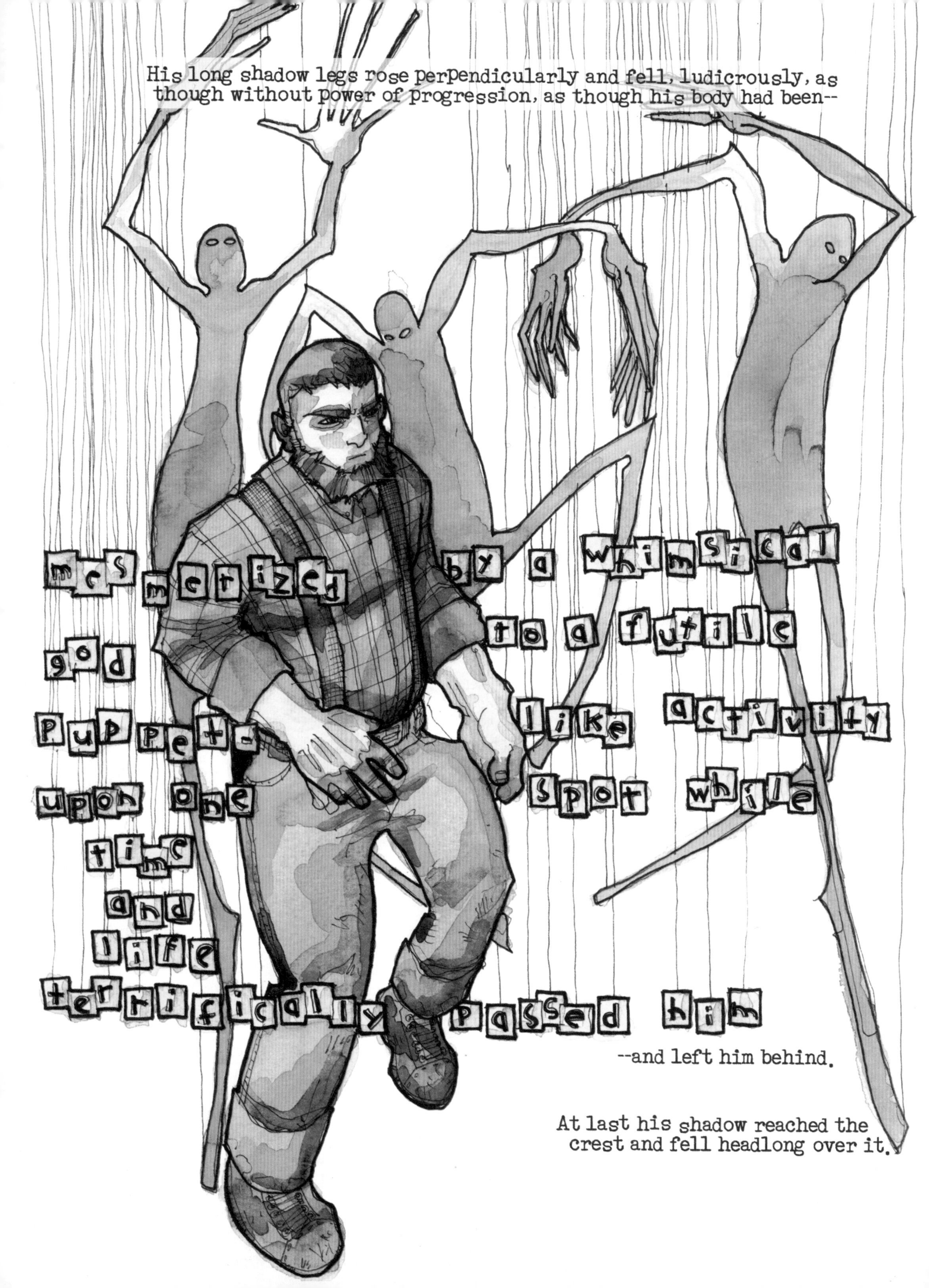
His long shadow legs rose perpendicularly and fell, ludicrously, as though without power of progression, as though his body had been--
mesmetized by a whimsical god
to a futile puppet-like activity
upon one spot while
time and life terrifically passed him
--and left him behind.
At last his shadow reached the crest and fell headlong over it.

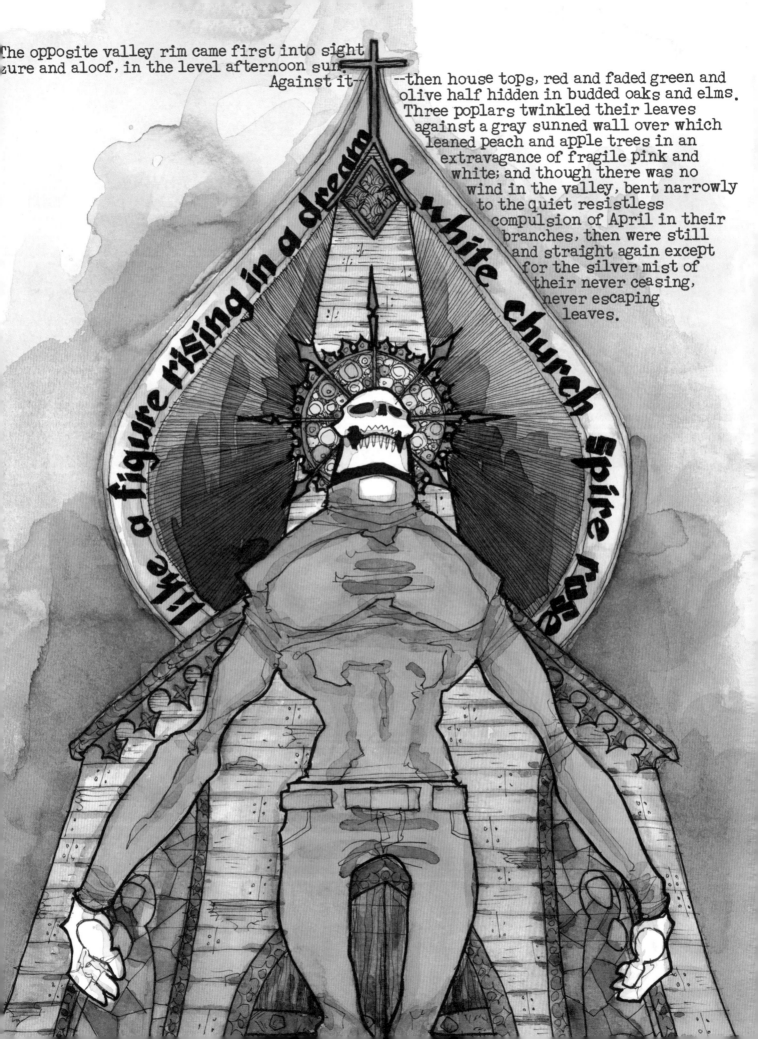

The opposite valley rim came first into sight
azure and aloof, in the level afternoon sun.
                    Against it—   —then house tops, red and faded green and
                                       olive half hidden in budded oaks and elms.
                                       Three poplars twinkled their leaves
                                       against a gray sunned wall over which
                                       leaned peach and apple trees in an
                                       extravagance of fragile pink and
                                       white; and though there was no
                                       wind in the valley, bent narrowly
                                       to the quiet resistless
                                       compulsion of April in their
                                       branches, then were still
                                       and straight again except
                                       for the silver mist of
                                       their never ceasing,
                                       never escaping
                                       leaves.

like a figure rising in a dream

a white church spire rose

The entire valley stretched beneath him, and his shadow, springing far out, lay across it, quiet and enormous. Here and there a thread of smoke balanced precariously upon a chimney. The hamlet slept, wrapped in peace and quiet beneath the evening sun, as it had slept for a century;

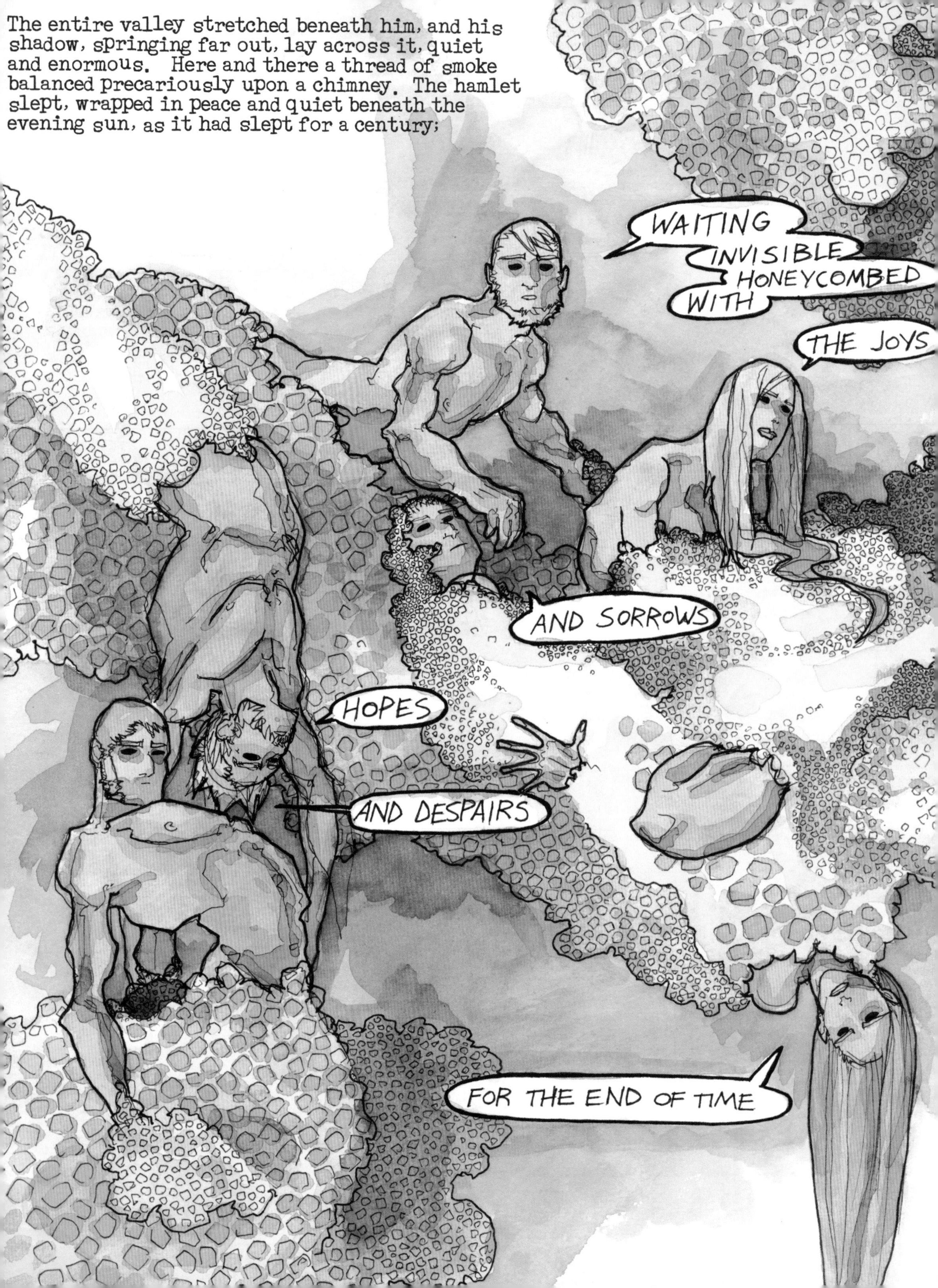
WAITING
INVISIBLE
HONEYCOMBED
WITH
THE JOYS
AND SORROWS
HOPES
AND DESPAIRS
FOR THE END OF TIME

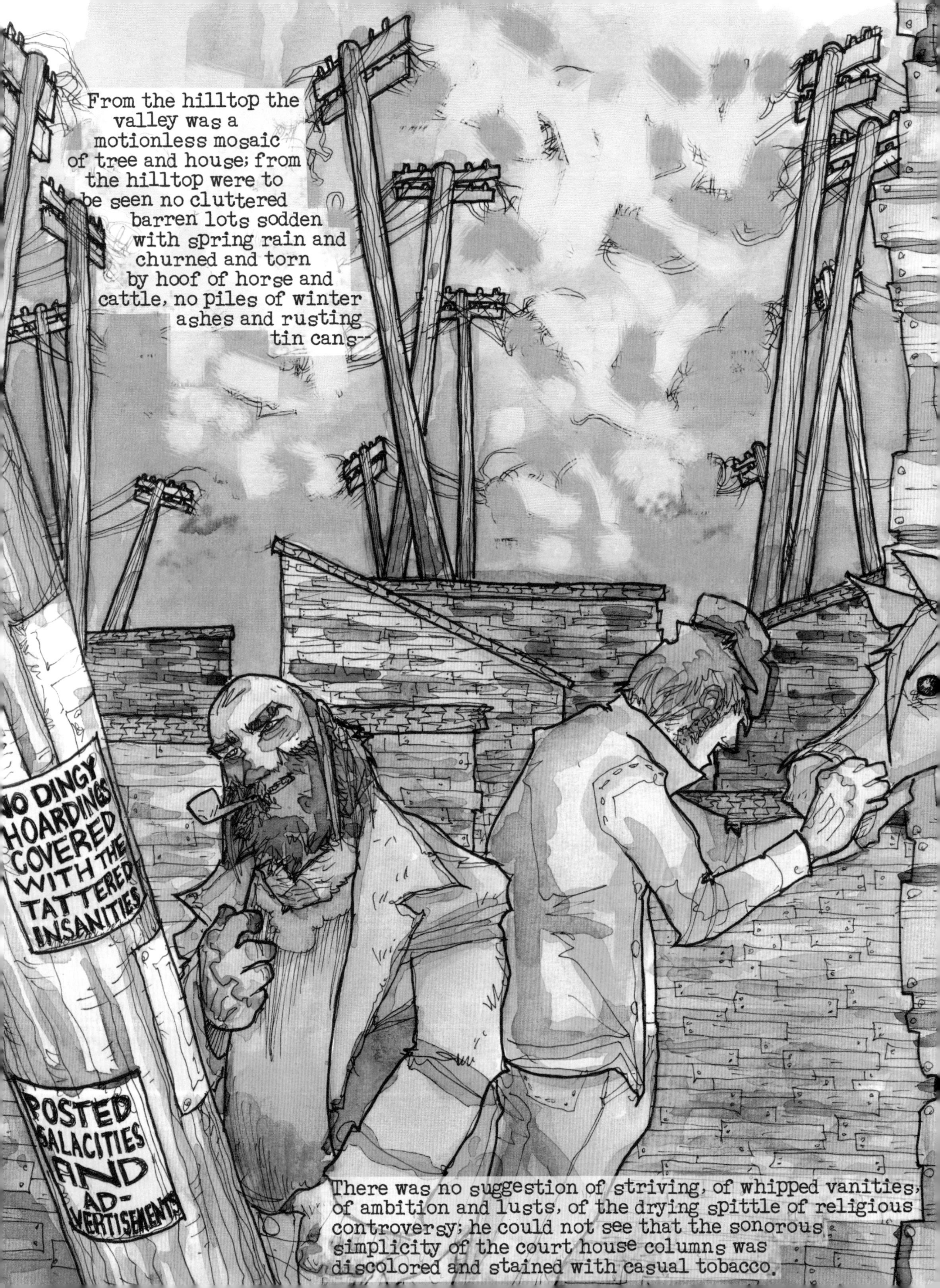
From the hilltop the valley was a motionless mosaic of tree and house; from the hilltop were to be seen no cluttered barren lots sodden with spring rain and churned and torn by hoof of horse and cattle, no piles of winter ashes and rusting tin cans--
NO DINGY HOARDINGS COVERED WITH THE TATTERED INSANITIES
POSTED SALACITIES AND AD-VERTISEMENTS
There was no suggestion of striving, of whipped vanities, of ambition and lusts, of the drying spittle of religious controversy; he could not see that the sonorous simplicity of the court house columns was discolored and stained with casual tobacco.

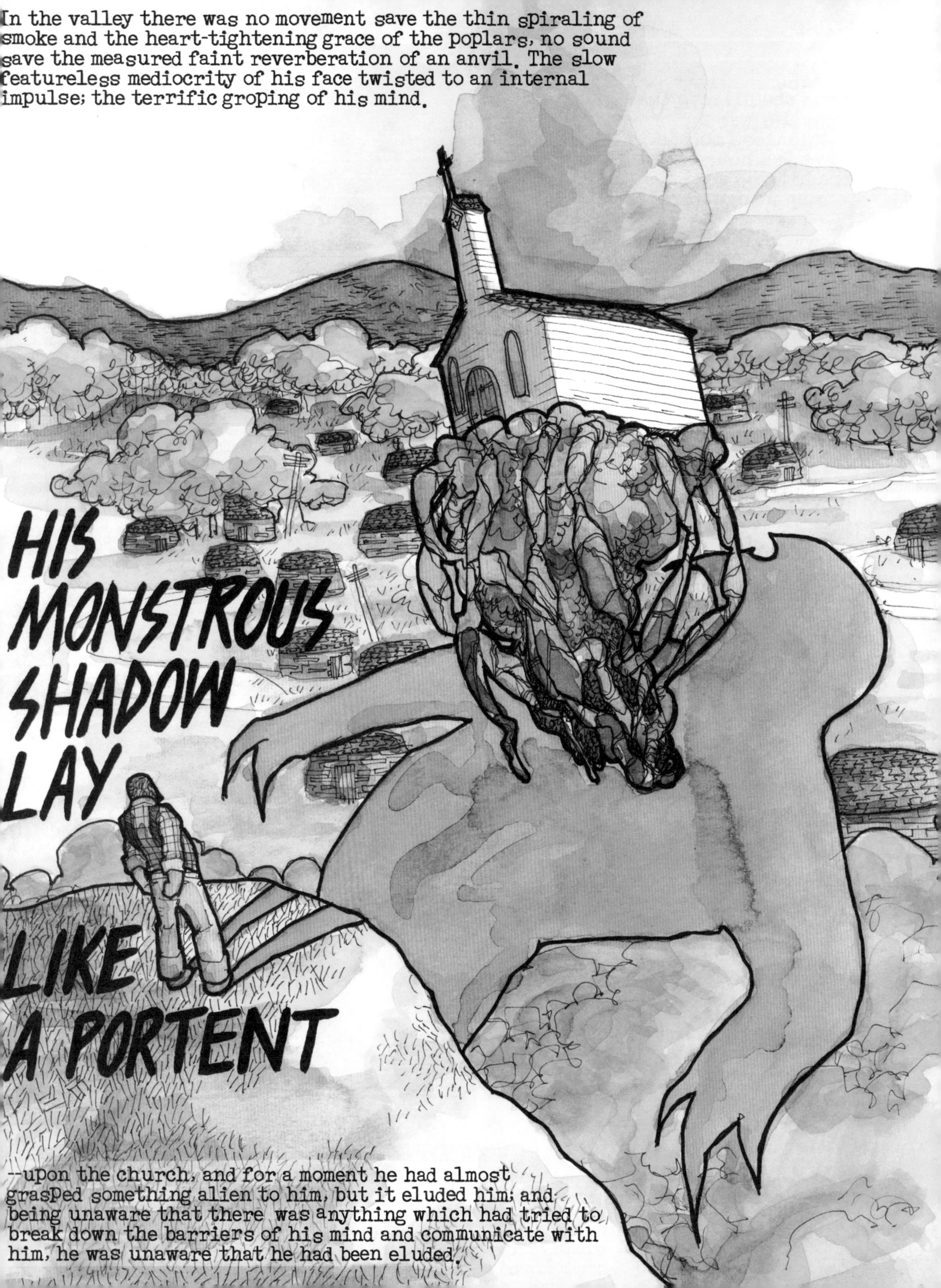
In the valley there was no movement save the thin spiraling of smoke and the heart-tightening grace of the poplars, no sound save the measured faint reverberation of an anvil. The slow featureless mediocrity of his face twisted to an internal impulse; the terrific groping of his mind.
HIS MONSTROUS SHADOW LAY
LIKE A PORTENT
--upon the church, and for a moment he had almost grasped something alien to him, but it eluded him; and being unaware that there was anything which had tried to break down the barriers of his mind and communicate with him, he was unaware that he had been eluded.

ehind him was a day of harsh labor with his hands, a strife against the forces of nature gain bread and clothing and a place to sleep, a victory gotten at the price of bodily tissues nd the numbered days of his existence; before him lay the hamlet which was home to him, ie tieless casual; and beyond it lay waiting another day to toil to gain bread and clothing and a place to sleep.

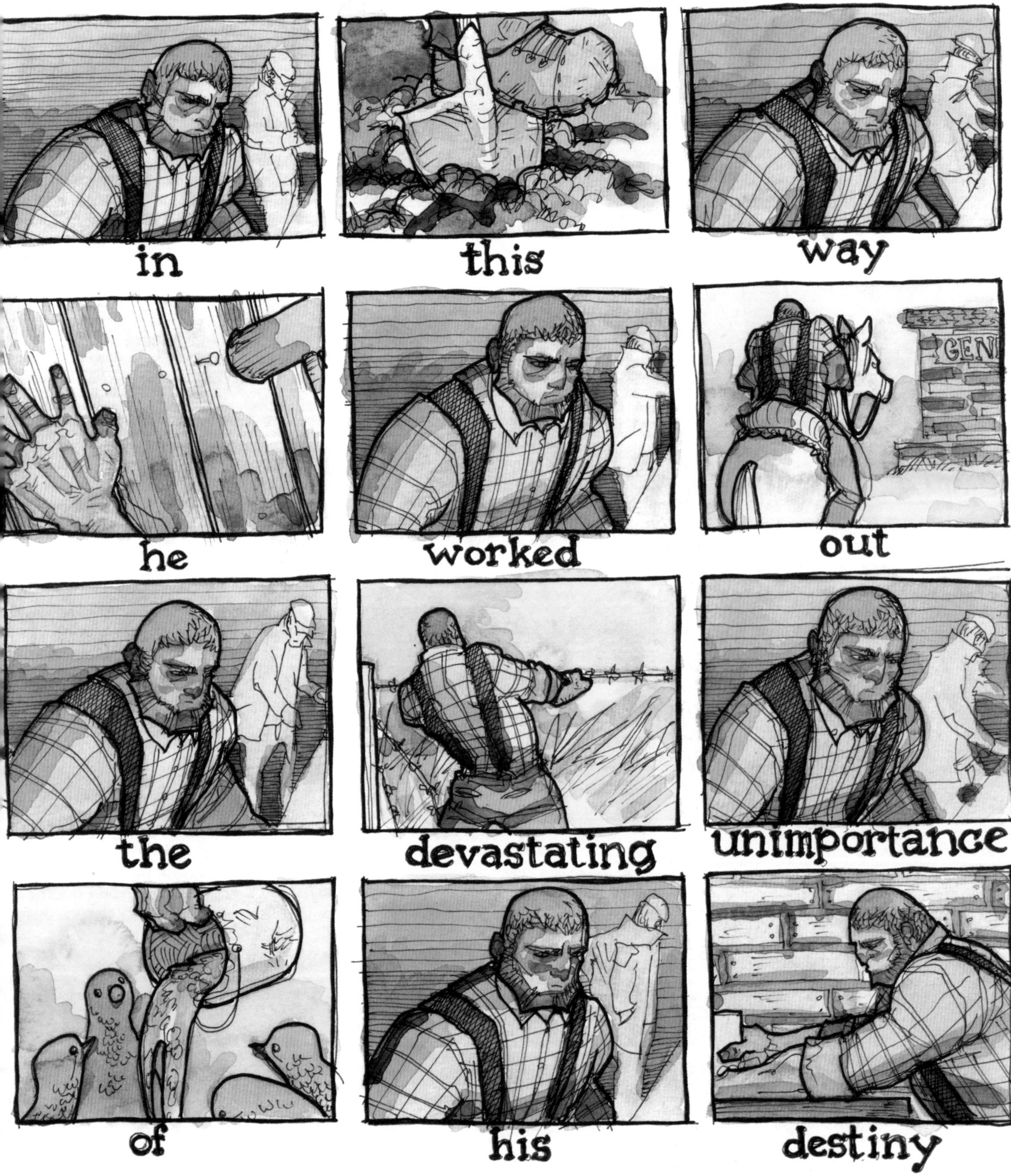
in
this
way
he
worked
GEN
out
the
devastating
unimportance
of
his
destiny

--with a mind heretofore untroubled by moral quibbles and principles, shaken at last by the faint resistless force of spring in a valley at sunset.

The sun plunged silently into the liquid green of the west and the valley was abruptly in shadow. And as the sun released him, who lived and labored in the sun, his mind that troubled him for the first time, became quieted.

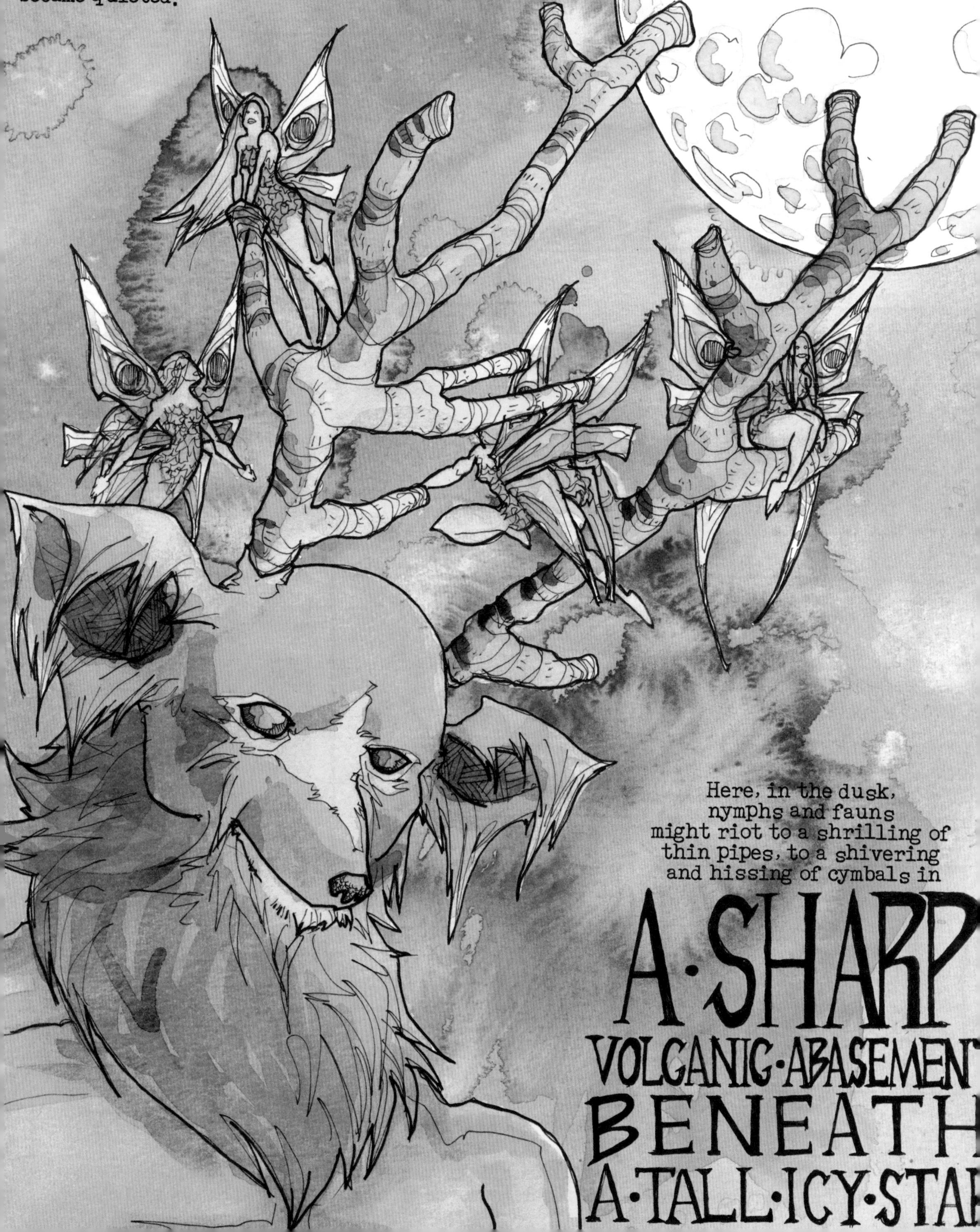
Here, in the dusk,
nymphs and fauns
might riot to a shrilling of
thin pipes, to a shivering
and hissing of cymbals in
A·SHARP
VOLCANIC·ABASEMEN
BENEATH
A·TALL·ICY·STA

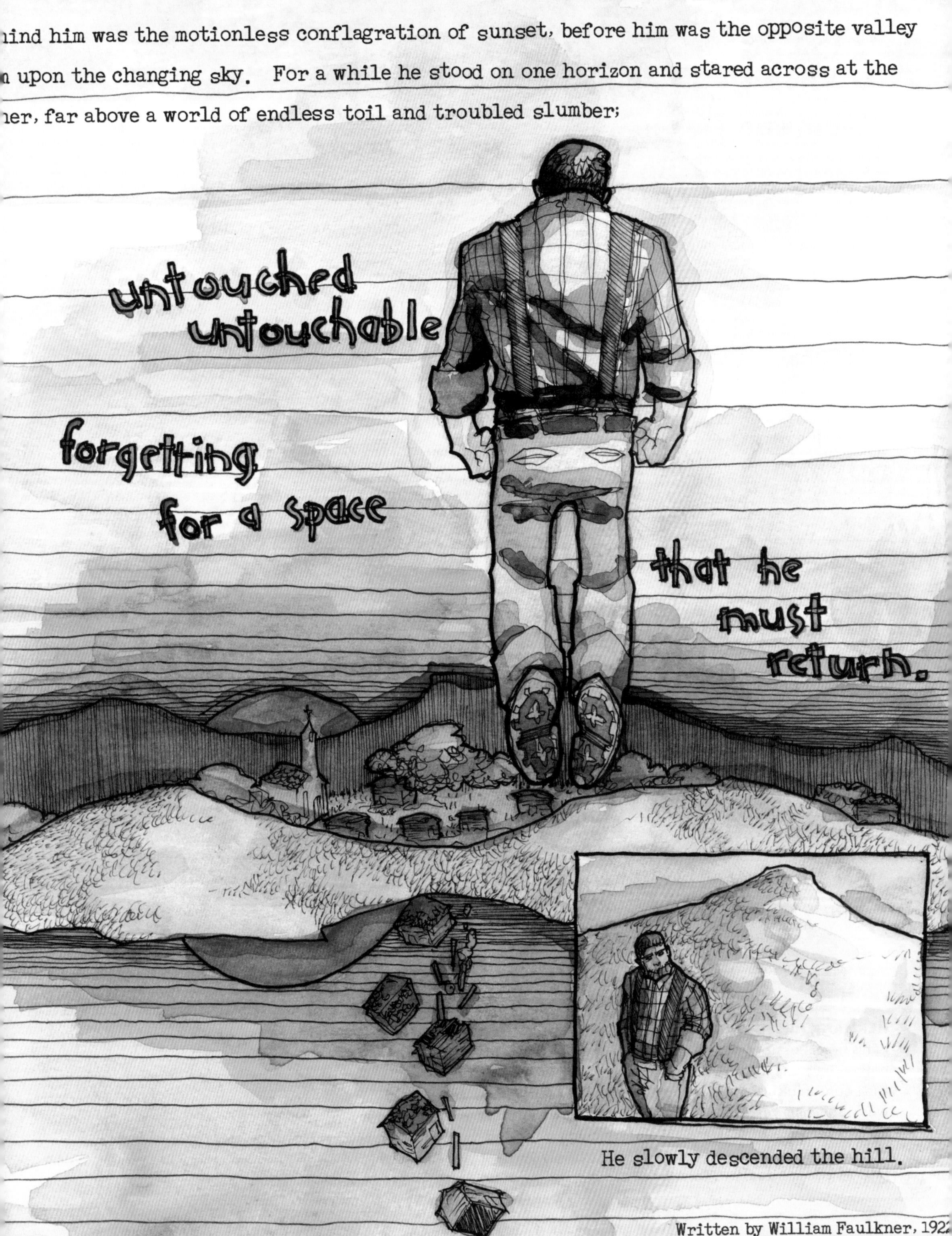
hind him was the motionless conflagration of sunset, before him was the opposite valley
n upon the changing sky. For a while he stood on one horizon and stared across at the
her, far above a world of endless toil and troubled slumber;
untouched
untouchable
forgetting,
for a space
that he
must
return.
He slowly descended the hill.

Written by William Faulkner, 192
Illustrated by Kate Glasheen, 201

Siddhartha

Hermann Hesse

ART/ADAPTATION BY **J. Ben Moss**

HERMANN HESSE WAS A GOOD FORTY YEARS AHEAD of his time. Possibly more. *Siddhartha* was published in his native Germany in 1922, but became a huge seller during the counterculture of the late 1960s and still reads like it was published yesterday. Based on Hesse's own interest in, and practice of, Eastern religion—including the biggies of Hinduism, Taoism, and Buddhism (mainly Zen)—it follows the spiritual progression of Siddhartha, a young Indian man living in the time of the Buddha. Born into the Brahmin caste, he rejects their bookish approach to spirituality, and tries to find something more authentic and direct.

In the following pages, J. Ben Moss—who counts this novel among his very favorite works of lit—adapts a crucial scene in which Siddhartha meets the Buddha himself and declines to become a disciple.

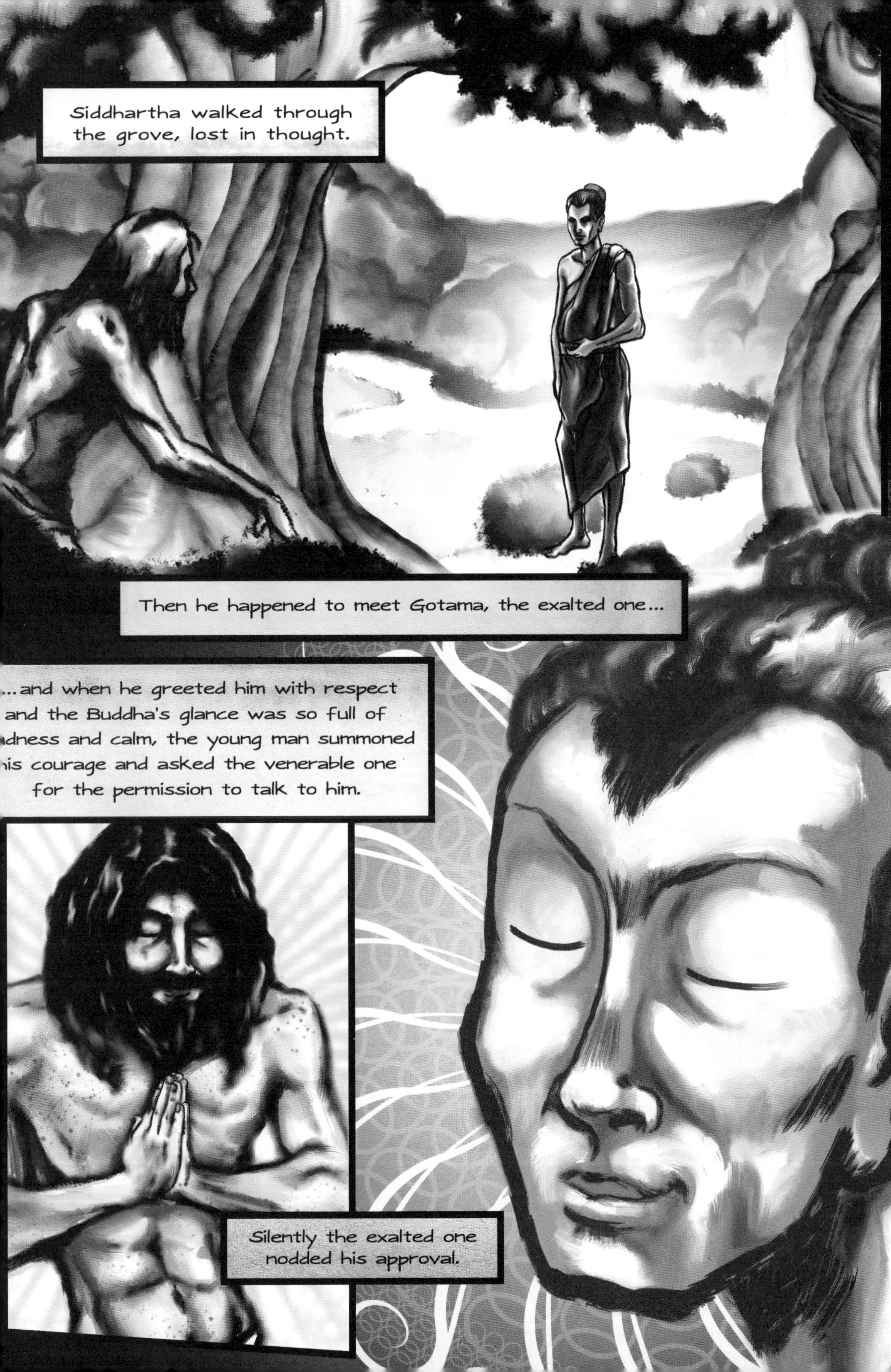
Siddhartha walked through the grove, lost in thought.
Then he happened to meet Gotama, the exalted one...
...and when he greeted him with respect and the Buddha's glance was so full of dness and calm, the young man summoned is courage and asked the venerable one for the permission to talk to him.
Silently the exalted one nodded his approval.

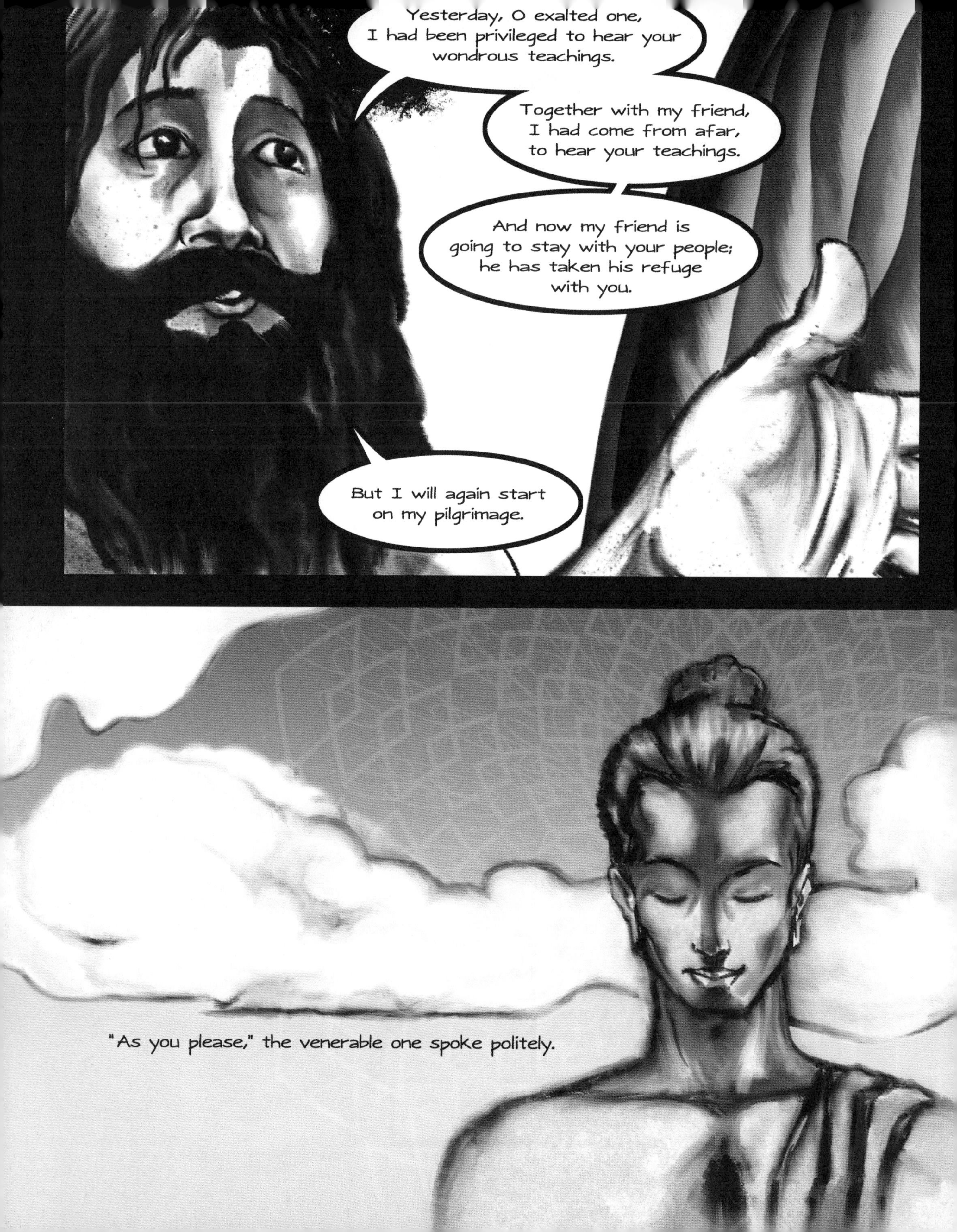
Yesterday, O exalted one, I had been privileged to hear your wondrous teachings.
Together with my friend, I had come from afar, to hear your teachings.
And now my friend is going to stay with your people; he has taken his refuge with you.
But I will again start on my pilgrimage.
"As you please," the venerable one spoke politely.

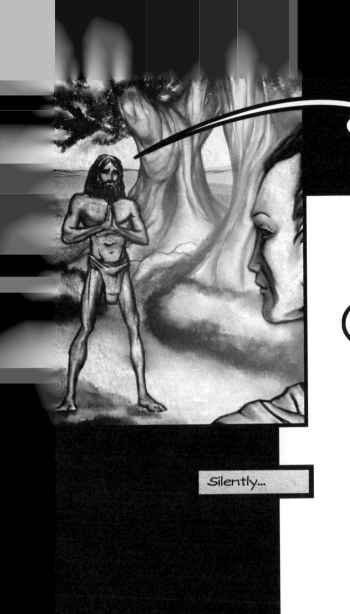

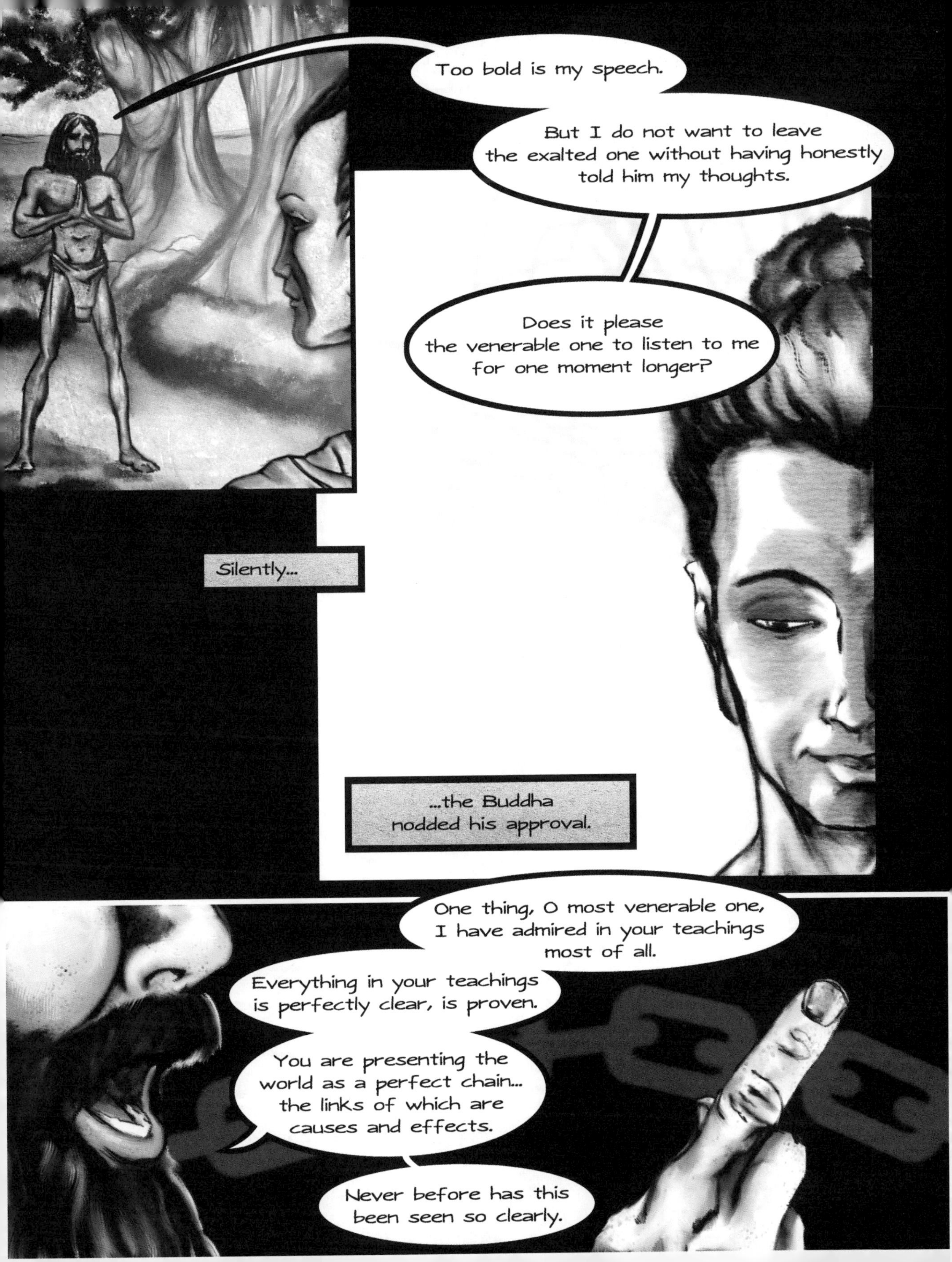
Too bold is my speech.
But I do not want to leave the exalted one without having honestly told him my thoughts.
Does it please the venerable one to listen to me for one moment longer?
Silently...
...the Buddha nodded his approval.
One thing, O most venerable one, I have admired in your teachings most of all.
Everything in your teachings is perfectly clear, is proven.
You are presenting the world as a perfect chain... the links of which are causes and effects.
Never before has this been seen so clearly.

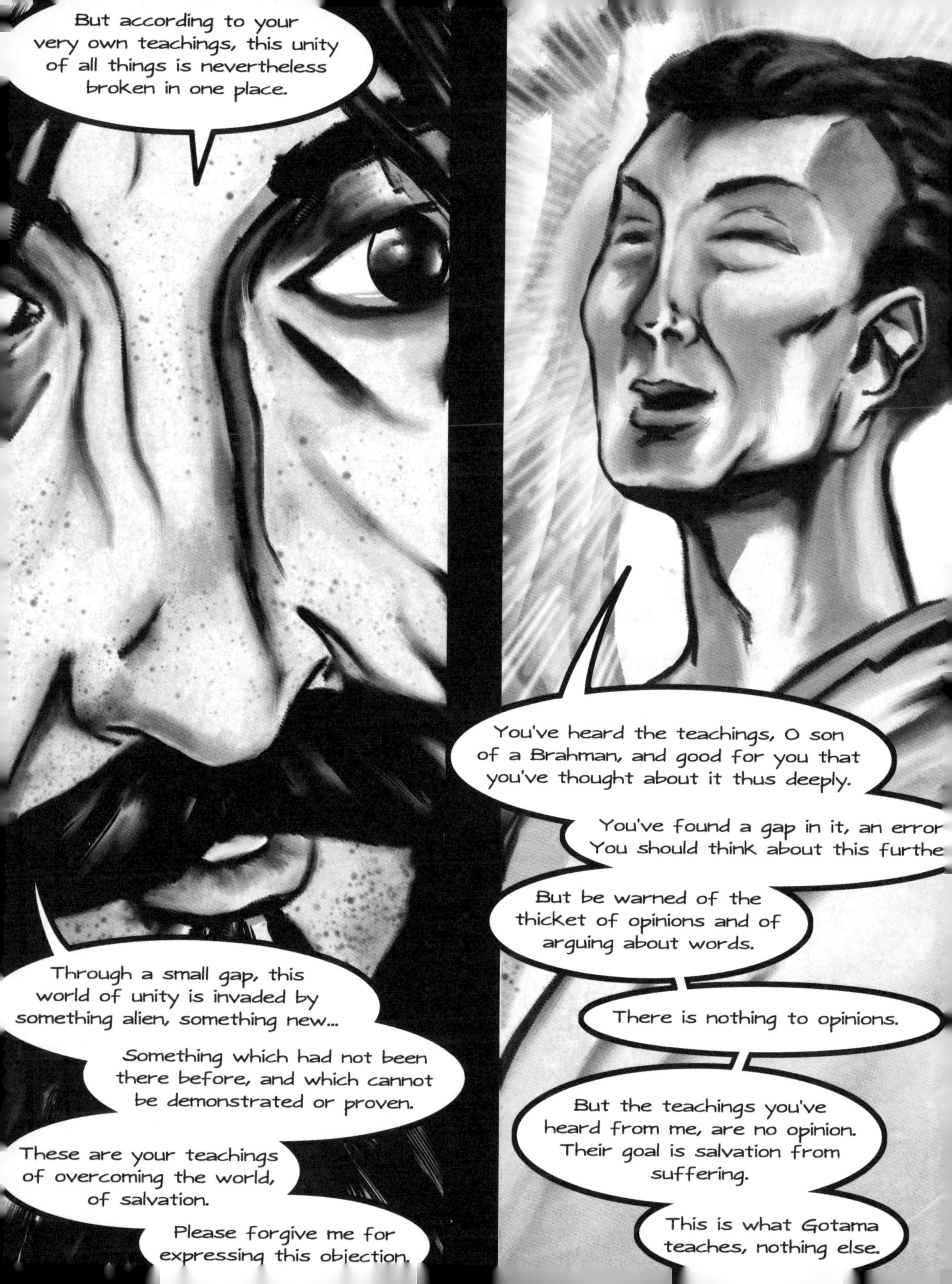
But according to your very own teachings, this unity of all things is nevertheless broken in one place.
Through a small gap, this world of unity is invaded by something alien, something new...
Something which had not been there before, and which cannot be demonstrated or proven.
These are your teachings of overcoming the world, of salvation.
Please forgive me for expressing this objection.
You've heard the teachings, O son of a Brahman, and good for you that you've thought about it thus deeply.
You've found a gap in it, an error You should think about this furthe
But be warned of the thicket of opinions and of arguing about words.
There is nothing to opinions.
But the teachings you've heard from me, are no opinion. Their goal is salvation from suffering.
This is what Gotama teaches, nothing else.

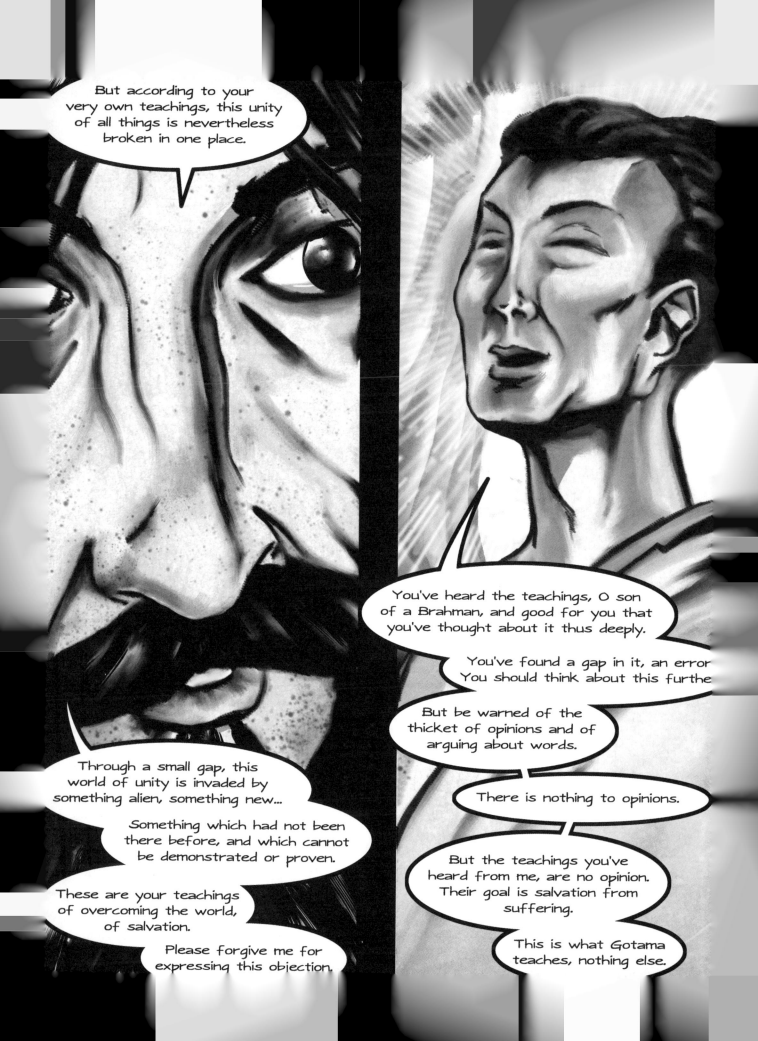

"The Waste Land"

T. S. Eliot

ART/ADAPTATION BY **Chandra Free**

OFTEN CONSIDERED THE MOST IMPORTANT POEM of the twentieth century, "The Waste Land" went a long way in disrupting poetry and literature in general. At the time it was written, massive technological, industrial, social, and economic changes were transforming the world in unprecedented, inconceivable ways, culminating in the carnage and chaos of the first worldwide war the human race had seen. The world was altered, and Eliot wanted to reflect this. He showed the fragmented, confusing nature of the modern world by writing a poem that is itself fragmented and confusing.

But Eliot didn't fill the poem with a jumble of randomness. The dark lines carry great significance, even when the meanings aren't clear. "The Waste Land" is jam-packed with obvious and obscure allusions to religion, myth, and esotericism, including Christianity, Hinduism, the Fisher King, and the Tarot. It's also rife with death, decay, and desiccation.

Additionally, there are enough literary references to have kept scholars digging since the poem came out around ninety years ago, in late 1922. Cynics suggest Eliot was showing off, but the references tie the poem to the past, in an attempt to bring the past into the present, but again, in

a fragmented way. We're presented with bits of powerful myths, with religious thoughts that are supposed to give comfort and meaning, with insights into the human condition from history's greatest literary minds. . . . But, Eliot is asking, do they still apply? Does "meaning" itself still have meaning? Or has civilization become a vast, barren waste land with no hope of regeneration?

As soon as I saw Chandra Free's gorgeous graphic novel, *The God Machine*, I was hoping she'd say yes to being in *The Graphic Canon*. The elongated figures, the angular faces, the lush colors, the otherworldiness. Her style practically oozes literature. She bravely chose to take on Eliot's complex masterpiece, zooming in on two related parts. The poem's shortest section, "Death by Water," is about the decaying corpse of a Phoenician sailor who died at sea. There is no resurrection. Death is final. This scene fulfills a prophecy made by one of the narrators of the poem's first section, Madame Sosostris, who uses a pseudo-Tarot deck to foretell the future. Chandra has artfully bookended "Death by Water" with Madame Sosostris's card-reading section.

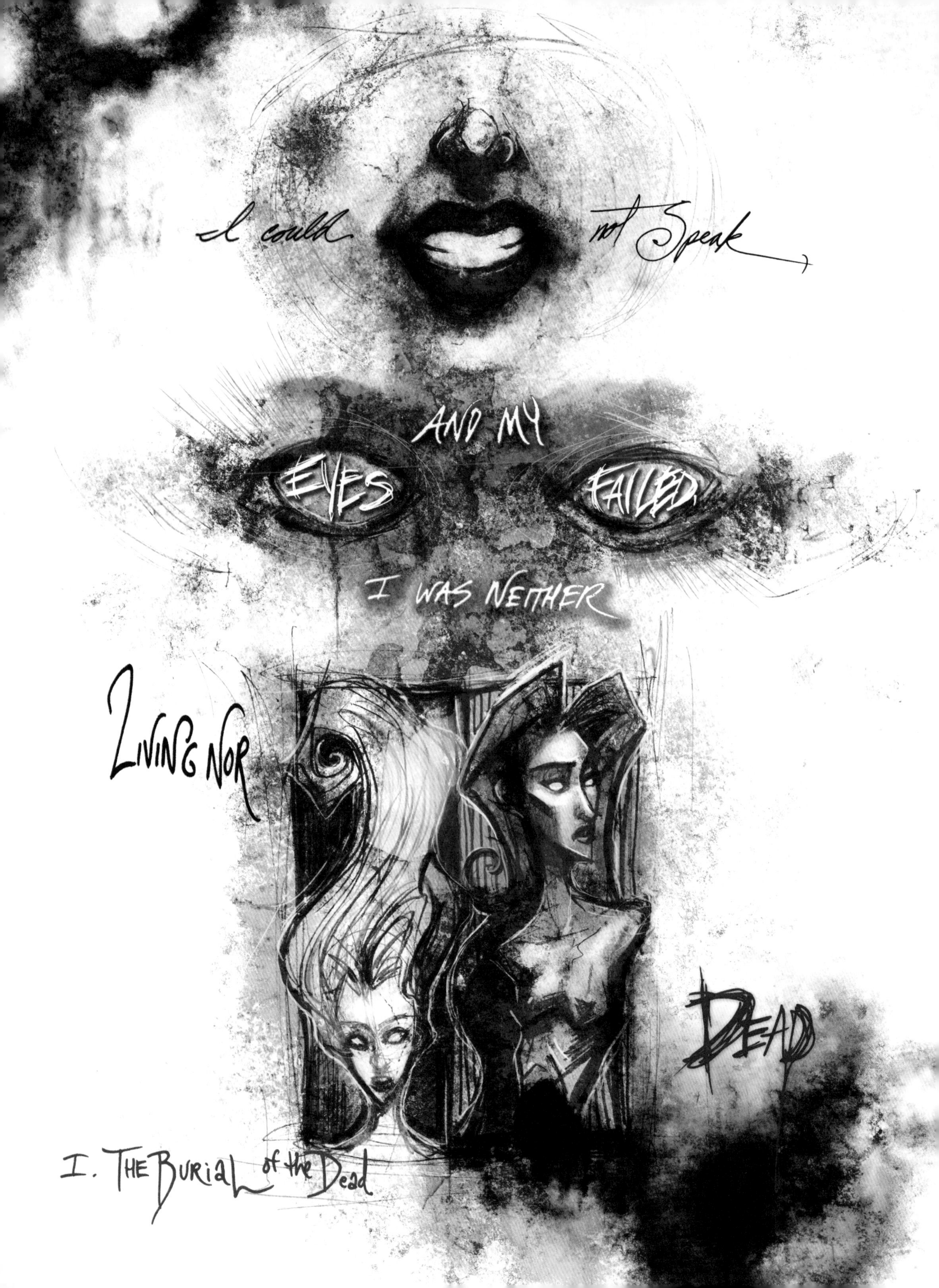
I could not Speak
AND MY
EYES
FAILED,
I WAS NEITHER
LIVING NOR
DEAD
I. THE BURIAL of the Dead

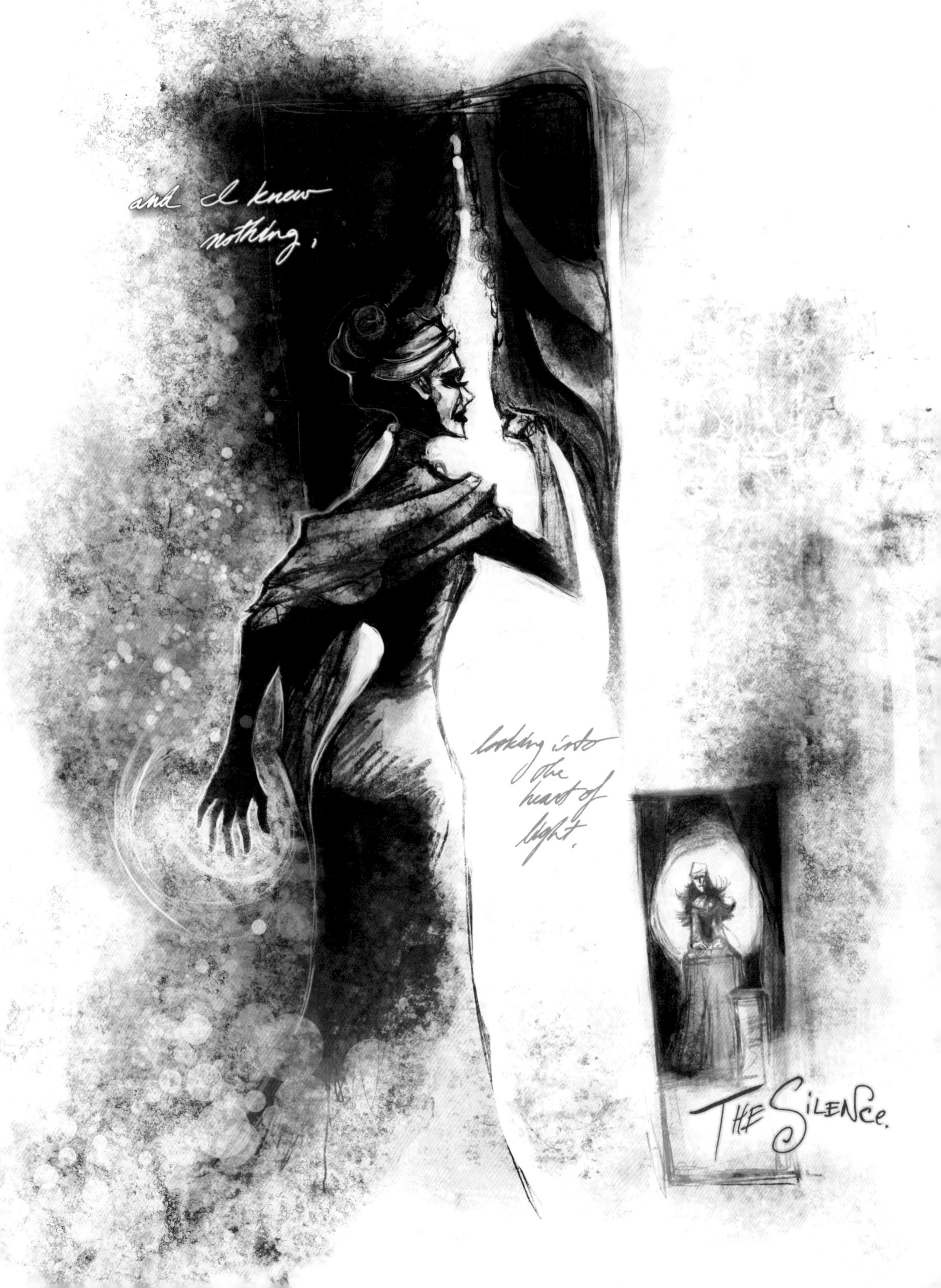
and I knew
nothing,
looking into
the
heart of
light.
THE SILENCE.

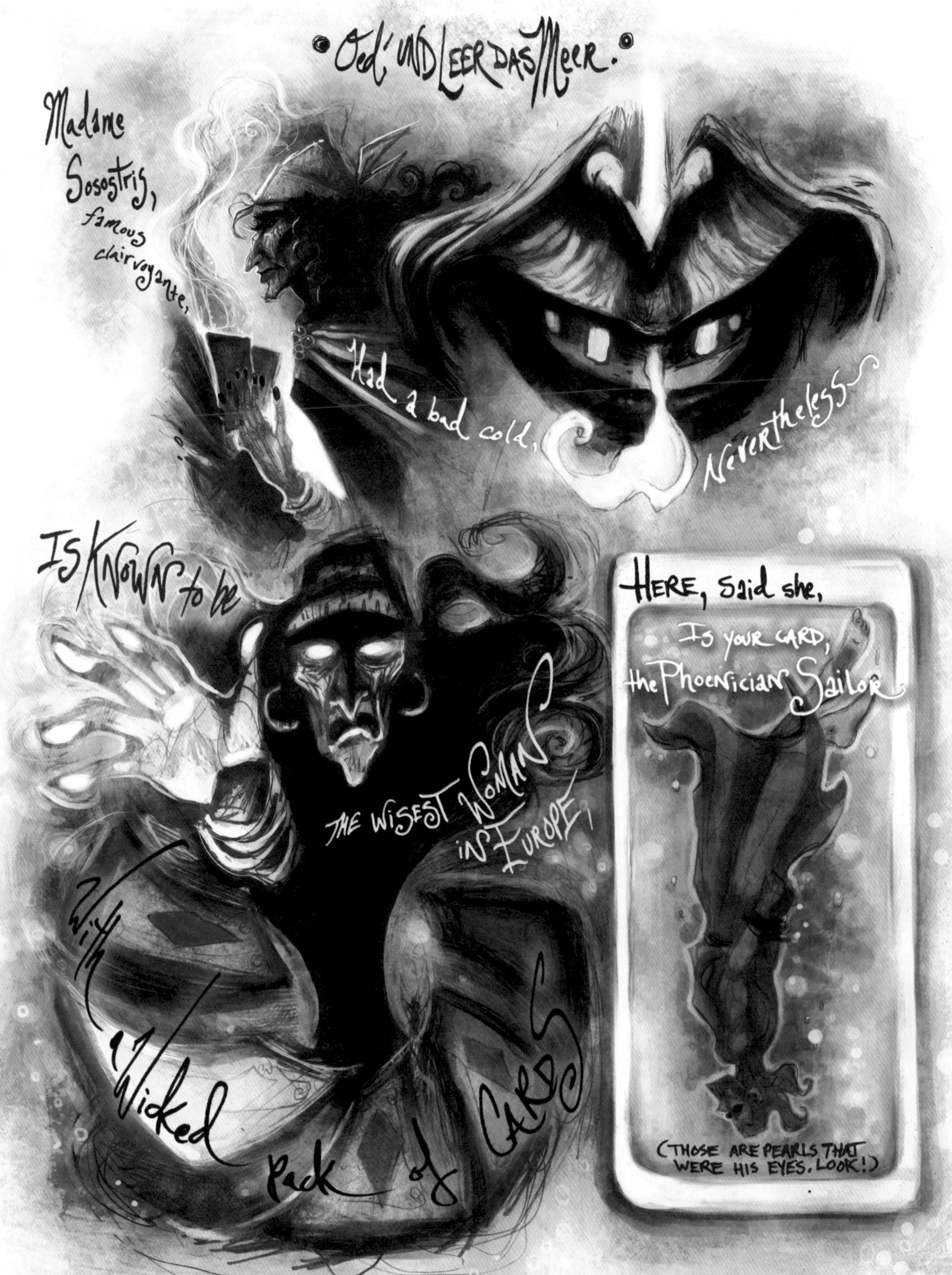
Oed' und leer das Meer.
Madame Sosostris, famous clairvoyante,
Had a bad cold, Nevertheless
Is known to be
the wisest woman in Europe,
With a wicked pack of cards.
Here, said she,
Is your card, the Phoenician Sailor
(Those are pearls that were his eyes. Look!)

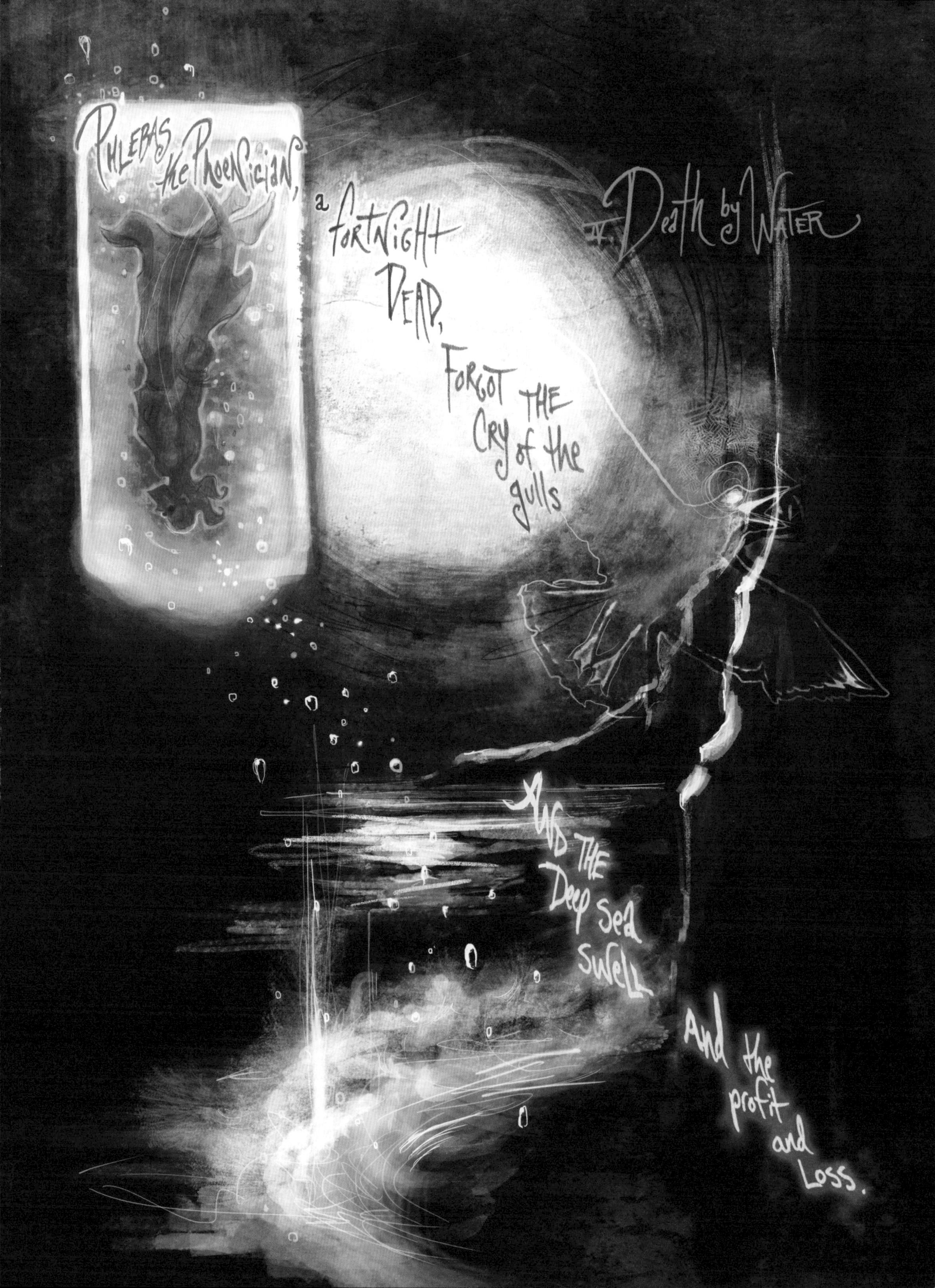
IV. Death by Water
Phlebas the Phoenician,
a fortnight dead,
forgot the cry of the gulls
And the deep sea swell
And the profit and loss.

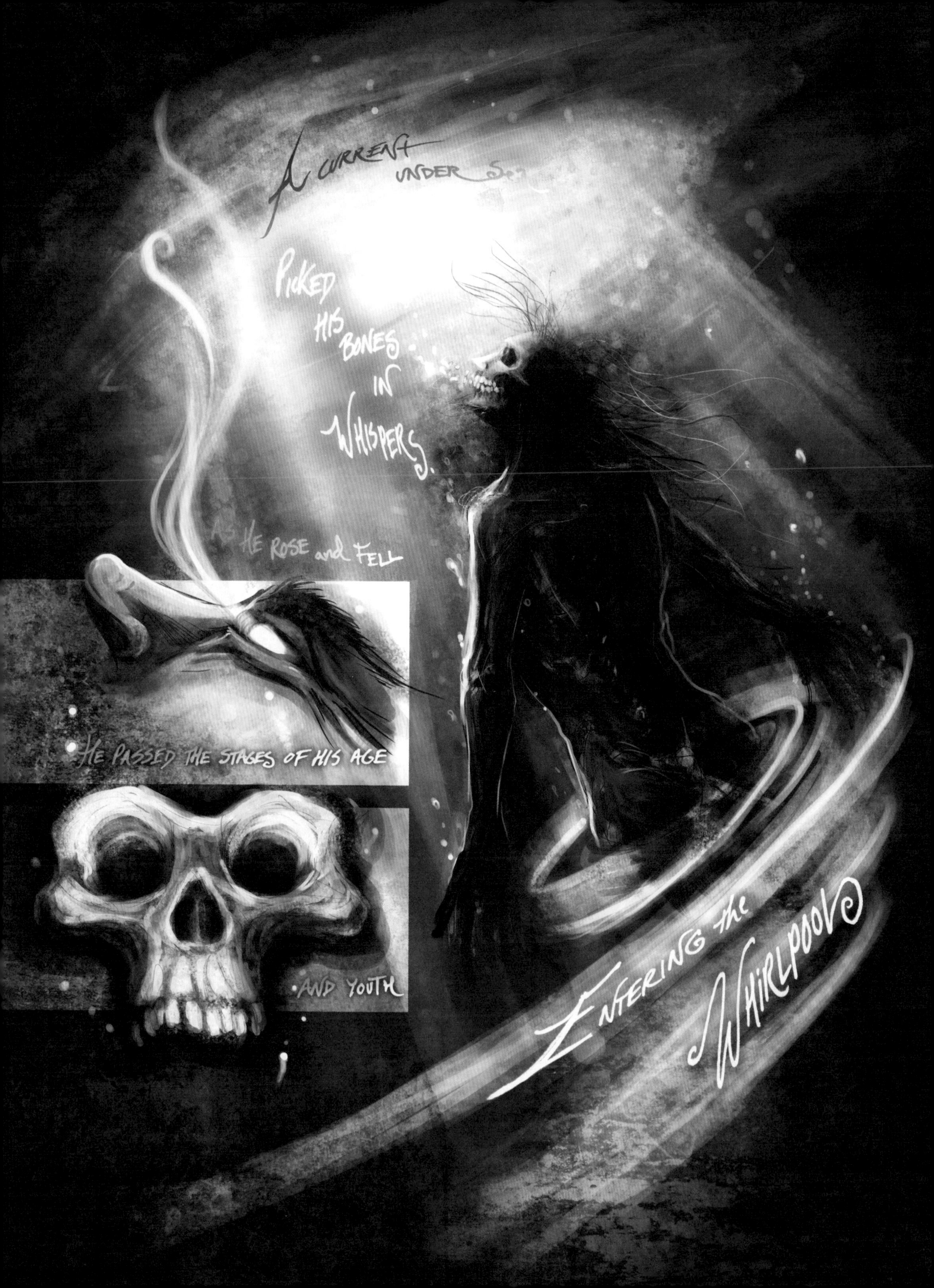
A CURRENT UNDER SEA
PICKED HIS BONES IN WHISPERS.
AS HE ROSE and FELL
HE PASSED THE STAGES OF HIS AGE
AND YOUTH
ENTERING the WHIRLPOOL

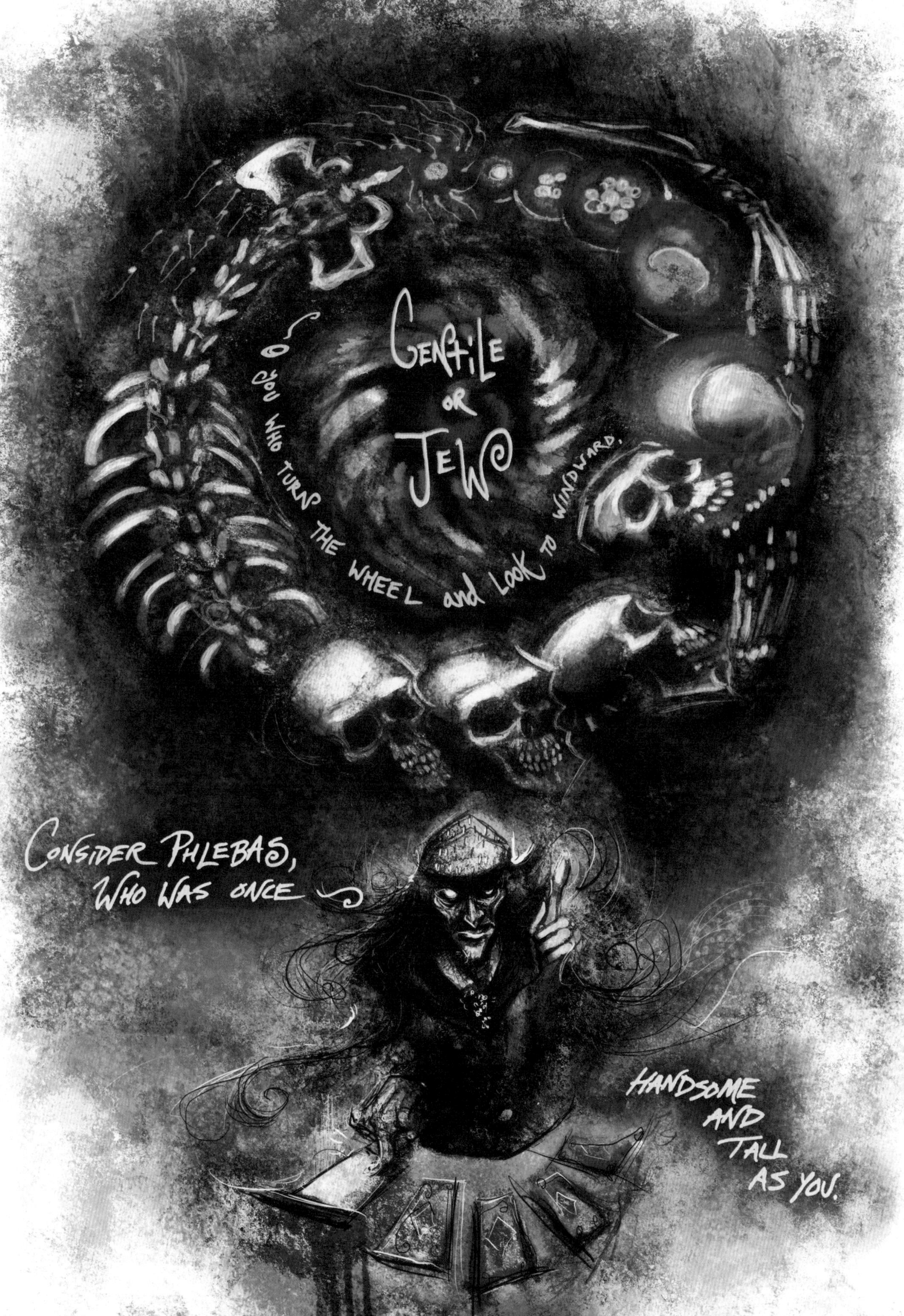
Gentile or Jew
O you who turns the wheel and look to windward,
Consider Phlebas, who was once
handsome and tall as you.

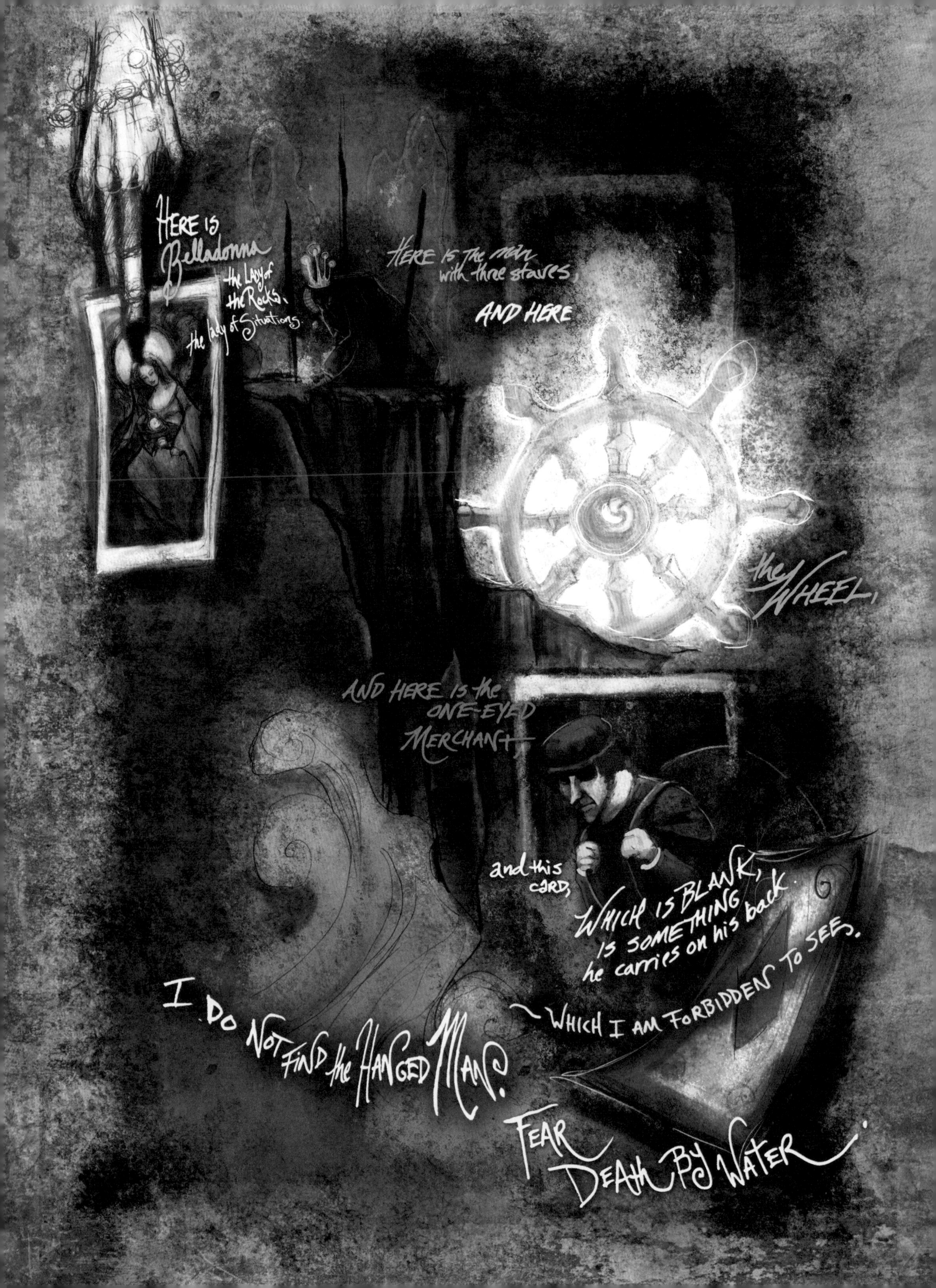
HERE IS Belladonna the LADY of the ROCKS, the lady of Situations.
HERE IS the man with three staves,
AND HERE
the WHEEL,
AND HERE is the ONE-EYED MERCHANT
and this card,
WHICH IS BLANK, IS SOMETHING he carries on his back,
WHICH I AM FORBIDDEN TO SEE.
I DO NOT FIND the HANGED MAN.
FEAR DEATH BY WATER.

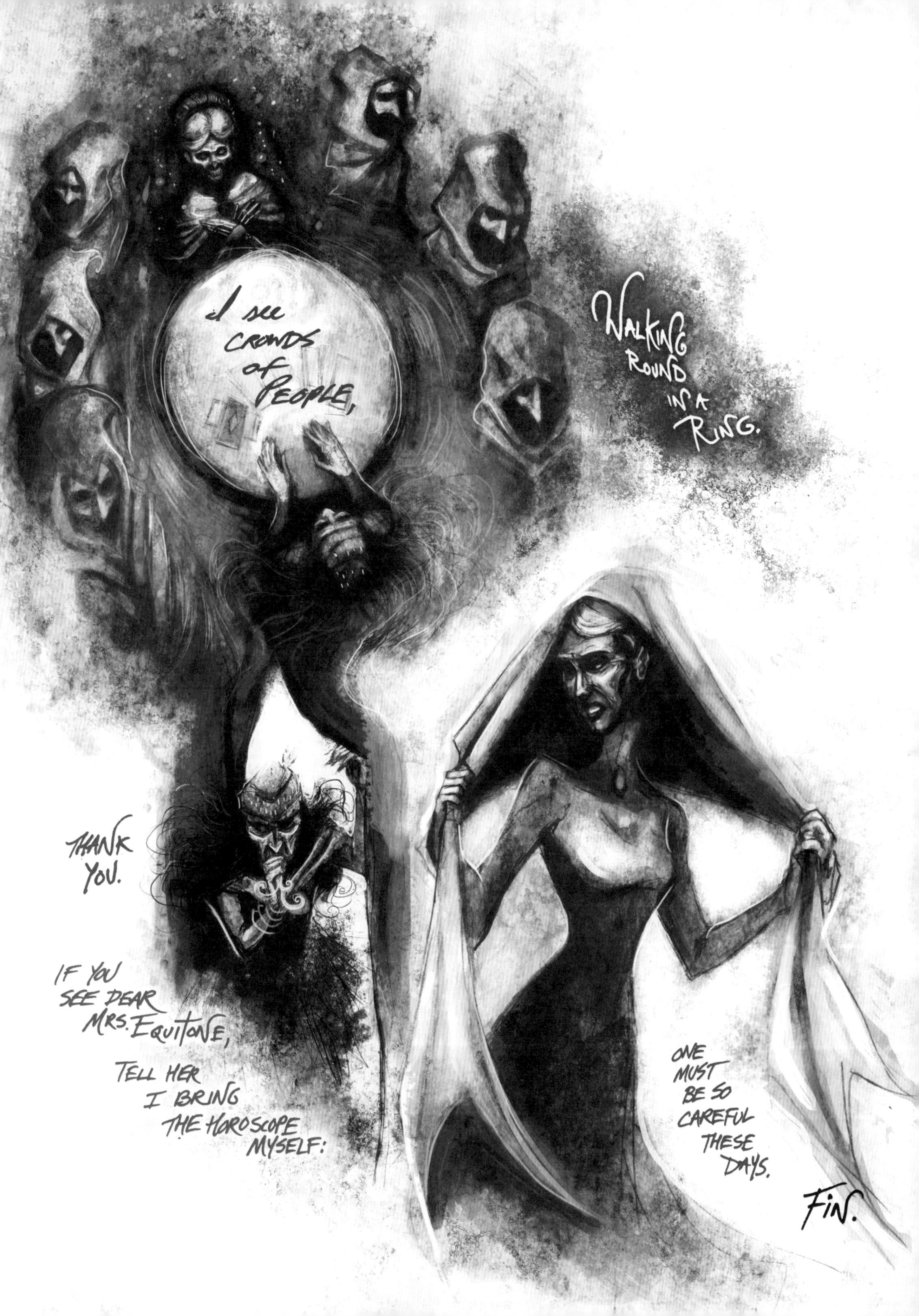
I see crowds of people,
Walking round in a ring.
Thank you.
If you see dear Mrs. Equitone,
tell her I bring the horoscope myself:
One must be so careful these days.
Fin.

The Great Gatsby

F. Scott Fitzgerald

ILLUSTRATIONS BY **Tara Seibel**

F. SCOTT AND ZELDA FITZGERALD WERE AVATARS of the glamorous Roaring Twenties, the "Jazz Age" (a phrase that Fitzgerald himself coined)—young, beautiful, and sophisticated. Fitzgerald wrote works that define this era in our minds, *The Great Gatsby*, from 1925, being the most famous. A wealthy, mysterious man who throws epic parties in his mansion in West Egg, Long Island, Gatsby is lovesick for Daisy, a married woman living across the bay in East Egg. The novel's narrator, Nick, is Daisy's cousin, who lives next door to Gatsby. One vehicular homicide later, things fall to pieces. *The Great Gatsby* is exquisitely written, a diamond-perfect little book where everything flows seamlessly, not a word out of place, and where so much more is hinted at than is ever revealed.

Tara Seibel brings her charming illustrations, beautiful colors, and inventive layouts to this complex, shining tale of love, money, and manslaughter.

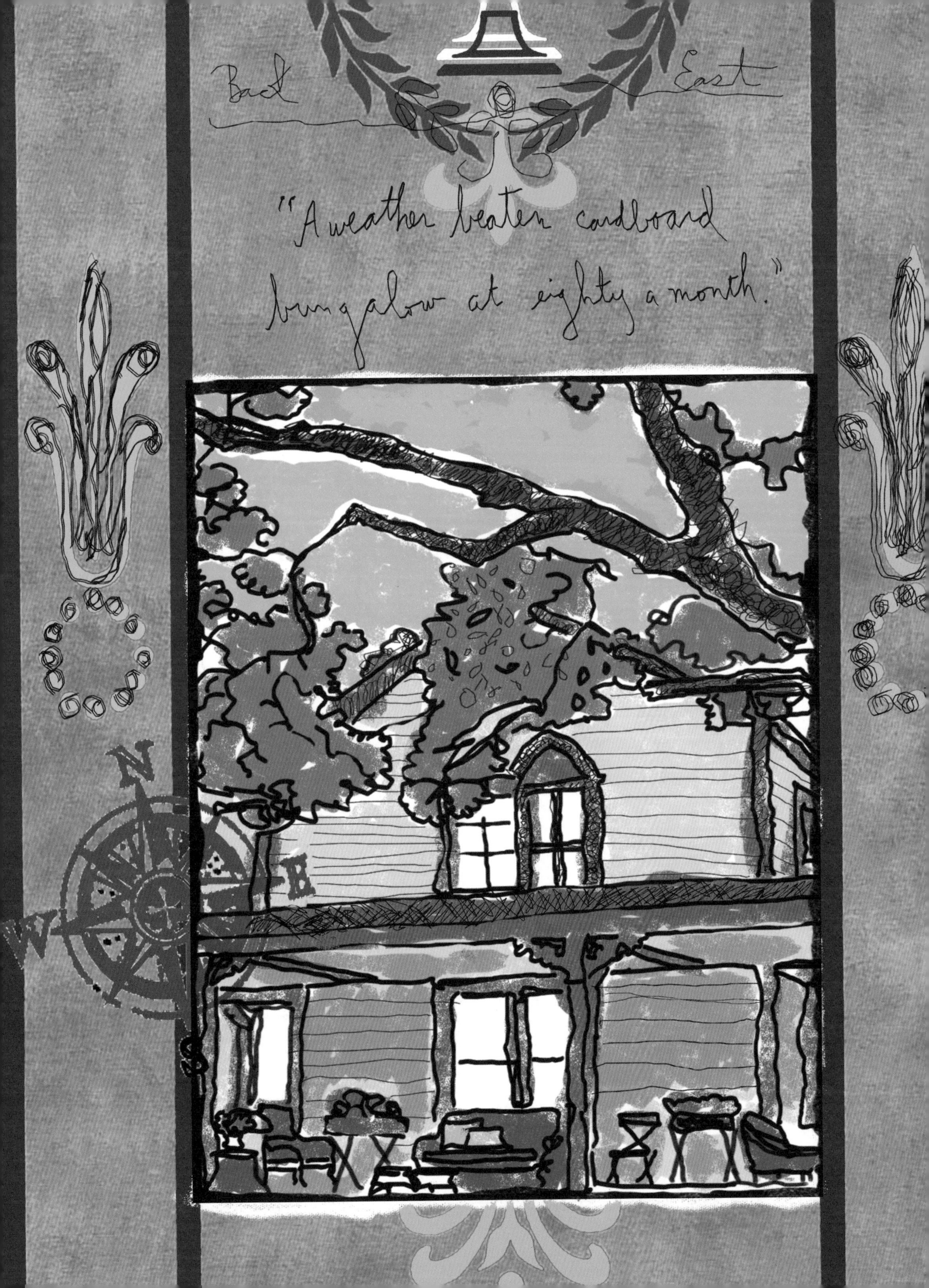
Back East
"A weather beaten cardboard bungalow at eighty a month."
N
W

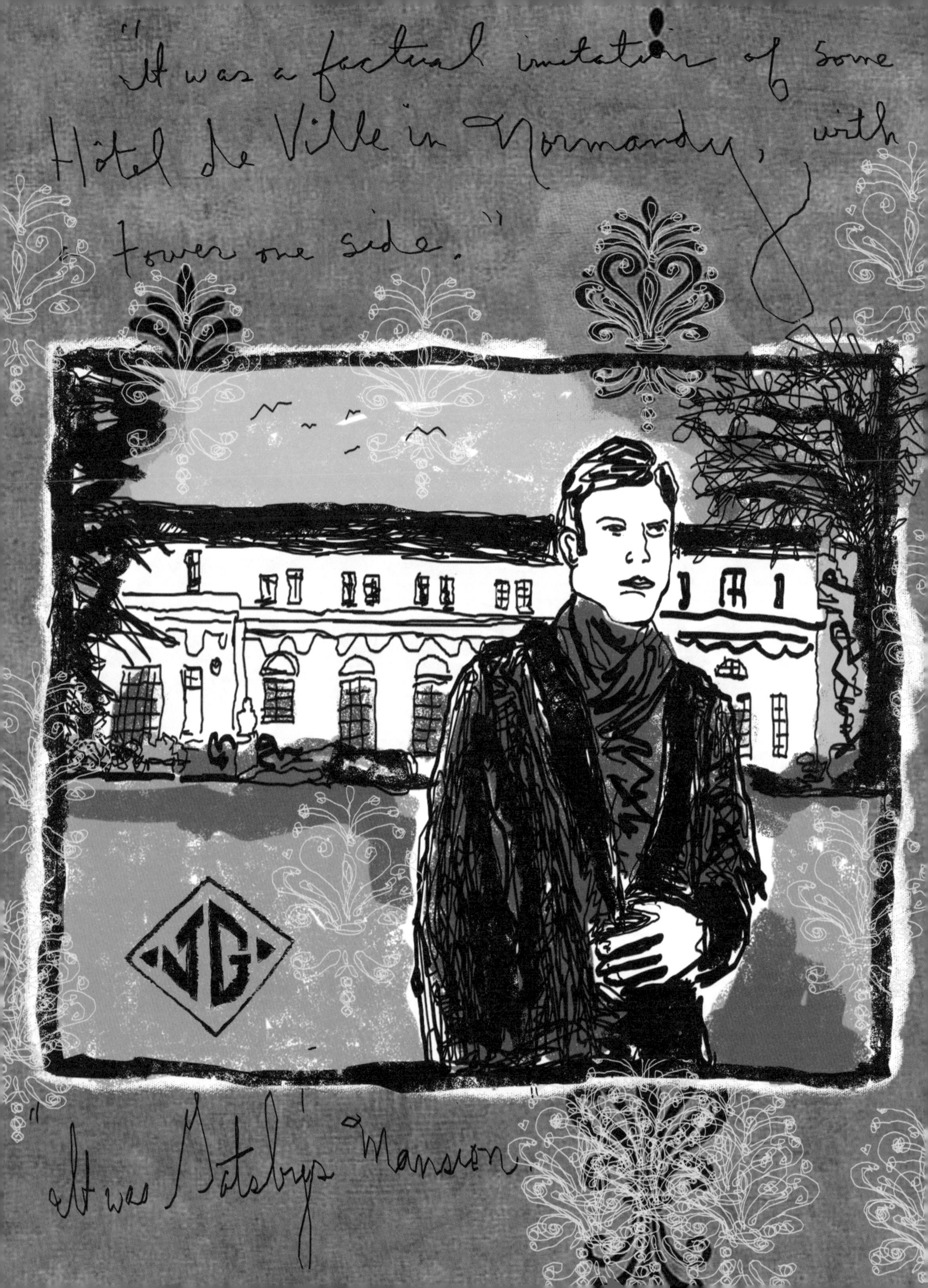
"It was a factual imitation of some Hôtel de Ville in Normandy, with tower one side."
JG
"It was Gatsby's mansion."

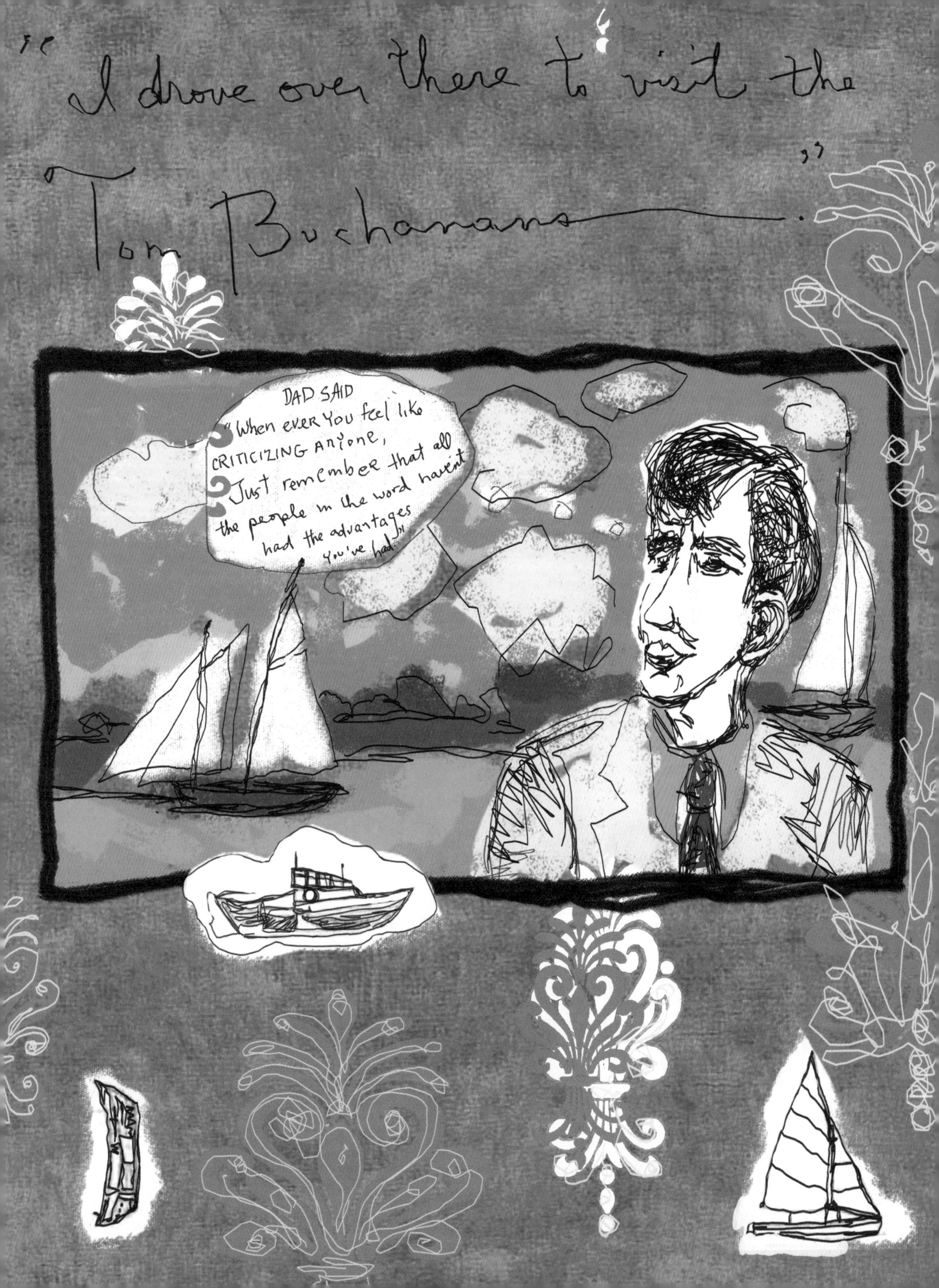
"I drove over there to visit the Tom Buchanans——."
DAD SAID "When ever You feel like CRITICIZING ANYONE, Just remember that all the people in the word haven't had the advantages you've had."

"The only completely stationary object in the room was an enormous couch on which two young women were buoyed up as though upon an anchored balloon.

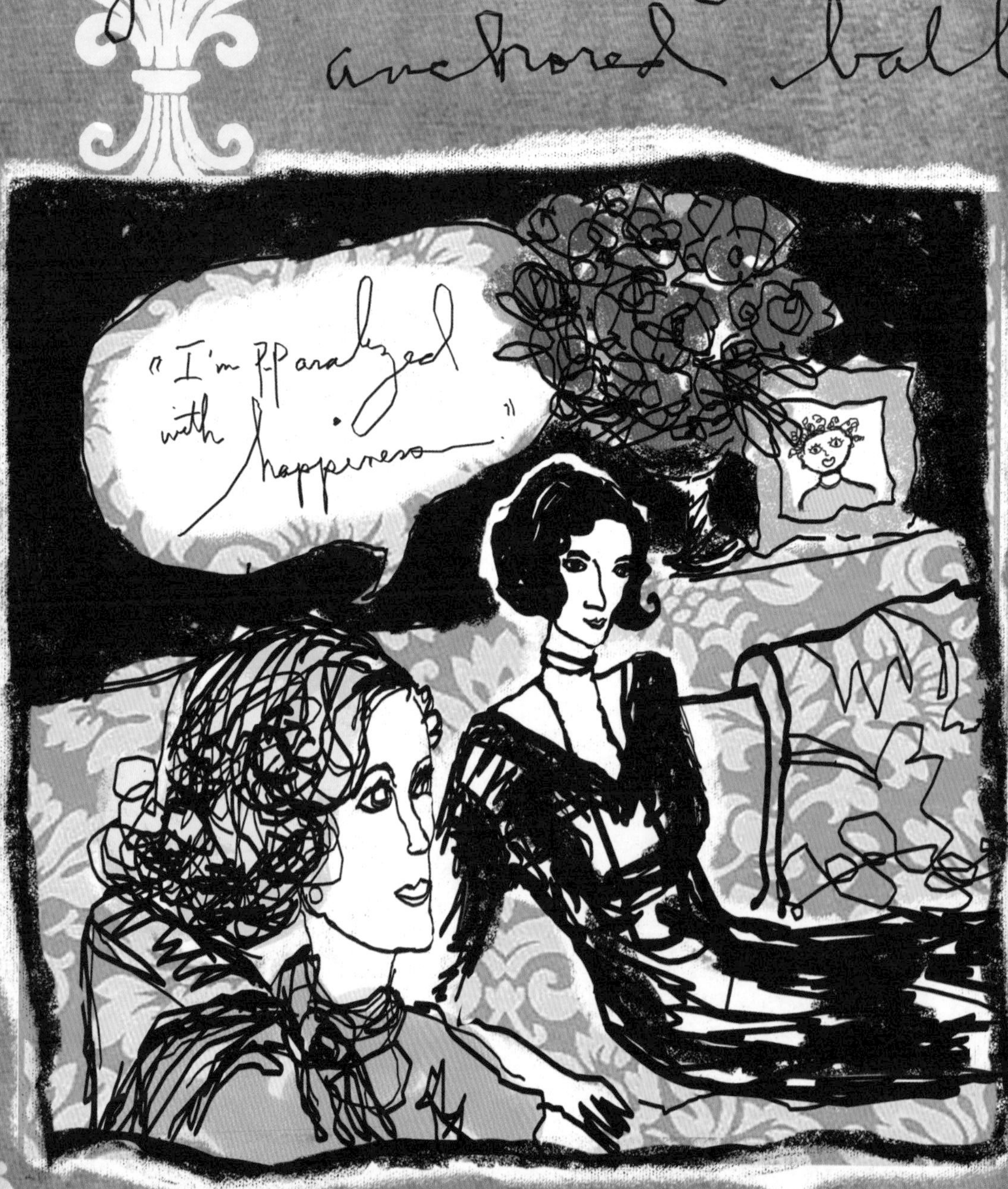
"I'm P-Paralyzed with happiness"

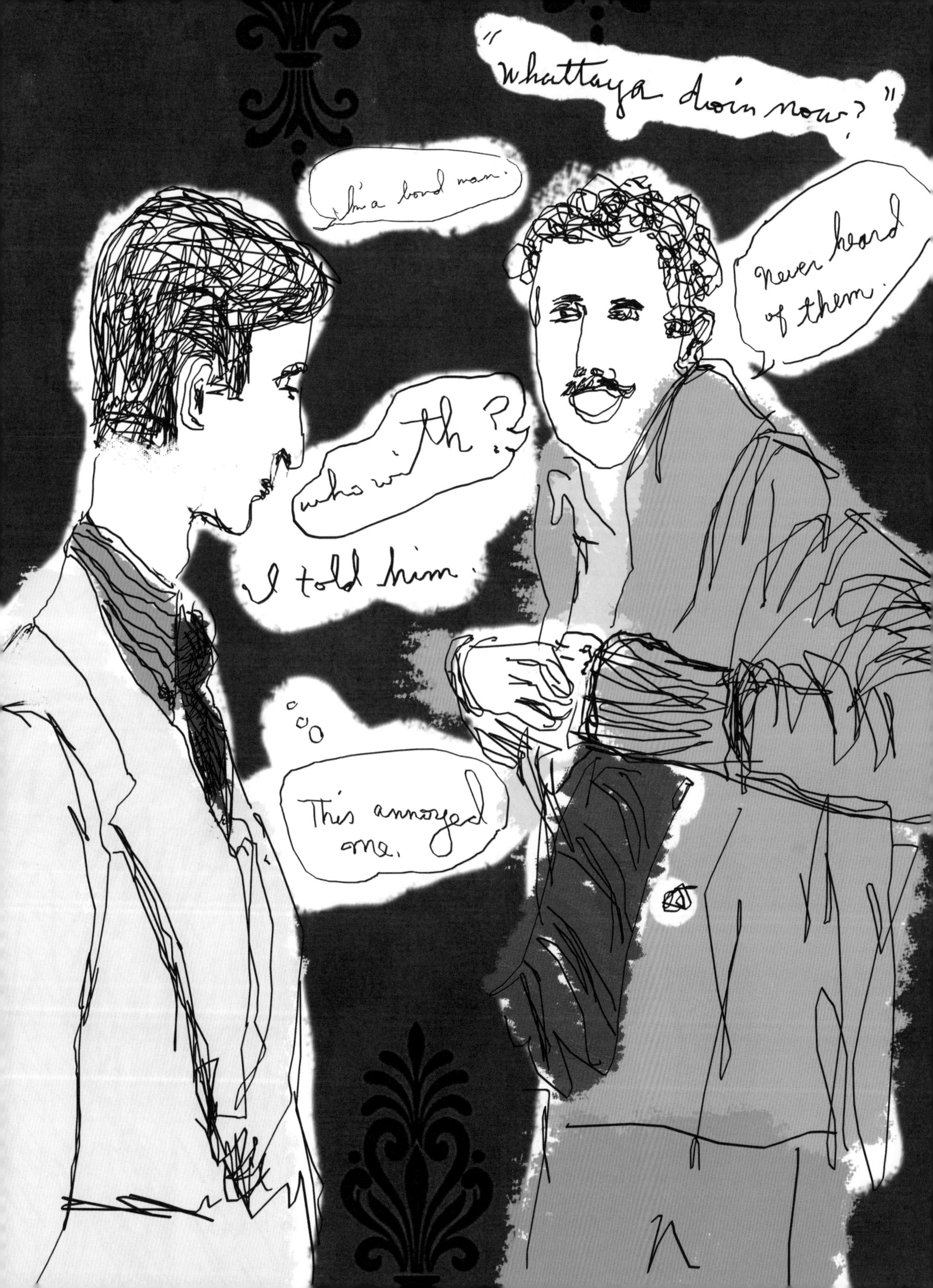
"Whattaya doin now?"
I'm a bond man.
Never heard of them.
who with?
I told him.
This annoyed me.

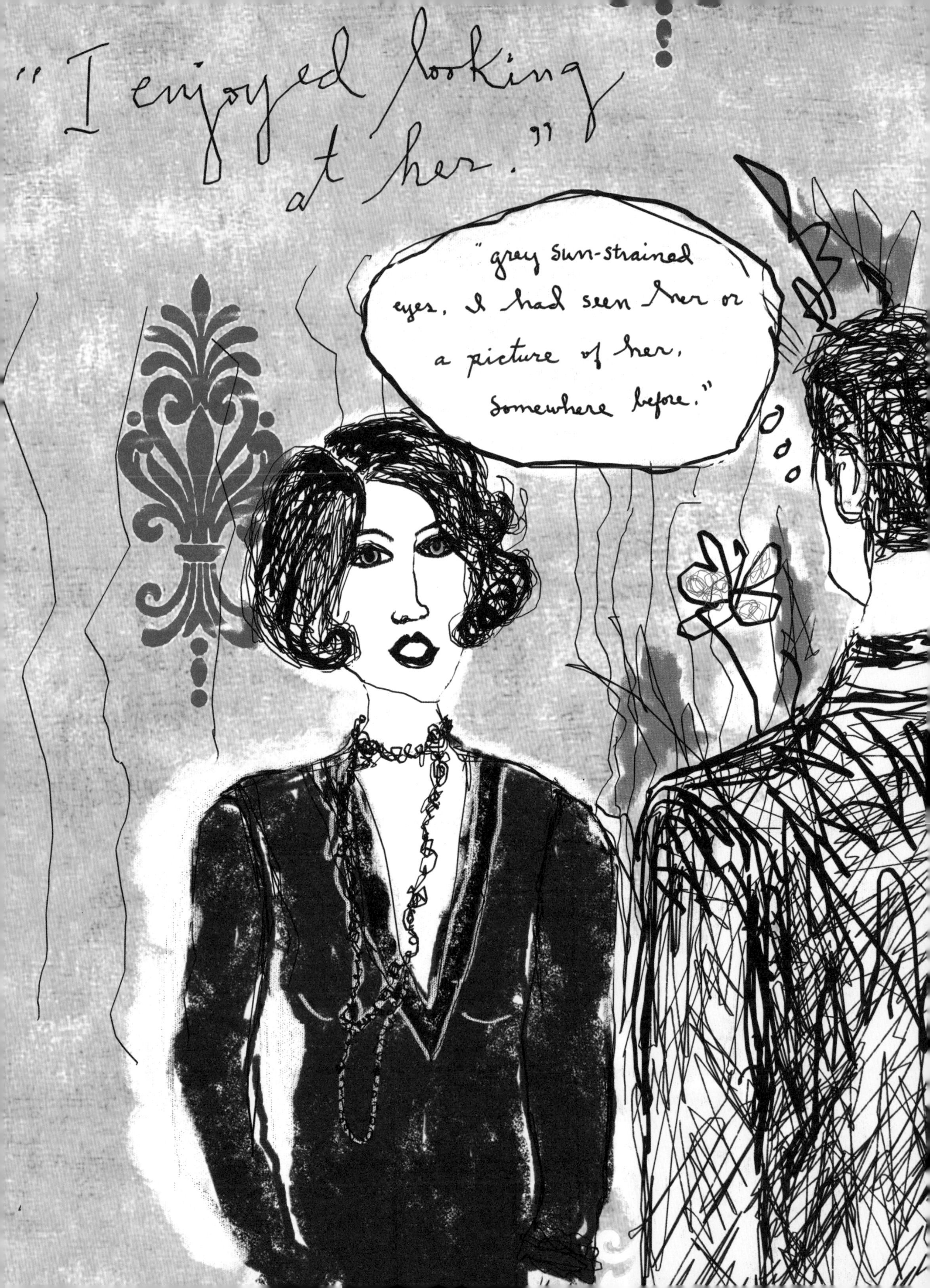
"I enjoyed looking at her."
"grey sun-strained eyes, I had seen her or a picture of her, somewhere before."

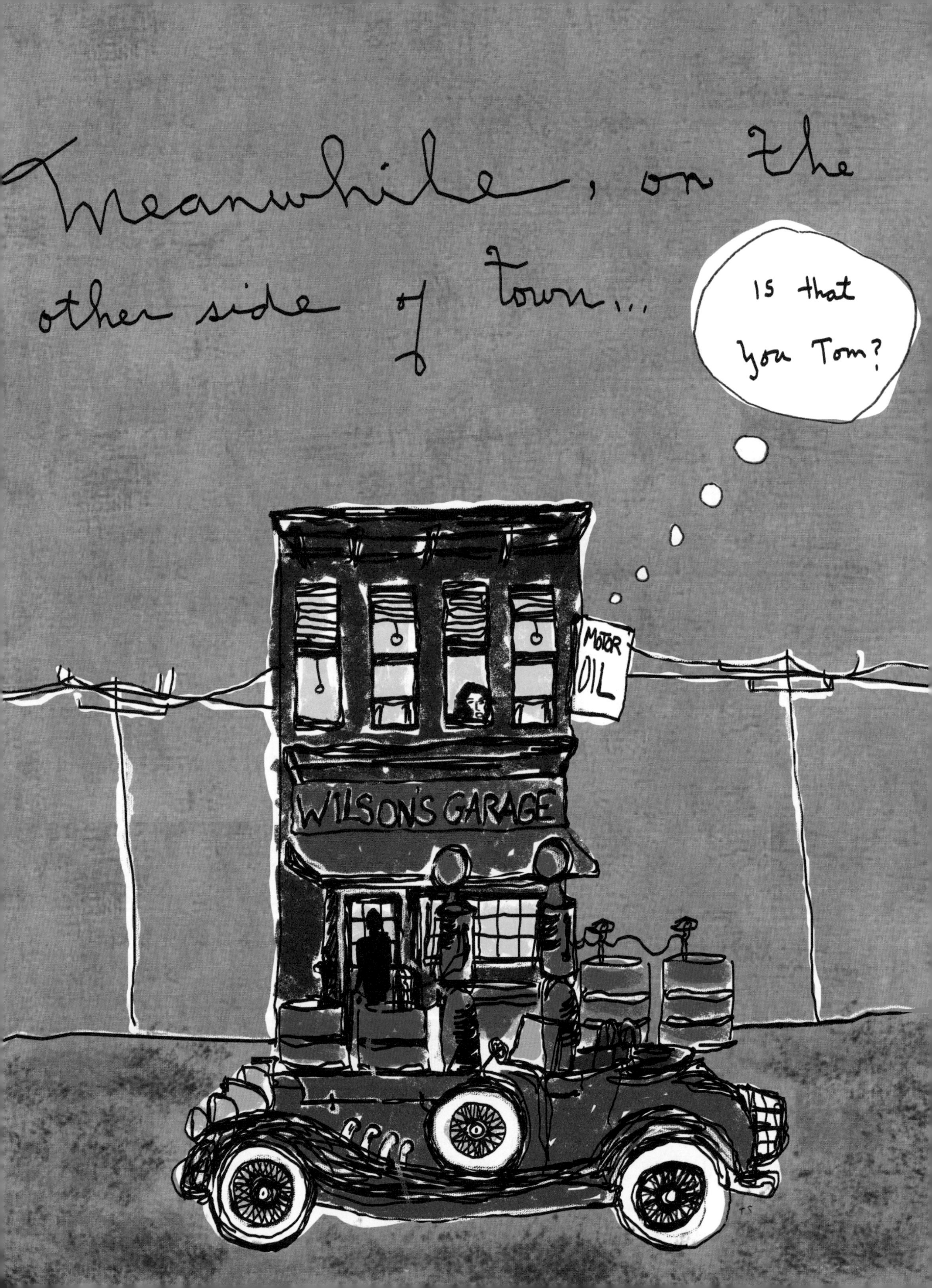
Meanwhile, on the other side of town...
Is that you Tom?
MOTOR OIL
WILSON'S GARAGE

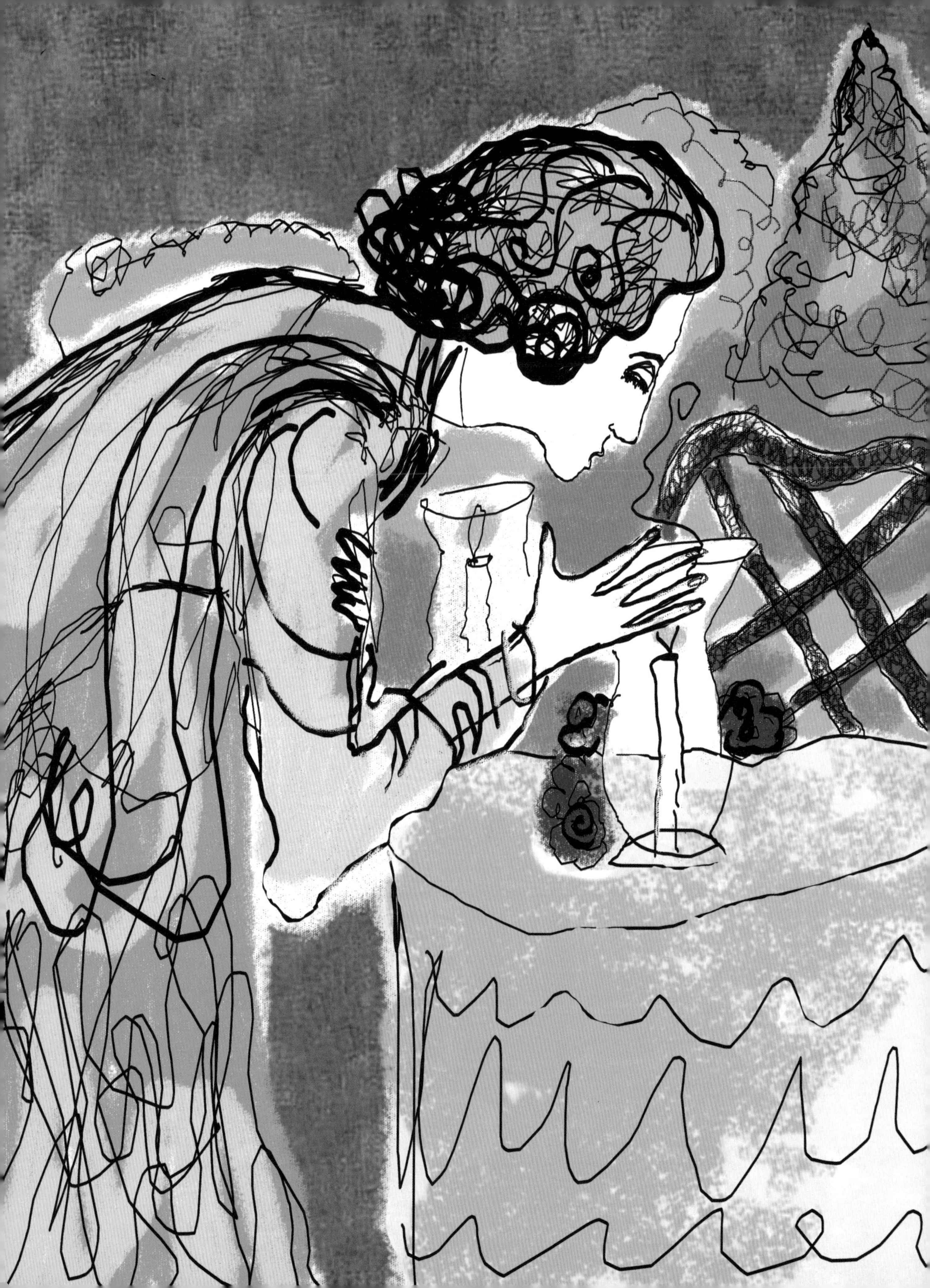

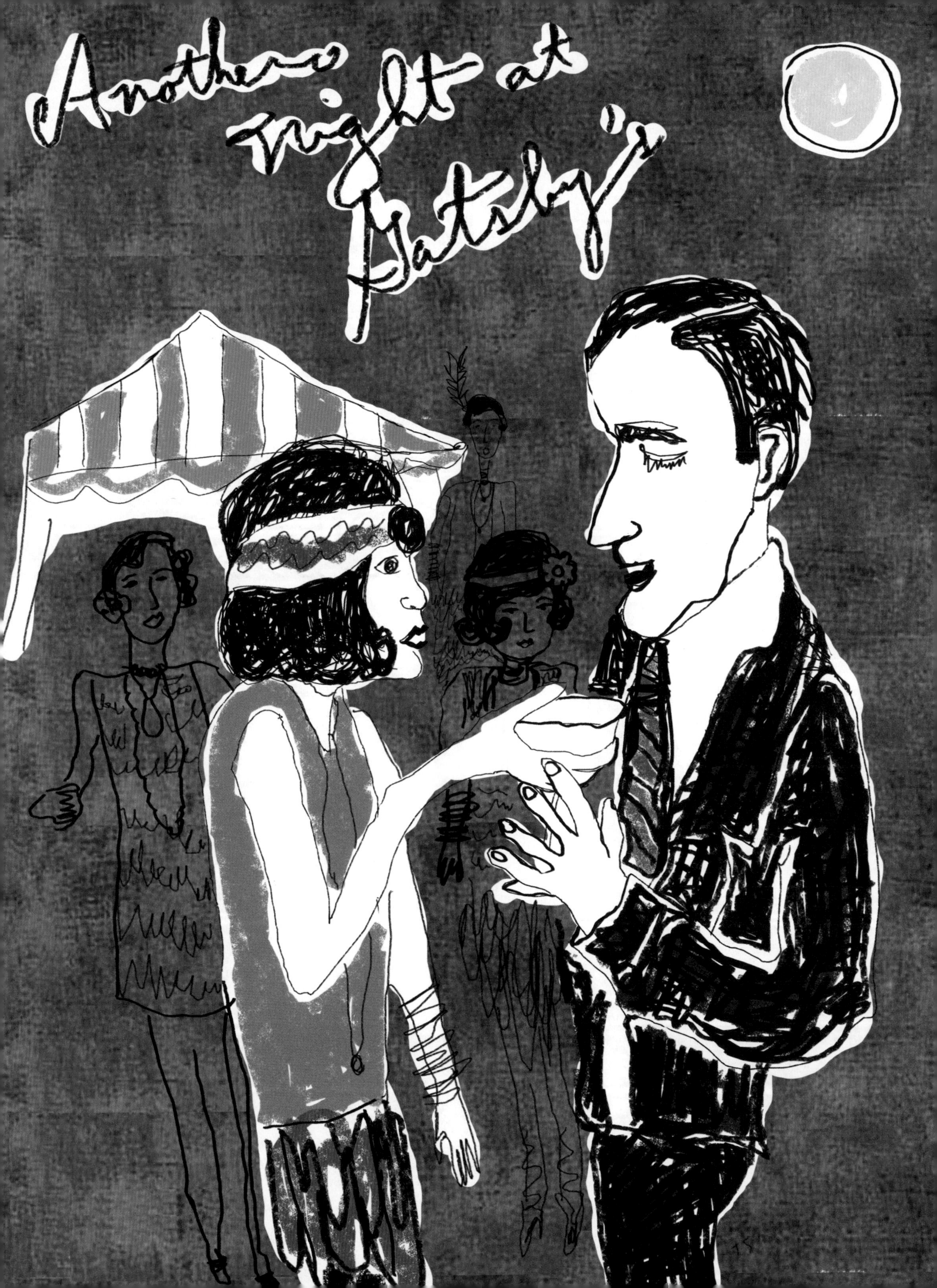
Another Night at Gatsby's

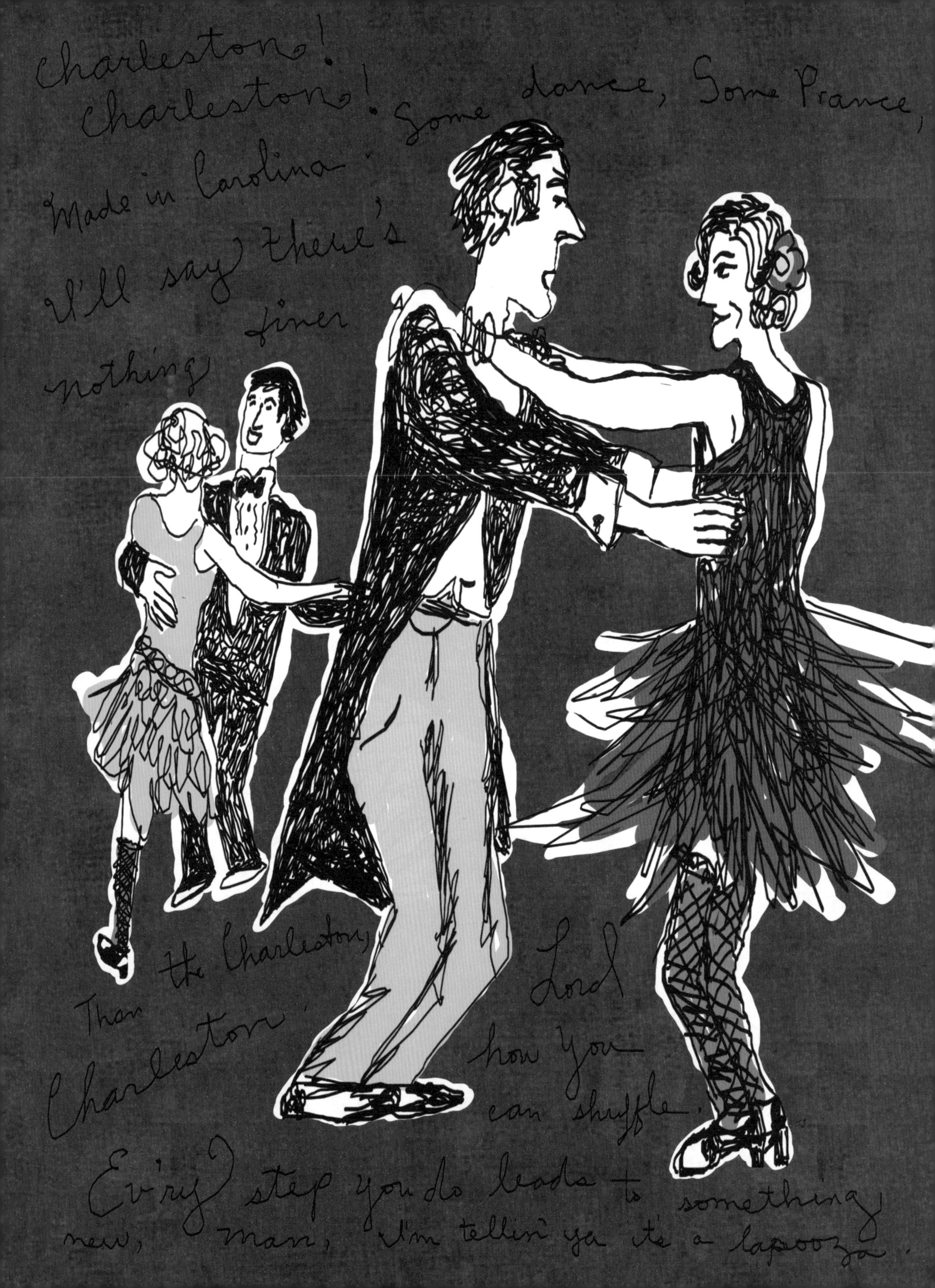
Charleston!
Charleston!
Made in Carolina.
Some dance, Some Prance,
I'll say there's
nothing finer
Than the Charleston,
Charleston,
Lord
how you
can shuffle.
Ev'ry step you do leads to something
new, man, I'm tellin' ya it's a lapazooza.

Steppenwolf

Hermann Hesse

ILLUSTRATIONS BY **John Pierard**

THE 1927 FOLLOW-UP TO *SIDDHARTHA*, *STEPPENWOLF* is another examination of a man's search for how to live, and how to deal with the different, seemingly incompatible aspects of existence. The middle-aged Harry Haller detests bourgeois life (even while attracted by aspects of it) and struggles to deal with his animalistic inner nature, the steppenwolf, or the wolf of the steppes. As an irreconcilable outsider, he cannot live in the intellectual, artificial world of the middle class, but he also can't let himself express his so-called baser instincts. He meets a woman named Hermine, who leads him down a wilder path, and he may or may not end up killing her—in fact, she may or may not even exist. He also meets a jazz saxophonist and bandleader, Pablo, who is devoted to enjoying the moment and doing, rather than theorizing. The final part of the novel is an extended scene in which Haller/Steppenwolf enters Pablo's Magic Theater, which manifests various aspects of his multilayered, fractured personality.

John Pierard—who adapted part of Jack London's auto-biography earlier in this volume—shows us Haller entering Magic Theater, with a series of fragmented illustrations.

Steppenwolf by Hermann Hesse

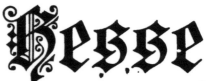

THE SHABBY OLD STEPPENWOLF...
THE SOLITARY, THE HATER OF
LIFE"S PETTY CONVENTIONS...

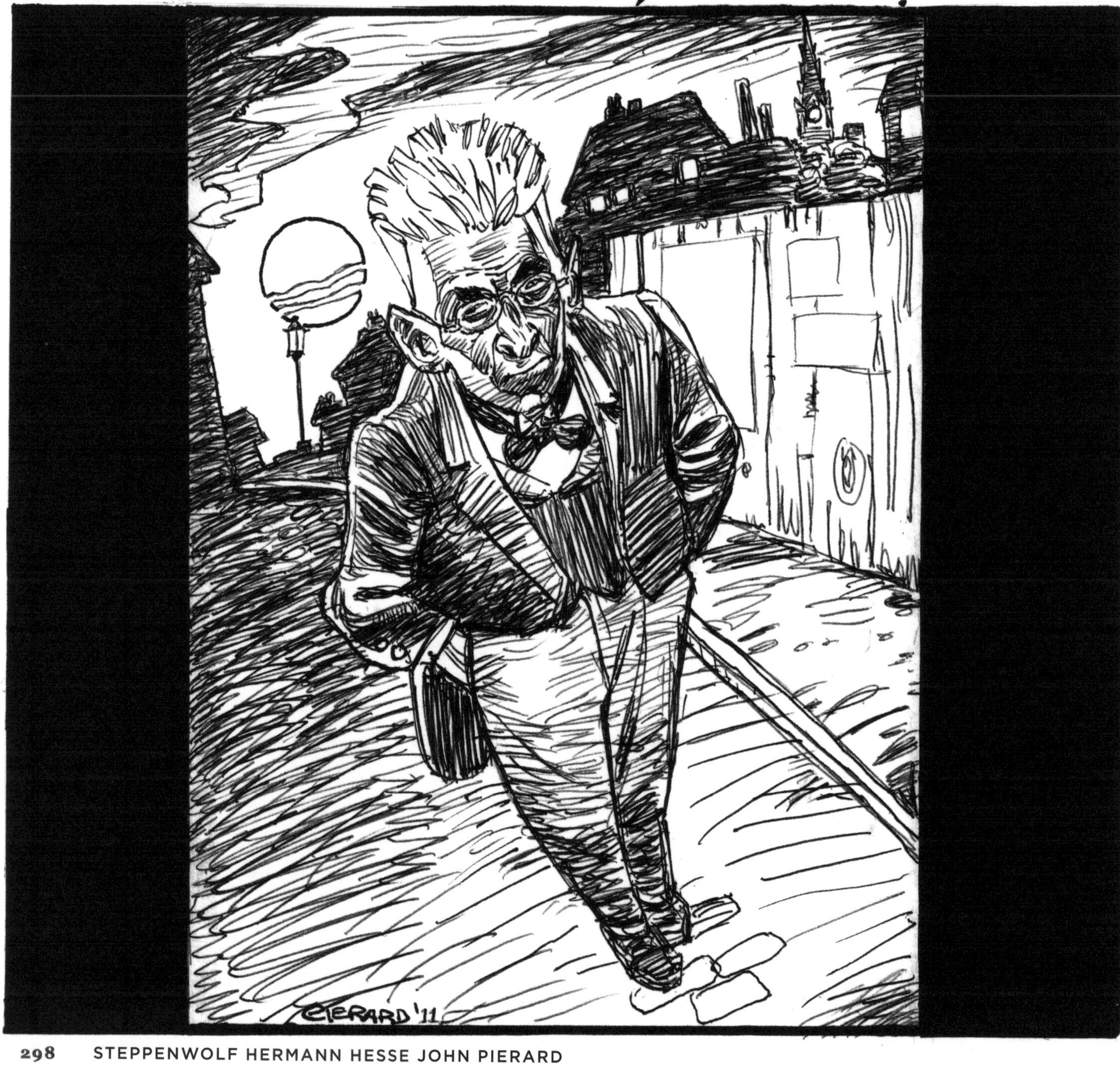

PIERARD '11

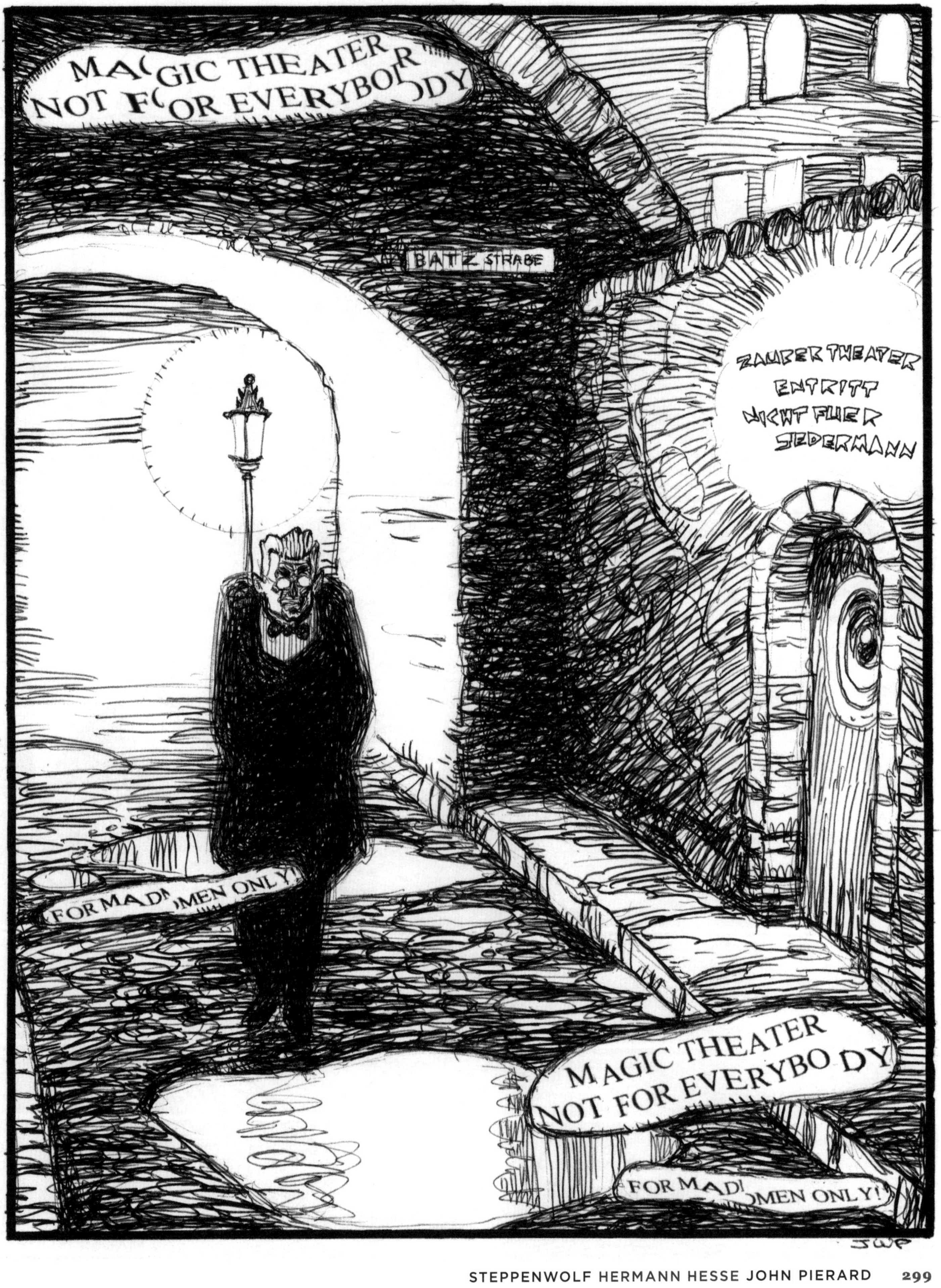
MAGIC THEATER
NOT FOR EVERYBODY
BATZ STRABE
ZAUBER THEATER
ENTRITT
NICHT FUER
JEDERMANN
FOR MAD MEN ONLY!
MAGIC THEATER
NOT FOR EVERYBODY
FOR MAD MEN ONLY!
JWP

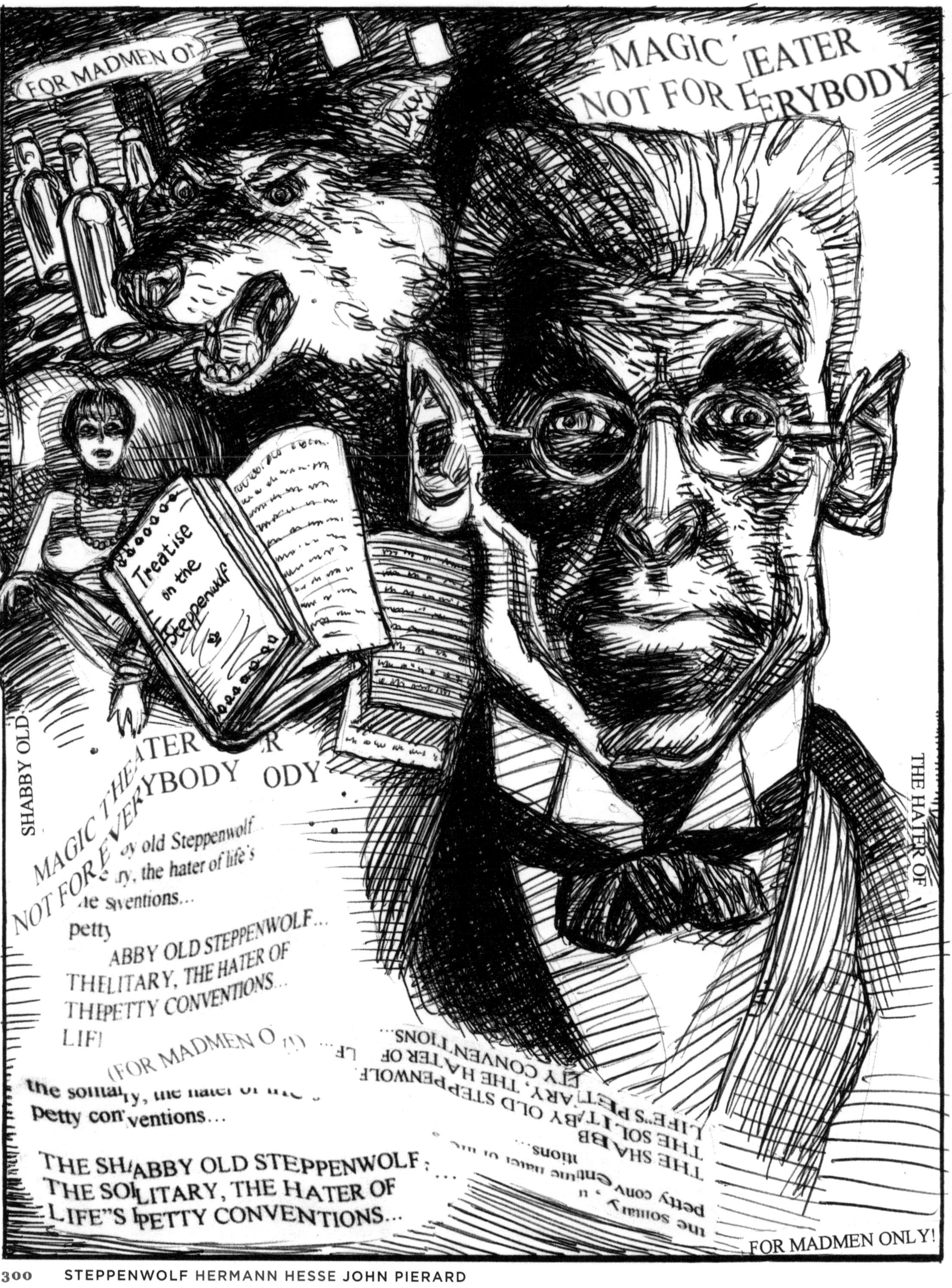
(FOR MADMEN O
MAGIC TEATER
NOT FOR E RYBODY
Treatise on the Steppenwolf
SHABBY OLD
THE HATER OF
MAGIC THEATER
NOT FOR EVERYBODY
ABBY OLD STEPPENWOLF...
THELITARY, THE HATER OF
THIPETTY CONVENTIONS...
(FOR MADMEN O
petty con ventions...
THE SHABBY OLD STEPPENWOLF...
THE SOLITARY, THE HATER OF
LIFE"S PETTY CONVENTIONS...
FOR MADMEN ONLY!

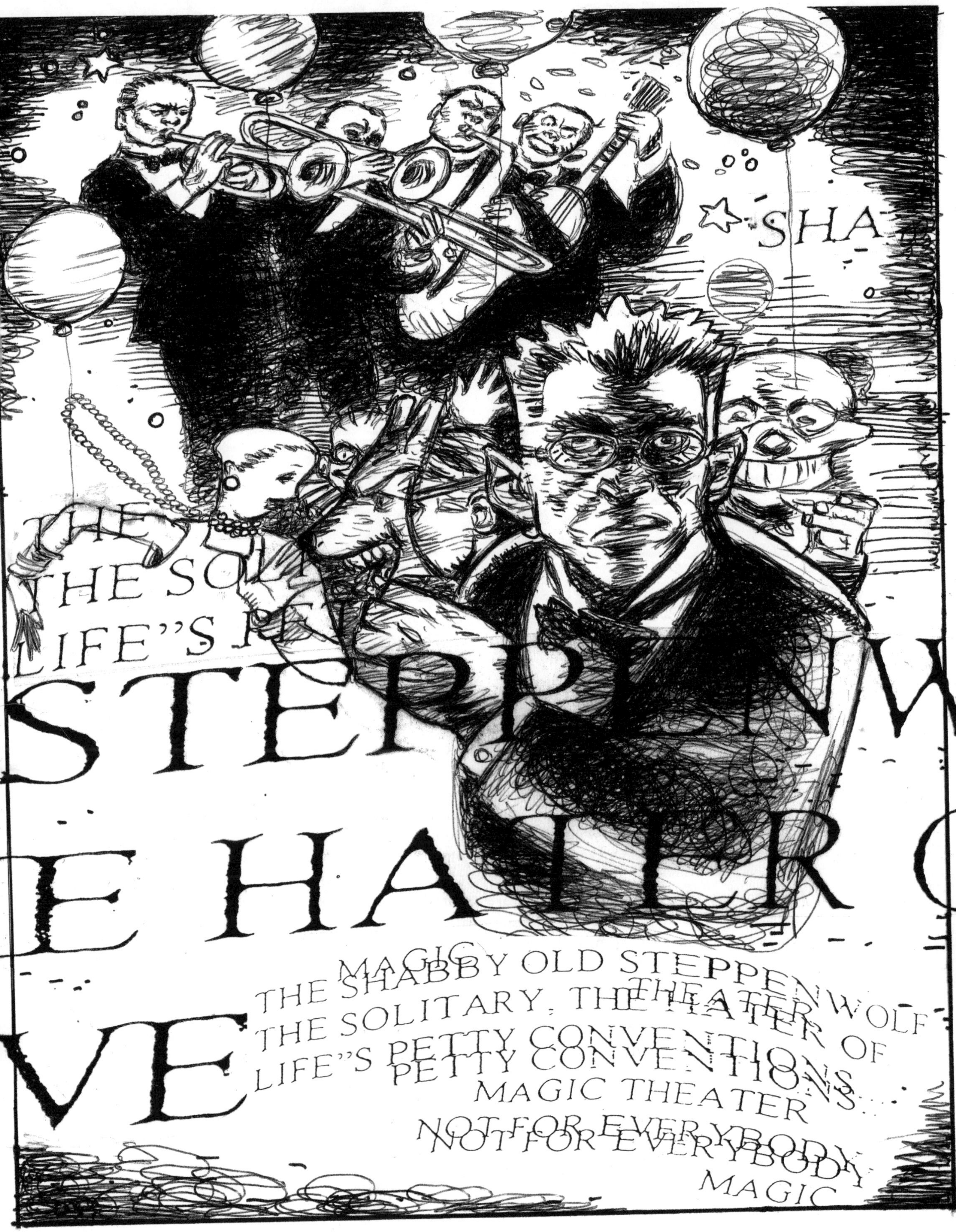
SHA
THE SO
LIFE"S
MAGIC
THE SHABBY OLD STEPPENWOLF
THE SOLITARY, THE HATER OF
LIFE"S PETTY CONVENTIONS
THEATER
PETTY CONVENTIONS
MAGIC THEATER
NOT FOR EVERYBODY
NOT FOR EVERYBODY
MAGIC

Lady Chatterley's Lover

D. H. Lawrence

ART/ADAPTATION BY **Lisa Brown**

ONE OF THE MOST NOTORIOUS NOVELS EVER published, *Lady Chatterley's Lover* spells out in explicit terms what's going wrong with society—the deaths of instinct, spontaneity, and hot-bloodedness at the hands of industrialization and intellectualism—and it prescribes the cure. Nobel-winning novelist Doris Lessing explained:

> Lawrence was preaching sex as a kind of sacrament, and more than that, one that would save us all from the results of war and the nastinesses of our civilisation. "Doing dirt on sex," he anathematised; "it is the crime of our times, because what we need is tenderness towards the body, towards sex, we need tender-hearted fucking."

Constance Reid has married the aristocratic Clifford Chatterley, but he's soon wounded in World War I, rendering him paralyzed and impotent. He becomes a successful writer and business owner—weak, cerebral pursuits. Constance eventually encounters Oliver Mellors, the game-keeper of the estate, a manly man in touch with the earth, with animals, with his body. At first he puts her off, but eventually they start having mind-melting, earth-shattering sex, complete with simultaneous orgasms and anal action. Complications ensue.

Lawrence and colleagues privately published the book in Florence, Italy, in 1928. Many British booksellers refused to carry it after learning of its scandalous contents. US Customs seized arriving copies. Pirated copies sold briskly, and to combat this loss of income, Lawrence arranged for a cheaper edition to be published in Paris the following year.

The unexpurgated novel wasn't openly published in the UK until 1960, and triggered a landmark freedom-of-expression case when the Crown hauled Penguin Books to court for "obscenity." The prosecutor's opening speech gave a laundry list of the novel's four-letter words: "The word 'fuck' or 'fucking' appears no less than thirty times . . . 'Cunt' fourteen times; 'balls' thirteen times; 'shit' and 'arse' six times apiece; 'cock' four times; 'piss' three times, and so on." One academic and literary titan after another defended the book, and Penguin's acquittal effectively ended literary censorship in Britain (and caused the novel to sell three million copies in the three months after the verdict). Across the pond, the US Court of Appeals overturned the ban on the novel in 1959, allowing it to be openly published by Grove Press.

Cartoonist and children's book illustrator Lisa Brown (*The Latke Who Couldn't Stop Screaming*) creates the clever *Three Panel Review* strips that festoon all three volumes of *The Graphic Canon*. Specially for this volume, she has created a cheeky, full-size take on Lawrence's final novel.

SOURCES

Lessing, Doris. "Testament of Love." *Guardian* (London), July 14, 2006.

Robertson, Geoffrey, QC. "The Trial of Lady Chatterley's Lover." *Guardian* (London), October 22, 2010.

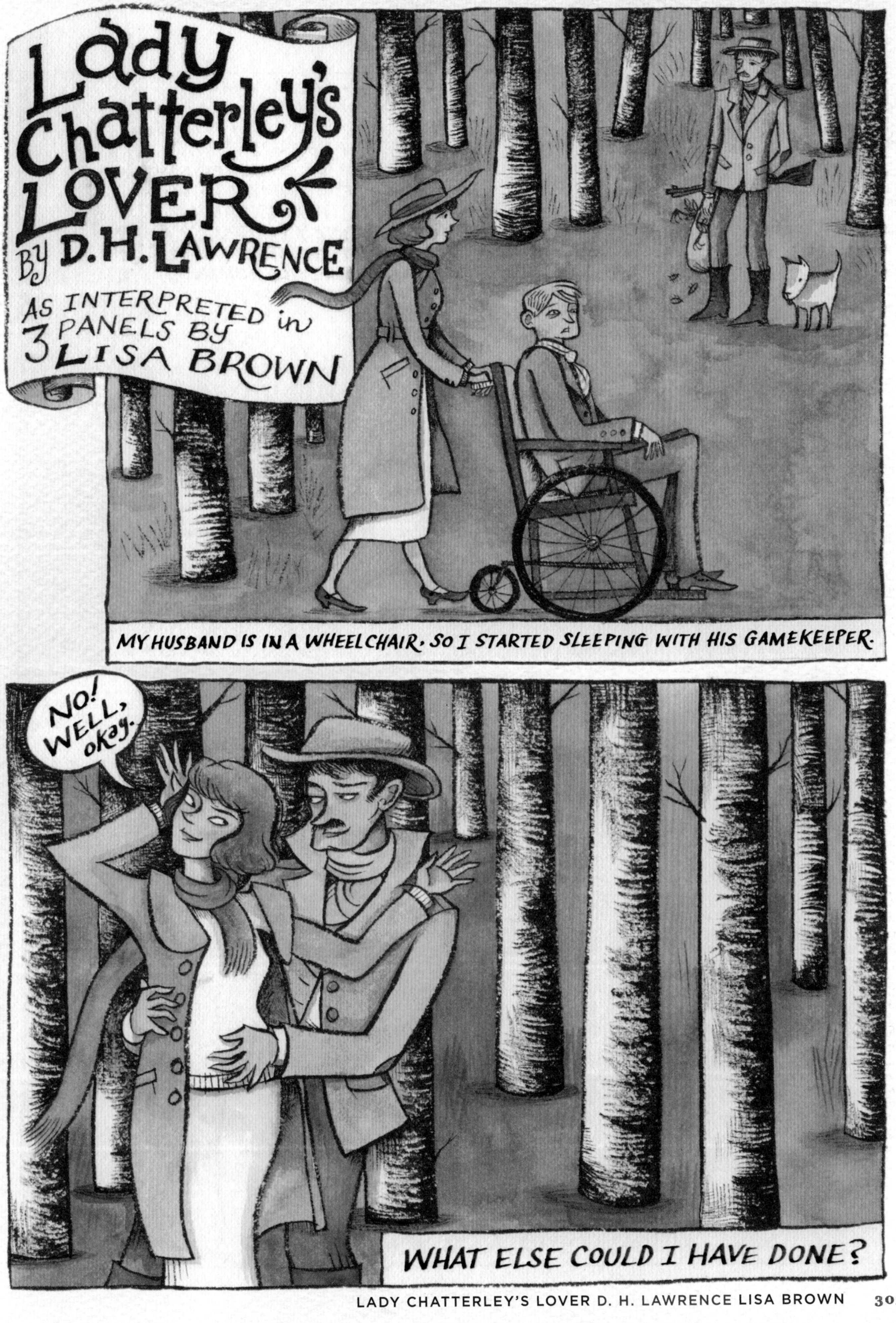
Lady Chatterley's Lover
By D.H. Lawrence
As interpreted in 3 panels by Lisa Brown
MY HUSBAND IS IN A WHEELCHAIR. SO I STARTED SLEEPING WITH HIS GAMEKEEPER.
No! WELL, okay.
WHAT ELSE COULD I HAVE DONE?

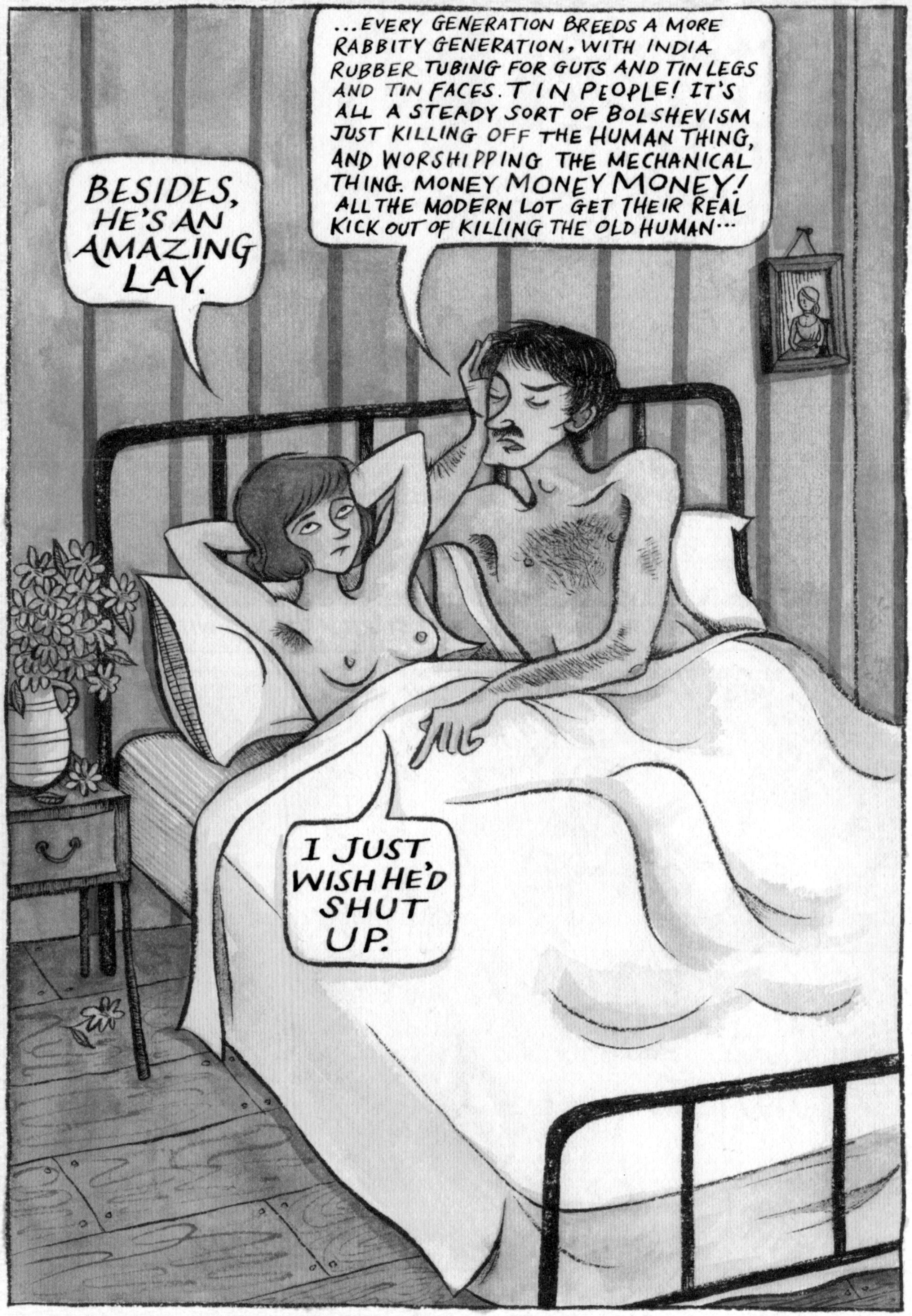

BESIDES, HE'S AN AMAZING LAY.
...EVERY GENERATION BREEDS A MORE RABBITY GENERATION, WITH INDIA RUBBER TUBING FOR GUTS AND TIN LEGS AND TIN FACES. TIN PEOPLE! IT'S ALL A STEADY SORT OF BOLSHEVISM JUST KILLING OFF THE HUMAN THING, AND WORSHIPPING THE MECHANICAL THING. MONEY MONEY MONEY! ALL THE MODERN LOT GET THEIR REAL KICK OUT OF KILLING THE OLD HUMAN...
I JUST WISH HE'D SHUT UP.

The Sound and the Fury

William Faulkner

ART/ADAPTATION BY **Robert Goodin**

AS MENTIONED IN THE INTRODUCTION TO "THE Hill," William Faulkner is generally regarded as the greatest American novelist of the twentieth century, and would certainly make anyone's shortlist for that honor. He rarely gave interviews, but in one of his rare exceptions, with the *Paris Review* in 1956, he showed himself to be prickly and uncompromising:

> The writer's only responsibility is to his art. He will be completely ruthless if he is a good one. He has a dream. It anguishes him so much he must get rid of it. He has no peace until then. Everything goes by the board: honor, pride, decency, security, happiness, all, to get the book written. If a writer has to rob his mother, he will not hesitate; the "Ode on a Grecian Urn" is worth any number of old ladies.

How many, then, is *The Sound and the Fury* worth? We'll leave that calculation for another day, but if one of Faulkner's novels must be named his masterpiece, it's usually this one.

Kaleidoscopically told by multiple narrators, who are usually unreliable, with the opening section told in stream-of-consciousness style by a man who has some kind of mental disability, it charts the decline and fall of the Compsons, a Southern aristocratic family. Faulkner's biographer Jay Parini said: "This was something new in American fiction, something strange, complex and disruptive, a work that attempts to articulate grief and loss while acknowledging, at every turn, the impossibility of recovery, the limits of articulation, as well as the pleasures afforded by repetition and incomplete reconstruction: the pleasures of the text itself."

Robert Goodin irreversibly planted himself on my radar with his barn-burning nineteen-page "The Spiritual Crisis of Carl Jung," which culminates with the bizarre vision that caused the Swiss psychologist to reject organized religion. Robert agreed to do a two-page spread, creating this appropriately complex crazy-quilt of images and fragments from Faulkner's 1929 novel. At the center is Dilsey, the mother of the servant family, who is truly the rock-solid, loving, selfless matriarch of the dysfunctional Compson family.

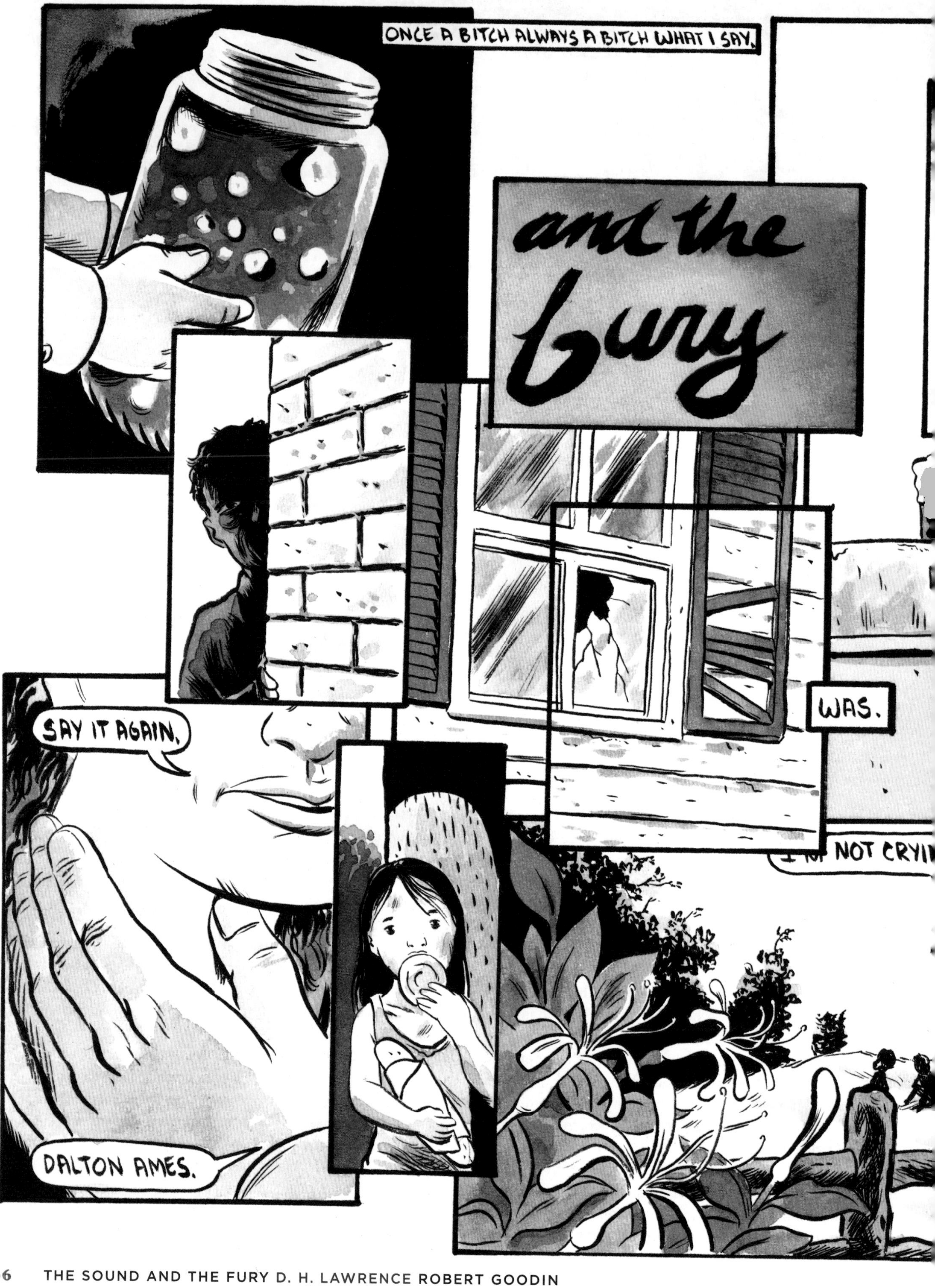
ONCE A BITCH ALWAYS A BITCH WHAT I SAY.
and the fury
WAS.
SAY IT AGAIN.
DALTON AMES.

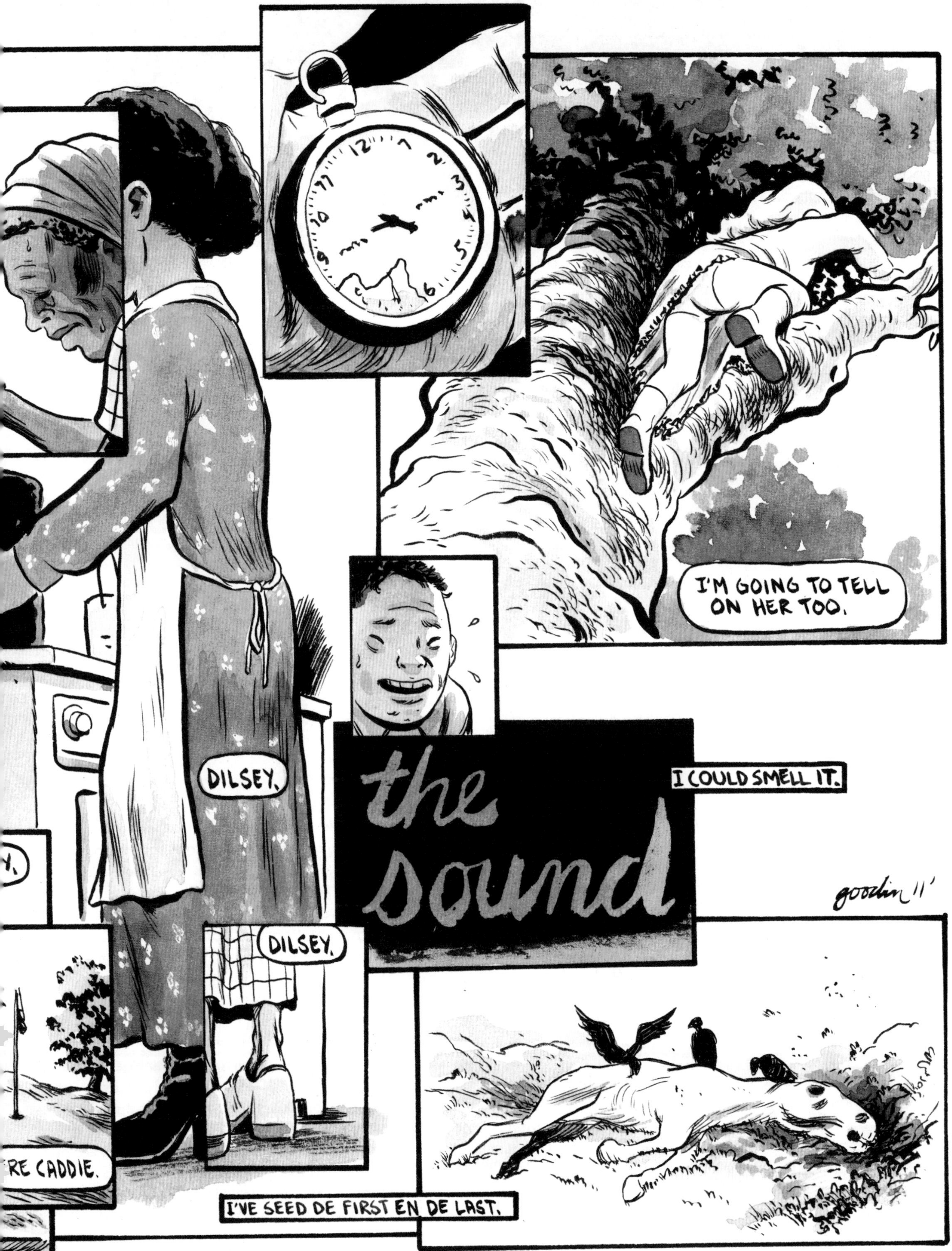
I'M GOING TO TELL ON HER TOO.
DILSEY.
Y.
the sound
I COULD SMELL IT.
goodin '11'
RE CADDIE.
DILSEY.
I'VE SEED DE FIRST EN DE LAST.

Letters to a Young Poet

Rainer Maria Rilke

DESIGN BY **James Uhler**

RAINER MARIA RILKE IS ONE OF THE GREAT GERMAN- language poets, but his appeal goes way beyond this—multiple English translations of his major works are constantly in print and can be found in the poetry section of basically every bookstore in the US. His appeal lies in his mystical and spiritual inclinations tempered with feelings of doubt, confusion, and loneliness. The first line of the first poem in his masterpiece, *Duino Elegies*, captures the dichotomy:

Who, if I cried out, would hear me among the angelic
orders?

So, angels do exist, says Rilke . . . but he's afraid that they'll ignore him. In 1902, *Duino Elegies* was still two decades away, but Rilke's early poems had come to the attention of a budding young poet who was attending the same military academy in Vienna where Rilke had been educated. Young Franz Kappus sent Rilke some of his own poems, asking for critique and guidance. Twenty-six-year-old Rilke responded with sage, beautifully written advice about ignoring criticism

and staying true to one's vision. The correspondence totaled just ten letters each by the time their correspondence ended in 1908. After Rilke's death, Kuppus published the older poet's letters in 1929 (in an admirable, egoless move, he left out his own side of the correspondence). We get Rilke's thoughts on love, relationships, loneliness, sadness, God, being a poet, and being fully alive. There are at least half a dozen editions of *Letters to a Young Poet* currently in print.

When I started compiling *The Graphic Canon*, I knew that it would be mainly comics and illustrations, but I wanted to include at least one piece that used radical graphic design as its medium. No images as such, only avant-garde use of typography and lay-out. Graphic designer and illustrator Jamie Uhler is an admirer of Rilke's missives and had decided to apply his craft to an unorthodox presentation of them, which he posted to the website Wonders in the Dark. He writes that this is "an attempt to guide your eyes as mine have been, and feel what I've felt. To articulate in white space and typography (mediums I love) what Rilke has beautifully rendered in word and thought." Here are the eighth and ninth letters.

I

L T A Y P
E O O O
T U E
T N T
E G
R
S

by **R** *ainer*
M *aria*
R *ilke*

translation by reginald snell
design by james uhler

I

LETTER EIGHT: *borgeby gard (fladie), sweden*

august

12, 1904

I WANT TO TALK TO YOU AGAIN FOR A WHILE,
dear herr kappus, ALTHOUGH I CAN SAY ALMOST NOTHING THAT IS HELPFUL, HARDLY
ANYTHING PROFITABLE. YOU HAVE HAD MANY GREAT SORROWS,
WHICH HAVE PASSED AWAY. AND YOU SAY THAT EVEN THIS PASSING WAS DIFFICULT
AND JARRING FOR YOU. BUT PLEASE CONSIDER WHETHER THESE GREAT
SORROWS HAVE NOT RATHER PASSED THROUGH THE MIDST OF YOURSELF?
Whether much in you has not altered, whether you have not somehow
changed in some PART OF YOUR BEING, *while you were*
sorrowful? Only those SORROWS *are dangerous and bad which we carry*
about among our fellows in order to drown them; like diseases which
are superficially and foolishly treated, they only recede and break out
after a short interval all the more frightfully; and gather themselves
in our inwards, and are life, are
UNLIVED,
DISDAINED,
LOST *life, of which one can*

DIE.

IF IT WERE POSSIBLE FOR US TO SEE FURTHER
THAN OUR KNOWLEDGE EXTENDS AND OUT A LITTLE OVER THE OUTWORKS OF OUR
SURMISING, PERHAPS WE SHOULD THEN BEAR OUR SORROWS WITH GREATER CONFIDENCE
THAN OUR JOYS. *For they are the moments when something new, something*
unknown, has entered into us; our feelings grow dumb with shy confusion,
everything in us RETIRES,
a STILLNESS *supervenes,*
and the NEW THING, *that no one knows*
stands SILENT
there
in the
midst.

I believe that almost all
our sorrows are moments of TENSIONwhich we experience as paralysis, because we no longer hear our estranged feelings living. Because we are alone with the strange thing that has entered into us; because for a moment everything familiar and customary has been taken from us; because we stand in the middle of a crossing where we cannot remain standing. Therefore it is, also, that the sorrow passes by us: the new thing in us, that has been added to us, has entered into our heart, has gone into its innermost chamber, and is no more even there, is already in the blood. And we do not realize what it was. We could easily be made to believe that nothing had happened, and yet we have been changed, as a house is changed into which a guest has entered. We cannot say who has come, perhaps we shall never know, but there are many indications to suggest that the future is entering into us in this manner in order to transform itself within us long before it happens. And therefore it is so important to be solitary and heedful when we are sad: because the seemingly uneventful and inflexible moment when our future sets foot in us stands so much nearer to life than that other noisy and fortuitous instant when it happens to us as if from without. The more patient, quiet and open we are in our sorrowing, the more deeply and the more unhesitatingly will the new thing enter us, the better shall we deserve it, the more will it be our own destiny, and when one day later it "happens" (that is, goes forth from us to others) we shall feel in our inmost selves that we are akin and close to it. And that is necessary. It is necessary-and in that direction our development will gradually move-, that nothing alien shall befall us, but only what has long been part of us. We have already had to think anew so many concepts of motion, we shall also learn gradually to realize that it is out of mankind that what we call destiny proceeds, not into them from without. Only because so many did not absorb their destinies and transform these within themselves as long as they lived in them, they did not recognize what went forth from them: it was so alien to them that they believed, in their bewildered terror, it must have just entered into them, for they swore that they had never before found anything similar in themselves. As we have long deceived ourselves about the motion of the sun, so we still continue to deceive ourselves about the motion of that which is to come. The future stands firm, dear Herr Kappus, but we move about in INFINITE
SPACE.

how
SHOULD
WE NOT

find

it
DIFFICULT

?

and, to speak again of solitude, it becomes
increasingly clear that this is fundamentally
not something that we can choose or reject.
we are **solitary**. we can delude ourselves about it, and pretend that it is not so. that is all.
but how much better it is to realize that we are thus, to start directly from that
very point. then, to be sure, it will come about that we grow dizzy; for all the
points upon which our eyes have been accustomed to rest will be taken away
from us. there is no longer any nearness, and all distance is infinitely far. a
man who was taken from his study, almost without preparation and transition,
and placed upon the height of a great mountain range, would be bound to feel
something similar: an uncertainty without parallel, an abandonment to the
unutterable would almost annihilate him. he would imagine himself to be falling
or fancy himself flung outwards into space or exploded into a thousand pieces:
what a monstrous lie his brain would have to invent in order to retrieve and
explain the condition of his senses. so all distances, all measures are changed for
the man who   becomes solitary; many of these changes
take effect suddenly, and, as with the man on the mountain top, there arise
singular fantasies and strange sensations which seem to grow out beyond all
endurance. but it is necessary for us to experience that too. we must accept our
existence as far as ever it is possible; everything, even the unheard of, must be
possible there. that is fundamentally the only courage which is demanded of us:
to be brave in the face of the strangest, most singular
and most inexplicable things that can befall us.

The fact that human beings have
BEEN COWARDLY IN THIS
SENSE HAS DONE ENDLESS
HARM TO LIFE; the experiences
that are called "apparitions", the
whole of the so-called "spirit
world", death, all these things
that are so closely related to us,
have been so crowded out of life
by our daily warding them off, that
the senses by which
we might apprehend
them are stunted.

To say *nothing* of God.
BUT THE FEAR OF THE INEXPLICABLE
HAS NOT ONLY IMPOVERISHED THE

EXISTENCE OF THE SOLITARY MAN;

IT HAS ALSO CIRCUMSCRIBED THE

RELATIONSHIPS BETWEEN HUMAN BEINGS,
as it were lifted them up from the river bed of infinite
possibilities to a fallow spot on the bank, to which
nothing happens. For it is not only indolence which
causes human relationships to repeat themselves
with such unspeakable monotony, unrenewed from
one occasion to another, it is the shyness of any
new; incalculable experience which we do not feel
ourselves equal to facing. But **only the man who is
prepared for everything**, who doesn't exclude any experience, even the
who excludes nothing, not even the most unintelligible, will live the relationship
with another as something vital, and will himself exhaust his own existence.
For if we think of this existence of the individual as a larger or smaller room,
it becomes clear that most people get to know only one corner of their room,
a window seat, a strip of floor which they pace up and down.

In that way they have a certain security. And yet how much more human is that insecurity, so fraught with danger, which compels the prisoners in Poe's Tales to grope for the shapes of their ghastly prisons and not to remain unaware of the unspeakable horrors of their dwelling. But we are not prisoners. No snares and springes are laid for us, and there is nothing that should alarm or torment us. We are set in life as in the element with which we are most in keeping, and we have moreover, through thousands of years of adaptation, become so similar to this life that when we stay still we are, by a happy mimicry, hardly to be distinguished from our surroundings. We have no cause to be mistrustful of our world, for it is not against us. If it has terrors they are our terrors; if it has abysses those abysses belong to us, if dangers are there we must strive to love them. And if only we regulate our life according to that principle which advises us always to hold to the difficult, what even now appears most alien to us will become most familiar and loyal. How could we forget those old myths which are to be found in the beginnings of every people; the myths of the dragons which are transformed, at the last moment, into princesses; perhaps all the dragons of our life are princesses, who are only waiting to see us once beautiful and brave. Perhaps everything terrifying is at bottom the helplessness

t   h   a   t
                seeks
our   help.

▬▬▬▬▬▬▬

So you must not be frightened, dear Herr Kappus, when a sorrow rises up before you, greater than you have ever seen before; when a
restlessness like light and cloud shadows passes over your hands and over all your doing.
You must think that something is happening upon you, that life has not forgotten you, that it holds you in its hand; it will not let you fall.
Why do you want to exclude any disturbance, any pain, any melancholy from your life, since you do not know what these conditions
are working upon you?
Why do you want to plague yourself with the question where it has all come from and whither it is tending?
Since you know that you are in a state of transition and would wish nothing so dearly as to transform yourself.
If something in your proceedings is diseased, do reflect that disease is the means by which an organism rids itself of a foreign body; you
must then simply help it to be ill, to have its full disease and to let it break out, for that is its development.
In you, dear Herr Kappus, so much is happening now; you must be patient like a sick man and sanguine like a convalescent; for
perhaps you are both.

And more than that: you are also the doctor who has to superintend yourself.
But in every illness there are many days when the doctor can do nothing but wait.
And that is what you, in so far as you are your own doctor, must now above all things do.

—

Do not observe yourself too closely.

Do not draw too rapid conclusions from what happens to you;
let it simply happen to you.
Otherwise you will too easily reach the point of looking reproachfully
(that is morally) at your past,
which is naturally concerned with everything that is now occurring to you.

But what is taking effect in you from the mistakes,

desires and longings of your boyhood is not what you

recall and condemn. The extraordinary circumstances

of a solitary and helpless childhood are so difficult, so

complicated, exposed to so many influences and at

the same time so untrammeled by all real connection

with life, that where a vice appears in it we must not

call it a vice and leave it at that.

**One must in general
be so careful**

with names; it is so often the name
of a misdeed upon which a life is shattered, not the nameless and personal action itself, which
was perhaps a quite definite necessity of that life
and could be taken on by it without trouble.
And the expense of energy seems to you so great only because you overrate the victory; this
] latter is not the "great thing" that you think you, have achieved, although you are right about [
your feeling; the great thing is that something was already there which you could set in place
of that betrayal, SOMETHING TRUE AND GENUINE. Apart from this even your victory would have
been only a moral reaction without great significance, but thus it has become a chapter of

YOUR LIFE.

DO YOU REMEMBER HOW THIS
LIFE HAS LONGED EVER SINCE
CHILDHOOD FOR THE "GREAT"?
I SEE HOW IT IS NOW LONGING
TO LEAVE THE GREAT FOR
GREATER. THEREFORE IT DOES
NOT CEASE TO BE DIFFICULT,
BUT THEREFORE IT WILL NOT
CEASE, EITHER, TO GROW.

AND IF I MAY SAY ONE THING
MORE TO YOU, IT IS THIS:
DO NOT THINK THAT THE MAN
WHO SEEKS TO COMFORT YOU
LIVES UNTROUBLED AMONG
THE SIMPLE AND QUIET WORDS
WHICH SOMETIMES DO YOU
GOOD. HIS LIFE HAS MUCH
HARDSHIP AND SADNESS AND
LAGS FAR BEHIND YOU. IF IT
WERE OTHERWISE, HE COULD
NEVER HAVE FOUND THOSE WORDS.

RAINER

MARIA

DEAR

HERR   ABOUT WHICH I AM THINKING

OF YOUR LIFE,   KAPPUS,   WITH SO MANY WISHES.   YOURS, RILKE

LETTER NINE: *furuborg (jonsered), sweden*

my *dear herr.* kappus, november 4, 1904

During the time which has passed without a letter I have been partly on the move, partly so busy that I could not write. And even today I find writing difficult, because I have already had to write a number of letters, so that my hand is tired. If I could dictate, I would say much to you, but as it is you must accept only a few words in answer to your long letter.

I think of you often, dear Herr Kappus, and with such concentrated wishes that it really must help you in some way. Whether my letters could be truly a help, I often doubt. Do not say: yes, they are. Accept them quietly and without many thanks, and let us wait to see what will come.

It is perhaps no use now to reply to your actual words; for what I could say about your disposition to doubt or about your inability to bring your outer and inner life into harmony, or about anything else that oppresses you-: it is always what I have said before always the wish that you might be able to find patience enough in yourself to endure, and single-heartedness enough to believe; that you might win increasing trust in what is difficult, and in your *solitude* among other people. And for the rest, let life happen to you.

Believe me:
life is right,

at all events.

9

And about feelings: all feelings are pure which gather you and lift you up; a feeling is impure which takes hold of only one side of your being and so distorts you. Everything that you could think in the light of your childhood is good. Everything which makes more of you than you have previously been in your best hours, is right. Every exaltation is good if it is in your whole blood, if it is not intoxication or turbidness, but joy into whose depths you can see. Do you understand what I mean?

And your doubt can become a good quality if you train it. It must become aware, it must become criticism. Ask it, whenever it wants to spoil something for you, why something is ugly, demand proofs from it, test it, and you will perhaps find it helpless and nonplussed, perhaps also aggressive. But do not give way, demand arguments and conduct yourself thus carefully and consistently every single time, and the day will dawn when it will become, instead of a subverter, one of your best workmen,— perhaps the cleverest of all who are building at your life.

That is all, dear Herr Kappus, that I am able to say to you today. But I am sending you by the same post the off-print of a little composition (THE LAY OF THE LOVE AND DEATH OF CORNET CHRISTOPH RILKE, WRITTEN IN 1899 AND FIRST PUBLISHED IN BOOK FORM IN 1906. -TRANS.) which has just appeared in the Prague *Deutsche Arbeit*. There I speak to you further of life and of death, and of the greatness and splendour of both.

yours,

RAINER
MARIA
RILKE

The Maltese Falcon

Dashiell Hammett

ART/ADAPTATION BY **T. Edward Bak**

EVERY TYPE OF "GENRE FICTION"—DETECTIVE fiction, science fiction, horror, Westerns, erotica—has its own classics, its own canon. Sometimes the absolute best works in these genres creep into the overall literary canon. The old guard reacts with disgust, sniffing that, for example, "Time Considered as a Helix of Semi-Precious Stones" by Samuel Delany, *At the Mountains of Madness* by H. P. Lovecraft, *Riders of the Purple Sage* by Zane Grey, or *Story of O* by Pauline Réage could never enter the rarefied confines of literature. Still, these works have their adherents, and certain works of genre fiction wriggle their way into college courses, literature anthologies, and the prestigious Library of America series.

The pioneers of hardboiled detective fiction—Dashiell Hammett and Raymond Chandler—are among this group of infiltrators. Although Chandler, creator of Philip Marlowe in *The Big Sleep*, is usually considered the finer writer, Hammett's pared-down, no-nonsense style recalls Hemingway, although Hem and Hammett both started getting published at the exact same time. Like calculus, their clipped style was developed simultaneously. Hammett put his to service writing about tough-guy detectives, like Sam Spade, the cynical, two-fisted gumshoe in *The Maltese Falcon.*

Spade and his partner, Miles Archer, are hired by a mysterious dame to tail some guy named Thursby. Archer ends up shot to death, and Thursby is soon dead, too. The police suspect Spade. It turns out that the femme fatale, Brigid, and two mooks were hired by a sleazeball named Gutman to track down a gold, jewel-encrusted figurine known as the Maltese Falcon. They found it, then double-crossed Gutman by trying to abscond with it, then double-crossed each other. **Spoiler Alert:** Brigid killed Archer to frame Thursby, her former partner in crime. The statue that led to all these murders is a fake; the real Maltese Falcon is still out there somewhere.

T. Edward Bak is working on an epic, meticulously researched graphic biography about the discoverer of Alaska, *WILD MAN: The Strange Journey and Fantastic Account of the Naturalist Georg Wilhelm Steller*. Between trips to that frozen state and in-depth study of natural history publications from the last two centuries, Ed did the seemingly impossible—creating a wordless adaptation of Hammett's quintessential 1930 work in two pages. And you'll notice that Spade actually resembles Hammett's description, looking nothing like Humphrey Bogart.

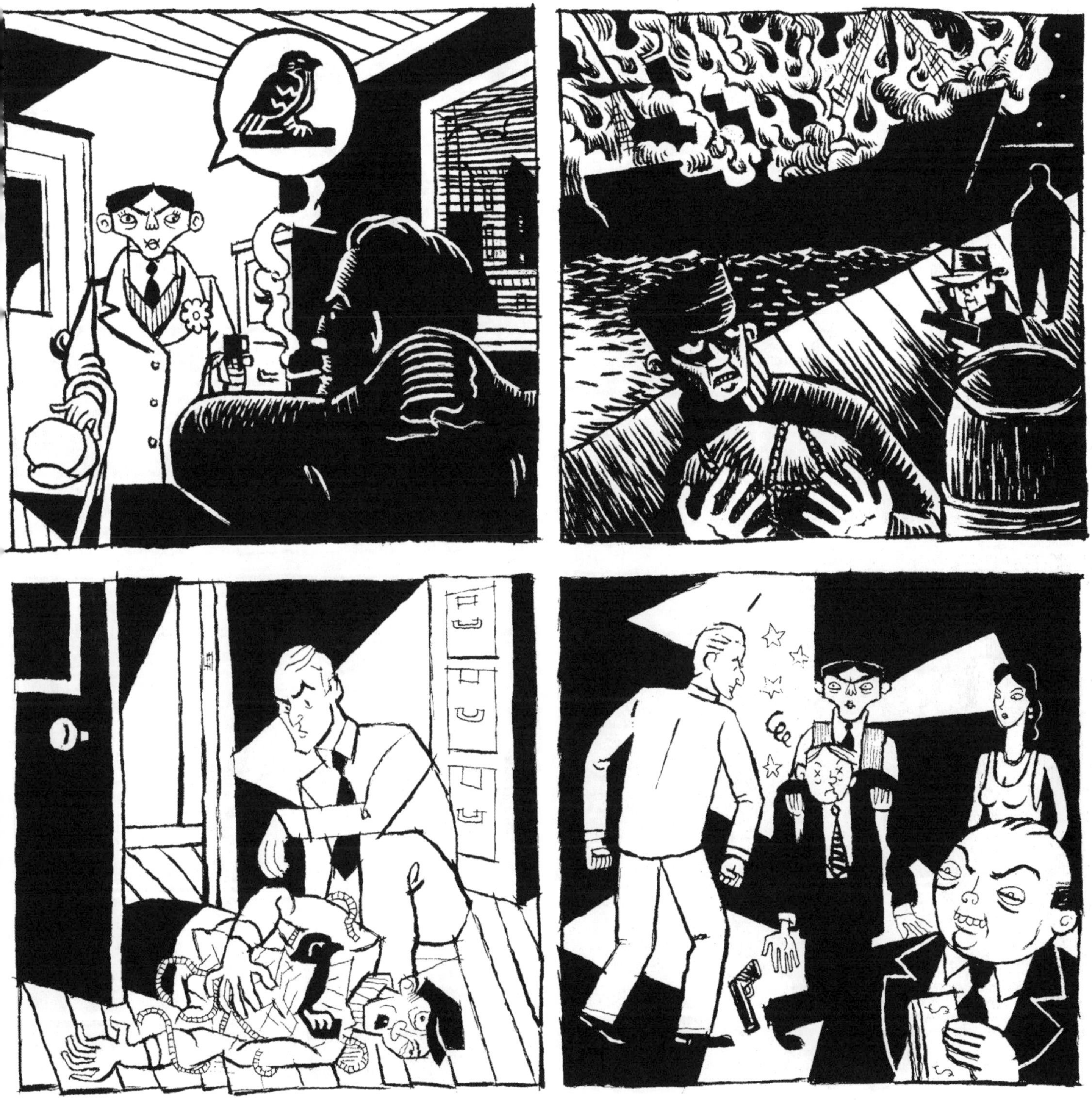

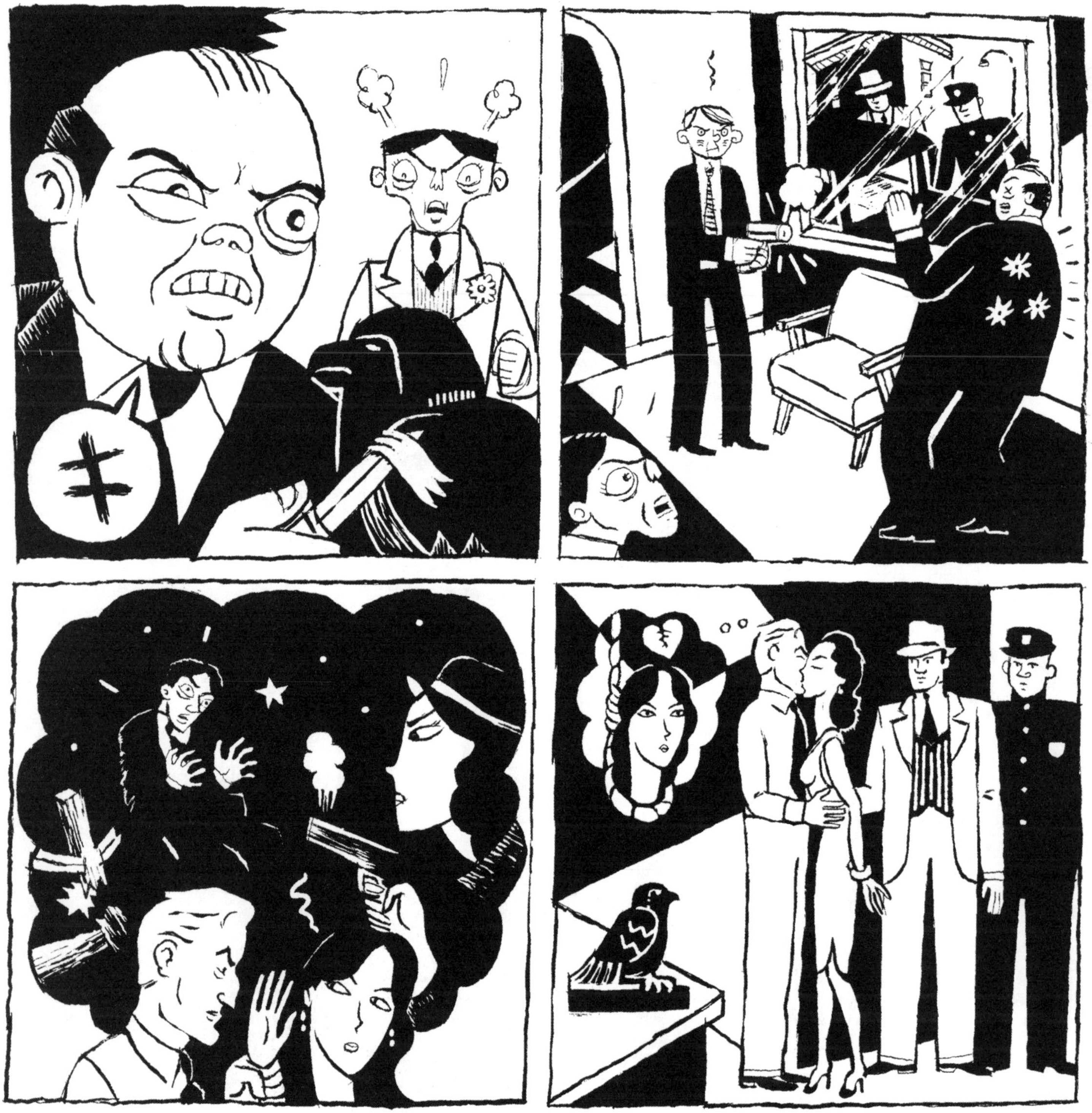

Brave New World

Aldous Huxley

ILLUSTRATION BY **Carly Schmitt**

ONE OF LITERATURE'S GREAT DYSTOPIAN NOVELS, *Brave New World,* published in 1932, imagines a World State where the populace is pacified through a drug called soma, as well as other methods, including "feelies" (movies that let you see, hear, and feel the action), discouraging committed relationships, and "hatching" and "conditioning" children. While the world of Orwell's *Nineteen Eighty-Four* is based on fear and enforced obedience, *Brave New World* mollifies, tranquilizes, and distracts.

Carly Schmitt has created her mesmerizing portrait of the main female protagonist, Lenina, with a halo of her beloved soma. On the medium, Carly explains: "It's all done with pencil on white paper, even the black space was painstakingly filled in (completely killing my drawing hand), and I used marker for the purple in the eyes."

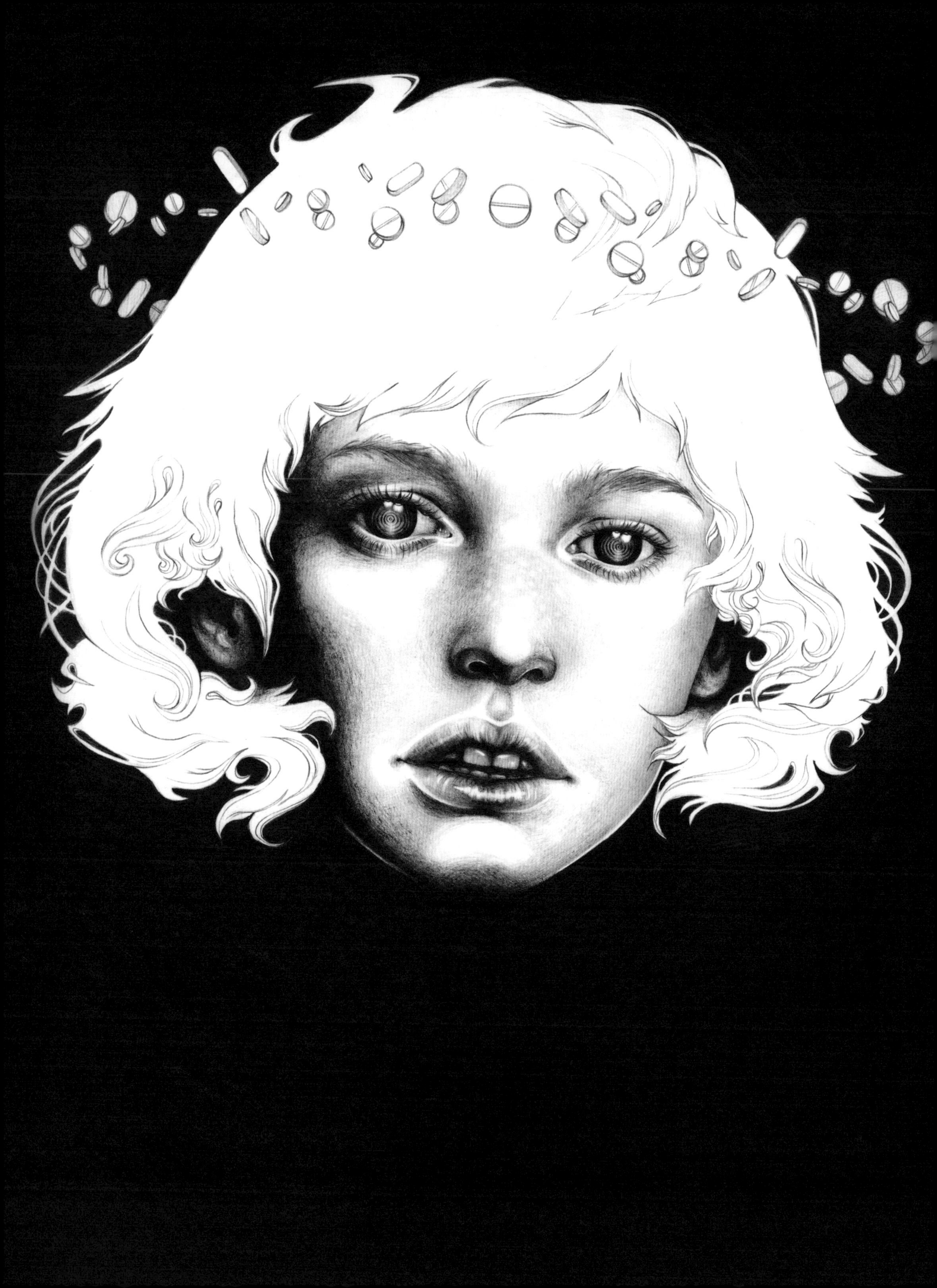

Poker!

Zora Neale Hurston

ART/ADAPTATION BY **Milton Knight**

ZORA NEALE HURSTON GREW UP MOSTLY IN THE all-black town of Eatonville, Florida. She studied folklore and anthropology under Franz Boas—and was classmates with Margaret Mead—and wrote some classic works in those fields. After moving to New York in 1925, she became one of the core members of the Harlem Renaissance, and is best known for the novel *Go Tell It on the Mountain.*

She also wrote plays, though the bulk of them remained unknown for decades after her death. The literati knew she had written a few plays, and that she and Langston Hughes collaborated on an unfinished drama, *Mule Bone*, which was a big cause of their famous falling out. But it turns out that Hurston wrote at least six full-length plays and four one-act plays or sketches that were never published or performed. They were finally discovered among manuscripts at the Library of Congress in 1997. Alice L. Birney, American literature specialist at the library, noted that this previously unknown cache "firmly establishes their author, an African-American woman, as a significant dramatist of the twentieth century." Most of the plays are humorous, sometimes bitingly so, and the short *Poker!*—probably written in 1931—is the very definition of gallows humor.

Milton Knight has drawn for lots of great publications—the *Village Voice, Heavy Metal, National Lampoon*, and *Screw*, among others—and he's worked with some legendary characters, including Richie Rich and the Teenage Mutant Ninja Turtles. He's also done animation work for Warner Brothers, Disney, MGM, and HBO. His highly dynamic, old-school style is just what this card game among heavily armed cheaters needs.

SOURCE

The Zora Neale Hurston Plays at the Library of Congress, http://international.loc.gov/ammem/collections/hurston.

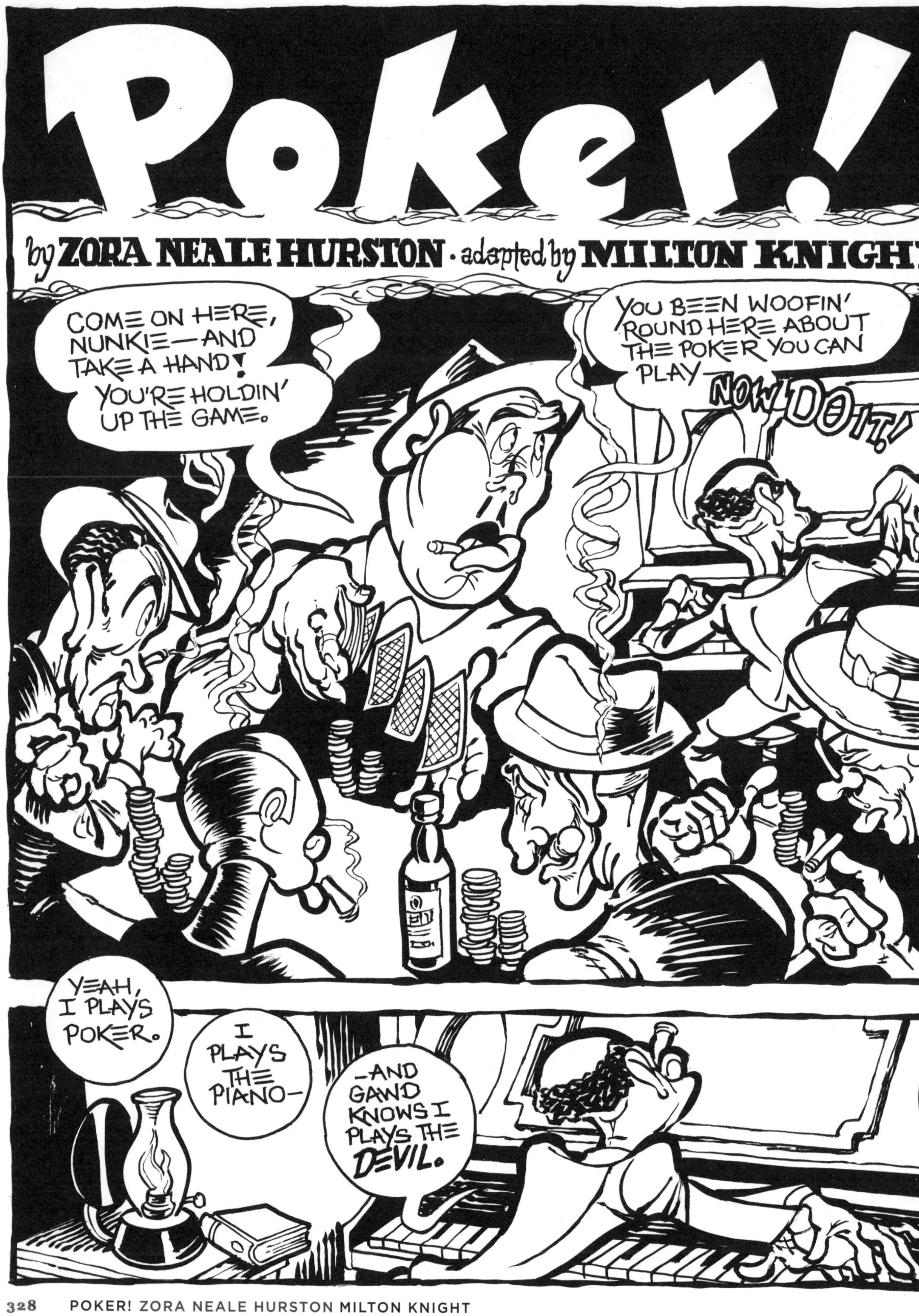
Poker!
by ZORA NEALE HURSTON · adapted by MILTON KNIGHT
COME ON HERE, NUNKIE—AND TAKE A HAND! YOU'RE HOLDIN' UP THE GAME.
YOU BEEN WOOFIN' ROUND HERE ABOUT THE POKER YOU CAN PLAY— NOW DO IT!
YEAH, I PLAYS POKER.
I PLAYS THE PIANO-
-AND GAWD KNOWS I PLAYS THE DEVIL.

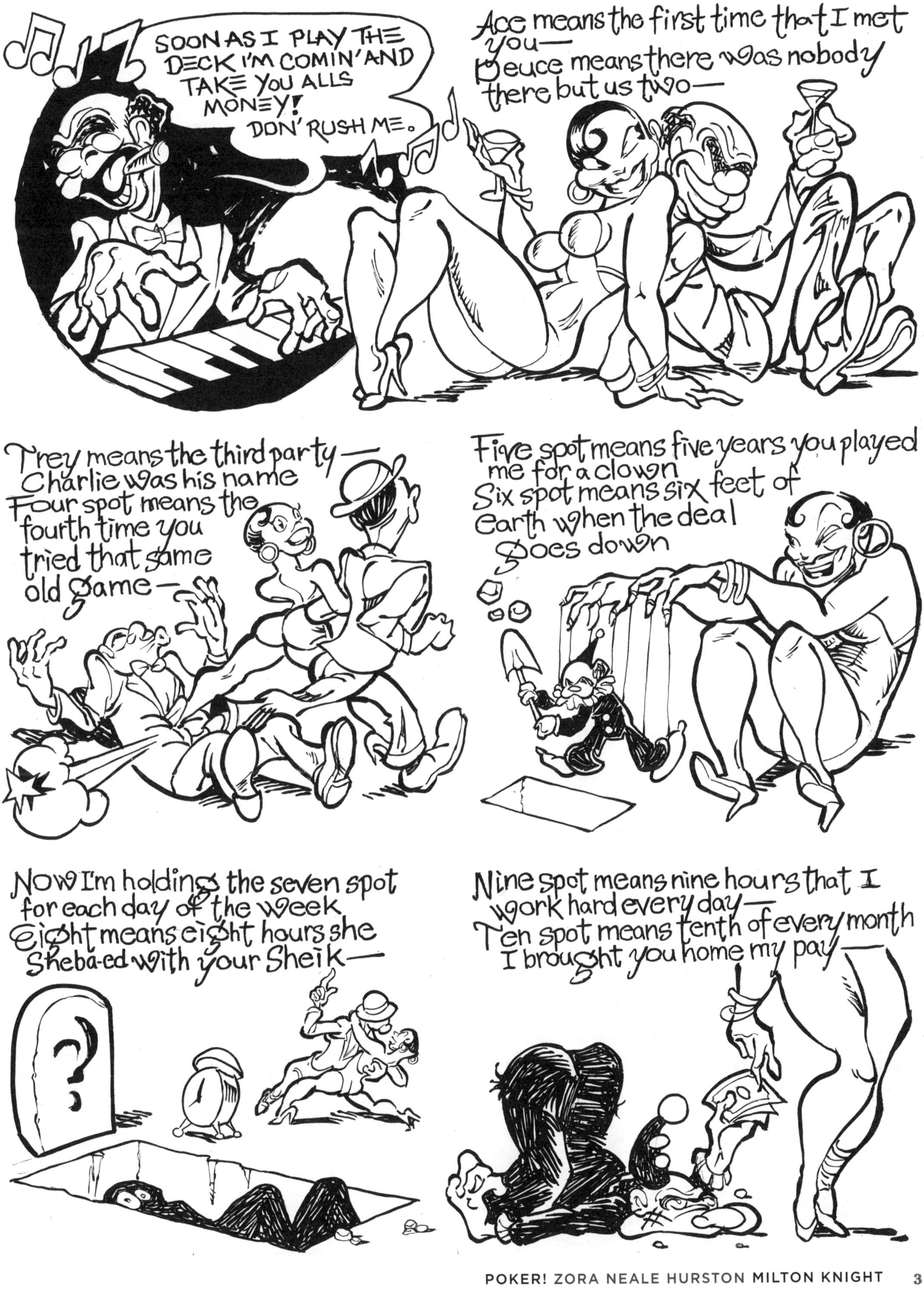
SOON AS I PLAY THE DECK I'M COMIN' AND TAKE YOU ALLS MONEY! DON' RUSH ME.
Ace means the first time that I met you—
Deuce means there was nobody there but us two—
Trey means the third party— Charlie was his name
Four spot means the fourth time you tried that same old game—
Five spot means five years you played me for a clown
Six spot means six feet of earth when the deal goes down
Now I'm holding the seven spot for each day of the week
Eight means eight hours she Sheba-ed with your Sheik—
Nine spot means nine hours that I work hard every day—
Ten spot means tenth of every month I brought you home my pay—

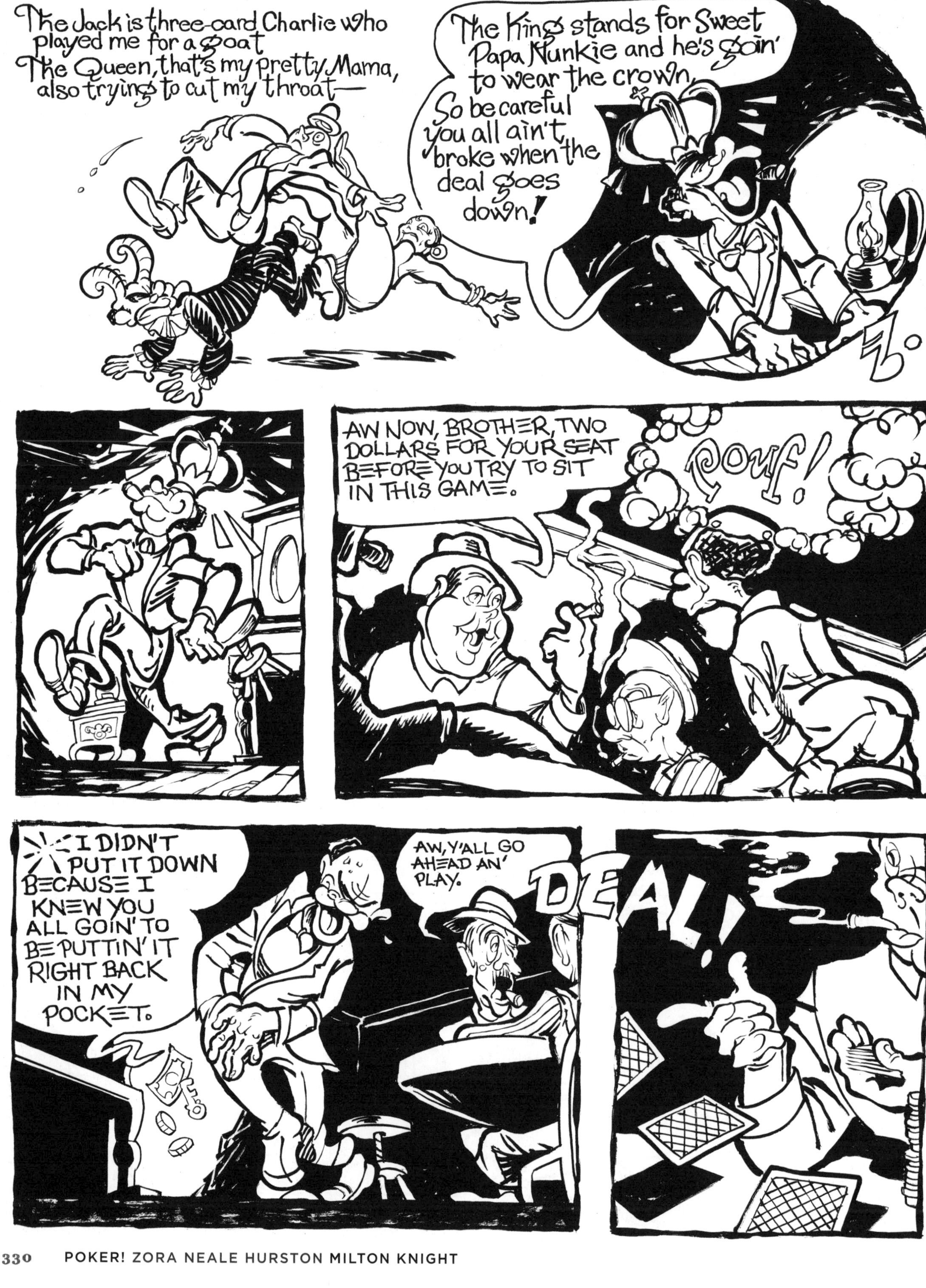

The Jack is three-card Charlie who played me for a goat
The Queen, that's my pretty Mama, also trying to cut my throat—
The King stands for Sweet Papa Nunkie and he's goin' to wear the crown,
So be careful you all ain't broke when the deal goes down!
AW NOW, BROTHER, TWO DOLLARS FOR YOUR SEAT BEFORE YOU TRY TO SIT IN THIS GAME.
POUF!
I DIDN'T PUT IT DOWN BECAUSE I KNEW YOU ALL GOIN' TO BE PUTTIN' IT RIGHT BACK IN MY POCKET.
AW, Y'ALL GO AHEAD AN' PLAY.
DEAL!

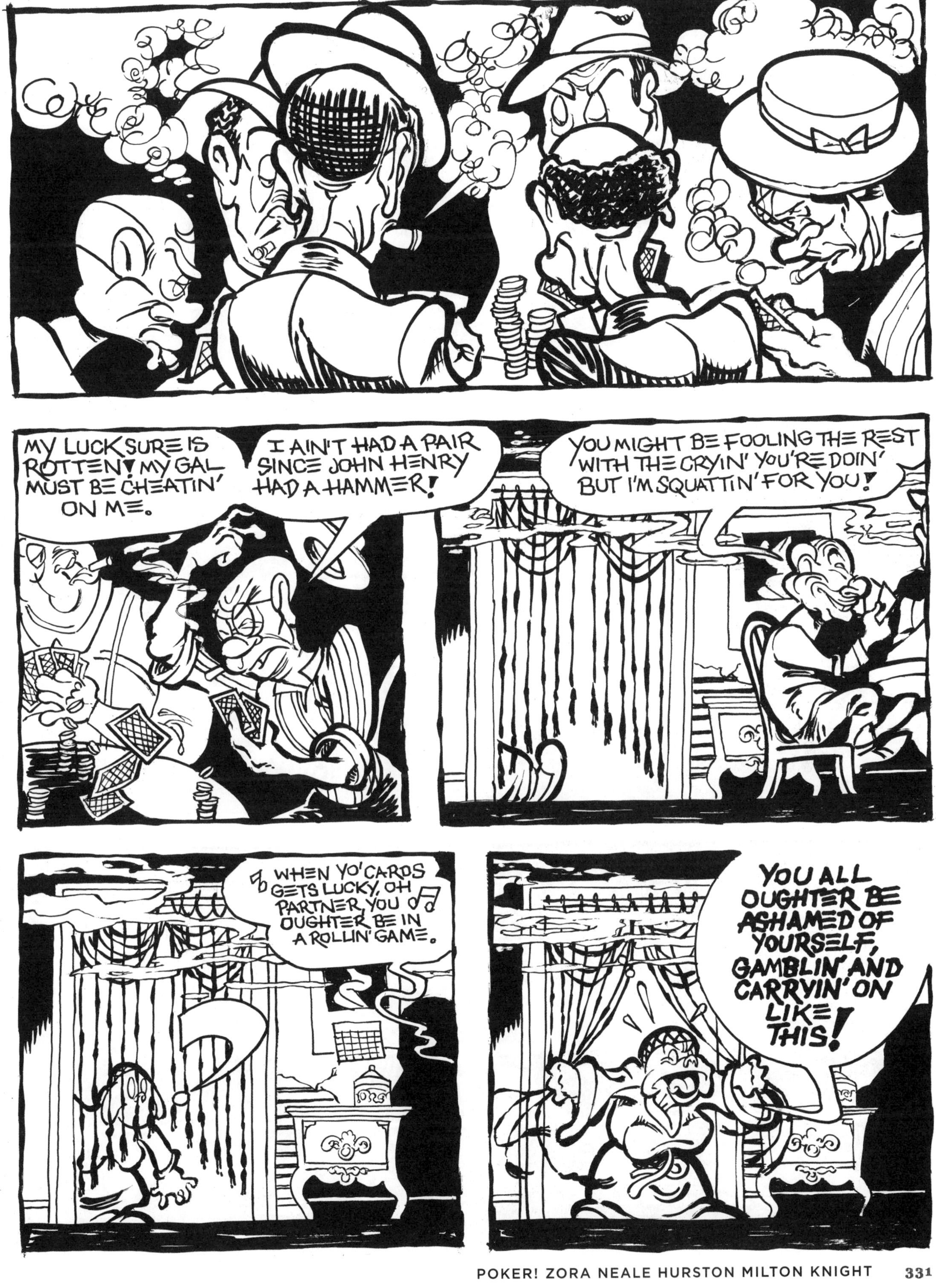
MY LUCK SURE IS ROTTEN! MY GAL MUST BE CHEATIN' ON ME.
I AIN'T HAD A PAIR SINCE JOHN HENRY HAD A HAMMER!
YOU MIGHT BE FOOLING THE REST WITH THE CRYIN' YOU'RE DOIN' BUT I'M SQUATTIN' FOR YOU!
WHEN YO' CARDS GETS LUCKY, OH PARTNER, YOU OUGHTER BE IN A ROLLIN' GAME.
YOU ALL OUGHTER BE ASHAMED OF YOURSELF, GAMBLIN' AND CARRYIN' ON LIKE THIS!

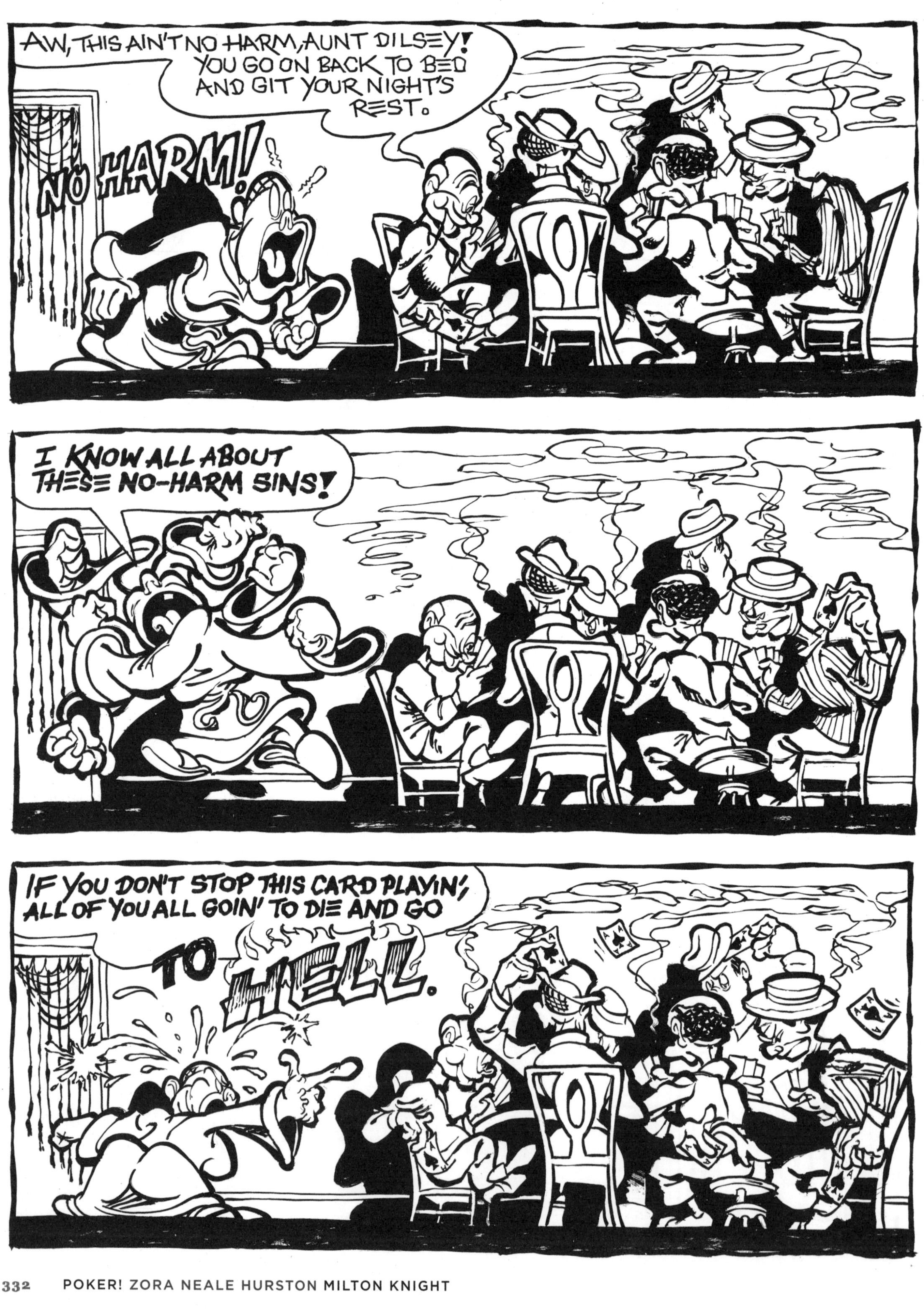

AW, THIS AIN'T NO HARM, AUNT DILSEY! YOU GO ON BACK TO BED AND GIT YOUR NIGHT'S REST.
NO HARM!
I KNOW ALL ABOUT THESE NO-HARM SINS!
IF YOU DON'T STOP THIS CARD PLAYIN', ALL OF YOU ALL GOIN' TO DIE AND GO
TO—HELL.

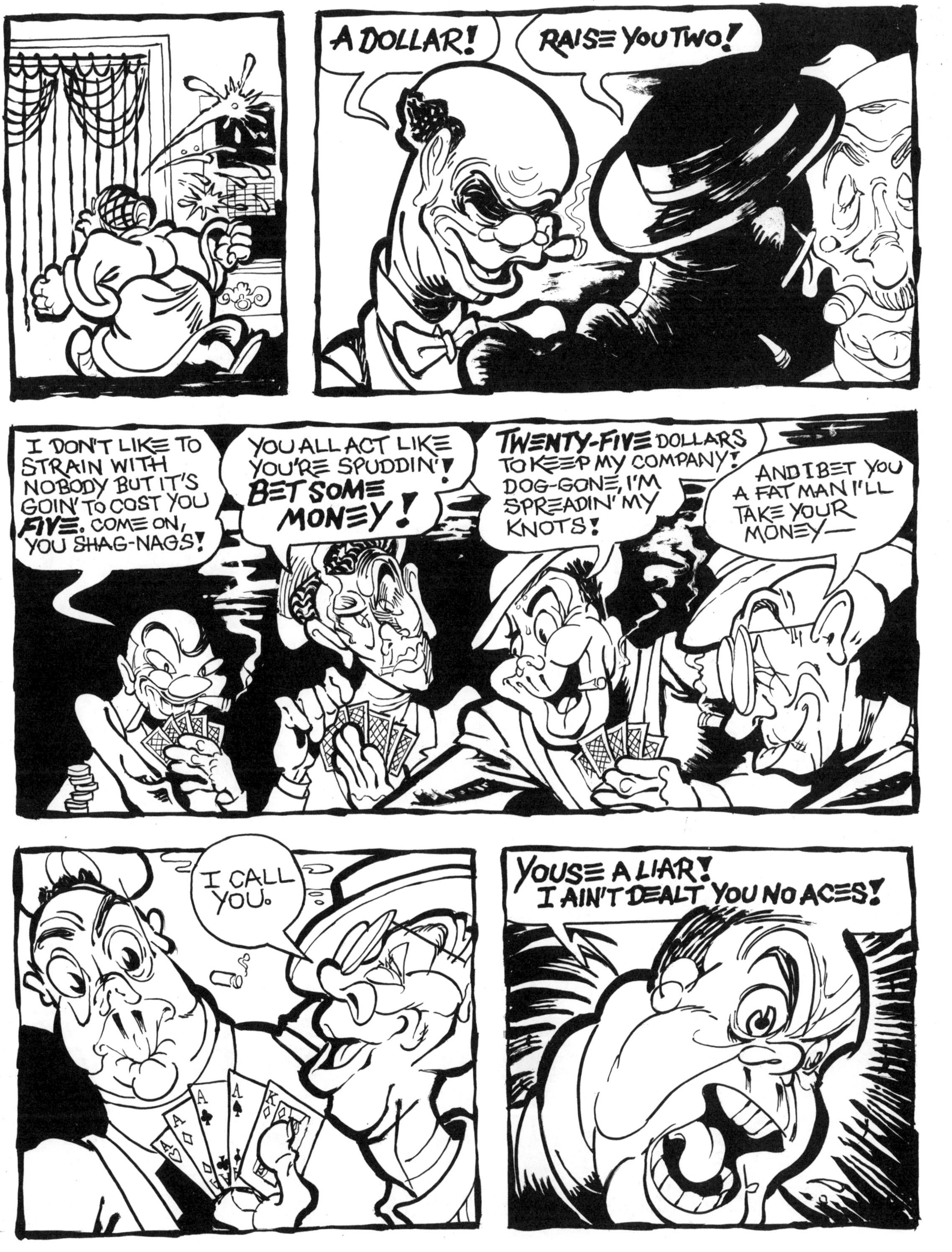
A DOLLAR!
RAISE YOU TWO!
I DON'T LIKE TO STRAIN WITH NOBODY BUT IT'S GOIN' TO COST YOU FIVE. COME ON, YOU SHAG-NAGS!
YOU ALL ACT LIKE YOU'RE SPUDDIN'! BET SOME MONEY!
TWENTY-FIVE DOLLARS TO KEEP MY COMPANY! DOG-GONE, I'M SPREADIN' MY KNOTS!
AND I BET YOU A FAT MAN I'LL TAKE YOUR MONEY—
I CALL YOU.
YOUSE A LIAR! I AIN'T DEALT YOU NO ACES!

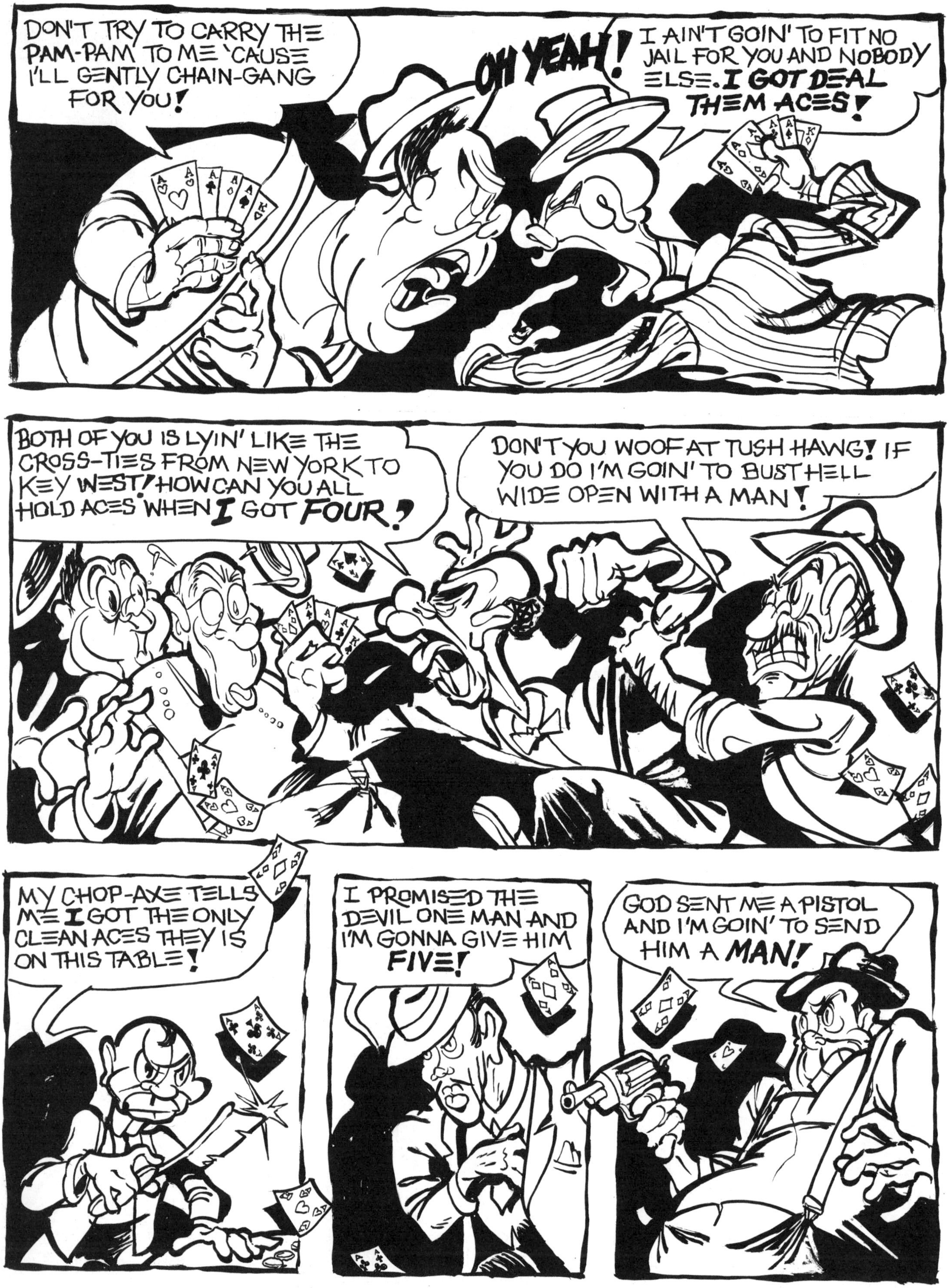
DON'T TRY TO CARRY THE PAM-PAM TO ME 'CAUSE I'LL GENTLY CHAIN-GANG FOR YOU!
OH YEAH!
I AIN'T GOIN' TO FIT NO JAIL FOR YOU AND NOBODY ELSE. I GOT DEAL THEM ACES!
BOTH OF YOU IS LYIN' LIKE THE CROSS-TIES FROM NEW YORK TO KEY WEST! HOW CAN YOU ALL HOLD ACES WHEN I GOT FOUR?
DON'T YOU WOOF AT TUSH HAWG! IF YOU DO I'M GOIN' TO BUST HELL WIDE OPEN WITH A MAN!
MY CHOP-AXE TELLS ME I GOT THE ONLY CLEAN ACES THEY IS ON THIS TABLE!
I PROMISED THE DEVIL ONE MAN AND I'M GONNA GIVE HIM FIVE!
GOD SENT ME A PISTOL AND I'M GOIN' TO SEND HIM A MAN!

THEY WOULDN'T LISSEN—
IT SURE IS GOIN' TO BE A WHOLE LOT TOUGHER IN HELL NOW!

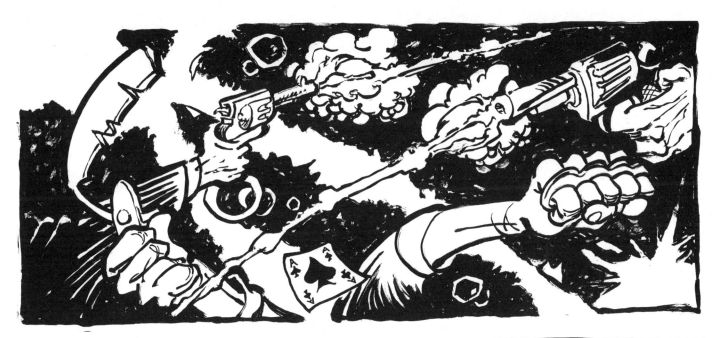

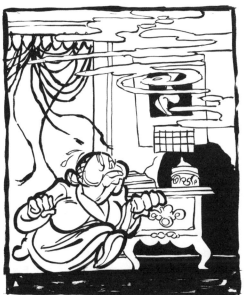

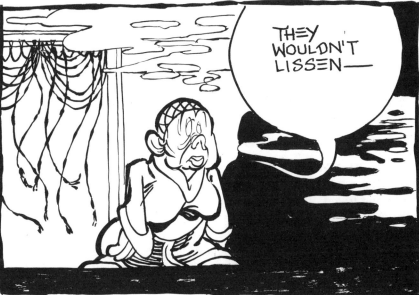

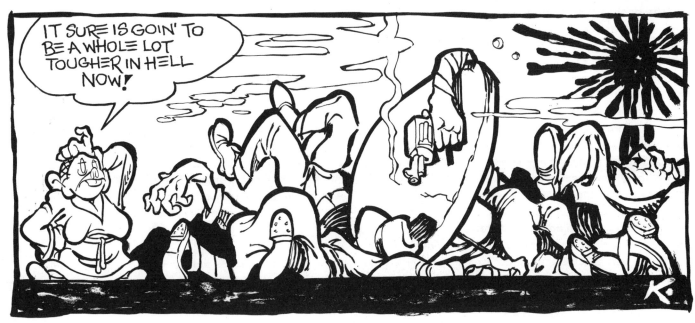

Black Elk Speaks

Black Elk and John G. Neihardt

ILLUSTRATIONS BY **Molly Kiely**

BLACK ELK WAS A SHAMAN OF THE OGLALA Lakota (also called the Sioux). Born in 1864, a second cousin and good friend of Crazy Horse, a teenage participant in the Battle of Little Big Horn, and a survivor of the Wounded Knee Massacre, Black Elk was a living link to history. His 1932 autobiography is regarded as a spiritual classic and remains the best-selling book by a Native American. It pays particular attention to Black Elk's visions and his role as a healer.

The book is complicated by the fact that it technically was not written by Black Elk. The author and poet John G. Neihardt—who researched and wrote extensively about the history of the Great Plains—interviewed Black Elk at length, with the shaman's son providing the real-time translation and Neihardt's daughter transcribing. Neihardt is credited on the cover as sole author (a situation I have changed in this volume). Through the decades, some observers have questioned or attacked his role as an outsider writing about/for an indigenous holy man. We now know that Neihardt did indeed make some changes to what Black Elk said. Yet it's obvious that the two liked each other very much, and Neihardt was more than accepting of Black Elk's beliefs. In the preface of the 1961 edition, Neihardt flat-out states, with no qualifiers, that this medicine man "certainly had supernormal powers."

For his part, Black Elk "adopted" Neihardt and his daughters, giving the writer the name Flaming Rainbow. Black Elk believed that this white man had a sincere desire to learn about the "Other World" and had been sent by the Great Spirit to record Black Elk's knowledge, so that others would have access to it. Black Elk's main concern, Neihardt tells us, was to preserve his Great Vision, the famous, life-changing mystical experience he had at age nine when he was in a coma, for unknown reasons, for twelve days. (If you'd like to read the raw transcripts of Neihardt's interviews with Black Elk, they're presented in full in *The Sixth Grandfather: Black Elk's Teachings Given to John G. Neihardt* [Bison Books, 1985].)

This vision is elaborate—the telling of it takes up twenty pages of the original book and truly deserves to be called epic. Molly Kiely—who has contributed to each volume of *The Graphic Canon*—commented that a graphic adaptation of the entire Great Vision would form a book of its own (and an amazing one at that). Her first illustration depicts a buffalo hunt that Black Elk describes; then we get two blazing depictions of the Great Vision. Molly asked that her illustrations be presented in landscape format, one per page, rather than as two-page spreads. She says: "I hope this modern white woman's interpretation of a white male writer's modified transcription of Black Elk's remarkable vision is presented with the respect and honor it deserves."

SOURCE

Neihardt, John G. *Black Elk Speaks: Being the Life Story of a Holy Man of the Oglala Sioux.* Premiere ed. Albany, NY: State University of New York Press, 2008.

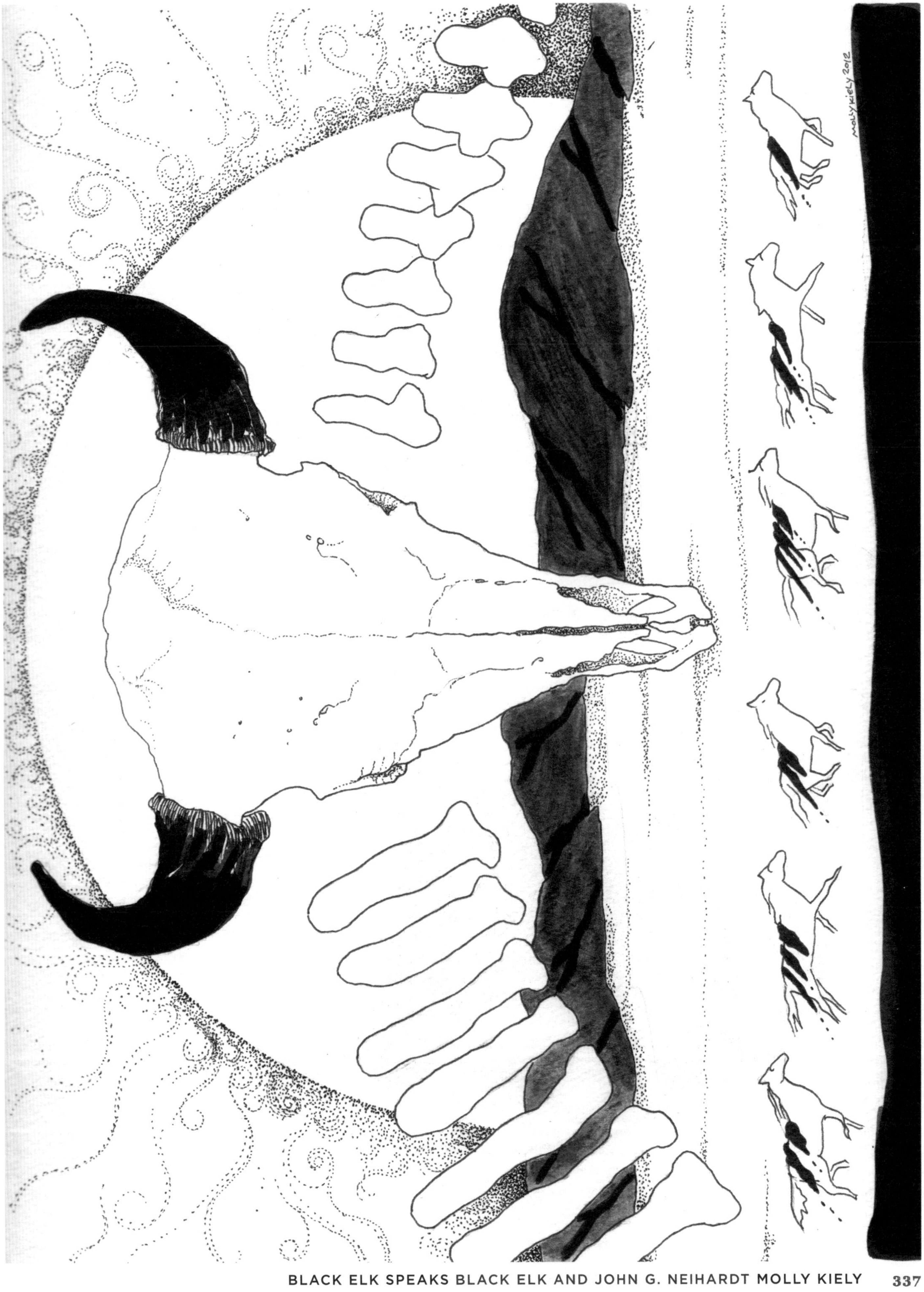
molly kiely 2012

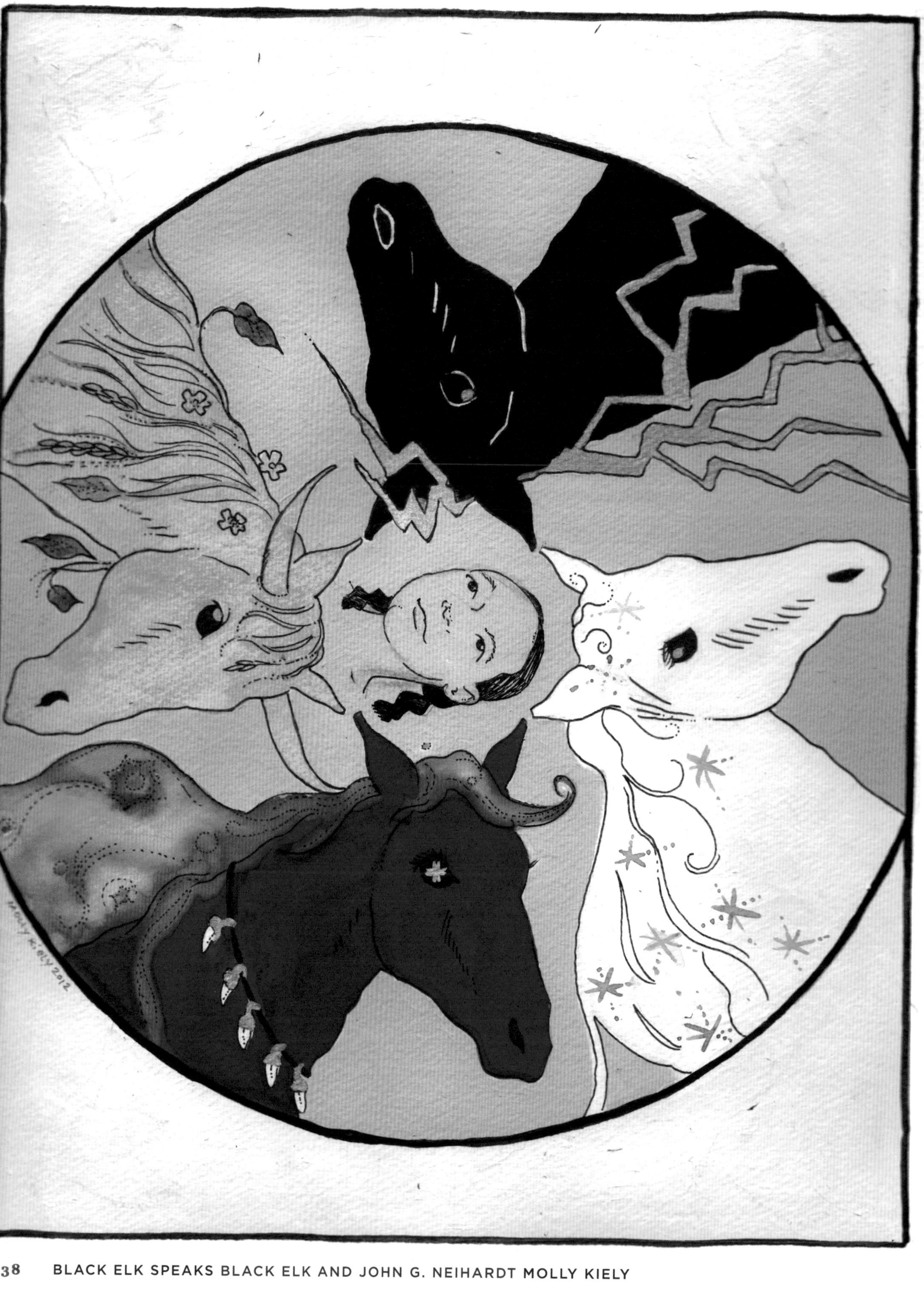

 BLACK ELK SPEAKS BLACK ELK AND JOHN G. NEIHARDT MOLLY KIELY

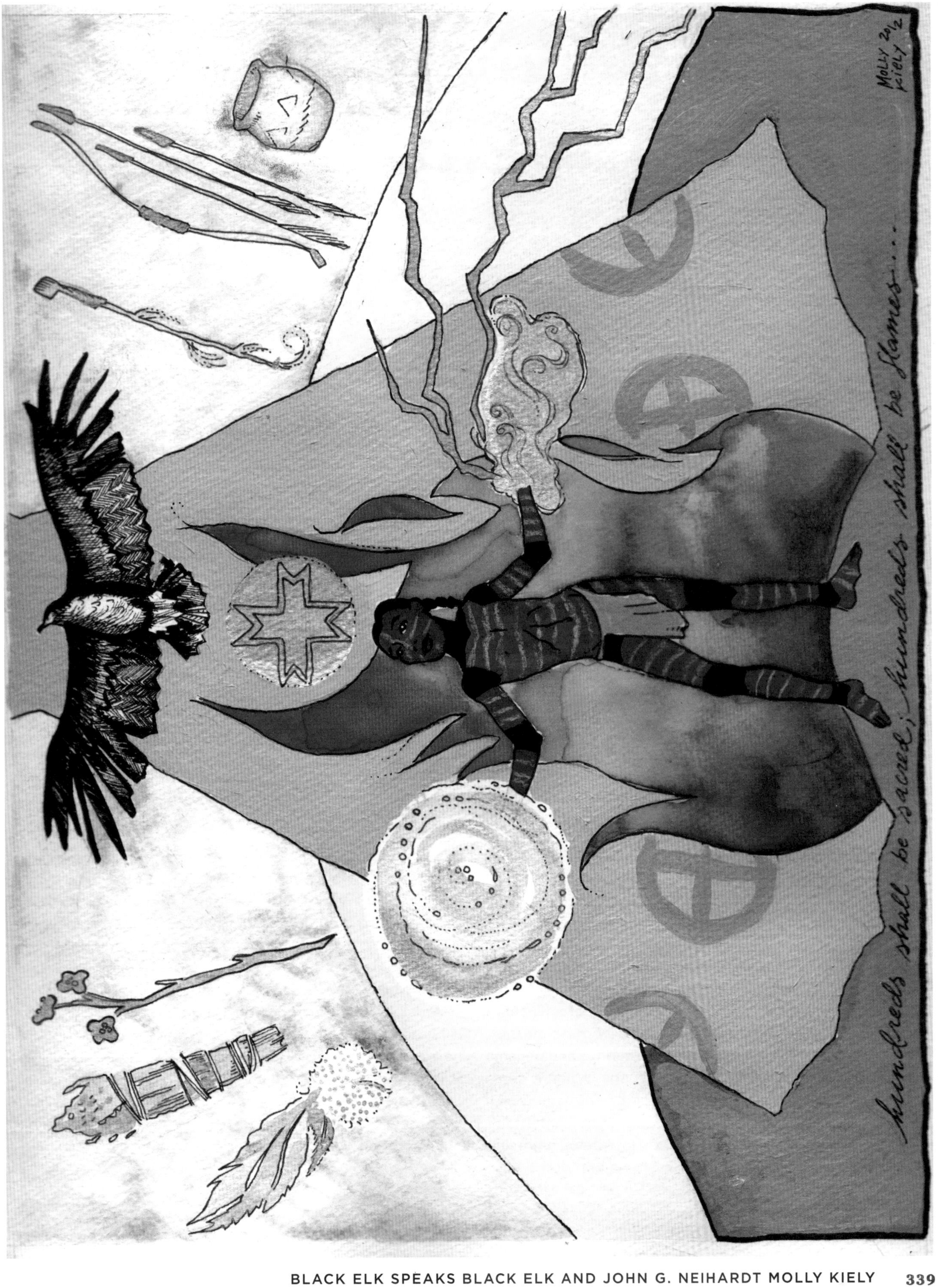
MOLLY KIELY 2012
hundreds shall be sacred; hundreds shall be flames . . .

"Strange Fruit" (a.k.a. "Bitter Fruit")

Lewis Allan

ART/ADAPTATION BY **John Linton Roberson**

THE SIGNATURE SONG OF THE LEGENDARY BILLIE Holiday, "Strange Fruit" is one of the all-time classics of jazz. It started as a poem, "Bitter Fruit," published in a union magazine, *The New York Teacher*, in early 1937. Abraham Meeropol (using the pseudonym Lewis Allan), a high-school teacher in the Bronx—and a member of the Communist Party who was surveilled by the FBI for decades—wrote the poem after being haunted by a photograph of a lynching. He was also a composer, and soon set his words to music; it was performed at various left-wing gatherings and became one of the earliest political protest songs. When it came to the attention of Holiday, she started performing it, with great trepidation, at the end of her shows at Manhattan's Café Society, the country's first racially integrated nightclub. Her record label, Columbia, refused to let her record it, so it was released on a small indie label, Commodore Records.

The poem/song is remarkable for the way it juxtaposes the beauty of the American South with the atrocities committed there. Even the title itself does this. Apples, pears, oranges, cherries, plums, and other fruit hanging from trees are pretty and enticing. But a horrible "fruit" also dangles from these trees—the twisted, broken bodies of black people lynched by mobs. Line after line reinforces this contradiction; for example, the smell of magnolia trees is followed by the "smell of burning flesh."

Artist John Linton Roberson has captured this dichotomy in his adaptation. John lives on the West Coast now, though he was born and raised in Charleston, South Carolina: "My family goes back to 1800 and used to have money and be landowners. They owned plantations and at least one was a Confederate officer. So my family has a lot of karma to work off." Adapting "Strange Fruit" is part of paying off this debt.

SOURCE

Margolick, David. *Strange Fruit: The Biography of a Song*. New York: Ecco Press (HarperCollins), 2001.

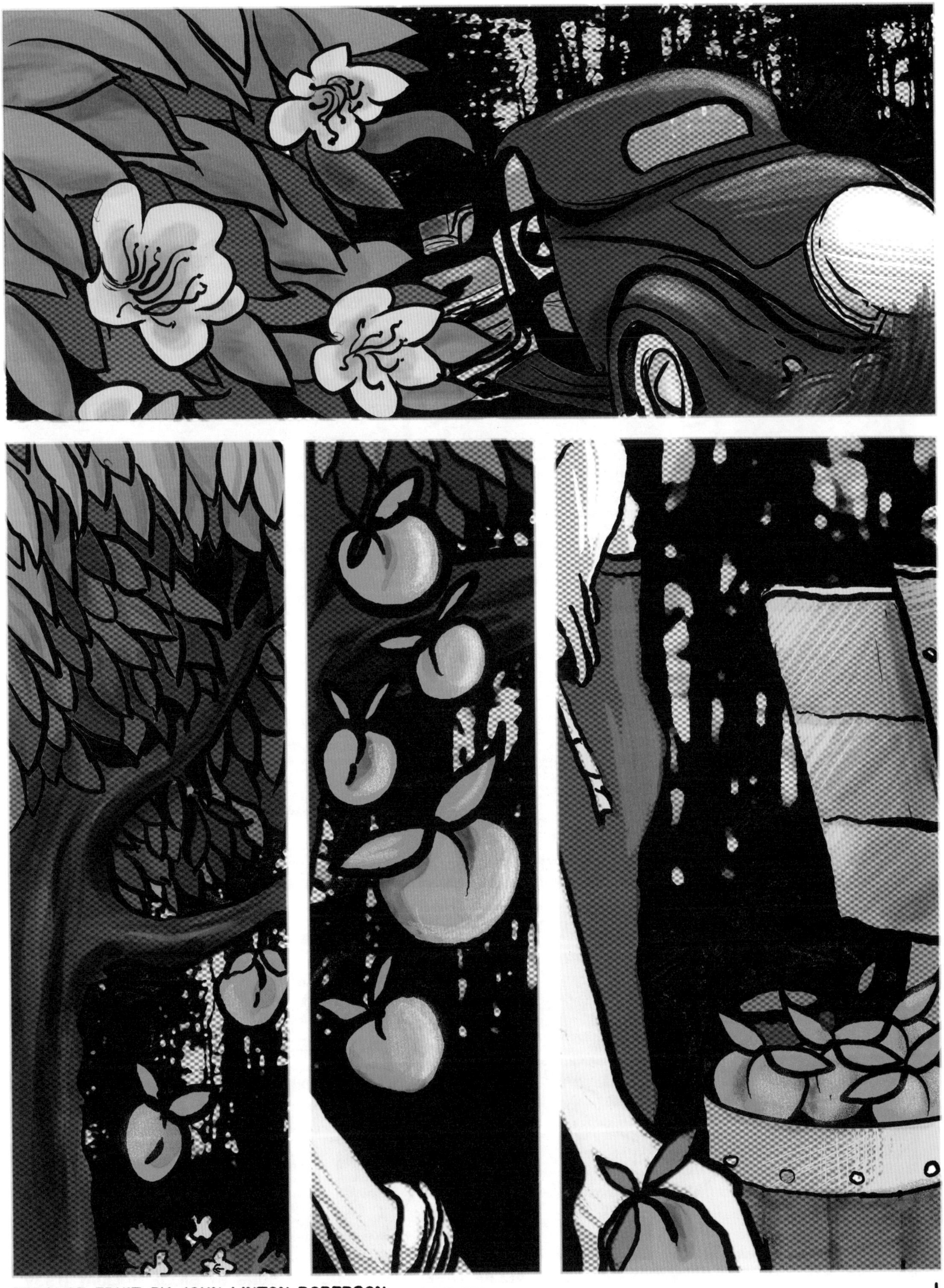

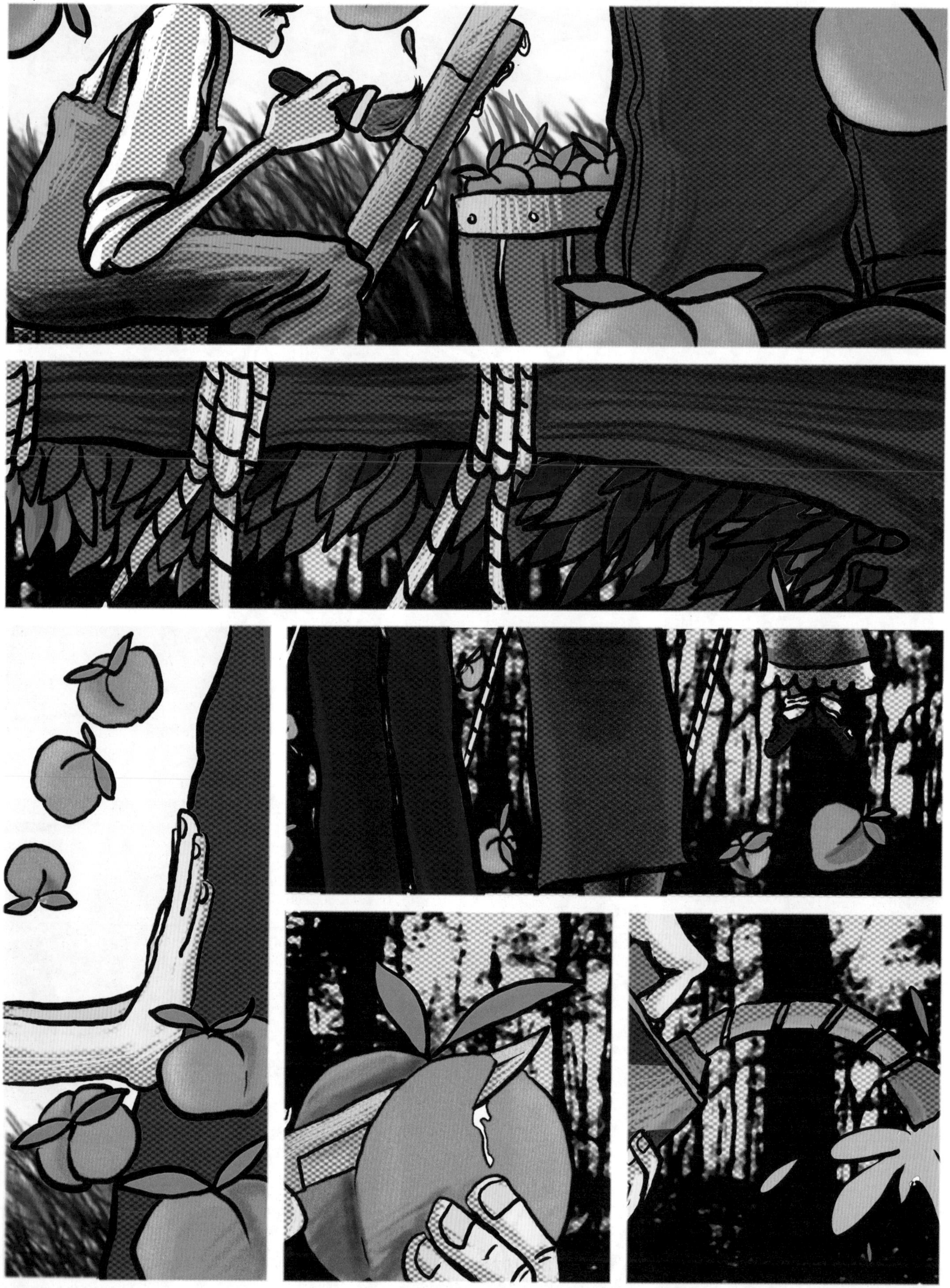

INTERPRETATION OF THE POEM/SONG BY LEWIS ALLAN (ABEL MEEROPOL) AS SUNG BY BILLIE HOLIDAY (1939)

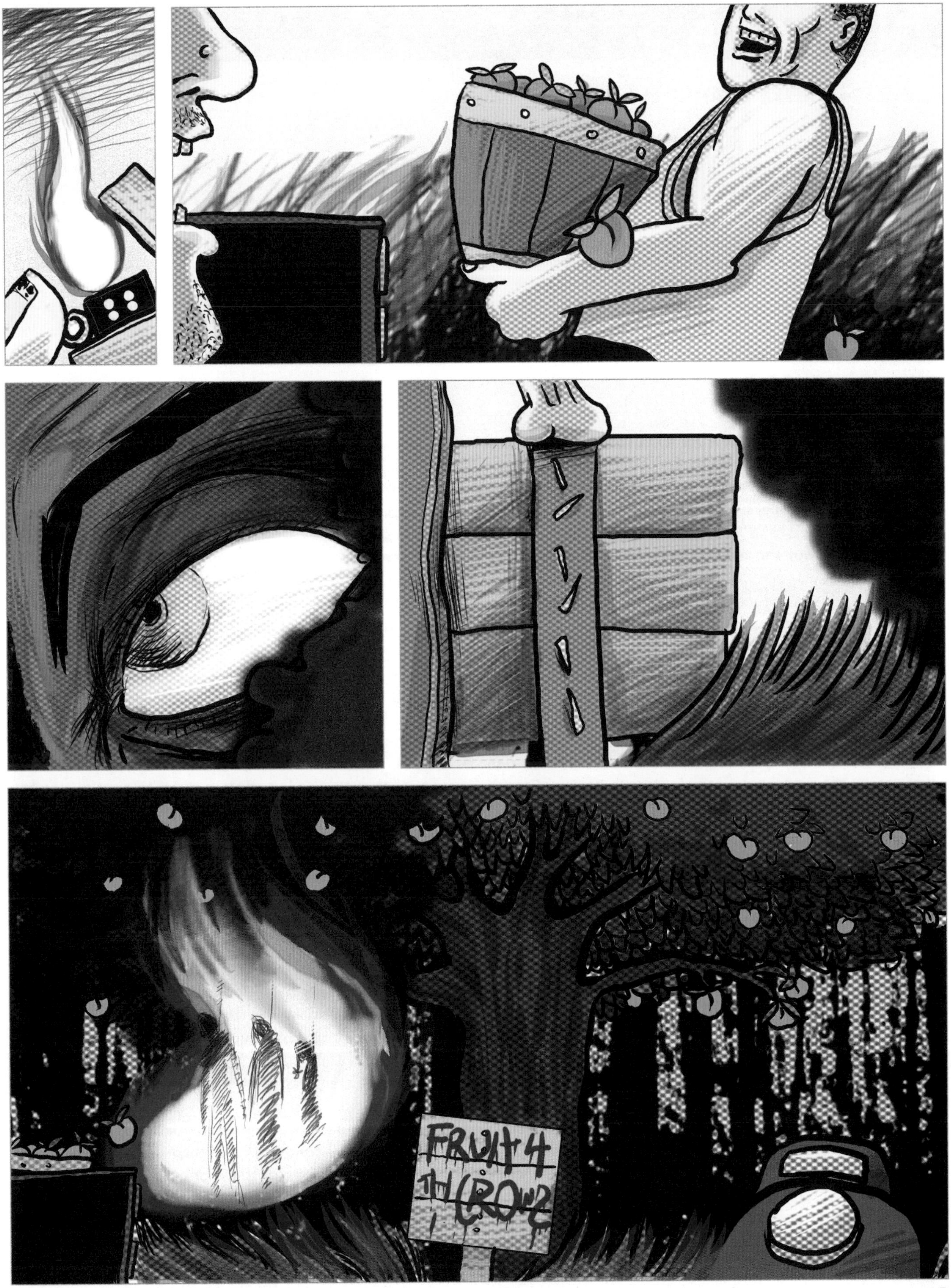
FRUIT 4
TH CROWZ

THE END

Nausea

Jean-Paul Sartre

ART/ADAPTATION BY **Robert Crumb**

THE PHILOSOPHY KNOWN AS EXISTENTIALISM WAS formally created and labeled by French superstar philosopher Jean-Paul Sartre. It had its forerunners, its supporters, and its fellow travellers, but really, Sartre's the guy. Trying to truly understand Existentialism, much less explain it, is daunting, but the oversimplified gist is that—as the name implies—we exist. That's all we can really say for sure. There's no reason we exist; there's no "meaning" to life. We're here. That's it. You cannot look outward for meaning, and you cannot look inward. You can't look to the past or to the future. You will not find meaning anywhere. Perhaps— and that's a big *perhaps*—you could maybe possibly give it your own meaning from moment to moment.

Sartre's 1938 novel in the form of a diary follows the existential crisis of Antoine Roquentin, a reclusive historian working on the biography of an eighteenth-century French aristocrat. Roquentin first becomes overwhelmed by the physical presences of the inanimate objects around him (it's hard to explain), and he increasingly realizes that his life has no inherent meaning, filling him with feelings of dread, anxiety, and disgust that cause nausea.

Most people reading this will probably be familiar with Robert Crumb, but for you others: he's a living legend, probably the most famous, influential, and controversial artist in comics, especially the alternative/underground wing. Nearly everything he's ever drawn or doodled has been lavishly published. Even his sketchbooks, from 1964 to 2011, have been published in twelve beautiful hardcover volumes, totaling 2,700 pages, in two boxed sets retailing for $1,000 each. (Speaking of which, Crumb bought his home in the south of France by giving the owner some of his original sketchbooks.)

Interestingly, his adaptation of part of *Nausea* remains one of his lesser-known works. To my knowledge, it has never been reprinted after originally appearing in the third issue of Crumb's comic series *Hup* in 1989. That might be because Crumb hand-lettered it in the original French.

In the scene here, Crumb's Roquentin looks an awful lot like Sartre as he has lunch with "the Self-Taught Man" (who looks a bit like Crumb himself), a local autodidact who's out to read every book in the local library. At first, Sartre is glad to see Crumb . . . er, I mean, Roquentin is glad to see the Self-Taught Man, feeling some need for human interaction. The Self-Taught Man mentions having been held as a prisoner of war during World War I, but when Roquentin asks him about it, the Self-Taught Man stares at him "with prodigious intensity." Roquentin looks around at the other patrons, scoffing at the farce they're all engaged in, so wrapped up in their personal difficulties that they don't realize that they exist. But Roquentin knows they exist, and he knows that he exists. He laughs out loud, and the Self-Taught Man asks why. Roquentin replies that everyone is eating in order to continue existing, but there is no reason for existence. The Self-Taught Man believes there is a reason: humanity. He claims that his experience in the POW camp taught him to love all people, to admire them, to feel that helping the human race is a worthy end in itself. Roquentin dislikes this philosophy of humanism, feeling that it's condescending and, more to the point, that it misses the fact that there simply is no reason for existence. You actually love humanity too, the Self-Taught Man tells him—we both do; we just say it differently. Something inside Roquentin snaps. Roquentin thinks: "People. You must love people. Men are admirable. I want to vomit—and suddenly there it is: the Nausea." He grasps a knife, thinks about the fact that it exists. Then he thinks about plunging it into the Self-Taught Man's eye. Everyone around him gets nervous—between his smoldering silence and his fondling of a sharp knife—so he leaves, noisily tossing the knife onto his plate. (To read the entire scene in English, look for Roquentin's journal entry labeled "Wednesday," starting on page 103 of the Lloyd Alexander translation published by New Directions.)

344

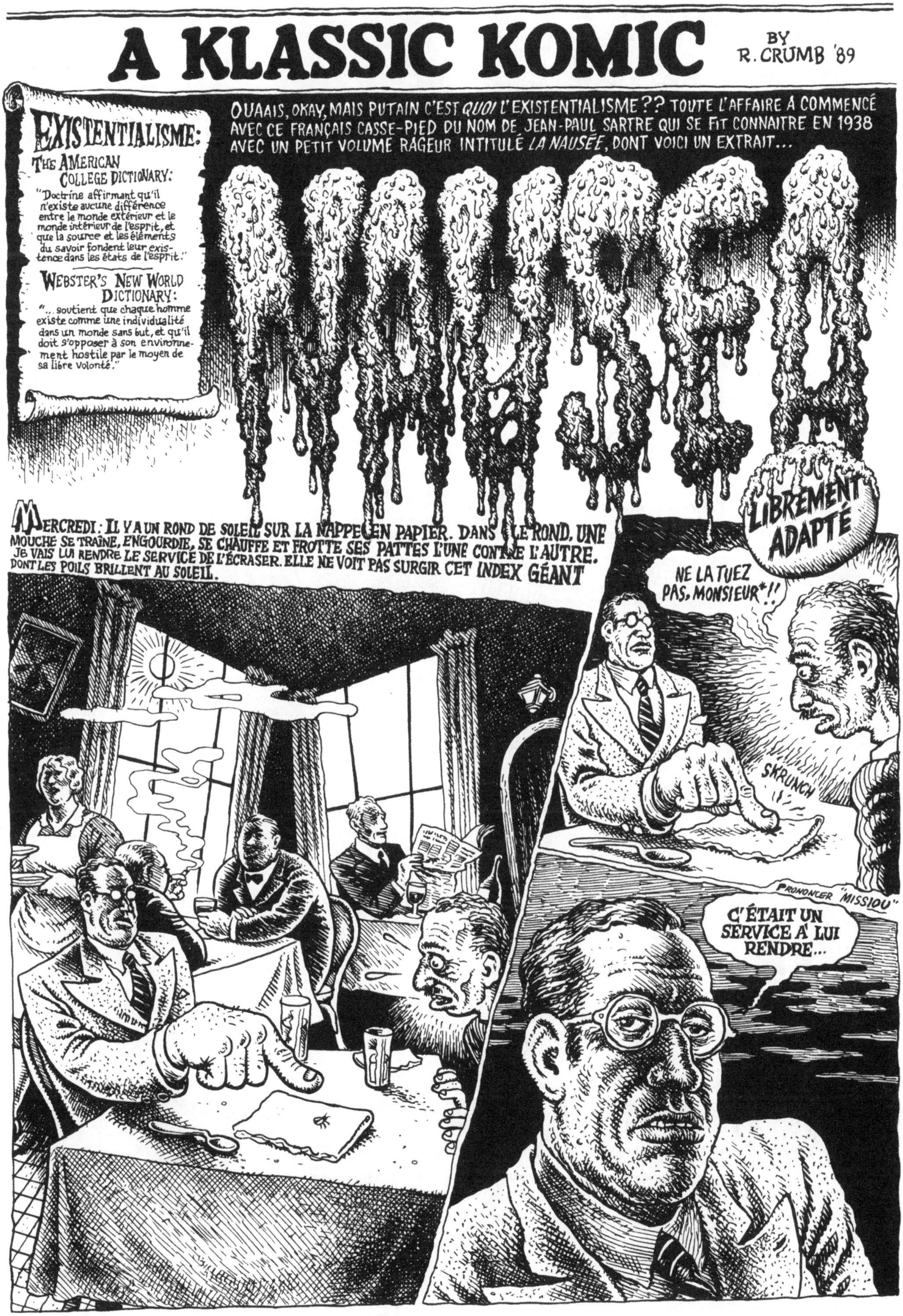
A KLASSIC KOMIC
BY R. CRUMB '89
EXISTENTIALISME:
THE AMERICAN COLLEGE DICTIONARY:
"Doctrine affirmant qu'il n'existe aucune différence entre le monde extérieur et le monde intérieur de l'esprit, et que la source et les éléments du savoir fondent leur existence dans les états de l'esprit."
WEBSTER'S NEW WORLD DICTIONARY:
"... soutient que chaque homme existe comme une individualité dans un monde sans but, et qu'il doit s'opposer à son environnement hostile par le moyen de sa libre volonté."
OUAAIS, OKAY, MAIS PUTAIN C'EST QUOI L'EXISTENTIALISME?? TOUTE L'AFFAIRE A COMMENCÉ AVEC CE FRANÇAIS CASSE-PIED DU NOM DE JEAN-PAUL SARTRE QUI SE FIT CONNAITRE EN 1938 AVEC UN PETIT VOLUME RAGEUR INTITULÉ LA NAUSÉE, DONT VOICI UN EXTRAIT...
LIBREMENT ADAPTÉ
MERCREDI : IL Y A UN ROND DE SOLEIL SUR LA NAPPE EN PAPIER. DANS LE ROND, UNE MOUCHE SE TRAÎNE, ENGOURDIE, SE CHAUFFE ET FROTTE SES PATTES L'UNE CONTRE L'AUTRE. JE VAIS LUI RENDRE LE SERVICE DE L'ÉCRASER. ELLE NE VOIT PAS SURGIR CET INDEX GÉANT DONT LES POILS BRILLENT AU SOLEIL.
NE LA TUEZ PAS, MONSIEUR*!!
SKRUNCH
*PRONONCER "MISSIOU"
C'ÉTAIT UN SERVICE À LUI RENDRE...

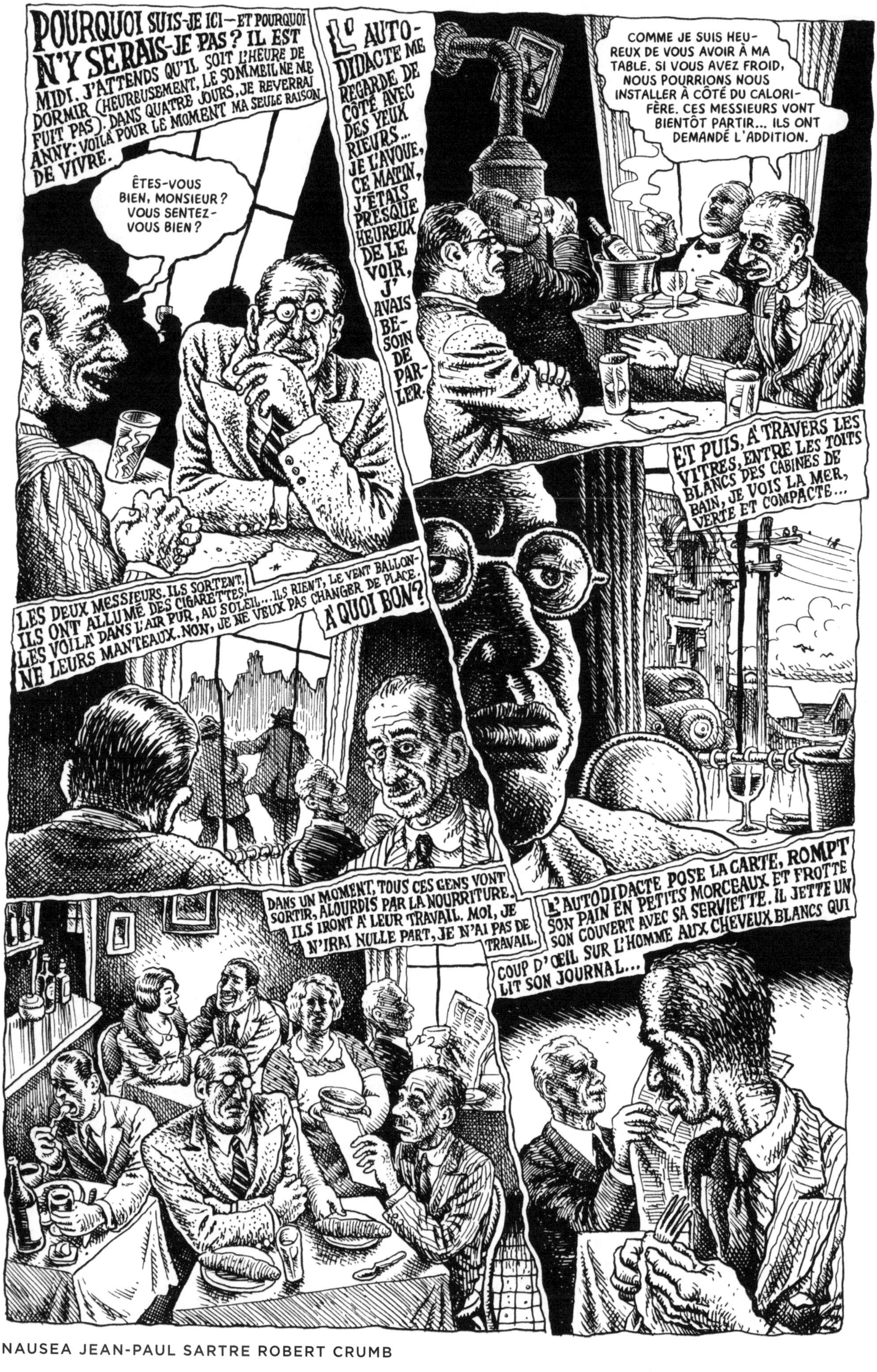
POURQUOI SUIS-JE ICI — ET POURQUOI N'Y SERAIS-JE PAS? IL EST MIDI. J'ATTENDS QU'IL SOIT L'HEURE DE DORMIR (HEUREUSEMENT, LE SOMMEIL NE ME FUIT PAS). DANS QUATRE JOURS, JE REVERRAI ANNY: VOILÀ POUR LE MOMENT MA SEULE RAISON DE VIVRE.
ÊTES-VOUS BIEN, MONSIEUR? VOUS SENTEZ-VOUS BIEN?
L'AUTODIDACTE ME REGARDE DE CÔTÉ AVEC DES YEUX RIEURS... JE L'AVOUE, CE MATIN, J'ÉTAIS PRESQUE HEUREUX DE LE VOIR, J'AVAIS BESOIN DE PARLER.
COMME JE SUIS HEUREUX DE VOUS AVOIR À MA TABLE. SI VOUS AVEZ FROID, NOUS POURRIONS NOUS INSTALLER À CÔTÉ DU CALORIFÈRE. CES MESSIEURS VONT BIENTÔT PARTIR... ILS ONT DEMANDÉ L'ADDITION.
ET PUIS, À TRAVERS LES VITRES, ENTRE LES TOITS BLANCS DES CABINES DE BAIN, JE VOIS LA MER, VERTE ET COMPACTE...
LES DEUX MESSIEURS. ILS SORTENT, ILS ONT ALLUMÉ DES CIGARETTES, LES VOILÀ DANS L'AIR PUR, AU SOLEIL... ILS RIENT, LE VENT BALLONNE LEURS MANTEAUX. NON, JE NE VEUX PAS CHANGER DE PLACE.
À QUOI BON?
DANS UN MOMENT, TOUS CES GENS VONT SORTIR, ALOURDIS PAR LA NOURRITURE. ILS IRONT À LEUR TRAVAIL. MOI, JE N'IRAI NULLE PART, JE N'AI PAS DE TRAVAIL.
L'AUTODIDACTE POSE LA CARTE, ROMPT SON PAIN EN PETITS MORCEAUX ET FROTTE SON COUVERT AVEC SA SERVIETTE. IL JETTE UN COUP D'ŒIL SUR L'HOMME AUX CHEVEUX BLANCS QUI LIT SON JOURNAL...

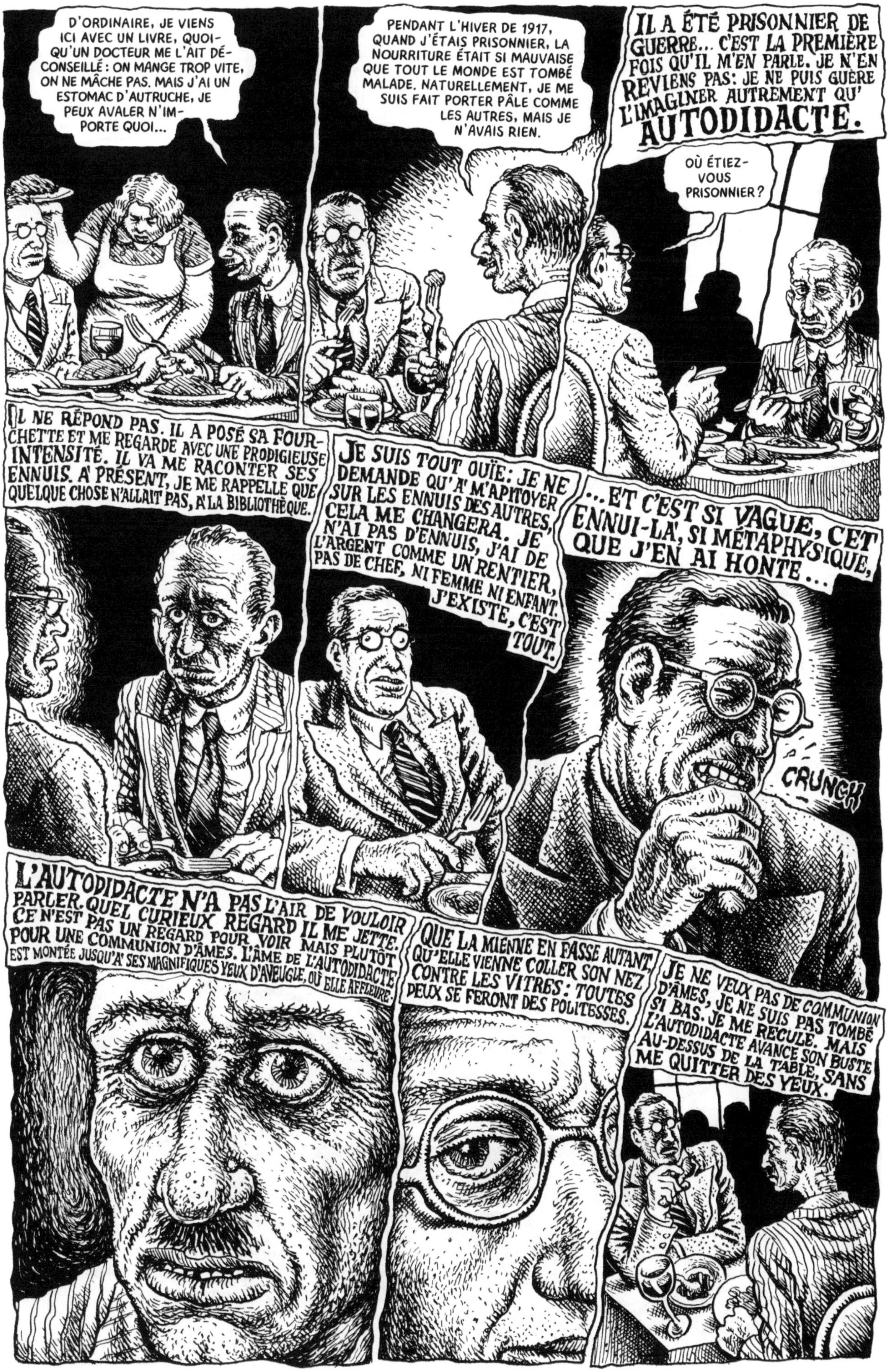
D'ORDINAIRE, JE VIENS ICI AVEC UN LIVRE, QUOIQU'UN DOCTEUR ME L'AIT DÉCONSEILLÉ : ON MANGE TROP VITE, ON NE MÂCHE PAS. MAIS J'AI UN ESTOMAC D'AUTRUCHE, JE PEUX AVALER N'IMPORTE QUOI...
PENDANT L'HIVER DE 1917, QUAND J'ÉTAIS PRISONNIER, LA NOURRITURE ÉTAIT SI MAUVAISE QUE TOUT LE MONDE EST TOMBÉ MALADE. NATURELLEMENT, JE ME SUIS FAIT PORTER PÂLE COMME LES AUTRES, MAIS JE N'AVAIS RIEN.
IL A ÉTÉ PRISONNIER DE GUERRE... C'EST LA PREMIÈRE FOIS QU'IL M'EN PARLE. JE N'EN REVIENS PAS: JE NE PUIS GUÈRE L'IMAGINER AUTREMENT QU'AUTODIDACTE.
OÙ ÉTIEZ-VOUS PRISONNIER ?
IL NE RÉPOND PAS. IL A POSÉ SA FOURCHETTE ET ME REGARDE AVEC UNE PRODIGIEUSE INTENSITÉ. IL VA ME RACONTER SES ENNUIS. À PRÉSENT, JE ME RAPPELLE QUE QUELQUE CHOSE N'ALLAIT PAS, À LA BIBLIOTHÈQUE.
JE SUIS TOUT OUÏE: JE NE DEMANDE QU'À M'APITOYER SUR LES ENNUIS DES AUTRES, CELA ME CHANGERA. JE N'AI PAS D'ENNUIS, J'AI DE L'ARGENT COMME UN RENTIER, PAS DE CHEF, NI FEMME NI ENFANT. J'EXISTE, C'EST TOUT.
...ET C'EST SI VAGUE, CET ENNUI-LÀ, SI MÉTAPHYSIQUE, QUE J'EN AI HONTE...
CRUNCH
L'AUTODIDACTE N'A PAS L'AIR DE VOULOIR PARLER. QUEL CURIEUX REGARD IL ME JETTE. CE N'EST PAS UN REGARD POUR VOIR MAIS PLUTÔT POUR UNE COMMUNION D'ÂMES. L'ÂME DE L'AUTODIDACTE EST MONTÉE JUSQU'À SES MAGNIFIQUES YEUX D'AVEUGLE, OÙ ELLE AFFLEURE.
QUE LA MIENNE EN FASSE AUTANT, QU'ELLE VIENNE COLLER SON NEZ CONTRE LES VITRES: TOUTES DEUX SE FERONT DES POLITESSES.
JE NE VEUX PAS DE COMMUNION D'ÂMES, JE NE SUIS PAS TOMBÉ SI BAS. JE ME RECULE. MAIS L'AUTODIDACTE AVANCE SON BUSTE AU-DESSUS DE LA TABLE, SANS ME QUITTER DES YEUX.

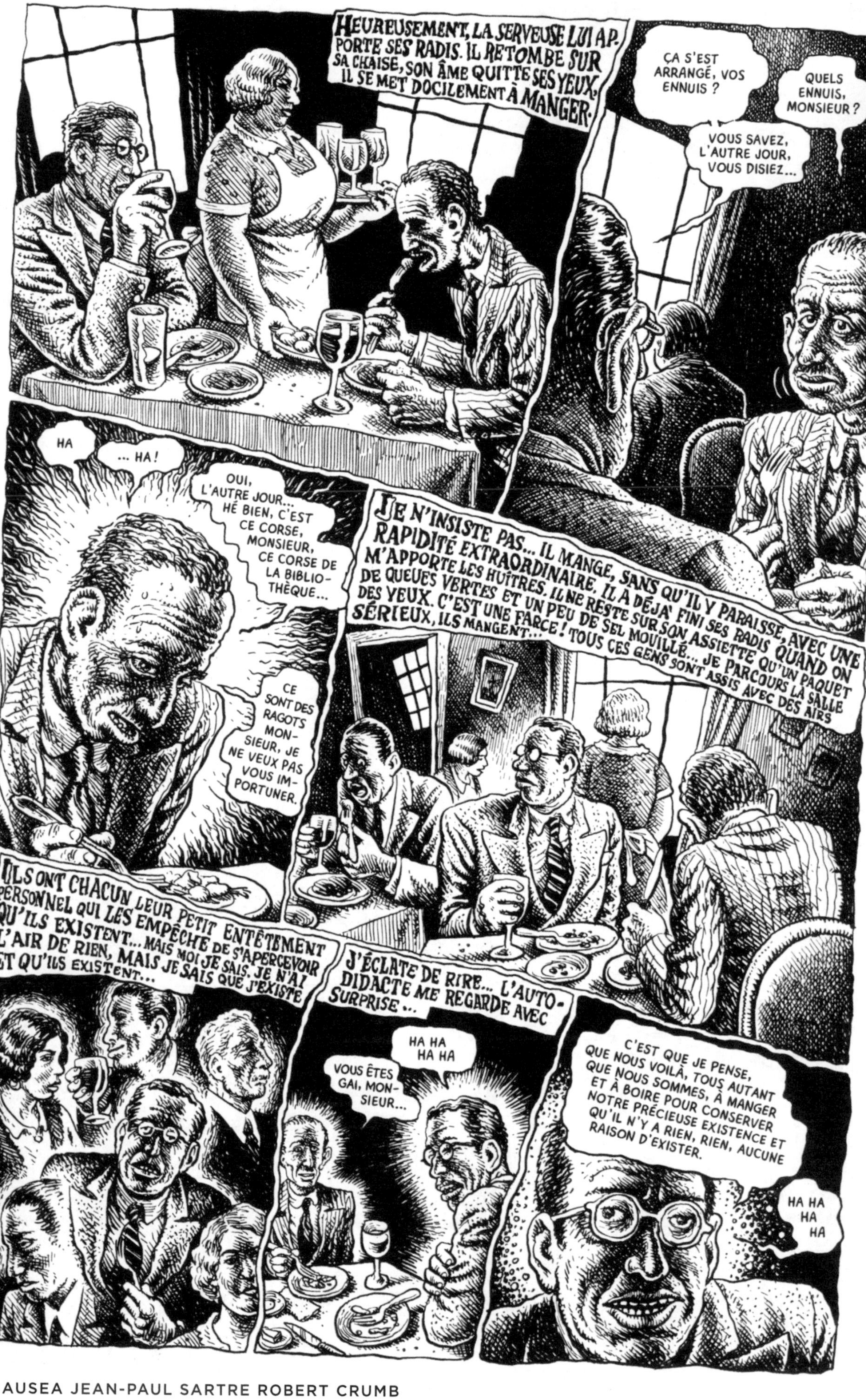
HEUREUSEMENT, LA SERVEUSE LUI AP-PORTE SES RADIS. IL RETOMBE SUR SA CHAISE, SON ÂME QUITTE SES YEUX, IL SE MET DOCILEMENT À MANGER.
ÇA S'EST ARRANGÉ, VOS ENNUIS ?
QUELS ENNUIS, MONSIEUR ?
VOUS SAVEZ, L'AUTRE JOUR, VOUS DISIEZ...
HA
... HA !
OUI, L'AUTRE JOUR... HÉ BIEN, C'EST CE CORSE, MONSIEUR, CE CORSE DE LA BIBLIO-THÈQUE...
CE SONT DES RAGOTS MON-SIEUR, JE NE VEUX PAS VOUS IM-PORTUNER.
JE N'INSISTE PAS... IL MANGE, SANS QU'IL Y PARAISSE, AVEC UNE RAPIDITÉ EXTRAORDINAIRE, IL A DÉJÀ FINI SES RADIS QUAND ON M'APPORTE LES HUÎTRES. IL NE RESTE SUR SON ASSIETTE QU'UN PAQUET DE QUEUES VERTES ET UN PEU DE SEL MOUILLÉ... JE PARCOURS LA SALLE DES YEUX. C'EST UNE FARCE ! TOUS CES GENS SONT ASSIS AVEC DES AIRS SÉRIEUX, ILS MANGENT...
ILS ONT CHACUN LEUR PETIT ENTÊTEMENT PERSONNEL QUI LES EMPÊCHE DE S'APERCEVOIR QU'ILS EXISTENT... MAIS MOI JE SAIS. JE N'AI L'AIR DE RIEN, MAIS JE SAIS QUE J'EXISTE ET QU'ILS EXISTENT...
J'ÉCLATE DE RIRE... L'AUTO-DIDACTE ME REGARDE AVEC SURPRISE...
HA HA HA HA
VOUS ÊTES GAI, MON-SIEUR...
C'EST QUE JE PENSE, QUE NOUS VOILÀ, TOUS AUTANT QUE NOUS SOMMES, À MANGER ET À BOIRE POUR CONSERVER NOTRE PRÉCIEUSE EXISTENCE ET QU'IL N'Y A RIEN, RIEN, AUCUNE RAISON D'EXISTER.
HA HA HA HA

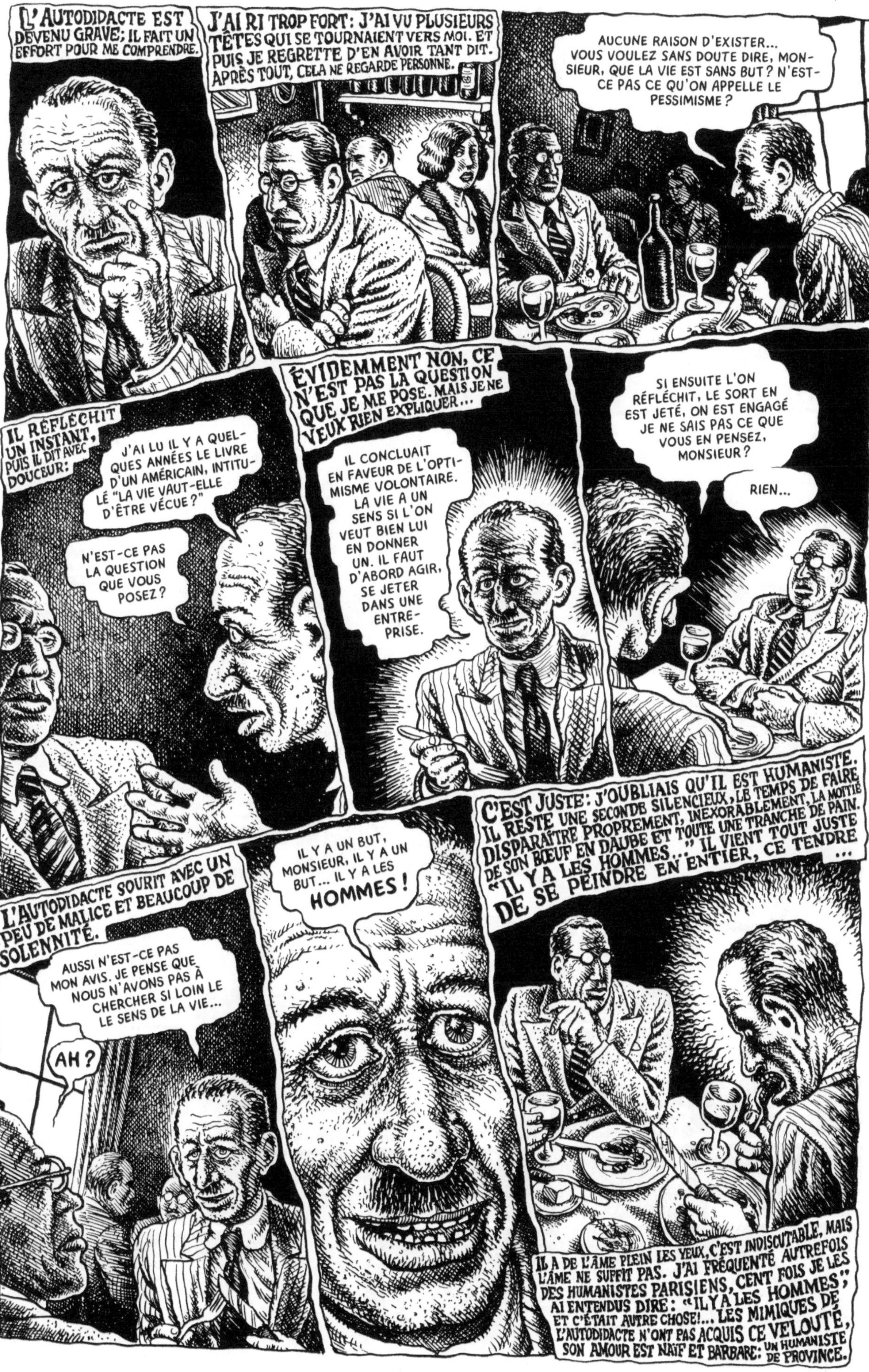
L'AUTODIDACTE EST DEVENU GRAVE; IL FAIT UN EFFORT POUR ME COMPRENDRE.
J'AI RI TROP FORT: J'AI VU PLUSIEURS TÊTES QUI SE TOURNAIENT VERS MOI. ET PUIS JE REGRETTE D'EN AVOIR TANT DIT. APRÈS TOUT, CELA NE REGARDE PERSONNE.
AUCUNE RAISON D'EXISTER... VOUS VOULEZ SANS DOUTE DIRE, MONSIEUR, QUE LA VIE EST SANS BUT? N'EST-CE PAS CE QU'ON APPELLE LE PESSIMISME?
IL RÉFLÉCHIT UN INSTANT, PUIS IL DIT AVEC DOUCEUR:
J'AI LU IL Y A QUELQUES ANNÉES LE LIVRE D'UN AMÉRICAIN, INTITULÉ "LA VIE VAUT-ELLE D'ÊTRE VÉCUE?"
N'EST-CE PAS LA QUESTION QUE VOUS POSEZ?
ÉVIDEMMENT NON, CE N'EST PAS LA QUESTION QUE JE ME POSE. MAIS JE NE VEUX RIEN EXPLIQUER...
IL CONCLUAIT EN FAVEUR DE L'OPTIMISME VOLONTAIRE. LA VIE A UN SENS SI L'ON VEUT BIEN LUI EN DONNER UN. IL FAUT D'ABORD AGIR, SE JETER DANS UNE ENTREPRISE.
SI ENSUITE L'ON RÉFLÉCHIT, LE SORT EN EST JETÉ, ON EST ENGAGÉ JE NE SAIS PAS CE QUE VOUS EN PENSEZ, MONSIEUR?
RIEN...
L'AUTODIDACTE SOURIT AVEC UN PEU DE MALICE ET BEAUCOUP DE SOLENNITÉ.
AUSSI N'EST-CE PAS MON AVIS. JE PENSE QUE NOUS N'AVONS PAS À CHERCHER SI LOIN LE SENS DE LA VIE...
AH?
IL Y A UN BUT, MONSIEUR, IL Y A UN BUT... IL Y A LES HOMMES!
C'EST JUSTE: J'OUBLIAIS QU'IL EST HUMANISTE. IL RESTE UNE SECONDE SILENCIEUX, LE TEMPS DE FAIRE DISPARAÎTRE PROPREMENT, INEXORABLEMENT, LA MOITIÉ DE SON BŒUF EN DAUBE ET TOUTE UNE TRANCHE DE PAIN. "IL Y A LES HOMMES..." IL VIENT TOUT JUSTE DE SE PEINDRE EN ENTIER, CE TENDRE...
IL A DE L'ÂME PLEIN LES YEUX, C'EST INDISCUTABLE, MAIS L'ÂME NE SUFFIT PAS. J'AI FRÉQUENTÉ AUTREFOIS DES HUMANISTES PARISIENS, CENT FOIS JE LES AI ENTENDUS DIRE: "IL Y A LES HOMMES"; ET C'ÉTAIT AUTRE CHOSE!... LES MIMIQUES DE L'AUTODIDACTE N'ONT PAS ACQUIS CE VELOUTÉ, SON AMOUR EST NAÏF ET BARBARE: UN HUMANISTE DE PROVINCE.

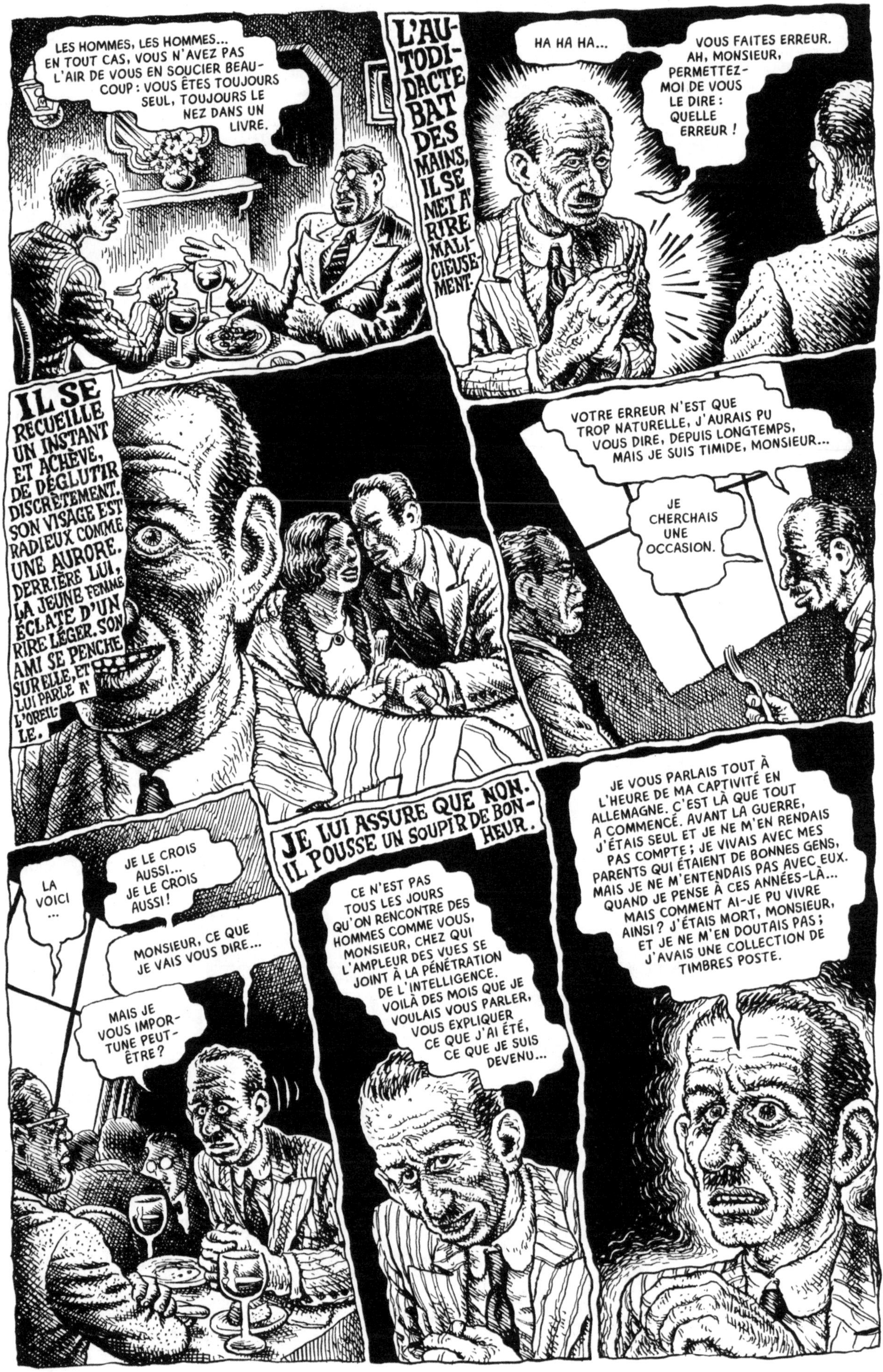

LES HOMMES, LES HOMMES... EN TOUT CAS, VOUS N'AVEZ PAS L'AIR DE VOUS EN SOUCIER BEAUCOUP : VOUS ÊTES TOUJOURS SEUL, TOUJOURS LE NEZ DANS UN LIVRE.
L'AUTODIDACTE BAT DES MAINS, IL SE MET À RIRE MALICIEUSEMENT.
HA HA HA...
VOUS FAITES ERREUR. AH, MONSIEUR, PERMETTEZ-MOI DE VOUS LE DIRE : QUELLE ERREUR !
IL SE RECUEILLE UN INSTANT ET ACHÈVE, DE DÉGLUTIR DISCRÈTEMENT. SON VISAGE EST RADIEUX COMME UNE AURORE. DERRIÈRE LUI, LA JEUNE FEMME ÉCLATE D'UN RIRE LÉGER. SON AMI SE PENCHE SUR ELLE, ET LUI PARLE À L'OREILLE.
VOTRE ERREUR N'EST QUE TROP NATURELLE, J'AURAIS PU VOUS DIRE, DEPUIS LONGTEMPS, MAIS JE SUIS TIMIDE, MONSIEUR...
JE CHERCHAIS UNE OCCASION.
LA VOICI ...
JE LE CROIS AUSSI... JE LE CROIS AUSSI!
MONSIEUR, CE QUE JE VAIS VOUS DIRE...
MAIS JE VOUS IMPORTUNE PEUT-ÊTRE?
JE LUI ASSURE QUE NON. IL POUSSE UN SOUPIR DE BONHEUR.
CE N'EST PAS TOUS LES JOURS QU'ON RENCONTRE DES HOMMES COMME VOUS, MONSIEUR, CHEZ QUI L'AMPLEUR DES VUES SE JOINT À LA PÉNÉTRATION DE L'INTELLIGENCE. VOILÀ DES MOIS QUE JE VOULAIS VOUS PARLER, VOUS EXPLIQUER CE QUE J'AI ÉTÉ, CE QUE JE SUIS DEVENU...
JE VOUS PARLAIS TOUT À L'HEURE DE MA CAPTIVITÉ EN ALLEMAGNE. C'EST LÀ QUE TOUT A COMMENCÉ. AVANT LA GUERRE, J'ÉTAIS SEUL ET JE NE M'EN RENDAIS PAS COMPTE ; JE VIVAIS AVEC MES PARENTS QUI ÉTAIENT DE BONNES GENS, MAIS JE NE M'ENTENDAIS PAS AVEC EUX. QUAND JE PENSE À CES ANNÉES-LÀ... MAIS COMMENT AI-JE PU VIVRE AINSI ? J'ÉTAIS MORT, MONSIEUR, ET JE NE M'EN DOUTAIS PAS ; J'AVAIS UNE COLLECTION DE TIMBRES POSTE.

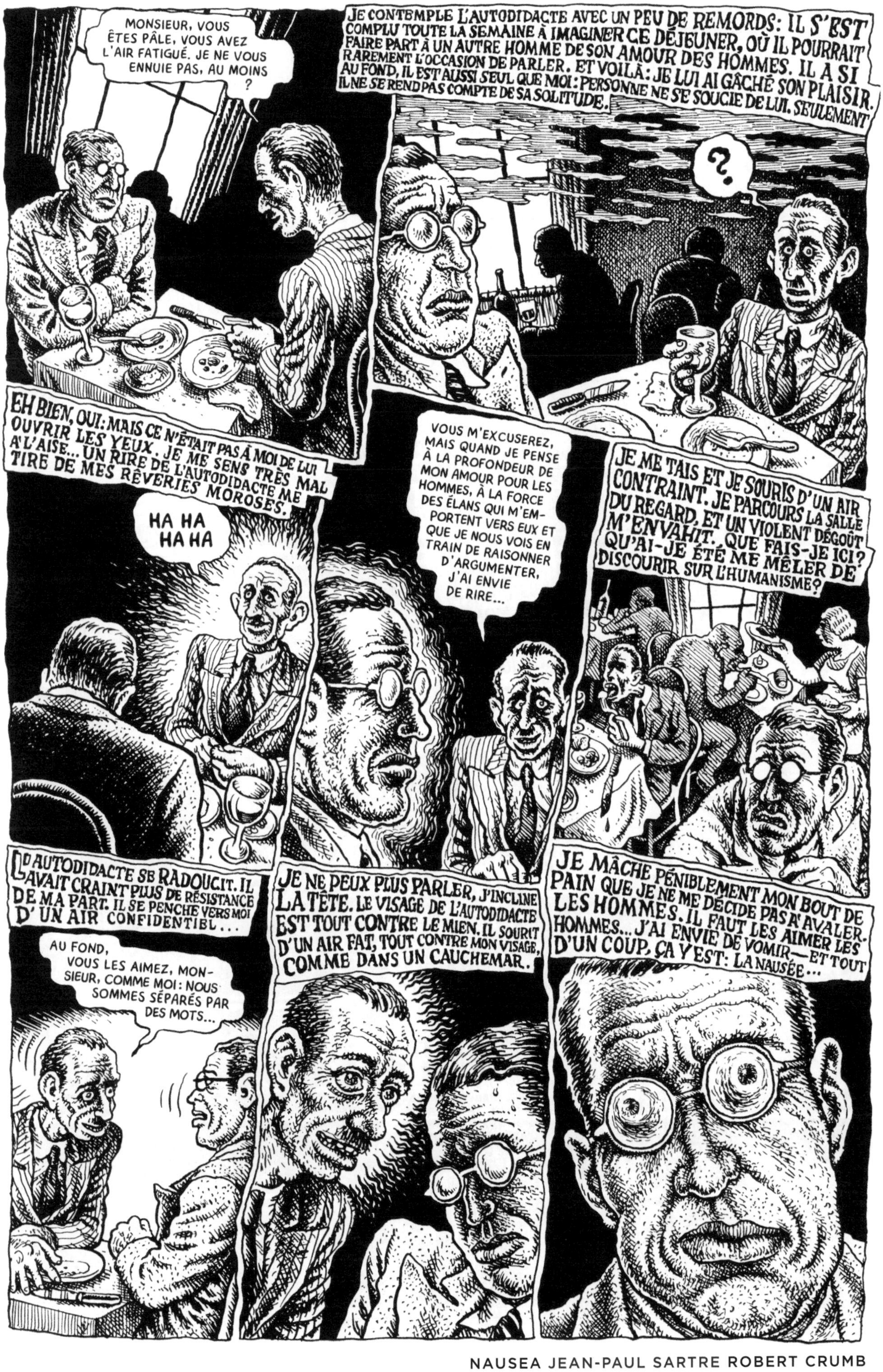
MONSIEUR, VOUS ÊTES PÂLE, VOUS AVEZ L'AIR FATIGUÉ. JE NE VOUS ENNUIE PAS, AU MOINS ?
JE CONTEMPLE L'AUTODIDACTE AVEC UN PEU DE REMORDS: IL S'EST COMPLU TOUTE LA SEMAINE À IMAGINER CE DÉJEUNER, OÙ IL POURRAIT FAIRE PART À UN AUTRE HOMME DE SON AMOUR DES HOMMES. IL A SI RAREMENT L'OCCASION DE PARLER. ET VOILÀ: JE LUI AI GÂCHÉ SON PLAISIR. AU FOND, IL EST AUSSI SEUL QUE MOI: PERSONNE NE SE SOUCIE DE LUI. SEULEMENT IL NE SE REND PAS COMPTE DE SA SOLITUDE.
?
EH BIEN, OUI: MAIS CE N'ÉTAIT PAS À MOI DE LUI OUVRIR LES YEUX. JE ME SENS TRÈS MAL À L'AISE... UN RIRE DE L'AUTODIDACTE ME TIRE DE MES RÊVERIES MOROSES.
HA HA HA HA
VOUS M'EXCUSEREZ, MAIS QUAND JE PENSE À LA PROFONDEUR DE MON AMOUR POUR LES HOMMES, À LA FORCE DES ÉLANS QUI M'EMPORTENT VERS EUX ET QUE JE NOUS VOIS EN TRAIN DE RAISONNER D'ARGUMENTER, J'AI ENVIE DE RIRE...
JE ME TAIS ET JE SOURIS D'UN AIR CONTRAINT. JE PARCOURS LA SALLE DU REGARD, ET UN VIOLENT DÉGOÛT M'ENVAHIT. QUE FAIS-JE ICI? QU'AI-JE ÉTÉ ME MÊLER DE DISCOURIR SUR L'HUMANISME?
L'AUTODIDACTE SE RADOUCIT. IL AVAIT CRAINT PLUS DE RÉSISTANCE DE MA PART. IL SE PENCHE VERS MOI D'UN AIR CONFIDENTIEL...
AU FOND, VOUS LES AIMEZ, MONSIEUR, COMME MOI: NOUS SOMMES SÉPARÉS PAR DES MOTS...
JE NE PEUX PLUS PARLER, J'INCLINE LA TÊTE. LE VISAGE DE L'AUTODIDACTE EST TOUT CONTRE LE MIEN. IL SOURIT D'UN AIR FAT, TOUT CONTRE MON VISAGE, COMME DANS UN CAUCHEMAR.
JE MÂCHE PÉNIBLEMENT MON BOUT DE PAIN QUE JE NE ME DÉCIDE PAS À AVALER. LES HOMMES. IL FAUT LES AIMER LES HOMMES... J'AI ENVIE DE VOMIR— ET TOUT D'UN COUP, ÇA Y EST: LA NAUSÉE...

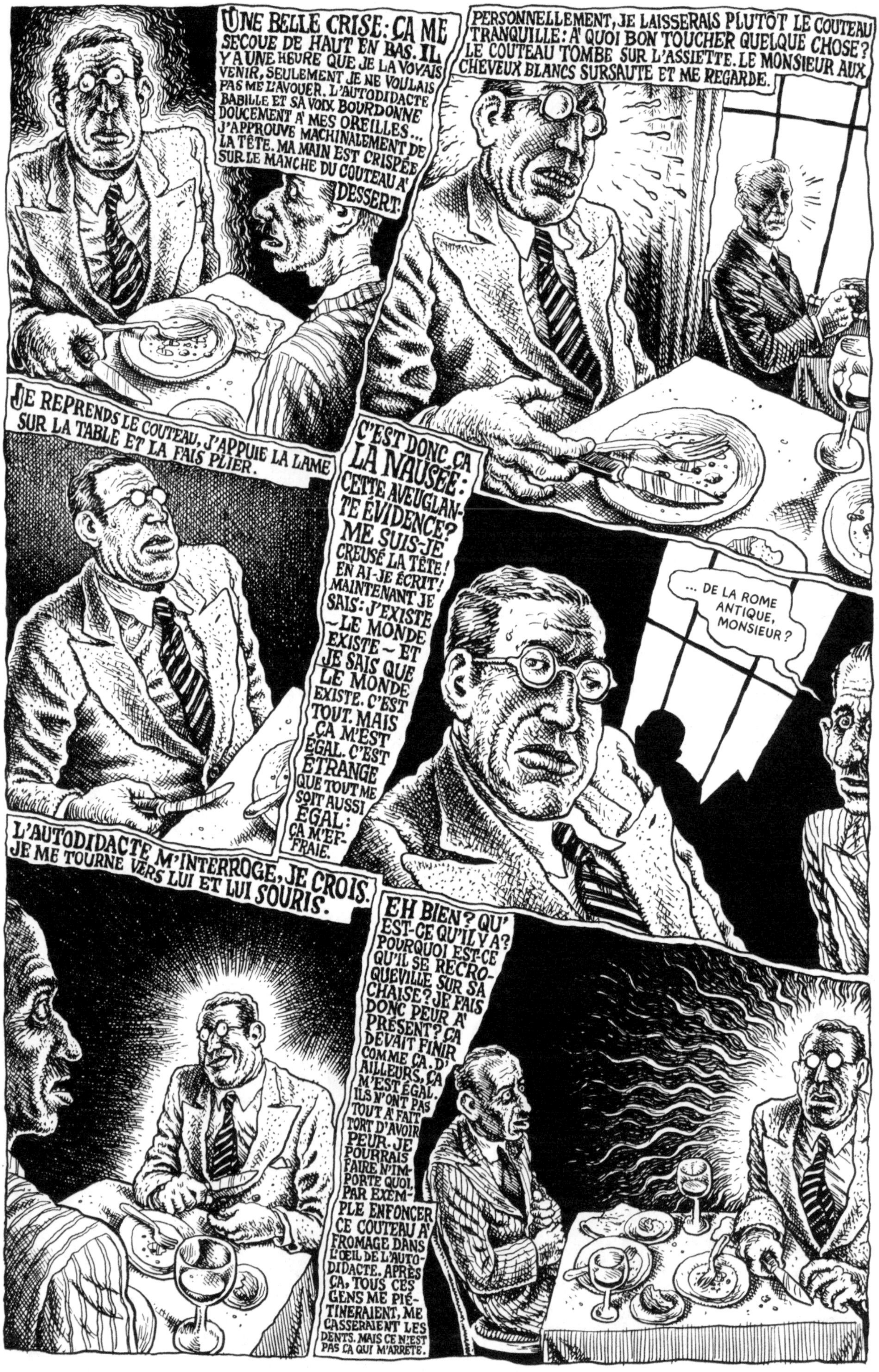
UNE BELLE CRISE: ÇA ME SECOUE DE HAUT EN BAS. IL Y A UNE HEURE QUE JE LA VOYAIS VENIR, SEULEMENT JE NE VOULAIS PAS ME L'AVOUER. L'AUTODIDACTE BABILLE ET SA VOIX BOURDONNE DOUCEMENT À MES OREILLES... J'APPROUVE MACHINALEMENT DE LA TÊTE. MA MAIN EST CRISPÉE SUR LE MANCHE DU COUTEAU À DESSERT.
PERSONNELLEMENT, JE LAISSERAIS PLUTÔT LE COUTEAU TRANQUILLE: À QUOI BON TOUCHER QUELQUE CHOSE? LE COUTEAU TOMBE SUR L'ASSIETTE. LE MONSIEUR AUX CHEVEUX BLANCS SURSAUTE ET ME REGARDE.
JE REPRENDS LE COUTEAU, J'APPUIE LA LAME SUR LA TABLE ET LA FAIS PLIER.
C'EST DONC ÇA LA NAUSÉE: CETTE AVEUGLANTE ÉVIDENCE? ME SUIS-JE CREUSÉ LA TÊTE! EN AI-JE ÉCRIT! MAINTENANT JE SAIS: J'EXISTE ~ LE MONDE EXISTE ~ ET JE SAIS QUE LE MONDE EXISTE. C'EST TOUT. MAIS ÇA M'EST ÉGAL. C'EST ÉTRANGE QUE TOUT ME SOIT AUSSI ÉGAL: ÇA M'EFFRAIE.
... DE LA ROME ANTIQUE, MONSIEUR ?
L'AUTODIDACTE M'INTERROGE, JE CROIS. JE ME TOURNE VERS LUI ET LUI SOURIS.
EH BIEN? QU'EST-CE QU'IL Y A? POURQUOI EST-CE QU'IL SE RECROQUEVILLE SUR SA CHAISE? JE FAIS DONC PEUR À PRÉSENT? ÇA DEVAIT FINIR COMME ÇA. D'AILLEURS, ÇA M'EST ÉGAL. ILS N'ONT PAS TOUT À FAIT TORT D'AVOIR PEUR. JE POURRAIS FAIRE N'IMPORTE QUOI, PAR EXEMPLE ENFONCER CE COUTEAU À FROMAGE DANS L'ŒIL DE L'AUTODIDACTE. APRÈS ÇA, TOUS CES GENS ME PIÉTINERAIENT, ME CASSERAIENT LES DENTS. MAIS CE N'EST PAS ÇA QUI M'ARRÊTE.

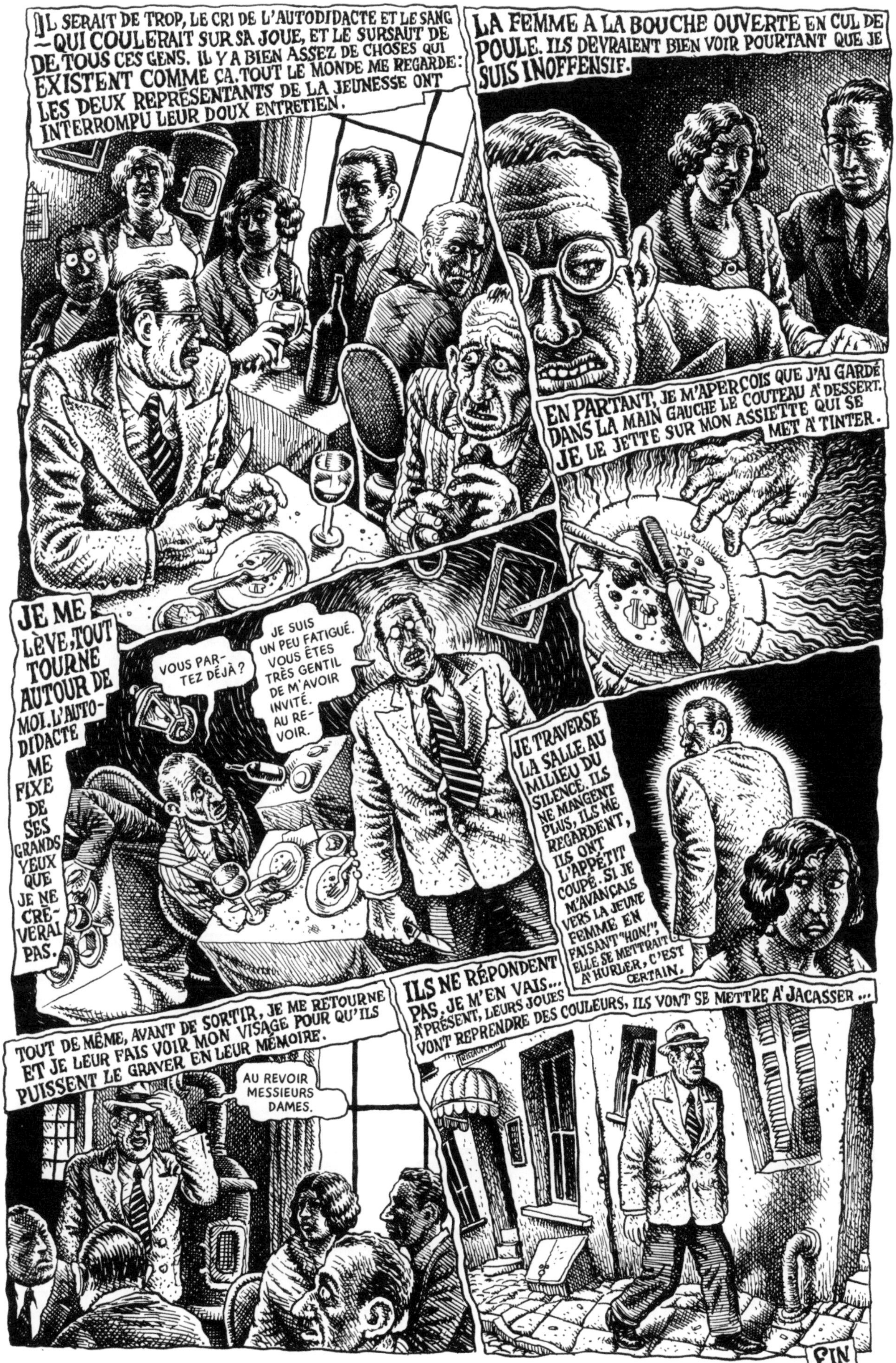
IL SERAIT DE TROP, LE CRI DE L'AUTODIDACTE ET LE SANG QUI COULERAIT SUR SA JOUE, ET LE SURSAUT DE DE TOUS CES GENS. IL Y A BIEN ASSEZ DE CHOSES QUI EXISTENT COMME ÇA. TOUT LE MONDE ME REGARDE: LES DEUX REPRÉSENTANTS DE LA JEUNESSE ONT INTERROMPU LEUR DOUX ENTRETIEN.
LA FEMME A LA BOUCHE OUVERTE EN CUL DE POULE. ILS DEVRAIENT BIEN VOIR POURTANT QUE JE SUIS INOFFENSIF.
EN PARTANT, JE M'APERÇOIS QUE J'AI GARDÉ DANS LA MAIN GAUCHE LE COUTEAU À DESSERT. JE LE JETTE SUR MON ASSIETTE QUI SE MET À TINTER.
JE ME LÈVE, TOUT TOURNE AUTOUR DE MOI. L'AUTODIDACTE ME FIXE DE SES GRANDS YEUX QUE JE NE CRÈVERAI PAS.
VOUS PARTEZ DÉJÀ?
JE SUIS UN PEU FATIGUÉ. VOUS ÊTES TRÈS GENTIL DE M'AVOIR INVITÉ. AU REVOIR.
JE TRAVERSE LA SALLE AU MILIEU DU SILENCE. ILS NE MANGENT PLUS, ILS ME REGARDENT, ILS ONT L'APPÉTIT COUPÉ. SI JE M'AVANÇAIS VERS LA JEUNE FEMME EN FAISANT "HON!", ELLE SE METTRAIT À HURLER, C'EST CERTAIN.
TOUT DE MÊME, AVANT DE SORTIR, JE ME RETOURNE ET JE LEUR FAIS VOIR MON VISAGE POUR QU'ILS PUISSENT LE GRAVER EN LEUR MÉMOIRE.
AU REVOIR MESSIEURS DAMES.
ILS NE RÉPONDENT PAS. JE M'EN VAIS... À PRÉSENT, LEURS JOUES VONT REPRENDRE DES COULEURS, ILS VONT SE METTRE À JACASSER...
FIN

Three Panel Review
Lisa Brown

ATONEMENT by Ian McEwan
I read something I shouldn't have.
World War II.
© 2010 LISA M. BROWN
Now I'm old and I make things up.

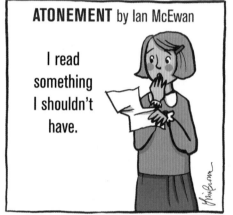

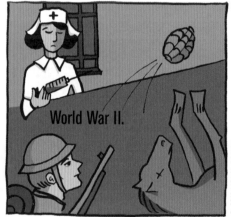

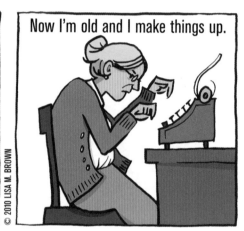

The Grapes of Wrath

John Steinbeck

ART/ADAPTATION BY **Liesbeth De Stercke**

JOHN STEINBECK'S MASTERPIECE WON HIM THE Pulitzer and was the main reason he later scooped up a Nobel. *The Grapes of Wrath* was hugely popular and controversial upon publication in 1939, and has been one of the core books taught in high school and college classes for decades. It's a history lesson, a slice of Americana, a radical political document, and a classic work of lit rolled into one. That said, it's often acknowledged that Steinbeck was no master of prose style or characterization. But what he lacks in finesse he makes up for with heart. This tale of the salt of the earth—heavy with biblical overtones—makes you feel something as you follow the Joads and other displaced Midwestern farming families on their exodus to the promised land of California, where vast, fertile fields ready for harvesting promise good wages and a good life. . . . Except that there's an overabundance of labor, and the corporate farming industry runs the show, violently quashing any attempts at worker organization.

I love the fact that an artist from Belgium has so absolutely, perfectly captured this very American novel. Liesbeth De Stercke employs extremely spare line work to the utmost effect. You can almost taste the dust. The lack of text adds to the already stark, empty feel of the proceedings, as we see Tom Joad—freshly paroled for manslaughter—get a ride to his parents' farm, which, like the rest of Oklahoma, is decimated by drought. He meets up with former preacher Jim Casy (J. C.—a Christ figure) and neighbor Muley Graves, and finds out that the Joads and many others have been forced off the land by the banks and landowners, which often send bulldozers to do the deed. The three men spend the night on the land, hiding from police because they're now technically trespassing. They catch up with the Joad clan at Uncle John's place, where they're picking cotton, and decide to head to California. Muley stays behind, while Ma, Pa, the grandparents, Uncle John, Tom, and his siblings begin their pilgrimage in a beat-up truck. . . .

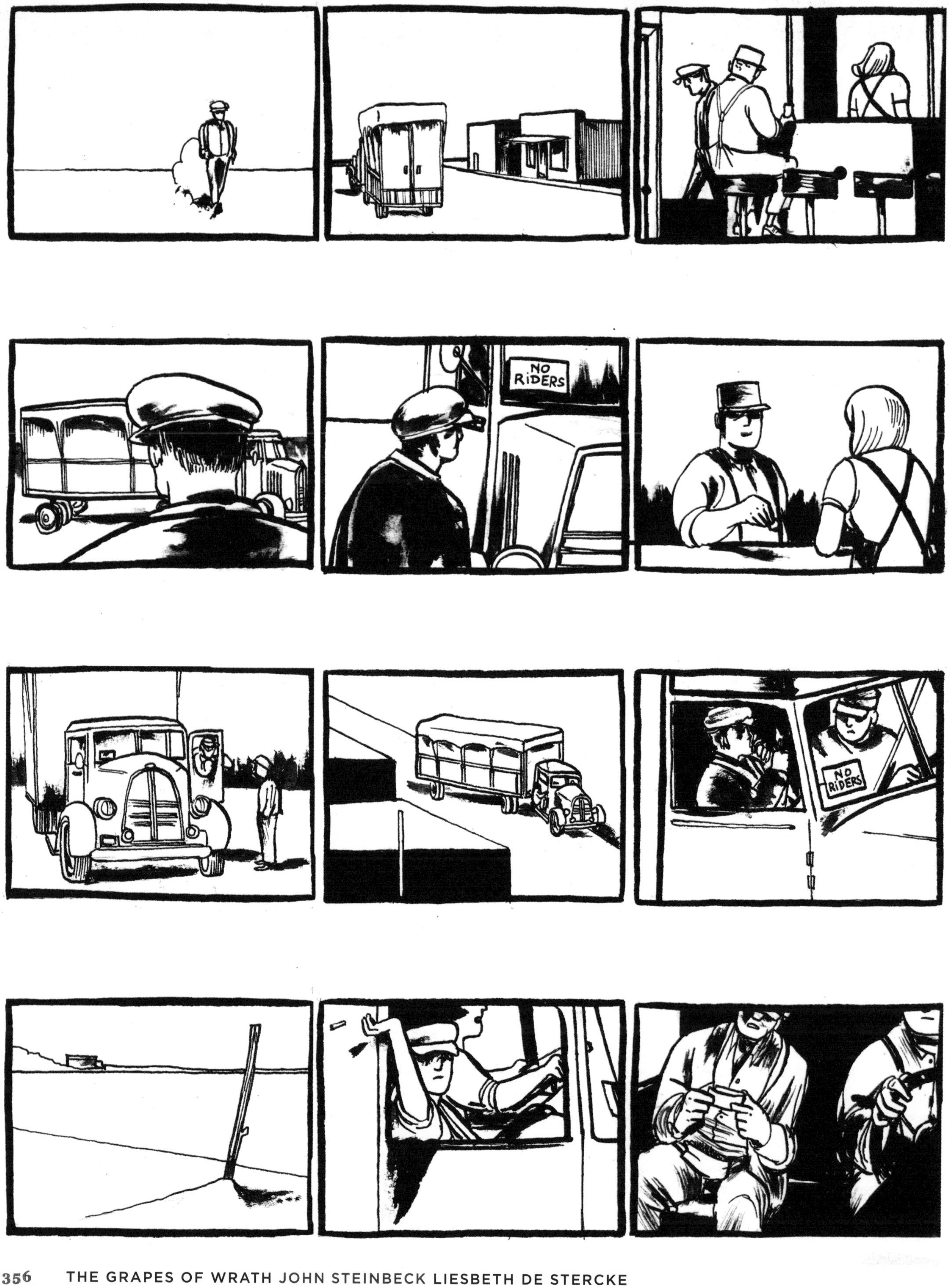
NO RIDERS
NO RIDERS

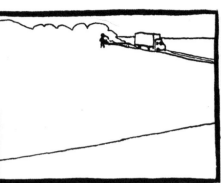

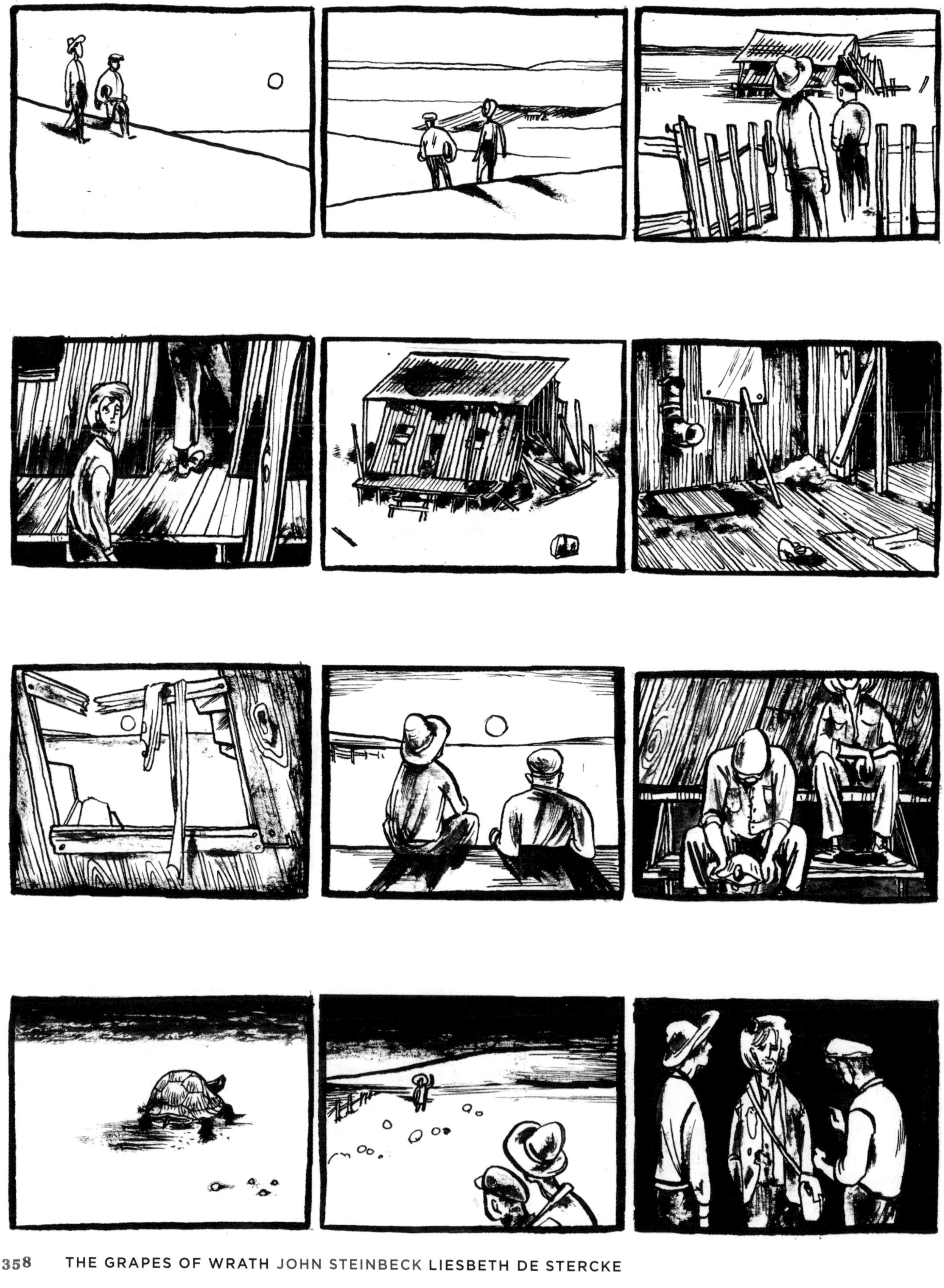

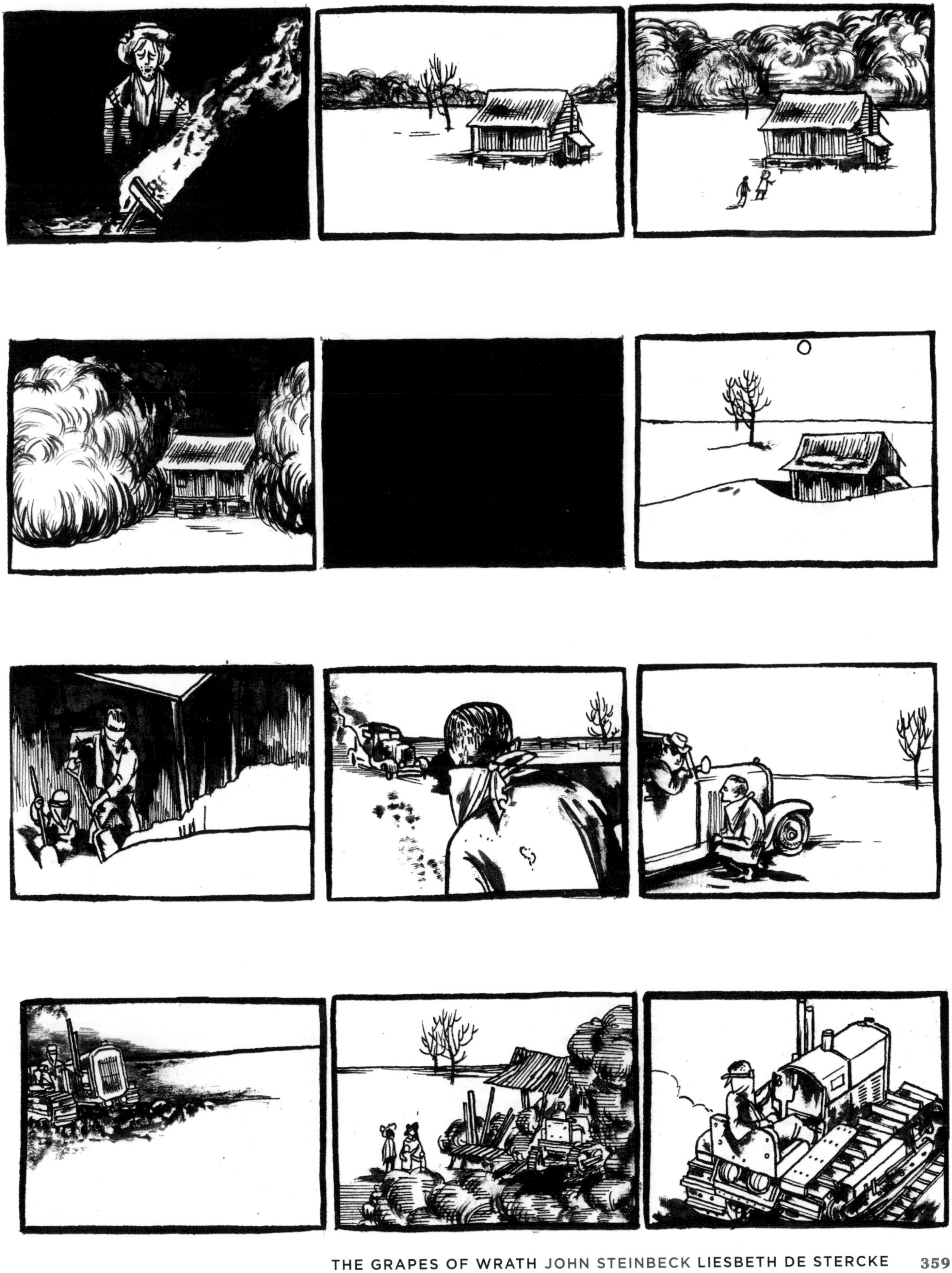

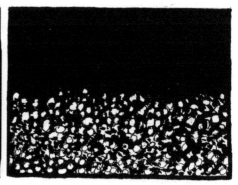

THE GRAPES OF WRATH JOHN STEINBECK LIESBETH DE STERCKE

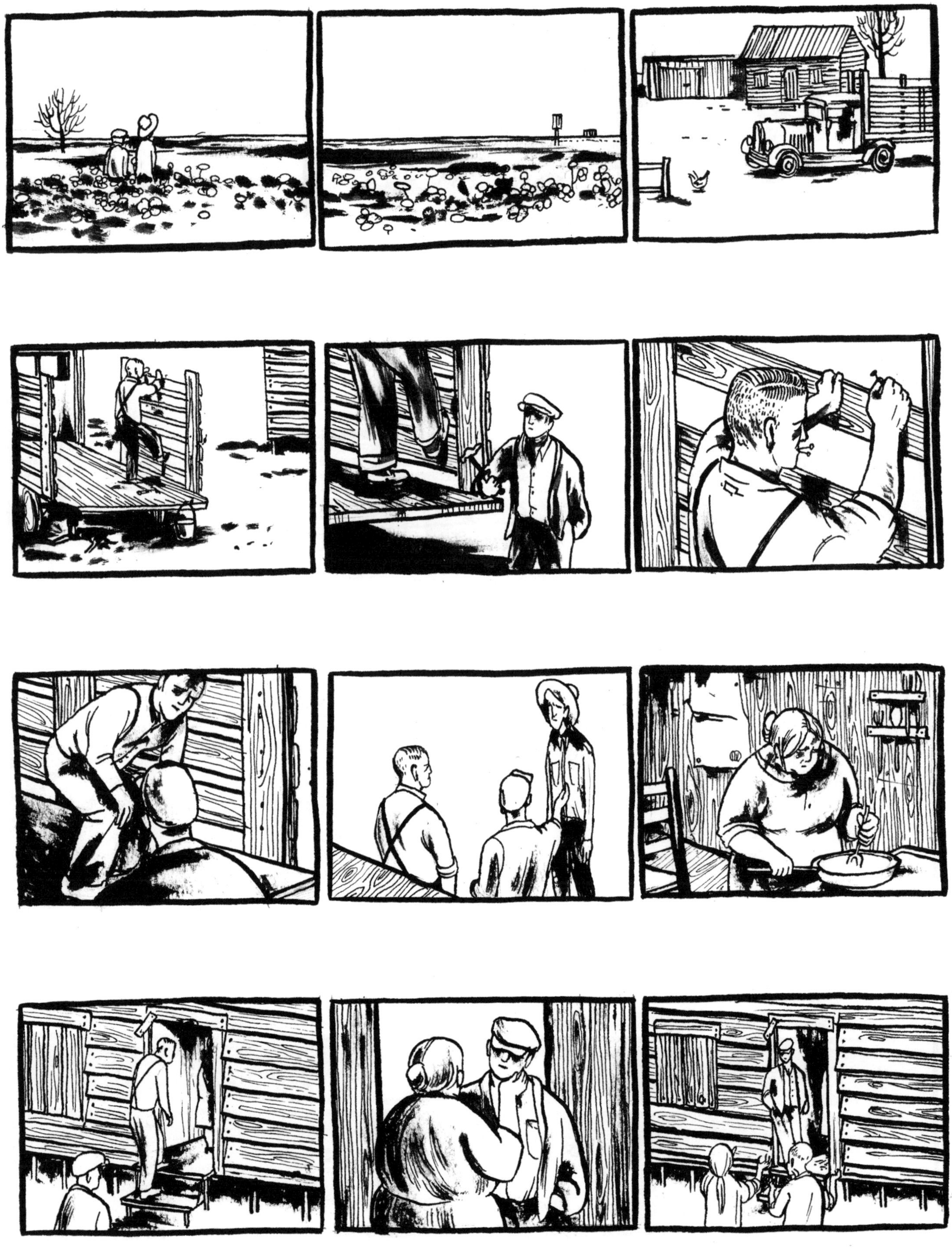

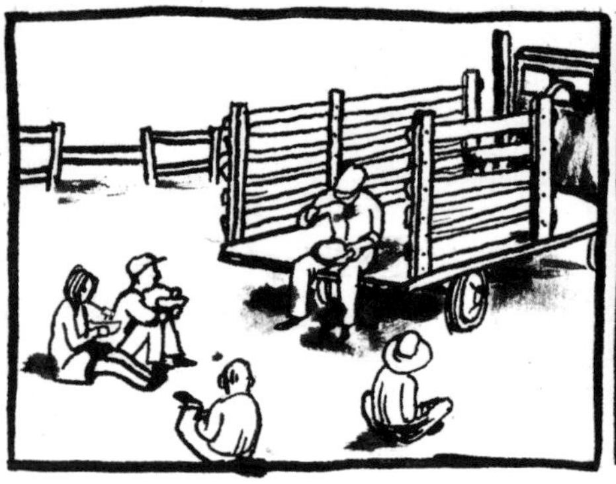
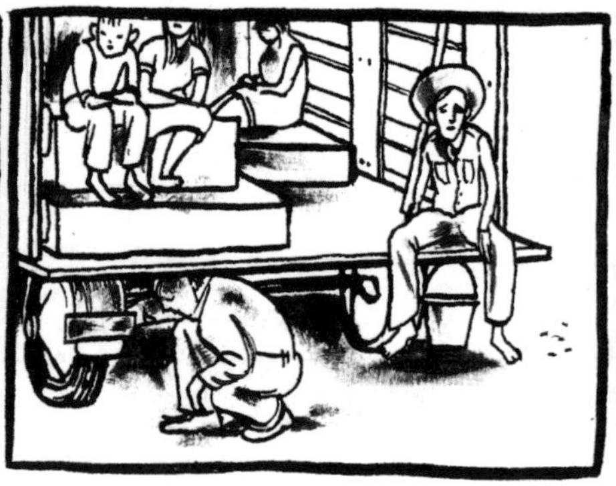
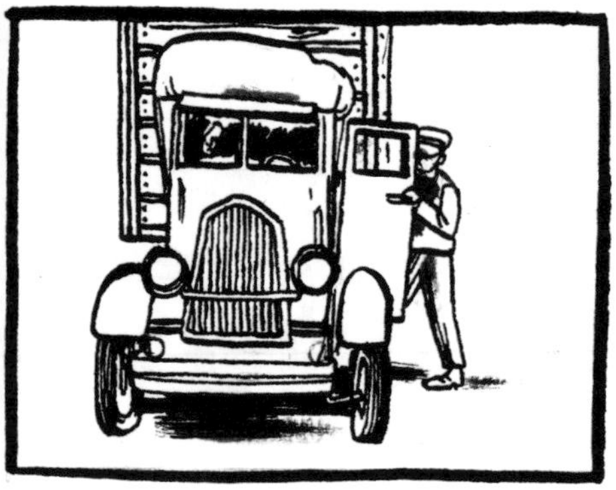
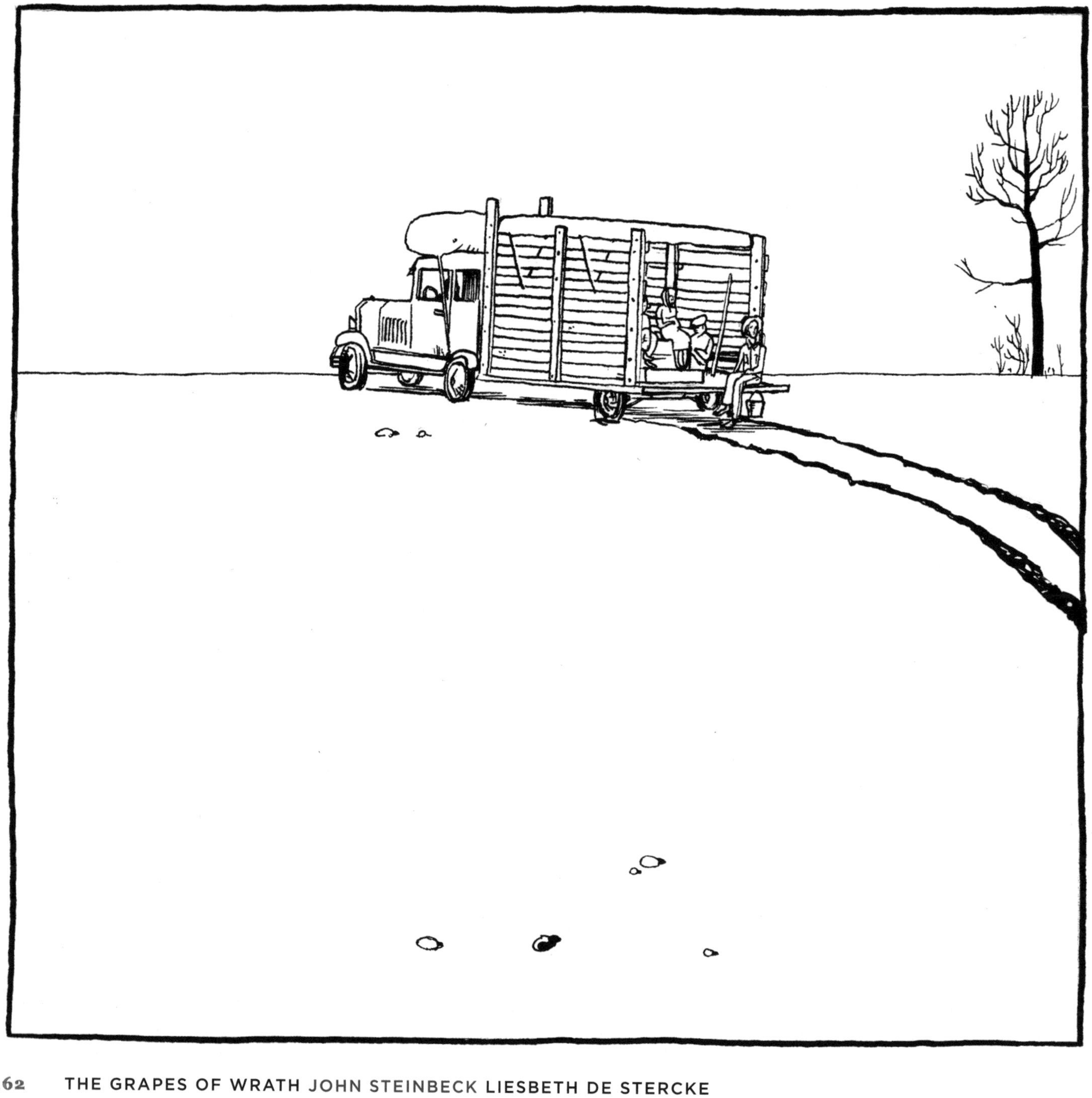

Three stories

Jorge Luis Borges

ILLUSTRATIONS BY **Kathryn Siveyer**

A LIFELONG RESIDENT OF BUENOS AIRES, JORGE Luis Borges started publishing poetry and essays in 1921, but international literary fame didn't come until exactly forty years later. As his short stories started appearing in more languages, including English, he was recognized as a genius creating small masterpieces that belong in their own category.

With Borges, you pretty much need to forget about notions of characterization and even, to a large degree, plot. The Argentinian legend is all about ideas. Big ideas. The nature of reality, time, self, truth. His stories are chock-a-block with dreams, mirrors, labyrinths, nonexistent books, real people taking part in fictional events, fictional people taking part in real events. Each of his brief *ficciones* is so dense with ideas, philosophical conundrums, existential riddles, and layers of meaning that they would normally risk burgeoning into novels. Hell, some writers would try to wring a trilogy out of a single Borges paragraph. But Borges took these epic ideas, these grand thought experiments that question the very fabric of reality in multiple ways at the same time, and compressed each one into a super-condensed little nugget that's on the short side, even for a short story.

Not only have numerous books been written that survey and probe Borges's fiction, but there's an entire book devoted to a single one of his short stories: *The Unimaginable Mathematics of Borges' Library of Babel* by William Goldbloom Bloch (Oxford, 2011) examines a story of less than 3,000 words. If another book focusing solely on one classic short story exists, I'm unaware of it.

Kathryn Siveyer has taken up the challenge of creating a full-page illustration for each of three of Borges's most famous stories, starting with his best-known, the aforementioned "Library of Babel," first published in 1941 and translated into English in 1962. In this *ficcione*, a honeycombed library as big as the universe contains every book that could possibly be written. Each book is 410 pages, with a set number of characters per page. Every possible variation of characters on all 410 pages exists somewhere. Most books are gibberish. A very small number have a meaningful sentence somewhere among the noise. Somewhere *Oliver Twist* exists, created randomly. And somewhere is *Oliver Twist* with one typo. And somewhere is *Oliver Twist* with the last page as total gibberish. And somewhere is *Oliver Twist* with a sentence from a physics textbook on page 89. And somewhere is your biography, completely right in every detail all the way to your death. And somewhere is your biography, completely right until your twenty-ninth birthday, after which it becomes fiction and/or gibberish. Somewhere is a book that contains the exact truth about the nature of reality, God, etc. And somewhere are countless books that contain almost the truth. And countless books containing endless variants of misinformation. The library is so vast that most people have only seen the barest fraction of books that exist, and almost all of them are filled with gibberish.

Professor Bloch did some calculating and found that the number of books in Borges's library would easily fill the entire known universe many, many times over. To give you an idea, imagine that there's a particular book that makes perfect sense; let's say it's a history of Ireland. This history also exists with a single mistake—the first letter of the book should be "A," but it's "B." There's also a version where the only error is that the first letter is a "C." And there's a version where the 202nd letter on page 45 is a "d" instead of what it should be, a "t." And there's a variant where that letter is an "x," though the rest of the book is perfectly correct. So how many variants are there with a single mistake? Well over thirty-one million! And how many variants are there of this single book containing a mere two errors? Almost five trillion. The numbers become inconceivable from there. And those are just the variations of one book. You can see why this story has excited the imaginations of countless mathematicians, philosophers, bibliophiles, and artists, including Kathryn.

She has also illustrated "The Garden of Forking Paths" (likewise published in 1941). On the surface, this is an ingenious cat-and-mouse WWI espionage thriller about a spy who must get his secret message to the Germans even though he's going to be captured in minutes. At its heart, though, this *ficcione* is about an ancient, unfinished Chinese novel in which every conceivable action—and its subsequent chain of events—happens simultaneously. The professor in the story explains to the spy:

> He [the novel's author, Ts'ui Pên] creates, in this way, diverse futures, diverse times which themselves also proliferate and fork. Here, then, is the explanation of the novel's contradictions. Fang, let us say, has a secret; a stranger calls at his door; Fang resolves to kill him. Naturally, there are several possible outcomes: Fang can kill the intruder, the intruder can kill Fang, they both can escape, they both can die, and so forth. In the work of Ts'ui Pên, all possible outcomes occur; each one is the point of departure for other forkings. Sometimes, the paths of this labyrinth converge: for example, you arrive at this house, but in one of the possible pasts you are my enemy, in another, my friend.

Kathryn's third pencil drawing is for "The Circular Ruins," Borges's 1940 story about a wizard who successfully attempts to create a human being by dreaming him into existence. Only, the ending is a bit trickier than simply that.

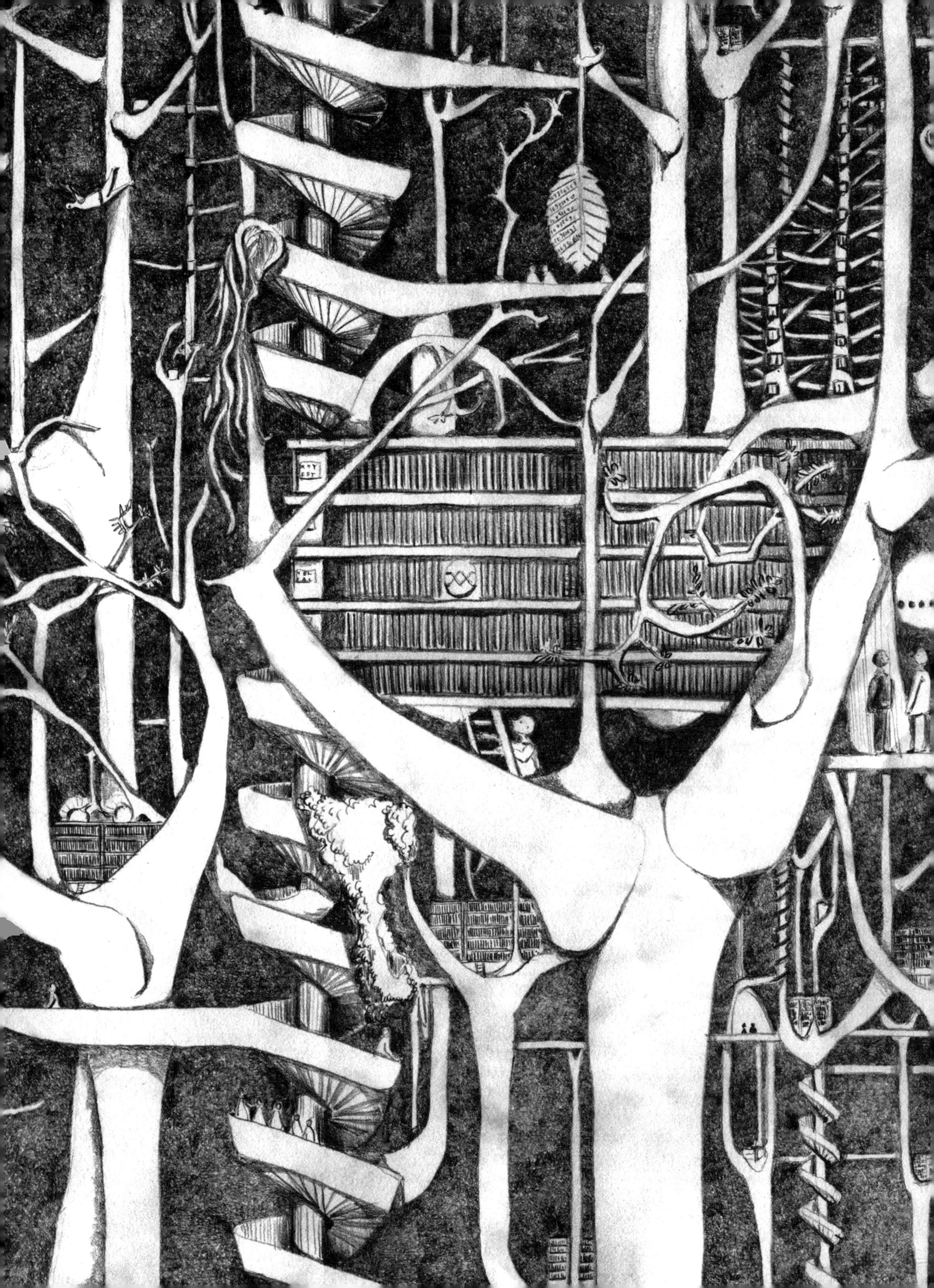

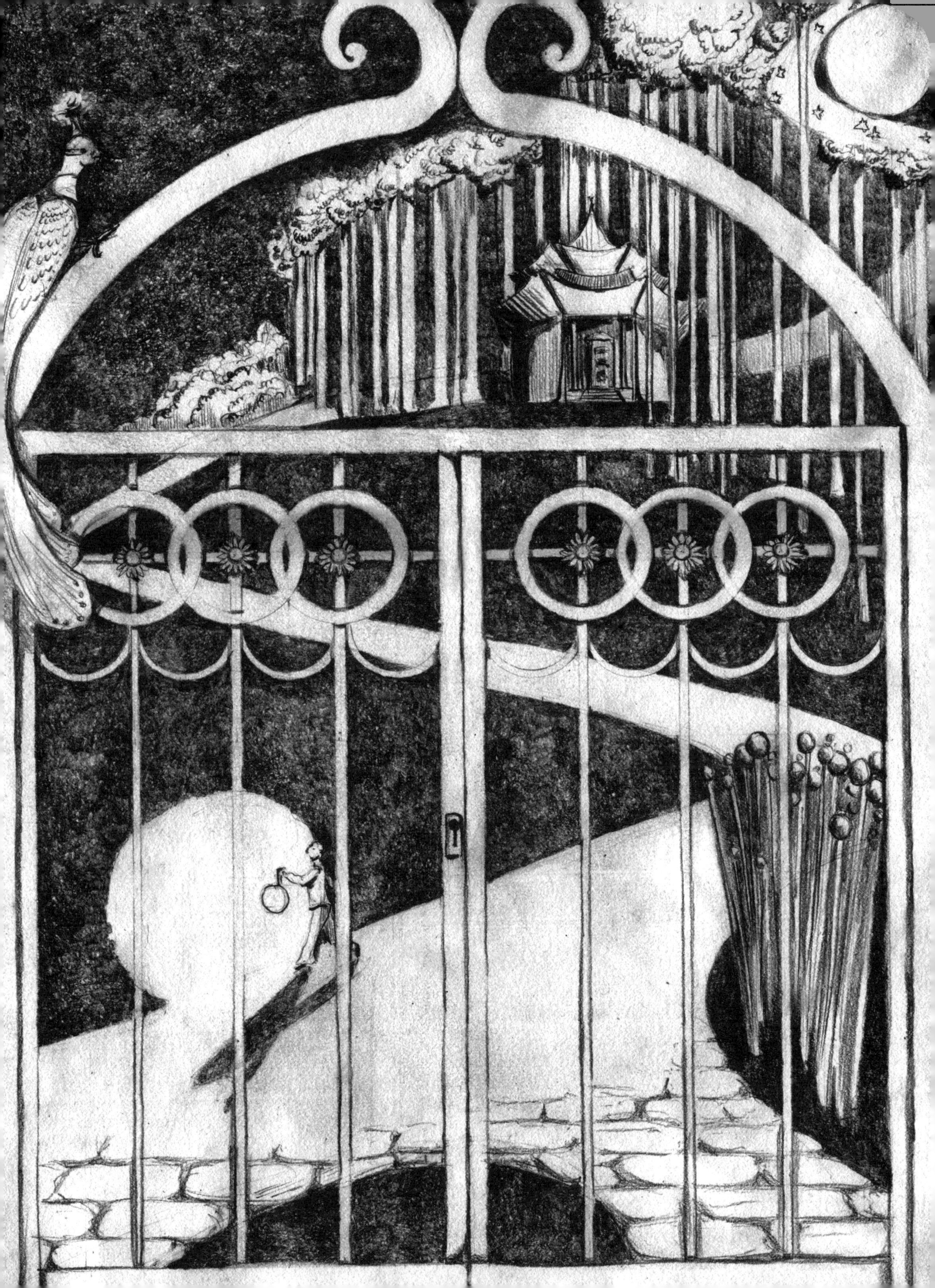

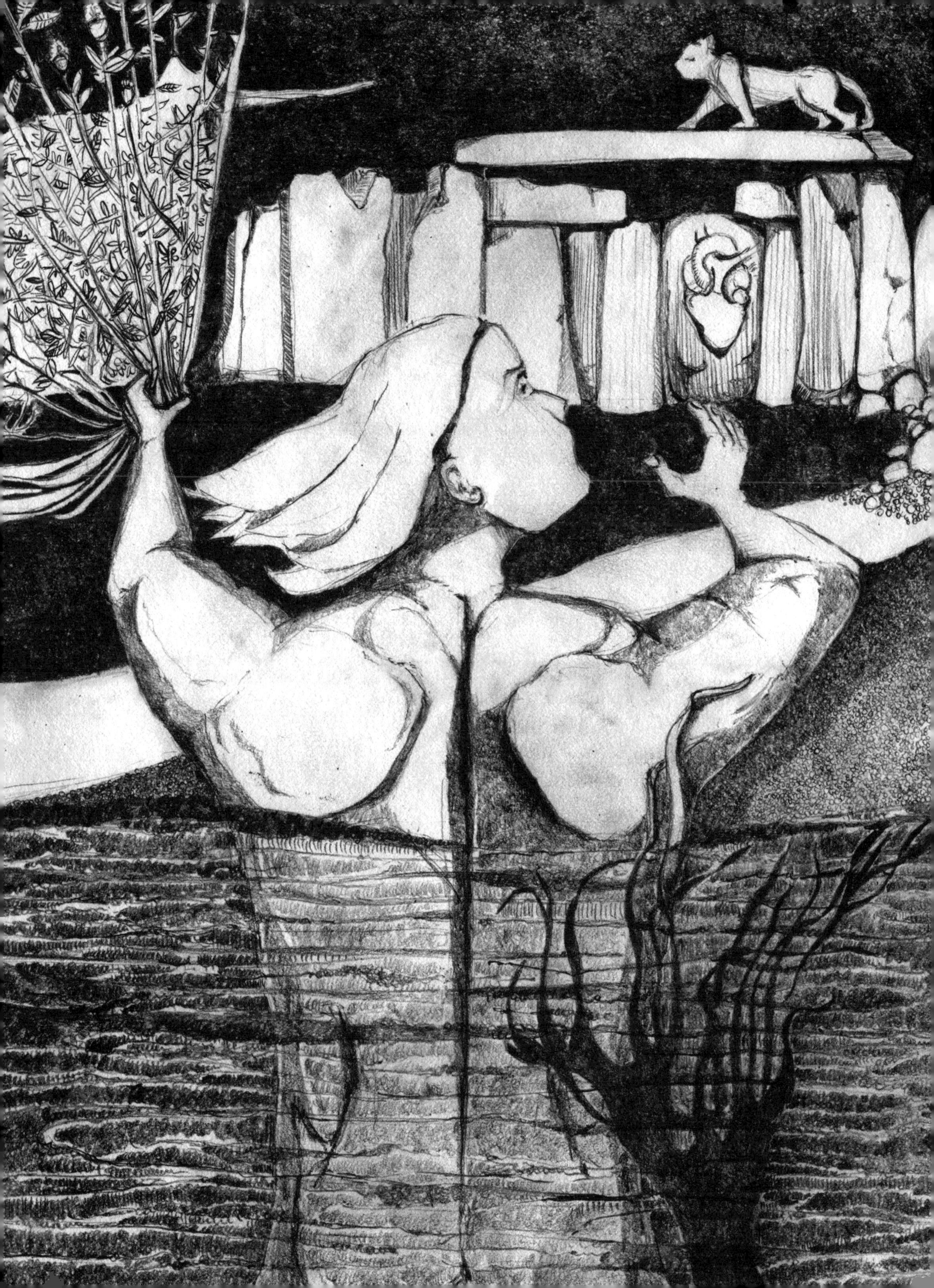

The Stranger

Albert Camus

ADAPTATION BY **Juan Carlos Kreimer**

ART BY **Julián Aron**

TRANSLATION BY **Dan Simon**

BORN IN ALGERIA—THE NORTH AFRICAN COUNTRY that was then a colony of France—Albert Camus became a lifelong promoter of social justice, pacifism, and anticolonialism. As a reporter for leftist papers, he focused on the plight of the oppressed. Living in Occupied France during World War II, he risked his freedom and probably his life by editing the resistance newspaper *Combat*. He wrote the short novel *L'Etranger* (*The Stranger*) while literally on the run from the Nazis.

Published in 1942, *The Stranger* remains a widely read classic of twentieth-century literature, and it does double-duty as a philosophical statement. Camus is often lumped in with the Existentialists—you'll hear him mentioned in the same breath as Sartre—but he himself flatly rejected the label. Instead, he proposed a philosophy of the absurd. *The Stanford Encyclopedia of Philosophy* explains:

> The essential paradox arising in Camus's philosophy concerns his central notion of absurdity. Accepting the Aristotelian idea that philosophy begins in wonder, Camus argues that human beings cannot escape asking the question, "What is the meaning of existence?" Camus, however, denies that there is an answer to this question, and rejects every scientific, teleological, metaphysical, or human-created end that would provide an adequate answer. Thus, while accepting that human beings inevitably seek to understand life's purpose, Camus takes the skeptical position that the natural world, the universe, and the human enterprise remain silent about any such purpose. Since existence itself has no meaning, we must learn to bear an irresolvable emptiness. This paradoxical situation, then, between our impulse to ask ultimate questions and the impossibility of achieving any adequate answer, is what Camus calls the absurd. Camus's philosophy of the absurd explores the consequences arising from this basic paradox.

The protagonist of *The Stranger* is Meursault, a man living in French Algeria. A more enigmatic, inscrutable character you will not find in literature. The book opens with his mother's death. He seems unmoved by the event. He then gets into a relationship with a woman who wants to marry him. He agrees, even though he sees no real reason to and doesn't seem to care one way or the other. In the novel's infamous, pivotal scene, he shoots to death an Arab on the beach, for reasons that are unclear . . . or perhaps for no reason at all. He is as indifferent to the murder as he seems at his own trial and subsequent death sentence. Camus never reveals Meursault's thoughts or emotions, and judging by what we have to go on, Meursault seems unmoved and unconcerned by the death, violence, and love swirling around him. This has caused a lot of debate, but the basic premise seems to be that he personifies the supposedly indifferent, pointless universe we live in. Trying to ascribe meaning to his actions is a fruitless trap.

A graphic novel of *The Stranger* has yet to appear in English, but the Argentinian publisher Ediciones de la Flor has put out a Spanish version. Juan Carlos Kreimer—novelist, cyclist, and editor of the For Beginners series in Spanish—provided the adaptation. Julián Aron, who has illustrated books on mythology, history, and warfare, put it into visuals. (For inclusion in *The Graphic Canon*, Seven Stories Publisher Dan Simon translated to English from the original French.) Here we see their take on one of the most famous scenes in twentieth-century literature. Earlier, Meursault and two of his companions were attacked by two Arab men who had a beef with one of Meursault's pals, who ended up getting cut. Later that day, Meursault is walking along the beach and unexpectedly comes across the knife-wielding Arab taking a snooze. . . .

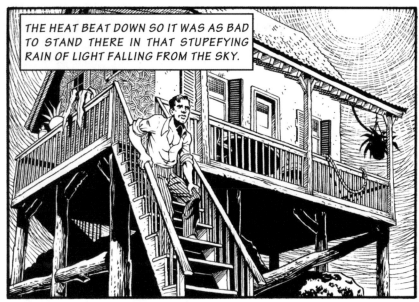

THE HEAT BEAT DOWN SO IT WAS AS BAD TO STAND THERE IN THAT STUPEFYING RAIN OF LIGHT FALLING FROM THE SKY.

TO STAY OR GO, IT MAKES NO DIFFERENCE.

SO MUCH HEAT PRESSING DOWN ON ME THAT I COULD BARELY MOVE FORWARD.

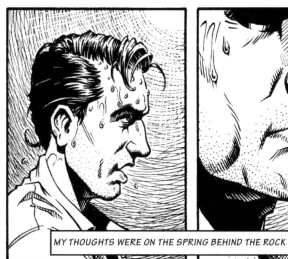

MY THOUGHTS WERE ON THE SPRING BEHIND THE ROCK . . .

TO GET AWAY FROM THE SUN, THE STRAIN, THE TEARS OF THE WOMEN . . .

TO REST AGAIN IN THE SHADE.

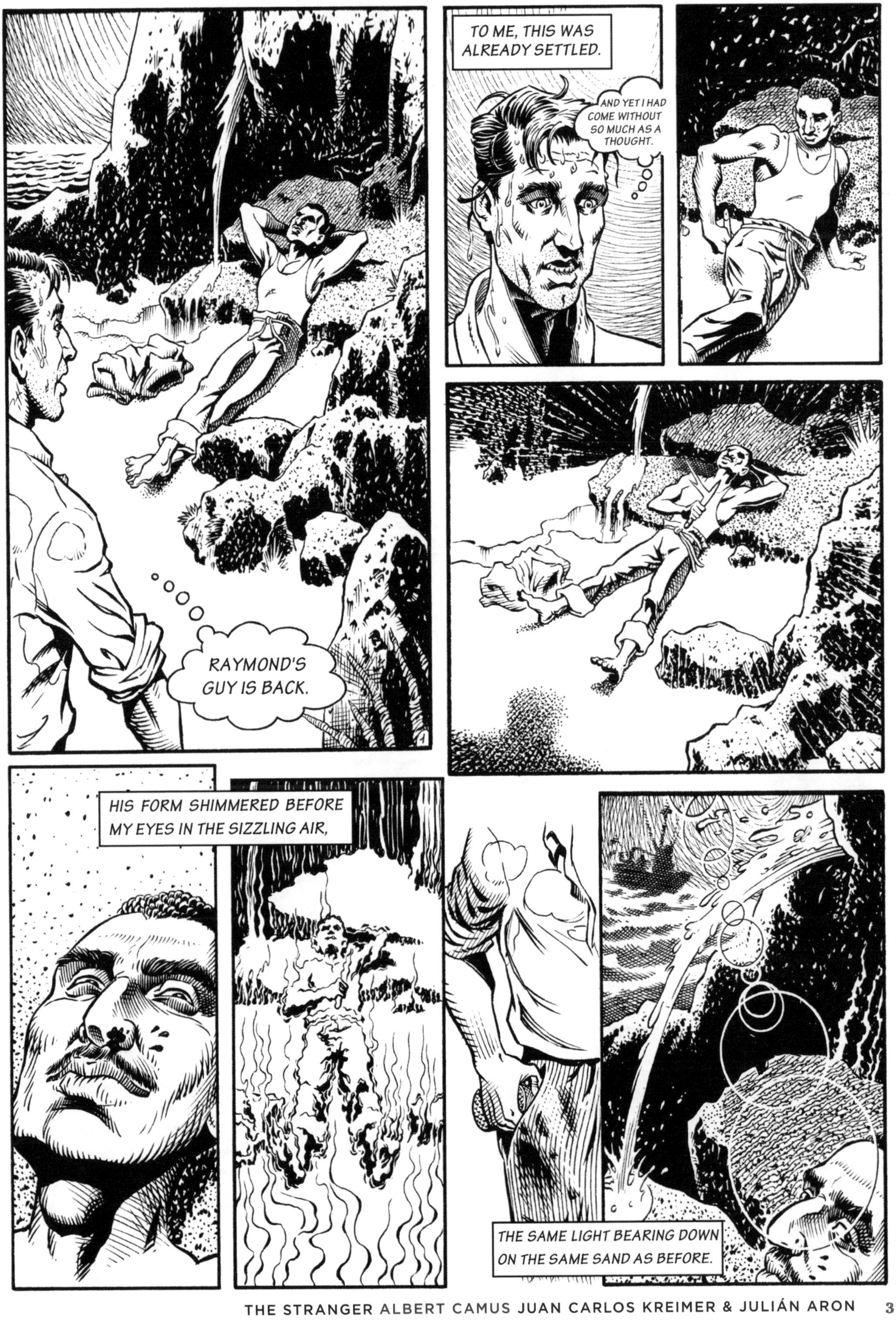
RAYMOND'S GUY IS BACK.
TO ME, THIS WAS ALREADY SETTLED.
AND YET I HAD COME WITHOUT SO MUCH AS A THOUGHT.
HIS FORM SHIMMERED BEFORE MY EYES IN THE SIZZLING AIR,
THE SAME LIGHT BEARING DOWN ON THE SAME SAND AS BEFORE.

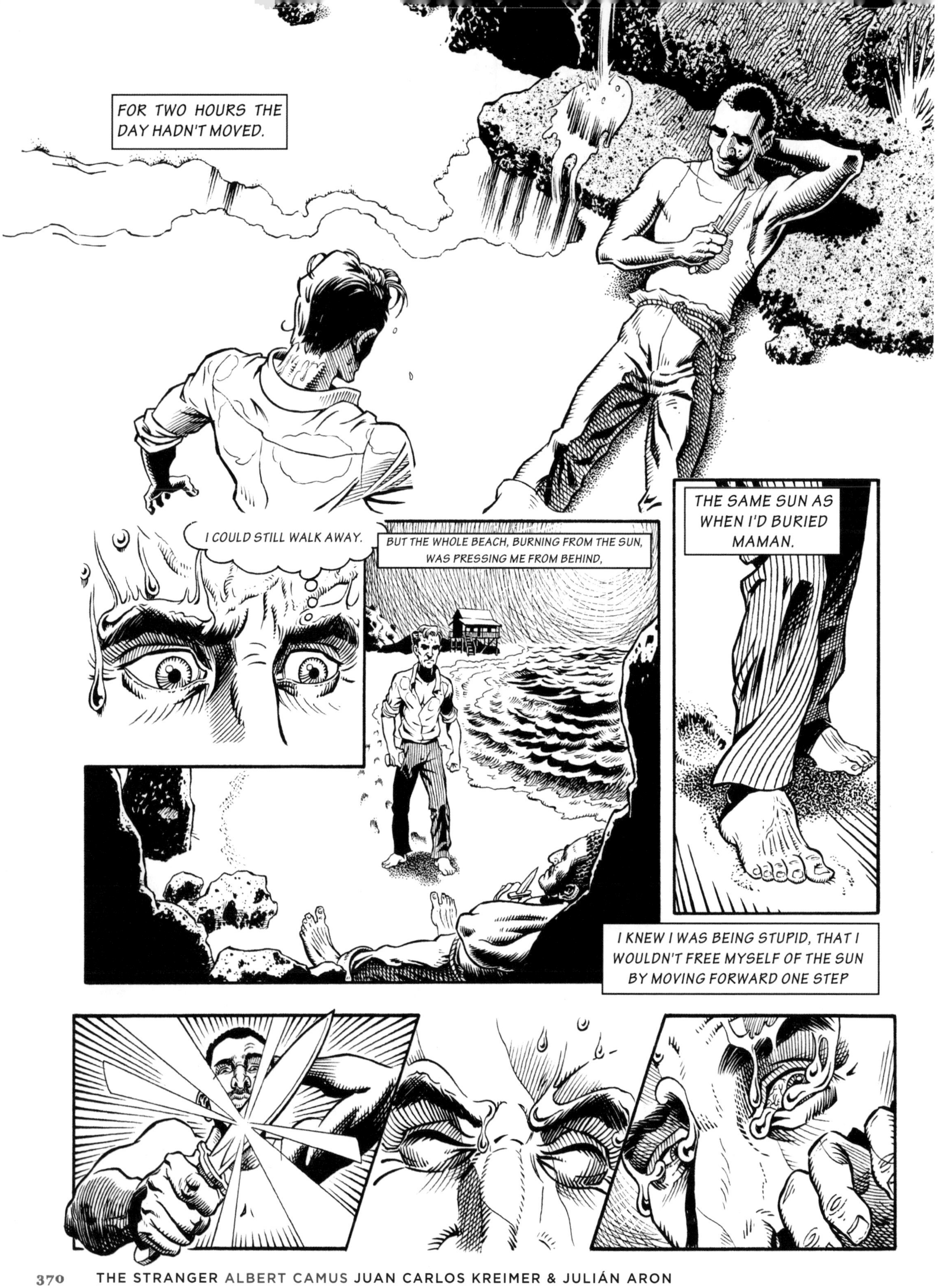
FOR TWO HOURS THE DAY HADN'T MOVED.
I COULD STILL WALK AWAY.
BUT THE WHOLE BEACH, BURNING FROM THE SUN, WAS PRESSING ME FROM BEHIND,
THE SAME SUN AS WHEN I'D BURIED MAMAN.
I KNEW I WAS BEING STUPID, THAT I WOULDN'T FREE MYSELF OF THE SUN BY MOVING FORWARD ONE STEP

. . . YET TAKING ONE STEP FORWARD.

IT HAD SEEMED TO ME THAT THE SKY BROKE OPEN FROM END TO END TO RAIN DOWN FIRE.

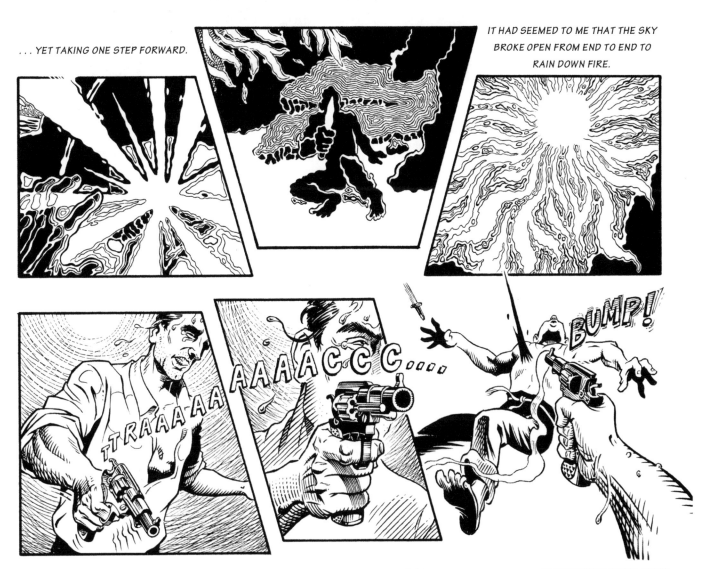

I HAD DESTROYED THE DAY'S EQUILIBRIUM, ITS RARE SILENCE IN WHICH I HAD FOUND MYSELF PERFECTLY CONTENT.

FOUR SHOTS, LIKE I HAD KNOCKED FOUR TIMES ON MISERY'S DOOR.

THE STRANGER ALBERT CAMUS JUAN CARLOS KREIMER & JULIÁN ARON

Animal Farm

George Orwell

PHOTO-DIORAMAS BY **Laura Plansker**

BRITISH JOURNALIST AND WRITER ERIC BLAIR WAS A socialist who fought with the Republicans against Franco's Fascist forces during the Spanish Civil War. Among the Republican factions were Communists taking their orders from the Kremlin who turned on Orwell's faction, accusing him and his wife—who was helping the cause with an administrative position in Spain—of being in league with the Fascists. The couple fled the country. Soured on Stalin's brand of authoritarian Communism, Blair (under his pen name, George Orwell) wrote an animal fable skewering the betrayal of Marxist ideals in the Soviet Union. In *Animal Farm*, published in 1945, two pigs, Napoleon and Snowball, lead a revolution of the animals, ousting the humans from the farm and ostensibly creating a worker's paradise where all animals are equal.

The two pigs assume leadership roles, and when they start disagreeing on courses of action, Napoleon ousts Snowball. As Napoleon amasses more and more power, rules that are supposed to apply to all animals don't apply to him and his circle; propaganda and outright lies become the order of the day; young animals are taken from their parents; the ruling pigs become increasingly decadent,

greedy, and ruthless. They exploit the animals under their control and form alliances with neighboring human farmers. At the end, you can't tell the pigs from the humans they rebelled against.

Artist Laura Plansker specializes in photo-dioramas, an often-overlooked artform that I love, in which scenes are physically created in miniature, then photographed. Her approach is sometimes cute and quirky (a beet drinking a glass of beet juice is one of my favorites) and sometimes sinister and dark (a Japanese woman whose long, thick hair is grabbing food to feed a giant mouth in the back of her head). She veers toward the dark approach in these three dioramas. In the first, immediately after vanquishing the humans: "The harness-room at the end of the stables was broken open; the bits, the nose-rings, the dog-chains, the cruel knives with which Mr. Jones had been used to castrate the pigs and lambs, were all flung down the well." Next we see Boxer, the simple workhorse who believes wholeheartedly in his dear leader, allowing himself to be worked almost to death building a windmill. (Napoleon will then sell the sick worker to a glue factory.) Finally, the pigs hit the bottom of their human-like decadence.

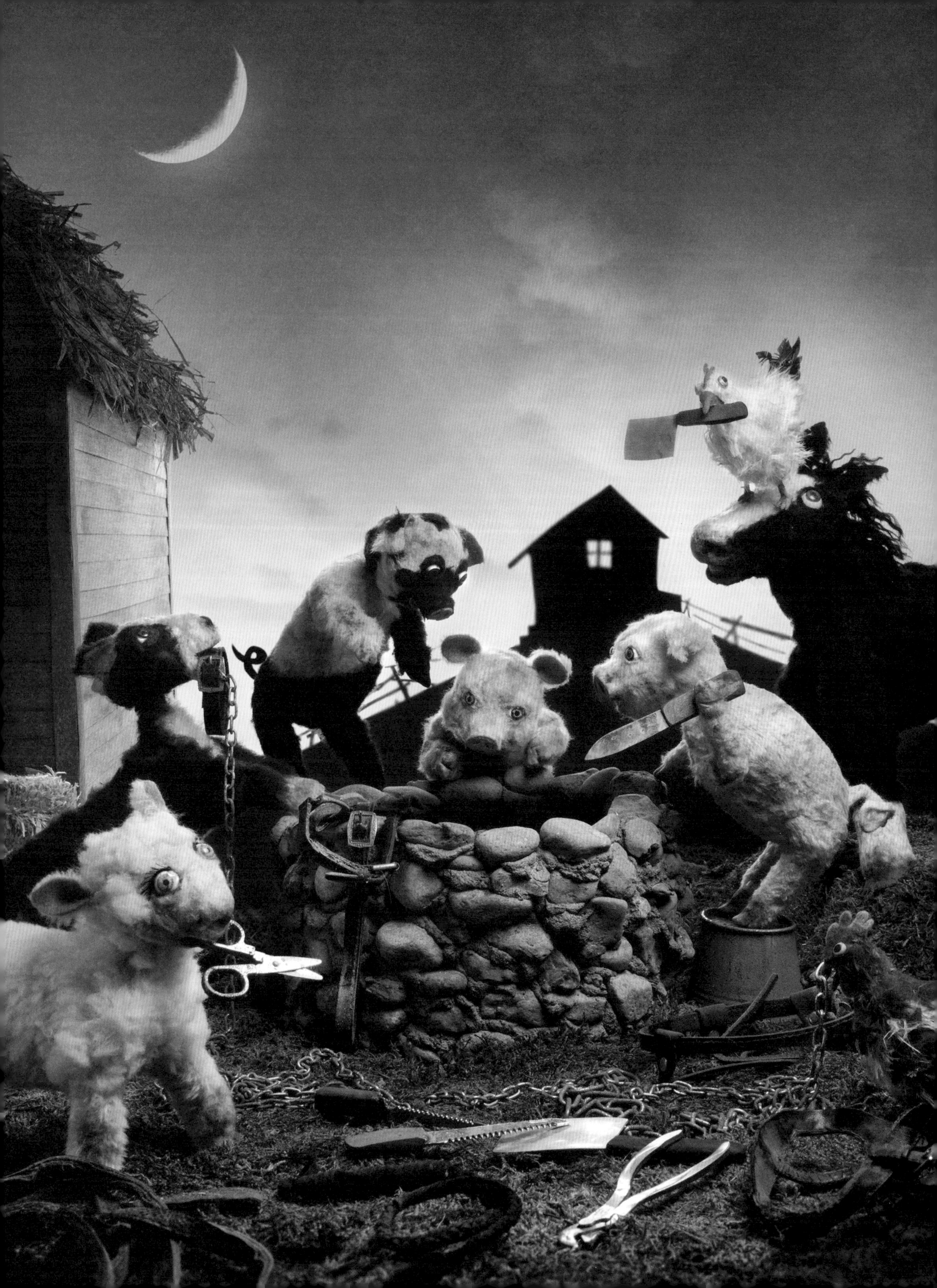

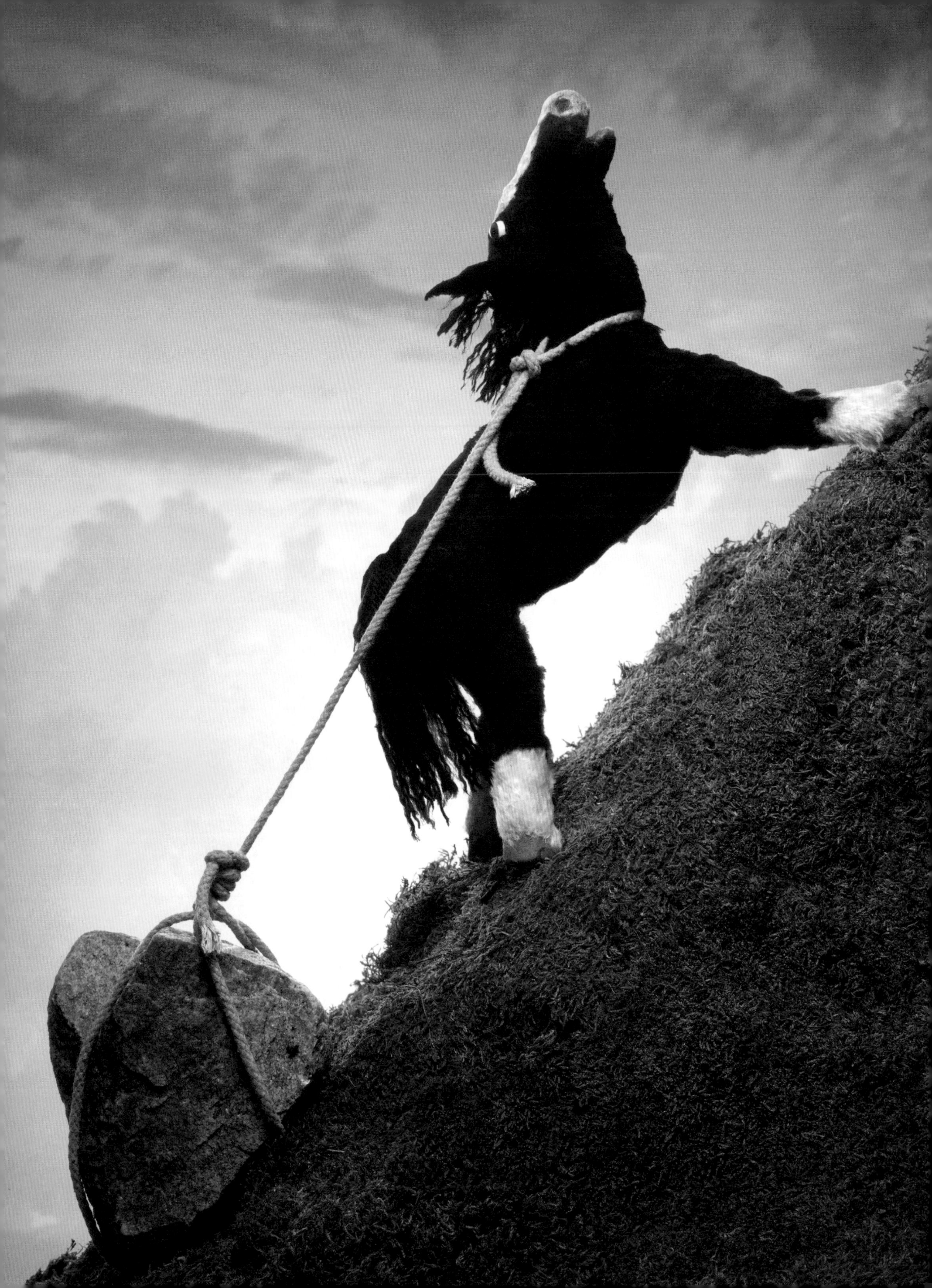

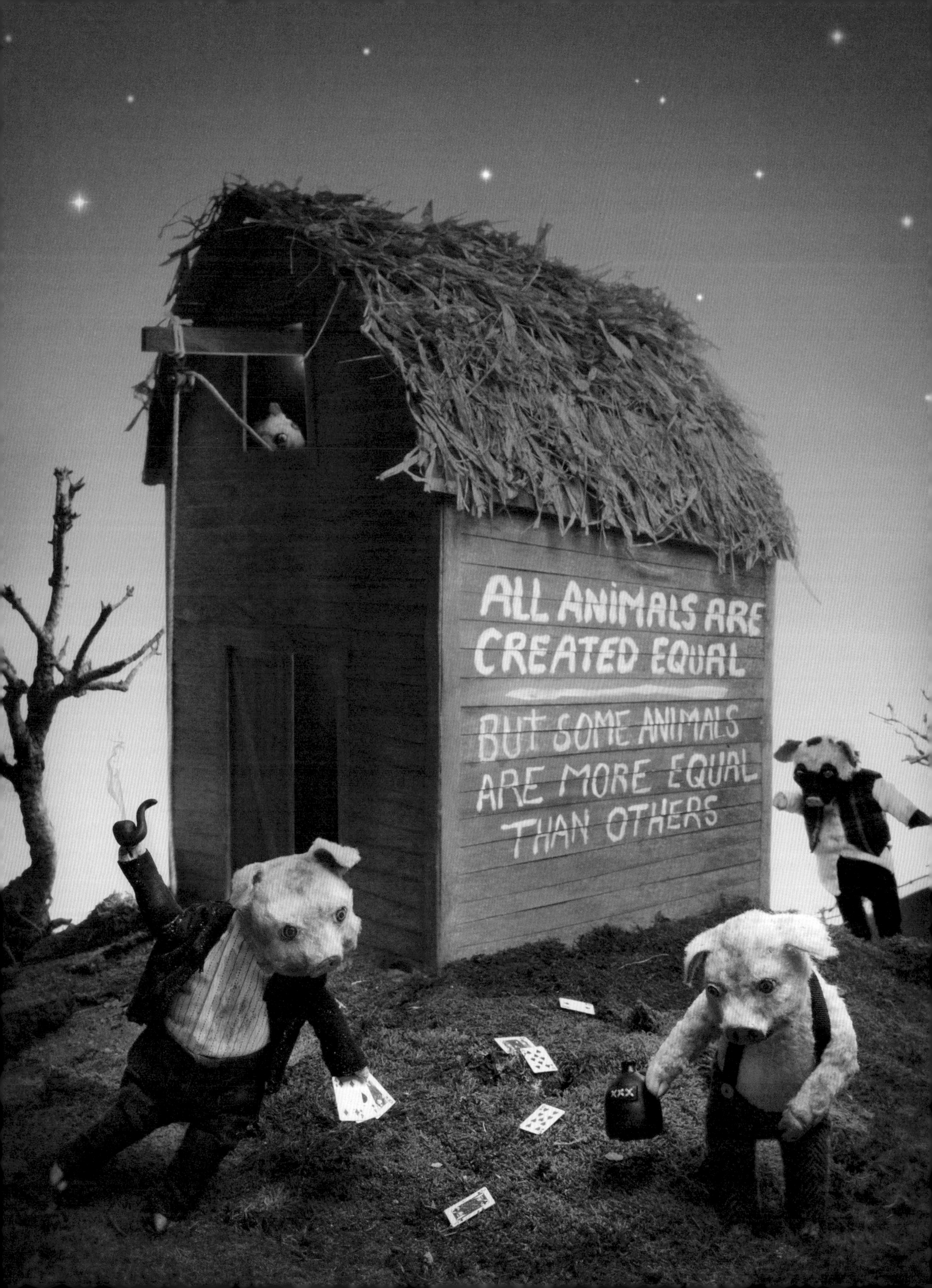
ALL ANIMALS ARE CREATED EQUAL
BUT SOME ANIMALS ARE MORE EQUAL THAN OTHERS

"The Heart of the Park"

Flannery O'Connor

ART/ADAPTATION BY **Jeremy Eaton**

FLANNERY O'CONNOR WAS BORN IN THE MAGICAL, otherworldly city of Savannah, Georgia. She was gaining firm entrée into the literary world in her early twenties, but a diagnosis of lupus sent the socially awkward O'Connor back to the family farm in Milledgeville, Georgia, where she wrote and raised birds—poultry and exotic species—until her death at age thirty-nine.

Her fiction—two novels and thirty-one short stories—is a uniquely personal, almost indescribable blend of grotesque, violent, cruel, wounded, eccentric, hypocritical, and fucked-up Southerners, with Catholic themes running strongly but invisibly throughout. After all, this is the South, where Protestantism dominates in the forms of Bible-banging fundamentalism and holy-rolling Pentecostalism, and that is indeed what most characters identify with. But O'Connor was Catholic, and this provides the hidden dynamic in everything she wrote. "All my stories are about the action of grace on a character who is not very willing to support it," she said, "but most people think of these stories as hard, hopeless, and brutal." Indeed.

Her short story "The Heart of the Park" eventually became part of her first novel, *Wise Blood* (1952). As a stand-alone story, it's quite cryptic, but that's part of its weird beauty. How is it that the two main characters—park security guard Enoch Emery and park visitor Hazel Weaver—already know each other? Why is Hazel so desperate to track down a married couple that the two of them met at some point? What is on display in the park's rinky-dink museum that Enoch is so desperate, to the point of insanity, to show Hazel? And what overwhelming significance does this object have for Enoch? We find out what the object is at the end of the story, but these other questions remain unanswered.

Jeremy Eaton's work—comics, illustrations, paintings, photography—has appeared in museums and alternative weekly papers including the *Village Voice*, on album covers for Sub Pop Records and in his collections from Fantagraphics. He decided to take a highly experimental approach to O'Connor's story: almost all of the visuals are built from basic geometric shapes or typographical symbols (letters, numbers, punctuation marks, and dingbats). I urge you to check out Jeremy's bold take on the story now, and if you have trouble following the action, return here and read the final paragraph, below.

Spoiler Alert: Enoch gets upset when the park guard who replaces him at 2:00 p.m. shows up late, as always. Now off-duty, he proceeds with the rest of his day, which involves hiding in the bushes to spy on women at the pool. As he watches, an old acquaintance, Hazel, unexpectedly arrives at the park. Hazel openly watches an unattractive woman, two children in tow, at the pool, but when she shows him some skin, he beats a hasty retreat to his car. Enoch runs after him, and Hazel says that he came to see Enoch and demands to know the address of the Moats. Enoch says he'll tell him if he goes to see the mysterious object. Hazel reluctantly agrees, but first it turns out they must go through Enoch's daily ritual. First, a malt at the park's cafe, where the waitress hates Enoch but takes a shine to Hazel, who doesn't feel the same. Then it's a stroll through the park's pitiful zoo, to see the animals whom Enoch "hates." They finally get to the museum, where Enoch excitedly shows Hazel the object that he's obsessed with—a mummified dwarf. Meanwhile, the woman and her two brats have followed the men, and she stands looking at the dried-up husk, too. Hazel again runs away, Enoch catches up with him, and Hazel once again demands to know the address of the couple. At this point, Enoch is in some sort of quasi-religious revelry from having revealed the mummified man to Hazel. (It holds a bizarre spiritual significance for him, which is revealed in the novel.) Hazel throws a rock that cuts Enoch's head and drives off.

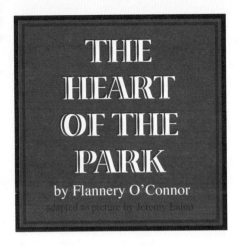

THE HEART OF THE PARK
by Flannery O'Connor
adapted to picture by Jeremy Eaton
CITY FOREST
CITY FOREST

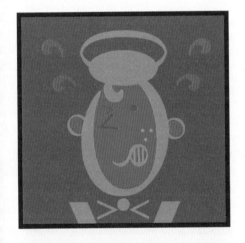

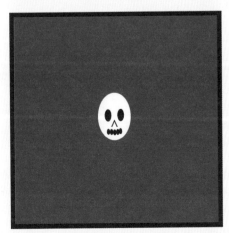

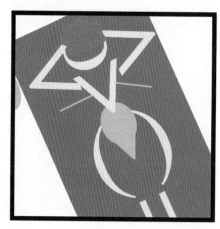

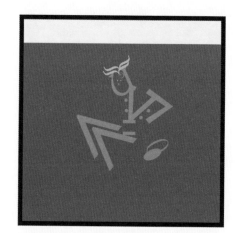

"THE HEART OF THE PARK" FLANNERY O'CONNOR JEREMY EATON

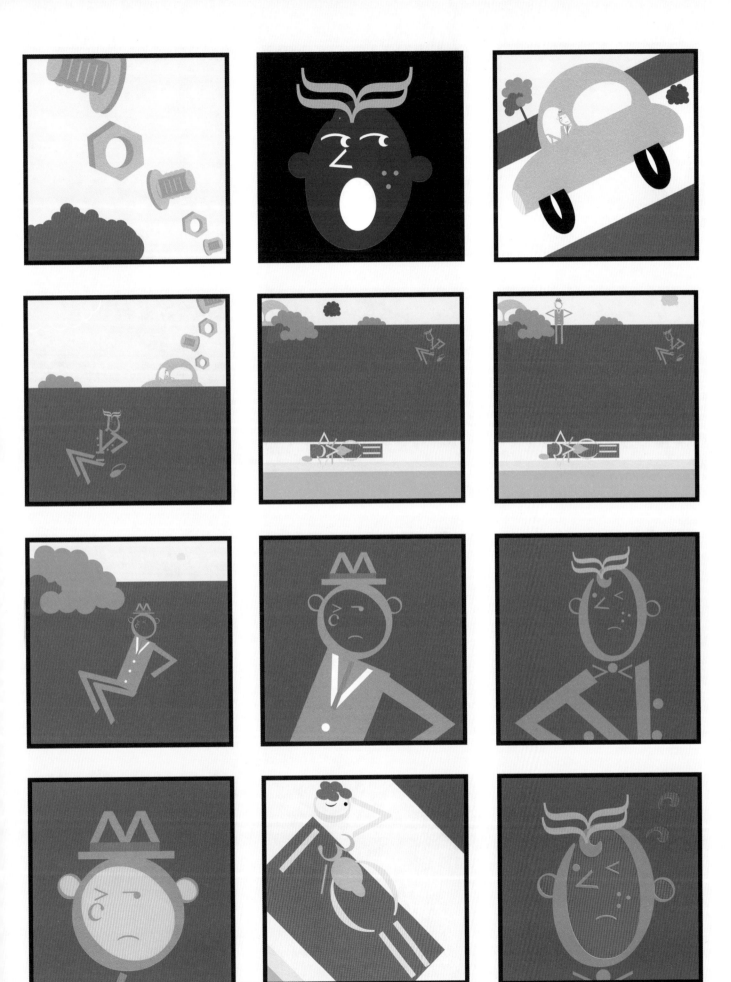

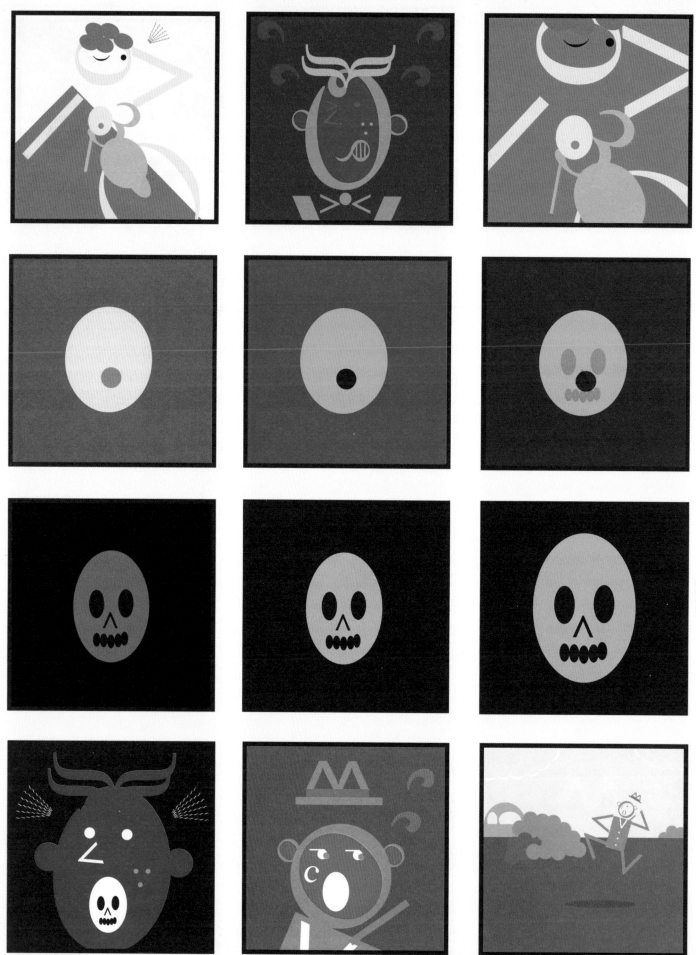

380　"THE HEART OF THE PARK" FLANNERY O'CONNOR JEREMY EATON

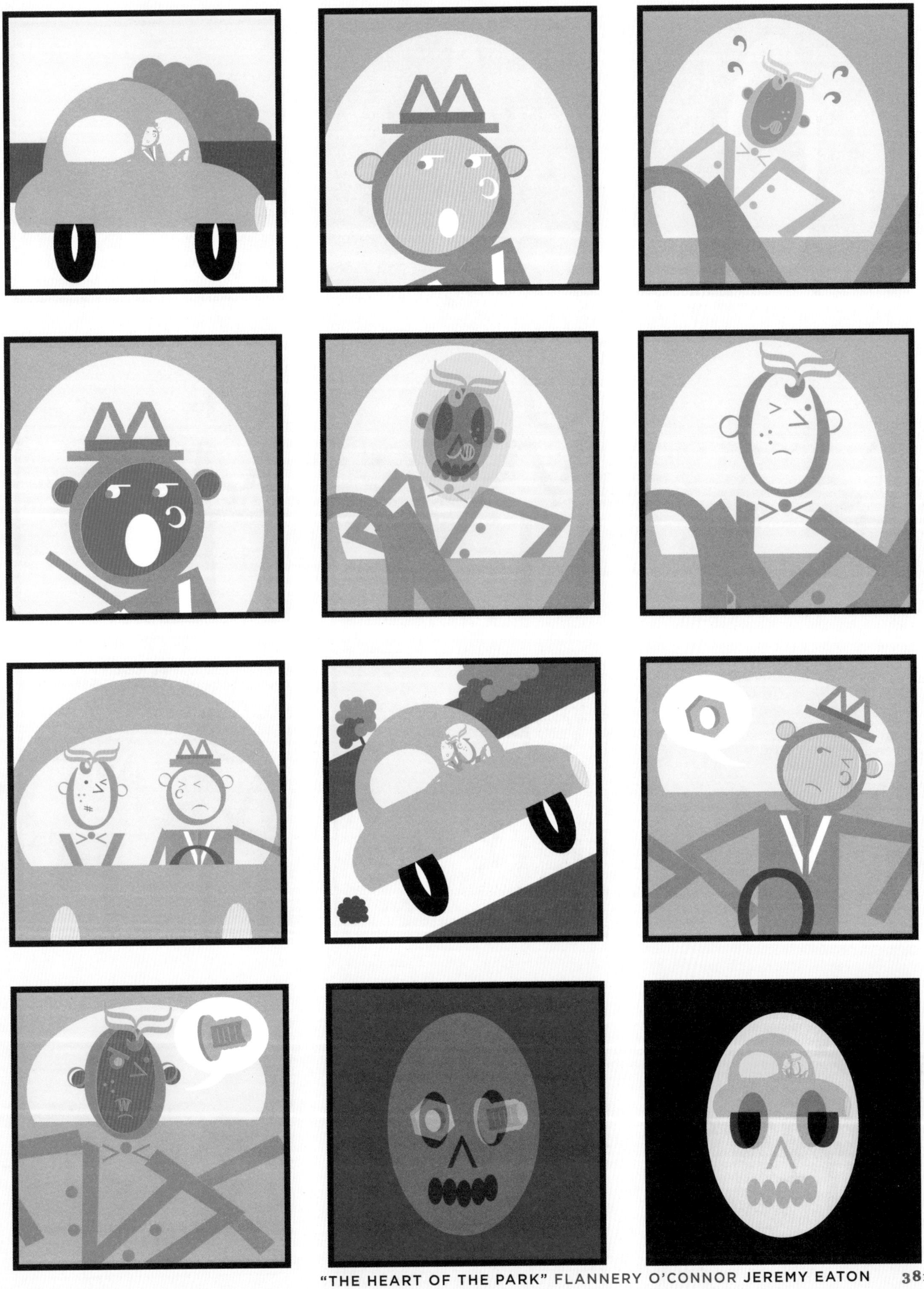

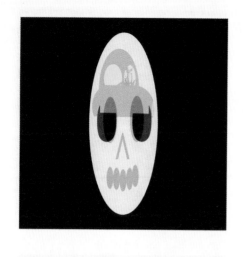

382 "THE HEART OF THE PARK" FLANNERY O'CONNOR JEREMY EATON

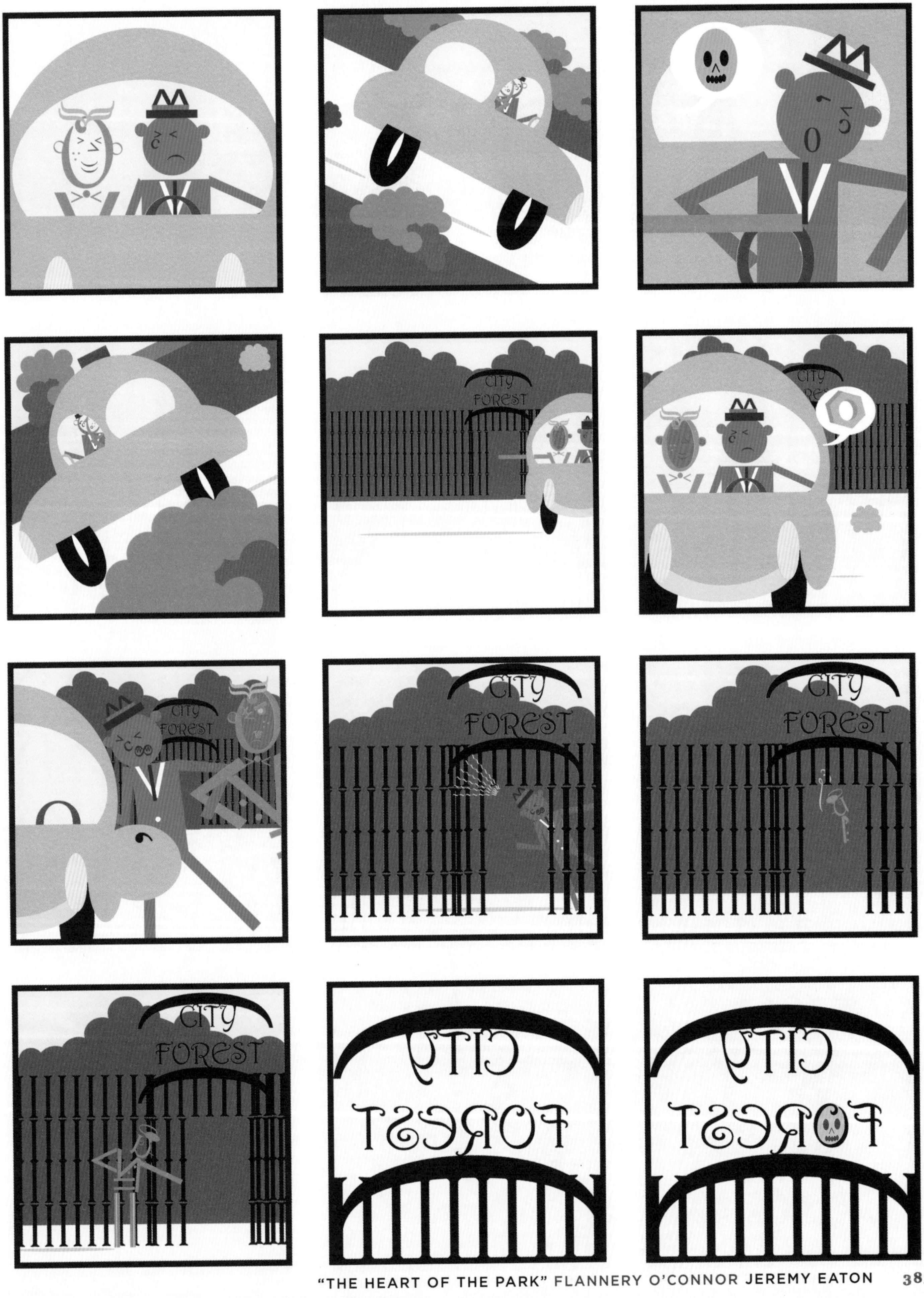
CITY
FOREST
CITY
FOREST
CITY
FOREST
CITY
FOREST
CITY
FOREST
CITY
FOREST

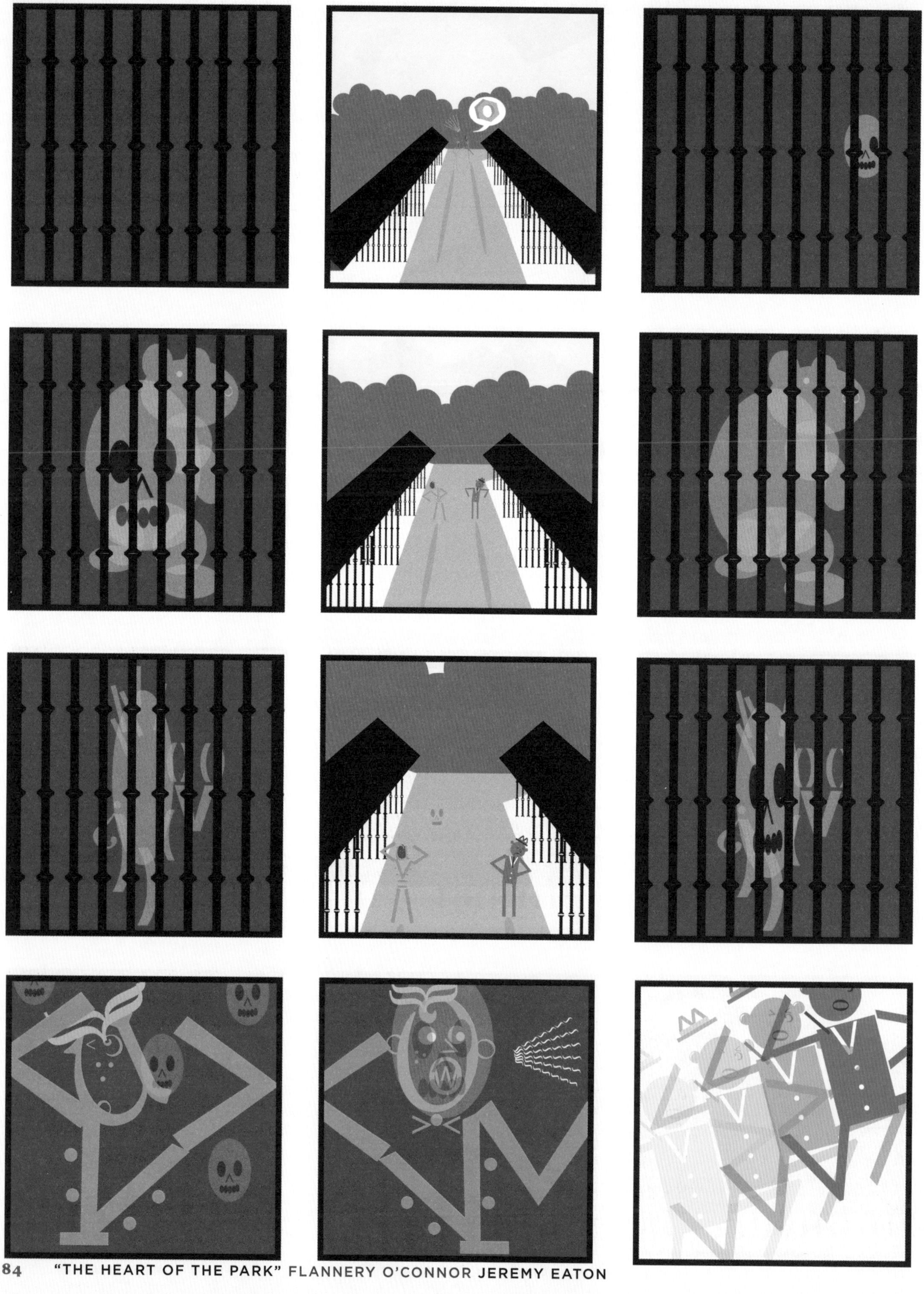

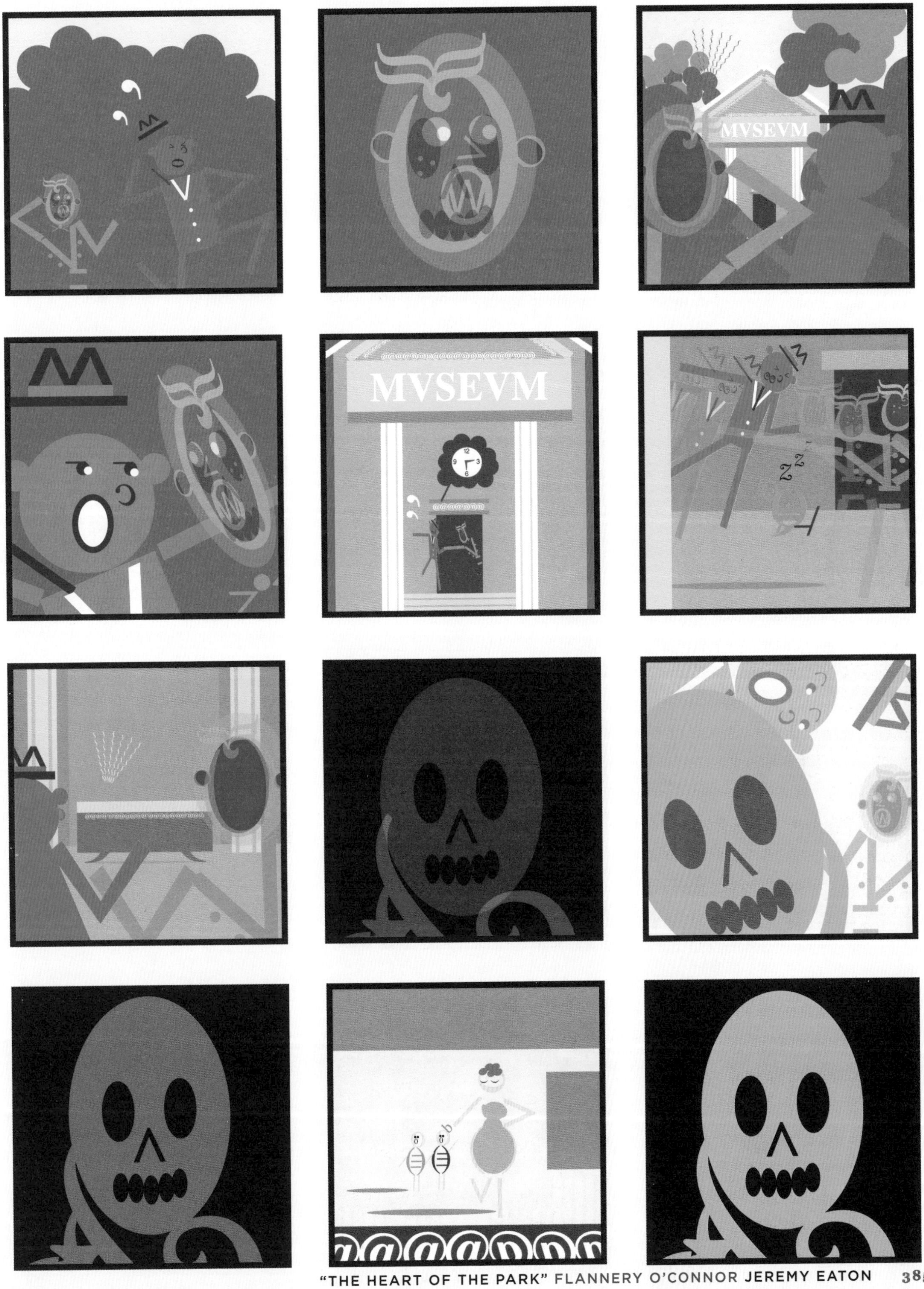
MVSEVM
MVSEVM
Z
Z
Z

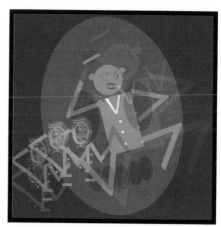

386   "THE HEART OF THE PARK" FLANNERY O'CONNOR JEREMY EATON

Nineteen Eighty-Four

George Orwell

ILLUSTRATION BY **Lesley Barnes**

IN THE 1949 NOVEL NOW SYNONYMOUS WITH dystopias, Eric Blair (George Orwell) imagined a nation-state with citizens under constant direct surveillance, where the media are merely organs of propaganda, the past is literally rewritten, language is dumbed down, war is constant, everyone is a snitch, subversive thoughts are illegal, and rebellion is a form of mental illness. A low-level bureaucrat in the so-called Ministry of Truth, Winston Smith starts questioning the political order and attempts to join the resistance with his girlfriend, Julia. But Big Brother always wins. Always.

Lesley Barnes has a gloriously intricate, colorful, geometric style that she brings to book and record covers, animation, giftwrap, window displays, fashion shows, *The Economist* . . . anywhere viewers' optic nerves need to be lit aflame. In her version of Winston's London, you are always under intense surveillance from endless eyes, but it's so gorgeous you almost don't mind. . . .

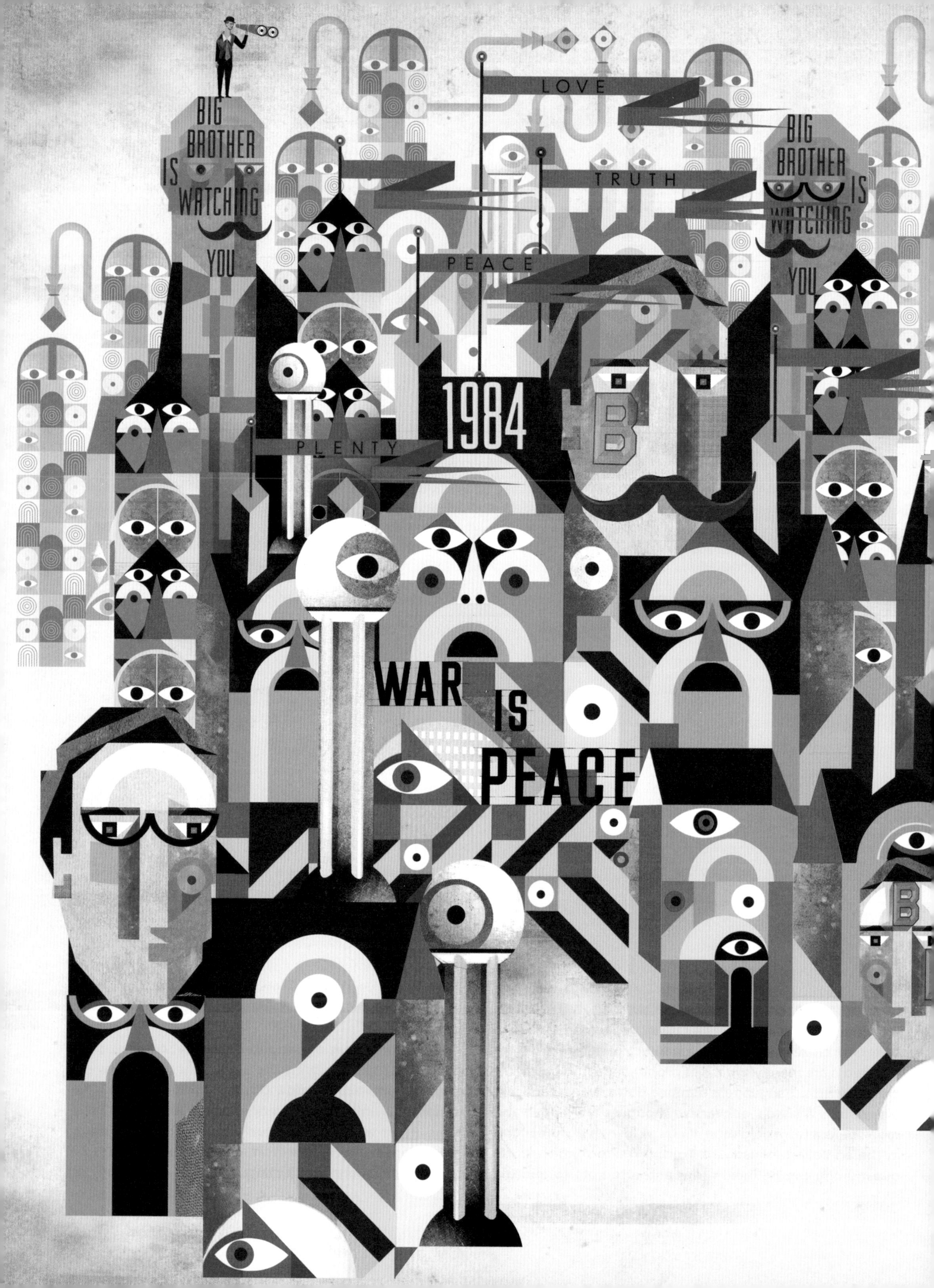
BIG BROTHER IS WATCHING YOU
LOVE
TRUTH
BIG BROTHER IS WATCHING YOU
PEACE
1984
PLENTY
B
WAR IS PEACE
B

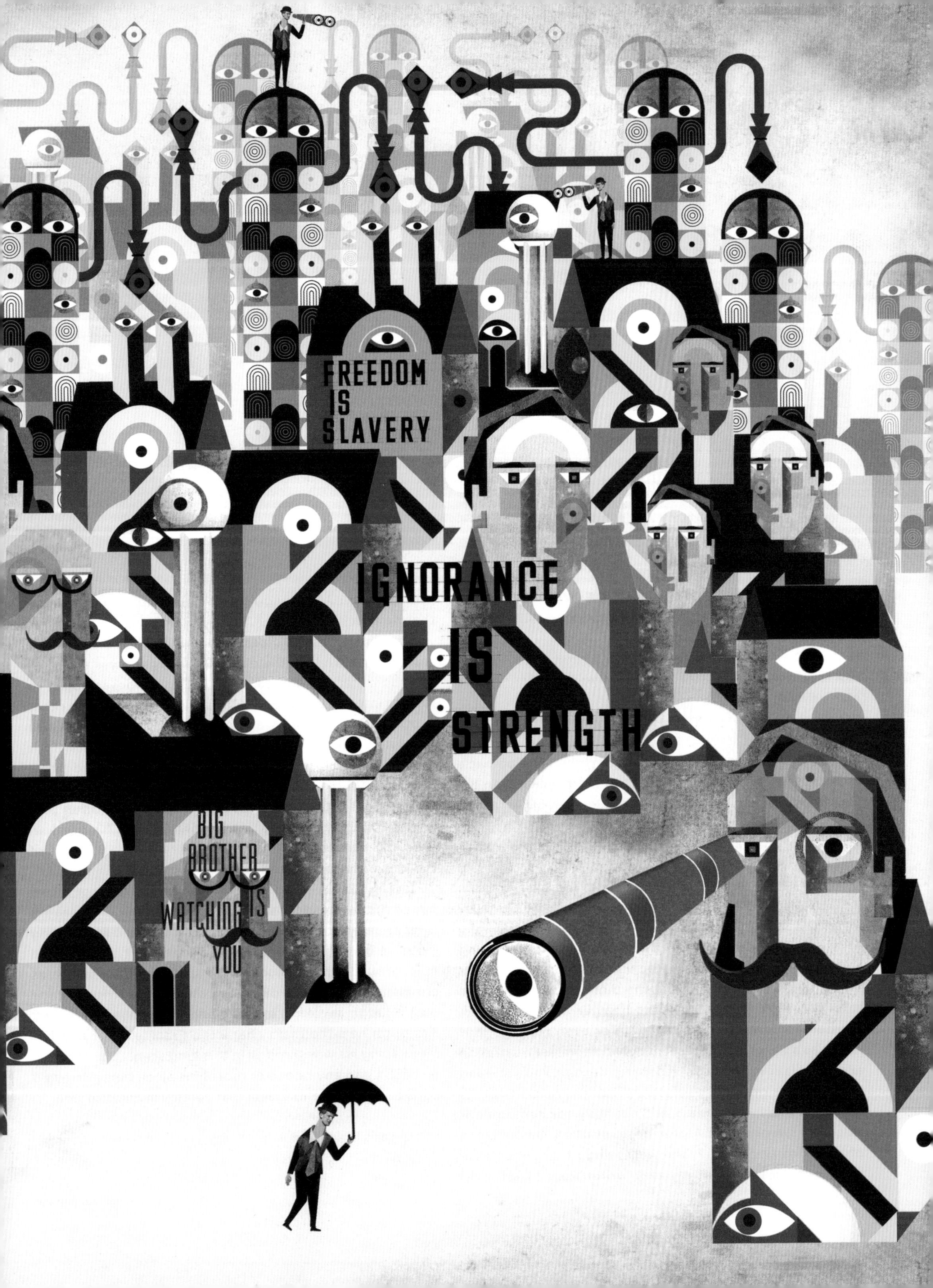
FREEDOM IS SLAVERY
IGNORANCE IS STRENGTH
BIG BROTHER IS WATCHING YOU

The Man with the Golden Arm

Nelson Algren

ART/ADAPTATION BY **Jeremy Eaton**

FOUR YEARS AFTER THE END OF WORLD WAR II —and fully six years before the publication of William Burroughs's *Junky*, during a period of stultifying conformism in America—Chicago author Nelson Algren wrote one of the true masterpieces of postwar American fiction, *The Man with the Golden Arm*. Algren may have been the last of the practitioners of what was once a thriving subgenre, the Proletarian novel, as written by Theodore Dreiser, John Dos Passos, and James T. Farrell. Algren reached the pinnacle of his artistry with *Arm*, published in 1949, which won the very first National Book Award for Fiction in 1950, an award Algren received at the Waldorf Hotel in New York City from none other than Eleanor Roosevelt. It was his third book and only his second novel.

Written in a dense, rich, lyrical style, *The Man with the Golden Arm* is situated in the lower depths of Chicago, a world inhabited by memorable coneroos and conmen, prostitutes, card hustlers, and addicts, with not a winning hand among them. Frankie Machine is a morphine addict trying to clean up his act, but the monkey on his back—a term Algren coined—only gets heavier and tougher. A murder is committed, not for gain or even revenge, but rather as an expression of seemingly bottomless frustration and humiliation. The novel resonates despair, and yet—and herein lies its greatness—also surprises the reader with its characters' self-awareness and capacity for companionship. The sweet regret Algren bestows upon the denizens of these lower depths is the wellspring of its undeniable grandeur. As the great mystery writer Ross Macdonald said: "Nelson Algren could talk about hell in such a way that he touched heaven."

The Man with the Golden Arm took the literary world by storm. For a while in the early 1950s Algren was the most famous writer in America. Then J. Edgar Hoover began to take an interest in Algren's political activities. Among other provocations, Algren was honorary cochair of the Save Ethel and Julius Rosenberg Committee. Hoover saw to it that a visa application from Algren was denied, and that a nonfiction book of his to be published by Doubleday was canceled.* Though Algren would write books, often brilliantly, for another thirty years, right up until his death in 1983, his moment as America's literary giant and voice of the voiceless had passed quickly.

Jeremy Eaton—who adapts Flannery O'Connor a few pages prior—presents a jumbled, blurry take on Frankie's brief appearance in court, after being pinched for stealing clothing irons ("eye-rons") at a department store. It's an epic, groundbreaking scene of despair and dark humor, as criminals and lowlifes of every conceivable stripe parade past a judge, invoking excuses and lies at every moment. Although he's the main character, Frankie's just another mook filing his way through in this long scene. The fact that he hasn't had any booze or morphine since being arrested adds to the disorienting feel that Jeremy invokes so well. . . .

---

* Many years later the book-length essay was published as *Nonconformity: Writing on Writing*.

—Dan Simon

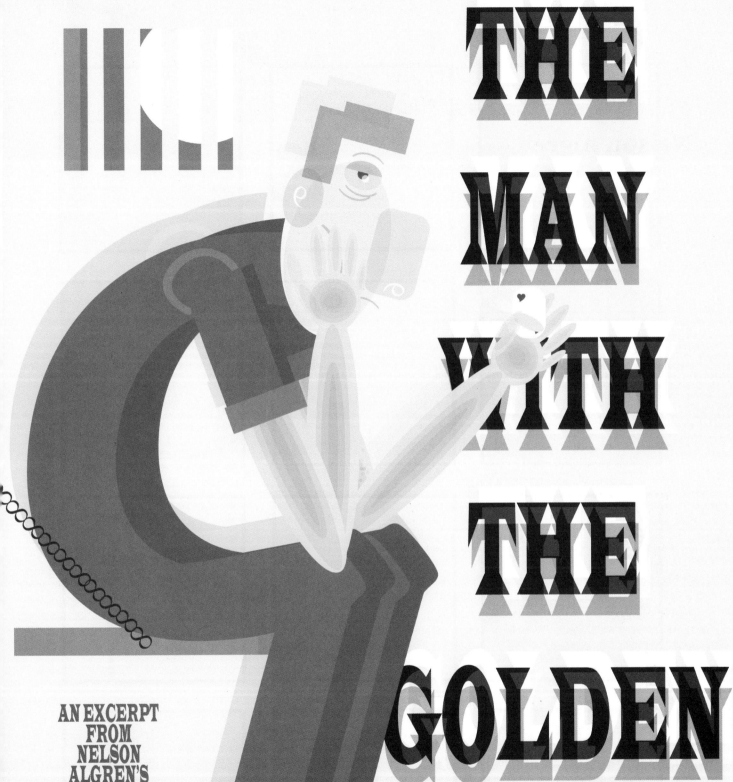

THE MAN WITH THE GOLDEN ARM

AN EXCERPT FROM NELSON ALGREN'S LANDMARK NOVEL, AS ADAPTED AND VISUALIZED BY JEREMY EATON

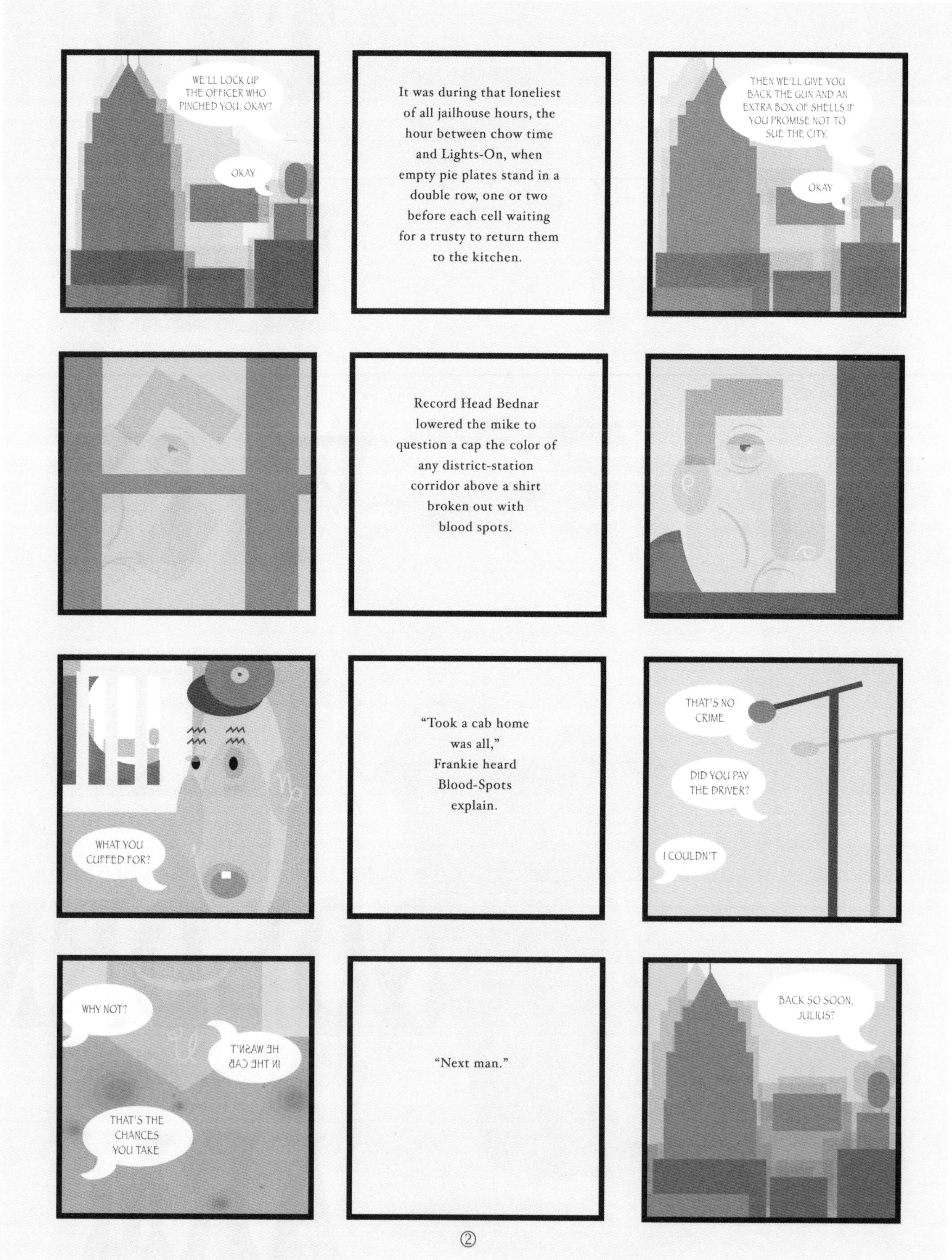
WE'LL LOCK UP THE OFFICER WHO PINCHED YOU. OKAY?
OKAY
It was during that loneliest of all jailhouse hours, the hour between chow time and Lights-On, when empty pie plates stand in a double row, one or two before each cell waiting for a trusty to return them to the kitchen.
THEN WE'LL GIVE YOU BACK THE GUN AND AN EXTRA BOX OF SHELLS IF YOU PROMISE NOT TO SUE THE CITY.
OKAY
Record Head Bednar lowered the mike to question a cap the color of any district-station corridor above a shirt broken out with blood spots.
WHAT YOU CUFFED FOR?
"Took a cab home was all," Frankie heard Blood-Spots explain.
THAT'S NO CRIME
DID YOU PAY THE DRIVER?
I COULDN'T
WHY NOT?
HE WASN'T IN THE CAB
THAT'S THE CHANCES YOU TAKE
"Next man."
BACK SO SOON, JULIUS?
2

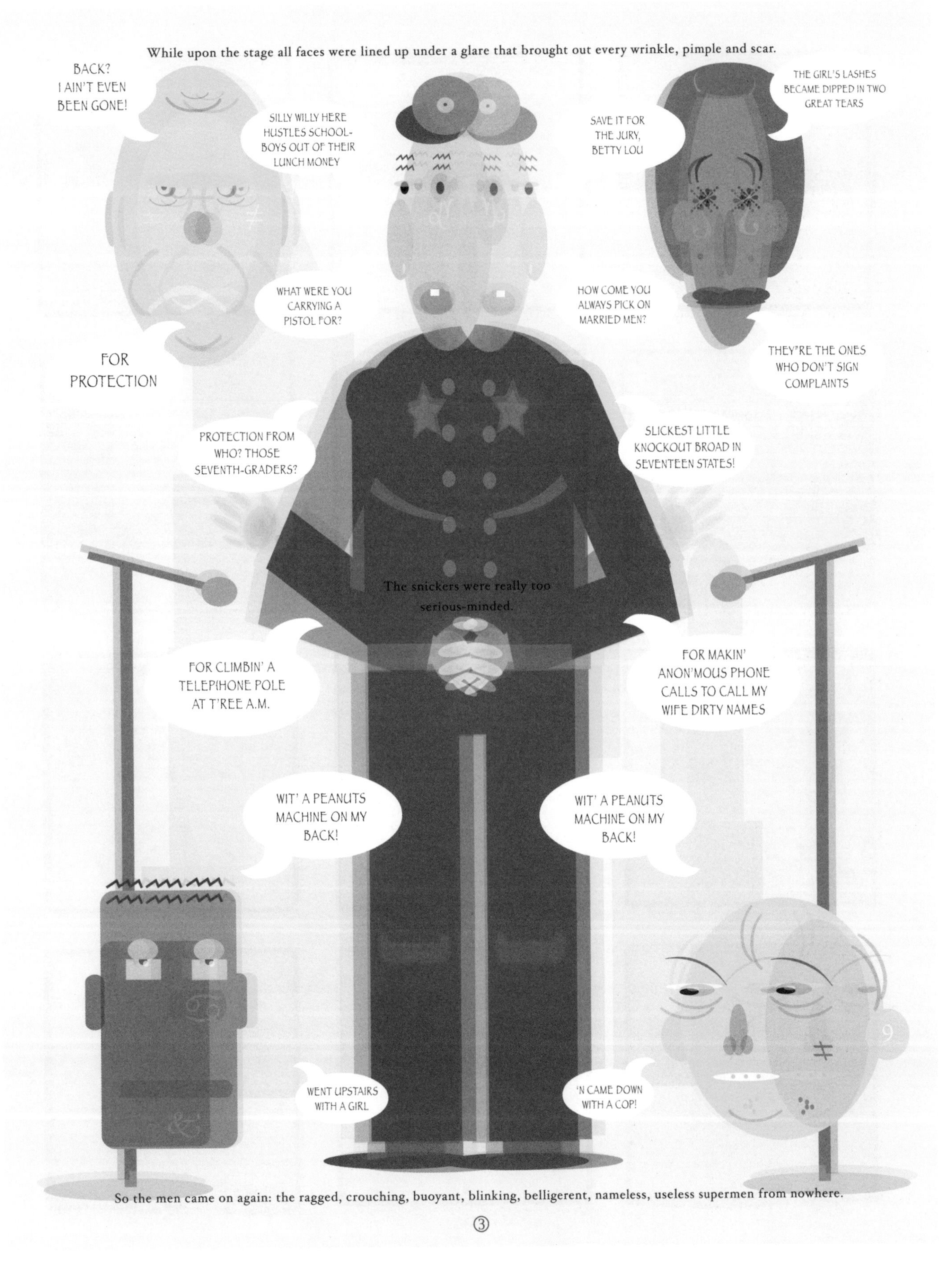
While upon the stage all faces were lined up under a glare that brought out every wrinkle, pimple and scar.
BACK? I AIN'T EVEN BEEN GONE!
SILLY WILLY HERE HUSTLES SCHOOL-BOYS OUT OF THEIR LUNCH MONEY
SAVE IT FOR THE JURY, BETTY LOU
THE GIRL'S LASHES BECAME DIPPED IN TWO GREAT TEARS
WHAT WERE YOU CARRYING A PISTOL FOR?
HOW COME YOU ALWAYS PICK ON MARRIED MEN?
FOR PROTECTION
THEY'RE THE ONES WHO DON'T SIGN COMPLAINTS
PROTECTION FROM WHO? THOSE SEVENTH-GRADERS?
SLICKEST LITTLE KNOCKOUT BROAD IN SEVENTEEN STATES!
The snickers were really too serious-minded.
FOR CLIMBIN' A TELEP(HONE POLE AT T'REE A.M.
FOR MAKIN' ANON'MOUS PHONE CALLS TO CALL MY WIFE DIRTY NAMES
WIT' A PEANUTS MACHINE ON MY BACK!
WIT' A PEANUTS MACHINE ON MY BACK!
WENT UPSTAIRS WITH A GIRL
'N CAME DOWN WITH A COP!
So the men came on again: the ragged, crouching, buoyant, blinking, belligerent, nameless, useless supermen from nowhere.
③

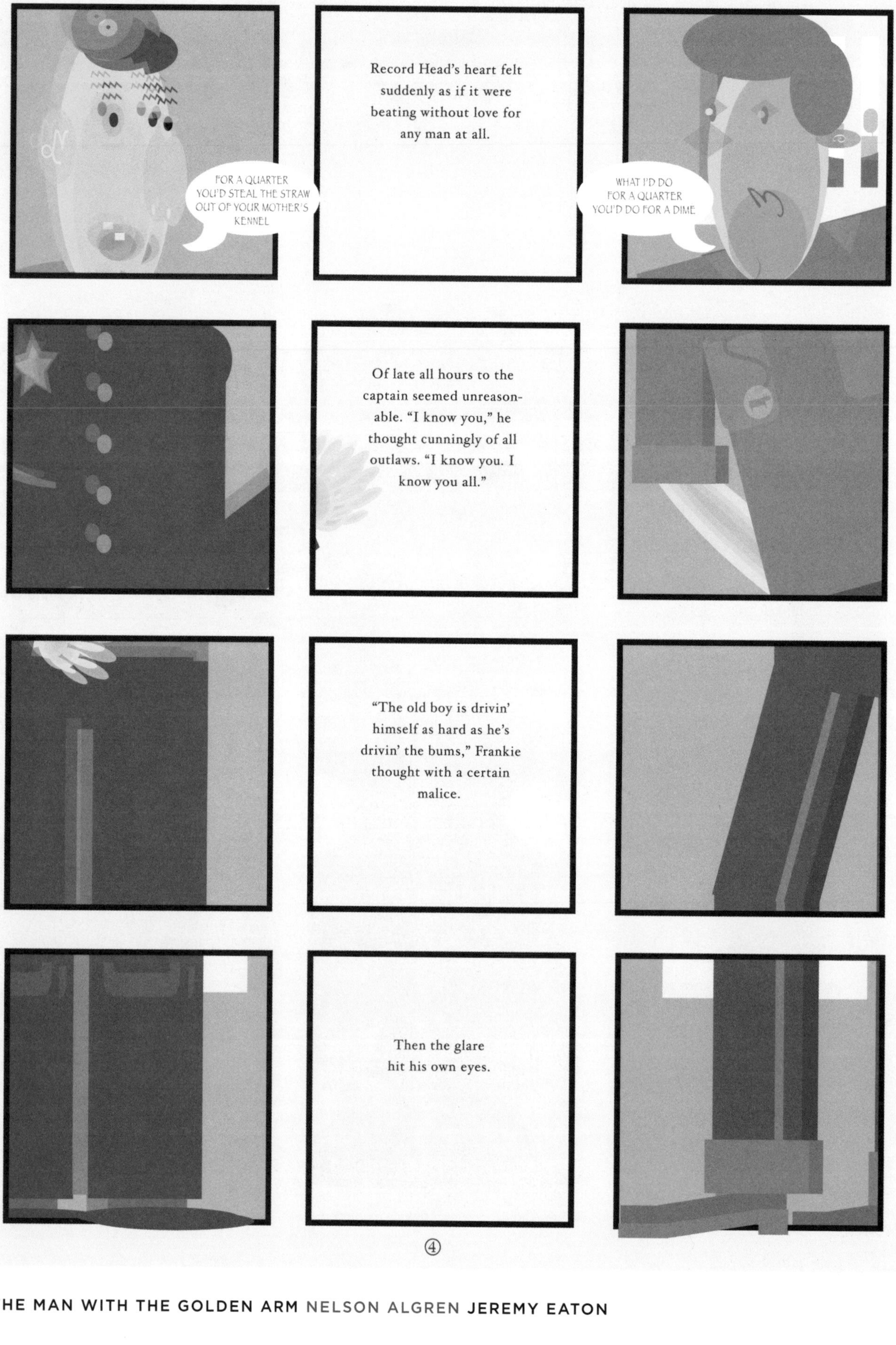
FOR A QUARTER YOU'D STEAL THE STRAW OUT OF YOUR MOTHER'S KENNEL
Record Head's heart felt suddenly as if it were beating without love for any man at all.
WHAT I'D DO FOR A QUARTER YOU'D DO FOR A DIME
Of late all hours to the captain seemed unreasonable. "I know you," he thought cunningly of all outlaws. "I know you. I know you all."
"The old boy is drivin' himself as hard as he's drivin' the bums," Frankie thought with a certain malice.
Then the glare hit his own eyes.
④

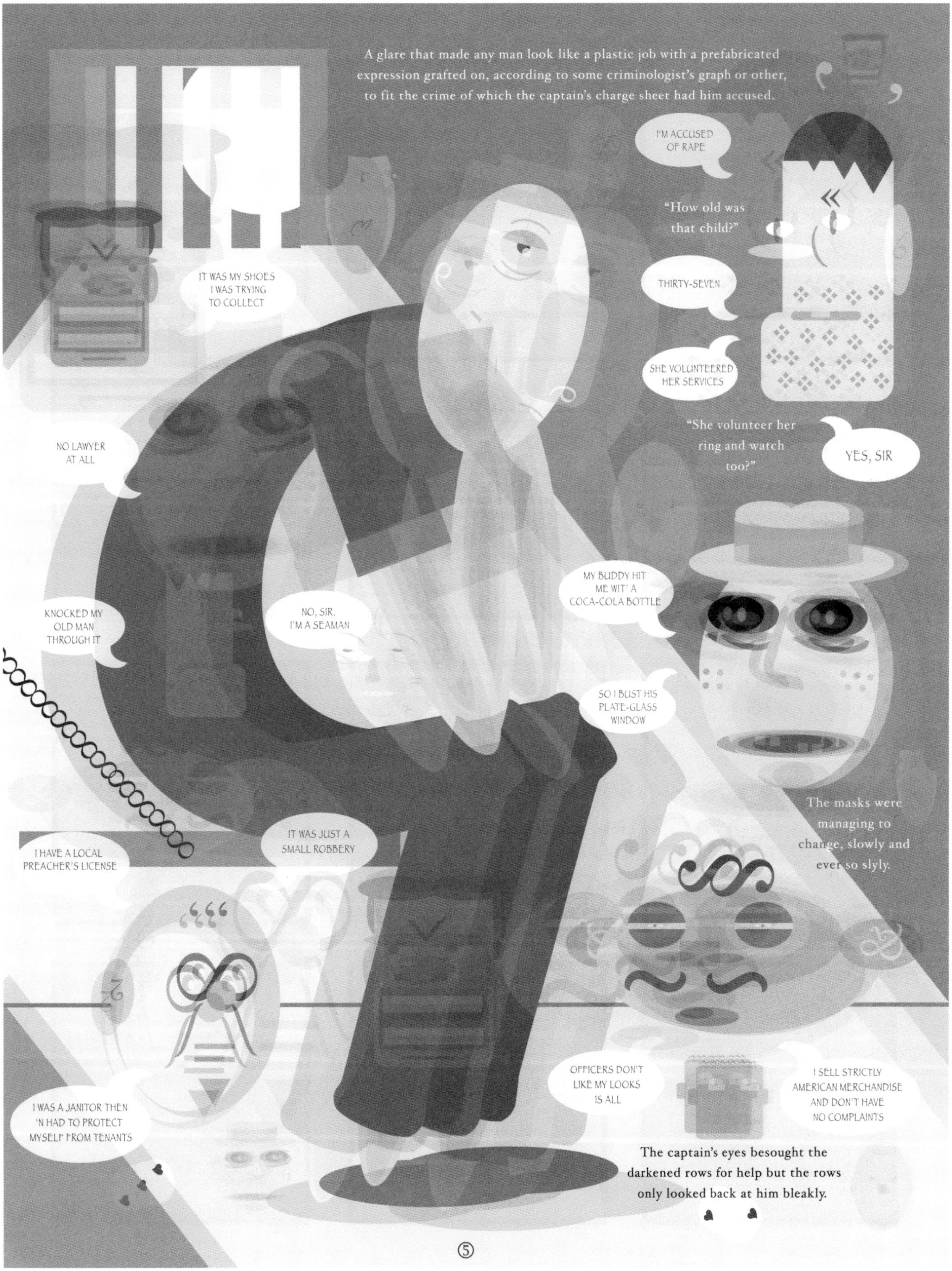
A glare that made any man look like a plastic job with a prefabricated expression grafted on, according to some criminologist's graph or other, to fit the crime of which the captain's charge sheet had him accused.
I'M ACCUSED OF RAPE
"How old was that child?"
IT WAS MY SHOES I WAS TRYING TO COLLECT
THIRTY-SEVEN
SHE VOLUNTEERED HER SERVICES
"She volunteer her ring and watch too?"
YES, SIR
NO LAWYER AT ALL
MY BUDDY HIT ME WIT' A COCA-COLA BOTTLE
KNOCKED MY OLD MAN THROUGH IT
NO, SIR, I'M A SEAMAN
SO I BUST HIS PLATE-GLASS WINDOW
The masks were managing to change, slowly and ever so slyly.
I HAVE A LOCAL PREACHER'S LICENSE
IT WAS JUST A SMALL ROBBERY
OFFICERS DON'T LIKE MY LOOKS IS ALL
I SELL STRICTLY AMERICAN MERCHANDISE AND DON'T HAVE NO COMPLAINTS
I WAS A JANITOR THEN 'N HAD TO PROTECT MYSELF FROM TENANTS
The captain's eyes besought the darkened rows for help but the rows only looked back at him bleakly.
⑤

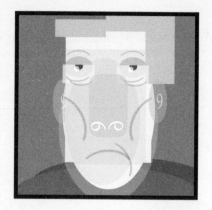

The flat-nosed, square-faced, tousled blond with the dark lines under the eyes was next.

FRANCIS MAJCINEK, DIVISION ARMS HOTEL

WHAT WERE YOU UP TO WITH THE SHOPPING BAG AT NIEBOLDT'S, DEALER?

WENT TO BUY AN EYE-RON

"With a shopping bag?"

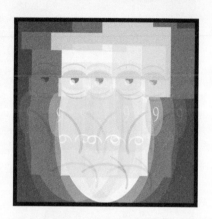

"Had to stop by the butcher's on the first floor."

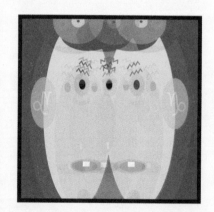

THOSE WEREN'T LAMB CHOPS FELL OUT OF THE BAG. HOW LONG YOU BEEN ON THE STUFF, FRANKIE?

I'VE KICKED IT

Frankie managed a look of blandest innocence.

NOT A NERVE IN HIS BODY!

NEXT MAN

⑥

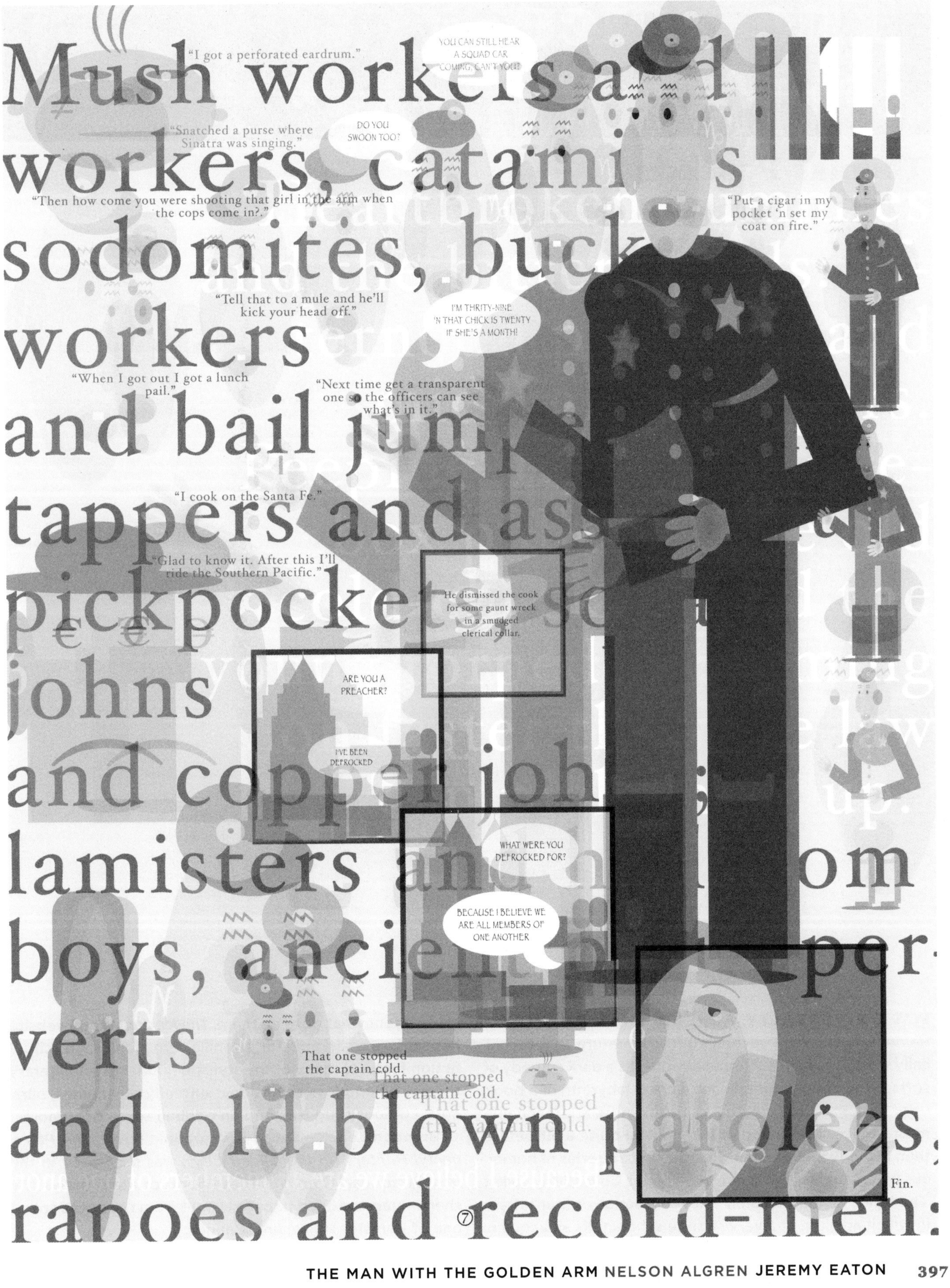
Mush workers a d
"I got a perforated eardrum."
YOU CAN STILL HEAR A SQUAD CAR COMING, CAN'T YOU?
"Snatched a purse where Sinatra was singing."
DO YOU SWOON TOO?
workers, catami s
"Then how come you were shooting that girl in the arm when the cops come in?."
"Put a cigar in my pocket 'n set my coat on fire."
sodomites, buck
"Tell that to a mule and he'll kick your head off."
I'M THIRTY-NINE 'N THAT CHICK IS TWENTY IF SHE'S A MONTH!
workers
"When I got out I got a lunch pail."
"Next time get a transparent one so the officers can see what's in it."
and bail jum
"I cook on the Santa Fe."
tappers and ass
"Glad to know it. After this I'll ride the Southern Pacific."
He dismissed the cook for some gaunt wreck in a smudged clerical collar.
pickpocke
ARE YOU A PREACHER?
I'VE BEEN DEFROCKED
johns
and copper joh
WHAT WERE YOU DEFROCKED FOR?
BECAUSE I BELIEVE WE ARE ALL MEMBERS OF ONE ANOTHER
lamisters a om
boys, ancie per-
verts
That one stopped the captain cold.
and old blown parolees,
Fin.
rapoes and record-men:
⑦

"The Voice of the Hamster"

Thomas Pynchon

ART/ADAPTATION BY **Brendan Leach**

IT'S UNIVERSALLY AGREED THAT *GRAVITY'S Rainbow* is Thomas Pynchon's gift to literature. Pyrotechnically written but almost impenetrable, it's a dark comedy of sorts, a towering mountain and a crazy labyrinth of a book. Prior to it, Pynchon created a smaller, more approachable masterpiece, *The Crying of Lot 49*. And quite a bit before that, in the 1952–53 school year, he wrote a series of humorous pieces for his high school newspaper. Collectively called "The Voice of the Hamster," they're a series of four letters in which an alum of a very strange school tells an acquain-tance about what goes on there. *The Modern Word* website has said: "Remarkable for juvenilia, Pynchon's high school fiction features many of the stylistic flourishes and literary themes he employs to this day: surreally silly names, para-noia, copious drug use, and an oddball sense of humor."

Brendan Leach—whose first graphic novel, *The Ptero-dactyl Hunters (in the Gilded City)*, was excerpted in the *Best American Comics* series—appropriately draws the shenanigans on lined paper, straight from the notebook of one of Hamster High's finest minds.

THOMAS PYNCHON'S

THE
VOICE
OF THE
HAMSTER

DRAWN BY

BRENDAN LEACH

Dear Sam,
    You may remember me — I don't know. I met you at that party in Huntington last August. I was the squat individual with the red crewcut who was doing the imitation of Winston Churchill. Anyway, you expressed interest in the school I go to and asked me to get in touch with you. So, here I am...

13 November 1952

Hamster High is located on a rock about a half-mile off the South Shore, and not a very big rock at that, as anybody can tell you who's been there at high tide. Nobody seems to know why they call the place Hamster High, other than the highly debatable rumor that its founder, J. Fattington Woodgrouse, had a strong liking for the fuddy little creatures. There is a statue of J. Fattington Woodgrouse in front of the school. He is a little baldheaded man with a pot belly, and he looks like a cross between the last Martian and a hungry barracuda. Last Hallowe'en some one wrote on this statue a very nasty word in bright orange paint. There was a big scandal. I was suspended for four weeks.

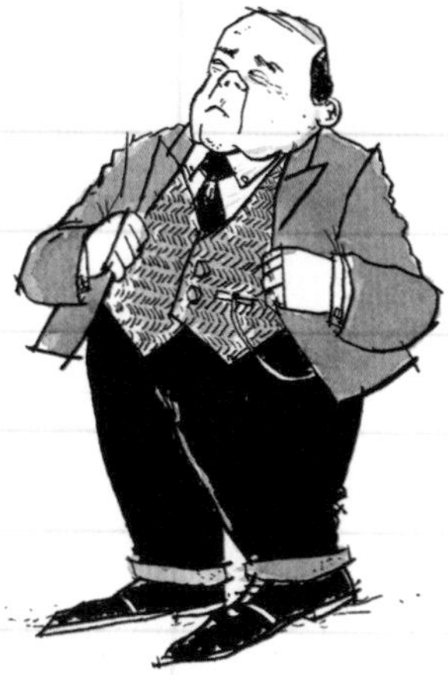

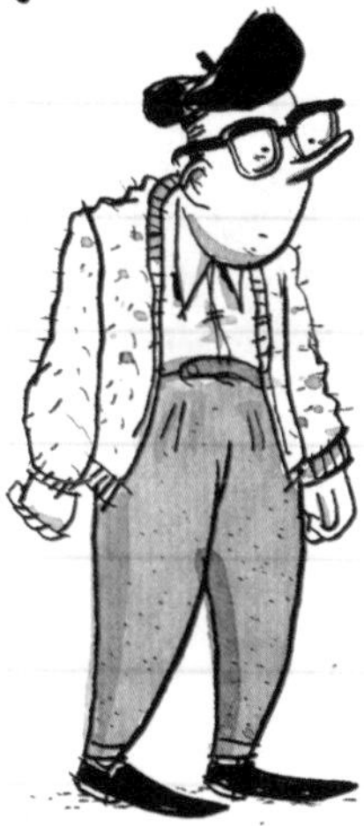

Maybe the fact that we're fairly well isolated accounts for why Hamster High is— well, not exactly crazy, but—slightly odd. Take for example our trig teacher, Mr. Faggiaducci. He's a quiet respectable young man who tears around in a long, baby-blue hotrod sedan, and he's always telling be-bop jokes in class. There's nothing actually wrong with him, it's just that he used to be a bop drummer, and now he wishes he were back with the boys at Birdland and Eddie Condon's. He talks to himself a lot and I've heard rumors he takes heroin. A real "gone guy."

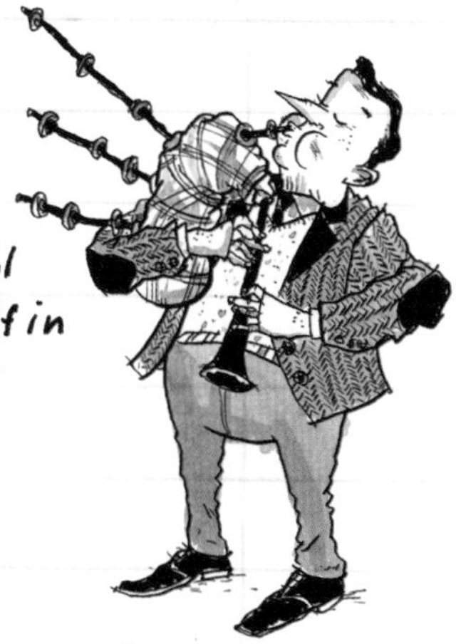

Then of course there's our principal, Mr. Sowturkle. This boy also has music leanings—he plays the bagpipes. The bad thing about it is that he uses school hours to practice. He's very devoted to the bloody instrument. He locks himself in his office for about an hour every day to play it. Somehow one gets the idea he doesn't like interruptions. He was born in the hills of Tennessee, and he still carries a shotgun with him, a nasty thing with a sawed-off barrel.

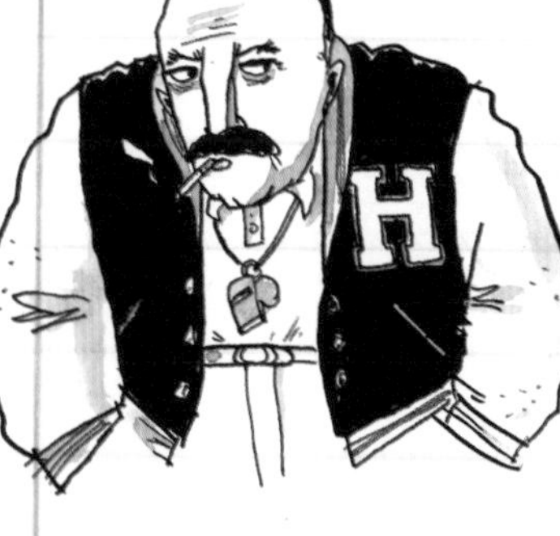
H

You might think we're pretty limited as far as sports go, being out on a rock like we are, but that isn't so. Of course, we can't have our own football fields, so we use the ones in the nearest town, Riverhampton. I feel sorry for Coach Willis. He turned down a chance to coach Football at one of the Big Ten Colleges and came to Hamster High instead. In the past three years we've lost every game except one, and that was a tie with some grade school. The only reason we were able to tie them was because the grade school team was continually being penalized for unnecessary roughness. Coach Willis drinks a lot.

But now I must say so long because I am getting tired, and I have a lot of trig homework to do. Not that it has to be done for tomorrow, as chances are Mr. Faggiaducci won't be there; he's out on another binge. Remind me sometime to tell you about the time the State Education Inspector came to Hamster High. Poor fellow—he's in an institution now.

Your drunken amigo,
Boscoe Stein

18 December 1952

Dear Sam,

In your last letter you mentioned that you wanted to hear about the time the State Education Inspector came to Hamster High. WELL...

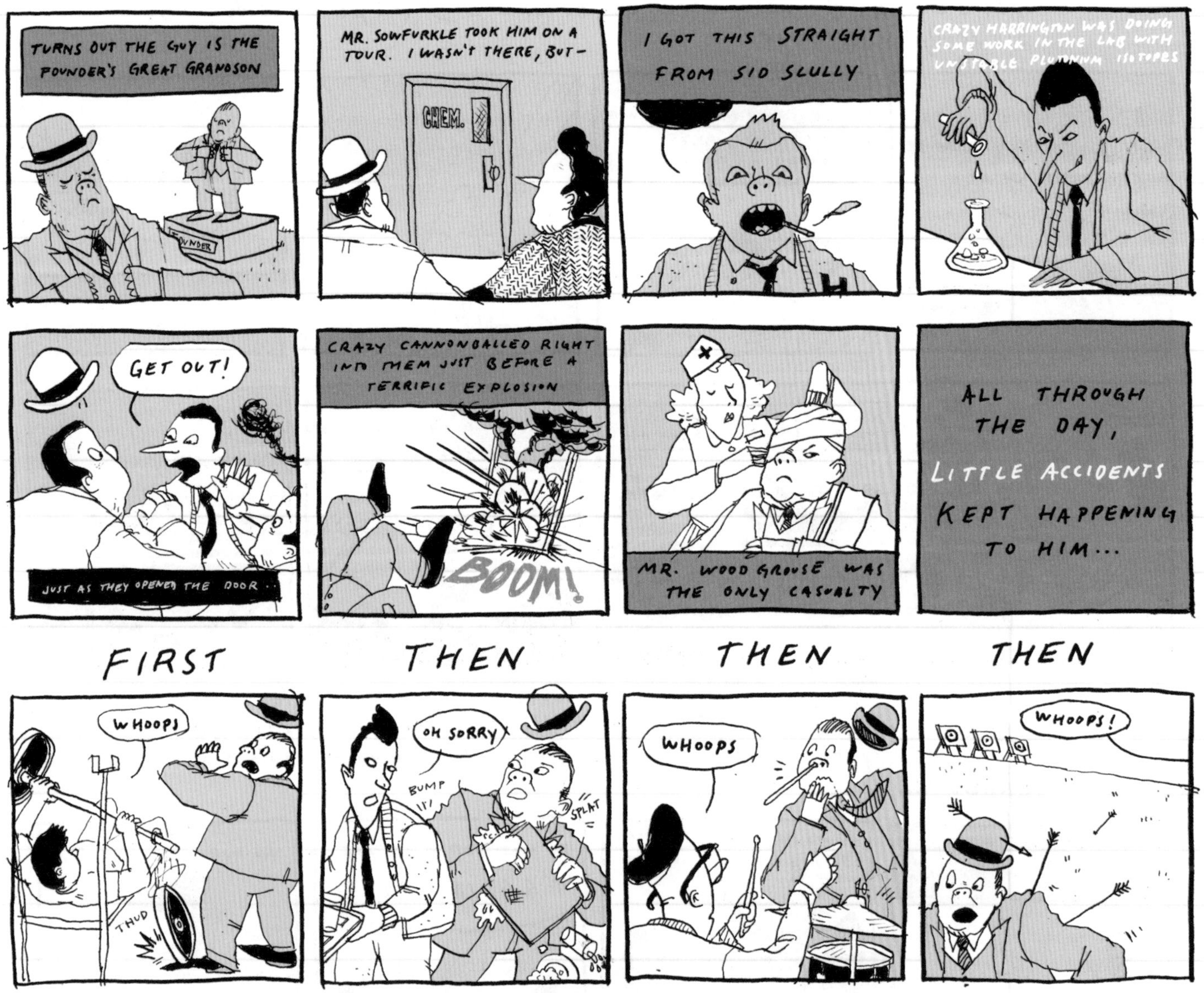

TURNS OUT THE GUY IS THE FOUNDER'S GREAT GRANDSON
FOUNDER
MR. SOWFURKLE TOOK HIM ON A TOUR. I WASN'T THERE, BUT—
CHEM.
I GOT THIS STRAIGHT FROM SID SCULLY
CRAZY HARRINGTON WAS DOING SOME WORK IN THE LAB WITH UNSTABLE PLUTONIUM ISOTOPES
GET OUT!
JUST AS THEY OPENED THE DOOR...
CRAZY CANNONBALLED RIGHT INTO THEM JUST BEFORE A TERRIFIC EXPLOSION
BOOM!
MR. WOODGROUSE WAS THE ONLY CASUALTY
ALL THROUGH THE DAY, LITTLE ACCIDENTS KEPT HAPPENING TO HIM...
FIRST
THEN
THEN
THEN
WHOOPS
THUD
OH SORRY
BUMP
SPLAT
WHOOPS
WHOOPS!

He would have left then, but Coach Willis wanted him to watch football practice. Everything went O.K. until Coach Willis caught wind of the fact that Mr. Woodgrouse had played collegiate football. Before he knew what was happening—

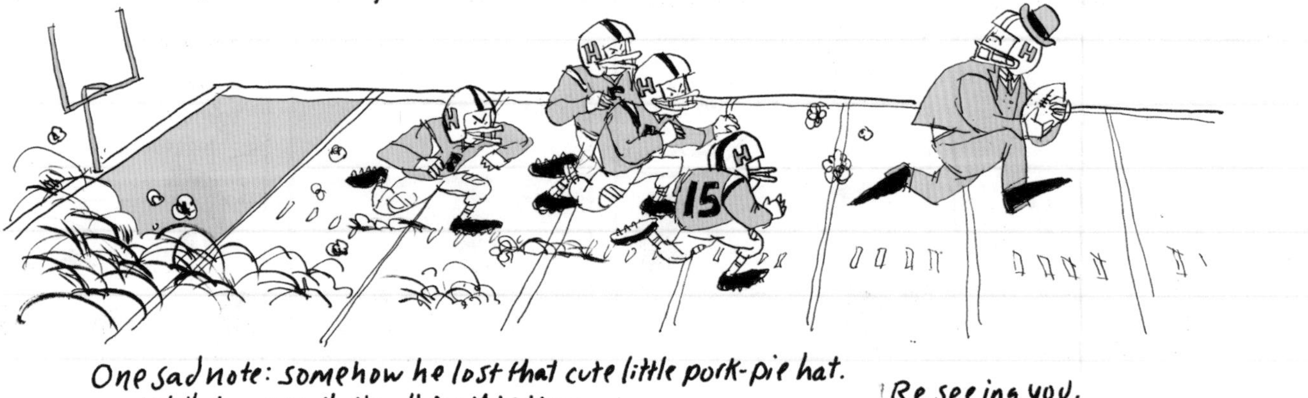

15

One sad note: somehow he lost that cute little pork-pie hat.
Well, I guess that's all for this time.

Be seeing you,
Roscoe Stein

22 January 1953

Dear Sam,

Sorry I haven't written sooner, but I'm in the midst of recovering from A NEW Year's Eve party. It was what can only be called a riot. The party was thrown by Sid Scully's sister Marge...

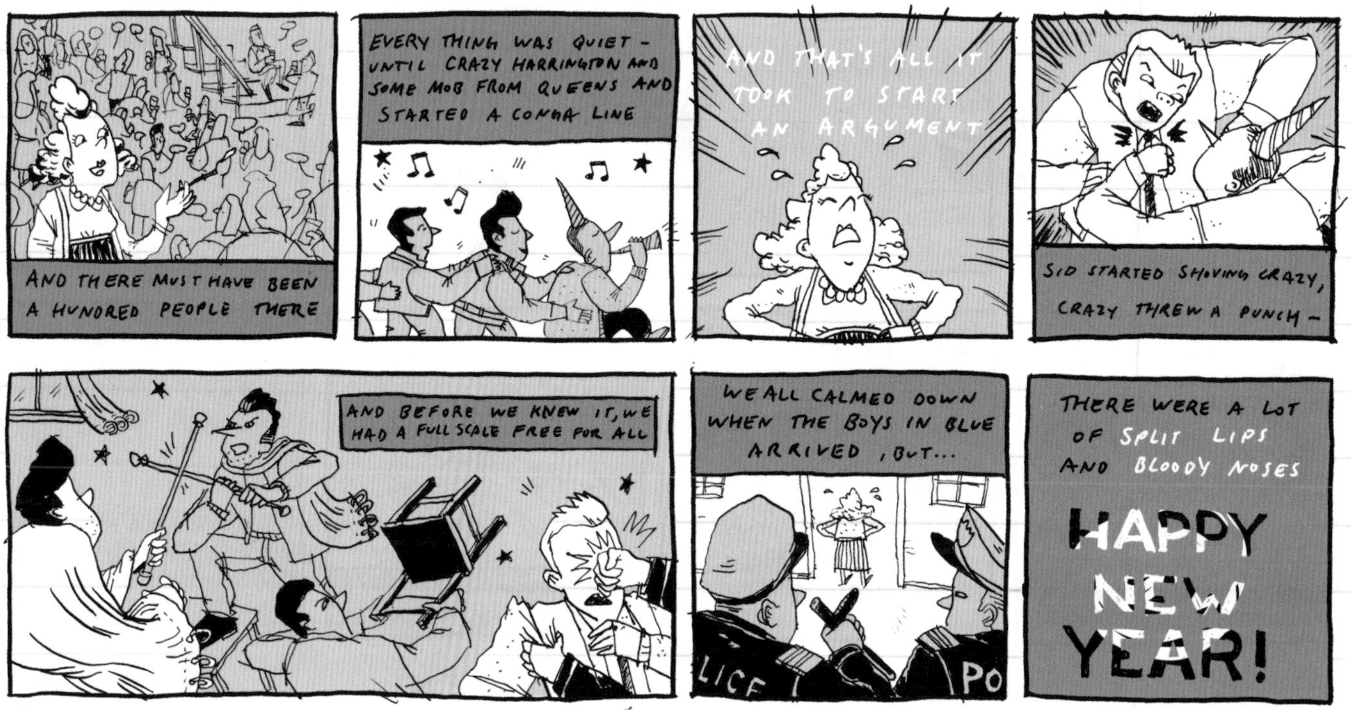
AND THERE MUST HAVE BEEN A HUNDRED PEOPLE THERE
EVERY THING WAS QUIET - UNTIL CRAZY HARRINGTON AND SOME MOB FROM QUEENS AND STARTED A CONGA LINE
AND THAT'S ALL IT TOOK TO START AN ARGUMENT
SID STARTED SHOVING CRAZY, CRAZY THREW A PUNCH -
AND BEFORE WE KNEW IT, WE HAD A FULL SCALE FREE FOR ALL
WE ALL CALMED DOWN WHEN THE BOYS IN BLUE ARRIVED, BUT...
LICE
PO
THERE WERE A LOT OF SPLIT LIPS AND BLOODY NOSES
HAPPY NEW YEAR!

In your last letter you said you wanted to know more about Mr. Rafael Faggiaducci, who teaches "trig." In that class, I sit with "the Boys" (capital B), a peculiar and very select group. We are engaged in a fascinating experiment in psychology...

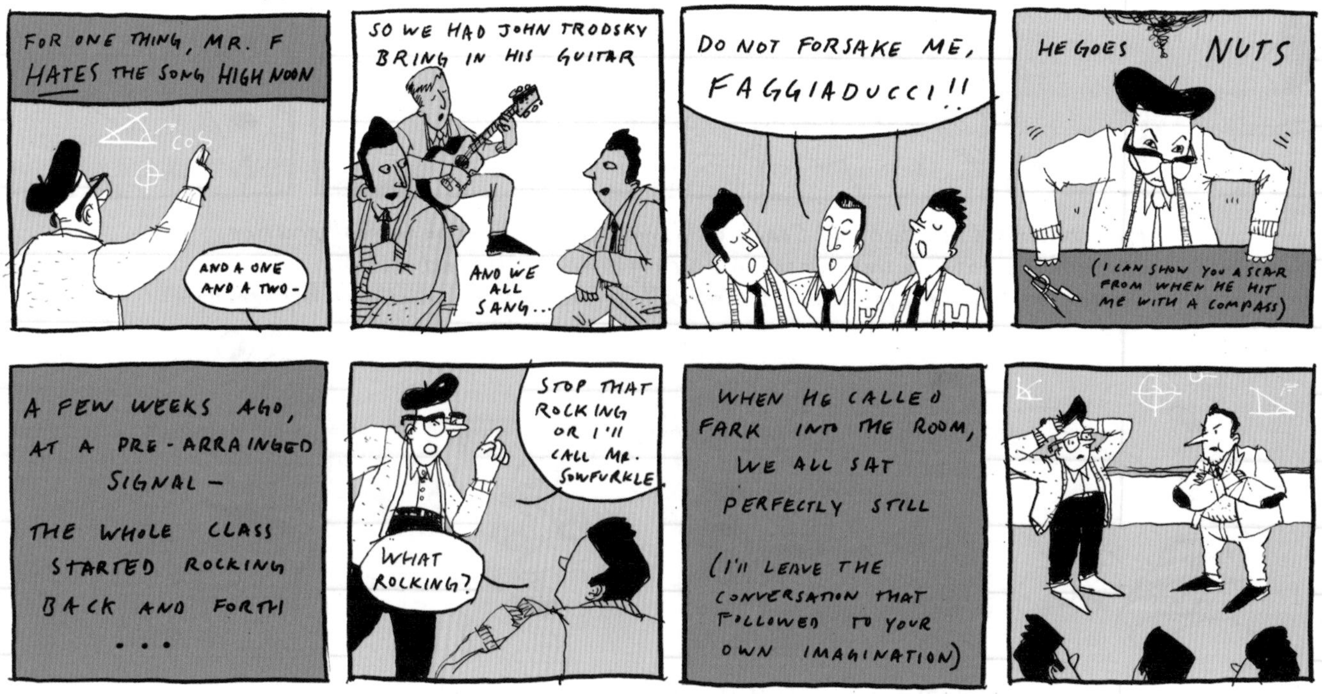
FOR ONE THING, MR. F HATES THE SONG HIGH NOON
AND A ONE AND A TWO-
SO WE HAD JOHN TRODSKY BRING IN HIS GUITAR
AND WE ALL SANG...
DO NOT FORSAKE ME, FAGGIADUCCI!!
HE GOES NUTS
(I CAN SHOW YOU A SCAR FROM WHEN HE HIT ME WITH A COMPASS)
A FEW WEEKS AGO, AT A PRE-ARRAINGED SIGNAL - THE WHOLE CLASS STARTED ROCKING BACK AND FORTH ...
STOP THAT ROCKING OR I'LL CALL MR. SOWFURKLE
WHAT ROCKING?
WHEN HE CALLED FARK INTO THE ROOM, WE ALL SAT PERFECTLY STILL
(I'LL LEAVE THE CONVERSATION THAT FOLLOWED TO YOUR OWN IMAGINATION)

Well, Sam, I guess that's about all for now.

As always,

Bose.

19 February 1953

Dear Sam,

I did it! I passed trig! The Boys and I succeeded in getting Mr. F completely fed up with us. He got so mad that he refused to proctor the Regents exam. So we were stuck with some neurotic Czech. Anyway, we started singing...

DO NOT FORSAKE ME, FAGGIADUCCI!!
SHUT UP OR I'LL KICK YOU OUT!
HE GOT PURPLE AND SCREAMED! (NOT YELLED LIKE MR. F)
THEN HE STARTED SWEARING AND INSULTING US UNTIL HE GOT US PRETTY RILED
AND YOU KNOW – THERE'S ONE THING MEANER THAN THE BOYS... AND THAT'S THE BOYS RILED
SID SCULLY CALLED HIM SOMETHING IMPOLITE AND CRAZY HARRIMAN HIT HIM WITH A RULER
THEN...
THE BOYS AROSE, EN MASSE, PICKED HIM UP BODILY AND STUFFED HIM IN THE DUMB WAITER
AND LEFT HIM THERE SO WE COULD TAKE THE EXAM IN PEACE

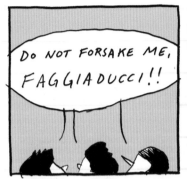

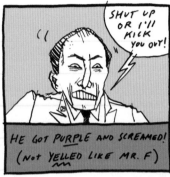

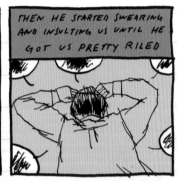

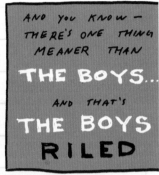

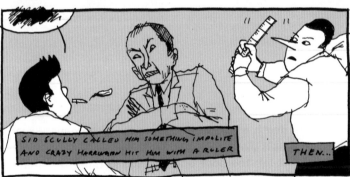

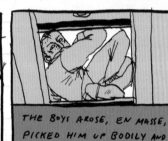

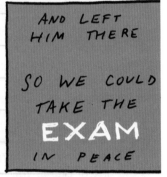

Faggiaducci had said that the best mark he had expected was somewhere in the low 60's; as it was, there was no mark lower than 92. (Don't ask me how we did it!) This, of course, had a severe psychological effect on Faggiaducci. He hasn't been to school in a week. I hear he had a breakdown. The Czech? Well, nobody uses that dumb waiter shaft anymore, and so we decided to leave him there. They may find him someday – I don't care much – he gets fed twice a week.

Must go now
Arrivaderci,
Bose.

Waiting for Godot

Samuel Beckett

ILLUSTRATION BY **Gustavo Rinaldi**

TWO TRAMPS ARE WAITING FOR ANOTHER man to arrive. He never does. End of play.

I've simplified *Waiting for Godot* a tiny bit here, but that is the gist of one of the most famous and debated plays since the days of Shakespeare. Written in French by the experimental Irish novelist and dramatist Samuel Beckett and first performed in 1953 (though written four years earlier), it involves Vladimir and Estragon waiting near a tree by the side of the road for a certain Godot, to whom they've made some kind of request. They talk about things, engage in some bickering and some slapstick, briefly talk about committing suicide, go offstage to urinate, decide to leave but never do. . . . They meet two strange characters who pass by, one of whom is apparently the slave of the other. A boy comes with a message from Godot, saying he's sorry he couldn't meet them but he's sure he'll be there tomorrow. End of Act One. The second act, apparently taking place the next day, is largely the same. We get hints that this has been going on every day for some time, and are left with the impression that it will continue.

Something vague yet seemingly profound is going on here. It must be an allegory. Godot is actually God, many people say, and these two people wait in vain for him to show up. The play is a Modernist, Existentialist comment on the death of God, the aloneness of humans. Except that Beckett denied this was what he had in mind. Sort of. Really, he left the door open, saying at times that maybe he subconsciously thought this. Others think Godot represents Jesus, and the two men are waiting for the Second Coming. Then there's the theory that Godot is Death, or that he, Vladimir, and Estragon symbolize the id, ego, and superego, as theorized by Freud. My favorite theory is a looser one proposed by professor Michael Worton: "He stands for what keeps us chained to and in existence, he is the unknowable that represents hope in an age when there is no hope, he is whatever fiction we want him to be—as long as he justifies our life-by-waiting."

Coming to us from São Paulo, Brazil, Gustavo Rinaldi uses splendid hatching to capture the loneliness of the scene—the empty setting, the broken, barren tree, the late afternoon light, the boredom of the two tramps . . . waiting . . . just waiting. . . .

SOURCE

Worton, Michael. "Waiting for Godot and Endgame: Theatre as Text." In *Bloom's Modern Critical Interpretations: Samuel Beckett's Waiting for Godot.* Edited by Harold Bloom. New York: Infobase Publishing, 2008.

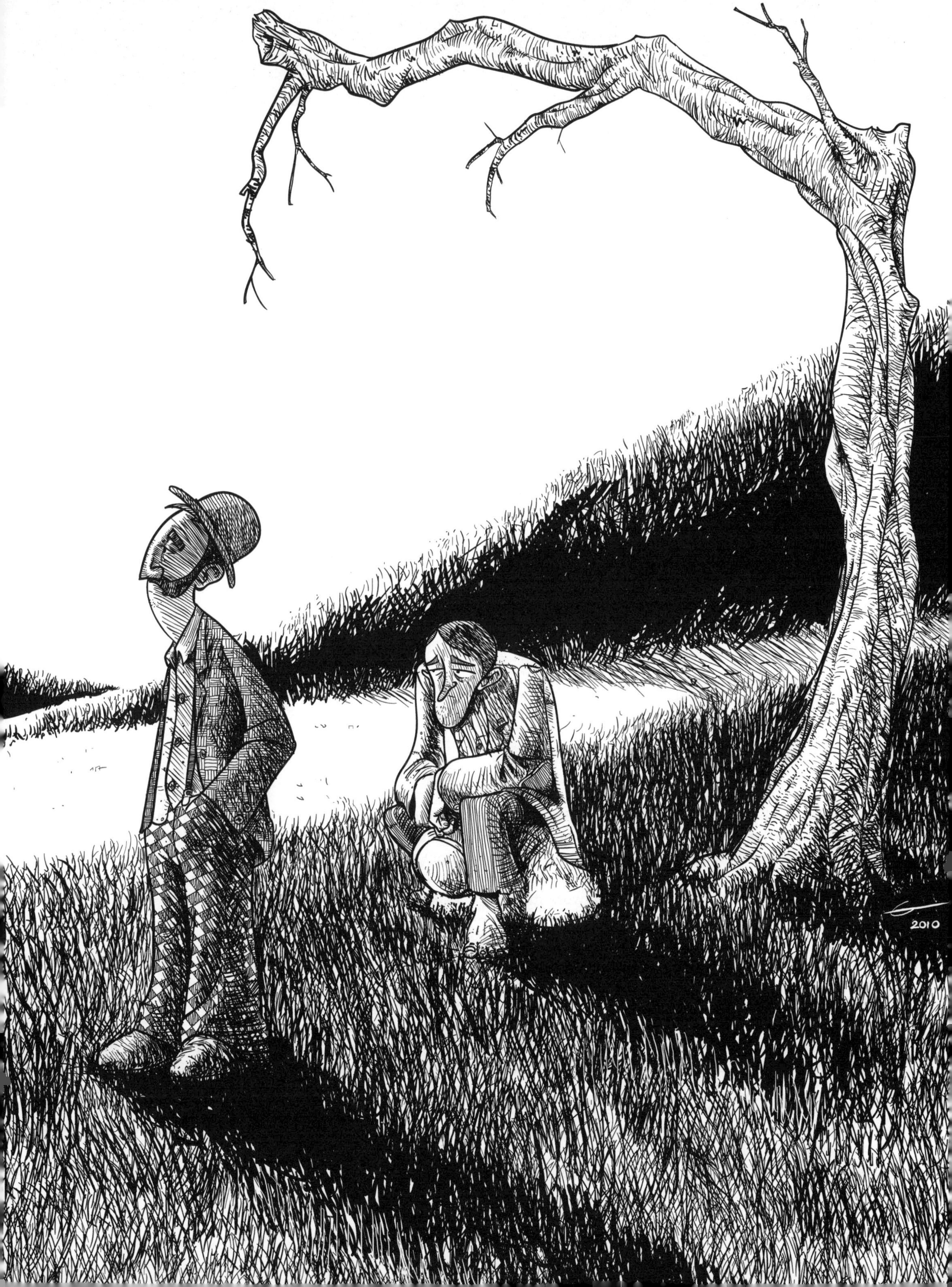
2010

"The Dancer"

Gabriela Mistral

ILLUSTRATION BY **Andrea Arroyo**

IT TURNS OUT THAT THE LEGENDARY PABLO Neurda was not the first Latin American to win the Nobel Prize for Literature. In fact, he wasn't even the first Chilean poet to win it. It was Gabriela Mistral who claimed the honor, winning in 1945. Unlike Neruda, she and her work strangely remain little known in the US. Of Basque and indigenous heritage, she was raised Catholic in a gorgeous, rural part of Chile, and all of these influences can be found in her work. Teacher, journalist, college professor, ambassador to the UN, autodidact, feminist, world-traveling expatriate, tireless crusader for social justice, Mistral led an amazing life. She appears on her country's currency, and to this day the Mistral brand of notebooks—named after her—remains hugely popular in Chile.

Like many observers, writer Ursula K. LeGuin—who translated a volume of Mistral's poetry spanning her entire output—said that even in her native country, Mistral has been watered down to make her safe for consumption. Her early poems about childhood and nature are given prominence,

the rest forgotten. LeGuin wrote: "I'd say that anybody who reads her might well be afraid of her. She can be frighteningly strange."

"The Dancer" ("La bailarina") is part of a cluster of poems called "Crazy Women" ("Locas mujeres") in Mistral's 1954 collection, *Winepress* (*Lagar*). Like many of Mistral's poems, it defies easy or possibly literal explanation. Essentially, the dancer is engaged in a powerful, highly transformative dance, "the dance of losing it all. / Whatever she had, she lets it go . . ."

Born in Mexico, New York artist Andrea Arroyo creates abstracted, vibrant paintings of women, which have been widely displayed. She often uses historical or mythological women as her basis, and has garnered a lot of attention for her *Flor de Tierra* series, which she explained as "an ongoing project in homage to the nearly 400 women of Ciudad Juárez, Mexico, that have been murdered since the early 1990s and whose deaths have not been brought to justice."

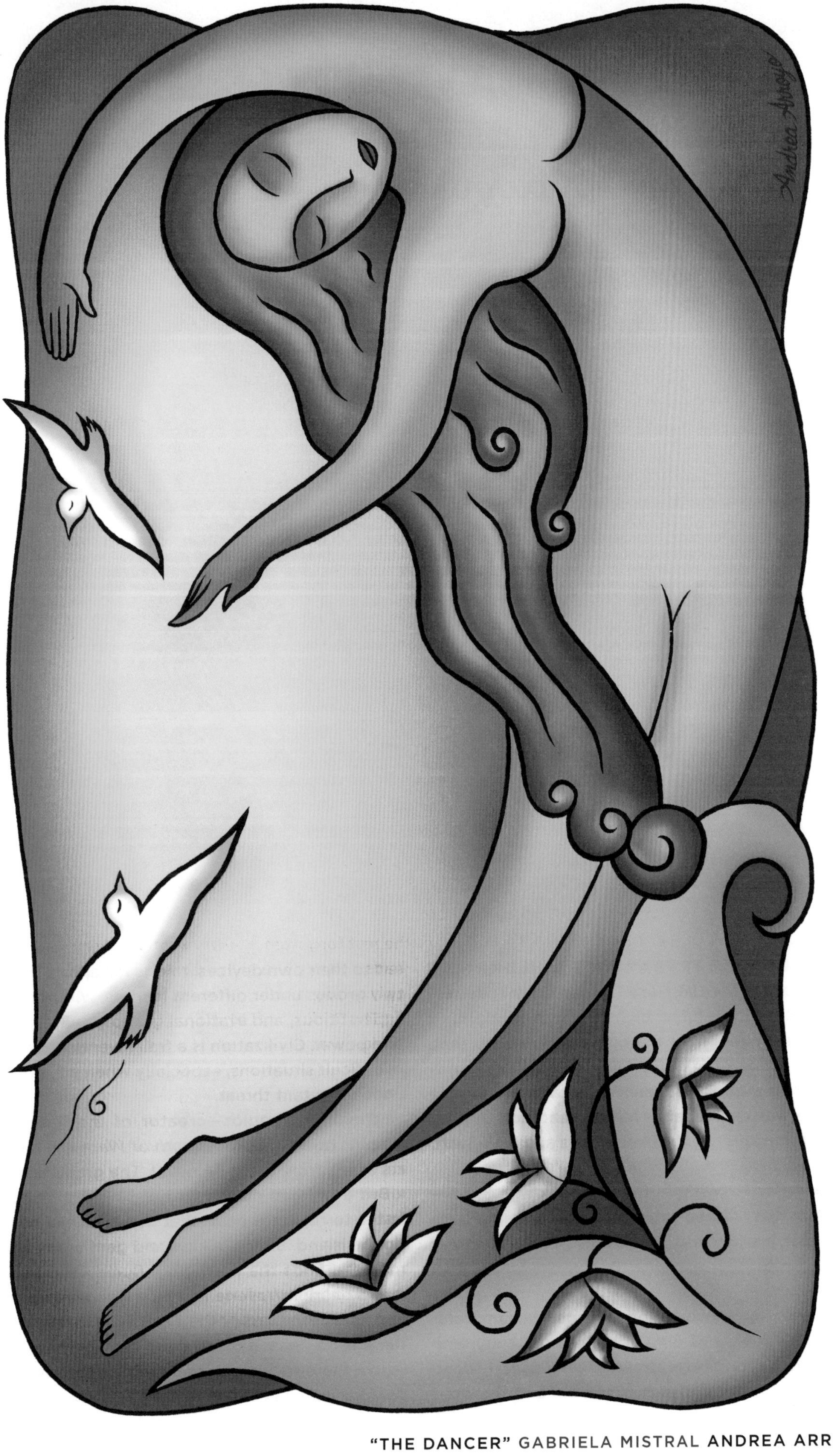
Andrea Arroyo

Lord of the Flies

William Golding

ART/ADAPTATION BY **Trevor Alixopulos**

PROBABLY BECAUSE IT FEATURES CHILDREN AS its characters, *Lord of the Flies*—like *The Catcher in the Rye*—is read and taught a lot in junior highs and high schools but pretty much disappears from the conversation after that. But make no mistake, *Lord of the Flies* is a nuanced, hard-hitting work of literature. Stephen King recalls reading the book when he was twelve, after having read nothing but boys' adventure novels like the Hardy Boys and Tom Swift:

> It was, so far as I remember, the first book with hands—strong ones that reached out of the pages and seized me by the throat. It said to me, "This is not just entertainment; it's life-or-death."

In this, his best-known work, Nobel-winner William Golding presents a bleak view of human nature and society, with a bunch of British schoolboys stranded on a desert island as his microcosm. With no adult presence, and the boys left to their own devices, things fall apart. They divide into two groups under different leaders, with the more violent, superstitious, and irrational group gaining more members and power. Civilization is a frail invention that dies quickly in difficult situations, especially when physical safety feels under constant threat.

Trevor Alixopulos—creator of the Ignatz-nominated graphic novel *The Hot Breath of War*—has adapted a critical scene from the 1954 novel. The group of wild boys has killed a pig and placed its head on a stick as an offering to the terrifying "beast" that they wrongly believe is living on the island. Simon, a kind and gentle boy with an innate morality, finds the horrifying, fly-covered head and goes into a delirium/reverie in which the head seems to talk to him. It is "the Lord of the Flies" and it reveals to him that there is no beast on the island but—perhaps more terrifyingly—there's a violent, untamable beast dwelling in every person, including Simon himself. He faints at this revelation.

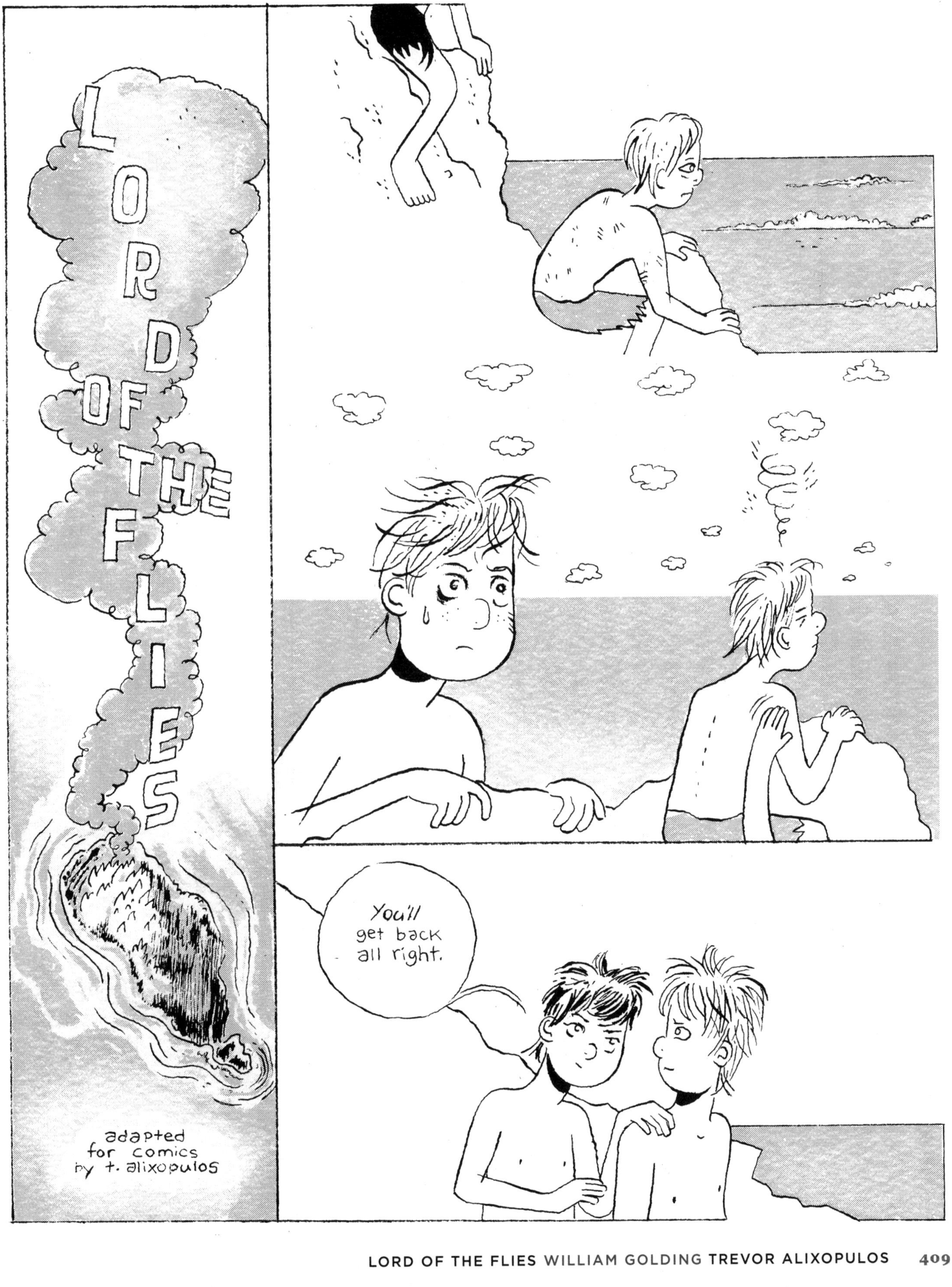
LORD OF THE FLIES
adapted for comics by t. alixopulos
You'll get back all right.

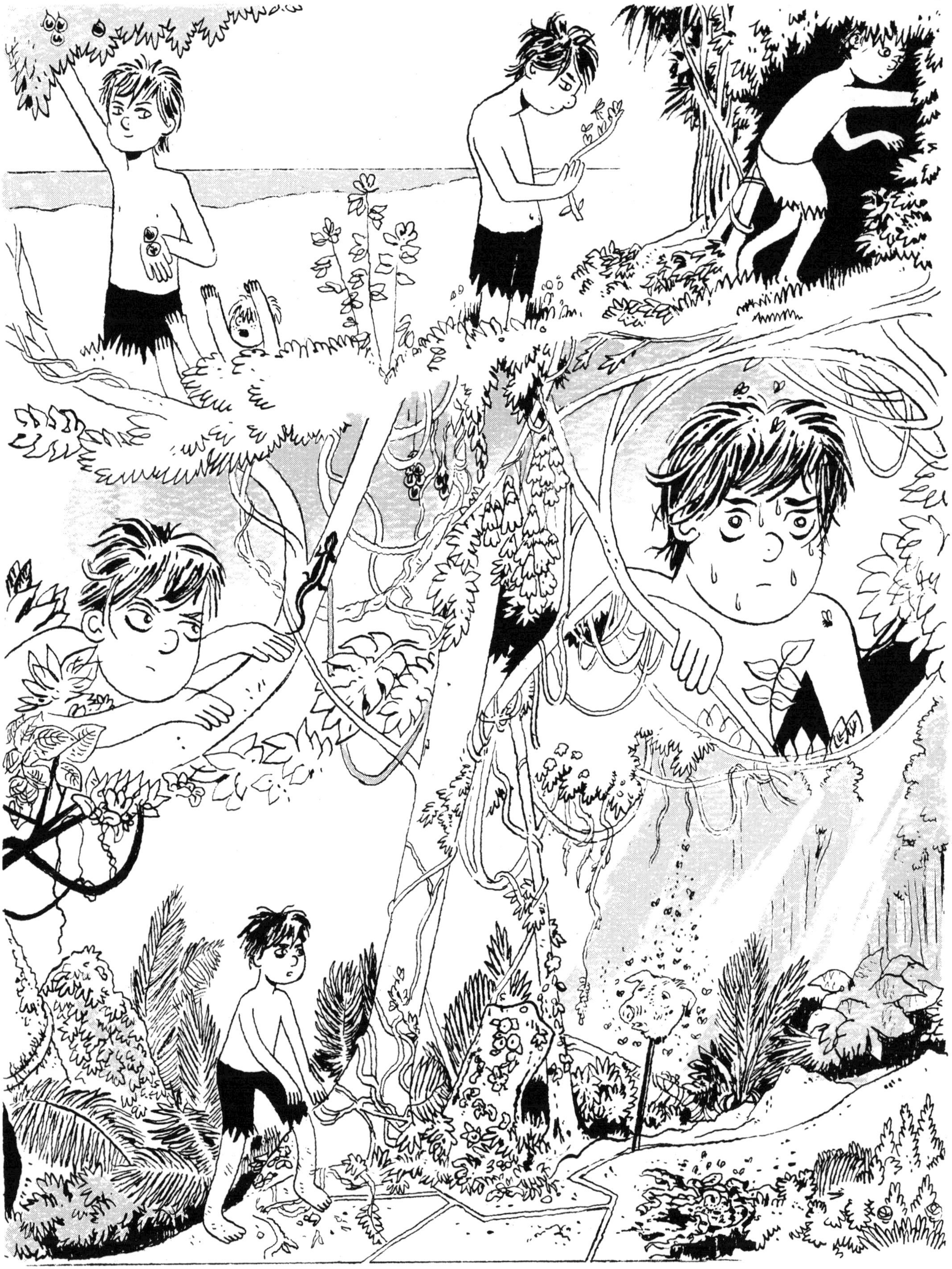

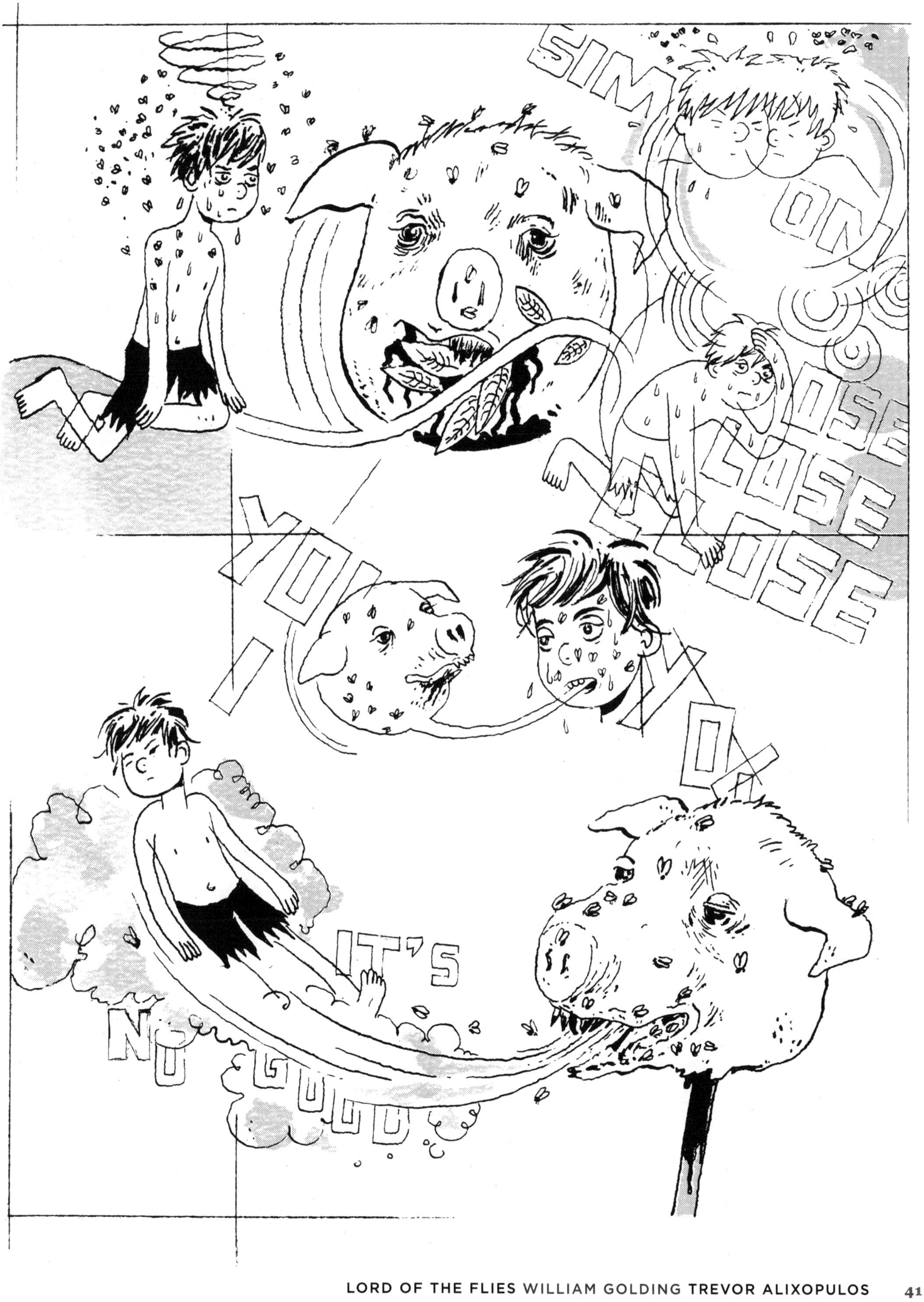
SIMON
LOSE
LOSE
LOSE
YOU
I
IT'S
NO GOOD

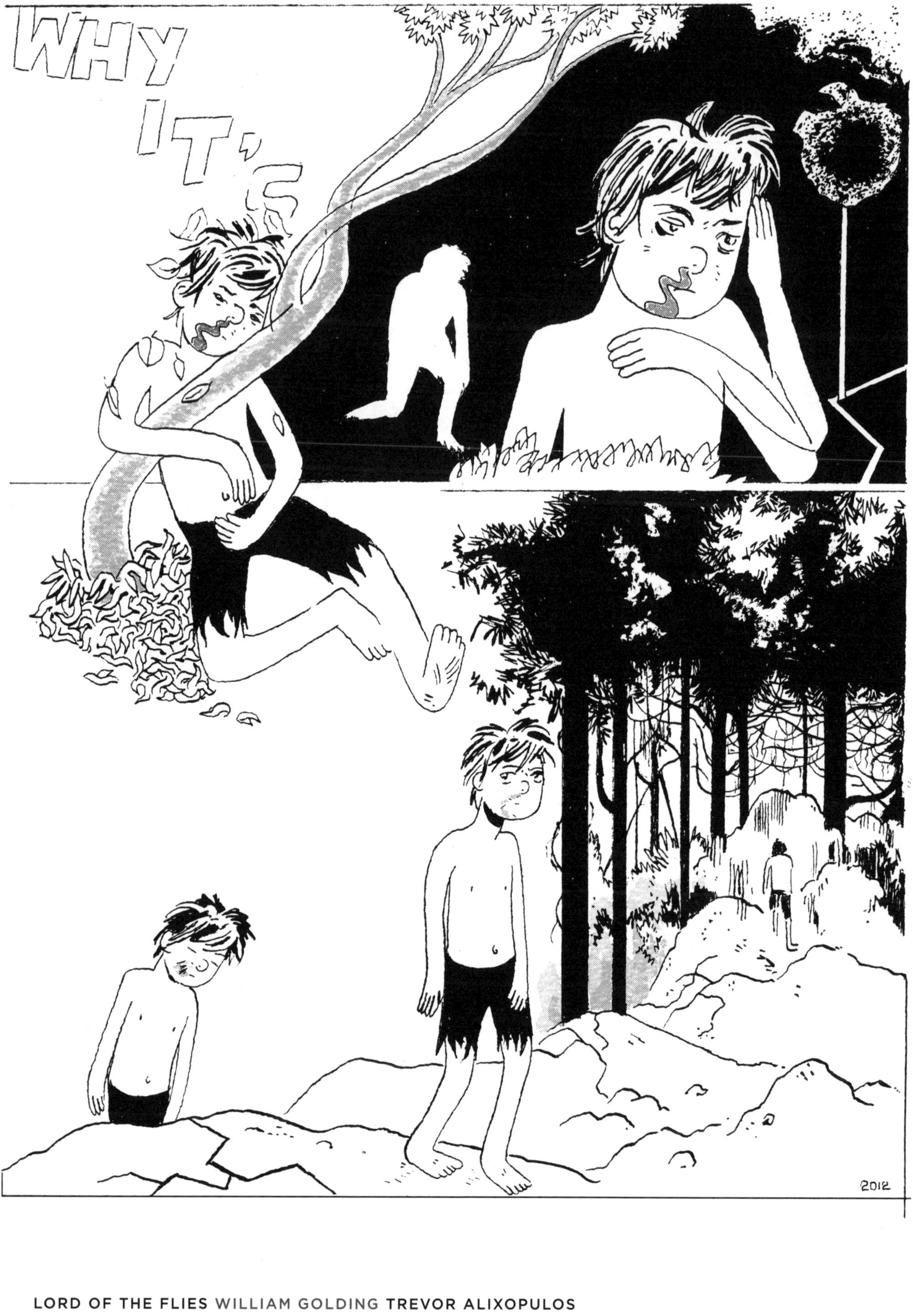
WHY IT'S
2012

The Doors of Perception

Aldous Huxley

ILLUSTRATIONS BY **John Pierard**

ALDOUS HUXLEY WAS THE VERY ESSENCE OF THE refined British writer-intellectual, yet, even with all the patrician education and superintelligent DNA oozing from him, he manifested a highly mystical side. His *Perennial Philosophy* is a twentieth-century spiritual classic that examines the direct encounters with the numinous that run throughout Eastern and Western religions. But the author of *Brave New World* wanted to do more than just read about transcendent experiences, including those triggered by psychedelic substances. He got his wish during a visit from Humphry Osmond, a pioneer of research into consciousness-altering drugs. In *The Doors of Perception*, Huxley wrote:

By a series of, for me, extremely fortunate circumstances I found myself, in the spring of 1953, squarely athwart that trail. One of the sleuths had come on business to California. In spite of seventy years of mescalin research, the psychological material at his disposal was still absurdly inadequate, and he was anxious to add to it. I was on the spot and willing, indeed eager, to be a guinea pig. Thus it came about that, one bright May morning, I swallowed four-tenths of a gram of mescalin dissolved in half a glass of water and sat down to wait for the results.

Published the following year, the rest of the short book is devoted to his experiences and impressions during this one time on the active agent from the peyote cactus. He was surprised to find that he wasn't tripping in the sense of seeing grand visions and vivid hallucinations. Instead, though he witnessed some interesting geometric patterns, he mainly found himself seeing the inner essences of things, their true natures, their numinous glow. Earlier that morning, when he had looked at a vase containing a rose, a carnation, and an iris, he had found the colors "lively." But under the influence of the mescaline, "I was not looking now at an unusual flower arrangement. I was seeing what Adam had seen on the morning of his creation—the miracle, moment by moment, of naked existence."

Earlier in this volume, John Pierard showed us the disastrous effects of alcohol on Jack London. Now we are treated to Huxley's transcendent experience on mescaline.

THE DOORS OF PERCEPTION

By Aldous Huxley

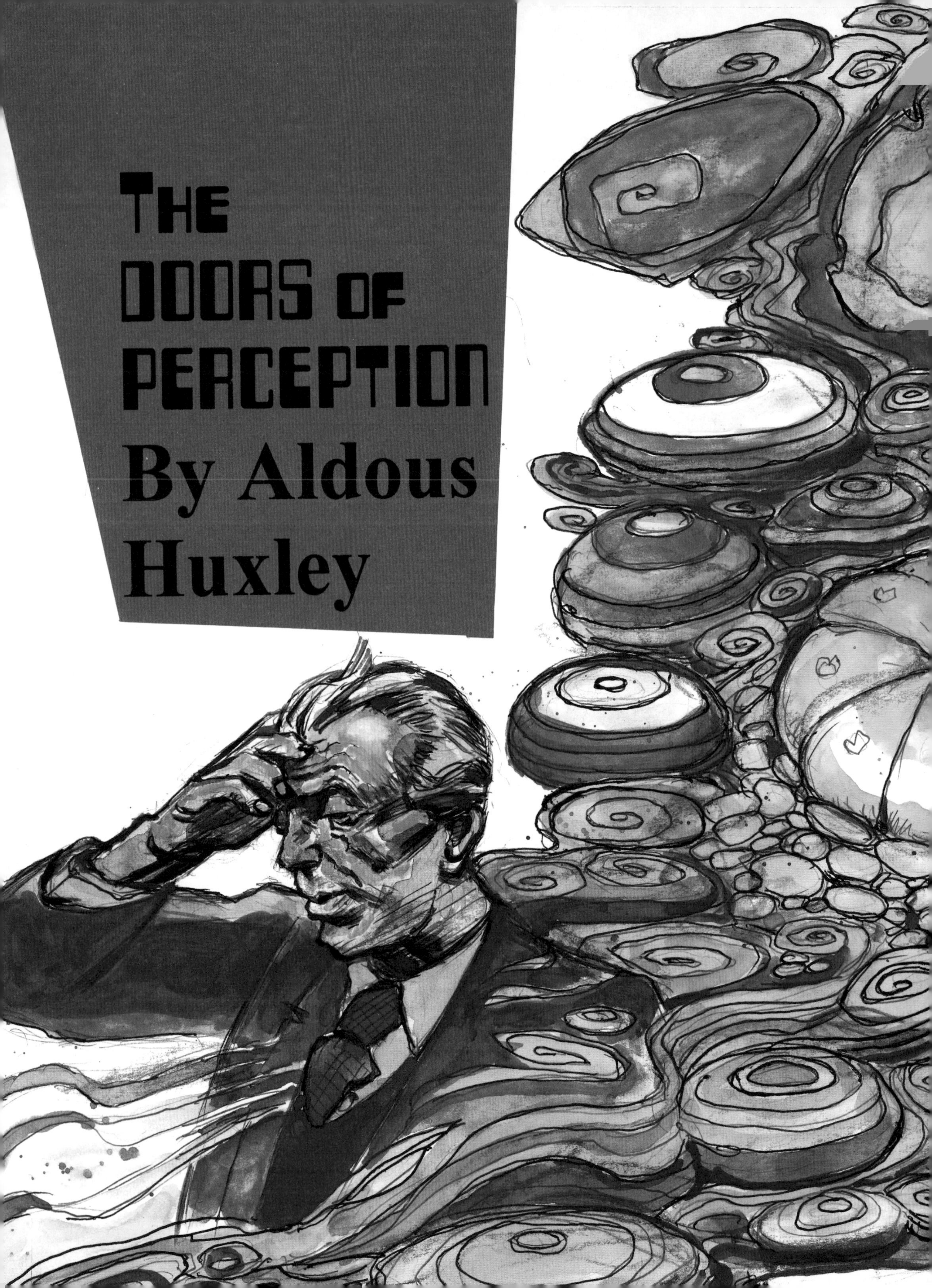

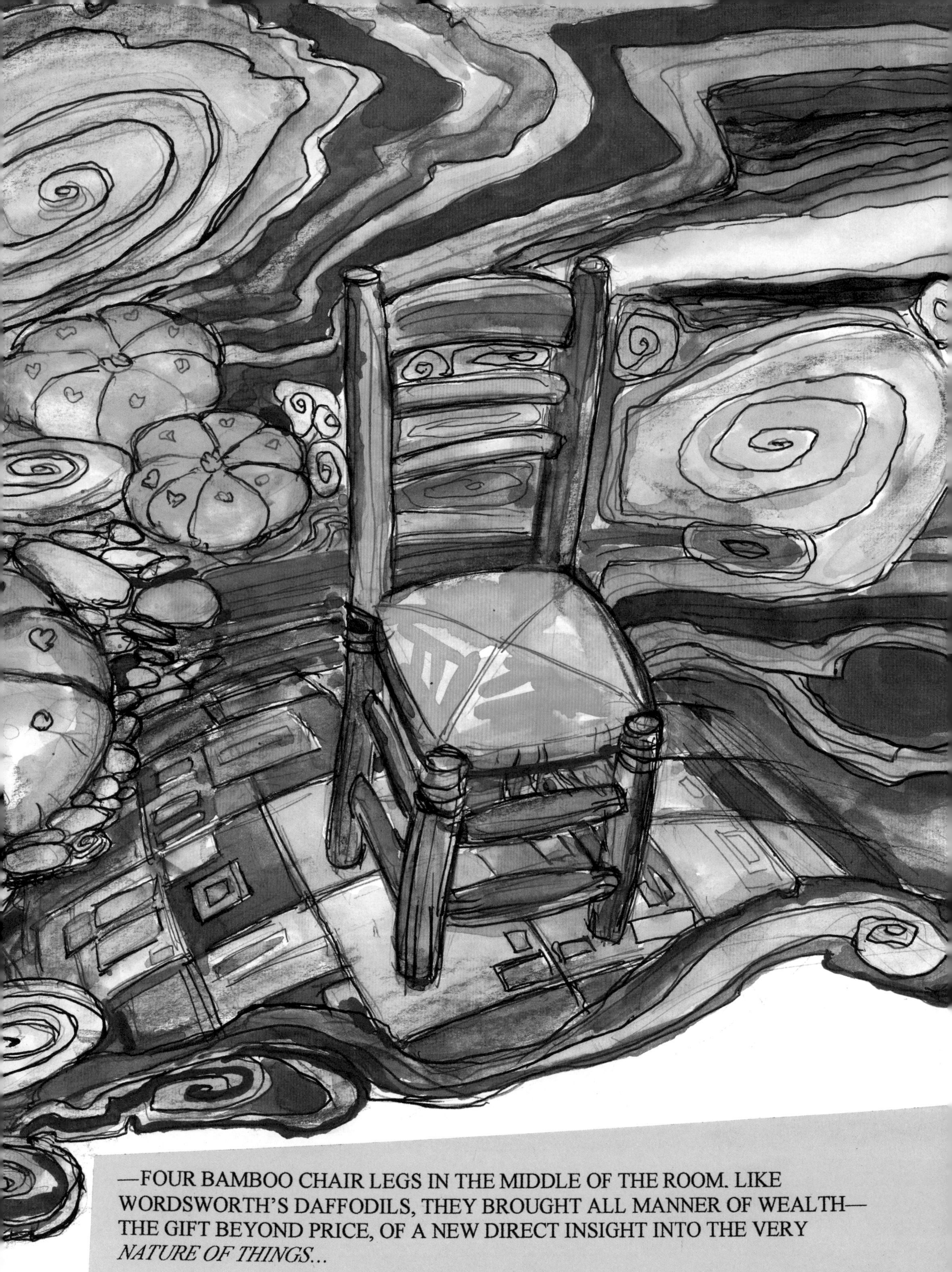

—FOUR BAMBOO CHAIR LEGS IN THE MIDDLE OF THE ROOM. LIKE WORDSWORTH'S DAFFODILS, THEY BROUGHT ALL MANNER OF WEALTH—THE GIFT BEYOND PRICE, OF A NEW DIRECT INSIGHT INTO THE VERY *NATURE OF THINGS...*

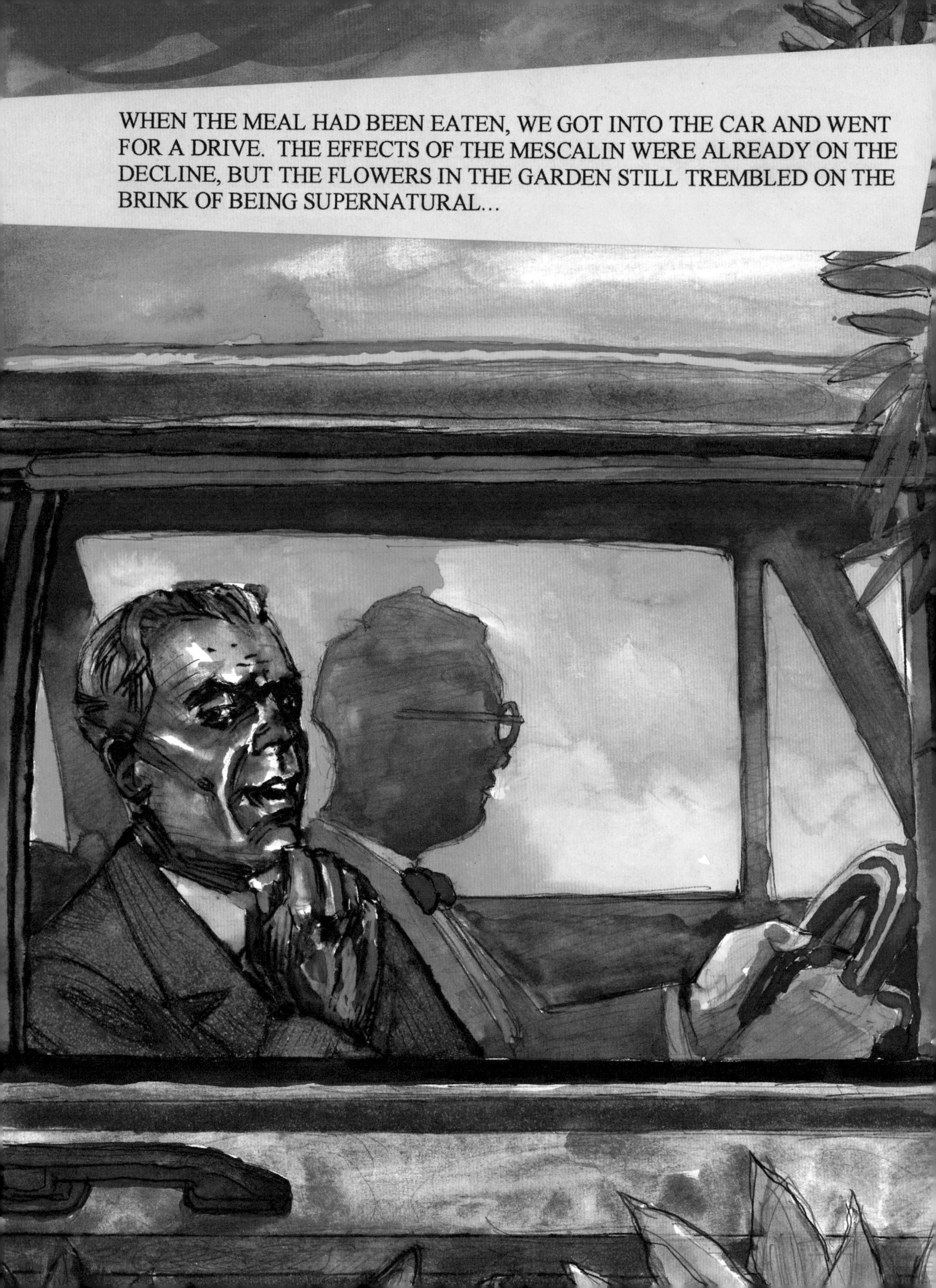
WHEN THE MEAL HAD BEEN EATEN, WE GOT INTO THE CAR AND WENT FOR A DRIVE. THE EFFECTS OF THE MESCALIN WERE ALREADY ON THE DECLINE, BUT THE FLOWERS IN THE GARDEN STILL TREMBLED ON THE BRINK OF BEING SUPERNATURAL...

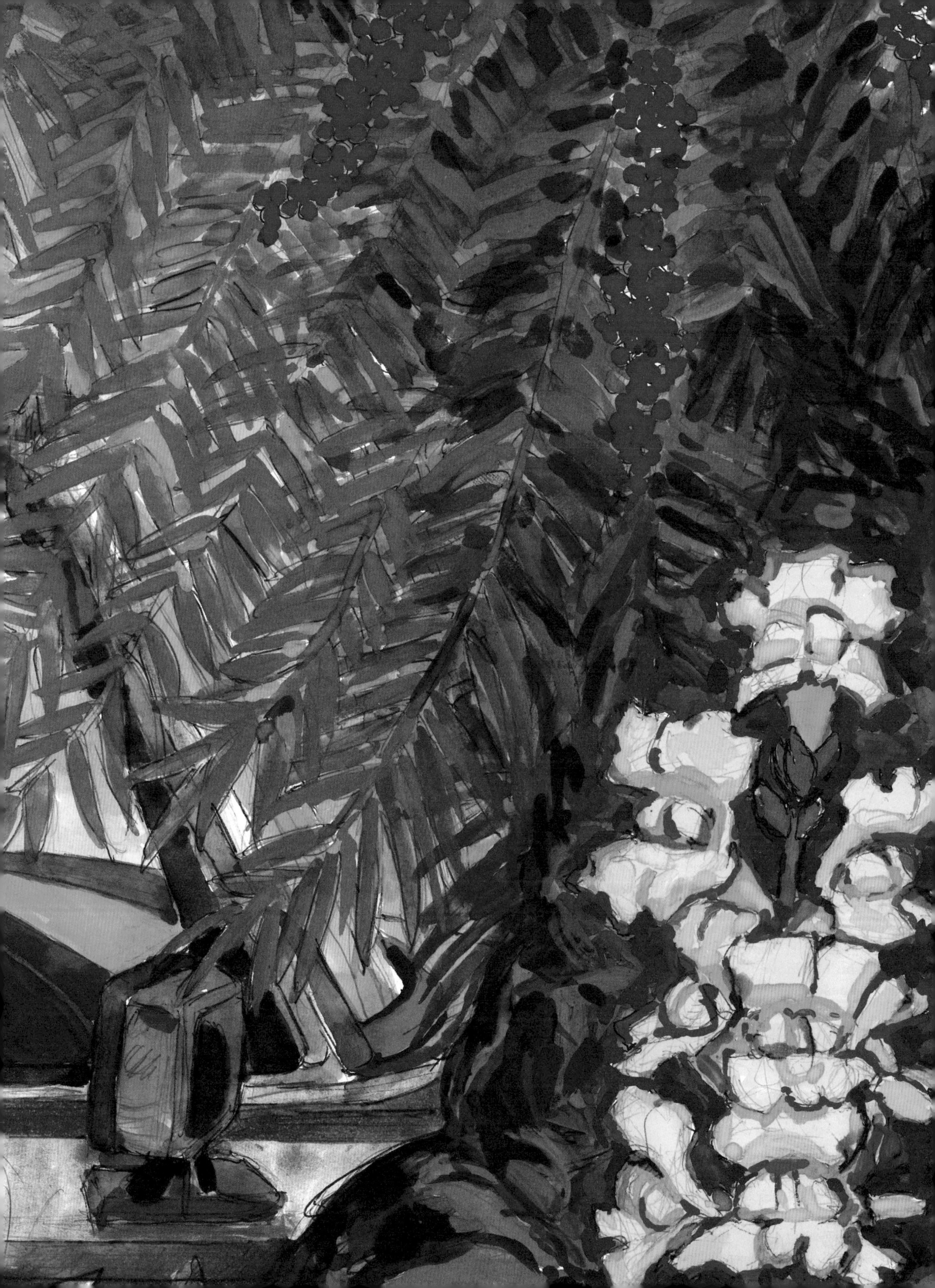

Lolita

Vladimir Nabokov

ART/ADAPTATION BY **Sally Madden**

HAS THERE EVER BEEN A NOVEL MORE MISUNDER-
stood by nonreaders than *Lolita*? It has a salacious aura
about it, but it's resoundingly nonerotic. Vladimir Nabokov is one of the towering figures of twentieth-century
literature, a Russian émigré who wrote his best work in his
third language, English, and *Lolita* is consistently ranked
as one of the greatest novels of the century, alongside
Ulysses, *The Great Gatsby*, and *In Search of Lost Time*. It
is gorgeously written. Harold Bloom marvels at the "endlessly dazzling paragraphs of *Lolita*." Nabokov essentially
challenged himself to write the most aesthetically pleasing
novel he could about the most horrid subject matter, with
one of the most reprehensible characters in literature as its
protagonist and narrator.

Humbert Humbert—a middle-aged literature professor
who has moved to the US from Europe—is attracted to
pubescent girls, and he marries Charlotte Haze solely to
get access to her twelve-year-old daughter, Dolores (a.k.a.
Lolita). He considers bumping off Charlotte, but she conveniently gets run over by a car, and Humbert takes Lolita on
the road, crisscrossing the US, never staying in one hotel
very long while he repeatedly molests his stepdaughter.
They fight about money and her desire to socialize with
boys. He dreams of using her as a baby factory in a few
years, cranking out daughters for him to molest for the rest
of his life. In one of the novel's most famous lines, Lolita
cries herself to sleep every night.

Despite the absence of any sex scenes, no US or UK
publisher would touch the novel. It was published in English
by the legendary Olympia Press, operating out of Paris.
Olympia published explicit erotic works as well as edgy
avant-garde literature, including *Naked Lunch* and Samuel
Beckett. *Lolita* languished until another great novelist, Graham Greene, named it one of the best books of 1955 in the
Sunday Times of London, igniting interest and controversy
on both sides of the Atlantic. *Lolita* was attacked by the
usual suspects and praised by the literati. Within three
years, publishers in Britain and America had found the nerve
to publish it. Like all of Nabokov's work, it's a luminous
puzzlebox, a self-referential, multilayered hall of mirrors
filled with allusions, puns, patterns, and the very definition
of an unreliable narrator.

Into this tinderbox, Sally Madden bravely walks. Taking
time out from her other projects—a book of folk tales and a
book of Catholic saints—she presents some of the highlights
of Nabokov's favorite novel, with a gorgeous palette and
an ingenious wordless approach.

SOURCE

Nabokov, Vladimir. *The Annotated Lolita*. Rev. and updated ed.
    Edited, with introduction, preface, and notes by Alfred Appel Jr.
    New York: Vintage Books, 1991.

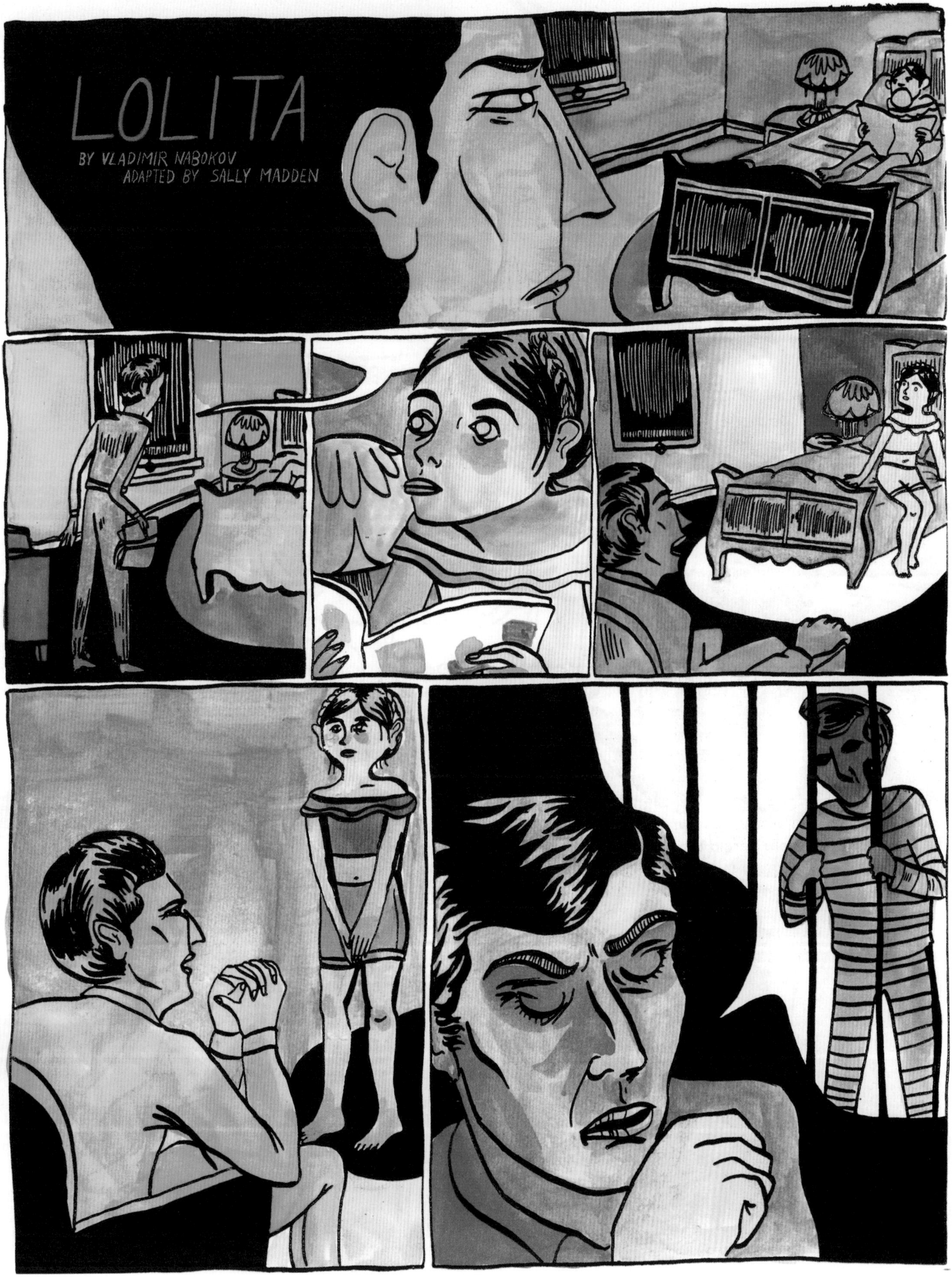
LOLITA
BY VLADIMIR NABOKOV
ADAPTED BY SALLY MADDEN

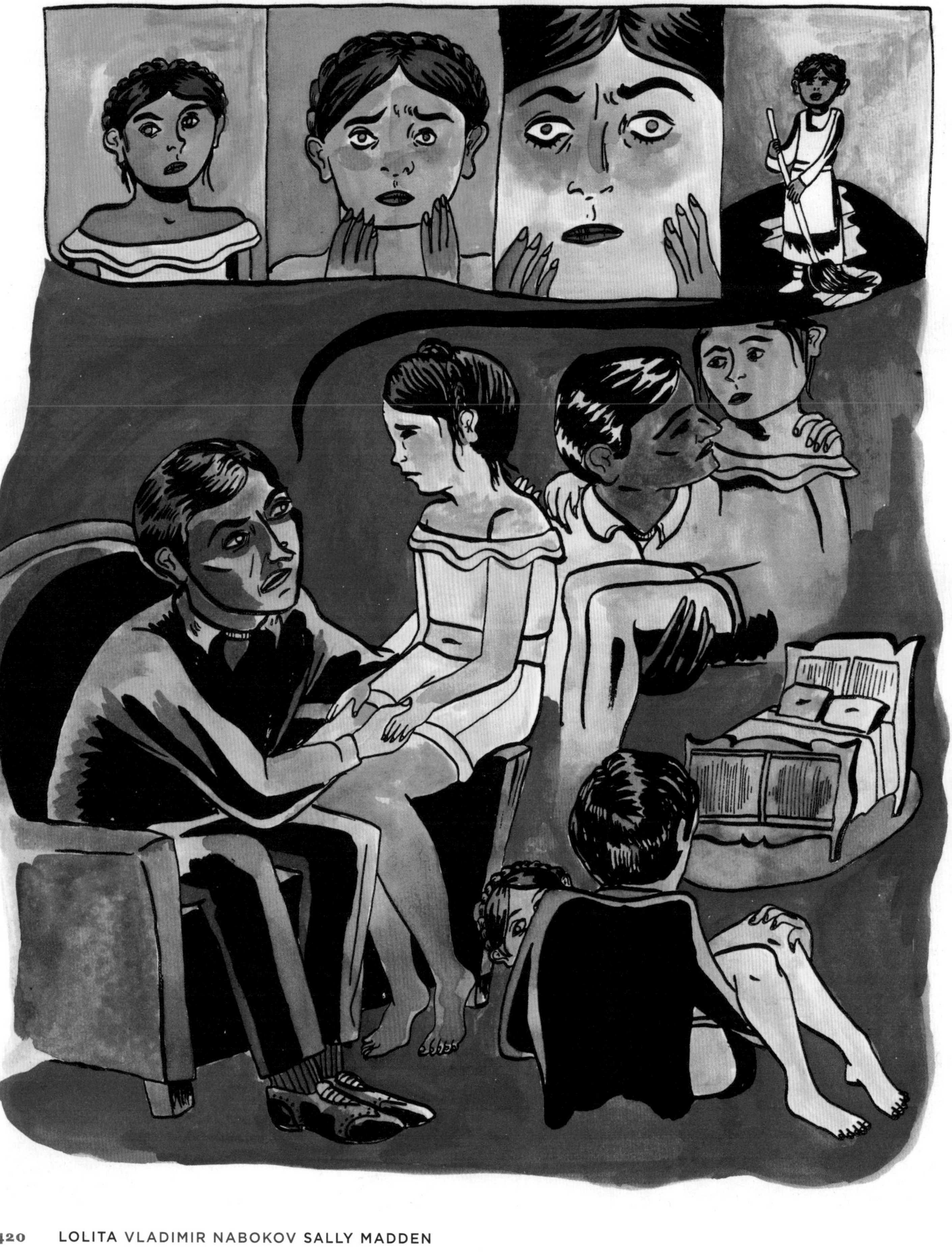

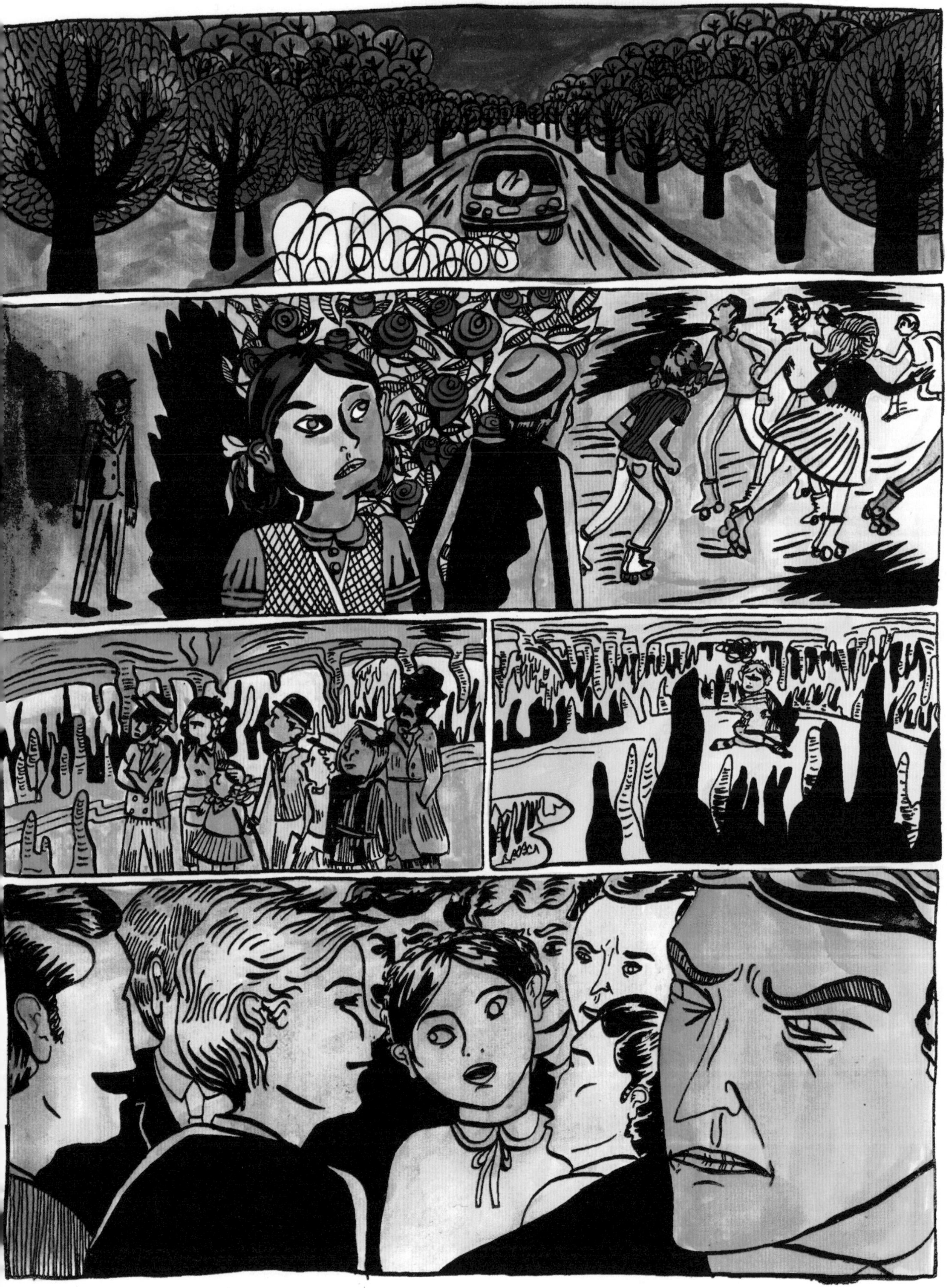

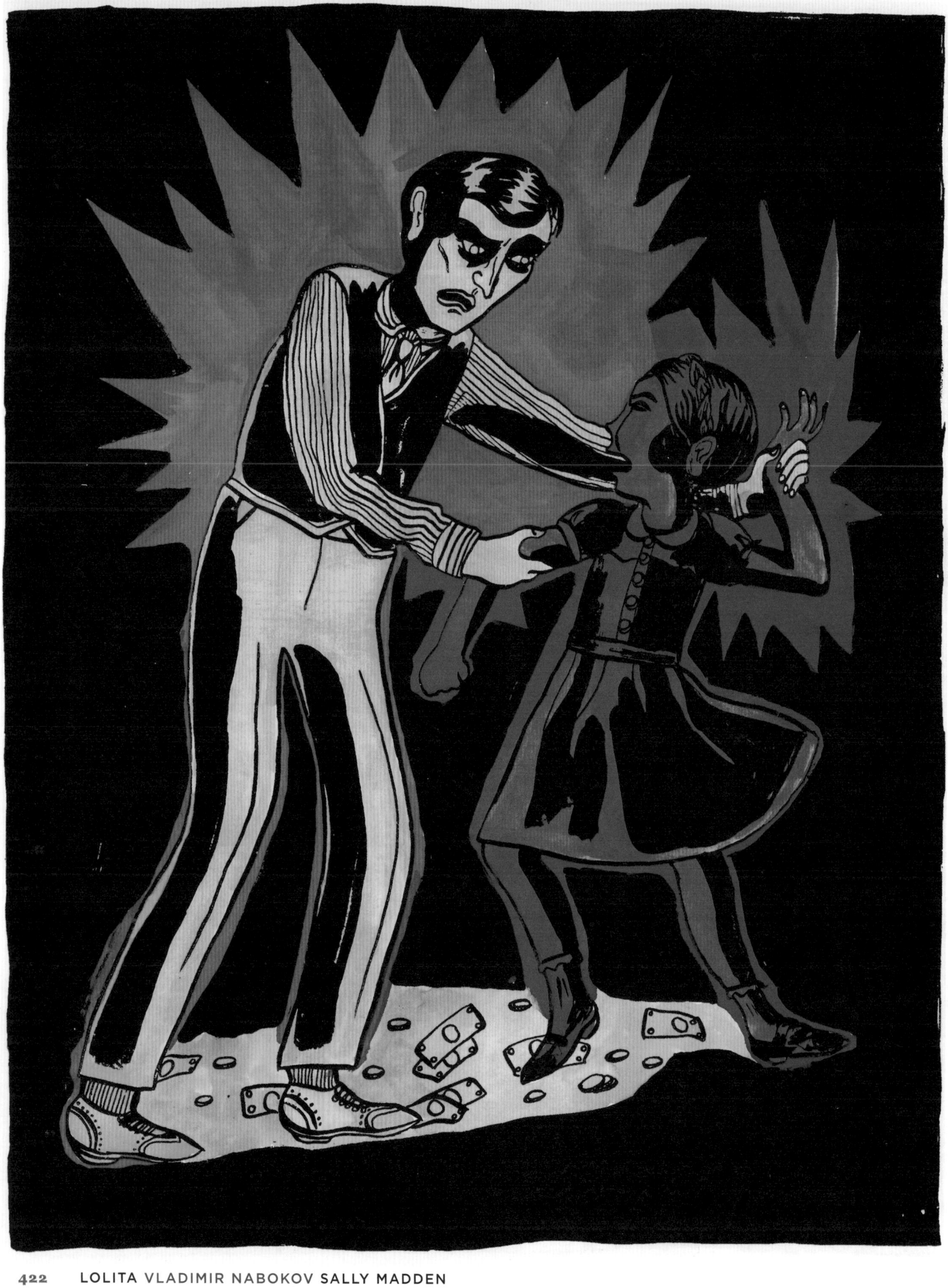

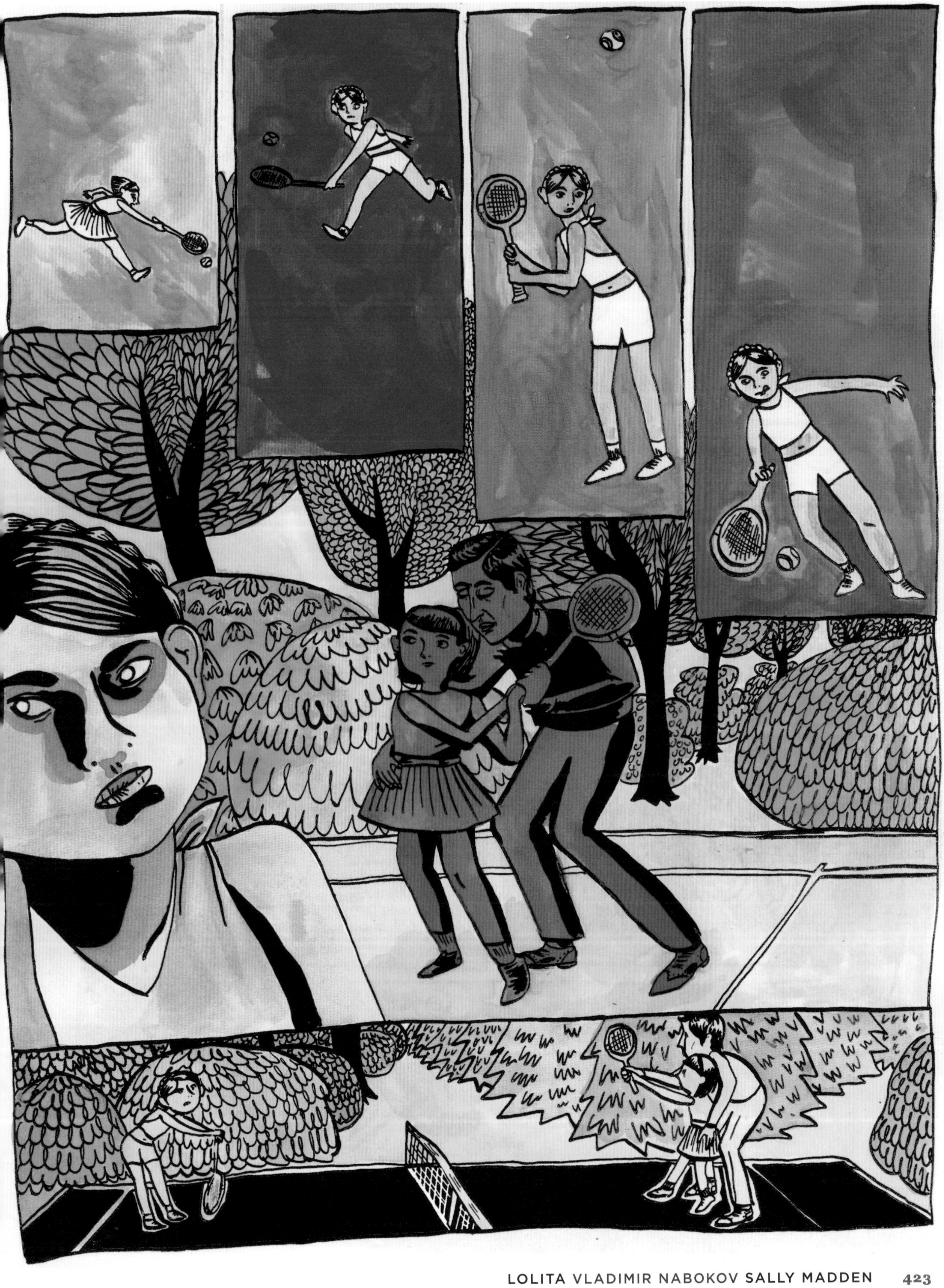

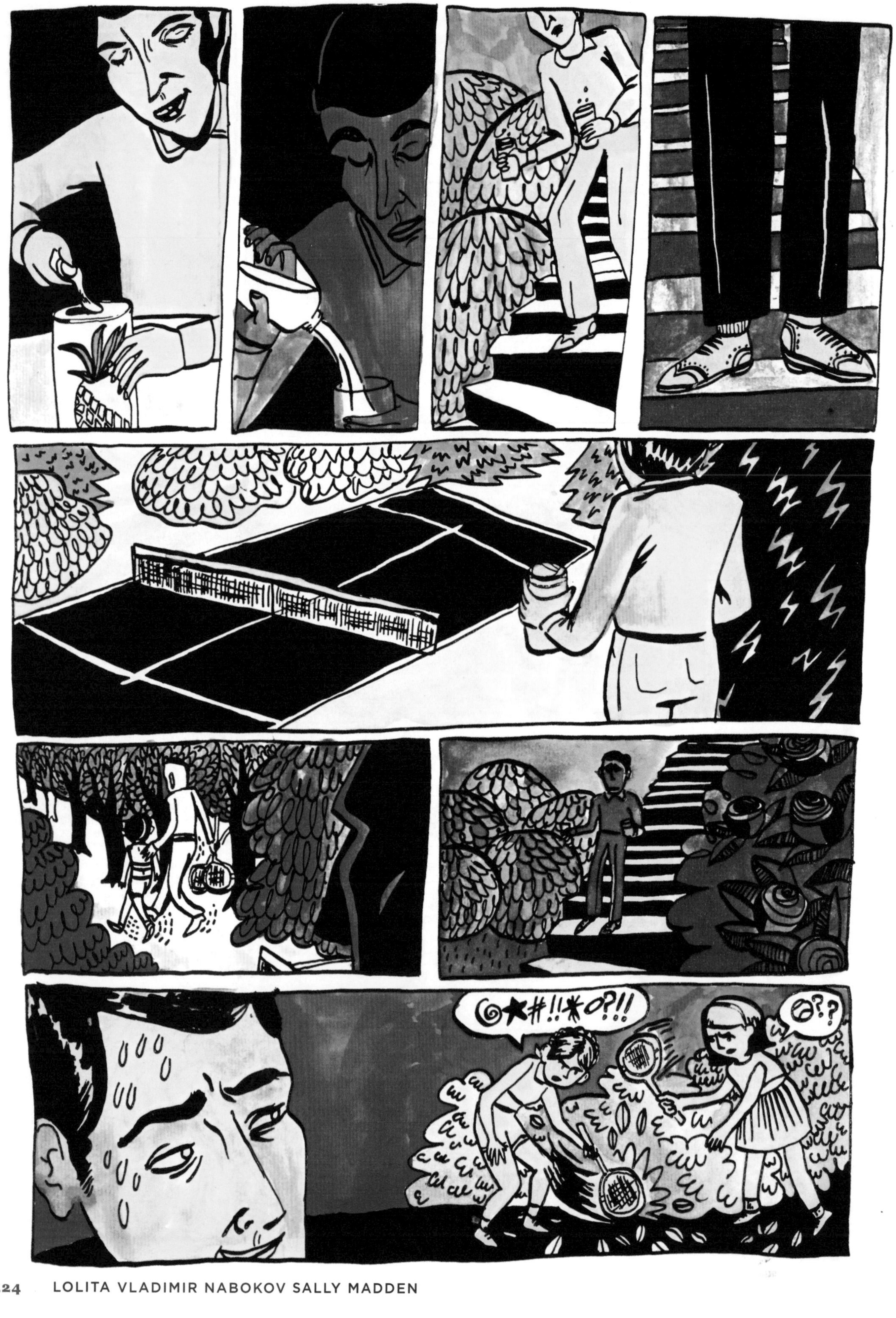
★#!!✱O?!!
??

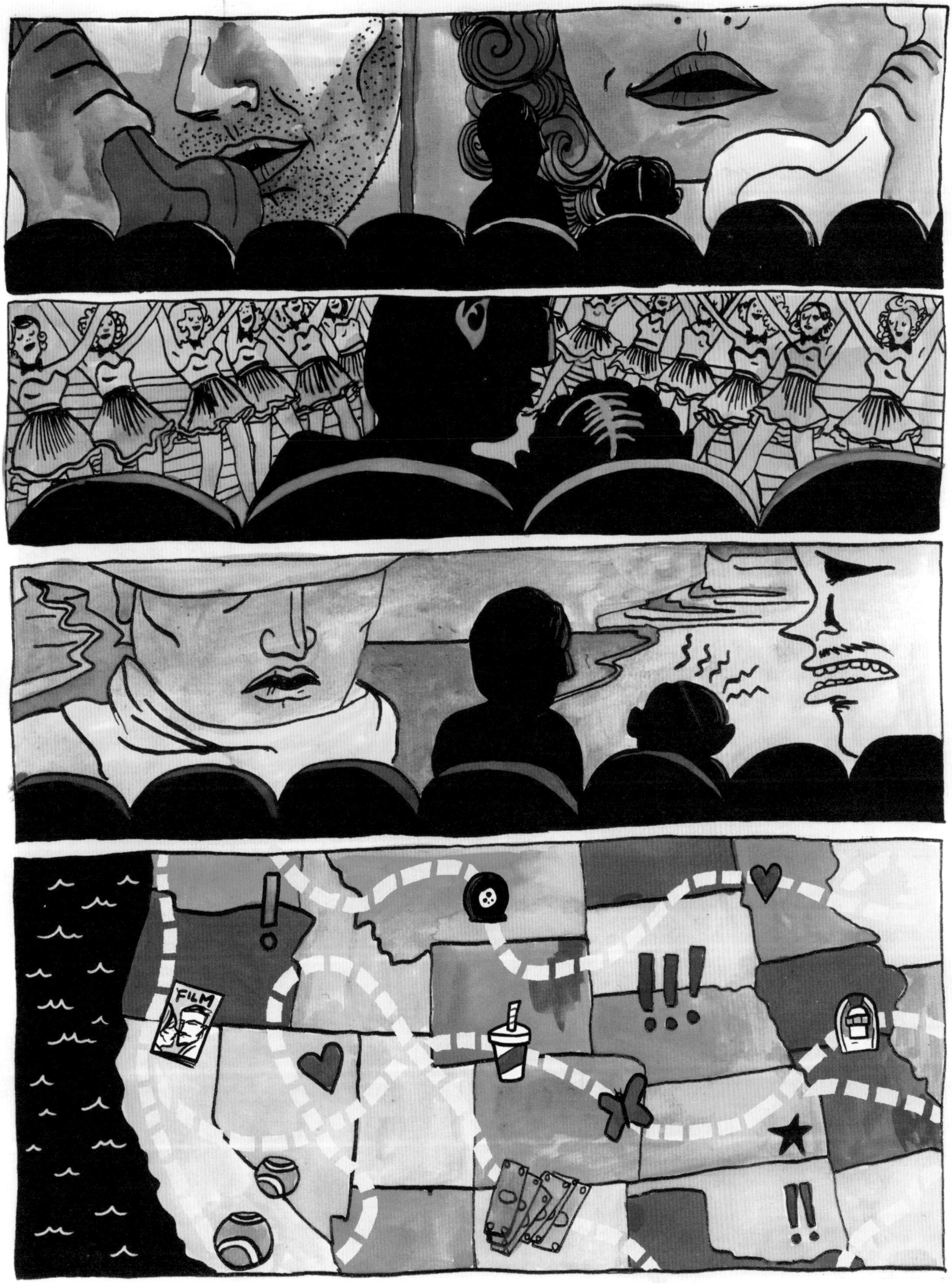
FILM

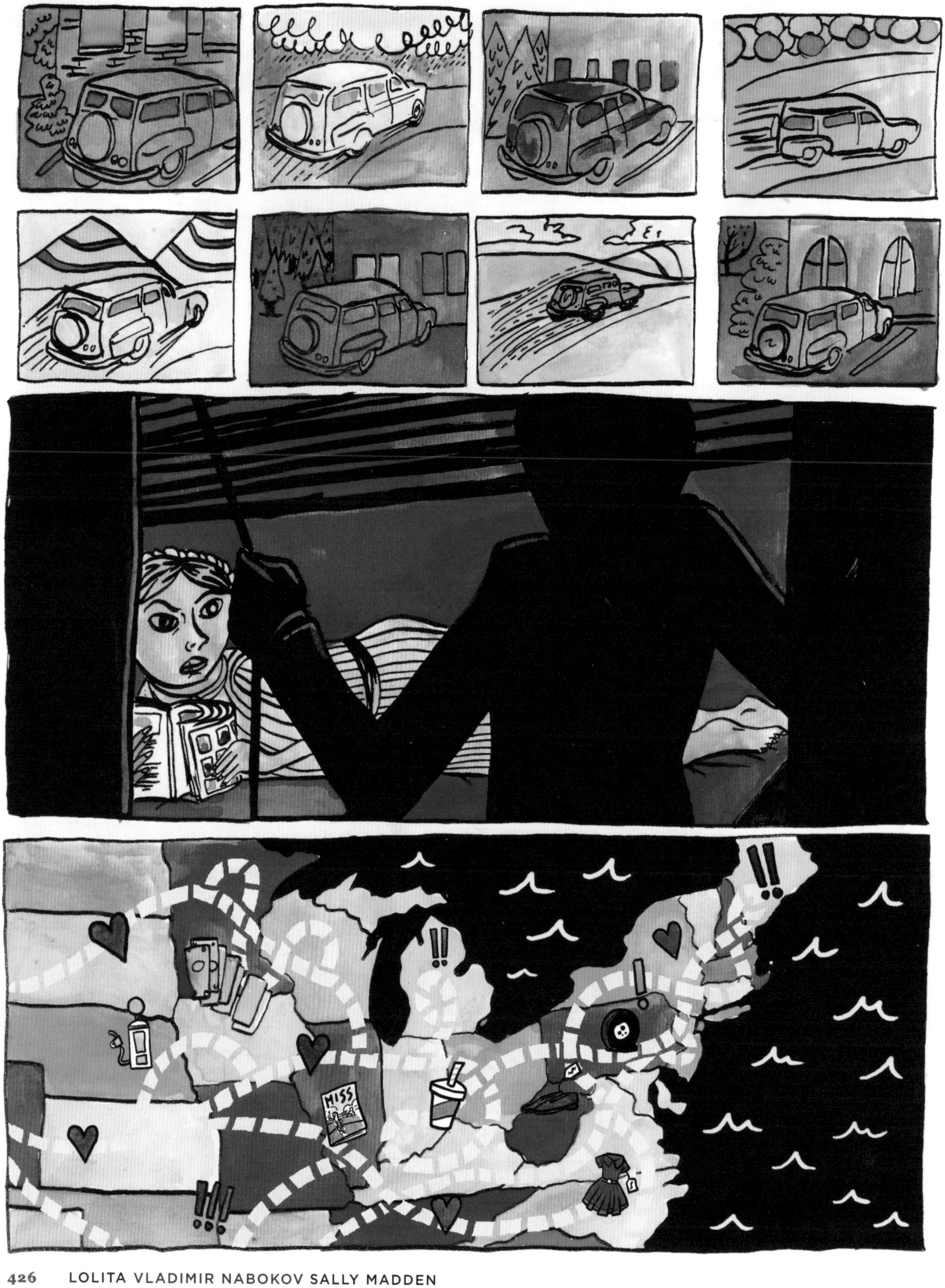
MISS

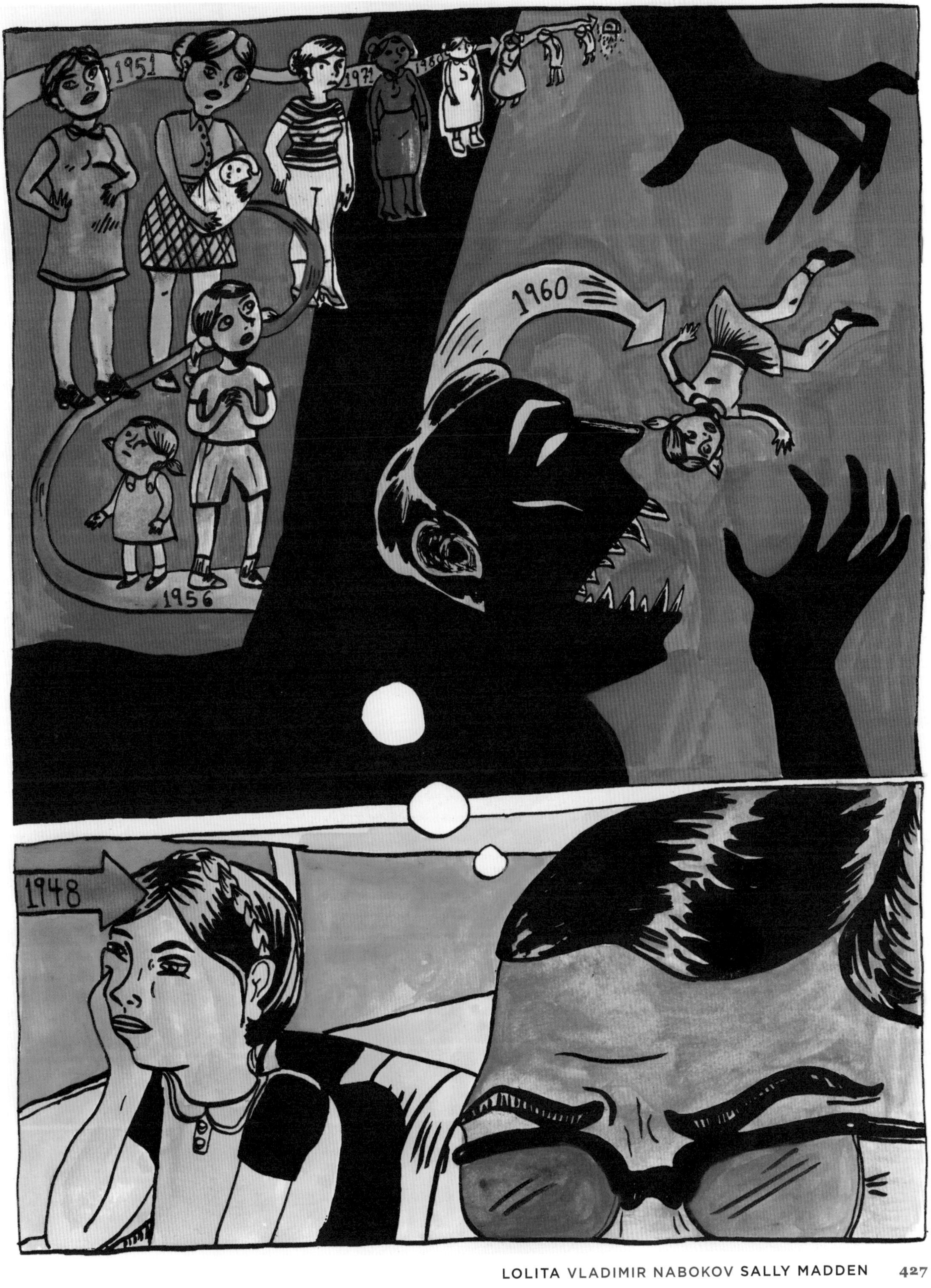
1951
1971
1956
1960
1948

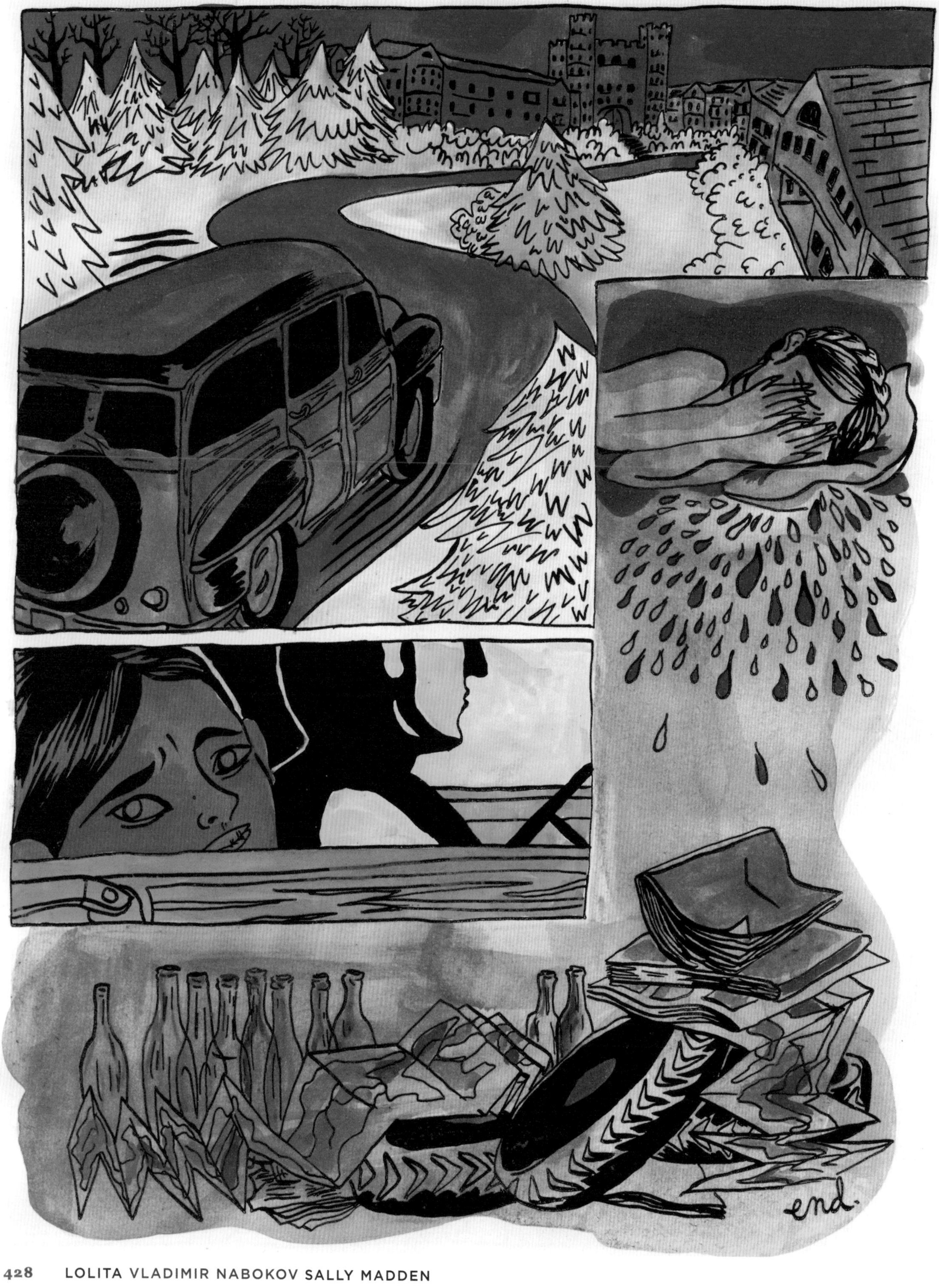
end.

Four Beats

ART AND DESIGN BY **Tara Seibel**

FOR A LITTLE CHANGE OF PACE, TARA SEIBEL USES her trademark combination of illustration, design, hand-lettering, and patterning to give us cool little bios of four writers from the Beat movement of the 1950s and early 1960s. Although "Beat" has connotations of tired or defeated, in a 1958 essay, Jack Kerouac—who had popularized the term—wrote:

> Beat doesn't mean tired or bushed, so much as it means *beato*, the Italian for beatific; to be in a state of beatitude, like St. Francis, trying to love all life, trying to be utterly sincere with everyone, practicing endurance, kindness, cul-tivating joy of the heart. How can this be done in our mad modern world of multiplicities and millions? By practicing a little solitude, going off by yourself once in a while to store up that most precious of golds: the vibrations of sincerity.

The big three are here: Kerouac, best known for *On the Road*; William Burroughs, whose masterpiece is *Naked Lunch*; and Allen Ginsberg, who lit American poetry aflame with "Howl." The Beat women often get short shrift, so it's great to see Diane di Prima, whose forty books of poetry and prose include the epic poem *Loba* (i.e., "She-wolf").

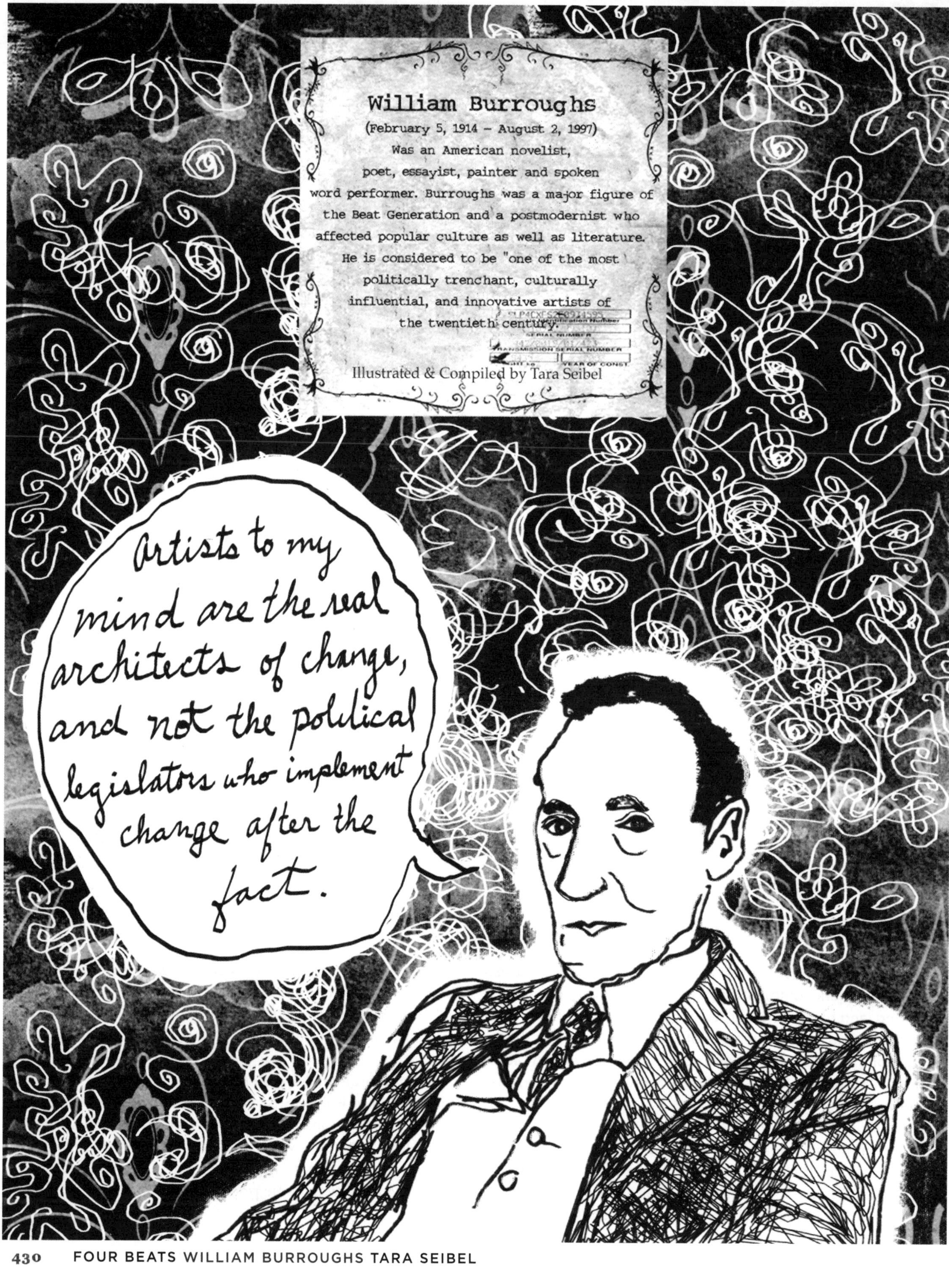
William Burroughs
(February 5, 1914 – August 2, 1997)
Was an American novelist, poet, essayist, painter and spoken word performer. Burroughs was a major figure of the Beat Generation and a postmodernist who affected popular culture as well as literature. He is considered to be "one of the most politically trenchant, culturally influential, and innovative artists of the twentieth century."
Illustrated & Compiled by Tara Seibel
Artists to my mind are the real architects of change, and not the polilical legislators who implement change after the fact.

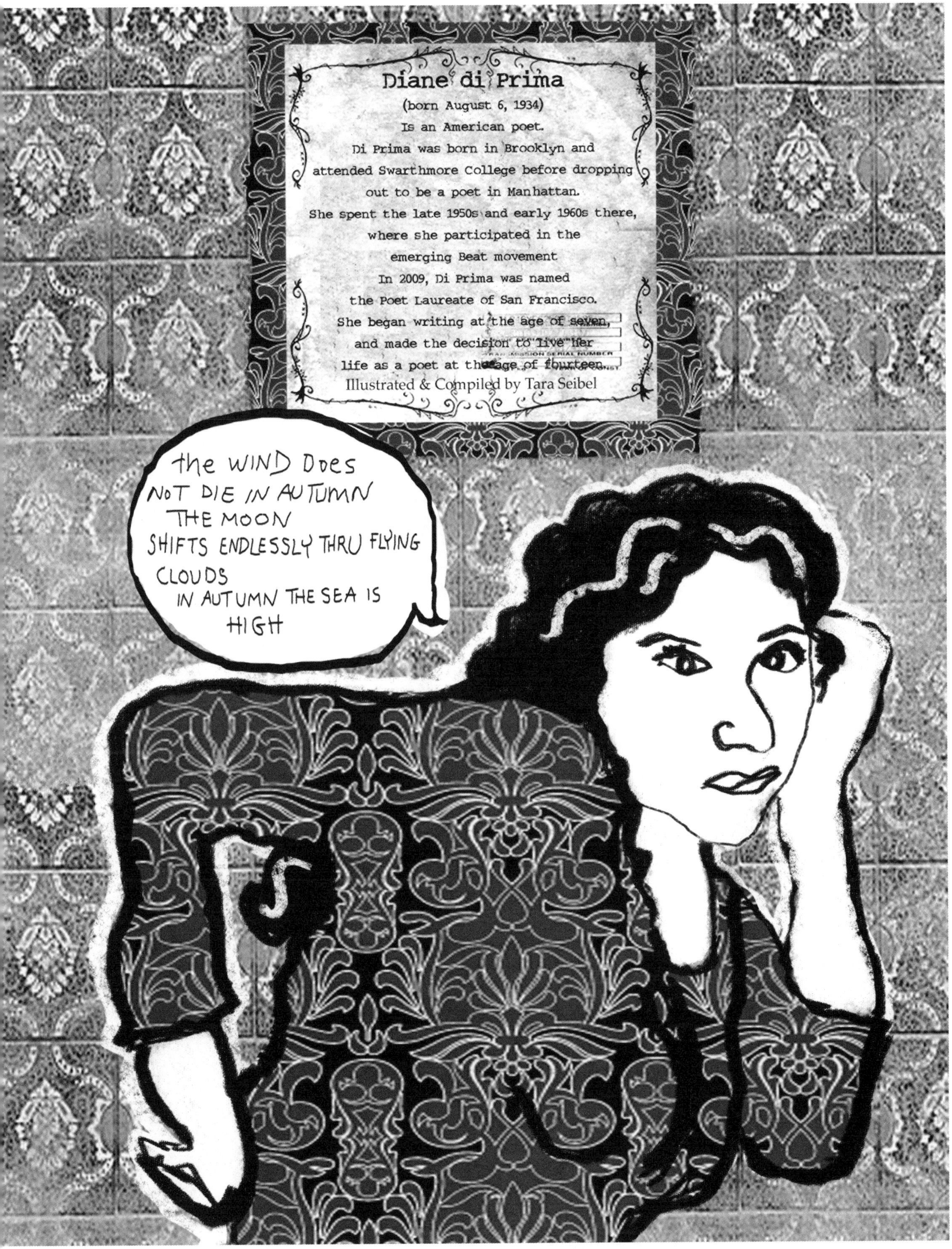
Diane di Prima
(born August 6, 1934)
Is an American poet.
Di Prima was born in Brooklyn and attended Swarthmore College before dropping out to be a poet in Manhattan.
She spent the late 1950s and early 1960s there, where she participated in the emerging Beat movement
In 2009, Di Prima was named the Poet Laureate of San Francisco.
She began writing at the age of seven, and made the decision to live her life as a poet at the age of fourteen.
Illustrated & Compiled by Tara Seibel
the WIND Does NOT DIE IN AUTUMN THE MOON SHIFTS ENDLESSLY THRU FLYING CLOUDS IN AUTUMN THE SEA IS HIGH

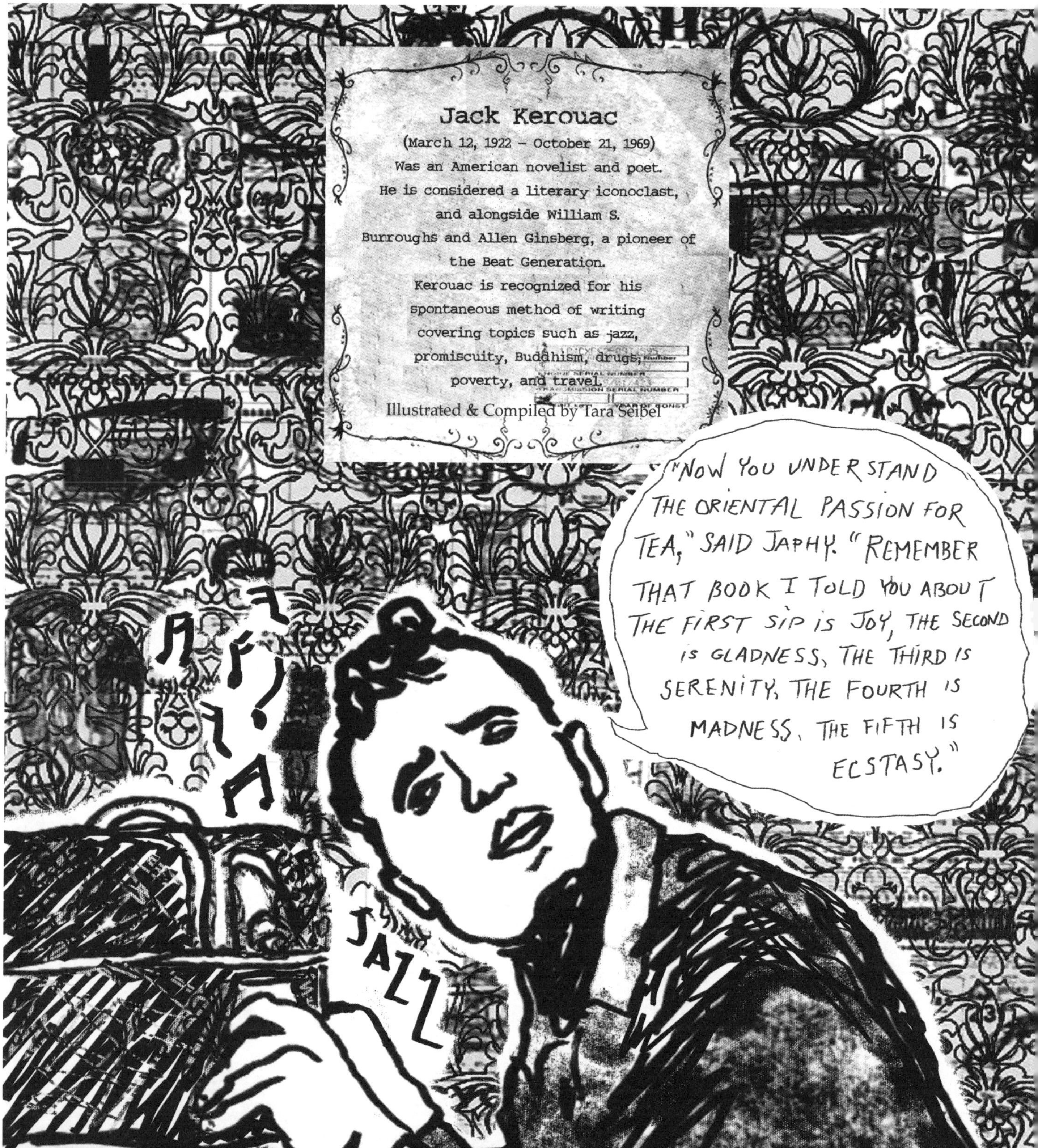
Jack Kerouac
(March 12, 1922 – October 21, 1969)
Was an American novelist and poet.
He is considered a literary iconoclast,
and alongside William S.
Burroughs and Allen Ginsberg, a pioneer of
the Beat Generation.
Kerouac is recognized for his
spontaneous method of writing
covering topics such as jazz,
promiscuity, Buddhism, drugs,
poverty, and travel.
Illustrated & Compiled by Tara Seibel
"NOW YOU UNDERSTAND THE ORIENTAL PASSION FOR TEA," SAID JAPHY. "REMEMBER THAT BOOK I TOLD YOU ABOUT THE FIRST SIP IS JOY, THE SECOND IS GLADNESS, THE THIRD IS SERENITY, THE FOURTH IS MADNESS, THE FIFTH IS ECSTASY."
JAZZ

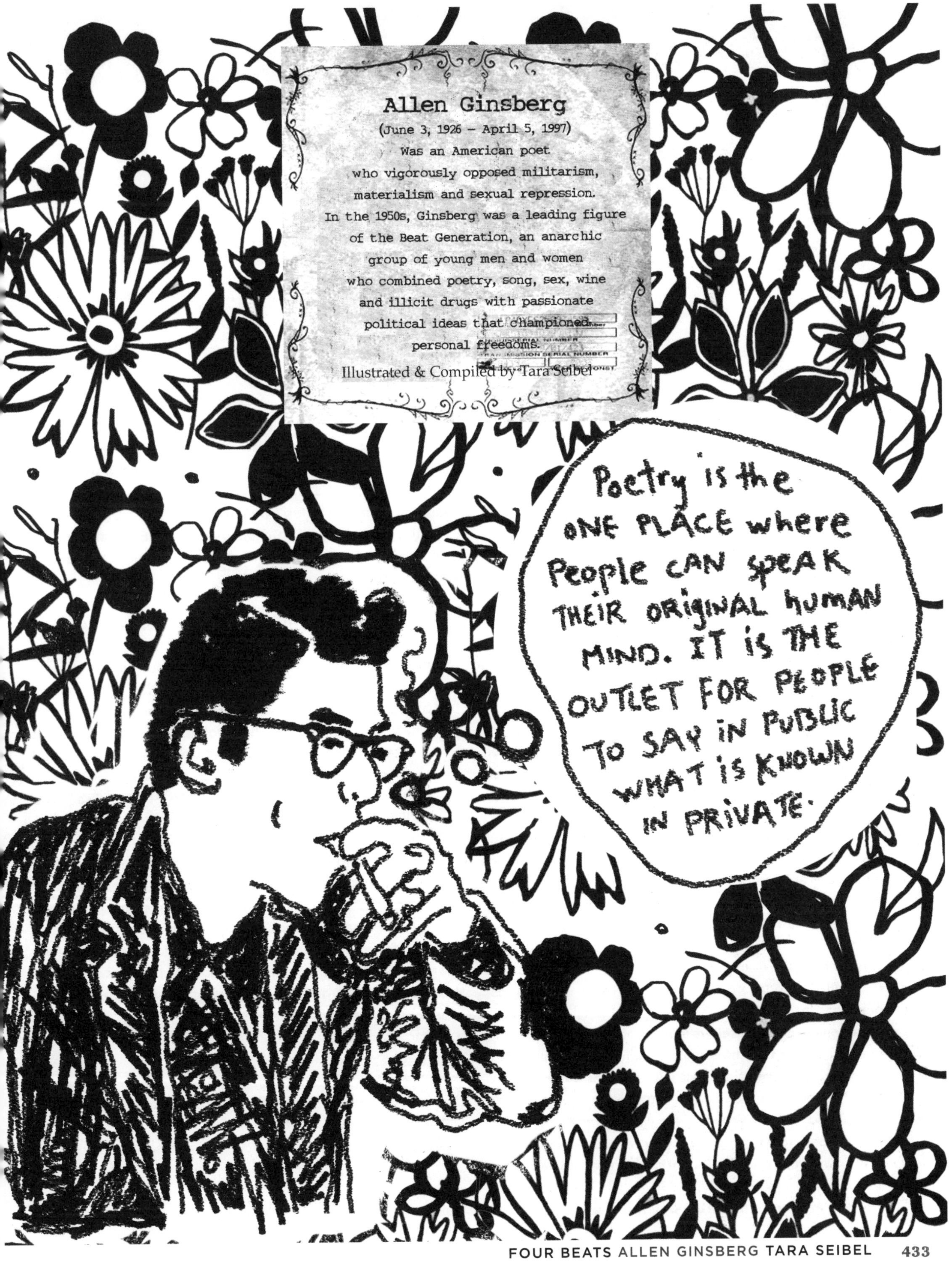
Allen Ginsberg
(June 3, 1926 – April 5, 1997)
Was an American poet
who vigorously opposed militarism,
materialism and sexual repression.
In the 1950s, Ginsberg was a leading figure
of the Beat Generation, an anarchic
group of young men and women
who combined poetry, song, sex, wine
and illicit drugs with passionate
political ideas that championed
personal freedoms.
Illustrated & Compiled by Tara Seibel
Poetry is the ONE PLACE where People CAN SPEAK THEIR ORIGINAL human MIND. IT IS THE OUTLET FOR PEOPLE TO SAY IN PUBLIC WHAT IS KNOWN IN PRIVATE.

Jack Kerouac

ILLUSTRATION BY **Yeji Yun**

THE PROCESS OF WRITING ON THE ROAD—BASED on Jack Kerouac's cross-country journeys with his buddy Neal Cassady from 1947 to 1950, during which they traveled restlessly in search of kicks, chatted up characters dotting every corner of America, and searched with every ounce of their being for the meaning of everything—is legendary in itself. In order to keep writing in a fast, unfiltered manner without having to change sheets of paper, Kerouac typed out the bulk of the book on giant rolls of thin tracing paper that he had taped together to form one long scroll, in just a little over three weeks, all while hopped up on bennies and sweating through shirt after shirt as his wife at the time, Joan Haverty, fed him a constant stream of pea soup—good lord! Before coasting on this surge of the crazy jazz energy he often craved, Kerouac had made several attempts to write his road novel in imitation of more conventional forms through his studies of Wolfe and Dreiser, but none of these quite worked until his mad dash to explain with little reflection. As John Tytell put it in *Naked Angels*:

> It was not merely what he saw, but how he perceived it and wrote it down that distinguished Kerouac from others who were able to register some of the ambiance of the new hip freedom. In his aesthetic of spontaneity, Kerouac extended the romantic tradition to its logical ends, far beyond the Wordsworthian idea that the writer's function was to recapture an action, a strongly felt emotion, in tranquility. Kerouac's model was closer to the opium transport that inspired Coleridge's "Kubla Khan," an ecstatic abandonment of conscious control of language, an intuitive response to the inner voice. Such a heightened state usurps normal consciousness with its filtering processes, soars beyond the intellectual capabilities of reason and choice and selectivity to achieve what Kerouac called "an undisturbed flow from the mind" or what Ginsberg termed in his own work an "undifferentiated consciousness."

Though Kerouac had written one novel prior, and com-pleted several afterward, *On the Road*'s appearance in 1957 (six long years after he wrote it) totally shook critics and readers of American literature, who heralded a new literary movement—the Beat Generation—with Kerouac as its avatar, and his pals Allen Ginsberg and William S. Burroughs as major contributors in their own right. Biographer Ann Charters wrote of the book's impact on both the public and its author:

> Kerouac was thirty-five years old when *On the Road* was published, and later it would seem he had spent the first part of his career trying to write the book and get it published, and the rest of his life trying to live it down. One problem was that he was supposedly the spokesman for a new generation. The other problem was that his portrait of "Dean Moriarty" in the novel was so exhilarating that reporters expected him to live up to its image, despite his insistence that he was the character "Sal Paradise," who had "shambled after" Dean in their cross-country trips.

Illustrator and self-described "memory collector" Yeji Yun interprets the book in a somewhat abstracted full-page illustration that you can view from the top or bottom. Here are Sal and Dean, or Jack and Neal, or even Kerouac the Homebody and Kerouac the Quest-Seeker, one with eyes aflame, the other with, perhaps, wings in his eyes. Between them is their playground, the United States, land of jazz, girls, and open highways.

SOURCES

Charters, Ann. "Introduction." *In On the Road* by Jack Kerouac. New York: Penguin Classics, 2002.

Tytell, John. *Naked Angels*. New York: Grove Press, 1976.

—Veronica Liu

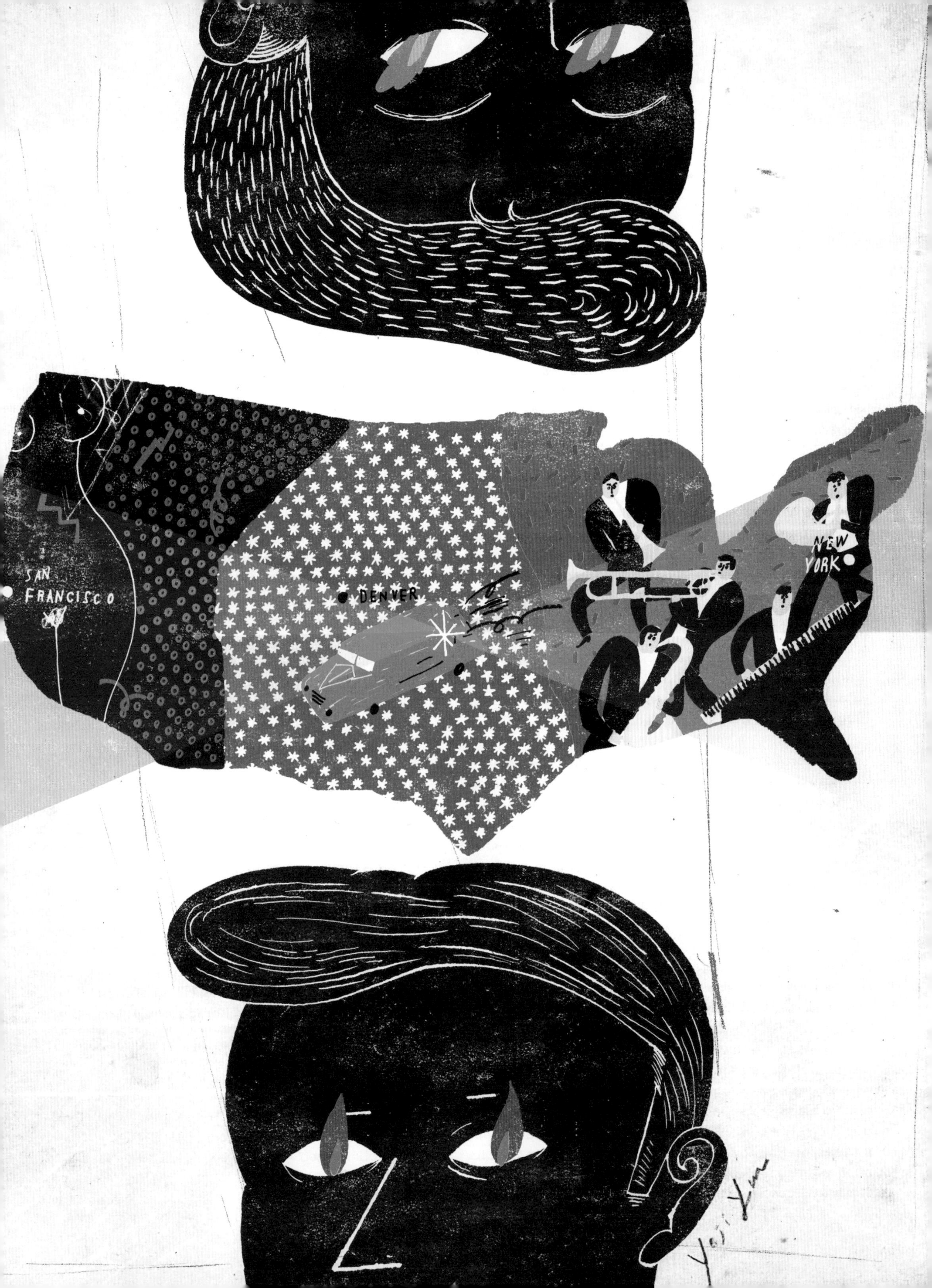
SAN FRANCISCO
DENVER
NEW YORK

Naked Lunch

William S. Burroughs

ART/ADAPTATION BY **Emelie Östergren**

WHEN WILLIAM S. BURROUGHS WAS SIXTEEN years old, he purchased chloral hydrate to "see what it's like." This dark, exploratory tendency never left him, shaped by vague remembrances of being sexually violated by a nanny's boyfriend when young, defined by a desperate need to reject his family's upper-middle-class lifestyle (his grandfather invented the modern adding machine, and so grandson William benefited from a trust fund), and aggravated by a society still unfriendly to his homosexuality. Born of a well-respected St. Louis family and educated at Harvard, Bill Burroughs would eventually be counted with his buddies Jack and Allen as one of the three foundational figures of the Beat Generation, become entrenched in a desperate junk addiction, and craft a novel so distressing to various government agencies that its landmark court victory became the case by which all future works were judged. *Naked Lunch*, in winning the right to be published and distributed by Grove Press, arguably ended literary censorship in the United States.

Unfortunately, this latter achievement was really only kick-started after Burroughs *accidentally* shot and killed his wife in a party-trick *accident*. As he recounted in a massive biography written by Ted Morgan:

> I am forced to the appalling conclusion that I would never have become a writer but for Joan's death, and to a realization of the extent to which this event has motivated and formulated my writing. I live with the constant threat of possession, and a constant need to escape from possession, Control. So the death of Joan brought me in contact with the invader, the Ugly Spirit, and maneuvered me into a lifelong struggle, in which I have had no choice except to write my way out.

The creation of *Naked Lunch* was a legendary ordeal: Burroughs typing page after page as the bizarre and grotesque scenes flow from his drug-fueled brain in his Tangiers apartment, throwing each sheet of paper on the floor; Allen Ginsberg eventually rescuing the food-encrusted, rat-gnawed pages and attempting to put them into some kind of order (although, as Burroughs later said, you can open up and start reading *Naked Lunch* at any point; it doesn't matter); Jack Kerouac helping type the manuscript for presentation to publishers and suggesting the title; its publication in 1959 by the notorious Olympia Press in Paris; and finally, the aforementioned obscenity trial. . . .

During and after the writing of *Naked Lunch*, Burroughs experimented with a technique, invented by his friend and fellow writer/artist Brion Gysin, called the "cut-up": cutting up newspapers and his own writing and others' writing, mixing up the strips of paper, then deciphering and typing out the new arrangements—effectively mirroring a trip. As John Tytell described in *Naked Angels*:

> [Burroughs's] novels are composed of scenes which are often without the narrative focus provided by recognizable characters, or the scenic unity provided by a particular locale. Characters metamorphose into other characters, appear without introduction only to disappear without explanation; scenes shift sharply from New York City to South American jungles without transition. Such difficulties are compounded by the presence of alien forms that seem derived from the world of science fiction—annihilating insects, viral parasites, succubi and other demons, all merging with humans, invading their bodies and manipulating their minds, acting through their beings bizarrely, disruptively creating what Burroughs calls nova: the aggravation of insoluble conflicts and incompatible political situations resulting in a planetary explosion.

Emelie Östergren's "Eat Me or You Will Be Eaten" . . . well, *goes there*, in fantastical panel after panel, in a colorful illustration style that recalls children's books—until you actually look at the content and realize that it's not for kids at all. This is the one piece in the entire *Graphic Canon* that squicks out everyone who reads it and has led to nightmares. From her home base in Sweden, Emelie explains that her piece is essentially a riff on the book, using some of its grotesque imagery, rather than an adaptation of any one portion. She believes that Burroughs wrote *Naked Lunch* as a way to deal with his accidental killing of Joan—that in some way the entire book is filtered through her. He was trying to meet Joan again and finally he does in a way, becoming reborn through her.

SOURCES

Morgan, Ted. *Literary Outlaw: The Life and Times of William S. Burroughs*. New York Henry Holt, 1988.

Tytell, John. *Naked Angels*. New York: Grove Press, 1976.

—Veronica Liu

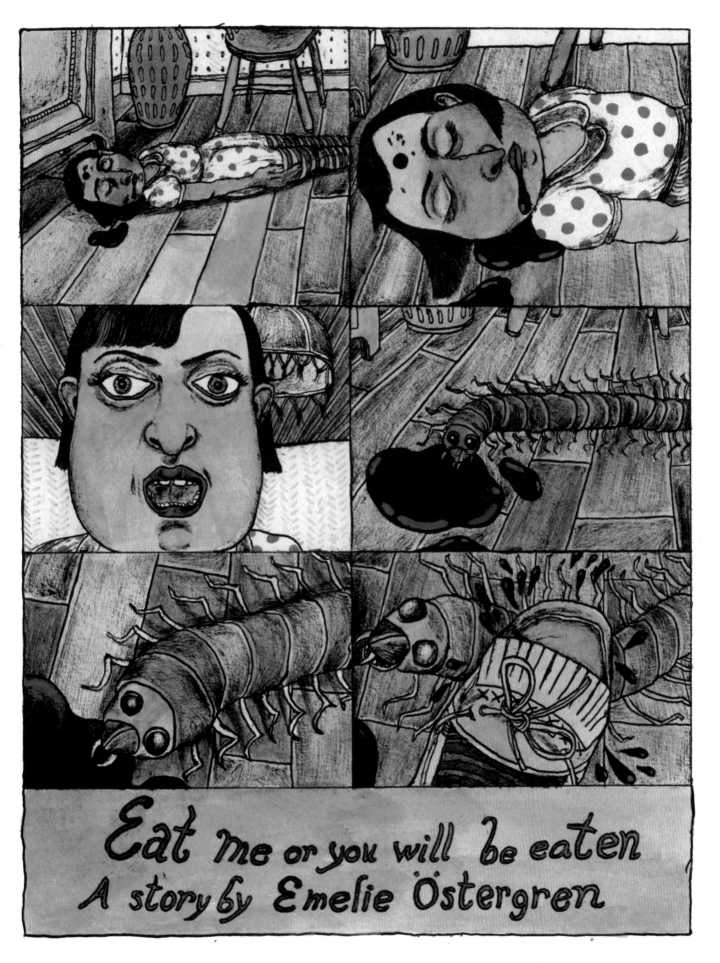

Eat me or you will be eaten
A story by Emelie Östergren

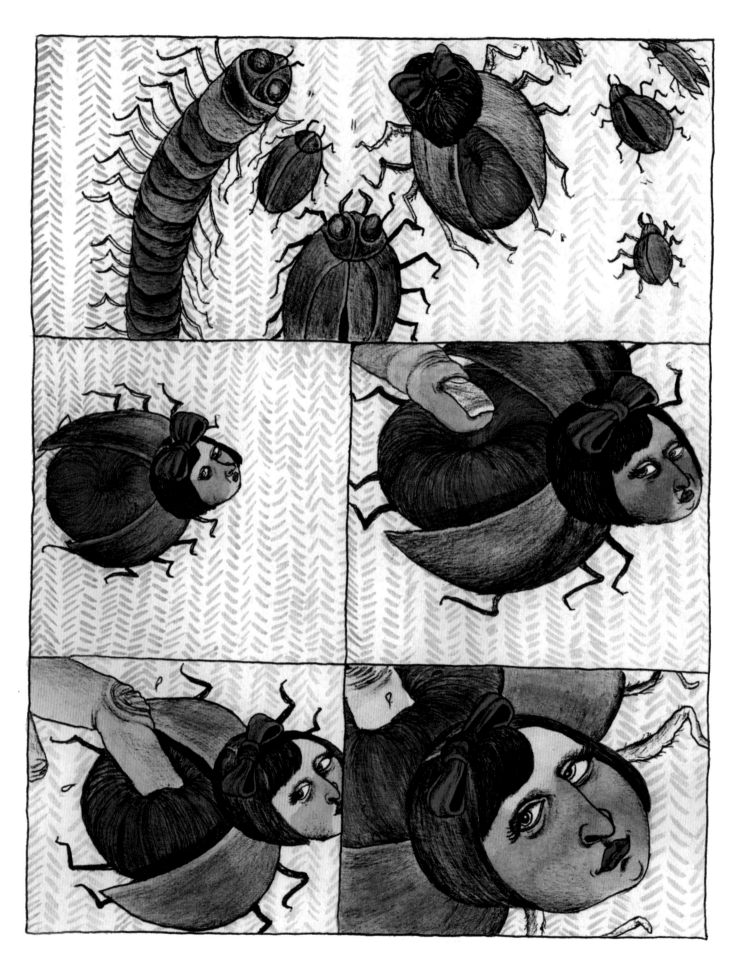

NAKED LUNCH WILLIAM S. BURROUGHS EMELIE ÖSTERGREN

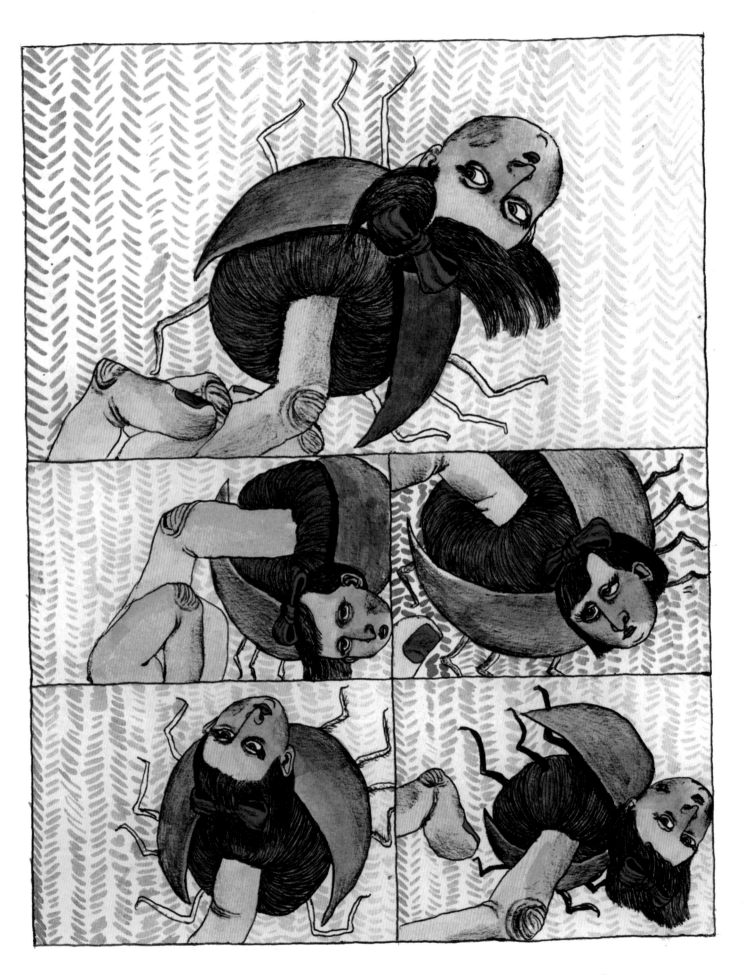

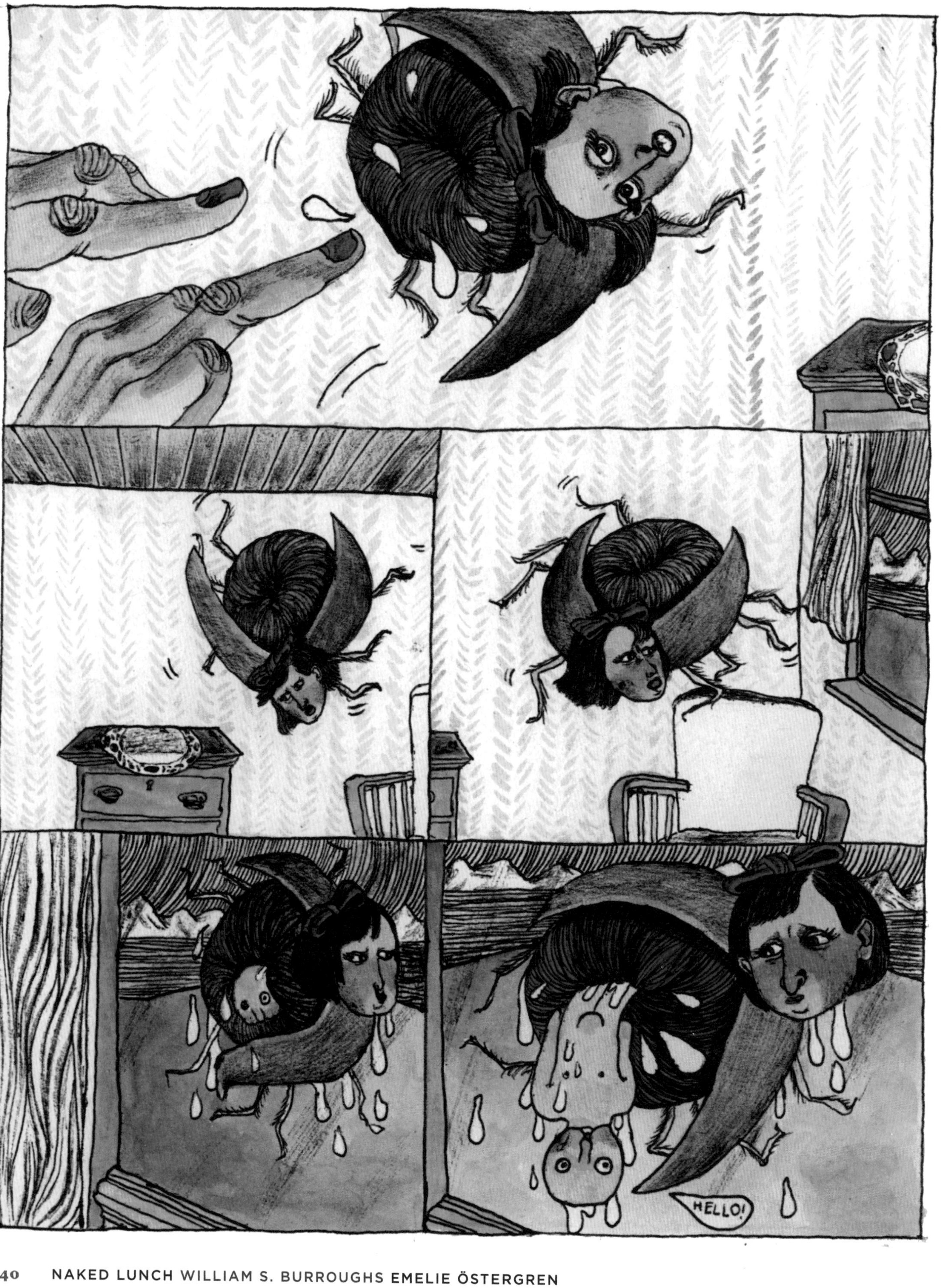
HELLO!

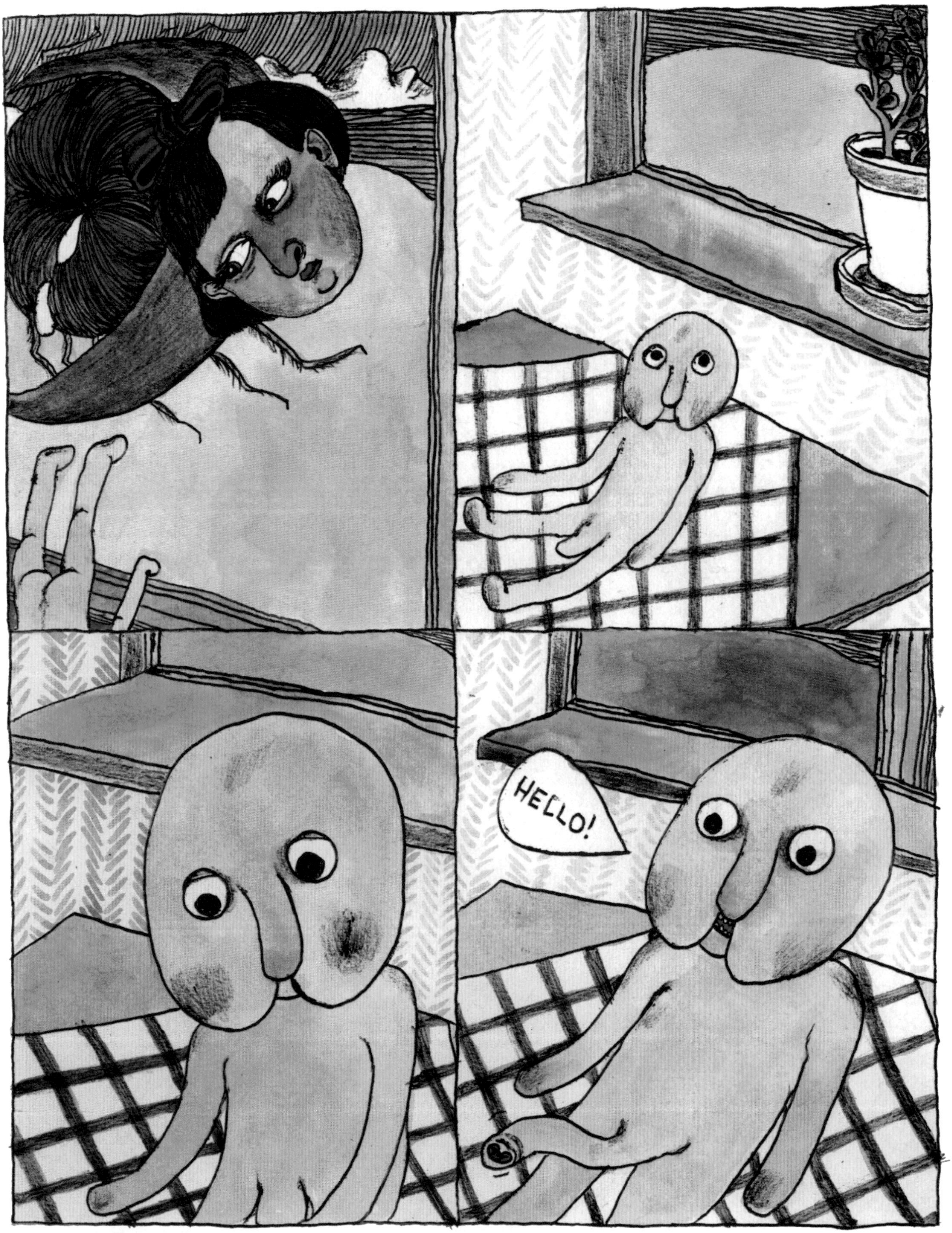
HELLO!

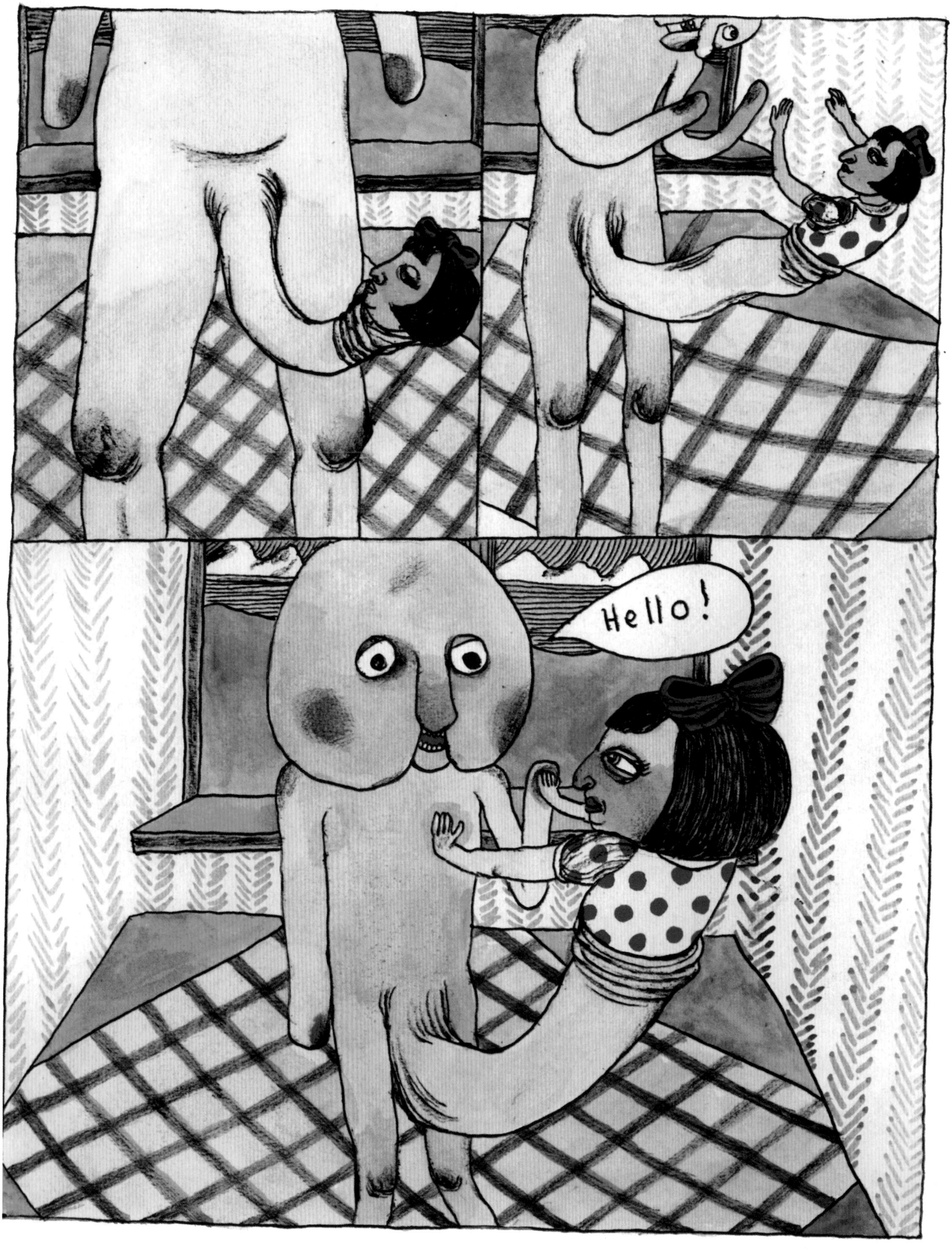
Hello!

One Flew Over the Cuckoo's Nest

Ken Kesey

ART/ADAPTATION BY **PMurphy**

PERHAPS MORE WIDELY KNOWN AS A CLASSIC, multiple-Oscar-winning movie—one of the high points of Jack Nicholson's career—counterculture icon Ken Kesey's 1962 novel *One Flew Over the Cuckoo's Nest* is itself a classic, named by *Time* as one of the greatest English-language novels since the magazine's founding in 1923, and recipient of the deluxe treatment from Penguin Classics.

Set in a mental hospital in Oregon—and based on Kesey's time as a night orderly in a psych ward—it's a parable for the way society crushes individuality, sexuality, and vitality. The boisterous, brawling, horny Randle McMurphy fakes insanity in order to serve out his prison time in the mental asylum. He finds a joyless, fear-ridden place ruled with an iron fist by the dictatorial Nurse Ratched, who keeps patients in line with sadistic orderlies, the threat of electroshock or isolation, and by turning patients against each other. McMurphy rebels, inspiring the others to follow his lead. The war between McMurphy and Ratched escalates. The climax comes when McMurphy hires a prostitute to sneak into the ward and take the cherry of the shy man-child Billy Bibbit. Ratched threatens to tell Billy's domineering mother what he's done, and the poor guy has a meltdown, killing himself by slashing his throat with scissors. In a rage, McMurphy assaults Ratched.

Spoiler Alert: This is a rare novel, like *Nineteen Eighty-Four*, where our rebellious hero doesn't triumph over the soul-crushing System. McMurphy is lobotomized, retiring into a permanent vegetative state. The novel's narrator—a schizophrenic Native American called "Chief"—mercifully smothers the defeated McMurphy, then literally breaks out of the asylum. Most of the other patients are gone—the ones who checked in voluntarily have left, and the others have transferred elsewhere. Ratched's reign of terror is broken. So, in a way, McMurphy wins, but at the ultimate cost to himself.

Artist PMurphy—no relation to McMurphy—has rendered key scenes from the novel in his trademarked exquisite palette. Or, to be more accurate, he has captured the just-before and the just-after of key scenes. In this masterpiece of quiet understatement, we first see the empty settings but not the characters. We see the window of the nurse's station after McMurphy has smashed it and grabbed the drugs for the party. We see the phone used to call the prostitute. We see the blood-soaked aftermath of Billy's suicide, and the empty restraining bed where McMurphy's frontal lobe was icepicked. In the final two panels, we see Chief just before the smothering and just after his escape.

One Flew Over the Cuckoo's Nest

The 1962 novel by Ken Kesey interpreted through a short series of drawings by PMurphy.

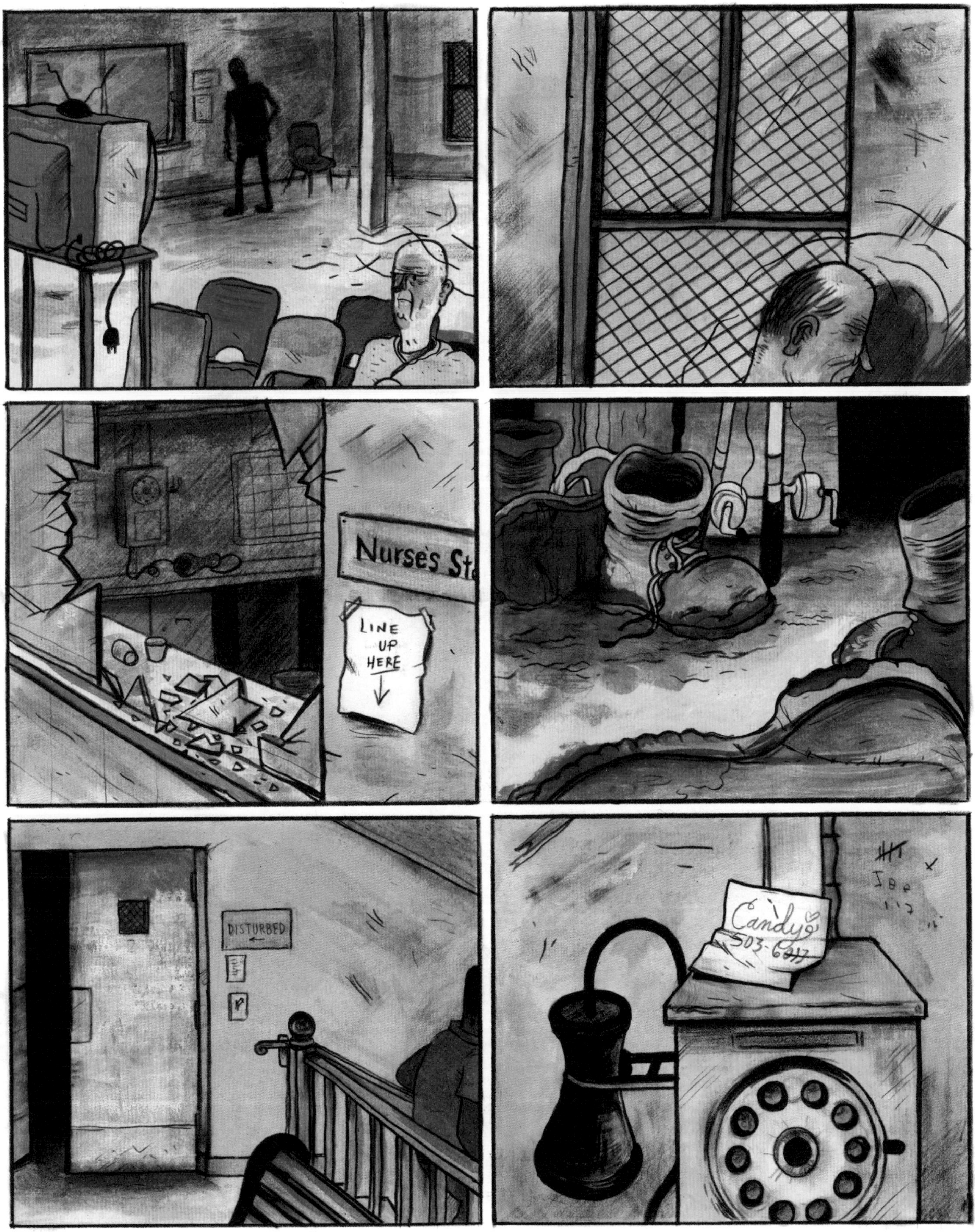
Nurse's St
LINE UP HERE
DISTURBED
Candy

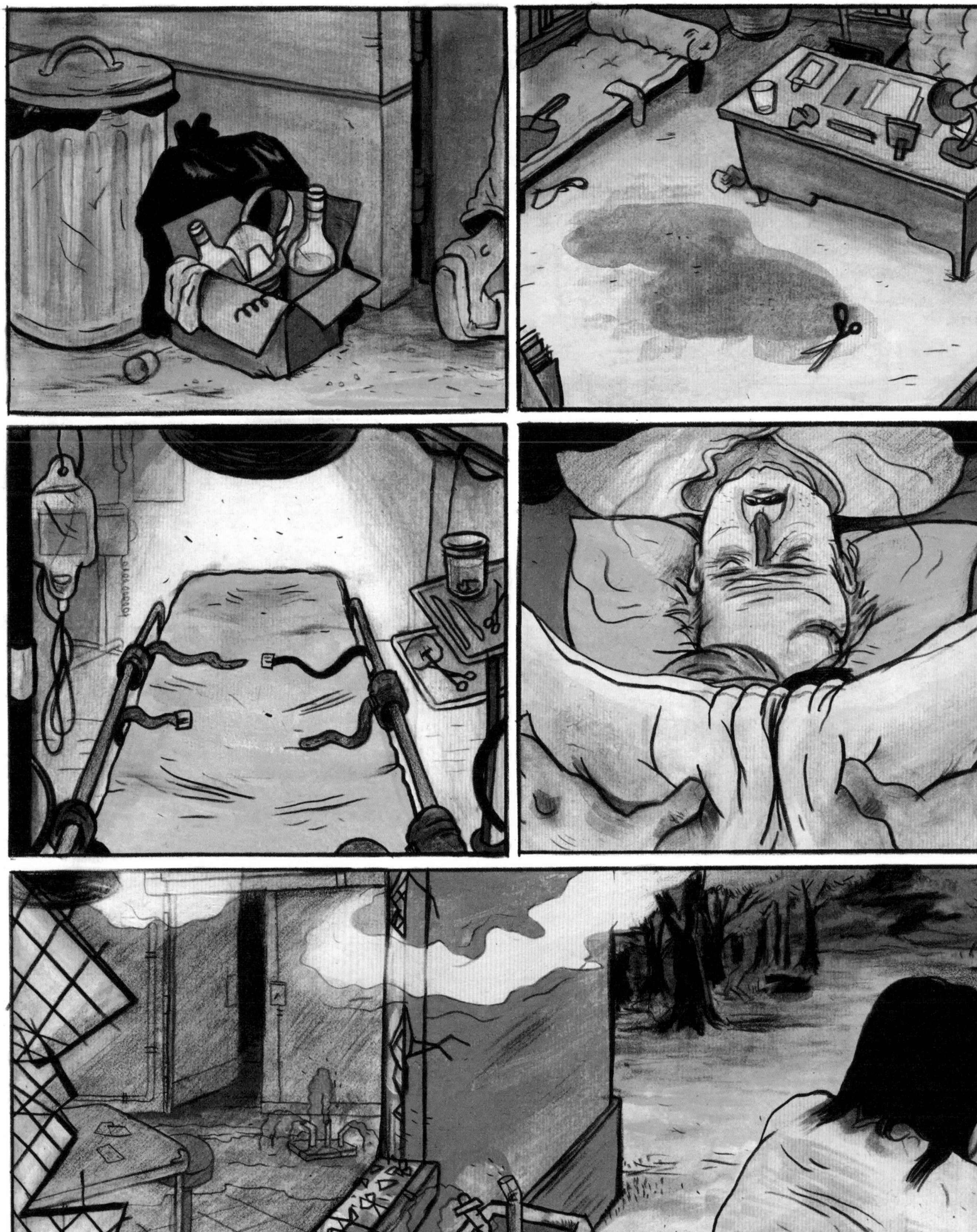

The Bell Jar

Sylvia Plath

ILLUSTRATION BY **Ellen Lindner**

IN A WAY THAT REMINDS ME OF JOHN KEATS, Sylvia Plath had a tremendous creative burst, writing most of her best, most lauded poems in the space of a month or so. They were collected in *Ariel*, one of the great poetry books of the century, which was published two years after she killed herself by putting her head in a gas oven. It was the end of a tumultuous life filled with academic achievement, literary success, multiple suicide attempts, electroshock therapy, and a stormy marriage to fellow poet Ted Hughes.

Just before her suicide in February 1963, her novel, *The Bell Jar*, was released. Largely autobiographical, albeit with a hopeful ending, it's become a touchstone for young women who feel ill-at-ease in the world. Ellen Lindner, editor of *The Strumpet* comics anthologies and creator of the graphic novel *Undertow*, reveals a jolting full-page illustration for Plath's only published novel. She notes:

> *The Bell Jar* has a reputation as a sour, depressing read. And it is depressing—it's tragic to read about someone who is intelligent, hard-working, and quickly succumbing to mental illness. But as in *Anna Karenina*, another work I adapted for *The Graphic Canon*, you get a sense of society at large from *The Bell Jar*—and it's a 1950s society full of girls like Esther, torn between the opportunity to be educated, to be intellectuals, and the overwhelming pressure to just be pretty and nice and look good in a dress.
>
> Plath tells the story in such a way that her character's disease feels less like a singular affliction and more like a generational epidemic—when Esther is joined in the sanitorium by a classmate (with rumors teeming of other victims), the reader starts to wonder whether there's something in the water, something in the air, that's turning young women into pale, dysfunctional, starkly self-destructive versions of themselves. Plath tells this story with plenty of ribald detail and amusing asides—as when Esther lies to a sailor about her real name, and what she's really doing in his city. But one of the major motifs in the book—electrocution—comes out in the first line of the novel ("It was a queer sultry summer, the summer they executed the Rosenbergs"), and recurs when Esther undergoes electroconvulsive therapy. That's why I chose this imagery for my illustration—I liked the idea of a young woman being struck by lightning and her smiling dates remaining unaware, somehow, that something's gone wrong with their night out on the town. I wanted to depict the moment when a blinding bolt of pain descends.

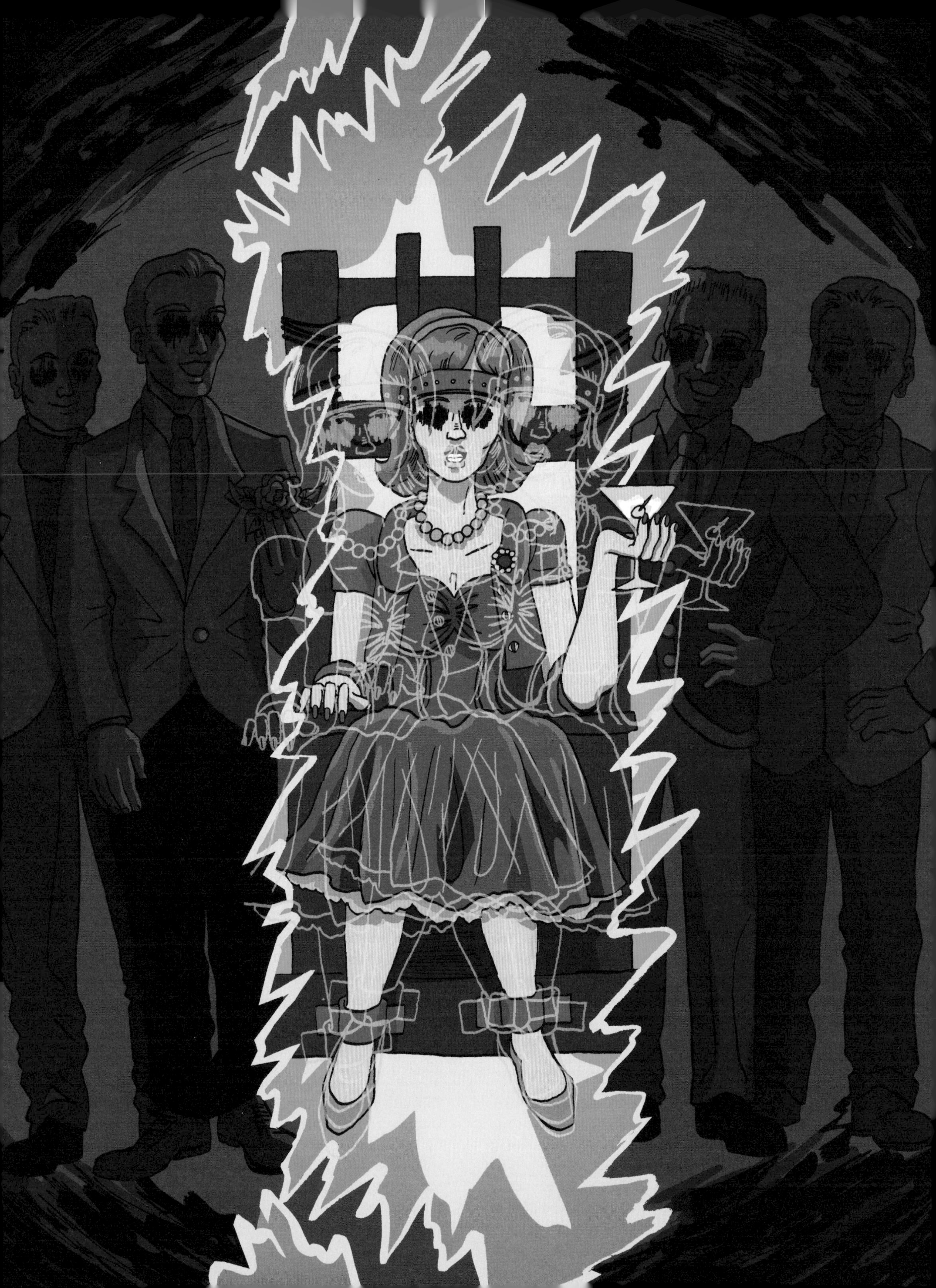

Last Exit to Brooklyn

Hubert Selby, Jr.

ART/ADAPTATION BY **Juliacks**

HUBERT SELBY, JR.'S 1964 NOVEL—ACTUALLY, A series of six interrelated short stories—is part of a literary tradition that takes a steely-eyed look at life among society's underclass: *Oliver Twist, Dubliners, The Man with the Golden Arm, Junky*. . . . Selby took this approach to the extreme, however, creating a raw, brutal work that's still disturbing as hell fifty years later. The look at street life among thieves, pimps, prostitutes, hoodlums, gangsters, pushers, addicts, poor laborers, gays, transvestites, and other outcasts in 1950s Brooklyn is unflinching and without a modicum of hope. Violence and drugs are the order of the day. Like James Joyce's Dublin residents, they long for escape and transcendence but can't seem to make it happen. *The New York Times* noted the legal problems the book triggered:

> "Tralala," one of the stories that make up the book, was the subject of an obscenity trial involving *The Provincetown Review*, which published it in 1961. And when "Last Exit," which consists of "Tralala" and five other loosely connected stories, was published in England in 1966, a jury found it to be obscene and fined its publisher.

The *Times* noted Selby's reaction: "The events that take place are the way people are. These are not literary characters; these are real people. I knew these people. How can anybody look inside themselves and be surprised at the hatred and violence in the world? It's inside all of us." The author himself had been a merchant marine, morphine addict, and alcoholic who lived in the Red Hook neighborhood in which *Last Exit* is set. "I lived their life," he said. "I wasn't looking in. I was in."

Selby—a fellow traveler of the Beat movement, but never actually a part of it—broke new ground with his writing style: no quotation marks (or anything else to indicate speech), slashes instead of apostrophes, lots of slang and dialect, very little correct grammar, and a conversational, stream-of-consciousness tone throughout.

In the chapter/story "The Queen Is Dead," the transvestite prostitute Georgette is hosting a prescription-drug party in her dingy apartment. Searching for a way to become the center of attention, she picks up a book of Poe's work and reads "The Raven" aloud. The assorted lowlifes and outcasts are transfixed by this classic poem of a man anguished over his dead love.

Juliacks's art often takes a multipronged approach, involving theater, film, performance art, installations, comics, and/or illustration. She brings her dense, page-filling approach—done with pen and ink and collage—to Georgette's mesmerizing reading of "The Raven." The artist explains:

> In the story the poem acts as this beacon of light—it draws everyone in and heightens Georgette's sense of grandeur—where Georgette feels herself to be the Queen—the one moment in the story where everyone feels themselves to be human. Then I think Selby makes the story itself act like the poem does—he uses the phrase "nevermore" to highlight the self-delusion of the characters.

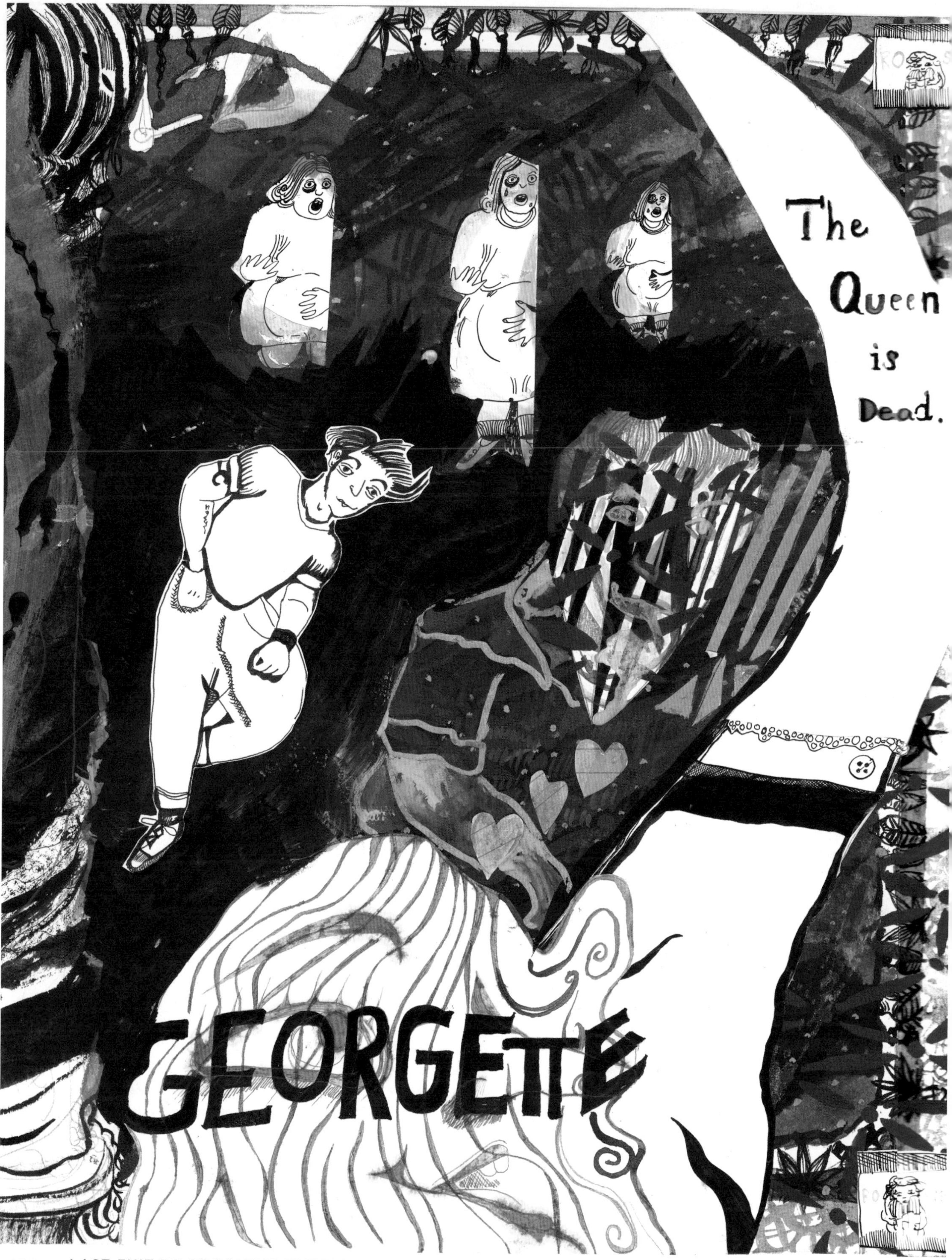
The Queen is Dead.
GEORGETTE

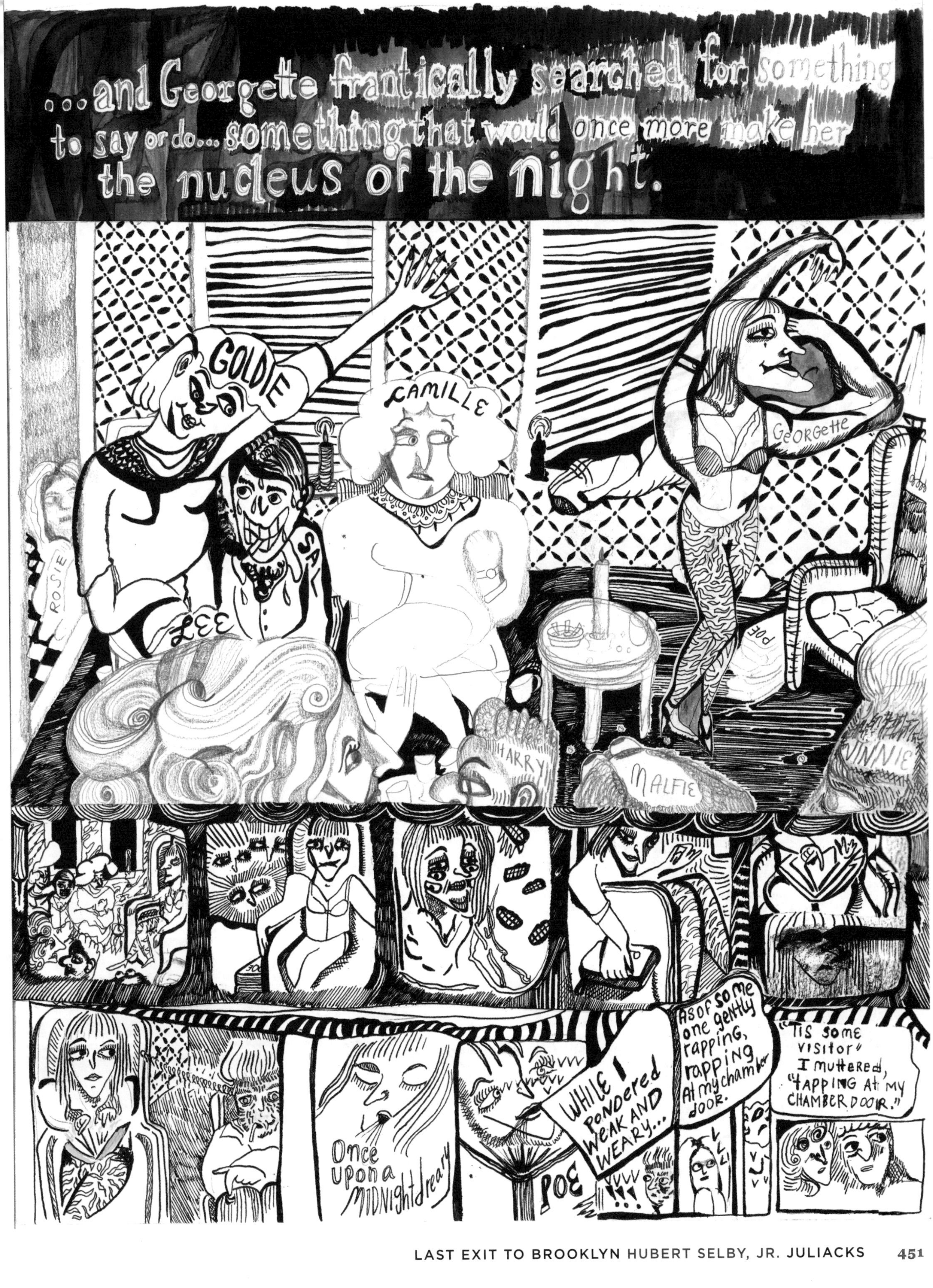

...and Georgette frantically searched for something to say or do... something that would once more make her the nucleus of the night.
GOLDIE
CAMILLE
GEORGETTE
ROSIE
SAL
LEE
POE
HARRY
MALFIE
VINNIE
Once upon a midnight dreary
POE
WHILE I PONDERED WEAK AND WEARY...
As of some one gently rapping, rapping At my chamber door.
"Tis some visitor" I muttered, "tapping at my chamber door."

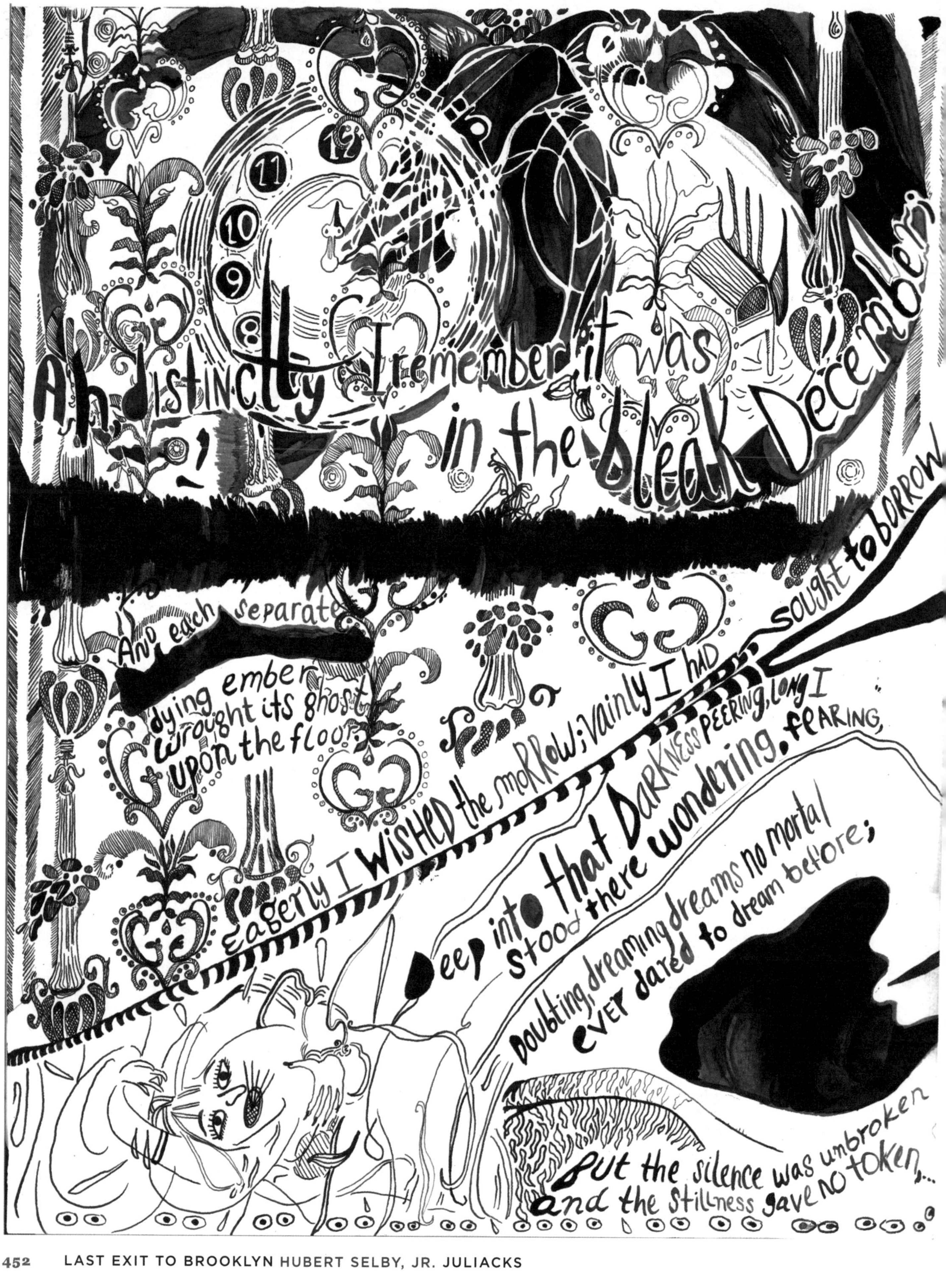
Ah, distinctly I remember it was
in the bleak December;
And each separate
dying ember
wrought its ghost
upon the floor.
Eagerly I wished the morrow; vainly I had sought to borrow
Darkness peering, long I
Deep into that Darkness
stood there wondering, fearing,
Doubting, dreaming dreams no mortal
ever dared to dream before;
But the silence was unbroken
and the stillness gave no token,...

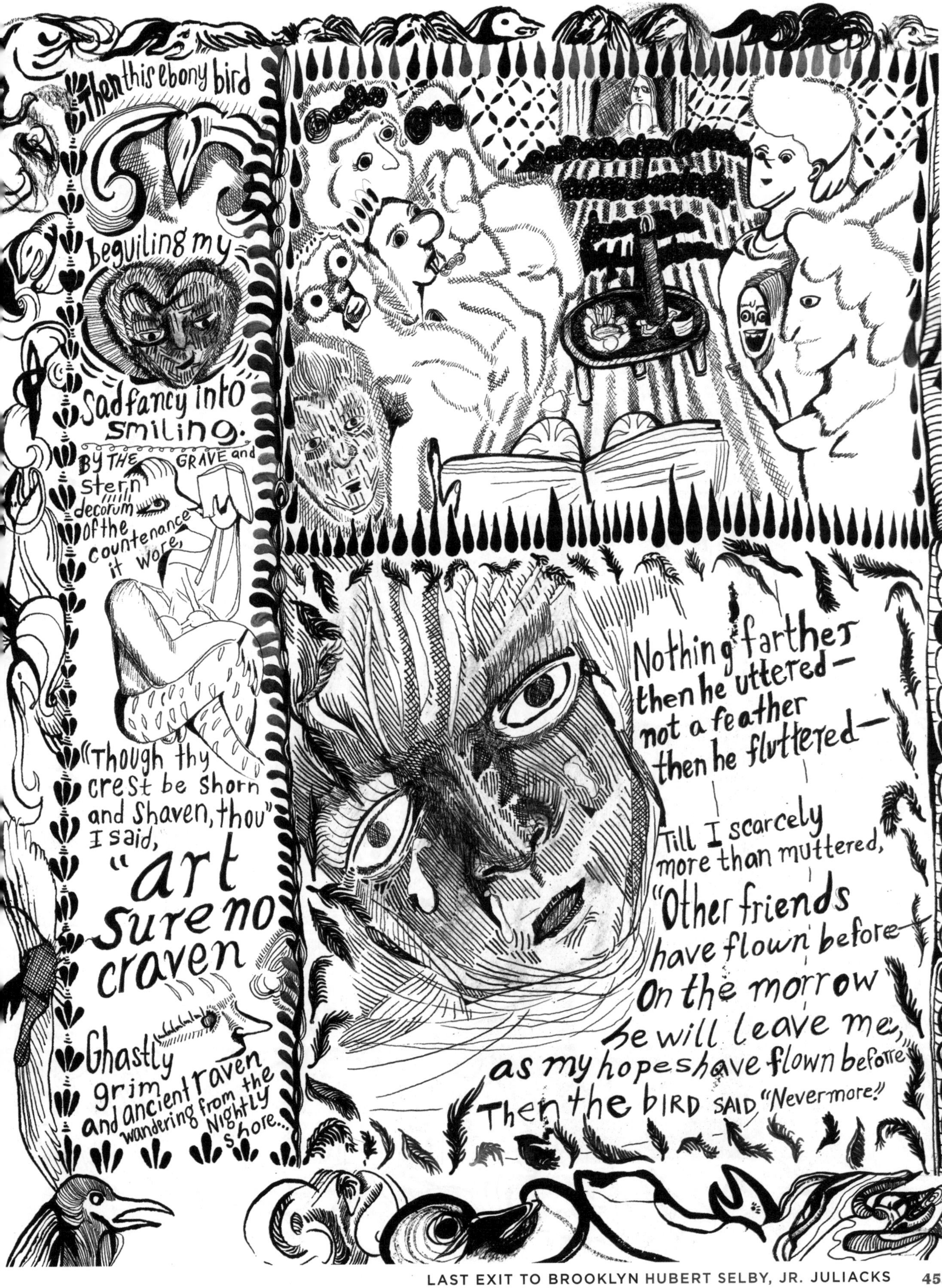
Then this ebony bird
beguiling my
sad fancy into
smiling.
By the grave and
stern
decorum
of the
countenance
it wore,
"Though thy
crest be shorn
and shaven, thou"
I said,
"art
sure no
craven
Ghastly
grim
and ancient raven
wandering from the
Nightly
shore...
Nothing farther
then he uttered—
not a feather
then he fluttered—
Till I scarcely
more than muttered,
"Other friends
have flown before—
On the morrow
he will leave me,
as my hopes have flown before"
Then the bird said "Nevermore."

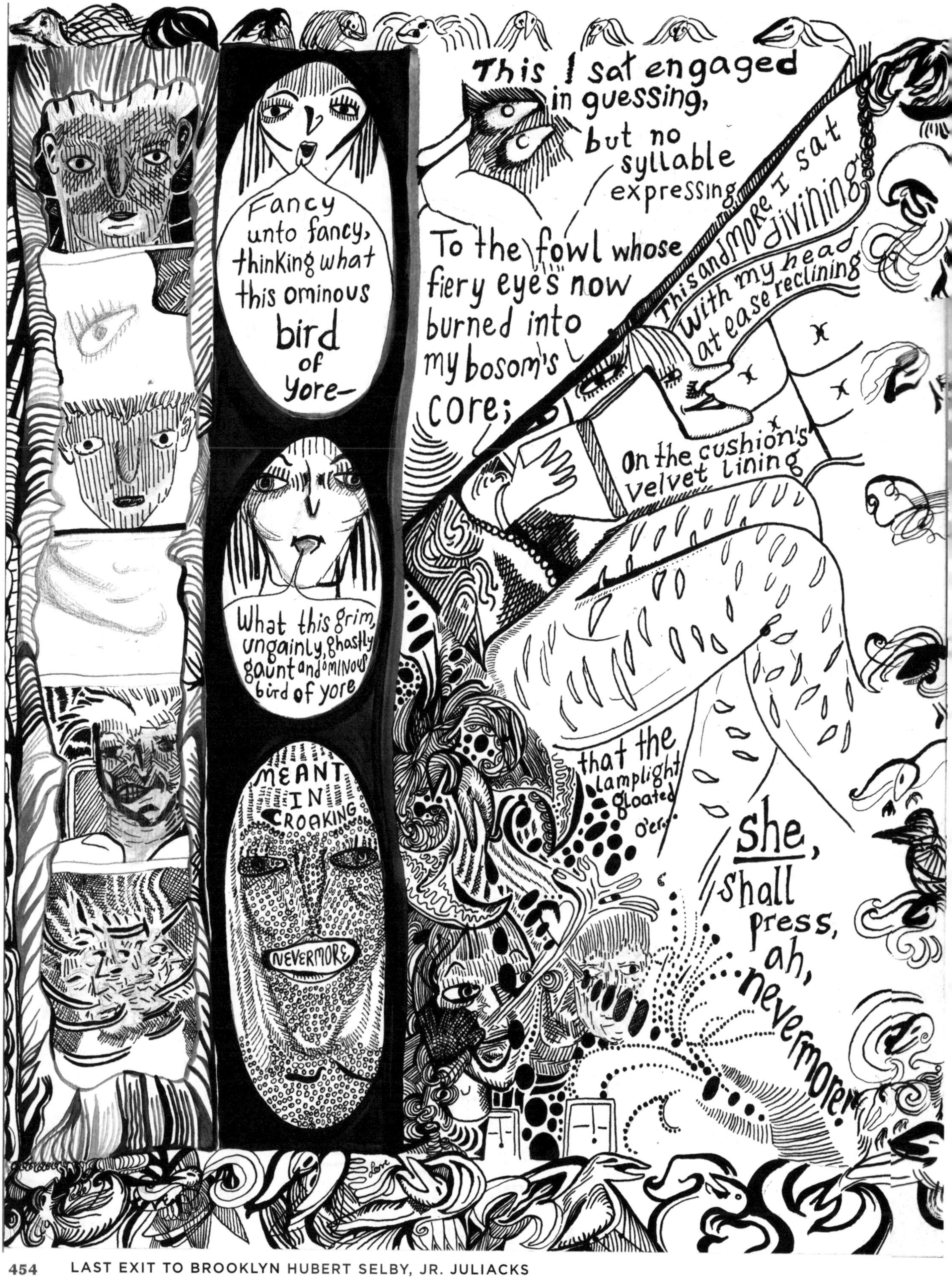

Fancy unto fancy, thinking what this ominous bird of yore—
What this grim, ungainly, ghastly gaunt and ominous bird of yore
MEANT IN CROAKING
NEVERMORE
This I sat engaged in guessing, but no syllable expressing
To the fowl whose fiery eyes now burned into my bosom's core;
This and more I sat divining, with my head at ease reclining
On the cushion's velvet lining
that the lamplight gloated o'er,
She, shall press, ah, nevermore!

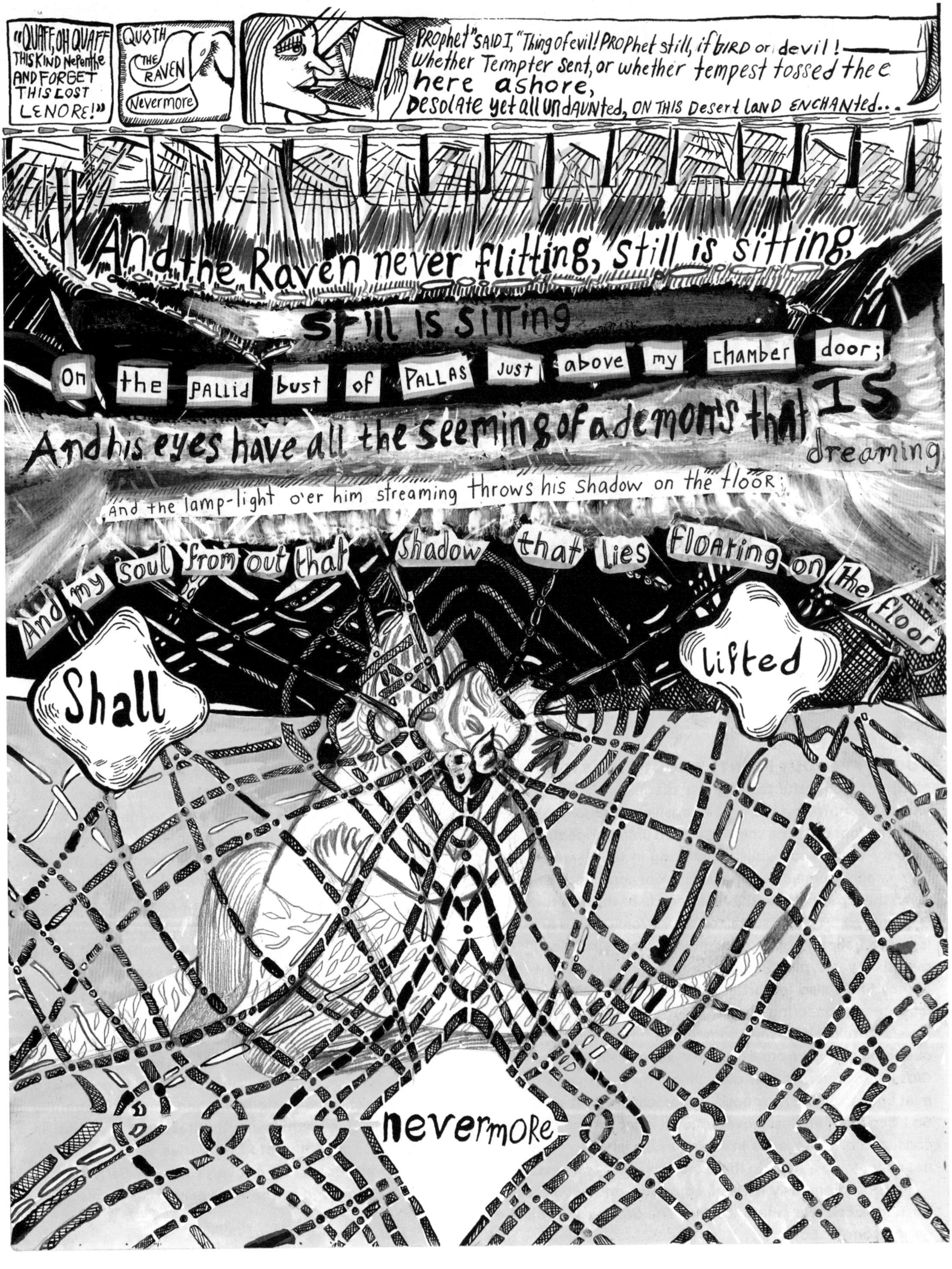
"QUAFF, OH QUAFF THIS KIND NEPENTHE AND FORGET THIS LOST LENORE!"
QUOTH THE RAVEN
Nevermore
"Prophet" SAID I, "Thing of evil! PROPHET still, if BIRD or devil! Whether Tempter sent, or whether tempest tossed thee here ashore,
Desolate yet all undaunted, ON THIS Desert LAND ENCHANTED...
And the Raven never flitting, still is sitting,
still is sitting
On the pallid bust of Pallas just above my chamber door;
And his eyes have all the seeming of a demon's that is dreaming
And the lamp-light o'er him streaming throws his shadow on the floor;
And my soul from out that shadow that lies floating on the floor
Shall
lifted
nevermore

Diaries

Anaïs Nin

ART/ADAPTATION BY **Mardou**

YOU'LL FIND OUT PLENTY ABOUT ANAÏS NIN FROM Mardou's delightful take on her diaries, so there's not a whole lot more to say. Nin's extensive personal journals—written from the time she was eleven until her death at age seventy-three, and published starting in 1966—are an epic literary achievement. It's hard to think of another artistic creation that spans all but the first decade of the creator's life. (*Peanuts*—a fifty-year sustained effort from Charles Schulz—is in the ballpark, but Nin wrote her diaries religiously for over sixty years, plus Schulz didn't start until he was twenty-eight.) She's also important—in my idiosyncratic view, at least—as a pioneering female writer of erotic literature. Her novels certainly have their admirers, although they're largely overlooked. She wrote of her five-volume novel sequence, *Cities of the Interior:* "The diary taught me that there were no neat ends to novels, no neat denouement, no neat synthesis. So I began an endless novel, a novel in which the climaxes consisted of discoveries in awareness, each step in awareness becoming a stage in the growth like the layers in trees."

Mardou graciously revised, colorized, and even redrew portions of her Nin adaptation for *The Graphic Canon*. She wrote from St. Louis:

I originally wrote the Anaïs Nin piece for an anthology I edited, *Whores of Mensa*. It fit the theme of that issue ("Ladies of Paris") and allowed me to indulge a literary passion. When I'd first read Nin, the *Incest* volume, ten years previously, I had become fascinated, though I disapproved of her too. I couldn't stop reading her journal and eventually she won me over. I happened to see online this (sort of trashy) comic strip someone had drawn for *The Big Book of Wild Women*, and it made me so mad. It was full of errors (the year of her death was listed as 1974, for example), and it just listed all her sexploits, one after the other. It made her sound like a crazy, brainless nymphomaniac. So I had that in mind when I wrote my own graphic story of her life. I wanted to express her as I knew her from her diary—flawed but brave, strikingly intelligent and unique. I hopefully captured some of that real Nin presence. She's like an old friend now, I dip into her diaries, and she's a real pick-me-up. Especially those years, the *Early Diaries* from 1927 through to the war years.

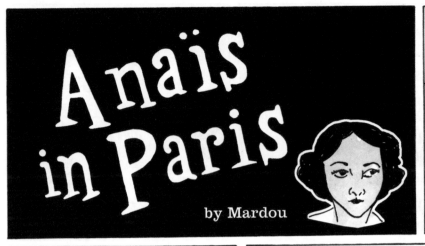

Anaïs in Paris

by Mardou

MUSE, GROUPIE, LITERARY LEGEND - ANAÏS NIN KEPT A DIARY FOR OVER SIXTY YEARS.

ALTHOUGH SHE STRUGGLED AGAINST THE FORM, IT WAS HOME TO HER BEST WRITING.

MERDE! WHY CAN'T I JUST WRITE A NOVEL?

LIFE - THAT WAS HER THING - AND THEN RELIVING IT IN THE "WHITE HEAT" OF HER JOURNAL.

PFFT!

'MAY AS WELL GO OUT...

A LIFE SHE LEFT IN MANY VOLUMES, BOTH REVILED AND REVERED BY READERS.

DIARY OF ANAÏS NIN

A WOMAN SPEAKS

ANAÏS NIN

INCEST

HENRY & JUNE

HEN

ANAÏS NIN

ANAÏS NIN

EARLY DIARY OF ANAÏS N.

LINOTTE

EARLY DIARY

SHE CONTINUES TO FASCINATE: FILM MAKERS, BIOGRAPHERS, CONTEMPORARIES, EVEN PERFUMERS HAVE TRIED TO CAPTURE HER 'GLAMOUR'.

A MINOR NOVELIST AT BEST!

SHE COULDN'T PRONOUNCE 'YACHT'!

A SERIOUS WRITER OF SOME IMPORTANCE.

AN ABUSED CHILD.

DEIRDRE BAIR

GORE VIDAL

MARIA DE MEDEIROS

EDMUND WILSON

NOEL RILEY FITCH

PHILIP KAUFMAN

BUT SHE REMAINS HER OWN GREATEST BIOGRAPHER....

BECAUSE I'M "INSAISSABLE".

HER FAVORITE WORDS

AND ALSO "ENSORCELLED".

IN THE 1924-39 DIARIES, THE PARISIAN YEARS, YOU CAN ALMOST HEAR HER HIGH-HEELED ONE-STRAPS CLICKING THROUGH THE PAGES.

BOULANG

CAFÉ TABAC

IT WAS THE PARIS OF JEAN COCTEAU, PAUL VALÉRY, JOSEPHINE BAKER, JAMES JOYCE .... AND OF A HOUSEWIFE WHO WOULD JOIN THEIR RANKS ...

Shakespeare and Company

EVENTUALLY!

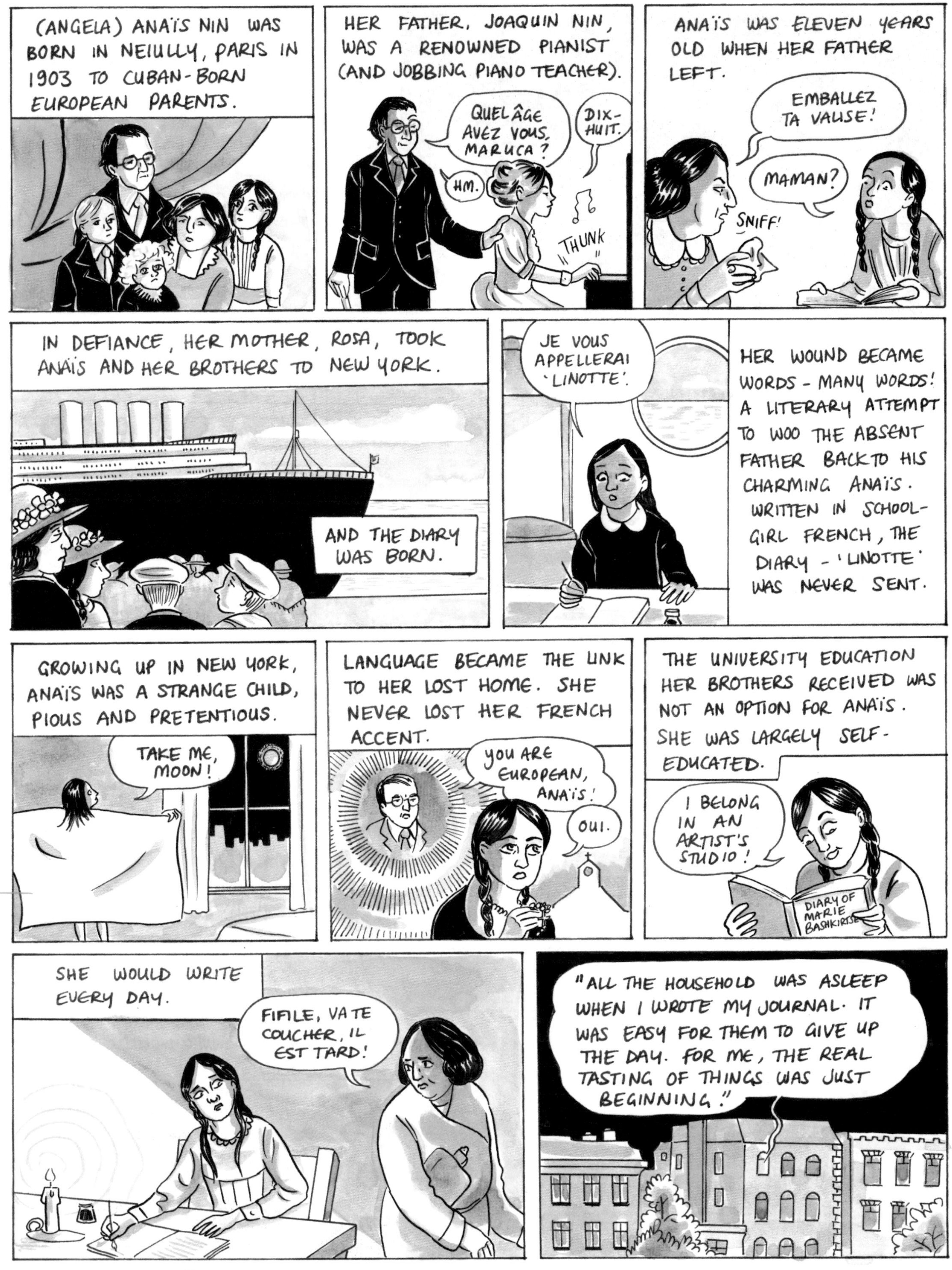
(ANGELA) ANAÏS NIN WAS BORN IN NEUILLY, PARIS IN 1903 TO CUBAN-BORN EUROPEAN PARENTS.
HER FATHER, JOAQUIN NIN, WAS A RENOWNED PIANIST (AND JOBBING PIANO TEACHER).
QUEL ÂGE AVEZ VOUS, MARUCA?
DIX-HUIT.
HM.
THUNK
ANAÏS WAS ELEVEN YEARS OLD WHEN HER FATHER LEFT.
EMBALLEZ TA VALISE!
MAMAN?
SNIFF!
IN DEFIANCE, HER MOTHER, ROSA, TOOK ANAÏS AND HER BROTHERS TO NEW YORK.
AND THE DIARY WAS BORN.
JE VOUS APPELLERAI 'LINOTTE'.
HER WOUND BECAME WORDS - MANY WORDS! A LITERARY ATTEMPT TO WOO THE ABSENT FATHER BACK TO HIS CHARMING ANAÏS. WRITTEN IN SCHOOL-GIRL FRENCH, THE DIARY - 'LINOTTE' WAS NEVER SENT.
GROWING UP IN NEW YORK, ANAÏS WAS A STRANGE CHILD, PIOUS AND PRETENTIOUS.
TAKE ME, MOON!
LANGUAGE BECAME THE LINK TO HER LOST HOME. SHE NEVER LOST HER FRENCH ACCENT.
YOU ARE EUROPEAN, ANAÏS!
OUI.
THE UNIVERSITY EDUCATION HER BROTHERS RECEIVED WAS NOT AN OPTION FOR ANAÏS. SHE WAS LARGELY SELF-EDUCATED.
I BELONG IN AN ARTIST'S STUDIO!
DIARY OF MARIE BASHKIRTSE
SHE WOULD WRITE EVERY DAY.
FIFILE, VA TE COUCHER, IL EST TARD!
"ALL THE HOUSEHOLD WAS ASLEEP WHEN I WROTE MY JOURNAL. IT WAS EASY FOR THEM TO GIVE UP THE DAY. FOR ME, THE REAL TASTING OF THINGS WAS JUST BEGINNING."

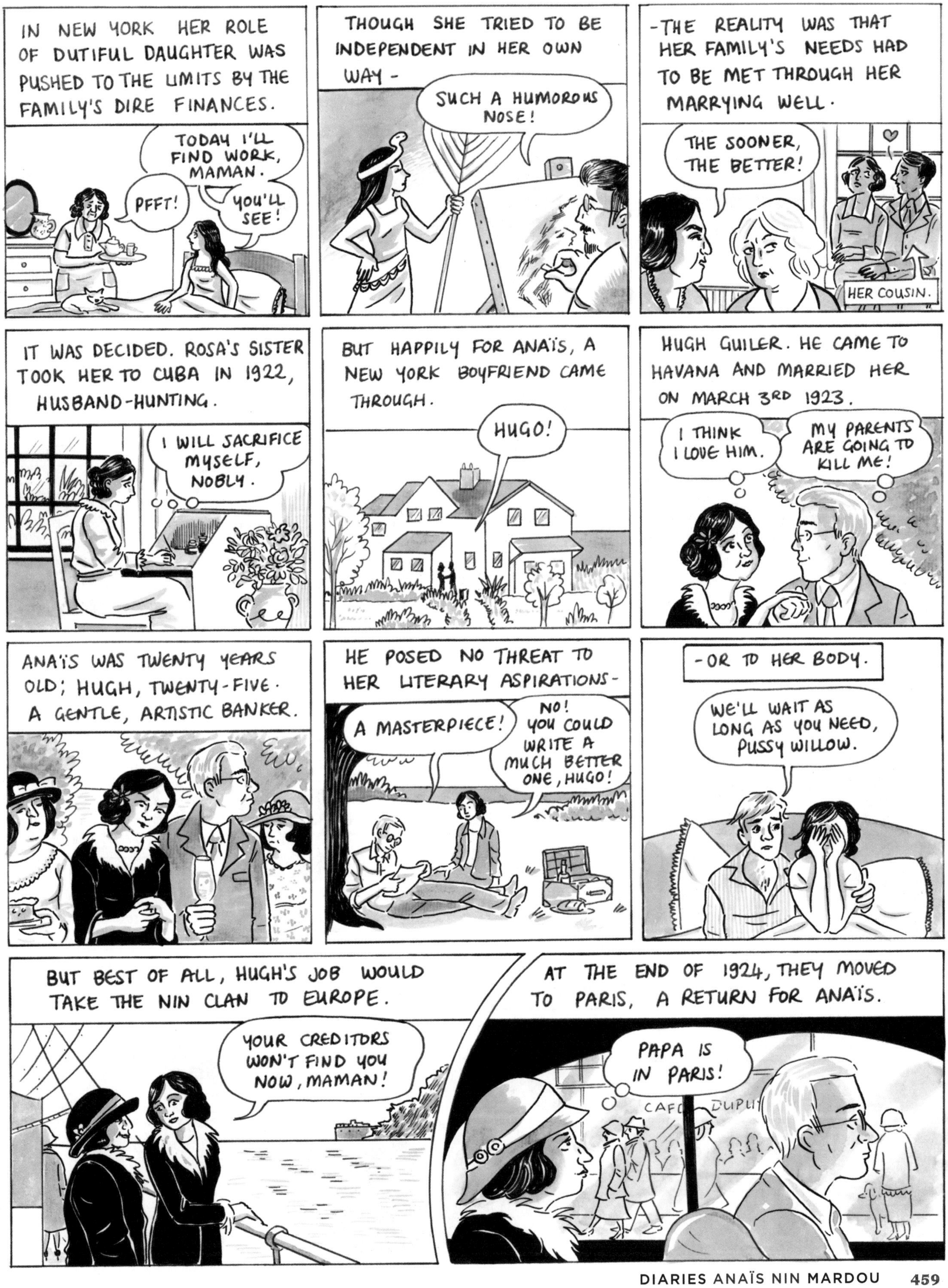
IN NEW YORK HER ROLE OF DUTIFUL DAUGHTER WAS PUSHED TO THE LIMITS BY THE FAMILY'S DIRE FINANCES.
TODAY I'LL FIND WORK, MAMAN.
PFFT!
YOU'LL SEE!
THOUGH SHE TRIED TO BE INDEPENDENT IN HER OWN WAY -
SUCH A HUMOROUS NOSE!
-THE REALITY WAS THAT HER FAMILY'S NEEDS HAD TO BE MET THROUGH HER MARRYING WELL.
THE SOONER, THE BETTER!
HER COUSIN.
IT WAS DECIDED. ROSA'S SISTER TOOK HER TO CUBA IN 1922, HUSBAND-HUNTING.
I WILL SACRIFICE MYSELF, NOBLY.
BUT HAPPILY FOR ANAÏS, A NEW YORK BOYFRIEND CAME THROUGH.
HUGO!
HUGH GUILER. HE CAME TO HAVANA AND MARRIED HER ON MARCH 3RD 1923.
I THINK I LOVE HIM.
MY PARENTS ARE GOING TO KILL ME!
ANAÏS WAS TWENTY YEARS OLD; HUGH, TWENTY-FIVE. A GENTLE, ARTISTIC BANKER.
HE POSED NO THREAT TO HER LITERARY ASPIRATIONS -
A MASTERPIECE!
NO! YOU COULD WRITE A MUCH BETTER ONE, HUGO!
-OR TO HER BODY.
WE'LL WAIT AS LONG AS YOU NEED, PUSSY WILLOW.
BUT BEST OF ALL, HUGH'S JOB WOULD TAKE THE NIN CLAN TO EUROPE.
YOUR CREDITORS WON'T FIND YOU NOW, MAMAN!
AT THE END OF 1924, THEY MOVED TO PARIS, A RETURN FOR ANAÏS.
PAPA IS IN PARIS!

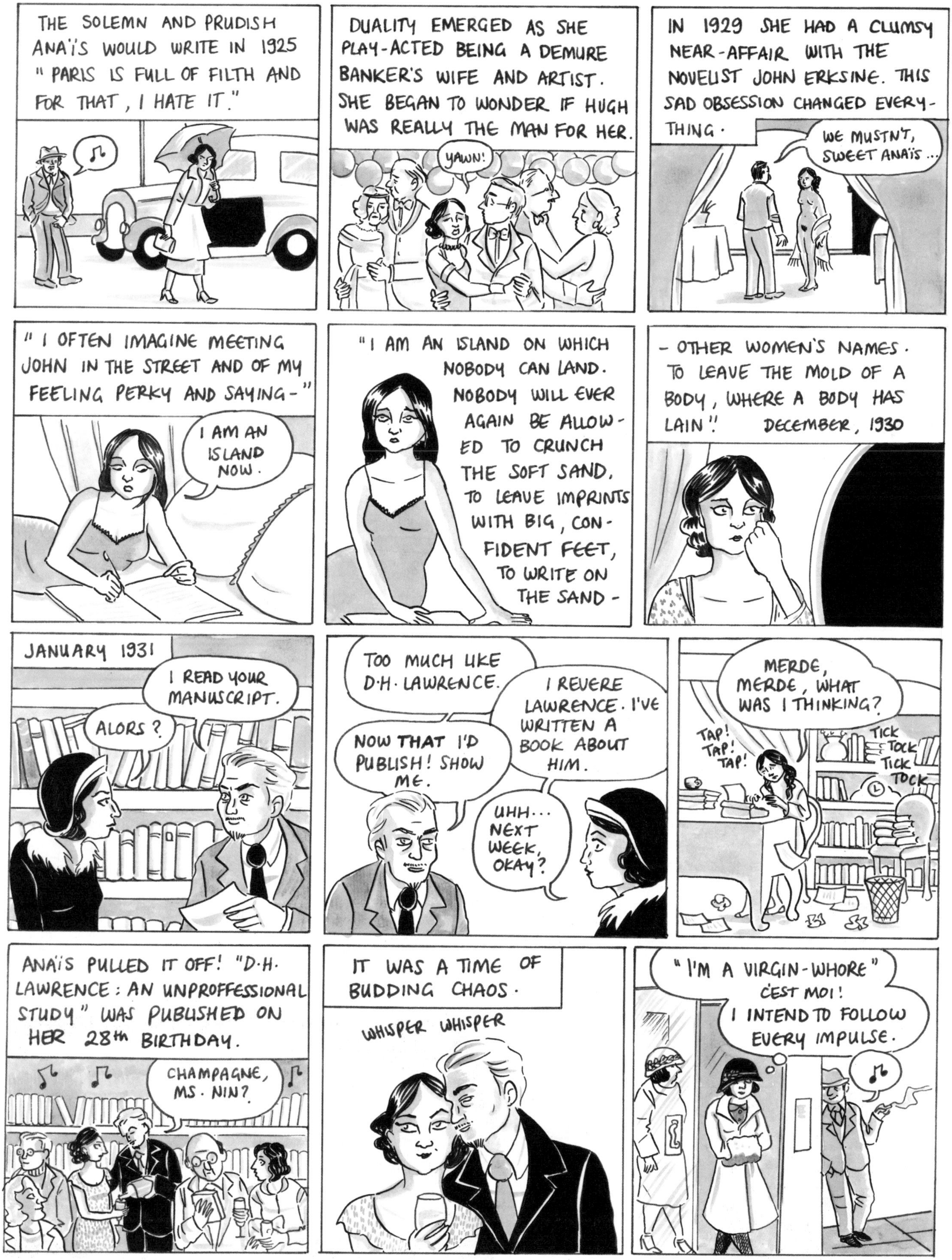
THE SOLEMN AND PRUDISH ANAÏS WOULD WRITE IN 1925 "PARIS IS FULL OF FILTH AND FOR THAT, I HATE IT."
DUALITY EMERGED AS SHE PLAY-ACTED BEING A DEMURE BANKER'S WIFE AND ARTIST. SHE BEGAN TO WONDER IF HUGH WAS REALLY THE MAN FOR HER.
YAWN!
IN 1929 SHE HAD A CLUMSY NEAR-AFFAIR WITH THE NOVELIST JOHN ERKSINE. THIS SAD OBSESSION CHANGED EVERY-THING.
WE MUSTN'T, SWEET ANAÏS...
"I OFTEN IMAGINE MEETING JOHN IN THE STREET AND OF MY FEELING PERKY AND SAYING-"
I AM AN ISLAND NOW.
"I AM AN ISLAND ON WHICH NOBODY CAN LAND. NOBODY WILL EVER AGAIN BE ALLOW-ED TO CRUNCH THE SOFT SAND, TO LEAVE IMPRINTS WITH BIG, CON-FIDENT FEET, TO WRITE ON THE SAND-
- OTHER WOMEN'S NAMES. TO LEAVE THE MOLD OF A BODY, WHERE A BODY HAS LAIN." DECEMBER, 1930
JANUARY 1931
I READ YOUR MANUSCRIPT.
ALORS?
TOO MUCH LIKE D.H. LAWRENCE.
I REVERE LAWRENCE. I'VE WRITTEN A BOOK ABOUT HIM.
NOW THAT I'D PUBLISH! SHOW ME.
UHH... NEXT WEEK, OKAY?
MERDE, MERDE, WHAT WAS I THINKING?
TAP! TAP! TAP!
TICK TOCK TICK TOCK
ANAÏS PULLED IT OFF! "D.H. LAWRENCE: AN UNPROFFESSIONAL STUDY" WAS PUBLISHED ON HER 28th BIRTHDAY.
CHAMPAGNE, MS. NIN?
IT WAS A TIME OF BUDDING CHAOS.
WHISPER WHISPER
"I'M A VIRGIN-WHORE" C'EST MOI! I INTEND TO FOLLOW EVERY IMPULSE.

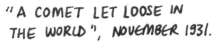
"A COMET LET LOOSE IN THE WORLD", NOVEMBER 1931.

ANAÏS NIN, HENRY MILLER; HENRY MILLER, ANAÏS NIN.

HE WAS AMERICAN. AN UNKNOWN HOBO-ARTIST, BUMMING AROUND PARIS.

YES, SINCE I WAS A CHILD.

YOU WRITE?

SOME PLACE YOU HAVE HERE.

THANK YOU!

THE FISH ARE MADE OF GLASS AND THE WATER'S DIRTY!

YOU SHOULD MEET MY WIFE!

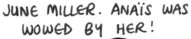
JUNE MILLER. ANAÏS WAS WOWED BY HER!

MYSTERIOUS AND EXOTIC - A MUSE AND ALTER-EGO.

JUNE TOLD YOU THAT?

ENCROYABLE, NON?

INCREDIBLY CHEAP, YES.

HUGO!

WHEN JUNE RETURNS TO AMERICA, ANAÏS AND HENRY ARE DRAWN TO EACH OTHER.

WELL?

YOU'VE NOT GOT HER, HENRY. IT TAKES A WOMAN TO WRITE JUNE.

IT COULDN'T BE HELPED, THEY LOVED ANALYSING JUNE. SHE WAS THE UNWITTING CATALYST THAT BOUND THEM.

HENRY!

ON MARCH 8TH 1932, THEY EMBARKED ON AN AFFAIR.

ANNÏS!

"I EXPECTED DOSTOEVSKIAN SCENES AND FOUND A GENTLE GERMAN WHO COULD NOT BEAR TO LET THE DISHES GO UNWASHED."

DIARIES ANAÏS NIN MARDOU   461

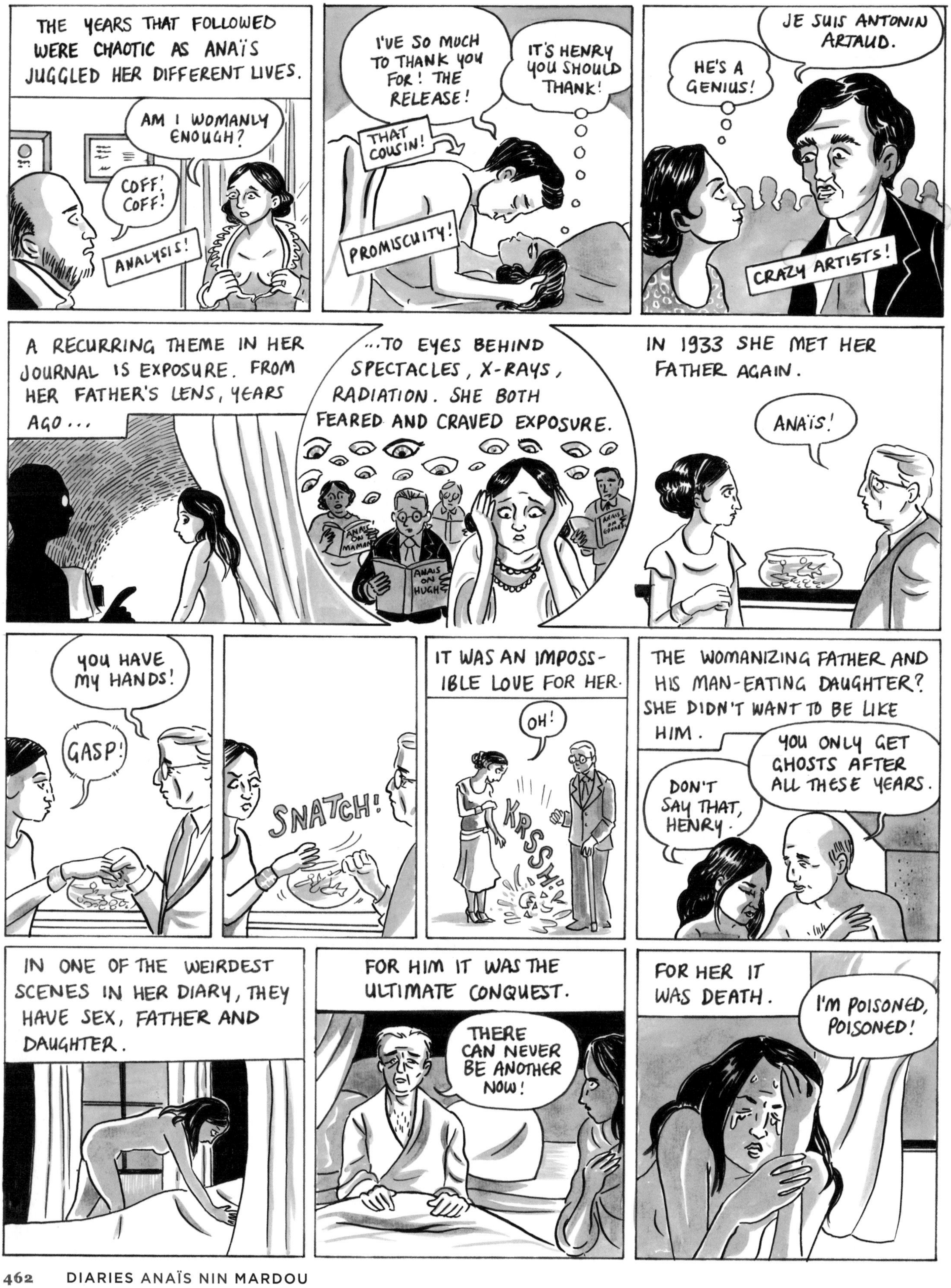
THE YEARS THAT FOLLOWED WERE CHAOTIC AS ANAÏS JUGGLED HER DIFFERENT LIVES.
AM I WOMANLY ENOUGH?
COFF! COFF!
ANALYSIS!
I'VE SO MUCH TO THANK YOU FOR! THE RELEASE!
IT'S HENRY YOU SHOULD THANK!
THAT COUSIN!
PROMISCUITY!
JE SUIS ANTONIN ARTAUD.
HE'S A GENIUS!
CRAZY ARTISTS!
A RECURRING THEME IN HER JOURNAL IS EXPOSURE. FROM HER FATHER'S LENS, YEARS AGO...
...TO EYES BEHIND SPECTACLES, X-RAYS, RADIATION. SHE BOTH FEARED AND CRAVED EXPOSURE.
ANAÏS ON MAMAN
ANAÏS ON HUGH
IN 1933 SHE MET HER FATHER AGAIN.
ANAÏS!
YOU HAVE MY HANDS!
GASP!
SNATCH!
IT WAS AN IMPOSS-IBLE LOVE FOR HER.
OH!
KRSSH!
THE WOMANIZING FATHER AND HIS MAN-EATING DAUGHTER? SHE DIDN'T WANT TO BE LIKE HIM.
YOU ONLY GET GHOSTS AFTER ALL THESE YEARS.
DON'T SAY THAT, HENRY.
IN ONE OF THE WEIRDEST SCENES IN HER DIARY, THEY HAVE SEX, FATHER AND DAUGHTER.
FOR HIM IT WAS THE ULTIMATE CONQUEST.
THERE CAN NEVER BE ANOTHER NOW!
FOR HER IT WAS DEATH.
I'M POISONED, POISONED!

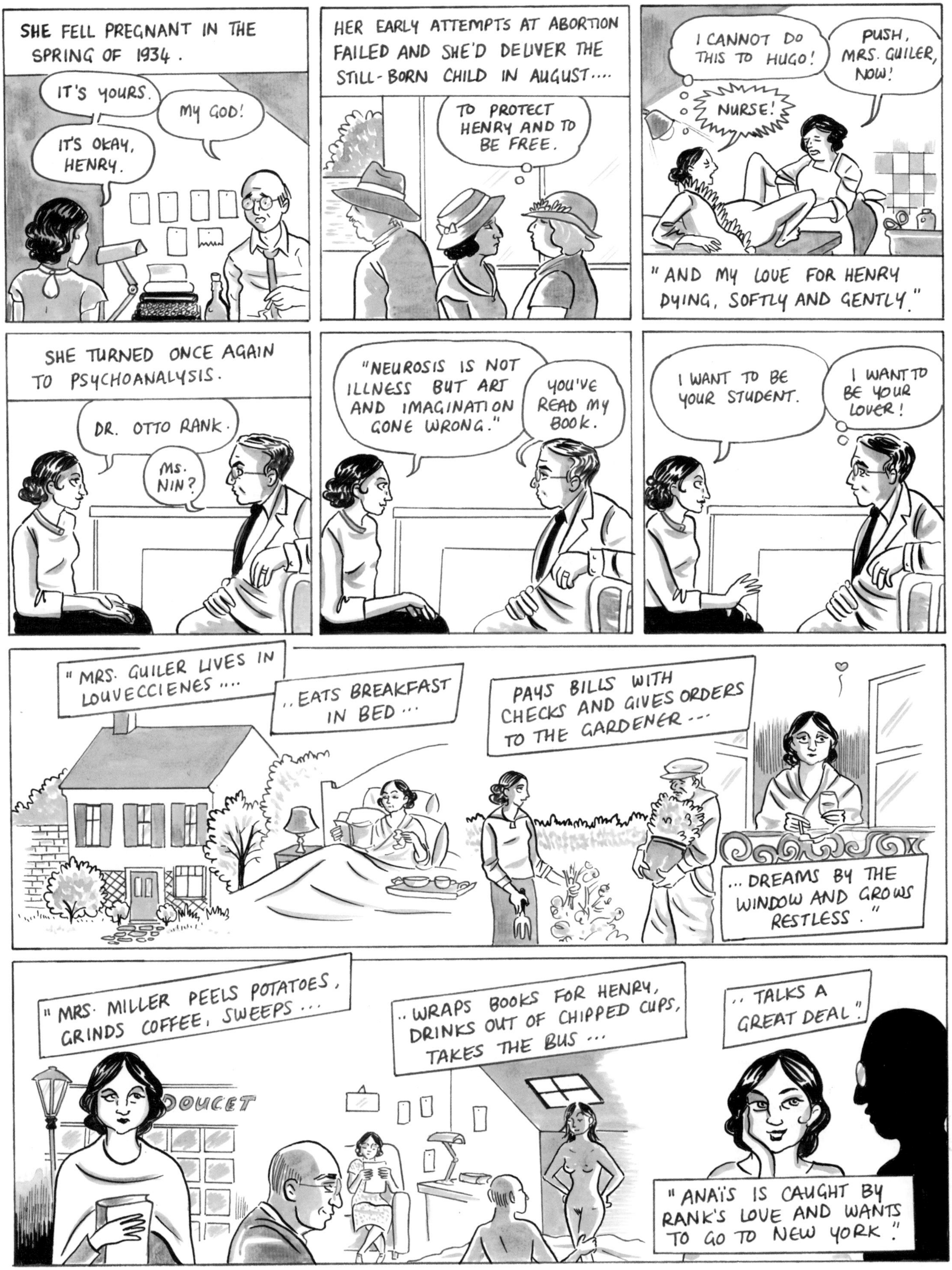
SHE FELL PREGNANT IN THE SPRING OF 1934.
IT'S YOURS.
MY GOD!
IT'S OKAY, HENRY.
HER EARLY ATTEMPTS AT ABORTION FAILED AND SHE'D DELIVER THE STILL-BORN CHILD IN AUGUST....
TO PROTECT HENRY AND TO BE FREE.
I CANNOT DO THIS TO HUGO!
NURSE!
PUSH, MRS. GUILER, NOW!
"AND MY LOVE FOR HENRY DYING, SOFTLY AND GENTLY."
SHE TURNED ONCE AGAIN TO PSYCHOANALYSIS.
DR. OTTO RANK.
MS. NIN?
"NEUROSIS IS NOT ILLNESS BUT ART AND IMAGINATION GONE WRONG."
YOU'VE READ MY BOOK.
I WANT TO BE YOUR STUDENT.
I WANT TO BE YOUR LOVER!
"MRS. GUILER LIVES IN LOUVECCIENES....
..EATS BREAKFAST IN BED...
PAYS BILLS WITH CHECKS AND GIVES ORDERS TO THE GARDENER...
...DREAMS BY THE WINDOW AND GROWS RESTLESS."
"MRS. MILLER PEELS POTATOES, GRINDS COFFEE, SWEEPS...
..WRAPS BOOKS FOR HENRY, DRINKS OUT OF CHIPPED CUPS, TAKES THE BUS...
..TALKS A GREAT DEAL."
DOUCET
"ANAÏS IS CAUGHT BY RANK'S LOVE AND WANTS TO GO TO NEW YORK".

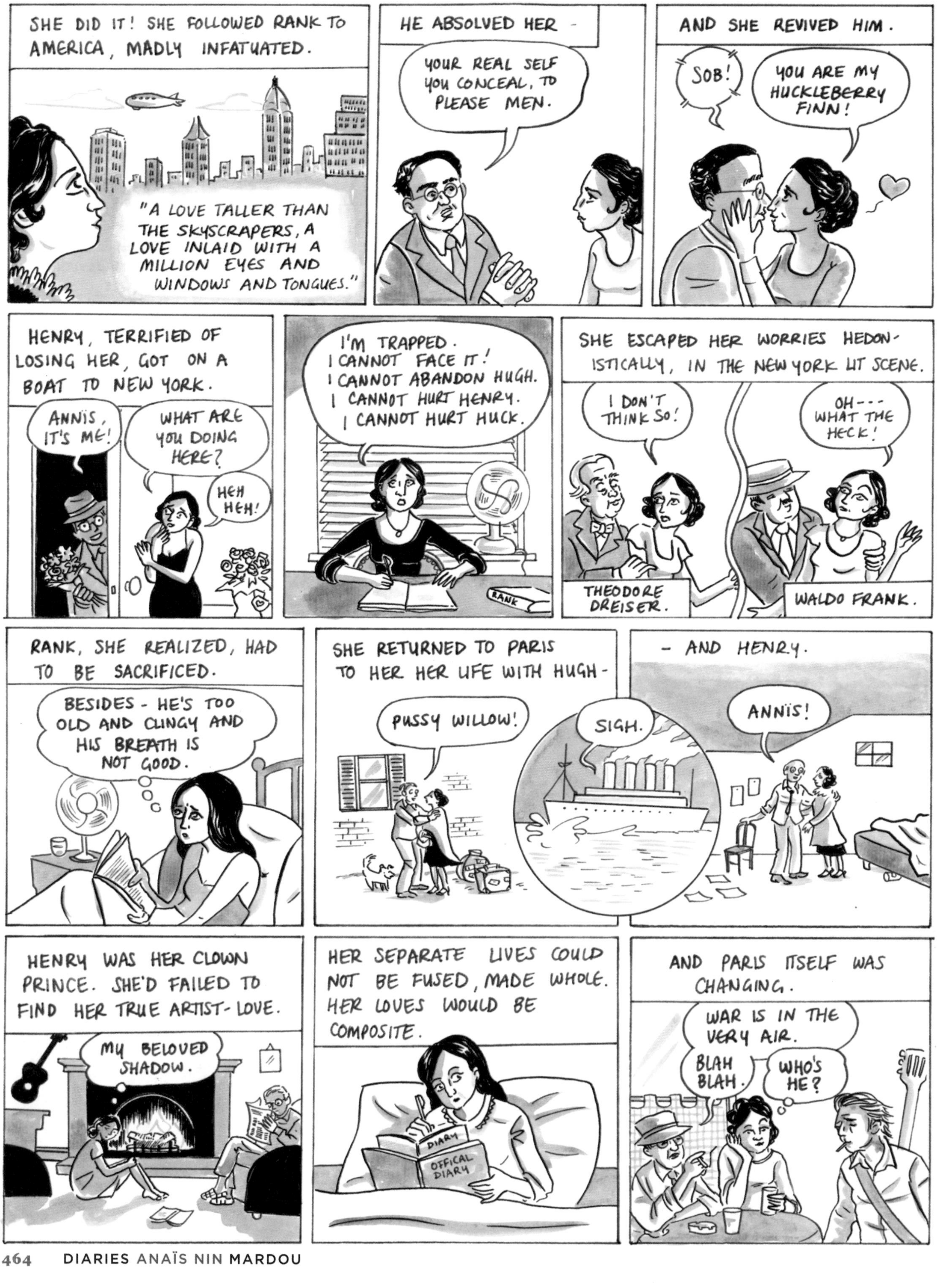
SHE DID IT! SHE FOLLOWED RANK TO AMERICA, MADLY INFATUATED.
"A LOVE TALLER THAN THE SKYSCRAPERS, A LOVE INLAID WITH A MILLION EYES AND WINDOWS AND TONGUES."
HE ABSOLVED HER -
YOUR REAL SELF YOU CONCEAL, TO PLEASE MEN.
AND SHE REVIVED HIM.
SOB!
YOU ARE MY HUCKLEBERRY FINN!
HENRY, TERRIFIED OF LOSING HER, GOT ON A BOAT TO NEW YORK.
ANNIS, IT'S ME!
WHAT ARE YOU DOING HERE?
HEH HEH!
I'M TRAPPED. I CANNOT FACE IT! I CANNOT ABANDON HUGH. I CANNOT HURT HENRY. I CANNOT HURT HUCK.
RANK
SHE ESCAPED HER WORRIES HEDONISTICALLY, IN THE NEW YORK LIT SCENE.
I DON'T THINK SO!
OH--- WHAT THE HECK!
THEODORE DREISER.
WALDO FRANK.
RANK, SHE REALIZED, HAD TO BE SACRIFICED.
BESIDES - HE'S TOO OLD AND CLINGY AND HIS BREATH IS NOT GOOD.
SHE RETURNED TO PARIS TO HER HER LIFE WITH HUGH -
PUSSY WILLOW!
SIGH.
- AND HENRY.
ANNIS!
HENRY WAS HER CLOWN PRINCE. SHE'D FAILED TO FIND HER TRUE ARTIST-LOVE.
MY BELOVED SHADOW.
HER SEPARATE LIVES COULD NOT BE FUSED, MADE WHOLE. HER LOVES WOULD BE COMPOSITE.
DIARY
OFFICAL DIARY
AND PARIS ITSELF WAS CHANGING.
WAR IS IN THE VERY AIR.
BLAH BLAH.
WHO'S HE?

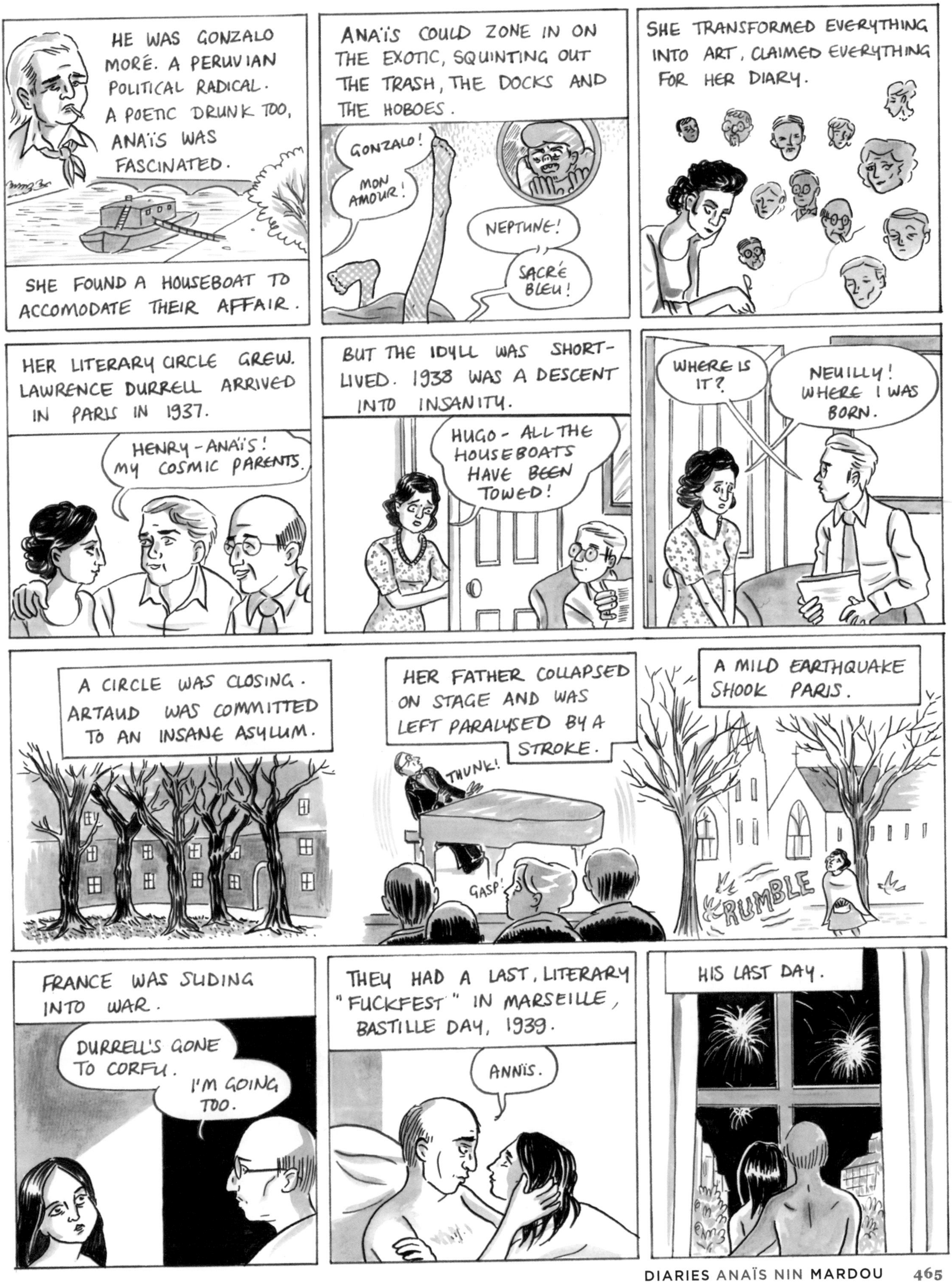
HE WAS GONZALO MORÉ. A PERUVIAN POLITICAL RADICAL. A POETIC DRUNK TOO, ANAÏS WAS FASCINATED.
SHE FOUND A HOUSEBOAT TO ACCOMODATE THEIR AFFAIR.
ANAÏS COULD ZONE IN ON THE EXOTIC, SQUINTING OUT THE TRASH, THE DOCKS AND THE HOBOES.
GONZALO!
MON AMOUR!
NEPTUNE!
SACRÉ BLEU!
SHE TRANSFORMED EVERYTHING INTO ART, CLAIMED EVERYTHING FOR HER DIARY.
HER LITERARY CIRCLE GREW. LAWRENCE DURRELL ARRIVED IN PARIS IN 1937.
HENRY-ANAÏS! MY COSMIC PARENTS.
BUT THE IDYLL WAS SHORT-LIVED. 1938 WAS A DESCENT INTO INSANITY.
HUGO- ALL THE HOUSEBOATS HAVE BEEN TOWED!
WHERE IS IT?
NEUILLY! WHERE I WAS BORN.
A CIRCLE WAS CLOSING. ARTAUD WAS COMMITTED TO AN INSANE ASYLUM.
HER FATHER COLLAPSED ON STAGE AND WAS LEFT PARALYSED BY A STROKE.
THUNK!
GASP!
A MILD EARTHQUAKE SHOOK PARIS.
RUMBLE
FRANCE WAS SLIDING INTO WAR.
DURRELL'S GONE TO CORFU.
I'M GOING TOO.
THEY HAD A LAST, LITERARY "FUCKFEST" IN MARSEILLE, BASTILLE DAY, 1939.
ANNÏS.
HIS LAST DAY.

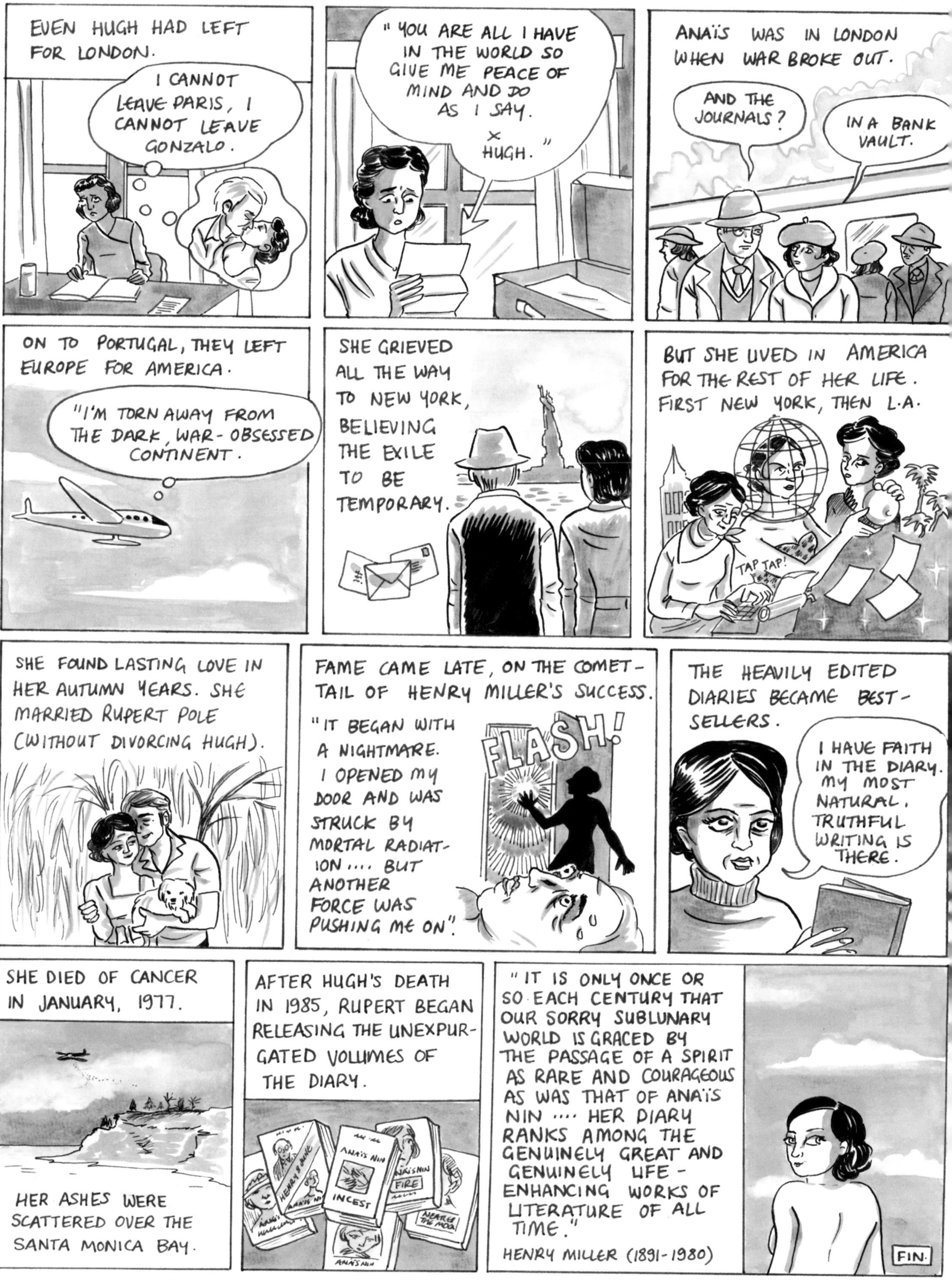
EVEN HUGH HAD LEFT FOR LONDON.
I CANNOT LEAVE PARIS, I CANNOT LEAVE GONZALO.
"YOU ARE ALL I HAVE IN THE WORLD SO GIVE ME PEACE OF MIND AND DO AS I SAY. x HUGH."
ANAÏS WAS IN LONDON WHEN WAR BROKE OUT.
AND THE JOURNALS?
IN A BANK VAULT.
ON TO PORTUGAL, THEY LEFT EUROPE FOR AMERICA.
"I'M TORN AWAY FROM THE DARK, WAR-OBSESSED CONTINENT.
SHE GRIEVED ALL THE WAY TO NEW YORK, BELIEVING THE EXILE TO BE TEMPORARY.
BUT SHE LIVED IN AMERICA FOR THE REST OF HER LIFE. FIRST NEW YORK, THEN L.A.
TAP TAP!
SHE FOUND LASTING LOVE IN HER AUTUMN YEARS. SHE MARRIED RUPERT POLE (WITHOUT DIVORCING HUGH).
FAME CAME LATE, ON THE COMET-TAIL OF HENRY MILLER'S SUCCESS.
"IT BEGAN WITH A NIGHTMARE. I OPENED MY DOOR AND WAS STRUCK BY MORTAL RADIATION .... BUT ANOTHER FORCE WAS PUSHING ME ON".
FLASH!
THE HEAVILY EDITED DIARIES BECAME BEST-SELLERS.
I HAVE FAITH IN THE DIARY. MY MOST NATURAL, TRUTHFUL WRITING IS THERE.
SHE DIED OF CANCER IN JANUARY, 1977.
HER ASHES WERE SCATTERED OVER THE SANTA MONICA BAY.
AFTER HUGH'S DEATH IN 1985, RUPERT BEGAN RELEASING THE UNEXPURGATED VOLUMES OF THE DIARY.
HENRY & JUNE
ANAÏS NIN
INCEST
ANAÏS NIN
FIRE
NEARER THE MOON
"IT IS ONLY ONCE OR SO EACH CENTURY THAT OUR SORRY SUBLUNARY WORLD IS GRACED BY THE PASSAGE OF A SPIRIT AS RARE AND COURAGEOUS AS WAS THAT OF ANAÏS NIN .... HER DIARY RANKS AMONG THE GENUINELY GREAT AND GENUINELY LIFE-ENHANCING WORKS OF LITERATURE OF ALL TIME."
HENRY MILLER (1891-1980)
FIN.

The Master and Margarita

Mikhail Bulgakov

ART/ADAPTATION BY **Andrzej Klimowski** AND **Danusia Schejbal**

IMAGINE WRITING A BOOK, KNOWING THAT THE discovery of the manuscript would get you arrested and either sent to Siberia or executed. That's what Mikhail Bulgakov dealt with during the entire ten or eleven years he worked on *The Master and Margarita*, now considered one of the greatest Russian novels of the twentieth century. He'd already had serious problems with The Man in the 1920s, when his plays and stories were decried by the press and officially banned. After pleading directly to Stalin, Bulgakov was allowed to have a job in the arts, as a director at the Moscow Art Theater, producing other people's works. During this time, the 1930s, probably the darkest decade in the Soviet Union's history, he secretly penned a dark comedy with occult overtones, a political satire skewering the Soviet elite (especially the writers and critics who toed the party line), a counterattack on atheism, and a fine love story. All in one novel.

Satan himself pays a visit to the USSR, disguised as the urbane professor Woland, bringing his diabolic retinue with him to ridicule the Soviet literati and wreak havoc across Moscow. Then there's the writer known only as "the master," who has written a novel about Jesus's trial from Pontius Pilate's point of view. No one will publish it, causing him to break down and enter a mental hospital. Meanwhile, his devoted mistress, Margarita, is hanging out with Satan and his crew—which includes a huge, anthropomorphic black cat and the angel of death—eventually becoming a witch and serving as the nude hostess of Woland's ball.

Bulgakov died in 1940, and *The Master and Margarita* would not be published for another twenty-six years. The fact that it was published in the mid-1960s, under Soviet rule, albeit in slightly censored form, remains a marvel; no one can explain how the publication was allowed to happen. It appeared in two installments in a Russian literary magazine and was an instant phenomenon. "The 150,000 copies sold out within hours," writes Richard Pevear, one of the novel's translators into English. "In the weeks that followed, group readings were held, people meeting would quote and compare favorite passages; there was talk of little else. Certain sentences from the novel became proverbial. The very language of the novel was a contradiction of everything wooden, official, imposed. It was a joy to speak." The full version was somehow published in 1973, still during Soviet rule.

Now a professor at the Royal College of Art in London, Polish artist Andrzej Klimowski has won many awards for his work over the last four-plus decades, which includes posters for film, theater, and opera, books covers, animation, and newspaper illustration for the *Guardian*. Danusia Schejbal creates art in such diverse media as paintings, movie posters, and theater props and costumes. They teamed up for a dark, full-length take on *Strange Case of Dr. Jekyll and Mr. Hyde* (excerpted in Volume 2 of *The Graphic Canon*). For *The Master and Margarita*, they divvied up the duties, with Klimowski rendering the main action in black and white, and Schejbal adapting the fantastical sequences and the Jesus/Pilate narrative in color gouache paints.

SOURCES

Bulgakov, Mikhail. *The Master and Margarita*. Translated by Richard Pevear and Larissa Volokhonsky. New York: Penguin Books, 2007.

Bulgakov, Mikhail. *The Master and Margarita*. Translated by Mirra Ginsburg. New York: Grove Press, 1967.

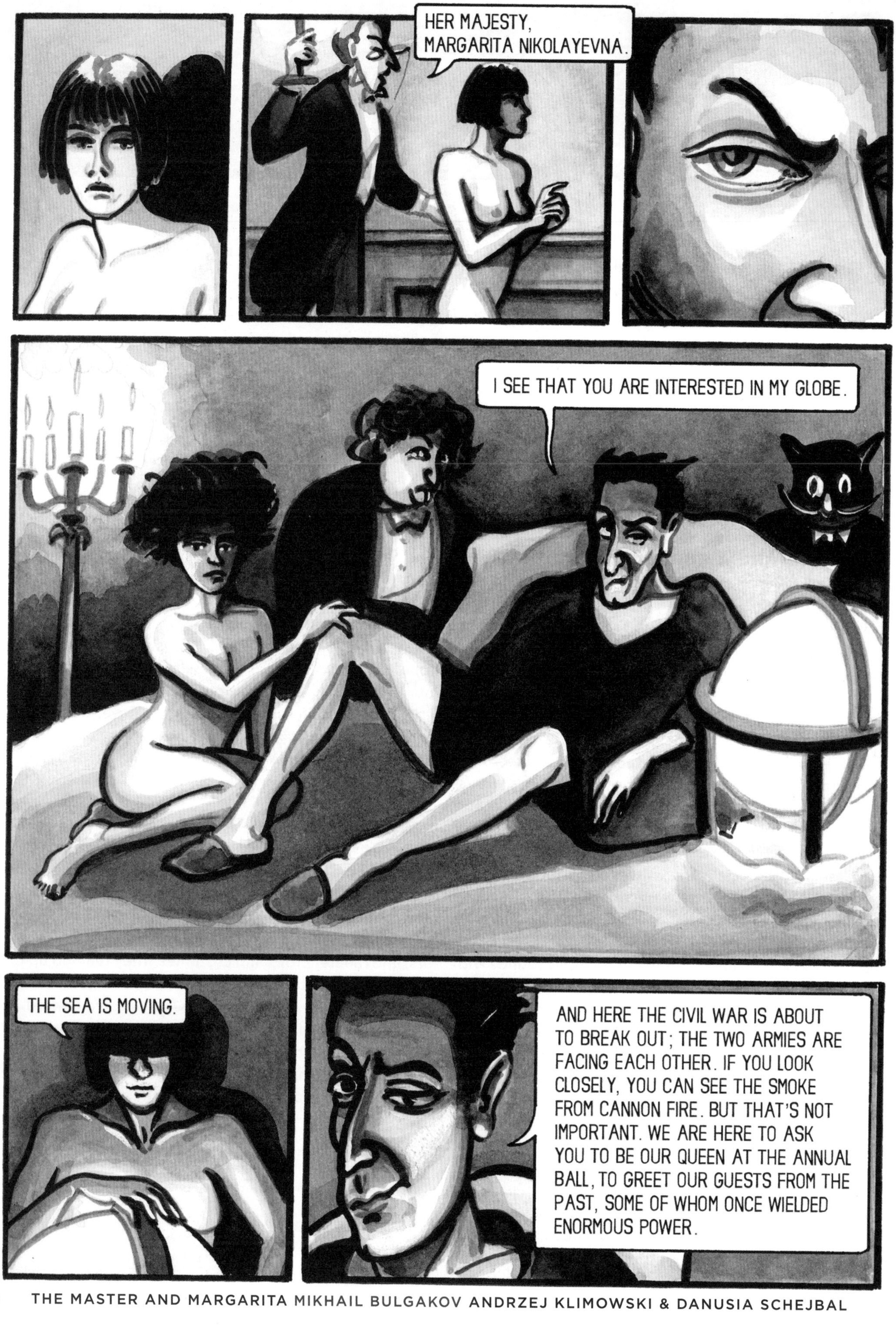
HER MAJESTY, MARGARITA NIKOLAYEVNA.
I SEE THAT YOU ARE INTERESTED IN MY GLOBE.
THE SEA IS MOVING.
AND HERE THE CIVIL WAR IS ABOUT TO BREAK OUT; THE TWO ARMIES ARE FACING EACH OTHER. IF YOU LOOK CLOSELY, YOU CAN SEE THE SMOKE FROM CANNON FIRE. BUT THAT'S NOT IMPORTANT. WE ARE HERE TO ASK YOU TO BE OUR QUEEN AT THE ANNUAL BALL, TO GREET OUR GUESTS FROM THE PAST, SOME OF WHOM ONCE WIELDED ENORMOUS POWER.

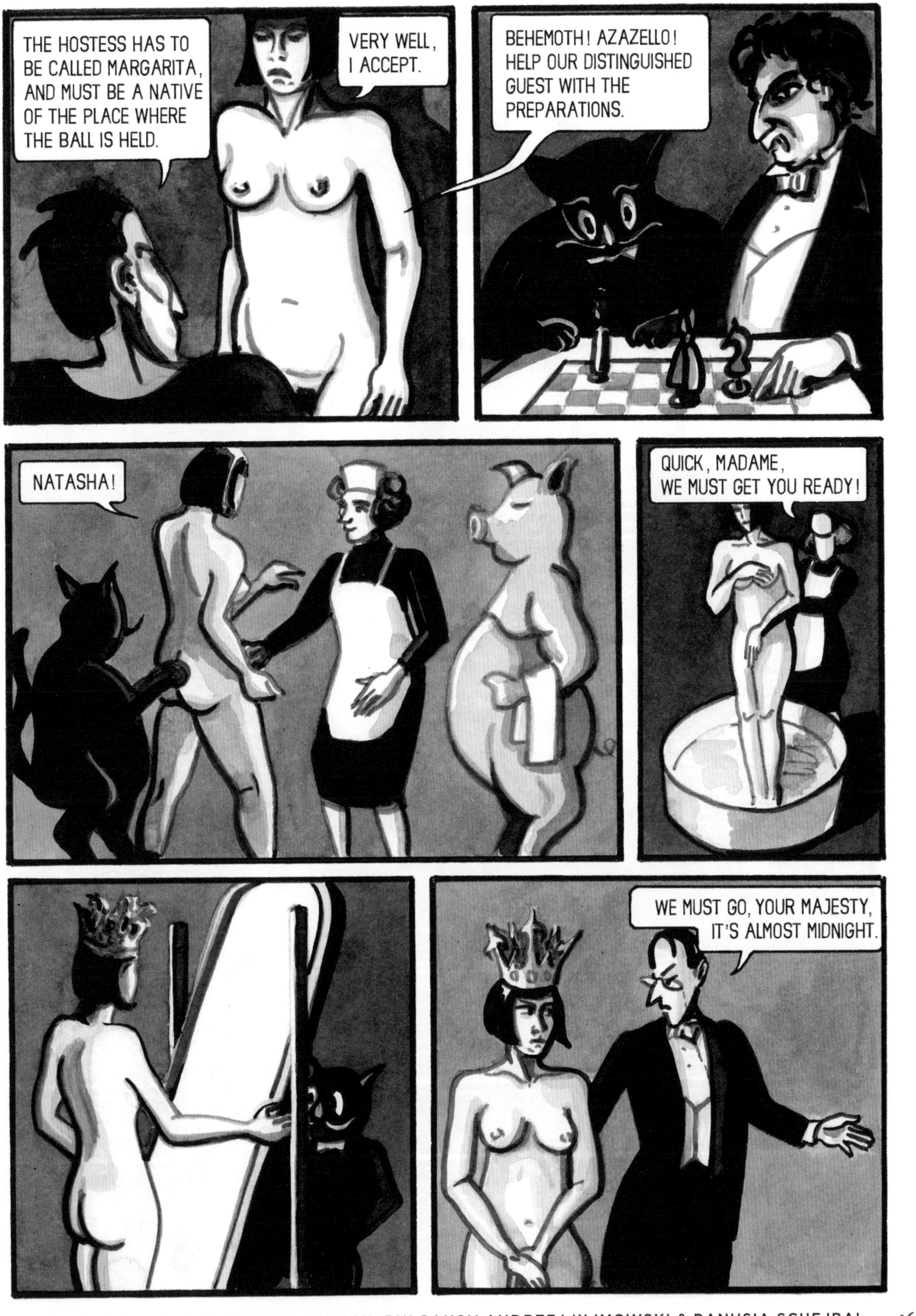
THE HOSTESS HAS TO BE CALLED MARGARITA, AND MUST BE A NATIVE OF THE PLACE WHERE THE BALL IS HELD.
VERY WELL, I ACCEPT.
BEHEMOTH! AZAZELLO! HELP OUR DISTINGUISHED GUEST WITH THE PREPARATIONS.
NATASHA!
QUICK, MADAME, WE MUST GET YOU READY!
WE MUST GO, YOUR MAJESTY, IT'S ALMOST MIDNIGHT.

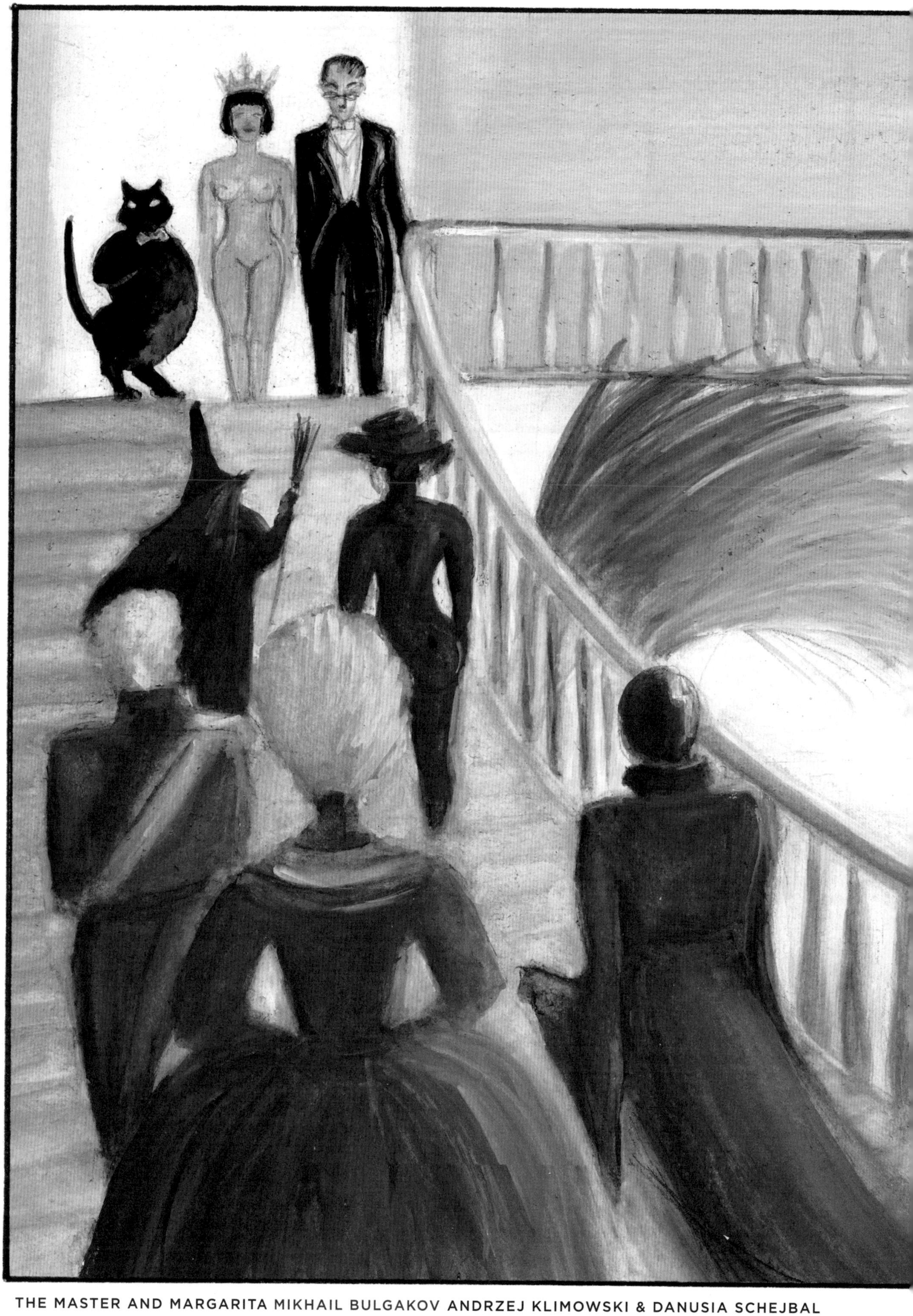

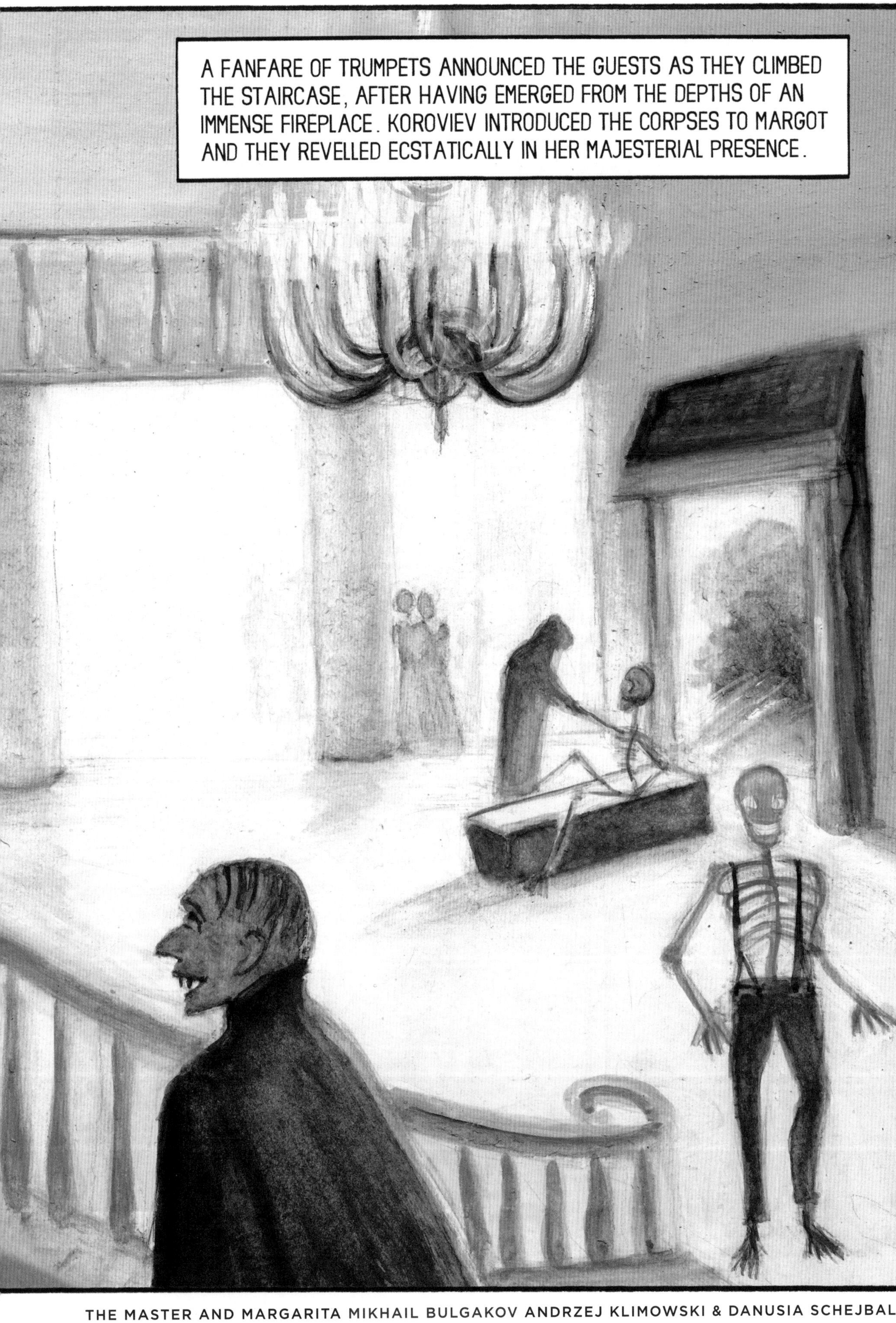
A FANFARE OF TRUMPETS ANNOUNCED THE GUESTS AS THEY CLIMBED THE STAIRCASE, AFTER HAVING EMERGED FROM THE DEPTHS OF AN IMMENSE FIREPLACE. KOROVIEV INTRODUCED THE CORPSES TO MARGOT AND THEY REVELLED ECSTATICALLY IN HER MAJESTERIAL PRESENCE.

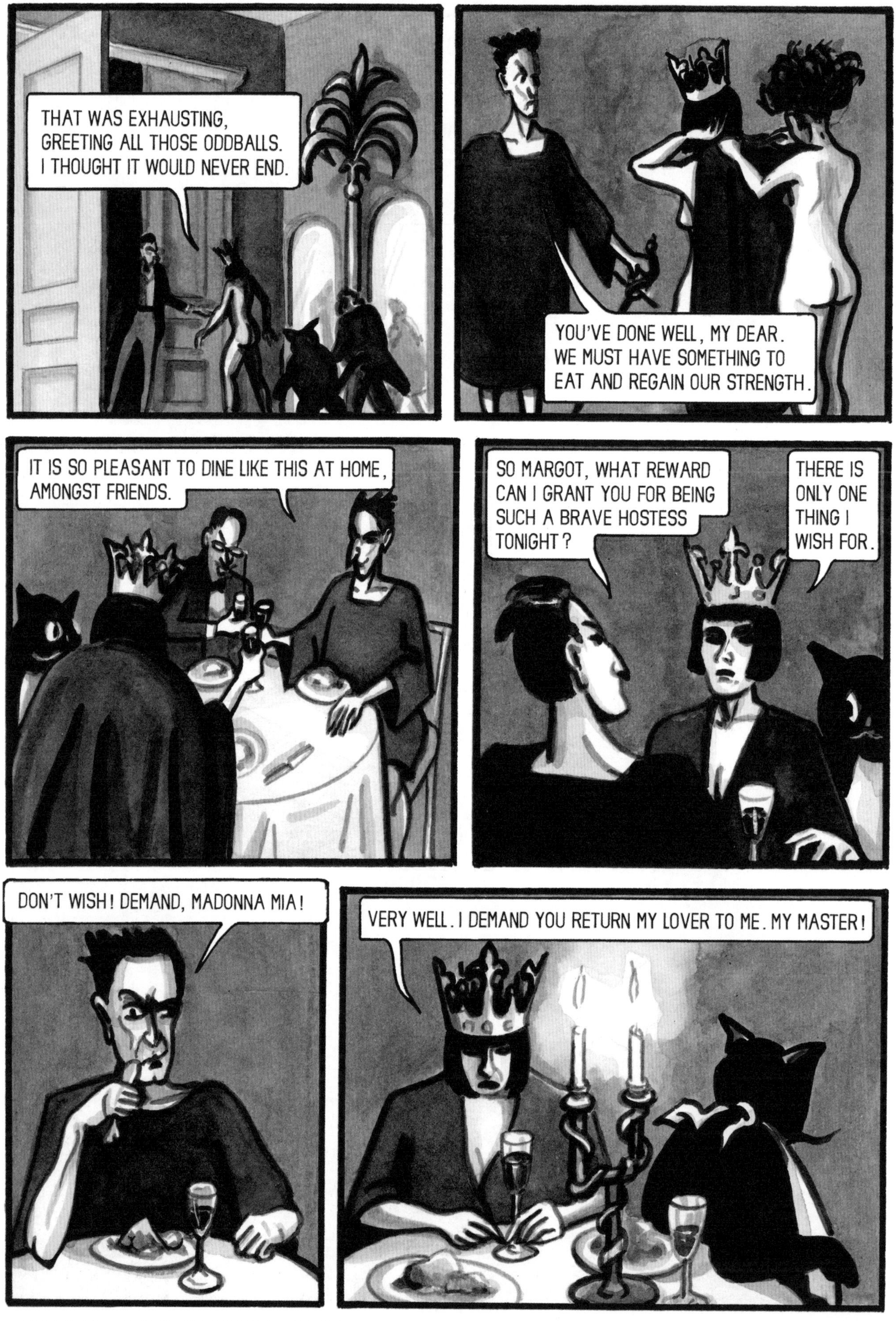
THAT WAS EXHAUSTING, GREETING ALL THOSE ODDBALLS. I THOUGHT IT WOULD NEVER END.
YOU'VE DONE WELL, MY DEAR. WE MUST HAVE SOMETHING TO EAT AND REGAIN OUR STRENGTH.
IT IS SO PLEASANT TO DINE LIKE THIS AT HOME, AMONGST FRIENDS.
SO MARGOT, WHAT REWARD CAN I GRANT YOU FOR BEING SUCH A BRAVE HOSTESS TONIGHT?
THERE IS ONLY ONE THING I WISH FOR.
DON'T WISH! DEMAND, MADONNA MIA!
VERY WELL. I DEMAND YOU RETURN MY LOVER TO ME. MY MASTER!

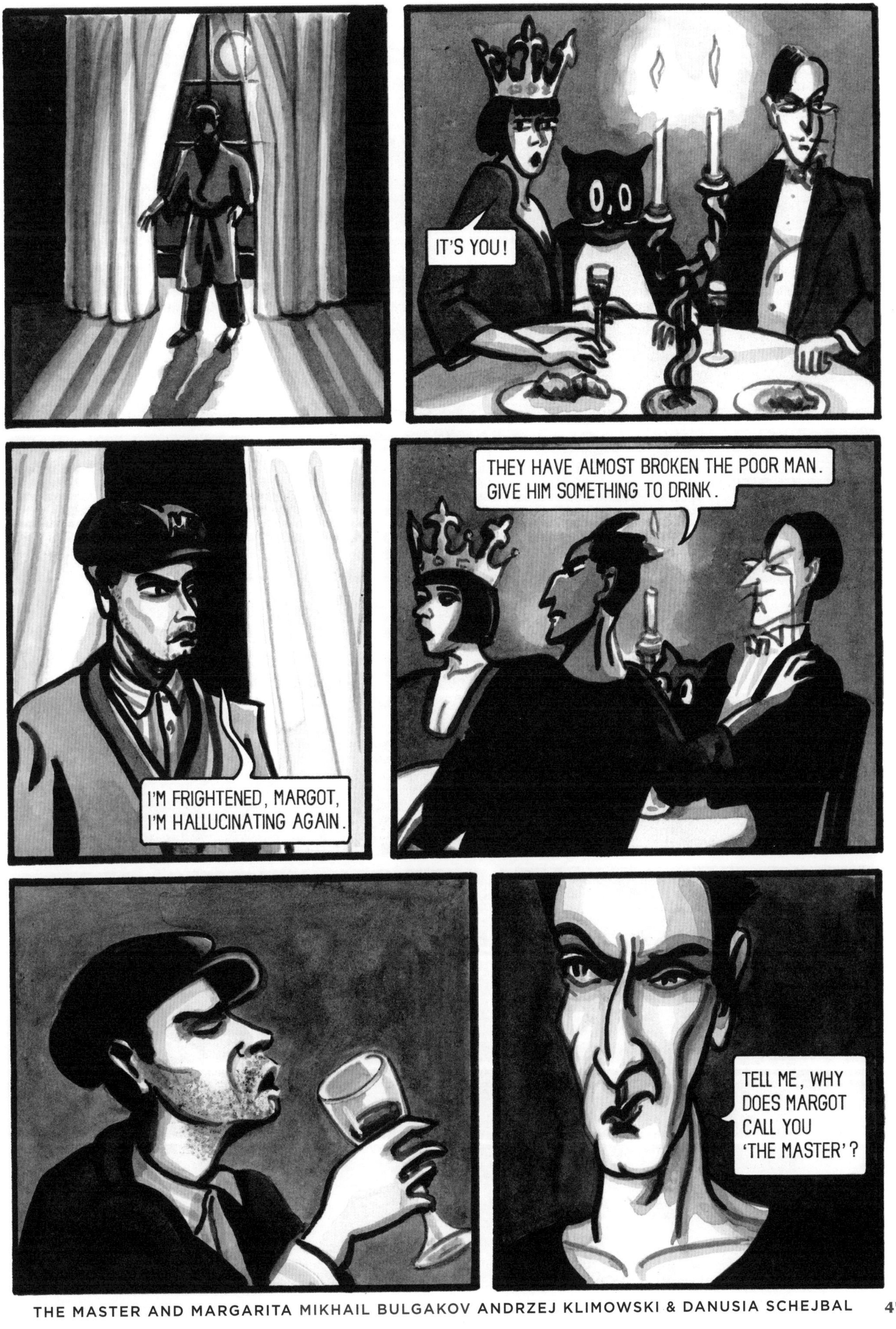
IT'S YOU!
I'M FRIGHTENED, MARGOT,
I'M HALLUCINATING AGAIN.
THEY HAVE ALMOST BROKEN THE POOR MAN.
GIVE HIM SOMETHING TO DRINK.
TELL ME, WHY
DOES MARGOT
CALL YOU
'THE MASTER'?

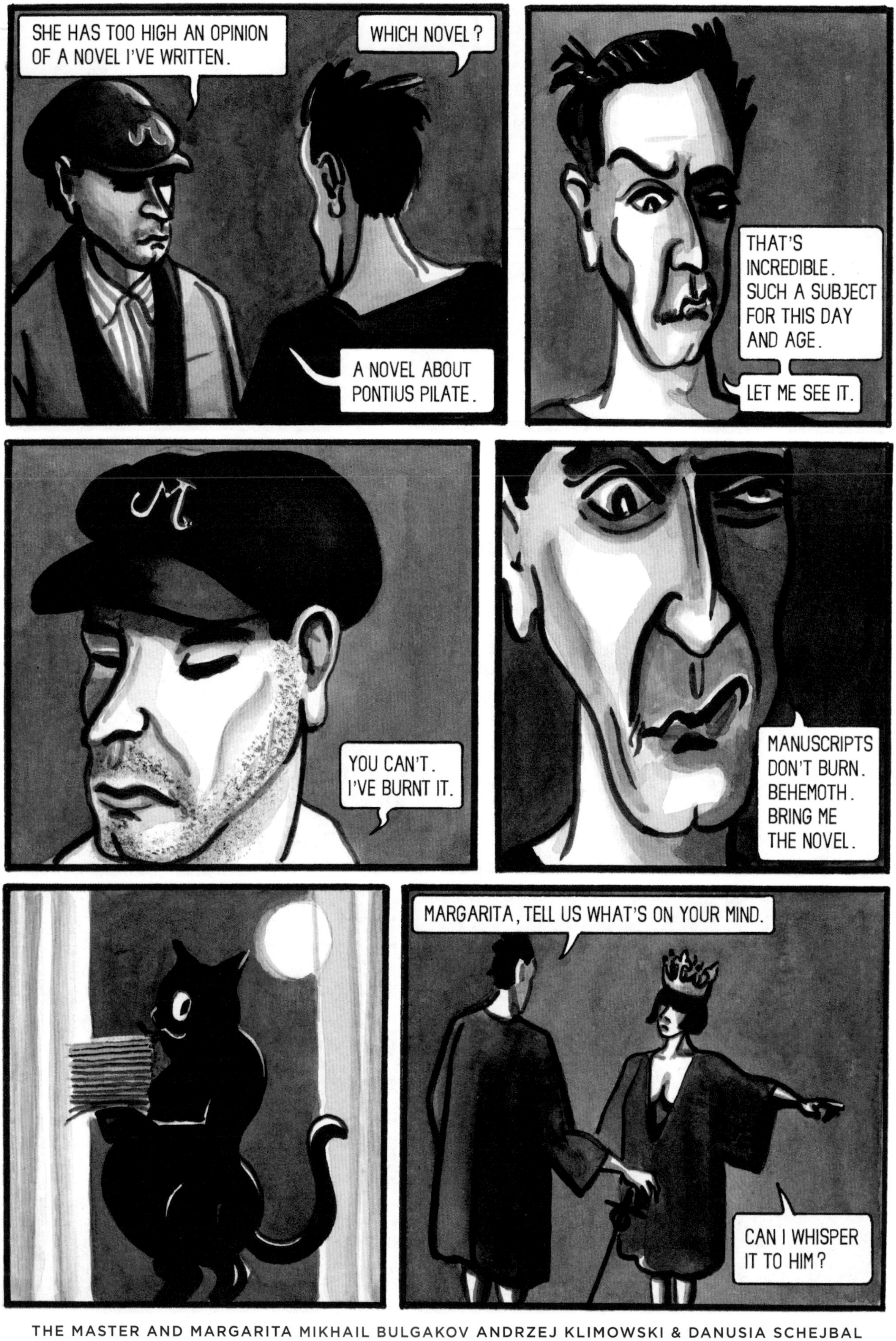
SHE HAS TOO HIGH AN OPINION OF A NOVEL I'VE WRITTEN.
WHICH NOVEL?
A NOVEL ABOUT PONTIUS PILATE.
THAT'S INCREDIBLE. SUCH A SUBJECT FOR THIS DAY AND AGE.
LET ME SEE IT.
YOU CAN'T. I'VE BURNT IT.
MANUSCRIPTS DON'T BURN. BEHEMOTH. BRING ME THE NOVEL.
MARGARITA, TELL US WHAT'S ON YOUR MIND.
CAN I WHISPER IT TO HIM?

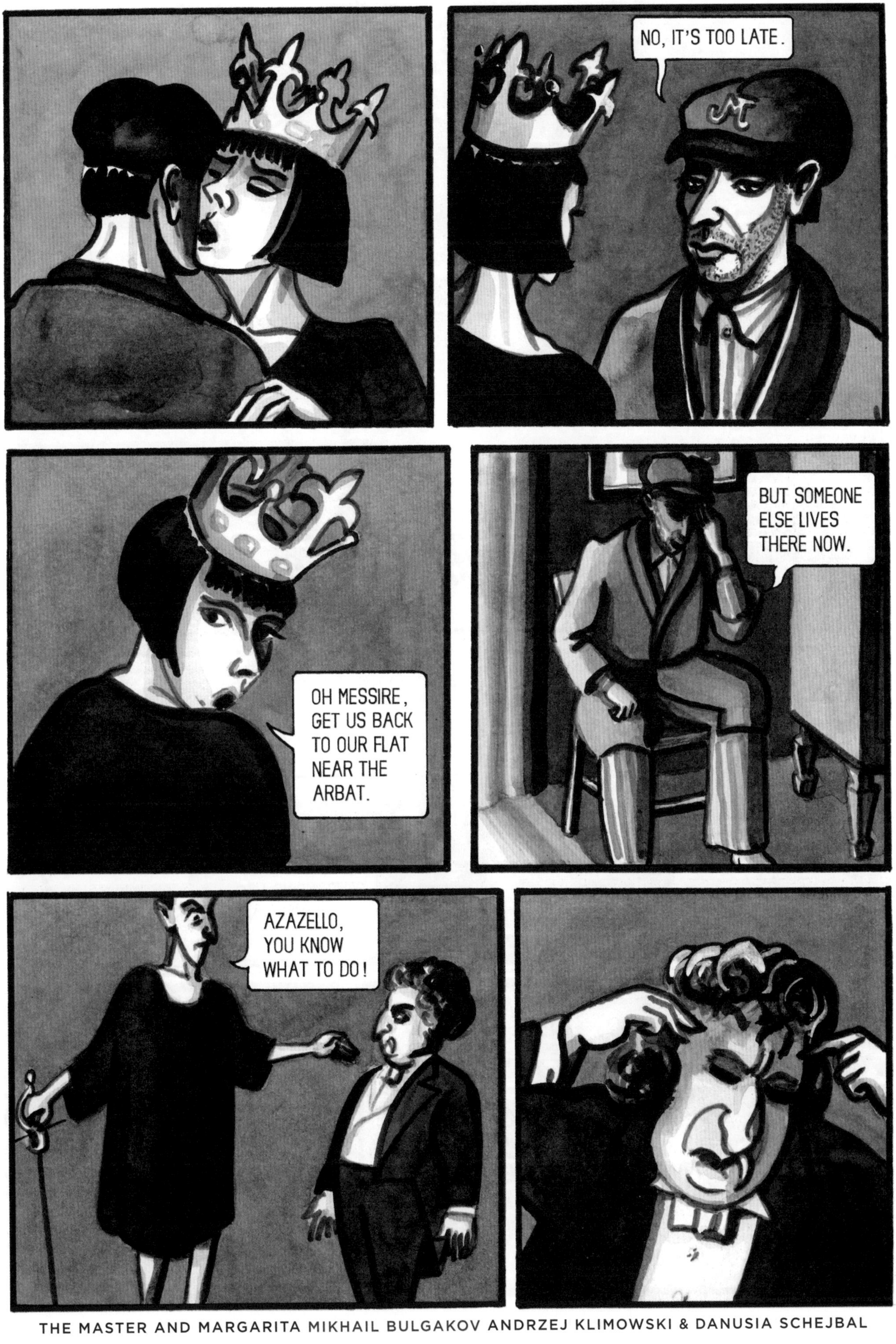
NO, IT'S TOO LATE.
OH MESSIRE, GET US BACK TO OUR FLAT NEAR THE ARBAT.
BUT SOMEONE ELSE LIVES THERE NOW.
AZAZELLO, YOU KNOW WHAT TO DO!

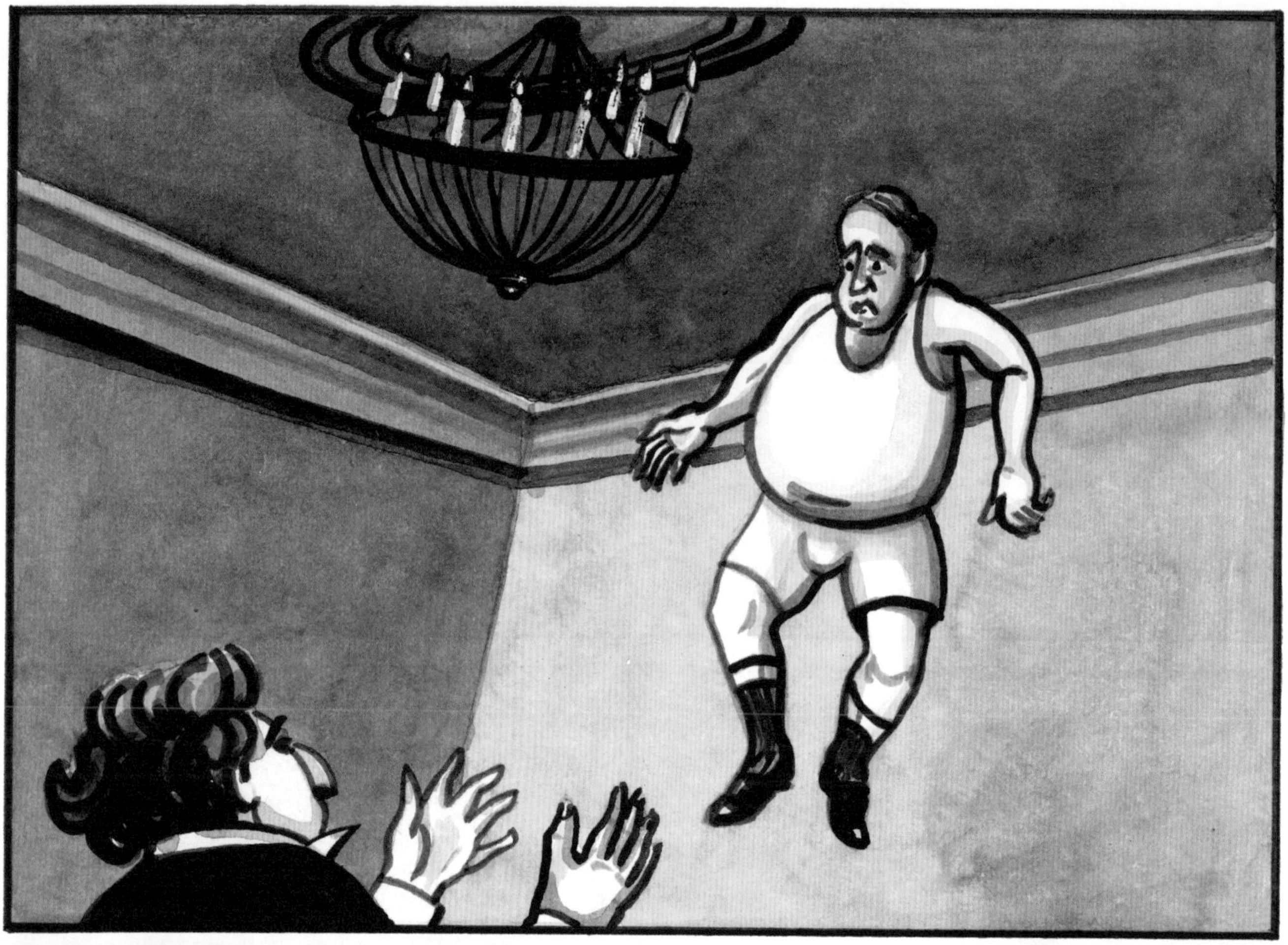

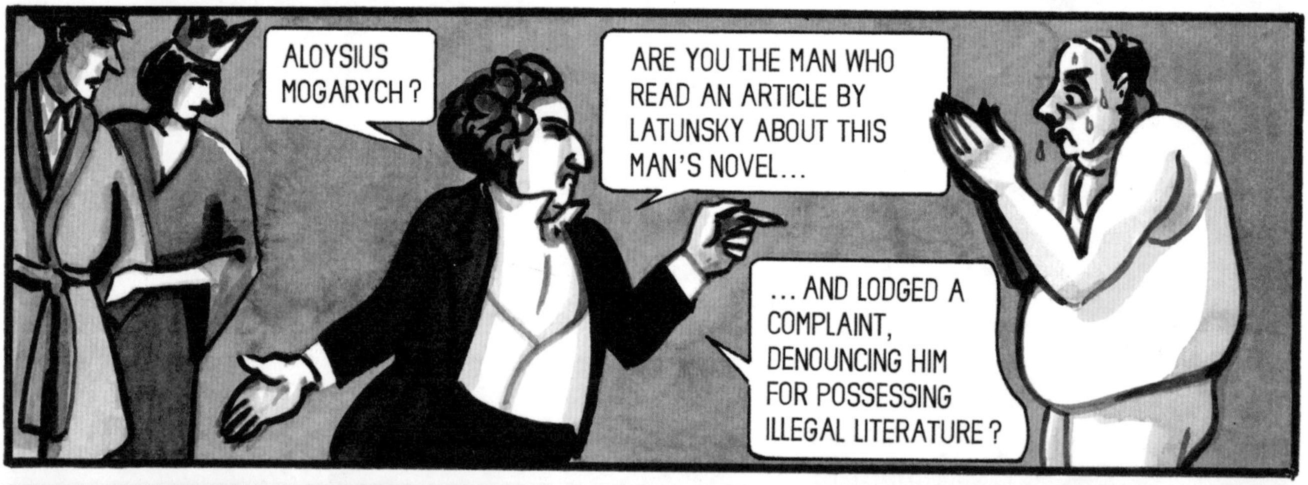
ALOYSIUS MOGARYCH?
ARE YOU THE MAN WHO READ AN ARTICLE BY LATUNSKY ABOUT THIS MAN'S NOVEL...
...AND LODGED A COMPLAINT, DENOUNCING HIM FOR POSSESSING ILLEGAL LITERATURE?

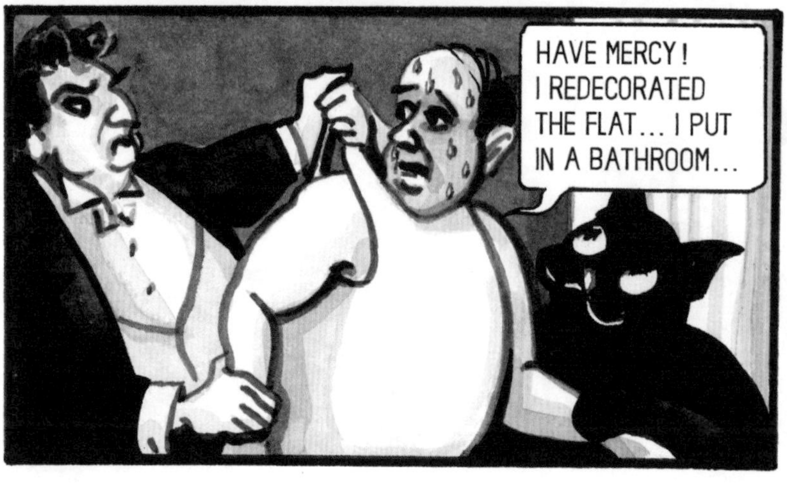
HAVE MERCY! I REDECORATED THE FLAT... I PUT IN A BATHROOM...

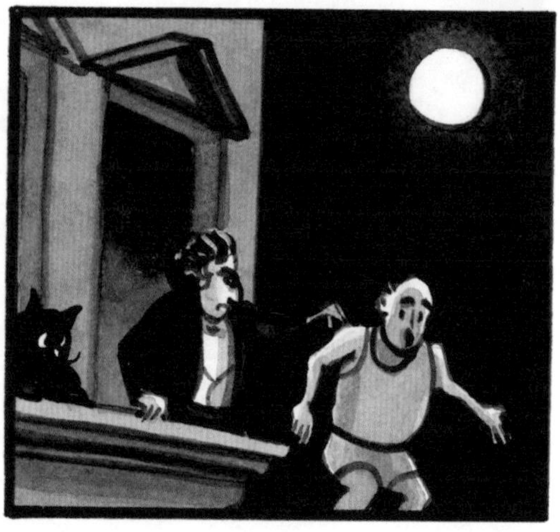

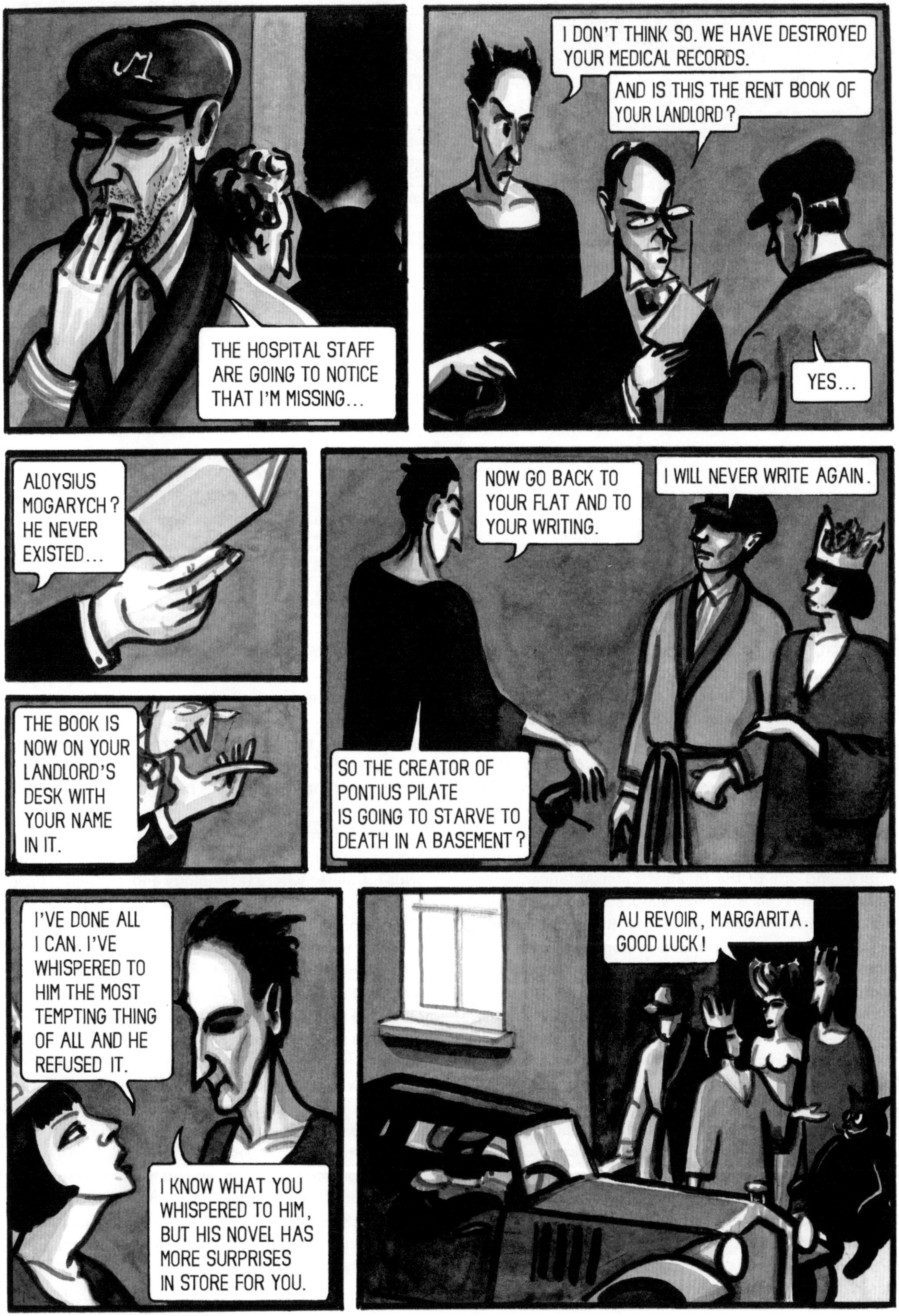
THE HOSPITAL STAFF ARE GOING TO NOTICE THAT I'M MISSING...
I DON'T THINK SO. WE HAVE DESTROYED YOUR MEDICAL RECORDS.
AND IS THIS THE RENT BOOK OF YOUR LANDLORD?
YES...
ALOYSIUS MOGARYCH? HE NEVER EXISTED...
THE BOOK IS NOW ON YOUR LANDLORD'S DESK WITH YOUR NAME IN IT.
NOW GO BACK TO YOUR FLAT AND TO YOUR WRITING.
I WILL NEVER WRITE AGAIN.
SO THE CREATOR OF PONTIUS PILATE IS GOING TO STARVE TO DEATH IN A BASEMENT?
I'VE DONE ALL I CAN. I'VE WHISPERED TO HIM THE MOST TEMPTING THING OF ALL AND HE REFUSED IT.
I KNOW WHAT YOU WHISPERED TO HIM, BUT HIS NOVEL HAS MORE SURPRISES IN STORE FOR YOU.
AU REVOIR, MARGARITA. GOOD LUCK!

One Hundred Years of Solitude

Gabriel García Márquez

ILLUSTRATIONS BY **Yien Yip**

ONCE YOU GET TO THE 1960S, IT BECOMES MUCH more difficult to figure out what's canonical. Classic literature stands the test of time, but not a whole lot of time has gone by, so how do we know which writings from the last fifty years are for the ages? Based on the usual measures such as acclaim, popularity, influence, academic attention, and *je ne sais quoi, One Hundred Years of Solitude* is one of relatively few post-1960 books to have a lock on classic status.

Nobel-winner Gabriel García Márquez is considered one of the greatest writers of the second half of the twentieth century—and one of the greatest Latin American writers of all time—and this is his sprawling, surging masterpiece. It tells the interrelated story of the Buendía family and the fictional town they found and populate, Macondo, a metaphor for Gabo's home country of Colombia (and, to a larger extent, South America in general).

We're there for the founding of Macondo, and we're there for its decline and destruction, and along the way we follow the adventures, trials, tragedies, loves, and deaths of six generations of Buendías, many of whom have the same names. There's not much characterization in the typical sense, not a whole lot of dialog. Just action, action, action. If you're going to get through a century of complex familial and geographical history in 430 pages, you need to adopt a new kind of writing. Lots of compression, just keep chugging along as lives get lived to the fullest. Oh, and then there's the dirt-eating, the incest, the ghosts, the civil war, self-mutilation, gypsies, capitalist exploitation, contagious insomnia and amnesia, bodily ascension. . . .

One Hundred Years is one of the key works of magical realism, a literary form in which fantastical, supernatural, deeply weird, and seemingly impossible things happen every day, right alongside "normal" events. None of the characters think there's anything strange about this, and the book's narration makes no distinction between the magical and the mundane. (Perhaps it's telling that magical realism flourishes in the literatures of less industrialized regions like Latin America and Africa, where folklore, "superstition," and various religions hold heavy sway, where the veil between worlds is thinner, where technology and capitalism haven't yet squashed the inexplicable undercurrents of life.)

Illustrator and textile artist Yien Yip has contributed to each volume of *The Graphic Canon*, and here she gives us stunning, swirling illustrations of two scenes from the novel. The first illustration captures one of the novel's most memorable moments. Remedios the Beauty—a member of the family's fourth generation—is literally the most beautiful woman in the world. Her mere presence is unbearable to men, driving them to the brink of madness and even to death, yet she cares nothing for love or sex, being a simple, childlike being who wears a sack-dress when she can be convinced to wear clothes at all. One day, while hanging laundry, she ascends to heaven and is never seen again.

The last illustration is the final scene of the book, one of churning destruction, as the second Buendías named Aureliano is finally able to translate the prophetic manuscript of the gypsy Melquíades.

The Ascension of Remedios the Beauty

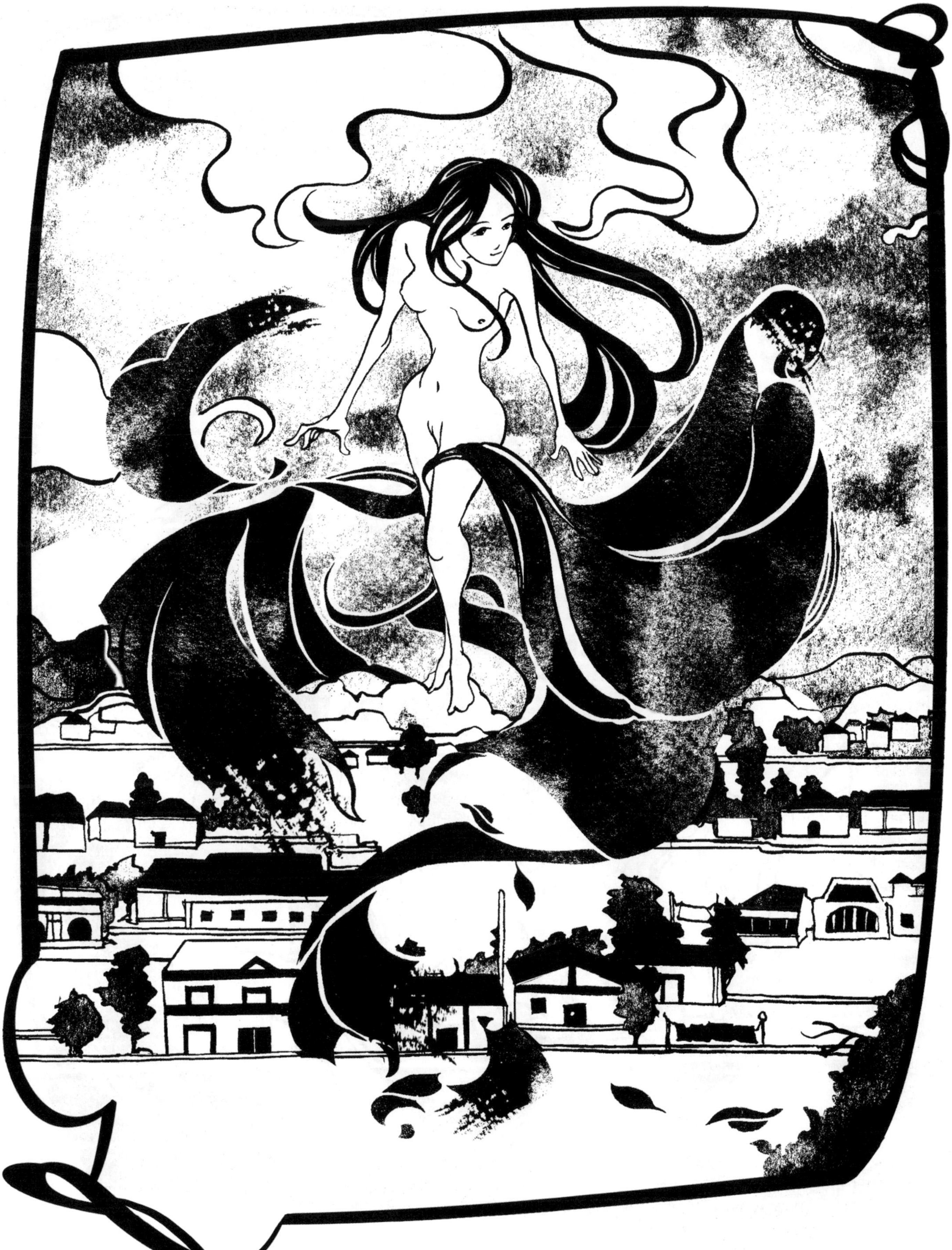

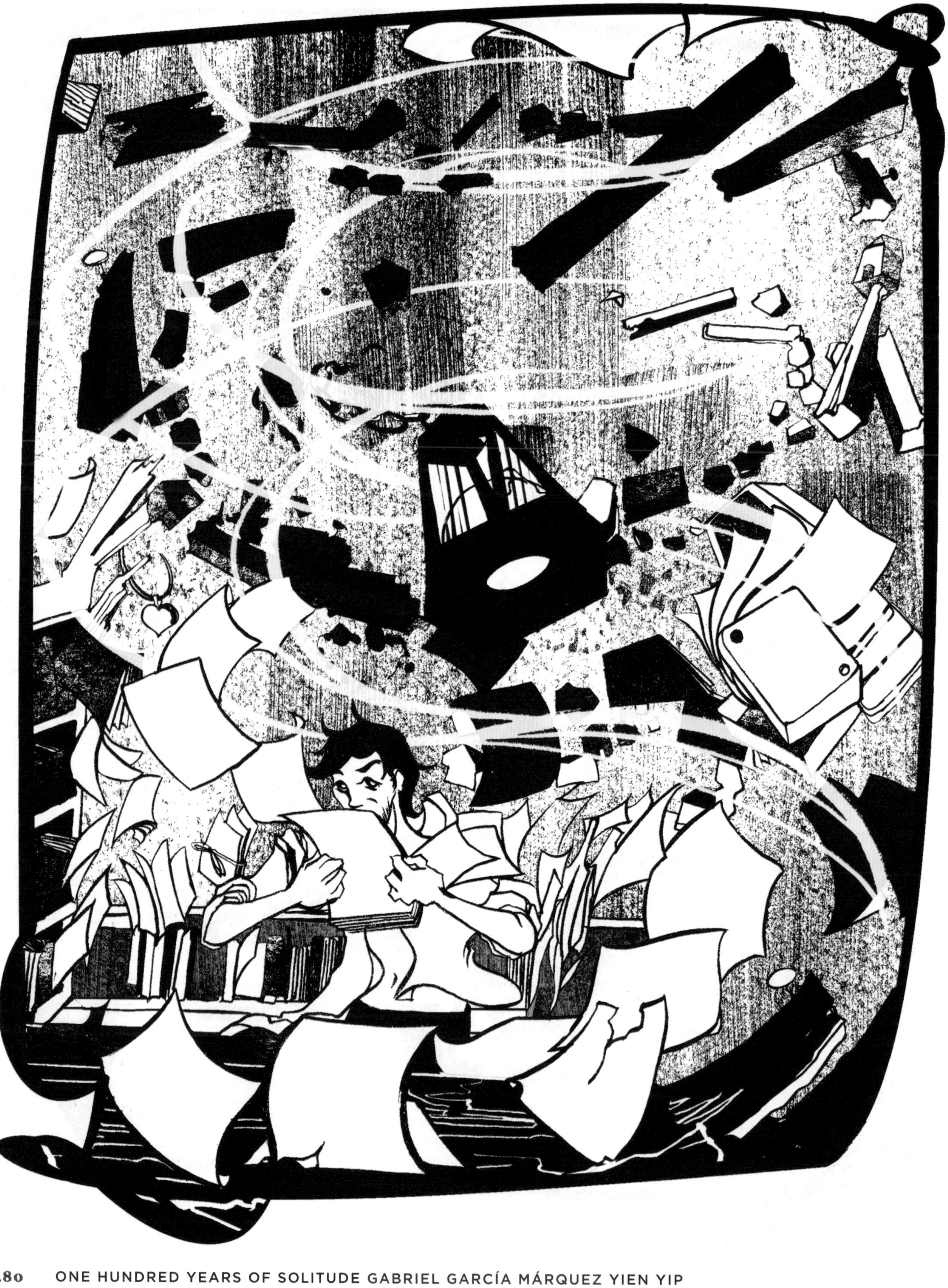

In Watermelon Sugar

Richard Brautigan

ILLUSTRATION BY **Juliacks**

RICHARD BRAUTIGAN'S POETRY AND PROSE ALIGN to some degree with the Beats and with the counterculture, but he really was of neither camp, though the latter often claims him. He's pretty much impossible to classify, wholly an individual who did his own thing, though, due to his sarcastic humor and his likeability, he has been compared to Mark Twain more than once. He had his biggest mainstream success with his second published novel, *Trout Fishing in America*, which the *Times Literary Supplement* called "a slender classic." All of his major works remain in print, and his readers remain fiercely loyal.

His third fiction book, the 1968 novella *In Watermelon Sugar*, is composed of single-page chapters, forming a surreal, fairy-tale–like, patchwork narrative. It centers around a utopian commune of gentle souls—iDEATH (that is, "I death," the death of the ego)—that forms after some kind of apocalypse. The inhabitants have learned to live in com-plete harmony with each other and with nature through a Buddhist-like practice of nonattachment. Most things in iDEATH are in fact made from watermelon sugar, and their fuel is oil from trout raised at the commune. Trouble comes when two characters are fixated on the past, clinging to the desire to have things go back to the way they used to be, on personal and societal levels. But it doesn't end the way you probably think it will.

The multitalented Juliacks has created this stunning, complex silkscreened spread based on Brautigan's hopeful tale. She explains:

> The image was made as a six-layer serigraphy print. I was inspired by how in the book, the sun shines a different color everyday—and that determines the color of the water-melons—the stuff of their lives. Each layer shows details from the book.

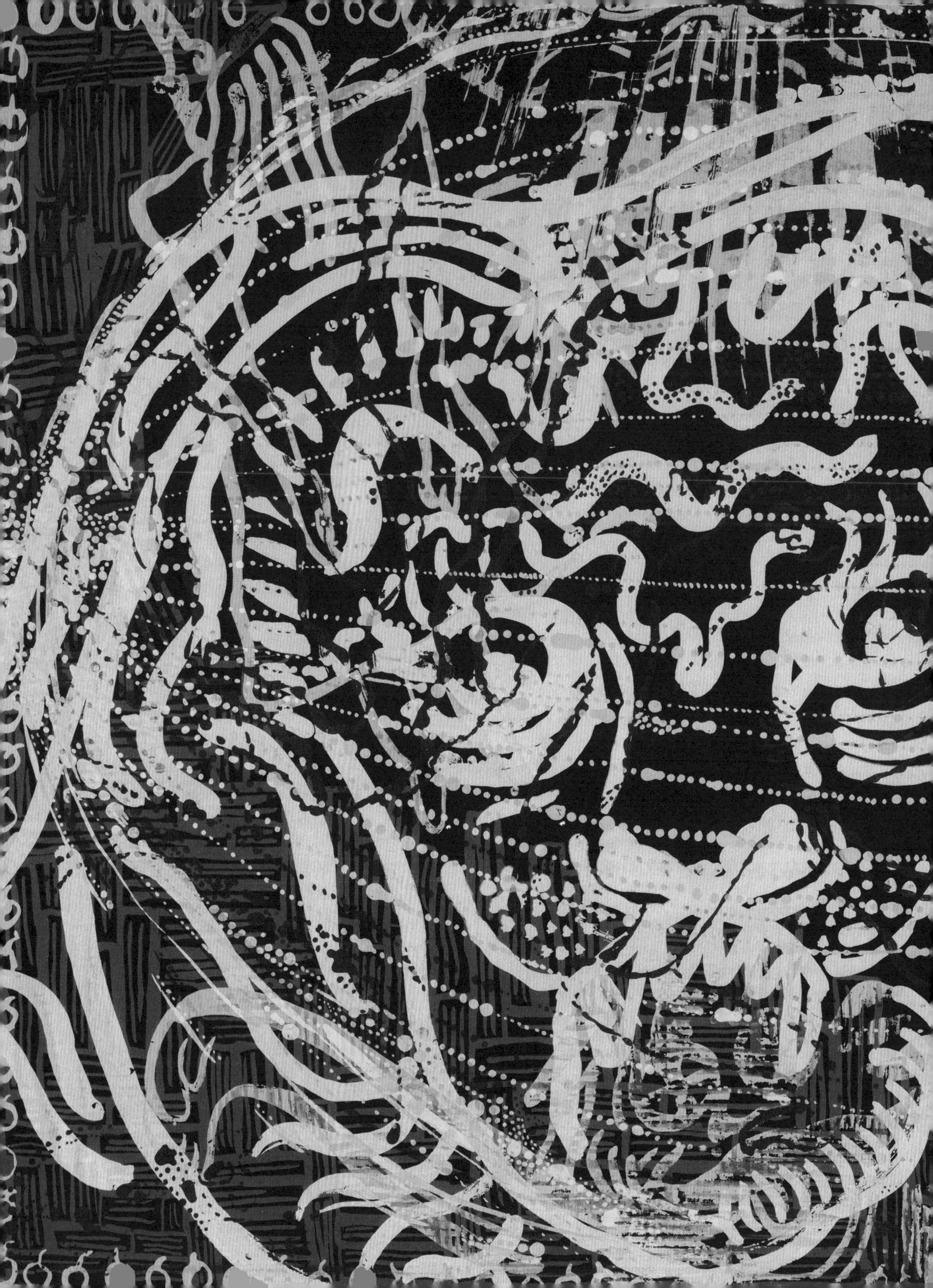

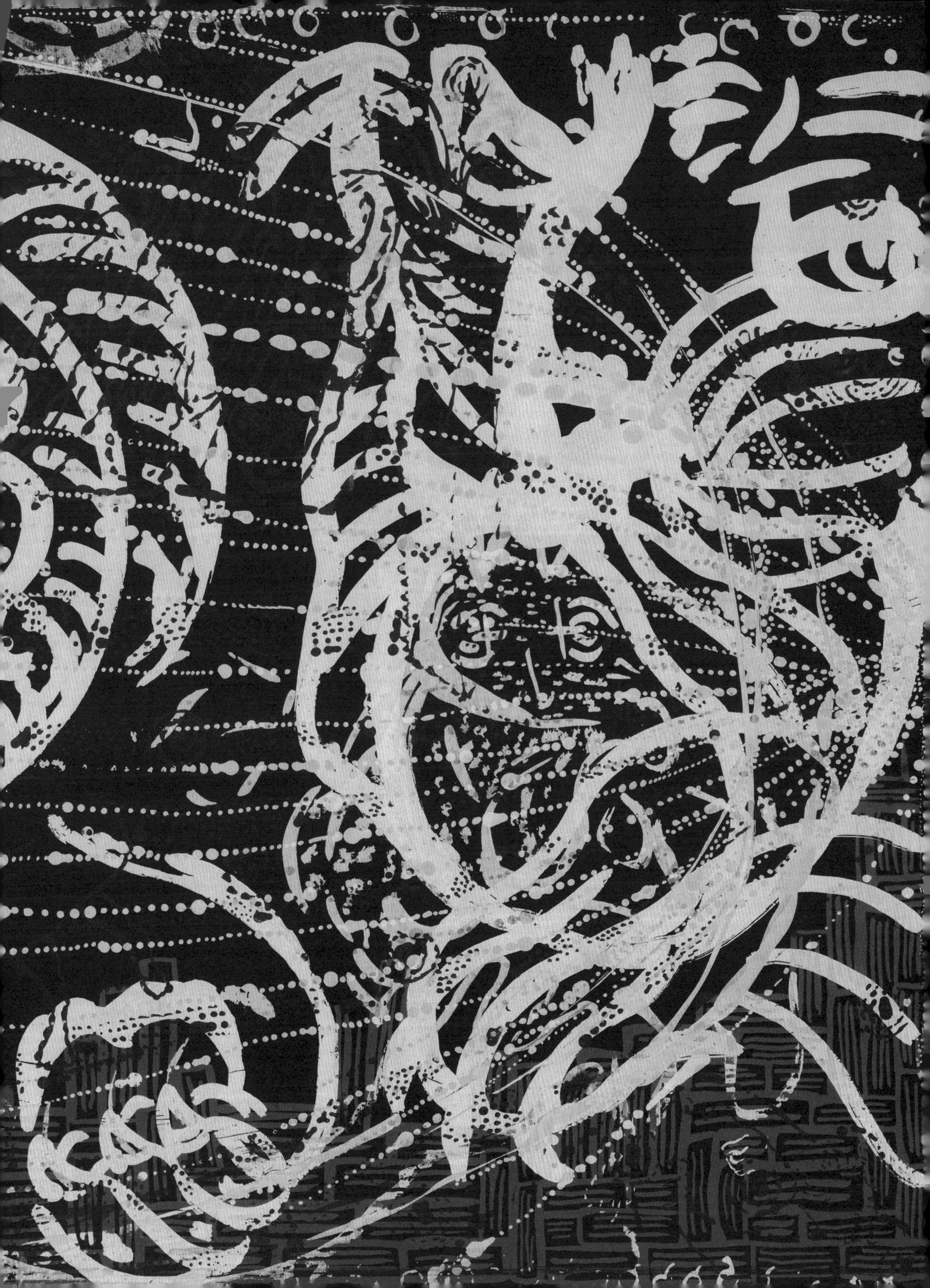

Thomas Pynchon

ILLUSTRATIONS BY **Zak Smith**

SO HOW DO YOU SUM UP *GRAVITY'S RAINBOW*, the intensely, purposefully convoluted novel universally regarded as a masterpiece of postwar literature, even if there's no way to understand it without a guide? I can tell you that the book more or less centers on Germany's V-2 rocket—the arc it makes from launch to target-strike gives the novel its title. To some degree, it turns out, the history of the twentieth century is the history of the development of rocket weaponry. But this, more or less, is simply the peg on which Pynchon hangs his elaborate, experimental, inconceivably intricate novel. Within its 760 pages, you'll find around 400 characters, numerous subplots coming seemingly out of nowhere, digressions and flashbacks that go on for pages, some of the most extreme, explicit sex scenes in all of literature, highly technical information, history lessons, pop culture references, and, um, a fight scene with an octopus. Paranoia, conspiracies, and the modern world's death drive are major themes. Rilke's poetry, the occult, and Christian holy days provide unexpected anchor points throughout.

In its review of the novel in 1973, the *New York Times* said: "'*Gravity's Rainbow*' is bone-crushingly dense, compulsively elaborate, silly, obscene, funny, tragic, pastoral, historical, philosophical, poetic, grindingly dull, inspired, horrific, cold, bloated, beached and blasted." ("Surreal" and "absurdist" also belong on that list.) Of the plot, the *Times* said: "If all this seems hard to follow, rest assured there's plenty more to unravel: There are dozens of false leads and characters who start out big, drop by the wayside and pop up hundreds of pages later for brief appearances." Add to this the extremely detailed real-world information Pynchon weaves in:

> His expert knowledge encompasses: spiritualism, statistics, Pavlovian psychology, London in 1944, Berlin, Zürich and Potsdam in 1945, chemical engineering, the Baltic black market, plastics, rocket propulsion and ballistics, economic and military complexes, international industrial cartels (GE, ICI, Shell, Agfa, I.G. Farben), Tarot cards and the Kabbala, witchcraft, espionage, Rossini operas, pop songs and show tunes of the thirties and forties, limericks, cocaine and hashish fantasies, and the history of American clothing styles and slang.

In his guide to the book, former lit professor Larry Daw began:

> It is a Jeremiad, an encyclopaedia of cultural minutiae, an historical novel, a catalogue of operas, an anatomy of illicit perversions and mindless pleasures, a book in which you are

as likely to read an equation describing the gyroscopic stabilizers of a V-2 rocket as you are to find a Porky Pig cartoon. Coprophilia and rooftop Banana gardens exist in a singularly bizarre harmony, repelling and enticing in equal measure.

Gravity's Rainbow—and all of Pynchon's oeuvre, including his smaller masterpiece, *The Crying of Lot 49*—is made all the more intriguing by the author's extreme reclusiveness. No interviews. No photographs. No public appearances. When *Gravity's Rainbow* won the National Book Award, Pynchon's publisher, Viking, sent comedian Irwin Corey to accept the award and make a (hilarious) speech in his stead.

Called "a leading exponent of punk-based, DIY art" by his publisher, Zak Smith caused a sensation when he decided to create an image for each page of the novel. He explained:

> So I illustrated *Gravity's Rainbow*—nobody asked me to, but I did it anyway. Most of the pictures are drawings—ink on whatever paper was lying around, but there are also paintings (acrylic), photos I took, and experimental photographic processes. I tried to illustrate the passages as literally as possible—if the book says there was a green Spitfire, I drew a green Spitfire. Mostly, I tried to make a series of pictures as dense, intricate, and rich as the prose in the book. The entire project was shown in the Whitney Museum's 2004 Biennial exhibition of contemporary art and is now in the permanent collection of the Walker Art Center in Minneapolis.

In an interview, he explained why *Gravity's Rainbow* led to this epic and, at the time, unprecedented art project:

> Well if your reading list is mammoth literary classics and comic books, then sooner or later you'll find out about Pynchon. So I checked out the first page of *GR* and was amazed. Just the style was gorgeous—it was intricate but also just barely out of reach—you were never sure you'd read what you just thought you'd read. I think that's why it's so haunting and why ten years later I decided I needed to pin all those images down. . . . I feel like *Gravity's Rainbow* had all these fleeting images that really sort of called out for this kind of treatment.

The project was published in its entirety (without Pynchon's text) in the brick-like book *Pictures Showing What Happens on Each Page of Thomas Pynchon's Novel Gravity's Rainbow* (Tin House Books, 2006). On the following pages are 28 of the 760 images, selected by Zak. (The corresponding page number of the novel is written somewhere within each image.)

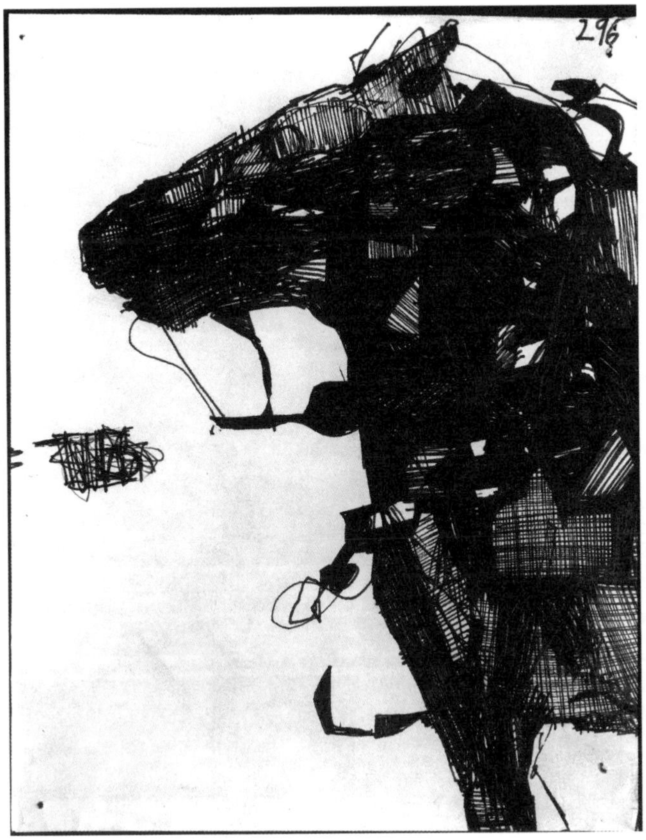
296

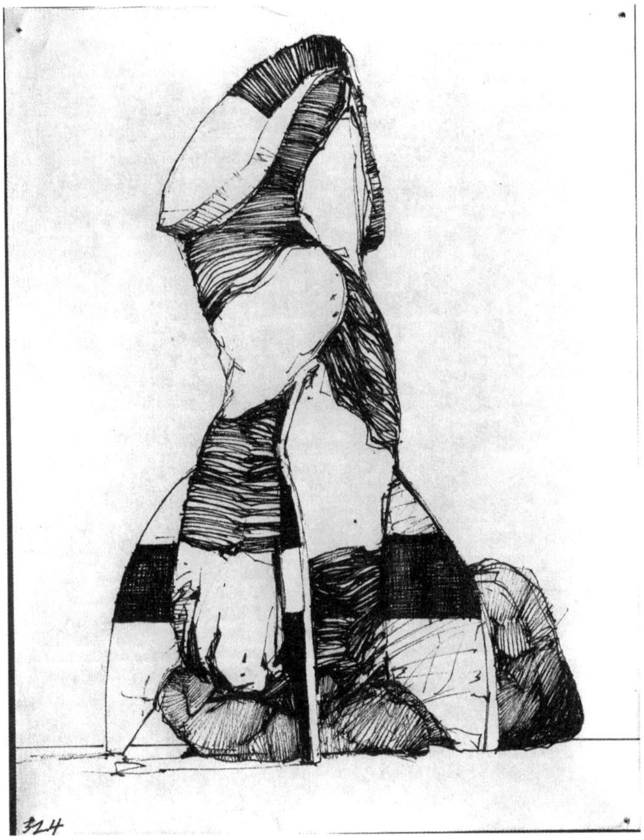
324

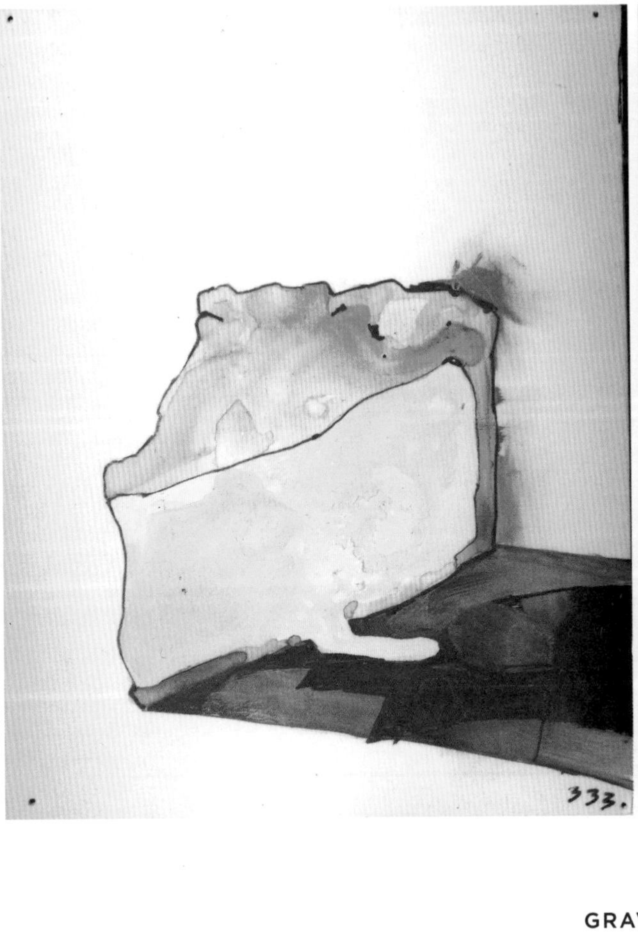
333.

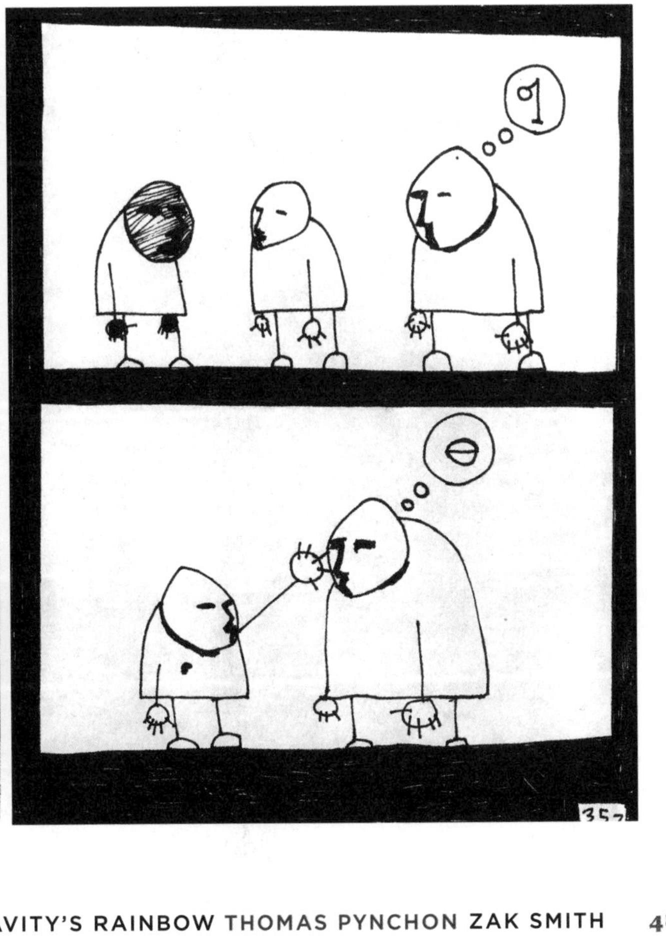

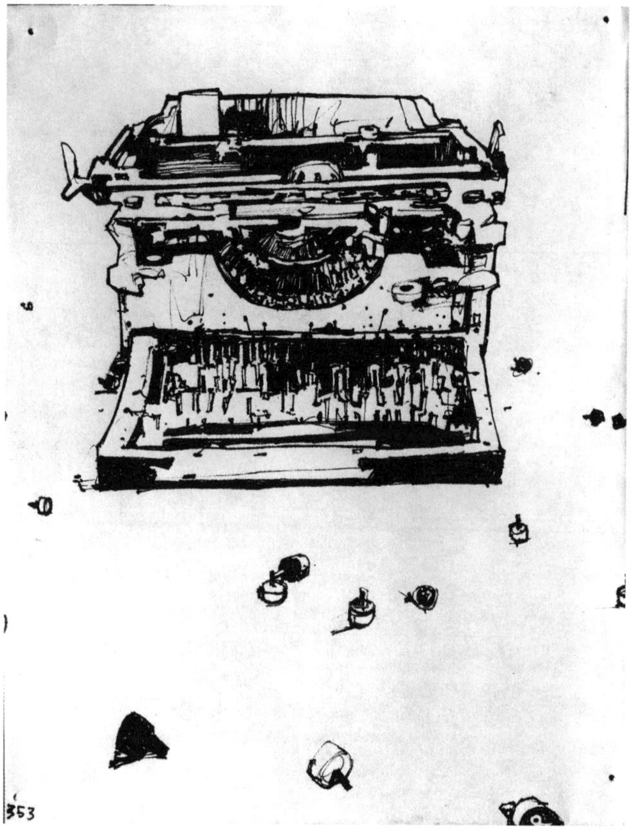
353

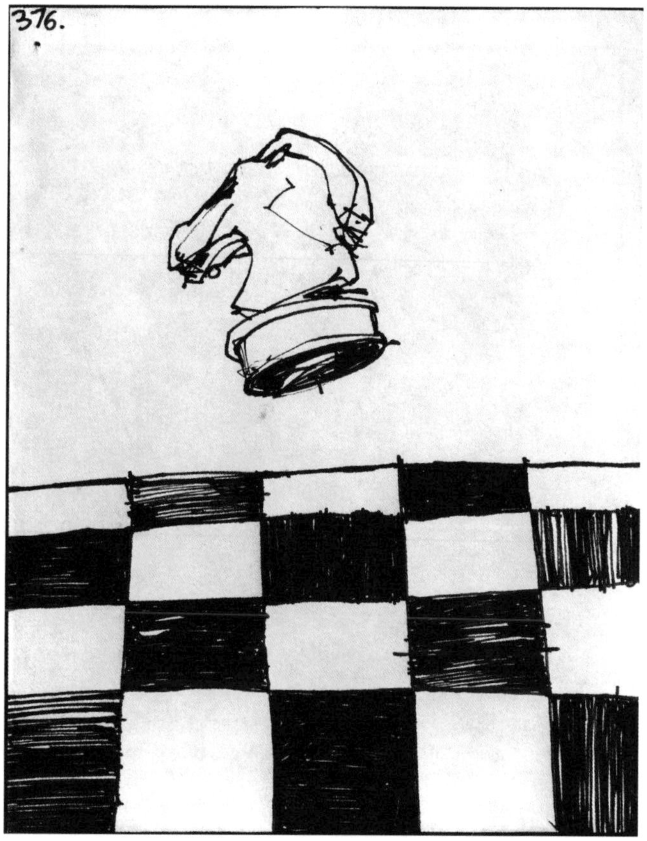
376.

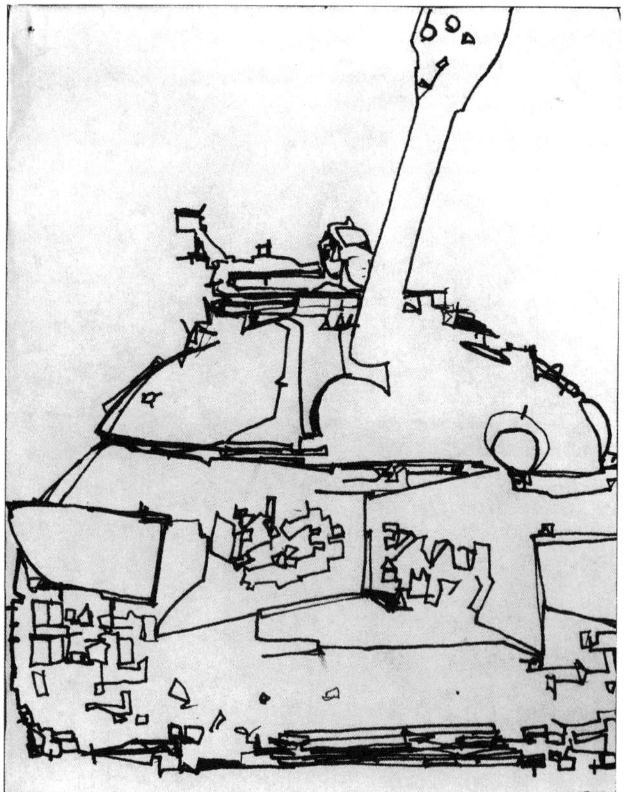
377.

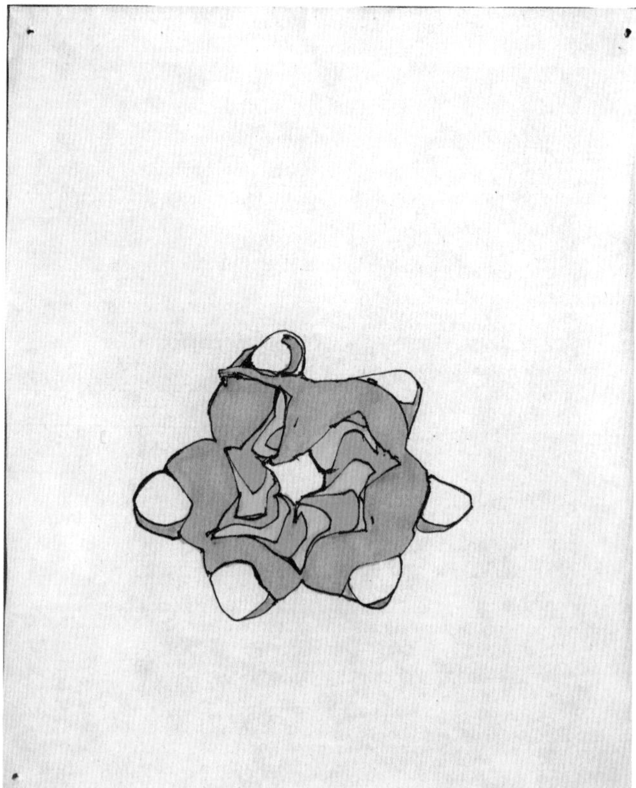
412

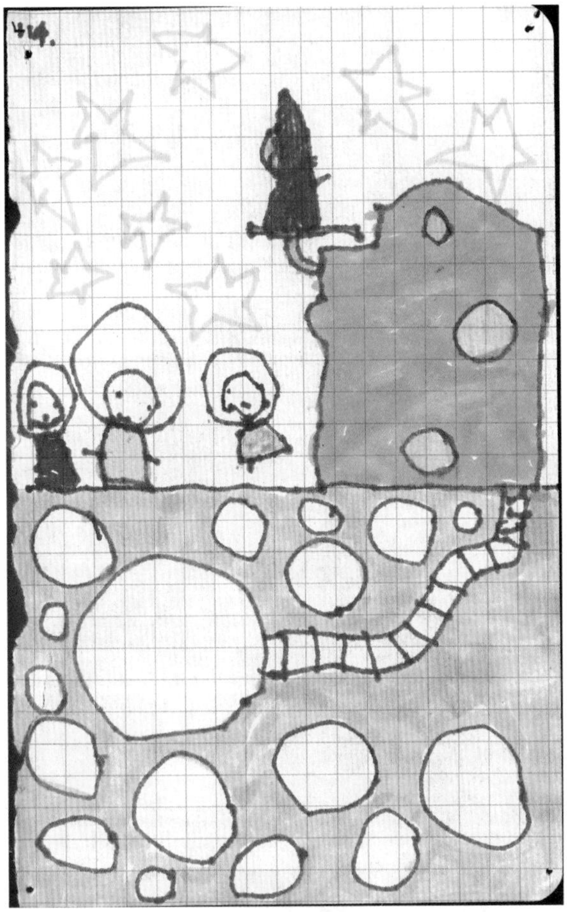

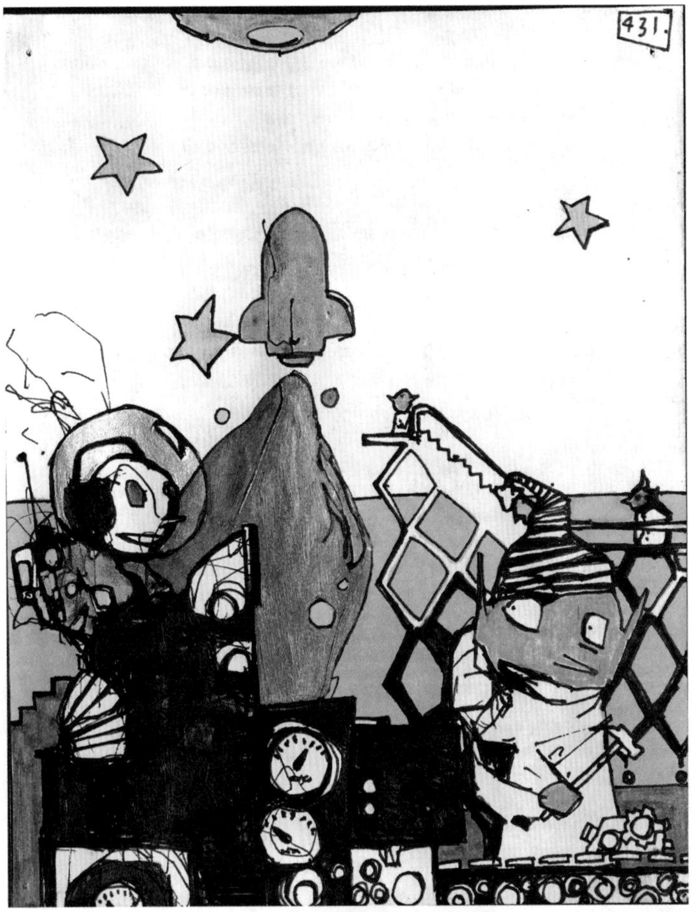
431.

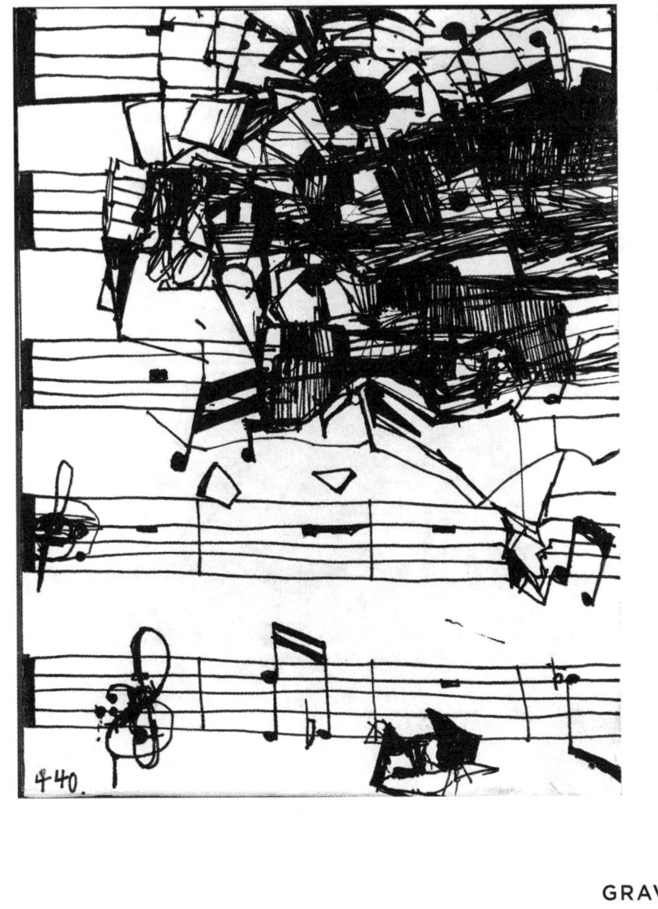
440.

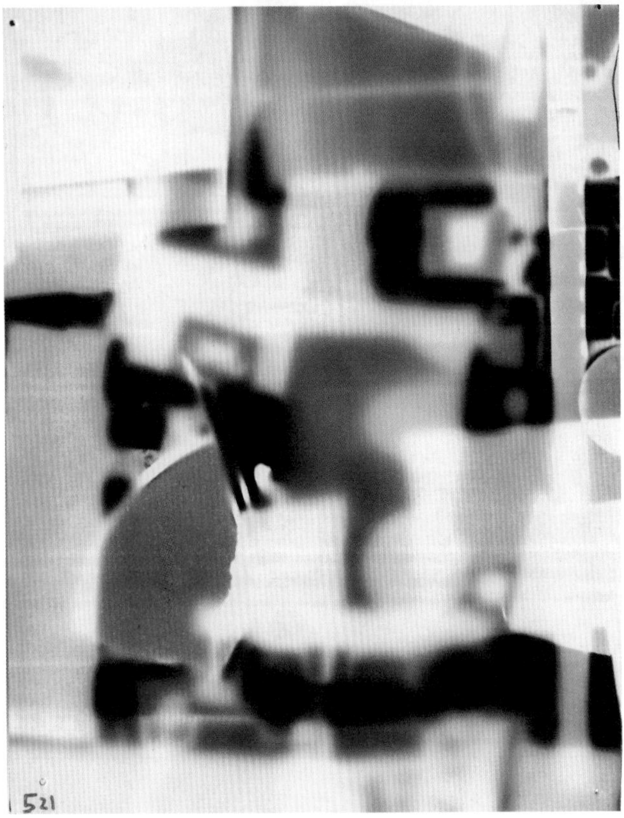
521

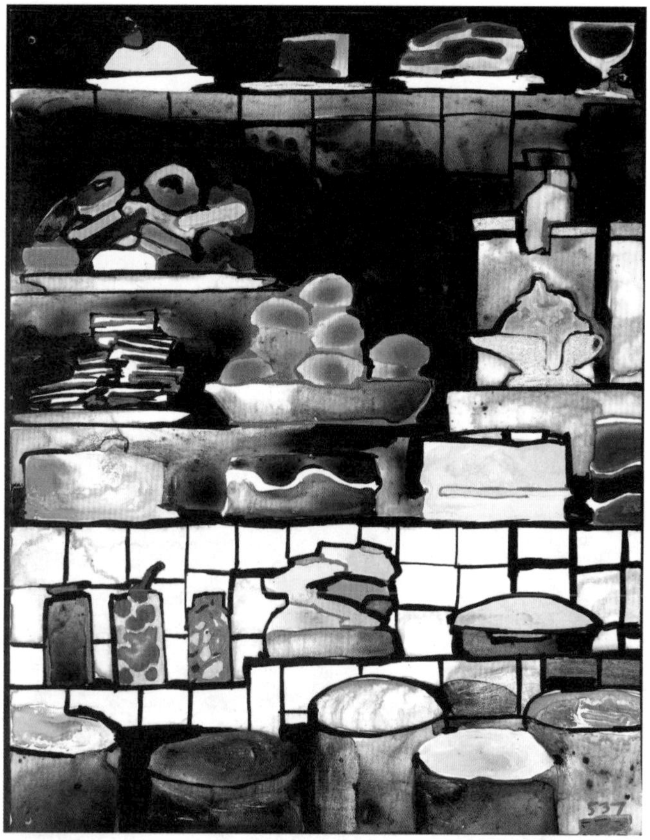
537

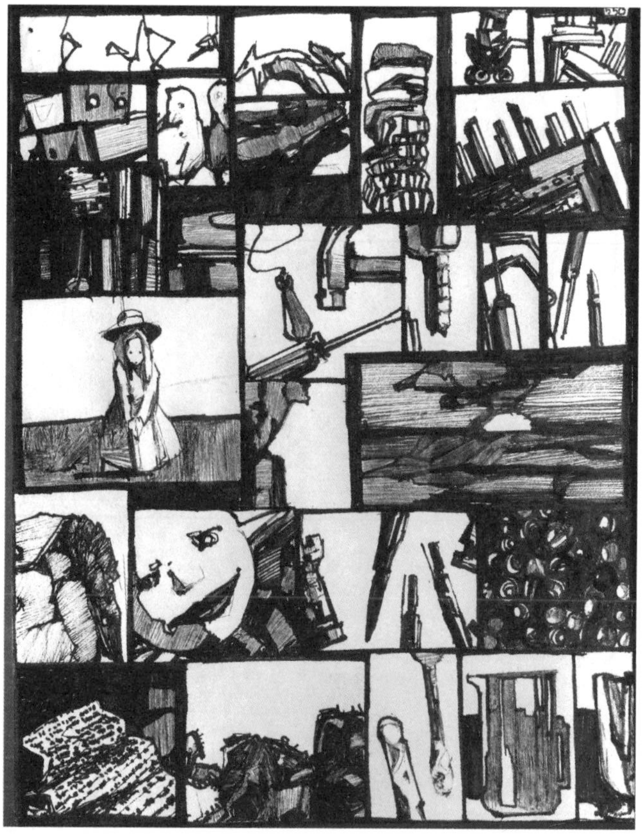

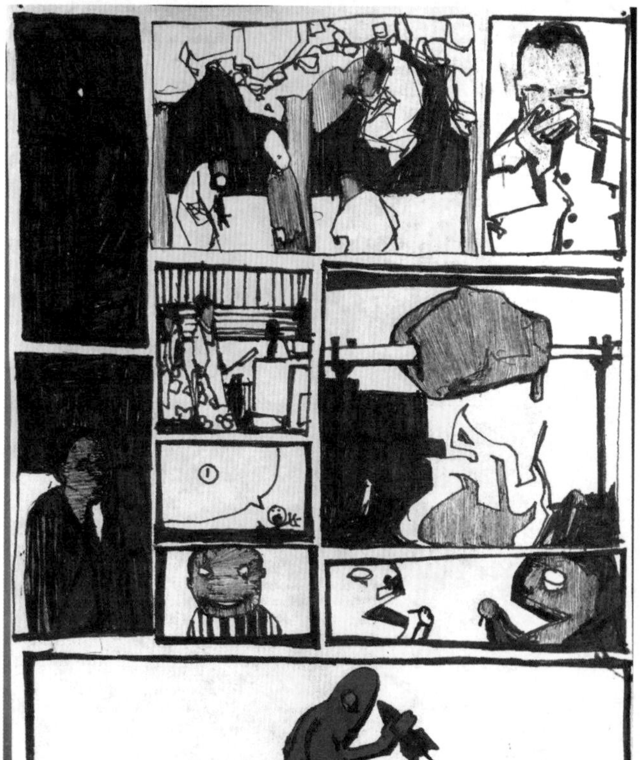
562

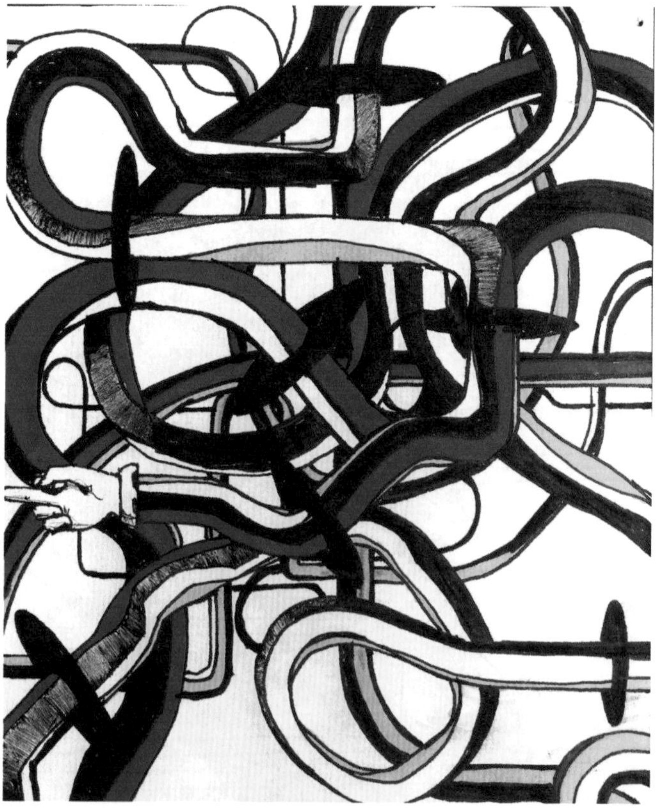

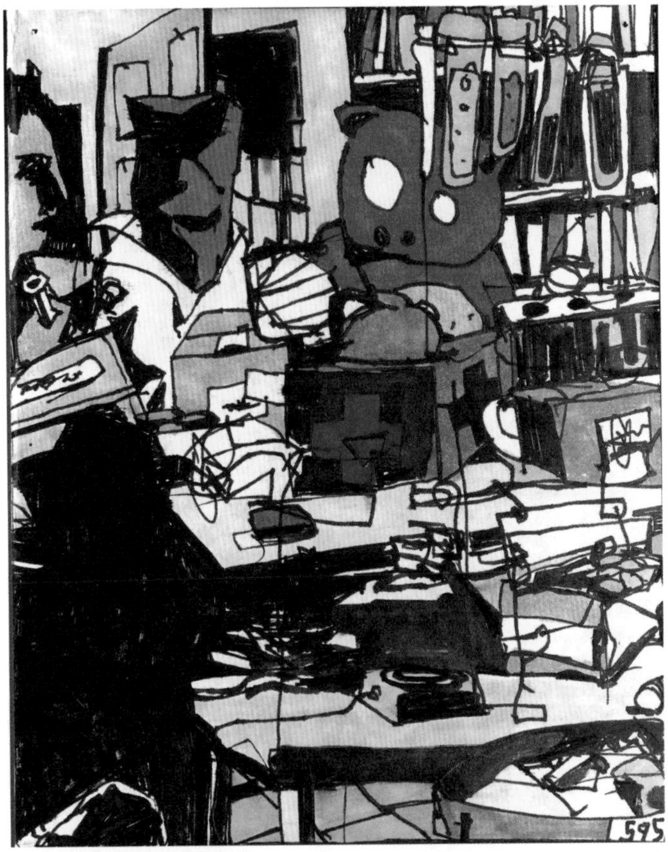
595

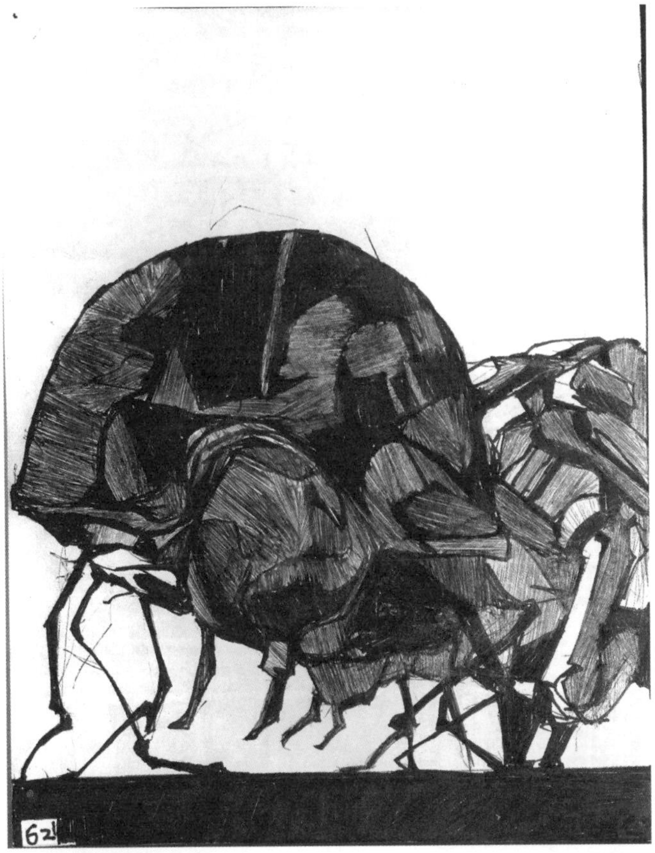

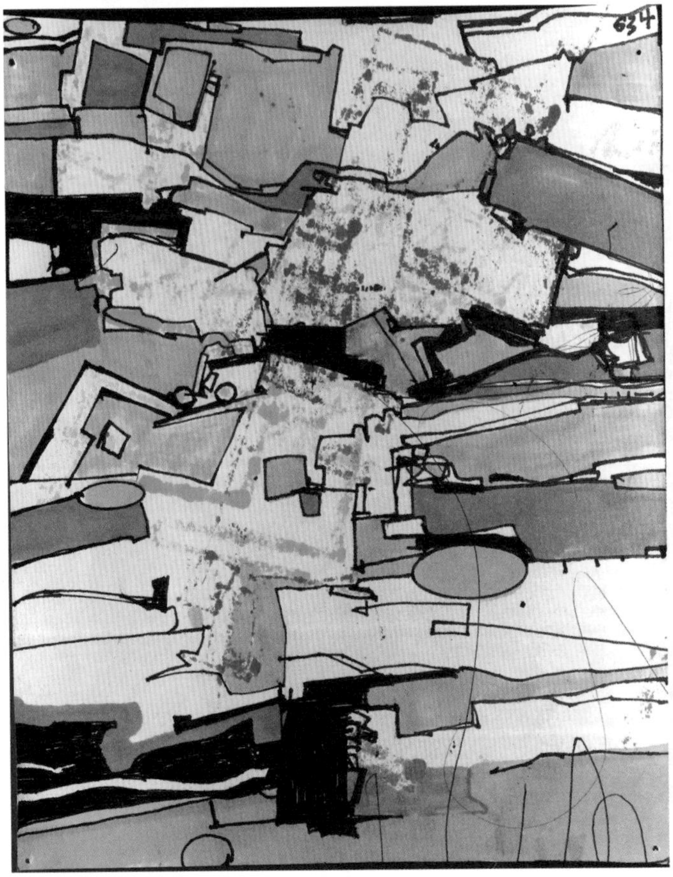
634

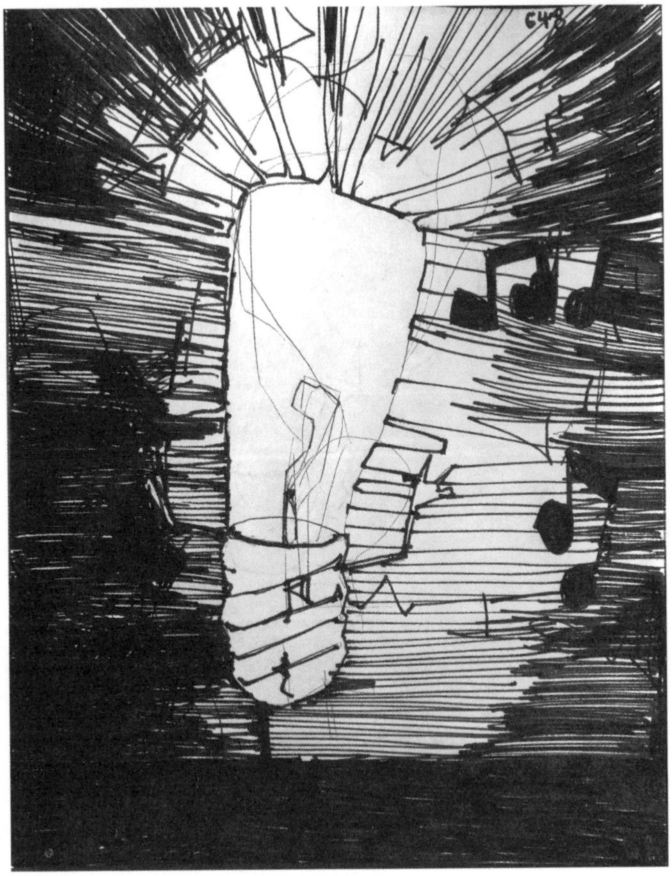
648

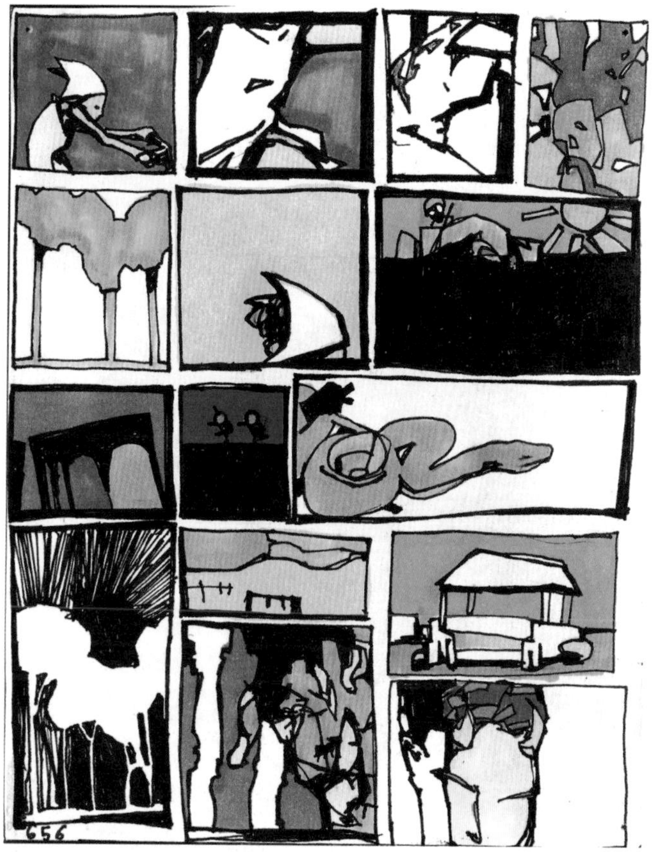
656

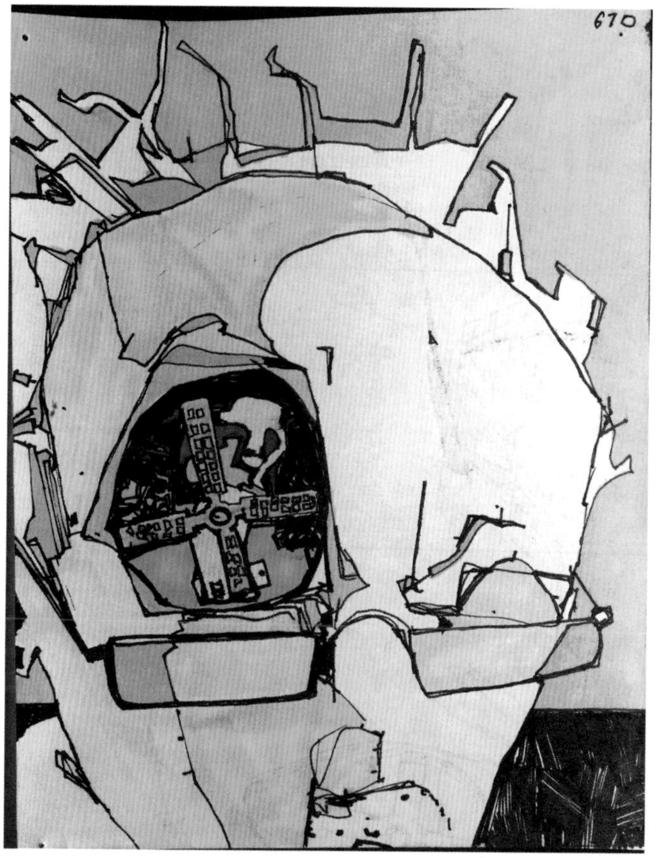
670

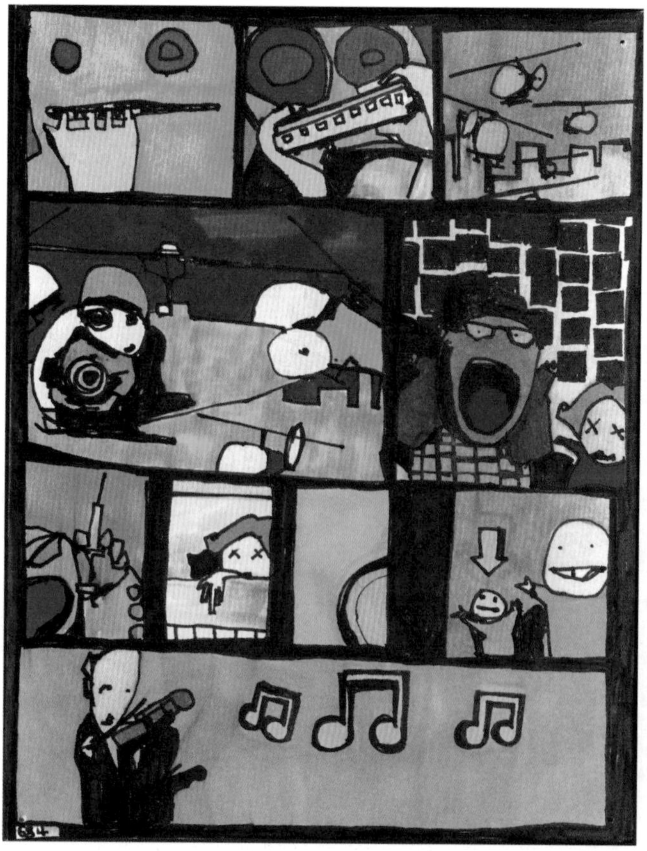

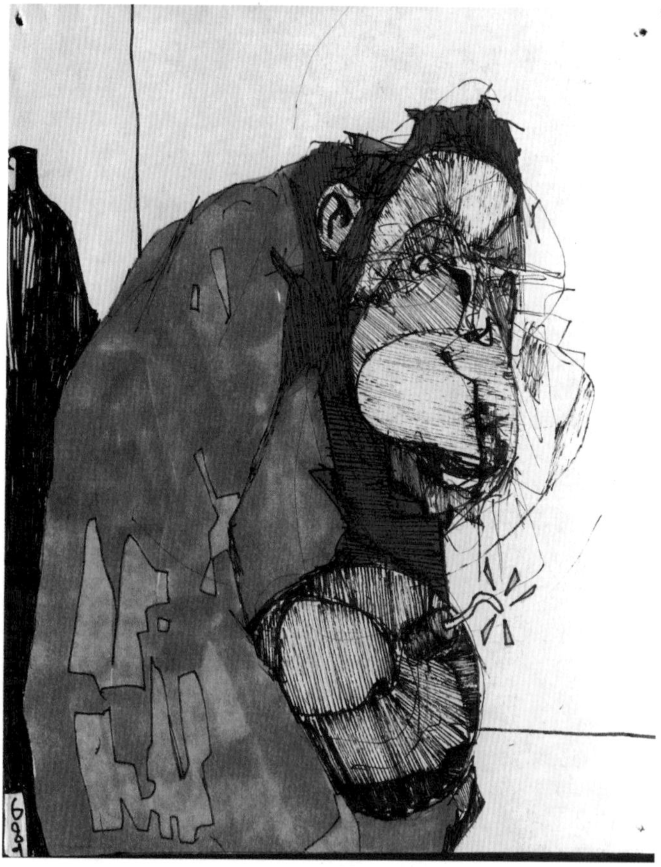

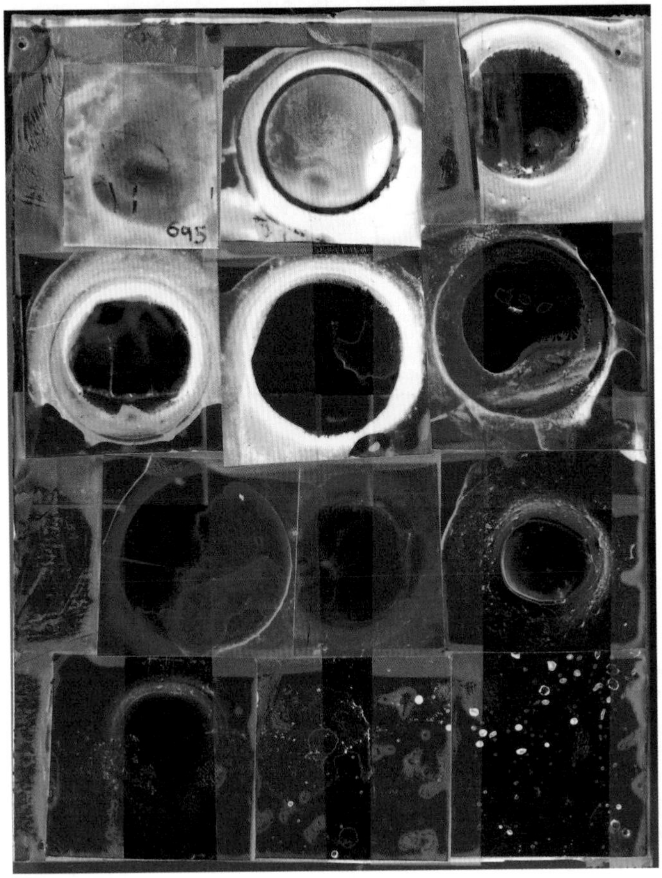
695

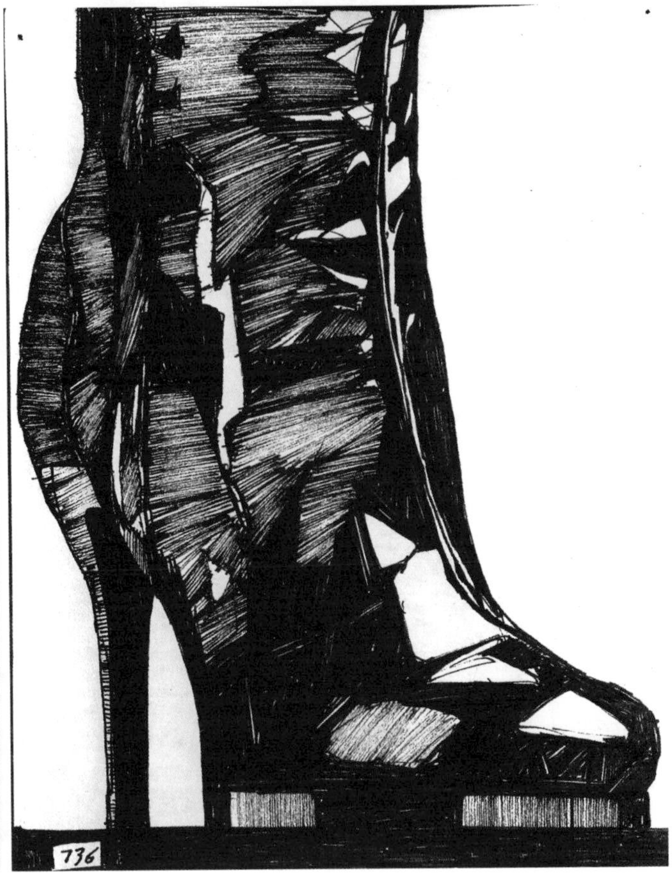
736

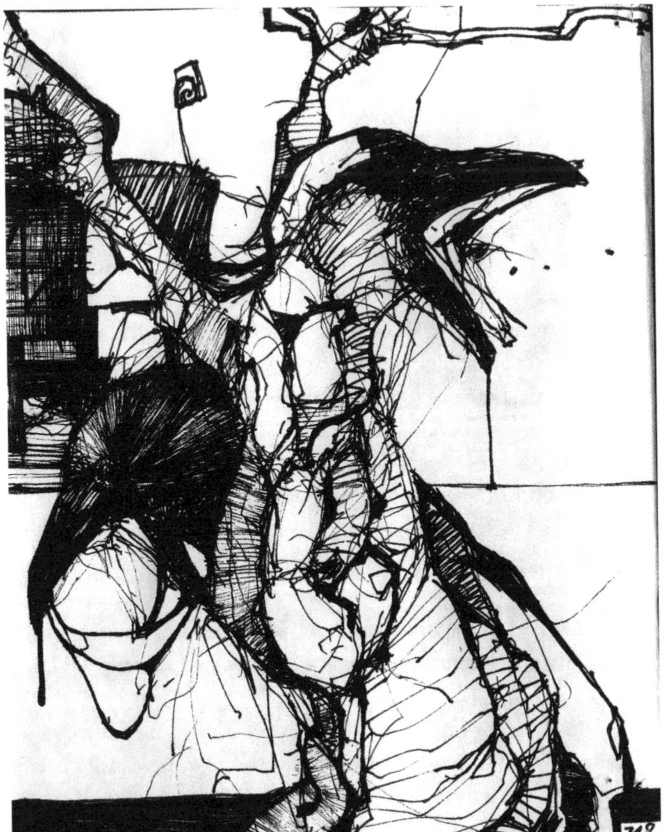
748.

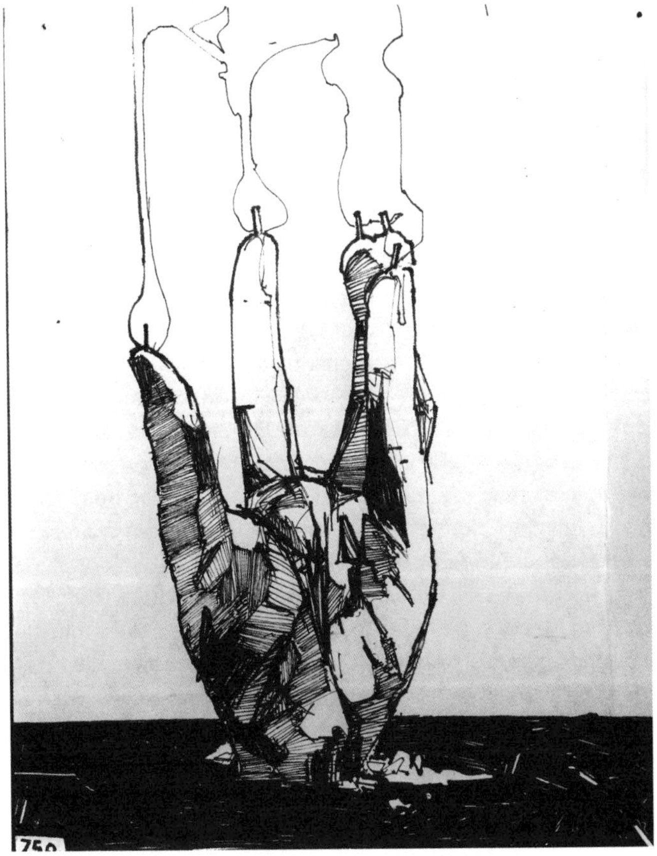

Crash

J. G. Ballard

ART/ADAPTATION BY **Onsmith**

CRASH **IS ONE OF THE BEST NOVELS TO COME OUT** of science fiction's New Wave movement of the late 1960s and 1970s, which tried to take the genre out of its "bug-squashing" (alien-fighting) clichés and show what it could really do. Writers such as Harlan Ellison, Samuel Delany, Tom Disch, Joanna Russ, Michael Moorcock, and Pamela Zoline brought literary and experimental styles, complex viewpoints, and mature themes (love, sex, gender, death and dying, religion, politics, etc.) to what they often preferred to call "speculative fiction."

Although J. G. Ballard experimented wildly with style, creating lots of avant-garde pieces like "The Assassination of John Fitzgerald Kennedy Considered as a Downhill Motor Race" and "Mae West's Reduction Mammoplasty," *Crash* is more an experiment with theme. It examines the hidden significance of car crashes, that very literal, painful interfacing of our bodies with technology. Much of the significance is erotic. The eroticism of car crashes? It's hard to grasp the concept—even after reading *Crash*, you'll probably have a

hard time explaining it, like much of Ballard's work. He was a radical interpreter, even something of a prophet, regarding the postmodern world, especially the less-obvious ways that media and technology are altering the physical landscape, our bodies, and our minds.

Onsmith—a comics artist, painter, and silkscreener residing in Chicago, whose work has appeared in Yale's *An Anthology of Graphic Fiction*—dived into this biomechanical thicket with a super-slow-motion take on a car crash through a Ballardian lens. He told me:

> I wanted to work within my own aesthetic interests while maintaining the overarching themes of the book. This is why I looked to the glorification of modernity in Futurism and Cubism and stylized it as such. I had a sort of inner logic working with the color so the last drawing works as a sort of exhaustion of both the energy (carnal and gas-powered) and the final manifestation of color itself.

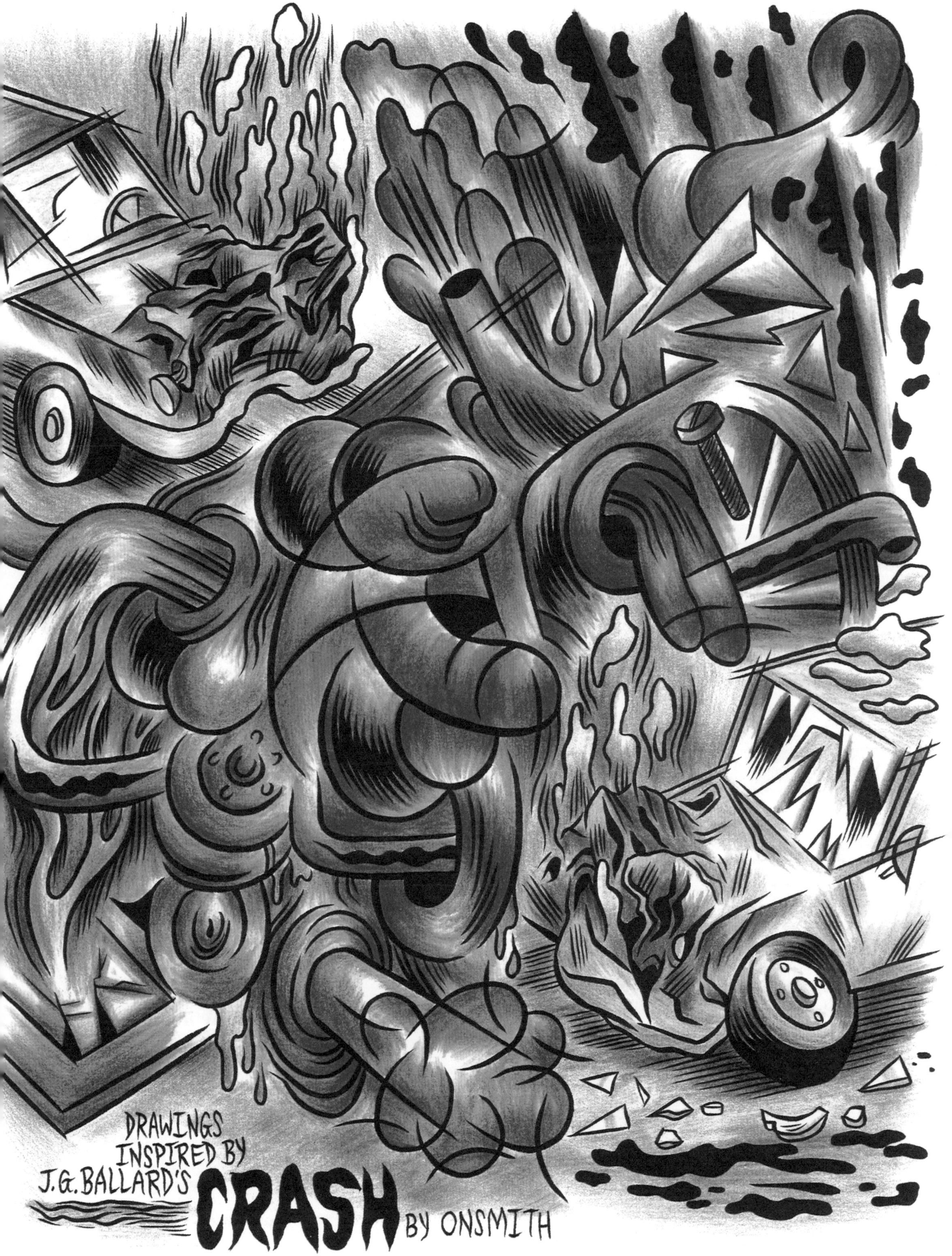
DRAWINGS
INSPIRED BY
J.G. BALLARD'S
CRASH
BY ONSMITH

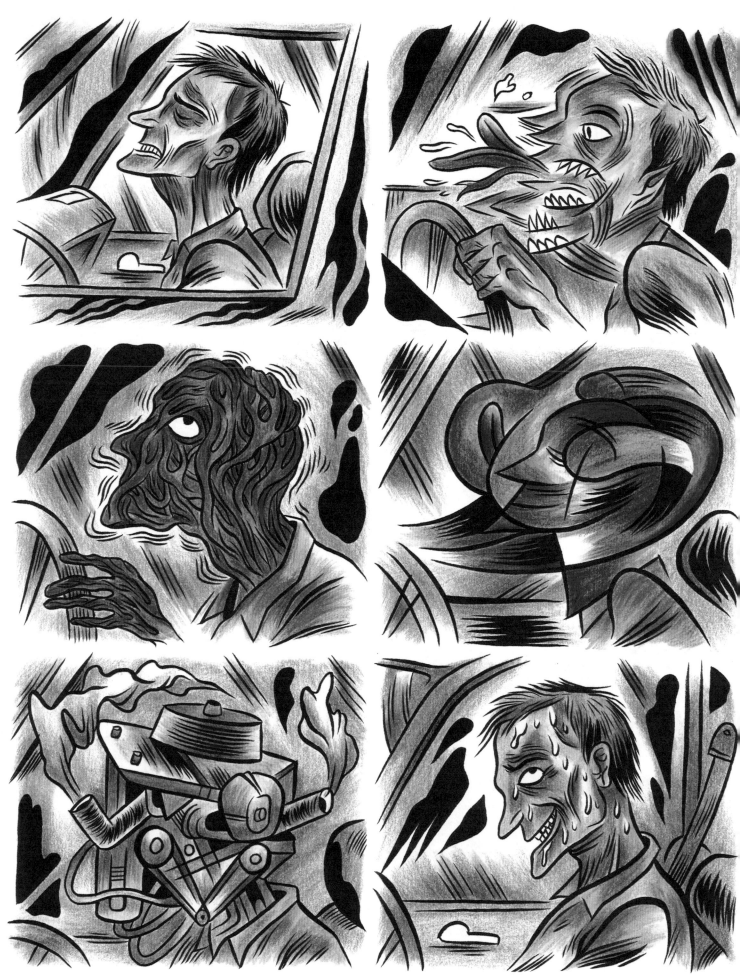

CRASH J. G. BALLARD ONSMITH

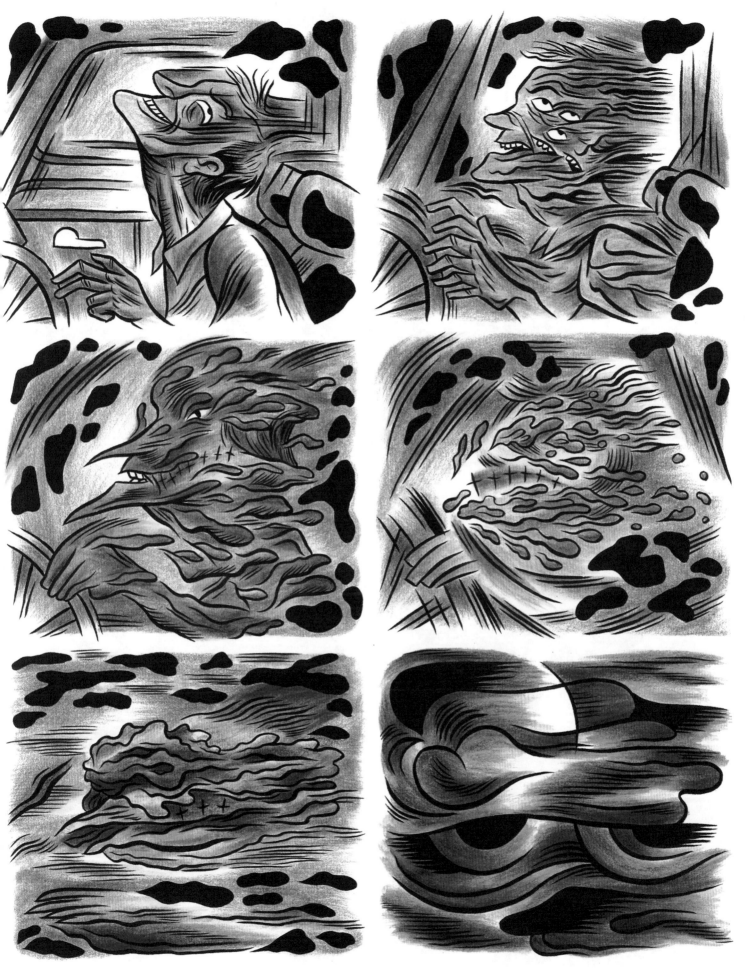

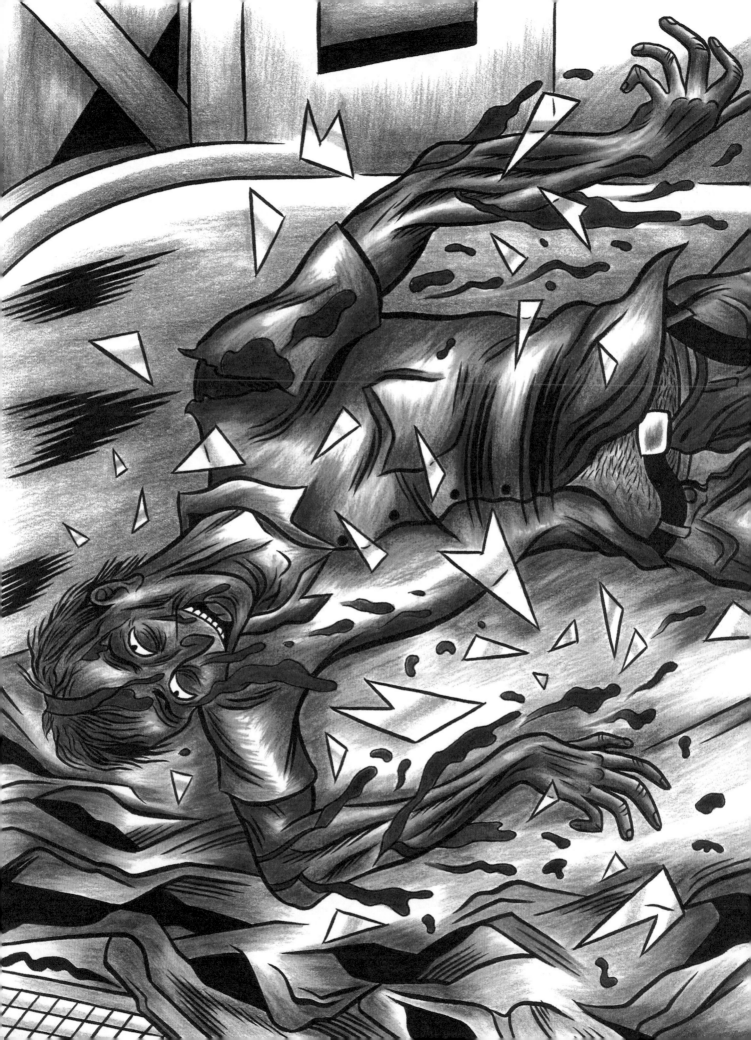

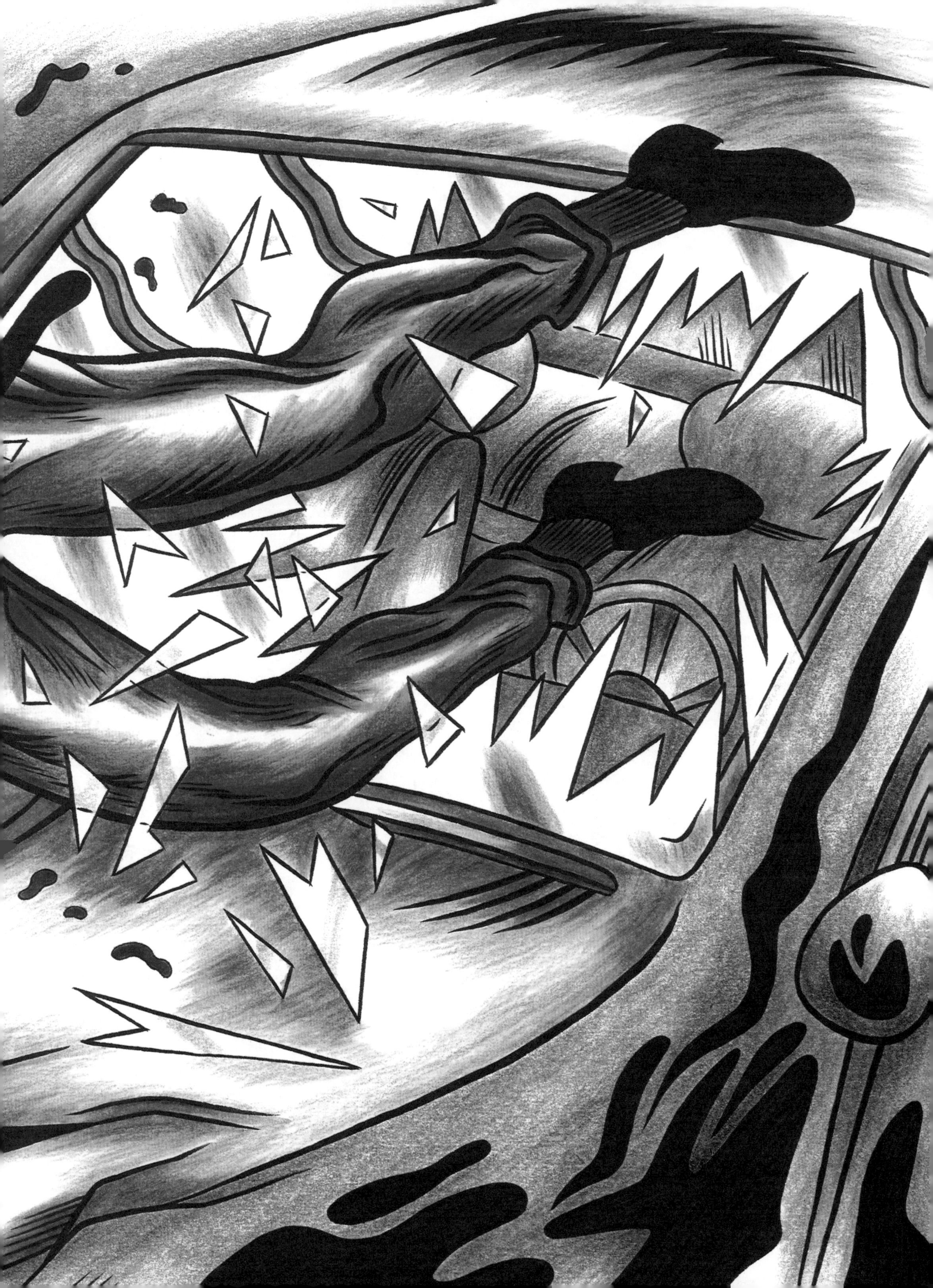

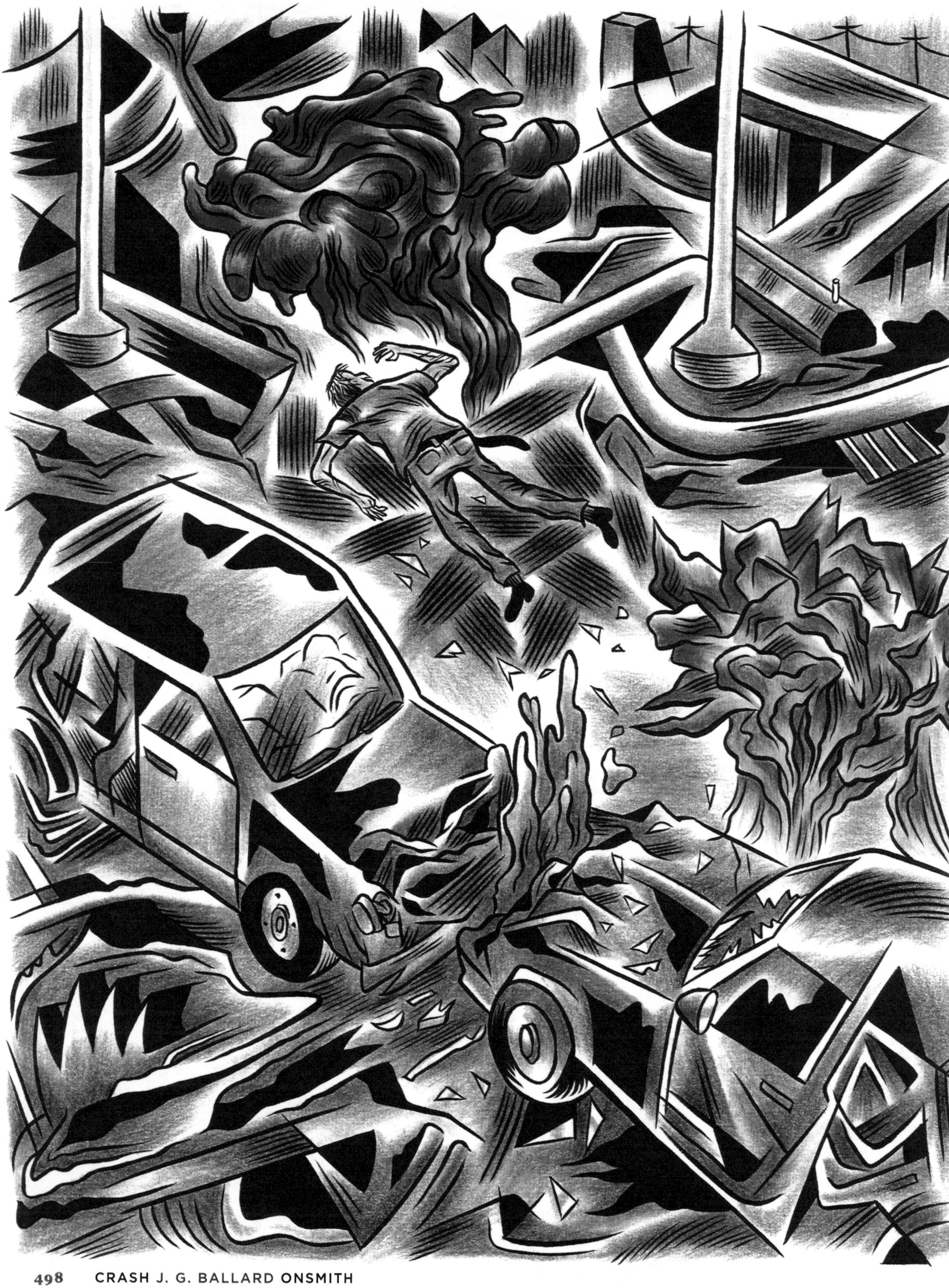

"I Bought a Little City"

Donald Barthelme

ILLUSTRATION BY **Andrice Arp**

ONE OF THE MORE AVANT-GARDE NEW FICTION stylists ever to gain a regular place in the pages of *The New Yorker*, Donald Barthelme wrote short stories that, according to writer James Wolcott, "weren't finely rendered portrait studies in human behavior, or autobiographical reveries à la Johns Updike and Cheever, but a row of boutiques showcasing his latest pranks, confections, gadgets, and Max Ernst/Monty Python–ish collages."

Born in Philadelphia in 1931 to an architect father also named Donald, Donald Jr. moved to New York City in 1962 and, while taking to a hard-drinking writer's lifestyle in the Greenwich Village of the 1960s, began to pump out tales that pushed Modernist fragmentation to limits that seemed at once playful yet precise. Filled with lists and odd tangents but also razor-sharp focus on the topics at hand, Barthelme seemed to be daring himself as a writer to get to a conclusion that would surprise even him. An editor for little magazines on and off throughout his career, he demonstrated a concern for form and style in his publication in 1960 of Marshall McLuhan's speech "The Medium Is the Message."

In his 1987 essay "Not-Knowing," published two years before his death from throat cancer, Barthelme wrote:

> Style is not much a matter of choice. One does not sit down to write and think: Is this poem going to be a Queen Anne poem, a Bieder-meier poem, a Vienna Secession poem, or a Chinese Chippendale poem? Rather it is both a response to constraint and a seizing of opportunity.

Andrice Arp's single-page illustration of "I Bought a Little City" (1974) shows an aerial view of the words and sentences piling out of the author's head. In the story, the narrator buys Galveston and proceeds to make changes—slowly so as not to disturb too abruptly—including the displacement of a small part of the population in order to raze the houses and build a park. Andrice draws the drawing of the accumulation of details—from the jigsawed land plots and the underground parking, to the fancy Galvez Hotel to where the displaced are relocated, as well as the positioning of the bongo drums in the park that displaced them and a somehow-even-more-tangential desire to shoot the dogs. Presiding over all is Sam Hong's, wherein the narrator finds his weakness till he eventually backs out of owning the city, because it's "like having a tooth pulled. For a year. The same tooth. That's a sample of His imagination. It's powerful."

SOURCES

Herzinger, Kim, ed. *Not-Knowing: The Essays and Interviews of Donald Barthelme*. Introduction by John Barth. New York: Random House, 1997.

Wolcott, James. "The Beastly Beatitudes of Donald B." *Bookforum.* Feb./Mar. 2008.

—**Veronica Liu**

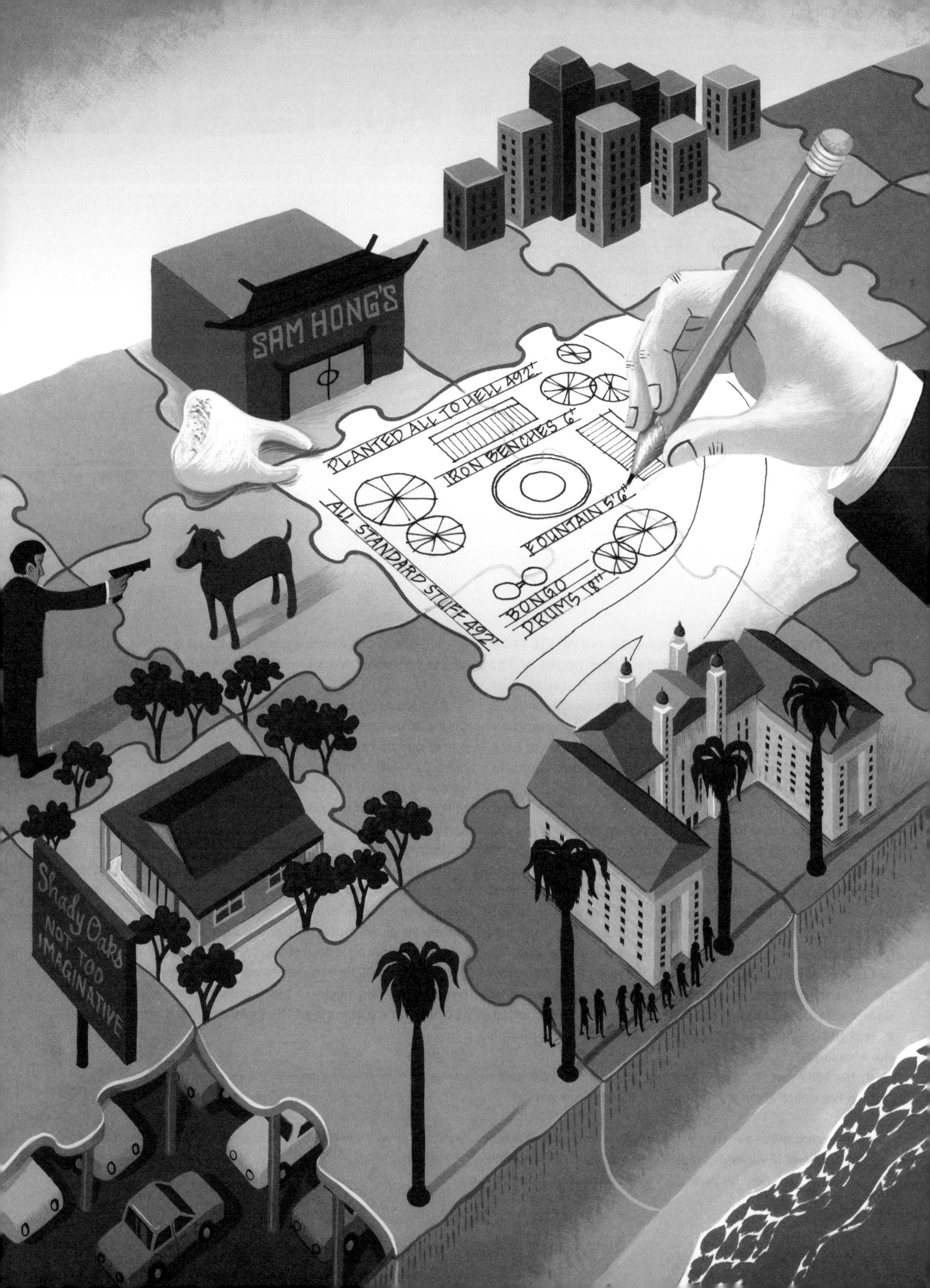
SAM HONG'S
PLANTED ALL TO HELL 492'
IRON BENCHES 6'
ALL STANDARD STUFF 492'
FOUNTAIN 5'6"
BONGO DRUMS 18"
Shady Oaks
NOT TOO IMAGINATIVE

"What We Talk About When We Talk About Love"

Raymond Carver

ILLUSTRATIONS BY **Annie Mok**

APPEARING REGULARLY IN *THE NEW YORKER*, *Esquire*, the *Best American Short Stories* series, and other prestigious spots, Raymond Carver was one of the 1970s–1980s masters of the short story. He typically employed an extremely lean, spare style that hinted at more than it showed about the sad, tragic lives of his middle-class and working-poor characters. (Though, it turns out—as everyone discovered much later—this skeletal style was largely the product of Carver's heavy-handed editor, Gordon Lish.) Carver's style was referred to as minimalism; his themes and content were called dirty realism or Kmart realism.

One of Carver's most well-known stories is "What We Talk About When We Talk About Love." Two married couples sit in a living room in the late afternoon, drinking and discussing the nature of love. Mel brings up one of the main sticklers of the evening, wondering what happens to the love we had for our former partners. He points out that every one of them was once seriously involved with—and deeply loved—someone else. His wife, Terri, brings up another main point of the story by insisting that her former boyfriend's homicidal and suicidal rages caused by her were expressions of his love. In the end, the sun has sunk, leaving the four in total darkness, and the gin has likewise vanished, leaving them drunk. The conversation stops and they sit in silence, no one knowing a goddamn thing about what love is, the issue more cloudy than ever.

Annie Mok gave us a cracking good sequential adaptation of "Araby" by James Joyce earlier in this volume. Here she presents a diptych based on Carver's 1981 story of love and disillusionment. The first illustration—ingeniously eschewing text—resembles a cover for the story or perhaps the short-story collection that bears its title. The other illustration uses a quote from the original manuscript version of the story (then called "Beginners") that was cut by Lish in the published version.

RAYMOND CARVER

WHAT WE TALK ABOUT WHEN WE TALK ABOUT LOVE

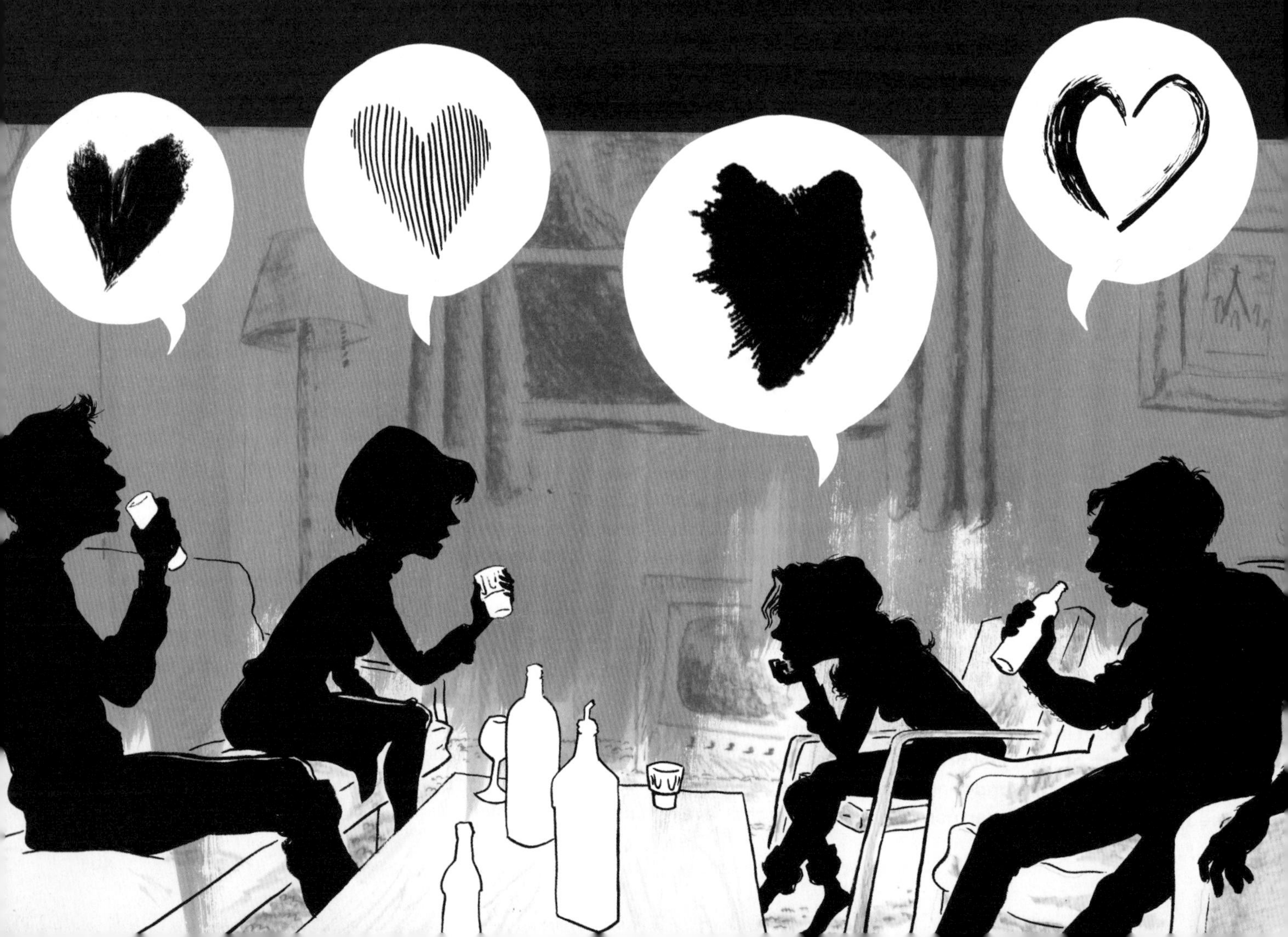

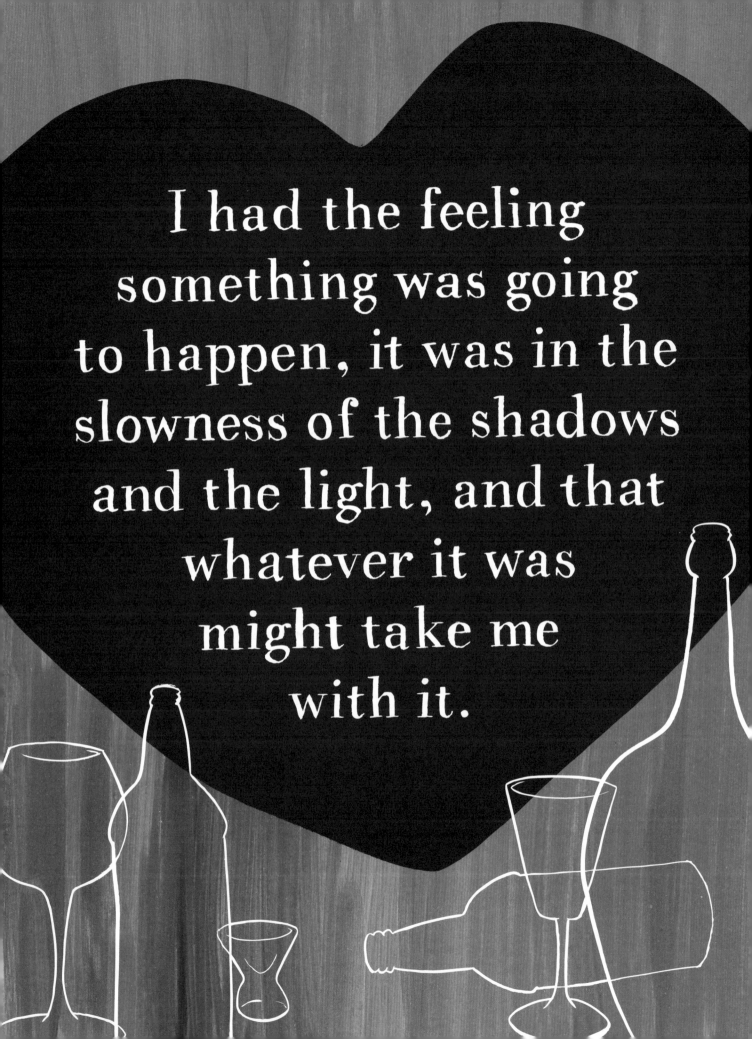

I had the feeling something was going to happen, it was in the slowness of the shadows and the light, and that whatever it was might take me with it.

Blood and Guts in High School

Kathy Acker

ART/ADAPTATION BY **Molly Kiely**

"LITERARY TERRORIST" KATHY ACKER CAME OUT of the New York punk/underground scene, initially as a poet, then really making her mark as a novelist. Her highly experimental works employ a variety of avant-garde techniques while the content strides into transgressive, often sexually violent territory, with sociopolitical overtones. Pornography and high literature are two of her many influences/sources, put into her postmodern blender of collage, cut-up technique, appropriation/plagiarism, and other radical approaches to text.

Mark Pritchard—a writer and publisher of groundbreaking, literary erotic fiction in the 1990s who knew Acker—summed up:

> Acker's work was a bundle of contradictions, an assault on sense, and a scream against convention. Capable of an exalted lyricism, she more often wrote deliberately "badly." Though she had a highly sharpened feminist and post-feminist sense, her female characters tended to express self-loathing and seek validation through offering themselves as pieces of meat.

. . .

Typical of Acker's work: Sex, violence and politics mixed up with characters and stories from literary classics and history. A character identifiable with the author (and sometimes called Kathy) who uses sex to manipulate people into loving her. A willingness to turn literature and narrative reality inside out. Acker's books are like those fantastic exploded-view illustrations of mechanical devices, in which you can see every part labeled and floating near the part to which it is connected. Like these drawings, Acker's writing explodes reality until you can see the underlying works; unlike them, the purpose is not to explain and make clear, but to create meaning through fantastic juxtapositions and bare, raw rendition.

She published from the early 1970s until her early death from cancer in 1997, with her most famous works coming out in the 1980s—*Great Expectations, Don Quixote, Empire of the Senseless*, and *In Memoriam to Identity* (1990). In the middle of that decade came her most well-known novel, *Blood and Guts in High School*, which had been written in the 1970s. In fragmented fashion, it tells of Janey, a girl who has a series of sexual relationships with her father, gang members, a Persian slave trader, and the French writer Jean Genet, among many, many others, before dying of cancer at age fourteen.

Although most of her large oeuvre is kept in print by the redoubtable Grove Press—publishers of Kerouac, Burroughs, Ginsberg, Beckett, Genet, de Sade, Borges, Paz, and other titans of avant-garde literature—Acker has never been fully accepted into the world of high-brow Postmodernism inhabited by Pynchon, Barthelme, Don DeLillo, David Foster Wallace, et al. She and her work are just too untamable and confrontational, her techniques too experimental and personal for the literati. Still, through sheer, raw power, she created outsider classics of Postmodernism.

Artist Molly Kiely—who has adapted *The Tale of Genji, Venus in Furs*, and other works for *The Graphic Canon* volumes—explains her final choice of literature:

> While *Blood and Guts in High School* is transgressive, I actually didn't find it repulsively violent—perhaps because it's a book, and not visual like a movie, and my mind's eye just chose not to get gruesome on me. I loved the incoherence and non-linear quality—again, because it's a book and my mind's eye did choose to bridge those gaps. I read it several times, picking up the story (if you could call it that—some passages are repetitive like a mantra, or nonsensical, or written out like a map) in a different place each time. I found it a very beautiful book—angry, unsettling, and violent, certainly—but very liberating; much more symbolic (each reader's own interpretation) than literal. The line "and then she was beautiful"—which I wrote (I hope) in Arabic on the fifth page of my adaptation—after being freed from her captor still resonates. This isn't the way women are supposed to write; this isn't what women are supposed to read.

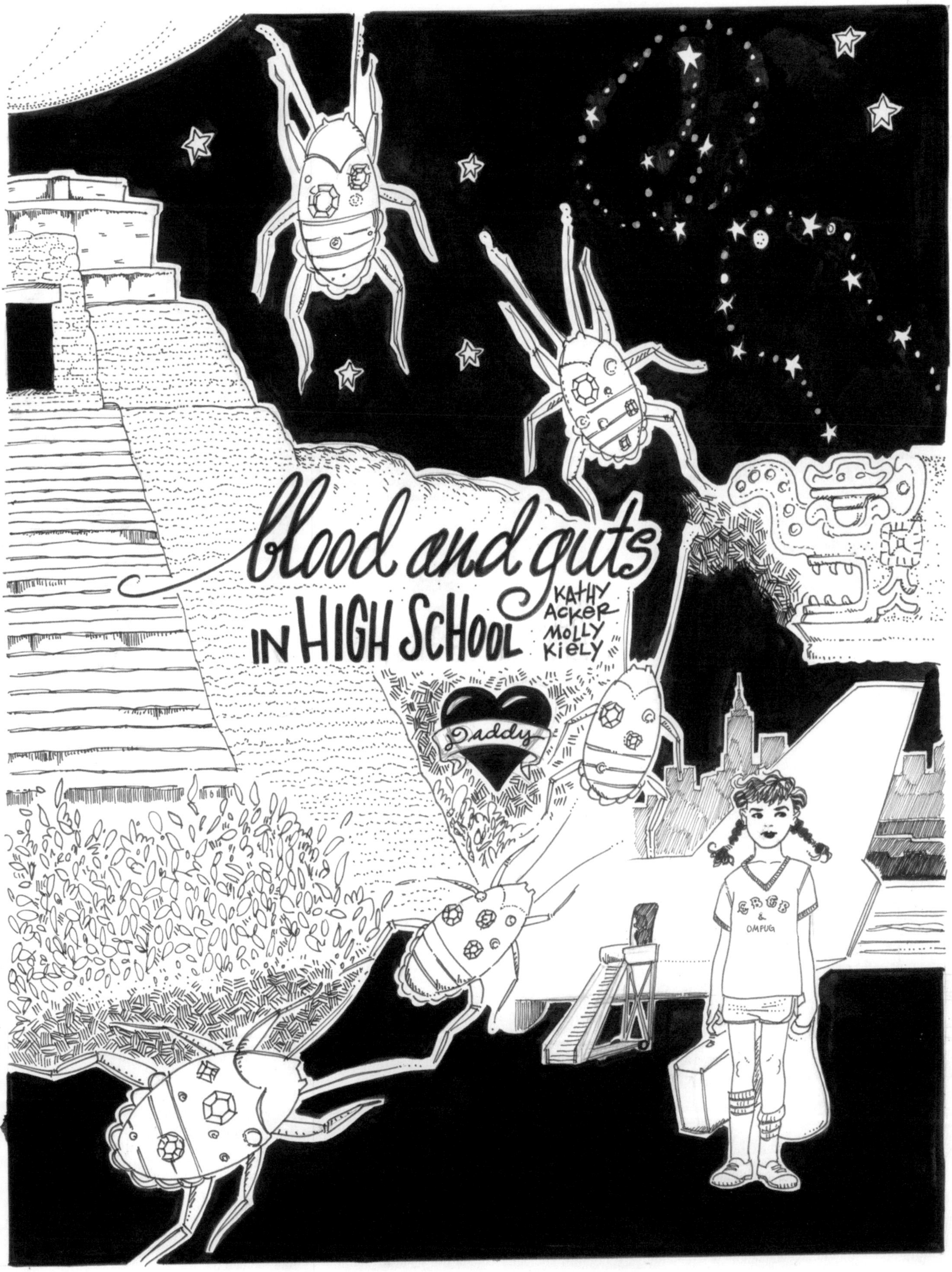
blood and guts
IN HIGH SCHOOL
KATHY ACKER
MOLLY KIELY
Daddy
CBGB & OMFUG

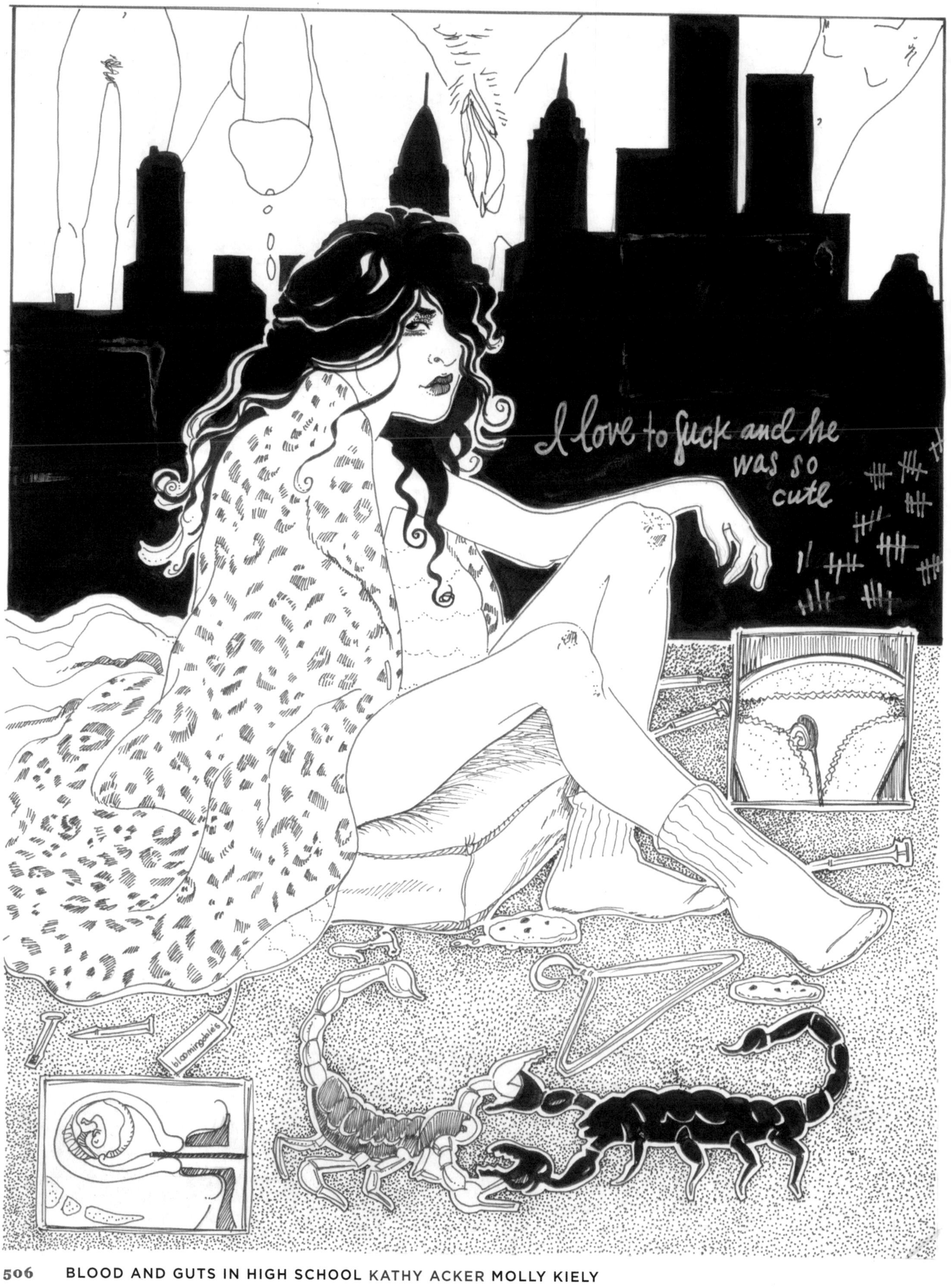
I love to fuck and he was so cute
bloomingdale's

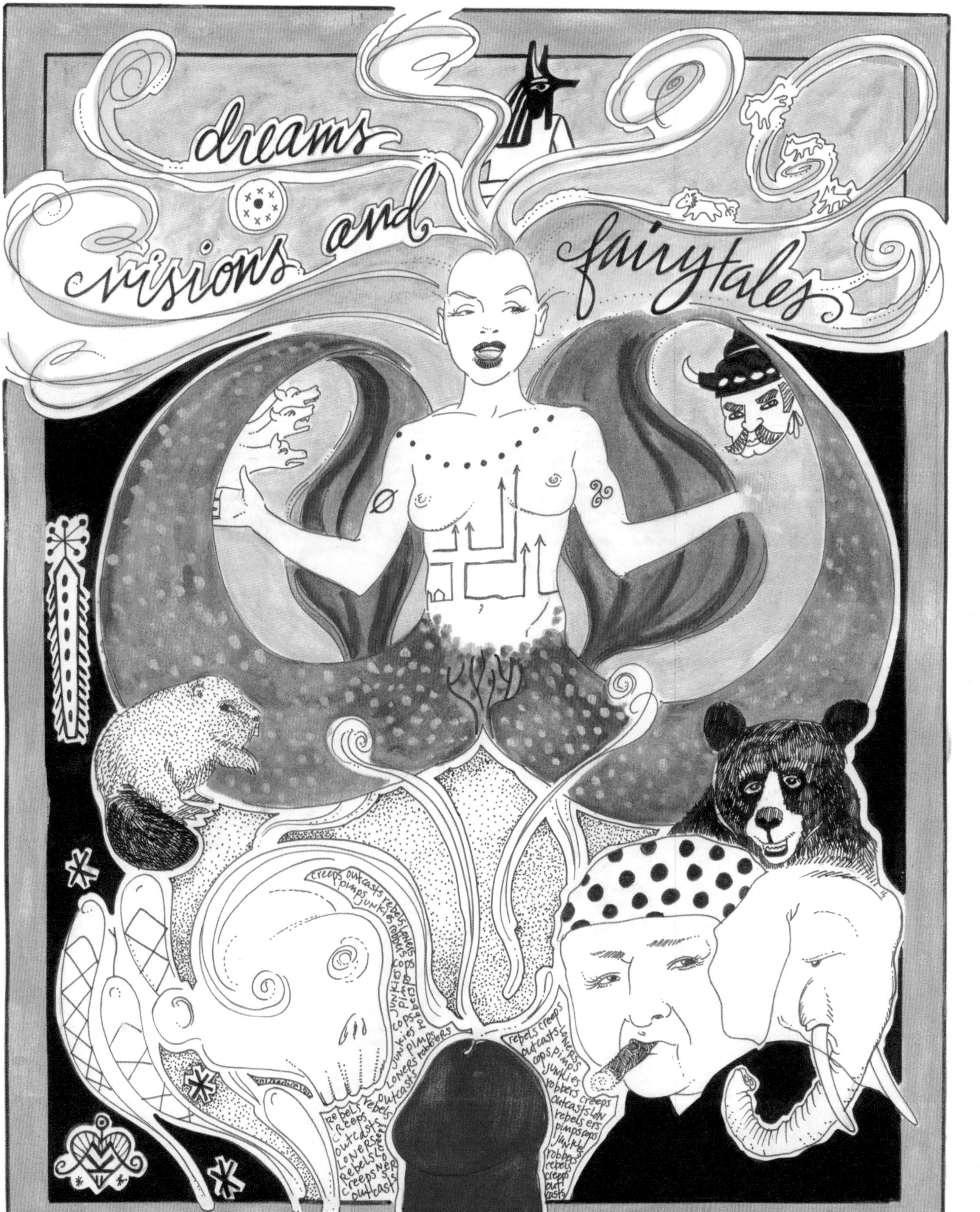
dreams
visions and
fairytales

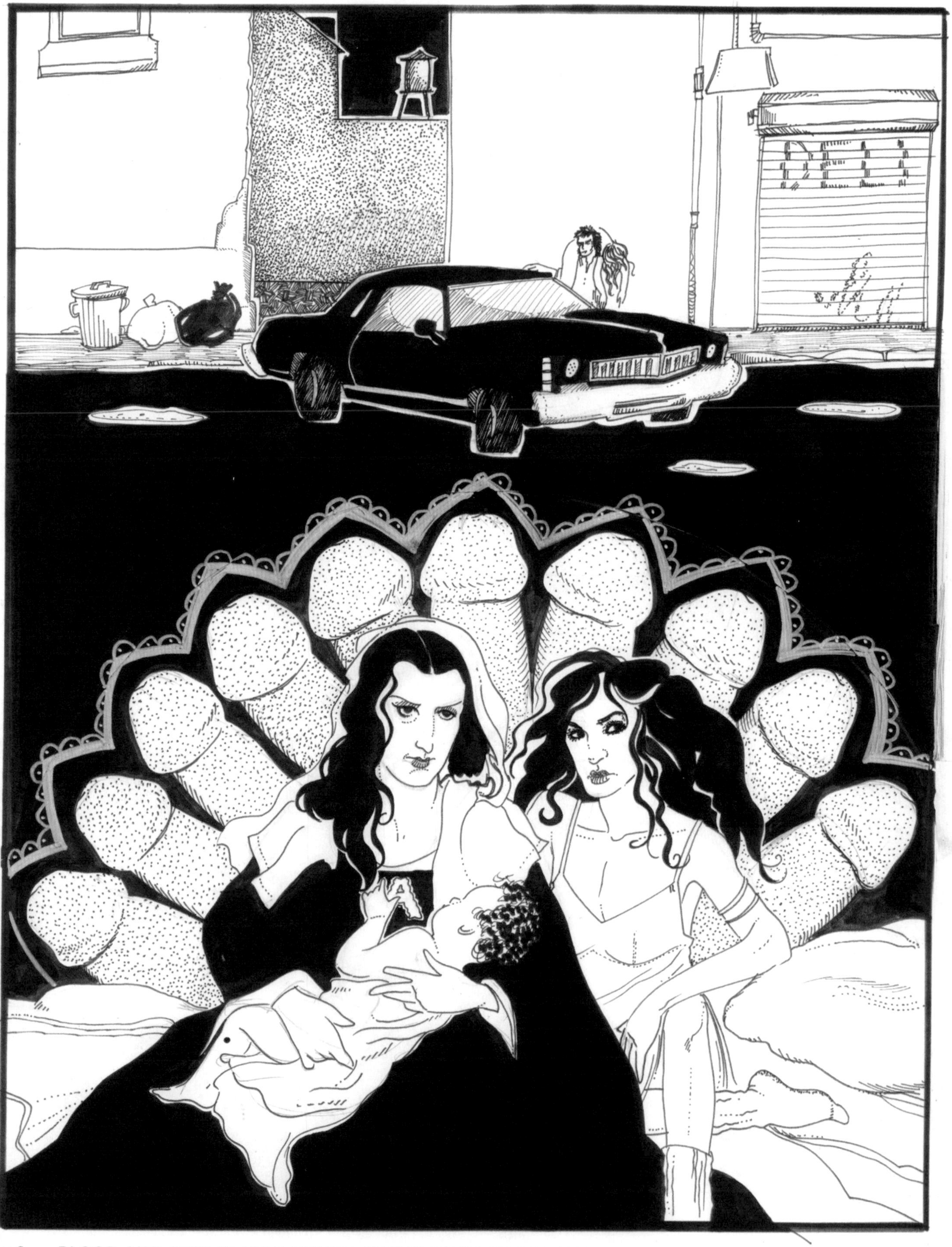

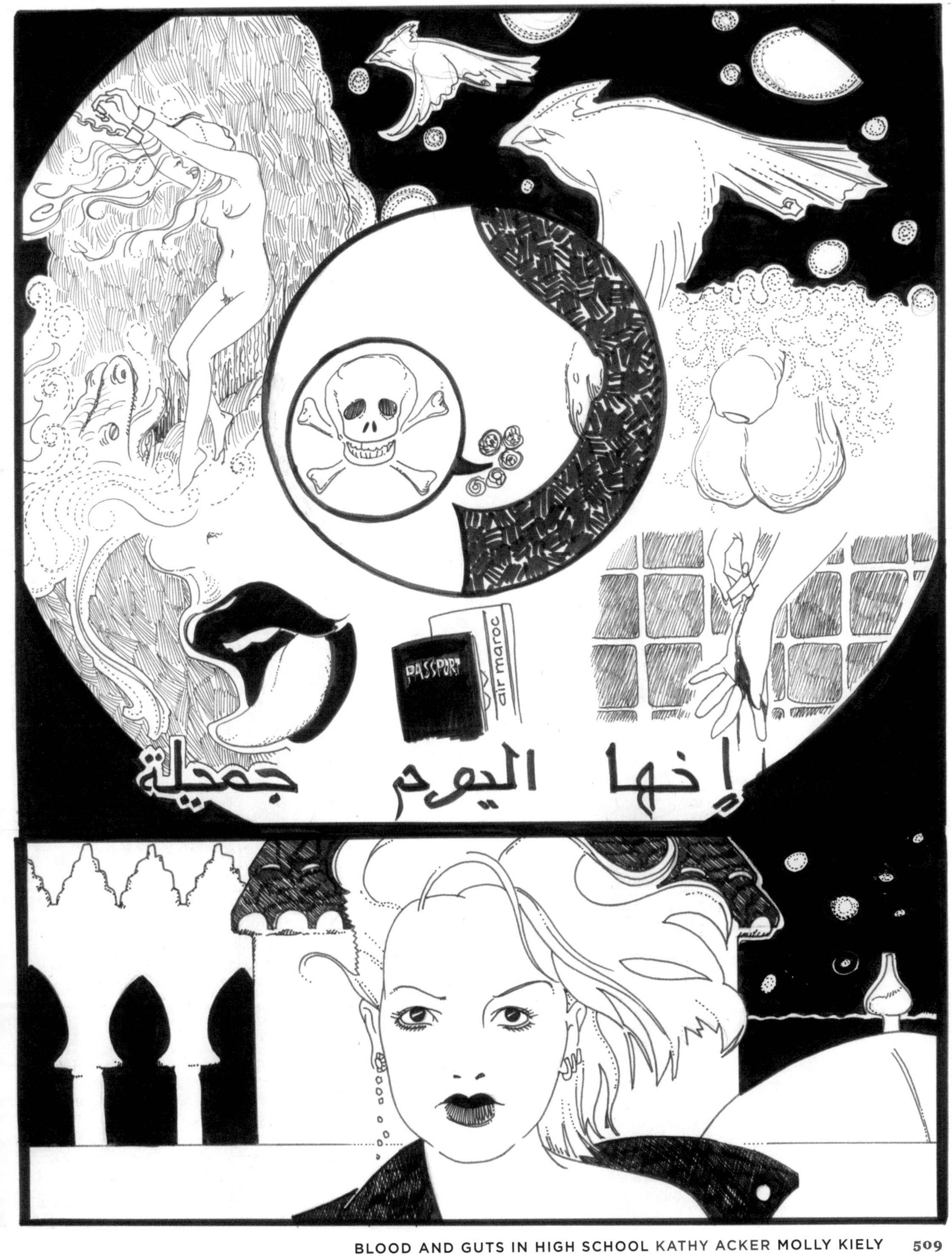
PASSPORT
air maroc
إنها اليوم جميلة

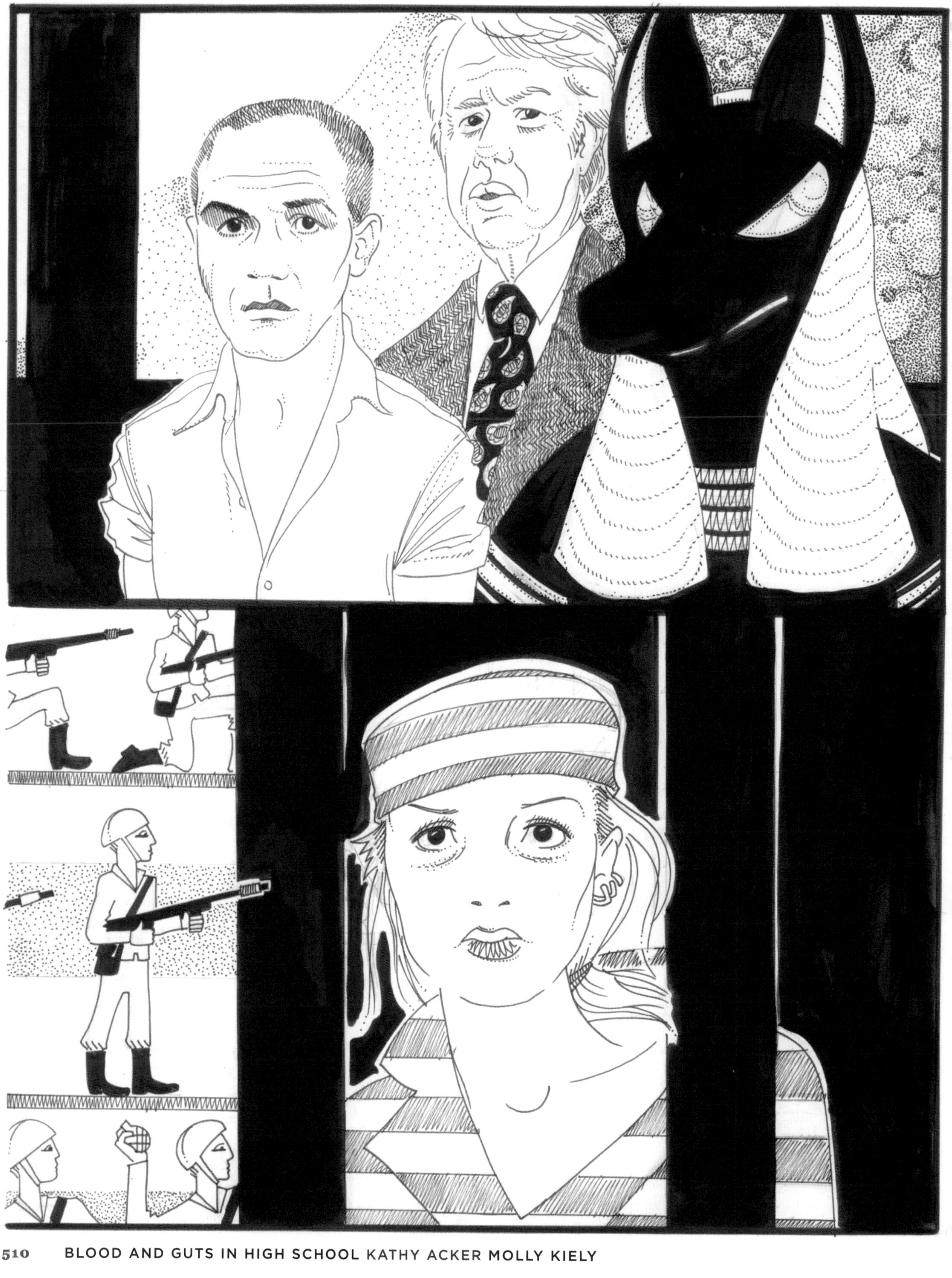

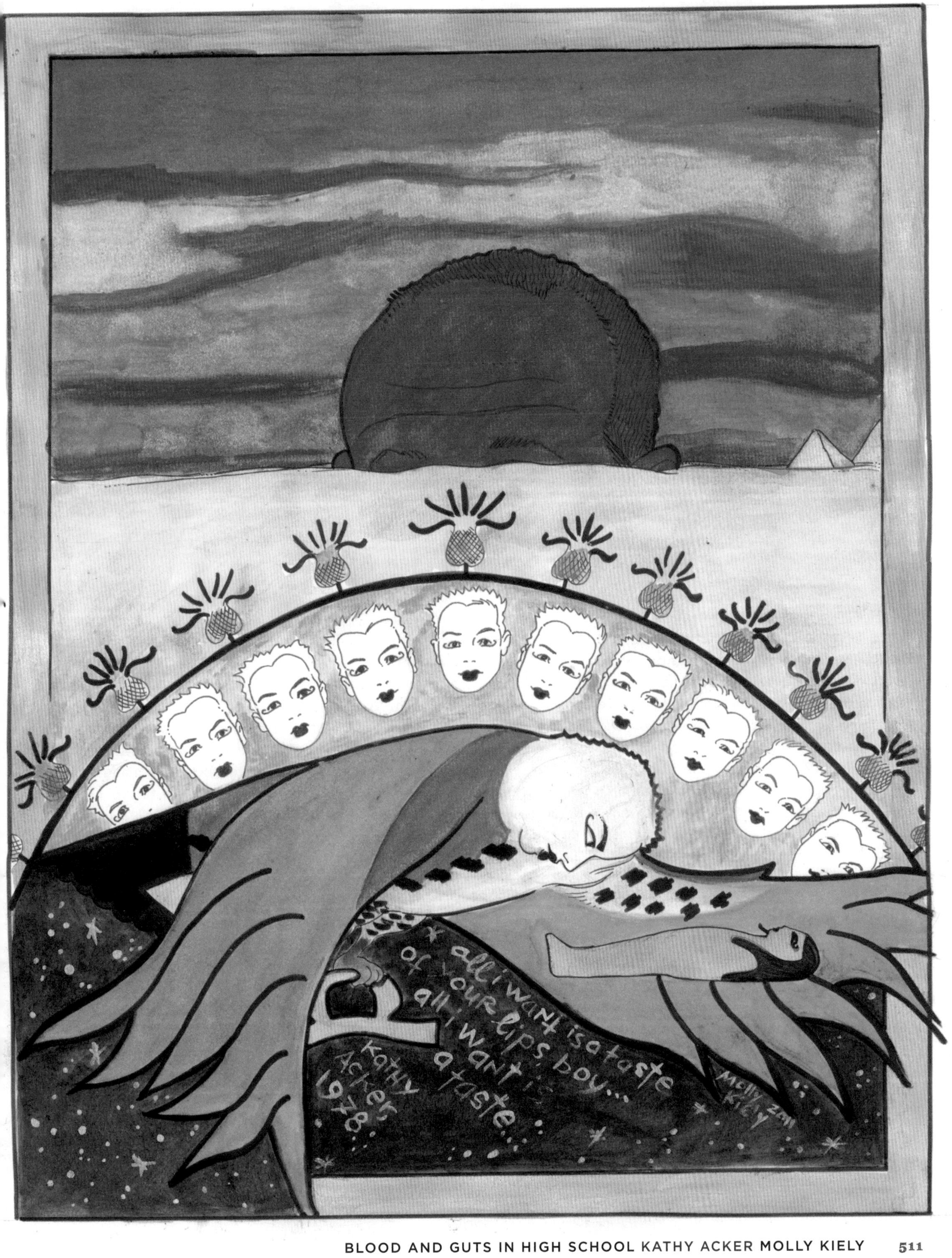
all i want is a taste
of your lips boy...
all i want
a taste...
Kathy
Acker
1978
Molly Kiely
2011

Blood Meridian

Cormac McCarthy

ILLUSTRATIONS BY **Dame Darcy**

IT'S MORE OR LESS AGREED THAT CORMAC McCarthy is one of a small number of living writers producing classic-level work. He's achieved mainstream fame due to the Hollywood adaptations of several of his books, including *All the Pretty Horses*, *No Country for Old Men*, and *The Road* (which also won the Pulitzer and was, somewhat strangely, selected for Oprah's Book Club).

McCarthy's 1985 novel *Blood Meridian* is widely considered his masterpiece. Harold Bloom, the most influential literary critic and theorist, has said that it's "the greatest single book since Faulkner's *As I Lay Dying*" and "is worthy of Herman Melville's *Moby-Dick*." It also has the deserved reputation of being one of the most violent, brutal novels ever written. Even Bloom says that at first he found the book "appalling" and had nightmares because of it.

The action is based on historical events involving the Glanton gang, who were paid to kill and scalp Apaches at the Mexico-US border around 1850. Vicious and bloodthirsty, they proceed to murder and mutilate peaceful Indians, Mexican civilians, and pretty much anyone else. Literally almost every page contains a barbarous act described in detail using McCarthy's lovely prose. Beautiful descriptions of the landscape and numerous allusions to the Bible, *Paradise Lost*, cycles of life, and the sun and other celestial bodies give the book mythical resonance.

Some commentators can only conclude that McCarthy was simply going for shock value—albeit wonderfully written—with the over-the-top litany of atrocities and violations, while others believe that he has written the only true Western novel, one that dispenses with John Wayne silliness and shows the Wild West in all its real-life savagery and horror. Some see it as the bleakest possible comment on America's manifest destiny and imperialism. Others counter that there is no sociopolitical message intended, though perhaps there is some kind of statement about human nature. Like most great works of literature, the ambiguities leave room for endless debate and contradictory interpretations.

Comics legend Dame Darcy knows a thing or two about the darkness. Her long-running *Meatcake* is an alternative Victorian Wonderland filled with outrageous violence and grotesquery. But there's always an undercurrent of whimsy, a bit of tongue-in-cheek in the proceedings. Not so with *Blood Meridian*, and Darcy captures this grimness in the following full-page illustrations of some of the book's most notorious passages.

First, one of the main characters—known only as "the kid"—enters a ruined church to find buzzards, mutilated bodies, and a statue of Mary holding a headless baby Jesus. In one of the novel's most talked-about scenes, an Apache war party is dressed in clothing taken from their previous victims, including white stockings and a wedding veil. Later, the kid and another character walk by a tree or a bush (McCarthy used both words to refer to it) "that was hung with dead babies."

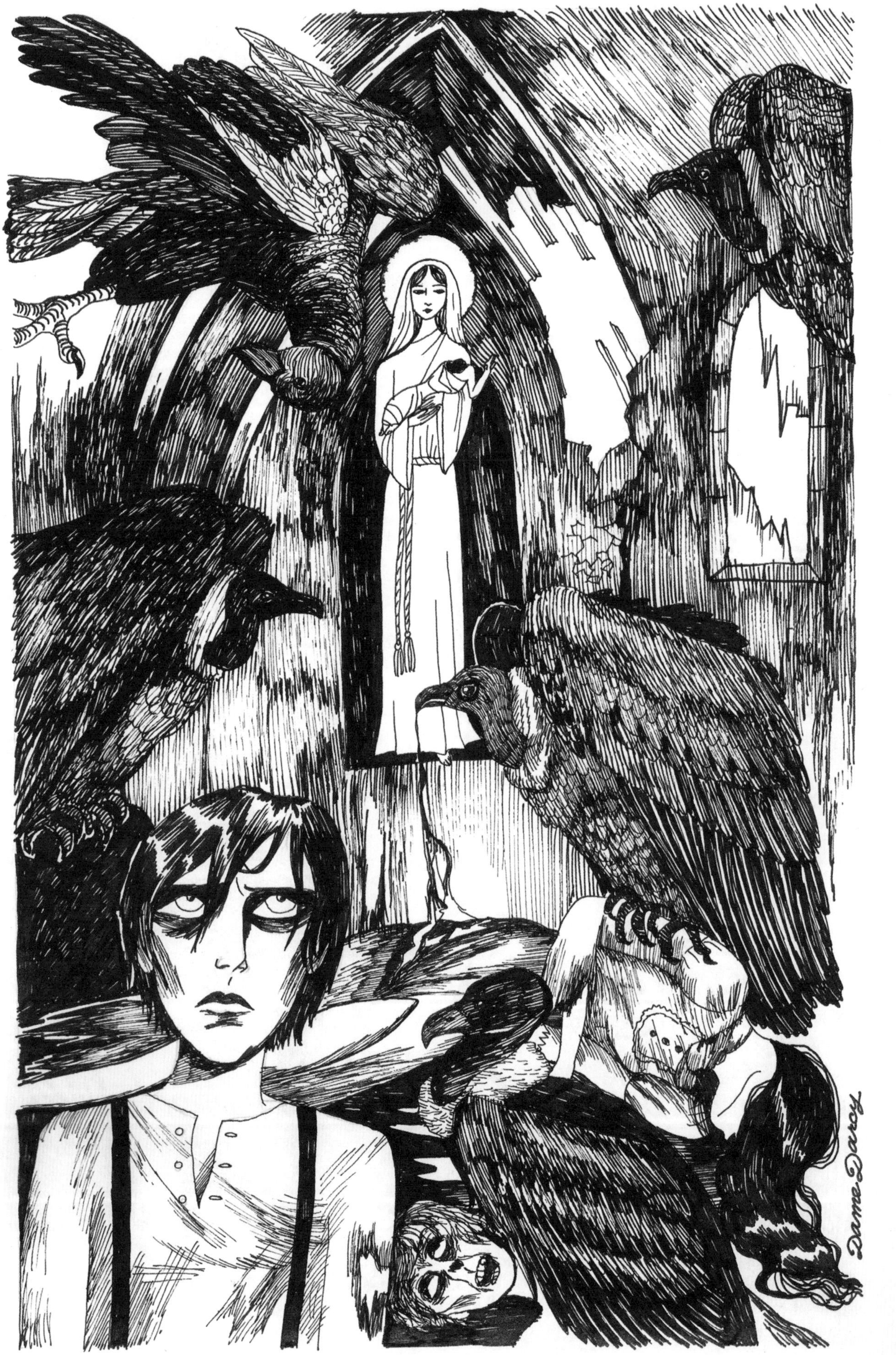
Dame Darcy

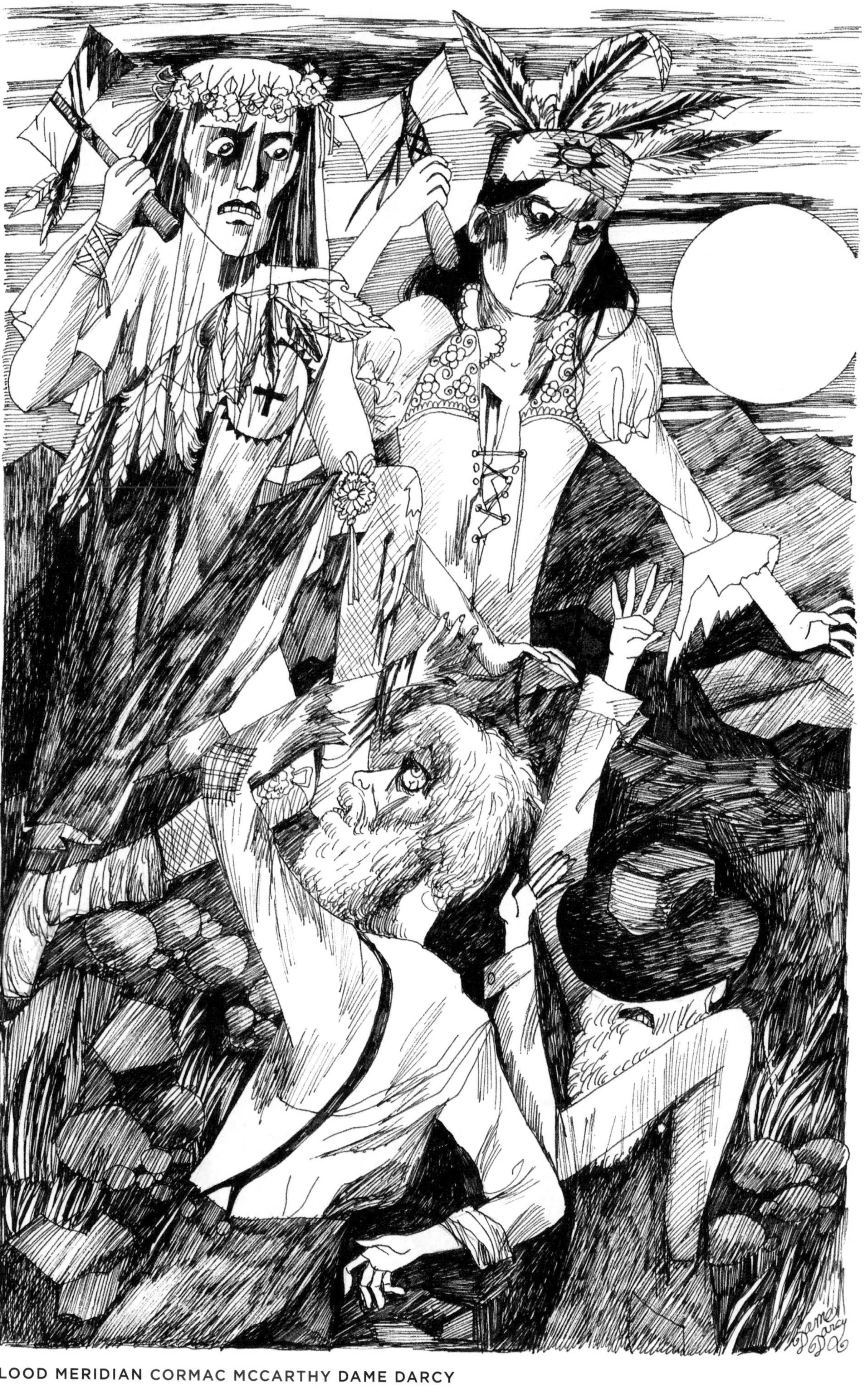

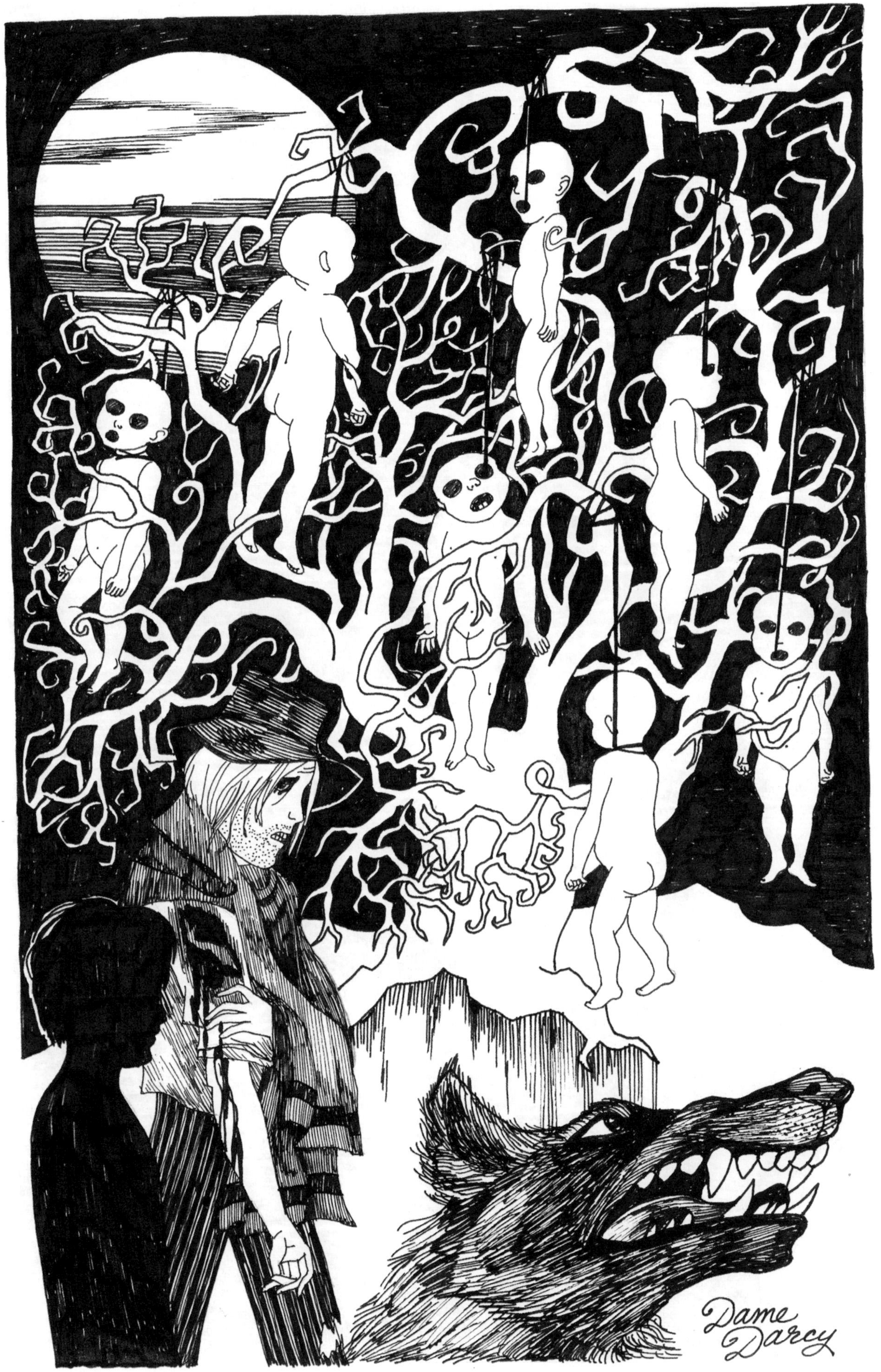
Dame
Darcy

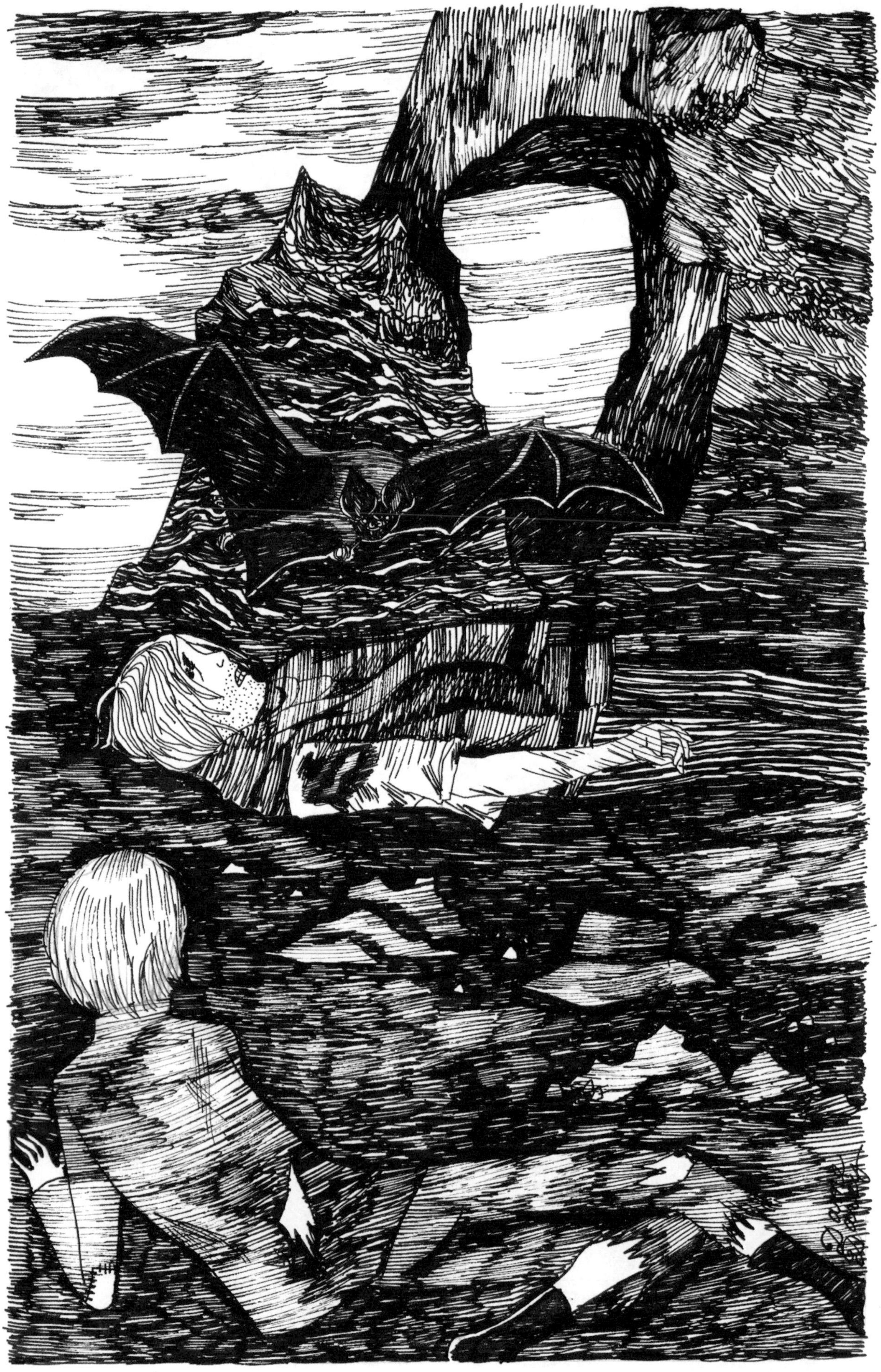

Foucault's Pendulum

Umberto Eco

ART/ADAPTATION BY **Julia Gfrörer**

UMBERTO ECO IS A SMART GUY. A PIONEERING professor of semiotics at the University of Bologna (the world's oldest university), he's also a highly regarded medievalist, as well as an art critic/theorist, philosopher, linguist, and plain old polymath. He writes children's books and graduate-level textbooks, and once curated an exhibition at the Louvre. As of 2008, his private library consisted of 50,000 volumes. According to visitors, lots of them look well-worn. "No man should know so much," Anthony Burgess, author of *A Clockwork Orange*, wrote of him.

In 1980, he penned a medieval monastery murder mystery, *The Name of the Rose*—with heavy doses of theology, philosophy, and shadowy Catholic history—that became an international megaseller (over nine million copies sold). Eight years later, he followed up with the crushingly dense *Foucault's Pendulum*. The three main characters work for a vanity publishing house in Milan, which any number of conspiracy theorists use to self-publish books on their theories. Bored, the three men decide to invent a grand conspiracy of their own, hinging on the Knights Templar but bringing in a huge number of widely scattered conspiracy theories and esoteric beliefs—including the Holy Grail, Kabbalah, alchemy, kundalini yoga, the Illuminati, the Assassins, Nazis, Francis Bacon, orgone energy—all of which Eco explains in extreme detail. A coded manuscript is involved, and even the Eiffel Tower has a hidden role in the conspiracy. They feed every bit of arcane info they can find into a computer to come up with their grand unified theory. However, strange things start happening, real-world events indicating that maybe this conspiracy isn't just a theory after all. (If this sounds a bit like *The Da Vinci Code*, which Dan Brown wrote fifteen years later, they do share some core elements, but what the authors do with them—and how well they do it—is on different orders of magnitude. It's the difference between a Big Mac and filet mignon.)

Publishers Weekly called the novel "a mixture of metaphysical meditation, detective story, computer handbook, introduction to physics and philosophy, historical survey, mathematical puzzle, compendium of religious and cultural mythology, guide to the Torah (Hebrew, rather than Latin contributes to the puzzle here, but is restricted mainly to chapter headings), reference manual to the occult, the hermetic mysteries, the Rosicrucians, the Jesuits, the Freemasons—ad infinitum."

Julia Gfrörer loves the esoteric, the mythological, the literary, and the darkness. She's created two highly regarded comics—*Flesh and Bone* and *Too Dark to See*—and has illustrated one of Oscar Wilde's fairy tales, "The Star Child," for Scout Books. She explains her process here:

> The excerpt I ended up choosing occurs about halfway through the book, the point at which the protagonists and the reader begin to suspect that the supernatural events described by the "diabolicals" aren't entirely the result of delusion. The main characters are attending a gathering of occultists, and the novel's narrator, Casaubon, witnesses an allegorical film (?) projection that describes the alchemical process.
>
> This passage stuck with me because it takes place outside the narrative, more or less, and the imagery is haunting, but to a reader unfamiliar with alchemical philosophy, it could also seem to be arbitrary, like a Marilyn Manson video or something: here's this creepy image! Here's another one! What about this?! Are you creeped out yet?! To me the alchemical metaphor described the process that Casaubon undergoes in the novel, from ignorance and cynicism, to knowledge and enthusiasm, to true awareness and the rejection of didacticism. But of course that interpretation may fall victim to the same error the protagonists of *Foucault's Pendulum* make: the facile assumption that everything can be connected to everything else.
>
> Symbolic analysis is a lifelong passion of mine, and extensive research went into parsing the allegory before I began to draw. I'd like to believe my understanding of it now is reasonably good for a layperson, but there are certain elements I was sworn to secrecy about, and some I think I would prefer not to know too much about. Or maybe it's all nonsense, in which case, you know, I hope it looks pretty.

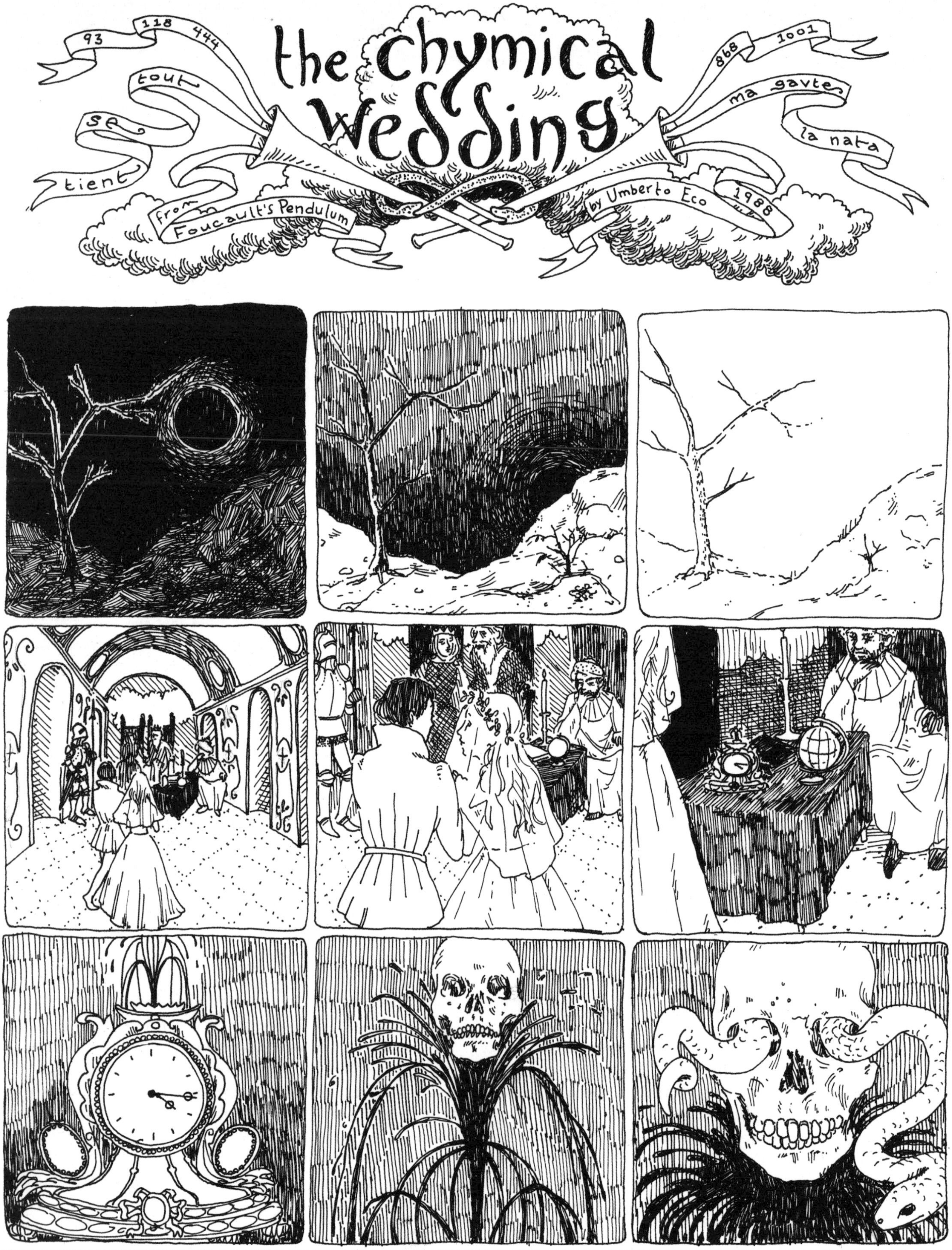
the chymical wedding
93
118
444
tout
se
tient
868
1001
ma gavte
la nata
from Foucault's Pendulum
by Umberto Eco
1988

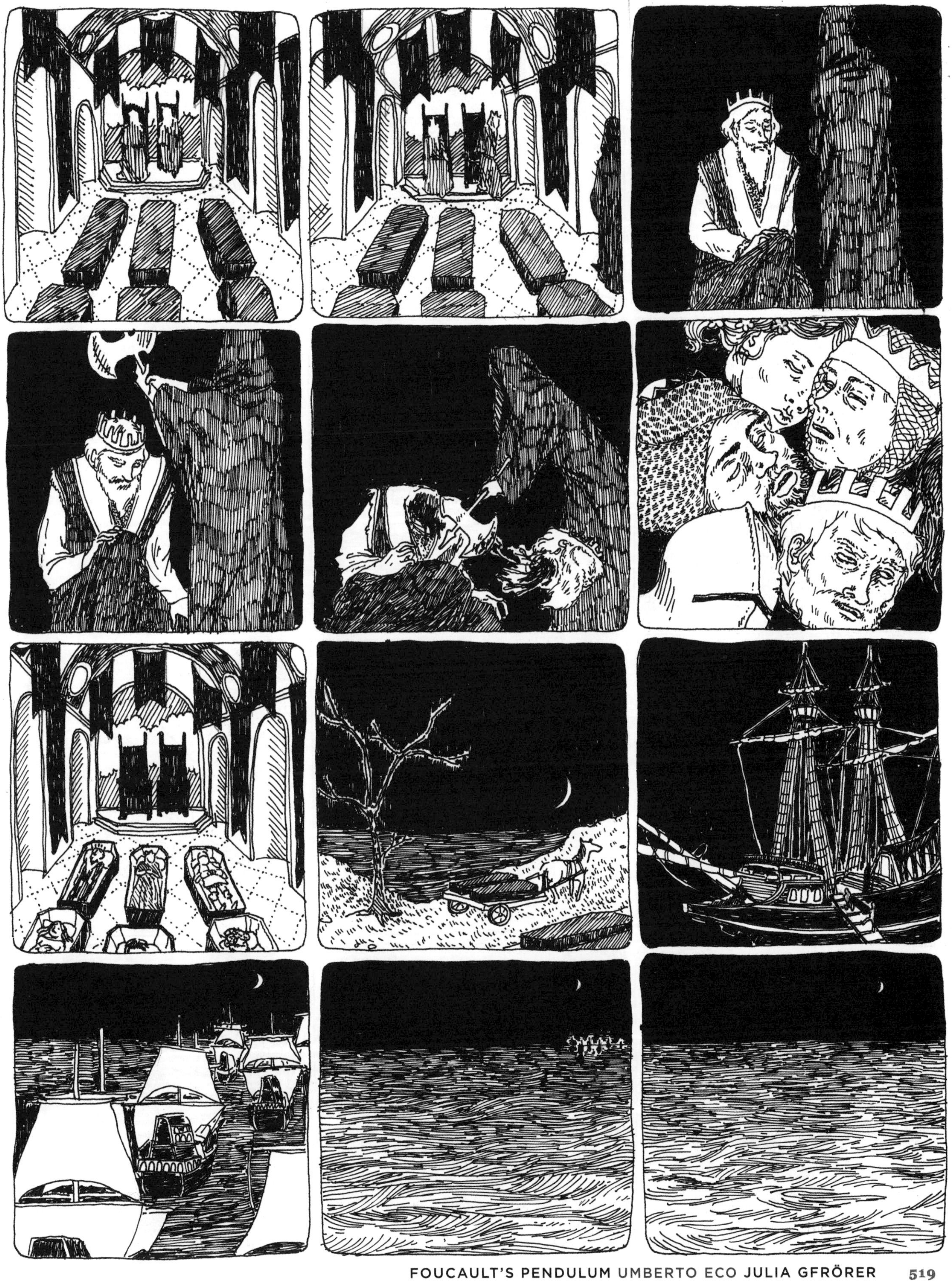

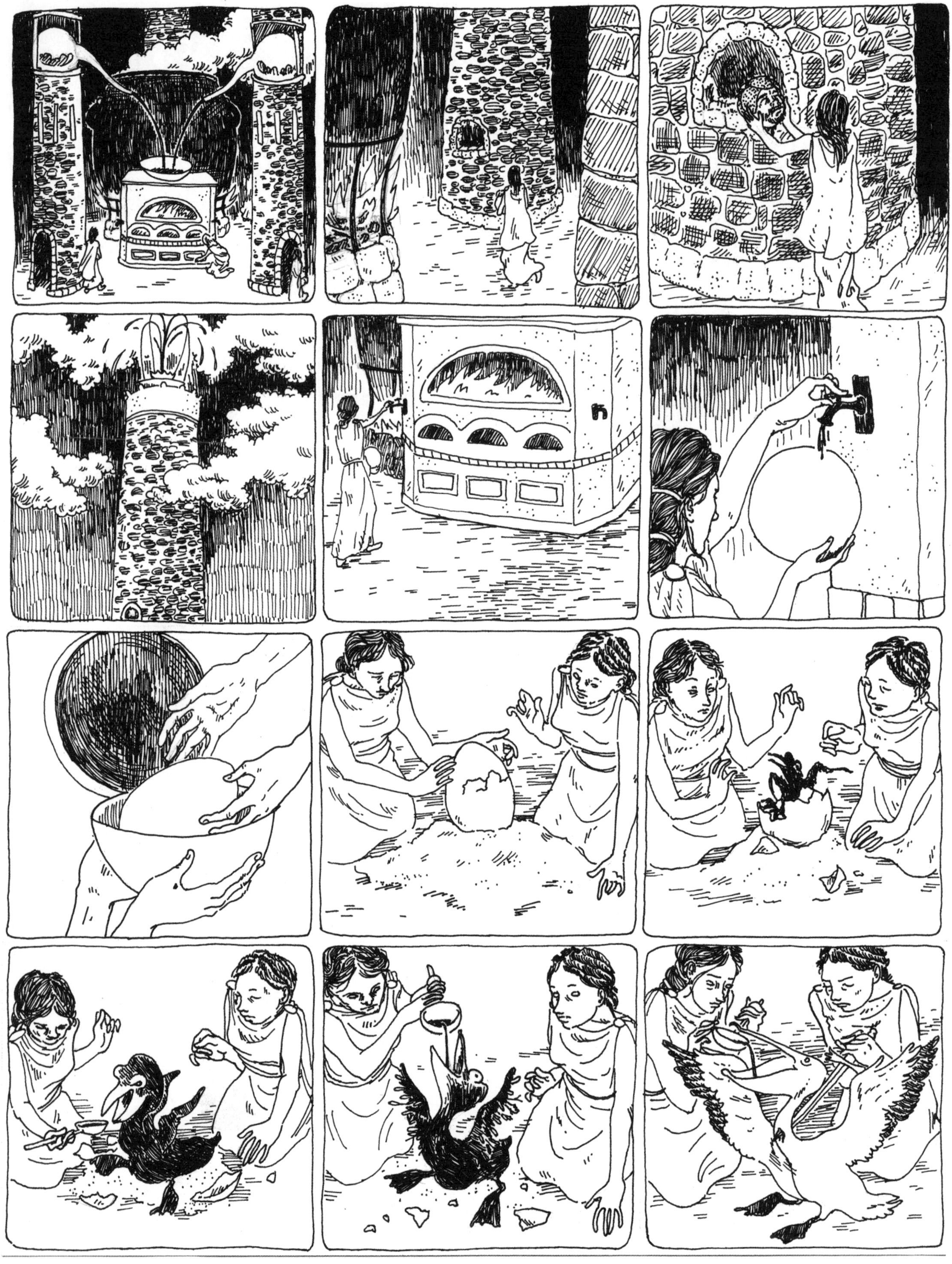

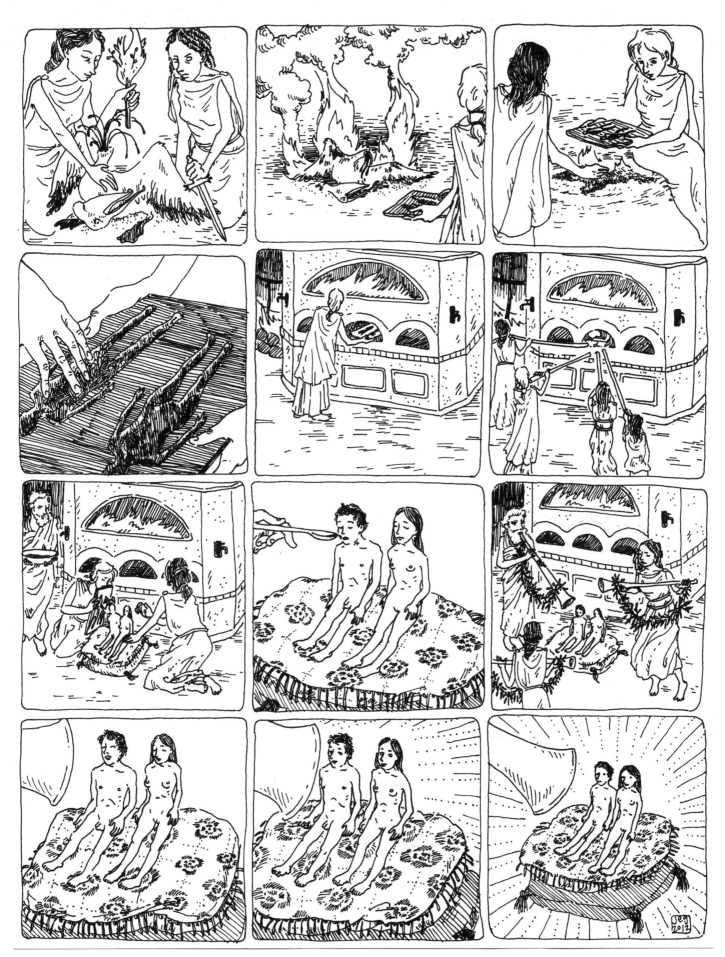

Wild at Heart

Barry Gifford

ART/ADAPTATION BY **Rick Trembles**

THERE'S A GOOD CHANCE YOU'VE SEEN DAVID Lynch's film *Wild at Heart*, starring Nic Cage and Laura Dern as "the Romeo and Juliet of the Deep South," Sailor Ripley and Lula Pace Fortune. Lynch was starting work on *Twin Peaks* when a colleague showed him the unfinished manuscript for the novel *Wild at Heart*—not just unpolished, mind you, but literally incomplete, lacking the final third. He immediately bought the rights and created his highly regarded film version. He changed quite a bit, adding the Elvis and *Wizard of Oz* elements and giving it a totally different ending.

Reading the book itself is a dizzying experience. It's mainly comprised of short chapters of dialog between Sailor and Lula and/or a cast of eccentric and violent characters. The action, plot, character development . . . all of it takes place via the high-octane, trailer-park dialog. The film brought Barry Gifford mainstream recognition after almost twenty years of writing novels and short stories filled with the downtrodden, penning poetry that's been published everywhere from *The New Yorker* to *Esquire* to the *Chicago Review*, and using his position as editor at Black Lizard to resurrect forgotten *noir* crime fiction. He followed up 1990's *Wild at Heart* with six more novels and novellas in the Sailor and Lula cycle. It's rare to read about the books without someone invoking Faulkner, that literary master of Southern weirdness. In fact, the series has been referred to as "Pulp Faulkner."

Andrei Codrescu has proclaimed: "Barry Gifford is both a cult writer and a great one." Jonathan Lethem said: "Barry Gifford invented his own American vernacular—William Faulkner by way of B-movie film noir, porn paperbacks, and Sun Records rockabilly—to forge the stealth-epic of *Sailor & Lula*. His accomplishment looks more and more like one of the permanent glories of recent storytelling . . ." And the *San Francisco Chronicle* chimed in: "Gifford has been the master of hip disenfranchisement for more than a quarter of a century, and American literature is much better for his efforts."

To adapt *Wild at Heart*, I turned to Rick Trembles, known for being wild at heart himself. For the last thirty-five years, he's been igniting Montreal with his raw, transgressive music, film, comics, and sculptures. Robert Crumb called him "even more twisted and weird than me," and said of his comic *How Did I Get So Anal?*: "I've never seen anything so disgusting. Interesting, but bleeeeechhhh!" Chester Brown (author of *Paying For It*, *The Playboy*, and others) cites him as a major influence. Since 1985, Rick's been producing cynical, hilarious movie reviews in the form of single-page comics called *Motion Picture Purgatory*, which have been collected in two volumes. Rick gives us the entire *Wild at Heart* in four pages, and it sails by at an even faster clip than the book itself, which hardly seems possible. Speed Pulp Faulkner.

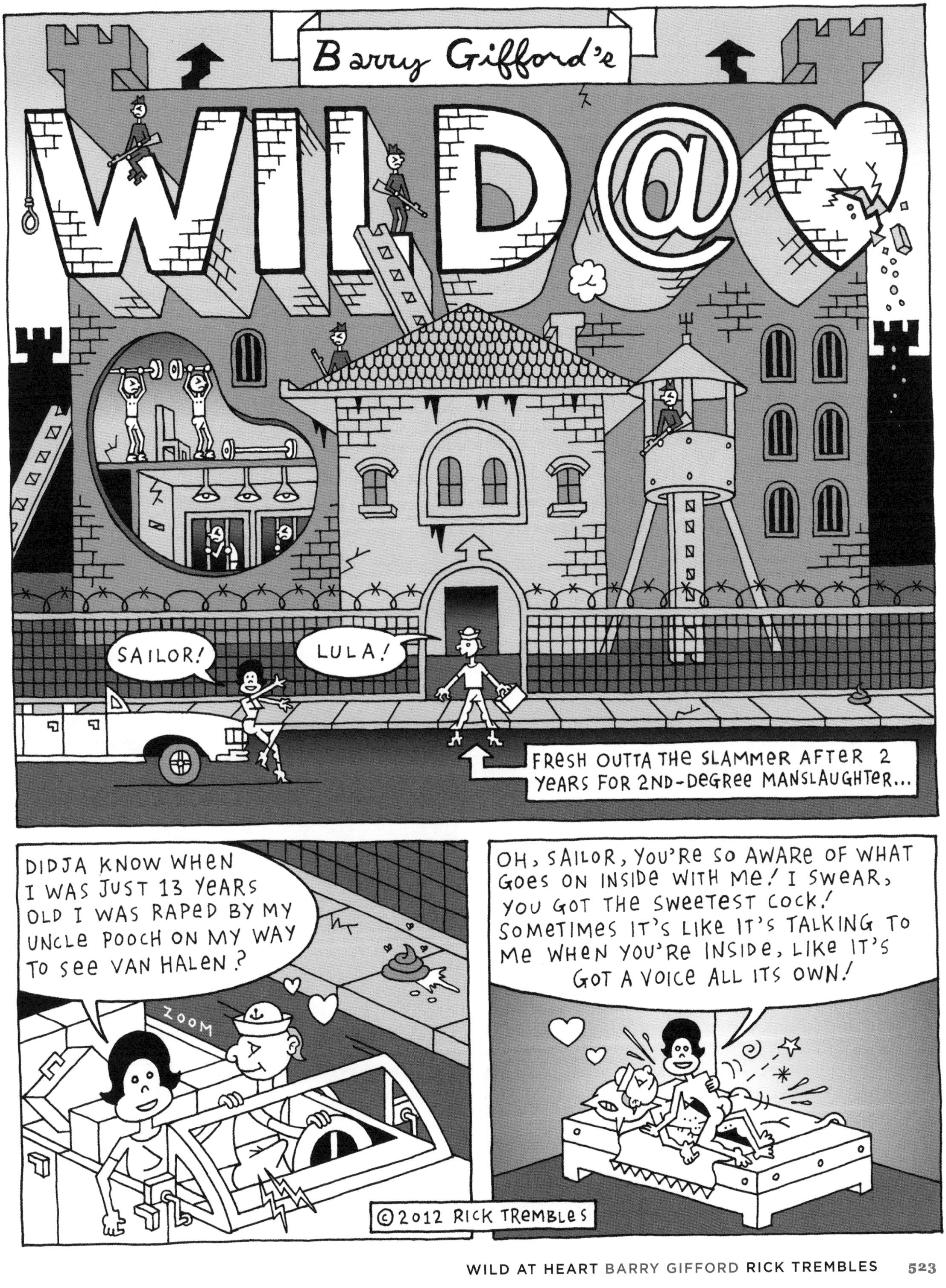
Barry Gifford's
WILD @ ♥
SAILOR!
LULA!
FRESH OUTTA THE SLAMMER AFTER 2 YEARS FOR 2ND-DEGREE MANSLAUGHTER...
DIDJA KNOW WHEN I WAS JUST 13 YEARS OLD I WAS RAPED BY MY UNCLE POOCH ON MY WAY TO SEE VAN HALEN?
ZOOM
OH, SAILOR, YOU'RE SO AWARE OF WHAT GOES ON INSIDE WITH ME! I SWEAR, YOU GOT THE SWEETEST COCK! SOMETIMES IT'S LIKE IT'S TALKING TO ME WHEN YOU'RE INSIDE, LIKE IT'S GOT A VOICE ALL ITS OWN!
©2012 RICK TREMBLES

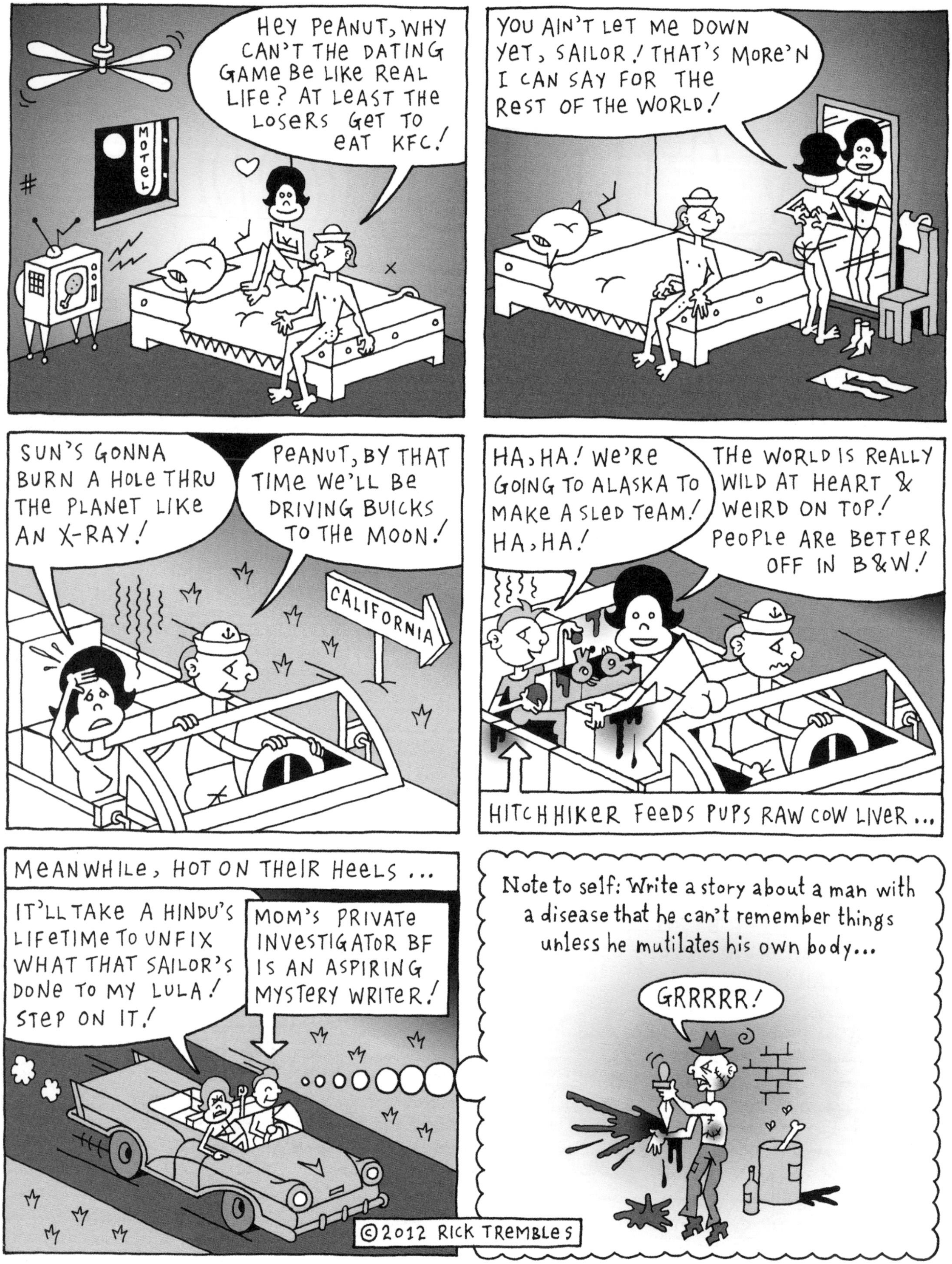
M
O
T
E
L
HEY PEANUT, WHY CAN'T THE DATING GAME BE LIKE REAL LIFE? AT LEAST THE LOSERS GET TO EAT KFC!
YOU AIN'T LET ME DOWN YET, SAILOR! THAT'S MORE'N I CAN SAY FOR THE REST OF THE WORLD!
SUN'S GONNA BURN A HOLE THRU THE PLANET LIKE AN X-RAY!
PEANUT, BY THAT TIME WE'LL BE DRIVING BUICKS TO THE MOON!
CALIFORNIA
HA, HA! WE'RE GOING TO ALASKA TO MAKE A SLED TEAM! HA, HA!
THE WORLD IS REALLY WILD AT HEART & WEIRD ON TOP! PEOPLE ARE BETTER OFF IN B&W!
HITCHHIKER FEEDS PUPS RAW COW LIVER...
MEANWHILE, HOT ON THEIR HEELS...
IT'LL TAKE A HINDU'S LIFETIME TO UNFIX WHAT THAT SAILOR'S DONE TO MY LULA! STEP ON IT!
MOM'S PRIVATE INVESTIGATOR BF IS AN ASPIRING MYSTERY WRITER!
Note to self: Write a story about a man with a disease that he can't remember things unless he mutilates his own body...
GRRRRR!
©2012 RICK TREMBLES

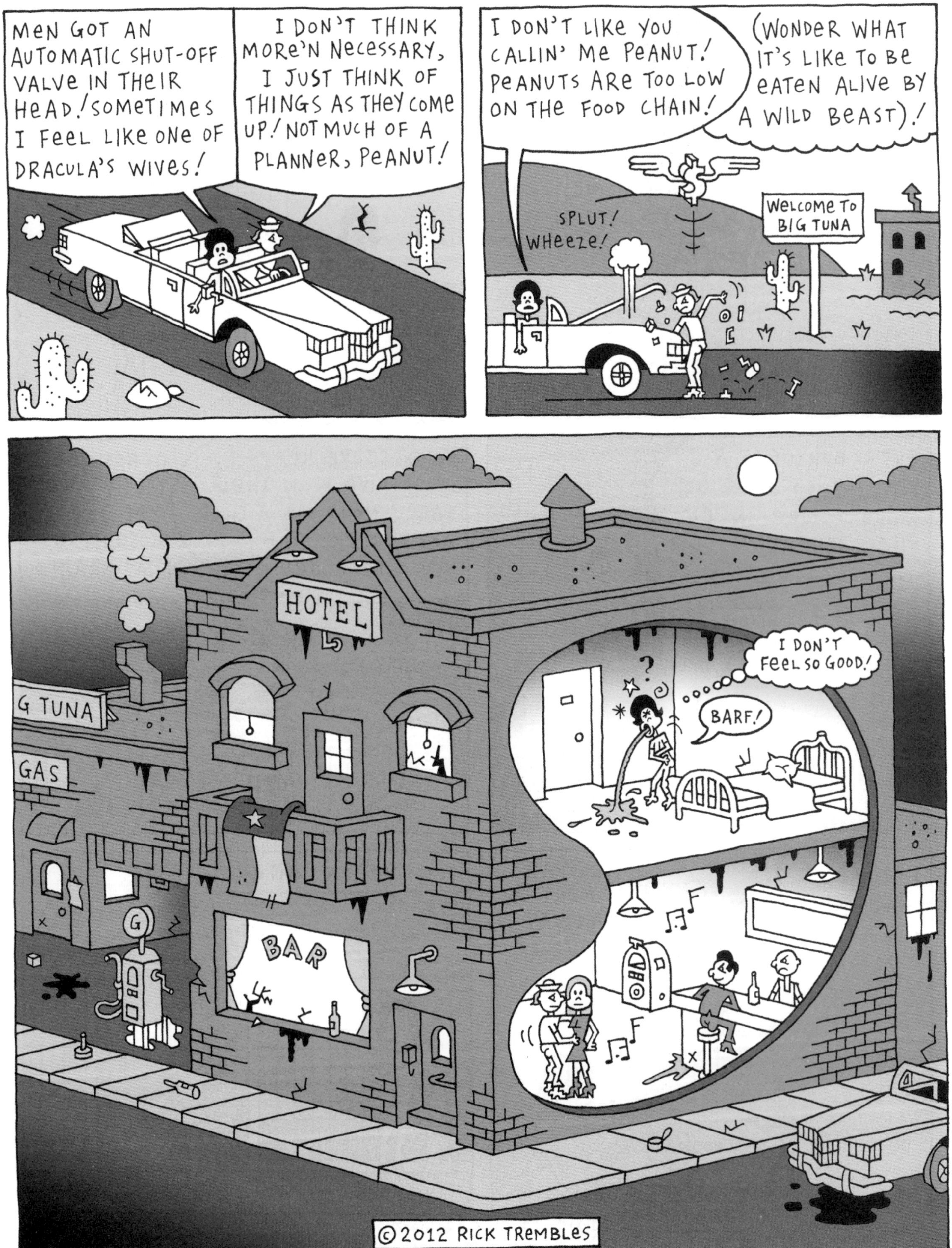

MEN GOT AN AUTOMATIC SHUT-OFF VALVE IN THEIR HEAD! SOMETIMES I FEEL LIKE ONE OF DRACULA'S WIVES!
I DON'T THINK MORE'N NECESSARY, I JUST THINK OF THINGS AS THEY COME UP! NOT MUCH OF A PLANNER, PEANUT!
I DON'T LIKE YOU CALLIN' ME PEANUT! PEANUTS ARE TOO LOW ON THE FOOD CHAIN!
(WONDER WHAT IT'S LIKE TO BE EATEN ALIVE BY A WILD BEAST)!
SPLUT!
WHEEZE!
WELCOME TO BIG TUNA
HOTEL
G TUNA
GAS
BAR
I DON'T FEEL SO GOOD!
BARF!
©2012 RICK TREMBLES

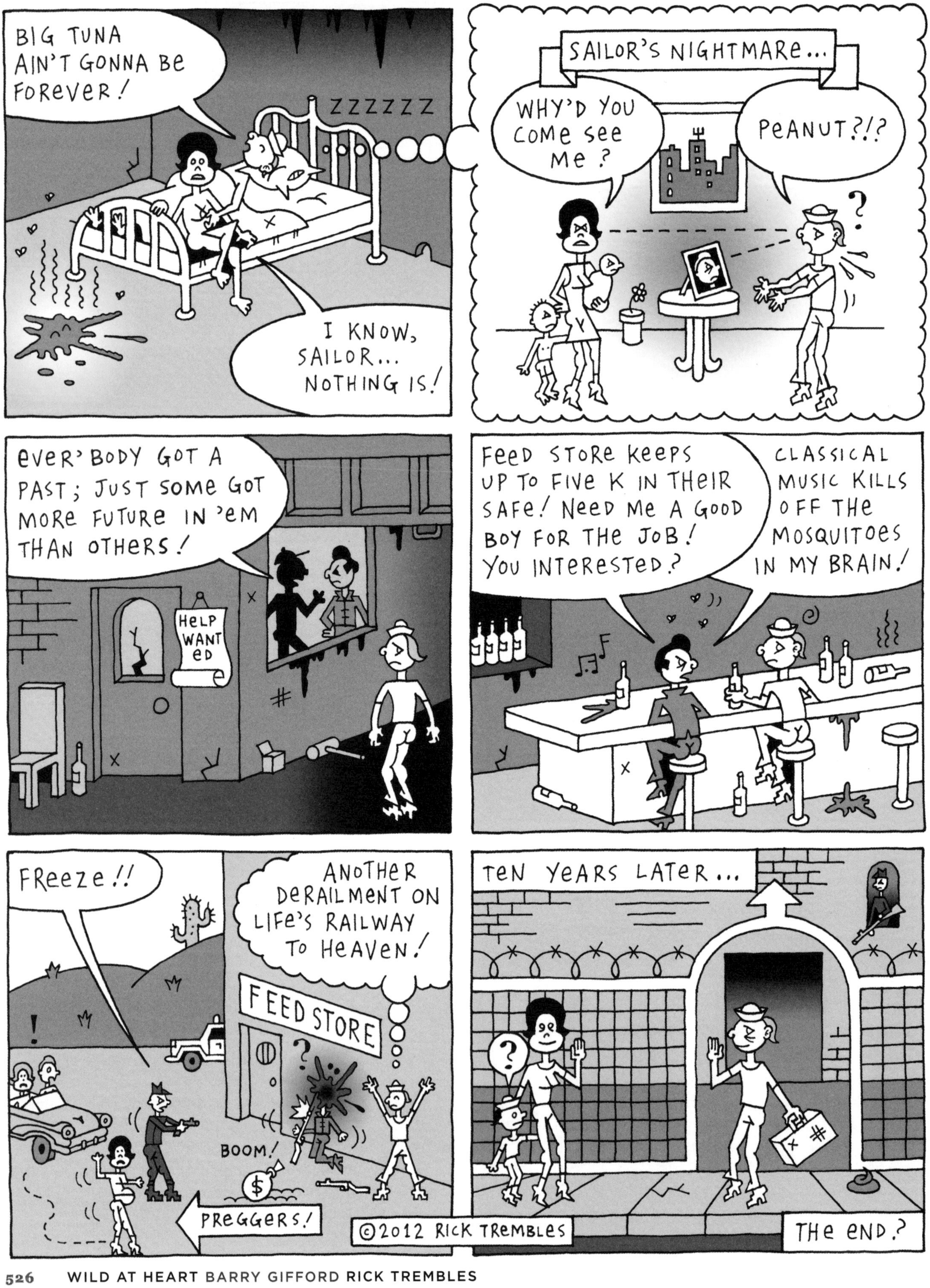
BIG TUNA AIN'T GONNA BE FOREVER!
ZZZZZZ
I KNOW, SAILOR... NOTHING IS!
SAILOR'S NIGHTMARE...
WHY'D YOU COME SEE ME?
PEANUT?!?
?
EVER'BODY GOT A PAST; JUST SOME GOT MORE FUTURE IN 'EM THAN OTHERS!
HELP WANTED
FEED STORE KEEPS UP TO FIVE K IN THEIR SAFE! NEED ME A GOOD BOY FOR THE JOB! YOU INTERESTED?
CLASSICAL MUSIC KILLS OFF THE MOSQUITOES IN MY BRAIN!
FREEZE!!
ANOTHER DERAILMENT ON LIFE'S RAILWAY TO HEAVEN!
FEED STORE
BOOM!
$
PREGGERS!
©2012 RICK TREMBLES
TEN YEARS LATER...
?
THE END?

The Famished Road

Ben Okri

ART/ADAPTATION BY **Aidan Koch**

BEN OKRI OF NIGERIA WRITES IN THE MAGICAL realist tradition pioneered by Gabriel García Márquez, Salman Rushdie, and Angela Carter. The Booker Prize–winning *The Famished Road*—one of the greatest African novels of the twentieth century—slips in and out of reality (it's up to you to decide where to draw the line) as it's narrated by Azaro, a "ghost child"—the Nigerian name for a child who almost dies at birth, then spends his life with a foot in both worlds, able to see the dead, demons, and other spirits. Azaro tells of violent, poverty-stricken life in his village and his struggle to not just chuck it all and return to the land of spirits. In a review on Goodreads, Justin Mitchell

says: "Imagine reading a David Lynch movie taking place in Africa with a script by Karl Marx and you've got some idea of what you're in for."

Aidan Koch likes to explore the interzones in her art—for Volume 1, she interpreted Shakespeare's gender-bending Sonnet 20; Volume 2 contains her version of William Blake's mystical "Auguries of Innocence." Here is her muted take on this hallucinatory, mythopoeic 1991 novel of life in post-colonial Africa.

"Beware of the stories you read or tell," Okri once said; "subtly, at night, beneath the waters of consciousness, they are altering your world."

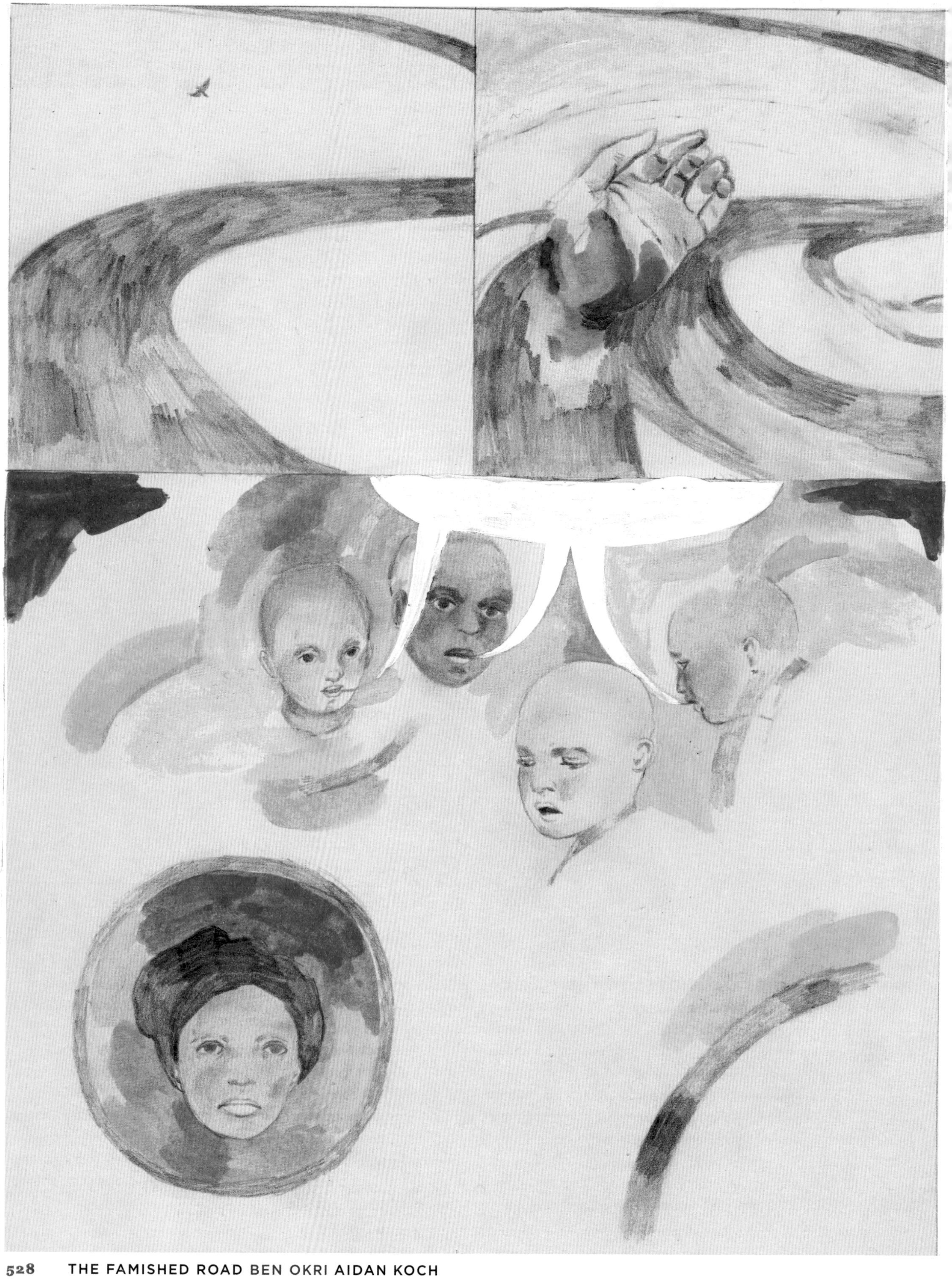

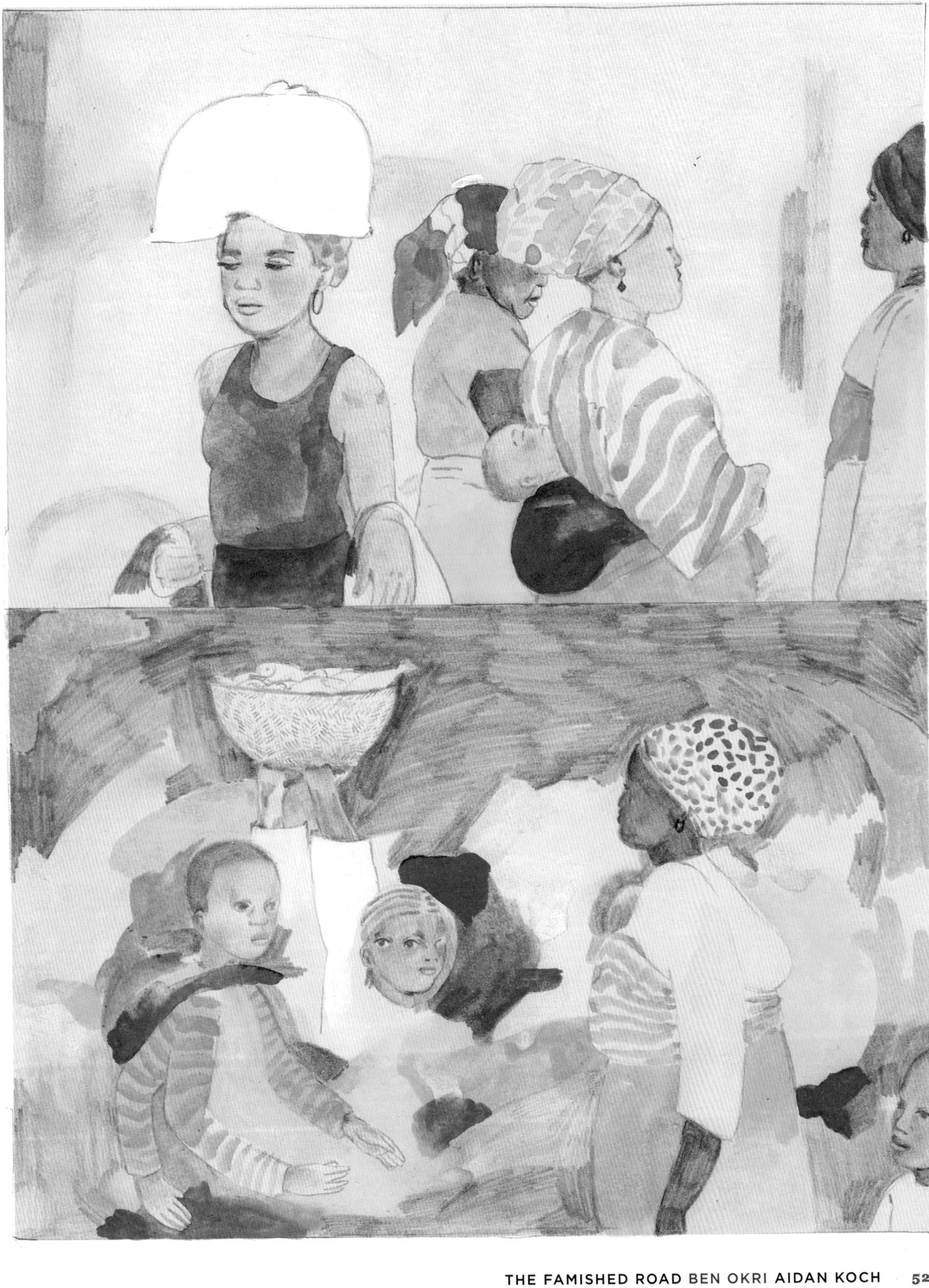

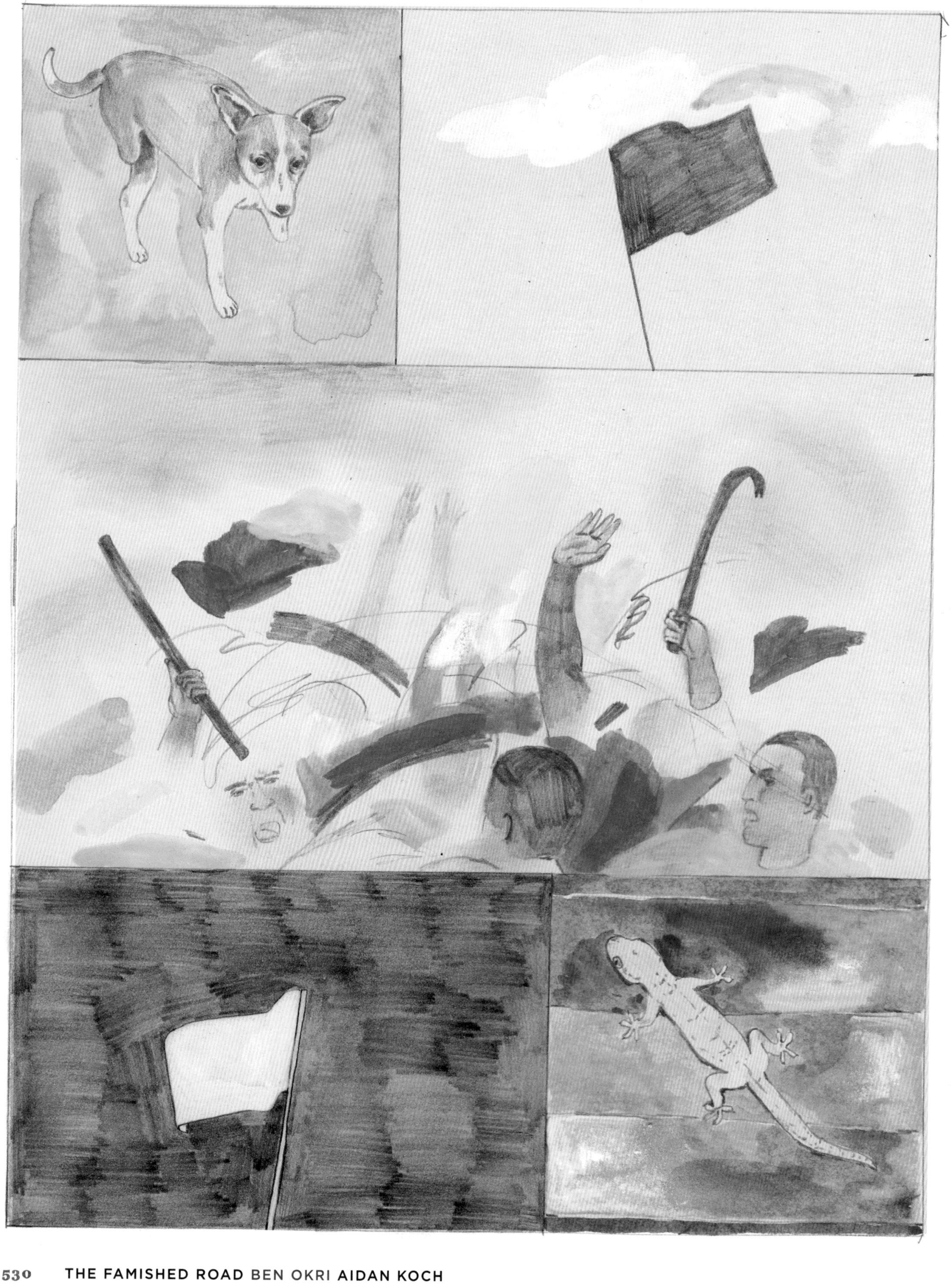

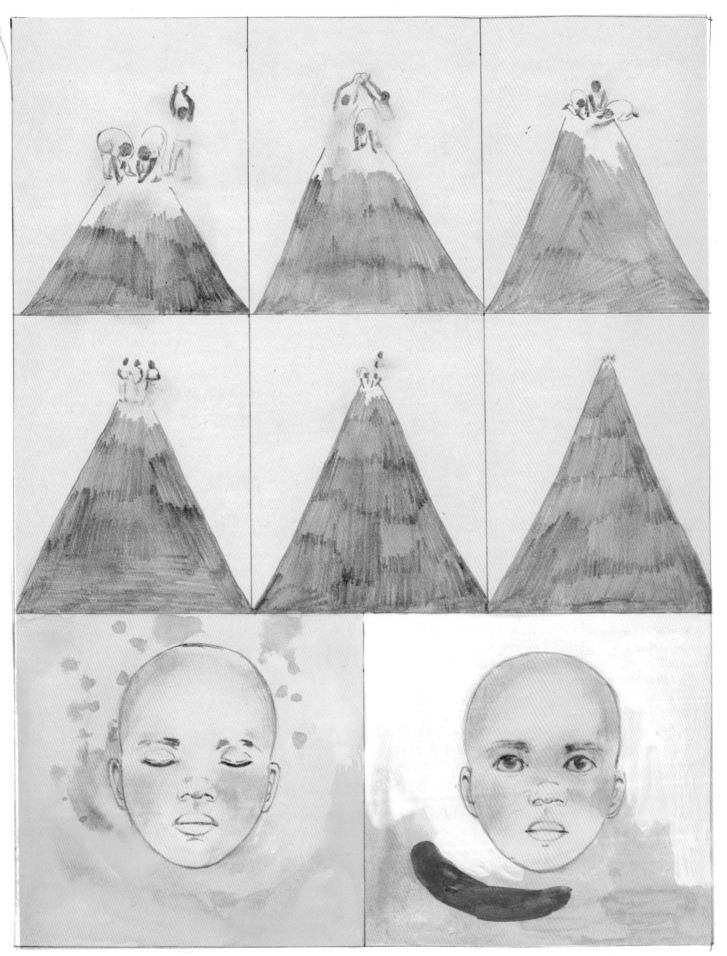

Einstein's Dreams

Alan Lightman

ART/ADAPTATION BY **Rey Ortega**

AS WE GET REALLY CLOSE TO THE PRESENT, determining which works are canonical—which will be considered classics decades from now—becomes much more of a judgment call. *Einstein's Dreams* is a controversial choice, but in twenty years, this slim volume has developed hallmarks of a classic—widely taught and studied in universities, an inspiration for works of performing and visual art, translated into thirty languages, often referred to as a masterpiece and compared to the works of Italo Calvino and Jorge Luis Borges.

We find Albert Einstein in 1905, still a patent clerk in Switzerland, his brain churning with this new theory of relativity that he's cooking up. The meat of the book is thirty dreams that Einstein has, lyrically written vignettes in which the nature of time is conceived in radically diverse ways. In one, "time is a circle, bending back on itself. The world repeats itself, precisely, endlessly." Later, Einstein dreams that every decision point creates precisely three forks, in which different timelines happen simultaneously. In other

dreams, time is frozen, runs backward, spirals, strobes, or goes at varying speeds depending on location; people live in an eternal now, not experiencing a past or future.

Now, if this were simply a collection of entertaining ideas about the possible nature of time, it would be a fun, brain-percolating read, but it wouldn't really be literature. MIT professor Alan Lightman lifts *Einstein's Dreams* above a mere theoretical physics textbook by using these thought exercises to examine the human condition, to look at how we live our lives. How do we use our time now, as we experience it? How would our lives, our memories, our actions, our priorities, and our society be different if time operated differently? Work, play, friendship, families, love and sex, death, joy, sadness . . . Lightman looks at how all of these would be affected.

Toronto's Rey Ortega brings his delicate colors to three of Einstein's time-dreams, nicely tied together by a flowing river. . . .

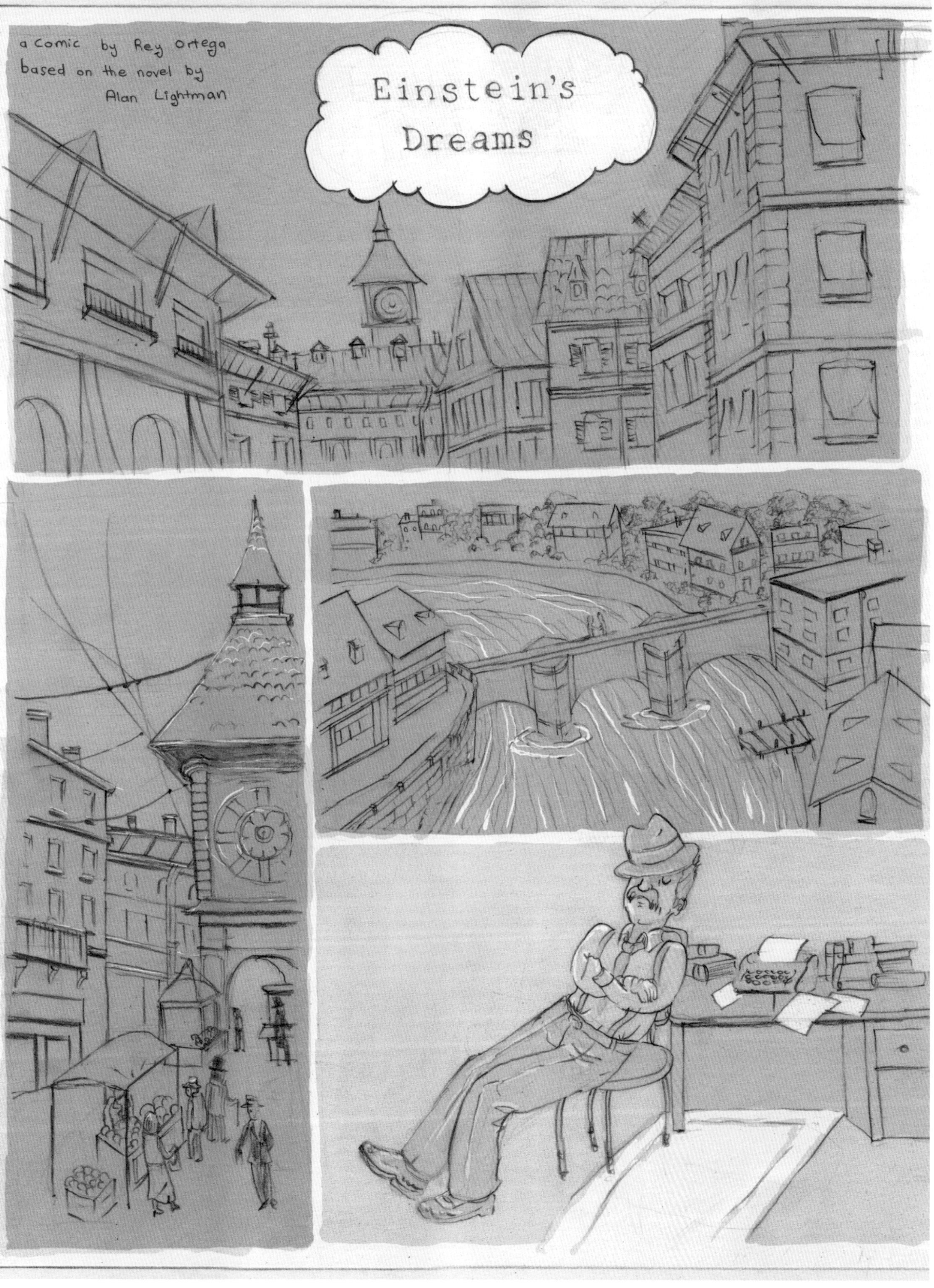
a Comic by Rey Ortega
based on the novel by
Alan Lightman
Einstein's
Dreams

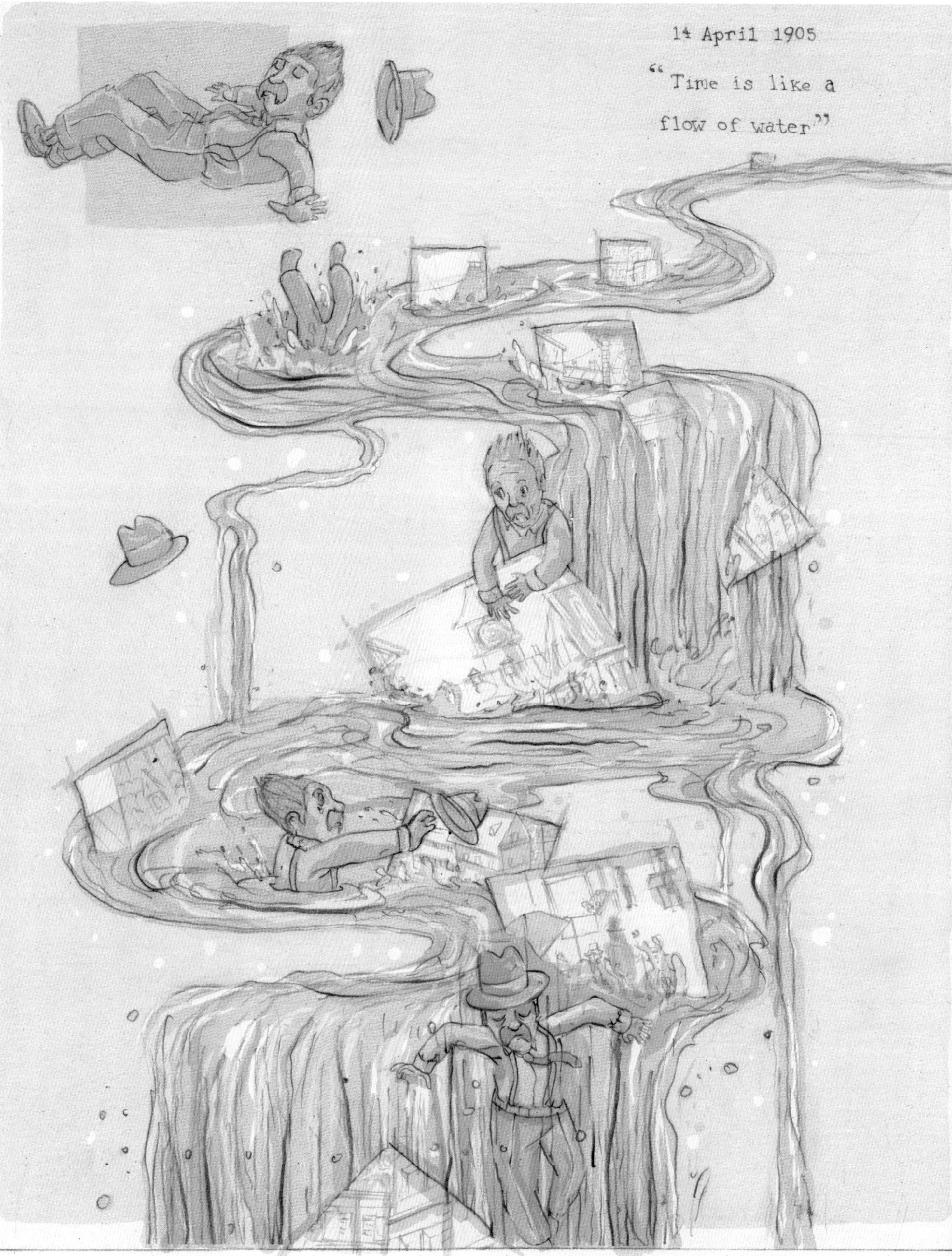
14 April 1905
"Time is like a flow of water"

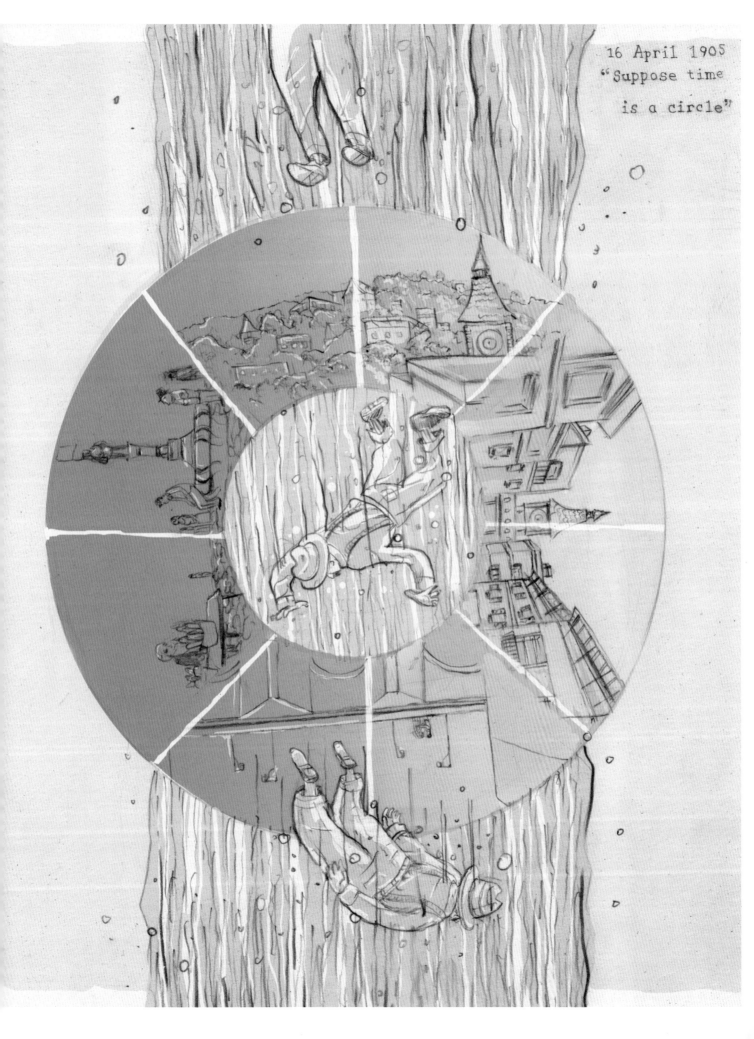

16 April 1905
"Suppose time
is a circle"

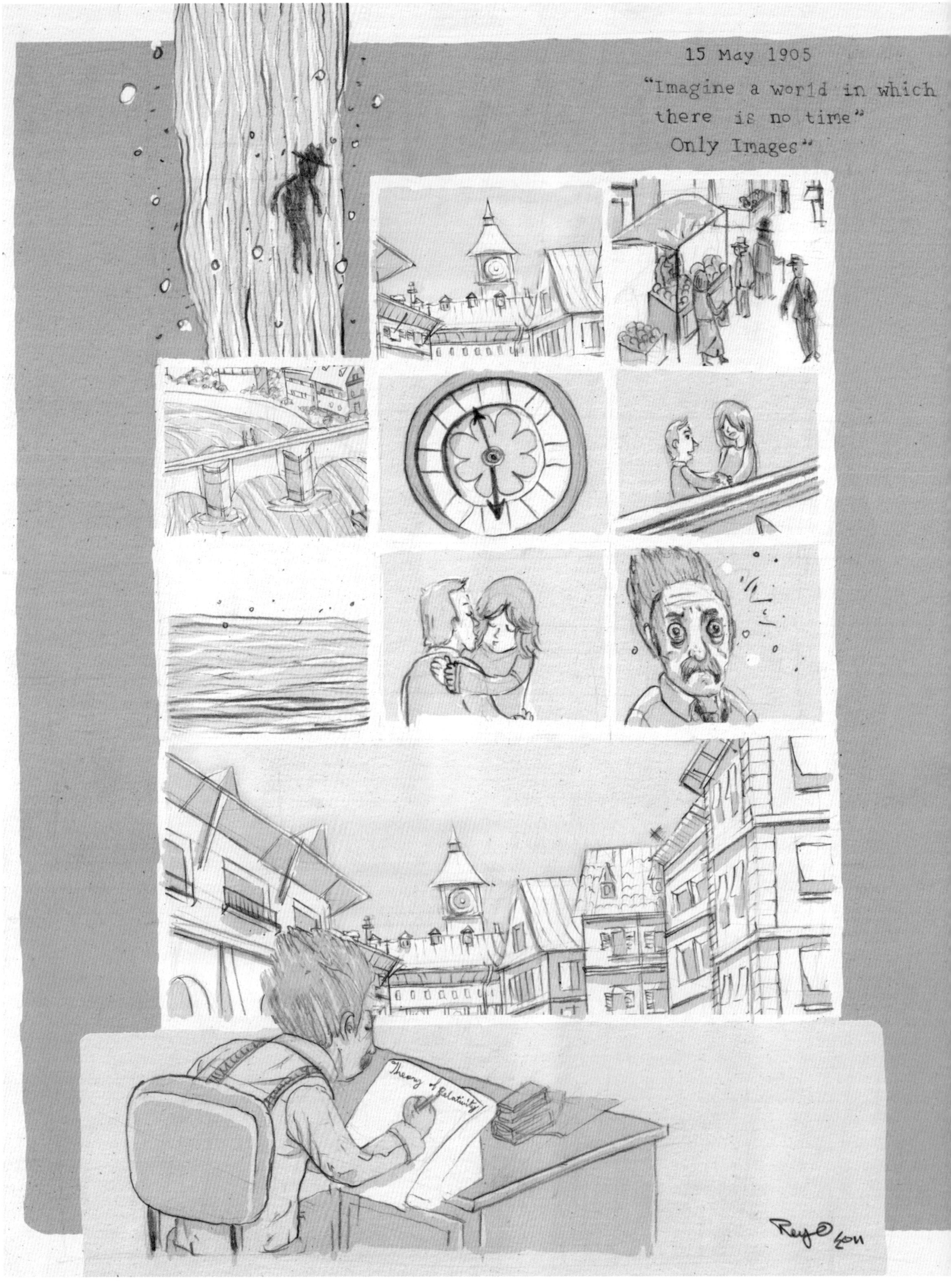
15 May 1905
"Imagine a world in which there is no time"
Only Images"
Theory of Relativity

The Wind-Up Bird Chronicle

Haruki Murakami

ILLUSTRATION BY **Rey Ortega**

HARUKI MURAKAMI IS JAPAN'S PREEMINENT author on the international literary stage. *The New York Times* notes: "Western critics searching for parallels have variously likened him to Raymond Carver, Raymond Chandler, Arthur C. Clarke, Don DeLillo, Philip K. Dick, Bret Easton Ellis and Thomas Pynchon—a roster so ill assorted as to suggest that Murakami may in fact be an original." The reviewer then goes on to identify elements of Hemingway ("bluntness"), Kafka ("alienation" and "waking dreams"), and James Joyce ("range of literary forms") in *The Wind-Up Bird Chronicle*, Murakami's breakthrough novel, published in three separate volumes in 1994–95. It hinges on Toru Okada, an unmotivated, unemployed milquetoast who meets a slew of oddball characters when he searches for his lost cat, then for his wife when she goes missing.

The novel resembles a dream, shot through with illogic, hazy strangeness, and mysticism. There's a touch of magical realism and some surrealism, too. Toru finds escape from the world by spending time at the bottom of a dried-out well behind his house. But even here the weirdness follows

him, as he seems to (or maybe not) find a passage to a hotel room where he has sex with a woman who gives him healing powers. "I had a dream," he says of this encounter. "But it was not a dream. It was some kind of something that happened to take the form of a dream." Someone pulls up the rope ladder he used to climb down, and he finds himself trapped.

Rey Ortega chose to illustrate this pivotal scene of Toru's transformative time at the bottom of a dark well. He says:

> *The Wind-Up Bird Chronicle* piece went through many different iterations before I settled on the one presented here. So much happens in the book that it would have been a mistake to represent it all in a single image. Instead I focused on the main character being stuck in a well, and how in that emptiness many thoughts, for better or for worse, can come unwarranted. I also wanted the figure to almost disappear into the well. So much of the book is about the deconstruction of this man, that it felt appropriate to have him lost here in nothingness.

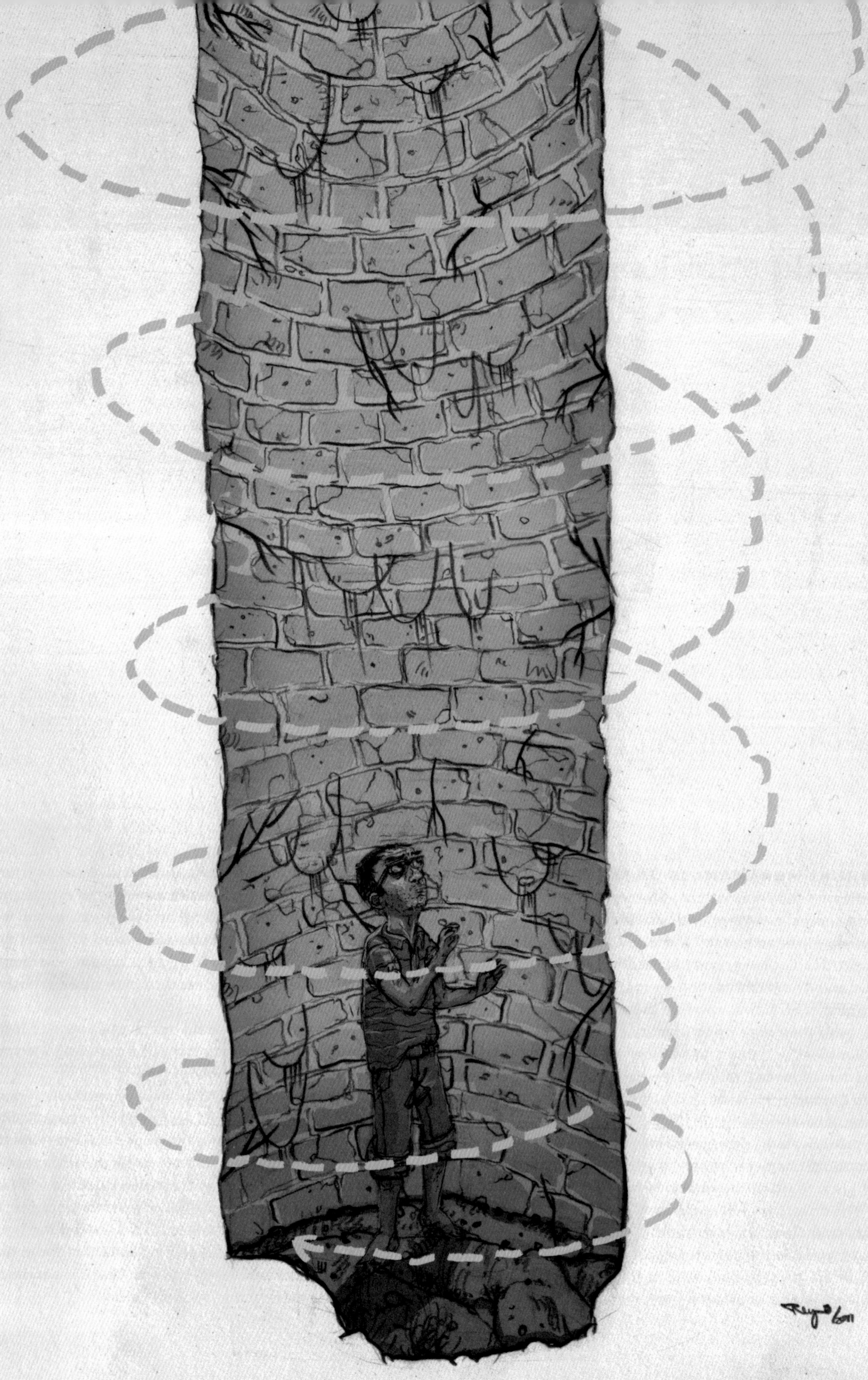

Infinite Jest

David Foster Wallace

ILLUSTRATIONS BY **Benjamin Birdie**

PRETTY MUCH EVERYONE AGREES THAT ONE OF THE latest novels to be assured of classic literary status is David Foster Wallace's 1996 magnum opus, *Infinite Jest*. When Wallace—a prodigy in academics, writing, and tennis, who struggled with depression most of his life—hanged himself in 2008 at age forty-six, the *New York Times* obituary described him thus:

> A versatile writer of seemingly bottomless energy, Mr. Wallace was a maximalist, exhibiting in his work a huge, even manic curiosity—about the physical world, about the much larger universe of human feelings and about the complexity of living in America at the end of the 20th century. He wrote long books, complete with reflective and often hilariously self-conscious footnotes, and he wrote long sentences, with the playfulness of a master punctuater and the inventiveness of a genius grammarian. Critics often noted that he was not only an experimenter and a showoff, but also a God-fearing moralist with a fierce honesty in confronting the existence of contradiction.

. . .

Mr. Wallace was best known for his mammoth 1996 novel, *"Infinite Jest"* (Little, Brown), a 1,079-page monster that perceives American society as self-obsessed, pleasure-obsessed and entertainment-obsessed. (The president, Johnny Gentle, is a former singer.) The title refers to an elusive film that terrorists are trying to get their hands on because to watch it is to be debilitated, even killed, or so it's said, by enjoyment. The main characters are a stressed-out tennis prodigy and a former thief and drug addict, and they give rise to harrowing passages about panic attacks and detox freak-outs. The book attracted a cult of fans (and critics too) for its subversive writing, which was by turns hallucinogenically stream of consciousness, jubilantly anecdotal, winkingly sardonic and self-consciously literary.

DFW could've put his virtuosic skills to work in the service of irony. Given the time period, it would've been a natural, predictable thing for a young, postmodern writer to do. Way before 9/11 had cultural critics emptily promising "the death of irony" (if only . . .), Wallace was forcefully rejecting that smarmy, hollow approach, and urging other writers to do likewise. He was not interested in being the cool, detached kid taking potshots at everything that he felt was stupid and beneath him in the world. Instead, he was about sincerity, about authenticity. Famously, he said: "Fiction's about what it is to be a fucking human being." He talked of fiction being "nourishing, redemptive"; by reading it "we become less alone inside." He wanted to write fiction that makes people feel emotions. He was very aware that he was risking being laughed at—ridiculed for being sentimental and naïve—for saying such earnest things, yet still he would tell an interviewer for *The Review of Contemporary Fiction*:

> Look, man, we'd probably most of us agree that these are dark times, and stupid ones, but do we need fiction that does nothing but dramatize how dark and stupid everything is? In dark times, the definition of good art would seem to be art that locates and applies CPR to those elements of what's human and magical that still live and glow despite the times' darkness. Really good fiction could have as dark a worldview as it wished, but it'd find a way both to depict this world and to illuminate the possibilities for being alive and human in it.

Benjamin Birdie gets the exuberance and humor of *Infinite Jest*. In these colorful full-page illustrations, the dark humor, bathroom jokes, and outright gags come through. In the first illustration, high-school tennis whiz Hal Incandenza, being grilled on his academic record by several deans and other administration officials at the University of Arizona, has some kind of horrendous seizure/breakdown that greatly disturbs everyone present. Next, Hal's older brother Mario has his "first and only even remotely romantic experience, thus far," with a large female tennis player. Then we see Hal's best friend, Michael Pemulis, the tennis academy's drug dealer, who also makes money selling clean urine to beat drug tests.

The final two images come from the book's epic fight scene, in which three members of a Quebec separatist/terrorist group try to forcibly kidnap one of the residents of the halfway house. Joelle Van Dyne is leaning out the window, yelling during the melee. She's so impossibly beautiful that men go mad when they see her (shades of Remedios the Beauty from *One Hundred Years of Solitude* earlier in this volume!); thus, she must always wear a veil. (Or maybe it's because she was beautiful but got accidentally scarred by acid. The reader never knows for certain.) The physically huge Don Gately runs the drug and alcohol treatment program and, feeling responsible for the tenants, pulverizes the Canadians though shot in the shoulder.

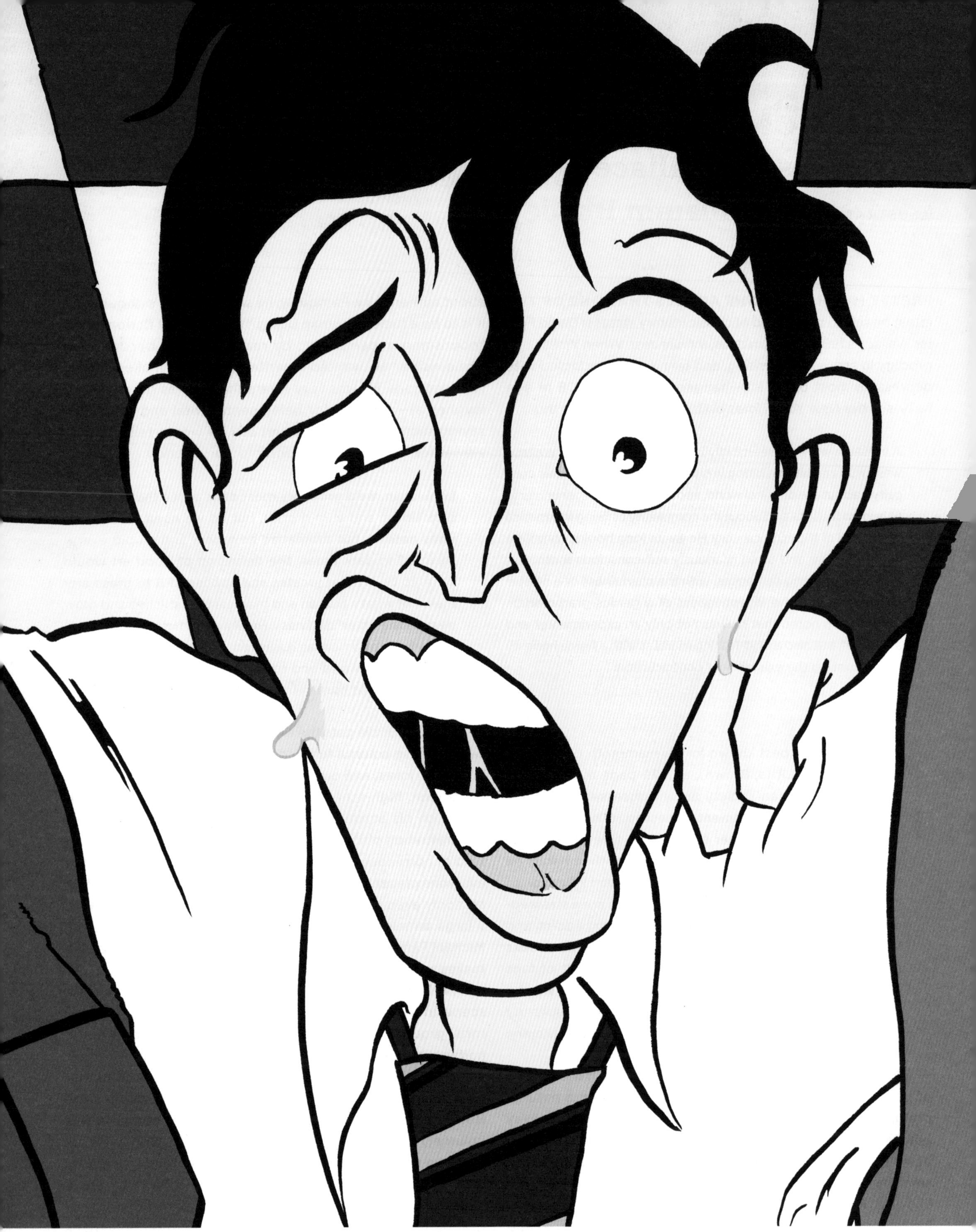

I am in here.

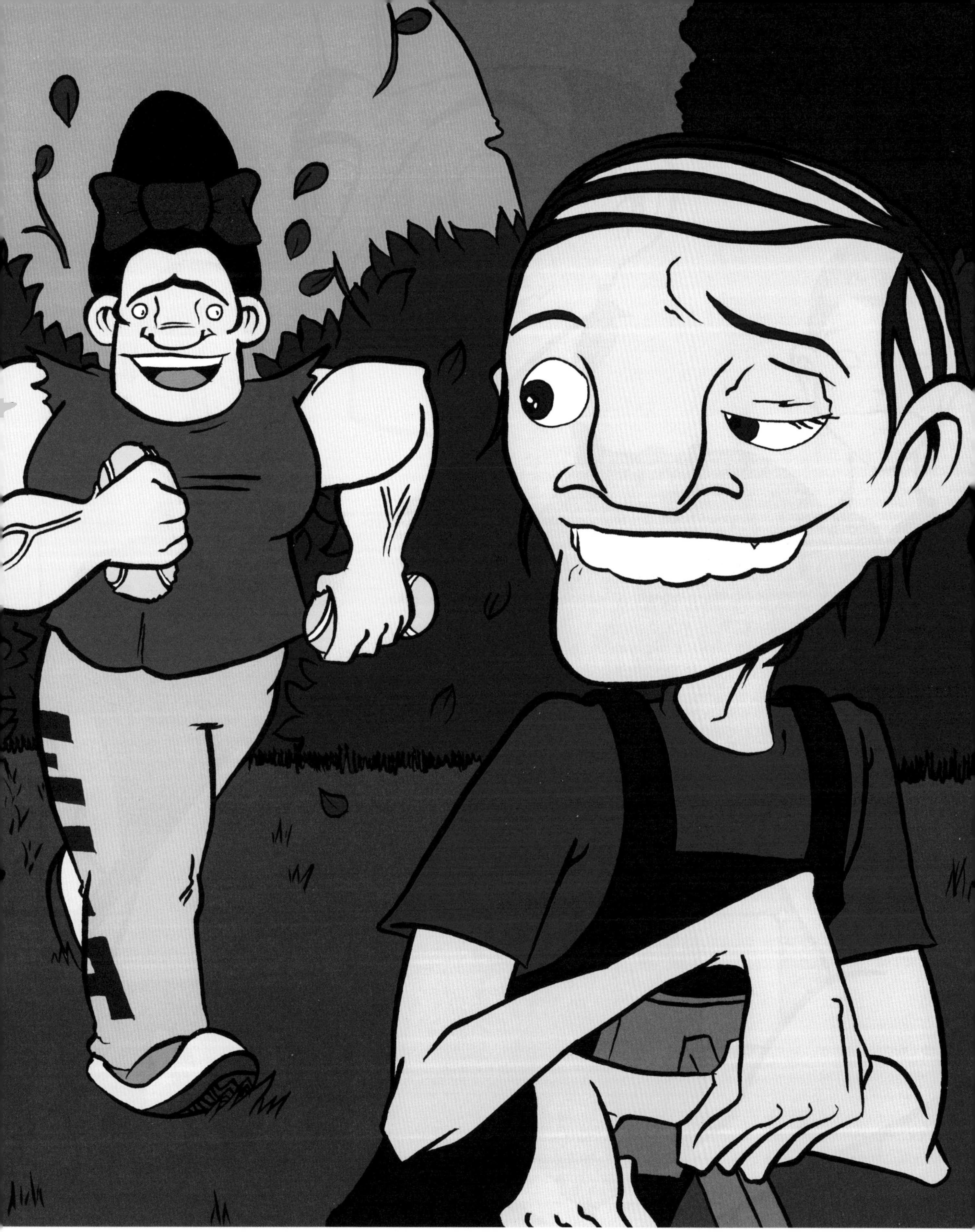

...and who should heave into unexpected view but the U.S.S. Millicent Kent...

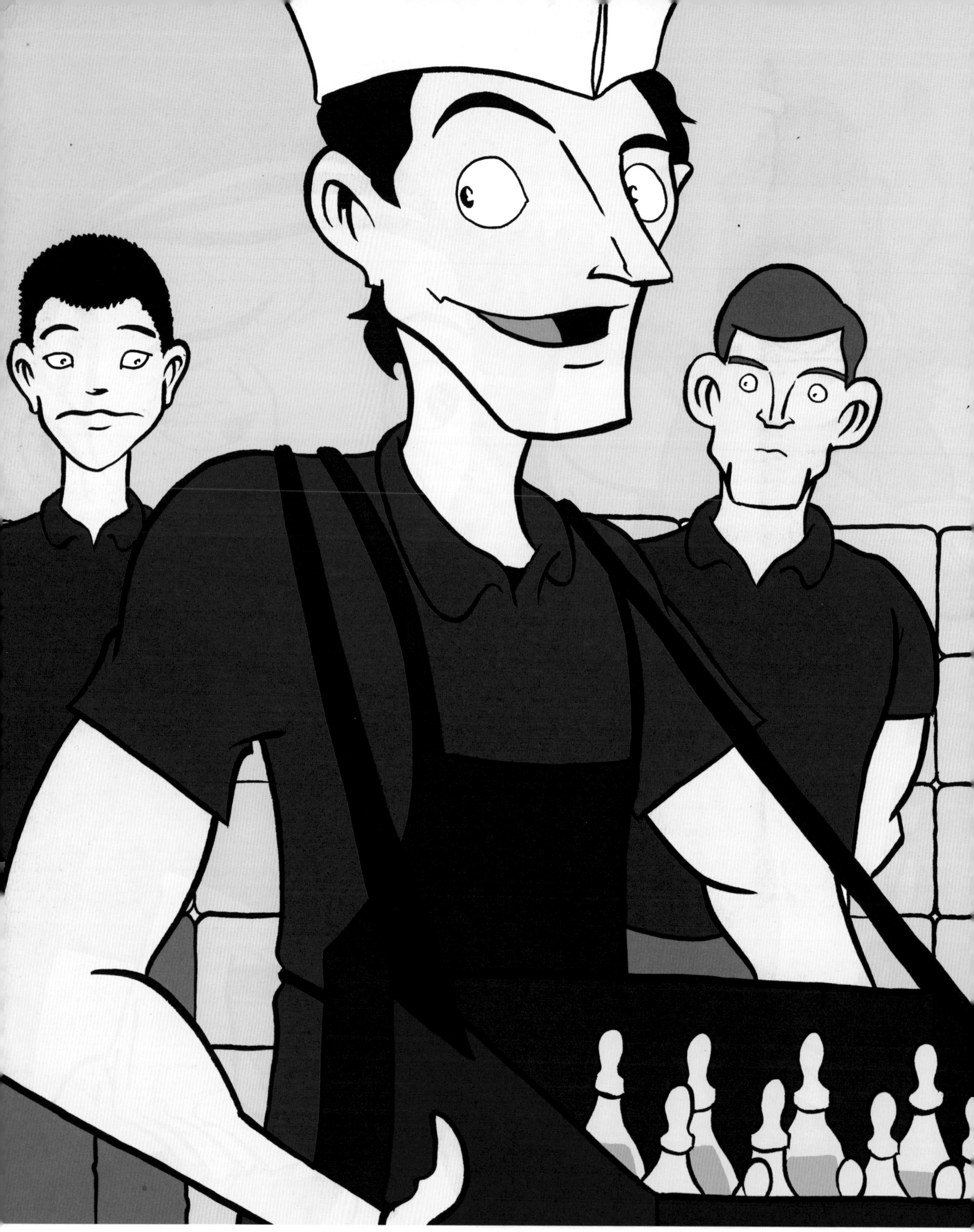

"Urine trouble? Urine luck!"

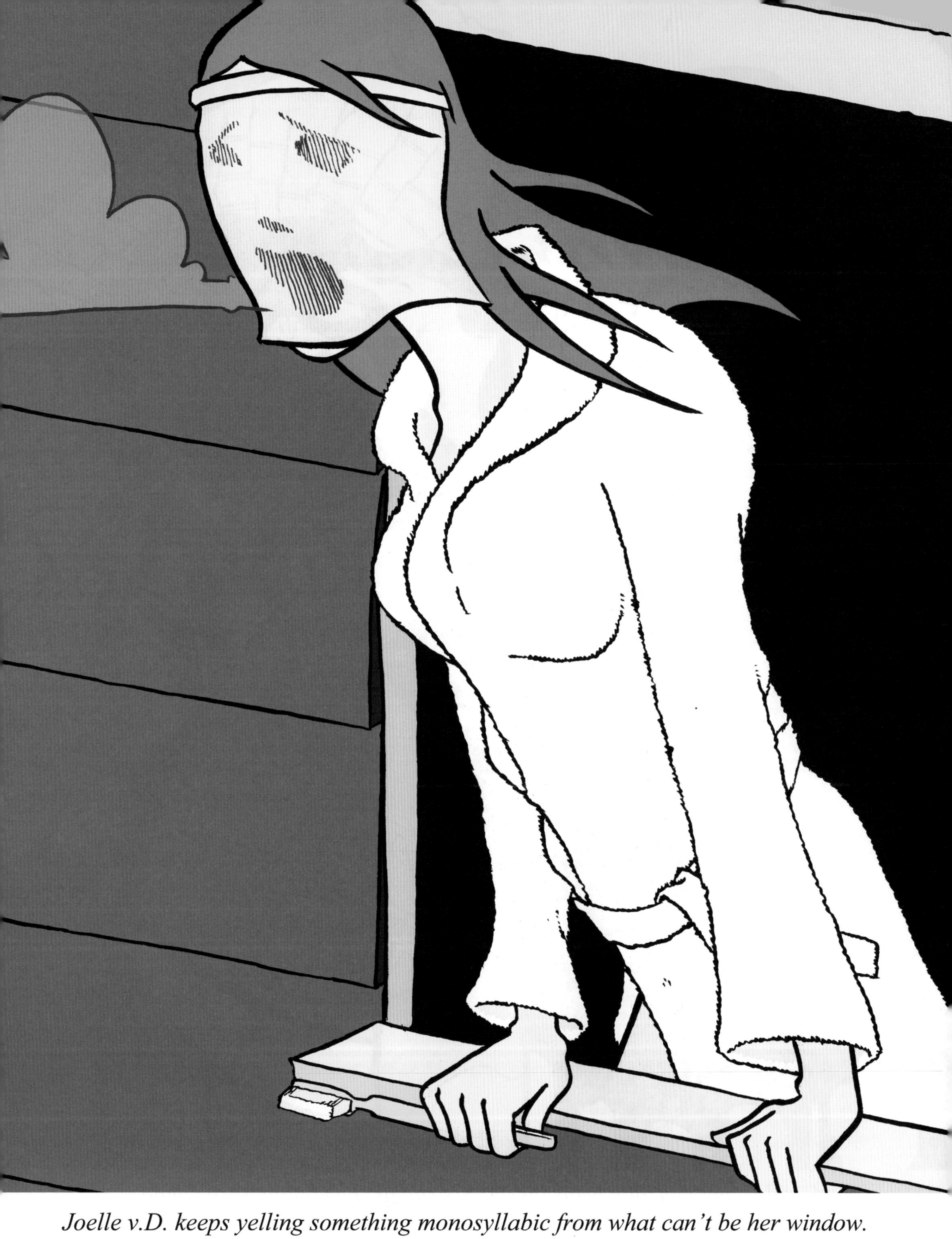

Joelle v.D. keeps yelling something monosyllabic from what can't be her window.

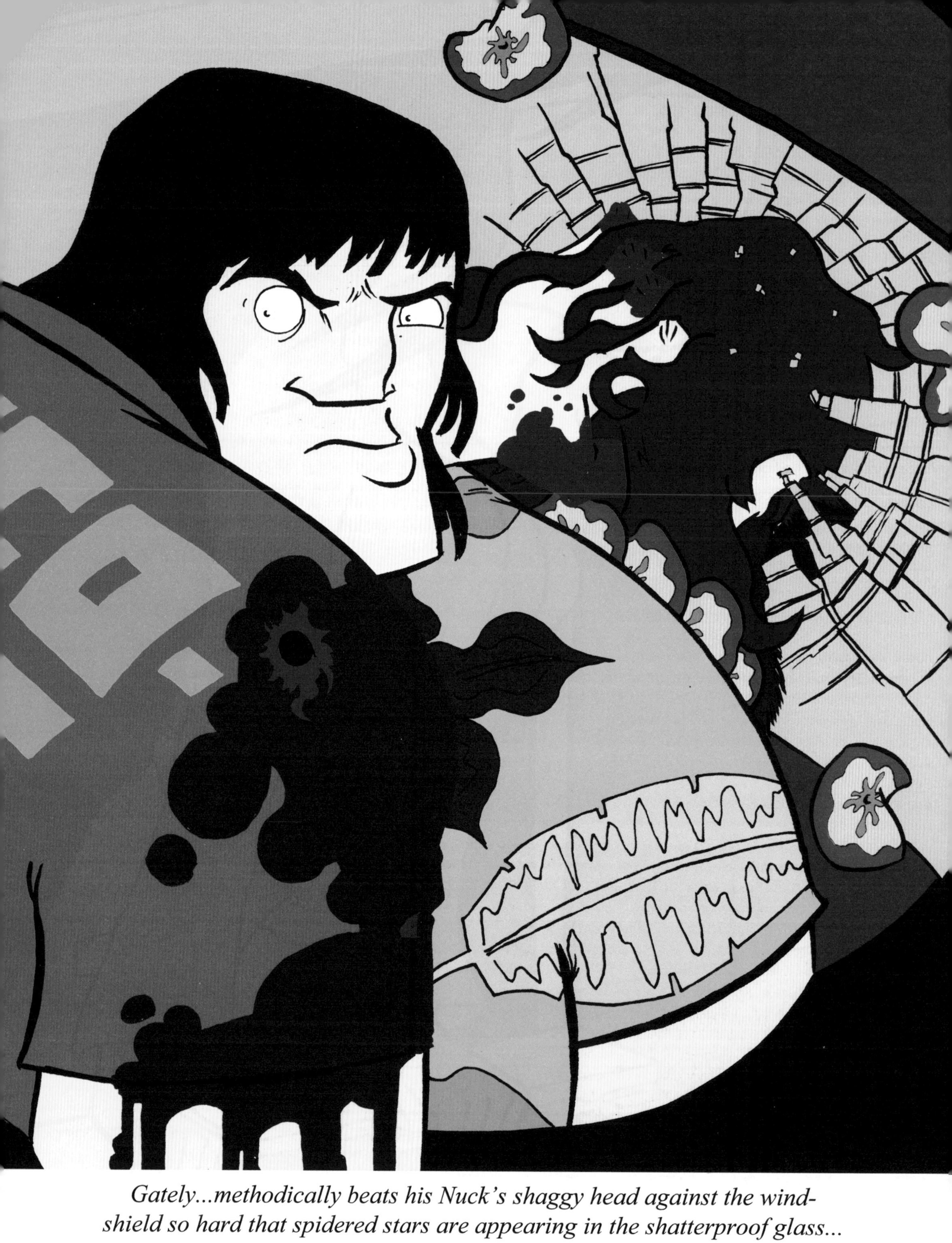

Gately...methodically beats his Nuck's shaggy head against the windshield so hard that spidered stars are appearing in the shatterproof glass...

FURTHER READING
JORDYN OSTROFF

HEART OF DARKNESS

Joseph Conrad's 1899/1902 novel *Heart of Darkness* sparked both a lively, productive debate about the portrayal of Africa in Western literature, and Francis Ford Coppola's 1979 film *Apocalypse Now*, starring Marlon Brando and Martin Sheen. No wonder it's a classic. Spring for the authoritative 1921 text prepared for UK publisher Heinemann, which is now available in Bedford/St. Martin's Case Studies in Contemporary Criticism Third Edition (2011). Edited by Ross C. Murfin, it provides contextual documents, and historical and contemporary criticism. For more of Conrad's racial and moral grappling, check out scholar Cedric Watts's *Heart of Darkness and Other Tales* (Oxford World Classics, 2008), which includes three additional stories, notes, and chronologies.

THE AWAKENING

Once censored for its frank depictions of female sexual desire and flouting of established social and gender roles, Kate Chopin's 1899 novel, *The Awakening*, has now earned a permanent place in high school English classrooms and inspired a long tradition of American Southern writing (see Tennessee Williams, Flannery O'Connor, Eudora Welty . . .). The Penguin Classics Edition (2003), edited by women's lit scholar Sandra M. Gilbert, includes a number of other Chopin stories, all for a good price. Also affordable is the student-friendly Bedford College Edition (2007), which contains notes, a glossary, an annotated bibliography, and other helpful materials. The true Chopin devotee should spring for the Library of America's handsome *Kate Chopin: Complete Novels and Stories* (2002), which collects all of Chopin's fiction for the first time.

THE INTERPRETATION OF DREAMS

Few works have so infiltrated our worldview—psychologically, literarily, and philosophically—as Sigmund Freud's *The Interpretation of Dreams*, first published in German in November 1899. *The Interpretation of Dreams: The Complete and Definitive Text* (Basic Books, 2010)—containing a translation by James Strachey, made in conjunction with Anna Freud herself in 1953—remains the most complete English-language translation in print. For a truly beautiful version, spend some time with *The Interpretation of Dreams: The Illustrated Edition* (Sterling, 2010), a lush, hardcover, coffee-table book which contains an introduction and essays by Freud scholar Dr. Jeffrey Moussaieff Masson, supporting excerpts by psychoanalytic writers like Jung and Lacan, archival photographs and reproduced documents, and gorgeous art from Modernist and Surrealist artists such as Dalí, Picasso, and Magritte. If you're hooked on Freud, consider adding the Modern Library edition to your library—*The Basic Writings of Sigmund Freud* includes *The Interpretation of Dreams*, *Psychopathology of Everyday Life*, *Three Contributions to the Theory of Sex*, and other texts, all translated by A. A. Brill.

THE WONDERFUL WIZARD OF OZ

If only all our parents could spin mundane everyday life bedtime yarns as well as L. Frank Baum could! But then *The Wonderful Wizard of Oz*, first published in 1900, wouldn't be as wonderfully unique. It can be had for a song from Signet Classics (2006), along with the original illustrations by W. W. Denslow. *The Annotated Wizard of Oz* (W.W. Norton, 2000), with notes by leading children's lit scholar Michael Patrick Hearn, provides a more immersive, luxurious trip to Oz, featuring previously unpublished illustrations, contemporary references, character sources, and more, all gorgeously leather-bound. This was only the first of fourteen tales set in Oz; it's packaged with two of the others in *The Wonderful World of Oz* (Penguin Classics, 1998), with an introduction from fairytale scholar Jack Zipes. Of course, there's always the 1939 film version, *The Wizard of Oz*—but be warned: the flying monkeys are particularly terrifying in live action.

"THE NEW ACCELERATOR"

"Father of Science Fiction" H. G. Wells presciently confronted everything from radioactive decay to dystopias to the dangers of scientific discovery. His 1901 short story "The New Accelerator" is a prime example of Wellsian time travel. The inspiration for the *Star Trek* episode "Wink of an Eye," it was also adapted for the premier episode of the 2001 miniseries *The Infinite Worlds of H. G. Wells*. The story can be found in print on the cheap amid a small selection of other Wells tales in *The Country of the Blind: and Other Science-Fiction Stories* (Dover Thrift Editions, 2011). Ursula K. Le Guin edited a more expansive selection, *Selected Stories of H. G. Wells* (Modern Library Classics, 2004), in which the stories are arranged thematically. She caps the volume with a brilliant introduction.

"REGINALD"

The influential short story writer Hector Hugh Munro—or Saki, as he was known on the page—introduced the reoccurring Reginald in the sharp, wickedly funny 1904 piece that bears his name. *The Complete Saki* (Penguin Classics, 1998) opens with the "Reginald" stories but contains the author's entire body of work, including his novels and plays—it is not a slim volume. For just the short fiction, *Collected Short Stories of Saki* (Wordsworth Classics, 1999) is a great value. If it's just the "Reginald" stories you're after, look into *Reginald* (Dodo Press, 2007).

MOTHER

Maxim Gorky was a son who loved his mother, and a comrade who loved his mother country. His two fealties merge in his 1906 novel, *Mother*, about a young son's and his mother's revolutionary struggles in Russia. The novel can be found in its entirety online, or in paperback from BiblioLife (2008). Citadel's 1992 edition is out of print, but *The Collected Stories of Maxim Gorky* (Citadel, 1998) contains an otherwise representative selection of Gorky's work, and demonstrates his capacity to spin his childhood poverty into pure literary gold. Don't forget to watch *Mother* in one of a handful of screen adaptations, including Vsevolod Pudovkin's 1926 silent film.

"IF—"

Rudyard Kipling's poem "If—" may spring from a somewhat shady imperial past, but it remains a cornerstone of British pride—and parody. First published in 1910, the poem's reach has endured, even becoming an icon of the Wimbledon marketing campaign. Peter Washington's *Kipling: Poems* (Everyman's Library, 2007) includes "If—" and a thorough selection of Kipling's other poetry, both well and lesser known. Of many editions, only one collects all the poems in an affordable paperback: *Complete Verse* (Anchor, 1988).

JOHN BARLEYCORN

Taking its name from an old British folk song of the same alcoholic theme, Jack London's 1913 memoir *John Barleycorn* depicts the highs and lows of the booze-fate. It quickly became a weapon in the American fight for temperance and thus the bane of liquor companies. A silent film adaptation was even made in 1914. The Oxford World's Classics edition (2009), edited and with an introduction by Professor John Sutherland, contains the text as well as a significant body of notes. Proof of Jack London's—and *John Barleycorn*'s—significance to the American canon comes in the form of the Library of America volume that includes the memoir, some of London's fiction, and fairly extensive notes.

DUBLINERS

First published in 1914, James Joyce's *Dubliners* is a surprisingly accessible collection of stories depicting the epiphanies of everyday life in the Irish capital. The story "Araby"—of longing and disillusionment—is one of the most well-known works in the volume. The revised edition *Dubliners: Text and Criticism* from the Viking Critical Library (Penguin, 1996) is edited by preeminent Joyce scholars and contains a significant body of notes and critical essays. For a more well-rounded reading, *The Portable James Joyce* (Penguin, 1976) contains excerpts from the author's other works as well as an introduction and notes from Harvard professor and Joyce expert Harry Levin. But for the full *Dubliners* sans bells or whistles, the Dover Thrift Edition (1991), at only two dollars, is the way to go.

"THE METAMORPHOSIS"

Rarely do cockroaches make good protagonists. Gregor Samsa in Franz Kafka's "The Metamorphosis" is the exception that proves the rule. First published in German in 1915, the novel's unique sentence structures and diction make for difficult translation. Still, options abound at any well-stocked bookstore. The preeminent English version is PEN Translation Prize–winner Joachim Neugroschel's *The Metamorphosis, In the Penal Colony, and Other Stories* (Touchstone, 2000). The Willa and Edwin Muir translation, through which many readers first came to know the novella, is available with all of Kafka's short fiction in the handsomely clothbound *Collected Stories* (Everyman's Library, 1993). For a graphically illuminating Kafka experience, check out the comic adaptations of "The Metamorphosis" and other tales in *Introducing Kafka* by R. Crumb and David Zane Mairowitz.

"THE TOP" AND "GIVE IT UP!"

When Kafka died in 1924, he left behind an assortment of shorter works—both published and unpublished, finished and unfinished.

Many have been published in English. The eerily existential "The Top" and "Give It Up!" are included in the deckle-edged *Franz Kafka: The Complete Stories* (Schocken Books, 1995), with an introduction by John Updike. Peter Kuper's graphic versions of these two stories, included here, appear beside seven others in *Give It Up! And Other Short Stories* (NBM Publishing, 2003).

THE VOYAGE OUT

Virginia Woolf's first novel, *The Voyage Out* (1915) presages much of her later work (it introduces Mrs. Dalloway, for example). Check out the Penguin Classics edition (1992), with notes and introduction by Woolf scholar Jane Wheare, or, for even more scholarly illumination, The Oxford World's Classics edition (2009), edited by Lorna Sage. The novel as we know it today was heavily edited before publication by Woolf herself, who wanted to tone down the potentially controversial material. Scholar Louise DeSalvo painstakingly reassembled the original text, published as *Melymbrosia* (Cleis Press, 2002). For more of the story behind Woolf's singularly gifted body of work, including the origins of *The Voyage Out*, see Dr. Julia Briggs's *Virginia Woolf: An Inner Life* (Houghton Mifflin Harcourt, 2005).

"THE LOVE SONG OF J. ALFRED PRUFROCK" and "THE WASTE LAND"

Is there a world more beautiful and angst-ridden than that of T. S. Eliot's 1915 "The Love Song of J. Alfred Prufrock"? Or a poem more impenetrable than his 1922 "The Waste Land"? Harcourt Brace Jovanovich's *T. S. Eliot: Collected Poems, 1909-1962* (1991) contains the poet's entire body of verse, while *The Waste Land and Other Writings* (Modern Library, 2002) is a superb, if not complete, selection featuring a stunning introduction by memoirist and poet Mary Karr. Of course, Eliot's verse is famously incomprehensible—rife with obscure allusions and symbols. You may want to keep B. C. Southam's line-by-line explanations, *A Guide to the Selected Poems of T. S. Eliot* (Mariner, 1996), handy as you read. And for further clues, check out Lyndall Gordon's *T. S. Eliot: An Imperfect Life* (W.W. Norton, 1999) for a window into Eliot's life—and flaws.

"THE MOWERS"

D. H. Lawrence's poetry might not be as controversial as his novel *Lady Chatterley's Lover*, but it is certainly worth reading on its own merits. The full range of his verse can be experienced in the conveniently sized and affordable *Complete Poems of D. H. Lawrence* (Wordsworth Editions, 1994). For a bit more guidance, the Penguin Classics *Complete Poems* (1994) comes with notes and an illuminating introduction from leading Lawrence scholars Vivian de Sola Pinto and Warren F. Roberts.

"SEA IRIS"

Some speculate that Ezra Pound created the Imagist movement explicitly to promote the poems of his friend, muse, and sometimes lover, Hilda Doolittle. True or not, H. D.'s poems—such as "Sea Iris," from her 1916 collection, *Sea Garden*—are uniquely powerful explorations of the often-erotic human consciousness via the tropes of nature. *H. D.: Collected Poems, 1912-1944* (New Directions, 1986), edited by Yale professor Louis L. Martz, is an excellent introduction to H. D.'s many poetic moods. Martz also edited *H. D. Selected Poems* (New Directions, 1988), a slimmer, cheaper volume that still includes a representative sampling. *Sea Garden* can be had in a complete, standalone volume from BiblioLife (2009). Award-winning poet Barbara Guest's biography, *Herself Defined: The Poet H. D. and Her World* (Doubleday, 1984) is sadly out of print, but definitely worth tracking down for a real glimpse into the life of a writer whose work influenced such poets as Adrienne Rich, Margaret Atwood, Robert Creeley, and Anne Sexton.

"A MATTER OF COLOUR"
Deep-sea fishing, big-game hunting, bullfighting—big animals populate the greater part of Ernest Hemingway's writing; yet, his writing is characterized by small things: simple words, short sentences, brief paragraphs. In fact, his career was built on his body of short stories, one of the first of which was "A Matter of Colour," a story about boxing that Hemingway wrote in 1916 while still a high school student. It was published in his high school newspaper, and is difficult to find in print. You can track down the slender, obscure *Hemingway at Oak Park High* (Oak Park High School Library, 1993) for all of his school writings or the chunky *Collected Stories* (Everyman's Library, 1995), published in the UK.

THE MADMAN
Kahlil Gibran is the third best-selling poet of all time—behind only Shakespeare and Lao Tzu. His first English-language work was *The Madman*, a slim book of parables and aphorisms first published in 1918. Find it in *The Collected Works* (Everyman's Library, Knopf, 2007), which features Gibran's own artwork as illustration. The most comprehensive volume of the Lebanese poet's work is *Treasured Writings of Kahlil Gibran* (Castle Books, 2009)—a hefty but reasonably priced edition. In honor of the seventy-fifth anniversary of his death, the Kahlil Gibran Research and Studies Project joined with Oneworld Publications to publish *The Essential Gibran*, edited by foremost scholar Suheil Bushrui to contain representative selections from all of Gibran's major works of Arabic and English poetry, letters, and selected criticism of his art. For more on the inspiring life of this timeless poet, consider Bushrui's *Kahlil Gibran: Man and Poet* (Oneworld, 2007).

"HANDS" (FROM *WINESBURG, OHIO*)
Sherwood Anderson played many roles in his lifetime: soldier, ad man, factory manager, and father. But he abandoned them all—including his family—to devote himself to a literary career that gave us such frank and unflinching accounts of small-town America as his 1919 short-story cycle, *Winesburg, Ohio*. The Signet Classics edition (2005) is inexpensive, and includes an afterword from none other than Dean Koontz. The Norton Critical Edition (1995) is also a bargain, featuring ample annotation from professors Charles E. Modin and Ray Lewis White, a selection of Anderson's letters, critical essays by the likes of John Updike, and much more.

THE DREAMING OF THE BONES
William Butler Yeats did not mess around. The Nobel Prize-winning Irish poet also served as a Senator, founded a theater,

and wrote plays. *The Dreaming of the Bones* (1919), one of his "Four Plays for Dancers" that are written in the Japanese Noh tradition, was first performed in 1931. It's not easy to get your hands on these plays about the dreams of the dead in print, but they can be found in *Four Plays for Dancers* (Forgotten Books, 2010). *The Dreaming of the Bones* can also be read in a standalone e-book edition from Digireads.com (2011).

CHÉRI
Modern women owe a debt to the boundary-busting bravery of French novelist and performer Colette, whose controversial works, such as *Chéri* (1920), flipped gender stereotypes upside down. Writers like Marcel Proust greeted the novel as a masterpiece. Check it out alongside its sequel, *La Fin de Chéri* (1926) in *Cheri and the Last of Cheri*, translated by Roger Senhouse and introduced by Colette biographer Judith Thurman (Farrar, Straus and Giroux, 2001). If you would rather experience this steamy novel on the big screen, rent Stephen Frears's 2009 film adaptation, starring Michelle Pfeiffer. For more on this larger-than-life author, page through Thurman's National Book Award finalist biography, *Secrets of the Flesh: A Life of Colette* (Ballantine Books, 2000).

THE AGE OF INNOCENCE
Gossip Girl has nothing on *The Age of Innocence*, Edith Wharton's 1920 novel about marriage and scandal in upper-class New York City. It can be had cheaply and with an introduction by novelist Maureen Howard from Barnes & Noble Classics (2004). If you need all the details you can get on this Gilded Age tale, check out the Oxford World's Classics edition (2008), edited by scholar Stephen Orgel, whose introduction and notes dissect the historical context and narrative technique. But for an edition that truly matches the sumptuousness of the novel, splurge on the deluxe *Three Novels of New York: The House of Mirth, The Custom of the Country*, and *The Age of Innocence* (Penguin Classics, 2012), which features striking illustrations from Richard Gray and an introduction from Jonathan Franzen.

"DULCE ET DECORUM EST"
How is it that the most effective pacifist writings so often come from the battlefields themselves? English soldier-poet Wilfred Owen's "Dulce et Decorum Est," first published in 1920, is such a poem. Owen died in battle at only twenty-five years old, but his writing is some of the most important in British war poetry. His entire body of work can be found in *The Collected Poems of Wilfred Owen* (New Directions, 1965), with an introduction by poet C. Day Lewis. *The Works of Wilfred Owen* (Wordsworth, 1999) is a narrower selection, but still contains Owen's most important works, as well as an introduction and notes by Professor Owen Knowles.

"THE SECOND COMING"
Artists ranging from Joan Didion to Chinua Achebe to Woody Allen have all taken inspiration from W. B. Yeats's 1919 poem "The Second Coming." Packed with portent, apocalypse, and Modernism, this twenty-two line classic can be found in the revised edition of *The Collected Poems of W. B. Yeats* (Scribner, 1996), edited by esteemed Yeats scholar Richard J. Finneran, and including Yeats's

own notes. For more scholarship (and at a very reasonable price), check out James Pethica's *Yeats's Poetry, Drama, and Prose* (W.W. Norton, 2000); with critical essays by Harold Bloom, Paul de Man, and Seamus Heaney, among many others, the volume is a must-have for budding Yeats scholars. *The Yeats Reader* (Scribner, 2002) is annotated and covers Yeats's work across genres.

"THE PENITENT" and "THE SINGING-WOMAN FROM THE WOOD'S EDGE"

Poet, playwright, political activist, and ravishing beauty Edna St. Vincent Millay wrote poems that were groundbreaking for their exploration of femininity and sexuality. "The Penitent" and "The Singing-Woman from the Wood's Edge" are from her 1920 collection *A Few Figs from Thistles*, currently available from Juniper Grove (2008). Like her poetry, St. Vincent Millay's life was impassioned, sensational, and unconventional; read about it in *Savage Beauty: The Life of Edna St. Vincent Millay* (Random House, 2002) by best-selling biographer Nancy Milford.

"THE NEGRO SPEAKS OF RIVERS"

In true improvisational jazz form, Langston Hughes wrote his 1921 "The Negro Speaks of Rivers" on an envelope as he traveled to Mexico by train—it would later become his signature poem. Read it and 867 others (300 of which had never before appeared in book form) in the definitive *Collected Poems of Langston Hughes* (Vintage, 1995), edited and with notes by Hughes biographer Arnold Rampersad. If you're more of a dabbler than a serious aficionado, you might try the slimmer *Selected Poems of Langston Hughes* (Vintage, 1990), containing a selection chosen by Hughes himself shortly before his death. For more on the author's life as an American poet, social activist, playwright, and novelist, consider investing in the two volumes of Rampersad's biography (Oxford University Press), or in the two-volume autobiography: *The Big Sea* and *I Wonder as I Wander* (Hill and Wang, 1993).

"RAIN"

W. Somerset Maugham had a special talent for turning real-life drama—World War II spy scandals, familial dysfunction, his many lovers—into profitable, best-selling novels, plays, and short stories. "Rain," a 1921 short story inspired by accounts he heard in his travels through the British Empire, can be found in the first volume of *Maugham: Collected Short Stories* (Penguin Classics, 1992), or in the beautifully bound Everyman's Library hardcover edition, *Collected Stories* (2004). Maugham was one of the first writers to turn a heavy profit on Hollywood adaptations of his work, so do him right by seeing one of the films based on "Rain": the silent *Sadie Thompson* (1928) starring Lionel Barrymore, or the talkie *Rain* (1932) starring Joan Crawford.

ULYSSES

There are numerous editions of James Joyce's 1922 Modernist masterpiece, each with minute differences. The most widely accepted version is the Gabler Edition, edited by Hans Gabler to include previously unseen text (Vintage, 1986). The Wordsworth Edition (2010), with introduction by Cedric Watts, is less than half the price. Navigate the notoriously dense text with

the guidance of *Ulysses Annotated: Notes for James Joyce's Ulysses* by renowned Joyce scholar Don Gifford (University of California Press, 2008). The novel is adapted endlessly for the stage, radio, and screen, and is relived, to varying degrees, each year on the day it takes place—June 16, a.k.a. Bloomsday.

"LIVING ON $1,000 A YEAR IN PARIS"

Hemingway may have been a sporting man, but he also knew how to enjoy the finer things in Paris with the rest of the Lost Generation—on mere pennies, no less. In 1922, Hemingway even wrote a short piece on how wonderful it was to be poor in Paris for the *Toronto Star*. That essay can be found in the slim *On Paris* (Hesperus Press, 2010) and *Ernest Hemingway, Dateline: Toronto: Hemingway's Complete Toronto Star Dispatches 1920-1924*, edited by William White (Scribner, 1985). Hemingway's true Parisian masterpiece, though, is his memoir, *A Moveable Feast*. It may not contain "Living on $1,000 a Year in Paris," but the restored edition (Scribner, 2010), with introductory material by Hemingway's son and grandson, is an exuberant evocation of Lost Generation Paris. For more on just how Hemingway—with the Fitzgeralds, Gertrude Stein, T. S. Eliot, and others—lived in the City of Light, page through Michael Reynolds's *Hemingway: The Paris Years* (W.W. Norton, 1999).

"THE EMPEROR OF ICE-CREAM"

American poet Wallace Stevens inspired such artists as James Merrill, Mark Strand, John Ashbery, and David Hockney with rococo yet meditative poems like "The Emperor of Ice-Cream," from his first collection, *Harmonium* (1923). All of Stevens's poetry, as well as his prose works, is collected into the lovely *Wallace Stevens: Collected Poetry and Prose* (Library of America, 1997), edited with notes by literary experts Frank Kermode and Joan Richardson. Nearly as complete is *The Collected Poems of Wallace Stevens* (Vintage, 1990). If you prefer your poetry pocket-sized, the affordable Everyman's Library edition (1993), with Harvard professor Helen Vendler's selection of Stevens's poems, is an excellent choice. Esteemed critic Harold Bloom is an admirer, as evidenced by his guide *Wallace Stevens: The Poems of Our Climate* (Cornell University Press, 1980).

"THE HILL"

Not even icons of American literature like William Faulkner spit out masterpieces when they first begin writing. "The Hill," one of Faulkner's first two short works of fiction, was originally published in 1922 in *The Mississippian*. The story never achieved the timelessness of the author's later works, and while it was reprinted once in *William Faulkner: Early Prose and Poetry* (Little, Brown, 1962), it is very difficult to find on the printed page today.

SIDDHARTHA

Popularized in the United States during the 1960s counterculture, Herman Hesse's *Siddhartha* is now simply a part of the culture. It has several enduring translations: Hilda Rosner's, from 1951, is still available in an inexpensive edition from Bantam Classics; Joachim Neugroschel's is fluid and readable, and bolstered by Hesse biographer Ralph Friedman's introduction in the beautifully designed Penguin Classics edition (2002); Susan Bernofsky's is highly regarded for its melody and faithfulness to the German original (Modern Library Classics, 2006).

THE GREAT GATSBY

F. Scott Fitzgerald's tale of lavish hollowness and moral decay in the upper classes, *The Great Gatsby*, has become the paragon of the American Novel. With a permanent spot on nearly every high-school reading list, the novel is a must-read. The most popular edition is Scribner's (2004). But it took Fitzgerald years of editing to arrive at the text we now know. Check out the original version in *Trimalchio: An Early Version of 'The Great Gatsby,'* which includes scholarly notes on the unedited text (Cambridge University Press, 2002). The sad beauty of East and West Egg is lovely on the page, but is done particular justice on the screen. Of several adaptations, the 1974 movie—starring Robert Redford and Mia Farrow, and with a script by Francis Ford Coppola—was the most famous. That is, until the release of Baz Luhrmann's version, starring Leonardo DiCaprio, in 2013.

STEPPENWOLF

Hermann Hesse complained that readers fundamentally misunderstood his tenth novel, *Steppenwolf*, first published in Germany in 1927. He thought their focus on the protagonist's suffering blinded them to the potential for transcendence. See what you think: Basil Creighton's 1929 translation is still the most popular, and can be found revised and improved in the Picador paperback edition (2002). Although the novel was far from popular upon first publication, the 1960s and '70s saw a surge of interest in its treatment of drugs and sex. Check out the 1974 film adaptation, directed by Fred Haines.

LADY CHATTERLEY'S LOVER

First published in Italy in 1928, the explicit descriptions of sex in D. H. Lawrence's *Lady Chatterley's Lover* prevented the novel from being openly published in England or the United States for over thirty years. Both countries ultimately decided the literary merit outweighed the "obscene" language. The lovely Penguin Classics Deluxe edition features an introduction by Doris Lessing, illustrations by Michael Squires, and excellent notes by Lawrence scholar Paul Popalawski (2006). If you're looking to spend a bit less, check out the (almost) no-frills Signet Classics edition (2011)—at under six dollars, it still includes an introduction by Geoff Dyer. Lawrence lived in self-imposed exile even before the *Lady Chatterley* scandal; read more about his lonely struggles in *D. H. Lawrence: The Life of an Outsider* (Counterpoint, 2007), by longtime Lawrence biographer John Worthen.

THE SOUND AND THE FURY

For years, readers have been mystified by the shifting stream-of-conscious perspectives in William Faulkner's *The Sound and the Fury* (as well as the pronunciation of the novel's setting, Yoknapatawpha County). But they have also embraced the 1929 book as one of the best of the twentieth century. Even Oprah's Book Club featured it in 2005. You can buy it with her seal of approval, and with Noel Polk's authoritative corrections, from Vintage (2001). But for more scholarly guidance, the Norton Critical Edition (1993), with notes from Faulkner scholar David Minter, is the way to go. It includes the corrected text, as well as critical essays by such stars as Jean-Paul Sartre, Ralph Ellison, and Irving Howe. Faulkner has, of course, received the full Library of America treatment, so *The Sound and the Fury* can also be read alongside the author's other first three novels in *William Faulkner: Novels 1926–1929* (2006), one of four lovely hardcover volumes.

LETTERS TO A YOUNG POET

You might think Rainer Maria Rilke was too busy producing some of the most significant poetry of the twentieth century to mentor a novice. In fact, for seven years the German poet exchanged letters with Franz Kappus, providing advice to the teenager soldier about how to remain a sensitive writer in a harsh world. Kappus published the letters in 1929 after Rilke's death. Seek Rilke's advice in *Letters to a Young Poet* (W.W. Norton, 1993), in which M. D. Herter Norton (cofounder of the publishing house) translates the letters and includes a chronology of Rilke's life at the time he wrote them. There are also newer, respected translations from Stephen Mitchell, in a clothbound Modern Library edition (2001), and Mark Harman, published with an in-depth introduction by Harvard University Press (2011).

THE MALTESE FALCON

The hard-boiled detective novel occupies significant real estate in most American bookstores, and it wouldn't be a stretch to say it all started with Dashiell Hammett's *The Maltese Falcon* (1930). Check out Vintage's popular 1989 edition. If you find yourself hooked, consider indulging in *The Maltese Falcon, The Thin Man, Red Harvest*—that's the Everyman's Library volume of three Hammett novels, with an introduction by noir expert Robert Polito. What's better suited for the silver screen than a good detective story? *The Maltese Falcon* (1941), starring Humphrey Bogart, is a classic of the genre.

BRAVE NEW WORLD

Aldous Huxley's *Brave New World*, first published in England 1931, continues to be widely challenged across the United States for its supposedly antireligion and antifamily ideas. Clearly, any book so controversial is worth a look. First, read the Harper Perennial Modern Classics paperback edition (2006). Then read *Brave New World Revisited*, written thirty years after the original, in which Huxley concludes that the world is moving towards his dystopic vision much faster than he originally thought (Harper Perennial Modern Classics, 2006).

POKER!

A central figure of the Harlem Renaissance, and, along with Langston Hughes and Wallace Thurman, a member of the intellectual group Niggerati, Zora Neale Hurston is famed for her anthropological renderings of the African-American experience. While her novels and short stories are well known, her plays, such as the short piece *Poker!*, are less so. They are brought together for the first time in *Zora Neale Hurston: Collected Plays* (Rutgers University Press, 2008), edited with an introduction by professors Jean Lee Cole and Charles

Mitchell. The Library of Congress also makes *Poker!* and nine other plays available digitally.

BLACK ELK SPEAKS

Poet John G. Neihardt's powerful 1932 account of his conversations with Black Elk, an Oglala Sioux shaman, remains in print: *Black Elk Speaks: Being the Life Story of a Holy Man of the Ogala Sioux*, The Premier Edition (State University of New York Press, 2008). The volume is annotated by anthropologist Raymond DeMallie and includes reproductions of the original illustrations by Ponca chief Standing Bear. The full transcription of interviews is available in *The Sixth Grandfather: Black Elk's Teachings Given to John G. Neihardt* (Bison Books, 1985).

"STRANGE FRUIT" ("BITTER FRUIT")

We are most familiar with Lewis Allan's poem "Strange Fruit" via Billie Holiday's haunting 1939 vocal rendition. Lewis Allan—who was really a Jewish high-school teacher named Abel Meeropol from the Bronx—first published the poignant verse in 1936 in response to the recent lynchings of black men in the South. *Time* magazine called "Strange Fruit" the song of the century in 1999, and the lyrics inspired artists from Caryl Phillips to Bob Dylan to Seamus Heaney. The song itself is available on *The Best of Billie Holiday: 20th Century Masters* (Hip-O Records, 2002). For an intriguing account of its long and powerful history, see *Strange Fruit: The Biography of a Song* by David Margolick and Hilton Als (Harper Perennial, 2001).

NAUSEA

Ever felt nauseated by existence? Wallow in *Nausea*—first published in France in 1938, it was Jean-Paul Sartre's first novel. Lloyd Alexander's 1949 English-language translation is available from New Directions with a new introduction by poet and translator Richard Howard (2007). Find Sartre's existentialism a bit depressing? Take the short course in *Sartre in 90 Minutes* (Ivan R. Dee, 1998), Paul Strathern's breezy, witty introduction to Sartre's life and work.

THE GRAPES OF WRATH

John Steinbeck's 1939 novel *The Grapes of Wrath* has been banned, burned, and debated—its impact is undeniable. See what the fuss is about in the Penguin Classics revised edition (2006), with an introduction by distinguished American literature scholar Robert DeMott. For more of Steinbeck's landmark works, consider investing in *John Steinbeck: The Grapes of Wrath and Other Writings 1936–1941*, the second Library of America volume devoted to the author. It features a newly corrected version of *The Grapes of Wrath* based on Steinbeck's own manuscript. The 1940 film adaptation, starring Henry Fonda, is a masterpiece in its own right.

STORIES BY JORGE LUIS BORGES

The entirety of Jorge Luis Borges's elusive, fantastical, and influential short fiction has been collected for the first time by Penguin, crisply translated by Andrew Hurley (*Collected Fictions*, 1999). The more limited *Labyrinths* (New Directions,

2007), edited by Donald A. Yates and James E. Irby, includes an excellent introduction by Borges scholar William Gibson, as well as biographical and critical material. Many say that *Ficciones*, faithfully translated by Andrew Bonner (Grove Press, 1994), is the best introduction to Borges's work.

THE STRANGER

Albert Camus's debut novel *L'Etranger* (1942) struggles with absurdism, human consciousness, and free will. Englishman Stuart Gilbert's translation reigned supreme for thirty years, but has arguably been supplanted by Matthew Ward's American touch in the 1989 Random House/Vintage version. If the novel leaves you feeling a bit alienated, cap your reading with a listen to one of the songs it inspired: The Cure's "Killing an Arab" or Queen's "Bohemian Rhapsody."

ANIMAL FARM

Sharp-eyed social commentator and influential English novelist Eric Arthur Blair—better known by his pen name, George Orwell—had a talent for allegory. Case in point: his famous 1945 novella, *Animal Farm*, depicting the events of Stalin's reign in the Soviet Union. Observe the revolution in the pigsty in *Animal Farm: Centennial Edition* (Plume, 2003), with an introduction by Ann Patchett. The Fiftieth Anniversary edition (Houghton Mifflin Harcourt, 1995) is an oversized hardcover affair, with Orwell's previously unpublished foreword, his rare foreword to the Ukranian edition of 1947, and color illustrations throughout by famed gonzo artist Ralph Steadman. For a view into the complex mind and life of this incisive writer, page through the detailed *George Orwell* by Gordon Bowker (Little, Brown, 2004).

"HEART OF THE PARK"

Flannery O'Connor's several dozen deeply elegant stories of the sacramental, the Southern, and the grotesque were collected for the first time in 1971's *Complete Stories* (Farrar, Straus and Giroux), which includes previously unavailable stories such as 1949's "The Heart of the Park." All of her work—stories, novels, essays, and letters—is in *Flannery O'Connor: Collected Works* (Library of America, 1988). Brad Gooch's *Flannery: A Life of Flannery O'Connor* (Back Bay Books, 2010) brings to life this fierce, mysterious writer, as well as her long-term friendships with such literary celebrities as Robert Lowell, Elizabeth Hardwick, and Elizabeth Bishop.

NINETEEN EIGHTY-FOUR

We have George Orwell's prescient 1949 dystopian novel *Nineteen Eighty-Four* to thank for phrases like "Big Brother," "Thought Police," and "Orwellian." Plume's paperback edition (2003) has a foreword by the elusive Thomas Pynchon, and an afterword by Erich Fromm. *Nineteen Eighty-Four* and *Animal Farm* are available together in one volume from Houghton Mifflin Harcourt (2003), introduced by Christopher Hitchens. The novel's influence on popular culture is pervasive, with themes and phrases popping up in songs, artworks, TV series, and cinema. The most popular film adaptation—fittingly released in 1984—features Richard Burton in his final role on screen.

THE MAN WITH THE GOLDEN ARM

Gritty and powerful, *The Man with the Golden Arm* earned its author, Nelson Algren, the first National Book Award for Fiction and begat a 1955 author-unapproved film starring Ol' Blue Eyes himself, Frank Sinatra. Seven Stories Press's fiftieth anniversary edition (1999) features an extensive critical appendix with contributions from Kurt Vonnegut, Studs Terkel, William Savage, and others. For more grit, see *Entrapment and Other Writings* (Seven Stories Press, 2009), which contains several previously unpublished or uncollected works.

"VOICE OF THE HAMSTER"

Elusive and ever-so-postmodern writer Thomas Pynchon got an early start: he wrote "Voice of the Hamster" at only fifteen years old. It was serialized in his high school newspaper, *Oyster Bay High School Purple and Gold*, in 1952–53. The story was later published in *Thomas Pynchon: A Bibliography of Primary and Secondary Materials* (Dalkey Archive Press, 1989), which is now out of print, but you can still find the text online.

WAITING FOR GODOT

Samuel Beckett's own English translation of his influential play *En attendant Godot*, which premiered in 1953, is published by Grove Press (*Waiting for Godot*, 2011). The obtuse text invites diverse interpretations. Find a guide in *Samuel Beckett's Waiting for Godot* by British professors Mark and Juliette Taylor-Batty (2009), published as part of Continuum's Modern Theatre Guides. Or splurge on the guide from Bloom's Modern Critical Interpretations (2008), edited by Harold Bloom. Beckett himself resisted offers to adapt the play for film, but many movies have followed its model, including *Waiting for Guffman* (1996) and *Clerks* (1994).

"THE DANCER"

The magisterial verses of Chilean feminist, teacher, and diplomat Gabriela Mistral is not as readily available in English as they should be. But *Madwomen: The "Locas mujeres" Poems of Gabriela Mistral; A Bilingual Edition* (University of Chicago Press, 2009), featuring Randall Couch's excellent translations of lyrically intense poems like "La bailarina" ("The Dancer"), offers a nuanced, succinct introduction that sets the works in biographical context. Famed author Ursula K. Le Guin has selected and translated her own anthology, *Selected Poems of Gabriela Mistral* (University of New Mexico Press, 2003). To learn more about the gender and political boundaries Mistral brushed aside on her way to success, consider checking out *Queer Mother for the Nation: The State and Gabriela Mistral* by Licia Fiol-Matta (University of Minnesota Press, 2002).

LORD OF THE FLIES

William Golding's iconic, controversial 1954 novel, *Lord of the Flies*, captures the complexity of human nature in dire circumstances, and has become a staple of the high school reading list. The Centenary Edition from Perigee (2011) is slim and lovely, and features an introduction by Stephen King. Even Harold Bloom has deigned to treat the novel with his critical eye, in *William Golding's Lord of the Flies* (Bloom's Modern Critical Interpretation, 2008). The novel has been adapted for film twice: by director Harry Hook in 1990, and by director Peter Brook in 1963; the latter has been released by the Criterion Collection. John Carey's recent biography, *William Golding: The Man Who Wrote Lord of the Flies* (Free Press, 2010), draws upon previously unpublished materials and information to paint a definitive portrait.

THE DOORS OF PERCEPTION

If you thought *Brave New World* was trippy, wait until you read Aldous Huxley's 1954 spiritual and aesthetic awakening. Harper Perennial's Modern Classics edition (2009) pairs it with Huxley's later essay on consciousness-altering drugs, "Heaven and Hell," and features for the first time an additional essay, "Drugs That Shape Men's Minds." If you're looking for more on Huxley's psychedelic experiments, page through *Moksha: Aldous Huxley's Classic Writings on Psychedelics and the Visionary Experience* (Park Street Press, 1999), which includes selections from his major works as well as magazine articles, letters, and scientific papers demonstrating the evolution of his ideas on mind-altering substances.

LOLITA

Until the 1955 publication of Vladimir Nabokov's classic *Lolita*, few readers expected to read such a beautiful, sorrowful, and complex portrayal of pedophilia. Read the novel in Vintage's 1989 fiftieth anniversary edition, or take a sampling of a wider range of Nabokov's prose from the slim, inexpensive *Vintage Nabokov* (Vintage, 2004). Library of America's *Nabokov: Novels 1955–1962* includes the author's own *Lolita* screenplay—compare it with the very different 1962 Stanley Kubrick film adaptation, and then the 1997 Adrian Lynne version.

FOUR BEATS

The sexual experimentation, anti-conformist attitude, and spontaneous creativity of the Beat Generation has pervaded nearly all corners of American culture, but its literary legacy is especially lasting. Check out the vital and exuberant work of Beats like Neal Cassady, Allen Ginsberg, and more in *The Portable Beat Reader* (Penguin Classics, 2003). The volume, edited by Beat expert Ann Charters, is not slim, but the excellent selection and biographical, historical, and critical essays make it well worth the heft. For the complete guide to all things Beat, consider *The Typewriter Is Holy: The Complete, Uncensored History of the Beat Generation* (Free Press, 2010) by leading authority Bill Morgan.

ON THE ROAD

First published in 1957, Jack Kerouac's inimitable *On the Road* is available today from Penguin Classics (2002) with an introduction by biographer Ann Charters. Before the novel was first published, the 120-foot scroll on which Kerouac wrote it was edited and the names of the characters changed. For the *On the Road* centenary, Viking published the rough, uncut, more provocative text straight from the scroll. Make your own comparisons in *On the Road: The Original Scroll from Penguin Classics Deluxe* (2008), which includes a critical introduction explaining the publication and compositional history, as well as the cultural context. (A facsimile edition of the original scroll is rumored to be in the works.) As usual, the Library of America offers the most handsome, inclusive, and expensive option: *Jack Kerouac: Road Novels, 1957–1960* (2007), which includes *On the Road*, *The Dharma Bums*, and more.

NAKED LUNCH

Nowhere is the relationship between art and obscenity more sensationally and explosively explored than in William S. Burroughs's *Naked Lunch*. Check out this seminal, controversial work in *Naked Lunch: The Restored Text* (Grove Press, 2004). Edited by longtime Burroughs editor James Grauerholz and Barry Miles, the text corrects many editorial errors, incorporates Burroughs's own notes and essays, and includes an appendix of new material and alternative drafts. For a bit more cash, you can own the deluxe fiftieth anniversary edition, in which the restored text is gorgeously clothbound and slipcased and clinched by a new afterword by David Ulin. Don't miss David Cronenberg's 1991 *Naked Lunch* film, which combines adapted material from the book with biographical elements of Burroughs's own life.

ONE FLEW OVER THE CUCKOO'S NEST

Merry Prankster Ken Kesey's *One Flew Over the Cuckoo's Nest* is a rip-roaring, rambunctious, and searing story about a mental institution, its inhabitants, and ultimately, society as a whole. First published in 1962, the novel was adapted in 1975 into a five-time Academy Award–winning film starring Jack Nicholson. Read the 2002 Penguin Classics edition, which features a new foreword and unpublished drawings by Kesey. Or, for only a couple dollars more, you can have the 2007 Penguin Classics Deluxe Edition, with a foreword by Chuck Palahniuk and cover by Joe Sacco.

THE BELL JAR

Sylvia Plath committed suicide only a month after the 1963 UK publication of *The Bell Jar*; perhaps writing this roman à clef about descent into depression was the catharsis she needed before leaving this world. Check out the Harper Perennial Modern Classics edition (2006), and then perhaps compare the breakdown of the fictional Esther Greenwood to the breakdown of Plath herself in *The Unabridged Journals of Sylvia Plath* (Anchor, 2000). *The Unraveling Archive: Essays on Sylvia Plath* (University of Michigan Press, 2007) presents a range of deep, scholarly essays on Plath's life, work, and impact.

LAST EXIT TO BROOKLYN

Like many cult classics, Hubert Selby, Jr.'s *Last Exit to Brooklyn* depicts society's outcasts: drug addicts, homosexuals, transvestites, and the down-and-out in Brooklyn. First published in 1964, it can still be found in Grove's 1994 paperback edition. Check out Uli Edel's grim, award-winning 1989 film adaptation. For a more critical approach to *Last Exit to Brooklyn* and Selby's other major works (including the famous *Requiem for a Dream*), page through the pricy, but illuminating, *Understanding Hubert Selby, Jr.* by Professor James R. Giles (University of South Carolina Press, 1998).

DIARIES OF ANAÏS NIN

Anaïs Nin hid little of her famous love triangle with American writer Henry Miller and his wife, June; she published groundbreaking female erotica and became famous for her published journals, which span nearly her entire life. Fifteen volumes of her diaries are available from Mariner Books, edited by Nin scholar Gunther Stuhlmann. Mariner also publishes unexpurgated narratives from the journals in standalone editions, like *Henry and June* (1990) and *Incest* (1993). *Henry and June* was adapted into a film of the same name by Philip Kaufman in 1990—it's just as titillating as the text itself. *The Portable Anaïs Nin* (Sky Blue Press, 2011), edited by Benjamin Franklin V, arranges excerpts from all of the diary volumes (including the later uncensored ones), Nin's erotica, her novels, and other works into a handy, annotated collection.

THE MASTER AND MARGARITA

If the gun-toting, vodka-swilling cat wandering around Moscow on two legs doesn't reel you in, perhaps the densely packed allusions to Stalin's Soviet Russia will. Mikhail Bulgakov's *The Master and Margarita*, first published in 1966, is a true satiric trip. Richard Pevear and Larrissa Volokhonsky, award-winning translators of *The Brothers Karamazov*, brought the novel into English from the unabridged, original Russian, and include an insightful introduction and notes that help identify the many Soviet allusions (Penguin Classics, 2001). Mirra Ginsburg's popular translation (Grove Press, 1994) is from the censored Russian text and therefore incomplete, while Michael Glenny's is known for its smooth flow, but also for the many liberties it takes with the original text (Everyman's Library, 1992). The Diana Burgin and Katherine Tiernan O'Connor translation is widely regarded as the most accurate (Vintage, 1996).

ONE HUNDRED YEARS OF SOLITUDE

One Hundred Years of Solitude, Gabriel García Márquez's epic, lyrical tale of birth and death in the mythical town of Macondo, has become an icon of magical realism and of Latin American literature as a whole. Find Oprah's insignia on the Harper Perennial Modern Classics Edition, translated from the Spanish by famed translator Gregory Rabassa (2006). For the inside story on the life of this brilliant, Nobel Prize–winning Colombian writer, check out the first volume in a planned trilogy of memoirs, *Living to Tell the Tale* (Knopf, 2003), translated by the estimable Edith Grossman.

IN WATERMELON SUGAR

Nothing is as it seems, and nothing stays the same in counterculture classic *In Watermelon Sugar* by Richard Brautigan. This novella, first published in 1968, can be found alongside two other major works in Richard Brautigan's *Trout Fishing in America*, *The Pill versus Springhill Mine Disaster*, and *In Watermelon Sugar* (Mariner, 1989). *Jubilee Hitchhiker: The Life and Times of Richard Brautigan* by William Hjortsberg (Counterpoint, 2012) captures this enigmatic poet and novelist of the 1960s.

GRAVITY'S RAINBOW

Epically postmodern and exhaustively referential, Thomas Pynchon's National Book Award–winning 1973 novel, *Gravity's Rainbow*, is available in a lovely deluxe edition from Penguin Classics (2006). Should you need a guide for this famously difficult and allusive text, see *A Gravity's Rainbow Compan-*

ion: Sources and Contexts for Pynchon's Novel (University of Georgia Press, 2006), by Steven C. Weisenburger. For a more graphic kind of guidance, take a look at *Pictures Showing What Happens on Each Page of Thomas Pynchon's Novel Gravity's Rainbow*, in which punk artist Zak Smith illustrates each hallucinatory, surreal page of the novel and writer Steve Erickson contributes an introduction (Tin House Books, 2006).

CRASH

J. G. Ballard's shocking, hypnotic novel *Crash*, first published in England in 1973 is available in paperback from Picador (2001). David Cronenberg transposed it into a controversially lurid film starring James Spader and Holly Hunter in 1996. Ballard's New Wave fiction has influenced the cyberpunk movement, and post-punk and industrial music—see Joy Division and the Normal, for starters.

"I BOUGHT A LITTLE CITY"

First published in 1974 in *The New Yorker*, Donald Barthelme's story "I Bought a Little City" is a perfect example of the writer's absurdist, playful fiction. It can be found alongside several other compact works from the 1960s and 1970s in *Sixty Stories* (Penguin Classics, 2003). The volume, with an introduction by David Gates, is the broadest Barthelme collection in print today, and contains several previously uncollected stories. Writer Donald Antrim—who openly acknowledges Barthelme's influence on his work—reads "I Bought a Little City" and then discusses it with *New Yorker* fiction editor Deborah Treisman on a New Yorker podcast, available online for free.

"WHAT WE TALK ABOUT WHEN WE TALK ABOUT LOVE"

Before Raymond Carver succumbed to alcoholism and heavy smoking, he revitalized the American short story with works like 1981's "What We Talk About When We Talk About Love." Hugely reduced by Carver's longtime editor Gordon Lish, it is included in the eponymous collection, Carver's second (Vintage, 1989). Recently, Carver's widow fought to have the collection published as Carver originally wrote it, before Lish's controversial alterations—this story, for instance, appears as "Beginners" in *Raymond Carver: Collected Stories* (Library of America, 2009), edited by William Stull and Maureen Carroll. The volume also includes Carver's other collections.

BLOOD AND GUTS IN HIGH SCHOOL

High school really sucks for Janey Smith, Kathy Acker's protagonist—she is ditched by her father/lover, conscripted by a gang, kidnapped and sold into prostitution, besides dying of cancer. *Blood and Guts in High School* is a metafictional collage exploring gender politics, writing theory, and capitalism. It was first published in 1984, and can be read in Grove Press's 1994 paperback edition. Grove also publishes Acker's other novels, including. *Empire of the Senseless* and *Don Quixote*. For a wider sampling, consider *Essential Acker: The Selected Writings of Kathy Acker* (Grove Press, 2002), edited by Amy Scholder and Dennis Cooper and with an introduction by Jeanette Winterson; it contains excerpts from nineteen of her novels.

BLOOD MERIDIAN

Cormac McCarthy's sparse prose glows with expansive myth and history in his 1985 novel of the American Wild West, *Blood Meridian*. Read the twenty-fifth anniversary paperback edition *Blood Meridian: Or the Evening Redness in the West* from Vintage (1992), or splurge on Modern Library's 2001 clothbound edition, which includes an introduction by McCarthy enthusiast Harold Bloom. To appreciate the true extent of the historical and biblical references in this bloody novel, you may want to consult *Notes on Blood Meridian: Revised and Expanded Edition* by McCarthy scholar John Sepich (University of Texas Press, 2008).

FOUCAULT'S PENDULUM

Umberto Eco's best-selling 1988 novel, *Foucault's Pendulum*, is sometimes known as "the thinking person's *Da Vinci Code*." First published in Italy as *Il pendolo di Foucault*, the novel was translated into English by William Weaver, and is available in paperback from Mariner Books (2007). Eco is a philosopher and prolific author of criticism, essays, fiction, and children's books. To get inside his mind, page through *On Literature*, a collection of his penetrating, often humorous, essays on his writing career, translated by Martin McLaughlin (Mariner 2005).

WILD AT HEART

In the spirit of the Beats, Barry Gifford's Sailor and Lula series features a pair of star-crossed, sex-crazed lovers who hit the road. The first novel in the series, *Wild at Heart: The Story of Sailor and Lula* (1990), caught the eye of director David Lynch, who adapted it into an award-winning 1990 film starring Nicolas Cage and Laura Dern. The complete series can be found in a compact volume, *Sailor & Lula: The Complete Novels* (Seven Stories Press, 2010).

THE FAMISHED ROAD

Whether you call it magical realism, animist realism, or just plain fantasy, there is no denying that Nigerian author Ben Okri's 1991 novel, *The Famished Road*, presents a powerful, mythic vision of modern-day Africa. It won the Booker Prize, after all. Immerse yourself in its fevered, hypnotic atmosphere in Anchor's 1993 paperback edition.

EINSTEIN'S DREAMS

Only a twentieth-century genius like Albert Einstein could make science so cool, and only a brilliant science writer like Alan Lightman could make a fictional book about Einstein's dreams an international best seller. First published in 1992, *Einstein's Dreams* has become a university reading list staple. Vintage is now in its sixth reprint of the novel (2004), and the story has been adapted for the stage several times.

THE WIND-UP BIRD CHRONICLE

The surreal, quirky fiction of Japanese writer Haruki Murakami has reached incredible international fame, especially since 1995's *The Wind-Up Bird Chronicle*. The English translation by Jay Rubin takes certain liberties with the text (for example, a couple of chapters are completed excised) but is still magnificent; it can be read in Vintage's paperback edition (1998).

The scholarly minded Murakami reader might want to consider investing in *Haruki Murakami's The Wind-Up Bird Chronicle: A Reader's Guide* by Professor Matthew Strecher (Continuum, 2002), a slim volume that includes an author biography, interviews, full-length analysis of the novel, and more.

INFINITE JEST

David Foster Wallace's tome *Infinite Jest* has a special place in many a hipster's heart. Sprawling, heavily footnoted, and by turns hilarious and philosophical, the 1996 novel is available in a chunky tenth anniversary paperback edition from Back Bay

Books (2006). No one would blame you for seeking guidance; see *David Foster Wallace's Infinite Jest: A Reader's Guide* (Continuum, 2nd ed., 2012), a conveniently sized volume by English professor Stephen J. Burn. For more on Foster Wallace, who tragically ended his own life much too early, check out the funny, moving *Although of Course You End Up Becoming Yourself: A Road Trip with David Foster Wallace* (Broadway, 2010), in which *Rolling Stone* writer David Lipsky records his conversations with Foster Wallace during a five-day book tour. The first book-length bio of DFW is *Every Love Story Is a Ghost Story* by D. T. Max (Viking, 2012).

Three Panel Review
Lisa Brown

DEATH IN VENICE by Thomas Mann

Famous author goes on vacation,

Becomes obsessed with a boy,

and eats some bad strawberries.

© 2011 LISA M. BROWN | DIST. BY TRIBUNE MEDIA SERVICES, INC.

CONTRIBUTORS

TREVOR ALIXOPULOS was born in Hawai'i and raised in California. His graphic novel, *The Hot Breath of War*, was published by Sparkplug Comic Books and nominated for the 2008 Ignatz Award for Outstanding Graphic Novel. Other short comics have appeared in *Study Group Magazine*. He also paints and occasionally works as a commercial illustrator. His home is Northern California.

JULIÁN ARON is an illustrator, comics artist, and graphic designer. Born in 1976, he studied at the Carlos Garaycochea School of Drawing in Buenos Aires under the legendary Argentine cartoonist Alberto Salinas. His work includes contributions to the illustrated anthologies *Joyas de la mitología* ("Treasures of Mythology") and to the comics *100% Lucha* ("100% Fight"), *Skorpio*, and *Lanciostory*. He has also designed book covers for Planeta in Spain and Alfaguara in Argentina, as well as a number of album covers.

ANDRICE ARP makes comics, paintings, illustrations, and small objects in Portland, Oregon. She was the coeditor of the Hi-Horse comic book series, which ran from 2001 to 2004, and *Hi-Horse Omnibus*, which was published in 2004 by Alternative Comics. Since then, her comics and paintings have appeared semi-regularly in the Fantagraphics comics anthology *Mome*, among other places. Her paintings have been in group shows

at Giant Robot and other galleries, and in a solo show at Secret Headquarters. She is currently working on trying to understand everything.

ANDREA ARROYO's work is exhibited widely and is in featured private and museum collections around the world, including the Library of Congress and the Smithsonian Institution. She has been named as one of the 21 Leaders for the 21st Century, Groundbreaking Latina in the Arts, Official Artist of the Latin Grammys, and Outstanding Latina of the Year. And she has received awards from Clinton Global Initiative, New York City Council, New York Foundation for the Arts, Northern Manhattan Arts Alliance, Harlem Arts Alliance, and Lower Manhattan Cultural Council. Her work has been published extensively, including in the *New Yorker* and the *New York Times*.

T. EDWARD BAK's illustrated natural history biography, *WILD MAN: The Strange Journey and Fantastic Account of the Naturalist Georg Wilhelm Steller*, was originally serialized in the Fantagraphics comics anthology *Mome*. The artist has conducted his own research in southeast Alaska and the Aleutian archipelago, as well as in St. Petersburg, Russia, where he has delivered presentations of his work for this ongoing project. He resides in Portland, Oregon.

LESLEY BARNES is an animator and illustrator from Glasgow. Her animations have shown in competition at film festivals all over the world and have won a number of awards. Lesley recently expanded into illustration, and her work has since been featured in publications such as *Grafik*, Puffin Books, *Time Out*, *Glamour*, and the *Sunday Times Style Magazine* and at institutions such as the Victoria & Albert Museum in London. See more at lesleybarnes.co.uk.

ROBERT BERRY left behind a career as an easel painter in Detroit ten years ago and moved to Philadelphia to make comics and stories. With his production partner, Josh Levitas, he's the cartoonist of *Ulysses "Seen,"* an interactive comic book adaptation of Joyce's great novel. His adaptation in Volume 1 of *The Graphic Canon*, of Shakespeare's Sonnet 18, is dedicated to his mother, who taught him everything he knows about Shakespeare, poetry, and the uncompromising drive it takes to make art.

BENJAMIN BIRDIE is the artist behind the popular webcomic *The Rack*, about a comic shop (with writer Kevin Church and colorist Joe Hunter). More correctly, it's a comic strip about the *people* who work in a comic shop, which means it's a bit soap-operatic and there's whole storylines that have nothing to do with talking about how Nova's helmet makes him look like a "ladies' massager." See more at agreeablecomics.com/therack.

JOHN BLAKE studied illustration at Middlesex University, after which he worked as a freelance illustrator for several years, providing images for a wide range of clients. He is currently employed at Sony Computer Entertainment and continues to work on various art projects, manga, and webcomics. In recent years, he has also moved into sculpture and now runs the tabletop miniatures range *Titan Wargames*. More of his work is available to view at johnblakeillustration.com.

LISA BROWN is a *New York Times*-best-selling illustrator, author, and cartoonist. She lives in San Francisco. You can usually find her at americanchickens.com.

JASON COBLEY lives with his wife and daughter in Norfolk, in the east of England, where he spends most of his days teaching English to high school children. He writes about mythical monsters and historical heroes, most notably in his Weird Wild West graphic novel, *Frontier: Dealing with Demons*, with artist Andrew Wildman (Print Media Productions, 2011), and his children's novel, *The Legend of Tom Hickathrift* (Mogzilla, 2012). He has adapted classic texts—*Frankenstein*, *Dracula*, "Dulce et Decorum Est," and *An Inspector Calls*—for Classical Comics; in 2009, *Frankenstein* won an Association of Educational Publishers award. Jason is currently working on an adaptation of Charles Dickens's *The Signal-Man* with artist David Hitchcock.

MOLLY CRABAPPLE is an artist, comics creator, and the founder of Dr. Sketchy's Anti-Art School, a chain of alt-drawing events that takes place in 140 cities around the world. She is the coauthor, with John Leavitt, of *Puppet Makers* (DC Comics) and *Straw House* (First Second Books).

For nearly four decades, **ROBERT CRUMB** has shocked, entertained, titillated, and challenged the imaginations (and the inhibitions) of comics fans the world over. In truth, alternative comics as we know them today might never have come about without R. Crumb's influence—the acknowledged "Father" of the underground comics could also be considered the "Grandfather" of alternative comics. Mr. Natural, Angelfood McSpade, Flakey Foont, and most especially, the hedonistic anthropomorphic version of Crumb's childhood pet, Fritz (a cat), have become cult icons. His voluptuous, acid-inspired romps of the 1960s gave way to comparatively sober, introspective dialogues and biting indictments of American culture. In 2009 he published—to worldwide acclaim—a complete adaptation of the Book of Genesis.

DAME DARCY is known worldwide as an illustrator, writer, animator, fine artist, musician, filmmaker, and doll crafter. She designs, animates, and produces music for and conceptualizes Paper Doll Dreams, an online game based on Meat Cake comix. She has collaborated with writers ranging from Alan Moore to Tori Amos, and her comic book series, *Meat Cake*, has been published by Fantagraphics Books for twenty years. Her most recent graphic novel, *Hand Book for Hot Witches*, was released in 2012 by Henry Holt and Company, and she's currently at work on the *Black Rainbow Ranch* graphic novel trilogy, a romantic dark fantasy based on Darcy's life as a teen. A musician with the band Death By Doll, and fashion illustrator for the likes of Anna Sui and others, Darcy is also the founder of the EZ Bake Coven Forum (ezbakecoven.com), a feminist place to connect with other artists and profile your own art, with a gothic Lolita flair. You can find out more at DameDarcy.com, where she can be contacted directly.

A graduate of the Joe Kubert School of Cartoon and Graphic Art in Dover, New Jersey, **DAN DUNCAN** is an illustrator, designer, and "storyteller" for the animation, movies, gaming, and comic book industries. Due to a zero-tolerance policy on snow, Dan now lives and works in Burbank, California, where the warm weather allows him to work without being hindered by stiff little fingers and a heavy coat. Primarily telling stories in comics and animation, he has also done a range of freelance work for clients such as Criterion, Blizzard, IDW, Film Roman, Image, Marvel, Boom!, and Hasbro. See his work at dan-duncan.deviantart.com or dan-duncan.blogspot.com.

JEREMY EATON is an alternative cartoonist and illustrator whose work has been published in more than a dozen comics and paperback collections by the likes of Fantagraphics Books, Chronicle Books, Kitchen Sink Press, and Black Eye Comics, major titles being *A Sleepyhead Tale*, *The Island of Dr. Moral*, and *A World of Trouble*.

C. FRAKES grew up on the ocean, but left home for funny book school. She was a member of the inaugural class of the Center for Cartoon Studies, and was awarded a Xeric Grant to publish her book *Tragic Relief* in the fall of 2007. In 2009, her second graphic novel, *Woman King*, won the Ignatz Award for Promising New Talent. Her most recent book, *Island Brat*, was published with help from Koyama Press.

CHANDRA FREE is the writer and illustrator of the graphic novel series, *The God Machine*. Born in Orlando, Florida, Chandra now resides in Brooklyn, New York, where she concocts her uniquely abstract and elongated art and comics. Intensely interested in the incorporation of psychology in her art, she focuses on the unconscious and human aspects of her characters. She has worked as a digital painter on the comic series Sullengrey, and as an illustrator on Jim Henson's *Fraggle Rock*, and has contributed paintings to Conspiracy of the Planet of the Apes. She is an art director at BLAM! Ventures.

JULIA GFRÖRER is an artist and letterpress printer from Concord, New Hampshire. She earned her BFA in printmaking from Cornish College of the Arts in Seattle in 2004, and moved to Portland, Oregon, in 2007. Her comic books include *Mundane Grimoire*, *Too Dark to See*, the series *Ariadne auf Naxos*, and *Flesh and Bone*, which was nominated for an Ignatz Award for Outstanding Comic in 2010, and was included in 2011's *Best American Comics*.

KATE GLASHEEN earned a BFA in drawing in 2004 from Pratt Institute in Brooklyn, New York. Since then, she has divided her time between her birthplace of Troy, New York, and Brooklyn—drawing, and collecting enemies like baseball cards. Other sequential works include the critically acclaimed *Hybrid Bastards!* written by Tom Pinchuk and published by Archaia Entertainment, and the self-published *Bandage: A Diary of Sorts*, her most personal work to date. Her portfolio can be found online at katiecrimespree.com.

ROBERT GOODIN spends his days working on *American Dad!* for Fox and his nights drawing comics. He has published stories in the Fantagraphics anthology *Mome*, and has had a solo comic, *The Man Who Loved Breasts*, published by Top Shelf Productions. He lives in Los Angeles with his wife and two dogs.

FRANK M. HANSEN is a cartoonist, artist, and writer living in Los Angeles. He creates original cartoons for various print and digital publications around the globe in addition to creating designs for the clothing and animation industries. He is currently working to bring sound and motion to his cartoons in what he hopes is a fresh and new way, and posting satirical cartoons at AnimaticPress.com. To quench his desire to merge design and expression further, he creates ink and paint pieces, which have been shown at several galleries, including Gallery Nucleus, WMA Gallery, and the Red Gate Gallery in London. You can see more of his work at fmhansen.com.

COLE JOHNSON lives in San Antonio, Texas. His first book, *Hush-Hush*, was released in 2009 by l'employé du Moi. His work has appeared in a number of anthologies and self-published minicomics. His website is colejohnson.net.

JULIACKS makes worlds with comics, performance-installations, film, and theater. Published internationally in independent maga- zines and anthologies including *Kuti*, *Windy Corner Magazine*, and *Unicorn Mountain*, in 2009 Sparkplug Comic Books published her collaborative comic book, *Rock that Never Sleeps*. While in Finland on a Fulbright grant for performance art, she made the comic art book and film *Invisible Forces*, which was taken on a mini-world tour. Her graphic novel *Swell* premiered as a play at Culture Project's Women Center Stage Festival 2012 in New York. Currently living in France, she's beginning a new film, performance, and comics project: Architecture of An Atom.

MOLLY KIELY is an artist, illustrator, underground cartoonist; Canadian-in-exile in Tucson, Arizona; and stay-at-home mom to a spitfire. She's been drawing erotic comix since 1991, including the *Diary of a Dominatrix* and *Saucy Little Tart* series, and graphic novels *That Kind of Girl* and *Tecopa Jane*. The Wapshott Press recently collected her works in *Molly Kiely: Selections 1991–2012*. See more at mollykiely.com or mollykiely.tumblr.com.

MATT KISH is a librarian in Ohio. Childhood obsessions with Jack Kirby, Philippe Druillet, and the *Monster Manual* led to this all. He talks to the planets, the results of which can be seen at spudd64.com.

ANDRZEJ KLIMOWSKI has exhibited internationally, with work collected by museums in Europe and the United States. During his acclaimed career, he has designed film and theater posters; directed short, animated films in Warsaw; and designed covers for Penguin, Faber & Faber, Everyman Library, and Oberon Books. His graphic novels include *The Depository*, *The Secret*, and *Horace Dorlan*. Klimowski is a professor of illustration at the Royal College of Art, London. In addition to his adaptation of *The Master and Margarita* for SelfMadeHero, Klimowski has also adapted *Dr. Jekyll and Mr. Hyde*, which his readers can see in Volume 2 of *The Graphic Canon*.

Born in Mineola, New York, **MILTON KNIGHT** has had work published in Graphic Classics, *Heavy Metal*, *High Times*, *National Lampoon*, and *Nickelodeon* magazines. His comics titles include *Hugo*, *Midnite the Rebel Skunk*, and *Slug and Ginger*. In addition to comics and writing, Milton has worked in animation since 1991 as a designer, animator, and director. He currently exhibits and teaches at The Colonnade Art Gallery and Studio in Pasadena, California. See more at miltonknight.net.

AIDAN KOCH is an illustrator and comics artist working out of Portland, Oregon. Her first graphic novella, *The Whale*, was released in 2010. See more at aidankoch.com.

JOY KOLITSKY is a freelance illustrator and storyboard artist. She also has a small greeting card company called Sugar Beet Press, which features her artwork. She started making comics after college at the encouragement of comic-loving friends and has continued to enjoy doing so to this day. After many years in Los Angeles and New York, she now lives by the beach with her husband and son in Ocean City, New Jersey.

JUAN CARLOS KREIMER is an Argentine journalist, writer, novelist, and editor. His most recent novel is *Quién Lo Hará Posible?*, and his book *Bici y Zen, Ciclismo Urbano Como Meditación* (*Bike 'n' Zen: Urban Cycling as Meditation*) is forthcoming from Planeta. Two of his nonfiction books have enjoyed continuous reprinting: *Cómo Lo Escribo?* and *Punk: La Muerte Joven*. He is the editor of the Spanish-language Para Principiantes (For Beginners) series, and is the author of *Krishnamuerti for Beginners* (Writers and Readers, UK) and *Counterculture for Beginners* (Zidane Press, UK).

PETER KUPER is cofounder of the political graphics magazine *World War 3 Illustrated*. Since 1997, he has written and drawn *Spy vs. Spy* for every issue of *MAD*. Kuper has produced over twenty books, including *The System* and an adaptation of Franz Kafka's *The Metamorphosis*. He lived in Oaxaca, Mexico, July 2006–2008, during a major teachers' strike, and his work from that time can be seen in his book *Diario de Oaxaca*. Kuper has been teaching comics courses for twenty-five years in New York and is a visiting professor at Harvard University.

DAVID LASKY has been a published cartoonist since 1989. Among his best-known work is the award-nominated *Urban Hipster*, in collaboration with Greg Stump, and *No Ordinary Flu*, in collaboration with King County Public Health. His first graphic novel is *Carter Family Comics: Don't Forget This Song*, the story of the first family of country music, in collaboration with Frank Young.

BRENDAN LEACH is an Ignatz and Xeric award-winning graphic novelist and illustrator. His comics have been published by Top Shelf Comics, Secret Acres, and Retrofit Comics. Brendan's illustration work has been recognized by the Society of Illustrators and *3x3 Magazine*, and his comics have been included in many collections and anthologies, including the 2011 *Best American Comics*. Brendan received his MFA in illustration from the School of Visual Arts. He used to drive a zamboni in New Jersey, but now he lives and draws in Brooklyn, New York.

SONIA LEONG is an award-winning manga artist and company secretary of the UK-based Sweatdrop Studios. Best known for *Manga Shakespeare: Romeo and Juliet* (SelfMade-Hero), she's worked with Tokyopop, Image, *NEO Magazine*, Channel 4, HarperCollins, Hachette, Walker and others on over eighty projects. She has taught manga at the *Guardian*'s Hay Festival, Victoria & Albert Museum, London County Hall, and internationally with the British Council, and her art's been featured in the Kyoto International Manga Museum and London Cartoon Museum.

JOSH LEVITAS shares the byline for *Ulysses "Seen,"* an annotated comics adaptation of James Joyce's *Ulysses*, with Robert Berry, handling the graphic design, web design, production art, and hand-lettering duties. He also handles the graphic design and app interface design for Throwaway

Horse's other iPad releases: Martin Rowson's *The Waste Land "Seen"* and Eric Shanower's *Age of Bronze "Seen."*

Born on Long Island, illustrator **ELLEN LINDNER** now lives in New York City after spending time in London, England. She is the author of *Undertow*, a graphic novel about Coney Island in the early 1960s, and the editor of *The Strumpet*, a transatlantic comics magazine showcasing art by upcoming women cartoonists. See more of Ellen's comics and illustration online at littlewhitebird.com, or take a peek at her sketchbook at ellenlindner.livejournal.com.

VERONICA LIU is an editor at Seven Stories Press.

After failing as a medical illustrator, **SALLY MADDEN** turned to comic book illustration in 2005, the same year she cofounded the discontinued but still financially exhausting anthology *Always Comix*. A member of the Partyka Collective, she is working on a series of folktale adaptations with fellow member Matt Wiegle. She is supposedly illustrating a book of the Catholic saints with Marvel science fiction writer Charlie H. Swift, who has been researching the book for over two decades with no end in sight. She has done cartooning work for Wide Awake Press and the online music magazine *If You Make It*. She lives in the city of her birth, Philadelphia, with her husband and no children.

MARDOU was born in 1975 and grew up in Manchester, England. She studied English Literature at the University of Wales and began making minicomics after graduation. She's currently serializing a graphic novel called *The Sky in Stereo*. Mardou now lives in St. Louis, Missouri, with her cartoonist husband, Ted May, and their small daughter. See more at mardouville.com.

STEPHANIE MCMILLAN has been a political cartoonist since 1992. In 2012, she won the Robert F. Kennedy Journalism Award for her work on the self-syndicated *Code Green*, a weekly editorial cartoon focused on the environmental emergency, and the Occupy cartoons collected in *The Beginning of the American Fall*. She also creates the comic strip *Minimum Security*. Her cartoons have appeared in hundreds of publications including the *Los Angeles Times*, *Daily Beast*, and the *San Francisco Bay Guardian*. She currently works with an anticapitalist/anti-imperialist collective called One Struggle. See more at StephanieMcMillan.org.

While toddling around on the patio unobserved, eighteen-month-old **REBECCA MIGDAL** ate several dead cockroaches. At three, mounted on her trusty tricycle, she attempted to ram head-first through the wall of the family garage in emulation of cartoon hero Mighty Mouse. (The consequences included five stitches.) Some years later, Rebecca would fashion a large and convincing-looking cockroach out of eggplant skin, stuck together with green icing, and eat it with gusto during a public performance. Today, Rebecca Migdal is a cartoonist. See more at rosettastonecomic.com.

ANNIE MOK is a maker, cartoonist, and illustrator. She received a BFA from the Minneapolis College of Art and Design in 2009 and currently lives in Philadelphia. She has previously published under the names "Eel" and "Ed Choy." She self-publishes mostly Risograph-printed comics; edited and published the Xeric-awarded anthology *Ghost Comics*; and recently contributed to 2D Cloud's *Little Heart* with "Roosterlegs," a collaboration with artist Sam Sharpe. Find her work at edsdeadbody.com and anniemok.tumblr.com.

The spiritual lovechild of Jack Kirby and Pablo Picasso, **J. BEN MOSS** is from the artistic no-fly zone called Shreveport, Louisiana. He is the star of many an internet profile "About Me" section, as well as the creator of a bajillion brain-babies that may or may not decide to surface in full light of day. J. Ben Moss is an actual, real-life literate Southerner who is pursuing his MLA with a concentration in animation and visual effects. He is also father to the two most brilliant and awe-inspiringly beautiful daughters to have ever existed in the entire multiverse. See more of his work at thecreativefinder.com/benmoss or squoog.com.

ONSMITH grew up in a small town in Oklahoma and currently lives in Chicago. His art and comics have appeared in numerous publications such as *Hotwire Comics* (Fantagraphics Books), *An Anthology of Graphic Fiction, Cartoons, and True Stories* (Yale University Press) and the recent *BLACK EYE* anthology (Rotland Press). He also exhibits his work in galleries and continues to create his own self-published books. See more at onsmithcomics.blogspot.com.

REY ORTEGA is an illustrator working out of Toronto, Canada. His work has appeared in magazines, art galleries, ad campaigns, and on his mom's fridge. If he isn't drawing/reading/sleeping/playing video games, then he's probably thinking about drawing/reading/sleeping/playing video games. Rey's work focuses on the intersection between reality and magic. His contributions to this volume, and the books they are inspired by, share this sensibility.

EMELIE ÖSTERGREN was born in Sweden in 1982. Her most recent publication, *The Duke and His Army: A Dream Revisited*, as well as her debut comics work, *Evil Dress*, were published by Sanatorium Förlag in Sweden. In 2010 and 2011, three volumes of *Mr. Kenneth* were published by Optimal Press. She has also participated in anthologies and magazines such as the *Believer* and *Kuti*. See more at emelieostergren.se.

JORDYN OSTROFF graduated from Brown University, where she studied comparative literature and art history. Originally from Miami, Florida, she now lives in Brooklyn and works variously in art and publishing.

CAROLINE PICARD is an artist and writer based out of Chicago. She is also the founding director and senior editor for the Green Lantern Press. Her work has been published in a handful of publications, most recently *Artifice Magazine*, *MAKE* magazine, *Ampersand Review*, the *Pinch* literary journal, and *Proximity Magazine*. She is a weekly contributor to the *Bad at Sports* blog. Her first collection of short stories, *Psycho Dream Factory*, was published in 2011. For more information, visit cocopicard.com.

JOHN PIERARD is an old pro: an Air Force brat until the age of thirteen, he was ejected from that existence and forced to seek work as an illustrator. Some of his main influences have included Ray Bradbury and Harryhausen; Alfred Hitchcock and Stanley Kubrick; Sams Fuller and Peckinpah; Robert Altman; Charles Willeford; and Jim and Hunter S. Thompson—Mort Drucker, Frank Frazetta, with a soupçon of R. Crumb and Vaughn Bode. John lives in Manhattan with his beautiful wife, Wendy, and two dogs, and he really likes it a lot.

Raised just outside of Detroit, Michigan, **LAURA PLANSKER** received a BFA from the College for Creative Studies. She continued her studies in New York where she interned at the Polaroid 20x24 Studio. Her work has been exhibited in Los Angeles, Detroit, Seattle, and New York. Plansker presently lives in Eagle Rock, California, and spends most her time surrounded by scraps of felt, fun fur, dried-up paint brushes, and clay eyeballs. Someday she will clean her studio.

PMURPHY is an illustrator, designer, animator, and all-around art tinkerer currently living in Portland, Oregon. Moving on from a six-year, full-time designer gig, he moved to the Pacific Northwest from the East Coast to pursue personal and freelance work. He is inspired by his friends, functions of the brain, the occult, and online documentaries. PMurphy is always interested in creative collaborations and can be contacted here: pmurphy.org.

TED RALL is a syndicated political cartoon and the author, most recently, of the acclaimed *The Book of Obama* (Seven Stories Press, 2012). He has twice been awarded the Robert F. Kennedy Journalism Award and was a finalist for the Pulitzer Prize. He is a regular contributor to the *Los Angeles Times*, *MAD Magazine*, and scores of other publications. Visit him at Rall.com.

GRAHAM RAWLE is a London-based writer, artist, and designer. His popular *Lost Consonants* series ran weekly in the *Guardian* for fifteen years. He has produced other regular series for the *Observer*, the *Sunday Telegraph* magazine, and the *Times*. Among his published books are the *Wonder Book of Fun*, *Diary of an Amateur Photographer*, and *The Wizard of Oz*, winner of the 2009 Book of the Year at the British Book Design and Production Awards. His acclaimed novel *Woman's World* was collaged entirely from fragments of text cut from 1960s' women's magazines. His latest novel, *The Card*, was published in June 2012.

MIKE REID has a degree in fine art from London Guildhall University. He is currently working on several projects in comics and animation and lives in Hastings. By the sea.

GUSTAVO RINALDI draws characters, illustrations, animations and storyboards and does illustrations for advertising agencies, books, and magazines. His clients include Ford, Coca-Cola, Citibank, Unilever, and Philips, among others. He graduated from the University of São Paulo in Brazil with a bachelor of arts in multimedia and intermedia.

JOHN LINTON ROBERSON is a Seattle underground writer, cartoonist, and illustrator, currently adapting Frank Wedekind's *Lulu* in his comic *This Sickness*. His past works include the graphic novels *Vitriol, Vladrushka, Rosa and Annalisa*, and *Martha*, the play *Suspension of Disbelief*, as well as collaborations with Charles Alverson, Janet Harvey, and Shane Durgee. He has been published by Fantagraphics Books, spark-online.com, Martian Lit, and his own imprint, Bottomless Studio. Since 2002, he has written the blog *I Didn't Write That!* He was also the regular illustrator for *Journey Magazine* in 2008 and 2009. See more at jlroberson.org.

STEVE ROLSTON has been telling stories in the comic book medium for the past decade and has illustrated a range of genres, from the spy series *Queen & Country* to the punk rock comedy *Pounded*, from the teen drama *Emiko Superstar* to the supernatural thriller *Ghost Projekt.* His comic book work has earned an Eisner Award and Cybils Award, as well as a couple Joe Shuster Award nominations. Beyond comics, he has provided illustrations for educational children's books and character designs for both TV animation and videogame projects. Steve lives in Vancouver, Canada.

Born in London, **DANUSIA SCHEJBAL** was awarded a British Council Scholarship to study stage design at the Academy of Fine Arts in Warsaw, Poland, and later studied fashion and textiles at Ealing School of Art, Design and Media, London. From 1976 to 1981, she designed sets and costumes for various theaters in Poland. Her career has subsequently seen her as a designer for the Cherub Company, which received the *Sunday Telegraph* Award for best production at the Edinburgh Fringe Festival for *Macbeth* in 1981. Schejbal has exhibited her critically acclaimed paintings across Europe. Her further collaborations with Andrzej Klimowski on *Dr. Jekyll and Mr. Hyde* can be seen in Volume 2 of *The Graphic Canon*.

CARLY ELIZABETH SCHMITT is a freelance illustrator currently living in Fort Wayne, Indiana. She was born in southern Florida in 1988. After moving to Indiana at the age of sixteen, she completed high school and began studying illustration at Moore College of Art and Design in Philadelphia, Pennsylvania. She attended the school for a year and a half before moving to Virginia, where she lived for a few years before returning to Fort Wayne. Her illustrations are mostly done in pencil, with fine attention to detail. She is currently working on personal pieces as well as commissions. See more at milkattack.tumblr.com and flickr.com/photos/milkattack.

TARA SEIBEL is an alternative cartoonist, graphic designer, and illustrator from Cleveland, Ohio, who is best known for her collaborations with underground comix book writer Harvey Pekar. Her work has been published in Chicago's *Newcity*, the *Austin Chronicle, Cleveland Scene, Juxtapoz Magazine*, the *New York Times*, and the *Los Angeles Times*, among other publications. After receiving a BFA from Edinboro University of Pennsylvania, Seibel illustrated covers for restaurant menus and food packaging, then later worked as a line designer and illustrator for American Greetings before becoming a freelance editorial cartoonist. Seibel has taught illustration courses at Ursuline College in Cleveland. She lives with her husband, Aaron, three children, and pets in Pepper Pike, Ohio.

R. SIKORYAK is the author of *Masterpiece Comics* (Drawn & Quarterly). He's drawn for the *Onion*, the *New Yorker, GQ, MAD, SpongeBob Comics*, and *Nickelodeon Magazine*, among many other publications, as well as the TV series *The Daily Show with Jon Stewart* and *Ugly Americans*. His comics have appeared in the anthologies *Raw, Drawn & Quarterly, Hotwire, Black Eye*, and *TYPHON*. He hosts the live cartoon slide show series, *Carousel*, and has taught at the Center For Cartoon Studies and in the illustration department of Parsons The New School for Design. For more info, see rsikoryak.com and carouselslideshow.com.

DAN SIMON is the publisher of Seven Stories Press. His books include *Run, Run, Run: The Lives of Abbie Hoffman*, coauthored with Jack Hoffman (Tacher/Putnam, 1995); *Van Gogh: Self Portraits* by Pascal Bonafoux, translated by Daniel Simon (Wellfleet Press, 1989); *Nonconformity: Writing on Writing by Nelson Algren*, edited by Daniel Simon and C. S. O'Brien with an afterword by Daniel Simon (Seven Stories Press, 1996); and the 50th Anniversary Critical Edition of *The Man with the Golden Arm* by Nelson Algren, edited by Daniel Simon and William J. Savage (Seven Stories Press, 1999). In 1996, Simon was named a Chevalier in the Ordre des Arts et des Lettres, by order of the French Minister of Culture.

KATHRYN SIVEYER is an illustrator and maker of things living very happily with a dachshund and some pencils in Canterbury, UK. Her drawings have appeared in the science journal *Nature*, and as part of a prominent BBC documentary series. See more at kathrynsiveyer.carbonmade.com.

ZAK SMITH's paintings and drawings are held in many major public collections worldwide including the Museum of Modern Art and the Whitney Museum of American Art. His books include *Pictures of Girls, Pictures Showing What Happens on Each Page of Thomas Pynchon's Novel Gravity's Rainbow*, and, most recently, *We Did Porn*, an autobiographical collection of drawings and true stories about Smith's experiences working as an actor in the adult film industry under the name Zak Sabbath. He lives and works in Los Angeles and writes a regular column called "Decoder" for *Artillery* magazine.

BISHAKH SOM abandoned architecture to focus on comix, illustraton, and painting. His work has previously appeared in *Hi-Horse* (a comics anthology of which he was a coeditor and contributing artist), the anthology *Blurred Vision*, *Pood*, and the academic journal *Specs*. He received a Xeric Grant in 2003 for his comics collection *Angel*. He is currently wrapping up a larger collection of new short stories, which will soon see the light of day. He lives in Brooklyn, New York. You can see more of his work at archicomix.com.

LIESBETH DE STERCKE was born in Belgium in 1987. She graduated from Saint Lucas School of Arts in Ghent. She currently has her studio in Ghent, where she spends her time filling sketchbooks, drawing comics, and printing woodcuts. Liesbeth is hungry for books and enjoys taking Thinking Walks.

JENNY TONDERA is a graphic designer and art director currently living and working in Philadelphia. Originally from the Detroit area, she received her BFA from the Minneapolis College of Art and Design. She has worked with clients such as University of Notre Dame, Mercedes-Benz, Urban Outfitters, Philadelphia Photo Arts Center, Topman UK, and Adobe. Her work has been exhibited at the Walker Art Center and the Cranbrook Academy of Art.

The coeditor of *African-American Classics*, **LANCE TOOKS** began his career as a Marvel Comics assistant editor. He has worked as an animator on 100+ television commercials, films, and music videos; self-published the comics *Danger Funnies*, *Divided by Infinity*, and *Muthafucka*; and illustrated *The Black Panthers for Beginners*, written by Herb Boyd. His stories have appeared in Graphic Classics volumes of Edgar Allan Poe, Ambrose Bierce, Mark Twain, and Robert Louis Stevenson, and he collaborated with Harvey Pekar on *The Beats: A Graphic History* and *Studs Terkel's Working*. Tooks's first graphic novel, *Narcissa*, was named one of the year's best books by *Publishers Weekly*, and his four-volume *Lucifer's Garden of Verses* series for NBM Comics Lit won two Glyph Comic Awards. Lance moved from his native New York to Madrid, Spain, where he's hard at work on a new and very original graphic novel. See more at lancetooksjournal.blogspot.com.

Montreal-based **RICK TREMBLES** has been self-publishing his comix since the 1970s, reprinted in anthologies such as Robert Crumb's *Weirdo Magazine* and Danny Hellman's *TYPHON*. FAB Press has published two volumes of his *Motion Picture Purgatory* comic-strip film reviews culled from the pages of the *Montreal Mirror*, where they've been published weekly since 1998 until the alternative weekly folded in June 2012. *The Guardian* called him a genius and Robert Crumb once said he was "even more twisted & weird" than him. Trembles's artwork has been exhibited at numerous art galleries, and his short animated films have won awards and toured festivals worldwide. He occasionally acts in counterculture films, tours with his comic-strip

slideshows as an onstage lecturer, and has been singing and playing guitar for his post-punk band, the American Devices, since 1980. Trembles is currently writing a book about the sticky creative process behind his autobiographical cartooning.

JAMIE UHLER is a graphic designer, illustrator, sometime painter, and amateur writer. A Cleveland émigré who now resides in Chicago, Jamie works in advertising and is currently attempting in his free time to birth courtesan design, a group assisting struggling artists and causes in getting their projects off the ground. See more at attractivevariance.com.

ANTHONY VENTURA has been working as an illustrator since graduating from Sheridan College, though he has been drawing and painting for even longer. He has done work for print, multimedia, advertising, and television, and he currently resides in a hamlet north of Toronto.

LAUREN WEINSTEIN is a cartoonist, teacher, and gardener who had a baby and moved to the suburbs of New Jersey. Her award-winning comics books include *Girl Stories* and *The Goddess of War*. Her work has been published in *Kramer's Ergot*, *The Ganzfeld*, *An Anthology of Graphic Fiction*, and *The Best American Comics of 2007* and *2010*. She is currently working on a sequel to *Girl Stories* for Henry Holt and Company, and is teaching comics at the School of Visual Arts. To keep herself amused during her child's naps, she draws comics that can be seen at laurenweinstein.com.

MATT WIEGLE lives in Philadelphia and draws things. He is responsible for the minicomics *Is It Bacon?*, *Ayaje's Wives*, and *Seven More Days of Not Getting Eaten*, and is the 2010 recipient of the Ignatz Award for Promising New Talent. He is cocreator of the webcomic *Destructor* with writer Sean T. Collins. When facing a deadline, he will draw during a hurricane. See more at destructorcomics.com, wiegle.com, and partykausa.com.

YIEN YIP is currently a freelance illustrator and screen-printing artist who was born and bred in Alberta, Canada. She has been drawing and painting ever since she was a kid; however, like every other member of her family, she decided to be "realistic" and took up accountancy for a bit. After five years in the field and one quarter-life crisis, she packed her bags and got her BAA in illustration at Sheridan College. With a deep love for drawing, screen-printing, some animation, and noodles, she is taking on the illustration world one step at a time.

YEJI YUN is an illustrator born and raised in Seoul, South Korea. She studied graphic design and illustration in Seoul, then Baltimore, and lastly in London, where she lived until recently returning to Seoul. She has produced illustrations for many different fields, including magazines, books, logos, posters, T-shirts, and advertising. She also makes her own zines and exhibits her personal projects. Yeji is influenced by poetic and nostalgic material and likes to draw inspiration from her own imagination and emotions. Her favorite color is turquoise. See more at seeouterspace.com.

ACKNOWLEDGMENTS

IT TAKES A LOT OF PEOPLE TO MAKE A BOOK, ESPECIALLY a gigantic anthology. Endless gratitude goes to Dan Simon, founder and president of Seven Stories Press, who immediately shared my vision for *The Graphic Canon* and, by his second e-mail to me, was already discussing the nitty-gritty details. I originally pitched an oversized 400-page book, but much later in the process, when I told Dan that it could easily be expanded to 500 or even 600 pages, he expanded it, all right—to two volumes. Then, weeks later, to three. From 400 pages each to 500. From some color to color throughout. From mostly reprints to mostly new material. We both like to think big.

Huge thanks to editor, main point of contact, and fellow night owl Veronica Liu, who was so much fun to work with that it didn't feel like work at all, even when she found loads of errors I had embarrassingly overlooked or when she lovingly cracked the whip as I let this or that task fall by the wayside. Liz DeLong did lots of heavy lifting in the editorial arena, while staying hidden behind the curtain. Stewart Cauley took on the Herculean task of designing this three-volume set, turning hundreds upon hundreds of digital files into the beautiful physical object you hold in your hands. Ruth Weiner and Anne Rumberger are the dynamic duo of publicity/marketing, doing everything from landing an illustrated review in *Reader's Digest* to making sure I have places to stay from Maine to Memphis. *Merci beaucoup* to the rest of Seven Stories' all-star team: Gabe Espinal, Jon Gilbert, Phoebe Hwang, Silvia Stramenga, Linda Trepanier, Crystal Yakacki, and all the interns. *Gracias* to Dave Kang for copyediting, Jordyn Ostroff for putting together a fantastic "Further Reading" section, Will Glass for fact-checking, and Ann Kingman, Michael Kindness, and everyone else at Random House Publisher Services for the distribution.

Hugs go to my parents, Ruthanne & Derek, Kiki, Sky, Terrence & Rebekah, Darrell, Billy Dale, Cat & David, Kelly & Kevin, Mary, Z, Hawk, Songtruth, Fred & Dorothy & Josh, Jeff & Christy, Jenny, Susan Maret, and Michael Ravnitzky. I raise a glass to Gary Baddeley, Ralph Bernardo, and Matt Staggs at Disinformation. I bow to the people who led me to artists—Paul Buhle, Molly Kiely, Annie Mok, Onsmith, and Zak Smith.

A tip of the hat to Ediciones de la Flor, Anne-Solange Noble at Éditions Gallimard, Catherine Camus, Lora Fountain at Agence Littéraire Lora Fountain & Associates, Clive Bryant at Classical Comics, Chad Rutkowski at Throwaway Horse LLC, Emma Hayley at SelfMadeHero, Kathrine at Fredericks & Freiser, and Charlotte Sheedy, Meredith Kaffel, and Mackenzie C. Brady at the Charlotte Sheedy Literary Agency. Major thanks are due to everyone who gets this book made and into your hands: the papermakers, the truck drivers, the printers, the distributors and wholesalers, the booksellers. . . . And of course the many trees who gave their all.

I'm grateful to all the authors, poets, and playwrights who gave us these works of literature. Many of them sacrificed their personal freedom, economic well-being, sanity, relationships, livers, and lives to illuminate the human condition. And I reserve a special place in my heart for all the artists and adapters, who enthusiastically produced amazing work. Without you guys, *The Graphic Canon* couldn't exist.

CREDITS AND PERMISSIONS

Heart of Darkness by Joseph Conrad was created especially for this volume. Copyright © 2013 by Matt Kish. Printed by permission of the artist.

The Awakening by Kate Chopin was created especially for this volume. Copyright © 2013 by Rebecca Migdal. Printed by permission of the artist.

The Interpretation of Dreams by Sigmund Freud was created especially for this volume. Copyright © 2013 by Tara Seibel. Printed by permission of the artist.

The Wonderful Wizard of Oz by Graham Rawle first appeared in *The Wizard of Oz* by L. Frank Baum and Graham Rawle (Counterpoint; Una Gft edition, 2008). Copyright © 2008 by Graham Rawle. Printed by permission of the artist.

"The New Accelerator" by H. G. Wells was created especially for this volume. Copyright © 2013 by Cole Johnson. Printed by permission of the artist.

"Reginald" by Saki was created especially for this volume. Copyright © 2013 by Sonia Leong. Printed by permission of the artist.

Mother by Maxim Gorky was created especially for this volume. Copyright © 2013 by Stephanie McMillan. Printed by permission of the artist.

"If—" by Rudyard Kipling was created especially for this volume. Copyright © 2013 by Frank M. Hansen. Printed by permission of the artist.

John Barleycorn by Jack London was created especially for this volume. Copyright © 2013 by John Pierard. Printed by permission of the artist.

"Araby" (from *Dubliners*) by James Joyce was created especially for this volume. Copyright © 2013 by Annie Mok. Printed by permission of the artist.

"The Metamorphosis" by Franz Kafka first appeared in *Raw* Vol. 2 #2. Copyright © 1990 by R. Sikoryak. Printed by permission of the artist.

The Voyage Out by Virginia Woolf was created especially for this volume. Copyright © 2013 by Caroline Picard. Printed by permission of the artist.

"The Love Song of J. Alfred Prufrock" by T. S. Eliot was created especially for this volume. Copyright © 2013 by Anthony Ventura. Printed by permission of the artist.

"The Mowers" by D. H. Lawrence was created especially for this volume. Copyright © 2013 by Bishakh Som. Printed by permission of the artist.

"Sea Iris" by H. D. was created especially for this volume. Copyright © 2013 by Bishakh Som. Printed by permission of the artist.

"A Matter of Colour" by Ernest Hemingway was created especially for this volume. Copyright © 2013 by Dan Duncan. Printed by permission of the artist.

The Madman by Kahlil Gibran was created especially for this volume. Copyright © 2013 by Matt Wiegle. Printed by permission of the artist.

"Hands" (from *Winesburg, Ohio*) by Sherwood Anderson was created especially for this volume. Copyright © 2013 by Ted Rall. Printed by permission of the artist.

The Dreaming of the Bones by W. B. Yeats was originally published in *Bookforum* (June/July/Aug., 2009). Copyright © 2009 by Lauren Weinstein. Printed by permission of the artist.

Chéri by Colette was created especially for this volume. Copyright © 2013 by Molly Crabapple. Printed by permission of the artist.

The Age of Innocence by Edith Wharton was created especially for this volume. Copyright © 2013 by C. Frakes. Printed by permission of the artist.

"Dulce et Decorum Est" by Wilfred Owen was created for Classical Comics UK. Copyright © 2013 by Jason Cobley and John Blake. Printed by permission of the publisher.

"The Second Coming" by W. B. Yeats was created especially for this volume. Copyright © 2013 by Anthony Ventura. Printed by permission of the artist.

"The Penitent" and "The Singing-Woman from the Wood's Edge" by Edna St. Vincent Millay were created especially for this volume. Copyright © 2013 by Joy Kolitsky. Printed by permission of the artist.

"The Top" and "Give It Up!" by Franz Kafka first appeared in *Give It Up! And Other Short Stories* by Peter Kuper (NBM Publishing, 1995). They were colored by the artist expecially for this volume. Copyright © by Peter Kuper. Printed by permission of the artist.

"The Negro Speaks of Rivers" by Langston Hughes was created especially for this volume. Copyright © 2013 by Jenny Tondera. Printed by permission of the artist.

"Rain" by W. Somerset Maugham was created especially for this volume. Copyright © 2013 by Lance Tooks. Printed by permission of the artist.

Ulysses by James Joyce was originally published as part of *Ulysses "Seen"* [ulyssesseen.com]. Copyright © 2012 by Robert Berry with Josh Levitas. Printed by permission of the artists.

Ulysses was originally published by David Lasky as a minicomic titled *Minit Classics Presents: Joyce's Ulysses*. Copyright © 2012 by David Lasky. Printed by permission of the artist.

"Living on $1,000 a Year in Paris" by Ernest Hemingway was created especially for this volume. Copyright © 2013 by Steve Rolston. Printed by permission of the artist.

"The Emperor of Ice-Cream" by Wallace Stevens was created especially for this volume. Copyright © 2013 by Anthony Ventura. Printed by permission of the artist.

"The Hill" by William Faulkner was created especially for this volume. Copyright © 2013 by Kate Glasheen. Printed by permission of the artist.

Siddhartha by Hermann Hesse was created especially for this volume. Copyright © 2013 by J. Ben Moss. Printed by permission of the artist.

"The Waste Land" by T. S. Eliot was created especially for this volume. Copyright © 2013 by Chandra Free. Printed by permission of the artist.

The Great Gatsby by F. Scott Fitzgerald was created especially for this volume. Copyright © 2013 by Tara Seibel. Printed by permission of the artist.

Steppenwolf by Hermann Hesse was created especially for this volume. Copyright © 2013 by John Pierard. Printed by permission of the artist.

Lady Chatterley's Lover by D. H. Lawrence was created especially for this volume. Copyright © 2013 by Lisa Brown. Printed by permission of the artist.

The Sound and the Fury by William Faulkner was created especially for this volume. Copyright © 2013 by Robert Goodin. Printed by permission of the artist.

Letters to a Young Poet by Rainer Maria Rilke was first published on the Wonders in the Dark website [wondersinthedark.com] and reworked especially for this volume. Copyright © 2010 and 2013 by James Uhler. Printed by permission of the artist.

The Maltese Falcon by Dashiell Hammett was created especially for this volume. Copyright © 2013 by T. Edward Bak. Printed by permission of the artist.

Brave New World by Aldous Huxley was created especially for this volume. Copyright © 2013 by Carly Elizabeth Schmitt. Printed by permission of the artist.

Poker! by Zora Neale Hurston was created especially for this volume. Copyright © 2013 by Milton Knight. Printed by permission of the artist.

Black Elk Speaks by Black Elk and John G. Neihardt was created especially for this volume. Copyright © 2013 by Molly Kiely. Printed by permission of the artist.

"Strange Fruit" ("Bitter Fruit") by Lewis Allan was created especially for this volume. Copyright © 2013 by John Linton Roberson. Printed by permission of the artist.

Nausea by Jean-Paul Sartre first appeared in *Hup* #3 by Robert Crumb (Last Gasp Comics, 1989). Copyright © 1989 by Robert Crumb. Used by permission: Agence Littéraire Lora Fountain & Associates, Paris, France.

The Grapes of Wrath by John Steinbeck was created especially for this volume. Copyright © 2013 by Liesbeth De Stercke. Printed by permission of the artist.

Three stories by Jorge Luis Borges were created especially for this volume. Copyright © 2013 by Kathryn Siveyer. Printed by permission of the artist.

The Stranger by Albert Camus first appeared in *El extranjero* by Juan Carlos Kreimer, Julián Aron, Albert Camus (Ediciones de la Flor, 2011). Copyright © 2011 by Ediciones de la Flor, Juan Carlos Kreimer & Julián Aron. English translation © 2013 by Dan Simon. Printed by permission of the artists and Éditions Gallimard.

Animal Farm by George Orwell was created especially for this volume. Copyright © 2013 by Laura Plansker. Printed by permission of the artist.

"The Heart of the Park" by Flannery O'Connor was created especially for this volume. Copyright © 2013 by Jeremy Eaton. Printed by permission of the artist.

Nineteen Eighty-Four by George Orwell was created especially for this volume. Copyright © 2013 by Lesley Barnes. Printed by permission of the artist.

The Man with the Golden Arm by Nelson Algren was created especially for this volume. Copyright © 2013 by Jeremy Eaton. Printed by permission of the artist.

"The Voice of the Hamster" by Thomas Pynchon was created especially for this volume. Copyright © 2013 by Brendan Leach. Printed by permission of the artist.

Waiting for Godot by Samuel Beckett was created especially for this volume. Copyright © 2013 by Gustavo Rinaldi. Printed by permission of the artist.

"The Dancer" by Gabriela Mistral was created especially for this volume. Copyright © 2013 by Andrea Arroyo. Printed by permission of the artist.

Lord of the Flies by William Golding was created especially for this volume. Copyright © 2013 by Trevor Alixopulos. Printed by permission of the artist.

The Doors of Perception by Aldous Huxley was created especially for this volume. Copyright © 2013 by John Pierard. Printed by permission of the artist.

Lolita by Vladimir Nabokov was created especially for this volume. Copyright © 2013 by Sally Madden. Printed by permission of the artist.

Four Beats was created especially for this volume. Copyright © 2013 by Tara Seibel. Printed by permission of the artist.

On the Road by Jack Kerouac was created especially for this volume. Copyright © 2013 by Yeji Yun. Printed by permission of the artist.

Naked Lunch by William S. Burroughs was created especially for this volume. Copyright © 2013 by Emelie Östergren. Printed by permission of the artist.

One Flew Over the Cuckoo's Nest by Ken Kesey was created especially for this volume. Copyright © 2013 by Patrick Murphy. Printed by permission of the artist.

The Bell Jar by Sylvia Plath was created especially for this volume. Copyright © 2013 by Ellen Lindner. Printed by permission of the artist.

Last Exit to Brooklyn by Hubert Selby Jr. was created especially for this volume. Copyright © 2013 by Juliacks. Printed by permission of the artist.

Diaries of Anaïs Nin was originally published in *Whores of Mensa* #4. It was then self-published in 2010 as a minicomic titled *Anaïs in Paris*. Mardou added color and reworked the piece especially for this volume. Copyright © 2008 and 2013 by Mardou. Printed by permission of the artist.

The Master and Margarita by Mikhail Bulgakov first appeared in *The Master and Margarita* by Mikhail Bulgakov, Andrzej Klimowski, Danusia Schejbal (SelfMadeHero, 2008). Copyright © 2008 by SelfMadeHero / Andrzej Klimowski & Danusia Schejbal. Printed by permission of the publisher.

One Hundred Years of Solitude by Gabriel García Márquez was created especially for this volume. Copyright © 2013 by Yien Yip. Printed by permission of the artist.

In Watermelon Sugar by Richard Brautigan was created especially for this volume. Copyright © 2013 by Juliacks. Printed by permission of the artist.

Gravity's Rainbow by Thomas Pynchon first appeared in *Pictures Showing What Happens on Each Page of Thomas Pynchon's Novel Gravity's Rainbow* by Zak Smith (Tin House Books, 2006). Copyright © 2006 by Zak Smith. Printed by permission of the artist.

Crash by J. G. Ballard was created especially for this volume. Copyright © 2013 by Onsmith. Printed by permission of the artist.

"I Bought a Little City" by Donald Barthelme was created especially for this volume. Copyright © 2013 by Andrice Arp. Printed by permission of the artist.

"What We Talk About When We Talk About Love" by Raymond Carver was created especially for this volume. Copyright © 2013 by Annie Mok. Printed by permission of the artist.

Blood and Guts in High School by Kathy Acker was created especially for this volume. Copyright © 2013 by Molly Kiely. Printed by permission of the artist.

Blood Meridian by Cormac McCarthy was created especially for this volume. Copyright © 2013 by Dame Darcy. Printed by permission of the artist.

Foucault's Pendulum by Umberto Eco was created especially for this volume. Copyright © 2013 by Julia Gfrörer. Printed by permission of the artist.

Wild at Heart by Barry Gifford was created especially for this volume. Copyright © 2013 by Rick Trembles. Printed by permission of the artist.

The Famished Road by Ben Okri was created especially for this volume. Copyright © 2013 by Aidan Koch. Printed by permission of the artist.

Einstein's Dreams by Alan Lightman was created especially for this volume. Copyright © 2013 by Rey Ortega. Printed by permission of the artist.

The Wind-Up Bird Chronicle by Haruki Murakami was created especially for this volume. Copyright © 2013 by Rey Ortega. Printed by permission of the artist.

Infinite Jest by David Foster Wallace was created especially for this volume. Copyright © 2013 by Benjamin Birdie. Printed by permission of the artist.

INDEX TO VOLUME 3

TITLE

AUTHOR/POET

ARTIST/ADAPTER

COUNTRY/AREA OF ORIGIN

Photo by Ross Smith

RUSS KICK is the editor of the bestselling anthologies *You Are Being Lied To* and *Everything You Know is Wrong*, which have sold over half a million copies. *The New York Times* has dubbed Kick "an information archaeologist," *Details* magazine described Kick as "a Renaissance man," and *Utne Reader* named him one of its "50 Visionaries Who Are Changing Your World." Russ Kick lives in Nashville, Tennessee, and Tucson, Arizona.

SEVEN STORIES PRESS is an independent book publisher based in New York City. We publish works of the imagination by such writers as Nelson Algren, Russell Banks, Octavia E. Butler, Ani DiFranco, Assia Djebar, Ariel Dorfman, Coco Fusco, Barry Gifford, Hwang Sok-yong, Lee Stringer, and Kurt Vonnegut, to name a few, together with political titles by voices of conscience, including the Boston Women's Health Collective, Noam Chomsky, Angela Y. Davis, Human Rights Watch, Derrick Jensen, Ralph Nader, Loretta Napoleoni, Gary Null, Project Censored, Barbara Seaman, Alice Walker, Gary Webb, and Howard Zinn, among many others. Seven Stories Press believes publishers have a special responsibility to defend free speech and human rights, and to celebrate the gifts of the human imagination, wherever we can. For additional information, visit www.sevenstories.com.